Appassionato!

The word describes the essence of the man Salvatore. He was a man of passion and pride, imbued with a burning sense of justice for his fellow man. No one who met him would forget him. There was something different— something very special—about Salvatore, something that elevated him above his countrymen and made him a hero.

His world was a much smaller one in the 1940s but one of great intensity. In it you will also meet:

Appolladora, she was Salvatore's goddess of love, a Sicilian beauty who'd give her very life for him . . .

Gina, the American journalist who couldn't escape becoming part of his destiny . . .

Antigone, his mother, a powerful matriarch who kindled and nourished his fierce love of family, honor, and country . . .

Stefano, the U.S. Army Intelligence officer who inspired Salvatore to pursue his heroic legacy . . .

Barbarossa, the Machiavellian Mafia chieftain whose relationship to Salvatore would haunt both of them . . .

Appassionato!

The spectacular story of a man caught in a time and place, amidst people and events that formed a crucible for greatness. History alone could not record Salvatore's story—perhaps this brilliant new novel does it best. Rarely does a writer blend such eloquence and violence, such love and rage, into a reading experience of such magnitude. You will remember the people in these pages, and you will know they lived and loved like no others . . .

Appassionato

by Gloria Vitanza Basile

PINNACLE BOOKS   LOS ANGELES

Woe to the nation whose politics is subtlety, whose philosophy is jugglery, whose industry is patching . . .

Woe to the nation that greets a conqueror with fife and drum, then hisses him off to greet another conqueror with trumpet and song. . . .

—Kahlil Gibran

APPASSIONATO

Copyright © 1978 by Gloria Vitanza Basile

All rights reserved, including the right to reproduce this book or portions thereof in any form.

An original Pinnacle Books edition, published for the first time anywhere.

ISBN: 0-523-40072-1

First printing, January 1978

Cover illustration by Ben Wohlberg

Printed in the United States of America

PINNACLE BOOKS, INC.
One Century Plaza
2029 Century Park East
Los Angeles, California 90067

For
my number two son, Robert,
and
the friendly Siculi demons
and
ghostlike apparitions
who
invaded my soul to keep me
company
while
writing this novel
and
to
the spirit of Salvatore
and
to
Louis A. Basile, Attorney
who
guided me
through endless
legal translations

TYRRHENIAN

Ustica Prison

Castellamare

Partinico

Montegatta

Trapani

Palermo

Mt. Erice

Monreale

San Guiseppi

Piana dei Greci

Jato

Godrano

Portella Della
Rosa

Corleone

Marsala

Villalba

Castelvetrano

Mazara

Mussimeli

Selinunte

Agrigento

kilometers

| 0 | 20 | 40 | 60 | 80 |

| 0 | 10 | 20 | 30 | 40 | 50 |

miles

MEDITERRANEAN

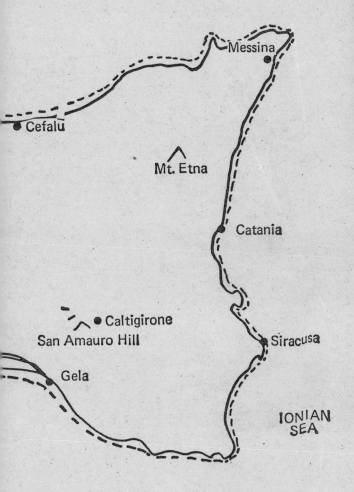

IN THE BEGINNING

He was seven years old. His father had died. Confused by death's mysteries, he wandered off by himself to sort out the confusion in his mind. Standing at the edge of the broken clay floor at the Temple of Cats, above Montegatta, he stood gazing down at the scattering of villages strung together like broken and runted rows of teeth, spilled along the limestone slopes of the majestic mountains.

Flushed and elated at the new secret hiding place he had discovered earlier, he marveled at how an enormous stone between two pillars had moved easily for him, as if a power, not his, had induced it to budge and reveal an opening to an inner grotto. Inside the cool, mysteriously compelling cave, he had stared wondrously at the strange signs carved into the walls. And when voices, whispering and tunneled, rushed at him in a language he didn't understand, he had gazed about in awe, but he hadn't been frightened. He had made a vow to keep this place as his very own secret hiding place; not even to Vincenzo would he confide the discovery of such a place. He had left the grotto, replacing the stone with equal ease, still baffled that he could move such a stone. It was incredible.

Now, as he glanced at the valley below, it seemed to change before his eyes. Windswept plains no longer contained villages as he knew them. Ancient temples and edifices of another century, with marketplaces and bazaars, replaced the former scene. There came a distant sound of trumpets, a call to arms. He searched everywhere for the source of the sounds. In the distance came a charge of horses; legions of men on horseback converged from all directions like a splendid pageant of antiquity. Chiefs and subchiefs in scant, colorful dress, with breastplates, armor, and shields that glittered in the blinding sunlight; gaily dressed horses with bright feathers and gleaming bridle regalia; standard-bearers, with vivid banners waving in the wind, rode swiftly alongside the vast armies of Greeks, Carthaginians, and Roman soldiers, coming together as one force. Just as quickly, the rattling of wheels, clatter of

1

horses, and eerie sounds of anguished trumpets faded and the scene restored itself to the present.

"Tori . . . Tori. . . ." He heard his name called, like the rustling of wind through bamboo thickets. Drawn seductively by the sirenlike voices, he stepped forward. God! He wanted to take that perilous step forward into the most exciting sight of his life. He hesitated, but not through any power of his own. His foot refused to obey his command. His energies tried to propel his foot forward, but it was useless. It was as if the same force that earlier had moved aside the rock now held him from pitching forward into eternity.

"Tori! Tori!" called Filippo and Marco. He turned to his older brothers with that same stunned expression of amazement on his face.

Filippo took one look at him and laughed. "The Siculis have called to him. See? It's written on his face. Don't be frightened, Tori. Legend claims they always call to their own."

"But I am not frightened," he told them. They paid him no heed. No one every paid much attention to boys his age. Except for his mother.

"The friendly Siculi demons won't permit you to be hurt, not if you listen to them," said Marco.

Taking his hands, they led Tori out the temple and back onto the winding road that led into their village.

"I wasn't really frightened," insisted Tori, his small face turned back to the scene as he stumbled along. His eyes compulsively searched the area, awe-filled, trying to understand all he'd been witness to. How could he tell his brothers he had wanted to go with whoever had called to him? They'd never understand—would they?

"You better tell Mamma, Tori," said Marco seriously. "It's time she taught him of more earthly things, Filippo. He's too impressionable at this age. He might have fallen to his death if we hadn't arrived in time. Now, with Papa gone, we'll have to devote all our time to the *campagna*."

Tori couldn't understand his brothers' concern. They didn't know what he knew. There was no way he could have fallen. Some force, something he couldn't begin to imagine, had held him back.

"Mamma, who are the Siculis?" he asked her one night weeks later.

"Where did you hear of them, Tori?"

"At the Temple of Cats. They called to me. Filippo told me."

2

"Did Marco also tell you?"

"Yes, Mamma, *bedda*. He said I should learn more of earthly things."

"I see. The Siculis, my son, were the first inhabitants of our island, whom God placed upon the land when he created it. Legend claims they call to their own."

"And what does that mean, Mamma?"

"It means—so claims the legend—that once upon a time you lived here before."

"I did?" he asked wonderingly. "Was I very good, Mamma?"

"Very, very good, Tori."

"Was I rich? As rich as the landlords?"

"Very rich, Tori."

"Was I important?"

"You were king!"

"Is that why they let me come back?"

"Perhaps."

"Will I be king once again?"

"You'll be whatever you picture in your mind."

"Are you sure, Mamma, *bedda*?"

"I'm sure."

"But—how do I make these pictures? Do I buy a camera?"

"The camera is already in your mind."

"Will I learn to use it?"

"You will learn. Be patient."

"Mamma—I already see pictures."

"Good. Then you already know how to use it."

"Mamma, if I see a splendid white horse, will I be a horse?"

"Tori. You are making jest with me."

"Or a tiger—a lion—or an eagle? What if I see them all?"

"And what if I see a broad paddle with which to warm your bottom?"

"Oh, Mamma, *bedda!* I truly love you."

"And I love you, Tori. Now run and play. But don't meddle with the Siculi. They are playful enough, but sometimes they don't know when to stop."

She watched him run out into the Sicilian sunshine to join his friends. Soon enough, he'd have to set aside these childish dreams and go to work with his brothers. Perhaps Marco is right, thought Antigone Naxos Salvatore. It's time to stop filling him with legends of his Greek and Roman heritage. He is growing up and is old enough to learn of earthly matters.

3

BOOK I

The *Mise en Scène*

Their national symbol is a funeral cortege. Their national anthem, a howling wail of soundless horror echoing in the blood-filled corridors of their minds. For seven years his existence on earth had proved threatening to them. His time had come. High officials in government, totally without conscience or humanity, had gathered to dispose of those who defied their edicts. An imperceptible nod, the slightest flickering of a power-saturated eye, a barely discernible movement in an upraised hand had decided it was time to put an end to a legend and bury his bones among the skeletons of the past.

CHAPTER 1

July 5, 1950
Castelvetrano, Sicily

At 2:30 A.M. on this Wednesday, there was no moon in the sky. No light of any kind flickered in the deserted streets. There was only a hollow silence in which there were no echoes, for the village at this time was dead, soundless. Villagers, exhausted and unable to sleep in the early evening hours, now entered their deepest slumber, unaware that ghoulish goings-on had already commenced in their village.

A three-day heat wave muzzled any breeze that might have escaped Mediterranean waters. It hung in a pall over the desperately hot village, where antiquated and delapidated houses with swan-breasted balconies jutted over narrow, cobbled streets, hardly more than alleys strung together by mean, sequestered courtyards, fetid and foul with the stench of animal excrement and waste waters.

But wait. There was a light after all, so faint it was barely discernible. In one of those shabby courtyards, at *numero* 54, Strada Sarina Madonna, two burly men worked feverishly against time, their faces dimly illuminated by weak, sputtering rays from a battery-powered hand torch lying on the ground at their feet. The men moved about their business with skillful dexterity, unaware that they unwittingly prepared the *mise en scène* for what would become the most bizarre drama ever to be enacted under the proscenium arch of Sicilian politics.

Earlier, a mule-driven lorry had deposited the body of a dead man with them. An aged driver with failing eyesight, amply paid for his services, was curtly dismissed. No one had to warn him not to breathe a word of his deeds on this satanic night. He knew full well the consequences: reprisal, even death.

Hampered by unabated heat, intolerable odors, and a deadline, the two men worked swiftly, as if prodded by Lucifer. The older man, dressed in shirtsleeves and trousers, propped the dead body up against the stone wall. For a split second, the faintest glimmer of triumph flashed in his intent dark eyes. He stared at the body, then he

7

brandished a submachine gun and fired several shots into the corpse.

The dead man didn't bleed.

Struck with amazement, the younger man marveled at the phenomenon. Damn! His captain was right. My, my, what skills one acquires in this line of work, he told himself. A profound respect shone in his eyes as he watched his superior officer scribble a name on a small card and press it into his hand.

"Run swiftly to this address," instructed the captain. "A man will give you what I ordered earlier. Make haste! We're fighting time."

As the aide left the courtyard, the captain glanced apprehensively at the pulsating eastern sky, at the fading, yawning stars, soon to be swallowed up in daylight. Shortly, peasants preparing for day labor at nearby feudal estates would be rising. *Vaccari* would fill the streets with their cows until all the milk in those swollen udders was sold. Bakers would fire their ovens. Goddamn! He had to move before the cocks crowed.

The captain, flushed with adrenalin, moved rapidly. Fleeting images came at him attempting to shatter his resolve. Methodically and meticulously, he shoved aside his scruples and adroitly blocked from mind all memories of the circumstances leading to this point. Four days ago, he'd made his decision. Despite certain drawbacks, he was fully committed to the act. It was too late to turn back.

Expertly, he turned the dead man over, sprawling him face down in the dirt, right knee drawn up slightly, right arm outflung to aptly display a large diamond solitaire on the third finger of his hand. He paused a moment to observe his handiwork. Everything had to be just right. There could be no errors—not at this point. He flashed the torch over the body, inspecting it against some inner design in his mind.

Probing dark eyes scanned the carefully creased beige Levis, spotless white undershirt, and spiffy dark mahogany sandals worn by the corpse. The four-day stubble on his face caused the officer a moment's consternation, but he had no time to worry over the incongruities. Perhaps no one will notice, he thought. Moreover, who'd contest the word of the Forces to Suppress Banditry, eh?

Satisfied for the moment, the captain wiped the rolling sweat from his face, moved closer, and with the aid of the flashlight attempted to read the inscription on the back of the golden scorpion amulet suspended on a gold chain around the dead man's neck. Unable to make it out, he

8

cursed himself for not bringing his reading glasses. He carefully placed the amulet in the dirt, inches from the lifeless face. Next he slipped a leather gun belt under the inert hips and secured into place an open gun holster. Midway between the man's face and his outflung arm, he placed a German Luger. With painstaking precision, he placed a .38 calibre Beretta submachine gun two feet from the bent knee.

Behind the body, next to a broken stone wall at the rear of the enclosure, he casually dropped a beige rucksack and scattered at random a German-made camera, three rolls of undeveloped film, two packs of unopened Pall Mall cigarettes, two Breda machine gun cartridges, a freshly opened box of shells for the Luger, and the last item found in the dead man's pocket, a white toy soldier on a white horse which he partially buried in the dust.

By then it was nearly 4 A.M. His aide, Private Foti, reappeared with a tin container which he promptly turned over to his superior officer. Total bafflement filled the incredulous eyes of the dark-skinned private as he watched his mentor's busy, skillful hands. Unsure of many things at this moment, Foti was certain of one thing: He was going to be sick. The bloodless wounds inflicted earlier on the deceased—two bullet holes in the right rib cage; two in the upper right arm; one in the inner elbow; several at the mangled wrist—now oozed with bright crimson blood injected into the empty craters with a hypodermic syringe. The captain's expertise both confounded and repelled Private Foti, but it also evoked an expression of profound respect.

Scrutinizing his handiwork with hypercritical eyes, the officer, dissatisfied with the overall picture, frowned. It wasn't complete. Resetting the body into its former position, sprawled face downward, he poured the remaining goat's blood over the right shoulder, spilling a trail of carmine outward past the outflung arm until the container was empty. Again, he surveyed the scene. Satisfied, he shoved can and container at Foti. "Get rid of these."

Container and syringe in hand, the bug-eyed private nervously negotiated his way out the rear entrance into an adjoining, deserted, inner courtyard abutting a neighbor's house. As his eyes searched the darkness, he tossed the empty can into a bed of myrtle at the base of a solitary almond tree and shuddered involuntarily at the syringe in his hand. A thought struck him. Sprinting lightly on the balls of his feet, he reentered the first courtyard and moved along the far side of the widow Grissi's house where earlier he had noticed a recessed sewer drain. Lifting the crude wooden cover, he tossed the hypodermic into it, then dropped the lid gently into place. He grimaced with disgust and wiped his hands on the seat of his trousers to erase the blood stains. He couldn't wait to tell his new wife the things his eyes had seen this day.

The next phase of this bizarre scheme was entered into when the captain let loose a short volley of machine-gun fire into one of the narrow stone walls at the right of the archway entrance. A crash of fire and chipping stones, as ricocheting bullets pinged and zinged loudly, caused no stir in the sleeping village except to send a few cats and rats scurrying for cover.

In the shifting shadows made by lights breaking in eastern skies, Private Foti failed to notice the muzzle of the gun turn subtly toward him. Before he guessed his fate, the officer's trigger finger squeezed gently and a burst of fire cut the private in two. Propelled backward by the force of the missiles, Private Foti's face jerked wretchedly. Shocked dark eyes widened in surprise. He groaned, "Why? Why? My lips were sealed." He fell to the ground like a limp rag doll.

"Now there can be no doubt," muttered the *capitano*, talking to a dead man. His watch read 4:15 A.M. He gazed warily at the horizon, now ablaze with spectral lights, and swore under his breath. The last phase of his diabolical plot should have been completed by now.

Quickly he pulled the aide's body out of the enclosure and dumped him onto the street side of the courtyard. He moved swiftly. Already he could hear the creaking of the rickety carts rolling along the cobblestones, as the village started to come alive. He wiped the sweat from his face and neck, buttoned his shirt, yanked his tie into place, and ran his fingers through his short black hair. In the light, he looked more formidable, like a well-muscled athlete. His face, free of humor, was one which most people took seriously. From the short end of the broken rear wall, he picked up his beige tunic and slipped into it. He squared a visored hat on his head and allowed his fingers to slide down both sides of the braided uniform, out of meticulous habit. He finished not a moment too soon, for already the cocks were crowing.

Running to the house at the right of the courtyard, he pounded furiously on the wooden door with balled fists and shouting authoritatively, he commanded, "Open the door! Open in the name of the Italian government! Water! I need water for a dying man! Open I say! I'm Captain

10

Franchina of the Forces to Suppress Banditry! I've just captured the bandit Salvatore!"

Inside the shabby house, the widow Grissi and her lover had been in the throes of sexual ecstasy when Manfredo first heard the crackling gunshot sounds like distant fireworks. *"Managghia, Giulietta,"* he whispered hoarsely. "I have always dreamed of hearing such sounds when making love, but I never dreamed I would experience such erotica!" He hugged her tighter and tighter, certain he had tasted eternal paradise.

"Ah, *che si beddu!*" she whispered. "Hold me tighter, *amore.*"

"Can you feel me now?"

"What is it you do to me? I feel like an animal, a cat!"

"Si, my little cat, kiss me again."

"Oh, Manfredo, Manfredo," she sighed. "We must get married so we can do this every night. You have the balls of a bull and an appetite to match."

"And you, my Giulietta, have the balloons of a cow, but so much tastier, *cara mia.* Lie back now and take what I have to offer."

"I'll take it. I'll take it. Quickly, Manfredo, before I scream so loud the neighbors will hear me and know I have a seed bull in my house."

"Giulietta . . . ah, Giulietta. Giulietta!"

"Stop, Manfredo. Stop. Listen, listen. *Santo Dio,* will you stop for a minute!" She pulled away from him and placed her slender hand over his lips. "There's someone knocking on my door. I knew it! I knew earlier when I saw strangers moving about in the courtyard, I shouldn't let you in. Pray it's not police."

"To hell with them! Tell them to go away!" he cried hoarsely taking her hands from his lips. Wild-eyed and frenzied, holding his aching and enormously swollen tumescence in his hand, he tried to find her honey pot.

"Listen, you son of a whore! That idiot—whoever he is—is jabbering something about Salvatore! Listen!" Giulietta's eyes lit up with wild lights.

Faintly the captain's voice was heard. It came in clear and carried well in the silence. "I am Captain Franchina of the Forces to Suppress Banditry! Open up. I need water for a dying man! I've just killed Salvatore!"

The widow Grissi stiffened imperceptibly, for both names rushed at her out of her past to fill her with a vile and contemptible hatred. Firmly and with new-found strength, she told her lover, "You stay here—out of sight,

11

Manfredo—while I go downstairs to see what this is about. I dare not close my ears to such authority."

"And what do I do about this, my little *gatta?*" Manfredo held his slowly deflating weapon in his hand, a pain-filled, unsatisfied expression on his face.

"Unload the bullets," she said with a glint in her eye. "I shall return to help you fire at your target." She slipped into a flannel robe and left him.

Downstairs, her heart· beating with unnatural excitement, the young widow peered through a narrow slit in the door and made out the khaki-colored uniform with shiny buttons. Even in five years, he looked the same. She remained in the shadows.

"I need your assistance, *signora,* for a dying man. Water, please, and a telephone," he told her. "I am Captain Giovanni Franchina of the FSB and I've just captured the brigand Salvatore."

Her face swollen with hostility as the face on the uniform came into focus, she scowled darkly and handed him the water jug. Beyond him in the growing light of dawn she saw a darkened form lying sprawled out in the courtyard. "Water, yes. *Telefono,* no. De Meo's house next door has a *telefono.*" She moved back into the shadows so he wouldn't recognize her. Earlier, waiting for her lover, she'd seen strange goings-on in the courtyard. But it was not her business—or was it?

Grabbing the bottle from her hands, with a false expression of anguish on his face, Captain Franchina returned to the dead man's side and made a pretense of trying to elevate the man's head. Naturally there was no response. With a certain *panache,* Franchina removed his snap-brimmed hat, inclined his head briefly, and crossed himself religiously. From the corner of his eyes he saw the woman's darkened figure peering at him. He heard an audible gasp as she, too, crossed herself. A self-satisfied smile tugged at the corner of his lips. Unfortunately, the officer didn't see the smile of satisfaction on the widow's lips.

Bolting her door securely, Giuletta Grissi scurried upstairs to her lover's side. Dismayed to find him snoring, she shook him vigorously.

"Manfredo! Manfredo! Wake up! They've just killed Salvatore! His body lies crushed in de Meo's courtyard, killed by that black-hearted mercenary, Captain Franchina. Sweet Jesus, my prayers have been answered!"

"Va, va," he told her sleepily, not fully hearing her. "Don't break my balls, woman! They'll never catch Salvatore. Never in a million years. He's in Brazil where he's

12

been for nearly six months." He rolled over and menced his snoring.

"Curse the devil, sweet Jesus. How sweet is the taste of revenge. How long I've waited for this. What justice! The memory of those men will no longer interfere in *my* life! Especially not my *love* life," she exclaimed, removing her robe and climbing back into bed. She began to prod her lover to renewed vigor. "Manfredo . . . Manfredo," she cooed lovingly.

By 5 A.M. a special squad of security police deputized by the FSB arrived at *numero* 54, Strada Sarina Madonna in response to the call made by Captain Franchina from the de Meo house. With them came the commander of the Forces to Suppress Banditry, Colonel Cesare Cala, a quiet, dignified, somber-faced man of forty-eight, with gray blue eyes and a perennial expression of apology carved into his features. His uniform was spotless, khaki-colored, with customary gold braid and buttons. His visored hat was tugged down over his expressive eyes. He stood to one side and watched without comment as the squad disposed of Private Foti's body—reported shot by bandits in the line of duty.

With official decorum, his hands clasped behind his back, the colonel lumbered through the stone arch into the courtyard, his keen, discerning eyes readily absorbing the scene. For the next twenty minutes he listened as Captain Franchina related the story of his successful coup against the redoubtable bandit Salvatore. He listened attentively as he usually did, asking no questions. This was not an unusual posture for the Italian intelligence officer who believed that listening, rather than talking, had paved the way for all his past successes.

The arrival of two police officers from the local office of the Security Police interrupted their tête-à-tête. Briefed on what had occurred and who lay dead in the courtyard, the duo were instructed to stand guard until men from the procurator general's office arrived to conduct their routine investigation.

"You are to guard this position, the body and all personal effects with your life, Corporal!" snapped Captain Franchina. "And button your tunic!" he added disdainfully. "Do you always dress so slovenly when on duty?"

"Yes, sir. I mean no, sir," retorted the corporal with a false brightness. Enmity between *carabinieri* and security police was a spreading cancer which the corporal tried to conceal in his response. Roused from barracks and a

13

sound sleep, he and his companion had been shuttled off in haste to this address, hardly awake. Now both policemen stood at attention until the FSB officers disappeared in the shadowy haze of dawn in the functional black Fiat.

Deliberately unbuttoning his tunic in the wake of Captain Franchina's stern admonition, the corporal glanced about the tricky shadows. His wary eyes met those of his companion and they both sensed silent, watchful eyes staring down at them from behind shuttered windows and sheltered balconies. With carbines held firmly in their hands, the two police officers moved slowly over the earthen courtyard and stared long and hard at the youthful corpse sprawled in the dirt amid a lake of blood.

At 6:30 A.M. the Eternal City of Rome had already yawned twice as the capital came alive. In an elegantly furnished baroque bedroom at the Villa Belasci, the Minister of the Interior, disturbed by the incessant ringing of the telephone, leaned over and reached for the raucous instrument on the nightstand. Disrespectful bastards! Who dared call his private number at such an ungodly hour?

He mumbled, *"Pronto,"* softly into the mouthpiece, hoping not to awaken the sleeping form next to him in the oversized bed. In moments his emerald eyes blinked open in astonishment. He sat up quickly, swung his pajama-clad legs over the side of the bed, and turned on the table lamp. He listened attentively and nodded from time to time. "Yes, yes, Inspector Zanorelli. You did the right thing to call. Contact Colonel Cala. Have him call my office at 9 A.M. sharp. Make sure all details are contained in the report." Belasci hung up.

Martino Belasci, cabinet minister in Premier de Aspanu's government, Minister of the Interior, and high-ranking political bigwig in the Christian Democratic Party, placed a hurried call to the villa of his premier. He blinked several times to force himself awake, reached for a cigarette from a decorative porcelain box, and lit it with a delicate, swan-shaped crystal and silver lighter. As Belasci inhaled deeply, his bright blue eyes betrayed an inner excitement.

When he had related the message to a joyous chief of state, Premier de Aspanu, he hung up and placed a second call to his personal secretary, Marcello Barone, and ordered a press conference in his office at 10 A.M. sharp that morning. He placed a third call to Don Matteo Barbarossa in Monreale, Sicily. Unable to get his call through, he hung up.

14

Twenty minutes later, by the time his manservant appeared with a tray of steaming hot coffee, Belasci had showered and shaved and stood meticulously dressed in a dove-gray double-breasted suit. He took the tray from his man and shooed him away. He poured the black beverage into a delicate bone china cup and gulped it down hurriedly. Satisfied with the image reflected in the gilt-edged oval mirror, the dark-haired, fair-complexioned state official, who wore custom clothing with a dashing flair, moved lightly toward the shadowy form under silken coverlets on the ornate bed, flushed with secret elation.

"Sorry to leave you, sweet. Important business. Everything we've been waiting for has just come to a stellar conclusion. I'll call you later for cocktails. Oh yes." Belasci adjusted his platinum and sapphire cuff links and gazed admiringly at them. "Thank you for the links. They are exquisite."

The sleeping form under the covers stirred slightly, opened a sleepy eye, and muttered huskily, "What is it this time? Hmmm?"

"They just got Salvatore. He's dead at last. Turn on the radio around 10 A.M. for the official announcement."

Prince Giorgio Oliatta sat up in bed wide awake. "Salvatore? Did you say Salvatore?" he asked wondrously. But Minister Belasci had already left.

At 8:30 A.M., under cover of an American diplomat, former U.S. Army Colonel Stefano Modica deplaned at Rome's airport. A compact fortnighter in one hand, olive green briefcase in the other, he limped noticeably through special customs provided for men with his credentials. In the deserted men's lounge, Modica paused to wash his hands, taking precautions to make certain he wasn't observed. He glanced casually at his watch just as the door opened and the shadowy figure of a man entered.

Morelli, former Italian aide attached to Colonel Modica's command during WWII, a man with the craggy countenance of a prize fighter, moved to the washstand next to him, nodded, and said, "It is done."

Modica heaved a relieved sigh. "His reply?"

"In this." Morelli placed an envelope on the briefcase.

Colonel Modica picked up both case and envelope and exited quickly.

Outside the terminal Colonel Modica was assisted to a waiting US Embassy Mercedes limousine, and in moments the auto sped easily through the morning traffic. He opened the envelope and read its contents:

15

SCORPIO AGREES. IT'S TIME WE HAVE DINNER.
FIVE YEARS HAVE BEEN TOO LONG. WILL MEET
YOUR PLANE IN PALERMO 7-5-50 AT 5 P.M.
AQUILO BRAVO.

By 9:15 A.M. Modica was seated at the large walnut desk in a sequestered office at the American Embassy attempting to learn from special agents Matt Saginor, Renzo Bellomo, and Len Salina what had gone sour on *Operation Red Star*, a highly involved anti-communist assignment.

Modica synchronized his gold pocket watch with the clock on the wall. He placed the timepiece open faced on the highly polished walnut desk next to several thick manila files spread open before him. He made a mental note to conclude the session by 11 A.M. to give him ample time to catch the 2:30 P.M. flight to Palermo. It was imperative that he make connections with Alessandro Salvatore, a young man for whose spectacular career Colonel Modica felt, in part, responsible.

ORS, the anti-communist project, was secondary to his purpose for being in Rome. Six months before, his support was enlisted in a highly covert plan to smuggle Salvatore out of Sicily. He had listened to Gina O'Hoolihan's proposal and in good conscience couldn't deny her aid. It took diplomatic know how, sheer guts, political muscle, plus a trunkful of special political favors owed him before he could begin to assemble the plan. An unblemished record of duty with the Office of Strategic Services, the Allied Control Council, and a stint as temporary legal sidekick to General Patton helped push the project through.

Colonel Modica, no stranger to the President, had worked for two years under the Chief of State's guidance, while the National Security Council was formed in 1947 to provide him with an advisory board on both foreign and domestic policy. This obscene embryo, nurtured and remolded by future administrations, would later become refined and formally named the CIA.

Due to the sensitivity of the subject and despite their acquaintance, Modica was compelled to wade through time-consuming protocol and reams of red tape before he could approach the President. Two additional months had dissolved before he put the question to General Patton, and a third month slipped by before General Eisenhower was briefed. Still, no oval office appointment.

On May 15, five months to the date after the original proposal had reached him, Modica, in a rush of excite-

16

ment, was ordered to "get his ass over to the oval office."

The President, familiar with Salvatore's anti-communist activities, which in spirit conformed to the Truman Doctrine, took into account the splendid work he had performed in crushing the Reds and his pro-American leanings. He recollected the letter sent to him by the Sicilian. Then he denied official sanction to Modica's "mad, mad plan" to slip Salvatore out of Sicily, with special reservations.

Before Modica deflated totally, Mr. Truman came to his rescue.

"Let me stress our position, Colonel. The White House can't overtly engage in plans which might alienate an Allied nation. Not now. Not at the height of the Cold War when we can't second-guess Russia's intent. However, you may—off the cuff—avail yourself of any government facility within your jurisdiction to bring your plans to fruition. But heed my words, bronc-buster. If this foolhardy plan fails and is exposed before its conclusion, any rumble from a foreign government will elicit a firm denial and formal statement disavowing our knowledge or implication in the matter. Is that clear? In short, Colonel, if your balls get burned, don't come crying home to Papa. Singed hair makes one helluva stink. Do you read me?" His Missouri accent thickened when making a point.

Ten minutes later, Modica, back in his office, had cranked gears and set his plan in motion. Gratefully, things moved ahead with amazing swiftness.

Now only one thing remained. He'd meet with Salvatore, provide him with necessary cover, passports and ID's, and together they'd fly to Rome, board an army transport, and fly to a pre-planned destination. Obviously, there was an alternate plan. Two fishing vessels, alerted to stand by in the Bay of Marsala, would on signal escort them to Lisbon, where another standby army transport would fly to a different destination.

Modica busied himself sifting through the bulky file containing a 400-page report, an update on ORS, including a dossier of photographs of certain high officials and their apparent involvement in the ORS project and frowned noticeably as he scanned the contents.

"Why have three top agents met with such obvious failure?" asked Modica, his eyes glued to the file's contents. "Is anyone on to you?"

"All right, Steve," began Matt Saginor. "You asked for it. We'll give it to you straight."

17

Slightly before 10 A.M. hordes of international and local news reporters, tipped off by highly paid collaborators who smelled newsworthy items miles away, milled restlessly through pillared halls and marbled corridors outside the office of the Ministry of the Interior like hungry pack rats, waiting to be fed the *official* version of Salvatore's death.

Minister Belasci finally emerged to address the reporters. Evasive in that maddening manner employed by politicians in making a point, his words brought smirks of disgust to the faces of seasoned pressmen. Minister Belasci's comportment, the self-containment of an overly ambitious man who'd do anything to attain his goal, after fifteen minutes of boring procrastination incited the reporters to press hard for answers. Belasci cranked out oratory considered to be the *official* statement. Some attentive newsmen, passionately provoked, began to scribble away in their note pads. Others, more astute, listened and stared unbelievingly at this audacious government official.

"Early this morning, at approximately 3 A.M., the bandit Salvatore was captured and shot to death in a skirmish with the Forces to Suppress Banditry while attempting to escape a stupendous dragnet deployed against him by Colonel Cesare Cala and Captain Giovanni Franchina, in the village of Castelvetrano," began Minister Belasci. "It is, therefore, with great pride that I announce the promotion of Colonel Cala to the rank of general. Captain Franchina, who inflicted the *coup de grâce*, is now promoted to the rank of major. I take this time to salute both these men, to whom we are indebted, the real heroes in our nation. The Forces to Suppress Banditry, initiated a year ago to combat this scourge, have served us well. Now that this mission has ended, Premier de Aspanu and I sincerely wish that you esteemed members of the press print no further reports to glorify that murderous and despicable criminal, Salvatore."

Minister Belasci posed briefly for photographers. Sensing their contempt, he curtly cut them off and retired behind hand-carved doors, aware that he left behind an assemblage of dissatisfied newsmen. There was no flurry of activity, no swift sprinting to locate phones in the usual race to scoop their competitors. These tough veteran reporters, most of whom were experts in their fields, felt terribly cheated. They had expected more from this heavyweight official who'd been at the center of a fiery controversy between Salvatore and the state, a controversy that had amounted to civil war for nearly seven years.

Within the hour their discontent took flight. Outraged

members of the fourth estate converged upon the airlines and all modes of transport that would take them to their hero—Salvatore. Dead or alive, one thing was certain, Salvatore wouldn't let them down. They'd get a story if it had to come from Salvatore's ghost.

It was 11 A.M. in Monreale, a suburb of Palermo. A gilded Roman warrior clock on the fireplace mantel struck the hour. Don Matteo Barbarossa, *capomafia* and the most influential feudalist in Sicily, numbly watched the six Roman warriors march out of a center door under the clock's face, rotate in a circle, and disappear inside the door by the time the last chime sounded. The Don had been sitting in the dimly lit study with drapes drawn against an inexorable sun all morning. He poured himself a stiff shot of whiskey from a decanter on the desk, threw it down in one swallow, and sat back listening to the soft sounds of music emanating from the small desk radio nearby.

Four days ago the Don had retired into a silence in his villa. Normally a vigorous, strapping giant of a man, on this day, he appeared haggard and aged beyond his sixty-eight years. White hair in wild disarray, shirt and trousers crumpled and unchanged in four days, face unshaven, he had the appearance of any old man, unloved, neglected, and unwanted. Where were the traces of the tough, two-fisted, hard, shrewd, and cynical Mazzarino bandit who once terrorized the entire island by killing his way to the top of the Mafia hierarchy? Would he ever pull himself together again to be *capomafia*? His dark eyes, swollen in their red-veined whites, had dimmed retractably.

Peppino Orafisso, a Palermo radio announcer and news commentator, interrupted the regular musical interlude to announce: *"People of Sicily! People of Italy! People of the world! Salvatore is dead! Long live Salvatore! This morning, before the break of. . . ."*

Orafisso's tremulous voice, overwrought with frenzy and emotion, began to describe the capture of the heretofore invincible Salvatore. Don Barbarossa, no trace of emotion on his heavy-jowled features, leaned forward in his chair and snapped off the radio. His face, lined with fatigue, paled noticeably. He turned off the desk lamp and sighed heavily, making audible grunts and groans as if something pained him terribly.

It had all worked out for the best, he told himself. Everything considered, he could have done nothing else. He reached for another bracer and gulped it down. He shoved his dark-tinted glasses to the top of his head and rubbed

19

his swollen eyes with his knuckles. Nothing eased his pain. Not even the whiskey coursing through to his intestines relaxed him. He fell like a sack against his chair, a giant tear spilling from his eyes. Angry that he couldn't take hold of himself, he groped in his rear pocket for a handkerchief and dabbed at his eyes as he tried to clear the thickness in his throat.

In that instant, the Don tensed. He cocked his head, as if listening to something. It was nothing outside himself he strained to hear. Something inside his brain nagged at him. His face screwed up reflectively. What was it the newscaster had said? An instant replay of the announcer's words tripped across his mind. He moved forward, turned the radio on, fumbled for several moments to erase the static, then picked up another newscast. He listened intently, his black lizard eyes staring motionless.

". . . *Captain Franchina of the Forces to Suppress Banditry inflicted the* coup de grâce *upon the dying Salvatore, who in his final moments begged the officer for water to sate his thirst. Utterly compassionate, the captain, out of the goodness of his heart and with deep sympathy for a dying man—even a bandit—obliged the mortally wounded man by supplying the water for which he desperately begged. . . ."*

In over sixty years of a life filled with indescribable crimes and violence, the *capomafia* couldn't recall when his senses had been so inflamed. Violent displeasure fired through him as he contemplated the man's words. So intent was he upon his hatred and loathing, he hardly heard the ringing of the telephone. It rang seven times before he moved to answer it. He lifted the receiver, and in a sudden transition, without emotion, he said, "Talk."

Chief Inspector Zanorelli's voice came over the phone, booming with melodrama. "Don Matteo—have you heard the news? They finally got that son of a bitch Salvatore! Goddamnit! That bastard is finally a thing of the past!" He was beside himself with the pleasure of his announcement.

The Don, who was not the *capomafia* for nothing, contained himself as if nothing had disrupted his composure.

"To whom are we indebted for such a service?" he asked with slow, measured words.

"But, of course, you must know? The FSB! They stalked him for a long time. Colonel Cala set the trap, Captain Franchina snared him, just as he always said he would. . . ."

"That's the *official* story?" The Don's deadly voice clearly transmitted foreboding.

Chief Zanorelli tensed. It wasn't the question that made him hesitate but the Don's cool, matter-of-fact tone. "*Mah*—sure. Sure it's official. No?"

"*Va bene, grazie*," muttered the Don as he hung up.

Startled by the curt dismissal and confused by the Don's attitude, the chief inspector was too cowardly to ring back and inquire why he should have been treated with such apparent lack of respect.

On the backside of the golden mountains, southwest of Palermo, in the village of Montegatta, Antigone Naxos Salvatore glanced up, wondering at the blatant invasion of her privacy. She sat in her garden, straining fresh tomato paste on bamboo trays. Two uniformed *carabinieri* had entered the rear terrace from a side entrance; two more had entered her house, strode boldly through it, and emerged at the rear door to join their companions.

Curtly, with no effort to disguise the triumph in their voices, they requested her presence in Castelvetrano to officially identify "the dead body of your son." Just like that! Without preamble, they had addressed themselves to her with skilled impertinence.

Hah! What will they think to do next, she wondered, watching them through hate-filled and contemptuous eyes. She told herself to be strong and defiant against these enemies. Inside her a small voice prayed, *it couldn't be true. Dear, sainted God, let it be a lie.* This was just another deception in a long line of lies and deceptions heaped upon her by these black-hearted mercenaries. She steeled herself against the bamboo frames on the wooden bench under the fig tree, pushed aside a few wisps of gray hair, blinked her pecan-brown eyes, and wiped her hands on the tomato-splattered apron.

She raised her eyes to meet the eyes of the spokesman, a young man about the same age as her son, hoping to read the truth in them. She saw only the official coldness of a man doing his duty.

"All I've been ordered to do is escort you to Castelvetrano to make the official identification," he told her without apology.

Ten minutes later, she had washed, changed into a black cotton shift, combed her hair, and draped a black mourning veil over her head. She picked up her rosary beads, a fresh white *fazzoletto*, and walked downstairs, hoping to disguise the sinking feeling at the pit of her

21

stomach. Just to prove them wrong, she had capitulated, condescended to make the trip. Just to show them.

Outside her front door, Antigone noted with alarm the gathering of sober-faced villagers who watched with mixed emotions as she entered the car. She reconsidered the situation with trepidation. News had an uncanny way of reaching interior villages with frightening accuracy, before the official news was aired. In that instant she felt her world disintegrate. If only Athena hadn't departed. Or her son-in-law, Santino Siragusa. Even Vincenzo. Where was Vincenzo? Surely her nephew would know what had happened to her son.

Pausing only to pick up Antigone's personal physician who'd been treating her for a heart condition, the *carabinieri* hastily eased their car in a southerly direction toward Castelvetrano. Antigone's watch told her it was 10:45 A.M. Why, she asked herself, was she concerned with the time? Of what use was it to her anymore? Only that it would take approximately an hour or two to reach the southern village and learn this was just another hoax. *It has to be,* she kept telling herself, trying to keep calm. *Tori must be in Brazil—or America by now. Dear God—isn't he?* Her mind was afflicted with a whirlwind of memories of the past seven years as they drove down off the mountains.

•

Vincenzo de Montana took a mid-morning shower in a luxurious marbled bath at the Calemi villa. Rubbing his hard, lean body vigorously with an oversized bath towel, the handsome, dark-haired young man of twenty-nine years reentered the sumptuous bedroom, toweling his curly black hair and glancing casually at the naked brunette lying on the bed.

He had tired of her. After four days he could barely stand the sight of her. She had served her purpose and, while it lasted, had been most accommodating. He felt able to face the ordeal of the coming weeks without his cousin Tori Salvatore. Thoughts of Maria Angelica Candela, a flaxen-haired girl with emerald-green eyes and a voluptuous body, whom he once intended to marry, stirred him into asking himself what the fuck he was doing, here, with this whore.

At the sound of his footsteps, the whore opened one eye, then the other. She fanned her long black hair over her olive-skinned shoulders and smiled invitingly at him. She snaked seductively across the wide bed, transmitting sexual and erotic thoughts to him. Vincenzo forced an artificial smile, barely tolerating her presence. Oh, what the

22

hell! In a pinch she hadn't been bad. Hadn't she satisfied his prurient longings? Why take out his frustrations on her, eh? She was only earning a living. All in all, if you discounted the dullness of perception brought on by the wine, in whose lights the whores of Lucifer would be appealing, she'd been pretty exciting.

What irked Vincenzo was the white powder she sniffed periodically. She had insisted it was balm for her hay fever. Fucking bitch! Did she think him a jackass, still suckling his mother's breasts? Her reaction to the powder was too immediate, too erotic, and for Vincenzo, a blow to his manhood. That a woman, any woman, might resort to stimulants to cope with his virility was shattering to his *maschiezzo*—his manliness. He recalled the effects of the powder had so inflamed her that within moments she became insatiable. His manhood taken into her hot, wet mouth began a series of wild and passionate responses in him; he could think of nothing else. In four days no thoughts of the outside world had penetrated his consciousness. Only the pyramiding excitement of her tongue, lips, and hands on his penis, inner thighs, and scrotum had pierced his awareness. Lost in this euphoric world, he'd thought of no one, not Maria Angelica or even his cousin Tori from whom he'd been inseparable for seven years.

Here at Calemi's villa where he temporarily hid from the world, he had truly been lost for a time. What the hell! She could—*hay fever*—him any time she wanted.

Yet, in the light of sobriety which always followed these sojourns, reality returned all too swiftly and with it came the agony of uncertainty. Wrapping the towel about his midriff, he moved across to the nightstand and reached for a cigarette. What the hell day was this? July 4? No, it was the fifth. He nodded to himself in reflection. Tori must be in Brazil by now. Or was it America? At the very last Tori hadn't been able to confide in Vincenzo except to say he'd be in touch with him. *Managghia!* Vincenzo looked for a match and thought, *I should have gone with Tori. It was stupid to remain behind. What is there for me, here, without Tori?* He lit the cigarette and inhaled deeply. He sat on the bed and lay back on the pillows.

Before he realized what was happening, the whore got to him again. At first he pushed her gently aside with a tolerant giggle. She persisted. As her hands caressed him, his insatiable flesh was aroused. He lay back without protest, listening to the soft romantic music coming from the the Palermo radio station. Well, damnit, why not? If it was up to Vincenzo, the whole world would be fucking every hour of every day. What else was there to do that was as pleasurable and worthwhile? He lay back contentedly, blowing smoke rings while the whore blew him.

Vincenzo swelled and grew harder, climbing higher and higher to that pinnacle of sweet forgetfulness. At that crucial moment, just before he began skydiving through fleecy clouds and came crashing to earth, the frenzied voice of Peppino Orafisso cut through the music to announce: *"People of Sicily! . . . Salvatore is dead! Salvatore, King of Montegatta, is dead! . . . Long live Salvatore!"*

Vincenzo's heart stopped. Wild-eyed and frenzied, he tried to swim through the euphoria. He cocked his head and strained to listen. Withdrawing from the whore, his manhood "plopped" out from between her lips like a soggy *cannolo*. He flung her from him roughly, sprang from the bed, and moved heavily across the floor to raise the radio's volume. Against the pouting protests of the slim-hipped prostitute, he listened with every nerve fiber in his mind, body, and soul.

". . . According to Minister Martino Belasci, the battle waged against Salvatore terminated before dawn in a bloody coup in which the Forces to Suppress Banditry emerged victorious. Salvatore is dead! Long live Salvatore!"

Vincenzo nervously pulled on his trousers, dug into his pockets, and peeled off a thick stack of lire from a healthy roll of bills. Stuffing them into the whore's hands, he told her to get lost. He'd learned never to disclose his true identity to such women. Always in the back of his mind lay the outside chance she could be a spy. He walked her to the door after she dressed, locked it behind her, and watched her drive off with her pimp who'd been waiting that morning for God knows how long. Giving them no further thought, he rushed back upstairs and listened as a newscaster described the capture of his cousin Salvatore.

He paced the floor, chain-smoked, wrung his hands, and slapped his thighs in nervous frustration until he was a total physical and emotional wreck. *Another trap,* he told himself. *Bastards! They'll try anything.* There was only one thing for him to do: beat it the hell out of there. He tossed a few articles into a duffle bag, and running downstairs into the butter rooms, he packed a few provisions and flung everything into the back seat of a dusty black Alfa Romeo parked in the courtyard. After a few bad moments in which the motor failed to turn over, it finally resounded with life. Breathing easier, Vincenzo kicked it

24

into gear, uncertain of his destination and headed away from Calemi's villa.

If it was true that Tori had been caught, he, Vincenzo, would be next. As cocaptain and second in command, he knew as much as Salvatore knew. *Think carefully. Plan your moves meticulously, step by step, until you hear from Tori or receive confirmation of his death.*

His enemies could be everywhere; at the moment he was uncertain as to just how many were involved. Past the Saracen Fort was another road off the coastal highway that few knew about. Vincenzo's decision to take this route away from Calemi Villa hadn't been made a moment too soon. Only a short distance from the villa, he noticed four squads of heavily armed security police pulling into the courtyard.

Very well, he thought, already he had been betrayed, just as Salvatore was betrayed. Only this time he had the jump on them. Accelerating quickly, he headed for the only place he could think of that might be safe: a deserted shambles of a Romanesque villa where Tori, Maria Angelica, and he had played as children. It had later been converted into a radio shack where the bandits had housed radio equipment for the past several years.

He almost missed the turn-off to the old villa, pondering what his Aunt Antigone might be thinking at such a time. What would she do? She had no one left. Guilt feelings took a stranglehold on him. How in God's name could he go to her without jeopardizing his own safety? There must be an all-out alert for him. The FSB had captured every other member of Tori's soldiers, hadn't they? The battery-operated portable radio on the car seat beside him squawked loudly with static interference, bringing him out of his reverie.

Fifteen minutes later, Vincenzo arrived at the old hide-out and hid the car under straw matting in the old stable. As he walked toward the villa, mental images of Maria Angelica and his cousin Tori came at him, but he shoved them neatly aside until his plans for survival were intact.

Thoughts that these radio announcements might be a trap to flush him out into the open were uppermost in his mind, especially when he considered the many amateurish and fraudulent schemes they'd been subjected to over the past few years. Vincenzo shook his head in a gesture of frustration and ran his fingers through his curly crop of hair as he tried to collect his thoughts. Something vaguely familiar played hide-and-seek in his mind. He walked past the rear entrance of the villa and skirted along the time-

25

eroded stone steps to the wildly overgrown and weeded area alongside the building. Gazing about, he finally located the entrance to a storage cellar beneath a layer of straw. He grinned with relief.

Goddamnit! That cousin of his was some man! He'd thought of everything! Stored in the cellar were enough provisions to last him a year. Tori had even thought to store fresh water! Vincenzo's spirits soared even higher when he located a cache of weapons and ammunition. If he'd uncovered a gold mine, he couldn't have been happier. And there was wine!

Moving cautiously about the shadowy interior, he sorted out a few tins of sardines, tuna fish, olives, artichokes, and other tasty morsels. Slinging an automatic rifle over each shoulder, he shoved two pistols into his belt, stuffed a few rounds of ammo into his shirt and several boxes of cartridges into his pockets. Then, gathering two blankets and a few candle tapers, he climbed the steps to daylight.

Depositing his booty inside the villa, he returned to secure and camouflage the cellar doors. Shading his eyes with his hands, he glanced cautiously about the area. No one could approach the villa without being spotted for a distance of at least 300 yards. What he needed now was an old hound to act as a watchdog. He made a mental note to acquire a dog somehow and returned to the house.

As he moved about the shabby interior trying to make it more livable, he uncorked a bottle of wine and began sipping it. Why hadn't he thought of this place before? Several such places of refuge, complete with stored provisions, had been provided by Salvatore in the event of unexpected emergencies. If he kept his head, he could survive for as long as he desired, or until he determined to show himself. He guzzled more wine. Next, he had to locate Salvatore's personal portfolio. Once before, it had bought time for Salvatore. It might do more for Vincenzo.

Spreading some hay for a makeshift bed, he turned on the battery-operated radio and zeroed in on a station from which an emotionally overwrought announcer described the famed bandit's seven years of glory. His bloodshot eyes began to well up with tears as the realization that his cousin was truly dead hit him. His swollen face engorged with blood and hatred and the tears spilled in a storm. "Goddamn them!" he moaned to the four walls. "Tori did nothing but good for his people! I tried to tell him! I told him not to trust those crazy bastards, but he wouldn't listen! By God their hour will come!" he raged aloud.

Convinced that his own life was in jeopardy, he

promised himself to be more careful, more calculating than Tori had been. There were many matters to be considered. He'd bide his time. He would trust no one! Certainly he'd not be as forgiving as Tori had been. Not by a damn sight! He, Vincenzo de Montana, would show these whoring sons of unchaste mothers they weren't dealing with an ignorant peasant dog!

Vincenzo fell into a drunken sleep, dreaming of the tasty nectars of vengeance.

Former U.S.A. Captain Matt Saginor, red-haired, freckle-faced and presently downcast, sat slouched in his chair with his polished boots propped up on the gleaming conference table. His right hand hung loosely over the arm of the uncomfortable wooden chair, absently twirling a golden eagle key chain. His dark probing eyes searched Modica's face, noting how his friend had changed over the past few years.

Modica's silent temperament kept him apart from the others. But it hadn't always been that way. Saginor, a captain with Army Intelligence during WWII, recalled many occasions when Modica's temperament had been more volatile than that of the Sicilians they'd been associated with. When Saginor noticed the decided limp made by the prosthesis Stefano wore in place of his left leg, he realized the change in Modica these past five years was irrevocable.

"This is serious, Matt. Nothing in a year?" asked Modica.

"Man, we're up against a slick combine, Steve," began Saginor in his thick West Texas drawl. "It's like an octopus with a hundred tentacles. "I tell you, man, no one knows where the orders originate."

"They're more organized then Luciano's drug army," said Renzo Bellamo, a craggy-faced, tranquil man in his thirties, recently transferred from Narcotics. "Whoever's at the helm of this gold slick is a mastermind first class!"

Len Salina, a sandy-haired, green-eyed former Marine commando with bushy brows over innocent but discerning eyes, shook his head. "Damn, we've planted good men in various agencies where official government documents are produced. Still the forgeries mushroom. No one will talk. They say the same thing anyway—like a broken record. They don't know where the orders originate. The small fry take their graft—peanuts compared to what the men higher on the totem rake in—and all are damned grateful for the dough!"

Len Salina moved his heavy bulk across the room,

turned up the volume on the radio, and dialed in some low-keyed music; it had been customary procedure since a microphone had been discovered hidden in the eyes of a golden eagle in the U.S. Seal hung decorously in one of the conference rooms at the Embassy.

"You can't believe how smooth things are run, Colonel. Too fuckin' smooth! There's not a rupture in the link, and I've tried finding a weak spot for nearly two years!"

Modica nodded mechanically. His watch read 11 A.M. He'd give it a few more minutes and then he'd wind it down to a lunch break. He had to make some excuses for not lunching with any of them today. Then, around 2 P.M., just before he boarded the Alitalia plane he would call Saginor and make some excuse to postpone their business until tomorrow. Tomorrow—well, he'd give that some thought after he had Salvatore safely out of Sicily.

He glanced at the men carefully. He knew them well and had recommended them for Project ORS. They were excellent. Top men in their fields. Tall, with athletic builds and crew cuts, all three agents were incessant gum-chewing, cigarette-smoking addicts who boozed a lot, loved a lot, and lived dangerously.

Modica, a handsome, well-tanned man with a touch of gray at the temples, looked much younger than his forty years. His startling azure-blue eyes dramatized his features vividly. A reserved intensity about him created a dynamic and forceful picture of a man who usually got what he went after. Once you met him you'd never forget him.

Saginor removed his boots from the desk, rose to his feet, stretched, and addressed himself to Modica. "From the moment orders for Cold War supplies are placed by Italian firms, everything follows strict procedure. Things grow uncontrollable when the materials arrive in port. To begin with, the country has too many rules, too many licensing procedures, and a crockful of senseless paper work that stretches to infinity. Just to secure a lousy permit! Add to our dilemma, poorly paid government employees who accept bribes as a matter of course to augment their shoddy incomes. For a lousy buck, they'll falsify, or sell, import and export permits, manipulate or ignore regulations—and we can't pinpoint any one of them. Men involved in narcotics traffic abandoned their work when they learned they could profit more by arranging for the false documentation of Cold War commodities behind the Iron Curtain."

Len Salina poured bourbon into his coffee cup from a slim silver flask. "Ever since America began pouring bil-

28

lions in economic aid into Europe, the racket has flourished," he told Modica. "Despite international agreements made by these companies to use the materials here, the practice persists. Incidentally, these same companies emphatically deny communist leanings."

Modica glanced uneasily at his watch. He had to wrap this up if he hoped to make connections to Palermo. Before he could bring the meeting to a conclusion, Saginor intervened.

"Man, just take a look at our inquiries. They're in the reports. We've conferred with the Embassy every step of the way. They pretend to be ignorant of the goings-on. 'No, no, no, no,' they tell us. To their knowledge there's been no infraction of agreements. Washington plays mute on laws governing foreign shipments. No one seems to give a coyote's hoot about what's happening. Isn't that a bust in the balls? It's a real *mishegass!* That the raw uranium moving into communist countries might one day be dropped on their heads as bombs doesn't disturb these larcenous and highly respected businessmen." Saginor's Texas accent thickened.

"Gotta admit to top cooperation from Belasci's office," said Renzo. He lit a cigar and grimaced. "Fuckin' cigars taste like camel dung."

Modica had listened intently. *Martino Belasci, Minister of the Interior.* He wrote the name and underlined it heavily with his pen. He clearly recalled the dapper, highly ambitious politician who had sat on the Palermo Grand Council with him in April 1945 and who had left to accept a position with Premier de Aspanu's government. He glanced at his watch. Just a few more minutes, he told himself.

Suddenly, something in the file caught his eye. A list of names, prominent men reportedly involved in this scheme to defraud the United States. The names of several Middle Eastern potentates—men who'd been driven from their palaces due to their immoral regimes—stood out. Learning these men were involved in such a corrupt affair incensed Modica: they were still receiving aid from both the State and Defense Departments! He read further, scanning the names of Greek shipping tycoons, French industrialists, and Italian diplomats. When he came across the names of two high-ranking American officials occupying two of the most important offices in the land, he gazed at Saginor with total disbelief in his eyes.

"You don't mean to tell me—" began Modica. He never got to finish his statement. At that precise moment, the music from the radio was interrupted by a special bulletin. The excited voice of a radio announcer, Peppino Orafisso, sliced through their conversation.

"People of Italy! . . . People of Sicily! . . . Hear this! Salvatore is dead! . . . I repeat, Alessandro Salvatore is dead! The King of Montegatta is dead! Long live Salvatore!"

His attention commanded instantly, Modica felt a chill sweep through him. He held up a restraining hand, gesturing for silence. He listened to each and every word as if it were a knife stab to his guts. The announcer's voice, tremulous and filled with emotion, continued:

". . . This morning, in the darkest hours of night, just before the dawn when fiendish demons prowl about the shadows and take earthly form, the Forces To Suppress Banditry encountered Salvatore. In a lengthy gun fight in which thousands of rounds of ammunition were expended, Salvatore fought valiantly against the hundreds of well-armed soldiers deployed against him. Finally felled and shot to death, his body riddled with bullets, he now lies in state at Castelvetrano. . . ."

Stefano Modica turned deathly white. His hands shook as he tried to light a cigarette.

"They got him!" Matt Saginor, listening intently, jumped to his feet. "The bastards finally got him! Damn!" he exclaimed. "I remember like it was only yesterday . . . newsmen from all over the world crammed into my office, demanding special passes to interview this Sicilian phenomenon! What a man!" Flushed with a curious exuberance, Saginor turned from the radio and caught sight of Stefano Modica's face. Noting the tight-lipped grimness, excessive paleness, the total incomprehension and shock etched into his features, he lowered his voice. "That's right, you knew him well, didn't you? Didn't Gina—" Saginor caught himself. He didn't complete the question, knowing it was a touchy subject with Modica. He just didn't know *how* touchy.

Bellomo's and Salina's interest piqued at the look of anguish on Modica's face as he nodded numbly and busied himself lighting a cigarette. Anything to keep from talking. Several moments passed before he was able to mutter, "I planned on flying to Palermo to renew our acquaintance this afternoon." He spoke economically, careful not to reveal his true intentions. Modica was crushed. He could feel his heart start up again as a series of mental images rushed at him.

The first time he had encountered Salvatore, at Allied

Command Headquarters in Palermo had been when the lad was twenty-three years old. Even at that age, Modica had recognized the greatness in him. Salvatore had exuded a compelling charisma, a peculiar naïveté, strong ethnic charm, and the most engaging smile he'd ever seen on a young man. This phenomenon, Salvatore, had risen out of the litter and rubble of a war-torn country to dominate the minds and imaginations of millions of people. In a land where bandits were held cheap and where thousands like him had passed unknown, unheralded, into obscurity, Salvatore had emerged a tremendously powerful man whose deeds would be recorded in Sicily's history.

In an unguarded moment, Modica muttered to himself, yet loud enough for the others to hear. "But why? Why now at this moment? Why, after all these years?" These were questions he hadn't intended for other ears.

His words drew surprised glances from the other three agents. Modica's background in politics and intelligence work precluded the asking of such unsophisticated questions. If anyone knew about the abrasive cunning and manipulative tactics employed in political coups, it was Stefano Modica.

Sensing his anguish, Renzo Bellomo said quietly, "Salvatore's been involved in political intrigue over his head for at least two years now—no, three. He's no match for that barracuda Belasci."

"You forgot to include the Mafia," said Renzo.

Modica glanced sharply at him, checked the impulse to say something, then busied himself collecting the papers spread before him. He shoved them inside the manila folder. God, he was numb from all this.

"You want to fly to Castelvetrano to see what's happening? Might be interesting to observe the end of a hero," suggested Bellomo.

That was all it took. Within the hour the Americans winged their way southward in a requisitioned U.S.A. army transport, never thinking their presence in the southern village would nearly cause an international incident.

Only when they were airborne did Colonel Modica realize he had inadvertently slipped the entire ORS file into his briefcase. About to mention this to the others, he changed his mind, telling himself he'd have to be careful with it and return it somehow.

31

CHAPTER 2

Castelvetrano, Sicily

Fifty miles south of Palermo, along the southwest shores of Sicily, shimmering Mediterranean waters wash up on the golden shores of Selinunte, where ancient empires once thrived and where Greek, Roman, and Carthaginian warriors who battled and died for the glory of their leaders now lie buried beneath the sands of time. Broken stones and a time-worn acropolis with pilasters and entablatures scattered on the ground covered with a mauve undergrowth are the only reminders of their existence. Temples erected to the worship of Venus and Apollo have long since disappeared; apathetic generations have permitted the area to become commonplace, a trap for tourists.

A little to the north of this oriental bazaar atmosphere of Selinunte lies Castelvetrano, a village that reeks of Arab ancestry and upon which has been applied a garish twentieth-century cosmetic to give the illusion that it belongs to modern day. Encouraged by the influx of tourists following the war, city fathers had built hotels and encouraged other accomodating businesses, but they were in no way prepared for the demands placed upon the town when, on July 5, the natives awakened to find the town's dull and monotonous routine interrupted. Long lines of traffic assaulted the desert oasis which was swollen beyond its capacity by international journalists, government officials, FSB brass, newly deputized recruits, and wide-eyed tourists. The middle-class village was baffled and conversely filled with dread when rumors spread that their village had been labeled *"Judastown."*

The American agents found disorganized chaos in that shabby, dried-up courtyard at numero 54, Strada Sarina Madonna. More than 300 people had jammed the narrow street, packed tighter than sheep in a branding corral. Renzo Bellomo dismissed the driver of their rented and immobilized Fiat a block away and the foursome snaked their way through the crowds to their destination. From the moment they were spotted, their presence brought immediate reaction from the Sicilians who parted the crowds

32

to make room for them. Their towering bulk and imposing features precluded the anonymity they had hoped for and gave rise to rumors that American retaliation for Salvatore's death was imminent.

Much to the Americans' amazement, it became an easy matter for them to enter the well-guarded courtyard without identification. Their presence was accepted as procedural protocol and, for reasons unknown to them, was acknowledged by snappy salutes from the posted guards who restrained others and permitted them entrance. Not about to press their luck, they moved to the left of the courtyard and stood quietly along the wall of the de Meo house, observing the activities of the incompetent investigators, keeping their thoughts to themselves, and watching the busy activity around them.

Modica, staring interminably at the body of the dead man, meticulously searching it for some identifying clue. The face was concealed by dust and caked blood was splattered all over the body. The corpse could be anyone. Damn! Why hadn't he considered this before? The thought gave rise to hope. Was it possible this *wasn't* Salvatore? Had he been so caught up in the news broadcast and what the others had said about Salvatore that he had accepted the death as gospel? He knew better! Christ! He wasn't this naïve! Yet ...

His eyes traveled to the faces of the somber men and women pressing in and about the crowded street, hoping to read the truth in their eyes. What he saw stirred his guts and filled him with foreboding and a sickening sensation.

Procurator General Maggio and his staff of investigators moved about with the clumsy theatrics of a neophyte disaster squad, taking endless measurements of the body. They inventoried everything in sight and huddled continuously over one apparent incongruity after another. Photographers had climbed the rear and front walls of the courtyard and balanced themselves precariously near the stone archway, shooting pictures from all angles.

For better than a half-hour the Americans scanned the all too perfect setting in disgust. They didn't utter a sound. The silent messages contained in their eyes as they exchanged glances indicated their awareness of the obvious inconsistencies existing in the scene laid at their feet. Unable to contain either his professional curiosity or the question he felt compelled to ask, Matt Saginor addressed himself to the procurator.

"Has this body been moved since the fatal bullet was inflicted?"

33

Procurator-General Maggio, a small wiry man with a cadaverous face, turned abruptly to Saginor and, with black squinting eyes under knotted brows, he shook his head. "My report indicates this is the position in which the deceased fell when he expired." He turnẹd his back on the American.

Just as quickly Maggio reconsidered and once again turned to face the man of whose presence he'd been oblivious until the question had been posed. His bird eyes focused on Saginor, taking in the lightweight Brooks Brothers suit, the white shirt open at the neck, the rumpled red hair and inquisitive brown eyes. "Who are you?" he demanded to know. Blinking his eyes, he saw for the first time the three Americans lined up against the wall behind Saginor, intently absorbed in the goings-on.

Feigning wide-eyed innocence, Saginor glanced to either side of him and asked, "Who—me? I'm no one."

After a long hard look in which the procurator drew his own conclusions, he turned away from Saginor and harshly commanded his men to speed up their work. Periodically, however, Maggio would pause in his duties, glance uneasily at the Americans, and scowl darkly. No one had told him there might be American agents on the scene. He knew them all. Oh, not personally, but since the war he could smell foreign agents a lightyear away. He had had his fill of them when he had engaged in procommunist activities. *"Allesti te! Allesti te!"* he urged his men. "Hurry it up!" He liked less and less the expressions on the angry reporters around him.

Saginor sidled up to Modica, expressionless, and muttered without a glancing at him. "It's all wrong, Steve. All wrong. There's something too pat in this fucking mess."

Modica nodded. "Tell me."

"What do you make of that massive bloodstain, as contrasted with the darker, purplish blood dried up from the two bullet wounds below the left rib cage?" asked Matt Saginor.

Modica shook his head, unable to speak. There was something unreal, totally false in all this. Yet, weren't all his memories of Sicily the same? Everything done in this strange land of antiquity was exaggerated to a larger-than-life reflection, too theatrical. But this sham was too much. At this point, something sparkling brightly in a ray of sunlight caught Modica's eyes. Squinting, he moved closer to the body and caught sight of the familiar golden scorpion amulet. His heart stopped. In that split second he tried to shut out the possibility that it might indeed be Salvatore lying dead at his feet. Images rushed at him, vivid images of Salvatore on the day Colonel Modica had presented him with the golden scorpion amulet. They had said their farewells at the Temple of Cats. . . .

"*You honor me much too much,* Colonnello. *I don't deserve such a tribute,*" Salvatore had told him. "*I truly wish I could be the man you see pictured in your eyes.*"

"*But you are, my friend,*" Modica had told him. "*You are a very special person. You have within you the power to lead your people out of bondage. You are Sicily's only hope.*"

He could still see the flush of self-consciousness coupled with the ineffable delight on Salvatore's face when he received the golden scorpion. . . .

Modica opened his eyes now and discovered he had broken into a cold sweat. His fists were tightly clenched, his nails dug deeply into his palms. He felt terrible. Waves of guilt swept through him. He quickly lit a cigarette with shaking hands. He noticed Saginor on bended knees, touching the fresh blood with his fingertips. Renzo Bellomo moved in and did the same with the darker, caked blood. Both men exchanged noncommittal glances.

Noting the differences, they kept their thoughts to themselves. Too many discrepancies, they felt certain, but without tests they couldn't be sure. One thing was certain, they didn't believe the scene.

"Don't touch! Don't touch anything!" screamed the procurator.

Instantly the men jumped back. Every eye was on them.

It became obvious to Modica that Maggio had formed several conclusions that didn't coincide with the information given him by Captain Franchina. Bringing focus upon himself, Maggio was instantly besieged now with countless questions thrust at him by angry and impatient reporters whom he'd banned from the courtyard. Time and again he refused comment and, in so doing, found himself the subject of many sullen, uncomplimentary remarks. Hoping to silence the hungry tigers, he now declared for the third time, with a tone of finality, "I repeat, I'll make no comments until *after* the autopsy, and only after the FSB has released the official statement to you!" He then ordered the guards doubled at all exits.

Procurator-General Maggio sensed the Americans had discovered the jarring inconsistencies and he grew increasingly nervous. He cursed inwardly. Why hadn't someone found the means to bar *them* from the courtyard? They had no business here! From time to time he glowered at them, hoping they'd take the hint they weren't wanted. As angry as he was at their presence, his ire was more heatedly directed toward the FSB. Why hadn't they posted their own men on this detail? Fucking smart of them! To make Maggio's office accept full responsibility for problems arising from this mess! Disturbed by discoveries made on this day, Maggio had let his mounting tension so cloud his judgment that he had forgotten this was *his* jurisdiction. He had but to open his mouth to deny entrance to anyone—including the Americans.

Speculation at their presence intimidated him more than the recriminating thoughts of his own participation in this distasteful conspiracy. The rewards? His cooperation would wipe the slate clean of all former procommunist activities enabling him to seek office with the Christian Democrats. Even this reward dimmed, however, when he learned that Private Foti had been shot with bullets from Franchina's machine gun, not by the Luger purportedly carried by Salvatore. Would his fate be the same as Foti's, he wondered? The thought provoked a rush of activity as he lit a rocket under his men. *"Avanti! Avanti! Subito!"* he prodded.

A cry arose from the men outside the courtyard. "An impostor lies here! The FSB lies! They can say what they will, but we know better!"

In Viterbo, a few miles from Rome, the trial of the People vs. Assassins at Portella della Rosa, held before a tribunal of judges, was in session. Presidente Umberto Ginestra, an impressive, highly polished aristocrat and presiding judge of the tribunal, glanced wearily at the clock on the wall opposite him. It was 11 A.M. In a half-hour he'd adjourn for lunch.

The prosecutor, interrogating Arturo Scoletti, one of the fifty bandits being tried for the Portella Massacre, glanced up at the sight of a federal courier entering the courtroom. He saw the slim blond court clerk accept a sealed envelope, and, signaling the *presidente* for recognition, the clerk approached the bench. He handed the envelope to the presiding magistrate.

The magistrate, a man with snow white hair and icy blue eyes, glanced down his slender nose to read the contents. He blinked several times, nodded to the clerk to rap for order, and, beckoning to the battery of lawyers to approach the bench, huddled with them for several moments. The president, with traces of irony, spoke to them in undertones, as spectators expectantly leaned forward in their seats.

The court was packed with prosecution and defense lawyers, as well as countless other *avvocati* who represented the fifty bandits individually to insure against a conflict of interest. Startled by the news imparted to them, the *avvocati* returned to their seats evidencing a variety of emotions, all colored by client interest.

President Ginestra now addressed himself to the entire court and to the *galleria* of spectators, most of whom were loyal to Salvatore and his men. He raised his head, lifted his voice, and announced without preamble, "This court is recessed. The bandit Salvatore has been captured and slain by the Forces of Suppress Banditry."

A hush swept through the stately halls of justice as the tribunal magistrates arose in a body and marched in single file out the courtroom into chambers. Fifty of Salvatore's men, all former brigands, sat deathly still in the witness cages without expression. A spectator's voice arose in a frenzied cry, *"Viva Salvatore! Long live Salvatore!"*

Tough, hard-nosed, and cynical, the exbandits exchanged silent glances, wondering and speculating over this latest development. Hah! What next? So many lies! So many betrayals! Who among them could express faith in this comedic arena of injustice where scapegoats were needed to satisfy the blood-lusting thirst of highly immoral, yet influential government officials?

Lawyers approached their clients and solemnly apprised them of the veracity of the president's words. "Word came direct from the Minister of the Interior. It's official all right," they were told.

Glaring in black silence, the exbandits spat contemptuously at the mention of Martino Belasci's name.

Fifteen minutes later, back in their cells, the men sat hunched over in their seats, ears glued to their radios, listening attentively to the bias of special commentators, the sad laments of the mourners, and the arrogant sarcasm of the celebrants. A few of the former brigands exchanged thoughts through the bars of their cells. Before lights went out that night, they told themselves that before they would believe this fable, Salvatore himself would have to appear in the flesh to tell them he'd been killed.

In Castelvetrano, Sicily, one of the American agents, Renzo Bellomo, overpaid for a camera and film and busied himself taking photos of the courtyard scene. He covered all angles. At one point, he nudged Saginor, unable to contain his contempt.

"I'd like to meet the dummy who staged this production. Look at this. A cartridge case of a Breda machine gun lying next to a Beretta .38 submachine gun. Shee—it! It's clear to see the cantaloupe-head who set this up was seedless."

"Patience," replied Saginor, tongue in cheek. "Let's not jump to conclusions. Let's wait for the official report."

At 1:30 P.M. Procurator-General Maggio gave the order to remove the body to the mortuary for autopsy. Instantly the stretcher bearers moved forward.

"Let's go," called Saginor. "This I gotta hear!"

Like most combat officers, Modica had seen many deaths during the war, but none had left him with the mounting guilt he experienced when he saw the men place the dead man's body on the stretcher. He felt wretched. The guilt continued to rise overwhelmingly. If only he hadn't urged Salvatore ahead. If only he had done as Matt Saginor suggested. "Let the fucking Sicilians play the game their own way!" he had advised. Why had Stefano interfered? If only he hadn't attempted to bring Salvatore into the twentieth century before he was prepared to tackle its complexities, the man might be alive today. If only he had arrived a week sooner—even a day. . . .

Modica, relentless in his self-persecution, was unaware that he had moved out of the courtyard. Somehow he found himself in the Fiat with the others. He had learned to mask his emotions during the hell of war, and later, in the agony that came ironically at war's end when he lost a leg by accidentally stepping on a mine in Berlin, he had wondered why God had permitted the accident to occur. For a time he believed it had been his punishment for interfering in another man's life. Intelligent enough to know a man's truth is ultimately what he believes it to be, he was just emotional enough to believe he wasn't guiltless in this monstrous tragedy. Behind that expressionless mask, he punished himself every moment.

Moving at a snail's pace, hampered by crowds on foot and the traffic jam at either side of them, the Americans removed their jackets and loosened their neckties, hoping for some relief from the prostrating heat.

"Craziest damn scam I've ever seen! The whole thing's staged like some demoniacal scenario. Someone's gone to a helluva lot of trouble to confuse the world—or else the corpse got up and messed things up," said Renzo Bellomo, wiping the sweat pouring off his face and neck.

"I'll lay odds on the corpse," said Saginor brightly.

"The Salvatore I knew wouldn't have fallen into such an obvious trap," murmured Modica half to himself, as he lit a cigarette from Saginor's.

The black sedan, heavily talcumed with layers of dust, traveled at moderate speed as it coursed along the narrow road winding down off the long mountain range. Antigone Salvatore noted the widening of the landscape. In the distance she saw the vast sweep of Mediterranean waters, sparkling and rolling like corrugated glass, mirroring the sun's glare. As stifling heat came at her, she stirred the air about her with a sweat-soaked *fazzoletto*. One hand speedily fingered her rosary beads. *Let them be wrong, dear God. Let them. It won't be Tori. I know.*

The mortuary at the Camposanto was overrun with disgruntled and morose members of the press, who cursed and damned the numerous delays. For a time the Americans cursed with them. Periodically a *carabiniero* appeared at the ornately grilled iron gates to issue bulletins. Entrance to the morgue had been denied them until the grubby little man they'd seen entering earlier had completed taking a death mask for the Palermo Criminal Museum. A variety of colorful expletives, articulated acridly by crusty press correspondents, echoed through the halls in a steady drone of dissatisfaction.

Irritated by the numerous delays and the conspicuous absence of the FSB officials, who they were told were being feted at a victory banquet held in their honor, Renzo Bellomo, who earlier advised his companions to underplay their presence, pressed them forward. "C'mon, let's use a little diplomatic clout!" He glided toward the khaki-clad *carabinieri* guards, flourished his ID, and beckoned to his companions.

"We'll be kicked out on our asses," said Len Salina.

Modica plowed on through, followed by Saginor and Salina, while Renzo Bellomo's voice bowled over the impressionable military police. Bowing respectfully, the *carabinieri* escorted them into the morgue, leaving behind an indignant horde of newsmen grumbling antagonistically over the preferential treatment accorded the foursome.

When the *carabinieri* returned to their posts, they were deluged with queries. Their lips, sealed until several dollars changed hands, mouthed a simple statement: "American agents with the State Department."

Their suspicions confirmed, the newsmen put two and

39

two together and came up with a highly explosive theory. A much-publicized letter written by Salvatore to President Truman, which had recently found its way into print in the communist press, was thoroughly discussed, and the reporters concluded there was some truth to the story of America's intention to support Salvatore in his anticommunist fight, after all. The story grew more explosive by the moment. Salvatore backed by the U.S.A.? When had the intrigue begun?

Inside, cool halls of marble lowered the temperature by several degrees. High-vaulted ceilings and *terrazzo* floors amplified sounds like an echo chamber. Under a concentration of spotlights, rigged like those in a surgical amphitheater, the nude corpse lay upon an oval slab of marble. The maskmaker, having completed his task, brushed away flecks of plaster from the deceased's hairline. The Americans approached the catafalque solemnly.

"My God! He was so young," whispered Bellomo.

"It *is* Salvatore, *isn't* it?" Saginor asked Modica. "They must be certain if they employed the services of a maskmaker."

Modica's hope sank. Saginor was right. "I'm not certain. It's been five years—longer than I thought. I never saw him in this position—" His sad eyes compulsively locked on the body. Five years *was* a long time. It was a crazy, wild affinity he felt with Salvatore, even with the dead body before him. From the first, there had been this same magnetism between them, an intangible, mysterious, and compelling force.

Reporters, finally admitted, swarmed like locusts and descended upon the raised dais without dignity. Light bulbs popped; cameras clicked with nerve-wracking monotony—without let up. Suddenly, without warning, the cavernous room became deathly still, as if the room's occupants realized they were in the presence of greatness. The youth of the dead man distorted the preconceived images of veteran reporters, who found it inconsistent with the reported ferocity of the highly lauded rebel whom most had written about but had never met. Recent reports of Salvatore had characterized him as a savage and ruthless murderer. Seeing him so young and handsome, bigger in death than in life, colored their reaction.

The Minister of the Interior's office had carefully spoon-fed them a sharply-defined prototype of a criminal. His terrifying and lawless nature had been grossly exaggerated, and this deception staggered them. Where was the Pancho Villa in him? How did he resemble Dillinger?

Which qualities could be likened to Al Capone's, they asked themselves? None of the hard-boiled correspondents who stood looking at the body in the cool marble room could hide their compassion or shock at the inexplicable tragedy. Irreconcilable contrasts made them study the body with microscopic intensity.

Attendants turned the body over and everyone saw that the right shoulder, from which the blood had seemed to flow endlessly, was devoid of injury. Not even a scratch could be found! A shocked hush swept through the room. They were ordered to stand back from the oval slab as attendants, under Dr. Alba's instructions, brought in large quantities of ice and began to pack the body. The coroner, a large-framed man noticeably intimidated by the hordes of newsmen, kept blinking at the persevering reporters, as if he didn't even see them. As they looked to the efficient man, who nervously cracked his knuckles as he directed his men, he seemed to sense what they were thinking and wanted no part of the questions he knew were coming. He was certain they'd pick up the flagrant inconsistencies—and he was right.

"Why all the need for ice," asked one reporter, "if, as the official report says, the corpse has been dead for less than twelve hours?"

Dr. Alba wiped beads of perspiration from his bald pate and deferred to the FSB officials. And when they persisted and asked why the blood seemed varying shades of red in the various wounds, Dr. Alba blinked his nervous eyes and ignored them. He waved all other questions aside.

While reporters harassed Dr. Alba, Modica sauntered by the table where the personal effects of the corpse lay with identifying tags. He studied the solid gold belt buckle with the Eagle and the Lion of which many ballads had been written. His eyes fixed on the golden scorpion amulet. His face flushed red with guilt. Sinking feelings churned his stomach. Picking it up, Modica turned it over in his trembling palms and read the familiar inscription: *"To Salvatore: May the King of Montegatta rule Sicily wisely— Colonel Stefano Modica U.S.A. 4-12-45."*

Stefano turned to the body on the slab, sighed heavily, and closed his eyes. His hand clutched the scorpion tightly. When he reopened his eyes, he stared into the dispassionate, suspicious eyes of a *carabiniero,* who motioned to his clenched fist. Modica smiled weakly, opened his fist, and replaced the amulet. "Just looking," he said huskily.

At 2:30 P.M. Antigone Salvatore arrived at the mortuary only to be told with blistering candor that she couldn't enter the premises until Colonel Cala and Captain Franchina arrived from the victory banquet held in their honor for the killing of her son. It was the first of many humiliations this iron-willed matriarch would endure on this scorching hot day of bitter trauma.

Cameras, thrust into her face, clicked incessantly. Reporters anxious to solve the riddle of her son's death tugged and pulled cruelly at her for a statement. Bewildered and revolted by their brashness, she shied from them. The nightmare wouldn't cease. She tried to shut out the cyclopean lenses and retard the predatory swarm of vultures who posed threats to her existence. Nothing eased her heartache, and her vulnerability frightened her.

She felt pushed to the edge, hardly able to breathe. The smell of death's putrefaction was all around her; the unbearable odor of unclean, sweaty humans, nauseating cigar smoke, the malodorous stench of dead chrysanthemums from nearby waste receptacles wafted toward her sensitive nostrils and sickened her. Overhead in the tall, black cypress, branches bent with clusters of noisy cicadas protested the intrusion of strange humans upon their routine siesta. In the distance, Antigone saw the North African waters like a thin strip of glass drawing her hypnotically. She closed her eyes and retreated to safety behind the wall of her eyelids, away from all that threatened.

If it's true my son is dead, I am truly alone. . . . Take courage, she told herself. *Don't let anyone see you crumble. These vultures wait only to gloat when you disintegrate. Don't share your tears with anyone. . . .*

"Please take those cameras away," she pleaded. "They distress me." *It's so hot. I feel dizzy, sick to my stomach. Dear God, don't let it be my son in there. Not my last child.*

"No cameras, please." She raised her hands to shield her burning, swollen eyes.

The sea of faces melted into many more, none fully distinguishable to her. Antigone felt herself slipping into a pit of terrifying uncertainty. Everything became a blur.

She felt strong arms at either side of her in a firm grip. Through fluttering eyelids, she glanced into the faces of two strangers, and suddenly felt both frightened and safe with them. But the blinding lights of popping flashbulbs didn't cease. The vultures swarmed closer and closer.

"Steady, *Signora,*" instructed the steady voice of Stefano Modica. "We'll get you out of this den of *animales.* Don't be frightened. We're friends of your son, Alessandro," he told her in well-schooled Italian.

Bellomo and Salina ran interference for them as Modica and Saginor, flanking Signora Salvatore, made for Dr. Alba's office. *"Fermate!* Stop!" shouted a guard. "Where the hell you going?" he asked in broken English. The *carabiniero's* rifle barred their entrance, until Bellomo and Salina shoved ID's under his nose.

"Go ahead, Colonel. We'll take care of this," snapped Bellomo in an authoritative voice.

Modica and Saginor propelled Antigone Salvatore through the iron gate and disappeared inside the open office where they helped her to a chair. She sank into it gratefully and studied them with questioning eyes.

"I can't thank you enough for rescuing me from those cretins. It took courage to brave that crowd. . . ." She lifted her wide brown eyes. "Is it really my son?" she asked softly of Modica.

"Only you can answer that, *Signora.* You must identify the body."

An enigmatic smile formed on her lips. "By now, my son is in Brazil, perhaps America. He'll laugh at the absurdity of these rumors. You'll see. He warned me something like this would happen. That I should be prepared. It's just that it came too soon. . . ." Her eyes glittered with anemic hope. "You'll see." Her breathing grew labored.

"Signora, are you all right?" Modica studied her intently.

"I tell you it's not him." She glanced from Modica to Saginor, wild-eyed. "But if I say it's him, identify the body as that of my son, they would stop hunting him down like an animal—wouldn't they?"

Saginor's eyes found Modica's. A trace of alarm flashed. "I'd better find her a physician. . . ." Leaning close to Modica, Saginor whispered, "She wouldn't do that, would she?" Modica shrugged and indicated he should find a doctor.

"I'm all right now," said Antigone, taking several deep breaths. A sudden Sicilian wariness crept into her eyes. She searched Modica's eyes for some sign of recognition. She felt certain she had seen him before.

"You said you are friend to my son, Tori?"

"Colonnello Modica. Stefano Modica. I was here during the war."

"Colonnello Modica?" She paled with excitement. *"Santo Dio,* you came, *Colonnello!"* She clapped her

43

hands together. "My son loves you like a brother. He talks of you always."

Concerned both by her peculiar choice of words and the possibility they might have been overheard, Modica gazed anxiously about the room. "I couldn't return at war's end to keep my promise to him. An accident—you see, I lost a leg." He waved his hands in the air aimlessly.

Out of curiosity, Antigone's eyes darted to his legs. A flush swept over her face, as she apologized for her rudeness and waved her hands in the air in a gesture of futility. As things jelled in her mind, she gave him an odd look. "But what are you doing here if you are supposed to be with Tori—"

Stefano, distressed by her abrupt question, frowned noticeably. "You know about that?" His voice was barely above a whisper.

She nodded. "Last year I confided my concern for Tori to a mutual friend. She wrote me months ago assuring me my deepest prayers would be answered the beginning of July. When you identified yourself, I assumed you were the man of whom Gina spoke."

Modica frowned again. "*Signora*," he began, "it's important that you do not speak of this—" The look in Antigone's eyes arrested him. She wasn't listening to a word he spoke. He followed her line of vision.

Beyond him on the large desk, Antigone saw for the first time, several articles of clothing; a pair of beige Levi's, brown sandals, a beige rucksack, and the other items recovered in the courtyard on Strada Sarina Madonna. Her body sagged heavily forward and her fingers groped for her rosary beads tremblingly.

"Steady, *signora*," said Stefano Modica in a hoarse voice. "Take courage. Take courage."

"Who the hell are you to disrupt our order of things?" bellowed Captain Franchina, directing his arrogance at Modica and Saginor.

The FSB officers burst into the room, followed by the sunken-faced procurator general, like ostriches hot in the pursuit of battle. Before either Modica or Saginor could respond, Captain Franchina addressed his anger at Signora Salvatore.

"—And who permitted you entrance to these chambers?"

Grossly offended by Franchina's manners and lack of taste at such a time, Modica, no slouch in handling these popinjays, leveled his blue eyes on the bombastic officer and asked icily, "And—just who are you?"

Watching Captain Franchina's discomfort, Antigone flushed with inner satisfaction, her memory vivid at their last encounter. She was certain Franchina hated her as much as he hated her son Tori.

Captain Franchina lost no time in introducing himself and his superior officer, Colonel Cala, to the Americans. He made certain that he explained with emphasis that Procurator-General Maggio was in charge of the investigation. These formalities over, he demanded imperiously, "Just who the hell are you and why are you here?"

Saginor moved swiftly. Bellomo and Salina had followed the uniformed peacocks into the room; now they all brandished their ID's. Saginor took the position of responding to Captain Franchina's queries himself, indicating they were Special U.S. agents on a security assignment in Rome. Then, with dashing aplomb, he introduced Modica to the anti-bandit detail's officers. In view of Franchina's pomposity, Saginor gave the introduction more importance than needed. "You may recall Colonel Modica was stationed in Palermo during the war," he began. "He was with the Allied Control Council—advisor to the Palermo Grand Council, wasn't it, sir?" He winked covertly at Modica.

Stefano merely glanced cooly at the officers, only the shadow of a nod coming from him.

The name struck Captain Franchina instantly. Flushing slightly, he conferred with Colonel Cala for several moments. The FSB chief listened with overt politeness, his blue eyes fixed on the cigar rolling between his tobacco-stained fingers.

"Consider us at your disposal, Colonel Modica. Accept my profound apologies for keeping you waiting." Cala, far more experienced in such matters, appeared overly cautious. He was uncertain of his position in this case. The presence of American agents in Castelvertrano intimidated him. He recalled vividly the headlines in the Communist press alluding to an American alliance with the anti-communist, Salvatore. Damn! What complications! He made a mental note to get to Minister Belasci in a hurry.

Modica, snuffing out his cigarette in a nearby ashtray, replied tactfully, "This is your case, Colonel. Your territory. Your country. Consider us merely as observers."

By minimizing the Americans' importance and their interest in the matter, Modica had unwittingly caused the FSB to interpret their presence on the scene as indicative of a subversive foreign plot. Prone to exaggerate their own importance at times, Italians, he knew, tended to assume

45

foreigners would do likewise. In this case, foreign agents understating their position meant only one thing to the Italians—a cauldron of trouble.

Modica suggested to them that they see *Signora* Salvatore who, he stressed, shouldn't be kept waiting and put through intolerable and agonizing delays. This brought an immediate reaction from Captain Franchina. His face swelled to a livid purple hue as he angrily ground out his cigar. He had no recourse but to do his superior officer's bidding as Colonel Cala nodded to him. Franchina, in turn, gave the nod to Procurator-General Maggio.

"You heard the *Colonnello*. Proceed with the *Signora*."

Colonel Cala's face twisted with worry lines. Why else would the Americans arrive so swiftly on the scene if America weren't in some sinister way involved with Salvatore? If their presence didn't justify rumors of an alliance, he didn't know what did. Dammit! Why should destiny complicate matters, now that Salvatore was dead and no longer mattered? Why hadn't Minister Belasci briefed him thoroughly in this matter? These, plus countless other questions, remained unanswered in his mind. By damn, he'd get answers someplace, he promised himself.

CHAPTER 3

Antigone's dark eyes were fixed upon the body as it lay in deep repose on the oval catafalque. His features, as handsome in death as in life, appeared more relaxed, as if he were finally at peace. The accumulated bitterness of recent months was gone—erased as if it never existed on his face. In that instant, Antigone's body swayed and trembled, as a tremor shot through her; she felt herself crumble. She could hear his sweet voice, just as he had called to her in the past, *"Mamma bedda. Mamma bedda."* She closed her eyes for a moment and saw in her mind's eye an array of faces superimposed over those of Tori's. Filippo and Marco, handsome in their new soldiers' uniforms, appeared in her vision along with Athena's beautiful face. They smiled, but not as infectiously as their sister. It was as if they stood in judgement of her. "We told you,

Mamma, not to fill his head with legends of gods and godesses. We told you it was time you taught him of earthly matters. . . ."

Superimposed over this scene in her mind was the face of her husband Antonio. His face was a mask of stone, cold and disapproving. The voices grew, tunneled in the caverns of her mind; nevertheless they were loud and clear. "Come, Mamma. We're waiting for you," they whispered seductively. "Come Mamma *bedda.*"

Antigone, overcome by grief, felt the blood drain from her. She fell heavily into the arms of Stefano Modica. From somewhere came the *strega*'s voice. *"He must be protected for seven years of glory."* Over and over, these words echoed in her brain until a merciful blackness enveloped her.

Instantly there was a flurry of activity around her.

"It's her heart," apologized her physician, who appeared from nowhere carrying a small black bag and a hypodermic needle which he quickly thrust into her arm. "Someone please bring a chair for the *Signora,*" ordered the rotund and balding Dr. Raffa.

Five minutes later, Antigone, showing a surprising composure, requested that they get on with the business at hand.

"Is this your son, Alessandro Salvatore?" asked Procurator Maggio?"

Now, for the first time, Antigone's eyes came to rest on the massive amounts of crushed ice packed around Tori's body. She scooped up a handful, refreshed by its cool properties, and allowed it to sift through her fingers. A sudden mad gleam of denial crept into her eyes. It flickered—and died just as quickly. Sighing heavily, she nodded. Saginor, nearby, drew a steady breath of relief. Modica exhaled evenly and unclenched his balled fists. Now, he too, looked closer at the body on the catafalque, aware of the squirming mass of nerves that knotted achingly in his stomach.

"You must answer the question, *Signora,*" said Maggio. "I can't accept the nod of her head as an answer."

"Yes," she said, throatily.

"Do you officially identify this body as that of your son, known as Tori, also known as Salvatore the bandit—the brigand?"

Antigone leaned in to stroke his face tenderly, brushing away a few particles of the plaster of Paris left by the maskmaker.

"Signora?"

47

She drew herself up regally, head held high. "Yes. I identify him. He is my son, Alessandro, hailed as king of Montegatta, born November 16, 1922." She turned to Modica and said softly, "You came too late, *Colonnello*."

Modica gave a start. Hadn't he made it clear she wasn't to say anything about his mission? His men gave no sign of having heard. He breathed easier.

In a room containing over a hundred sophisticated newspapermen, and photographers, not a sound could be heard. Only the tremulous voice of the Procurator-General, rising and falling in rhythmic cadence like a high priest reciting low mass, was heard as he continued to ask all the questions for which the law, required answers before the deceased could be pronounced officially dead.

The formalities had ended.

Antigone Salvatore looked up and around at the vast circle of faces she'd never seen before, and, after a long and dreadful silence during which every eye in the room was upon her, she flung herself down beside the corpse. She lifted his cool head and pressed it to her feverish bosom: hot flesh cooled by dead flesh. She seized his hands and pressed them to her lips with an abandoned passion. She kissed his cheeks; his cold unresponsive lips. "My magnificent son," she whispered in a broken voice. Her passionate whispers filled the room. She was a woman whose child had been murdered; a woman mourning the death of her son. She was all grief and despair. Yet, over it all, she managed to maintain a certain majestic dignity.

There were no maudlin histrionics; no beating of her breasts; no lingering lamentations of sorrow; no martyr's affectations. The crowd who moved in closer, anxious to document her final words, felt both cheated and astonished by her control. They watched as she released her hold on him and crossed his hands over his chest. These words they heard as she spoke clearly and firmly: "Now, my beautiful son, you truly do belong to the world, *Sanguo del mio sanguo* blood of my blood."

Hardly anyone there fully understood these cryptic words. Later they'd talk about this, talk and wonder and probe. But for now, they only watched this matriarch who appeared as invincible as her son had seemed. She was a magnificent woman of strength, courage and fortitude.

Suddenly there was pandemonium. A cry arose from the spectators, and the strangers moved in on her. The magic had ended. The legend had let them all down by being a mere mortal. Given priority, the reporters broke the spell. Earlier they had strained to hear her words, and now they asked one another, "What did she say?" They had to know if they intended to record her grief and loss for posterity. Once again the flashbulbs popped. Cyclopean camera lenses blinked incessantly all around her.

Antigone, shielding her raw, sensitive eyes from the flashes of blinding lights, asked the Procurator-General to be allowed a few moments alone with her son. Her request was denied by Captain Franchina. Recalling his initial encounter with the formidable matriarch, the arrogant officer glared at her with a perverse sense of triumph.

Undaunted, Antigone said," Very well, then, permit me to view my son's personal effects."·

In Dr. Alba's office, Antigone seemed a different woman. Stronger, more composed and in full command of herself, she let her dark eyes scan the articles collected on the table in reflective silence. Watching her, Modica got the feeling that she was assessing the items individually with some diabolical plot in mind. He sensed something was wrong. But what?

He was right. Something caught Antigone's eye as she examined the articles, touching nothing for the moment. Catching sight of the golden scorpion, she glanced up at Modica. She picked it up tenderly in her hands and handed it to him. "It's made a complete circle. I'm sure he would want you to have it, *Colonnello.*"

The FSB Officers tensed and nudged each other. Modica caught their reactions, and mumbled a "thank you."

"But there was another amulet—" began Antigone.

Maggio handed her another, the *Eye of God.* "It was in his pack." He handed her the fabled gold belt buckle, the diamond ring, and the other articles.

". . . And his gold watch?"

Reporters, speedily scribbling down what they could hear of the conversation, moved in closer.

"There was no watch. . . ."

"He was never without it," she said firmly, fingering the toy soldier and horse.

The FSB Officers exchanged glances, and turned to Maggio for guidance.

"I tell you there was no watch." Maggio mopped his brow.

Antigone's eyes were on the leather holster and Luger. "My son carried *this* gun? In *this* holster?" she asked scornfully.

"I personally removed them from his person," admitted Maggio. "The gun lay alongside his body where he dropped it."

"I've never seen these items before in my life. My son carried a Browning automatic. He was never without it." She picked up the Pall Mall cigarettes and tossed them aside in disgust. "My son smoked Camels!" She turned to the FSB Officers to ask, formally, "When may I take my son home for burial?"

"That's impossible!" countered Maggio. "The time limit has expired. Now, he must be buried in Castelvetrano."

"Impossible? What time limit? What are you telling me, man? You still insist on playing the jackass? My son belongs to me. Tell me when I can expect to have him, and let's be finished with these disgraceful charades and infamy!" She tensed, prepared to battle to the end for her son.

Maggio looked to the FSB Officers for help. They were remote and impassive; it was up to him. "I regret, *Signora,* you cannot have him. The law clearly states—well, after so many hours, he must be buried here," he sputtered. "Besides, we haven't performed the autopsy yet. Our rules are explicit. . . ." Sweat poured off him.

Outraged, Modica intervened. He spoke evenly and slowly, so he wouldn't be misunderstood. "Are you saying, she can't have her son even *after* the autopsy?"

Antigone placed a restraining hand on Stefano's arm. "We'll see about these explicit rules," she said, directing her remarks as much to Captain Franchina as to Modica. "I shall return to claim the body of my son, after the autopsy, through the efforts of a man whose word will not be contested. They will not dare to deny me." She walked to the door held open by a mocking Captain Franchina, who, in bowing slightly, added salt to her wounds.

Burning memories of her first meeting with him, five years before, spurred him on. "Well, *Signora,*" he said, "It is finished. Now, who rides the ass?"

In Antigone's eyes burned the fires of a volcano. She stopped abruptly, lifted her dark eyes to meet his, and gave him a look that chilled him to the marrow. "But, *is* it over, *Capitano?* The final curtain has not descended." She moved on past him.

Outside, the desert heat rushed at her with its ovenlike intensity. Reporters converged upon her and hurled provocative questions at her while the Americans ran interference for her on her way to the waiting sedan.

"Have you nothing to tell us, *Signora?* What brought your son to Castelvetrano? Where has he been these past six months of silence? Did you expect him to be so brutalized by his enemies?"

50

Because she remained silent and unbending and comported herself with imperial dignity, the goading began. "Justice reigns at last, eh *Signora?* He finally got what he dished out for so long. The invincible Salvatore is no longer invincible—eh? What do you say to that, *Signora?*"

At the car door, Antigone turned and leveled her inscrutable eyes upon the assemblage. She stood before them, gaunt, gray-haired, but magnificent, a matriarch of power and dignity. Gazing at them, she spoke without preamble: "My son lies upon the marble *catafalco,* dead. You can simply say—he was betrayed."

She entered the car and it moved forward off the mortuary grounds, leaving a stunned mass of reporters, baffled and curiously moved by her provocative statement. *He was betrayed!*

Those three insidious words, like a lever, were to pry open the lid of a putrefying cesspool of political secrets and covert acts engaged in against the dead man, and swell in the minds of the newsmen like blistering boils to threaten the very network of the Belasci-Barbarossa-Christian Democrat combine.

Four hours later, the Coroner, Dr. Alba, made a limited statement to the press: "The missile causing Salvatore's death entered the heart chamber of the rear, directly under the left shoulder blade, perforating the heart itself. The lethal wound was inflicted by a .45 calibre revolver. Two bullets grazed his forehead, causing no serious damage. Frontal bullet wounds on right arm, wrist, hand and rib cage were made by machine-gun fire. Bleeding was comparatively slight." The gentle doctor spoke economically, and, visibly shaken, he evaded all further questioning under the usual shelter of "no comment." The FSB would release further facts later, he added before he disappeared behind closed doors.

There was enough ammunition in his words to pose a serious problem when the official statement was issued. This autopsy report, never printed in its entirety, disappeared shortly afterward from the coroner's office. Obvious to the reporters was the fact that both Coroner and Procurator-General had been forced into silence by the mounting discrepancies between the facts they uncovered in their investigation and those furnished them by Captain Franchina.

Alba and Maggio, in turn, brooded over the contradictory evidence. The most blatant inconsistency lay in the fact that the fatal wounds to the heart had been sustained several days before the bullet holes inflicted by a machine gun penetrated the body. The time span between these bullet wounds posed a serious problem. Why shoot a corpse *after* it was dead? Unless. . . . Neither man dared to speculate. Both preferred living to dying.

CHAPTER 4

Unable to believe what had been done couldn't be undone, Antigone wondered to whom she could turn for the strength needed to take her through these next few days? She ordered her driver to take her to the villa of the one man of power and influence who couldn't dare deny her the right to bury her son as she wished—the most powerful figure in Sicily, Don Matteo Barbarossa.

Four hours later she emerged from his villa in Monreale, white-faced, tight-lipped, agonized and shaking from the heavy burden inflicted upon her during her visit. No one had witnessed her terror, the black hatred she had felt, the crushed spirit she had endured in his presence. Yet, through it all, she had emerged victorious! She had gotten what she went after, the release of her dead son and the right to bury him where she chose.

Mah-Santo Dio at what cost? She had learned the identity of her son's murderer; his assassin! Bearing the heavy burden of this knowledge, she knew now that she could never reveal the assassin as long as she lived—if she wanted to live!

Don Matteo had been brutally exact, exceedingly precise in his assessment. "If this information leaks, who will the world believe? A deranged hysteric? A crazy, wild woman overwrought with the guilt of her son's criminal life? Or the official words of the Italian government? It would serve you little, *Signora*, and might even mar the image of the good deeds your son accomplished. My advice is to leave well enough alone."

Antigone had listened, dead inside. It was too much for her to contemplate, too much for her dazed, medicated mind to grasp. She knew he was right, and his power too formidable to contest. Slowly, as she made preparations to leave, she turned to the Don and said wearily, "There's one thing more, please."

He replied quickly, "Ask, and its yours."

Antigone picked up the bronze figure of a snorting bull from his desk. It was heavy and exquisitely carved. "I should like to have this, please."

"Consider it yours. Your, son, too, was fascinated by it," he said. "Has there always been such a passion for bulls in your family?"

She glanced sharply at him. Then, quicker than the eye could follow, she flung the bull from her, hurling it against the stone fireplace behind her where it struck with terrific force, cracking legs and horns and splintering the figure from its base, and fell to the hearth in several pieces. She removed the toy white soldier from her pocket and, having seen its companions on the large table behind him, she placed horse and soldier on the desk before him. She lifted her dark, anguished eyes to meet his.

"Now, Matteo Barbarossa," she told the startled *capomafia*, "it is finished!" She left him staring after her, confounded by her actions. She could hear his voice echoing through the halls as she took her leave.

"Porco diaoro! Devilish pig! Women! Always illogical! What the hell did she have against this poor defenseless bull? Where did she get this white soldier?" His eyes darted to the scale model she had left him. His eyes narrowed in thought.

Antigone returned to Montegatta, to her house where she bathed and rested and collected her thoughts. Tomorrow, she'd follow the Don's instructions to prepare for the burial of her son. For tonight, though, she wanted to mourn and release from her soul the grief collected over the past seven years.

However much Antigone had learned from Don Matteo, he, too, had learned a great deal from her—enough to force him to forego his personal despair and return to the business of *capomafia*. He had no doubt that he had aptly impressed Antigone with the need for secrecy, the need never to reveal the identity of her son's murderer.

He scribbled the names of two men on a slip of paper and rang for his personal bodyguard and emissary of confidential business. Mario Cacciatore, a frog of a man who bore a frightening air of malevolence about him, and who had been associated with the Don since their early Mazzarino days, entered the study and stood by until the Don finished his writing. The former bandit and cold blooded killer, whose skill and dexterity in carrying out executions was second to none, watched his Don through gloomy, disturbed eyes. Armed with the knowledge of the past five days' happenings and what had caused Don Matteo to sequester himself, Cacciatore, a brute of a man, had sensed a moment of black foreboding when he had earlier denied entrance to the shrouded woman dressed in black who had sought audience with the *capomafia*. Given the usual brushoff, the woman who gave her name as *Signora* Salvatore, had refused to leave. Shrugging indifferently he had motioned her to a highback chair in the foyer.

An hour later, Cacciatore had approached her, to suggest that she leave, since the Don was granting audience to no one. At that point, the woman had caught the *sicario*—the assassin—off guard for perhaps the second time in his life: she brandished a pistol!

Che demonio! A gun in the hands of a frantic, emotionally overwrought woman could prove more dangerous than one in the hands of a trained killer: you could always, after all, second-guess the professional killer's move. In the split-second he had taken to determine how to humor her, she had shattered his composure with another surprising move. Antigone had turned the gun around, butt-first, and handed it to him.

"Here, take it," she had urged. "Go ahead. Take it and shoot me! It's the only way you'll get me to leave this villa without seeing Don Barbarossa. He must give me what I came for. He must. Do you hear?" Her voice, raised in acrimonious discord, had echoed through the cavernous villa and reached Don Barbarossa's ears. In moments, Cacciatore had heard the Don's voice calling, assuring him it was all right to show the woman to his study. Horns of the devil! Would anything ever right itself again?

Now, Cacciatore turned his attention on Don Matteo, who displayed a remarkable recovery of composure since the woman's visit.

"Take care of these two," ordered Don Matteo. He was composed now, and had regained his usual self-sufficiency. He handed a slip of paper to his body guard. "Understand, they are not to live long enough to enjoy their blood money. When you finish, return here to me. We may be busy again as in the old days, my friend. Call Ruggero's Funeral Parlor, arrange for a limousine to be at *Signora* Salvatore's disposal for as long as she needs. She is not to pay for her son's funeral. They are to bill me."

Cacciatore nodded dutifully and left the study. Pausing in the corridor long enough to read the instructions, he let

54

a wicked gleam of satisfaction creep into his eyes as he read the names—Don Nitto and Natale Solameni. The perusal of instructions etched into his ugly features a look of diabolical glee.

"Is this Don Matteo Barbarossa speaking?"

"Yes, this is me."

"One moment please for Minister Belasci . . ." said the operator.

"Minister Belasci speaking. This is Martino P. Belasci, here."

"All right, I believe you."

"Ah—Matteo, how good to talk with you. I've tried to call you all day. Too many busy terminals. . . ."

"*che se decci,* Martino? What's going on?"

"Haven't you heard? They got Salvatore."

"Uh . . . *who* . . . got Salvatore?"

"The FSB. My sweet brainchild. Oh, yes, Captain Franchina."

The Don was silent.

"Matteo?"

"Ummmhum."

"What's wrong? Something's wrong, isn't it?"

"Do you buy their story?"

Belasci tensed. Something *was* wrong. "Shouldn't I?"

"Have you released anything to the press?"

"Yes. At approximately 10 A.M. today."

"What did you say?"

With measured words, Belasci filled the Don in on the press conference. Once again the lines fell silent.

"Why would four American agents from the State Department be interested in Salvatore?" asked the Don.

"American agents? I've no idea. Why?"

"They're in Castelvetrano, snooping around."

"Incredible! But—how? Is your source of information reliable?"

"The best."

"I'll look into it immediately. I can't understand. I've issued no special permits for Sicily in a long time. We've had agents looking into that . . . other matter, Matteo. But they know me as a strong anticommunist force, dead set against the Reds. What they could possibly want with Salvatore is. . . ."

The Don cut him off. "You remember *Colonnello* Stefano Modica with the Allied Control Council during the war?"

"From the Grand Council? Certainly."

"It's him, with three other agents, in Castelvetrano. Is Modica working on something special in Rome?"

"I had no idea he was here. I'll look into it immediately."

"Sure that no one in your office has issued special permits?"

"No, Matteo. I'm not sure. But our contacts at the U.S. Embassy have said nothing to me. Not a hint. You know there's been pressure from the U.N. about economic aid—that's all."

"I don't like it that Modica is in Castelvetrano. He was a *pezzonovante*—a big shot—in the war. He must have some position of high authority in his government. Modica's no fool, Martino. He was tough. A hard nut to crack in the Grand Council. If Roosevelt hadn't died when he did and if they hadn't transfered Modica to Rome. . . . He was too well informed, like a machine. Besides, he *knew* Salvatore! You know what must be done," said the Don.

"Yes, I know. You're sure he knew Salvatore?"

"I'm sure. Now, tell me what happened to Santino Siragusa? Is he to be deported from America?"

Belasci faltered. "None of our contacts through Genovese or Luciano located him in America. It was a false alarm. For all we know he might be dead."

"Martino, listen. For your sake he'd better stay dead."

"Calm yourself, Matteo."

"I'm calm. Tell me about Salvatore's personal portfolio. *Managghia!* Why didn't you tell me about Santino Siragusa sooner?"

"Matteo. I may have good news for you. It appears there is a duplicate portfolio in circulation. With Salvatore dead, we'll have no difficulty laying our hands on it. It may cost us a few *lire*, but once it's safely in our hands we shall ignite it. Then, we'll celebrate. *Va bene?*"

Don Matteo took time to light a cigar. He puffed on it hard until it was well lit. Listening to the inhalations at the other end of the line, Belasci took a moment to pour himself a stiff drink from a nearby decanter, grateful there was no one around to see him sweating.

The Don's voice was cold and contemptuous. "A duplicate, eh? Now, there's more?" He snorted. "What about Salvatore?"

"What about him?" Belasci's voice was guarded.

"They wouldn't permit his mother to claim the body," The Don's tone was deadly. Belasci recognized it and knew there was more to come.

"Why not?" he asked cautiously.

"You're asking me? I didn't hire those two *cappicolli*, Franchina and Cala. You did! Stupid shitheads? *Mah*, tell me something, Martino—where do you find these braying jackasses?"

"I'll take care of it immediately. . . ."

"No need. I just did. The mother came begging for her son's body. I made the necessary calls and finished it."

"Fucking idiots! I can't imagine what they were thinking of. . . ."

"*Allora*," said the Don, unable to resist the snide remark, "read the newspapers and find out."

"What's wrong, Don Matteo? There *is* something else. . . ." Belasci tensed.

"Tell me, how much did you pay Solameni? Was the reward ample?"

Belasci's blood turned to ice. He forced bravado. "You are simply a genius, Matteo. I've always said so. You know everything before I make a move to do it. Can't I ever keep a secret from you? It was the usual—I forget how much."

"It's not necessary to be clever with me. Fifty thousand dollars you paid. You realize when the autopsy report is complete, you'll all look like asses tied to the sun. . . ."

"I'm not in swaddling clothes, Matteo. I've taken care of that."

"How? A payoff? Another murder?"

"Does it matter? You've handled things in the past."

"*Amico*, I put you where you are to use your head. If I wanted a butcher for your job I would have used Cacciatore. Murders will no longer cover your blunders. Perhaps I should have put Salvatore in your place—given him the advantages I created for you. He used the brains God gave him, with talent."

"It wasn't I who fouled up Portella Della Rosa," blurted Belasci. Instantly he contemplated swallowing his tongue. In person or on the phone, Belasci could feel the Don's menacing presence and it chilled him instantly.

"I see. I see. When the hawk grows old, even the sparrows mock him."

Belasci felt the earth move under him. Following a testy silence, Don Barbarossa made no move to hide the contempt in his subdued voice.

"It was your puppet, Chief Semano, who hired the men for the attempted assassination. Before their guns had cooled, the deeds were announced to the world. Both sides

57

sit in Viterbo ready to spill their guts. Now that Salvatore's dead—don't think they won't!"

Belasci froze. He couldn't speak. He couldn't move. The phone felt as if it had turned to dry ice that stuck to his hands, searing through the flesh. The past flashed before him. Here they sat, the boa constrictor and the mongoose, in silent challenge.

"*Allora*—are you there?"

"Yes. I'm here. Strange isn't it? We've waited a long time for the capture or death of Salvatore. Now, dead, he presents more of a threat than when he ever did alive." Belasci's voice dulled perceptibly.

"It displeases me to think that wherever he is he's laughing at us!" The Don's voice, usually devoid of emotion, took on color. "It wasn't enough you had him dead. You could have turned him over to his mother for burial and ended it! No! Your arrogance and pride forced you to concoct a stupid story just to justify the existence of that infernal FSB. You had to take credit and bask in false glory! Hah! *Porco Diaoro!* You expose yourself to the snooping of highly sophisticated foreign journalists whose worst reporter is more expert than any man on your staff. You construct a mountain of fables and expect the world to believe your bullshit? Martino . . . Martino! When will you face reality? How much longer can I extend my arms to cover your ceaseless blunders? I'm growing old. I'm no longer young enough to put up with needless errors. Humor an old man, eh? Take Cala and Franchina in hand, before their balls are hacked off and ground up for vultures' bait. Eh?"

"Yes. Yes, right away. Immediately. I'll fly to Castelvetrano. . . ."

"No, Martino, no," sighed the Don wearily. "You stay in Rome. Send for them. Coordinate your stories, before you all step hip-deep in your own stinking shit and sink in it."

"It shall be attended to immediately. Anything else?"

"There is no time left for cleverness, Martino. Only action. *Ciao!*"

"*Si, ciao*, Matteo."

The seeds of discontent, germinated, began to sprout rapidly.

Concerned with Antigone Salvatore's well being and even more concerned by the fact that she appeared to know his mission, Stefano Modica left his companions, rented an auto, and motored to Montegatta.

Stefano Modica found Antigone, seated in the solitude of an amethyst twilight in her garden, wretched with dry tears of despair as she reviewed the events of that day. She was astonished by his presence and, despite her heavy heart, she tried to be cordial.

"It's not necessary, *Signora*," insisted Stefano. "I didn't come here to be entertained. It's just that you shouldn't be alone at such a time. Is there no one else who can remain with you at such a time?"

"No. There is no one. I'm quite alone. *Natura aborret saltum*. Sudden changes are painful and this pain is greatly minimized by the appearance of a friend," she told him.

They chatted for a time, and Stefano, detecting a tremendous loneliness in her in addition to a desperate need to speak, allowed her to ramble in any direction.

"He was special, you know," she began. "How can I explain? Things meant more to him. He had more questions for me than I had answers," she smiled in reflection. "From the first, the mid-wife who delivered him prophesied his greatness. Oh, I didn't believe her," she blurted flushing with self-consciousness. "I'm too much of a realist to believe in potions and spirits and the supernatural even though she possessed real prophetic powers—"Her hands flew to her forehead. "I'm confused. Perhaps the medication is stimulating me to talk so much," she rambled.

"I had to make certain you were all right. There's something else, *Signora*," he began lighting a fresh cigarette from his butt. "Even though my original mission failed, I must impress upon you the importance of saying nothing to anyone."

Antigone lowered her eyes to her callused hands, picking on a hangnail, then smoothing it into place. "You came too late," she sighed.

"*Signora*. If the slightest hint of those plans get into the wrong hands, it could create severe problems for innocent people."

"Destiny is a cruel mistress. She has a voracious appetite," she muttered, hardly aware of his presence.

Modica, concerned, detected in her manner a suppressed hysteria that threatened to burst at any moment. She rambled about Tori's life. If only he, Stefano, hadn't encouraged Tori to pursue his destiny, he might still be alive.

"The *strega* warned me—but how could I have known for sure? Antigone began to rock to and fro, intent upon some inner vision." For twenty years there'd been no sign in his life to foretell the violence that would come in his seven years of manhood—of the glories that would come

59

to him—of the treacheries and betrayals for which his education hadn't prepared him. How could I believe that the *strega*'s prophecy would come to pass? That his impotency would be caused by a bull?"

Possessed by his own guilt and submerged in his own mortification, Stefano hardly heard her words, at first. "Your son was a spectacular man, *Signora*. He was both loved and feared by enemies and friends alike. He had personal power—enough to shake up the world." He sighed heavily. "One thing is certain. He left imprints on the sands of time and they'll not be washed away. His spirit will live in the hearts of his people." He inclined his head in a mark of respect for her grief.

Antigone shook her head sorrowfully. "No, *Colonnello*. Your emotions blind you. Powerful politicians won't permit his spirit to live. They'll take careful means to destroy his image. Those men, high in government—those men who intrigued to kill his flesh—will now annihilate his spirit."

Modica glanced at her, curious lights sparking his blue eyes. "Not if we keep him alive, *Signora*. Not if we keep the spirit of Salvatore alive."

As Antigone's eyes darted towards him in an effort to fathom his remark, Stefano became conscious of her earlier words as they replayed in his mind. "*Strega*'s prophecy?" He turned to her. "What are you saying—witchcraft, black magic? How the devil could a bull influence your son's life?" Stefano was aghast. Surely she wasn't in her dotage?

Antigone kept her inscrutable eyes on the American for several moments, as if she were assessing him in a most curious manner. Then, rising to her feet, she asked him to follow her into the house, where she proceeded to bolt to the door. She led him upstairs into the modest sitting room. "Please be seated," she said cordially, gesturing to a comfortable sofa before excusing herself.

Modica's eyes instantly darted to the framed photograph that dominated an entire wall. Salvatore, seated on his white Arabian stallion, *Napoleono* was a spectacular sight. *By God, what a champion*, he thought; then, remembering what had happened to that magnificent beast early that afternoon, he felt as he had earlier, terribly saddened by the spectacle.

When Antigone returned she held in her hands the *Eye of God* amulet he'd seen earlier at the morgue and a frayed, yellowed folded paper. She set them on a nearby table and from a crystal decanter poured two *bicchierini* of anisette. She handed him one and took the other in her hand. They drank a silent toast to the dead man. Now, for the first time, she began to speak with coherence. *"Allora,* Stefano, please feel at ease. Don't be concerned that I possess certain information about the activities you engaged in with Tori. My lips are sealed. Because my son felt towards you like a brother—because you came despite the failure of your plans—and because of Gina, I shall entrust to you, certain explosive secrets. Let this be a legacy for Gina in her darkest hours of need," she said cryptically.

He didn't understand her words and couldn't guess where they were leading, so he remained silent, hoping to learn what her glittering eyes conveyed.

"I speak from love in my heart and through the memories of my son, be they bitter or sweet," she told him. "When you were here during the war, you knew a different man than the one he became in five years. *They* caused the changes in him. They made him what he became. They were afraid of him—those politicos in Rome and Palermo. If one—only one—of those men had kept their promises to him, he'd have been a king."

"I've never forgotten the potential greatness he possessed, *Signora.*"

"Va bene. I will start at the beginning. . . ."

CHAPTER 5

It would have been easier for Lucifer to enter the gates of heaven than for Minister Belasci, or anyone else for that matter, to place a telephone call to Castelvetrano in the next few days. In desperation the Minister sent a courier to the *"Judastown"* to order Colonel Cala and Captain Franchina to beat a hasty retreat to Rome for a regrouping of forces. Unfortunately for many concerned, the courier didn't arrive until well after the FSB Captain held the eagerly awaited press conference.

Baring their fangs like tigers at bay, an angry horde of reporters, waiting greedily for meat to be flung at them, refused to be pacified with milk. Mixed emotions surged through them as they awaited the "official" report. Gathered noisily in a special room set aside for them at the Selinus Hotel, the journalists, a heterogeneous lot, ignored the lavish display of wines and liquors set up for their benefit. For the most part they seemed short-tempered, incensed by unnecessary delays, and highly offended at the manner in which they had been treated. When finally Captain Franchina mounted the dais in the crowded ballroom, dressed in a brand new uniform with glittering brass buttons, and prepared to address the pressmen, their antagonistic presence was felt in overpowering waves of hostility. Undaunted, Captain Franchina got to the point.

"At approximately 3:15 A.M. on July 5, 1950, two armed men were seen walking along the Strada Sarina Madonna. Four specially deputized *carabinieri* went towards them and ordered them to halt. I was not far away when I heard the commotion, including the many shots they fired in their attempt to flee. One of the armed men took off in one direction, and evidently escaped. The second man ran in the opposite direction. I had a choice to make. Which mán to follow? I chose the one who tossed aside his jacket, and made an attempt to escape in the narrow alleys off Strada Sarina Madonna. Apparently, I made the right choice, for as luck would have it, the man I followed turned out to be Salvatore. The other man is presumed to have been Vincenzo de Montana. But, this is not known for certain."

"Then, it was you who shot Salvatore, fatally?" asked one reporter. The others moved in closer to the dais. Perhaps they would get a straight story, after all.

"Yes, it was I, Captain Giovanni Franchina of the Forces to Suppress Banditry. It was a tough fight. Salvatore fought well, making use of a special invention of his that permitted him to keep an extra magazine of forty rounds in the butt of his submachine gun. The fight for his life lasted approximately thirty-five minutes. He zig-zagged in and out the many courtyards on that street, firing in excess of fifty-two rounds of ammunition.

"He was losing much blood from his many wounds, and I felt certain he couldn't last much longer. Finally, he threw himself into the courtyard at *numero* 54, Strada Sarina Madonna. Twisting and turning like a madman, he never noticed the machine gun set up to fire at him. With my own hands, I opened fire. He fell, riddled with bullets, before he could use the Luger he pulled from his holster. Salvatore didn't die instantly. He groaned and moaned and begged for water. Unable to stand by and watch his suffering, I knocked on a few doors. One woman, a saint, the widow Grissi, supplied the water. Even a dying bandit is entitled to mercy, to sate the terrible thirst that comes upon him. . . ."

The reporters pressed Franchina for more facts. "Why were you here in the first place? What tipped you off that Salvatore would be here, so far from his own territory?" they asked.

"Colonel Cala knew Salvatore's weaknesses—arrogance, egotism and women." began Franchina.

The disgruntled horde of reporters booed him loudly. Franchina raised his arms, gesturing for silence. When they quieted down, he proceeded to explain that the FSB had set a trap for Salvatore. They had circulated a rumor that a motion picture company from Cinecitta, eager to make a film on Sicilian life, wanted Tori for a starring role. "In addition," continued the Captain, "the bandit leader's favorite prostitute was in the area. Unable to resist passions of the flesh, he was easily lured to this area, and thus sealed his fate."

Discerning reporters ridiculed Franchina's last statement, verbalizing their discontent with loud boos. "What the hell do you take us for?" they shouted hostilely. When he was alive, even Salvatore's distrust of prostitutes had been legendary. He had punished his men for their lack of discretion in affairs of passion too frequently for the newsmen to believe such a story. Goddamnit! Was there no truth in this preening peacock?

' Franchina raised his arms, hoping to stay the tigers. "And in addition," he said, "we were tipped off that an escape plan was under way. Colonel Cala had learned Salvatore was planning to leave Sicily, either from the old war airport here or through the fleet of high powered motor boats which mysteriously congregated near Selinunte and flee to America. . . ." Franchina gazed at them, perverse satisfaction glittering in his dark eyes.

A hush arose in the ballroom. So! America had come to Salvatore's aid, after all? The reporters pressed in closer, prepared to deluge Franchina with a barrage of questions. However, before they could pose the first of these, Captain Franchina's press conference was cut short by the arrival of Minister Belasci's courier, who quickly escorted the two FSB officers out of the Selinus in a whirlwind of secrecy, and flew them back to Rome without a hint of apology or explanation to the press.

The FSB's unexplained absence from the arena of action increased the discontent among the more scrupulous reporters, who were unable to fit together the distorted facts and downright lies spoonfed to them. They all agreed that a mere child could see through so flimsy a sham. It was a cover-up all right, they agreed. But why? Damned if they weren't going to find out!

Some reporters took off immediately for Viterbo to question former bandits. A few went directly to Montegatta to question the villagers. By late afternoon of the same day, Minister Martino Belasci's attempts to underplay and cover the facts of Salvatore's death boomeranged. Around the world, newspaper editors, hungrily awaiting the true facts of the story, were forced to reprint canned coverage of the famed bandit's seven-year career of glory, thereby bringing a spectacular rebirth to the legend and more prominence to Salvatore in death than he had enjoyed in life.

In Rome, Captain Franchina's "official" story was followed by a declaration from Belasci's office. There would be no further investigation in the matter of Salvatore's death: the case was closed. This should have satisfied the world and the international pressmen. But it didn't!

Banner headlines appeared in the Communist press:

WHO SPEAKS TRUTH? BELASCI IN LIFE OR SALVATORE IN DEATH?

INCONSISTENCIES IN SALVATORE'S DEATH BRAND FSB AND BELASCI AS LIARS!

"What is the grotesque secret behind Salvatore's death that Minister Belasci attempts to hide?" one newspaper demanded. "Reporters attest that the official version of the death of the Montegattan King is the poorest, most unbelieveable scenario written in Italian history, full of contrivances a child can detect and packed with blatant deceit. Why is the truth being withheld? The People of Italy and Sicily demand to know!"

Reporters remaining in Castelvetrano refused to abandon Salvatore to posterity, or to permit history to claim this as his final curtain. He had lent spectacular color to their dreary lives for seven years—should his death be less spectacular? *No!* they told themselves as they entrenched themselves firmly at the Selinus to organize a bit of team work to compare their findings. Certain there was treachery underfoot, aware that their presence would be met with stiff resistance, they watched and waited.

Then it came—subtly, with hinted innuendos. Six licensed prostitutes, imported to service the area, were suddenly withdrawn. Sex-starved newsmen, ready to give vent to the oldest and most primal of instincts, were told the women were for the exclusive use of the *carabinieri,* soldiers, and FSB.

Veterans among the press corps got the picture immediately. They sniffed out the procedure instantly, and, knowing their presence was no longer desired, they prepared themselves for that eventuality. Before the FSB closed down the liquor kiosks that day, the reporters had laid in a healthy stock of tobacco and liquors and a banquet of food. They offered to share their booty with the three American agents, who were cooling their heels, waiting for Modica's return.

"Damn!" griped Saginor to Renzo Bellomo, who sat cooling himself with a bamboo fan purchased in the Selinus lobby. "I wish we could stick our noses into *this* case."

"Yeah," retorted Renzo with a degree of preoccupation, moving the fan with rapid movements. They listened for a time to the excited chatter amongst the newsmen.

Saginor glanced casually at his friend, his eyes alert to the changes in him. "You're too quiet. You on to something?"

Renzo shrugged indifferently and accepted a drink thrust into his hand by one of the reporters. Saginor, unable to let it alone, guided Renzo towards the edge of the room close to the hallway, out of the hearing of the disgruntled newsmen. "Listen, pal, the *official* story stinks. You know it. I know it. They know it. Why didn't they just bury the poor bastard? Why all the *tsimmis?*"

Renzo stopped fanning himself. He stared at Saginor as if seeing him for the first time. "If I knew that . . . if I knew *that*—well, I could solve the riddle. The motive behind this is what baffles me." He commenced fanning himself, pausing now and again to punctuate his words with the woven bamboo.

"You that close to doping it out?"

"Franchina's version is a crock. How the bloody hell would he have time to set up a machine gun if, as he said, he was only out roaming the streets at that ungodly hour? And we both know a dying man with a bullet in him doesn't become thirsty until *after* fever sets in. And something else doesn't set right. Did you get a gander at Salvatore's sandals? There wasn't a speck of dust on them. Now how the hell could that be possible if, as Franchina says, he chased him through several courtyards? The dust would be that thick." He raised a hand, showing a wide space between thumb and forefinger. "Look, pal, let's get the hell outa here," he said impatiently. "I've had enough post-mortems and conjectures and repetitious allegations to last a lifetime." He guided Saginor out the door into the corridor, leaving the swarming hordes of reporters behind them. "Besides," he added. "I've had a bellyful of this hot box." He swatted angrily at the flies in the air with his fan. "Sonofabitching flies! These talk-filled jerks are gettin' to me. Whaddya say we beat it the hell back to Rome?"

Something else was itching Renzo, but he wasn't ready to scratch the itch yet. "Where the fuck is Modica—will you tell me?" he said sourly.

Saginor's attention was taken by a fresh gathering of news-hawks just alighting from the elevator. "So many leave, so many keep coming," he observed thoughtfully. "Why the hell do you suppose they're hanging around?" His endless fascination with the reporters had turned into morbid curiosity. "They got the official statement. What more do they expect from those jackals? The carcass has been plucked clean. Dead is dead; don't they know that?"

Renzo butted his cigarette on the tile floor with the heel of his shoe. "Ain't no more gonna happen here." He too was taken by another flock of journalists scaling the stairwell. "What else *can* happen?" he muttered weakly.

"Then why the hell don't the press get the hell back to where they came from?" commented Saginor.

"Beats me," muttered his companion. "Fuckin' reporters! That built-in radar of theirs can track a story across a fuckin' ocean." His heavy lidded eyes stared dourly at the men filing past him into the hospitality room. He plugged his ears with his fingertips to dim the tumult of conversation and busy drone of voices. "They're like a pack of buzzards watching a woodpecker chip away at a hangman's noose, waiting for the moment they can swoop down to their banquet and pick the carcass clean."

Matt Saginor nodded in agreement.

"Let's get outa here," urged Renzo in a voice that bordered on hysteria. "Look, buddy, do we have to be concerned with Modica?"

"He knows Sicily better than he knows the States. He'll find us."

Renzo rang for the elevator. In their absorption with the reporters, the lift had gone on to another floor.

"What do you make of Franchina's reference to an escape plan for Salvatore? Wouldn't we have heard a rumble if our side had planned it?" Saginor wiped the sweat rolling off his freckled face.

Bellomo's face turned a beet red. "Ya hadda bring it up, eh? I've been trying to ignore that ever since I heard it." He pushed the elevator button savagely.

"You *know* something." Saginor became intent. His eyes were riveted on the darker man. "You're on to somethin', aren't you? I can tell. When you get mad, good buddy— you're close to something."

"Does it matter? The poor bastard's dead. C'mon, for Christ's sake, elevator—work!" Renzo pushed the button again. "Let's take the fuckin' stairs! This elevator won't be here till Christmas!"

At *numero* 54, Strada Sarina Madonna, madness ensued. Bellomo, rushing ahead to observe the curious activity and milling crowds jostling each other, craned his neck to see over the heads of the people. Saginor, bewildered by the rush of activity, circled in behind his friend, and, making his way to the edge of the crowd, he saw the bent figure of a woman shrouded in a black shawl, sprawled over the body of what appeared to be a dead man lying in the position Salvatore's body had been in two days before. The woman appeared to be sucking up blood from the ground, in a reenactment of a scene in which it was claimed the mother of Salvatore had drunk his still-warm blood in an act of vendetta, swearing to be avenged for the death of her son—when, indeed, she had been nowhere near this courtyard at the time of his death.

Camera shutters clicked incessantly. Reporters scribbled in their note-books and the frenzied scene continued. On cue the woman got to her feet and stepped aside as photographers took photos of the young actor who played the part of Salvatore. Matt Saginor turned away in revulsion. He glanced about for Renzo, unable to find him. They'd been pushed apart by the swarms of curiosity seekers, and Matt, flung against the courtyard wall, scraped his nose sharply against the rough concrete. About to move away, he was struck with an idea. Turning, he searched the wall carefully in all directions. He heard Renzo calling to him, anxious to be leaving. Matt nodded, and, waving, acknowledged him over the heads of the mob.

Unable to press through the hordes of people, Saginor let his curiosity about the wall take priority for the moment. He continued to hug it closely as he followed a path along the outer perimeter of the courtyard, alongside the de Meo house, to the rear of the stone wall. Moving along, flush with the widow Grissi's house, he was unable to locate a bullet hole, except for those he'd seen to the left of the archway wall. Of the four possible places random machine gun fire could have hit, the least likely to have been struck by stray bullets was that narrow area of stone wall. *Man oh man!* Saginor, no dummy, reasoned these bullets had to have been purposely fired at the wall. His mind went back to Captain Franchina's words. How many rounds of ammo had Salvatore fired? What was it Franchina had said? He stopped himself. What the hell? Why get upset over the lack of bullet holes in the right places, when the whole fucking mess was an outright phony! Disgusted at himself for having even attempted to disprove Franchina's outright lies, he began to elbow his way through the crowds, with a grim determination to escape this insanity.

Flung back by the pressing horde, Saginor fell off balance, caught his boot on something, and held on to the drainpipe for support. The heel of his boot, caught between two wooden slats of the drain cover, wouldn't free itself. He gave it a kick and accidently dislodged the cover. In a shaft of light something glistening caught his eye. He ignored it until an after image flashed into his consciousness—something incongruous to the setting and unlikely to be found in such a setting distorted his senses.

The red-haired American shoved hard, pushed several people from him, and, falling to his knees, he saw lodged in the rim, between the crudely cut wooden frame and copper tubing of the drain itself, a bloodied hypodermic syringe. He reached into his pocket for a handkerchief, leaned in, lifted the syringe out, placed it on the white square of linen, and stared at it, unmindful of the glares and angry curses hurled upon him for his rudeness. On his feet, he continued to examine it with avid curiosity. Finally he wrapped it carefully, slipped it into his pocket, and pushed through the crowd to join Renzo.

They were some pair, these two. The most casual eye would assume they weren't acquainted with each other as they moved towards the *piazza*. Saginor grew introverted; Bellomo brooded, his mind intent on the morbid scene in the courtyard. They walked in the sultry heat, on antiquated streets too narrow for a car to traverse, past the better shops where business flourished. It became obvious there were now more arrivals in the village than departures, and everywhere hawkers had set up roadside stands to deal with the newfound prosperity the town had found in the vending of photographs and souvenirs. Photographers of the death scene in the courtyard had printed an enormous quantity of the photos and were selling them at dear prices. Women draped in black shrouds—women who bore little or no resemblance to *Signora* Salvatore—posed for tourists and sold amulets at prices dearer than gold. The American found the scene incredible.

At the edge of the *piazza,* they found a *gelateria* and seated themselves at a sidewalk table where they watched the ceaseless flow of pedestrians coming and going in the carnival-like atmosphere that descended on the village. Served their *gelato alle fragole*—frozen strawberry ice cream—in silence, they ate the cooling refreshment in silence, until Len Salina, having spotted them both from across the *piazza,* joined them, his face flushed with the relaxation of a sexual interlude. His companions brightened at his appearance and the mood broke.

By the time their coffee arrived, Saginor had taken out the hypodermic syringe and placed it before them on the table. "What do you make of this?" he asked quietly.

Bellomo stared at it with profound interest. "Where the hell did *that* come from?" He was perpetually angry of late.

Saginor explained.

"No sense asking Dr. Alba to run tests on it," said Renzo dryly. "It would probably disappear like the autopsy report."

"What do you *really* think, Renzo?" pressed the Texan. "I've never seen you without some theory to offer. Can't you make a guess?" Matt removed his jacket and lay it on a nearby chair.

"C'mon, supersleuth," urged Salina. "Make a guess. We ain't playing games."

Renzo felt wilted in the heat. His crumpled suit and sweat-soaked shirt didn't help his disposition. He liked things orderly, and he had a tendency to be skittish when they weren't. "Why pursue it, Matt? It won't do Salvatore any good. He's a dead man. Nothing will resurrect him. The days of miracles are long gone. Besides, who'd believe what we've stumbled on in this land of insanity?" Renzo stared off at nothing in particular.

Saginor shook his head regretfully. "Damn shame, when a man gets knocked off and no one gives a damn. . . . Steve knew Salvatore much better than he's led us to believe," he said thoughtfully. "I know him well enough to know something's eatin' at him."

"Is that why he went to Montegatta?" asked Salina, devouring the tasty strawberry cream.

Saginor lit a cigarette and inhaled deeply. "I suppose. The woman has no one."

"You don't think it strange that Modica chose this particular time to make this trip?" Renzo toyed with the melted cream running from his spoon. "Why Modica at this time? Nothing really pressed on ORS. Something else, good buddy. Something *Signora* Salvatore said bothers me. 'You came too late,' " she told him.

"What devilish brew is boiling your brains?" laughed Saginor. Then, he got the full implication. "You mean about that stuff Franchina refered to—boats in the harbor, a special plane awaiting Salvatore? All that mumbo-jumbo Franchina made up about an escape plan? C'mon buddy, you don't believe all *that* crap?"

Renzo merely raised his brown eyes and met Saginor's. Salina got the picture. He whistled low. Saginor sobered. His face screwed up with thought. "Nah," he scoffed. "You're off base. Even if you're right—what's the good of any plan, now? The operation's been snafued. . . . Besides, I'm more interested in learning for what devilish purpose this damned hypodermic was used." He was suddenly concerned for Modica.

"Only that I'd hate to be here if Italian intelligence has broken the case and it's learned that Modica is the key, *numero uno*, behind the plan.

"Oy vey!" muttered Saginor.

"Oy vey, my ass!" exclaimed Salina. *"Butana u diaoro* is more like it!" He rose to his feet, picked up the check. . . .

Saginor placed the syringe into his jacket pocket, slung the coat over one shoulder, and followed the others down the street. They turned off the square onto the Strada Vittorio Veneto, walking past delapidated houses and old buildings on whose peeled, faded and cracked walls were plastered electioneering posters touting *political* parties who had faded from prominence years before.

A poster of Salvatore dressed as a General, lauding the Partitionist Party, caught Renzo's eye a block away from the Selinus. He stopped, stared at it hard, and, wiping the sweat from his face and neck, opened up with a stream of consciousness. "Now, wait the hell until I'm finished before you burst the bubble. It's only a theory, from what I've observed, and without supportive data. I'm stretching it—believe me, you guys, I'm stretching it. Hear?"

Saginor brightened. "Listen, I only asked for an educated guess."

"O.K. How does this grab you? Dr. Alba stated death resulted from .45 calibre bullets entering a rear perfo-

70

ration of the heart chamber where we all noticed darker, caked blood. My theory is Salvatore wasn't killed the morning of July 5th. Probably not in Castelvetrano. Judging from the quantity of ice used to preserve the body, I'd say two—maybe—three days before. Got that? I think he was brought here and dumped into the courtyard, where someone then pumped extra bullets into him. Whoever killed him, whoever set the stage, came prepared knowing he wouldn't bleed. They bought fresh animal's blood. Goat's, or perhaps chicken's, blood isn't hard to come by. In Sicily such shops are open in the middle of the night. Then, with that needle you found, the bloodless holes were filled with crimson blood. . . ."

Saginor and Salina whistled low, trying to conceal their astonishment.

"The pool of crimson we saw concentrated over the right shoulder was probably made by pouring a moving container of blood over it into the dust. That explains the defiance to gravity—the uphill slant of the blood and the differences in the coagulation properties—and the variety of hues. It also explains the too-perfect positioning of the corpse. *Signora* Salvatore attested the guns were not her son's, that she smoked Camels not Pall Malls. So it proves someone hastily put the scene together. The weight of evidence that the murder was committed long before the official time is overwhelming in my eyes. . . ."

"You've got it narrowed down pretty well," Saginor said, "except for *why?* Why couldn't he have been found dead wherever he had been killed? Why manufacture so many obvious lies and distortions? It makes no sense at all, man!"

"It would if we knew all the facts leading up to the staging of the act. And we ain't gonna *get* no more facts," insisted Renzo. "So, we'd better haul ass back to the Selinus, pay our bill, and get the fuck back to Rome before we get our asses kicked in—or worse. Knowing you, Matt, I've already said too fucking much. That Jew head of yours will figure it too close!"

"Renzo"s right. We've got no business in this," said Salina, glancing cautiously over his shoulder. We've got more than we can handle with ORS."

"We can't leave the Colonel," protested Saginor.

"He's a big boy. He'll know where to find us. And you know something else?" said Bellomo, his dark eyes flashing. "I don't appreciate the sonofabitch not telling us what risks we might be taking down here."

71

"Christ! You don't know if it's even true!" admonished Saginor.

"Yeah. Maybe you're right." They picked up momentum as they walked back to the hotel. "Maybe I've been in the business too long."

"If Franchina didn't kill Salvatore, damnit, who did? And why would he admit to such a thing? Why would a man like Colonel Cala be a party to such a thing?" Saginor's perplexity alerted them.

"Oh! Oh!" lamented Renzo. "He's off and running. I knew I should have kept my big mouth shut!"

At the Selinus Hotel, mingling with the seasoned reporters up in their suite were a fresh batch of reporters who had arrived that morning. Fresher and shrewder in their questioning, they were echoing Saginor's thoughts. The grave conflicts at issue had caused such consternation among the men that they had gone out and interviewed twelve witnesses. All told the same story, and all disagreed vehemently with Captain Franchina's official story.

These reporters took a better look at the man—Captain Giovanni Franchina—professional soldier, injured in action, who had risen in the ranks of the *carabinieri* by promotion. Educated at Naples Police Academy. His thesis on Psychological Behavior of Criminals had earned him a special niche in forensic criminology. For establishing *modus operandi* in the behavior of certain types of elusive criminals, his opinions were sought after by several police units. The reporters could hardly believe such a man would string together such a flimsy story with so many loose ends. These actions were not worthy of such a man. Yet, on the other hand, this apparent carelessness on his part might have been deliberately planned to imply that he was an impostor, with the authority to claim the reward for executing Salvatore. If nobody believed him, this might ward off an onslaught of Sicilian vengeance.

The reporters now focused on Colonel Cala. Cesare Cala. Distinguished service in both World Wars. A long list of formidable successes throughout the world during his service with Italian intelligence, and every command a success. Slow, precise, painstaking and methodical, with an uncanny way of doing the right thing at the right time, Cala was a man who shied away from the kind of publicity in which Martino Belasci thrived. He hardly gave thought to the immense powers conferred upon him, which elevated him upon occasion to third man in a power structure of authority in the nation. Cala evidently lacked the inflated superego and flagrant audacity that commanded authority. Most of all he lacked that special quality of dishonesty that becomes requisite to overly ambitious politicians. He was at most a staunch Italian patriot, a man who took orders and executed them exceptionally well.

Why, then, would such a man be party to such obvious fraud? Promotion? A man who'd exposed himself to countless dangers all his life, who lived free of ostentation, needed no such encouragement. What then? The reporters were baffled. What was this crude conspiracy endorsed by these officers?

In Rome, both these men had emerged from their meeting with Minister Belasci, strained, red-faced, and filled with an inner turbulence which they held surprisingly in check. More surprising was the fact that the bombastic Capt. Franchina, whose pride and arrogance in the past had been a deterrent to his success, had refrained from mouthing off to Minister Belasci. How he wanted to tell the pompous ass what he could do with the FSB.

For hours they had kept silent while they pleasured themselves at the famed Madama Roulettini's bordello. Several weeks of pent-up emotions and self-denial had exploded in the aftermath of their visit with Belasci and they had to seek sexual outlets. But Franchina had continued to brood unrealistically.

It wasn't until they had retired to the Turkish baths and prepared themselves for the ordeal they both faced in Castelvetrano that Captain Franchina let loose a torrent of volatile expletives and a loquacious rhetoric to which even Cala hadn't been subjected to in the past.

"You should have told that cocksucker off, Cesare!" he began. "Where does that limp-wristed pansy come off, ripping our insides apart? Who does he think he is? Dandified asshole! He asks the impossible. When we deliver it, he sounds off like a harem of dissatisfied whores." Franchina craned his neck and struck vigorously at his nude body with a bouquet of birch branches tied together.

"He's our commanding officer in this special assignment," said the Colonel wearily. "That's who he is." Sitting hunched over on the wooden benches, naked, he appeared much older than his forty-eight years, and seemed completely cowed by the enormous burden carried on his shoulders. "We are simply good soldiers taking orders. Remember that. . . ." He pulled on a long cord at his side. Instantly, inundated by a forceful gush of steam, they basked in it for moments in silence.

"We're in it up to our necks. You know what'll happen if we get sucked under," said Franchina, trying to locate the Colonel in the vaporous air.

"Giovanni," said Cala patiently. "I've been an army man too long to change my ways. Wrong or right, I've taken orders all my life. In that time I've learned a lot. I've learned that no matter how much shit hits the fan, sweeping it up while it's fresh will only make one hell of a mess."

Franchina refused to be assuaged. "After the copious bungling and mishandling of our assignment and his constant interference with the press for his own self glorification, Belasci has a nerve calling us idiots!

"Bastard! Wasn't it he who demanded the blood of Salvatore? *'Bring me the blood of Salvatore!'* he ranted that day in his office. Now we've done it, and *this* is the thanks we get? Hah!" He struck at himself with alarming brutality, until he winced at the welts raised on his body by the birch branches.

"What's done is done. We must go forward with what we have. No tears or laments over errors and wrongdoings. Next time we'll both know better. . . ."

"Next time? Are you insane, Cesare? There may never be a next time for us. I've seen what happens to people who know too much. They're shipped to a foreign land, where they evaporate into thin air—or are done in mysteriously by unseen forces in unforeseen accidents. Loyalty to these vultures earns no rewards!"

"You should know," said the Colonel. "The expiration of a certain Private Foti. . . ." He cut a reproving eye towards his companion.

"He knew too much!" retorted Franchina defensively. "He saw enough to crucify us."

"You mean *you;* to crucify *you*," said the Colonel beating his body with birch branches to stimulate circulation.

Colonel Cala's point was well taken. Franchina's face became engorged with blood as waves of anger surged through him. Noting the mounting fury in his fellow officer, Colonel Cala tried to make light of the situation. "Come, come, take hold of yourself. You heard the Minister. Our main objective is to learn what the Americans are up to. Belasci assured us he can handle the press. In a month's time Salvatore will be forgotten. He guarantees this. Already he's requested the press to tone down their interest in the bandits. Their propagandists, the radio stations and the Christian Democrats' control over all such

74

platforms will insure his orders will be obeyed or they'll lose their licenses. Just think positive. Belasci will attain his goal. Remember he's an ambitious man who plans to be Premier. Let's look to ourselves. It pays to be on the winning side, eh, *Capitano?*"

Franchina nodded his head knowingly. "Come anything save an earthquake, we stick to our original story, is that it? What if the rumors are true—that the Americans represent President Truman?" he asked his superior officer.

Belasci will handle it," repeated the Colonel. "Look, our job is to make the Americans aware that they aren't welcome and are considered trespassers in our domain. To escort them out of town if necessary. Belasci has already lodged complaints against them with the American Embassy. You heard Belasci."

"Si," nodded Franchina, sullenly. "I heard that forked-tongued viper, all right. I also recall vividly that Salvatore warned you we'd be betrayed. He told us he'd neither be captured nor killed, and that Belasci intended to seduce us both and leave us as scapegoats, with both cock and balls exposed to the world. Cesare, I'm telling you now, I'll not stand for the same fate meted to *Il Duce* and his mistress! If I'm left alone in this, I swear I'll sing an aria that will straighten the Tower of Pisa!"

Precisely at that moment, the doors burst wide open and a blustery faced, irate madam, holding on to a waif of a girl, entered the *verboten* Turkish bath on the warpath. The young prostitute had been badly beaten around the face, neck and upper torso, and ugly swollen weals and bruises on her face had formed welts, half closing the girl's eyes. The madam confronted Captain Franchina. *"Signore!"* she shouted. "I demand restitution for the *infamia* you hurled upon this sweet, innocent bloom of youth."

The astonishment on his face turned to a blustery, red-faced embarrassment. Under heavy lids his eyes darted in the direction of his stunned superior officer. Colonel Cala, by nature a mild-mannered man, who had, in a career devoted to the military, probably strayed from the nuptial bed no more than a dozen times, and who, despite his reputation as a hard-driving man, was as gentle as a dove in bed, was shocked at what he saw. He averted his eyes, flushed with embarrassment for Franchina.

"It couldn't be helped," offered Franchina by way of explanation—not apology. "I was so furious—so fucking mad at Belasci. . . ."

". . . That you took it out on this poor child. Well, *Sig-*

75

nore," stormed the Madam. "For this you'll pay! I tell you you'll pay, or I'll go directly to the Minister and tell him what a devil he has on his hands!"

"Va bene!" shouted Franchina. *"Va bene!* I'll pay. As soon as I dress, and leave this damned establishment. . . ."

Colonel Cala reached up to pull the cord, to rid himself of these gawkers. Instantly the room filled with eddies of scalding steam, so hot that Franchina cried out indignantly.

"Dio Malodetto! Turn off the fucking steam! Aren't we in enough hot water already without you scorching us? *Butana u diaoro!* Whore of the devil! Come along and I'll pay you! Only for Christ's sake, shut your serpent's face!"

The Captain stalked out of the steam room, his mustache drooping like that of a giant walrus.

Colonel Cala shook with livid rage. *What else will go wrong?* he thought. *What am I teamed up with—a crazy psychopath, a sexual pervert?*

CHAPTER 6

Colonel Cala sat behind the hand-carved oak desk in the office of the Prefect of Police in a drab and badly-lit room of an ancient building. Captain Franchina sat next to him in a stiff high-backed chair, still intent on his reaction to Martino Belasci's excoriating effrontery and his own sadistic bent.

"Please come in, gentlemen," said Cala, rising as the trio entered. A glance at Saginor's red face and surly manner convinced him the American had been drinking.

"You wanted to see us?" asked Bellomo, with a tone of formality.

"Please be seated. But . . . aren't there four of you?" asked Cala.

"We've lost one. He's out sightseeing like a tourist," said Matt.

The Americans took the stiff high-backed chairs indicated and refused the English Ovals offered them. They lit their own cigarettes.

"What brings you to Castelvetrano?" Cala got to the point.

"Curiosity," replied Saginor.

"Official business?"

"No."

Cala and Franchina appeared to relax.

"You've no business in this area at all?"

"If we did, we'd have presented ourselves to the Prefect."

"How well do you know *Signora* Salvatore? You intervened on her behalf quite gallantly," Cala smiled tactfully.

"Correction, uh—*General*—Cala. It was Colonel Modica who intervened on her behalf. Not that we wouldn't have done the same for any woman given such shabby treatment by your men and all the ravenous reporters who clawed at her like vultures."

"Then it was merely an act of chivalry?" asked the Colonel tapping the tips of his fingers together, tentatively.

"That's what it's called? Funny you Italians get credited with chivalry. In America our women think we are grossly lacking in these graces." Saginor winked at his companions, both of whom refrained from winking back, uncertain where his impudence would lead.

"I hope you understand, uh—*Captain*—Saginor," said Cala clearing his throat apologetically. "There was no time for gallant behavior that day."

Sonofabitch, thought Saginor, *catching the reference to his past, the bastard probably knows the last time I took a healthy crap. Ooooooh Kaaaay! He called me Captain!* From this Saginor deduced that Cala knew all about them.

"None of us has enjoyed a good night's sleep since the FSB was formed," continued Cala. "That loathsome bandit led us a merry chase. Our efforts finally ended his tyranny. The books are closed, once and for all. It's over," said Cala making his point.

"Over?" Saginor mocked scornfully. "It's only just begun—hasn't it?"

Bellomo and Salina angled their heads sharply towards Saginor. *Goddammit!* that Salina. *He's had too much to drink.* Bellomo cursed softly and inclined his head in disgust. As if there weren't enough problems already. Damn!

"What do you mean?" asked Franchina, rising to his feet. His craggy face was swollen with anger and he didn't give a damn if it showed. "Explain yourself, *Signore!*"

"Uh—what my associate means," interrupted Len Salina, shaken by Saginor's impertinence, "is that the difference between the way you perform the anatomy of a murder

77

. . . uh, death . . . uh, slaying, is, if you will, so diverse from our methods that your work appears to begin where ours would have already ended "

"Is that so?" Colonel Cala regarded Saginor with interest. "Since when do American agents with the State department concern themselves in the anatomy of murders, deaths, *or* slayings," he asked under a mask of polite affability.

"You'd be surprised, Colonel at the things we State Department ogres get involved in from time to time. . . ." Saginor beamed syrupy smiles at them.

Bellomo intervened. "Colonel Cala, We came only in curiosity, to examine the methods used by your law enforcement agencies. We've no personal interest in Salvatore. That *is* the reason for your questioning?" He wanted to get the hell out of town before irreparable damage had been done. As it was, they had stayed too long, said too much. . . .

"Oh come now, Renzo," Saginor smiled indulgently. "We wouldn't be hospitable if we didn't give the *General* and the *Major*, here, the benefit of some advanced techniques. Now, would we boy?"

Saginor had some balls! Here in Sicily where a man's life wasn't worth the clothing he wore, anything could happen, thought Salina. Renzo consoled himself with the thought: *they wouldn't kill Americans—would they?*

Saginor began his litany. Drunk, his accent thickened. His friends slunk down into their chairs, like whipped puppies.

"Well, sir, take the position of the body. Yes, that's as good a place to begin." He talked for several moments, pointing up all the weak spots and distortions and pitfalls. He directed his remarks more to Captain Franchina than to Cala. "You said Salvatore fired fifty rounds or more? Man, I looked and looked, and I couldn't find a bullet rupture in those walls, except in the southwest corner of the courtyard. But take the wounds of the deceased." He shook his head and clucked his tongue against his teeth. "That Salvatore must have been one super human being, to maintain such an unusual blood supply. More than two, perhaps even three types of blood poured from his veins and arteries, all with contrary properties of coagulation. Now, where we all come from, a man has only one kind of blood—red! But on Salvatore—man ,oh, man!—I saw red, purple, blue, some dried and caked and some bright crimson. . . ." His voice rose and fell in west Texas cadences.

78

Colonel Cala had paled to the color of paste. Captain Franchina's face had reddened deeply and his moustache twitched nervously. His eyes darkened with a scowl. "You were able to determine all that in a superficial examination?" he asked icily.

"I doubt the layman could discern the inconsistencies. But, you see, we're all experts. Well trained."

Some of the deathly pallor lessened on the Colonel's face. He recovered fully and grimaced distastefully. "You're drunk! Wine loosens the tongue. Sober, you wouldn't have the guts to fart in our presence. But since this is pure conjecture and since you seem to feel the need for catharsis, go on, if it suits your nature. You might provide us with enough imagination to convert this into a fairytale to tell our grandchildren on a rainy night."

Compelled to pause, Saginor wished he could tell them how he *really* felt. Sickened at the sight of such men, who simply followed orders and had no guts to speak the truth, he felt the trials at Nuremburg should have taught such men a lesson about executing orders for which they might have to answer. He made an instant transition, affecting a shyness, a rush of modesty. "I don't wanna appear presumptuous."

"I find your theory profoundly provocative. That's what it is, isn't it? A theory?" Colonel Cala's polite inquiry had an edge to it, now.

"Nope!" Saginor's brow wrinkled almost as apologetically as Cala's. Franchina considered Cala had lost his senses to pursue this. Bellomo groaned inwardly, and Salina inclined his head, to one side and propped it into his hand.

"If you insist, Colonel. But only because you insist. You take the deceased's skin tone. The degree of *rigor mortis*. We feel Salvatore was dead long before the alleged confrontation took place. With all due respects to your contrived story," he told Franchina.

Bellomo felt sick. His features suffused with mortification and dread. Salina paled and remained speechless. Captain Franchina seemed turned to stone, a look of offended dignity frozen on his face. Colonel Cala stared intently at Saginor, testing his many years experience against the brassy American.

"Then, there was the question of so much ice. When does a freshly-killed body have to be packed in so much ice? Not as soon as you did to Salvatore, if he was dead at 4 A.M. that morning. . . ."

"You've gone too far!" Franchina kicked back his chair.

With burning rage and humiliation, he turned to face his superior officer. "How dare he suggest that I'm falsely proclaiming to the world to be . . . It's too much! This is too much! To take these insufferable comments from a—"

"I'm sure you misunderstood my good friend, Captain Franchina," interrupted the cold and formal voice of Stefano Modica as he entered the room. He turned to Saginor. "Matt. Apologize, instantly!" he ordered.

All heads turned to him. The Americans breathed in relief. Saginor affected to be crestfallen. "Apologize? For an educated opinion?" He walked to Franchina and jabbed him playfully in the ribs. "I could be wrong, but I'm not. Am I? Between us cops, I'm not wrong, eh?"

Captain Franchina pushed Saginor's hand aside as if it were contaminated. "Colonel Cala! I demand an immediate apology from this foreigner. . . ."

"Matt! This has gone far enough." Modica, appearing strained, addressed himself to Colonel Cala. "I regret my associate has seen fit to be utterly thoughtless. Totally without sense and decorum. To intrude upon a matter of no concern to us is appalling to me. I can't apologize enough, Colonel."

Matt Saginor spun around and studied Modica askance. Was this the same man who had promoted eyeball confrontations with the voracious General Patton? Bellomo and Salina breathed easier. Saginor sulked.

"We've all been drinking a bit too much, sir," apologized Salina.

Modica nodded to Bellomo, who began to guide Saginor out the door.

"He meant no disrespect," said Modica, slipping a pair of binoculars around his neck.

"Oh, yes I did!" shouted Saginor. "You goddamn well betcha I did." He shrugged off Bellomo's restraining arm, adjusted his seersucker jacket, and, mustering a bit of dignity, he walked towards Captain Franchina. A moment's reflection might have saved Saginor from committing his greatest folly. But he didn't reflect. He reached into his pocket and handed the Captain the linen-wrapped hypodermic. "A parting gift. Just for you—*Major!*" Saginor was elated and exquisitely amused at the menace he saw in the other's face, as he wagged the object under the other's nose.

At a quick nod from Modica, Len Salina and Renzo Bellomo moved in. Saginor felt both arms in a vise-like grip as he was lifted bodily off the floor and whisked out the room, his toes barely touching the floor. Saginor turned his head back toward Franchina, eyed him reprovingly and clucked his tongue at him. He broke free of one arm and wagged his fingers reprovingly at the FSB officer.

The Americans left with the echo of Saginor's zany laughter ringing through the halls of the old building.

"He's crazy! That sonofabitch is crazy!" shouted Franchina with blood-engorged veins pulsing over each temple. He opened the linen square and stared dumbly at the bloodied hypodermic syringe. A red flush crept up his neck into his face.

"No, he's not crazy," said Colonel Cala simply. "How can a man be crazy when he speaks the truth?" He leaned wearily back in his chair and glanced up at the thunderstruck figure of his captain. "What's wrong? What do you have there?" He leaned forward and glanced into Franchina's outstretched hand. When he saw the syringe, he sat back in his chair heavily, as if the life had been drained from him. He shook his head and his eyes grew maniacal.

"Colonel! This is no time to show weakness. No time for second thoughts! We're in this up to our necks and you sit there moralizing. We had no other choice!" insisted Franchina.

"It's beginning to appear that Salvatore reigns supreme even from the grave. . . ." reflected Cala.

"Va! Va! Don't hand me that shit. He's dead! What does it matter how he died?" stormed Franchina tossing the syringe on the desk angrily.

"Salvatore was right, after all. I'm the scapegoat, just as he told me I'd be. Why didn't I leave well enough alone?"

"You know why! We'd have been left holding the bag. Belasci would have made *cafone* of us. We followed *your* plans, didn't we?"

"And *your* suggestions," countered Cala.

"Still, we took orders. We have no reason to fear. Our superior, the Minister of the Interior, commanded us and we obeyed!"

They stared at each other in a grim silence.

"Why? Why are we talking to each other like this? Some stupid meddling American dared to insinuate. . . .".

"Basta! Basta!" interrupted the Colonel. "You and I know the truth! Don't try to convince me of your innocence, nor of your notion that the American is stupid! He's not. The blood of Salvatore is on *our* hands—not because we're guilty of his death, but because we insisted on taking credit for it! Belasci must be told of this incident so he can control it from Rome." Cala was all business. "Now, we'd better get on to the mortuary. Someone signed

the necessary papers for Salvatore's mother to claim his body and I, for one, want to know who dared defy our authority!" snapped the FSB Chief. He was unusually upset. His usual calm had evaporated.

"You stupid bastard! What the fuck's wrong with you? If you think nothing of your own neck, you could have considered Len's and Renzo's," admonished Stefano Modica, trying to contain a smile.

Renzo drove at breakneck speed until the Fiat sputtered and wheezed.

"Sorry," grinned Matt. "Couldn't resist it." He sipped from a container of black coffee they had insisted on to sober him up. "You don't know the half of it, Steve. You should have been there to hear what I told him . . . ugh, this coffee is awful! Goddamnit! You trying to poison me? . . . Hey, did you get a good look at Franchina's face when I gave him the syringe?"

"Yeah, sure—hero—at the expense of our fucking lives!" smirked Salina bitterly.

"What syringe? What's he talking about?" asked Stefano Modica.

The men explained their findings, Renzo's theory, and all that had transpired in Stefano's absence, while Modica sat in an attitude of remote contemplation. Antigone Salvatore's words began to make sense, he thought as he listened.

Stefano Modica had come away from the Salvatore house with dynamite in his possession—the personal portfolios of Alessandro Salvatore. Bound by his solemn promise not to share his findings nor his plans with another soul. Modica had, as a matter of wise judgement, stopped off in Palermo to pack and mail the explosive material including the ORS file to Gina O'Hoolihan in the USA. He had also sent her a wire. Simple and direct, he hoped it would explain his failure: *"I could have taken on any power—even God's—but never destiny. Package to follow. Keep safe for me."* It was signed, Steve."

"Pull that shit again, Matt, and I swear I'll put in for a transfer! I hate to think what's waiting for us in Rome!" yelled Renzo Bellomo, piercing Modica's thoughts.

"Aw, go to hell!" mumbled Saginor. He felt awful. The heat, the alcohol, and the criticism filled him with nausea. Coffee hadn't helped. Low laughter formed deep in his throat and he smiled mischeviously. "What I'd give to wire those two FSB's for sound. They sweat bullets up there. Their skins blistered under the strain of my words. . . ."

Renzo impatiently sounded the horn on the rented Fiat. Milling traffic had thickly congested the area of the mortuary, next to the *camposanto*. "Bastards! *Avanti! Avanti!*" he shouted to the pedestrians who blocked their way.

Absorbed with angry thoughts over Saginor's outrageous behavior, the agents had forgotten about Modica's prolonged absence. Grateful for the diversion and knowing he'd found the means to be evasive, Stefano glanced out the car window, wondering at the milling crowds.

"Can't you go faster, Renzo?" He prodded impatiently.

"There's a bottleneck up ahead . . . packed with people. . . ."

Saginor stuck his head out the window, shaded his eyes, and peered about the area. Bellomo sat on the horn. The raucous sounds made no dent in the converging masses up ahead. They could feel the electric vibrations in the sultry air.

"Kill the motor," ordered Modica. "We aren't moving. Might as well park it, and we'll walk to the mortuary up ahead. Something's happening."

Bellomo complied instantly. He locked the car and left it standing and followed the others who'd begun to carve a path through the congestion. The Americans glanced at either side of them as they snaked forward. Lines of people having spilled off the road had fanned out into the open fields for as far as Modica could see. It was impossible not to sense that something exceptional was about to happen. On the faces of the people were fixed expressions of reverence or awed superstition. Men reverently uncovered their heads. Shawled women knelt on both knees. They blinked their eyes from time to time, muttering incoherent prayers and rocking to and fro. Brown fingers formed the sign of the cross in vigorous repetition, their words gibberish, unintelligible.

The whole thing began to resemble a giant pilgrimage as people chanted indiscernible mantras, but every now and then the word *Salvatore* was clear and audible.

Modica's point of focus was directed to the top of a grassy hill, ringed a quarter of the way up by marble headstones of the cemetery opposite the marble halls in which Salvatore's body lay in repose.

Outlined against a fiery blue sky, there stood a magnificent, riderless snow-white Arabian stallion, adorned with a black leather saddle studded with a profusion of silver ornaments which splintered in the blazing light into myriads of brilliant colors, so bright in the sunshine that people were forced to avert their gaze from time to time.

83

From the saddle dangled a pair of shiny black boots. It was an electrifying scene, and a moving one.

"What's going on?" Salina asked of a genuflecting peasant. "What is it? What's happening?" He received no answer he could make out.

"Follow me," said Saginor, gazing at the strange reaction at either side of him as he followed Modica through the mob. "I don't know what the hell's going on."

"*Paesano*," Bellomo asked of an elderly man. "*Che c'e?* What's happening?" He slipped several lire into the man's trembling hands.

Tugging off his beaked cap, white hair standing on end like snowy pine needles, the old man crossed himself religiously time and again.

"*The Spirit of Salvatore! The spirit of Salvatore and his Napoleono!*"

They all heard. Instantly the Americans turned their attention on the spectacular sight of the stallion standing in an attitude of uncertainty on the hill. They watched with mixed emotions for several moments, then wound their way through to the mortuary in full view of the spectacle, leaving behind them hordes of supplicating Sicilians.

Several squads of *carabinieri*, ordered to disperse the immovable hordes, gave up and watched, in open-mouthed fascination, the awesome sight and its effect on the masses.

"What's going on out there?" shouted Captain Franchina, emerging from the mortuary. "What's the trouble?" he asked the guards, who pointed to the scene at the top of the hill. Shading his eyes, Franchina peered at the proud and stately stallion, whose arched tail and long silky mane fluttered slightly in the breeze.

"Looks like Salvatore's ghost has returned to haunt you, eh, Captain," needled Matt Saginor standing a few feet away, unable to resist the urge.

Bellomo and Salina groaned internally and gave Modica a helpless look.

Livid with rage, Captain Franchina bridled indignantly and scowled at him. "You six men," he called to a squad of *carabinieri*. "Go up there and bring that damned animal down to me!"

Shuffling awkwardly on the pebbled walkway, the men individually resisted his command and glanced uneasily at each other, each reluctant to be the first to move. Unsure of what was happening, they obeyed the instinct which told them not to budge. Enraged at their insubordination, Franchina, frustrated, snorted like a charging bull.

"Sniveling cowards! Understand this, you're on report!

84

Very well, then, come with me! I'll fetch him!" He called to another squad. "You six men over there, and you six here, all of you accompany me!"

Flanked on either side of the Captain, a total of twelve men moved in a body across the narrow road, past the courtyard, beyond the tricolor flag of Sicily set on a standard at the center of the compound.

"*Avanti! Avanti!*" shouted Captain Franchina as they began the ascent past the gravesites and the wooded area onto the denuded breast of the hill.

Modica, in adjusting his binoculars, observed the activity of the reluctant soldiers without comment. He raised the powerful lenses to his eyes, focusing on the stallion. He saw candy-glazed eyes of ebony flaring instinctively at the approaching strangers. The stallion's powerful head angled sharply in a nearly human response as he warily watched these uniformed men. Suddenly he reared on his hind legs, his velvet-pink nostrils pulsating as he clawed the air with his forepaws. He whinnied, flinging his head from side to side, snorting several times as if he sensed these enemies.

Light refractions bouncing off the glittering silver saddle momentarily blinded the advancing officers, obliging them to shade their eyes.

Forced at one point to avert his head from the glaring brightness, Captain Franchina lost his footing on the rocky terrain, stumbled, slipped back and fell several yards, rolling down the hill, landing with a hard fall against a marble headstone, totally disheveled, in what was perhaps the luckiest fall in his life.

One *carabiniero* braver than the others, cooed to the stallion who had resumed his original, silent and unmoving pose. His arms outstretched, the officer moved in closer, beckoning the animal. *Napoleono* eyed him hesitantly. Reaching him at last, the *carabiniero* triumphantly grasped the reins firmly, pulling the animal towards him.

Suddenly, the earth exploded! The booby-trapped stallion and twelve *carabinieri* shot up into the air, to the accompament of loud explosions!

CHAPTER 7

Stunned! The American agents were stunned when, with the setting of the sun on July 10, blistering orders arrived from the American Embassy, demanding the immediate return of the agents to Yankee soil. The very network of the Christian Democratic Party had been visibly shaken by their findings in Castelvetrano, and the lives of the American agents, now worth less than the price of a shoestring, had to be protected to avert an international incident.

The next several months brought about a series of events explicable only to those deeply involved in the matter of Salvatore. Major Franchina accepted with pompous affectation the quasi-martyrdom accorded him by the loss of one arm, together with the national acclaim as a hero who had brought about the demise of Salvatore, thus hopefully ending banditry in Sicily.

General Cala, with modest reservations, showered consolation upon the convalescing Major and both men basked in the glorious limelight afforded them by a grateful Premier de Aspanu and fawning Minister Belasci who demanded, with his usual panache, the need to bask in the spotlight alongside his victorious officers of the Forces to Suppress Banditry. He made what he hoped would be his final words in the Salvatore matter: ". . . *I fully confirm the version of Salvatore's death as reported by General Cala and Major Franchina, and can state with authority there was no conspiracy involved in the bandit's death other than routine business expended in the normal course of FSB operations. Once again, it is the profound wish of Premier de Aspanu and myself that the people of this great nation put Salvatore behind us and allow us to move forward to more important business. . . .*"

In the United States, things moved swiftly for the agents. Following time for proper indoctrination, Bellomo, Salina and Saginor were transferred to Japan, where it had been learned that American currency was being counterfeited in abnormal sums. Stefano Modica, greatly distressed by both the course and coincidence of events, grew incensed and more introverted over the dastardly affair. However, both Bellomo and Salina, well aware of how close they had come to giving up the ghost, welcomed the transfer, feeling safe only when they heard the reassuring sounds of Japanese music and Geisha girls.

Matt Saginor, taking transfer in his stride and accepting his new role with vigor and daring, paid little attention to those dark and sinister shadows accompanying him wherever he went. If he had, he might have been spared the agony of a bloody and gory death meted him while relaxing in the indolent luxury of a geisha house. So that his death would be recognized for exactly what it was—a silent warning to others—Saginor, slaughtered by means of a butchering knife thrust into the jugular by unknown assailants, was found floating in a bath of crimson, his face blown off by a shotgun. At the far end of a carmine pool, a portion of his face, upon which had been placed a dead, withered hummingbird, was found adrift, affixed to a slab of cork.

But, on August 28, months before this atrocity took place, Stefano Modica's disillusionment with the State Department had reached the breaking point. Having sent his letter of resignation four days before, he sat, sober, suspicious and hard eyed, in the air-conditioned halls of the State Department in Washington D.C., waiting to be heard, at a meeting of the National Security Council advisory board, by the very men who'd given birth to his functions with the bureau.

Their quick departure from Rome—shuttled off like criminals—and the swift transfer of his men out of his jurisdiction had thoroughly rankled Modica. In addition to the countless unanswered questions plaguing him, there lay deeply imbedded in his mind the remotest possibility that he'd been done in by his own government. God knew how he tried to dispell such nagging thoughts, how he fought to reject them from mind. Why would his own country be a party to such fraud? he asked himself. He knew he'd done his best in the Salvatore matter, yet something had come apart. What? How? Where? Each time he dissected every step of his involvement, he came up blank. Modica was about to learn he had overlooked the most obvious factors in the appalling treachery.

"Colonel Modica?" Summoned by a nattily-dressed page, Modica nodded, picked up his briefcase, and followed him into an oval-shaped room where twelve men sat comfortably around a mirror-polished oaken conference table against a stately decor of Colonial stuffiness. Tight-lipped, Modica seated himself at the end of the table, barely acknowledging the others.

Two hours later, Modica, ready to commit murder, emerged from the room, revolted by what he'd heard and incited to the point of madness. In all his life, he'd never come as close to doing physical violence as he had while seated in that austere office, where everything dovetailed and added up to a stinking mess of political immorality, with himself—him, Stefano Modica—at the center of the contemptible betrayal of Salvatore.

Washington, D.C. sweltered in the stifling August heat wave. Yet Modica, seated in his broiling apartment, killing off the best part of a pinchbottle, felt nothing except the dull uncertainty that he'd been sold out by his own government. Nothing, not their words, the scotch, or his own attempts to minimize the situation eased his pain or removed the guilt. Yes, he thought, that's what it was—guilt. His personal guilt in the Salvatore matter would never be assuaged, and he might have to live forever under its strangling weight. Stretched out on the sofa, he chain-smoked and watched the disintegrating rings drift off into nothingness as he reflected on the previous few hours—two and a half hours he'd never forget.

Earlier, Richard Bixby, an obnoxious, self-righteous, prissy-assed Presidential aide, had attempted to explain the vast complexities of international politics. Even the Council, in refusing to accept Modica's resignation, had told him, "Reconsider. Take a long rest. Gain a new perspective. Then reassess your position."

Modica, no fool, sensed their rejection. Most of the consortium had resented his appointment because he was commonly referred to as a "hyphenated American of Italian descent." Before the war the bigotry had been incalculable. But since so many sons of Italian parentage had fought for America and returned as heroes, these WASPs couldn't be as obvious in their hatred of Italians as they had in the past. However, in their sly, subversive and covert ways, they nipped any promising political careers in the bud if the aspirant was of the Italian-American persuasion.

He paid little heed to their false expressions of florid patriotism; he knew all of them too well, with their empty chatter and redundant rhetoric. But as they spoke, and while Stefano listened, there began to form between the lines a hidden message, which at first he rejected as ridiculous, unfounded and without basis. They offered him scraps in appeasement, and he saw through them.

When it came together in Modica's mind, a wave of shock swept through him. Yet, there it was—proof to corroborate his deepest suspicion. He, Stefano Modica, had been set up in the Salvatore matter! Salvatore's planned expatriation had been a sham! Uncle Sam's protective umbrella had collapsed under a hailstorm of betrayals that led from the Italian High Command to the White House and that had ended with Stefano buried neck-deep in the putrefaction of their corrupt seduction.

The way Modica figured it, even *Operation Red Star* had been a sham! Tremendous interest in the de Aspanu-Belasci-Christian Democratic Party had been heightened in the past two years, especially since the war. American Ambassador J. H. Steele had been keeping the White House and certain Wall Street interests well informed on the internal business affairs and growing conditions in Italy. Modica's costly file on ORS confirmed his government's apathy in the matter; their reluctance to take necessary action to retard the cancerous spread of graft in Italy was indicative that some—or many—were profiting enormously . . . and the trail of bloody dollars led directly to the White House.

There was more. Stefano asked himself, what could possibly be the interrelationship of these various far-flung interests? Viewing it internally, Modica could see the emblem of the Christian Democrats, the cross itself, standing upright with the Presidential seal atop it; upon it, in his mind's eye, was superimposed the American dollar sign. The shadow of this ignominious cross fell across a bloody background of stinking politics and insatiable ambitions, beneath which had been buried, in hopeless obscurity, the seven-year reign of Salvatore.

The appalling, manipulative chain linked Ambassador Steele to the President; the President to Wall Street; and Wall Street to de Aspanu, Belasci and the papacy. The last three would insure the nation would remain in capitalistic hands, where Wall Street would find Welcome mats spread over the wealth of Sicily. A capitalistic nation had no use for the rebel Salvatore. He had served his purpose. All their loyalties to him had ceased. As the only link left to their bloody misdeeds, Salvatore had become expendable. Bloodstained hands of the government officials had been scrubbed lily white, leaving no trace of their gross misdeeds.

But Salvatore, that enigma of redoubtable power, hadn't

been an easy mark. Three thousand soldiers, sent to liquidate him, had failed. What was left for these trembling, ambitious politicians? If they convinced him to expatriate and promised no further action against him and his mother, would Salvatore believe them? There had been so many false promises. . . . But . . . suppose a skilled agent of a cooperating government, sworn to uphold his duties for the glory of his country, a man with a stellar background, and one who could be trusted in such circumstances, could be found? And suppose this man was the only man whom Salvatore would trust? What then? Only one such man would fit the bill—one man, whom the outlaw Salvatore would trust, Stefano Modica! *Colonnello Stefano Modica!*

What a fool he'd been not to recognize this at the outset! With Salvatore out of the way there'd be no further threat to the Christian Democrats. No further strife and complications for these sanguinary and overly-ambitious vipers. Having created Salvatore, their monster, they now had an obligation to remove him from their midst.

But how, if everything else had failed? Of course, with the cooperation of a powerful and protective nation, how could they lose? They didn't. Biding their time, they moved decisively, using Stefano as their pawn.

Within this sphere of machinations, when it was learned that Modica had conceived the lofty ambition of secreting Salvatore out of Sicily, there arrived through another arm of the National Security Council, unknown to Modica, information that certain foreign diplomats sought the annihilation of Salvatore. Certain officials, then, arranged for both ideas to flower simultaneously, yet, out of necessity, to remain independent of each other. In mid-May, red tape suddenly swept aside, Modica was permitted license to set his plans in action.

"Bastards!" cursed Stefano jumping to his feet and pacing the floor in a sorry limp. "I should have known! I should have guessed when things moved ahead so swiftly," he said aloud as if to convince himself. He had killed off the rest of the pinchbottle, and, reaching for a fresh one from his back bar, he peeled off the foil, lifted the snap spring of the tightly fitting cap, and poured himself a stiff shot without ice. He gulped it down, made a wry face, and continued to whip himself for the next few hours. His subjective involvement had precluded his second-guessing the real reasons behind the abnormal velocity with which the operation moved in mid-May.

Well, there it was. Modica, fall guy personified, had

been had! In a life filled with uncertainties, rotten politics, death and the dangers of war, even the loss of his leg hadn't made him feel as impotent as he had in that moment of truth when, earlier, he had faced Bixby and the other devils of deception. Modica had been admonished by Bixby when he clearly indicated his gross displeasure at having become an unwitting ploy to entrap an old and trusted friend, and at the dangers to which he and his co-agents had been subjected. He could still hear that insufferable dolt's stinging words: "What does the life of one man matter when the security of our grand and glorious nation is at stake?"

Modica, unable to contain his anger, had countered savagely," Would you be so charitable if your life was the one to be expended?"

He'd listened to these State Department ghouls with a sense of death hovering over him. Arguments, offered as balm to soothe his fierce reactions of shame and humiliation, had only increased his agony. None of the flimsy, glossed-over cliches or patriotic euphuisms compensated for the terrible loss he felt. Judas Iscariot would have hanged himself on the first available tree instead of delaying the act as long as he had, if he felt what Stefano felt in those moments.

Very well. He'd been the Judas goat! But it hadn't ended. Modica would have his victory. It might only be a microdot of victory, overshadowed by the unwarranted death of Salvatore. Nevertheless, it would be a victory to show these supercilious whoremasters, wrapped in their cloaks of respectability, that they couldn't continue to manipulate and expend human lives for their own self-serving purposes. Stefano Modica had promised himself such a victory when he had addressed the twelve-man council brass earlier.

"You have my resignation, gentlemen," he'd said. "Accept it. But before I go, I want you to know your deceit is transparent. You think I need explanations for the complex and diabolical manipulations of men in government who, in their god-like superiority, snuff out lives needlessly, bury their heroes in disgrace, and hail with hallelujahs the vicious criminals in their midst? The shroud of political expediency and ruse of government security no more deceive me than do the files stamped *confidential* or *top secret* when they in fact mark the cover-up for greed, graft and immorality prevailing among power-hungry, salacious and self-serving men in office—men whom an unsuspecting public place on pedestals next to gods!" Stefano had to catch his breath before he bombarded them with his wrath.

"I've seen it all, from the unique position I held—the power plays and mad struggles for supremacy when nation pitted against nation in the stinking cancer of war play corrupt games. But when my own nation takes part in such vile practices, knowing in advance the rules of the game have been rigged, and they condone wrongdoings— well, I grow appalled! I shan't be a party to such action. I refuse to serve a government for whom I feel disrespect!"

Reflecting bitterly as he left the conference room, he noticed several of the room's occupants were red-faced, speechless and sputtering with indignation. Those hardnosed politicians might have suffered a momentary setback due to his caustic remarks, but Modica knew them all too well. Before he left the austere building those twelve men would clear their aristocratic throats, light fresh cigars or cigarettes, guzzle from bourbon-spiked water carafes and make recommendations for his replacement. He suffered no delusion that he'd be missed, or that the council would suffer from the loss of his expertise and experience.

Modica was unaware there was one exception amidst this covent of political ghouls—Roger Cutter. This man, who would one day be President and gain prominence as the most corrupt public official to hold public office of such magnitude, read the contents of Modica's file with profound interest. His beady eyes scanned the contents and held at the following passage:

Stephen Modica, L.L.B. Born Palo Alto, California. Educated: Stanford University. Entered U.S. Army in 1941, commissioned Captain. Transferred to Army Intelligence. Attached to Office of Strategic Services. Served under General George Patton in North Africa. . . .

Roger Cutter, an ambitious party man, briefly read the information dealing with Modica's OSS activities and those with the Allied Control Council. It was impressive, and his service record was outstanding. He'd been recipient of the Silver Star and Purple Heart and other high citations and recommendations. However, it was the medical reports compiled by Orthopedic, Neurosurgery and Psychiatric chiefs at Letterman General Hospital that caught his attention. These reports he read more critically:

Emotional trauma as result of BKA (Below knee amputation) considerable. Patient shows signs of acute depression. Extensive therapy, both physical and psychological, recommended."

He read a fourteen-month progress report indicating it had been slower than expected. Cutter's eyes stopped at the word, *Prognosis:* "Favorable if patient can be remotivated and guilt syndrome reduced."

Further notation indicated that all charts and X-rays had been transferred to one Bartholomew T. Baines, M.D. in Georgetown.

The man who'd one day become President smiled internally. Who'd believe the wild rantings of a former mental patient if he did elect to talk? He could be discredited by any neophyte lawyer. Half way through a self-satisfied smirk, Cutter gave a start. In his hand was a resumé: a subsidiary file on the *Operation Red Star* project. Included were the names of those men, both here and abroad, who had either promoted communism or fought against these forces during the wartime and postwar period. Cutter studied these names with undisguised interest. The far-reaching implications in these papers was enough to jolt him.

Always a wheeling-and-dealing man, Cutter wasn't about to miss an opportunity that could springboard him to national attention and public acclaim. Ambition dripped from his greedy jaws. Hadn't Dewey had his Tammany Hall and Lucky Luciano battles to elevate him to prominence? Why couldn't Cutter find his ladder to help him scale those slippery slopes to political fame? Buried in this file was enough ammunition to shoot down many potential competitors. *Goddamn!* As excitement mounted in the presidential aspirant, sweet visions of political persuasion winked out at him from that pregnant file in total seductiveness.

He pored through the file. Suddenly he tensed. There was enough in the file to send him into borderline shock! The extensive probe on the Italian affair revealed enough ammunition to hammerlock certain political enemies of his, all right. But, in addition, the file contained weaponry that could shoot him down as well, and deter his own progress. He mopped the beads of perspiration forming on his forehead, hoping the others wouldn't notice his discomfort. By damn! If this subsidiary file contained dynamite—what would the *original* contain? Roger Cutter didn't know how or when he could pull it off, but he had to have access to the original ORS file before it got into the wrong hands. With the original tucked away into his private vault, he'd be free to drape himself in saintly robes and impart his knowledge and guidance to the man who'd next occupy the presidential office. Time now to collect on a large debt owed him by his Roman friends. Hadn't he just done them an immeasurable service? They'd get that file for him—or else!

On September 30th, after Modica had floundered about, infected by a growing depression, he leased an apartment in Sausalito, overlooking a colorful bay of sloops, yawls, yachts and other seaworthy craft in California waters. He joined the reputable law firm of Bally, Bowls, Baccardi and Schwartz hoping to bury himself in trials and the tribulation of others.

Nothing eased his conscience or removed the guilt he felt in the Salvatore affair. Nights spent in seclusion in the labored perusal and tedious translation of Salvatore's personal portfolios intensified Stefano's guilt feelings, Modica's continuous impression that he'd sent an unsuspecting victim into murky waters, where voracious *piranha* thrived, refused to abate.

On December 5, word of Saginor's brutal murder arrived. Confusion swirled around Stefano like black storm clouds. Uncontrollable outrage and a venomous anger took possession of him and Modica felt waves of insanity engulf him as his self-assigned guilt multiplied. The death of two friends worked on his conscience to drive him like a powerful dynamo. Unconsciously there began to form in his mind a plan, one of which he wasn't fully aware and wouldn't be for a while.

Driven by that inescapable urge that grips a man of conscience, a man who finds life intolerable until he makes amends, he took time to have the Salvatore portfolios microfilmed. These he placed in a bank vault along with the original manuscripts, retaining the transcribed copies for himself. On the previous advice of Antigone Salvatore, he'd written letters to specific people, taking the precaution to cover his actual whereabouts. Answers to these inquiries began to arrive periodically.

Shortly before Christmas Stefano knew what he had to do, and presented his empty-sounding excuses of resignation to Bally, Bowls, Baccardi and Schwartz. His special knowledge helped him acquire the necessary passports and IDs for the new identity he intended to assume. No shelter of diplomatic immunity would protect him if he were found out. The risks were immense: the reward—his sanity. For

94

security he held fast to the ORS file. It received the same treatment as had Tori's portfolios.

Modica reasoned that the clandestine operation to smuggle Salvatore out of Sicily had failed. Very well, his next move was to make certain Italian officials hadn't learned who authored the script. At top-level priority, it would be no problem for them to obtain the information. He had to work fast.

He contacted a loyal friend in the Bureau in Washington, asking him to pull the Salvatore file and delete his names from any portion of the operational proposal. A few days later Stefano got his reply. His friend was unable to comply with the request, due to the fact the entire file was missing. Despite the ramifications and complications this discovery presented, Stefano forged ahead with his plans. In response to an inner compulsion he could no longer ignore, he returned to Italy to learn more about Salvatore's involvements. The jaws of deception, firmly locked on its prey, had to one day open and release its victim. Then, the truth would out, Modica reasoned. He planned to be there when it happened.

He was, and it did—up to a point.

CHAPTER 8

Viterbo, Italy

This medieval village north of Rome, once the home of Popes, now the judicial seat of a military tribunal where the trial of *People vs. Assassins of Portella Della Rosa* was in progress, rocked with the latest development in the Salvatore affair.

On December 5, 1950, six months to the day after Salvatore's demise, Vincenzo de Montana, first cousin, blood brother, and former co-captain to the bandit, shocked an entire nation of citizens and police officials by surrendering himself into custody. A month later on January 7, 1951, banner headlines appeared in every major newspaper in the nation, above this astonishing text:

"I, Vincenzo de Montana, assassinated Salvatore in his sleep. This act was done by personal ar-

> rangement with the Minister of the Interior, Martino Belasci, in the government of Premier de Aspanu."

Was that all there was? wondered Modica as he read the news account. Was it purely and simply a matter of betrayal by his most trusted companion—his blood relative? Modica was baffled. Viewed without its fullest implications, it was a statement of simple betrayal. Examined against a background of political intrigue among crafty Sicilian mentalities it carried ominous and serious implications.

If it were taken at face value as a true statement, Vincenzo de Montana had just signed his own death warrant. Unwittingly he had slipped into the same position held by Salvatore before his questionable demise. Why? Now why would de Montana kiss his life away?

Three months later in March 1951, Stefano saw Vincenzo de Montana enter the courtroom for the first time, where he remained under a gag order imposed by the Tribunal, restraining him from speaking. As he studied the handsome young man, Stefano still wondered why. Why had he put himself into so vulnerable a position? He'd have to wait and see it out.

The daily excitement of personality clashes between tribunal magistrates and the battery of lawyers fighting for their clients stretched into tedious, repititious testimony, encased in reams of denials and accusations bordering upon boredom. The dull testimony, moving at the pace of a tortoise, wore at him and Modica began questioning his sanity at coming to Viterbo. It began to appear that the truth would never be told.

In August 1951, Modica returned to San Francisco on pressing business. When he returned Viterbo was in festival. The Santa Rosa *festa* had attracted thousands of tourists in addition to the galaxy of news reporters who attended the trial. Since they had appropriated every available hotel room in the ancient city, Stefano was forced to seek lodgings at the Villa Etruria, at the outskirts of the city, where he remained until the trial's end in October. Countless times he had considered interviewing Vincenzo, but to do so would blow his cover and expose him to unnecessary dangers.

Modica slept badly on the night after the trial ended. Early next morning, before dawn, he ordered breakfast sent to his room as he packed and prepared the next leg of his journey. He'd shaved, showered, and rubbed soothing ointment on his knee stump before slipping it into his artificial limb. Built into the prosthesis was a small compartment containing his real ID and a small firearm, a single-shot derringer, used in WW II by the OSS. He checked the firearm, replaced it, and finished dressing. He wore beige khakis with a short sleeved bush jacket. A wide brimmed Aussie-style hat with a leopard band lay on a nearby chair.

Bags packed, ready for departure, Stefano waited for his breakfast. He moved across the room, flung open the French doors, and inhaled the fragrant aromas of the sweet-smelling countryside as he walked into the patio. His azure eyes veiled in thought. Something in addition to the trial results nagged at Stefano and provoked his decision to meet with Antigone Salvatore before leaving Europe. The only way of saving the remaining bandits, including de Montana, from the kangaroo-court edicts which sentenced them all to life at hard labor was to persuade the *Signora* to permit him to publish Salvatore's portfolios before the time previously agreed upon.

There was more. Modica was troubled by something more personal. Experience in clandestine operations had conditioned him to know instinctively when he was under surveillance. Certain that Minister Belasci had recognized him one day in court when their eyes locked, Modica knew there'd be a tail on him sooner or later. It came sooner than expected. Immediately following the tragic and mysterious death of *Principessa* Gabriella Rothschild, proprietress of the Villa Etruria, an incident which left him shaken, he began to experience the familiar feeling of being watched. He had expended considerable caution to avoid bringing attention to himself. He wore dark glasses wrapped around his eyes and dressed in the garb of a local citizen. He'd even adopted several ethnic mannerisms. In court he remained in the background, swallowed up by the hordes, as he attempted to take notes in his high-school shorthand. Nightly, in the confines of his hotel room, he'd transcribe his notes and mail them the next day to a post office box in northern California.

Three weeks before, the faces of two strangers had appeared at the Villa Etruria. Was it coincidence they kept the same hours he did? That they entered the dining salon when he did, and left when he did? From time to time he had spotted one or both men in the previously deserted courtyard, under a domed archway or behind a stately pillar. It had occurred to Modica he might be overly sensitive, so he'd pushed them out of his mind for a time.

One day, after court, he had stopped at his favorite to-bacco kiosk. The sight of their faces peering into the shop window had filled him with annoyance. He'd remained in the city that night, taking dinner at Zia Giulia's on the Via Tuscanese. Was it coincidence that these swarty-faced brutes had also picked the same night to dine on spit-rost-ed game? Still coincidence when he'd seen them in court, never too far away, observing with increasing curiosity the notes he took? Stefano thought not. For him it had stopped resembling coincidence after the first four days. He'd taken precautions to avoid them and confuse them and, on several occasions, he'd gone out of his way to lose them in traffic. Only yesterday, after outfoxing his watchdogs, Ste-fano had managed to smuggle the last of his writings out of the villa and mail them safely back to the United States.

Why hadn't they approached him to make their business known? Under normal circumstances, Modica would have taken the offensive. Confronting them, he'd have extracted from them their reasons for tailing him. But, without a backup crew or an aide, it would have been suicidal for a BK amputee to jump the gun. He wasn't ready to kiss off his life—not yet.

Absorbed in these thoughts when a soft knock sounded at the door, Modica called from the patio, "Avanti." It would be the room steward with his breakfast. "Set the tray on the table, please," he called out in Italian. "I'll serve myself."

The instant he sensed his error and started to turn around, he felt his arms gripped in a vise-like grip. A black hood was slipped over his head. He struggled. A coarse hand chopped him across the nose. He heard the soft crunch of bones and a warm flow of blood as it gushed from his nose and ran down his lips and chin. An-other hand struck a severe blow to his solar plexus, and he doubled over. A knee rammed into his groin. Modica felt little after that. A pressure exerted at a vulnerable point on his neck rendered him unconscious.

But Modica was lucky. He was still alive.

He heard voices, faded and tunneled. His eyes, speckled with blood clots across their whites, refused to focus, and he thought he was blind. His body ached excruciatingly in the hour it took a physician to motor in from Viterbo. Modica felt like he'd been crushed by one of General Pat-ton's former Iron Ladies—those turreted, creeping crawlers of the desert that destroyed everything in their path. Uncertain of anything, Stefano slipped in and out of consciousness for several hours, unaware that silent eyes watched over him.

It was 4 P.M. before he regained consciousness. Trying to pierce the haze before his eyes until they focused, he felt the room spin beneath him. As focus returned to him, he could see his luggage ripped apart, its contents torn to shreds; the room lay in a state of wild disorder, a total shambles. His briefcase, picked clean, was damaged beyond use.

"*Signore*, are you all right?"

Modica recognized the voice. Now, if only he could see the blur standing over him. . . . Images blended into several before they formed one figure. He recognized *Avvocato* Luigi Basile, de Montana's lawyer.

"The entire hotel speaks of nothing save this disgraceful *infamita* done to an American citizen, *Signore*. How can we apologize for so deplorable an act done to you?" asked the dapper young lawyer, indicating his grave concern.

Stefano winced with pain and, trying to pull himself up to a sitting position unsuccessfully, fell back against the pillows, groaning with pain. His hands flew to his face. His nose, swollen beyond its size and magnified far more in his mind, dazed and distorted his perception, creating a problem in breathing.

"You'll be fine in a few days," consoled Basile. "No doubt you've suffered a broken nose. The doctor gave you morphine and left you several pain tablets. You're a fortunate man, *Signore*, lucky, as they say in your country."

"Yeah," muttered Stefano through pain-filled jaws. "Damned lucky."

Basile appeared superficial for several moments as he explained, "I was leaving for Rome when I was apprised of this calamitous and most regrettable affair. In good conscience, I couldn't leave until I assured myself you didn't need some assistance." He leveled his perceptive hazel eyes on the blue-eyed American; then, suddenly, dropped his defenses. "Look, who the hell are you, eh? What interest do you have in the trial—in my client, de Montana? Don't bother to deny it," he wagged a finger at the bedridden man. "I've seen you constantly for many months. Now, after all this, I'm more than curious."

Modica, silent and sullen, didn't reply.

Basile nodded his head tentatively; then he shook it, his teeth biting his lower lips contemplatively. "Was this

Belasci's handiwork?" he indicated the disordered room, Modica's.

"Belasci who?" asked Stefano superciliously.

Basile shook his head tolerantly. "All right, play your games. It's your life. I've instructed the local *questura* to post an officer at your door and afford you protection until you're well enough to leave. We Italians can't permit such reprehensible treatment to our American allies. Or is it Irish?"

"No! Stefano shouted, trying to raise himself again. "Send them away." He sank back on the pillows, prostrate with pain, his face reflecting his agony.

Avvocato Basile moved in swiftly, forcing him to stay down. "Is there anyone I can summon for you?" he asked with concern. He lit a cigarette and slipped it between Modica's lips. Stefano acknowledged it gratefully.

"I'll be fine." said Modica. "Thanks."

Basile glanced anxiously at his watch. "I'm due in Rome—overdue. Won't you reconsider talking to me about my client? I'll need all the help I can get if I'm to save Vincenzo's life before the next trial comes due."

"What makes you think I can be of help to you?" Modica tried not to be obvious. A thousand aches and pains shot through him, and he grimaced sharply.

Basile smiled enigmatically and paced the floor like a man driven by time. "Someone thinks you know too much to remain alive. You think they won't try again?" scoffed Basile. "By the looks of this place and your face, they nearly finished the job. What the hell were they after?" He regarded the disorder in silence. "Salvatore's personal portfolio—is that it?"

Modica feigned innocence. "What gives you the idea I had anything to do with Salvatore?"

Basile laughed good naturedly. "If you'd been on this case as long as I, you'd be paranoid. To enumerate a few curious entanglements, my office has been broken into, my wife and children threatened with bodily harm. I've even been offered a handsome bribe to abandon de Montana. Lately, I've come to maintain a stable of bodyguards. . . . Basile paused. "Speaking of bodyguards, I insist on the loan of two of my most trusted men, until you leave Italy—or at least until you can handle yourself." He stared at Stefano's game leg, prone on the bed. "You must be mad to engage in whatever you're engaging in without benefit of an aide—with *your* handicap. And I refuse to take no for an answer."

In the time *Avvocato* Basile left the room, Stefano

raised himself with great effort and retrieved the Derringer from his prosthesis. He slipped the small weapon under the coverlet at his side just as the dapper young lawyer re-entered the room in the company of two burly men built like Primo Carnera, with faces that contained a hundred different twisted curves and angles and deadly eyes that could send chills up your spine.

"Borsini and Morelli will remain with you until you no longer need their assistance," said Basile. He glanced at Modica's rumpled trousers—at the partially exposed prothesis—and a glimmer of distortion flickered in his eyes. "You've got guts, my friend."

Modica hardly heard the lawyer's words. His eyes were fastened on the man, Morelli. Morelli's black eyes, rounded to steel points, registered surprise when he recognized Modica. The man, Morelli, Colonel Modica's Italian aide during the war—an undercover agent, the same man whom he had met at Rome's airport and to whom he had entrusted the special job of delivering a letter to Salvatore on July 5, 1950—stood before him, staring in astonishment. Before Modica could signal him into silence, he blurted,

"*Colonnello* Modica! *Managghia*! It's you? What the hell have they done to you?"

Observing this new development through cautious and alert eyes, *Avvocato* Basile instructed his men to wait in the corridor for him. Alone he confronted the American.

"So!" exclaimed the lawyer. "It's not *Signore* O'Hoolihan, but *Colonnello* Modica. "Please explain the charades."

"Nothing to explain," said Modica evasively. "Very well," he added, noting the chagrined expression on Basile's face. "I'm using an alias for personal reasons."

"Suit yourself. I can either be a friend or your worst enemy," retorted Basile. "You think it will be difficult to inquire at the Embassy?"

Modica cocked an eyebrow. "I wish you wouldn't. I'm not here officially. If it's bandied about that I'm using an alias, my presence will be misconstrued."

"Then tell me, so I won't be prompted to jeopardize your position."

Modica wondered how far he could trust Basile. He'd seen the stuff the lawyer was made of in court. His style, fearlessness, and astute legal tactics had impressed Stefano. Despite this, there was always that old guarded instinct which precluded Stefano from babbling freely. Using the utmost discretion and speaking with measured words, he stated only that he'd met Salvatore during the war and had been taken with him; that his presence in Castelvetrano at the time of Salvatore's death was purely coincidental; and that his interest was only one of simple curiosity. The closest expression of truth were the feelings he imparted about the sham—and the attempted conspiracy to cover up the facts—that surrounded Salvatore's death.

Avvocato Basile, no fool, sensed the avoidance of truth. He smiled tightly. "Yet, you've attended the trial from the outset, *Signore*? Very well, will you answer at least one question? Do you believe de Montana killed his cousin?"

"You don't believe the admission of your own client?"

The lawyer gave him a look that could have meant anything. "If it's only Salvatore you knew, what brings you here? Why is your curiosity so stirred? You'll forgive me, but I feel compelled to ask this."

"I had hoped to uncover the mystery surrounding Salvatore's death. Perhaps one day I might write a story about the brigand's life. . . ."

"You intend to pursue such a goal—after all *this*?" Basile waved his arms in the air about him. It was too incredible to him.

"If anything, this demonstration has only reinforced my determination."

The lawyer rose to leave. "I wish you good fortune, *Colonnello*. Guts, you have in surplus. *Pero*—I would reassess my capacity for brains, if I were you. A man would have to be crazy to pursue the course you've embarked upon." They shook hands.

"Good luck in your coming trial, *Avvocato*," said Stefano. He reached into his shirt pocket. "Here's my card. One day in the near future, I might like to converse with you about your client. Presently my hands are tied." The morphine was taking its toll.

Basile took the card, glanced at it and raised his hazel eyes in surprise. "You're a lawyer, also?" He shook his head regretfully. "I'd have considered it an honor, Colonel, if you had approached me prior to this. We could have exchanged a few experiences . . . but I forget, you are here *incognito*. Well, again, accept the apology of a humiliated Italian at the treatment you have received in our country. I'd enjoy remaining here. Unfortunately, I am already late for many appointments in Rome. *Buona fortuna*—good luck, to you. *Ciao!*"

After Basile left, Stefano made an attempt to sit up. He could not. He sank back against the pillows and closed his eyes. For a time he wafted in and out of a drugged euphoria.

Only vaguely did he become aware of another presence. His sixth sense, forever at work, nudged him, and he blinked his eyes and focused on the shadowy form of Morelli.

"I am distressed to find you in such a state. Tell me what I can do to ease your pain, *Colonnello*." The former aide moved in closer to the bed.

"Ah, it's you, Morelli," sighed Stefano relaxing. "I'm tired, my friend. Exhausted. Done in. Good to see a friendly face, though." The drug haze thickened. "So many times I've tried to reach you. So many times. At least you saw him. At least that, eh? Did the 'brave eagle' say anything to you? Anything at all to indicate what might have happened?"

"Rest, *Colonnello*. Rest. *Allora*—it took many weeks to reach him. Such complications. Phew! Those Sicilians are too clever. They guarded him well. He said nothing to me. Nothing. I gave him your message. I delivered his reply to you in Rome, remember?

Stefano turned his face away from him and sighed once again. "He was so young, Morelli. So young. What a waste." He couldn't keep his eyes open.

"Si, *mi colonnello*. He was young."

"I tried to save him. You know I did." He fought the drug, unsuccessfully.

"Si. You tried."

Modica grimaced in pain. His eyes took on unusual bright lights. Feverishly he cried out, "You'll tell no one, Morelli. I have your word! You're the only link between Salvatore and me. I can't impress how vital your silence is in this case!" His words were slurring and his mouth turned cottony.

"I will say nothing, *mi colonnello*." Morelli moved in closer to the bed. His right hand moved forward to pat Stefano's lean shaking hands reassuringly. In his left hand, behind his back, he held a .45 with a silencer affixed to it. "You have my word, and, out of respect for our former alliance, my lips are sealed."

Stefano fixed his drug-dazed eyes on his former aide and blinked them several times. Something he saw reflected in those piercing black orbs coming closer to him made him slowly grope for the gun beneath the coverlet. But his will dissolved, his strength dissipated. Before Morelli could bring his left hand around to fire point-blank at Modica, before Stefano discerned the intent, and before his hand touched the pistol at his side, the dull *pppphhhfffttt* of a gun fitted with a silencer pierced the room. Morelli's body

103

jackknifed, then fell back. A startled expression was frozen on his craggy face. His gun hand jerked up and the weapon bounced out of his hand, falling to the floor with a dull thud. He pivoted in a startled daze, crashed into a chair and went reeling uncontrollably into the wall before falling to the floor, dead.

Enveloped by a drugged stupor, unable to move a muscle, Stefano allowed everything to wind down into slow motion before he blanked out entirely.

He awakened in strange, shabby surroundings, in a dark, shadowy room barely discernible to him. Recollections of what had transpired earlier, mirrored intermittently in his mind came to him now in bits and pieces.

"Do not be alarmed," a voice said. "You are among friends. We transported you to a safe place until you can travel. I am Santino Siragusa. My friend here is Angelo Duca. Will you trust us? Place yourself in our hands?"

The voice came from a small man of medium build—a man dressed in the garb of a Franciscan Monk—who hovered over him.

Stefano elevated himself on one elbow, shook his head, and winced painfully. "I've no choice, have I?" The priest, a man with bushy, curly hair, had kind grey eyes and an expression of grave concern on his face. The other man, smaller more wiry, seemed familiar to him, but Modica couldn't place him. Memory returned slowly.

"What happened to Morelli?"

"I killed him," said Duca.

Modica blinked his eyes hard. "How easy you say it. Why?"

"It was you or him. He intended to kill you. The gun in his left hand was promised to your heart."

Modica, speechless, lay back on the sofa, stunned, shattered, distraught. "Not Morelli. I trusted him with my life . . . with—" He stopped. He had trusted him with *Salvatore's* life! "Oh God! Sainted God!" he moaned.

"Listen, *Colonnello*. Since the war a man does anything for money." said Santino. The subject was closed. A betrayal was so easily accepted by them!

"Where has loyalty, honor and fidelity gone?" asked Stefano rhetorically.

"To the man with dollar-lined pockets. Where else?" reflected Santino, bitterly. "Morelli has been Minister Belasci's man for some time. When we saw him acting as Basile's bodyguard, we had him checked out. His days were numbered. Now it's over for him."

Stefano watched Siragusa, the former "priest," removed

his cassock and busied himself making fresh coffee. Duca removed his jacket to reveal a shoulder holster with a .38 Beretta slung into it. On the table close by lay a Colt automatic and a German Luger. He studied the smaller man and something jelled in Stefano's mind. "I was instructed, if we encountered each other to mention *Terra Diavolo*," he managed between painful spasms.

"Who gave you such words to speak?" asked Santino moving in closer. He nodded to the man, Duca, assuring him it was all right.

"*Signora* Salvatore."

Nodding, Santino pulled up a chair, sat closer to him and spoke in subdued tones. "One can't be too careful, *Colonnello*. For five months we've seen you in court. Word from *Signora* Salvatore verified that you were in Viterbo. Behind those dark glasses and the clothing you wore, we couldn't spot you, and I only had a vague memory of your face seen on the day of my betrothal to Salvatore's sister. Through the *Principessa* Rothschild, we made the connection. Duca took a job at her hostelry and learned where you were quartered, and from that moment you've been under our protection, watched by our friends. We picked up on your recent escorts from the moment they tailed you, and kept them under surveillance. This morning Duca attempted to deliver your breakfast. He forgot to remove the sleep balls from his eyes. Caught off guard, he was hustled into a broom closet. Very fortunately, for all of us, the custodian discovered him within moments following the assault upon you. They rushed into your room in time to frighten off your assailants, who, sad to say, escaped through the open courtyard."

Duca reached into his jacket pocket and placed a thick, bushy false moustache under his lip and grimaced humorously at Stefano. Modica recognized him and smiled wanly. "I'm grateful for your help."

"What are you doing here in Viterbo?" asked Stefano. "Aren't you concerned that someone will recognize you? Do you still maintain contact with the other members of Salvatore's gang?" He addressed himself to Duca.

"Who me? How is it possible to communicate with them? You saw them in court. They wouldn't complicate our lives by writing to us. Our being here, in their time of need, gives them moral support. Santino and I have racked our brains to determine a way we can help them escape. There is none. The security is too tight. Why do you think they moved the trial out of Sicily—eh? They suspected that someone might be tempted to help them escape.

Besides, I only know a few of these men. I was with Tori only a year before I got too many of these." Duca opened his shirt, bared his chest. "See! Fourteen bullets! Go ahead, count the scars," he said proudly, showing off his battle wounds.

He went on. "Fearing the fifteenth might prove fatal, Salvatore, our chief, insisted I was more valuable alive than dead. I was never enamored of guns, you see. Me, I'm a lover. *Capeeshi?* The men who joined Tori after 1945, only Santino knows. When they needed a job from Duca only the paladins approached me. Vincenzo, Santino or the Scoletti brothers. I'm here only because Santino needed me. How did you know me?" Duca arose to see if the coffee was ready.

"From the History of the Bandits," Stefano told the expert forger.

"History of the Bandits? Where did you obtain such documents?" asked Santino, guardedly. Duca paused frozen to the spot.

Modica explained.

Only then did Duca move to the small stove to get the coffee. Santino lit a pipe and puffed on it evenly. "Why are you really here, *Colonnello?* After what happened in Castelvetrano and later in Rome, we never considered you'd return."

Stefano sighed and fixed his pale blue eyes on the former priest. "To find Tori's murderer. I swore an oath to write the truth about him and his men."

Duca almost dropped the boiling hot coffee pot. It was hot! But not as hot as the words he'd just heard from the lips of the *Americano.* "Whores of the devil! You will write the truth? The real truth? Colonnello—are you some crazy man! Tell him, *padre!* Tell him he's crazy! *Pazzu! Demonio!*" Duca shook one hand as if it was on fire. "If word leaks out that you're here for such a purpose, you'll never see your country again. You'll be given a house of Sicilian concrete, a mausoleum, six feet above the ground! You saw what happened to the men at the trial," exploded Duca. "They were railroaded, *amico.* See how equitable is our justice? Hah! Those men were as innocent of the charges as I am. See how it is? The Mafia is everyplace. They see everything, they know everything, and they bide their time to strike. One has no chance with them."

Before Stefano could ask what the Mafia had to do with the trial, Santino asked, "Do you know the identity of your assailants?"

"I can only guess. Please call me Stefano." He accepted the steaming cup of black coffee from Duca.

"Belasci or the Mafia?" asked Santino.

"Belasci or the Mafia?" exclaimed Duca. "What's the difference, *padre*? They are one and the same. Barbarossa is Belasci's benefactor, and Barbarossa is Mafia." His array of hand gestures fascinated the American.

"Barbarossa? Is that old goat still around?" Modica forced a tight smile.

Duca regarded the American with awe and stupefied curiosity. "You call the most powerful man in Sicily an old goat?" He swallowed hard and glanced at the noncommittal former Jesuit. "You must be crazy!" he said in a voice above a whisper. "Listen, Barbarossa knows everything. Even when a cockroach relieves himself that is known to the *capomafia*. Nothing escapes him." Duca wiped the sweat from his brow. "But, why do I chatter like a machine—*puta boom, puta boom*? It's Santino who knows everything. What I know is but a thimbleful compared to the barrelful Santino has written in his lifetime."

"My guess is your assailants were hired by the Minister of the Interior," said Santino, taking his cue. "The Minister and the *capomafia* disagree rarely, although there have been times when they are not in accord. Don Barbarossa, the perfectionist, creates political masterpieces. Minister Belasci, the 'reasonable facsimile,' the bungler, is a strange, crazy man. For instance, Don Barbarossa's men wouldn't have left you alive. *Capeeshi?* But, then, he wouldn't have been so foolish as to make an attempt on your life. You think he would have chanced killing an American in Sicily or Italy? Never! If you posed a threat to him, their arm would reach across the oceans to your country, *mi siente?* You hear?"

Stefano got the picture. "I wasn't aware that Don Barbarossa held the Sicilian sceptre in his hands. I recall vividly, however, that one can't play the fool with that devil." He reached for a pain pill on the table near him.

"Are you feeling badly?"

"The pill will help."

"Why are you really here, *Colonnello*?"

"I thought I made myself clear. To write Salvatore's memorial—the truth. Will you help me, Santino? I had hoped for your cooperation."

Santino aghast, reacted passionately. "You know what you ask? The death of all who remain. No," he shook his head emphatically. "No, you ask too much from me. I

107

don't want the deaths of my former companions on my conscience!"

He doesn't want *their* deaths on *his* conscience, thought Stefano, listening. *If you only know how I feel, Santino Siragusa.* He cleared his throat. How could he explain? "Their deaths are what I hope to prevent," he began. He explained further his intent to contact Antigone Salvatore and secure a release from his promise to wait twenty-five years before publishing the portfolio. "If I can arrange to make public the contents of the portfolio right away, all those who were badly railroaded at the trial can be saved. Don't you see, Santino? Only the truth will save them now!"

Santino stared at him in disbelief. "The truth will kill them! Their only hope is escape. If you published the truth in the papers, tomorrow—that is if you knew the real truth—I guarantee those men would be dead in less than a week. The government would find some way to discredit you and deny the story, even if it meant producing another set of false documents. They could confuse and distort the truth until even you wouldn't recognize their handiwork. Believe me, Stefano, they wouldn't hesitate resurrecting your past, including the fact that you spent time in a mental hospital."

"I what?" Modica was stupified that Santino should know this.

With that, without waiting to hear more, Santino excused himself, retired to the next room, and returned moments later with a photostatic copy of a report, which he handed to Stefano. The American's stupefaction grew at the sight of the medical report from Letterman General Hospital. Underlined particularly was the report by the psychiatrist.

"How did you come by this?" he asked with insatiable curiosity.

"What does it matter how we got it? We got it, all right?" He saw the stony-faced expression on the American's face. "All right, one of our men works in the Minister's office in Rome. This is how we learned of Morelli's treachery. He arrived in Viterbo in the stable of *Avvocato* Basile—"

"You mean *Avvocato Basile* is part of this infamous conspiracy?"

"No, no, no, no. I doubt Basile knows about Morelli's double—or was it triple?—life."

"What a sweet setup, infiltrating the camp of the defense counsel. A possible assassination scheduled for Basile if he didn't stay in line? And God knows what else?" Modica's mind shifted into high gear.

A clear mental image of the twelve-man security council rushed at him. One of these men was linked directly to Martino Belasci. Which one? How could they have known about Morelli? Had they known all the time? Even to the sending of the message to Salvatore? Morelli—had he been a double agent during the war, too? The only way the civil government could have tied Morelli to Modica, had been through U.S.A. Army files; the OSS or ACC. Someone had leaked Top Secret information. Goddammit! Modica had taken such pains to button down every possible connection to him—except the one through Morelli!

Modica felt sick. He wanted to scream out at those conniving, double-dealing bastards in Washington who had craftily steered him towards these ends—and at Morelli, the man who, ironically, had once saved his life. The insurmountable guilt of his own culpability tore at him. Through his own negligence he had led Salvatore to slaughter. God! Where would he begin to sift through this labyrinthian maze of intricate scheming? Where?

He began by explaining to Santino that he wasn't mentally deranged, that mental trauma is a natural by-product of the kind of injury he sustained.

Santino nodded his head knowingly. "But, you see, Stefano, how much the information could be used against you? With such documents, they could brand you insane, and insist you concocted the story you want to publish, for self-glorification or for whatever reason they invent to discredit you with."

"Not if I release the story in America. I have influential friends—honest, God-fearing men that despise conspiratorial politicians who plot to elevate themselves to power and fill their coffers with blood money. I've more reasons to promote the truth about Salvatore."

"And they are? . . ."

Modica didn't reply. He grew wary and, uncomfortable.

Santino glanced at Angelo Duca. "We're getting into deeper waters, *amico*. Perhaps deeper than you should involve yourself."

Duca took the cue. "I have no ache to know more than I know. It's not my affair. Already I've stayed too long." He packed a duffle bag in the corner of the room. "I will go to my house in Bagheria, Santino. You know where to reach me if the need arises."

Duca held up a restraining hand. "Please don't get up, Stefano. We say, *Ciao. Va bene?*" They shook hands. "I make only one request. When you write your book—it would please me if you forget my name. I wish to live long enough to read this story, by some *crazy* man, so I can smile and recollect those early days. It is not necessary for my children to inherit the sins of their father and forever live under the fear of exposure or possible *vendetta.* I've grown accustomed to breathing, and at my age a man shouldn't have to change his habits too abruptly." He embraced Santino. After glancing out the window several times to see if it was safe, Duca left.

Santino bolted the door after him and moved to the window, to peer cautiously behind the blinds at the street below until Duca was safely lost in the crowd. He stoked a pot-bellied stove in the corner of the room, slipped into a heavy coat sweater, and prepared a dish of cheese, bread and tomatoes for them to munch on. In no time Santino began to ramble, just as Stefano hoped he might.

"There was no one like him, Stefano. Salvatore was a giant among men. Men loved him and feared him. Women throughout the world fantasized over his sexuality. People from all walks of life sought his favor. There were those who sought to emasculate him. Sheer distortions of the truth have been written about him since his death. But—only his mother and I know the real truth. Right up to the very—" He sighed. "It *hasn't* ended yet, has it?" Santino puffed thoughtfully on the cigarette he had lit moments before.

"It's plain to see you loved him."

"It was more than love—and in a way I cannot explain. When I had to suffer all the lies and distortions told about this man, I wanted to go out and kill every last sonofabitch responsible for his death. Why is it, Stefano, that the best are always cut out of the flock and destroyed? They even dared intimate that Russia was behind him, that all the coups he'd perfected against the Reds had been a put-on—that he'd worked for them all the time! The nerve of them! The Reds had the audacity to accuse America. *They* spread the rumor that America planned to expatriate him! What a laugh that was! With Belasci and the *Mafia* so close to those politicians in Washington—how could that have been possible, eh?"

Stefano Modica's heart stopped. He moved stiffly forward on the couch, towards his host, his thin voice cracked. *"Belasci and the Mafia, linked with Washington politicians?* How?" He tried not to show his stupefaction.

110

"Ahhh. *That* you won't find in Tori's papers, only because *he* didn't know the truth. Or maybe he learned the truth too late to be recorded in the portfolio." Santino paused. "I never considered this, Stefano. I've been perplexed, wondering why, after such lengthy negotiations, after the expenditure of so much money and men, they took his life? You see what I mean? Well, in any event, I learned much during my stay in America. Much in the same way I came into possession of your medical report, I also stumbled on the name, Cutter. . . ." Santino stopped. "*Pero*, I'm getting ahead of myself. Perhaps between us, Stefano, we can find the truth, eh?"

Stefano didn't hear him. His mind stopped earlier at the mention of Cutter. *Roger Cutter!* His throat thickened with bitter bile. He couldn't swallow. The man about to occupy one of the highest offices in the land—he was in collusion with the *Mafia?* How was this possible? His senses reeled. Unfortunately, Modica knew little about this sanctimonious, double-dealing snake. Modica found himself saying, "Why don't you begin at the beginning?"

"Yes, of course. Between my Italian, Sicilian and broken English, if I don't paint the proper picture, please stop me and I shall try to make myself clear." Then, in an almost laughable cloak-and-dagger manner, Santino rechecked his pistol and automatic weapons, rebolted the door and tested it several times. He went into the adjoining room, returned with a blanket which he wrapped around Stefano, a box of .38 cartridges which he placed on the table, and a thick manila file. He blew the dust off it and wiped it with a cloth, then opened it. Inside, among many loose papers, lay a foolscap notebook like the ones in Stefano's vault in Sausalito. He handed it to Modica.

"It's the personal diary of Salvatore."

Modica frowned. "I already have it—don't I? How the hell many more are there?"

"Perhaps you have his personal portfolio, the one explaining his political involvements. This contains a personal biography, encompassing all phases of his life as written and set forth in his own hand. The date of the last entry is June 30, 1950. Without this, Stefano, the story can never be told."

While Santino refilled an oil lamp and set out a few more candles to accommodate his temperamental eyesight, Stefano, book in hand, was hesitant to open it. Perhaps it would be best not to stir up the hornet's nest. Who knew the nature of this explosive? Already, many lives hung in the balance—even his own. He didn't relish the thought of

111

living the life of a recluse as Santino did, or living with the pervasive fear Angelo Duca felt. It was possible they might find something better left buried with Salvatore. Yet, there was still the score of settling Matt Saginor's death—and Salvatore's. The attempt on his own life couldn't be ignored, either.

Stefano drained his coffee cup, sat back on the sofa and with trembling hands turned the page. In Salvatore's handwriting, he read: *The Biography of my Life. A. Salvatore.*

For an instant, he paused. This was different than the previous manuscripts. He could sense it. There could be no turning back. Committed, he could only go forward, despite the contents—or perhaps because of them. His eyes dropped reluctantly to the page. He swallowed hard.

"Thus begins the story of Salvatore," said Santino. "It's all there in the book. Go ahead, read it. But bear in mind, not until after the trials have ended can you hope to know the full story. Then again, perhaps the full story will never be known."

"Oh, but it will, Santino. I've just made a covenant with myself. I promised myself I'll find out and I will. You have my word. But—I'll need your help. Do I have it?" he asked somberly.

Santino Siragusa, former priest, Jesuit, scholar, and historian to Salvatore, paced the floor, his pale face creased with furrows of thought. It took several moments before he replied. Finally he said, "Yes. God help us both. I'll try to explain things only a Sicilian could understand. But first, Stefano, you must firmly fix in your mind an understanding of the complex political system in Sicily—or you will never understand Salvatore enough to write about him. Understand this also. Its been nearly two years since his demise, no? *Va bene,* the spirit of Salvatore endures. Most of the purposely distorted rumors about Tori were circulated with the intent of discouraging the legend of Salvatore from perpetuating itself in the hearts and minds of our people. Iron-fast rules of the Mafia, Church, nobility and government—the people who set themselves up as paragons—had been violated by Salvatore's power. God forbid any young men should take it upon themselves to emulate Salvatore! None of them, *mafiosi,* landbarons or politicians, is prepared for another Salvatore to spring up and proliferate the gnawing cancers in their bellies planted by Salvatore himself."

Santino sipped a glass of wine, refilled his glass, and poured one for his guest. "*Capeeshi,* Stefano?"

"*Capeeshu,* Santino."

"Very well, my friend, I shall begin by telling you there has never been a Sicily without bandits. Sicily has always been the dumping ground their slaves, who were put to work in the sulphur mines, in the building of underwater conduits, and in farming by conquerors.

"Those persecuted slaves who escaped the jaws of oppression took to the many grottos in the honeycombed mountains and became brigands to survive. Over the centuries these brigands, supported by a strong conviction that breaking the law was a respectable activity, never cooperated with the police, and between them prevailed a strict code of silence—*omertà*. Soon the Feudalists, the landlords, enforced the practice of hiring bandits to settle their disputes with the peasants and among themselves.

"Banditry came to be known as national character of the island. No conquering nation has ever succeeded in wiping out the existence of bandits. The governments most successful in dealing with the situation were those who suppressed their indignation and came to terms with members of the underworld, underground and bandit leaders. Setting a thief to catch a thief achieved some success, but it set a precedent which reached far into the 20th century. Notorious criminals—men for whom the people had no respect—were employed by police forces. Men, I might add, for whom the people had even less respect. Thus, a regard for law and order diminished rapidly."

"I see," said Stefano. "Then the problems faced by successive governments were not necessarily the isolated gangs of highwaymen, but rather a way of life shared throughout the society."

"Exactly," replied the former Jesuit. "Sicilians evolved into a tribal society, where the relationship of patron to client was more important than the State—and where the family counted most of all. You see, almost everyone carried arms in those early days and was prepared to use them in an underground conspiracy against the law. Later, these lawless forces, bandits, brigands and criminals were refined into what today is known as the Mafia.

"You have to take into consideration, Stefano, that Sicily's foreign invaders left behind them uncodified legislation extremely difficult to understand or apply. Many laws contradicted each other. For this reason public justice was disobeyed, even derided. In a world of overlapping and contradicting jurisdictions, of privileged exemptions from ordinary courts, of judgeships being sold and of witnesses intimidated, frequently the local boss or landowner was

113

more important to law enforcement and law making than a central government."

Santino paused momentarily and, moving towards the window, glanced cautiously about the street area below. Satisfied there were no imminent dangers, he stoked the fires and refilled the wineglasses. "Even viceroys complained then that the law was positively discredited by its deviousness. Its complexities and delays forced individuals to seek other means of redress. The poor were ruined by protracted lawsuits, and this put a premium on gangsterism for everyone. Peasant or landlord, priest or business man, even criminals had an added incentive to commend themselves to quasi-legal organizations which proved more practical and effective than the regular forces of law.

"The courts imposed harsh and deterrent penalties on any action they settled—penalties which included branding, public torture, and the strangling and disembowling of criminals. But, all this, including a permanent display of severed heads hung on hooks like so much meat, was a futile effort to conceal the ineffectiveness of these same courts in supporting law and order.

"Believe me, Stefano, this was the situation in 1600—and in 1700 and in 1800. There had been little change except for the burgeoning poverty of the peasants and the increasing wealth of the Feudalists. By the end of the 1800 the Mafia controlled most of the bandits, and crime became just one method of obtaining wealth and power. Political revolution was another."

Modica popped a pain pill into his mouth and gulped it down with water. He said, "I suppose each nation has had such a history to contend with, a way of life to guide them. But why hasn't any attempt been made to better the life here?"

"We are an old, old nation. All of Europe is old, for that matter. It isn't easy to teach the people a new way of life. Even Fascism, which Mussolini introduced and which promised so much, was greatly lacking. The most corrosive legacy of Fascism to Italy was World War II, which it strenuously advocated and finally brought about, but for which few preparations had been made. Sicily, especially, suffered gross hardships, as you very well know, Stefano."

"How well I know," said the former colonel." Reflective, he lay back to let the opiate take effect.

Santino's voice grew wistful as he recalled. "Once Montegatta, the village of Salvatore, an inland mountain village with an imposing Norman tower that lights up like a citadel of fable at night, had been noisy and colorful by

114

day; romantic and melancholy by night. Along its cobble-stoned streets and from the antiquated houses, there echoed mournful songs saturated with a special poetry of a haunted, spectral breed of Sicilian. Over the centuries this remote village became a refuge for a strange and oppressed people of Greek, Arab, Saracen, Spanish and Norman heritage: women with thickly fringed lashes over dark smoldering eyes that can kill, with wit that can blister or please, with love phrases that can infatuate or assassinate; men who became either young gods or nonentities. You've seen what's become of it. They are a people without hope.

"In the summer, an inexorable enemy, the sun, afflicts them with a prostrating force which Montegattans greet with remorseless and resolute silence. There follows a suffocatingly hot time when the tumultuous *sirocco* arrives. This sweltering North African wind gathers momentum from across the sparkling waters of the Mediterranean and with unbearable, pulsing, raw heat, blows gales of dust—blinding dust, as white as milk and powdery as ground glass. When the *sirocco* erupts, it scatters a devastating dust whimsically; sometimes gentle and insidious; sometimes in surly white clouds that snake and writhe with a vengeance only Boreas, God of the North Wind, could have created when he abducted Orithia, daughter of the King. . . ."

Santino paused to nibble on some cheese, then continued, "Spawned by the equatorial heat in this land of desolation, the people fall into a total despondency with their lot in life and the struggle for survival is usually no more than a day-to-day existence." He slapped his thighs with an air of finality. "*Va bene*, this was Tori's life. Montegatta was his village. Amid these surroundings and against this background of human misery, this exceptional Sicilian, Salvatore, was born. No man in contemporary history was so influenced by his environment as was Salvatore. He belonged absolutely to Sicily, was as much a part of her as if he had sprung from her loins. I tell you this, so you will better understand him.

"And now for the more pertinent facts. . . ."

CHAPTER 9

Two weeks later Modica came away with more information than was stored in his vault in California. Would the story never end? Wherever he turned, a new branch sprang from the tree—a branch on which new blossoms sprouted into a complicated maze of design. It was exhaustive work marking time, and compiling such data, but he felt certain in the not too distant future this labor would produce enormous results. He had one more stop in Montegatta to see the *Signora* Salvatore, and then—home. God, would he be glad to get back to the U.S.A.!

Modica, on the flight to Palermo, caught a few hours sleep and by the time he arrived in Palermo and checked into the *Albergo-Sole*, he felt refreshed and invigorated. Modica wasn't in his room ten minutes before the phone rang. A man's low voice, speaking meticulous accented English, came over the instrument.

"If this is the American *Colonnello* Stefano Modica who was stationed here in the war, would he join Don Barbarossa for lunch at his villa? For the *Colonnello's* convenience, a car and driver awaits him at the hotel entrance."

It was a subtle request, one which precluded refusal.

Moments later Stefano Modica, American citizen, sat in the back seat of the vintage Mercedes someone had kept in mint condition, trying to assure himself that he wasn't intimidated by the expressionless, scarred face of Mario Cacciatore. Earlier, when he'd caught sight of this gargoyle-faced man, he had instructed the desk clerk to convey his regrets to the deputy from the American Embassy. He made it a point to convey that he was lunching with the Don at his villa. Of course, Modica had no appointment with the Embassy deputy. If he'd known that the *Albergo-Sole* was a sacred Mafia institution, he'd have saved his breath.

On the silent ride to Monreale, Stefano found himself focusing on the rights of the American citizen abroad, something he'd never paid heed to before and to the coming meeting. In moments he'd come up against an indestructible force, a titan, a giant, the formidable overlord of Sicily—a man who'd given him many bad moments seven years ago, a man who, he hoped, would no longer intimidate him.

Don Matteo Barbarossa stood casually at the entrance gates of his villa awaiting Stefano's arrival. In his customary garb—shirtsleeves, his trousers held up by suspenders—and with three frisky English hounds playing at his feet, he looked exactly as Stefano had remembered him: a man much like any simple, hillside peasant found everywhere in Sicily. It was difficult for Stefano to reconcile in his mind, that here, indeed, was a power broker extraordinaire.

"Benvenuto, Colonnello! Welcome to Villa Barbarossa. Come. Come into my house," the Don spoke up with unexpected hospitality. "It is yours for as long as you wish to remain." He was the quintessence of cordiality, a perfect host, an amiable, warm and gentle man who prepared an excellent repast for a long-lost friend. He spoke his thick Sicilian dialect as usual.

They reminisced for more than an hour, following a superb luncheon of hot sausage, a variety of fresh, garden grown vegetables, and the pride of any Sicilian table, eggplant *parmesan,* and freshly baked bread as light as angel's hair.

"Let us do away with the many years in which we've not seen each other," began the Don. "Do you recall those exciting days during the war? Truly, the pulse of Sicily pounded with great excitement and hopeful promises as the tempo set by you Americans spread throughout out land." He sighed despondently. "When you left, it became the Sicily of old—antiquated, a bit stodgy, and without life." The overture had ended, Don Barbarossa went straight to the aria.

"I should be offended by your quick departure, *Colonnello.* You didn't take the time to say *adieu* when you left. But the war with its uncertainties was the culprit, so I forgave you. *Allora,* what brings you to Palermo?"

"I'm travelling. Unable to settle down after the war, I thought if I revisited Italy and other parts of the European theater I might find my lost years and glue myself back together again."

"Your leg, does it complicate your life?"

"Not physically." Stefano tapped his forehead.

"Ah. *Capeeshu.* That pain can be more complicating."

117

Without preamble he asked, "Did you find the trial at Viterbo enlightening?"

"You know I was there?" Stefano affected to be surprised. "Were you there? You should have made your presence known to me. It was rather lonely all those months."

"What kept you there if it was lonely?" The bull tiger bared his fangs.

"Why would the presence of an old friend—anywhere—interest you?"

"It pleases me to know where my friends are and what they are doing. I can offer better protection. Don Barbarossa permits no casualties to occur to his friends."

"Protection, Don Matteo? Ah, I see. Too bad you weren't around when I was attacked by unknown assailants. See—they broke my nose. Oh, it will heal in time. It's just damned inconvenient. I'm puzzled why they picked me. I carry little of value, if robbery was their motive." He played his part well.

Don Barbarossa sniffed out the game Stefano played. In addition, his memory served him well. Modica, his own man, wasn't an easy man to convince. During the war he had had to play a crafty game with the American. But, then, he had been only a newly resurrected Mafia Don. Today he was *capomafia* of all Sicily, with far reaching influences in Rome and abroad. At that time Modica had been the illustrious conqueror, the American colonel, the power. Today he was a plain American citizen, Stefano Modica. Even in this pose, too many complications could be reaped, if he didn't proceed with caution.

"Listen, *Colonnello*, out of respect to each other for our former association, let's be straight with each other. *Va bene?*"

"*Si, va bene.* Very well."

"In July 1950, you and three American agents, in Castelvetrano when Salvatore died, caused a big noise—eh?"

"You know that, too?" Stefano's blue eyes twinkled, dimming his indignation.

"You were difficult to convince in 1944. You haven't learned much since then, eh?"

Modica burned in silence.

"I'm getting old, *Colonnello*. Humor an old man. I have no time for games, symphonies or concerts—*capeeshi*? No longer do I dance the tarantella, either with my enemies or my companions. I no longer fox-trot to a fast-paced tune as I did in my youth. Now, I'm lucky if I can mark time to a funeral dirge. But, mind you, in my head there are no

118

spider webs. There is no softness, no faded memories. My pictures are quite clear, as sharp as they were during the war, and I remember you perfectly. *Colonnello* Modica of the Grand Council was direct, concise, and to the point. I liked you. Admired you. Never mind the differences between us. Never mind the difficulties my irrational companions caused you. With me you were straight. You spoke your mind. That's the way I remember you. Please permit this old man to hold such a picture of you now, even if we speak of disagreeable things."

"Perhaps I haven't learned as much as I should have learned, Don Matteo. I, too have clear recollections. Tell me, did you realize all your ambitions?"

Don Barbarossa nodded his head, and regarded the American through his darkly tinted glasses. "My observations have offended you? Please, take no offense. It confuses me to see you in such a light. Perhaps the *Colonnello* has indeed changed. In a uniform you were a real *pezzenovante*—a big shot who knew everything. Why you insist playing the man who is ignorant of my sovereignty amuses me. Tell me, my friend, did you permit me all those extravagances—all those privileges—without knowing for *whom* they were granted? They were not concessions accorded *every* man in the street," he said indulgently.

"During the war I took orders. My superior officers directed me to give Barbarossa whatever he required. Operation Redbeard—your code name—was a valuable asset to the Allies, and they simply reciprocated," said Modica.

"You asked no questions?"

"Question my superiors?" Modica laughed. "If they didn't know what the hell they were doing, I shudder to think what the war's outcome might have been." He managed a small rush of laughter.

"*Va bene. Va bene.* That's how it should be. One *capo*—the rest take orders." The Don made a sudden transition. "How long did you know Salvatore? You worked close—under Truman's orders, no?"

By now, Modica had had it. It hadn't been his posture during the war to be cowed by the Don, and he couldn't gracefully assume a different attitude now. He spoke crisply. "What's on your mind, Don Matteo? Sicilian intrigue has never been my cup of tea—or did you forget? Ask me what you wish to know, and if I can I'll try to answer. Now, what's this nonsense about Salvatore?"

"Why are you here?"

"I told you. I'm not a repetitious man."

"You have no interest in Salvatore?"

"In a dead man? Why? Should I?" Modica lied with a pleasant expression.

"Only you can answer."

"I've no interest in the dead. What must I do to convince you? Only the living can influence my life."

"Did you find Salvatore to be—special?" The Don meticulously unwrapped a foil covered cigar, careful not to tear it.

"You mean when he was alive? Of course. He was exceptional. You knew him much better than I. Didn't you find him an exceptional man?" Modica temporized. "As a matter of curiosity perhaps you can tell me what went wrong? What circumstances brought about his death? In 1945 he held much promise." Stefano continued to play the game well.

The Don grew silent and thoughtful, fully absorbed in twirling the red and gold cigar band around his finger. He nodded. "*Si.* He was exceptional. He deserves that much. *Pero*—he was stubborn. Unfortunately, he knew too much. And *caro mio,* death is the inevitable fate of men who know too much, and use the knowledge unwisely."

If Modica detected the silent warning couched in the Don's words, he shrugged them off. Impulsively, he affected a bright smile. "By the way, while I'm here I wish to pay my respects to the *Signora* Salvatore. Why not come with me, Don Matteo? Having such an important man visit her might help cheer her up. I understand she is quite a lonely woman since the death of her last son."

His words, expressed with such innocence, caused the Don to temporarily set aside his warring armor. *Perhaps,* he thought, *the Colonnello doesn't know as much as we give him credit for knowing. Would he have asked so foolish a question if he were in possession of the truth?*

"Permit a gesture of friendship, *Colonnello.* I shall have my driver escort you to Montegatta. It's been rumored there are a few desperate men in the hills, who might prey upon you, if you travel alone."

"Bandits, Don Matteo? *Still?* My, my, I thought Captain Franchina had put an end to banditry in Sicily."

The Don removed his dark glasses and glanced at Stefano. In that moment, all the things he'd ever heard and what he'd learned from Santino about this formidable *capomafia* rushed at him. If he'd been incautious, he regretted it instantly. "But of course how can I refuse your gesture of friendship, Don Barbarossa?"

They left the dining salon and the Don ordered coffee and wine brought into his study by his servant.

"Sit a while before you leave. It is seldom that I receive guests." He indicated a chair opposite his desk and sat down heavily in his leather chair. Stefano sat down.

He glanced about the room, gave a slight start. Perhaps the Don had forgotten. It might have slipped his mind. Or having lived with it, he might have grown used to it, never thinking it could set another man to thinking. Perhaps the Don had no reason to concern himself with the thoughts of others. Whatever it was, he failed to consider that the wall behind him contained a rash of faded newspaper clippings and worn photos of Salvatore astride his stallion. Modica tried to suppress his astonishment, until he recalled that this man was Salvatore's Godfather. Why wouldn't he have collected such trivia on his Godson?

Drawn blinds kept out the early afternoon sun, and shadows shifted frequently about the cluttered room. They sipped coffee in silence. Finally the Don began to talk.

"What decided you to write about Salvatore? And don't bother to deny it." He tossed a bundle of papers at his guest across the desk. "Work sheets collected from your trash bins from both hotels in Viterbo."

One thing in Modica's favor, the bundles had contained a mass of shorthand scribblings, for which only he knew the code. Affecting distress that his privacy had been violated, he confronted his host squarely. "Why are you pressing me? You should know I don't make a move without the full approval and sanction of my government," he bluffed.

"Bullshit! You resigned your post in August, 1950. Four months later you arrived in Viterbo, rented a writing machine, and proceeded to beat the hell out of it, stopping only to attend the trials, eat, sleep, and relieve yourself. It will be a simple matter to turn these over to Italian intelligence. But, listen, *Colonnello*, out of respect, I don't wish to boil the hairs off your ass, *pero*—its best you speak truth with me. Every minute of your time since you arrived in Italy has been documented. Now, suppose we talk, man to man, and cut out the bullshit, eh?"

Tense, stiff backed and doing a slow burn. Stefano pulled his prosthesis into a better position, then lit a cigarette. What else could he do, seated before this formidable tiger?

"*Va bene. Va bene.* I knew you as a man of understanding, good sense and reason. Where is Salvatore's portfolio?" The Don spoke easily as he began to decant two bottles of wine in Stefano's presence. "Which do you prefer? Red? White?"

"With your permission, white." Stefano couldn't pretend to know nothing of the portfolio. Any man attending the trials would have had that subject shoved at him three times a day. "What makes you think I might know?"

"Do you know who has it? Into whose hands it was left?"

"No." Stefano watched in utter fascination, the steadiness of the Don's hand, the manner, like an artist's, in which he prevented the sediment from mixing into the new crystal decanter.

"I thought we decided to be straight with each other?" Finished with the red wine, the Don proceeded to decant the white. "You saw what happened to its author, his associates. Ah—it is finished." He placed the old bottles on a sideboard and opened a *credenza* to remove two glittering wine goblets with a flourish.

"Certain powerful men would pay substantially for the return of this damaging document. Not because it rings of truth, understand." The Don used the decanter stopper to punctuate his words. "When malicious propaganda in the wrong hands causes too many complications. And you remember how Don Matteo dislikes complications? Consider my words, *Colonnello*."

"Please, call me Stefano. *Allora*, Don Matteo, is this your doing? Do I detect a hint of a threat towards me?— or—are you merely the voice for other men?" Stefano watched the artistry as the Don chilled the glasses in a bucket of ice.

"Never chill the wine, Stefano. You see? I teach you a long known art. Only the glasses. I speak for a number of men who will protect what they have, with anything it takes to silence the words of Salvatore." He poured a little red wine into a glass, picked it up, swirled it and tasted it. "Ahhh! *Che bello sapore!* What exquisite flavor. You sure you don't wish the red wine?"

"The white, please. Even if I had the portfolio, it wouldn't be for sale. Is that why you invited me to lunch and question me relentlessly?" Stefano clucked his tongue against his teeth. "Why didn't you ask me straight?"

"You *know* where it is?" The Don paused in his labors, feigning surprise.

"No. Not directly. At the trial, I heard rumors."

"Yes, yes, what rumors?"

"The portfolio has been microfilmed and remains in a vault, safe, someplace in America."

Don Matteo glanced at him through tilted eyes. The room grew silent.

"How do you know this—and don't be clever with me."

"Sorry. It's privileged information."

"What is this—privileged?" The Don glanced suspiciously at his guest.

"It means I can't reveal the source of my information."

"Or . . .?"

"Or I could be disbarred for breaking the confidentiality between lawyer and client. I'd not be permitted to practice law," he added at the Don's questioning glance.

"A client of yours has Salvatore's portfolio?"

"Possibly."

"Who is this client?"

Stefano laughed lightly. "You know I can't reveal such information."

"Or you'd be disbarred, eh?"

"Exactly."

"What if you don't live long enough to be disbarred? Oh, not by me, Stefano." He wagged a finger at him. "No, no, no, no. You have nothing to fear from me. It's been a long time since I've done the job of a hired killer. Others should concern you. I heard they almost did a first class job on you in Viterbo."

"All this for a portfolio?" Stefano's words were spoken slowly and clearly.

"All this." Having finished his decanting and pouring, the Don wiped his hands on a towel, and made no move to serve Stefano the glass of wine, yet.

Stefano, raging internally, grew braver. "Earlier you asked if I intend to write about Salvatore. Very well—straight as an arrow—yes. I plan to write a suitable memorial to him. The pity of it is, I've given my word, my solemn promise, not to publish it for twenty-five years. Uncertain of where my loyalties lay, up 'til now, I've quarreled with myself in assuming so large a burden. But, suddenly Don Matteo, your words have convinced me, stirred me into making a decision." Hs eyes grew electric.

The Don lit his cigar, puffed on it to conceal his rising anger. "My words—eh, Stefano? *Pe d'vero?*" *Before this stubborn mule is finished, my words will seal his tomb.*

The game grew interesting. It became the Don's move to estimate just how inculpating were these papers Salvatore had written and how much Modica really knew. In the next half hour, he asked a series of seemingly irrelevant questions. When Stefano, on guard, responded by purposely placing too much importance in some replies, and not enough in others, the Don concluded there were many truths in the Salvatore affair of which this cunning fox and slick American lawyer was totally ignorant. And without these truths, there could be no story, no memorial, no book. He kept these conclusions to himself.

"How long do you estimate such a memorial will take for you to write?"

"Two—perhaps three years. Why?"

"And if you shouldn't live so long?"

"Another threat, eh Matteo?"

The Don wagged a finger at him, "*Allora*, you know the entire story?"

"With Salvatore's death, the story ended. No?"

Don Matteo held the wine goblet containing the white wine in his hand, ready to set it before Stefano. He paused, glass in midair, and studied his guest. It was at this moment that Don Barbarossa made a decision.

Modica, sensing the immediate change in him, wasn't certain what had brought about the transition. His keen eyes fixed on the Don skeptically.

"It *is* over with—ended, is it not?" queried Modica.

The Don made a fumbling move; the glass slipped from his hand and fell crashing on the tiled floor. Stefano moved to retrieve the pieces, only to be stayed by his host.

"No. My servant shall attend to it. Here, I shall pour you another.

Fully aware of how quickly the Don bounced back, and that he poured the white wine from another decanter without the previous panache, Stefano accepted the wine and raised his glass along side the Dons, in toast.

"*Cento anni*, Stefano.

"*Cento anni*, Don Matteo."

During this time spent in mental gymnastics, neither man sold the other short. Having once engaged in very secretive matters of State, both men knew each other well. But it became apparent that Don Barbarossa held the trump card in this display of skill and technique. His demeanor changed, and so did his speech.

"Too bad we do not see eye to eye in this affair, *Colonnello*. It appears I cannot convince you of the folly in pursuing such a risky task, so I wish you well." Inwardly the Don felt a sense of relief. *This pezzenovante is spinning his wheels. He knows nothing*, he told himself. Then he said something inconsistent to his character, which might have given Stefano more insight on what would follow, if he'd known the key to his thinking.

"This story is one worth telling, and if it could be told

124

in its entirety it would be most spectacular. *Pero*—you will never write it, because you do not know it."

Sonofabitch! How easy he says it. Well, he won't get a rise out of me, thought Stefano as he steeled himself against a sharp reply.

"Humor an old man, eh?" the Don continued." Tell me why you, an American, with no business in our country or our culture, should wish to champion Salvatore after his death?" An expression of interest, rather than one of cunning or duplicity, shone in his eyes.

Stefano hesitated, uneasy at the change in him. "You wouldn't understand. Men of your stamp could never hope to understand a great man like Salvatore."

The Don wanted to say, "If you only knew. If you only knew." Instead he said, "Ahh. Now insults. Is that it?"

"I don't give a fig if what I do sits well with you or not. As an American citizen, I resent your intimidation. When I return home, I shall write the story of Salvatore, and neither you nor anyone else will prevent it. Just so you and your unholy coterie of holstered gunmen don't make the mistake of thinking you're dealing with a prize jackass, you tell your *compares* that the personal portfolio and all relevant papers of that remarkable Sicilian have been microfilmed, and lie in a vault to be opened if I don't arrive at my destination within a specified time. This information, which includes my personal observations, will be viewed critically by both American State and Defense departments. Such information, in the hands of scrupulous men, can cause repercussions that will break down the machinery of economic aid from the U.S.A. to Italy and cause it to shut down tight. Then where will your government be?"

"That's straight?" asked the Don, chewing his cigar benignly as if all this really made no impression on him. "Are you such a *pezzenovante*?"

"You can believe it!" retorted Stefano checking his temper at the Don's mocking tone.

"*Allora*—you have me by the short hairs, Stefano. The first round is yours. Once in awhile, like a wounded virgin, I must retreat into a corner, hoping no one learns of my *pecato*."

This transition left Modica speechless—and incensed.

"As long as we understand each other, Don Matteo, I'll take my leave. Thank you for your hospitality, especially for the use of your car and driver."

The Don merely nodded and watched Stefano leave.

After Stefano left, the Don, no fool, reflected on his meeting with the American. He had no reservations about putting out a contract on Modica. He'd do it in a moment if it would reap rewards. The consequences of killing an important American on Italian soil, however, were too numerous. In addition, such an act would be most imprudent and foolhardy. No way would he jeopardize the accomplishments of an entire career. Everything they had worked for could blow up in their faces and take them along with it. Hadn't he painstakingly explained this to the emotionally overwrought Belasci? That thoughtless, alcohol-crazed asshole had almost wrecked his own chances at the Premiership when his men had attacked Modica in Viterbo. No. Once Modica was safely back in his own country, means to erase him could be taken, *if* he still posed a threat. The arm of the Mafia had stretched across oceans before this, and would continue to do so.

But what was this crazy ambivalence? This hesitation? Scruples? Doubts? This inclination he had to become immortalized?

By the unholy sperm of Satan! Had he lost all perspective earlier? What the hell was he thinking to present the American with the white elixir of death? It had been a long time since he used his decanting skills to prepare a cup of instant eternity for a man, eh? *Allora*—no sense crying over spilled wine, eh? The Don laughed aloud. That was a good one: 'crying over spilled wine.' He'd have to tell Martino that the next time they spoke.

Something else nagged at the Don, causing a violent itch he couldn't scratch. And knowing he wouldn't have to wait very long before he could relieve the infernal itching, he made certain preparations, then lay back on his sofa and took a short nap, hoping as he did to resolve many conflicts.

An hour and a half later, Stefano Modica returned to the Don's villa, ready to commit murder if provoked. Tossing all caution to the wind, he raved at the Don in a manner quite inconsistent with his own character.

"You fatuous son of a bitch! You set me up. You knew what would happen if she saw me in your car, with your driver. And you let me destroy the woman! Hasn't she suffered enough indignities? You black-hearted son of a reprehensible whore!"

Stefano Modica paced the floor of the Don's study, not fully certain of why he had returned except that he had to get the last word in. He shook with rage in recollection of the catastrophic encounter.

Antigone Salvatore, that stalwart matriarch, both pleased and gravely disturbed by his presence in Montegatta, yet ready to accord him her most cordial hospitality, had caught sight of the familiar car and driver in her courtyard and recoiled. Her reaction, instant and complete, had struck her into insensibility. Shattered at what she misconstrued to have been a unification of forces between the American and Don Barbarossa, she had lashed out at him like a wounded tigress.

Unprepared for the burst of hostility and suspicion, Stefano Modica had been rendered impotent by her reaction. There had been no way for him to assure her of his fidelity, of his innocence, in this well-calculated and provoked encounter. And because he didn't know all the facts, there was no way he could hope to understand.

His attempts to secure her permission to publish her son's papers before the specified time had sent her into hysterics. She had damned herself for having trusted him, for having been so imprudent in turning the papers over to him at the outset. Highly emotional, she had ranted and raved like a madwoman, and when she had begun to hyperventilate, Stefano, fearing she might have another stroke, had been at a loss to know what to do for her. Nothing he had said could assuage her hysterics and he had made little of her thick, garbled mountain accent. The gist of her concern had been that, in a moment of weakness, she had entrusted the fate of all who survived her son to a double-dealing, black-hearted viper who was certain to betray them all. This much he had grasped.

He'd been helpless, stunned into full bewilderment by such erratic behavior, unsure of what he'd done to deserve such treatment. He had intended asking so many questions—about Vincenzo's testimony, about Santino's statements, about many other things. He had left, shaken and saddened. He'd ordered the driver to return to Palermo, where he could pack and leave this land of hopeless insanity.

He had ample time to consider why the sight of Don Barbarossa's car and driver had turned Antigone Salvatore into a madwoman. His brain roiled with suppositions. Sure, several parts of the puzzle were missing; he knew this. Hadn't they all told him so? Siragusa had made this apparent right off. Don Barbarossa had implied the same thing. What had eluded him? What? Everyone concerned knew more than they were telling—he knew it.

Goddamnit! Here he was at the center of a seemingly insoluble puzzle, straining to build an edifice with which to support it. What to do? What to do?

During the ride through the arid saffron mountain desolation, portions of the puzzle had come together in his mind and dovetailed to a logical conclusion. Instantly, Stefano had rejected these as being forcefully contrived, too fanciful and highly imaginative. He had concluded he was just groping for straws. Yet, he'd come this far, and having already risked a great deal including his life, why not press for the right answers? What could he lose? He had instructed the driver to return to the Don's villa. He had dealt with this self-inflated, high-and-mighty cock o' the walk before and won. Why not now? So here he was, more courageous perhaps than at any other time in his life, a bit too incautious, but still determined to do combat with this imperturbable feudal overlord.

Seated in a meditative, impenitent silence, watching Modica give vent to his fury, the Don let his face relax into lines of fatigue. It seemed he aged ten years. The Don raised his hand, gesturing for silence, but Stefano wouldn't comply.

"There's nothing you can say to me, that will excuse your lack of humanity and inconsideration for a poor woman pushed to the end of her rope!" he bellowed. "I wanted you to know that I understand what you did. And I shall keep this foremost in my mind when I do my writing—*Don* Matteo!"

"Sit down, Stefano, eh? When you were here earlier—we exchanged words. Now, we talk, man to man. *Va bene?*" His entire demeanor altered.

"You have nothing to say to me. I'll never forgive such brutality. Suppose the woman had died of a stroke? Would you have wanted this on your conscience?" he demanded hotly.

"We talk—eh? So that you understand me better, you should know that I made an attempt on your life earlier. It was easy. You were totally unsuspecting." He indicated the broken glass still on the tiled floor. "It would have been so easy. A few drops of strychnine. . . ."

Stefano faltered a moment in total disbelief. "I don't believe you."

The Don opened a drawer, withdrew a small vial and tossed it at him across the desk. Stefano hesitated before fixing his eyes on the label. *Strychnine!* His stomach gurgled uncomfortably. He lifted his eyes to meet the Don's.

"Why are you telling me this? What curious quirk in your character made you reluctant to snuff out another life?" he snorted contemptuously.

"It's not necessary to insult me. Once I permitted you to leave, I knew you'd return. All my moves are carefully plotted and with good reason. *Allora,* I want you to sit down and listen. I want no interruptions until I am 'finished. This is not easy for a man of my calibre, *capeeshi?*"

Don Barbarossa commenced. He talked into the hours of the night, and when he finished, he stood before Stefano, stripped of all pretense, totally without guilt, free from duplicity, a simple, vulnerable old man.

If Stefano had been moved by what he heard, he gave no outward indication. Because he was stunned, because the information had staggered his imagination, because he felt confusion,, torment and an inner wretchedness, rolled into one—a wild compulsion urged him to go out and get blind, staggering drunk. He wanted to leave. He craved to return to America, to leave this crazy madman's land behind and retreat into some sanctuary where he could think straight. Dear God! He'd been better off before a portion of the riddle was solved for him!

"Understand, Stefano. Certain machinery which I am unable to halt has been set into motion. You must guard yourself, take every means to protect yourself at all times, from the moment you leave my villa."

Numb, still unable to grasp all his mind had recorded, he prepared to leave the Don's villa. Totally out of character, Stefano found himself saying, "When you visit America, I'll be offended if you do not visit me in San Francisco."

The Don wagged a finger at him. "San Francisco? No, no, Stefano. Don Barbarossa will not leave this villa. I am nearly seventy years old, now—I am no longer a young buck. In my lifetime I've seen and learned many things. These things, not the years, have aged me. I've been powerful, invincible, and unbreakable. I was fortunate. Having sprung from the loins of Sicily, I knew all its secrets. Destiny, my tenacious mistress, that most clever of clever matriarchs, will never permit me to leave. She will cling to me, clutch me to her bosom, until I draw my last breath. The pity of it all is there is no one to whom I can leave such a legacy. You see what irony?"

The Don removed his glasses, lifted his swollen, red-rimmed eyes, and fixed them piercingly on the American. "You understand all I've told you? There will be—can be—no further communication between us. Your gesture of friendship will be remembered the rest of my days. I accept your word, my friend. Nothing for twenty five years. *Capeeshi?* I wait for only one more achievement. In February, Martino Belasci will hold the highest office in the land. Only then will I retire in my beloved *Sicilia*, away from public life. I will tend my horses and grow my roses, and smell the fragrance of orange blossoms again, in the season of planting. You know, next to harvest time it's the most romantic time in the year." His eyes grew soft.

Under the spell of his power-saturated eyes, Stefano was unable to avert his eyes, until the Don reset his glasses into place and broke the connection. For the first time since he'd first met the Don, he no longer resembled a marble institution of power.

They shook hands in parting. The Don startled him by embracing him warmly; a rare gesture on the part of this iceberg of a man. Precisely at this moment, distracted by something he saw on a mahogany console along one side of the wall, Stefano caught sight of a Belgian-made Browning lying next to a leather holster. Next to it, covered by a glass dome on an elevated base, he saw a gold calendar watch displayed. He gave a start, sucked in his breath, then, as quickly, breathed out.

Why wouldn't a Godfather cherish such memorabilia— eh? Why wouldn't he? Oh God! What a crazy bit of intrigue was this!

"I will see that *Signora* Salvatore doesn't fret over the misunderstanding of this day," Don Barbarossa told him in parting.

In Rome, Stefano suffered through a two-hour stopover before he could make connections to San Francisco. He paced the airport terminal, smoked incessantly, stopped in the bar for a few belts, and finally, bored with the delay, retired to the men's lounge to take care of a few physical needs, hoping to relieve his mind of the churning thoughts running rampant.

A peculiar feeling swept through him. He peered about the confines of the semideserted lavatory. There it was again—that inescapable feeling of being watched. Damn! He'd packed his gun away—hadn't thought to hide another on him. Taking the usual precautions, he failed to detect anything unusual. He finally convinced himself he was imagining things.

Bent over the washstand, washing his hands, he reached for a towel. A dull thud at the base of his skull turned on an array of colored lights in his head. Under the impact of the blow, he went reeling against a concrete wall, and everything became an enormous blur. A powerful fist struck the side of his head. From then on everything happened in split-second timing. He became aware of a confrontation between four men, who, ignoring him, commenced to exchange blows. In the scuffle, his assailants, immobilized, were left bloodied and brutally beaten on the tile floor.

He felt himself pulled up bodily off the floor. Apologies and concern for his well being, expressed sincerely by his benefactors, only added to his mental confusion. Between these burly brutes, he was eased out of the men's lounge. He became clearly aware that as one man hastened to steer him out of the area, the second man fumbled with a container the size of a match box and tossed it inside the men's room—then ran like hell in the opposite direction, through the lumbering crowds.

A loud explosion shook the airport terminal. Hysteria prevailed, as people scattered in every direction. Glancing over his shoulder, Stefano saw the outer lavatory wall crumble into rubble, smoke and debris. Joined by the second man, he was steered to the terminal gate where his plane was readied for departure. His benefactors tipped their fedoras politely.

"To whom am I indebted for saving my life?" he asked shakily.

"Don Barbarossa wishes you a safe journey and imparts a word of advice. Stay in your own country, *Signore, Colonnello*. It is not safe for you here. It matters not who nearly did you in. Only that we arrived in time to retard their efforts—only this should concern you. Outside this country, the Don's protection ceases. The Don wishes to impress this upon your mind, and he urges you to take proper precautions."

Between their valiant rescue and the silent threat couched in their message, Modica got the point. He thanked them, nodded and boarded his plane. Seated on the starboard side, nursing his lumps and bruises, he peered out the window and noticed his benefactors watching the plane. They remained until the plane was airborne.

Almost two years had passed.

Incredibly, he was home. More incredibly, Stefano was still alive.

His first impulse, when he had arrived safe in the confines of his Sausalito home had been to gather up all the

131

files on Salvatore—the portfolios, the diaries, the biography and all similarly explosive material—and toss it into the fireplace—to burn every last shred of Salvatore's existence on earth, along with his own bad dreams and nightmares. But, judging from the condition of his house, he had felt sure someone had beat him to it.

He had found it a total shambles.

Whoever had desecrated his property had known his business; not an item was left untouched. Thank God, he had forwarded all materials to a special post office box in San Mateo, miles south of San Francisco on the Peninsula. For a time he had moved about in a daze, staring at the interior of his house in full dismay.

How much more violence, how many more deaths would be forfeited before this snowballing force of depravity could be stopped? Modica had seen enough violence and death in the war, enough to leave him fearless of the things he could perceive. Fear of the unknown was what eroded his guts. Never certain of when an unseen hand in the darkness might reach out and strike, or when a swift bullet aimed at him from some remote hideaway when he passed along the street might find its mark, he had reasoned this was no life for a man as vital as he.

He leased another house overlooking the sea in Marin County, under a fictitious name, and for the next three months, as he furnished the place, he entered into a heated debate with himself. On the one side was honor, respect, integrity, and a firm resolve which rebelled at the liars, traitors and cold, hard, ambition-driven hypocrites who'd shown him their true colors. Someone had to let them know they couldn't get away with their corrosive and corrupt politics. Someone had to stand up to them.

On the other side was the accumulation of all that had happened, and the concern that even more could happen. The deaths of his friends, the brutality, the torment, the lack of justice done at the trials—all of it, having grown to phenomenal proportions in his mind, simply couldn't be swept aside and forgotten. He couldn't remain blinkered and silent the rest of his life and let his overwhelming hatred and resentment grow. He couldn't. He wouldn't. He, Stefano Modica, had the ammunition with which to crush them all, balled tightly in his fist, ready to hurl.

With no one close to him to suffer the consequences of his acts, he reasoned, he could lose nothing—save his own life—if he pursued the task he set for himself. Modica knew such a mission might prove suicidal, and that he stood alone; one man against a two-nation, political criminal cabal.

A newborn cynicism and a growing resentment prodded him to show contempt for those men who had betrayed his trust and now sought to annihilate him. In Stefano's mind, there was only one way to match the treachery of those self-righteous, self-serving jackals who had used him to entrap Salvatore, those satanic louts who had made a Judas out of him: *extinction!* Oh, not by aiming a weapon at them and slaughtering them as they so justly deserved. Nothing so simple for them. Uprooting their diabolical plots and plans, their selfish ambitions and foul lives, that was the ticket. Political slaughter of these treasonous bastards by the most public and efficient means. Exposing their deeds to the world so they could be seen in their true light. Regardless of which side of the Atlantic the chips might fall, the President's Palace in Rome or the White House in Washington, he was convinced that those who were culpable of the recent crimes must be exposed. This was his dream, his hope, his reality.

God plagued Stefano with an unrelenting conscience and increased his own personal guilt to a point where the pain became unendurable. It was enough to drive him mad. For Stefano the pain would grow, until, out of necessity to preserve his sanity, to absolve his guilt, he'd be forced to move in the right direction. It wouldn't take a day, a week, a month or a year. It would take time. It would take another death, another near-successful attempt on his life, before he would be moved to decision.

On a foggy day in the Bay Area, as the mist rolled into the bay in thick banks, a telephone call to Stefano from Fred Chall, deputy director of the Security Council's archives division, elicited a polite exchange of words before Chall zinged in with the real reason for his call. The entire ORS file had been missing from the Rome office since 1950. Did Modica know anything about it? Where the hell had he been all this time? Incessant calls to him—calls which failed to reach him—had gravely worried the bureau. Could he enlighten them on the possible whereabouts of this Top Secret file? Modica couldn't. Len Salina and Renzo Bellomo indicated the files had been seen last in Modica's possession. Modica expressed his regrets. He personally had turned over the file to Matt Saginor. *Let them go either to hell or heaven for verification of this,* thought Modica. He hung up the phone before bothering to ask how they had got his new telephone number or tracked him down.

133

Firmly entrenched in his new quarters with ample provisions to last a while, he kept at his side a newly purchased Browning and an old service pistol, plus an army surplus M-1 rifle, which he'd field-stripped, cleaned meticulously, oiled, and loaded. Having already microfilmed the entire ORS File and locked it in his vault with the rest of his treasure, he retrieved the original file and began an immediate, detailed and systematic perusal of it, never having previously had the opportunity to critically assess its contents and familiarize himself with them in the past.

Somehow, somewhere in all this mess, Modica would find the tie-in with Martino Belasci's office, someone willing to pawn one life for another to satisfy his own greed. Who was the logical man? Was it Roger Cutter, as Santino Siragusa had unwittingly mentioned to him? If so, he would need a complete make on the man—and, for additional insurance, one on every man in the Council. Chall had dropped the information that Len Salina and Renzo Bellomo, back many months from the Japan detail, were in the San Francisco area. He would trust them with his life—and did.

Five days after the call from Chall, Stefano Modica lay in the intensive care unit of the University of California Hospital in San Francisco, more dead than alive. He was alive due only to his ability to sense danger. A split second before Modica had been shot through the head by unknown assailants, he had been sitting at his desk immersed in his work. He made an instinctive move as the bullet sped along the trajectory and tore into his cranium at an angle striking the left temple and exiting the upper portion of the skull, missing the optic nerves and vital grey matter. A second missile punctured his left rear shoulder and exited through his throat, miraculously missing vital parts.

Simultaneous to the shots, the phone on his desk rang. Somehow, he managed, as he fell over the desk, to jar the phone from its cradle.

Salina's filtered voice came through the phone. "Steve! Steve! Be careful. There's a contract out on you!"

Modica tried to mouth the words, "Too late!" as he toppled over in a heap and fell into a coma.

Len's voice, frantic came through the instrument. "Steve! Steve! Are you there?"

He wasn't; and Salina, less than a block away when he decided to impart to Stefano the volatile information he had received an hour before from Bellomo, left the phone dangling from a hook in the public telephone booth and dashed to Stefano's house. Unable to enter the well-secured house, he used his gun to blow off the front door lock and ran up the cantilevered steps that hugged the glass-walled house to search the rooms until he located Stefano's body.

Salina had no way of knowing that whoever had gained access to the house had wiped the desk clean of the entire ORS file. During the month Stefano remained in a coma, Salina and Bellomo went over every possible reason for the assault of their former chief. Renzo Bellomo decided—it had only been speculation on his part up to now—that this was still part of the retaliation extending from the Salvatore affair. What else would have brought about such desperate ends? Neither agent had forgotten Saginor's fate, and often wondered why they'd been spared. Was it only a delayed time bomb? Would they taste the bite of vengeance, too? One thing, they sure as hell weren't about to waste their time worrying about it. Too many things needed doing.

Their skillful training and their long-standing friendship for Stefano made their next steps easy. They transferred Stefano to the University of California hospital, obscured his whereabouts, and gave him a new identity. Obvious to both agents was the fact that someone wanted Modica dead. Very well, dead he'd be. His death, reported to the San Francisco *Examiner* as the result of a mysterious malady, was posted in the obituary column. A coffin was ordered and a burial took place, so the world would believe him dead.

Prognosis for Stefano's health wasn't promising. For a time his life would be touch and go. His friends took turns staying with him, until Salina returned to Washington or until they could find a suitable, trustworthy nurse or companion.

Modica regained consciousness on the morning scheduled for Salina's departure. Dazed and partially confused by the time gap, he was still unable to speak coherently, and it took several moments before his brain started up and worked with enough efficiency to absorb what Salina told him about that fateful night. Questioned about the nature of his involvement, Stefano only shook his head. He couldn't tell Len Salina.

"Never mind. Don't overtax yourself, Stefano. Relax. Renzo will be here soon. Talk with him. I gotta go, pal." He glanced at his watch. He reached over and gripped Stefano's frail hands. "You'll be okay. Next time we see

135

each other we'll have a few blasts and thumb our noses at death. There's a gun under your pillow, if you need it."

Len Salina left just as a rush of nurses and doctors entered the room, excited about Stefano's return to consciousness, and set about an exhaustive examination of their patient.

Salina stepped out the door of the hospital into a dazzling daylight, and descended the steps to the concrete pavement. He ambled down Parnassus Street to where he had parked his rented black sedan. It was quiet this time of the day, before visiting hours. He paused to stretch his large frame, yawned and shook himself to wakefulness. He'd lost a lot of sleep this past month, he thought as he unlocked the car door. He sat down in the driver seat, lit a cigarette, and puffed on it for a few moments, hoping he might see Renzo before he left. Inserting the key into the starter, he thought, *Renzo had better learn what the hell Stefano was involved in before it was too late.* He turned the key, stepped on the accelerator, blowing himself to kingdom come.

The explosion knocked out windows in several of the nearby buildings. What was left of Len Salina; both arms severed from his body, his intestines splattered on the nearby pavement, decapitated and decimated beyond recognition, was growing cold by the time the hospital crew arrived to search for all his remains.

Renzo Bellomo, whistling happily and blinking his eyes against the bright sunlight, made a right turn on Parnassus Street and drove up the incline to approach the hospital area and the crowds gathering at the parking lot. He parked his car a block away and snaked through the crowds as the stretcher bearers loaded sections of the battered body into a canvas receptacle. Gazing away from the ghastly sight, Renzo let his eyes focus on the remains of the black sedan. His eyes narrowed with clinical detachment. Wasn't that the car Salina had driven away from the motel this morning? God, no! Not him!

Reluctantly his eyes moved towards the canvas where portions of the body were being fitted grotesquely together as into some obscene jigsaw puzzle. Only a long-ingrained discipline and years of training prevented him from collapsing over the state to which his dearest friend had been reduced. He turned a chalky grey and crumbled internally. He glanced about uneasily and peered at the horrified faces of the shocked onlookers, who instructed to leave by the police, had refused to budge.

When the homicide squad infiltrated the area, Bellomo

136

exchanged a few words with the officer in charge, showed him his credentials, and waited patiently until they located Salina's ID. The identity substantiated, Bellomo requested they keep the information under wraps until he was contacted later in the day, either by Bellomo or by the Bureau Chief. God! How would he explain to Salina's wife? How?

"Before there are none of us left, Stefano, you'd better tell me what the hell you've been involved in," insisted a brittle-voiced Bellomo, evidencing immeasurable sorrow at the death of their friend. He faced him in the hospital room.

"Not Len! Goddammit! Not him!" yelled Modica hoarsely in a violent reaction. He turned his face from Renzo and tortured himself for several moments. Hands, balled tightly into fists, struck at the bed at either side of him. "How can I tell you what I'm doing after this? It would only mean trouble for you."

Bellomo laughed sardonically with harsh overtones. "Len *didn't* know, and it seems to me he reaped plenty of trouble."

Stefano's bloodshot eyes and his swollen face contorted into a look of diabolical hatred. "You'd better leave, Renzo—while you're in one piece. Damn them! Damn them all! They think they can kill and maim and cheat and twist the minds of men because they sit in lofty positions and construct laws to make themselves immune to prosecution for the crimes they commit, while lesser men pay with lives and property. Have they no human decency? No respects for the rights of others?" he cried.

"Stefano! Stefano! What the hell's wrong with you? What the hell are you talking about? Calm down, man. You aren't home free yet!"

"Why the hell did we fight that fucking war? We paid a helluva price—the blood of innocent young men—just so we could perpetuate a breed of inhuman politicians who pile up mountains of gold and oil and riches for themselves, made available to them by the blood, sweat and tears of fools like us!" His eyes glowed unnaturally and he sat up in bed, shaking uncontrollably. He ranted on.

"I swear, Renzo, I shall light burning crosses for Salvatore, Matt Saginor, and Len Salina and I'll plant them on the White House lawn, so they can see what they've done!"

Bellomo rushed to his side, to hold him down. "Stefano, stop talking, man. You're raving!" He shook him. "Cool it. You're in no condition to work yourself up like this!"

Modica, spent, fell back on his pillows, his face wet

137

with perspiration, unable to control his shaking. Bellomo lit a cigarette and placed it between Stefano's lips. He lay back smoking, trying to calm himself. "This is my doing," he said, at last. "I'll make restitution for their deaths and these brutal atrocities. They can't stop me now!" His voice, deadly, was without expression. "How far do these tentacles of power reach? Between the ORS and the Salvatore story lie a dozen hangmen's knots, waiting to be stretched around the necks of the guilty. Those knots stretch from the White House to the Italian High Command, and I swear, Renzo, on the deaths of all three, Salvatore, Saginor and Salina, I'll find those nooses and prepare them for those men whose necks are tailored to fit them, if it kills me."

"You're already a dead man, Steve," said Renzo who pointed out how Len Salina had planted Modica's obituary and held a mock funeral.

Stefano glanced swiftly at his friend. "Good," he said after a moment. "Now perhaps I can work in peace."

"Can you use a partner?"

"No, no, no, no. *No!* I can't ask you to subject yourself to all this!"

"So don't ask. I volunteer. Besides, you need someone with my talents."

"You're right. I do need your talents, friend."

And so it went. Stefano Modica, a dead man, working diligently with Renzo Bellomo for several years, was finally ready. Bellomo resigned from the Bureau.

In a remote fishing village off the shores of Baja, California on the Bay of California, a few miles south of Palmia, a tall, distinguished American with piercing blue eyes stood on shore with his wife, an attractive brunette with pale lavender eyes and a soft smile, dressed in casual jeans and a shirt, watching as their son waved to them from the decks of Grand Banks fishing scow. Standing close by him, Renzo Bellomo watched as the huge prize marlin was loaded on a dinghy headed for shore.

Native fishermen, stripped to the waist, their skins sunbaked to the color of clay pottery, with toothless grins and straw hats, wearing pants wrapped like diapers around their lean hard, well-muscled bodies, moved into the water towards the approaching dinghy.

"Every day he grows, he looks more and more like his father," said Stefano with an undisguised smile.

"I hope we've done the right thing, Stefano," said his wife with worry lines creasing her forehead.

"We've done the right thing, Gina," he said turning to her. "It's the only legacy he'll have. A son should know his father."

That evening, as they sat in the open-aired portico of the Spanish hacienda. Renzo Bellomo handed Gina and Stefano their usual after-dinner drinks, *Damiana* on the rocks. Stefano sipped the silent toast made by his friend, placed it on the nearby rattan table and opened the manuscript on which both men had labored for so long and for which so many lives had been expended.

"Appassionato," began Modica. . . .

BOOK TWO

1943

The Beginning of a Legend

CHAPTER 10

September 27, 1943

> . . . *Before this day ends, tragedy will strike and*
> *effect the lives of countless people. My life will*
> *take an irrevocable turn and I will no longer be*
> *the same person I was when dawn broke on this*
> *day. Nothing in my childhood could have*
> *predicted what was to be in the early days of my*
> *manhood. For me, it all began on this day,*
> *shortly before my twenty-first birthday.*
> —*Alessandro Salvatore*

It was desperately hot. The *sirocco,* blowing aprons of white dust, fine, sharp as ground glass, had darkened the day, sealing off all vestiges of sunlight. At 1:30 P.M. it seemed like dusk. Early this morning Tori Salvatore and his friend Pallido, a bridegroom of two weeks, had hiked 20 miles to Jato to buy cheese with their hard earned money. Taking the usual precautions not to be caught, they found themselves nevertheless trapped only moments from home. They had no weapons, knowing if they were caught it would go hard on them.

To make matters worse they were surrounded on all sides by *Guardie Campestre* (Agriculture Police) and *carabinieri,* who promiscuously shot their Mannlicher-Carcano rifles at random into nearby wheat fields and bamboo thickets, hoping to flush out the culprits—or kill them. What did it matter which? Hot on their heels from Borgetto and from the dry waterways marking provincial borders, the police were rapidly converging upon them.

They tried to tell themselves not to worry, that it only made matters worse. But, as bullets pinged and zinged overhead and at either side of them, so close they felt rushes of hot air whizzing past their ears, they knew they could be easily killed, and they were crazy out of their heads thinking what to do next.

They asked themselves why they were treated like ferocious beasts and escaped murderers. Why? Hunted by police, shot at, because they bought and paid for food with their own money to feed their families? What irony was this? What mad scheme had the devil conjured up this time? They could understand an intensive manhunt if they'd been vicious killers who robbed and murdered for profit. But all this for buying food? Was it to be believed?

The sound of shrill police whistles split the air overhead. The shooting suddenly stopped. Tori and Pallido froze. They didn't breathe. They didn't move. What miracle had happened? Voices shouting in the wind, muffled and barely discernible, suddenly rang loud and clear.

"Firmate! Firmate! Stop firing! We've caught them!"

They exchanged startled, confused glances. Moving forward under the weight of their cumbersome packs, they saw through a clearing countless policemen waving rifles over their heads in a gesture of capitulation. Now, nodding to someone beyond their view, the policemen retreated into their jurisdictions.

Santo Dio! Their present and immediate danger far from over, and fully aware that much had to be negotiated before they arrived safe in their village, Tori and Pallido still expressed relief at the sudden reprieve. Sweat poured freely from Tori's handsome face. He wiped it with a red kerchief, then tied it Indian-fashion about his forehead to keep the salty sweat from running into and stinging his eyes.

He took stock of their situation. To the north lay terraced buckwheat fields, affording no cover. Directly east, running north and south, the winding, corkscrewed road from Castellammare Valley snaked through villages all the way to the summit of Monte d'Oro, where graft-filled *carabinieri* scouted the area, prepared to extort bribes from submissive peasants. Less than twenty feet from them, across the road, stood a straw hut—a *pagliao*—converted into a *carabiniero* checkpoint.

Peering from behind a thick cluster of cactus and bushes, Tori recognized two young lads from their village. Johnny and Joey Russo, ages eleven and twelve, had been caught by two khaki-clad *carabinieri* dressed in summer shorts and shirts, wearing desert forage caps and neck protectors.

The youths, both wearing beige shorts, shirts and ankle boots, were arguing heatedly with the *carabinieri* over the meager backpacks they carried.

Tori and Pallido, a small, wiry, dark-eyed youth of eighteen, with sun-baked features the color of mud, stared at the activity without feelings of personal involvement. It wasn't their affair. Their only concern lay in finding an avenue of escape. There was none. Stuck, unable to move, they watched the activity, unaware that these two obscene *carabinieri* were Gucci and Molino, the swinish sons of whores who had maimed and killed half the youth in Montegatta.

Gucci, a swarthy-faced brute with owlish eyes, the nose of a killer hawk, and the toughened skin of a behemoth, pressed the lads. He asked where they had come by the food they transported. In true Sicilian style, the lads professed ignorance. Threatened with jail, the eldest boy, Johnny, protested that his family had no money with which to buy their release from jail.

"Then we take half your goods," said Gucci. "Mind you, I'm fair!"

"The boys protested loudly. "No. Our family needs the food."

"No, eh?" roared the gargoyle whose powerful torso and upper arms set into the misfitted body of a bandy-legged gnome bordered on the grotesque. "You'd like it better, I suppose, if we took all your goods and clapped you in jail as well."

"All right," said Johnny, reconsidering. "I'll permit this injustice."

"Now, there's a smart peasant dog," said Gucci grinning evilly. His grin quickly dissolved and he commanded his partner, "Take it! Take it all!"

Molino, a bland looking man under whose face lurked the brain of an imbecile, did as he was told, while his companion Gucci raged aloud.

"I'll teach you misbegotten sons of a pig-eyed rhinoceros not to be so greedy. It doesn't pay to be so insolent to the *carabinieri!*" He struck the lad a powerful backhand blow and knocked him off his feet.

Tori's apathy disintegrated. He lunged forward, jolted by a spurt of rage. Encumbered by his back pack and unable to sprint forward fast enough, he found himself held in check by the bantamweight Pallido, who in an instant developed the strength of an ox.

"Fool!" he hissed. "Do you want to get us killed? This isn't our affair! Those trigger-happy sons of two-holed cunts would like nothing better than to cut us in two before we crossed the road. What purpose would our deaths serve, eh?"

Tori strained hard against him. Oh, how he wanted to give that bastard a sample of his own fare! Pallido was right. Knowing this only angered him more. His left ear began to throb like a giant kettle drum. Since he knew

145

what caused this phenomenon, he paid it little heed. His attention, caught by the strange lights in Pallido's eyes, shifted back across the road.

"You said *half*," came a storm of protests from young Johnny, who, for no apparent reason fell into a crouched position opposite the crazy brute as if he intended to do *mano a mano* combat with him.

"What's this? What's this?" snarled Gucci. Raising his gun butt high, he brought it down, full force, and struck the boy, catching the side of his head. Stunned by the blow, the boy reeled back with an insensible and idiotic look in his eyes. Blood spurted from both his nose and mouth. Holding his head between his hands, he twisted and moaned. Judging from the sounds he made, his pain must have been excruciating.

His younger brother, Joey, frozen under the gun of Molino, stood by helpless. Once again Gucci brought the gun butt down heavily upon the shoulders of the hapless victim. He struck him time and again, without mercy, until the lad no longer screamed, or moaned, or moved. Or breathed.

"Let me go, goddammit!" gurgled Tori hoarsely. "I said, let me go!" Pallido's strength, from wherever it came at that moment, increased. By now, he fairly sat on Tori and placed a hairy hand over his friend's mouth.

"Stay here!" he hissed. "I said, stay here! They'll kill you before you come within a yard of them! Goddammit! Calm down and I'll take my hand away," he told the wriggling squirming mass under him. "You know who I think they are? Gucci and Molino!"

Tori stared at him in disbelief. Held down by the damnable backpack and Pallido's leverage, he stopped struggling. Angry at Pallido, angry at the weighty backpacks, angry at the two beasts across from him, and angrier at his sudden impotence, he felt sick. Pallido cautiously removed his hand, ready to clamp it back on Tori's lips if he were to yell. For all his eighteen years, the lad showed wisdom.

"*Va bene,*" he said softly. "There are other ways to handle such matters, *amico*. Now is not the time."

There's a *bastinada* you won't forget!" yelled the bull moose, Gucci. He turned to the younger lad. "Now, move! Move! Get your brother out of here! Move before I do the job on you! And if you're thinking to report me, remember, I know your name and your face and I'll come looking for you!"

Startled by their sudden reprieve, Joey Russo pulled, and tugged at his brother's deathlike form. Dragging him

146

by the arms, legs, or anything he could grasp firmly in his young hands, he stumbled, fell, tripped and lost his footing, only to scramble compulsively to his feet again and labor breathlessly along the dusty road until they were mercifully swallowed up into the eye of the *sirocco*.

Salvatore felt wretched. His ear throbbed relentlessly. He continued to ignore the built-in device God had given him to alert him of impending dangers. What good was it? Pallido and he had brought no weapons. If caught, they'd be helpless. "Bastards!" he muttered, followed by a string of curses that expressed his feelings towards these black-hearted mercenaries infecting their land—the *carabinieri*. His ear wouldn't let up.

Shame-filled for not having aided the Russo boys, he took out his wrath on Pallido. "You should have let me go! Why did you hold me back? They were young babies," he hissed bitterly. "Goddammit! We should have brought a *lupara*—handguns—anything!" He reached up to worry his earlobe, as if that might stop the throbbing, and, unable to control his rage, he cursed aloud. "*Botta de Sanguo!* Why, God?" he supplicated, "Why do you see fit to warn me of trouble when you give me no wisdom or strength to combat the evil? You provided Moses with a staff containing your power. Me, you provide with a sensitive ear that plays a minuet. What good does it do a man to know of such things if he can't alter the conditions?"

Pallido's head swivelled around to stare at his handsome friend as if he'd lost his senses. Before he could ask why the hell Moses had entered their conversation, they were propelled forward by an unexpected shove from behind, and they both landed unceremoniously, scrambling forward into the middle of the road.

Alerted by a glimpse of Tori's red neckerchief, spotted when the winds blew through the thicket, Officer Molino had craftily crept in behind them and caught them off guard.

Towering over them stood that demon, Gucci. Tight lips pulled back fiendishly over yellowed teeth; scornful, hating eyes that could challenge a herd of charging bull elephants without flinching; everything about him told Tori that Gucci was capable of killing them both.

"Your identity cards!" bellowed the bull moose.

Tori took his time in pulling himself off the ground. He assisted his friend, who'd been thrown off balance by the backpack weight. He dusted off his trousers, clenched his teeth until his jaws ached, and, against his will, complied with Gucci's order. They both handed him their cards.

147

"What the hell is it with you ignorant Sicilians? Can't you read or write? Haven't you seen the notices? It's against the law to transport food over provincial borders. What's in your packs? Goddammit! Move! Move, I said, and remove those packs. We haven't got all day!"

"Cheese," said Tori, his eyes intent on the guns of their obstructors.

"Where did you buy the cheese? I suppose some vendor just happened along the road," snorted Gucci. "You all tell the same story." He studied their identity cards with marked interest.

"That's right. That's just the way it happened," replied Tori with a false brightness that drew a dumb look of surprise from Pallido's face. They slipped off their backpacks. Where the leather straps had cut into Tori's arms, angry welts had blistered and opened. He ached all over. Every muscle and nerve in his body felt swollen and he was consumed with thirst. He uncorked his goatskin. "Mind if I sip some water?" he asked pointedly.

Gucci hated handsome men who reminded him of his own ugliness. His eyes burned into Salvatore's and slowly assessed the peasant's physical potential. In his prime, suntanned and in perfect physical condition, Tori stood a hair under six feet. Broad shoulders, strong arms and thickly muscled thighs strained through khaki colored trousers and shirt. One strong hand held the goatskin to his lips; the other, thumb hooked through his belt, gave him the appearance of a relaxed, fearless man, one unconcerned with the presence of an obstructor. Warm brown eyes masked the inner fury of a man bent on destruction. Nostrils at the end of his straight nose flared, and his jaw line rippled as he clenched his teeth.

Gucci saw all this and more. None of it was in Tori's favor. He growled wrathfully. "Impertinent bastard! Be quick with those packs!" Gucci fingered his gun a little too eagerly. ". . . Or do I need my trusty little friend to persuade you?"

"There's two cheeses in each pack," volunteered Pallido.

"I didn't ask for an inventory, you son of a humpbacked turtle. I gave you an order!"

There came a sound of fast riding. Through clouds of dust came a squad of seven riders and their horses—raspy-throated, coughing men who braved the sweltering North African winds. The riders, coming to a stop, pulled up sharply on their reins. Their leader, a well-muscled officer flamboyantly-dressed in the *Napoletano* style, yanked hard on the reins of his lathered horse and let it dance a bit. Birds of such rare plumage, rarely seen in the interior villages, drew instant attention. Even Tori and Pallido seemed impressed by such a uniform.

"I'm Lt. Franchina of Bellolampo," he shouted at Gucci who saluted him smartly. Molina quickly stood at attention and saluted. "We're looking for two young lads carrying backpacks. . . ."

Lt. Franchina, a sharp bird, glanced at the Montegattans as if they were something utterly abhorrent to him. He inspected the *carabinieri* with discerning eyes, silently taking note of the lorry full of confiscated foods. His eyes assessed with more curiosity the large cache of weapons stacked against one wall of the straw hut. This, he surmised, was dirty business.

As the *carabinieri* exchanged words, Tori paid them no heed. More intent on watching the brutal Gucci, he wondered at his and Pallido's fate. The guns enticed him. Should he make a dive for them? If he were fast enough, he might bag both his obstructors. Pallido's earlier words deterred him: *There are other ways to handle such matters.* Tori bided his time.

"Is there another entrance to the village?" asked Lt. Franchina, shouting above the wind to be heard. He ignored the man's obvious salute of dismissal.

"Only along the dry waterways guarded by those ferret-eyed *Guardie Campestre*," answered Gucci. "I tell you those *birbanti*—those sharpies—don't let a flea escape. Nothing gets past them, *Tenente*, hear?"

"*Va bene*, I believe you," replied the peacock Franchina, who couldn't resist adding, "If they get through, then, it shall have been through your negligence, eh?"

Preoccupied with his own thoughts, Tori heard none of this conversation between the peacock on horseback and the vile obscenity, Gucci. Obviously something the peacock said had angered Gucci. By the time they had exchanged salutes and the officer and his squad of men had disappeared into cornucopias of dust, Gucci, tense, irritable and seething, was ready to turn his wrath on the men he detained. For a moment he listened to his partner make small talk.

"Is this good cheese?" asked Molino. "I've not seen anything worthwhile in these times," he added, his mouth watering for a taste of the cheese.

"We've had no opportunity to sample it," said Tori in the manner of a dandy. "Our auto broke down, you see. We sent our man for help—" He stopped abruptly, sobered by the name-tag on Gucci's shirt which came into clear focus. So! *This was Gucci!* He lifted his inscrutable dark eyes slowly, fixing them steadfastly on the brute.

Instantly Tori got the distinct impression that his testicles had exploded. He jacknifed forward to catch his breath. He'd been struck front, and nearly bull's-eye, by Gucci's rifle. Tori was lucky. Gucci had missed his manhood by a hair. That's not to say he wasn't in pain. He took his time drawing himself up to his full height. Without the weight of his backpack he towered over Gucci. He saw little else now, except the devil in his path.

One look at the menace in Tori's dilated eyes spurred Pallido into action with the antics of a court jester. He grinned broadly: "Here! Take a look! See what *fantastico* cheeses! Twenty pounds each, and orange as a harvest moon. Go ahead, take one and let us be on our way." He put on a good show, avoiding Tori's contemptuous glare, and moved about the area like an agile dancer. What did he care if Tori was angry? He had a new bride waiting for him at home, and he aimed to get there in mint condition. For now, he was all gaiety. He smiled falsely and did a side-stepping cakewalk to distract the police.

"You want us to look the other way and let you pass. Is that it?" asked Gucci. "Very well—two." He held up two grubby fingers.

"Take one and be satisfied," bargained Pallido. "We don't mind if you wet your beaks as long as there's enough to go around."

Gucci drew his service pistol. "Two—or jail for both."

"*Allora*—two," said the crestfallen bridegroom, with no help from Tori.

"Go on, move. Move!" yelled Gucci. "Move before I change my mind. I said move, mules, move. *Move!*"

Food in Sicily, more precious during wartime than money, could buy anything, even life. Food had become a vital weapon to ward off the sword of Damocles and death's invincible warriors. Which atrocity affected Tori most—the brutal *bastinada,* or the loss of their food—was hardly important now.

"I should peel you like a prickly pear for being so generous," he told Pallido as they scaled the rocky incline to their village. "Chop you at both ends and slit you down the middle!"

"*Allora*—that was really Gucci? That ruthless obscenity who's cut the lifeline of our youths? *Managghia!* And did you see all the artillery? Rifles, handguns?"

"I saw them. Do you realize the back-breaking sweat

150

that paid for those cheeses? How long we saved to buy them?" Tori wouldn't ease up.

"Whores of the devil! They have no feelings except for themselves. What do they care for us, eh?" Pallido, on his own tack, hardly heard his friend.

"They had no right to confiscate our cheese. I hope they choke on them."

"Listen, *professore*, be grateful we're alive—eh?" Pallido was exasperated.

"Be grateful we're alive?" Tori repeated in scornful mimicry. "Thieving bastards! Instead of bringing us relief, the Allies and their goddamned laws brought us doom. We cross borders, risk our lives for food paid with our own money—*our own money*, mind you—and we become felons. Is that justice? Blood sucking *carabinieri!* They bleed us dry with tributes we're forced to pay, then they steal our food and capriciously shoot us down. Next they'll steal our lands!"

Pallido lost all patience. "*Cazzo!* Did you want to go to jail? End up like your cousins, murdered in cold blood? You forget the de Montanas?"

"They'll never steal or cheat Salvatore again!" he glowered angrily.

"*Cafone!* Goddammit! There was no other way!" shouted Pallido, infuriated by the other's stubborness. "*Allora*—you go ahead. Be a hero! Anytime! *Pero* not with me around. I don't ache for a bullet in my belly. . . ."

Ping! Zing! Ping! Ping! Cracking sounds of rifle fire burst around them in small explosions.

"Get down, Pallido!" shouted Tori in warning.

Pallido, a look of insane bewilderment in his eyes, pitched forward and fell into his friend's arms.

"Pallido! Pallido!" Tori fell to the ground over his friend's body, searching frantically for the source of gunfire. In the distance, he saw those murderous monsters, Gucci and Molino, firing at them. He ducked, but not before a bullet creased his skull. Instantly blood dripped down on his forehead. He reached up, touched the warm sticky fluid, and stared dumbly at the crimson splotches in his hand. A surge of madness crept through him as he dove to the side of the road and shed his backpack. Crawling forward in the dust bowl, he grabbed Pallido's body and, pulling him closer, he prayed Pallido's wound would be as superficial as his own. He tore off his friend's backpack, flung it savagely aside, loosened his shirt, and placed his ear over the lad's heart. Heartbeats, faint and irregular, worked hard to keep him alive.

Out of range of those gun-crazed devils, he uncorked Pallido's goatskin and forced wine through his pale lips. Only when he removed his hand from Pallido's back and felt the warm blood oozing from an open wound did his hatred for those butchers multiply, and his concern for his friend intensify. He stroked the dirt-smeared face, pushed Pallido's hair off his forehead. "Talk, Pallido. Talk! Sonofabitch, you can't die! You hear? You can't die!"

Pallido's eyes fluttered opened. He smiled wanly. "It will pass, *professore*. It will pass," he said, and died.

Tori leaned over, feeling dead inside, and picked up Pallido's body in his arms. He lumbered through the *sirocco* towards the village, and with every step he told himself, *Pallido is wrong. It will not pass. Things will get worse. A wrathful Lucifer has entered Montegatta, bent on holocaust. Things won't right themselves without help and for all appearances there is no help for his people.*

He kept telling himself it wasn't his affair. Why should he court trouble? He was a pacific nature, that of a young scholar who had rightfully earned the title of *professore*. He had plans. After the war he intended to become a senator, a legislator, a lawmaker. This was his dream, his hope, his life. He was not, and never had been, a violent-tempered juvenile delinquent who'd go off half cocked to support a cause not his own.

Yet, Alessandro— "Tori"—Salvatore, who was not twenty-one years of age on this day when he first was feeling the irrevocable stirrings of his destiny, found himself, thirty minutes later, huddled across the road from Gucci and Molino's Checkpoint Two, where earlier he and Pallido had hidden. Pallido was dead; but Tori wasn't alone. His companions were a trigger sharp wolf gun—a *lupara*, a deadly weapon—and two loaded Beretta pistols—just in case.

Watching the vipers divide their collected graft from the lorry, Tori was uncertain what he'd do or how he'd do it. For a time, forced to wait until several villagers passed Checkpoint Two and paid their tributes to those dishonorable swine, Tori wondered if Destiny was attempting to dissuade him from his intended task.

At last, when the roads appeared deserted and he was readying himself for a move, he was once again deterred when Molino disappeared behind a roadside shrine and reappeared, holding two young lads by the scruffs of their necks. Tori, his blood boiling, watched them like a hawk.

He recognized the Giunta lads from his village, cousins

to the lads he and Pallido had seen stopped only that morning when they left Montegatta. Caught, the boys were made to part with a kilo of pasta. Like others before them, they protested the unfair treatment. Then, as the remorseless Gucci had done in the past—and would continue to do unless he was stopped, Tori reflected—he bullied the lads and threatened them. Their refusal to back down to him brought on the officer's specialty with the butt of his rifle. Time and again, he struck the impertinent child until blood ran freely and the lad reeled like a crazed animal.

A gust of wind rolled across the valley at them, lifting dust from the ground and swirling it about into a congested mass. When the dust settled, Tori stood at its center, *lupara* held firmly in hand, poised like a young god out of hell. He crept forward stealthily. His eyes, the wary eyes of a golden eagle, veiled the angry volcanic fires that maddened him.

Officer Molino saw him first. He froze. Young Frankie Giunta, a quick-witted lad of twelve years, saw Tori and made a fast grab for Molino's gun, but he wasn't fast enough for Gucci, who paused in his destruction to draw his service pistol and fire point-blank at the boy. The bullet caught the lad between the eyes. He gasped in surprise, screamed loudly, and fell back onto Molino, clutching his face and clawing at the officer with his last ounce of strength. He left a trail of carmine on the *carabiniero's* shorts. Blood gushed from between Frankie's horrified eyes. Tori couldn't believe what he was seeing.

Molino had turned into a dumb statue of immobility. Gucci neither saw Tori nor sensed him until he followed the inert expression on the face of his partner, and his line of vision. Recognition filled Gucci's eyes. Tori could almost see the wheels turn in the *carabiniero's* mind as he extended his pistol in a gesture of submission and permitted it to fall off to one side of his hand where it swung impotently from his trigger finger. His other hand let go the rifle. It fell to the ground at his feet. Tori nudged Gucci back a few steps to enable him to kick the weapon out of the way.

Gucci, collecting his wits, began to argue his case. "Listen, you don't hold all this against us, do you? Your people have been warned. Look, I don't make the laws. The Allies are the conquerors."

He was a cold, unfeeling, self-inflated ass, and his words rasped across Tori's nerves like a knife scraping the bottom of a kettle. Another gust of wind came at them. The

153

neck protector on Gucci's forage cap flapped savagely against his shoulders. In that instant Gucci might have had an opportunity to twirl the revolver back into place and fire at Tori; but the definitive menace · with which the Montegattan held his ground precluded any foolishness on Gucci's part. He smirked, shrugged, and tossed the gun forward into the nearby lorry with an attitude of resignation.

With the tip of his *lupara*, Tori motioned Molino in closer to Gucci. The man, rigid and embalmed with fright, was unable to move.

"What do you want, eh?" asked Gucci with false benevolence. "You'd best lay that elephant gun aside before someone gets hurt. I know you're a good lad. If you had intended to kill us, you'd have done it before this. What do you want, eh? Your cheeses? Go ahead, take them. No hard feelings, eh? Listen, take all you want from the lorry. And don't say we aren't generous."

Tori stared at him murderously, unable to express either his thoughts or his feelings, as the brute bargained for his life. Tori's outward calm and silence concealed a storm of inner rage and turbulence. Mistaking his silence for a reluctance to shoot, Gucci took courage and continued to bargain, obsequiously. "Listen, I've collected a handsome bundle of lire today. You want it? Take it all." He made a furtive effort towards his hip pocket, halted only by Tori's compelling voice.

"I wouldn't be that foolish," he said slowly and deliberately, so as to leave little doubt as to his intent. "Make one more move and you'll be dead before I permit you to make peace with the devil who spawned you. Now, move, both of you. To your knees. You've one minute to ask forgiveness for the butchery you've done to the youth of my village. One . . . two . . . three . .. four. . . ."

"You're going to shoot us in cold blood?" Molino, coming to life, accosted his partner. "Do something, you child-molesting son of a whore! You've been so big in the past. So brave! Where's your guts, now that you face a real man?"

"Be quiet, you sniveling son of a horned-toad whore," snarled Gucci.

"Thirty five . . . thirty six . . . thirty seven. . . ."

"In God's name, be human," shouted Gucci, his parched voice cracked.

"What's that? What did you say?" asked Salvatore, brightly.

"I said, in God's name, be human!"

154

Tori thought for a moment. "Very well. That seems a reasonable request. *Va bene*, Gucci." He nodded in seeming agreement. "I'll be as human as you've been. Can that be more equitable? Fifty-nine . . . sixty. . . ." Tori pulled the trigger and blew off Gucci's head.

The blast of a *lupara*, diffused by the sounds of the howling *sirocco*, sounds much like the discordant blast of a small cannon; its effects equally as devastating. Tori watched Gucci's face disintegrate and leave a gaping hole exposing portions of splintered bone fragments on the skull. Shreds of flesh hung like rent fabric. Gucci's body, propelled into the air from the force of the blast, sailed back and fell several yards from them.

Molino urinated in his shorts, unaware that the yellowish fluid soaked through him and ran down his hairy legs. Frightened, he fixed his eyes on Tori, staring like a raving madman. He began to rant and rave and methodically curse Gucci, the *carabinieri*, the day he had accepted duty in Sicily, and the blackest day of all, the day when he had gone against his wife's admonishments and warnings: "You told me not to be a party to Gucci's corruption, Maria Rosa. Did I listen? 'What you do to others will be done to you,' you told me. *Santo Dio!* Why didn't I listen? Why didn't you make me listen?" he squealed like a freshly slaughtered piglet. "Now, it's too late. *Arrivederci, mi amore.*" Molino closed his eyes and clasped his hands over his heart in a deathlike pose. *Carabiniero*, Antonio Molino waited—and waited—and waited. At last, one eye cocked open, he squinted at Tori.

"On your feet, dog!" commanded Tori. "Today is your lucky day—one you'll remember as long as you live you misguided son of a cross-eyed buzzard. You may deserve to die, but not at my hands. Now, hurry, load the lorry with the bodies of those two young innocents. *"Move!"* Tori borrowed Gucci's words and liked their effect. "Move!" he repeated, finding satisfaction in the way Molino moved his tail to the tempo he set.

When he finished, Tori ordered him to remove his service revolver and his boots. He pointed him in the direction of Borgetto with the admonition to run like hell and keep his mouth shut about the incident. "If I as much see your shadow I'll blow you apart as I did Gucci!"
Gucci!"

"I promise. I promise never to return. I swear! I swear. You hear, Maria Rosa? This Sicilian isn't an animal after all." His hope, thus reinforced, strengthened his thoughts of reprieve.

155

And Tori strengthened his warning. "If I see your face in my village, I'll not take time to count. *Butana u diaoro!*" yelled Tori. "Move!" And Molino moved. Before he was out of sight, Tori did to him what he and Gucci had done to Pallido. The second pellet in his *lupara* blew off the back of Molino's skull.

"This is Salvatore's brand of justice!" he said aloud. "You've been avenged, Pallido!"

Twenty minutes later, he deposited the bodies of the Giunta lads at the house of Doctor Raffa, where earlier he had left Pallido. Tori, unable to speak, made a gesture of hopelessness. Understanding, the doctor patted Tori's shoulder and promised to handle everything.

Outside, Tori welcomed the bleakness of the *sirocco* and the deserted streets which darkened by the moment. On a borrowed mare, he rode swiftly to the Temple of Cats to hide the weapons in his secret hiding place.

Having dumped the bodies of Gucci and Molino over a precipice into a deep ravine like a seasoned murderer, he realized only later that his lack of experience in such matters had precluded the removal of their identification. Because he felt no different after the killings, than before, he examined his conscience now, asking himself what it felt like to be a murderer. He had no answer. Inwardly he nursed a sense of secret joy, knowing that unless Gucci was reincarnated, the youth of the village would be no longer molested, abused, maimed or killed.

The clock in the Norman tower at the *piazza* of Montegatta struck the half hour. It was 3:30 P.M., and yet it seemed like midnight. He couldn't go home, yet. Not now. How could a man announce to his mother and sister that he'd just killed two men?

CHAPTER 11

Tori found her where they usually met, in the loft of the stable at the deserted Romanesque villa to the north of the village. He'd never killed a man before, let alone two. The soul-searching experience began to tear at him about a

156

half hour after he had performed the deed. On this unforgettable day he didn't feel his usual self.

Maria Angela Candela—medium brown hair, green siren's eyes, a voluptuous and most desirable body—had just turned eighteen. She was in her prime. Reaching for Tori, she pulled him eagerly towards her throbbing body. "You promised to be here sooner," she pouted. "Five minutes more, I'd have left and you would have found the place empty and the straw cold."

Mistaking his silence for a rebuff, she caught sight of the tight, hard lines on his face. "What is it? Is something wrong? What's happened?"

Unable to reply, he clutched her to him roughly and they both lay back on the matted straw, searching, greedily for each other in the silence. Only their heartbeats sounded above the force of the *sirocco*. The skies continued to darken until they could barely make each other out in the shadows.

Sensing his need, Maria Angelica clung to him even more tightly than usual. She guided his hands over her breasts until she felt him harden against her. It always gave her a sense of power to feel a man respond to her femininity. Tori felt a strange excitement, unlike any he'd experienced in the past with her. He kissed her as the savagery in his soul unleashed. Always, always in the past, he'd been gentle with women. His touch, tender and light as if they were fragile porcelain dolls, was like a whisper of love. Now he ravaged her, tore at her, lifted her breasts from her low-cut blouse, kissed them and sucked greedily as if he never could get enough of them. Tense, he generated a fierce excitement in himself as well as in her.

Maria Angelica moaned and groaned in ecstasy. Never had she been so alive and filled with passion. They didn't recall how or when they removed their clothing, but there they were, suddenly a tangle of arms and legs wrapped about each other. He prepared to enter her, and she strained upward to meet him. Her eyes, like those of a bitch in heat, luminous, lust-filled, rolled upward. They both made those low-voiced animal noises as they tossed and tumbled in ecstasy.

They moaned, writhed, and twisted deliriously, filled with erotic pleasure. Fifteen minutes later, fully spent, exhausted and incomplete, Tori slipped out of her broiling loins, his mind filled with perplexing curiosity. Impotence in any form was frightening. If Tori's puzzlement was profound, the hurt and disappointment in the girl's eyes was more devastating to him. Red-faced and embarrassed, he sat back, filled with burning humiliation and lit a cigarette.

"What did I do wrong ,Tori?"

"It's not your fault. I'm tired. Exhausted from the trip." How could he tell her he'd just killed two men, or that he'd seen Pallido killed before his eyes, or that he'd witnessed the brutal beating of the Russo and Giunta lads?

She didn't believe him. He saw the frustration and self-blame in her eyes, so he looked past her, through the broken walls, out at the dark skies, and tried to shut out the events of the day. Her fingers on his upper thigh traveled upward until she found his manhood, limp and as lifeless as a honey-soaked *pinolatto*. Determined, she moved her hands rhythmically until he responded. He felt a tingle, and a surge of excitement swept through him again. He felt her move silently over him, place her cool, feverish body between his legs. His eyes closed. New sensations rushed at him. He still held a lit cigarette between his fingers during this period of uncertainty. New hope sprang to life. Alien feelings of impotence melted under the fluttering of her hot tongue, and his erection responded in a confused excitement.

Straining forward, he lifted himself on one elbow, and watched her head bob up and down. In that instant he filled with both revulsion and ecstasy. Before he could do anything about either, he felt a surge of power spring from his loins and shoot out through his manhood. For what seemed an eternity of painful pleasure, he sighed and moaned with uncontrollable orgiastic release.

Pleased with her newfound powers, Maria Angelica sensed a strange inner excitement as she watched Tori's face during his release. She wiped her lips on her petticoat and snaked towards him, removed the dead ash from between his fingers, tossed it aside, and snuggled against him, unprepared for the stinging blow of his hand across her face, or for his caustic tongue.

"*Butana!* Whore!" he said, savagely. "Where did you learn to do a thing like that?" Shaken by her brazen sexual act, he rose to his feet and gazed down at her as if she were a vile animal. He couldn't believe what she'd done. "Only the whores in Palermo know of such things!" He let loose a string of expletives, followed by a rash of accusations which sprang from feelings he had harbored for too long, he realized later. But, at the moment, he was revolted. Her tears left him unmoved.

"I've never done such a thing before. I just thought—well, I thought when you love someone the way I love you. . . ." Maria Angelica paused. She didn't understand.

158

She knew he had felt a strange excitement—knew he had experienced orgasm; then why did he strike this attitude? "Oh, Tori, I love you so much. Can't you see? That's why I did it. You were hurting, and I wanted you to feel better." She couldn't have felt worse.

He didn't believe her. She was too well-practiced. In that moment he felt betrayed, defeated. Yet, even as he asserted his mid-Victorian *maschiezzo*, something inside him chanted a different lyric. Confusion overwhelmed him. And in this confusion he grew protective of her. Under this blanket of protection he told her, "You mustn't be in love with me, Maria Angelica. I can love no one. I regret slapping you. And I thank you for sensing my need." He drew her close to him, held her affectionately in his arms. "But you must never do that for a man unless he is your husband, and only if he instructs you to do such a thing. . . ."

Her brain stopped at his previous statement. "Why can't you love me? All this time I thought you felt about me as I feel about you. . . ."

"I don't know why I can't, only that I can't."

"There's someone else. You love another. Oh, I'm so ashamed now. Why didn't I see it before? No wonder you're impotent with me. You love someone else. You do!" she repeated incredulously.

"There is none other, Maria Angelica. Not in the way you think."

"Then, how, Tori? Tell me so I can understand."

"Since I don't know, how can I explain?"

"There's another woman, I know."

"Perhaps you're right," he said in an attitude of remote contemplation. Outside the howling winds abated. The *sirocco* would soon leave them.

"Who is she? Tell me. You owe me that at least."

He lit a cigarette, inhaled the smoke deeply, and exhaled it with a resigned sigh. Tori turned to her. "If you insist, I'll name her. But you won't understand what I say, and you won't hear what I tell you." He reached over, kissed her forehead lightly, sprang to his feet, and pulled on his pants.

"Her name is Destiny. . . ." he said.

Tori left Maria Angelica to the self-destruction that ravages a woman scorned.

Outside he battled the winds all the way back to his house. He mentally regarded Maria Angelica and his cousin Vincenzo de Montana, as they had been three years ago, before Vincenzo had left for the army. They had used the old villa for their numerous escapades. Maria Angelica, a hot little bundle of enormous passions whom no one, including her parents, suspected of entertaining prurient longings, had exuded sex from every pore the moment she blossomed into womanhood.

Calf-eyed, love-struck, and possessed of rampant emotions, Tori had worshipped the girl as one might a goddess. Each night during his adolescence he had serenaded her with love songs of his own creation, accompanied by friends he'd cajoled into assisting him musically. Marriage might have been the next step. However, Tori quickly came to learn that the intoxication of youth, stronger than the intoxication of wine, grows less addictive with time.

He thought back to the time, not long ago, when he and Maria Angelica had taken their pleasures in this same villa, when suddenly Tori heard the voice of his cousin, Vincenzo de Montana, call to him. As he'd been about to withdraw from the girl, Maria Angelica had protested loudly and vehemently. "Don't go, Tori. Not now. Don't leave me in the middle—like this."

Tori had laughed aloud, good-naturedly. They'd been at it for nearly two hours and she wanted more? She had clung to him fiercely. There'd been little he could do except continue with those well-practiced movements familiar to lovers since the beginning of time, until he could detect familiar overtones of impending orgasm. He had waited until she had quieted down.

"Now can I go?" he had asked tolerantly as she came out of the euphoria.

One eye had cracked open, then the other. Focusing on his expression of amused patience, she had become enraged at his total discipline and control. She had jackknifed her legs, shoved them hard against him, and pushed him off balance and he'd fallen, laughing against a bale of hay. That he found the whole thing humorous had brought forth a series of expletives from her lips. "I hate you! I hate you!" she had cried. "Always so smug! You act like you're doing me a favor!" She had pointed to the hardness between his legs. "Look at you—still hard! Why aren't you like the others?"

Tori had risen to his feet, pulled on his trousers, and gently stuffed his erection into them and buttoned his fly. He had patted the sizable bulge affectionately. "Why? Because I'm not a rabbit? *Cara mia,* when Salvatore attends

160

a ball, he is a star who gives unforgettable performances," he'd grinned proudly.

"Vincenzo can keep me happy for hours!" she'd pouted.

"*Va bene*. Then, go fuck Vincenzo."

"But it's you I want, Tori. Can't you show me the excitement, emotions and affection Vincenzo shows me? Must you always be so calm? So studied?"

He'd walked to where she lay, taken her hand, and placed it over his tumescence. "Does this hardness indicate I am calm, without emotions?" Her greedy hands had grabbed at him and began to unbutton his fly.

"Oh, no you don't, you hot little whore. You've had your share for the day. I need my strength. I've work to do."

"You make me so mad! You're like a frozen statue," she'd said with spite. "Who wants to fuck a statue?

Tori had left her in the hay, pouting and angry.

That day, Tori hadn't been gone five minutes when he filled with remorse at having left her so abruptly. Returning to the loft with apology on his lips, he had been arrested by the sight of two shadowy forms thrashing about in the hay.

By God! There they were, both of them, engaged in those familiar frenzied erotic movements. He'd been able to see that Maria Angelica and Vincenzo were really enjoying themselves. Momentarily startled as he'd been at the sight of them, there had been a split second when Tori considered he should be angry—that he should demonstrate his artful manliness with a sudden outburst of temper and utter a string of violent curses upon them both. But, at the sight of such abnormal vigor expended by his cousin Vincenzo, he hadn't been able to contain his laughter. Vincenzo, a sexually insatiable lad with only one thing in mind, would have been content if the walls in his house had consisted of a thousand cuntholes. His craving for what lay between a woman's thighs had been more enslaving than an addict's to drugs.

Sounds of Tori's laughter had startled the lusty couple. Maria Angelica's stifled cry of shame had had no effect on Vincenzo, who, at the point of no return couldn't and wouldn't stop, and, in his frenzied erotic state, every struggle against him had only heightened his arousal. Tori's face had creased with laughter, infecting Vincenzo with a need to prove his *maschiezzo* and his staccato thrusts had accelerated. Turning her face away from him, the girl had made the best of the situation, for, in Tori's mask of laughter, Maria Angelica told him later, she had clearly seen the end of her affair with him.

As it happened, she had been psychic, afterall. Their relationship had eroded. Vincenzo had left for the war. Tori had seen little of her. Recently in July, one night, after learning of the deaths of his two older brothers, he'd gone to the villa alone, never thinking he might encounter anyone. But, there she'd been. In a nostalgic moment he had surrendered to her sexuality. He had made it clear there could never be anything more between them than the fulfillment of baser needs. She had agreed to those terms.

One day she had confessed to him that it was easier to pretend affection for a man who fulfilled her sexually, even if her tortured soul longed for another—whom she loved.

"You see, Tori, I'm insatiable. There's a name for some-one like me, for someone who indiscriminately craves for sex. All my life I'll be compromising. . . ." She had added also that when Vincenzo made love to her, she closed her eyes and pretended it was Tori. "Skillful and re-warding as my imagination can be, I wasn't prepared for the devil who punished me. You see, I couldn't transform the touch, taste and feel of Vincenzo into the touch, taste, and feel of you, Tori. It's true, one can't have everything."

Lately, Maria Angelica had begun to hope again. Tori knew he had to cut it off with her for good. He promised himself now that it would be the last time he'd be with her sexually. Grateful to have cut it off without the usual false expressions of mutual affection and slim promises, he had made it back to his house wading through the *sirocco*.

No sooner had Tori arrived at his house than his mother, Antigone, informed him he was wanted at the workshop of Candela the cooper. Annoyed at the prospect of having to brave the *sirocco* again, and still not at peace with himself over the tumultuous emotions he'd experi-enced on this day, he dreaded the thought it might have something to do with Maria Angelica. He needed no such domestic tribulations on this day. "Is it necessary?" he asked his mother. "Can't it wait?"

"For me it matters not if you go. It must be important, else who on his right mind would venture outside in this weather?"

"Yes, Mamma. Who in his right mind?" had been his reply.

Antigone Salvatore must have remained at the door staring out at the rear terrace for a hour after Tori re-turned from Candela's with the shocking news that Don Matteo Barbarossa, the man she'd so foolishly palmed off on Tori as his Godfather, wasn't dead these many years! Instead he was more alive than before—and a hero at that. She'd been outside in the yard, rearranging trays of drying figs when Tori had come home and exploded that bombshell. If Tori had noticed his mother's sudden pallor, he hadn't remarked over it. His own excitement over the news superseded all else.

She had entered the modest kitchen at the moment Athena, her extraordinarily beautiful daughter, had entered the room. The girl suffered from a mysterious malady which caused a rash of severely painful migraine headaches in recent months, rendering her helpless for days. Then, as mysteriously as the symptoms appeared they'd vanish. Attracted by Tori's joyous voice, she had come in search of him.

Athena, an enchantress with wide and exotic dark eyes and a flawless ivory skin, had been instantly swept up in her brother's arms. He had planted an affectionate kiss on her lips as he'd twirled her around. They'd begun chattering like clucking chickens while their mother scanned the contents of the newspaper article Tori had brought with him, substantiating the fact that Don Barbarossa still lived.

The article bore a glowing account of the unquestionable aid Barbarossa had given to the Allies during the Sicilian invasion. For these special services the Don had been the recipient of many favors and courtesies extended by the Allied forces.

If Antigone had ever been strong-willed in her life, it was at this moment, when she had been forced to conceal the growing disturbance she'd felt at this new development. Moreover, she had been greatly distressed at the near hero-worship she'd seen in her son's eyes when he had rushed out to tell her the stunning news. She'd begun to feel pangs of remorse over the grotesque lies she had perpetuated these many years. In addition to these shaky feelings, a native wariness provoked her next remarks.

"Tori, for the love of God, you didn't mention to Candela or the others that Don Barbarossa is your Godfather?" It had been a painfully posed question, to which she had quickly added, "I mean with all the *fascisti* lurking around we don't need added problems. We must be cautious these days. . . ."

Tori would have had to be obtuse now, not to notice the changes in his mother. Just as he'd observed the aggravation and concern etched into the faces of the men gathered at Candela's when he read them the article of

Barbarossa's resurrection, he saw the disturbance in his mother. "I said nothing," he told her. He noticed the remark had brought approval to her face. He told himself he might be too sensitive this day, for many things had happened to color his outlook. Yet despite this, something nagged at him.

"How is it, Mamma, you were so misinformed about my Godfather?"

Antigone shrugged. "After the Mori holocaust, when Mussolini purged the island of the *Mafiosi*, I presumed him dead. That butcher was intent on killing all of them. There was so much carnage and confusion in those blood-letting days. Who knew from anything?"

"What will happen now that he's powerful again? What was his political persuasion?" he asked, chomping on a piece of cheese.

"I'd hesitate to speculate on the politics of Matteo Barbarossa," she said, feeling her stomach churn. "A man can change. It's been many years. . . ." Antigone's eyes narrowed in thought as she moved about the kitchen. She paused to light a gas burner on the stove to warm the coffee, her thoughts roiling with the sudden changes in her village. Perhaps she should have kept her thoughts to herself, but she didn't. "I wondered how it was that suddenly from nowhere, Don Florio becomes mayor of Partenico. Those rumors about Don Russo in Piana dei Greci must also be true."

"Why should such things concern you?" asked Tori, studying her inscrutably.

She shrugged indifferently. "I thought it peculiar that these hard-core *Mafiosi* should move so swiftly back into power. After twenty years in obscurity? Only Barbarossa could have effected such a coup." She clapped her hands together in a gesture of sudden awareness. "*Allora!* Now it begins!" she said cryptically. Then, as it all came together in her mind she exclaimed, "Those foolish Americans! *Pezzi de shekki!* Jackasses is what they are." She continued to upbraid the Allies with stinging rancor, shouting uncomplimentary expletives in a voice loaded with irony as she moved about the kitchen, preparing a small snack for her children.

She paused a moment, breaking her concentration, and glanced at Tori and Athena. "Don't you see what I'm driving at? They've been duped. The Allies have been duped, *figghiu beddu,* my beautiful son."

Tori straddled the chair next to Athena, fully bewildered, unsure of what had set his mother off. "Truly, Mamma, you have me confused."

"Confused? You don't understand?" Antigone paused. "Why can't you see—" Again she paused, suddenly recalling that her children, like the rest of their generation, really knew nothing tangible about the Mafia. Why would they? The past twenty years of fascism had been devoid of *Mafiosi*. The Mafia was to them like a bad dream that never existed. She calmed down and set the coffee pot on the table, and tried to explain. "If the Americans allowed the Don Matteo to aid them in this conquest, the price they'll have to pay in return for his special services will have made their victory worth less than—uh—*merede*," she said flatly.

Tori laughed. "Mamma, no one dictates to the United States."

"No one dictates to the United States, eh?" scoffed Antigone. "No one? Hah!" she smiled tightly. "You'll see. Just give him time. Just give him time, *caro mio*."

The room hung heavy with uneasy silence. Somewhere in the neighborhood an old Victrola played a Neapolitan love song. Shadows lengthened in the dimly-lit kitchen. Tori exchanged confused glances with his sister; then he raised dark, chaotic eyes to study his mother's face as she sat pouring coffee.

"Why do you attack my Godfather?" he asked in a crushed voice, dazed by the inexplicable vindictiveness by his mother.

"Because I know them—all of them!" she retorted in a rash moment. Incited by fires neither of her children could know about, she halted only when she saw the silent questioning in their eyes. Antigone faced a terrifying dilemma. How could she tell Tori? He was no longer an impressionable child. He'd grown up, and only expected the truth from her. She made a disorganized gesture. "Forgive me. I forget you never lived in those times. Perhaps it's as you say, no one dictates to America. I allowed foolish, womanly emotions to cloud sound judgment."

Tori's dark eyes lost their intensity. His face flooded in relief. In moments he and Athena, filled with youthful exuberance, pored over the newspaper article and were lost to their mother. Antigone retreated into the pantry, leaving her children to talk. She leaned her head against the cool concrete wall as tears sprang into her eyes. *Matteo Barbarossa, alive after all these years!* How was it possible, sainted God of the universe? How? She felt like a caged animal, silent, frenzied, hesitant to give rise to the muffled screams lodged in her throat, afraid to claw her way out of her inner torment.

Subtle changes in her village as old *Mafiosi* were restored to their former positions of power should have indicated something to her—and it did. But, never in her wildest dreams could she have guessed that Don Barbarossa had been resurrected! More than the rebirth of the Mafia instilled stark fear into her heart. That Barbarossa himself was alive terrified her.

What was she to do? Now that Barbarossa lived, she couldn't permit Tori to equate him as a hero with the godlike qualities she'd painted so vividly over the years. If she were to tell Tori the truth—he'd have every right to hold her in contempt. He'd be lost to her forever. Once she'd lied to her children—once for the love of God. Hadn't she paid the penalty? One husband and two sons dead! Wasn't that enough penance for one indiscretion, for an involuntary act done when the lives of her children were at stake?

Antigone took out her frustration on the risen bread dough. She punched savagely into the aerated mass, deflated it with her fists, pounded it, and kneaded the clumpy mass until it was reduced considerably in size. Finished, she slipped it back into the pan, covered it, and told herself to stop worrying. It was not for nothing she was considered an iron woman by her neighbors. Hadn't she always said that worrying never helped matters? She told herself to take courage. The chances of their ever meeting were remote. *God, let it be so. . . .*

For some strange reason she kept getting fresh images of Dona Sabattini, the village *strega*. The old woman was a seer, a prophet with an uncanny talent for prophecy. Antigone was too intelligent, too well educated, to give credence to such obvious fakery, despite the compliments bestowed on the *strega's* ability by her neighbors. Under no circumstances would she revive that old prophecy the *strega* had prepared for *Tori* at his birth. Not Antigone, not her. Recently, giving in to a weakness following the deaths of her two older sons in July, she'd given in to an urge and revisited the old sorceress, only to have Tori's prophecy resurrected along with the old uncertainties, fears and anguish of the past. She had received no balm. Why, then, should she even consider the old crone?

The sound of her son's voice calling to her stilled her thoughts. She skillfully erased all traces of her tears and moved back into the kitchen. "Yes, my son?"

Her paleness and distraught appearance was obvious and Tori asked himself how he could conceal the deaths of the

166

Russo and Giunta lads. There was no way to spare her, so he explained what had happened to the lads, adding only that he was leaving to pay his respects to their families. He told her about Pallido and how he met his death.

"Tori," she addressed him calmly looking him in the eyes. "Are there any other surprises you've forgotten to mention?" she asked in all candor.

He blinked to avoid her piercing gaze and reached over to the table to pick up a *biscotto* and began chomping on it. He shook his head. How could he mention Gucci or Molino? How would she take it when she heard he'd killed them? She was shaken enough over Pallido's death, and how it left his new bride a widow.

"Be careful, Tori," cautioned Antigone. "If you're caught aiding and abetting others it will go equally as hard for you and us."

"Can I turn my back on children trying to be men in the absence of their fathers and older brothers?" he asked.

"We must look to ourselves, Tori. This is the beginning of the end for a soil-tilling people. It's best we don't delude ourselves into thinking times will improve.

"We must be patient. The Allies will do something. It just takes time," Tori insisted.

"Like the laws they enforce to kill off our men? We can't permit you to take more chances, Tori. You expose yourself to too many dangers. One day—" Antigone's voice cracked. "One day, you may not return. We value your life more than a sack of flour or a tin of olive oil. God!" she agonized. "I feel we are all poor lambs in a field, disporting under the eyes of a fickle butcher who chooses, first one then another, until we are all gobbled up."

Athena and Tori had never seen their mother so distraught. She turned to him, her eyes fired with peculiar lights. "No! I won't let it happen. You mustn't allow anything to interfere with your dreams, my son. You must educate yourself, involve yourself in politics. The future of our world rests in the hands of young, strong, thinking men like you. Help restore to our people our God-given rights. *Misericordia!*"

Tori slipped off the chair he'd straddled. He stretched and yawned and patted his hard stomach at the waist. "Destiny decrees the war must end before the future of this *giovanotto* can be decided upon." He forced a weak smile. "Until the schools are rebuilt, Mamma, what can we do, eh?"

"I can go to work in Palermo," said Athena defiantly.

"Many girls are there working and making good money. It's important you go to school, Tori."

Confusion struck at him. He stared at them outraged and pulled himself up to full height. "Stop!" he shouted. "Stop this minute .Are you crazy? Have you both taken leave of your senses?" He stormed about the kitchen with the emotional outrage of a proud Sicilian male, directing his fury at Athena.

"Get this straight, sister dear. If the day ever came that you sold yourself on the streets like a common whore, I'd put a bullet through my head after killing you, first. I promise! Never let me hear such disgraceful words again!" He turned to his mother, angrily. "Not from you, either. It's not worthy of you and what you've taught me all my life. As head of this family I'll provide for you both. My future can wait until the war ends."

Antigone shrank away from him, and felt the worse for mentioning such a foolish plan. "Very well, my son," she said resignedly. "Speaking of plans, you'd best prepare yourself for an encounter with Don Pippinu Grasso."

Tori's dismay was readily apparent. "Not again? How much in arrears is he this time?"

When she replied, "Six months," her son asked why she'd waited so long before telling him. She explained that she'd expected to see the payment in the mail each month, and suddenly time had flown. She added, "But we can't wait for his convenience any longer."

"Are we in such dire straits?" he asked pouring a fresh glass of water.

Antigone nodded. "I have no heart left to nag at you— to remind you of our predicament."

He assured her she needn't worry, that he'd manage and he'd attend to Don Pippinu. "I'll go tomorrow to Mt. Erice and straighten him out." Tori's face took on a peculiar expression, one his mother couldn't hope to understand. To have explained what was in his heart would have brought her face to face with a stranger at that moment.

She watched him leave the house with a heaviness in heart that grew unbearable. In the last three months things for the Salvatore family had significantly collapsed. Inflation, sky high prices and a toppling economy had drained their savings to nearly nothing. The fragmenting of her world began in July with news of Filippo's and Marco's death. Now news about Barbarossa had caused an erosion to set in and she grew fearful—fearful that all would be lost soon. And then there was this crazy malady

168

of Athena's! Dear God, what else could happen to the Salvatore family?

For a time she remained framed in the doorway, glancing at the valley beyond the terrace. Swirls of cloudy dust in abstract shapes and form moved across the open sea at Castellammare in the far distance, giving pale illumination to the sun-scorched wastelands. The *sirocco* was leaving at last. She watched the raw, hot lights of a beginning sunset filter through the grey-white mist flooding the land with an incandescent glow, giving a fertile appearance to the broken clay of her back yard where little life had imposed itself in years. Once a few chickens ran around clucking their silly heads off. Now there was no sign of them— nothing.

At forty-five, the petite, gray-haired matriarch looked older because she had neither the interest in cosmetics nor the time or money to support the vanity. Her hair was worn pulled back into an unbecoming bun, speared through with tortoiseshell hairpins. Her high, wide forehead and piercing pecan-brown eyes, set wide, gave character to her spectacular bone structure. Her nose was straight and turned up slightly, complementing her strong, honest face. The beauty of her youth was indelibly stamped on these classic Greco-Sicilian features.

Being a sagacious woman, she'd wasted little time in grief, for the chaotic duties of raising her children, after the death of her husband, had been fulfilled with the matriarchal fervor of a woman intent on a vital mission; this was something she couldn't have accomplished if her time had been wasted in maudlin martyrdom. She was an iron woman all right, but none of these qualities were at her disposal in these next moments, as she reflected on her earlier behavior. Her dark eyes, filled with brooding, stared out at the panorama.

Whatever had possessed her to blurt out her feelings to her children earlier? She'd never lied to them. She had bent the truth, but never lied intentionally. There's a difference, she told herself. One day she'd have to reckon with the truth, consider the consequences. *Oh, God it isn't fair*! she thought. Why did he have to be alive after all these years? Why?

She had no one to talk with—no one to whom she could pour out her heart. She shivered involuntarily as if struck by an icy wind. Her mind began to settle slowly. *So, you struck a sensitive chord for which only you are responsible. So what? Get back inside and prepare your*

169

family's supper, she told herself firmly. She closed the door and returned to her mundane chores.

Outside the winds continued to tear at him, blowing gales of dust—that insufferable dust that stiffens clothing to cardboard consistency, enters your nose and eyes and ears until it parches your brain, refusing to let up. The perennial smell of Sicily, *Stratto*, a tomato paste concentrate, clung to his nostrils, stimulating Tori's appetite. Why didn't he think to wait until after supper to break the news to the unfortunate parents? About to heed that inner voice, Tori was arrested by the crackling sounds of *carabinieri* rifle fire, followed by muffled sounds of scurrying feet at the far end of the deserted street.

He cocked his head to listen. Dust stung his eyes and Tori, drawing his head in like a turtle and turning his back on the inexorable winds, continued to walk in that manner, wondering if he'd actually heard rifle fire or if his imagination had been overworked.

Turning left off Via de Grande onto a narrow, wormlike alley, Tori cocked his head once more to listen. His left ear throbbed with dull precision and he shook his head despairingly. Not again! Damnit to hell! Three quarters of the way into the alley he stopped dead in his tracks. Black clouds drifting overhead created a mass of shifting shadows. *But there!* He heard it again—rifle fire: *rat-a-tat-tat-tat rat-a-tat-tat-tat*. Moved by intense curiosity, he hugged the buildings and slowly crept forward cautiously, his dark, furtive eyes everywhere. Muffled voices grew more distinct. The sounds of horses, snorting and wheezing, came at him. Somewhere there was trouble.

He flattened himself against a shabby building, peering ahead of him into the swirling density of dust at the end of the *cul de sac*, edging in closer. Moments later he came upon the devastating scene. The bodies of two young lads, sprawled face down in the gutter, turned his stomach. He felt a rising nausea, his body sagging heavily against the doorway of a house. Touching his forehead, he found it ran cold with sweat. His dark eyes moved slowly around at the circle of somber-faced men standing over the bodies, reading the horrifying effects at the senseless deaths at their feet.

Would it ever stop? Would this limitless design of death never cease? cried Tori internally. He had shot Gucci and Molino just to end this continual killing. How many more Guccis and Molinos were there? He felt like vomiting.

Finished with their killing, the *carabinieri* stood to one

170

side of their prey like triumphant hunters flushed with the success of a fresh kill, while sobbing, wailing and grief-stricken parents picked up the lifeless young bodies and sober-faced neighbors, resigned to such a fate, assisted them and carried them into their house. Behind them, left lying in the street, two small backpacks, slit open by bayonets, were strewn about, spilling a handful of corn meal and flour. For *this*, thought Tori, two young lads, yet to reach manhood, had been slaughtered?

Moving in closer to the crowds to observe the goings-on, Tori gave a sudden start when he recognized that sleek, well-preened vulture, the dark-haired predator with the fancy uniform he'd already encountered twice that day; first at Gucci's Checkpoint Two and then later he'd been stopped by this same Lt. Franchina, who had demanded he produce his identity card. Asked by the officer if he knew anything about a black market ring operating in these parts, Tori had replied, *no*. Had he encountered anything unusual that day? *No*. Had he seen lads with backpacks in the past hour? *No*. Those questions, superficial enough, had given Tori a few bad moments. Had the deaths of Gucci and Molino been discovered? he asked himself.

Volunteering no information, Tori had been permitted to pass, but not before the officer had studied him carefully and asked if he hadn't already encountered him that day. Tori had shook his head indifferently and gone on his way before the carabiniero recognized him.

Now, less than ten feet away, the preening vulture raised his voice to the solemn gathering in stern reprimand. Authoritatively, Lt. Franchina asserted himself. "Let these deaths be a warning to one and all. You can't continue to defy the Allied laws without suffering the consequences. The laws are clear. Whoever breaks them shall be punished to the fullest. . . ."

Lt. Franchina turned from the stony-faced villagers, whose hatred of him and men like him was masked by a bland passivity, and all at once he caught sight of Tori's fiery eyes, arrested by the pure venom in them. Glittering dark eyes—eyes that spelled compelling messages—and a firm jaw line caught Franchina's casual glance and held.

"You again, Salvatore?" his eyes narrowed thoughtfully. "What business brings you here? Your card states you live on Via de Grande. . . ."

Tori, noting the man's retentive memory, tried to conceal his own hostility. "Is it now against the law to go

171

visiting in my own village without being questioned by the *carabinieri?*"

"I suppose you will know your rights," retorted the officer, bowing slightly.

Tori, resenting the attention brought to him, frowned and fixed his eyes on Lt. Franchina, who, without comment, mounted his horse. From his saddle, the officer turned to study Tori with intensity. Perceiving the silent menace in the young man's eyes, he retreated wordlessly. He had no real desire to tangle with him. He permitted his mare to dance a bit; then, wheeling her about, he called to his men, *"Avanti! Avanti!"* He spurred his horse on and, in passing Tori, he took another long, meaningful look at the lad. It wouldn't be difficult for Franchina to remember this young man: "His face stood out among the other villagers like a princely white panther in a den of black mice," he would tell the distinguished members of a Tribunal nearly seven years later.

At the right of the *piazza,* Lt. Franchina directed his tired, sweaty and thirsty squad of men to a *birreria.* After such a day they were entitled to refreshments before the long, nerve-wracking ride back to Bellolampo Barracks.

He stretched his legs after he dismounted before the tavern. Placing his hands in the small of his back, he arched it and stretched it as his men filed into the tavern. For a brief second, he felt a chilling tremor shoot through him as a clear mental image of their being served strychnine flashed through his mind. What a perverse flight his imagination had taken on this, his first day in western Sicily!

For Salvatore this day hadn't ended. For Lt. Franchina the nightmare was about to begin, one that would haunt him until his dying day.

CHAPTER 12

Tori had just sat down to a Spartan supper a half hour after his encounter with Lt. Franchina when the hair-raising blasts of a *lupara* shook their house. The blasts, known to literally crumble the walls of houses, were followed in rapid-fire order by the unmistakable staccato of *carabinieri* rifles.

"Stay here," Tori commanded his mother and sister as they exchanged terrified glances. "I'll see what it is." Kicking back his chair, he ran through the house and out the front door, which bore a bright purple mourning band with gold letters reading: *For Our Beloved Sons and Brothers.*

Across the street, at the house of his uncle Gianna de Montana, crowds of curious male neighbors had formed. Women, not permitted on the streets after dark in keeping with ancient customs inherited from the Moslems, stared out from shadowy doorways, their dark, inquisitive, terror-stricken eyes peering through shuttered windows, their lips moving soundlessly in prayer. Even the noisy, boisterous street *ragazzi* were subdued in the presence of death.

"Keep back, all of you," ordered a haughty, Turkish-looking *carabiniero*, wielding his rifle like a Lacrosse stick, "or we'll arrest the lot of you."

At that moment the bodies of two dead *carabinieri* were carried out of the de Montana house, much to the gloating satisfaction of the aged spectators.

"At least Gianni got two of those bastards," cursed the father of Maria Angelica, spitting hard into the dust.

Tori moved forward. "Permit me to pass. This is the house of my uncle," he told Lt. Franchina who turned sharply at the sound of the familiar voice. Surprise was etched into the officer's features as he recognized Tori.

"No one's permitted inside," growled another officer, obstructing Tori.

"If you're as intelligent as is rumored," said Tori, subduing his rage, "You'll not obstruct me."

At a nod from Lt. Franchina, the officer lowered his rifle and let Tori pass. Inside, sprawled face down in a pool of blood on a spotless kitchen floor, lay the inert body of his uncle. Tori, kneeling on one knee, stared solemnly at the motionless form. He couldn't believe what his eyes registered. *Demonio!* What violence this day had wrought. Filled with a mixture of flaring emotions, Tori turned the body over gently, closing the sightless staring eyes, and for several moments he watched the older man turn into an effigy of waxen features. A peculiar isolation gripped him. Tears spilled from his eyes onto the face of his uncle. He reached in and wiped the dead man's face off tenderly and whispered huskily, "For all the good it does, you've been avenged, *Ziu* Gianni."

173

Tori wondered how he could explain any of this to his cousin Vincenzo, when he returned from the war.

In this house one month had seen the death of four people. Two cousins, his aunt, and now his uncle. It just wasn't possible! Only last week he'd begged his uncle to ignore the constant harassment inflicted upon him by these despicable *carabinieri* who had made his life unbearable after he lodged complaints against the butcher, Gucci. Gianni had gone to the security police over the brutal, unprovoked attack on his sons who were obstructed for carrying food across provincial borders. "One day they'll tire of their persecution and give up,' he had told his uncle.

"Today, they came," rasped the voice of Tomasso de Montana. Tori looked up at the bleary-eyed brother of his uncle. "Like they have each day for the past month, just to torture my brother. *Annunca.* Today he was ready for them. When they broke in the front door, your uncle, *lupara* in hand, gave it to them. Poor soul! How could he have known that another son of a demented whore would enter the rear door and blast him from behind? Oh, if only Vincenzo were here. He'd show them!" Tormented, the brother of Tori's uncle shuffled about the room as his neighbors filed in to view the spectacle of death.

"Goddammit! The man never hurt a fly!" Tori's fists balled tightly and he pounded the nearby wall, hurting his hand. Hardly noticing the pain, he turned to Tommaso and spoke gruffly. "Get a blanket. Cover your brother. Let him lie in the dignity he deserves until the mortician arrives." He picked up the *lupara* at his uncle's feet and stroked the weapon lovingly. Countless happy hours spent at *caccia*—hunting—with his beloved uncle, a second father to him, were carved into the shotgun. He set it aside as he took the blanket from Tommaso's hands and covered the bullet-riddled blood-splattered body. For a moment he watched the older man pour wine for the others in true Sicilian fashion so that Gianni de Montanna's friends could drink to his departed soul.

"Bloody assassins murdered my brother!" cried the brother of Tori's uncle wailing and sobbing with torment.

Tori could hear the tremulous voice pitched high out in the street as he made his way through the crowd to his house .

"Salvatore!"

He turned abruptly in the direction of Lt. Franchina's voice.

"It's incredible to me that I've seen you so many times in one day. If I were a superstitious man I'd begin to think it an omen. You see I don't happen to view these encounters as mere coincidence," said the officer reeking of whiskey. "I'm beginning to think—"

"Goddamnit to hell, man! I don't give a shit what you think!" Tori turned his back on the red-faced, blustery *carabiniero* and strode boldly across the cobblestone street to his house, where for a few moments he stood talking with his mother and sister. He didn't give a damn if the entire army of *carabinieri* obstructed him, at this point. Tori was incensed; he was crazy with hatred as he'd never before felt in his life.

"He's dead," said Antigone. No one had to tell her.

"*Si*. He's dead," replied Tori, checking his emotions. "Four deaths in the family, because like all humans they couldn't escape the habit of eating."

"Now, all our cousins are dead," said Athena sotto voce, her sorrowful eyes searching her brothers.

"Not Vincenzo!" Tori turned to his mother. "Don't tell me that, Mamma. Not him!" He was visibly shaken, his momentary anger replaced by stark fear at the prospect.

"We've had no word from him in two years."

"But no word came from the Ministry like it did for my brothers—"

"No."

Tori sighed. "*Allora*, there's hope. We must believe Vincenzo will return safe from harm. We must." He lit a cigarette, his eyes moving across the street towards the bustle of activity. He had quieted down a notch, but his voice was empty and dead. "Look at us. Have we no tears left to shed? Are we all damned here in Montegatta? Is this decaying village truly the house of Lucifer?" He made a disorganized gesture. His throat thickened and, unable to hold back the burning tears, he went into the house followed by his mother and sister.

Lt. Franchina glanced at his watch. It was nearly 7:30 P.M. "How soon before this mess is cleared up, Marino?"

"It's not your mess, '*tenente*. You're free to leave. I can give you a brief run down, however, if you feel obliged to make note of this in your report."

"Suppose you brief me tomorrow?" Franchina wiped the sweatband of his snap-brimmed hat and his forehead before resetting it on his head. "God Almighty, I've felt heat before, but this is more like the bowels of hell. Is it always this hot in the interior?"

"Always. You get used to it in time." Marino saluted the officer and watched him idly as he mounted his mare and gave orders for his squad to follow him.

Lt. Franchina led his squad back along Via de Grande in a brisk canter, as the horses' hooves assaulted the cobbles and led them out past the winding road above the Camposanto which led to the summit and Rigano Pass. On the return trip he brooded inwardly, hardly aware of the magnificent twilight of amethyst ribbons, shot through with white fire as the sun slipped behind a mass of electrifying colored clouds. The violent *sirocco* had finally spent itself over the Tyrrhenian Sea.

Lt. Giovanni Franchina had no way of knowing that, through a curious twist of fate, his squad of men would be totally demolished before the clock struck ten, or that he'd be the sole survivor of an ambush directed at them. Nor did he have any inkling that his life, from this day forward, would be inextricably caught up in the life of one exceptional Sicilian, Salvatore, or that for the next seven years, perhaps for the remainder of his life, he'd come to know little peace. If he'd known in advance the hand that destiny had dealt him, he might have recharted the course of his life by fleeing Sicily. But then this hardnosed, seemingly indestructible bulwark, a man possessed of driving ambition, might not have heeded the danger signs even if they were spelled out for him in large block letters. Enroute to Bellolampo Barracks, Lt. Franchina concentrated his mind on the events of the day and how they'd figure into his report.

At 10 A.M. that morning, acting as second lieutenant of the Italian military police presently under the jurisdiction of AMGOT (Allied Military Government of Occupied Territories), Franchina had stepped out into the sun-bleached courtyard of the command post at Bellolampo, a military *caserne* some 2,000 feet above Palermo to the southwest. He had mounted his mare and waved his squad of six men forward heading for the summit at Rigano Pass. A backward glance at the vast sweep of sapphire waters in the bay and at the golden basin of fertility known as the Conca d'Oro in which Palermo nestled reenforced his courage. He could always return, coudn't he?

The contrast between what greeted him and what he had left behind had transported him back into the Middle Ages. The heat had been stifling. Outlined against a brash sun, slowly fading from sight in the path of an impending *sirocco*, an eagle whirled arcs in an empty sky; he had filled with premonitiion at the time, but shook himself out of it. It would be nearly twelve hours later before Franchina would learn the merits of trusting to his intuition.

Once through the narrow pass, they prepared for the steep descent on the rear slopes of the limestone mountains. He'd noted where portions of the road, destroyed by Allied bombs, ended abruptly and the alien terrain grew harsh, rugged and unpredictable, the vegetation scant. Approximately an hour out of Bellolampo, Franchina had risen in his stirrups and turning in his saddle observed his men. Both horses and men had projected a marked inner turbulence. No one had to tell him; he could tell by the uneasy manner in which his men surveyed the area that they were in bandit country. Franchina had paused to mark these events in his notebook. He was a stickler for reports and their accuracy.

As their skittiness continued, Franchina unconsciously felt for the security of his service revolver. He also fingered his Mannlicher-Carcáno rifle nervously. The feeling persisted. He felt that hundreds of eyes stared out at them from behind white boulders and the countless grottos nestled in the honeycombed mountains, watching, waiting, silent and hating; he grew wary of every second spent in this guerrilla paradise where boulders took on the shapes of men and the prickly pear cactus leaned over the narrow, impassable roads in silhouette and became ominous and threatening.

The horses, spooking, and rearing at the presence of porcupines, had trampled over *esparta* grass so sharp it could cut through horseflesh. It was at this point that Lt. Franchina had shouted to his men. *"Avanti! Avanti!* Forward—on the double!" He was anxious to move on to some form of civilization—anything but to remain here, in this living cemetery, where death was a heartbeat or two away from every turn in the road.

His discerning eyes made note of every possible area that could germinate an ambush. From time to time, he'd make further notes in his small book, much to the annoyance of his men who were even more anxious than he was to escape this treacherous land.

His first glimpse of Montegatta, as they passed a Greco-Roman ruin identified as the Temple of Cats, lay beyond the buckwheat terraces at the end of a narrow, corkscrew road which dove precariously into a series of right-angled turns and emptied into the mean poverty-stricken village. He couldn't help recalling his first impression that it resembled a giant centipede, with its tangle of narrow, squiggly streets running the hump of one main *strada* that stood silent, incubating in malignant concrete. By the time their clattering horses' hooves cleared the deserted streets of the village there was no life, no activity to be seen. It hadn't occurred to him that earlier, when they'd heard a bleating of oxhorns, it might have been a signal to herald their coming. He couldn't wait to leave this village of brooding concrete, where sullen people had hidden from his sight.

At noon, the clock in the Norman tower had struck the hour. The sweating, agitated *carabinieri* left through the south entrance and rode into the eye of the *sirocco,* shielding themselves as best they could from the tempest, eager to arrive in Borgetto. He had completed his business in the small village and by 2 P.M. they were riding swiftly back towards Montegatta in pursuit of the alleged black marketeers. It was then he'd encountered Salvatore and Pallido at Checkpoint Two where they were being detained by Gucci and Molino.

Lt. Franchina had paid little attention to Salvatore then; he had been interested in the activities of the two corrupt *carabinieri.* He had disliked Gucci on sight, and when he saw this pretentious, ugly man wink slyly to his partner, Lt. Franchina had sensed these two were involved in some immoral activity. There was no question he intended to put them on report for retaining an enormous amount of contraband with no visible prisoners in sight. And that cache of weapons! Certainly it hadn't all been collected that day.

He'd gone about his business and in Montegatta at approximately 5 P.M. he'd encountered Salvatore walking along Via de Grande in a fresh change of clothing. Then later, he had confronted him at the *cul de sac* where the two youngsters had been apprehended and shot, and, of course, at the house of his uncle, de Montana. Although Salvatore's activities that day had piqued his interest, he still had no reason to suspect the lad of anything subversive or illegal.

Yet, for inexplicable reasons, his thoughts had centered on Salvatore. He'd been so concentrated on Tori that he failed to take normal precautions before advancing his men through the bottleneck at Rigano Pass.

It happened so swiftly. Suddenly they were halfway through an unprovoked ambush, with bullets zinging and pinging all around them, and all around him he saw his men falling like ducks at a shooting gallery. Stunned by the chaotic order of events, with no time to order his men into a counterattack or a retreat, Lt. Franchina had spurred his horse and galloped swiftly through the fusillade of bullets and miraculously escaped. Riding a whirlwind, he had arrived at Bellolampo and recruited a relief squadron, but by the time he returned to the bloody scene the ambushers had fled, taking with them all the horses, weapons and men's clothing, leaving the denuded bodies of the dead *carabinieri* floating in lakes of their own blood.

Lt. Franchina, solemn, somber-eyed, the very life drained from him, sat low in his saddle, observing the deathly scene. Pale shafts of moonlight illuminated the area between two mountain peaks, adding an eerie quality to the wooded basin as he pondered the reason destiny had spared him. He found no solace to comfort his wildly beating heart.

Later, in the confines of his meager office at Bellolampo, he paced his small room with the ferocity of a wounded tiger, appalled and incensed at the utter disregard Sicilians displayed for law and order. Finally, he sat down at his desk and began to write his report. He guzzled from a whiskey bottle periodically, and when he finished he glanced over the report.

Underlined several times was the name: *SALVATORE*. Even as he read the name he wasn't aware of why he had underlined it—only that he had. He was too upset to contemplate the reason for this. He was anxious to lay all this before his C.O., Major Carrini, immediately—regardless of the late hour.

Major Carrini, a lusty, physical man of medium build, was furious. Was this Franchina out of his mind? It was nearly midnight when his orderly had interrupted his sojourn with a prostitute imported from Neptune's Daughters in Palermo. And at a most inopportune time. *Sonofabitch!* Had he no regard for his superior officers? Major Carrini had no intention of leaving his warm bed, where the woman had been servicing him in a way that made him forget this lousy duty in a land of barbarians. His aide, however, insisted and when he mentioned that six men had been killed in an ambush, he put the girl off, whispering he'd return in moments.

There was another reason why Major Carrini decided to talk with Lt. Franchina. He disliked the man intensely, and itched to get something on him. Even at their first encounter, Franchina had recognized the gross resentment in the Major's eyes. The hard-bitten, scrappy officer pulled on his trousers and a shirt now, recalling how rankled he'd been by Franchina's natty appearance when they met. The preening peacock dressed meticulously, bringing into focus his own sloppiness, to which his apathy and conditions of the war had reduced him. He wasn't used to a man of Franchina's breed, whom he branded instantly as a stuffy, stodgy social climber, an ambitious fanatic, highly dangerous to the regulars because such men with their social notions couldn't be trusted.

He was grumpy and out of sorts when he entered his office to find Lt. Franchina seated in the cramped quarters chain-smoking. For all his libertine persuasions, the Major knew his duty, and he listened patiently to Franchina's impassioned report, trying to suppress his yawning boredom. Finished, Franchina waited to hear the Major's reaction. Carrini shrugged indifferently.

"Listen lieutenant, don't get your ass kicked out of shape. Here in Sicily you don't always follow the letter of the law. You give a little, you take a little, *capeeshi?*" He yawned and scratched his crotch, anxious to get back to that bundle of dynamite warming his mattress.

"Just so I don't misunderstand you," said Franchina stiffly, "Tell me more so I understand you." He refused the drink offered him.

The Major glanced impatiently at his watch. *Managghia! Is this prick to be believed?* He lit up a cigar and puffed on it with agitation. "Look, these Sicilians are strange birds. They resent outsiders. Why? Who knows. They consider us their mortal enemies. There's no way, no way at all, we can make them obey laws unless we shoot them. And I mean every last accursed son of a whore in sight! It's either that or we jail them. *Pero*—who has enough jails? We can't justify shooting them—so, we join them. *Capeeshi?* When we catch them violating our laws, we play their game and make them divvy up the booty. This way we go about our business and they go about theirs. Everyone is content."

Franchina didn't like what he heard. "You mean you condone felons? How the hell can we enforce Allied laws if we become a party to the torts? Major, by condoning these offensive practices, you're endangering the life of every *carabiniero* who does duty in this island. We're sitting on a time bomb that could explode without warning. How long do you think these people will tolerate such shabby treatment?" He then proceeded to relate to Carrini the reactions of the people he'd seen that day, the vile hatred in their eyes, the loathing and contempt and murder in the air. He mentioned the lorry filled with confiscated weapons he'd seen at Checkpoint Two. "Then all the undercurrents of pure vitriol I felt from them had some basis after all," he shouted angrily.

Major Carrini's face turned a ghastly purple. "Goddammit, Franchina! What the hell song are you singing? You're no cherry. You know the ropes. Don't give me that shit. You can't tell me you haven't wet your beak. In these times you're telling me this is all new to you?"

Franchina saw it did no good to repudiate Carrini's statement. Indignant at the suggestion he'd be party to the abominable acts, he pulled himself to his feet, boiling with resentment. In his mind it all fell into place. The laxity at the checkpoints, the general apathy of the mounted police, all of them. Why should they arrest a wrongdoer when they could share in the thriving graft, sit back, and live off the blood, sweat, and terror of another man's plight?

As he saw it, the ambush in which his men had been slaughtered could be justified when viewed through the peasants' eyes. Since these lawmen, sworn to uphold the law, were more lawless than the brigands who roamed the hills, how in the name of the Lord Jesus could they command respect?

Franchina said tersely, "I haven't wet my beak, Major, but I understand more than I did this morning. You should have explained things to me before you placed me and my men in such jeopardy. I hold you personally responsible for the deaths of those six men. You didn't squeeze the triggers. You didn't fell them with your own gun. You didn't even plan the ambush. But, by the soul of Satan, you're as guilty of their deaths as I am for not acquainting myself with such rank conditions beforehand."

A volcano erupted in the Major. He jumped to his feet, kicked back his chair, and snarled fiercely, his face swollen to a black-hued purple. "Where the fuck do you come off being so high and mighty—so disrespectful to your superior officer? You stupid sonofabitch! These are hard times, man! With the war on, we don't even know who's side we're on, you brainless orangutang. You dare spout morals and ethics to me? We're goddamn lucky the Allies chose us to enforce their laws. They could have tossed us into the *gaoletto*—jail—and declare us their enemies. We could have been left there to rot during the occupation. Tell me, omnipotent one—do you know what's happening on the mainland? I don't. We've not been paid in months. How do we live, eh? How do we feed ourselves and our families? Look! You don't like it here? *Va bene*. Then transfer the hell out of here, and don't bust my balls! Don't look down that supercilious, holier-than-thou nose of yours at us. Wait until you've been here a year like the rest of us. You'll play the game soon enough."

"With your permission," said Franchina bracing himself. "I'll put in for a transfer.

Major Carrini picked his chair off the floor and set it

181

back into place. He growled, "Put in for a transfer. What the hell do I care? Don't play the fucking game. See where it gets you. You'll be here for at least three weeks until the transfer comes through. Make the best of it."

"With your permission I'll make arrangements for the bodies of my men to be shipped home to their families."

Carrini's head swiveled towards the other. "You'll do what?"

Franchini repeated his statement and was cut off in mid-sentence.

"Never mind," exploded the major. "I heard you. I heard you but I don't believe you. You're a real *citrollo*, Franchina, you know that? A real cucumber. Where the hell do you come off thinking we offer first-class ac-comodations in wartimes, eh? Goddammit, we're under Occupation! Have the burial detail dispose of the dead in the customary manner. Now we've six mouths less to feed."

"But—"

"Yes, lieutenant?" the Major's voice was deadly.

Franchina saluted him, a protest dead on his lips. "With your permission, I'll withdraw."

"So, withdraw," muttered his C.O., flinging his soggy cigar into a nearby spittoon. "Meanwhile you take the same detail tomorrow. And don't go around infecting the other men with your crazy ideas, or, so help me, I'll write you up for subordination and dereliction to duty, and by the unholy balls of Satan, I'll make it stick."

All the way back to his quarters, Lt. Franchina was thinking that his superior was probably capable of any-thing. If he'd been a mere fanatic, he surmised, he'd have been no threat to Carrini. Long ago Franchina had learned to adjust to outside conditions while inwardly re-taining his own principles. Never a joiner, he was his own man, a prodder, someone who kept books and profited from his mistakes, but always preparing methodically for some future day when he would receive his own command and reach the goal he had set for himself.

Still stinging from the Major's words it was the last thing the major said to him that stirred his *cuglione*. "You don't belong here," the Major fired at him. "You belong in Rome, Florence or Naples with the rest of the *carabini-eri* snobs who articulate anemic policy that we red-blooded men put our lives on the line for. All you holier-than-thou, self-righteous men, out to save the world, never take into consideration that the world was fucked up by men like you in the first place!"

Franchina was filled with countless doubts as he undressed for bed that night, but one thing was certain. As his commanding officer, Major Carrini called the shots, and he had to obey. Before he fell asleep that night, he put in for a transfer, unaware that destiny had already begun to formulate other plans for him.

The next morning, stuck on this detail until his transfer was approved, Lieutenant Franchina awakened to a bright, clear and sunny world devoid of *siroccos*. The temperature, having dropped several degrees, brought some relief to the west. Given command of a new squad of men, he left the military barracks for Borgetto, where he was required to fill out several reports.

The day was uneventful until they passed Montegatta and Checkpoint Two, where they found no officer of the day. Gucci and Molino were nowhere about. Making a note to report this oddity at Borghetto, the *carabinieri* contingent proceeded south at a leisurely pace.

Lieutenant Franchina noticed, as they descended the narrow twisting roads towards Castellammare Valley, the eastern sky filled with several buzzards, wheeling arcs over a lonely gulch. Fascinated, he watched these flesh-eating predators through binoculars, wondering what tasty tidbits these sable-plumed gourmets had spied. Somewhere in these time-eroded mountains, beneath them, they sensed a banquet of death had been spread for them. He watched them slowly, very slowly descending to the feast, spiralling lower, lower, until they disappeared behind limestone ridges out of sight.

Lieutenant Franchina galloped ahead swiftly to catch up with his men, who were already at the entrance to Borgetto by the time he closed the distance between them. At HQ's he handled the lengthy red-taped reports of the previous day, had lunch, and after reporting the absence of a detail at Checkpoint Two, he and his squad of men headed back up the mountain towards the summit.

Converging towards them, at a slow pace over a lonely mountain road from Piana dei Greci, several *carabinieri*, escorting two horse-driven lorries over the tedious, rutty roads, waved to Lt. Franchina. He ordered his men to halt, and with an aide rode forward to greet the newcomers. Exchanging salutes, Lt. Franchina introduced himself asking, *"Che passa?"*

Young Corporal Greco raised his arms, halted the lorry drivers, and introduced himself. He explained that the lorries contained dead bodies found in a ravine where his men had seen vultures circling overhead and pointed to the area where Franchina had seen the predators earlier.

Lt. Franchina spurred his horse and rode to the end of the lorries to inspect the bloodied carnage, mutilated beyond recognition from the long fall against the jagged rocks and from the pickings of vultures. "Who were they?" he asked as the corporal rode up alongside him.

Corporal Greco reached inside his tunic and pulled out several identity cards. Two of them—I'm not sure which—were fellow officers: Gucci and Molino," he read from their IDs. "The others, the young lads must be those missing from Montegatta these many months. Listen, Lieutenant, will you take the lads to Montegatta? We'll take the officers to Borgetto. Their deaths will have to be investigated. They were both shot with a *lupara,* an ethnic firearm, according to the nature of their wounds."

"You surmised that in their condition, Corporal Greco?"

"My specialty, Lieutenant. One day I hope to transfer to Naples to work in Intelligence."

"My, my," commented Franchina. "I wish you good fortune."

He accepted the identity cards and watched as the men transferred the bodies of the dead youths to one lorry. Once again the officers exchanged salutes and each contingent went its separate way.

It was dusk by the time Lt. Franchina deposited his lorry of death with the security police in Montegatta and returned with his men to Bellolampo without incident. That night, he was totally exhausted and unwilling to fraternize with the other officers. He retired to his room and slept like a baby, unaware that in other parts of the land there brewed bits of intrigue that would give him many a sleepless night for the rest of his life.

CHAPTER 13

The very same day that Lt. Franchina reluctantly began his second day of duty in western Sicily, Tori had arrived in Mt. Erice. Having scaled the spotless stone pavement up the hill to the quaint village from Trapani on his horse,

184

he dismounted, tethered it to a hitching post, and strode boldly into the Naxos Weights and Measures *negozio*, ready for his encounter with Don Pippinu Grasso. He was annoyed to learn that the Don was out lunching with Allied officials and wouldn't return until after the noon siesta.

A toad-faced clerk directed him to a small table to partake of a cup of *espresso* or whatever suited his appetite while he waited. He chose instead to wander about the *negozio*, fully irked by the delays. *Managghia!* He'd intended to take care of the pressing business and return with the overdue payments owed them by this cousin of his mother. The chore, distasteful enough because this distant cousin had a penchant for making him feel like a poor relative who came begging for something to which he wasn't entitled, further aggravated him when he caught sight of the phenomenal amount of food stores stocked in the shelves. *Porco Diaoro!* Damn the devil! Where were the food shortages here? Black market goods abounded in this place. Most Montegattans hadn't tasted or seen pasta in years. Here, boxes of that precious commodity were stacked from floor to ceiling. This very fact set Tori to wondering about such special privileges. His senses were assaulted by the appetizing aromas of the soul-stirring foods. His mouth watered at the sight of the *prosciutto,* cheeses, salamis, and other delicacies; yet he felt compelled to swallow his hunger pangs and avert his eyes, lest he give in to temptation. Who in Montegatta would believe him when he described such a display of food? The prices were prohibitive; nonetheless the food was sold openly. Imagine—sold openly!

Earlier, when he had arrived in Trapani, the sight of the recent aerial bombardment given the city had shaken him into a fit of depression. Yet nothing had astonished him more, when he had ridden among the Greco-Spanish and Norman-influenced village of Mt. Erice, than to see it had escaped unscathed by Allied bombs. His spirits had been elevated considerably because he loved the birthplace of his mother, where, she'd always assured him, "the most beautiful woman in Sicily come from Mt. Erice." It was a game they played. Tori would respond to this declaration by telling her, "Since they are all descended from gods and goddesses, isn't it fitting they should come from Mt. Erice?" Tori had yet to encounter these creatures of legendary beauty, and he teased his mother about this. Always ready with a reply, Antigone would insist that the men of the village kept their women hidden, and with good reason. With such hedonistic stallions as Tori and Vincenzo around, she would say, the women had to be safeguarded. Then Tori, with sparkling deviltry in his eyes, would laugh, insisting it wasn't necessary to see them, because to him *she* was the most beautiful woman in the world, Athena included.

He laughed internally now, for he always recalled these anecdotes each trip he made to this quaint village. He sauntered over to a counter and picked up a newspaper, growing more restless by the moment, the puzzle of so many foodstuffs sticking in his craw like bitter bile. Later he was to learn why this village had earned such privileges not granted to his province. It seemed that the Mafia, under the able guidance of his godfather, Don Barbarossa, assisted by those members of the Honored Society, had been instrumental in assisting the Allies by painting the tops of buildings housing Axis arsenals, strategic stronghold, and ammunition dumps with luminous paint to facilitate the aerial bombardment. For these services, Mt. Erice had been spared and an abundance of food had been released. A neat exchange, he thought when he heard this story. It had also set him to thinking about the wheeling and dealing that went on.

The sound of a young woman's voice, cool and disdainful as she crisply ordered the toad-faced clerk about, caused him to glance up from the newspaper into the face of the most beautiful creature he'd ever seen. Dressed simply in a navy blue skirt with a pale blue sweater that revealed a body of voluptuous curves, she was purchasing what to him seemed an abnormal amount of groceries, for which she overpaid with a staggering amount of *Am-Lire* (the new occupational currency) She appeared to take perverse delight in flaunting the money.

Toadface moved in closer to Tori and, with whispered innuendo and animated gestures, indicated she was a member of the world's oldest profession. *"Managghia!* Does this whore make money! Phew!"

Tori noticed the forced, sullen respect for money indicated by the clerk's attitude. He also noticed that the faces of a few inquisitive shoppers had screwed up with a superior attitude: here and there a raised eyebrow, envious stares, bold and haughty attitudes, while others stood by quietly with prudent reserve, avoiding the girl as if she were a leper. For some unknown reason Tori had to check the sudden impulse he had to change the sniggering expression on the toad's face with an upraised fist. Just as quickly, he asked himself why he should feel personally

186

affronted. After all she wasn't his girl—or his property. *What's the matter with me?* he asked himself, shrugging in annoyance.

Yet when she brushed by him, accidentally dropping a parcel, he didn't back off or mind his own business as he'd been taught to do all his life. He gallantly retrieved the parcel and bowed in a cavalier manner. "Permit me to assist you *Signorina*," he said, hoping to disguise a rising excitement. Before she could refuse him, he relieved her of another parcel. The girl flushed with a mixture of pleasure and self-consciousness at his gracious manners. Her eyes caught sight of the eye-popping stares of those around her who gawked openly at them.

With a toss of her coppery gold hair, she gave them a *go fuck yourself* look and, fixing her electric green eyes alluringly on the accommodating man, she smiled dazzlingly. "*Signore*, how kind of you. I'd be most grateful for your assistance," she purred with an angel's voice that caused his heart strings to quiver.

"Tell Don Pippinu, Salvatore will return," he told Toadface as he left.

Good God! Is she beautiful! Tori felt a sense of pride as he walked alongside this angelic beauty, despite Toadface's candid observation. Her skin, the texture of a baby's, was soft and white, with a tinge of pale blush to her cheeks. Her red-gold hair, worn cropped in a mass of curls, danced glowingly in the sunlight. Her eyes, incredible to behold, looked unreal, more like precious jade and turquoise jewels. Within them, he saw unfathomable emotional depths; perpetually haunted, like those of so many female victims in a war-ravaged country.

Tori wondered, could she be a love goddess of legend his mother had told him about? The idea titillated his senses, caused his heart to beat faster, and filled him with indescribable joy.

They stopped before a run-down apartment, and he appeared dismayed that such a beauty should live in a place short of a palace. He was unaware that his thoughts were scrawled boldly, across his face, like graffiti.

"What did you expect, the palace of a queen?" she asked defensively.

"Why—uh—I—er—uh," he stammered at her perception. "I didn't mean to appear impolite or unmannerly, *signorina* . . ."

His eloquence of speech threw her off balance and she glanced hesitantly at him.

"May I carry these to your apartment?" he asked pleasantly.

"No!" she grew defiant. "No one comes to my house—unless they pay." Her voice, no longer soothing and angelic, turned acrimonious.

Salvatore smiled indulgently. "Even the delivery man?"

His tone and manner forced a smile upon her lips, which suddenly bloomed into a sunshine of laughter and infected him with her spontaneity. . . .

"My name is Apolladora Felice," she told him later. "I'm eighteen. Until three months ago, I lived in Jato with my parents, four sisters and three baby brothers. My family had always been poor. The war made us destitute. My friend, Concetta, sent me a bus ticket and told me I could earn more money than my family would need to survive. Could I stand around watching the children die of starvation and other illnesses? Knowing what I had to do, my father refused to talk with me or kiss me goodbye. I cried all the way to Mt. Erice.

"A week later, when I returned with food, medicine, and clothing, I no longer cried. Into my father's hands I pressed enough money to support them for months. Weekly I make the trip to bring them food and money. My parents never ask, 'Do you have a place to sleep? Enough to eat?' They just ignore me. My father turns his back on me. He eats the food I bring, drinks the wine, and smokes the cigars like a royal pasha. But he doesn't talk with me. I'm a stranger to them. It's as if Apolladora Felice no longer exists for them. I'm a phantom who comes weekly to attend to their needs.

"I'm an outcast because I sell my body to the British and American soldiers to keep my family alive. I no longer try to convince my family that if what I do keeps nine humans alive and well-fed, could it be so wrong? . . .

"It wasn't all sunshine and morning glories for me, Tori. My first night was a nightmare. What drove me were the haunted faces of my younger brothers and sisters. Even my cherished dreams of being deflowered by the man I love—these, too, dissolved. In the wake of poverty, how quickly one learns to adjust. The feel of so much money in my hands and knowing the good it could do erased all sentimental thoughts of my virginity. . . .

"Three times a week, I go to Naxos Weights and Measures to buy groceries, which I take to Jato each week. Something compels me to make those weekly visits, like a penance I must pay for the life I lead.

"One Saturday, an American GI drove me to Jato to save petrol costs. Everyone on our street noticed the American machine. Filled with shame, my father wouldn't come into the sitting room. His caustic voice, shouting vile names at me, echoed through the streets. "*Disonorata! Butana!*" Oh, the things he called me!

"The American, furious, wanted to tell my father a thing or two. I implored him to pay the old man no heed, and assured him it didn't bother me. But in truth I felt dead inside. My friend boiled at the shabby treatment I had received. But how can a foreigner hope to understand the fierce pride of a Sicilian father? The disgrace at having a prostitute for a daughter? Such stigma too deeply planted in their minds can never be erased.

"And so it was that today, when I went to Naxos and met you, I felt sure it was Destiny that pushed me. Earlier I had awakened with such a headache I told myself I'd not go shopping on this day, that tomorrow would be as convenient. But something prodded me, pushed me into getting up, and I ended up at Naxos. When I saw you standing there, looking at me in that special way, I felt a warm flush inside me. I am not so eloquent with words that I can describe what I felt, but it seemed I'd known you all my life. Did you feel what I felt? That we might mean something to the other? *Allora*—I dropped my package. Then I heard you ask in that voice that sent shivers in me, " 'May I assist you, *Signorina?*' "

Apolladora giggled like a naive child and sat up in bed. The sheets fell from her milky skin and her full breasts trembled slightly from the excitement that swept her body. "So, I said in my most seductive voice, 'I'd be grateful for your assistance, *Signore*,' and here we are, three hours later, as if we'd known each other all our lives." She was breathless, vibrant, and trembling.

"Yes," he said huskily. "Here we are."

"So!" She sprang from the bed and returned with a fresh pot of coffee she'd made during her oratory, and pouring a cup for him and one for herself, she said, "Tell me about yourself. Are things bad in your village?"

"Yes." His eyes devoured her nakedness and he was delighted at her lack of embarrassment. He was as breathless as she was, and equally astonished by his own actions. Such women were to be used—not revered.

"From where do you come ?"

"Montegatta."

"Are you married?"

"No."

She smiled at that. "Are you here on business? Do you come often?"

"Yes, business. No, not often."

"I love it here. To me Mt. Erice is like a fairyland. Do you like it here?"

"*Do I like it here?*" He rhapsodized. . . . "I am enchanted with it. Part of my ancestry lies in Mt. Erice. Do I like it here? Ah, *Signorina*, besides being the birthplace of my mother, it was here that Hercules challenged the King. Here Venus arose from the sea and, with a legion of cupids, built her temple high on the rocks, 2500 feet above the sea. And it was here that I meet you. What's not to be enamored of Mt. Erice?" he whispered, trying to subdue his own excitement.

She listened with wide-eyed wonder as he told her of the lore connected with this village. For a while they made small talk, none of which mattered. What did matter to Tori were the strange and unique feelings that shot through him when he set eyes on her copper-colored hair, the color of an amber sunset, and her jade-green eyes that gazed right into his soul, it seemed. She had a voluptuous body, unlike any he'd ever seen, with everything worked into the right places. Just to feast his eyes upon her left him with a strange and peculiar breathlessness. "*Cara mia*," he cooed softly. "I'm happy you dropped your parcel . . ." he told her huskily, pulling her close to him again.

Before they got around to drinking their coffee, they melted into each other's arms as if it was the most natural thing to do. For Apolladora, the experience with Tori was fascinating and terribly rewarding. For the first time in her sexual life, she hadn't exacted a fee from her lover, and it gave her an entirely different outlook on the sexual act. She found the passive role profoundly exciting and unendurably delicious. Later, the breathlessness and trembling and shaking wouldn't cease.

"You like it?" she felt impulsed to ask.

"Apolladora—Apolladora," he replied huskily. "What's not to like?" His greedy young body swelled and strained against her softness, and she giggled self consciously, filled pleasurably by his soft caress. He cupped her breasts gently, ever so gently, and with the faintest touch flicked his hot moist tongue over her nipples. Apolladora sighed, delirious with ecstasy, and wondered what else she had been missing.

He had a marvelous way of teasing her by rubbing his large erect penis against her vagina in soft light touches, until she felt she was losing her mind. Gently, lightly, like the touch of a feather, he caressed her until the juices ran freely and she climaxed time and again until she seemed unable to endure the precarious heights to which he propelled her. Clutching at him she begged him to enter her. "Please! Please!" she cried hoarsely.

She raised her body up to meet his. "I can't wait any longer, Tori. I'm begging you. I'm going to burst wide open if you don't enter me!" She pleaded, frenzied and wild-eyed.

Slowly, like an artist creating a masterpiece, Tori entered her a bit at a time, teasing, until she gasped and grew more frenzied by the moment. Slow, sensual thrusts brought alive every nerve in her body, and suddenly they both tensed. Like bursting rockets, time and again they soared into space, until smaller rockets burst from these into a fan of tiny explosions. Their heads pounded, and their hearts—their delirious hearts—could no longer endure the delicious strain. Finally, in the gigantic stillness, they lay back, breathless and motionless.

Faint sounds of a radio playing in another apartment, filtering through the thin, shabby walls for several moments, became their first awareness of reality. Slowly, moving forward through the erotic euphoria of sex, other natural sounds became discernible.

"I've never known such feelings," whispered Apolladora. "When I began my work, I promised I'd never feel anything. It's only a job, I told myself, a job to support my family. I would save my feelings for the man I'd one day marry, God willing. But, now, Tori, all that is finished. I'll not be able to keep my promise, for you've stirred up in me such feelings I shall never forget. With you I feel no shame. You make me feel like someone very special. Very very special."

"You are special," he told her. "Truly, like no other I've met." he found himself saying, almost against his will. "I've never been with a woman who had the power to make me forget everything except being here with you." He wasn't being dishonest, as men were prone to be with whores. He had never felt the love, the tenderness and erotic feelings, he had experienced with Apolladora. Not with Maria Angelica, not with anyone!

Apolladora melted against his lean muscular body and breathed in deeply, inhaling the clean, fragrant smell of his body. This in itself served to arouse her erotically. Tenderness, the key to her soul, made her highly vulnerable. She experienced an overwhelming desire to reciprocate his love, to make him feel as he'd made her feel.

Totally without inhibitions, throwing all modesty to the winds, she exposed herself to him by engaging in highly sensual movements he'd never permitted the girls at Neptune's Daughters to do to him.

She moved her body sensuously over his and began to caress his manhood and inner thighs until he quivered under her expert touch. In the past he'd been indifferent to oral copulation, and on occasion, as with Maria Angelica only yesterday, he'd been terribly offended by the act. He could take it or leave it, and Tori, who loved as sensually as he lived, still preferred the feel of a woman's loins. Now, as Apolladora performed the act, he was consumed by an overwhelming feeling of love; a tenderness shook him deeper than the astounding force of the subsequent orgasm, which rendered him prostrate for more than a half hour. He wanted to reciprocate her love, but couldn't. He was spent. He was replete.

Side by side they lay, naked, silent and unmoving. He reached for a cigarette, lit it and lay back on the bed. She hadn't moved. He looked down on her face and pushed a damp curl off her forehead. He thought about all she'd told him, and, recalling all he'd told Athena yesterday, wondered what he'd do if she ever turned to prostitution; an involuntary shudder passed through him. Apolladora stirred in his arms. He straightened the slim silver crucifix around her neck and stroked her face tenderly. Life was hard. Life was very hard, he thought.

Her spectacular green eyes fluttered lazily and opened. She smiled indolently at him. In a wonderously inspired voice, he whispered, "Apolladora, where did you learn to make love so exquisitely? With you it's an inborn art. Truly you must be descended from all the nymphs of Venus. Here, in Mt. Erice, where her temple still stands, have you come to me as the reincarnation of all the love nymphs she kept at her side . . . ?" As he spoke a flush of warmth flooded his loins, and once more he felt himself give rise to the feelings of sexual exigency.

He also felt Apolladora stiffen and pull away from him. On her marble-like face he saw the same cold defiant shield of protection he'd seen at Naxos when she was bargaining with hostile clerks.

"Where?" she asked icily. "Working at the *fattoria* canning tuna fish! Where else?" Profound hurt surfaced into her eyes at what she mistook to be an insult. Unfamiliar with the gods and goddesses of mythology that were commonplace to Tori, she didn't understand his words.

Needless to say, the mood splintered. Nothing Tori

could say would appease her. He stopped trying and grew silent. She ranted on. "You had me believing you were different than the other men I've met. But I was wrong. *Managghia!* Was I ever wrong! Animals—all of you! You lie and cheat and deceive and flatter until you get what you want, and then it's *Va Futta!* Go fuck yourself! No?"

Tori's face blanched with indignation. Tight-lipped and livid, he'd gone to the bathroom, cleansed himself, then returned in silence to finish dressing. "How dare you classify me with all these promiscuous, lust-filled soldiers? How dare you? No matter what you think, I'm unlike any man you'll ever meet. But don't fret. Knowing how you feel, I shall not see you again." He had to have the last word. His Sicilian *maschiezzo* was at stake. There was nothing left for him but to leave.

"Hah! As if I care!" she retorted indignantly.

"If I did, you'd never see another man but me!" said Tori, unhearing.

"What makes you think I'd want to see you again?" she countered hotly.

He smiled enigmatically and walked to the door. "Goodbye my love goddess," he said softly.

Her aim was expert, and Tori barely ducked in time to avoid colliding with a bottle of French perfume. It connected with the door, broke, and spilled over his clothing. He smiled and closed the door behind him.

Long after he left, Apolladora cried bitterly and berated herself for allowing Tori to walk out of her life, for not making some move to stop him. No one had ever touched her as he'd touched her. For all time he was committed to her memory, for he had taken with him the best part of Apolladora Felice. Why hadn't she stopped him? But how? She was a whore!

Try as he did, he couldn't remove the fragrance of her perfume from his clothing. He hastily returned to Naxos to keep his appointment with Don Pippinu Grasso. As it was he had lingered too long with the girl.

Don Pippinu Grasso, heavily paunched and, with a wide, flat nose set deeply in swollen flesh and nostrils resembling a pig's snout, sniffed the air gingerly at the reeking aroma of perfume and grinned lasciviously.

"Ah, Salvatore! What a strong young stallion you've become!" He grinned revoltingly. "I see Apolladora has serviced you, also. . . ."

Tori froze. She couldn't have! Not with *this* pig of a man, who stank of garlic, wine and strong Romano cheese, and of the putrefaction of male uncleanliness. He wanted to retch. Speechless, shattered, dazed by the pulsating venom boiling his blood and searing his soul, he took hold of himself. *What the hell's wrong with me? She isn't my property. Why do I take this so personally? Hadn't she admitted being a whore?*

"She knows her stuff, eh?" suggested the snorting lump, never knowing how close he came to having his face smashed in.

Mental images of Apolladora lying naked in the arms of this uncouth brute rushed at Tori. He fought for control. *Goddammit! Stop this,* he told himself. *She's a whore! A whore! Stop acting as if she were Sheba reincarnated!*

"*Allora*—what brings you to Mt. Elice?"

"What always bring me here?" he asked tightly.

"Ah, *si*. Payment on the leases. You will tell that generous and most understanding of cousins, your Mamma, an angel if I ever saw one, that I shall be late with the payments. Business is bad. With the war it's intolerable!" He shook his head in a woebegone manner.

"No, no, no, no." Tori's sudden hatred for the man fell into organized articulation. "I shall tell her no lies. I've seen the business you do. One look at the prices you charge tells me the entire story. If it hadn't been for the weights and measures leased to you by my mother, you'd be what you were twenty years ago, a mere beggar without enough backbone to do an honest day's work! Now, I've come to collect what's legally hers by virtue of the agreement you made with her." Never had Tori spoken so boldly before.

"How dare you?" Don Pippinu's fat lips hung open, in indignation. The cigar had fallen from between his lips, spilling ashes down his vest. "How dare you?" He shook with rage. "You the son of a pitiful sheepherder, dare come to my house and treat me, Don Pippinu, with such disrespect!"

The power-saturated glance transmitted to the young man remained totally ineffectual, for Salvatore had been raised to fear no man, not even a *Mafioso*.

"This pitiful son of a sheepherder happens to be the man to whom you are presently indebted" he said mockingly, taking a step towards the *Mafioso*. "But, you misjudge me," cooed Tori with cunning. "I speak with more respect than to which you are entitled. If I didn't respect you . . ." he paused within inches from the fat man's face and averted his head at the distasteful odor reeking from him. He placed his hands on the man's

194

grimy lapels, grasped them firmly, and pulled the Don in towards him. ". . . I would have smashed your face in long ago. Are we in accord?" His dark fiery eyes sent clear messages to the Don.

Instinctively Don Pippinu averted his head and flinched as if to ward off an imaginary blow. "You're crazy, you know—crazy in the head. No one dares treat Don Pippinu with such foolish craziness! You must be insane. Perhaps the desert *sirocco* has broiled your brains, eh?"

Tori continued to sniff and squint as if he'd stepped on something distasteful and backed away. The stench emanating from the man was intolerable. The Don, meanwhile, glanced apprehensively at the son of his third cousin, related to him through marriage, and, with nicotine-stained fingers clasped to his chest in supplication, he decided to tread carefully. Something about the lad. . . .

"Because I cannot meet my payments, am I to be treated so disrespectfully?" he wailed. "In these trying times, even Satan would extend credit to a man unable to keep up with payments."

"I'm not interested in the ethics of Satan, only my own," temporized Tori. "*Allora,* I don't like coming here any more than you like having to be reminded what a *schifoso* you really are. What do you say we strike a bargain? Make me a flat offer of six thousand American dollars for an out-and-out sale of the weights and measures. Then we won't have to see one another again."

"You're crazy! I knew it, you're crazy! Demented! Out of your head! You must have fucked yourself crazy and drained the brains from your head!" roared the Don. He paced the floor with mounting agitation.

"Where the fuck will I get six thousand dollars?" He turned the pockets of his trousers inside out in a gesture symbolic of poverty. "What money do I have, eh? I have no money. I can barely support my family, and you ask me for a fortune. You're crazy! Like I said before, crazy!"

Tori's mind functioned with an adroit cleverness that surprised him. "Very well," he said in a deadly calm. "The weights and measures go up for sale in—what's customary—three, five days, a week? Can you vacate the premises by then?"

"For sale? What the hell are you saying? What is this 'for sale'?" The Don, stunned, had never contemplated such an eventuality. He should have—but he didn't, because he had decided long ago to somehow cheat Antigone Salvatore out of the business and property as well.

Yesterday, Salvatore had learned his Godfather was

195

alive. Contemplating this now, he grew bolder, bluffing his way. "I've been assured by Don Matteo Barbarossa of Godrano that his people are willing to pay a great deal more for the lease than you are paying now. When approached, I indicated, out of respect to you, that I'd be obliged to give you first refusal in the matter."

"*Don Matteo Barbarossa?*" The Don's obesity in no way interfered with the swiftness with which he pivoted on one foot, did an about-face, and stared with utter disbelief. Black pig eyes narrowed to slits, glittered insanely. "Your Godfather?" The wheels turned swiftly in his mind.

"Yes. My Godfather."

"*Mah*—how the hell is he your Godfather?" scoffed the obnoxious Don.

For a second Tori faltered. "How many ways are there for a man to become a Godfather?" he asked evenly.

They locked eyes. Don Pippinu read the truth in Tori's eyes and made an impatient gesture. He poured himself a glass of wine, gulped it down, and wiped his lips with the back of his wrist. He made a half-baked gesture at the wine, indicating Tori should help himself.

Standing in a careless pose, thumbs hooked into his belt, he watched the high-strung *Mafioso*, who hadn't thought enough of the encounter to keep a muscle man at his side, and smiled internally, at the other's distress and at his unmanly comportment.

Don Pippinu's pig eyes jumped here, there and everywhere with erratic intensity. As he waddled about the *negozio* he shouted, outraged, "Six thousand dollars! Where the hell will I get that sum in these impoverished times?" He stopped abruptly and, in a quick transition, struck a bargaining note. "Oh, no you don't! Not a cent over five thousand—and that's tops!"

Tori remained steadfast. "Six. Take it or leave it. Where you get the money isn't my concern." He glanced at his watch. "You have an hour to decide. If it's not ready then, I'll deal with Don Barbarossa. One hour," he said firmly. "And another thing, Don Pippinu, don't plan anything clever if you desire to live," he said lightly as he might have said a greeting.

Ten minutes later Tori walked among the temple ruins of centuries past, high above Mt. Erice where the fabled Rock of Venus had materialized and where legends claimed that over 200 soldiers once guarded the fabulous treasures given as gifts by the many enchanted visitors who had enjoyed the ingenious and amorous rites performed by the sacred, nymphlike prostitutes, those constant companions of the goddess Venus. Hitching his horse to a nearby post, Tori looked about for the caretaker he usually encountered when he came here. He lit a cigarette and for a time glanced out from these Cyclopean Phoenician walls at the magnificent spread of ocean—at the Egadi Islands at his feet, overrun with countless medieval castles and picturesque grottos, at the magnificent panorama of antiquity.

Never in all his youth had Tori felt such explosive forces within him. He felt as if a sleeping Hercules in his subconscious mind, aroused, had been born in these past few hours spent with Apolladora. This plus the events of the past twenty-four hours had caused an emergence of some inner force he'd never recognized before. He was a different man. Forceful and cunningly direct as he'd been in his dialogue with Don Pippinu, he now found that the change in him both confused him and intrigued him.

Quaint salt-grinding windmills turned in the wind below him along the shores of Trapani, and for a time he watched them absently. As he turned about, gazing at the Rock of Venus, his imagination ran rampant. Before his very eyes everything seemed transformed back in time to the era when Venus had been worshipped. The ruins had disappeared and the temple had been restored as it had been when the Greeks ruled the island; resplendent with mosaic water fountains, marbled pillars, graceful statues and friezes of dancing nymphs—and one added delight; the face of Apolladora took form on the faces of the dancing girls.

Wherever he looked he saw Apolladora; he saw her face, her body, heard her laughter and felt her presence. His clothing, saturated with her perfume, continued to stir his senses. Earlier, in the presence of the despicable Don Pippinu, the aroma had so engulfed him that he could hardly concentrate on the business at hand. Now, as he fought off the impressions the girl had left behind, he found there was no escaping her. She'd taken possession of him. *What the hell's wrong with me?* he asked himself. Closing his eyes and turning from the pulsating scenes of the floating, gyrating dancers around him, all replicas of Apolladora, he shouted internally, 'She's a whore! A common whore! Whores have their place in the world—but not in mine!"

Despite every logical reason Tori formed in his mind to turn from her, there was no escaping her or the overwhelming feelings taking possession of him. He'd never felt such sensations. He was in agony; he was in pain; he was in a confusing world of new excitement—but he also felt ecstasy, joy and a lightheaded, wondrous feeling that could fly him to Venus and back if he but willed it. *What to do? What to do?* he asked himself, over and again. A glance at his watch told him he was due back at Naxos.

Tori's disillusion with Don Pippinu amounted to distrust and active dislike. He hated duplicity or impropriety, and he abhorred men who made stupid and improper remarks without foundation. But to his surprise, when he arrived back at the end of the hour and found the money waiting for him, all these negative feelings dissolved.

Tori, astounded, had expected an excuse, a temporary payment—anything to appease the serious default, but, never six thousand dollars! No question that it was the best possible solution to a nagging situation, but the sight of so much money dimmed Tori's usually excellent judgment. In his entire life he'd never seen so large a sum of money at one time.

Don Pippinu, craftier than Tori, watched him, urging, "Go ahead, count it. It's all there. I know I overpaid you," he lamented. "To show you my heart's in the right place, I wish to make further reparations."

"And what does that mean?" asked Tori, too engrossed with the money count to pay him much mind.

"Only that I took the liberty of having my men saddle your horse with a few extra tokens of my respect for that angelic mother of yours, my wife's third cousin. All prewar stuff, *capeeshi?* Oil, sugar, flour—you know, a few extra tidbits, to show we're in accord. . . ."

Tori completed the money count. He lifted his eyes to meet those of the fawning man. He said politely, "I assure you that whatever you send will be accepted with sincere appreciation. It will bring tears of joy and happiness to the eyes of my mother to think that the husband of her third cousin would be so generous and thoughtful. She has always held Don Pippinu in the highest esteem." He gave the Don a bit of his own kind, then packed the money into his saddle bags as the Don watched him through veiled and sinister eyes.

"She's an angel, that woman—an angel!" The Don's oratory, loaded with all the venom collected in a serpent's tooth, burned him like a malignant infection as he studied the assured *Mafiusu* attitude, that arrogant cocksure manner ascribed only to such *men of respect*. Unquestionably, beneath Don Pippinu's fat face lay a vicious brain, a petty man with overinflated ambitions. Burning at the fact that he'd been bested by a *montanaro*—a peasant hillsman, he cursed inwardly. *Fucking upstart! I'll get the sonofabitch yet. Insolent dog!* Words stuck in his throat like impassable gall stones. Acid sprayed his intestines as he watched the proud young eagle, born under the sign of Scorpio, proudly tuck away the money in a money belt.

Exquisitely delighted at the unexpected victory and more possessed each moment with thoughts of Apolladora, Tori failed to detect in the Don the obvious signs of craft, guile, and hatred fermenting in his bowels. Amid strained farewells he departed, leaving the Don staring after him in the night.

In minutes he was knocking at Apolladora's door.

."You came back," she cried joyously with abandon. "You came back to me!"

"Did you really think I wouldn't, Apollodora?" he asked hoarsely, his eyes boring into hers, causing the excitement to begin inside her all over again. She fell into his arms. "I'll never let you go, *cara mia,*" he said breathlessly with the impetuosity of a youth struck through the heart by a love dart from Eros.

"Yes," she cried. "No. Oh, I don't know. What matters is that you're here."

They clung together in silence, adoration and a rising desire. Tori had to push her away from him reluctantly. He walked to the balcony and drew the blackout drapes.

He made certain the door was locked. Opening the saddle bags, he removed all the money, counted out five hundred dollars, and set it aside. On a small white card, he scribbled the name of a priest in Palermo and instructed the girl to go to the Church of St. John and present herself to Father Capellino. "Tell him you'll need shelter. In three days I shall come for you to take you to the house of my mother. Then we'll be married." He handed her the five hundred.

"All this money? It's a fortune," she explained flabbergasted. Ecstatically delirious over his proposal, she muttered, "You're crazy, *caro mio.* Completely crazy!" Tears of joy blurred her vision, and she trembled rapturously.

"I know. I know I'm crazy in love with you. I've never known such joy," he confided passionately. "Never!"

"Knowing what I am—what I've done—you still want to marry me?"

He placed his strong hand over her trembling lips tenderly. "You are my *adorata*—my beating heart—my life. We've never lived before today, when we both came alive in the magic of our love." He pressed her close, and Apolladora uttered a low cry and melted in his arms.

199

"*Carissima*, my time is limited. I must leave you for now," he said softly.

"Oh, Tori. If we never saw each other again I'd die content to know that at least I've known your love, *amore mio*," she whispered huskily. "I will go to Jato on Saturday. From there I will go to Palermo."

He nodded in agreement and explained that he needed certain items. Did she have any tissue paper, envelopes, stamps and glue? She did. Moving about the room collecting the items, Apolladora brought them to him, then sat and watched in total fascination as he counted out the balance of the money. He wrapped three thousand dollars carefully in tissue paper, slipped it into an envelope, sealed it, stamped and addressed it to himself. He then counted out four hundred more, which he placed into the toe of his sock before slipping his foot back into his boot. He placed a hundred into his pocket and divided the remaining two thousand into three stacks. He then wrapped them in tissue paper and glued them to the inside of his belt.

Glancing into the puzzled and enthralled eyes of Apolladora, he smiled and explained. "Bandits would make short order of me if they caught me with so much money. They'd never think to look here," he said, fastening the belt into place.

"Tori—you didn't—" She hesitated. "What I mean is—you didn't—"

"Steal it?" He laughed amiably, nibbling on the sandwich she'd made for him. "No, *Cara mia*, I didn't steal it." He told her the story and for a time, they both laughed.

Apolladora sobered instantly and reflected. "You must be careful in your dealings with Don Pippinu. He's a demon, that one. An evil animal. He's not to be trusted, Tori. He's in league with the old Mafia. Even the Allies detest him, yet treat him with much respect. Among the girls who work the streets, it is rumored that his enemies disappear mysteriously. Recently one of his *sicarii* attempted to extract compensations from the girls. Several who were approached refused, protesting the unfairness of such demands. Three that I know of, Tori, will never earn another lira as they did in the past. They were so badly mutilated, they can only beg on the streets as side-show freaks. . . ."

Tori stared at her in disbelief, then gathering all his *maschiezzo*, he drew himself up and in bold *pronunciamento*, declared, "He wouldn't dare harm me. I am Salvatore!"

The logic of his words was lost in the pomposity of his

200

attitude. His departure saddened Apolladora and filled her with pangs of dismay. Only their renewed vows to meet in Palermo, no later than the following Monday, brought a smile to her lips and happiness to her jade eyes.

Tori rode swiftly to the post office in Trapani, deposited the envelope containing the money, and headed out into open country.

At midnight, at Bellolampo Barracks, a desk orderly ran into Lt. Franchina's quarters and awakened him from a sound sleep. A military warrant issued at Allied HQ in Mt. Erice for the arrest of one Alessandro Salvatore of Montegatta, necessitated the lieutenant's immediate attention. The charges: grand larceny, and the transport of stolen and illegal goods.

Pulling on his trousers, a sleepy-eyed Franchina made a quick telephone call to Officer Nino Marino in Montegatta. Salvatore, it was reported on good authority, should be approaching Montegatta shortly before sunrise. Therefore Marino was instructed to prepare an ambush with a special detail to insure the felon's capture.

"I knew it! I knew it all along!" Lieutenant Franchina's excitement was transmitted to Nino Marino. "It *wasn't* sheer coincidence that I encountered the blackguard so many times on Monday," he bellowed. "I should have followed my intuition and locked the bastard up!"

"What the hell are you saying, Franchina?" Marino yawned sleepily, but he hadn't missed the self-accusatory remark. It would take more than Franchina's say-so to convince him that Salvatore was a felon, and he spoke out and said so. "Salvatore's no criminal. He's a straight young man who possesses morals you or I might fall short of."

"Listen, Marino," boasted Franchina. "I've a good nose for criminals. They can't fool me. The sonofabitch might just turn out to be head of the black market ring that's plagued Borghetto. Hell, now that I consider it, he might even be guilty of murder—perhaps two. I've nothing to go on except a policeman's hunch. . . ." Franchina thought about Gucci and Molino. Hadn't he seen Salvatore in their company that first day?

"*Va! Va!* With all due respect, *'Tenente,* you can shove that theory up your ass. I've been here a long time. I know these people. This young Tori is a religious acolyte whom the villagers respectfully call, *'il professore'.* Goddammit, man, he doesn't involve himself in criminal activities. There's not a dishonest bone in his body. Look, it must be another man with the same name. So many people are named Salvatore in these mountains."

201

"Listen, Marino. You think your way, I'll think mine. I tell you there's more than meets the eye here. We'll know soon enough. You just make sure the ambush is set up. I want no excuses. If he's innocent, he'll have enough time to prove himself. We'll compare notes later."

"Yeah, sure," said Marino under his breath. "Fat chance."

"What's that, Marino? Speak up. I can't hear you."

"I said, yes sir! I'll attend to it immediately."

CHAPTER 14

P—i—n—g! . . . *P—i—n—g!* The whistling, cracking sound of rifle fire burst all around him. A bullet, then another, and still more whizzed overhead and around him. Tori's stallion spooked, bolted, and reared uncontrollably for several moments until he managed to check rein the beast. Wheeling him around, Tori's eyes squinted in the bright sunlight of dawn, but he saw them. Every last one of them came at him. He was at the center of a circular ambush, and *carabinieri* converged on him from four points on the dial. They came at three, six, nine and twelve o'clock, with rifles aimed at his heart.

"*Firmate*! Stop!" shouted officer Nino Marino, galloping swiftly to Tori's side. "Dismount and identify yourself!"

There was no time to think. His hands were raised over his head in submission. Once again Marino shouted to him.

"I said, dismount!" commanded the feisty *carabiniero*.

Tori was in a daze. He listened to Marino snap out orders to the rest of them, dismissing them and keeping with him only another officer named Fabrizio. "This man is known to me. Two of us can handle him. We'll meet at Bellolampo, later," he told his men. To Tori he shouted even louder. "Goddammit! I said dismount!"

Tori complied. He was ordered to turn over his identity card. "And no funny stuff! One false move and you'll find yourself separated from half your body," added Marino.

All of this seemed false to Tori. Even as Marino walked to the rear of his stallion, identity card in hand, it seemed to Tori he was playacting. With the tip of a knife, Marino slit open the ropes tying the foodstuffs to his saddle and sliced away the tarp exposing the goods. Marino snorted contemptuously.

"Black marketeering too, eh? Don't bother to explain. You can tell it to Lt. Franchina at Bellolampo. In case that lawyer's head of yours questions my orders, I've a warrant for your arrest. Now make it easy on yourself—tell me where you've hidden the money."

"The what—?" In all this confusion Tori hadn't given it a thought.

"Stop stalling. Turn it over, Salvatore. It'll go easier for you in my report, you hear?"

Tori was stunned as it all came together in his mind. So this was the game Don Pippinu played! The bastard reported him to the police. Now he'd get his money back and jail Tori on a trumped up charge. He should have known better.

"Listen, Marino," he began, "I can explain all of this—" He was so intent on his hatred for the despicable Don that he wasn't prepared for the next jolt.

"I said tell it to Franchina. Now hand over the belt!"

For Tori this would be the blackest moment of his life. He could only stare dumbly at Marino. *Santo Dio!* Only one person knew of the belt. *Apolladora! Apolladora! Sweet merciful God tell me I'm wrong.* Don Pippinu and Apolladora working together! His legs turned to water. Shaken, disorganized and stunned by the sequence of events, he moved as if in a dream; his stiff, cumbersome hands fumbled with his belt buckle, unhitching it and handing it to the officer. His mind had stopped, gone blank.

He vaguely heard Marino's words of chastisement. Something to the effect that he'd argued with Lt. Franchina about the question of Salvatore's involvement, certain the lad wouldn't have been involved in a reprehensible crime. "My faith in you is shattered, Sicilian," said Marino. "Grand larceny and black marketeering!"

Tori, numb from shock but not too stunned to berate himself, waded through the mental fog that enveloped him. What a jackass he'd been! *Un pezzu de shekko!* Trusting two people that an idiot of three years wouldn't have given the time of day! Moving robotlike, bewildered by the deception foisted upon him, Tori vaguely heard Marino's words: "Get on your horse and don't try anything funny or I'll give it to you through the head!"

Five minutes later they were mounted and climbing the narrow corkscrew road to the summit. Confusion blistered

Tori's mind, yet in this confusion he caught sight of the *lupara* in his saddle holster, which Marino had failed to remove earlier. The treacherous road was narrow, and they were approaching a tortuous hairpin bend in the road where his keen eyes discerned that, judging from the distance between him and his captors, as soon as he made the U-turn, he'd be facing the officers. He had to make a split second decision, and he did. Once past the U-turn, Tori moved fast. He pulled up on the *lupara* and got the drop on the *carabinieri*, taking them by surprise. And then, the unexpected happened—a freak accident.

Pursuant to regulations when escorting a prisoner, Officer Marino carried his Mannlicher-Carcano slung under one arm. The sight of the *lupara* aimed at him had caused him to rein his horse; the antique rifle misfired and sent a bullet spiralling through Tori's left shoulder. The sudden impact of the perforating missile, ripping into Tori, caused an involuntary reflex action as his trigger finger squeezed tightly exploding the *lupara*. A blinding ball of white fire caught Marino between the eyes, and with a loud, agonized groan of pain he went flying off his saddle, toppling to the ground, his hands clutching blindly at his head where blood oozed and spurted like a fountain. Marino's horse, an army mare, spooked for a moment, then retired to a distance a few feet away from the scene.

Fabrizio's horse, a squeamish, quivering mass of animal flesh, shuddered under him as the neophyte took random shots at Salvatore before he panicked and rode off in a whirling cloud of ocherous dust. Most of the shots went wild, but one struck Tori's left arm inches below the shoulder wound.

Wincing at the pain in his upper arm and shoulder, Tori clutched at the area of shooting fire and saw a thick glob of warm blood seep through his fingers. Despite his injuries, he rode to Marino's side, and springing from his saddle, sickened by the ghastly sight, he stared numbly at the faceless mass where portions of the skull had exploded, exposing sections of the cranium and the skeletal structure of bones and teeth. There was no mistaking it, the man was dead.

Tori reeled unsteadily as the faces of Gucci and Molino superimposed themselves over the bloodied mass of Marino's body. Sickened by the rapidly evolving order of things, he couldn't believe his senses. He felt dizzy, flushed with burning sensations and considerably weak. Dimly his eyes made out a cloud of dust riding at him from the distance. How many were there? Four. Four uniformed *cara-binieri* approached him.

Without thought of the moneybelt or his identity card, he mounted his stallion, wheeled him about, and rode off the road beyond several large boulders. He found a secluded grotto and h͟i͟d from sight.

He could hear their voices dimly. Too weak to scale the boulder that overlooked the scene, he lay his head on the cool stone and remained motionless.

"Where's the money?" asked a voice vaguely familiar to Tori. "The six thousand." Lt. Franchina's voice rang loud and clear.

"I swear, it's all he had on him," insisted Fabrizo.

"Take Marino's body back to Bellolampo. Go to Salvatore's house and wait for him. Bring him back with the rest of the money, or *you'll* be swinging from the nearest tree. The charge in addition to grand larceny is murder, now."

Tori couldn't see them, but he heard this portion of their conversation. Moments after he heard their horses ride off, he returned to the cool grotto and sat down. He removed his shirt, ripped off the sleeves, and bound his upper arm as best he could. He found a twig and made a tourniquet to halt the flow of blood. Using a torn sleeve to stuff the bloodied hole in his shoulder, he tried to find something to bind it and couldn't. Sweat rolled off his face as the pain intensified. It being so early in the morning, he didn't dare chance an escape in broad daylight, only to be picked off by roaming *carabinieri*. No. He'd have to wait until nightfall before chancing it. He 'lay back against a cool rock, his head roiling with violent and uncontrollable thoughts.

The effect on Salvatore of this bewildering and rapid succession of events struck him with a sequence of alternating reactions. First, blind fury and outrage at Apollodora's betrayal and Don Pippinu's obvious treachery. Then came concern over his family. What must they be thinking? Would his mother believe the charges of grand larceny—the murder of Nino Marino? God! What had happened to him these past forty-eight hours? Had he suddenly been possessed by a demoniacal monster? He didn't recognize these strange emotions coursing through him. From where had they sprung? Had they always been there inside of him, lying dormant waiting to be unleashed?

Only last night, after he had left Apolladora's apartment he'd been like a man returning to a warm hearth after a long and glorious journey to far and wondrous places he'd never forget. He'd galloped with the speed of a meteor along the winding roads, through barren orchards, past olive groves older than those in biblical Babylon with their gray whorled trunks like spiralling goat horns. Thoughts of Apolladora had saturated his mind, body and soul, and love had oozed from every pore in his body. The tableau of love he'd created with Apolladora had dazzled his senses and occupied most of his thoughts, diffusing all thoughts of that devil, Don Pippinu.

It was his own fault for trusting in a whore. Yes! That's what she was—a whore! How could he have been so blind? He had even pushed aside the nagging thoughts that had attempted to pierce his mind, trying to warn him. What could happen to him? Just before midnight, he had paused at the Greek ruins at Segesta to rest his horse and nibble at the *companaggio* prepared for him by Apolladora. Seated at the base of one of the enormous pillars of the temple, Tori had felt his left ear throb. It had come to him at the time that the matter with Don Pippinu had been too easy.

Moving quickly, he had pulled the *lupara* from his saddle holster and loaded it with pellets. He'd slipped it back into place, then checked his Beretta automatic. At least he'd had the good sense to take the warning in good stead. He had even detoured to Castellammare, where he'd awakened a keeper of stables and bargained for the black stallion, which he had exchanged for the chestnut mare by adding a few lire to the bargain. He had thought if anyone lay in ambush for him they wouldn't be looking for a black stallion. . . . Well, a lot of good it had done!

The sun had just been rising when Tori had paused in the plains of Partenico to water his horse from the cascading crystal waters spouting from the jaws of open-mouthed serpents constructed by the Romans centuries before. Back on his horse, he had galloped through wheat fields, suddenly very tired, hungry and saddle sore and unduly irritated by the creaking bridle paraphernalia—a sound that he found grating on his nerves. The familiar throbbing in his ear had commenced once again, causing Tori to become wary and edgy. Even the snorting, labored breathing of the stallion had alerted him, as if he, too, sensed the impending dangers. In the distance Tori had seen vultures circling overhead against the eastern skies, and he had suddenly recalled the deaths of Gucci and Molino. Just before the shots rang out, he had felt the beast quiver under him and snap his powerful head from side to side, his nostrils flaring and ebony eyes darting wildly about. He had grown skittish, resisting Tori's control.

Hah, thought Tori reflecting on this. Even the beast had been more intelligent than he'd been when he rode into the ambush.

By mid-afternoon, Tori became increasingly feverish. He needed water to slake his thirst. Hunched over, he let his head fall heavily into his right hand. He felt miserable, defeated. Worse, he was sick. He'd smoked incessantly and had no more tobacco left. The pains he felt were sheer agony. His eyes grew swollen and distended, his bloodshot eyes frenzied and maniacal. In the raging fever his madness increased. His heart shriveled at Apolladora's deception.

"Don Pippinu!" he shouted with satanic exhaultation. "Watch yourself carefully. Your days are numbered. And you, Apolladora, to whom I gave my love, my heart and soul, there's a place for traitors. You'll not live to enjoy the fruits of this day's treachery. By, God, I shall be avenged for the betrayal you wrought upon me this day, you Delilah!" Tears of humiliation stung his eyes as he recanted his misery aloud.

"How you must have laughed at me! I stood before you, a simpering shadow of a boy, parading his tumescence like a badge of honor! A jackass is what I was. A foolish adolescent! All cock and no balls! A foolish joke of a boy, trying to impress the world with his manliness. *Cafone! Cafone!*" As bitterness and self-condemnation eroded his guts and sapped him of strength, he succumbed from sheer exhaustion, slipping in and out of fretful consciousness.

Dreams. Nightmares. Recollections came at him. The events of the past two days wouldn't quit in his mind. The faces of Gucci and Molino were etched sharply on each eyeball. He'd never killed before. Not from squeamishness or fear, but because he'd felt this a violation of human dignity. Yet in three days he'd killed three men. The faces of those brutalized youngsters, helpless at the hands of Gucci—even Pallido who had died in his arms and his uncle Gianni dead at their hands—faded into the recesses of his mind while the faces of Gucci and Molino remained vivid in his memory to torment him. Finally he fell mercifully unconscious.

Tori awakened in high fever. Shaken by chills, consumed by fire and unable to hold to a clear thought, he struggled to his feet holding his head in his hands in an effort to unscramble the chaos in his brain. A dullness of perception struck him. Memory came and went with alarming frequency. He staggered and stumbled about in the darkness, confused by a body that refused to do his bidding. Yet somehow, miraculously, he managed in this confusion to strap himself onto his horse and head out into the night towards a destination he had never dreamed would be his home.

Irrevocably drawn by unseen forces towards a particular place and a specific people to fulfill some predestined plan, he slumped over the saddle of his satiny stallion and, guided by an instinct older than time, he moved slowly over the craggy terrain of boulders and stones of antiquity.

A swarm of stars hung over the desolate land with fierce intensity, as if they'd purposely been turned on to illuminate his path and guide him forward into the blackness. No matter how he tried to retain consciousness, he found himself outwitted by a raging infection and an all-consuming fever which broke down his resistance. Through the murky haze he vaguely heard a voice calling. "Apolladora . . . Apolladora. . . ."

Lieutenant Franchina had had no time to compare notes with Nino Marino. The next time he saw the younger man, Molino was dead at Salvatore's hand, and this had been attested to by an eyewitness, *carabiniero* Fabrizo. Franchina needed no further proof. He had in his possession Tori's identity card and a belt containing only a portion of the six thousand dollars allegedly stolen from a Mt. Erice merchant, and the dead body of Nino Marino. In his eyes, now, Salvatore was guilty beyond a shadow of a doubt. He'd turned all this evidence over to Major Carrini at Bellolampo late that afternoon, and to his astonishment was instructed to charge Salvatore only with the murder of Nino Marino and the stolen foodstuffs. He was instructed under oath to say nothing about the money or grand larceny charges. He complied with the orders of his superior, keeping his thoughts to himself.

For the next several days Lieutenant Franchina launched an exhaustive search for Salvatore. Nothing turned up. It was as if those infernal mountains had swallowed him up. On Sept 29 he presented himself at the Salvatore house. Greeted by Athena who was ill with one of her nagging headaches, he asked to speak with her mother.

As he departed, leaving the woman and her daughter shaken and distraught over the information he had imparted to them, he requested their cooperation in the matter of apprehending Tori. He was annoyed by the unusual strength and fortitude the woman displayed. Earlier when he had thrust the warrant into Antigone's hands and told her he was looking for 'that murderer, Salvatore,' Antigone had insisted he must be mistaken. He assured her they had an eyewitness to the felony.

"Who?" Antigone had queried. "Another *carabiniero?*" She had displayed her contempt.

"When will you peasants learn you can't continue to violate the laws?" he'd asked.

"The same time you learn that we Sicilians have stomachs that need feeding as regularly as yours," she had replied scathingly.

By then his aides had searched the Salvatore house thoroughly and returned, announcing they'd found no one. "He can't have gone too far with two bullets pumped in him," he said aloud, watching the reaction on the women's faces.

Lieutenant Franchina touched his cap politely and informed them the police and *carabinieri* would be watching their house with the eyes of hawks. "When a man needs shoes he goes to a cobbler," he told them in parting. "And when a man needs his family—well, we'll be here to grab him." He and his men left immediately, leaving the women to their despair.

"Mamma, oh Mamma," cried Athena. "Our world has collapsed. First, Filippo, then Marco, now Tori." She buried her face in her mother's shoulder. "Two bullets shot into him! *Two!* How will he live? Who'll care for him?"

"Don't cry, *cara mia,*" said her mother soothingly. "Don't cry. If crying helped, I'd be the first to shed tears. Don't believe their lies. Tori's no murderer."

"I can't help it. I'm not as strong as Tori or you."

"All right then, cry if you must, dear heart."

Athena pulled away, blew her nose, and dabbed at the tears.

"That's my girl. Dry your eyes. You'll only aggravate your pain if you cry. Wherever Tori is now, God watches over him. He's fully protected now—" Antigone gave a start. She had stopped in mid-sentence, horror-struck. She blinked hard as if to help sharpen her mind.

"Mamma, you're truly made of iron," said Athena, impervious to the changes occurring in her mother until she glanced at the terrified expression on her face. "Mamma? What's wrong?"

Antigone ran from the kitchen with the frenzied eyes of

a woman possessed. She ran up the stairs and groped along the wall of her bedroom until she located the key to her hope chest. She moved across the room, inserted the key, and turned it in the lock. She lifted the cover and removed from the chest both the prophecy and the amulet, sinking to her knees in a crumpled heap. Sighing deeply, as if to catch her breath, she read and reread the *strega*'s prophecy, her eyes spotlighting certain portions: *"He musn't be without this protection. Already there are strange webs of entanglements in the fires of his life...."*

She told me there'd be trouble," wailed Antigone softly. "I didn't listen. Oh God of all that's sacred and holy, what have I done? *Santo Dio*, what have I done?"

Athena stood at the door watching her mother, wondering at this peculiar behavior. Who'd told her there'd be trouble? What had she done by not listening? She caught sight of the glittering disc in her mother's hands, and, unable to make it out, she decided it was the wrong time to invade her mother's privacy. She retreated back to her room and placed a vinegar-soaked cloth over her forehead. The fumes in some way helped to alleviate the pain.

On October 3, a Saturday, Lieutenant Franchina, filled with an inner restlessness and an increased loathing for Bellolampo and the growing apathy he discerned in his fellow officers, gathered together a squad of men and ventured forth in the direction of Rigano Pass, where only five days before his men had been massacred. Drawn back to the area by a profound curiosity and a desire to avenge the deaths of his former companions, he was eager to find those responsible for the atrocity.

During the course of the past few days, Lieutenant Franchina, on his own initiative, had sought the services of a special breed of man who for a price would spy for him and report their findings. Most of these leads, however, turned up without the much sought after results. However, the knowledge that such men existed among this clannish withdrawn society was filed away in his mind for future reference.

For three hours the weary, overheated *carabinieri* wove in and out of the few accessible grottos and came up with nothing. Finally, from the southern-most point of the pass, Lt. Franchina gave his men the signal to remount and return to Bellolampo.

Bandits approaching the Pass from the north had the advantage of spotting their enemy first. Had any *carabini-*

ero at Bellolampo Barracks been walking idly about the military *caserne* and glanced up in the distance, they might have wondered at the small puffs of smoke rising in the distance. Even the faint popping of rifle fire might have captured their attention. If any of them might have been discerning enough to realize what was happening and thought to ride swiftly to Rigano Pass, they might have caught up with the bandits and finished them off.

But unfortunately it was Saturday, a day most officers already in Palermo had begun to wind down in preparation for a gala weekend, partying with the British and American soldiers and the influx of prostitutes abounding in the city. What few remained on duty at Bellolampo were playing cards and drinking sociably, never once thinking about their foolish companions whom that crazy Franchina had encouraged to go out scouting on a Saturday. A Saturday—imagine!

In the bottleneck at the Pass five bandits picked off Franchina's men, one at a time, felling a man with each bullet they expended. Once again Lt. Franchina's star must have been in the ascendancy. He escaped death in the ambush. But this time he felt no stirrings of immortality surging in his loins. He wasn't as fortunate as he'd been on September 28. A heartbeat or two away from death's greedy claws, he hung on desperately to his saddle, his body riddled with bullets and spouting rivulets of blood. He reached the barracks miraculously and was rushed to the Palermo Hospital, more dead than alive—but still alive

CHAPTER 15

An early Sicilian sun splintered through a webbed network of upper branches on tall pine trees. He saw portions of a fiery blue sky in a cross-illumination of light outlining dark foliage. He had awakened to such profound weakness that he thought for an instant he was paralyzed and blind until he blinked his burning eyes and the milky film over his vision cleared and lightened enough for him to discern familiar objects, like trees, leaves and branches. Forced to

211

blink time and again, he stretched his eyelids until his vision cleared entirely.

Life first came to his mind in short electric bursts while his body lay immobile. But for Tori, it was enough to know he was alive! The smells of clean earth, pine needles, and fresh coffee invigorated him and he knew he was coming to. Slowly, his eyes gazed about the confines of his shelter. He wondered where he was. The shadowy form of an older man with wrinkled skin the color of smoked leather, propped sleepily against a tree trunk, caught his eyes. Wearing a brown beaked cap with flaps tugged down over his ears, the old man made grumbling noises as he snored. Intermittently, he'd nod as one did in fighting off sleep. Beyond him, through a small clearing, Tori saw a scattering of idle men, moving about a campfire sipping hot coffee.

Perplexed, he tried to wade through his mental confusion, and found to his dismay that his memory wasn't anxious to obey him. As more life stirred in him, he grew aware of bandages around his left shoulder and a sling around his neck in which his left wrist lay supported. A blanket wrapped warmly about him to ward off the early morning chill fell away as he moved. Then, like a rolling fog bank, a tunneled voice cut through his numb and hazy brain and pulled him back into reality.

"*Buon Giorno. Buon Giorno, aquilo bravo.* I see the brave young eagle has returned from the mountain," grinned a toothless old man, before he hawked up phlegm from his throat and spat it into a nearby bush. He cast off his poncho-shawl, and Tori saw a curiously misshapen man, bent from a crippling form of arthritis, move with remarkable agility and approach him. He helped to sit him up, and propped Tori against a tree trunk.

Tori glanced warily at him. He wanted to ask a thousand questions. He felt his lips move, but no sound came for several moments. Finally he asked with difficulty, . . . What day is this?" Tori leaned forward as pain spasms tore at him. He winced, gasped, and grimaced painfully.

"*Santo Dio!*" shouted the old man. "Mother of Satan! Lie still! Two bad bullets were pumped into you! Might as well have been a dozen, for all the trouble they caused. Don't you remember? *Managghia!* What the hell hit you—a *carabiniero's* relic of a gun?"

Instantly, Tori froze. He disliked questions. He became suspicious of anyone prying into his business, and drew away from the old man with an animal wariness.

"Don't worry, you're safe with the rest of us, here in the

212

macchia. I've had enough experience with *carabinieri* bullets to know their story. If the shot doesn't get you, infection from their rusty bullets will destroy you. Imbeciles! Haven't the sense to use proper bullets in their guns. You'd think Mussolini would arm his soldiers correctly, no? Imagine—they use World War I relics! They deserve to lose this goddamn war! Junk is what they use. Junk! 1891 Mannlicher-Carcano's and ancient Vetterli Vitale's, rebarreled for 6.5 mm rifles. What a disgrace, eh? *Allora,* would you believe these same guns are used for .22 calibre training rifles by the *carabinieri*?"

As the old man spoke, he peered critically under the dressings in Tori's arm and shoulder, and nodded in satisfaction. *"Molto bene . . . molto bene. . . ."* He replaced the bandages. "One day, *Il Duce* will wake up to learn he lost this fox trot with Hitler because those goddamn weapons blew up in the faces of those soldiers who accompanied him in the grand ball of war. I am called Giacomo. What are you called?"

"Alessandro," he began, surprised at the weakness of his voice. "Alessandro Salvatore. My friends call me Tori."

"Benvenuto, Salvatore. Welcome to the Mountain of Cats. This is Thursday. For two days, you've been embraced by the arms of death, *aquilo bravo."*

"Aquilo bravo? Me?" Tori forced a smile. "I doubt that I resemble a brave eagle. I feel more like a plucked goose." *So,* thought Tori bitterly, *I ended up in the bandits' camp.* He grew more guarded until he realized that in his condition there was little he could do to defend himself.

"Listen," confided the old man, rubbing his hands together to warm them, before he lit a cigarette, which he handed to his patient. "When I found you, fighting to sit tall in the saddle, in the darkness, where only the whites of your eyes and those of your valiant horse's were visible, and your body raging with fever as the angels of death fought over your bones, you brought to mind a magnificent golden eagle I once saw felled by hunter's bullets. It was too dangerous to approach, and I was forced to keep my distance. Daily I brought food and water to that king of flying creatures. He lasted eight days. If only I could have gotten closer without him savagely clawing me to death I might have saved his life. You reminded me of this *aquilo bravo,* for you too, fought me off. In your delirium you cried out, 'Let me die! Let me die!' Just as quickly, I told God he'd better not listen to you, that you were crazy out of your mind. That if he listened to you, he'd have to reckon with me. So, knowing my wrath, he

213

wouldn't argue with old Giacomo. I told God, 'This time I think we saved an even more magnificent eagle than before.'" The old man became a symphony of hand gestures.

Touched by the man's words, Tori nevertheless felt bitterness at his plight. Thoughts of Apolladora and Don Pippinu seared his soul. He glanced about the wooded area, beyond the makeshift campsite, noting the many unsightly and bearded men in their midst.

"You want to meet the others?"

"No." Tori's prompt reply brought a questioning look from the other.

"Later, then. Don't be concerned if there comes upon you a peculiar dizziness. I have medicated you with the wondrous sulpha drug I stole from the American dispensary in Palermo. *Allora*—rest for now. Soon I will bring you first class coffee. Phew! What I found in your saddle bags! *Managghia!* Such luxuries. But, do not worry. I shall not permit these thieving buzzards to steal them. What a joy to taste real coffee—" He rambled.

About to protest the brazen appropriation of his precious cargo, Tori shrugged it off. Who was in a position to argue? He neither possessed the strength or the desire to challenge a flea. In his misery he watched as Giacomo limped off towards the campfire, shuffling and dragging his arthritic leg behind him.

Tori's outward calm masked an earthquake of *vendetta* and vengeance. Unshaven for days, weak and far from healed, he'd made his plans. On Saturday when Apolladora arrived in Jato to bring food to her family he'd be there to greet her—unless that, too, had been a crock of deception! He didn't think so, though. Armed with the knowledge that he'd be settling the score shortly, Tori tried to get to his feet in Giacomo's absence. The earth suddenly moved from under him, and the sky whirling above him changed color. He lost his footing, and, falling heavily against a tree, he remained there until Giacomo returned with the coffee.

"Are you crazy?" shouted the old man. "By the balding black balls of Satan, are you trying to kill yourself? Get back down and stay put. Crazy fool!" He set the steaming mugs of coffee on the ground nearby and helped steady his patient.

"I want to walk," insisted Tori weakly. "It will make me stronger. Just a few feet. I have to—I must."

"All right. I'll walk with you," said Giacomo sensing the other's resolve. "But, by the beard of my sister's husband twice removed, you're a stubborn mule! *Testardo!* Lean on me, fool. I've ten times your strength."

"Thank you for taking care of me," said Tori as they walked.

"Balls! You'll thank me by getting off your feet—not by empty words. Why do you push yourself? You'll walk in time."

"Tell me—who are all these men?" Tori tried to change tack. It worked.

For a time he listened in courteous silence as Giacomo pointed out first, one then, another. Most were petty offenders who had run from the *carabinieri* for transporting food over provincial borders. The old man's eyes lit up suddenly as if possessed with a mighty secret. "These are only a few men," he added. "See those men up there—high on the ledge?" He pointed to a wooded area overhead, against the great mountain. "Up there are hundreds of men I've not met as yet. Prisoners of war, they say. Dangerous men, young eagle. True criminals. Damned tough, I hear. I tell you straight, *aquilo*," he whispered conspiratorially. "Those men have an arsenal of guns that could run the Allies out of Sicily. I do not lie!" he exclaimed crossing his heart. I personally have seen these weapons.

"Are they in the Grotto Persephone?" asked Tori sparked with interest.

"You know this place?"

"I know it." Tori paused to light a cigarette from a burning stick in the campfire. Finished, he tossed the twig back into the heart of the fire and inhaled deeply on the cigarette. "Listen, *amico*," he said, *sotto voce*. "If I desire to get a message out of the *macchia*—"

"Leave it to me, *aquilo bravo*," Giacomo interrupted boldly as if he read the other's thoughts. "It shall be done."

"Not now. Soon, perhaps, but not now. I'm tired. For now we sit down, eh?"

A few heads turned in their direction, most of them apathetic, paying them no importance. Tori felt better. Weaker, but better. He could feel his senses come alive, and that was better than the insensitivity he'd felt these past days. In an hour he'd take another walk. For now, he lay back against the trunk of a tall cypress, bundled warmly against the cool mountain air.

Still searing his heart and soul were the burning images of Apolladora and Don Pippinu. Until their fate was settled in his mind, Tori was determined never to forget the infamy done against him.

A few days rest and concentrated exercise would work wonders for him. On Saturday—in Jato, he'd settle the score. He'd killed before, this time it would be easier. The time passed swiftly, with revenge firing his emotions.

CHAPTER 16

"Padre!" called Tori for the fourth time.

The bent figure of a middle-aged parish priest, working vigorously in an unprolific garden, finally glanced up. *Padre* Francesco Voltera, a craggy-faced man with grey streaks in his wiry dark hair, possessed dark, angry eyes, smoldering under a shelf of bushy brows that expressed his outrage and the dark, brooding thoughts he harbored. Without thinking the uncordial man cursed aloud. *"Ma che cazzu voi?* Speak up! Speak up! I haven't all day."

Startled by the tart language uttered by priest at the Church of Santo Crocifisso, Tori stared at him in silence, aghast at the holy man's comportment.

Sensing his error, the priest lowered his shovel, dropped his anger a notch or two, and squinted up at the stranger who wore a sling around one arm. He sighed aloud, set aside his garden tool, tugged at a handkerchief from his rear pocket, and commenced to wipe the sweat from his face and neck. He ambled to the gate, grumbling and scolding himself for both his uncalled-for rudeness and his damned lumbago. He rubbed his back, gingerly.

"Come, come, my son," said the scowling priest. "Come. Sit down." He walked, leading the way to the *pergoda*, and continued his compulsive oratory. "Yesterday, our village was struck with the most deplorable atrocity in its history. Horrifying! Simply horrifying! Who can preach piety or turn the other cheek from the pulpit tomorrow—eh? Not after this. Please, take a seat. See?" He made a wide sweeping gesture with his arms. "Nothing grows here. Our people die from unproductive lands and intolerable *siroccos.* Nine months out of each year we pray for rain. When it comes it washes away half the village. Now—the

216

abrasiveness of war with foreigners once again. Most inhuman. Most inhuman! There's no hope for Sicilians, I tell you. No hope at all." He broke wind without apology.

"Uh—I—uh, Padre," interrupted Tori, in no mood for long-winded speeches about centuries-old grievances and inequities. He knew them by rote.

"Forgive me. I've come on an urgent matter. I'll not take your time if you will kindly direct me to the house of Felice, to the family in which there's a daughter, Apolladora."

The priest, suddenly aloof and suspicious, asked, "Who are you?"

Tori avoided the cleric's eyes. "A friend of the family," he replied.

"Ah, then you're here for the funeral. I tell it straight," said the priest relaxing somewhat. "It's unbelievable. Poor Abruzzi. What a job for the mortician. It'll be a closed casket, of course," rambled the agitated priest.

"Please direct me to the proper house," insisted Tori impatiently, as he pressed a stack of *Am-lire* in the man's hands. "For the poor box." he added.

Reacting to the money, Padre Voltera replied eagerly. "Better still, I'll take you there, personally." He was instantly cordial and obsequious.

"No, no, no. It's not necessary," said Tori, visibly irked.

"Nonsense. It's my duty. I want to apologize for my rudeness. . . ."

Before Tori's voice raised in protest, he found himself guided through the most depressed area he'd ever seen. They passed through narrow alleys, past hovels unfit for animals, yet occupied by humans. He sidestepped filthy gutters, gurgling with fetid waters. He saw dull, half-starved faces peering at him from behind dirty curtains: hungry children, brown from the sun, standing on thresholds dressed in rags. In the air was a feeling of doom, desperation and depression.

Revolting odors of animal excrement, heat and dust thickened the air. Stale foods, sickness, disease and the putrefaction of death appalled him. Was there no humanity in this wretched village? He could scarcely breathe. Tori reached for his handkerchief to cover his nose.

"I hardly notice the foul odors any more. One gets used to them," said the priest.

Tori wondered, as he'd wondered many times in the past. what good were priests? Was their role directed to the sole purpose of hypnotizing people into accepting such miseries in life without encouraging them into something better?

The alleys became more littered with refuse, and he felt the awareness of pain, fear and starvation pulsing in the atmosphere. Here and there a solitary figure approached them and paused to stare, then passed on, nodding to the priest. There was something ominous in their silent presence, and when he looked into their eyes they seemed not the eyes of humans, but more like those of wary animals, hating, suspicious and hostile.

He wondered: *Why are they like this? Is this why Apolladora had left this land of hopelessness?* Had all the interior villages crumbled to such decay? In his village, shabbily dressed men roamed the streets, but there the resemblance ended. Or was this the first time he had taken a good look at his country? Had the dreams and fantasies been suddenly stripped from his eyes, permitting him to see things as they'd always been, revealing X-rays of the shabby and deplorable life to which his fellow man had been reduced over the ages? He asked himself candidly if his sensitivity to these conditions had been heightened by his own inescapable dilemma. No answer came to ease his torment.

They stopped before a grubby, run-down shanty, generously called a building. A hand-lettered sign, in bold script, graced the door: *"Abruzzi's Funeral Parlor—A. Abruzzi, Mortician."*

"Be a good lad, stop with me for a moment. I must bless the body," urged the frocked man giving Tori no time to refuse. He disappeared inside.

Before Tori could grope for an excuse, there was no one left to listen. *Damn it to hell!* he cursed inwardly. His wounds pained him; his stomach felt queasy, nauseated from the lack of nourishment. He wanted to complete his mission and get the hell out of Jato. Reluctantly he followed the priest's footsteps inside the dismal and intolerable building. Odors of bland paraffin, intermingled with formaldehyde and death, clung cohesively to the air and mixed with the decaying stench produced by the dead, humans as well as flowers; Tori felt more nauseous. His eyes, adjusting to the interior, took in the familiar scene.

Death and God! God and Death! Always the immaculate white altar, upon which was displayed a profusion of statues; the Virgin with Child, Santa Rosalia, St. Anthony, St. Sebastian. Floral offerings, burning candles, incense—all of it stood in complete incongruity to the earthen-floored room with its leaky walls and leprous ceilings, where open sections of the roof allowed an ample view of the sky. Bowled over by the stench, Tori's first impulse was to run.

From the back room came the fat-jowelled, owlish mortician, wearing bloodstained rubber gloves, and a rubber apron, splattered crimson, around his rotund belly. Telltale lines of irritation creased his sweaty face. Recognizing the priest, the mortician Abruzzi took license to express himself and beckon them both inside.

"Ah, it's you, *Padre*. I can do nothing! Nothing!" he pushed his bifocals into place over the bridge of his nose.

"Abruzzi, this is Salvatore. Friend of the family."

The men nodded to each other. A protest lay on Tori's lips, unspoken. Death appalled him. His line of vision, partially obstructed by the priest's body, enabled him to see only a portion of the nude body lying on the marble slab, next to the bloodstained sewer drain. Quickly Tori turned his attention out the window, unsure of which sight was worse; the lifeless, skeletal structures abutting the buildings, or the lifeless cadaver on the slab. He heard an exchange of words between mortician and priest.

"You see? The heart's completely excised. See the gaping hole? The worst cadaver I've ever seen. Who'd do such an infamous job in these civilized days, eh, *padre*? Is there no more morality in our world?"

The priest, tight-lipped and grim in the presence of such atrocity, was speechless and visibly shocked. A swarm of black flies, attracted by death's stench, zeroed in through open windows and buzzed peskily about Tori's ears. Annoyed, he brushed them aside, dabbed at the air, and turned to avoid them. In that instance the priest moved aside, affording Tori a better view of the cadaver. He caught sight of the pale, waxen corpse, covered with a mass of swollen, discolored welts and purplish bruises. The body, barely recognizeable, did allow Tori to see instantly the mortician's dilemma. A rusty pipe two inches in diameter protruded from between the legs of the cadaver, from the vagina. Sickened at the sight, Tori turned away. God Almighty! What an obscenity! Who in his right mind would do such a brutal, inhuman thing? Who, indeed?

"That's how they found her, my son. Impaled upon this pipe, stuck into the ground, outside her parents' house like a slaughtered baby lamb skewered through for roasting. Fiendish devils! Did you know Apolladora well?"

Tori's agonized eyes snapped open. Everything converged into a wild moment of disbelief. "Apolladora?" He

219

could barely mouth the name. *"Apolladora?"* Horror turned him into a frozen statue of ice.

He forced himself to gaze upon the fragile, mutilated remains. Steadying himself upon the priest's arm, he uttered a low gasp, a savage moan at the incomprehensible violence done to the remains on the marble slab. His eyes lingered on every inch of the body and came to rest upon the silver crucifix at her neck, as if this symbol could finally make it all real for him, make him believe this to be Apolladora. *Apolladora! Oh My God!* A thousand images of their intimacy flashed before his eyes. It was incredible, this. Too grotesque, and unreal, too horrendous to be believed.

He moved in slow motion towards her. He felt as if his stomach had been ripped open and his guts lay sprawled upon the floor. Pressures in his head and chest wanted to explode with his feelings. Gently, he reached in and pushed aside tendrils of blood-clotted hair off her swollen and distorted face, unaware that the priest and mortician watched all this with mounting curiosity. Tori wanted to gather her in his arms, kiss her, and blow the breath of life into her lifeless body. Her last words echoed through his mind: *"Caro mio, if we never saw each other again, I'd die content—"*

"Who did this to her?" he asked the priest later at the rectory.

"You think I know? Only Satan keeps books on these malevolent acts. Did you know her long?"

Tori couldn't reply. His throat had thickened and felt parched, and he felt the violence of the past days rush at him like a cancer. He listened to the cleric as the man rambled.

"She was to have been married soon. She had sent her parents a tidy sum of money. There was a letter from her. But, come, we'll go to the house of her parents."

"No. Not now." Tori's voice trembled. He couldn't pull himself together. "You mentioned a letter. What sort of a letter?"

Father Voltera studied the young man, whom he'd have cause to remember in the not too distant future. There was something about him. . . . "I have the letter here. The family is illiterate. Wait here," said the priest. He disappeared inside his house and returned in moments with the letter and handed it to the grief-stricken Tori.

The letter was simple and written in a childish scrawl. It explained that she was to meet her future husband in Palermo, where they'd be married. It told Salvatore she hadn't willingly betrayed him. How then did the *carabinieri* learn of the moneybelt? Don Pippinu knew they had spent time together. Had Tori been followed to the apartment of Apolladora? Had they tortured her to reveal the hiding place of the money? Had she been forced to betray him? The answers to his questions lay dead on the marble slab in Abruzzi's mortuary. He reread the letter, bit the back of his hand, and fought off the impulse to scream.

There came upon him the relentless urge to kill; to strike back at those murderers. How much longer could he control this unfamiliar voice of violence and destruction which threatened to rise out of him? *God help me!* He sagged forward and stared at the letter in his left hand. His right hand fell limply between his legs in an atttiude of utter futility, all the strength, courage and manliness, drained from him. Tears fell from his eyes.

"Do you wish to make a confession?" asked the priest.

At the very heart of Tori, a voice warned. *"Trust no one, not even a priest.* "I'll confess to my confessor in my village, *Padre.* With your permission, I'll be on my way," he said with stiff politeness. *Sainted God of the Universe! God of all that's merciful and just!* Apolladora didn't deserve such a fate! No one had to tell him at whose hands the atrocity had been effected. Tori felt like bursting.

Father Voltera studied the man as he lit his pipe. Surely it wasn't all grief he thought. *He's too somber. His face and angry eyes fill with too much menace.* He puffed on the pipe and extinguished the match.

"If I didn't offer a few words of solace I'd be remiss in my duties," he began. This isn't my affair. True, you haven't solicited expostulation. Yet, I feel compelled, at the risk of being called a meddling hypocrite, to tell you that vengeance belongs to God."

I've no idea why Apolladora was subjected to these atrocities, and I don't burn with a desire to know. My son, close the book on this shocking act, turn away from it and forget it," he held up a restraining hand. "What I'm trying to say is that was no ordinary death. This form of torture, reserved for prostitutes and other women who through their sexuality earn a living by collaborating with an enemy, is a typical Mafia atrocity dating back to the days of the Sicilian Vespers. The bloodiest massacre in all Sicilian history. Sicilians, summoned at the first stroke of—"

"—a vesper bell," interrupted Tori. "Arose en masse to massacre all the French on the island, dethroned Charles I of Anjou, that tyrannical king who overburdened the citizens with unjust taxation and oppressed them, beyond all endurance. The underground's battle cry was *"Morte a Francia, Italia Anela: M.A.F.I.A.* Mafia! And so it was born!"

Unable to hide his astonishment, Voltera said, "What a strange young lad you are. My bones shudder at the savagery of your soul. You seem so intelligent, different than most young peasants—" He sighed. "I see it's futile to talk. You've not heard a word I've spoken."

Stimulated by Salvatore's silence, the priest flung off his cassock, removed his cleric's collar, rolled up his sleeves, and trudged back to his garden and, with his shovel, picked up where he had left off earlier. He resembled a wind-up toy gone haywire as he dug, turned over earth, and repeated the process with short, jerky, uncoordinated movements.

"Would the family object if I kept the letter?" Tori asked him.

"Take it! Keep it! If it helps your pain—it's yours!" snapped the irrate priest. He didn't pause in his work, because he saw death reflected in Tori's eyes.

"Perhaps, *padre*," said Tori as he moved towards the gate. "If I might suggest—"

"Yes?" growled the laboring cleric.

"—if you poured love into the earth instead of working out your hostilities, the land might prove more prolific."

Voltera straightened up, placed a hand in the small of his back and grimacing peered at Tori. "That's a strange suggestion coming from you. All I see in your heart is burning hatred, violence and pure vengeance," he retorted.

Salvatore shrugged. "Until a few days ago, there was only love in my heart. What you claim to see in me is of recent birth, caused by all this inhumanity I see around me. Something inside me rebels at all this. Stirs me with alien forces. . . ."

The priest set aside his shovel, wiped his brow and spoke. "We're all born with base feelings of hatred, an urge to do violence—even murder. Only through the power of love which God pours through our hearts can those demons of evil remain asleep in our subconscious. Remove that love and demons will spring forth, unchecked in their malevolency, to conquer and be conquered. . . ."

Tori turned back to the priest. He took a cigarette from his pocket and, holding a match box in his left hand, struck a light with his right and brought it to the tip of his smoke. After a few puffs he exhaled thoughtfully.

One day, Tori would recall this conversation with this *padre*, who was soon to become a vital part of the Palermo Grand Council; but, not as much as this priest, who would rise to be Archbishop, would recall with clarity every moment spent with this phenomenon that the world would come to know as Salvatore.

Tori groped for the words, the proper expression to put his thoughts across.

"If that's the case, I haven't the strength to keep these feelings buried. God's love has gradually thinned, paled and diminished by these foul conditions. Where was God's love when he permitted Apolladora to be brutalized? And don't insult me by trying to tell me she was punished for the way she earned money to feed seven hungry mouths!"

"Look, *Padre* . . . Look around you, here in your garden? Is it God's love that strips it of nourishment and renders it barren? Is God responsible for a government which refuses to bring water inland to the people? Oh, *Padre*, we are indeed a forsaken people!"

The sweaty priest studied him in a somewhat comatose state. Too much had happened this day. Too much. "Young man," he began. "If I were your father, of the same flesh and blood, I couldn't offer you more solace in your grief than what you are prepared to accept, more suggestions than your mind is willing to embrace. Every man is the seeker of his own destiny. Don't lose sight of God's love, or the sleeping demons within you shall rise to consume you as they have every other man in history who has ignored God."

Tori turned from him, somberly, and mounted his horse.

On this day, this unforgettable day carved out of the life of Apolladora, Alessandro Salvatore left in San Guiseppe Jato the soul and spirit of his adolescence to be buried with her, the *inamorata* of his destiny.

Facing the worst predicament of his life, Tori detoured to the Temple of Cats, his refuge in a storm. Seated astride his horse, he stared out at the stunning panorama, his brain churning with thoughts of the day's events—of Apolladora, of Don Pippinu, of the despicable events leading to this day.

That Apolladora's death would be avenged was a fore-gone conclusion. The liquidation of the Mt. Erice Mafia Don was inevitable—only the time and place of the *Mafioso*'s demise hadn't been firmly fixed in Tori's mind. There'd come a time for him to set the ball in motion, and when he did, he'd seek the cooperation of one special person, his Godfather, Don Mattèo Barbarossa.

Below him the lights went out on Montegatta, Montelepre, Borgetto and Alcalmo. He filled with an unendurable melancholy. He strained to hear the familiar sounds of the ancient trumpets announcing the presence of the *Siculi*. Hearing nothing only multiplied his sadness. He thought: *here in the temple among the caves and high cliffs and brooding mountains of timelessness, I must find and come to terms with my destiny.*

Giacomo had upbraided him like an errant child in the tone of a scolding father when he had discovered Tori's wounds reopened, pus-filled and bleeding with infection. Despite his patient's uncooperative nature and marked depression, the faithful old man's diligent care, the laborious cleansing of the wounds and the application of sulfa revived the eagle. In the coming weeks, Tori came to miss his mother and Athena more than he could bear. When he could no longer endure the melancholy, he sent a messenger to his mother with a note. Upon the lad's return, he anxiously asked if his mother had sent word. The boy shook his head. Never had Tori felt so despondent until he considered, she might have prudently exercised caution. Yes. That was it. His mother was no fool. He'd wait.

During his convalescence Tori grew keenly observant; his eyes and ears went everywhere, and his keen interest in the character and idiosyncrasies of these men forced together into similar circumstances intrigued him. He missed none of the goings-on in the camp.

Sharpened by the recent fever, his mind brought all these men into clearer focus. All of them—bandits, brigands, murderers, thieves, petty criminals alike—wore haunted expressions, all despondent at their lot in life, bitter towards an uncaring, unfeeling government which had turned them into hunted criminals. The inescapability of their common predicament and its effects upon those dear to them weighed heavily on their conscience, just as it did on Tori.

Dimly he began to see these men as a contingent force of power that might conceivably cause a decentralization of the present political system—such as it was—and through them, the liberation of his people.

The metamorphosis in him came gradually, not overnight. Embryonic stirrings of the sleeping Hercules he had felt in Mt. Erice continued to disrupt his tranquility. The more he considered the predicament of the men confined to the grottos, the more feasible became his plan. Was it possible that together they could minimize inequities, even stabilize the economy in some indirect way, until such time as reparations could be made to his people for all that had been taken from them? It stood to reason that a more sympathetic government would come to power. The way Tori viewed the political turmoil and unrest in his nation, everything was up for grabs. Only dimly in his mind did an idea begin to form—a powerful idea, through which he could equalize or reduce the problems that beset his people.

In coming days, Tori grew more critical and discerning. He studied the men, mentally selecting those who, he felt, would work into his plans. For a time he stared at those men on the upper ridges who remained shadows to him, and he wondered: Were the men in the Grotto Persephone a different breed of men than those in the lower grottos? What Giacomo had told him about those escaped prisoners intrigued him. As soon as he felt up to it, he intended to amble up there and look around.

Of late, burning thoughts of his cousin Vincenzo de Montana nagged at him. How many times he'd wondered, trying to imagine where that rascal could be.

"Vincenzo! Vincenzo," he'd cry out into the night. "Tell me where you are—that you're safe. . . ."

CHAPTER 17

Little did Tori know that his cousin, Vincenzo de Montana, was physically less than ten minutes away from him in the upper reaches of Grotto Persephone. Tall, slender, badly emaciated, his features pale with prison pallor, Vincenzo bore little resemblence to the army conscript who, in 1941, had left Montegatta as a handsome, proud and gallant cock o' the walk whose bulging biceps, staunch vigor and endless vitality had resembled that of a Roman centurion. His large, dark eyes, sunken in their deeply shadowed hollows, retained few traces of their former laugh-lines. Like that of other *Terra Diavolo* inmates, his dark curly hair had been shorn close to retard body lice. Look close, and you'd detect a peculiar hardness in him, the bold, cynical shrewdness of a man who'd seen too much and experienced untold horror.

Prison, for Vincenzo, had been an endless round of nightmares. Beaten half to death for his repeated attacks on the sadistic prison guards and starved when he had aired grievances on behalf of the other prisoners, he'd emerged from *Terra Diavolo* during an Allied bombing raid and miraculously escaped with other inmates possessed of a morose phobia, a fear of enclosed places and defiance to authority. He vowed repeatedly that he'd never be caught alive, if it meant he had to be returned to such a place—even if it meant his life and the lives of those who dared to obstruct him.

It was from this that Vincenzo had developed a form of paranoia which had triggered off a curious behavior in him. In addition to a tubercular lung, contracted in prison, it was his mental attitude that perplexed his friends now. He hallucinated at times, and displayed a perverse hostility towards those very men who he considered to be his obstructors, considering them his mortal enemies. Yet his friends understood. They held him in high esteem, and viewed this strange behavior as something which would pass as soon as he was back in his home.

And why wouldn't they revere Vincenzo? He was a hero! True—a real hero. If it hadn't been for his clear thinking, his wits, and the latent forces of which heroes are made, none of them, including Vincenzo, would have been alive or in Sicily, today.

God! Good God! How anxious he was to see his home. He knew nothing of the tragic catastrophies that had plagued his family. Standing at the edge of the Grotto, staring down at the lights in his village, he felt his heart and thoughts center around a deep longing to be with his dear ones. Deeply ingrained in his mind was a stark fear of leaving the bandits' sanctuary. In his condition, in these perilous times, it was unthinkable. If he were caught—well, he wouldn't think about this.

To contemplate the future at this time was difficult for Vincenzo. Uncertain as he was of the present and unable as he was to handle the past, his ambivalence disconcerted him. Yet, on this evening, early in October, if Vincenzo could have gazed into a crystal ball to see what destiny, working hand in hand with his cousin Tori, had in store for him, that together they'd make their mark in the nation's history, he might have done much to expedite such a fate.

Wrapped warmly in a sheepskin jacket, collar pulled

226

high around his neck, Vincenzo stomped the ground with his thick mountain boots and shoved his trembling hands into fur-lined pockets to ward off the oncoming chills produced by his erratic body temperature. One moment he'd sweat bullets; the next moment, those beads of sweat would turn into icicles.

He moved back towards the mouth of the grotto, now, and sat down on a boulder. Behind him, straggled about the reflecting fires, hundreds of men, desperate and haunted, made up a weird spectacle which could have been a scene designed by Federico Garcia Lorca. Closest to the fires sat the *Terra Diavolo* escapees, who never seemed to get enough warmth.

Two years had changed him drastically. Two years had changed Tori, too, so that when he walked among the men in the upper grotto, no one recognized him, not even Vincenzo. As was the custom, each man kept to himself, unless he was fortunate enough to have formed a coterie of friends or had the distinction of belonging to the *Terra Diavolo* fraternity. And on this night Tori was perhaps ten feet away from his cousin, jotting down names in his foolscap notebook as he'd taken to doing of late. Giacomo was at his side, as usual. He'd become Tori's mascot, a fountain of information and knowledge, he seemed to know nearly all the men in the camp, and if he didn't, give him a few hours and he'd return to Tori, fully oriented on the others in question. At times he possessed startling revelations.

Tori's tablet contained the names of several men whom he'd observed lately, noting a few of their characteristics and habits, he'd wanted to learn more about them. He'd remain quietly in the background, and, from time to time, he'd ask Giacomo about this one or that. On this night he'd paused slightly and, for the first time, took a good look at the scrawny-faced, skeletal man who sat at the mouth of the upper grotto, dressed in such heavy garments.

How could he know this was Vincenzo, when the man didn't bear the slightest traces of resemblance to the cousin he remembered and missed so much? When he nudged Giacomo to ask him who he was, the old man shrugged in vexation.

"Don't bother with him. He's crazy—that one. *Managghia*, I was told he was their chief in prison." He shuddered and moved forward along with Tori, dismissing the strange haunted fellow from mind—as did Tori.

Seated on a boulder, with his knees drawn up for a time, Tori leaned back to resume his observations.

Arturo Scoletti moved towards the grotto entrance in an apelike fashion, carrying a cup of steaming coffee to Vincenzo. He was accompanied by Santino Siragusa, who leaned over and asked Vincenzo solicitously, "Feeling better?" He accepted a light from a burning stick in the hairy, apelike hand of Arturo Scoletti, then stood for a time watching him wrap his brother Miguel in a blanket.

Suddenly for no apparent reason Vincenzo jumped to his feet and accosted Santino. "Goddamnit! Leave me alone! Stop busting my balls, *padre!*" he shouted in what seemed an irrational moment of confusion.

All eyes including Tori's turned in his direction. Others jumped to their feet, gawking, straining to get a better view of the activity. They saw Vincenzo fall to a crouch position, like a cornered animal, and back away from Santino. His dark, glazed eyes, shining unnaturally in the reflected firelight, were fixed on the former cleric as if he were some underworld demon. On a signal from Santino, Arturo moved in swiftly, pinning Vincenzo's body against the grotto wall, until Siragusa moved in from behind with a thick blanket to wrap around their friend.

Observing all this, Tori marvelled at their loyalty. He glanced at the others. They were tough and cynical and trained to mind their own business, yet they shook their heads regretfully. He listened to the comments among them. Apparently they'd seen this strange behavior before, wondered at it, and refrained from commenting on the patience demonstrated by this man's friends.

Reluctantly he agreed with Giacomo's observation—the màn, whoever he was, did seem crazy out of his mind. As Tori listened, it seemed that the crazy man had subjected his friends to vile and contemptible language and constantly shouted obscenities at them. Tori learned even more. Ever since these prison escapees had arrived in the *macchia,* looking like haunted skeletons—and there were hundreds of them—they'd kept to themselves. Little was known about them except that they'd brought a formidable cache of weapons with them and guarded them zealously. When the "crazy bastard" had moments of lucidity, he seemed to be in command. Imagine, taking orders from a crazy loon! Oddly enough, although many of these men weren't escapees from the prison, they had somehow gravitated towards each other as if an affinity of a predestined nature bound them together.

They had begun to converse now, wondering why the

man Santino Siragusa, a former *priest*, had given up the cloth and found himself in the company of brigands.

"Ask the *padre*, himself," spoke up Arturo, a pint-sized titan who once had broke chains with his biceps in a carnival he and his brother had owned before the war. "It's best you get the word straight from the horse's mouth."

"Are you crazy?" asked Bastiano Terranova, a handsome young man. "It's not our business. Besides such talk can be dangerous with the Reds and anticlerics around. Are you sure he isn't a communist?" he asked dubiously.

"Not our business!" Arturo snorted contemptuously. A shock of black hair, straight and wiry, grew low over his forehead, giving him an apelike appearance. His nose, like a bird's beak, was sharp and hooked, and a slight protrusion to his jaw line accented his primate appearance. "Listen, you porcupine, when this business of war ends, things had better be different for us or there *will* be revolution. I don't know about communists, and I don't care. Up north, where men aren't afraid to speak out, there's talk of labor unions. Labor unions and strikes. Up there the men are getting smart."

"Labor unions? What hell is that? Labor unions and strikes?" Fidelio Genovese, a dark, Moorish-skinned Sicilian with compelling black eyes that intimidated most men, was perplexed. Perhaps the most politically oriented of the lot, he knew the score. In this young man, as with most of the men gathered here, was the desperation of the illiterate who felt deeply the urge to speak out, but hadn't mastered the articulation of these feelings. It was enough to drive a man crazy!

With the superior aloofness of one possessed with great knowledge, Vincenzo, suddenly in perfect control of his faculties, spoke up. "Unions are organizations where the men think and act as one body. Fifty men, even a hundred, agree on one thing and fight for their rights in an organized way."

"Fifty men agree on one thing?" Fidelio Genovese's face knitted into a scowl. "*Mah*—how the hell is that possible? I've heard of everything, now!"

Tori leaned forward eager to listen to this strange young man, who now seemed as normal as the others.

"It works like this," began Vincenzo. "The landlords and peasants sit down and discuss their problems. Once the workers agree on certain terms, they tell the landlord straight out what they want." Crazy or not his words commanded their full attention.

"It's that easy?" asked Dominic Lamantia, another young, very handsome lad with startling green eyes.

"Let me put it this way," responded Vincenzo, lighting a cigarette. "If the landlord disagrees with what they want, he offers alternatives. Somehow it all works. One man alone can't instigate changes, but many men, united together, become a powerful force."

"I don't know what the hell you're talking about," insisted Fidelio Genovese, impatient with all this talk. He pulled out his holstered gun. "See this gun?" He patted it suggestively. "This is my labor union. With this little piece I can make everyone agree with me. So, who needs these goddamn labor unions?"

Turridu Nuliano, another handsome young man, outrageously ostentatious in manner of dress as well as behavior, twirled his six-shooter in the air before him. "That's the way it is, here. Power is the man with a gun. *K'pow! k'pow!*"

Terranova addressed himself to Vincenzo. "Your words stir my stomach to disquiet, and I find them too fanciful to give them importance. You're sure these things are possible?"

Vincenzo nodded. Arturo bobbed his head up and down.

"By the unholy balls of Satan! What wonders there must be on other lands. Labor unions, eh?" Terranova was impressed.

"If the peasants and landlords fail to agree, the peasants don't work—not until the landlord and they come to terms," said Vincenzo growing more articulate.

"Now I know you're crazy!" Fidelio Genovese shouted in rebuttal. "You know what would happen here? Landlords would import workers from other estates, then where would we be? We'd starve. Are you so crazy not to see such perils?" He wagged a finger at Vincenzo in reprimand. Then as his eyes narrowed suspiciously, he asked, "Listen, you aren't a political agitator—a communist, are you?"

Ignoring Genovese, Vincenzo turned to the others. "If all the workers on the island agree not to trespass on any lands under protest, it's possible. It works elsewhere."

Genovese holstered his gun and shrugged when he saw the expressions on the faces of his companions seated around the campfire. "*Allora, amico,* Genovese is no fool. He'll listen to such ideas if they are possible. Labor unions, eh? It makes sense, saying that one hundred voices, saying the same thing, make a bigger noise than

230

one voice. But by the belly of a sterile whale, tell me how so many can agree on one thing? Here each man is for himself. *Carabinieri* come to arrest a man. You think his neighbors help? *Mah—quando?* Afraid their own families will suffer or go hungry or that they'll be punished in other ways, they keep to themselves. Their neighbor's business isn't their affair. So tell me how so many long-eared men can agree on one thing?" The contest was between him and Vincenzo.

"They take a vote and the majority wins."

"What if my voice isn't one of the majority?"

"Your voice will be caught up in the majority."

"*Buttana u shekko!* We're back to guns again. See,—it wouldn't work!"

."Believe me, Genovese, you'd be convinced."

"How—with guns, bombs and artillery?" He scoffed openly.

"No. With words and common sense."

"What of my common sense? Why should another man's common sense be more prominent than mine? If I think the majority is wrong, why should I go along with them? You see, it wouldn't work." He patted his holstered gun affectionately. "I'll make my unions with my gun. My strike is my gun. This way we'll all be content."

This time the men's laughter was complicated by thoughtful speculation. Vincenzo had given them food for thought. What to do with this food was another matter *Demonio! Why be cursed with such brainwork? Such crazy ideas are dangerous*, the men told themselves Uneasy in the midst of revolutionary concepts, they glanced uneasily about the fires. Who knew what enemies lurked around them?

Tori glanced about, noting the reaction of the men and the kind of thinking they were used to. Some of the men got up and moved about, getting coffee or talking in groups. Giacomo indicated he wanted to return to their campsite. He was bored with such rhetoric. "Only action counts," he grunted. "You'll see, *aquilo bravo.*"

A few minutes later, Tori, shivering in the wind, considered he'd better leave. His attention was caught by the "crazy young man" who'd been struck with a coughing seizure. He began to bark and rasp and hawk convulsively and, rising to his feet, he swept past Tori, heading for the ledge on the rocks. For a split second their eyes met without a glimmer of recognition.

Tori decided to return to the comfort of his own fires, giving no importance to the coughing young man, who

231

sounded as if his insides would burst. Just as he began to descend the rocky incline, Tori stopped, uncertain of what it was that had deterred him. Turning to glance over his shoulder in the darkness at the prison escapee, Vincenzo's plaintive cry reached him.

"Tori! Tori! Where are you? Don't you know I'm up here in the mountains? Can't you hear me calling you?"

Tori's heart stopped. Had he heard correctly—or was the whispering wind deceiving him like the *Siculi* often did? *Dio Buono!* Could this shadow of a man be Vincenzo? He retraced his steps, slowly, inching towards him, careful so as not to startle him. When he was within two feet of him, he called to him softly. "Vincenzo—"

His cousin turned around, a fierce scowl on his face, ready to pounce, his hand on his knife worn in a sheath at his waist. His eyes had turned into those of an animal's, his body into a low crouch.

"It's me—Tori. I heard you calling. By the sainted balls of Christ, I heard you calling me."

Vincenzo searched the other's face, in disbelief and wonderment. "It's you, Tori? *Pe d'avero*—it's really you?"

"It's me. It's me," shouted Tori excitedly as the two cousins embraced. They slapped each other on the back and stared in wonderment at each other. In moments Vincenzo seemed a new man. They jabbed at each other playfully with broad swipes and rough caresses. Incredulity and disbelief were followed by gestures of affection. Then they sat back and talked for a while, until Vincenzo dragged Tori back towards the grotto to introduce him to his friends.

Inside, the men were discussing present conditions in Sicily. Most of the men wore dark trousers and shirts, with leather and sheepskin jackets. All wore one or two guns at their hips, with a knife or two in sight. They looked up when Tori and Vincenzo entered, aware of the change in the "crazy" man.

Tori let his cousin make all the introductions and he sat down to enjoy the comfort of men and their idle talk. It was Marco Genovese, Fidelio's younger brother, who started the ball rolling. Marco contrasted his brother's swarthy looks with his round, cherubic face, smooth as a baby's buttocks. Marco was a man who believed in no order except his own. His blue-eyed expression of innocence belied his true nature. He was a born thief, who laughed a lot and cried convincingly if it suited his purpose. This consummate actor, under whose face there aways lurked some ulterior motive, some scheme, was as shrewd as they came. He didn't believe most of these Terra Diavolo inmates, and thought that since they were all together he'd put the question to them.

"How did you all escape? How did you get through the Italian and German lines? Better still, how did you cross the seas, crawling with Allied battleships and marine patrols? *Managghia,* the whole of the British and American fleet lie warming their bellies in the water surrounding us since the Occupation—"

"Yes," echoed the others, "Tell us how."

Tori's presence had sparked Vincenzo with new life, and his friends were the first to see these changes. He drew himself up and, taking center stage, he began to speak.

"The first week in September, I filled with premonition. I was nervous, edgy, short-tempered, and I must have driven my cellmates crazy. I awoke one night when a vision of my aunt came to me in a dream so real I could feel her presence. *Mizzica!* I can still feel my flesh crawl the way it did that night. No, not the way those lice who made such short order of my body crawled. This was different. I leaned over to wake up the *padre.* Santino didn't want to hear my *baccano.* 'Listen,' he told me, 'in the middle of a good dream you have bust my balls!' But I insisted that I heard strange noises. Again he cursed me. 'You crazy fool,' he told me. 'Each night for a week it's been the same with you. Goddammit! Roll over and go to sleep.' I suppose I should have been mad at him. But who had the strength to challenge him, eh? I closed my eyes and told myself I was dreaming. But, then, suddenly there it was again. This time I didn't have to awaken Santino. One by one, all the men in our complex came alive, asking what had happened.

Then, there came a rumbling, groaning sound like an earthquake. It shook the walls and caused tremors under our feet. *Maronna!* The men screamed. They yelled and cried for assistance. We could see nothing through the barred windows except a patch of black sky. 'Earthquake! Earthquake!' cried the men. It was Santino who fell to the ground, his ear glued to it listening. 'No,' he screamed. Not an earthquake! *Bomba! Bomba!*"

Vincenzo paused and, looking at Tori, said solemnly, "You know what it's like to be in such a place, knowing no one would come to save us?" His voice dropped in volume and he stared hauntingly into the fires. "I can still hear their voices, calling the guards to come and help them. 'For the love of God, don't let us die,' they cried. 'Not like this!'

"Then came the bombs. From the bowels of those flying machines they erupted. *Boom! Boom! Boom!* Flame, like lightning, struck all around us, as the heavens opened up and reined its fury on us.

"*Allora, caro mio,* the earth roared, buckled and trembled, exploding everything in sight. The walls of the prison crumbled in a shower of rocks as devastating as the bombs themselves. They wouldn't stop, those bombs. *Dio Maledetta!* All around were the dead bodies of the men whose time was up.

"So many things to be negotiated in the dark! Dead and dying bodies, the broken rubble, the bombs themselves. We ran. God Almighty, did we run! We scattered like lizards, every which way. Then, through it all I heard Santino, the *padre* here, call to me. He told me to follow him to the arsenal. *Va bene.* I could hardly make him out in the congestion of dust, but I did the best I could. It was the same all over. More bombs. Explosions that shattered our ear drums and confusion! *Managghia,* none of us knew what to do. The men awaiting execution in death's row had been freed too. Liberated, they ran every which way, like ferocious animals, picking up weapons from the dead guards and shooting their way out when obstructed.

"As for us, the Sicilians in our complex managed to dance our way through that tarantella of hell! So many were killed. You know what its like to see a man's leg or arm torn off before your eyes? *Ayeee,*" he sighed.

"One of the men—" he paused and glanced towards a hulk of a man built like a bull tiger, with the muscle-bound look of a Samurai warrior—Ross Rizzuto, nicknamed *Sporcaccione*. "*Allora,*" continued Vincenzo. "He led some men from another building and we all converged on the arsenal. With a Beretta submachine gun I took from a dead guard who had no further use for it, I sprayed the lock with bullet fire. Sporcaccione kicked in the door and the men poured in. I shouted, 'Grab all the weapons you can carry!' *Managghia!* They went wild, strapping on automatic rifles, carbines and submachine guns—all they could carry, including small arms, which they shoved into every inch of their clothing.

"I ordered the men to run swiftly across the courtyard through the openings in the broken walls as they rushed out the door past me.

"While they were running for their lives, clearing the marble quarries some distance from *Terra Diavolò*, another load of bombs fell. We suddenly faced another enemy, more lethal than the bombs. The air rained pellets of marble, slag and sharp stones. Then, having dropped their loads, the bombadeers moved on into the darkest of skies. Behind this came ear-splitting explosions, one after another, until what remained of the arsenal, ammunition and warheads blew up, including what remained of *Terra Diavolo*.

"For a time we all stood on the lower slopes of the Tuscany hillside, weak from hunger, exhaustion and overexposure, to observe the spreading fires. *Demonio*! The stench of burned flesh, with its sickeningly sweet odor, fairly knocked us out. With the light of dawn came the realization that we couldn't stay in open country and risk being spotted by enemy patrols. So, I led them to another location, a spot cradled between the breasts of two hills where we could spot any approach. In prison we'd heard little of the outside world, so we didn't know what to expect.

"To tell the truth," continued Vincenzo, somberly, "I was dismayed by the number of escapees who clung to us, refusing to run off to the many avenues of freedom. I made my thoughts known to the *padre* here, wondering how we'd fare with so many men. There were at least six or seven hundred. *Managghia*! The *padre's* answer was, as usual, 'God will show us the way!' *Allora*, I didn't have the *padre's* faith. . . ."

Vincenzo paused at this point, weak and without energy to continue the story. He urged Santino Siragusa to finish the tale so that his cousin Tori would know all the facts. He rose to his feet and, walking to the water cistern, sprinkled his face with cool water. He returned and sat down next to Tori and lit a cigarette with shaking hands. Then all eyes were riveted on the former Jesuit as he relit his pipe. Pushing his glasses on the bridge of his nose, Santino ran his fingers through his thick, curly dark hair, corkscrewed like little mattress springs, settled himself more comfortably, and picked up the story where Vincenzo left off. In perfect Italian, his gentle voice grew reflective. It rose and fell with dramatic pauses. We knew absolutely nothing of the war's status, not even that the Allies had landed in Sicily, or that on July 25, King Vittorio Emmanuele had ordered Mussolini's resignation and formed a new government with Marshal Badoglio at its head, or that the liquidation of the fascists had followed. We certainly didn't know that the peace negotiations were already underway between Italy and the Allies, or that on September 3 a secret armistice had been signed with Italy."

"What has all this to do with you ex-prisoners?" asked Tori, eager for him to get along with the story.

"Just this," said Santino patiently. "It meant that a furious race had commenced between the Germans and Allies for possession of territories, bases, arms and supplies, communications, and other war facilities under Italian control. Where we suddenly found ourselves—in Northern Italy—the land, unbeknownst to us, was overrun with Nazi patrols. Those bloody Nazis could have been anywhere. Behind every boulder, curve and bend in the road, and in all the villages not burned down by partisan guerillas."

The men sucked in their breaths. They listened to this man with every nerve-fiber in their bodies. Marco Genovese and Bastiano Terranova interrupted at this point, to relieve themselves just outside the grotto, and returned anxiously to their places. These were the kind of stories Sicilians loved and could recount for generations to anyone who'd listen.

"None of us was free from the terror we experienced," continued Santino. "It's not to be believed that we finally arrived here in Sicily after the nightmares were endured. . . . *Allora*, as I was saying, six hundred of us trudged through Tuscany. We wondered at the flooded fields, frowned at the idle valleys, despaired at the fallow lands and stared solemnly at the ruined *fattorias*. We were outraged at the deserted farmhouses. *Misericordia*! Not a morsel of food was to be found any place. Only God and Vincenzo could have seen us through what was to follow.

"Starved, weakened from exposure, we needed something to inspire us—some life—something to assure us all wasn't lost! No life greeted us anywhere; not a bird, a lizard, a dog, a rabbit—not even an insect. We covered ten miles in what seemed to be the stillness of death. Finally, below us, in a fork in the road, we caught sight of a road sign. Vincenzo ordered the men to rest on the slopes of the hill while he and I went below to investigate. The sign read: *Cecina—4km.* I knew then exactly where we were: a few miles from the Ligurian Sea. Elated at the prospect of reaching the water after the stunning effects of the near-desert lands we'd crossed, I attempted to infect Vincenzo with my optimism. By then the lice began attacking my body and to alleviate the aggravation I began scratching myself. Watching me, Vincenzo laughed good-naturedly, 'They got no respect, even for a man of God, eh, *Padre?*'"

The men laughed at this. Santino tapped his pipe alongside him on the boulder and continued, "Wrapped in my discomfort, I trudged on ahead of Vincenzo, still scratching at my body, only to be pulled back by my shirttails. Annoyed, I turned to Vincenzo, ready to challenge him, only to be arrested by the look in his eyes. That man with cat's ears had angled his head sharply, listening to something that hadn't penetrated my ears. All at once he raised his rifle high above his head signaling the men on the hill to halt. His fingers over his lips silenced what protests I might have offered at this point.

"Then Vincenzo loudly shouted, 'Take cover, men. Take cover, *Padre!*' He waved the others off the road and back up into the hills. 'Pass the word, *Padre*. Tell the men to take cover and be ready for anything I might do. And tell them to stay out of sight, goddammit!' I moved swiftly to obey his instructions, scrambling up the nearby slopes, passing the word to anyone and everyone in my path. *Allora*—the men moved! *Managghia*—how they moved. They came to life and hid behind bushes, stone walls, tree stumps and any blade of grass that offered protection. They crouched down on all fours, out of sight. Along the sloping hillside, the newly liberated men lay still as death, with rifles, submachine guns, hand pistols and grenades, clutched in one or both hands, ready for anything. I saw the sweat pour off their faces, necks and underarms. Their dilated pupils reflected the terror in their hearts. Their tongues darted over parched, cracked lips, and it seemed their heartbeats, mine included, pulsed as one giant heartbeat. Sitting and crouching like wooden puppets, hunched over in fatigue until our muscles ached and our legs twitched from being in one position so long, we all prayed that whatever had disturbed Vincenzo would either cease or erupt.

"Those moments for us were an eternity. Then, suddenly, it all happened. We all heard what had penetrated Vincenzo's ears earlier. Approaching us was the sound of motors, straining and shifting gears—muffled at first, then more audible. It was the erratic sputter and cough of motorcycles in the distance. Then, there they were, pouring into the basin below us.

"From around the bend in the worm-like road came the largest detachment of Nazis we'd ever seen—even in the height of battle. More than five hundred—many more! They came in open touring cars, containing high-ranking Nazi officers, followed by countless trucks, supply wagons and other vehicles in a full troop train. So many—who took the time to count? Motorcycles zoomed up ahead and

237

at either side of the train and several brought up the rear.

"Vincenzo, meanwhile, never took his eyes off this stunning display of military strength. His mind worked swiftly, with rare perception and know-how. As they stretched out before him, filling the flatlands, Vincenzo became aware that we were in a perfect ambush position to annihilate the Nazi convoy. With no time to speculate, he quickly shouted orders to me: 'Tell them to get the grenades ready, *Padre*. When I move—they move! They are to hurl the grenades into the convoy, without hesitation.' Naturally, I bridled at the orders. 'You're crazy! We'll all be wiped out to the last man!' I shouted. Whereupon Vincenzo countered, 'Impossible! They're outnumbered. Move your ass, *Padre*, or we will be slaughtered.'

"*Allora*. I pulled in my neck and snaked along the sloped repeating my orders to the Scoletti brothers, who were now securely entrenched. 'Watch for Vincenzo's signal and do what he does,' I told them.

" 'That crazy bastard has lost all senses,' Arturo shouted, but he moved. He and the rest of the men—they moved their asses right on down the line. On and on they went until the hillside came alive, charged with the electricity of their fear and excitement. Below us the Nazis began to gear down, pacing the rest of the convoy until, suddenly, there it was, both ends of the convoy spread out across the valley. . . . The unsuspecting Nazis never knew what struck them. Nearly three hundred grenades hurled into their midst exploding them straight to hell. Trucks, cycles, autos and troops shot up into the sky taking half the countryside with them. Gasoline exploded and caught fire. It was an incredible sight, a scene so shattering to us that none of us will forget it until our dying day."

Santino wet his lips with a tankard of wine and continued. "When the dust settled we saw that what had been a flatland was now filled with enormous craters, and the road had vanished completely. Landslides occurred all around us, throwing our men off balance, some of them sliding down the hill, luckily unhurt. A few Nazis who had miraculously escaped the holocaust were instantly felled by blasts of machine gun fire from our men. The ambush was a total success—not one Nazi was alive to boast of his luck. Never have we seen such carnage. The land was littered with bloody, screaming, kicking, torn and dying bodies. For a moment we all stood in dumb stupefaction as silence descended upon us. For a second only—then there was bedlam. Desperate, hungry men, all who had been in prison for so long, rushed forward like a swarm of ravenous locusts to salvage what we could out of the rubble. Anything for survival! It was a ghastly sight. Decapitated bodies, whose severed heads lay close by attached by bleeding tendons and bearing expressions of demonical horror, arched brows, popped eyeballs and leering grins, with wet teeth glistening in the sunlight—these hardly intimidated the scavengers. Survival was all that counted and the men looked everywhere for food—rations—anything to fill their swollen and empty bellies. Unable to stomach their reactions I expressed my feelings to Vincenzo. 'Wild savages! Have they no respect for the dead? What an atrocity!'

"For a time Vincenzo's black, burning eyes jumped from one point to another as the predatory scene unfolded, and with an astonishing and mystical power of recuperation he replied vigorously, 'Better them than us!' "

The men came to life after listening to Santino's story. They reacted vigorously to Vincenzo's assessment of that scene, as Santino wrapped up the final portion of the story.

"Shortly after that, Vincenzo split the men into four groups with instructions to meet at the most southern point on the beach at Piombo. By the grace of God we all met again and crossed to the Island of Elba where, with the aid of some friends, we gained passage on fishing boats. In October, at intervals of a week, less than four hundred of us landed along the northern and western shores of Sicily, disguised as fishermen. And here we all are," said Santino wistfully, "here in these honeycombed mountains we met, and are unable to conceal our disappointment over the wretched conditions we find in our beloved Sicily."

Tori turned to observe his cousin Vincenzo, who had come to life, revived by the contents of a wine bottle. "A real hero, eh?"

Vincenzo flushed with a mixture of embarrassment and pleasure at his cousin's assessment.

"What are your plans, now?" asked Fidelio Genovese with a newfound respect shining in his eyes for the "crazy" man. "You don't intend to stay in these mountains until the war ends?"

Vincenzo didn't answer. He felt a self-consciousness permeate him, a sickening paranoia, a need to hide from them.

Santino came to his rescue. "He'll let you know. He must get well, first. In his condition—" he paused. He didn't have to explain. They all knew and understood. Hadn't they seen his strange behavior?

"It's not the way it was three years ago, *padre*," said Dominic Lamantia.

Santino nodded. He'd seen these conditions and detested them.

"And the Americans—what of them?" asked Arturo, whittling on a piece of wood. "Is there no help from them?"

"What can they do? Besides, what the hell do they want with us? All they want is to waltz on to Berlin, to the tempo of a fox trot, and finish with Hitler."

Tori listened as they talked—and noticed there was a better *camaraderie*, now, than there'd been earlier. As the natives described the shabby conditions in Sicily, a few of the *Terra Diavolo* escapees, whose homes were in various other parts of Sicily, grew disconsolate, and when Dominic Lamantia told them that Sicily had become a free-for-all, a lawless and chaotic land where every man was for himself and where the women of the villages had taken to the streets, whoring to keep their families alive—whoring for the benefit of foreigners—they grew restless and angry. Jumping to their feet to express their Sicilian *maschiezzo*, they huddled in small groups talking among themselves.

The next morning, several approached Santino Siragusa, expressing their desires to leave for their villages. The shocking and distressing news of conditions in their homeland tore at their emotions. They were incensed and, physically, nervous wrecks. It was then that Tori suggested that an expert forger whom someone had mentioned might prepare identity cards for these troubled men, to facilitate easy travel to their villages. The idea so intrigued them that they looked to Tori, questioning him about several matters and finding his answers satisfactory, and left their names and addresses with him in the event they were ever needed—for anything.

Tori, in a manner that seemed easy and natural, turned the names over to Santino, and, although no words were spoken, it was as if he relegated to the former Jesuit the duties that were later to be given him officially.

For the next few days Vincenzo and Tori bridged the gap between them. Tori had waited to find the right time to break the news to Vincenzo. How did you tell a man that his entire family had been murdered by men whose duty it was to uphold the law and enforce it? It didn't come easy to Tori, but in accepting the responsibility he

240

was only grateful that he was there for Vincenzo to lean on in his heartbroken moments of anguish.

Fiery tears escaped Vincenzo, and cries of savage vengeance burst from his swollen and engorged lips. The loathing and violence he felt was like the unleashing of a tempestuous storm. Only after Tori confided that he'd personally taken the lives of the brutes responsible, did Vincenzo calm himself. Consoled by his friends, he remained in a debilitated state. They left him alone for a while, to mourn in silence. If the bond between Tori and Vincenzo had been strong once, it was now like steel.

There remained little emotion to be wrung from both Vincenzo and Tori. Thoughts of the injustices in Sicily infuriated them both to borderline madness; yet Tori took it entirely different than Vincenzo. The difference between them was to become quite apparent in the near future.

CHAPTER 18

"Will you forgive me for bringing disgrace upon our house?" Tori asked his mother after their reunion was over.

She stroked Tori's face lovingly. If she harbored dismay at her son's predicament, she covered her feelings and became solicitous of his wounds, his pale and wan appearance. "You did what had to be done. What matters is, you're alive! We prayed for you—Athena and I were crazy out of our heads after we learned what happened. To think you were forced into a gunfight over food!"

You don't know the extent of the charges against me?" he asked. "Aren't you concerned? They're true, you know."

"What charges?"

"What charges?" Tori stared at her. "What precisely did the *carabinieri* tell you?"

Up ahead of them, Giacomo trundled the mule-drawn cart she'd ridden up the mountain to the Grotto Persephone as she and her son walked the short distance to the campsite. Antigone stopped in her tracks. "That you were stopped for transporting food over provincial borders. You were obstructed by Nino Marino, and in a skirm-

241

ish, you killed him. In my heart I know you bore him no malice. It was an accident, no?"

"What about the money? Didn't they mention the money?" Veins at his temples pulsed like writhing eels. "The charges of grand larceny?"

She was flabbergasted. "What are you saying? What money?"

Very quietly Tori led her to a felled tree and sat her down some distance from the others. He wasn't ready to share her with his cousin, not just yet. He lit up a cigarette and told her the whole story from beginning to end, including the deaths of Gucci and Molino. He especially told her about Apollodora, omitting nothing, not even the fate meted her. Antignone listened in stupefaction. If she felt one way or another about her son's adverse circumstances, she gave no sign. Reaching over, Tori took both her work-worn hands into his forcing her eyes to gaze into his.

"Mamma, I've sworn vengeance on him. I vowed to kill Don Pippinu."

"No!" she retorted, hastily withdrawing her hands from his. "You've not been raised in the ways of *vendetta*. If he's brought no further charges against you, his feelings may have been softened."

He was appalled. "He cheated us out of money. Because of him, my world has collapsed—yours too. He murdered an innocent person—and you say, 'let it be!'"

Antigone studied her son inscrutably. "You've punished yourself too much," she observed. After a moment's silence she added tersely, "*Mafiosi* don't go to the authorities with their grievances."

"This one did," countered Tori hotly. "He reported me to the Allied military police and they to the *carabinieri*. I walked into a planned ambush!"

She shook her head adamantly. "Let it be, Tori. I want no trouble—not for you, not for me, not for anyone. Certainly not from a *Mafioso*."

"It's too late. I've pledged my vow of vengeance," he said with finality. Then, as an after thought, he scoffed with indignation. Hah! *Mafiosi* don't go to the authorities. Where did you hear such goat dung?"

"Don't scoff. It's true. They don't violate the code of silence."

"*Omerta* or no *omerta*, Don Pippinu violated the code."

Antigone shrugged. She couldn't believe her ears. It was legend that the Mafia settled their own matters. "What do you make of this deception? Why would the *carabinieri* refrain from making formal charges against you? It makes no sense."

"No sense, eh? To line their own pockets—what else?"

Antigone gasped. "For this?"

"Now they can shoot me on sight and keep the money they found by eliminating all traces of me." After explaining the hard and bitter facts to his mother, Tori instructed her to claim the letter he'd sent from Mt. Erice containing the money. "Those protected thieves would sell their souls for so much money. By damn, they shan't have it!"

She stared at her son in a confused silence. In a short space of time her son had become a man she didn't recognize. Words of retribution and vengeance pained her, for in her mind the laws of *vendetta* were as alien as her son's present predicament. A twinge of sadness exploded her heart at the ends to which her son had arrived. When he had first confessed to the slaying of those two obscenities, Gucci and Molino, she had exclaimed, "Good! They deserved it." This was the justice of her people—the only kind they'd ever known. Inwardly she'd experienced a tinge of pride that it had been her son who had put an end to those two evil creatures. With this knowledge locked in her heart, she could approach the Lord in her nightly prayers to beg His forgiveness. She'd point out to the Deity that He must take into account that it had been a just killing, before He sat in judgment of Tori.

So caught up in her thoughts was Antigone that she hardly noticed Tori had left her side and returned with a tall stranger with a pale and gaunt countenance. She shuddered inwardly as she glanced about the camp—at the desperadoes who'd become her son's companions.

"Now for a surprise, Mamma," said Tori with Vincenzo at his side.

"I doubt I need any more surprises," she said tersely.

"Don't you know me anymore, *Zia?* I'm Vincenzo," he told her with a sheepish grin on his face.

After a hailstorm of emotional greetings subsided, Antigone's role became a motherly one as she plied them with the banquet of food she brought with her in the cart. From time to time Antigone's hands would fly to either side of her face and cupping it she'd shake her head in disbelief. "Look, Tori, look what they did to him—those beasts! How thin you are, Vincenzo. Eat. Eat, my nephew."

"I'm not the bull Tori is," exclaimed Vincenzo, admiring Tori's physique. Tori's upper torso, covered only with a sheepskin vest cut deep in the armholes, revealed two livid scars healing on his shoulder and upper arm. "Is that where the *carabinieri*'s bullets hit you?" he asked his cousin.

"Eat," urged Antigone. "You can talk later." She leaned in closer to them. "First tell me who are those strangers staring at us?" She indicated to Santino Siragusa and the Scoletti brothers, who stood a short distance from them with eager-eyed expressions on their faces waiting to be drawn into their circle.

"*Demonio!*" cursed Vincenzo. "I forgot about them. He signalled to his friends and drew them closer. Vincenzo made the introductions. Antigone nodded at them, barely hearing the names "Well, what do you think, *Zia?*" said Vincenzo, trying to make light of a serious situation. "Imagine, now Tori is a fugitive and, like us, is hiding from the law." It was a bad joke, and he realized it too late.

Antigone glanced sharply at her son. The statement stunned both of them. It was Tori's turn to become aware of this truth. At first he thought, *me, a fugitive?* It was still new to him. Whether or not it agreed with him, one thing was certain: the sooner he got used to this truth, the better off he'd be. In these next moments, Tori told himself, *forget your dreams, caro mio. You're a fugitive with a price on your head—and there's no mistaking it.* Tori retreated into a silence, mulling over this startling revelation, and for a time he sat back and watched the others, solemnly.

Arturo Scoletti kept his eyes on his brother Miquel as he hungrily devoured three plates of food. "*Prego, Signora,* excuse my brother's gluttony," he apologized. "Some men can take the horrors God keeps tightly clenched in his left hand. Others can't. My brother's been very ill." He reached over and slapped his brother's thigh playfully. "You see, Miquel? Didn't I tell you to have faith? Didn't I tell you the *Signora* would cook for us again one day?"

Antigone, as well as her son, raised an inquisitive eyebrow as Arturo, noting their astonishment, hastened to explain. Apparently Antigone had once bargained with them to play their carnival at an orphanage by promising to cook a banquet of food for them.

"You are Arturo and Miquel?" she exclaimed in astonishment. "I would have never known you. *Dio buono,* you are thin as toothpicks. Here," she pushed more food at them. "Eat. Eat all you want."

Then, beginning with Vincenzo's next few words, a strange story began to unravel. He'd expressed his joy at his reunion with her and Tori and added. "I knew we'd see each other again, like this. I knew it. I kept seeing

244

your face in visions, *Zia*," he told her. "Just before the bombing at *Terra Diavolo*, your face came to me in a vision. It was an omen, *Zia*. An omen that we'd be together—don't you see?"

Santino Siragusa's face blanched as he set aside his plate of food. A strange expression crossed his face. "*E a verida*? Is that the truth?" The former priest turned to Antigone. "Will you believe it I, too, saw your face before we encountered the Nazi's. I used to speak to you from the pulpit, *Signora*—Padre Siragusa—do you recall?"

Before she could respond to all this, Arturo chimed in. "—And I, also saw the *Signora*." He turned his ape like head towards her. "Just before the bombing at *Terra Diavolo*, before we crushed the Nazis." His voice dropped to a whisper.

"What can it mean?" she asked, as confounded as the others. Sicilians, predisposed to visions, omens and superstitions, didn't take lightly to them, for in them, they felt, lay their destinies. They must decipher them early in their existence, or life might pass them by and make of them another army of mankind who just didn't count. "It must be destiny, no?" she whispered, half afraid to speak aloud.

It was at this point that Tori came alive. From wherever it came—the power, insight and courage—Tori grasped the moment. His mind shifted into high gear, and when he broke the austere silence, no one, not his mother, or his cousin guessed at the awareness he possessed. They had no idea of the ingenious ability he had to perceive situations and make the sound judgments he'd shortly come to demonstrate. When he opened his mouth to speak, his opening words captured their attention and held it through sheer animal magnetism and a sharp articulation they'd never forget.

"Yes," he began. "It's Destiny's doing. Why else would she have sent you all safely back to me? I listened to your harrowing adventures—all you endured before returning to Sicily—to me." The magic commenced with these outrageously bold words, and he held them all under a spell for over an hour.

"The fate of our people is in our hands. You—you—you . . . and me," he gestured to several men. "It's our responsibility to lift Sicily out of this evil lethargy. Men like us, men of the soil, of the mountains, of the plains, we are the oppressed. We must unite as one and fight for our rights and rid our lands of these black hearted mercenaries. You've returned to your homes only to find them robbing, stealing and arresting our people and if we resist or protest, throwing us into jail. What can we to do to help our starving families? Nothing. Our hands are tied because we never had a voice."

Moved by profound curiosity and drawn by his princely posture and burning words, a small group of eavesdroppers began to gather about him. His voice had reached them. The more he spoke of conditions in their lands and because he spoke the truth, the more magnetic he seemed to them. He was one of them—a peasant! He knew of what he spoke. He didn't resort to florid patriotism; he didn't march them through fields and into battle with raised colors; he didn't hark back to Garibaldi's fame and triumphant conquests. No. He spoke little of history, and spoke instead of man's human rights.

"The time has come for us to break the chains of our desperate past. We must bring new ideas to this, our land. Let our voices be the voice of the future!"

The power of Salvatore's words and the contagious excitement he generated held them in rapt fascination. He strutted before them boldly, with precise animal movements, strong and sure of himself, without arrogance or the conceit that usually afflicted self-serving men.

Before Tori had finished speaking, hundreds of men, lured by the activity at first, had gathered around him, held only by the honesty and straight-forward manner in which he spoke. He had spoken to them, man to man—Sicilian to Sicilian—in a way none other had done before.

"Who is he?" asked many of the men. "What's his name? Is this brave young man running for public office—what? From what village does he come?" They muttered wondering and marvelling at him.

"His name is Salvatore," said Giacomo, proud as a jaybird as he circulated among the crowd, his chest inflated with a stirring excitement. "He is Alessandro Salvatore, *un' aquilo bravo.'* . . ." They turned their attention back on the young "brave eagle" to hear his next words.

"It's true the Allies and their abortive attempts to control prices have succeeded in making criminals of every decent Sicilian. I can understand farmers holding back their grain to take advantage of higher prices. But I ask, why isn't the graft stopped higher up, where it starts? The Allies or lawmakers could certainly consider this. But do they? No! What's worse, the Allies employ *carabinieri* to enforce their laws. Having worked for the *fascisti*, these men have become nothing but unscrupulous mercenaries, to be bribed and outsmarted according to the capacity of those who are obstructed." Tori paused dramatically then continued.

"I resent living in an atmosphere where violence is the order of the day. Where shooting, coupled with unnecessary brutality, prevails. Where youngsters are shot for transporting a pound of butter or a kilo of pasta, or are jailed if they can't pay a bribe. I resent, most of all, the fact that a Sicilian cannot walk his land free from fear, where strangers have always and still continue to walk our lands with more authority than we who are born to the soil." He hooked his thumbs into his belt and moved among them.

"If there's any man among us who doesn't feel the resentment *I* feel at having become a criminal due to forces beyond my control, let me hear from him. Let him step up here to tell us where we have erred and I'll listen." He glanced earnestly into their knowing faces, watching them nod in agreement.

"Is our crime simply that we have become habitual eaters? Drinkers? Let someone show us how to survive *without* food in our bellies and *without* water to nurture us, and I'm willing to bend to his will. But, until such a time, no one tells Salvatore he's a criminal for struggling to survive in these extraordinary circumstances of war!"

This exceptional young man, who commanded the attention of hundreds of men that day, continued to outline a plan. As he talked, they came to realize this plan wasn't a spur-of-the-moment, wild figment of his imagination, but, a well-planned and clearly articulated blueprint of hope—by a man who was one of them, a *paesano,* a compatriot, a Sicilian.

From across the campfire, Antigone stared at her son in marvelous wonder. Never had she seen him in such a pose. Vincenzo de Montana angled his head from time to time, unable to convince himself that this young man, speaking with silver tongued oratory, was his young cousin, with whom he'd grown up and played with not long ago. Santino Siragusa, perhaps the most literate man among this group of men, assessed him critically. He lit his pipe with lingering inhalations, studying Tori's comportment and evaluating his words. Arturo Scoletti tapped his brother's shoulder and commented, "You hear, Miquel? Listen to this *picciotto;* he has plenty to tell us. He makes sense—no?"

"Well, what do you think?" asked the calculating Marco Genovese of his brother Fidelio, feeling the electricity in the air.

"What do I think of what?" Fidelio replied with a tinge of annoyance.

"About this man—this Montegattan."

"What should I think, eh? He makes sense, no?"

"Phew," whistled Marco shaking his hand limply. "He makes much sense, *caro mio*. Just like those labor unions make sense." Marco stared at the cigarette he rolled between his fingers. "You know what I see, Fidelio?" he asked quietly. "I see a man who lights fires in the eyes of the men. I see a chance for us to make a lot of money for our nest egg, *capeeshi*?"

Salvatore paced about with long, striding movements. His thigh muscles strained against his khaki pants. His thumbs were hooked into his belt. His back was to the sun at the edge of the grotto. The late afternoon sun splintered through the tree tops, and where shafts of light converged, curious patterns of light of a bright intensity heightened the supernatural effect of power emanating from him.

Santino Siragusa, spellbound by the Montegattan and as captivated by his words as the others around him, felt certain that Salvatore possessed some magic of communication in that he articulated what the others had felt and hadn't been able to express in words. He turned his full attention on this young prince.

"If we unite," temporized Salvatore, "and strategically plan all our maneuvers, travel together, and become of one mind, not only will we outnumber the *carabinieri* and the security police, we can send them packing! We'll become our own police force and end this blood-sucking graft and corruption. If we don't unite, *amici*, we'll be picked off, one at a time and jailed, or killed by any thieving sonofabitching *carabiniero* who roams the hills."

"You see, Fidelio? What did I tell you? I see good times for us!" Marco's green eyes gazed over the thickening crowds of men. "Flies to honey, brother. Flies to honey," he muttered in exquisite delight.

"Be quiet, you crazy bastard! You've been drinking too much wine!" cautioned his brother hotly, gazing about uneasily for eavesdroppers.

"Not as much as I *will* be drinking, brother. Not as much."

The men moved in closer. Now nearly three hundred men had gathered, to listen to the "brave eagle."

"I have a plan, my friends, one as ancient as the laws and basic principles of feudalism afford us. In the situation we find ourselves, in times of war, anyone who can seize power has the right to govern. The ruler isn't restricted in his right to judge or interpret the law. Laws will be made to meet the situation at hand, with no concern for permanency, and those subject to our laws must obey, regardless of any other circumstances. When the war ends and our government is reestablished, we shall turn over the reins of our province to the State. Meanwhile we drive the *carabinieri* from our lands—or we dig our own graves."

"*Caspita!*" murmured Marco Genovese, delighted and chuckling with immense approval. "It's our lucky day! I can see it all! We drive out the *carabinieri* and we collect the loot. Think of those rich barons who'll tremble on their chamber pots when they see us coming! The tide is turning!"

"Shut up!" glowered Fidelio, grabbing his brother's arm roughly. "Goddammit! Go sober up! Get some coffee in you. Stop drinking the grape. For once start thinking with your brains instead of your balls!"

". . . If we unite," continued Salvatore, oblivious to the scenario enacted between the Genovese brothers, "I'll put an end to the starvation among our people. Foodstuffs will no longer be hoarded among our people until prices are suitable for higher profits. I'll make sure the Allies understand our problems. If they don't, I promise not to be as ineffectual as they. We shall protect ourselves until a proper government is formed, one which will treat Sicily with justice and restore to her the lands, livestock, and years the Italians have stolen from us. A Sicilian shall no longer endure the humiliations of the past!"

"*Bravo*, Salvatore! *Bravo! Bravo!*" shouted Santino Siragusa, cheering the loudest of all. He removed his sunglasses and studied Salvatore inscrutably. *He speaks like a revolutionary,* he told himself. *Per larme dio! This is what the people need! A revolutionary!*

They talked of arms and ammunition. And while Vincenzo took his cousin to the upper grotto to inspect the cache of arms, Antigone Salvatore remained at her son's campsite, besieged with alien thoughts.

Earlier, when Tori had moved across the rocks and stood with his back to the sun in a penumbra of power, in a play of golden lights, he had resembled a magnificent golden idol. She had felt the electricity generated by her son's words and his presence and found the whole thing incredible. Yet hadn't he grown in stature since she last saw him? He appeared much taller, loomed larger than life. Was it merely her imagination? Sainted God, everything was moving too fast. She didn't know anyone or anything, anymore. Her world had suddenly become a world of strangers, she told herself sadly.

Tori had seen the cache of arms before, and had acknowledged them mildly. But this time, when he reexamined the wealth of weapons through different eyes, he was delighted at the array of Lugers, Mausers, snub-nosed carbines, M-P 38's and .40 calibre Beretta submachine guns. There was an abundance of cartridges, and grenades, and ammo belts, enough to fire him with encouragement.

He picked up a few of the weapons, examined them critically, manipulated them expertly, and held them in firing positions. He even checked the gun sights, reversed them and peered into their barrels. He tested triggers, pulled back on bolts, and, slipping them back into place, he glanced excitedly at his cousin. He was impressed. Pausing momentarily he took notice of a Belgian-made Browning automatic, a 9mm weapon containing fourteen bullets. Such a gun with so many bullets? *Phew!* Awed by such a weapon, Tori laid claim to it. Later it was to become the symbol of Salvatore, an instrument immortalized by balladeers.

Tori grinned and addressed himself to his cousin. "What no Messerschmidts? Guns and horses must be given more consideration than you give yourself. They can be your friend or your worst enemy. . . ."

In these few moments, Alessandro Salvatore became their uncontested leader. Readily apparent was the fact that he knew, more intimately than they did, the problems they faced, and because he was a born leader the role suited him well. He struck a pose of bold authority.

"When we're ready we'll move on the prison at Monreale to liberate the prisoners. . . . We'll need all the manpower we can find to liberate our people!"

Everything moved forward with such staggering momentum, Antigone Salvatore wasn't prepared for it. This hadn't been the future she had planned for Tori. But then, death hadn't been the future she had planned for either Filippo or Marco, either. . . .

On this day, her son proclaimed his plans to reshape their world, Antigone had watched the phenomenal conversion of defeated men into super-charged warriors, infected by the words of Salvatore. The rosary beads in her brown, work-worn hands sped rapidly to the accompaniment of countless *Our Fathers* and many more *Hail Marys*.

That night, in the confines of her bedroom, she read

and reread the *strega*'s prophecy, hoping to make some sense out of it. Sainted God! It had taken her twenty years to work up the courage to visit the *strega*. Could she now set aside her foolish pride and present herself again, to ask the witch to explain the prophecy?

She sat rocking to and fro, holding both the prophecy and the Eye of God amulet clenched in both her hands. Let Tori laugh or ridicule me, she thought. She had never used feminine wiles or maternal ploys upon him in the past, and she had enough tears tucked in reserve to influence her son to humor her. He'd *have* to listen to her. *Dear, sainted God! Show me how to make him listen, to make him understand,* she prayed.

She closed her eyes and reflected upon her life. . . .

CHAPTER 19

Antigone's great grandfather, Plato Naxos, had come from the island of Naxos—midway between Greece and Turkey, one of the Cyclades—and settled in the romantic medieval village of Mount Erice where he had perpetuated farming skills and raised a fine family. One of his sons, Aristotle, had resisted farming. Through his personal ways, political inclination and enterprising spirit he'd managed to secure the highly prized Weights and Measures license in his village. Once secured, the Weights and Measures would remain in the family in perpetuity, or until such a time as they might be sold, leased or forfeited. There was the possibility of enriching oneself, and the tremendous prestigious benefits were far reaching. Through these means a less scrupulous man might make a fortune, just as Don Pippinu was now doing ever since the business had been leased to him.

Antigone's three brothers had joined the priesthood, and because she'd been a precocious child and displayed a bright intelligence, they'd convinced their father to educate her. She had become a school teacher, teaching privately for a year, before she'd met and fell in love with Antonio Salvatore, a husky, well-developed young man, a handsome shepherd from Montegatta who had come to Mt.

Erice to sell his wool. The dark-eyed, flamboyant mountaineer had lost his heart to her instantly.

Their sudden chemistry had turned to magic, and their love had broken her father's heart. He'd had visions of marrying her off to a wealthy nobleman who'd have provided her with an easy life crowned with an abundance of culture; but this dream had evaporated for Aristotle. Nevertheless, with a father's love and pride, he had provided Antonio with a handsome dowry which had helped them purchase more cattle. The happy couple had married and moved into the Salvatore house in Montegatta, on Via de Grande, and had planned a rosy future. Things had been simply marvelous at first for the enchanted couple whose lusty appetite for one another had turned Antigone into a prolific mother. They'd been so in love. . . .

The birth of each son had added to their joy, and Antonio had burst with pride at his good fortune in having so fertile a wife, for nowhere in civilized lands were young boys adored by adults as they are in Sicily. Boys were treated like gods and were treated to unrestrained emotional worship by their parents. In this idolatry came the strength needed for them to mature into a relationship that colored their entire life. Beauty in the male, considered a double blessing, invoked a near reverence from their neighbors, and as the lads grew into exceedingly handsome adults they had been critically assessed by eager mothers hoping to make good marriage contracts for their daughters. The fourth child, a daughter, hadn't been deprived of beauty. Doted on by her brothers, she had in turn became devoted to them.

How wonderful it had all been for so long—until the war. The boys had learned things of the farm, and manly ways, from their father. They had looked to their father for the development of their bodies, to their mother for the development of their minds. After all she'd been a schoolteacher—no?

Each night on their return from the farm where they went daily after school they'd become Antigone's to feed, pamper, and make over. She would gather them about the hearth with their cousins, the de Montana children, and spin tales of their Greek and Roman heritage until these mythological gods and goddesses and masterful earthlings had occupied their daily lives with as much ease as their everyday companions.

Perhaps she'd been wrong to teach her sons the philosophies that kept their heads in the clouds. She'd stimulated their mentalities and caused their imaginations to soar beyond the environs of Palermo, into the world beyond Sicily itself, instilling them with an intensive restlessness. How disillusioned her oldest sons had been to discover their real world lacked the idealistic concepts given birth to in their minds! The death of their father, when Tori was seven, had contributed in part to their rude awakening into a world of grim reality. Her sons, industrious farmers, had conformed to their mundane world until *Il Duce*'s power interrupted their lives to show them what little control they'd had upon their own destinies.

"How generous of *Il Duce* to leave me a son and a daughter," Antigone had told the officers who conscripted Filippo and Marco. "After taking all our sheep, every last head of cattle, all our crops, to feed alien soldiers, they take our blood, too!" There were many times when Antigone had wished she'd been born a man. She'd have made some politician, this woman, this bulwark of strength, this matriarch of wisdom.

Her sons, named Filippo for Philip of Macedonia and Marco for Marcus Aurelius, had taken their Greco-Roman heritage in stride. Once past their adolescence, they'd occupied their minds with healthy masculine longings until their stint in the army had turned them into statistics as casualties of WWII.

Alessandro, named for Alexander the Great, unique to begin with, had displayed an exceptionally bright and curious mind. In his formative years a squabble had ensued between his schoolteacher and parish priest in an unending rivalry over Tori's future. "He must become a priest," the Catholic cleric had insisted. "No," the school teacher had urged, "he must become a scholar." Neither realized there had already formed in Tori's mind the nucleus of a life's ambition, one their restricted intelligence couldn't have hoped to grasp.

At age twelve, Tori had been introduced to the incredible feats of the great Alexander, his namesake. Overwhelmed by the conquests of this ancient leader, he wondered how a man living in so primitive an era could have engendered loyalty from the vast armies he commanded. He had asked his mother this question one day. "Truly, he must have been a supernatural being. They *should* have declared him a god!"

Antigone had attempted to explain. "Only a man educated in the ways of men, one who understands their passions, comprehends their mentalities and can measure both the good and evil in them, one who's driven by a force superseding that of the gods can become such a leader."

Tori had stared at her, uncomprehending, until his mother hastened to add, "Bear in mind, Tori, that Alexander had for a tutor Aristotle himself. From this great scholar and master philosopher, he amassed a vast knowledge of history, literature and rhetoric. He created for Alexander a thirst for science, medicine and philosophy, all of which dovetailed into his own unique system for inspiring his men to follow him in battle. As he conquered, Alexander spread his ideals."

Because Tori had dared to dream a dream his contemporaries hadn't, he had immersed himself in a solitary world of ancient greats and, for a time, lost touch with the real world. During his adolescence, his cousin Vincenzo had pulled him away from his studies long enough to enjoy the real world. Following Vincenzo's conscription into the Italian Army, Tori was lost and turned more and more to books.

But with the war and the changes occurring in his land, there had begun to form a new awareness. Daily his subconscious mind had stored a warehouse of injustices he'd seen perpetuated against his people. One day he'd boldly announced to his family that he wanted to be a lawmaker, a *senatore* perhaps, someone high in government. He had feverishly declared that there should be equal justice for all men, something greatly lacking in his own environment. He had grown ardently impassioned over the works of several American authors—John Steinbeck, for example—and one book, *In Dubious Battle*, had held his interest at length.

In July the deaths of his brothers had caused him to take another look at the horror of war—at his environment, and at what the results of war had wrought upon his people. He had felt lost again, like a man poised between two worlds, shackled to one, while aching for another; one which remained as elusive as a faraway dream. Tori had expressed his concern to his mother numerous times since July, but she had nothing left to say to him. All her hopes for her sons had been shattered by influences over which she had no control, and she had withdrawn in near panic from external involvements. . . .

Nothing she'd ever intended for Tori, she thought now, could compare with the display of power she'd seen on this day. She was still stunned by his comportment, his strength and his silver-tongued oratory.

Antigone sighed. She stopped rocking and reexamined the articles in her hand. How long had it been since she'd first encountered Donna Sabattini? Twenty years? As long as she lived she'd never forget that night of November 16, 1922 when the *strega* officiated as midwife. How could she have known what was about to explode from her womb?

Every facet and event of that night stood out now in her mind as if endowed with some mystic significance, for on that night, at the birth of her third son, Antigone had been highly impressionable. On that night of unusual twilight, pulsating skies the color of blood had been streaked with white and gold fires. Radiations of a crimson-tinged purple had fallen like congealed blood in vast blanketing shadows over the desolate village. The wind, having risen, had whispered through the nearby trees with increasing momentum while she, Antigone, having drunk from a copper vessel filled with a drugged potion concocted by the *strega* to ease her troubled soul, had fallen off into a labyrinth of disturbing dreams.

In one of these dreams the fate of her unborn son was being determined by two redoubtable powers, Destiny and History, who, majestically draped in ethereal robes hotly contested claim over him until a third and more powerful force, Sicily, appeared in a blinding radiance of light to voice protestations. Dulling the luster of the golden-robed History and dimming the brilliance of the argent. Destiny, Sicily claimed jurisdiction over the unborn child. Antigone could still hear the seduction of Sicily's voice as it filled the room. "Interfere with my plans for him and no one will claim him. I will end this charade once and for all."

Antigone had awakened from that dream, soaked through with perspiration, screaming, "He's mine! He's mine! None of you shall have him. He's mine, I tell you!" So intense had her memory and that dream been that she had opened her eyes expecting to see the three throned monarchs before her. In the flickering candlelight she'd seen only the face of Donna Sabattini staring at her with those burning black eyes. Terror gripping Antigone, she had shouted hoarsely, as one in a raging fever, "They can't have him, you hear? He belongs only to me. He's all mine!"

She had remembered nothing after that until she had awakened to the sounds of howling winds and peals of thunder erupting against black skies as lightening split and cracked drunkenly across the skies. Her eyes had fluttered and her gaze fell upon the newborn baby squirming wet and hot on her pulsating belly; a tangle of squirming legs and hands. The *strega*'s eyes, reflected in the oil lamp, had shone like two black suns.

"Your son, born in a caul, will be someone special," she had prophesied. "One day—he will be Sicily."

Antigone's eyes fell upon the mass of bloodied caul. As lucidity had returned to her it had all registered. Why *wouldn't* this son be different? She'd had plenty of time to calculate the time on the calendar, now there'd been no mistake. She'd shook her head in near panic, and the word "no" had tried to form on her pale, parched lips. Her eyes had met those of the *strega* and the rare smile on the older woman's lips had dissolved. Arrested by the terror reflected in her patient's eyes and the wild-eyed denial transmitted to her in that instant, the *strega* had turned from her, for in that moment, Antigone had unwittingly communicated to the mind of the clairvoyant the full extent of her *peccato*. The one sin she'd kept locked tight in her bosom and dared not tell another soul, not even her confessor, had been communicated to Donna Sabattini.

She had not been the village *strega* for nothing, this strange, mystic woman who mixed love and death potions on request and whose powers of perception brought respect and reverence to her from the superstitious villagers over the years. On that night she had learned Antigone's secret.

Antigone, a well-educated woman with an intelligence beyond that of most men, disputed the supernatural powers attributed to the *strega*, and anything that hadn't fallen into the pattern of logic and reasoning had cast aside the strega's words giving them no importance. Yet, something that night, when Tori was born, had filled her with portents of impending disaster. For a long time afterwards she had continued to experience a tangle of hazy dreams and burning prophesies which left her in a state of unrest. For this reason she had refused to see the *strega* again after Tori's birth, and, when Athena was born, she had deliberately selected another midwife to assist in the birth.

"*My son will 'be' Sicily!*" she had scoffed. "*Indeed!*"

Yet, with every scoffing denial there had remained in Antigone a inner brooding, and, as Tori grew into manhood without incident, she had begun to breathe easier. Certainly if any prophecy were to come to pass, it would have shown up in twenty years. Antigone reasoned, if the *strega* knew her secret, she hadn't revealed it to another soul in all these years, or there would have been rumors and these rumors would have been certain to find their way back to thwart her. . . .

And so it was, because she had had no other recourse that fatal night Tori had come home with the earth-shattering news that Don Barbarossa was alive, Antigone had had to once again trust the *strega*—or go mad. The need for prophecy, never greater, had had to offset the insurmountable pressures and uncertainties and the heartaches caused by the death of the de Montana family and of her own sons. Pushed beyond the realm of reality, she had needed assurance that this stark terror facing her wasn't true. That Matteo Barbarossa wasn't alive!

Donna Sabattini, considerably changed in twenty years, with a heavy, cartilaginous face and snow-white hair, had sat crosslegged before an open brazier at the center of her shabby, one-room, dung-odored house, staring with turbid eyes under heavy lids into the fires. Considered by most not to be of this earth, the *strega* had used her amazing powers of prophecy judiciously, and her reputation had grown immeasureably. She hadn't resorted to sham or trickery and hadn't frightened the simple-minded peasants with fakery or sorcery although she was an expert in the art. Yet Antigone's presence after all these years stirred a perverse wickedness in the old crone. She experienced a diabolical desire to shake up this unbeliever.

Cackling through the distortion of a distended goiter, the *strega*'s voice, parched and brittle, had cut through Antigone's thoughts: "Why do you come now, after all these years? Once I could have saved your husband—even the lives of your sons."

The statement had struck Antigone between the eyes. Yet, not daring to speculate on her meaning and with more intent desire to reenforce her own courage, the matriarch had replied coolly, "I came not in mourning for the dead, but with grave concern for the living."

"For prophecy?"

"For prophecy."

Once again the old crone had cackled in a voice that sent shivers through Antigone.

Donna Sabattini, bent on tormenting the woman, had caused the fine hairs on Antigone's neck and arms to stand on end; her flesh had begun to crawl when, suddenly out of the fires there had come a hissing serpent. Slithering, slimy, with evil green eyes shining opalescent in the firelight, it had flicked its tongue between open jaws in short, darting movements, staring at her transfixed. Rooted to the spot, Antigone had stared, spellbound. Whether actuated by sheer chicanery or by the phenomenon of reality, she had been unable to circumvent the paralytic fear gripping

257

her as she held her ground. Through it all she had reminded herself that the *strega*, a sorceress, could mesmerize her into seeing what she willed her to see. Was this the catechism for which she'd come? *Demonio!* It had taken superhuman strength to force her eyes away from the apparition. It had been hell in those few seconds, but Antigone fought against the sorcery, valiantly.

Finished with her playful torment, the *strega* had got down to business. She'd made no mention of Antigone's deep, dark secret, and in the wake of what followed, Antigone had nearly forgotten what initially had compelled her to visit the *strega* in the first place. She had come away from the old crone's house gravely troubled and filled with a deeper ambivalence than before the *strega* had handed her the prophecy she'd fought against for twenty years.

The prophecy, set forth on yellowed paper so many years ago, was heavily couched in a jargon that made little sense to her. In addition she had been given an amulet of exquisite proportion, a spectacular piece of metallurgy referred to by the *strega* as the Eye of God—a circular disc, sightly larger than a silver dollar with a fireballing sun at its center surrounded by lightning bolts. Within the sun's center was carved an eye.

Stubborn pride had foiled her attempts to make herself ask the *strega* to interpret the prophecy. Even after the witch had asked emphatically if she had understood the contents of that yellowed paper, Antigone had simply nodded and left the woman's house.

How could she have discussed either with Tori or Athena the things she'd seen and heard in the *strega*'s house? How? Could she have offered them an explanation of either the prophecy or amulet without creating the impression she was in her dotage? After all her teachings and admonishments against belief in the supernatural, they'd have teased her unmercifully and shamed her into silence. She'd taught them too stringently. That night she had crept soundlessly into her room and undressed for bed, and fought every sensible reason in her own mind for not throwing the items away. Yet, she had no intention of discarding them, and before she'd placed them in her hope chest out of the reach or sight of her children, she had reread the prophecy.

Seated in her rocking chair, in a chenille robe, her long hair unpinned and hanging loosely around her shoulders, Antigone lit the candles before the wall portraits of her late husband and sons. She turned up the oil lamp on the table next to her and commenced to read:

Mother of the child, the one child, you are for-
given. For he shall belong to the world. The chil-
dren of one father shall soon cease to be. The
double sting of the scorpion gives flight to the
eagle and power to the lion. Beware. Beware!
The eagle is rendered impotent by the fury of
the bull. Beware the scorpion, keep the fires of
heaven and earth to protect you. The Eye of
God shall forever be upon you. Only this shall
be your invisible protection in the Seven Years
of Glory. There shall be a white horse, reined in
silver profusion, which must be protected. The
amulet must never be rendered impotent. After
the third year, it must be crafted in solid gold
for added protection—for SEVEN YEARS OF
GLORY. Son of the World must never be with-
out the Eye of God.

Antigone had permitted the paper to fall to her lap.
She'd held the Eye of God amulet in her hands, staring at
it in fascination, unable to break her gaze. She had felt a
strange, tingling sensation, as if it, in some mysterious
way, generated an energy of its own. She had refused to
accept so precious an amulet, because she hadn't the funds
to pay for it.

The *strega* had retorted with an offended dignity: "Who
speaks of money? He can't afford to be without it. Already
there are strange webs of entanglement in the fires of his
life. You do understand what I've told you? It's of dire importance to the Son of the World." At that moment,
Donna Sabattini had raised her enormous black eyes and
fixed them on Antigone. And the mother of the Son of the
World had shuddered and felt as she had the night Tori
was born, as if the *strega* had reached into her soul and
held it up for scrutiny and with her gnarled old hands
dissected it, piece by piece.

The prophetic clairvoyant had continued her litany, and
the words still burned vividly in Antigone's mind: "The
prophecy as I repeated this night, written twenty years
ago, hasn't changed. In all these years, I'd hoped you'd
swallow a most stubborn and foolish pride and come to
me, where working together we might have been able to
dissuade Destiny. Now it's too late. He's been seduced by a
voracious mistress, a designing Destiny, and stands deeply
entrenched in the path chosen for him. Pray we're in accord. You understand all I've said . . ."

259

Before Antigone could reply, the *strega* had commenced her meditations and stared into the fires in a gesture of dismissal.

If she'd wondered once, she'd wondered a thousand times what it all had meant. On that night the line in the prophecy reading *Mother of the Child, you are forgiven* had struck her. A surge of blood had shot through her veins as the warmth of guilt spread through her. "I'm forgiven," she had shouted, as if these very words had suddenly lifted a burden from her shoulder. "I'm forgiven!"

That Tori belonged to the world was something she had neither understood nor given credence to at that moment.

On this day, Antigone had seen her son become another person before her very eyes. The *strega* had predicted he'd *be* Sicily—hadn't she? What did it all mean? she asked herself over and over until she was nearly crazy with worry. All those references to the scorpion—the eagle—the lion and bull! What was this mention of Seven Years of Glory? Did she dare sit quietly with Athena and sort out these seemingly insoluable bits and pieces and put them in some order she could understand? Did she dare show Tori the prophecy? Certainly not now. To whom could she turn, then? The *strega*? If she could only swallow her stubborn pride of intellect. . . .

She reflected a moment. *Santo Dio*—what power Tori generated among those men in the mountains! *Managghia*—was this her son, the young, gentle lad she'd raised? She hadn't had time to discuss his actions with her daughter yet, uncertain as she was how to describe the magic that had taken place in the *macchia* that day. Besides, how would Athena believe the picture she'd describe, of a magnificent young prince with spectacular oratory? Her own sweet, loving brother? Never!

Antigone fell asleep that night, replaying all those scenes she'd seen that day and wondering more about this girl Apolladora whose influence, it seemed, had been the turning point in her son's life.

CHAPTER 20

The next six weeks saw a metamorphosis taking place in the Mountain of Cats. That whirlwind, Salvatore, let no grass grow under his feet. He became a brilliant organizer, with the keen ability to place the men in the positions to which they were best suited—and with ease. It wasn't easy. There were times when another man might have thrown in the towel and given up. But Tori's resolve was unshakable. His cousin Vincenzo, voicing his cynicism, thought Tori to be daft for attempting to unify the men. One day when he could no longer hold back his anger Vincenzo cursed aloud.

"You expect loyalty from such *cafone?*" he exploded one day. "To make these mules follow orders will take the power of an earthquake. They don't understand unity. They all want to be boss, but lack the balls to organize. That day, Tori, you lit fires under us and in that instant we were ready to move heaven and earth. *Allora,* it's already tomorrow and it's another day, *capeeshi?*"

They were seated around the fire, Vincenzo, Santino and the Scoletti brothers, drinking coffee after an exhaustive day. Santino softly added to Vincenzo's comments. He studied a troubled Salvatore, watching with fascination the smoke curling from his cigarette.

"Make no mistake, they're rough and tough men, self-centered and cynical, and they make no apologies for themselves. Brother fights brother in decades of *vendetta.* Some would sell his neighbor to put food on his own table. It's true, their loyalty is to themselves and they trust no one. What can you expect from such men? To hear an agreement reached between them is a matter for a tribunal."

"Listen," began Tori. "I reject your cynicism. It's natural that men should differ in opinions. As for a lack of trust, who blames us—any of us—for distrusting the men that have been shoved down our throats as leaders, eh? To whom could we go to air our grievances—to ask for justice? Our mayor? That insipid rabbit who hides behind the skirts of women? Our Parish priest—that spineless Victrola who plays the same words over and over and says nothing?" Tori laughed and glanced beyond the men at the setting sun melting into a flaming twilight of orange pinks, ribboned with white and golden fires. "Enough for such talk—we have important business," he exclaimed.

"You four men, Vincenzo, Santino, Arturo and Miquel, I name as my trusted paladins. To you, I, Salvatore, will incline myself and entrust the gravest responsibilities. You first duty will be to help me unify the men."

"What you propose is a helluva tough order," temporized Vincenzo.

"What in life isn't tough, cousin? And while I'm at it, you I name my co-captain. Any man who has the balls to evaporate the Nazis with such quick thinking shall be my right hand, *capeeshi?*" Vincenzo flushed pleasurably. "But first," added Tori, you go to Palermo—to the doctor. I have a friend, a most discreet physician."

"And take the chance of being recognized? Oh, no," retorted his cousin.

Tori glanced sharply at him, concerned by the alarm in his voice. Santino, striking his pipe against the palm of his hand to empty it, hastened to explain.

"You see, Tori, none of us could survive if we were caught and sent back to prison."

Tori rolled the cigarette between his thumb and forefinger thoughtfully. "You said the prison was destroyed. Files, records, all else must also have been destroyed. Why then are you concerned? The war is still going strong. Who will question your presence here? With no records to substantiate that you deserted the army and were jailed— why do you keep a frog up your ass, eh? You mentioned the expertise of, uh, what's his name, the forger?"

"Angelo Duca."

"Si, him. *Allora.* He'll make up identity cards for you. You could have been injured and sent home—"

Vincenzo was aghast. "All the time we've been hiding in these hills for nothing?" He slapped his thigh in a mixture of vexation and delight.

"At least until the war ends, and some *birbante* decides to check the central records in Rome. Even then, who pays attention to the Italian army?" He laughed easily. "Who'll know you didn't die in the bombing, unless your ghosts walk around to tell the others what happened?"

"Why the hell didn't we figure this out? You, *padre*—you should have figured this with your intelligence."

Before Santino could react, Vincenzo gave his cousin a bear hug. "*Managghia!* Not only have you grown into a roaring stallion, but, *caro mio,* you don't lack for brains. What a ball-buster! My cousin! Imagine, my little cousin with such brains!"

Tori laughed at his cousin's antics and took the compliments in his stride. Once again he got back to business. "In addition to you paladins, I will select from among the men twelve men to become my Inner Circle. To them shall be entrusted the responsibilities that the five of us can't accomplish without their support. *Va bene.* The task isn't simple. I'll work you all until your asses drop in exhaustion. To be Salvatore's men means they'll have to be the best goddamn fighters and soldiers on the island. Shirkers and troublemakers are to be weeded out from the beginning. When Salvatore plants sweet corn, he doesn't intend to reap bitter husks."

The paladins fell silent and reflective. He was tough, this Salvatore. And demanding. How the others would take to this thunderbolt after the tinsel of his oratory wore off would be something to see, thought Santino Siragusa, repacking his pipe with tobacco, his gray eyes intent on the human dynamo before him.

"Is this man, speaking with such powerful persuasion, my cousin Tori, who only a few years ago ran around with his head in the clouds, composing love sonnets and musical ballads? Has that passionate young cock, who sent the girls of our village into rapturous tailspins, turned into a powerful young god whom I recently saw seducing thieves, murderers, brigands, and army deserters into pledging their allegiance to him?" extolled Vincenzo in a picturesque manner. "Imagine! My cousin, Tori! *Managghia,* you're something else, *professore. Professore?* To hell with that nonsense. *Generale* is more like it!'

They all laughed heartily at his antics. He was a clown, this Vincenzo. A real clown. A *pagliaccio,* a court jester.

"Enough. Now, tell me, who among all these men have you observed to be the possessor of much *fegato*—guts?" asks Tori.

"Besides you? . . . Me," replied Vincenzo mischievously. Then he sobered. "What I might see in a man might not equal your idea of guts."

"What about *Sporcaccione?*" asked Santino subtly. "You considered him most capable once." This drew a deep scowl from Vincenzo.

"Why do you call him *Sporcaccione*—the filthy one?"

263

asked Tori, catching the look of annoyance that crept over his cousin's face.

Vincenzo didn't reply immediately. His eyes traveled across the campsite searching the faces of the men until he came upon the solitary figure of the man, Ross Rizzuto, the convicted murderer, that bull tiger of a man from whom the others shied away.

Tori's curious eyes fixed critically on the bronzed skin of the Samurai, who sat chain smoking and staring into the fire's embers. He turned in fierce profile, unaware he was the object of attention for several men,

"I suppose you couldn't pick a better man—to follow orders." He began, explaining *Sporcaccione's* background. "With partisan guerrillas in Trieste, he plagued the Nazi's, retarded their progress, and did heavy damage to supply depots. Some high ranking German officer—or an agent, I'm not sure who got on to him—set a trap. Somehow the tables were turned, and it was the Nazi who ended up at the end of *Sporcaccione's* garrote." Vincenzo shuddered involuntarily.

"Trouble was," added Santino, "Rizzuto was caught— *flagrante delicto,* in the act. Jailed and tried, he was sentenced to death. Rumor has it, he's killed three or four hundred men. If he feels remorse, he doesn't show it. He's cool. Never talks about it . . . only Lucifer knows the fires of hell that burn inside him. . . ."

Salvatore felt a stirring in him. He liked the bull tiger, fangs or not.

"He's a master at commando tactics," marveled Arturo. "You should see, him, Tori. Goddamnit, he's got the strength of ten bulls! A real Hercules." Arturo's zeal communicated itself to Tori instantly.

"Is that straight?" Tori's fascination mounted incurably.

"Sometimes he and Gambo Cusimano do *Mano a mano* combat for exhibition to keep the men entertained. *Lotta Giapponesa*—Japanese wrestling, they call it. It's something to see!"

The smell of fresh earth and fire, of sweating men and horses, of wines and various foods cooking over several campsites permeated the twilight. At the center of the Grotto Persephone, in the bright illumination afforded by the giant fire, two men prepared themselves for a wrestling exhibition. Salvatore leaned over a saddle slung over a boulder and kept his attention on the two men.

"Who's the elephant with *Sporcaccione?*" he asked, watching the two men stalk each other like animals.

"Gambo Cusimano, a deserter like the rest of us. He

was in charge of small arms and ammunition in my unit. I tell you he was a real talent."

"You say he knows guns? Well?"

"As well as I used to know the whores at Neptune's Daughters!"

"And probably treats them the way same way! Screws up real good! I'm not interested in amateurs, Vincenzo. Old Giacomo really knows his business."

"Listen, Tori. This man is first-class. He was in the service with me. I saw how he complicated war for the Germans and Italians. He's changed the course of many a bullet by realigning the barrels; he's made duds of many a godless bomb; he's jammed the bolts of thousands of rifles. And cousin, if he can do that, he could perfect our weapons to hit bull's-eyes!"

"He did all this, eh?"

"And more. . . ."

"And more?"

"And more! But don't take my word. Talk with him. He can make bombs from bottles. The powers of which would amaze you!"

Their attention was drawn to the arena of action, not far from where they stood.

"*Ayiiiiieee yi yi!*" shouted Vincenzo, joining the excitement of the others. "Did you see that, Tori? Did you see the way he tossed the elephant? Look! There! He did it again!" A murmured wave of astonishment swept the campsite. No matter how often they witnessed the feat, they still felt amazement as if it were some sleight of hand, a trick, an illusion.

Both men stood, stripped to the waist, their sweating upper torsos gleaming like copper satin in the fire's glow. Cusimano, a man twice the size of *Sporcaccione,* wore a red kerchief around his forehead, Indian style. They seemed totally mismatched for such a contest. Vincenzo whooped and yelled with gusto.

More than a hundred men clustered about them, watching the combatants, shouting their approval or disapproval depending on where their loyalties lay. Tori grew more fascinated by the moment. He found the exhibition incredible. Bound with insatiable curiosity over what appeared to be a battle of wits, skill and artistry, it became apparent that physical strength was secondary. Three times in succession, Rizzuto, the smaller of the two, felled his opponent in swift, deliberate moves employing the principle of leverage. Gambo took his time in premeditating every move; yet once he reached a certain point, he became powerless to ward off the other's incredible attack. No matter what strategy he employed, he was unable to bring it to a conclusion, and ended up victimized by a thrust or fall that came before his eyes could discern it. •

"Amazing," muttered Tori. "Incredible!" He called out to that powerhouse *Sporcaccione*: "Rizzuto—can you show me commando tactics?"

Sporcaccione nodded. Quicker than the eye could follow, he slipped behind the unsuspecting Turridu Nuliano, held his upper torso in the viselike grip of a half-nelson hold and, wrapping his right leg around his victim's left leg, immobilized him. A sharp stiletto appeared from nowhere, nearly puncturing the skin of Turridu's throat. Nuliano, a strong, crafty, quick-witted fighter, was unable to move or struggle free. *Sporcaccione* released him easily, helping him restore his equilibrium. Scowling and rubbing his neck gingerly, Turridu stretched his left leg and arched his back in a less than bemused manner. "Bastard!" he muttered, his ego sorely wounded.

Before Arturo Scoletti realized *Sporcaccione*'s intention, a garrote had been slipped around his neck and his body had been manipulated to a position where, with little effort, his back could be easily broken. Slowly, he, too, was released and helped to his feet, as the men watching sucked in their breaths with wonder.

Sporcaccione, pausing in his demonstration, placed a cigarette between his lips and asked Uccidato for a light. The other obliged, and as he did he observed the champion with an animal wariness. However, *Sporcaccione* moved with such swiftness and dexterity, with both hands raised over his head, that he managed to pull the other man's head down to his chest, and connect with a knee to Uccidato's groin. The victim doubled over in mortification rather than pain, allowing time for Rizzuto to grab his wrist and flip him expertly to the ground. Instantly his thick black boot moved into place at the man's neck, nailing him to the ground. Then he reached down and helped Uccidato back to his feet. Stunned by the display, Uccidato moved away from him, a frown on his face, unsure of what to make of the other's prowess.

Now the others, too, backed away from him, sullen, angry and somewhat frantic, almost like clucking chickens hoping to escape the axe. Their mouths hung agape at such cleverness demonstrated before their eyes, and they reflected a healthy respect for this hulking loner of a man. His felled victims vigorously rubbed their sore spots and,

266

blinking their eyes at him, were uncertain of the steam-roller's next move.

"Bravo! Bravo!" shouted Tori clapping his hands in appreciation.

The others hesitantly eyed both the victims and their assailant and slowly acquiesced that they'd witnessed something special in those few moments. *"Si, bravo,"* they muttered with mixed feelings. *"Va bene. Va bene."*

"Basta," shouted Tori, good naturedly. "Stop, *amico.* before you put our men into the hospital." Moving closer to the arena of activity, Tori patted one of the victim's back consolingly. "It was for a good cause," he told him.

He called to Rizzuto. "Come with me, my friend. We have many words to exchange."

Calo Azzarello picked up his flute, and in moments the air filled with sweet, haunting sounds. Vincenzo picked up a mandolin and Duca a guitar, and soon a mood of gaiety filtered through the wooded area where Tori and *Sporcaccione* sat on a felled tree trunk, talking.

"You're pretty damn good, you know that, Rizzuto?" he told the former commando. "You think you could teach me and about fifteen men what you know?" He offered him a cigarette.

"Perhaps, if they are not too stubborn, *mi Capitano.*" he said in a surprisingly gentle voice, filled with profound respect.

"How long would it take for them to learn enough to get by with, say in the event of a surprise attack?"

"It depends on how much they have up here." He touched his forehead. "Force is secondary to a man's wits."

"I see. I see, *amico.* A practised skill, eh?"

"—And an art. *Pero*—you can kill your opponent too easily. It is very, very important to know how far you can go to merely disable a man."

Salvatore took to *Sporcaccione* instantly. He was big and tall and straight and tough. A real sonofabitch of a man! Short on humor, but long on action. He could do with his hands and brains what others did with a cannon. "Tell me, who among those men would you select to learn this *como si chiama*—what do they call it? Hand to hand combat?"

Rizzuto studied the men across the campfires and, without hesitation, he named his choice. "The Genovese brothers, the Nuliano's and Gagliolo's."

Salvatore smiled internally, for he had already selected

these same men, plus a few others. "Why these above the others?"

"Why? Because they think with their heads like foxes instead of their balls."

"What about de Montana, Siragusa and the Scoletti's?"

"De Montana?" *Sporcaccione* shrugged and made a vague gesture.

"Why not?" Tori tensed. He experienced a slight sinking sensation.

"That one's been sick a long time—plagued with consumption."

"How long?" asked Tori glancing with concern across the fires at his cousin.

"A year—perhaps longer. I do not keep records."

"Then, we must see to it that he gets to a doctor, eh *amico*?"

"Why? It is no concern of mine if a man wishes to die, *capitano*."

"It should be the concern of all of us," he said quietly. The other shrugged noncommittally.

"Back to business—what about Gambo Cusimano, Terranova, Azzarello and Lamantia? What do you say to them?"

Sporcaccione quietly considered these men. "*Va bene, mi capitano*."

"There's one more, *amico*." Rizzuto raised an inquisitive eye. "Me," added Tori, grinning.

The ex-guerrilla flushed with pleasure. "You, *mi capitano*, I'll teach privately, and with the deepest of honor." And he did.

From that point forward, Tori's interest in anything this bull tiger had to teach him would become his strength. They shook hands that night and the former commando returned to his campfire, where the men, previously kept at a distance, suddenly converged upon him and engaged him in conversation.

"Whores of the devil!" exclaimed Vincenzo at the amazing spectacle. "That's the first time the others had considered him one of them."

"Then, it's a beginning," Tori smiled. "See how unity is born?"

And so began the thunder over the mountain. Deep in the heart of the golden mountains an idea, once born, began to stir and come alive amid the utmost secrecy. Tori organized things swiftly once he shifted into gear. First, came a special squad of carefully chosen men, selected to

procure food supplies and clothing. They acco[...]
Tori on carefully planned raids, and never [...]
empty-handed. The other men were separated int[...]
of twelve men and put under the command of [...]
trained soliders who knew their business; these[...]
leaders took orders directly from Salvatore.

Amid a perilous and most provocative situa[...]
which a rash of daily uncertainties and unique cha[...]
thwarted the men, the most frustrating chore of [...]
was to convince them of the necessity of unity. He e[...]
ed the best from these men and fought with every trick [...]
could devise to exact it. Subjecting them to a rigid discipline, he aimed at separating the men from the boys in a
hurry. It was the greatest education Tori could have had
about human nature, one which would serve him well in
the coming years.

At the *campagna* belonging to the Genovese brothers,
abandoned by the police who had once confiscated it when
the brothers had been involved in smuggling of contraband, the men were run through additional maneuvers
performed under simulated battle conditions. Once the
grounds were properly staked out, the men were ordered
to crawl, slide, snake or weave their way across a predeter-
mined area while squadron leaders shot live ammo expertly around their bodies.

Immediately the men voiced their indignation with
shocked resentment against such suicidal practices. Dominic Lamantia sputtered indignantly at his superior officers,
de Montana and Gambo Cusimano who meticulously enforced the maneuvers! "You're all a bunch of crazy
bastards! That's what you are."

Uccidato, better known as Giovanni Gagliolo, glowered
fiercely. He was a stocky, well-paunched man, hulking and
beetle-browed and built like a bull moose. This man
nicknamed Uccidato—killer—was all the name implied. In
his eyes could be seen the history of Sicily. On this day he
was at his fiercest. "If you think we'll let you shoot us like
pigs led to slaughter, you've another guess coming," he
snarled angrily.

Pietro Gagliolo, his brother, at fourteen a red-haired lad
with a face peppered with freckles and a laughing, happy
go lucky disposition, pulled his beaked cap down over his
forehead and agreed with his brother. "This is fool's play.
We'll all get killed. *Cazzu!*"

"Get back to your positions," ordered *Sporcaccione* with
fiercer intimidation. "*Subito*—right now."

o, your ass!" shouted Marco Genovese, accompa-
n obscene gesture.

ll have to kill us first. This is crazy, you know? Id-
aid Lamantia, planting his feet firmly into the
nd pointing his rifle at Sporcaccione's heart.

foolish performance continued for an agonizing
strating half hour before Vincenzo lost all patience.
he told Tori it would be useless? To convince these
it and egotistical infants the merit of conforming to
army training had become a feat worse than extract-
g venom from a serpent's tooth. "Better call Tori," he
growled. "Sonofabitches! If it was up to me I'd let the
cowards have it, right now."

Dressed in American combat fatigues like his men, Salvatore arrived and stood nearby on a small cluster of boulders a bit higher off the ground so they had to look up at
him. For a time he listened as they aired their grievances.
All the remarks made earlier to Vincenzo and *Sporcaccione* were repeated with more added.

"Either you shoot blanks at us or we quit and go
home," called one of the men.

"Why should we play this silly game and risk getting
shot up for nothing?"

On and on went the complaints. When they finished Tori
spoke up. "What do you think the *carabinieri* will shoot at
you—cotton balls?" He gave them no quarter. "Anyone
who thinks this is fool's play had better pick up his toys
and return to his mother's suckling breasts. There's no
room for cowards or Mamma's boys alongside Salvatore.
This is a job for real men."

He waited. No one moved. He stared at them inscrutably until they began to shuffle about, uncomfortable and
ill at ease under the sweltering brash sun. "If you've nothing to say, then, quit wasting time. Get back to your
business."

They didn't like it. Nevertheless, the grumpy, sullen and
resentful men returned to their places soaked with sweat,
dirt smudged, keeping their humiliation to themselves.
They sprawled out and, hunkering down, they began their
belly crawling bivouac as *Sporcaccione* and Arturo shot
live rifle fire all around their moving bodies. Tori watched
them quietly for nearly an hour inwardly pleased for,
despite such protestations, they had become more cautious,
more concerned and remarkably agile, their senses honed
appreciably. They had hardened up in that space of time
and become stouter of heart and more vigorous in their
participation. Even *Sporcaccione* noticed the improvement.

"They'll do anything you ask of them, *mi capitano*. It's as if they need reassurance from you—no matter what *we* tell them."

When next Tori ordered a rectangular pit to be dug, cemented, and filled with water and the squadron leaders ordered the men to jump in and maneuver their way across the pool with live ammunition exploding about them, the men rebelled again. It was highly perilous, to say the least. This time the men decided, while preparing their protest, they'd outsmart Tori by offering a foolproof argument against the continuance of such folly.

When Tori was once again called before the striking men, Uccidato became their spokesman. "Show us where there's water like this any place in Sicily—where we'll be required to fight over a box of cement—and we'll continue with these foolish and dangerous exercises," he challenged, the livid scars on his face shining like pink fire in the sunlight. He glanced smugly at his fellow conspirators.

Tori countered, "Show me where it's written that men like us should be shot down for trying to feed our families and I shall turn myself in to the authorities. I'll ask all you men to join hands with me and follow me to jail."

"You have an answer for everything, don't you?" retorted Fidelio Genovese.

"Would you think more of me if I had no answers?" He held Fidelio's power-saturated stare with his own dark eyes. "Would you follow such a man who offered no explanations except to command you blindly to follow his rule?"

The men had been bested again. Antagonistic over their lot, they retired to their tasks with continued sullen behavior. Tori sighed resignedly. It began to look as if Vincenzo and the others were right. It would have been easier to move the golden mountains than to convince these men of the intelligence behind these tasks. These men, bright, quick, with the ability to comply skillfully with these rigorous routines, also possessed the willful stubbornness of spoiled adolescents who wanted their way and refused to risk anything in return for promising rewards.

Two weeks later, at the end of a gruelling day, the men fell exhausted, eager to partake of their evening meal. Sporting an adhesive bandage over his left temple, Turridu Nuliano, a man with mocking brown eyes who was perpetually dismayed that he wasn't able to keep up his meticulous peacock appearance, threw himself down at the edge of the fire and devoured the rabbit stew hungrily. "Tough bastards! Those Terra Diavolo devils must have sprung from the loins of an iron tank! Ball busting seeds of Satan!"

"You mean *Sporcaccione*—don't you?" glowered his brother Calo, better known as "the fox," due to his strong resemblance to the animal as well as his skill in avoiding the *carabinieri*. He was boiling mad. "Incestuous fucking son of a whore has no nerves at all. Nothing scares him!"

Uccidato had had it. "You jackasses can take all this spoonfed horseshit all you want, but no one's gonna make Giovanni Gagliolo less than a man. I'm no *mammalucco* who intends to hand over his sword to another conqueror." His scarred left hand, run through with a pitchfork by a landlord who had caught him stealing a few oranges, brandished a cup of wine, which he guzzled noisily and in prodigious gulps. He wiped his mouth sloppily and resumed eating.

"You don't intend to do anything foolish, do you?" asked his kid brother the red-haired Pietro. "You swore loyalty to Salvatore," he said hesitantly. "A Gagliolo never goes back on his word," insisted the lad, who'd begun to display an idealistic worship for Tori.

"*Sta zitto!* Shut up!" ordered his brother. "I'm still boss in our family, *capeeshi?*"

"Working under live rifle fire has its hazards," remarked Terranova, the *Casanova*, who'd been sneaking off nights for romantic interludes with hot-blooded peasant girls. "*Pero—*" he grinned. "The food's great."

"What's the good of food if we aren't around to enjoy it?" complained Lamantia.

"Trouble is, Tori tries to run us like a bull runs a pasture," said Turridu.

"Why don't you all shut up, eh? Either stop complaining or do something about it! All you do is talk, talk talk, *putapoom putapoom putapoom,*" complained Calo Azzarello, the handsome shepherd lad who had confessed to copulating with sheep, "For the past two weeks I've heard the same record played over, and over, and over. Yet every day you get up and do exactly what you say you won't do each night. Stop your griping so we can get someplace or change the fucking record!" He tossed aside his food and grabbed his guitar. He began to play and sing loudly to drown out the other voices of protestations. "*Io sono nu maritu fortunato . . . Io sono un marito con amore. . . .*"

He grinned and adopted a lighter tone, and in moments the men forgot their laments and began to sing along with him. And as the spirit moved them they began to clap their hands and stomp their feet. Vincenzo and Arturo leapt into the circle and began to dance feverishly with abandon, bringing smiles to the onlookers. There was a sudden change of tempo as other men joined in with guitars and mandolins and a *tarantella* began. The dancing grew frenzied and ended abruptly an hour later when Vincenzo, the wind knocked out of him, fell to the ground in a faint, and began a coughing seizure.

He was taken inside the small farmhouse, where Tori was speaking with the Genovese brothers and carried to a bunk where his coughing seizure finally abated. Tori studied his pallor with stern reprimand. "Goddammit! Tomorrow, without fail, you go to the doctor *Capeeshi?* This is the final time I tell you. Next time I'll toss you on a horse and take you in myself."

It was almost over. The men entered the final phase of training. The final maneuvers consisted of the simulating of actual ambush tactics in which two sides would oppose the other.

Pietro Gagliolo was struck right off; a bullet grazed his forehead. Another grazed his right arm. Instantly he flung his rifle into the air. Seeing this, the next man followed suit. On it went until they all lay down their arms in submission.

"Get back to your posts, and be quick about it," ordered *Sporcaccione* gruffly.

The Genovese brothers grabbed their M-1 rifles, aiming them at the Samurai's heart. "Who the hell do you think you are—Salvatore's enforcer? You gonna make us play this comedy if we refuse?" growled Fidelio resentfully.

Vincenzo and Arturo stood by helplessly, unsure of their next move. They didn't want to hurt any of the men. Yet they didn't want Rizzuto to be hurt. They tensed as *Sporcaccione* inched closer to the Genovese brothers.

What the hell was he thinking of walking into that trap? they wondered. The Genovese's egged the Samurai on. These were tough, hard men, intimidated by no one. They'd reached the end of their rope in patience. As the paladins watched, they wondered at *Sporcaccione*'s daring. Was he so fearless that two rifles aimed at his heart by two expert shots didn't deter him? The others moved in closer, intent on the scene, some with smug grins, hoping the two-fisted guerrilla would get a sample of his own fare, others eager for blood; the rest wondering where all this would lead.

"Come closer and you'll taste the bite of our bullets," threatened Fidelio.

Sporcaccione pressed forward as if he'd heard words of

encouragement instead of threats, until he reached a point equally distant from each man. He dropped his Beretta sub-machine gun in a gesture of submission, taking his assailants off their guard for a split second. Triumph glittered in their eyes. Then, quick as a flash, *Sporcaccione* disarmed Marco on his right by pushing up on the man's gun while simultaneously shoving down on Fidelio's, dislodging the weapons from both their hands. Next in a surprised move, he drove a swift kick into Marco's groin, bringing him to his knees. Another rapid-fire movement and he had caught Fidelio from behind, wrapping one leg around him and felling him before he knew what struck him. He scooped up the weapons and tossed them to Miquel Scoletti, who, grinning wickedly, watched in exquisite amusement.

Before the other sympathizers could move into action they were covered by Tori's paladins. "No, you don't," warned Arturo sternly. Two against one was bad enough. *Sporcaccione* isn't finished yet."

With another body twist *Sporcaccione* released Fidelio and helped his brother off the ground. "Now, we're even.

With no guns, I'll take on the two of you, by myself," he told them. He stretched out his hairy arms in a wide gesture beckoning to them. "*Allora*—for why do you wait, eh? You wanted action—and here I am."

The Genovese brothers rubbed their aching spots with sullen and withdrawn faces, at the same time they backed off away from the ex-commando. Fidelio cursed bitingly. "Enough. This is the end. *Basta e fine!* Over and done with, You'd best call Salvatore. We'll tell him to his face."

Sporcaccione straightened from his crouch position and looked with distaste and disgust at the small crowd of dissenters forming a ring around the brothers. He nodded resolutely, signalling Miquel Scoletto. "It's best you call our *capitano*. Even I grow weary of changing diapers and wiping the noses of these spoiled, snot-nosed adolescents."

When Tori stood before them, he allowed himself to be verbally assaulted by their emotionally charged voices, knowing it was best to let them air their feelings.

"Dictator! You're worse than Mussolini. How do you justify exposing us to such dangers? Black-hearted despot! You want to kill us off, don't you? I'll bet you're in league with the *carabinieri*. You'll probably claim a reward for killing us off!" 'The fox' wasn't called that for nothing. His brain roiled with a complication of intrigues. If one didn't work, he'd think of another dart to aim at Tori.

Only the ruffling of an early winter wind was heard whipping through the bamboo rushes and the heavy scent of lemon and orange blossoms permeated the crisp air. Tori remained silent, in his usual pose, until they all had their say. Damn it! Why didn't this strange Montegattan get mad at them? Why didn't he yell at them and shout obscenities, so they could get angry at him and expurgate the acid that churned and twisted their guts. They'd never known anyone like him. In the silence, they began to shuffle about with disquiet.

They weren't likely to forget his words this day. "You're tired, overwrought, and need a rest," he said quietly. He took off his pith helmet and tossed it on the ground nearby. "Perhaps it's as good a time to get everything out in front so you all understand, eh? Because of what we've been through, I felt all of us had become men with a purpose—to rid Sicily of its blood-sucking enemies." He unstrapped his Beretta automatic rifle and dropped it with a dull thud in a careless gesture, too careless for even these men to understand. They stared, ill at ease and raised their eyes from the fallen weapon to Tori's impassive face.

He extended his arms in a helpless gesture. "I was wrong. It's not easy to admit, but when you are—you are. *Allora*— it's ended."

The men were stunned. They had expected an argument, a protest—not capitulation.

"You think we can discuss it?" suggested Fidelio Genovese. "It's little the men ask. Just that no live ammunition is used on maneuvers. Isn't there a half way place—some middle ground at which we talk?"

"There's no middle ground in war," snapped Tori. "Make no mistake, *amico*. Once we declare ourselves to our enemies it's out and out war. With Salvatore, nothing is half-assed. I know what's out there, what to expect. If you think I'd send anyone into combat without preparation, you're crazy, half-witted cretins who deserve to be shot up. If you don't care enough to protect yourselves in every way, I'm damned if I accept the responsibility for your stupidity! I want no part of such idiocy!"

He paced before them with bold strides, his thumbs hooked into his belt. "You think I've spent my time training a suicide squadron? If I permitted you to think that fighting our enemies is a game—it *would* be suicide. I'll take no part in a comedy of errors where one life is sacrificed for another."

"But be reasonable, Tori," protested Lamantia. "We can outshoot anyone." He looked to the others for support. Hadn't they all killed at least one *carabinero* in their lifetime?

"Si," agreed Terranova blinking his green eyes in the bright sunshine.. "We're expert shots. We can shoot the balls off a bull at a hundred paces."

"Ahhh," said Tori nodding as if he understood. "I see. Because you can shoot a gun makes you powerful, eh? Is that your measure of a man? The gun he carries?" He stared at them with contempt.

"It's the only talk our enemies understand," spoke up Uccidato.

Again the men's voices murmured their approval.

"Because our enemies are imbeciles—you wish to be classified as such?"

From the start, these brooding men knew they were powerless to match wits with him. This was logic and reasong you couldn't dispute. He had a way with words. They felt Tori's seduction all right, yet they all felt it was an honest seduction in which they'd all share and share alike. For this reason they had listened to him as they'd never listened to another man. They watched him as he lit a cigarette and smoked a few minutes, with one leg raised up on a boulder. "We've banded together to preserve life, not snuff it out," he continued. "You think because we possess enough guns and ammunition to blow us all to hell and back we'll do it? It's best you learn the power behind the gun, *cari amici*. A gun in the hand of a coward makes no hero of him. A man is what he is, with or without a bullet stinging machine. A gun in your hand doesn't mean you should shoot up your enemies at will. A gun is merely a symbol of strength, not strength itself."

"Symbol or not, Tori, it comes in goddamn handy when a *carabinero* aims his rifle at you," said Turridu Nuliano.

"What will you do if you find yourself in a position where you've been disarmed? Give up and surrender meekly, because you've been relieved of your strength? Any jackass can find a gun and run off half-cocked to shoot his fucking head off in battle, to the end. A real man is one who wants to live, not die. If he keeps his wits about him, trains himself to become fearless, and uses his brains to think, he'll know when he's been disarmed, he has lost merely a firearm, not his power."

"If a gun isn't power, what the hell is?" snarled Fidelio. "In my lifetime, the man with a gun has been the most feared." These were strange and alien words to his ears. Tori confused them made them feel uneasy, even though they sensed the truth in them.

Tori grew weary. They were indeed children, who lived by instinct alone. It was hard to reeducate them in so short a period of time. "We were drawn together for a purpose and must stay together as a team. If one man fails, we all fail. Which among you wants it on his conscience that he's responsible for the downfall of his people? Speak up. Tell me now and I'll excuse you. Any of you. Return now to your villages. Risk the chance of being captured and imprisoned. Or if you escape capture you can accept the oppression of our people without contest and live forever with a yoke around your neck, thinking of the glorious days when you might have been responsible for promoting a needed change in your country and were too chicken-livered to take that chance."

Tori's words, like the sting of a scorpion, were sharp and infectious. "I repeat, all you defanged and declawed tigers who think your stripes alone will paralyze an enemy are excused. The rest of us are in to the end—and victory."

The men lowered their shame-filled eyes and, walking off the rolling hills of the *campagna*, retired to their temporary housing along the side of the ancient farmhouse, a ghost of a centuries-old villa. The men cursed. They flung their weapons from them like petulant adolescents resentful of authority. Bullheaded and obstinant, as they were, they let their fiery tempers clash to explode their reasoning.

"Why should we get killed playing silly games for that power-crazed madman? Who made him our leader? Did we take a vote, eh? Who does he think he is?" came the genre of remarks.

After an hour of this, young Pietro Gagliolo jumped to his feet in disgust. "I've never seen anyone like him! If you beat me up you won't get me to abandon Salvatore," he told his brother with audacious bravado.

Uccidato gave his younger brother a withering look that normally would have sent shivers down his spine. This time, the young redhead picked up his gear and strutted across the dirt yard. With the tip of his bayonet, he drew a line down the center of the confine. "I'm with Salvatore all the way. I'll sit on this side of the line. Anyone who wishes can join me," he announced boldly.

For a time the fiery-headed youth remained by himself. The older men, those in their late teens or early twenties, ridiculed his youthful zeal and loyalty. The next day the men awakened and went about their usual routine, conforming to the rigid schedule imposed upon them. The end of each day, for the next week, found them vowing each night would be their last. Then, the very next morning they'd report to their squadron commander. This frenzied on again, off again behavior lasted a week. They went through the frightening ritual of bivouac, not sure of why they complied and angry at themselves for not punching Tori in the mouth. At the end of the week Pietro Gagliolo had been joined by twenty-six men.

Finally it was over—the six weeks had ended and a miracle had taken place. The men felt a deep sense of achievement, and it reflected in their behavior. A new *camaraderie* sprang up between the men, and an expression of care and concern for one another manifested itself. It was a good feeling, they told themselves, to know someone cared what happened to them.

The men Tori chose for his inner circle turned out to be those same men to whom he'd entrusted *Sporcaccione* to teach commando tactics. Of these twelve men, two were placed on probation. Terranova, with his hazardous collection of paramours and excessive promiscuity in sexual matters, had given Tori cause for alarm. He had explained his feelings to the Castellamarese and wasn't surprised that the young stallion hadn't taken too kindly to his ultimatum. Dominic Lamantia was the second man, and his probation came about due to his excessive drinking.

"Women," argued Tori, "can innocently, unintentionally, or if provoked, bring about the betrayal of any man. Wine loosens the tongue and causes the strongest of men to boast and do foolhardy deeds they wouldn't consider doing when not under the influence. I can't afford to take chances with such men who haven't the will power to control their weaknesses."

Terranova and Lamantia both protested the points of their probation but Tori remained steadfast in his decision. They complained and argued that Calo Azzarello should be placed on probation. That sonofabitch fornicates with sheep!"

Tori shrugged. "Sheep are less treacherous than women. They can't betray a man," he retorted walking away from them, leaving them with his thoughts.

Tori appointed Santino Siragusa his personal historian and the biographer of the bandits. He stressed only one thing. "You are to keep the records accurate. In years to come, I don't want some half-crazed historian to distort the issues at hand, nor the work we do. No matter what our involvement, Santino, I insist you record it in truth. And you can be certain I'll check on your work periodically to insure this, understand?"

At the time, the former holy man took all this in his stride, but in days to come he'd have time to think heavily on these prophetic words from Tori. They would one day return to haunt him.

And so it was that Santino Siragusa, the Scoletti brothers, the Genovese, Nuliano and Gagliolo brothers, plus Lamantia, Terranova, Azzarello, Rizzuto, Duca, Cusimano—and, of course, Vincenzo—became the nucleus of Salvatore's band, which would later grow into an army of three thousand men. All were to remain close and well-protected through the most unusual and complex political situation—only Sicily could have produced in its day—and were to remain as such to the very end of Salvatore's miraculous seven-year reign.

Tori had instructed his men patiently and groomed them with considerable care. Now, he was ready to see if they had absorbed anything besides *pasta fazule.*

CHAPTER 21

It was 4:15 P.M. the following Friday. In a faint drizzle of rain, a modest crowd of villagers gathered before the ancient jail in Monreale, a few miles from Palermo. They stood by silently, watching as *carabineri* locked chains on the ankles of twenty new prisoners who'd been recently apprehended for minor infractions of the law—stealing food to keep their families alive. The prisoners ranged from 12 to 23 years of age and were covered by two officers holding rifles aimed fiercely at them, while four more sat about swiftly clamping on the locks and chains about their ankles. Something in the air—something intangible—caused a restlessness among the *carabinieri.* From time to time they'd gaze about with apprehension, without comment, and subdue the rising nervousness they felt as their guts churned. Nearby a large truck waited to transfer the prisoners to a Palermo jail.

Overhead a mass of storm clouds drifted in a congealed mass of darkening gray mist, threatening a long-overdue rain. The stony grey limestone mountains in the distance reflected the somber black moods of the peasants, who stood motionless and staring at the officers. It was all too pat, too much like a stage setting where anything could happen—most likely the unexpected, one of the officers told himself as he scanned the area with guarded and suspicious eyes.

Four men who blended easily with the crowd stepped forward, not too noticeably so as to bring undue attention to themselves, but enough so that six additional men who cautiously inched forward, moving into a preplanned position at both sides of the low stucco building, would know they were in readiness. The air was charged with electricity, and none sensed it more than the agitated police officers, who asked themselves what in hell was happening.

From out of the crowd, Salvatore stepped forward, wearing a white trenchcoat with its collar pulled up around his neck in a debonair fashion. Under it, and concealed at the moment, he wore the elegant riding habit of an English Lord; breeches, gleaming black leather boots, a black turtleneck sweater and a tweed patch-sleeved jacket. He grinned easily tossing the *carabiniero* nearest him a mock salute. For a moment the crowd moved forward with him.

"Get back, *contadino* pigs!" snarled the nervous officer.

"Are you addressing such vile language to me, my good man?" asked Tori in the manner of a dandy.

"No, excellency, not you," said the *carabiniero* speaking politely to the clothing Tori wore. "It's these filthy beasts. Go on, get back with the rest of the dogs," he snarled savagely at them, poising the rifle with menace.

"Pigs? Dogs?" said Tori playing with him. "My, my, there's a difference." Meanwhile his eyes were everywhere, taking in the entire scene.

"Excellency, I beg of you, get back. With your permission I beg you not to toy with me. I've work to finish here with these *bruti cani—dirty dogs.*"

Tori recognized officer Fabrizio, the one who had shot him when Nino Marino had fallen accidentally under the blast of his *lupara.* A kneeling guard glanced up, shaken by the peasants unusual behavior, only to be admonished by Fabrizio. "Mind your business. *Fa presto!*" snarled Fabrizio, anxious to get these prisoners out of his jurisdiction as swiftly as possible.

Tori let his coat fall open. He hooked his thumbs into his belt, standing well-braced with a benign look on his face. Officer Fabrizio was coming unglued by Tori's steady gaze. When Fabrizio's eyes were leveled on him, Tori elected to stare at a point above the officer's head. Certain that this move had been duly noted by Fabrizio, he moved his eyes a few feet to the right and fixed his gaze at a distant point. Tori repeated these movements twice after that.

Less sure of himself, Fabrizio took a firmer grip on his Mannlicher-Carcano and gazed beyond Salvatore's head; he saw the peasants move their eyes now in the same manner Tori had done. Fabrizio, sweating bullets, wouldn't take time to wipe his face. Some inner sense warned him of impending danger. The arrogant, cocksure pose of that damnable man with a grin on his face alarmed him. *What devil's game is this?* he asked himself. His stomach continued to churn. He'd never seen anything like this. Usually the stinking peasants yelled and screamed in a display of histrionics designed to break a man's heart as they cried for mercy and the release of their loved ones. Now that Fabrizio recalled it, this was the first time since he'd begun duty on the island that none of them had offered him a bribe. That alone should have tipped him off that something unusual was underfoot.

He disengaged his attention from Salvatore and, under the pressure of all those stares, he turned to observe what they were so interested in, almost afraid of what he'd see. His jaw opened in astonishment as he counted four men dressed in combat fatigue of American soldiers complete with pith helmets. They stood on the roof of the jail aiming guns. Slowly, Fabrizio released his grip on the rifle, and as it rolled out of his hands Tori reached in to retrieve it.

Things moved swiftly after that. Fabrizio's partner released his hold on his weapon, and on cue Tori's men moved in quickly from out of the crowd and, in sure-fire order, discarded their coats and set to work unlocking the chains from around the prisoners' ankles.

Vincenzo and Santino and a few of the other men ran swiftly inside the jail to unlock the cells and release the ecstatic inmates, who rushed out past them as fast as they could run, yelling and shouting triumphant yells. Arturo and his brother, Miquel, together with the Nuliano brothers, began the destruction of the prison files. In a matter of moments the file drawers had been emptied and the desk compartments torn open, and, together with every chart, official paper and wanted posters in sight, the men heaped them into the center of the room where Michele set fire to them.

Marco and Fidelio Genovese had rounded up all the *carabinieri* and, after snapping chains around their ankles, marched them into the jail where they proceeded to lock them into the cells. The Gagliolo brothers and *Sporcaccione* had broken into the arsenal and confiscated every weapon and box of ammunition in sight.

Outside, the prisoners hugged and kissed their family

members and loved ones, wondering to whom they owed such a debt of gratitude for their freedom. They searched with curious and inquisitive eyes to find the leader of this motley group. They stared at Salvatore, noting his impeccable dress and manners. Some approached him with marked respect, coupled with great puzzlement for his deed.

"Who are you? From where do you come? Why do you take it upon yourself to save us?" they asked at random.

"I am Salvatore," he replied. "I come from Montegatta to liberate our people from their enemies."

An older man, more wise in life's ways, peered at their savior with suspicious eyes. "What do you propose to extort from us in return for your valorous deed?"

Tori's eyes on the man, filled with icy disgust—until he realized the poor man, robbed all his life, cheated and unprotected by his government, swindled by feudal landlords and kept in bondage, wouldn't recognize a kindness if he saw one and moreover he'd be suspicious of such an act.

In a princely manner, Tori addressed the gathering.

"Salvatore takes nothing from civilians. Ours has been a cause for survival for centuries. Until now, we've not had an opportunity to stand up and be counted. Any man among you who wishes to join our cause against a government who has abandoned its people can sign up with my men. With Salvatore you'll earn a small salary, plus the ability to feed your families and yourselves. . . ."

"*Bravo*, Salvatore! *Bravo*, Montegattan!" the people cheered, pledged their support.

"If we join you and become bandits we are as good as dead!" spoke up another concerned citizen. "You know the penalty imposed upon bandits! They'll kill us all!"

"We are not bandits, *paesano!*" proclaimed Salvatore with the majesty of a king. "Rebels, yes. Rebels who've united to fight a tyrannical and ineffectual government which must be made aware of our existence. Hear me well. Only the bravest of men are wanted. Those who still suckle their mother's breasts need not join. Return to the jails where you'll remain in the comfort of servitude, like animals chained to the ground!"

The villagers cheered with bravado. As he moved among them, the crowds parted to let him pass. They grabbed at him, kissed his hand.

"*Dio de benediggi,*" they shouted. "God bless you!"

"Salvatore? Who is this Salvatore?" they asked themselves as he passed among them. From that day forward they were never to forget the name.

The Genovese and Gágliolo brothers remained behind

to recruit volunteers for Salvatore's army. An hour later, Tori put into action his second surprise attack. He and his men rode to the government granaries at the edge of Palermo and pulled off a daring coup in broad daylight. Leaving the premises with truckloads of flour, wheat, pasta, olive oil, and a few food staples they hadn't seen in ages, the men returned to their bandit's lair.

From this point on, Salvatore struck with the speed of a meteor. Before the *carabinieri* could recover from the blow dealt them at Monreale, Tori and his men working in clockwork precision attack the jails in Partinico, Alcamo, Borgetto, Castellammare and other villages in the interior. Finished with the jails, where he had freed the prisoners and burned all records as he had done in Monreale, Tori selected as his targets the government granaries and warehouses, where he politely removed the foodstuffs to fill the warehouses of Salvatore with the precious commodities.

"Strike while the iron's hot!" he instructed his men, and they did just that. Their unanticipated moves began to unnerve the police network throughout western Sicily.

"Who can he be?" asked the titled landlords, appalled that the police offer no aid.

"Who is this Salvatore? How dare he defy law and order?" asked Chief Inspector Semano of the security police in Palermo when reports flowed into his office of the daring deeds perpetrated by this unusual band of brigands.

"Who dares strike at the heart of the *carabinieri?*" the head of the Sicilian Division of the Italian military police, demanded to know. "Who is this outrageous outlaw who dares set himself above the law?" demanded General Brancuso. "How dare he defy the laws of the Church?" asked Cardinal Rumalino.

On and on came the queries. The more people asked, the less they knew of this phantom who began to resemble a gallant Robin Hood. Salvatore's ostentatious generosity to the poor and his stern sense of justice, coupled with his handsome *maschiezzo* and his uncanny flare and sense of publicity, caught the attention of an admiring press, who succeeded in making a hero of him.

If it appeared that Salvatore took special care to set the stage and judiciously select his cast of players to act out in the most intriguing drama ever played in Sicily's political history, he did so as if gifted with insight. It began to appear, when he took certain precautions, as if he knew

283

years in advance the ending of the script and the forces which might one day betray him.

From the first, Salvatore and his men were unique, distinct from all the other brigands who roam the countryside. Considerable care, taken to mold his men into something special, prepared them for the role they were to play. The untenable position held by the *carabinieri* as they perpetuated the greed and corruption made them the target for Tori's wrath. It was against these black-hearted mercenaries that he aimed his rebellion and directed his hostilities, hoping as he did that someone in Rome's government would take note of the intolerable conditions in Sicily.

His manner of food distribution was adopted by his people as being most equitable and increased their dedication to him. Soon the cause of Salvatore became the cause of every Sicilian in his province. Vital to this young renegade's purpose was the importance he placed on not being hailed as a self-serving brigand, or a common thief. God forbid he should be equated on par with the *carabinieri!*

Salvatore never doubted the support of the people. He was one of them. He cried their tears, felt their pain, talked their talk. He identified with them. They were the men he knew, loved and needed as much as they knew, loved and needed him. They, both of them, were the people of Sicily: the despicable and destitute peasants; the landless *contadini*; the old men begging in the slums of the cities; the poverty-stricken; the needy; the laboring peasant who'd hardly known a moment's rest from birth; the women whose bellies were swollen with growing embryos whom they couldn't feed; the *ragazzi*, begging in the streets, yet filled with a peculiar pride and arrogance—the infinite throngs of Sicilians, exploited, cheated, browbeaten, shunned, trampled on, degraded and submissive. They were all Salvatore and he was all of them.

In the next two years, if he needed reassurance, he received it from the people. He would become a genius in the art of guerrilla warfare, unequaled as yet in the history of man. Salvatore would also come to the attention of a most scurrilous sect of feudalists, politicians and government officials, a genre of bloodthirsty men who had written the history of the ages with the blood of their fellow man. From their festering bowels will come the hatefilled battle cry—*Bring Me the Blood of Salvatore!*

All this because he will not bend to their whirlwind.

BOOK III

Two Years Later
February 1945

CHAPTER 22

Allied Command HQ
Palermo, Sicily

The island of Sicily trembled with excitement and a keen awareness, knowing something fresh and daring had come alive in these ancient lands. Without a doubt this awareness struck the feudal land barons first, since they were the ones who had the most to lose. They had gathered this day to discuss their grievances with the only man capable of resolving the issue of Salvatore.

Don Matteo Barbarossa sat at one end of the oval table in his penthouse suite at the *Albergo-Sole*, a hotel commandeered by the Allies as their headquarters for the duration, trying to act civilized. Once, as the most dreaded of *Mazzarino* bandits, he'd have found other means to deal with these laughable members of Sicily's nobility. One swift bullet for each man would have ended the idiotic small talk and then, by hell, decisions would be made. However, since the Don had become *civilized*, he had been sentenced to suffer the delays and compromises to which all civilized men were committed.

By design rather than choice the Don was quiet, attentive, soft-spoken, and restrained in the face of dangers, to the point of being impervious. He was ordinary of face, with no outstanding facial characteristics to distinguish him from most white-haired men in their sixties, and could walk the street unrecognized as the redoubtable *capomafia* of Sicily. Unrecognized, that is, until he removed his dark tinted sun glasses and the people saw his eyes; black burning fireballs, dilated and power-saturated, Matteo Barbarossa's were the eyes of Sicily.

He'd been a spectacular-looking man in his youth, with a flaming red beard and coal black hair the color of anthracite, as startling a contrast as it took for this tyrannical barbarian with the glittering jet eyes of Lucifer to terrorize the countryside. Barbarossa had perpetuated a legend of violence that no one, including all the baronial feudalists gathered in this room, had ever forgotten—and which, of course, was tactfully never discussed in his presence. Don Barbarossa's crude, coarse and illiterate peasant's voice had once thundered through the hills and valleys in the stony mountains of Sicily, shaking up the ancient skeletons of his forefathers buried under the substrata of the land. The Don could roar, did so on occasion, but only as a last resort, when he lost all composure at his wit's end.

He was a tough, hard-hitting, shrewd manipulator of men, a born predator, a man who made and broke his own rules, an exponent of Machiavellian politics who ruled absolute. He had but to flicker an eye, and one man, or a hundred men, would die; he had but to cough apologetically and a nation would legislate his slightest desire. A power-saturated glance from him inspired nations to march to his tempo. Because of Don Barbarossa, men had been elevated to great power. Because of him, these same men could be crushed before tasting the fruits of this power. Formidable political giants with the balls of a bull stood impotent before him when he held them by the testicles and squeezed until his will—not theirs—was done.

Since the Don had become refined in manners and social graces, no hint resembling a threat passed his lips now. There was no need. A reputation, a legend unlike that of any Sicilian before him, stood on its own merit with few daring to contest him.

This implacable power broker moved behind the scenes like a giant, omnipotent shadow. No longer the ignorant peasant of his birth, he grasped many things long ago when Destiny turned a light on in his mind. Stumbling about in the darkness of life was not a role to be played by this chosen son of Destiny. Yet, with all he'd accomplished, the Don was not replete. Something, he felt, was lacking in these winter years of his life.

Don Matteo Barbarossa, who had maimed, killed and murdered in a bloody path of violence all the way to the top of the political totem pole, had no doubt sired many a bastard in his day—none of whom ever came forward to claim kinship. His procreative powers, as an indifferent spouse in a marriage of convenience to a woman he could scarcely tolerate, had brought forth three issues—all daughters—for whom he'd contracted excellent marriages and who now lived many miles in the north with husbands of refinement and social prestige.

This widower of nearly eighteen years had sought no other companionship. Except for the torrid love affair he maintained with power, his *inamorata* was Sicily. Saddened by the fact there was no son of his seed to whom he could leave a legacy of omniscience and power, no one to carry on his teachings or further his powerful acquisitions Don

Barbarossa was satisfied knowing he was the only man of his kind, that Sicily's history would document him as such. He invested in several proteges periodically, out of a need to promote and extend his own ego.

So on this afternoon, early in February, at this gathering of the Palermo Grand Council, a group of formidable politicians selected by the Allies upon the recommendation of their advisor, Don Barbarossa, to restore some semblance of governing order in the chaos of war, it became evident the men were bent on discussing a subject alien to Grand Council business, one hot on the lips of nearly every Sicilian on the island—Salvatore. Much to his consternation and annoyance, he permitted the tiresome chatter, only because this was the *civilized* way.

He indulged this coterie of dignified nobles and politicians, knowing well in advance that his word would be adhered to in the end. *Santo Dio!* He detested these time-consuming moments. Valuable time could be better spent attending to matters of consequence. However, if the Don had learned anything during his twenty years of impotence under fascist rule, he had learned patience. Twenty years of being less than a nothing, during which time he hadn't raised his voice even to a chicken, had taught him that patience was the greatest of all virtues. Twenty times a day, for twenty years, he had practiced patience.

And with considerable patience, he masked a rising frustration in permitting these petulant nobles and ecclesiastic princes to voice their grievances.

"Just who is this impertinant upstart? This—uh—what's his name?" asked Duke Federico de Gioia, a corpulent giant of a man weighing close to three hundred pounds. As one of the wealthiest nobles, the Duke figured prominently to be crowned King in the future Monarchy of Sicily.

"You see?" shrugged the Don, making his point. "This Salvatore is a nothing. He's no one. Outside his province, he's unknown. Why do we waste our time discussing this *capo comedia*?"

"You call him a comedian when he controls the land west of Palermo?" asked Cardinal Rumalino. "A man who controls the people as he wishes?" The red prince expressed mild surprise at what he considered a rash statement. He sipped water from a delicate crystal goblet held between slender, jewelled fingers, while his lime-green cat's eyes moved furtively under a shelf of knotted brows and lingered longingly on the wine enjoyed by the others seated around the oval table.

"He's a champion to his people and he wields frightening and abnormal influence for so young a man," added the Archbishop, blinking his dark eyes. He'd never forgotten that strange brooding man he met in San Giuseppe Jato.

"My dears," sighed the obese Duke de Gioia, "Don Matteo is right. Why waste time discussing an annoying peasant—a mere passing phase who must be tolerated in these troublesome times."

"Exactly. My words exactly," echoed Mayor Cesare Tedesco, an egg-shaped man whose bald pate glistened like the freshly oiled buttocks of a baby, a man who hadn't expressed an original thought all his life.

"I don't agree with you, Excellency," interrupted the Archbishop, addressing himself to the Duke. "Two years of a man's life don't constitute a passing phase. Salvatore has become a god to his people. Never has an outlaw inspired such love and superstitious worship and profound obedience as had this—uh—passing phase."

"Are you personally acquainted with this upstart, Francesco?" asked the Don quietly, glancing at the black prince behind his dark tinted glasses.

"Matteo," interrupted the Cardinal, "it's come to our attention that Salvatore commands legions of men, armed better than the Italian Army, who don't blink an eye unless Salvatore nods." He watched Voltera refill his water glass. "Inspector Semano's been ineffectual in controlling this menace. He and his security police are a laughing stock. . . ."

"No more than the *carabinieri*, Eminence," muttered the Don, tightly.

"We learned Salvatore has formed some alliance with the bandit Barone, from Caltanisetta. Would revolution be a possibility? In a matter of hours they could march in unison, nearly a thousand strong, and take Palermo, if they had a mind," suggested the Cardinal coolly.

"Is this why you insisted we meet before the Grand Council convenes, Eminence?" The Don tried to hide his contempt. What was wrong with these idiots? Didn't they realize the Allies could crush a revolution in less time than it took to speak the word? A wall of reserve veiled his thoughts. The others present, leaned in closer to watch these figureheads lock horns.

The Cardinal shrugged imperceptibly. "The Vatican, concerned with his growing influence against the background of rising anticlerics in Rome who, under the very nose of the Church, promote communism. feels impotent while conquerors patrol our lands. Already in Salvatore's

290

province the vibrations of anticlerical sympathies are heard. We requested this meeting, to present a clearer picture of the nation's pulse," said the Cardinal tactfully. "Strange rumblings have been heard beyond the mountains."

"If that's all that disturbs your Eminence," began the Don, drumming his fingers on the table in a manner that belied his easy voice, "forget it. It's not possible. You think my people are sleeping? I guarantee, if such rumblings were taking place in the belly of Sicily, I'd be the first to know and offer bicarbonate of soda, to remedy the belching. Take my word. Perhaps fantasy dims your judgment in this—eh? No offense meant, Eminence.

"*Annunca*, who the hell gives a fig about this—uh—Salvatore? Few victories hang from his trophy belt. What is it he's called by the foreign press? Robin Hood? A man who steals from the rich and gives to the poor? Hah! If this is his story—why do you permit acid to spill into your bellies? Only a demented man would pursue such folly in our lands. I should know, eh?".

The Don paused dramatically. "Have we finished with this pesky, insignificant fly? Shall we progress to more important business? Or must I take measures to destroy the honey pot? Crush the house to kill the fly? Is that what you'd have me do?"

Within this melting pot of impatient ambitions, steeped knee-deep in political intrigues, every man seated at this austere gathering harbored secret, personal aspirations. Sketching grand designs of enormous power, prestige and riches in their imaginations, no matter how corrupt or illicit their involvements might prove, each man held hope for holding offices of high esteem and dominion in the Sicily they all dreamed of owning and controlling.

First among such schemers and undoubtedly the most ambitious was the Don's protegè, Martino Belasci. Smooth, slick and bombastic, this colorful man, glib of tongue, skillfully employed his legal background.

"With your permission, Don Matteo," interrupted Belasci in a well-modulated voice reeking of oratorical pretentiousness. He addressed himself quickly to the Cardinal and asked in respectful tones, "Do you have proof to substantiate such allegations, Eminence?"

"Surely *you* place no stock in such nonsense, Martino," asked the Don.

Belasci shrugged slightly; his aquamarine eyes were fixed on the red prince, whom he saw nod to the black prince. On cue Archbishop Voltera recited as if by rote:

"In 1943, Alessandro Salvatore, known as Tori to his

men and people, released over seven hundred prisoners from jails surrounding Montegatta. In 1944, that figure doubled. He burned prison records. Put the *carabinieri* out of commission. Recently, it's learned, he gives himself airs of omnipotence. He grants pardons! He places himself above the law, as if none exists. Don't you call this setting a precedent? What if this idea catches hold and spreads across the land? What will we do, then?"

"Are you really concerned about this nonsense, Eminence?" asked the Don, directing his attention only to the Cardinal.

"My concern is not the issue, Matteo," replied the Cardinal with dignified patience. These Allies are a strange breed of men, who turn Italy into a land of dubious intrigue. The Papacy grows uneasy. If the Vatican is concerned enough to make inquiry they must know something. Would that worry you?"

"Eminence, Don Barbarossa worries over nothing. *Pero*—on this desk are vital issues to be settled before we meet with the American *Colonello* Modica. The end of our long negotiations; the control of Sicily is at hand. Only because I, Matteo Barbarossa, have worked at great length, with much fatigue, for the past two years, against all odds and with much fervor, under enormous pressures, is it possible to navigate this crazy ship. Need I tell you what's at stake? We must play our chosen roles with great artistry— in perfect tune with one another, in full accord. *Capeeshi?*" Aghast at their shortsightedness, the Don puffed with exasperation, "And you giants sit there stewing over a mere *contadino* whose life can be erased at the nod of my head. I do not understand such thinking." He clucked his tongue impatiently, as if to chastise a child.

Martino Belasci shrugged skeptically. "You must admit, Salvatore has succeeded in doing for his people what the government's failed to do. He's kept them well-fed and alive. I hear crime in his province has vastly decreased since he eliminated all *carabinieri* from his province."

"Don't tell me you've heard of this punk as far as Rome?" snorted the Don glancing at the sleek, well-polished politician seated next to him.

"The papers write of nothing else. Even the Communists champion him. I hope this isn't an ominous prediction, Matteo." Belasci's handsome face grew taut and grim. "Of late I can't open a newspaper without the image of Salvatore staring out at me." He leaned in closer to the Don and spoke in hushed tones. "Tell me, Matteo, what's really going on with this audacious renegade? What a Sicilian—

eh?" He selected a choice cigar from the humidor extended him by the Don. He sniffed it appreciatively, then unwrapped the tinfoil, savoring it each step of the way.

"Believe me when I tell you, he's a nothing," whispered the Don. "A nothing! Outside his province he's unimportant except to these *cafone!*" he glanced dourly at the others. "For some reason our associates are impressed with him, like obstinate children awed by a new toy."

Belasci lit his cigar as clouds of blue-white smoke spiralled over head and drifted towards an open window. "Rome is outside his province, and we've heard of nothing else but Salvatore, Salvatore, for months." He clicked shut his lighter.

"Propaganda, my dear Martino. You should know how that works."

Belasci, presently employed in the Office of Propaganda, smiled knowingly and, turning his head towards the Archbishop, he listened intently as that wiry, energetic and compulsive talker spoke.

"If Salvatore succeeds where the government has failed, shouldn't the government intervene to set the score straight, before this brigand's worth increases far more in the eyes of his people, to the point where he can do no wrong?"

"An excellent point, Francesco. An excellent point," said Belasci drawing on his cigar. "Unfortunately at this time I must ask—*what* government? We are still in utter chaos in Rome. Ferrucio Parri's government recently formed the National Liberation Committee from a coalition of all parties. *Pero*—without peace settlements on matters such as frontiers and reparations and the status of the colonies, his government will become a little more than a stopgap regime. Parri is unable to grapple with the economic, social, and political problems that beseige him daily. Truly, I don't envy his task. Poor fool! Wrong timing will do him in."

Don Matteo took his cue. He placed his cigar in the ashtray and leaned back in his chair, leveled his eyes on them. "Of *course* the Parri government won't last! Listen—I'll try to explain. Right now, we are small fish, grabbing for a few crumbs. But they are *our* crumbs, *amici. Our* crumbs! Not crumbs the Allies toss up out of kindness and respect for our cause. These are crumbs I've had the balls to take. Crumbs for which I ingratiated myself, for which I even risked my life to grab and cling to. From these crumbs will come the land, the power, and the riches that spring from our beloved Sicily—and she will be ours. Bought by my blood, sweat and brains," said the Don, without the slightest hint of modesty or apology. "And your cooperation of course," he added.

They recognized the bitter truth. No one contested the Don's words. He winked slyly, with the confidence of one possessed with an enormous secret, and stated their position firmly and with a tone of finality. "For the present we shall keep the people happy playing with their toy hero. This—uh—Salvatore will content them with his vainglorious escapades, while we complete our business and victory is secure in our pockets.

"Once we succeed in forming a separate Sicily with full autonomy and the Monarchy of Sicily is firm with the Duke De Gioia as king, and when finally the premiership of Italy is handed to Martino Belasci, this Salvatore can be crushed. Meanwhile he serves an excellent purpose by diverting the interest focused upon us."

Unmindful of his rumpled trousers or the ill-fitting suit jacket he was forced to wear during these *civilized* affairs, Don Matteo rose to his feet with his wine goblet clutched firmly in his hand. "To the Monarchy of Sicily," he toasted, hoping to end the talk of Salvatore.

"To the Monarchy of Sicily," came the echoes, one at a time, as they rose to their feet to drink.

The room swelled with a comforting silence. Then, like a plague, talk resumed.

"They say Salvatore has an arsenal of weapons double what the Italians used in the war," reflected Mayor Tedesco, a real Humpty Dumpty of a man.

"Yes," agreed Archbishop Voltera nodding. "That's confirmed in my report."

"*Managghia!*" exploded Don Matteo. "It appears you are bent on boiling this issue! What is it? Is there some personal grievance that needs a quick solution?" he asked the Archbishop.

"Double the arsenal of what Italians used in the war doesn't say much," interrupted Belasci. "*Pero*—if you suggested double what the Nazis used. . . ." Belasci winked playfully at the Archbishop, who saw no humor in his facetiousness.

The Cardinal, fond of his assistant, recognized the den of foxes closing in on the rabbit. He gave the black prince the business with his cat's eyes. Voltera, his face tinged in color, sat back in silent submission.

None of this interplay was missed either by Don Barbarossa or Martino Belasci. More curious than cautious, Belasci persisted, unabashed. "On the contrarly, Eminence.

If Francesco has become fanatical over this *contadino*, Salvatore, and has something to report, let him do so. If, at some future time, problems evolve over this peasant, Francesco will have every right to tell us, You wouldn't permit me to speak when I tried to warn you. . . ."

Voltera asked himself why he bothered with these smug, arrogant, power-crazed men. Were it not for the confidence inspired by Cardinal Rumalino, he'd tell them all to become guests of Satan, where they were certain to fit into the design of things.

Don Barbarossa fumed inwardly and wondered why Martino persisted in this *tarantella* of controversy. He twirled a red and gold cigar band aimlessly around one finger, and told himself there'd better be a good reason for such idiocy.

"Don't be disturbed, Francesco," soothed Belasci with purring tones, at the black prince's silence.

"For now, Salvatore may be an annoying fly in the honey pot, but, in truth I share Don Matteo's feelings. This peasant and his activities are nothing compared to the issues at stake before the Grand Council. We're involved in matters far greater than the life of any one man, an outlaw at that. Within our grasp is the future fate of Sicily—and of ourselves, too. It's essential we remain diligent and do the right thing. Don Matteo's reasoning is not only intelligent, as usual, but wise. Let the people be content with their toy. We can take their pleasures from them—*after* we're in control."

Archbishop Voltera turned livid. As usual this compulsive talker couldn't resist the opportunity to assert himself. "Of course, you're right," he said silkily. "I keep forgetting that Jesus Christ was never looked upon as a prophet in his own land. He was merely the lowly son of a poor carpenter. The Sadducces and Pharisees were too busy in more important matters of the government to concern themselves with the brazen upstart son of a mere handyman's son." His voice dripped sarcasm.

"Francesco!" reprimanded the Cardinal. "Surely you don't equate our Lord Jesus Christ with this—uh—this Salvatore!"

Voltera made a disorganized gesture. "Forgive me, Eminence. The plots are so similar, I get carried away."

Mayor Tedesco poured garnet Valpolicella over crushed ice, and reflected. "Inspector Semano has offered rewards in these hard times that would have tempted the Angel Gabriel to betray Salvatore. This fact alone instills him with a sense of immortality."

"Such audacity," muttered the Duke de Gioia, fingering his gold watch fob in the manner of a coffee-house dandy.

"It's my understanding that the Chief Inspector came to some understanding with this brigand," spoke up Prince Giorgio Oliatta, a handsome, grey at the temple, *avant-garde* progressive who'd been silent and reflective for the most part. Dressed impeccably in a dove-grey flannel suit, he fingered his waxed moustache. "What was it—oh yes, 'The security police will not bother' Salvatore if Salvatore permits them to go about their other business."

With the exception of Don Barbarossa, the room's occupants suppressed smiles. The Don's patience had thinned considerably, to the point of losing his patience.

"If anyone says Salvatore to me once again I shall dismiss this council! *Porco Dio*! Enough is enough! By the tainted whores of Satan!" He waved an apologetic hand at the Cardinal and flushed with annoyance he subdued his anger. "Forgive such disrespectful words, Eminence. But, I refuse to permit this farce to continue. Why do we waste valuable time discussing this sheepherder?" He drew a bead on the gathering and addressed himself to them. "Once and for all time, understand that *nothing* happens in Sicily without my sanction or approval. *Capeeshi?*"

They should have known better than to be concerned, each man there told himself after the Don's outburst. In truth, the Don was right. Nothing *did* go on without his knowledge and permission. The rudest awakening came to Archbishop Voltera who, up until that moment, hadn't known the true identity of Sicily's real ruler. Now he knew. Why hadn't the Cardinal seen fit to explain such matters? he wondered.

In a more civil tone, Don Barbarossa continued. "Who can tell? in time we may need Salvatore and his rebel army. I'm watching . . . I'm watching, you can be sure. Nothing is settled yet with the Allies, nothing." The Don wanted to say—and of course didn't—that if he were to wait for *this* nest of capons to fertilize the eggs nothing would get done. He glanced at his watch, noting the time, and, slipping it into his pocket, he pushed his tinted glasses into place.

"In a few moments we convene with *Colonnello* Modica. Are we agreed on the points to stress? Complete separation from Italy. Full autonomy. We can't risk allowing another nation to rule us and pass new land reforms. His Eminence is correct about the growing threat of communism spreading like a pox in the north." He paused, sipped his wine and continued with the cunning of a fox. "In the

East, our people toss kindling on the fires of insurrection in a rebellion of loyalists opposing nationalism under Italy's skirts. Oh, don't concern yourselves yet. Everything is under the control of experts in such matters. The man, Canepa, is not my choice, you understand. You all chose him, you and the Allies. Just remember my admonishments regarding this man, eh? *Annuncia*, for now we sit, we wait, we watch like the great bird circling overhead watching a stray baby lamb. When the time is right—" *Wham*! He struck the table a hard blow with his fist "—Sicily will be ours!"

Twelve startled heads, including Martino Belasci's, shot up and stared inquisitively at their redoubtable leader. The Don was up to something. What? He leaned in closer, in a movement noticed by the rest. They leaned forward in their seats, eyes on the Don. Enjoying the attention, the Don continued.

"Massive spread of communism distresses our Allied friends *more* than it annoys us. *More*, in recent days," The Don paused, searched their faces, surprised they didn't pick up on the point he made. "You don't see eh? If Italy goes communist, America will be forced to support Sicily's separation from Italy, if only to keep an ally in the Mediterranean. You see what a big stick Sicily carries? A real weapon is in our hands."

Belasci uttered a low, knowing gasp. *"Ahhhhh."* Profound respect and admiration shone in his bright blue eyes. Lucky was the day when destiny had brought him to Don Barbarossa's attention, he told himself.

Needless to say the Don's words weren't lost on the others. Recognizing as they did the far-reaching power they would soon wield, they now let visions of personal involvements and future rewards transport them to another world of dreams, in which they could envision themselves a sovereign power, a new autonomous nation.

This Sicily had been Matteo Barbarossa's dream. By his own hand he'd carved and shaped its future and soon, through means of a supreme ego and sheer political genius, Sicily would become his monument for all eternity. These feudalists were certain to share in the power and its glory and all the profits. *Well, Well,* they told themselves. This Sicilian mongoose has gone and done it! *Mizzica!* Who would have believed it possible?

Twenty years stuck back in the womb of obscurity had sharpened his wits, heightened his ambitions and recharged him with a greater power than they had imagined. *Va bene*, Don Barbarossa! *Viva Sicilia! Viva Don Matteo! Managghia!* He was beyond belief!

Salvatore and his band of brigands, immediately expunged from mind, dwindled and shrank in importance in a wave of omnipotence that permeated the room and occupied the minds of each man on the Palermo Council. Don Matteo smiled internally as he watched their reactions.

The Don rose to his feet and waved them on. "Go into the Chambers ahead of me. Explain to *Colonnello* Modica that Don Barbarossa will arrive in five minutes."

"Is there anything wrong, Matteo?" asked Belasci solicitous of the Don, remaining behind after the others exited the sumptuous suite.

"Why is it so difficult to find intelligence among the nobility—eh, Martino?" asked the Don, sighing. "Such children. Always used to having things handed to them. Not one among them possesses an ounce of brains."

"Because they've not had to scratch for their bread, the dust collected in their minds has dulled their perception. Who knows?" Belasci shrugged, anxious to catch up with Prance Oliatta. "I'll see you downstairs, Don Matteo."

The Don nodded and waved him on. Alone, he gazed about the penthouse suite, nodding to himself as if to convince himself of his worth. For his monumental contribution to the Allied War effort, Don Barbarossa had been appointed official advisor to AMGOT—Allied Military Government of Occupied Territories. No one, not even the American gangster Vito Genovese who'd backed Mussolini with his American racket dollars until it became obvious Il Duce was drowning in his own semen, could match the honors bestowed upon the Don by the Allied High Command. Nick Gentile, a deported gangster who had professed loyalty to King Victor Emmanuel, had never reached the heights to which the Don had been elevated in postwar Sicily.

There was more. In the days before fascism, Don Matteo had been the most powerful feudal overlord and *capomafia* in Sicily, whose mighty power reached across oceans and made itself known. Mussolini's war on the Mafia and the subsequent holocaust orchestrated by his hatchet man Cesare Mori, brought about expert maneuvers on the part of the *capomafia*.

Secretly he'd imprisoned himself in Palermo's Ucciardone Prison, a Mafia stronghold. One day, a few years later, no one the wiser, he disappeared, his criminal file tucked under his arm. If you had viewed the situation through the eyes of government officials who searched in vain for him, you'd have thought no such man as Don Matteo Barbarossa ever existed.

Twenty years later, in paving the way for a successful Occupation for the Allies, the Mafia was reborn. Don Barbarossa was to enjoy a power greater than any he had imagined in those hard years of struggle up the ladder of the Mafia heriarchy. Historians, analyzing the man and these circumstances, would swear Destiny had brought about the Second World War simply for the convenience of this super power broker. As advisor to AMGOT, he recommended, for putting into key positions as Mayors in all principal cities and villages in Sicily, men whom he guaranteed to be antifascist; these were favorably accepted by the Allies. Probably the only truthful statement he had ever uttered was when he faced his Allied benefactors, American and British top brass officials, in an eyeball confrontation and passionately declared, "I swear by God and on the dead bodies of all those loyal Sicilians sacrificed in this ungodly and monstrous war, that the names of the men I submitted for these important political posts are all antifascists! No one could be more anti-Mussolini than these men and myself, who suffered grave injustices under fascism."

"We believe you. We believe you," admitted the Allied Officials, noting the prison pallor on the faces of those who stood humbly before them on that fateful day. Their belief was so profound, they bestowed limitless powers on this power broker.

Through the efforts of an intricate underground network of Mafia spies whose talents had been perfected over the many past years into a slick, well oiled machinery, Don Barbarossa had learned almost immediately of Salvatore and his activities.

Bandits abounded in Sicily, prior to and during World War II in greater quantities than in Sicily's history. Under normal circumstances Don Barbarossa might have controlled these mushrooming hordes, but not now. Not when he might need them. . . . Not since visions of a new Sicily took priority in the Don's mind. He couldn't be bothered with such petty offenders who'd never reach the glory of his Mazzarino days.

Rumors of Salvatore's philanthropy hardly fazed him. His credo was, take care of *numero uno*, first. He reasoned that while this idiot, who hadn't the sense to line his own coffers, first spent time feeding a thankless, worthless people in his province, he, Don Barbarossa was involving himself in the creation of an empire. It was purely a matter of priorities. Which came first? Salvatore's prominence diminished in the Don's mind.

A soft knock at the door brought the *capomafia* out of his reverie. "Matteo?" Belasci opened the door, intruded in his privacy, concerned with his well being. "Are you all right? Is something wrong? Colonel Modica awaits your presence."

Don Matteo sipped the remainder of his wine, rose to his feet and nodded. "I'm fine, *excellency*. I'm coming."

Martino Belasci faltered. Puzzled, he leveled his eyes on the Don. "*Excellency*? Why do you call me *Excellency*?" Confusion scrawled on his face.

"Didn't I mention it? Hummmm," said the Don nonchalantly tapping his forehead. "Confirmation of your appointment as Minister of the Interior arrived this morning." He spoke as if it were an everyday occurrence. "You'll be in the cabinet of the new Premier when he assumes office. Well, well, come along, *Excellency*. Let's not erase the smile from *Colonnello* Modica's face, yet."

Astonishment on Belasci's face was indescribable. Jesus Christ! He trembled at the prospect. In a few years the nation would be his! Martino Belasci! All this at the hands of this super powered *mafioso* who stood before, him looking like a simple *contadino* himself. *Managghia!*

Archbishop Voltera burned with indignation throughout the Council meeting. He hardly heard the words being spoken, either by the American Colonel Stefano Modica or by the redoubtable Don Barbarossa.

He glanced at the others, felt an extravagant desire to shake them and awaken them to the vigorous rumblings echoing from the hills of Montegatta, where, from the bowels of the earth, came emanations proclaiming the coming of their savior Salvatore. What supercilious conceit these foolish men contained within their addlepated brains!

Their actions proved them foolhardy and immune to storm warnings. They were like cocky, confident sailors, foolish enough to think they could outsmart Poseidon, without knowing first his contradictory and unpredictable nature. Very well, he told himself, let them drown in the juices of their own masturbations.

Right now, in those connecting grottos of the honeycombed, golden mountains Salvatore claimed as his own, there must be cauldrons of intrigue boiling, with Salvatore himself stirring the brew, thought Archbishop Voltera. *God! Good God!* What he would give to make himself the size of a fly so he could watch and listen and know what they were plotting. When he found himself praying that Salvatore would as usual emerge victorious, he felt uncomfortable, like a traitor. He glanced anxiously about at that moment, wondering if anyone had read his thoughts.

At that moment, he caught Don Barbarossa's glance and shuddered inwardly. He swore in that instant, the Don's eyes had focused on his thoughts and read them clearly. ·

CHAPTER 23

The very man whose name was bouncing off the tongues of Palermo's most formidable politicians was riding swiftly towards the Grotto d'Oro high above the golden mountains. Tori sat taller in his saddle than did his companions, Vincenzo de Montana and the Scoletti brothers. He rode with a quiet pride, for something unmistakably primitive was demonstrated as horse and rider fused into one unbroken rhythm. Tori was enroute to meet the rest of his men, and now, having crossed the shimmering topaz wheat fields in the plains of Partenico, they galloped up the twisting road towards the summit, turning off the road at a certain point where they slowed down to a canter in their approach to the grotto.

Overhead and behind them a glittering of mirrors flashed in a cross ray of blinding lights across azure skies, signalling their approach. Shepherds scattered here and there on the grazing lands, only a few in that vast, silent army of many in Tori's employ, sounded ox horns and waved excitedly to him in passing. There were more armed sentries standing like lonely sentinels on the ledge above the grotto, waving their rifles overhead in greeting. Santino Siragusa left the grotto to run down an incline to greet the approaching riders. A few men appeared from the lower meadow to take their lathered horses, and, when the riders dismounted, steered the animals to water troughs.

Vincenzo ambled towards his cousin Tori, slapping him

301

on the back affectionately, pleased at the outcome of their mission.

"How did it go?" asked Santino.

"How do you think it went?" asked Vincenzo, strutting to the nearby water cistern to slake his thirst and wash down the dry dust collected in his parched throat after the long ride. "If you hear the loud croaking bellowing through these mountains, you can bet your ass it'll be that crocodile, Chief Inspector Semano, when he learns the outcome of Tori's meeting with Director Umberto Rocca, today."

"You mean," interrupted Miguel Scoletti, jiggling his Adam's apple effectively, "He'll *maaaaaaahhhhh* like a judas goat!"

Arturo laughed like hell, slapping his thighs. "That's more like it. A judas goat. That's what that sonofobitch was—a judas goat! He thought he had you, eh, Tori?"

"You can bet that jackass Director Rocca will never pull another stunt like that," laughed Vincenzo, stimulated by his memory. "*Managghia*, you should have seen Tori. He is something else, *amici*. Something else." As he led the others back into the grotto, Tori laughed tolerantly at his cousin's generous praise and walked towards Santino's makeshift desk in the grotto to glance through the accumulations of bulletins and messages.

Once Tori had laughed with gay and infectious humor; now he smiled occasionally, and then with a sort of impatience. These past two years had taken their toll on him. He was in the prime of his manhood now, not quite 23 years old, and he'd matured into the handsome Apollo of his Greek ancestors with the physical beauty of Michelangelo's *David*. His forehead was broad and high, his nose straight with just enough of a curve to make him exceedingly handsome. His full lips, turned up at the corners, were set into a firm jaw line. His broad arms and upper arms bulged muscularly through his olive drab pinwale corduroy jacket and his thighs under the slim breeches bore an unmistakable *maschiezzo* about him. He stood in a nonchalant but power-packed pose, his thumbs hooked securely into his belt, his hands never far away from the holster encasing his fabled Belgian-made Browning. His mirror-polished boots at the moment tapped an impatient staccato against the flat stones of the earthen-floored cave as he glanced through the collection of memos—none being of great importance.

Tori's large velvety eyes, more cautious of late, were careful and cynical. He was a man in every sense of the word, always in command of emotions; rarely losing his temper. He believed with conviction that a man unable to control himself was a nothing, just as he believed that a man who boasted of his virility was without loins.

As Vincenzo related to the eager men the course of events that took place that morning, Tori sat on the edge of the desk to listen.

"Listen—will you tell us what happened?" asked Fidelio Genovese. "Or must we wait until the wheat is harvested before we taste the bread?"

"All right. All right," said Vincenzo, puffing expansively on a cigar. "Yesterday two thousand workers were dismissed without reason from Prince Oliatta's lands. *Alora*, this morning two hundred of these men arrived at Tori's house, pleading for his help. *Va bene*, we rode to the Prince's estates to find Director Rocca in his office. A more surprised man couldn't have existed. He was a pleasant enough chap, and when Tori asked politely, after introducing himself, what had happened, the bloke told us the story right off. 'Look,' he tells us. 'I want no trouble, not for the Prince or myself. But, what am I to do when Chief Inspector Semano orders me to cancel the work contracts with your people, eh? I was ordered to starve Salvatore and his people off and out of those infernal mountains that offer him sanctuary.'

"*Allora*, then he tells us that if he didn't cooperate with the police inspector, things would go rough on him. 'And believe me, that porcupine throws plenty of quills,' he told us. Semano demanded his cooperation, and the fool agreed to go along with him."

Vincenzo grinned wildly. "Then what do you think our *capitano* did, eh? I'll tell you," he said with pure delight and a flair for storytelling. "Now picture this, this fat slob seated at his desk as Tori walks towards him nonchalantly. To begin with, seeing Salvatore in person nearly caused him to wet his pants. . . ." Vincenzo laughed as the others joined in. "*Allora*, then, Tori took out his Browning and politely and quite easily shoved it into Rocca's ribs until his fat shaking belly did a dance with nervousness. Then in a soft voice to soothe a baby he said, 'With your permission, *Signore Direttore*, there are many moral reasons why I could insist that you alter your decision and resume business relations with my people. However, time, unfortunately, doesn't permit our entering into dialogue, so I'll limit myself to the fourteen solid arguments contained in this gun. Are we in accord?' "

A mixed reaction of astonishment, pride and gay laughter echoed through the grotto. Tori's men grinned with pleasure; their eyes twinkled in amusement and they filled with a firece pride for their chief. They glanced at him, nodding in approval as if they had anticipated victory. Hadn't he always uncannily been victorious?

Tori flushed with a modest self-consciousness and shook his head tolerantly at the overblown antics of Vincenzo. Subconsciously, his hand slipped under his open jacket to pat the holster of the Belgian Browning.

Vincenzo's voice cut through his thoughts. "The director's belly shook like jelly. His beady eyes never left the gun in his gut, and sweat rolled off him like the hot piss of a dog. He agreed to revoke the order immediately. 'You think I'm crazy to go against the word of Salvatore?' He promised to honor the original work contracts instantly. *Mah*—" interjected Vincenzo, with appropriate hand gestures. "You should have seen that pig's face when Tori said, 'No, *direttore*, the original contracts shall not be honored. It now becomes necessary for you to increase their compensation to allow for time lost. Let's say by one third more than that originally agreed upon. *Va bene?*' What could the old bastard do, but agree?"

Delighted, Tori's men chuckled and voiced their approval at his astuteness.

"How's that for swift justice?" asked Vincenzo.

"It beats legislation," retorted Santino Siragusa, his eyes twinkling in amusement.

Tori acknowledged Santino's compliment and moved outside the grotto. Earlier he'd been disheartened when so many peasants had gathered at his house with their problems. Having listened to their laments, he had instructed them to go home and eat a hearty dinner and leave the rest to him. The men had cheered and applauded him as smiles formed on their fearful and hard-lined faces. They knew Salvatore's promises weren't empty. His word to them was like iron—like steel—as strong as God's.

Demonio! Tori had brooded for a long while after that. No matter how difficult he'd made it for his enemies to harass his people, they kept up the farce, which only made matters worse. Filling his life with petty complications, it succeeded in only taking up his time, preventing him from going on to more important work. This act, however wasn't a petty one. It was the first time his people had been directly targeted for wrath and to Tori this became a point of concern.

Whose deviltry had planned so crafty a move? If suspicion lurked behind Tori's smoldering eyes, it wasn't without foundation. His distrust of men who spun empty promises like intriguing spiders had become strong in him. It was enough to cause him to lose faith in all mankind. Tori, however hadn't reached that plateau of immunity, yet. He'd learned to deal with each treachery, one at a time, as he'd done on this day.

Inwardly he felt contented at the outcome of this confrontation; a deep, glowing inner satisfaction surged through him for the first time in two years. He'd finally done something significant for his people. He wasn't simply putting bread on their tables, as he'd done in the past. Today he'd succeeded in buttering that bread. His action today had given them hope for the future.

Santo Dio, it had taken two years of his life to accomplish a feat that now took but a few moments to put into operation. Now, the mere mention of his name permitted bargaining in the right direction; with a little help, of course, from his trusted Browning. It was times like these, that his heart took wings. Perhaps with willingness, arms, and the force of justice behind him, Salvatore might stir this drowsing giant, Sicily, awake to take its true place in the world.

Tori moved out along the ledge of the cliff, gazing out at the magnificent panorama. In his eyes was a vast shadow. By now there should have been some word, he told himself, on another matter, quite vital to him and his companions. He retraced his steps past the grotto's entrance to where his horse grazed contentedly and, swinging to his saddle, he wheeled the beast around and rode swiftly to a point closer to the summit, absorbed in thought. Seeing him take off, Vincenzo followed suit. Wherever Tori went, his cousin was right alongside him.

Watching them ride off together, Santino grew thoughtful. Between those two was a vast difference, he concluded. Vincenzo, the eldest of Tori's fraternal aunt, bore only a superficial resemblance to his first cousin. The marked difference between these two grew more distinct each day. Vincenzo's mentality, however complex and intelligent, was superficial compared to the labyrinthian compulsions which were to propel Salvatore to soar to fantastic heights and rise above his fellow man. More at home on the ocean floor of intrigue and negotiations, Vincenzo was totally unencumbered by the plaguing conscience, the morals and ethics which periodically handicapped Salvatore. Having lived by his wits for several years, Vincenzo had learned well what benefits lurked behind a facade of smiles. He was a natural born actor, who with the *degage* of a moth turning into a butterfly could adjust easily to quickly evolving circumstances.

Where Salvatore had become the King of Montegatta to his people—the strategist, the greatest exponent of guerrilla warfare in history, their prince of justice, and for a time their Messiah—Vincenzo, the administrator of Tori's planning, became the facile politician, the temporal handler of internal complaints within the organization—and their treasurer. Vincenzo was darker-skinned, more exotic in appearance, and wore his neatly-brushed, curly black hair off his face like a lion's mane. His nose was straight and well-formed; his lips, full and sensual like a woman's, were covered by a thick moustache. Two years of good living had erased the former prison pallor. Now, he stood tall and straight and strutted about with unmistakable Sicilian *maschiezzo*. He was addicted to well-tailored clothing and ostentatious gold jewelry, and when not on duty he dressed impeccably. He and Marco Genovese were nicknamed 'movie stars' by the others.

Vincenzo laughed a great deal, and was more prone to view the world through rose-colored glasses. The attitude wasn't necessarily inborn; rather, it was one he'd adopted after his stint in prison and embellished by the self importance he'd engendered as Tori's co-captain. Things for Vincenzo couldn't have been better, except for the recurring ailment of a tubercular lung which at times knocked him flat on his back, into a period of insensibility and pain.

Between Salvatore and Vincenzo, there was a fraternal closeness, a bond renewed with fresh loyalties, which no one or nothing could tear asunder. Vincenzo never failed to humor Tori, who always laughed the hardest and loudest at his clownish capers and humorous antics.

All these revelations, Santino Siragusa had duly noted and documented in his History of the Bandits, which was growing to sizeable proportions over these past two years. His thoughts were interrupted by the sound of Fidelio's voice as the man approached him on the bluff.

"Well, Santino, what do you think, *padre?*" asked Fidelio.

"About what?"

"About what? About us, of course. See that bull in the pasture below us? I tell you that bull has more excitement than we do, anymore," muttered Genovese, gazing down on the rocky slopes at the focal point of his remark.

Santino laughed. "You don't like living the life of a

gentlemen anymore? Wasn't it you who said all he wanted to do was live in his house like decent folk?"

Fidelio turned to gaze into Santino's eyes as he twirled a straw shaft between his lips. He tried to see behind Santino's tinted glasses. "Look, *padre*, there's a whisper in the wind. Talk of a big revolution. Things are happening in Sicily and I feel we should be a part of it. We should all participate before we're castrated, *capeeshi?* How much longer can this existence remain tranquil for us? Something is ready to bust wide open, and I, for one, prefer being the propeller rather than the propelled."

"Tori knows what he's doing," insisted Santino. "He'll be back soon. Talk with him. Ask him. He'll tell you straight." He ran his fingers through a mass of curly brown hair that stuck out like untied mattress springs, and began to walk back to the Grotto Persephone, skirting past the spiny thistles planted at the mouth of the cave to deceive interlopers. Fidelio, not to be dissuaded, fell into step alongside of the former Jesuit.

"There's talk of insurrection," he blurted.

"Yes, I know."

"Will Tori drag us into it?"

"Ask Tori."

"But he must tell you something. You're historian to Tori."

"Listen," retorted Santino impatiently. "In two years when has he confided in any of us? He's brought us through terrible times, so why should we change his ways?" Santino lit his pipe, drawing on it deeply. He hated questions for which there were no immediate answers.

"He's obsessed with pardon, *padre*, and that should be all our business. You think when this mazurka of war ends, the central government in Rome will thank us for all we've done? Hah! Fat chance! They'll throw us into jail or shoot us. I'm for taking all we can, while we can, and skipping the country with our necks intact. Brazil—perhaps. We could live like kings."

Tori has something else in mind," said Santino tersely. "Pardons for all, in addition to several hundreds of acres for each man. Then we can live in our own country, on our lands, with our own kind of people. It's not as far-fetched as you might think, Fidelio."

"You know something, *padre?* You're crazy. Just like Tori. You're both *pazzi*—crazy out of your heads! The world that Tori dreams up doesn't exist," exclaimed Genovese, fully exasperated. "But since I'm here, I'll have to stick around to prove you both wrong." He wagged his finger at Santino and entered the grotto to join his companions, who were just beginning a card game.

The grotto no longer looked homey or lived in. It was merely a place of convenience now. In two years little had changed. The men had grown more civilized. They no longer lived in the wilderness without a roof over their heads like ferocious animals. The headhunting expeditions once engaged in by the *carabinieri* no longer affected them, nor did the thought of getting shot intimidate the men. Salvatore had changed all that. Now, the men ate well and fed their families and kept them alive and clothed. They no longer dreaded awakening to each dawn with the fear they might be dead by nightfall. They drank a lot, laughed too much, fornicated like rabbits in heat, and otherwise led complacent lives, while the grinding gears of Rome's central government slowed down for retooling during war time and floundered amid the complexities of restoring law and order throughout a war-torn nation.

You'd think they'd be satisfied, reflected Santino. But no, the men grew more restless each day. A potpourri of intrigue was brewing erratically in Sicily's political arena. Conditions changed so swiftly, in the confusion of war, that one couldn't be certain of the day-to-day reports they received. Santino was certain that Tori planned something. But—what? Tori, always a private person, permitted no one to become privy to his thoughts—not even Vincenzo, who knew him best, knew what went on inside his head. They'd have to wait until Tori made up his mind before they learned his plans.

Santino began to make entries into his notebook behind the makeshift desk, as the voices of the men chattered incessantly. The feverish excitement of those early days, filled with uncertainties, when they had matched wits with their enemies had leveled off into a dull routine of boredom, creating an incurable itch in these young men, an itch relieved only by continuous story-telling, and this they did in colorful profusion of animated hand gestures and a body language all their own.

Santino glanced at his watch. Tori should have been back by now. The voices of the others interrupted his thoughts.

"You tell me how he does it—Tori never sleeps," said Fidelio.

"With what he has on his mind, would you?" muttered Lamanita, guzzling his wine.

"Damn!" muttered Terranova, the hedonist. "How does

308

he do without the warmth of a woman's buttocks? *Marrona!* I'd end my life if denied this pleasure."

"You would," grunted Lamantia. "Women, to you, are like drugs. You think the gates of heaven lies between their thighs. By now, Lothario, you should own all of Neptune's Daughters."

"Goddammit!" shouted Fidelio, pausing in the card game. "No wonder I've been losing every hand. We're missing an ace in the deck." He slammed down the card on the rickety table and began sorting through the cards.

"Speaking of Neptune's Daughters, have I told you what new innovations have been made since the British and Americans soldiers have become *Madama*'s best clients?" asked Terranova rolling his eyes suggestively. "*Madama* Neptune has converted her house into a real League of Nations!"

"League of Nations? Now, what the hell is that? Goddammit! You always come up with something or another. Next you'll tell us she's a Nazi spy!" snapped Fidelio Genovese. "Come on, let's play."

"Spy?" Terranova didn't make the connection. "What the hell has that got to do with sex?"

"Sex? What the hell are you talking about. Listen are we going to play *scoppa* or do we play with ourselves?"

"Go on, Terranova, tell us about the League of Nations," urged Lamantia.

"Yes, yes, tell us," insisted the excited redhead, Pietro Gagliolo.

"It's like this," began Lamantia. "All the rooms are named after a country. Inside each man gets fucked in the manner and customs specialized in each country. *Managghia!*" he howled gleefully sparked by fresh memories. "What a crazy dance-hall! It makes you wonder why you stay in one country when the whole world is waiting to delight a man's senses."

"Is that all? Is that all you can say? You get us all excited. You stop a good card game and you don't tell us the secret pleasures you yourself have experienced?" teased Fidelio, winking his eyes at the others. "*Allora*—tell us. Which country is the best, Terranova?" he asked with aplomb.

The lascivious grin disintegrated from Terranova's face. "*Capeeshi*, not all are pleasure rooms. Not to me, any way. The things some people do for pleasure shames me," he glanced uneasily towards the former priest, unsure of how far he could go in Santino's presence.

"Listen if you're concerned about me, Terranova. Forget it. I've forgotten more than *Madama* Neptune could tempt you hot studs with."

"*Allora*," began Terranova hesitantly. "One room's called Turk Arabia. Here a man can do the job on mares, sheep, goats anything he wants for as long as he wants." He gazed towards Calo Azzarello who sat back smoking with little reaction to all this immature talk. "Sometimes they let the animals do the job on women. Even children."

The men sat forward testily. Copulating with animals was nothing new, but to hear women permitted this activity piqued their interest. The thought of involving children in such games, however, appalled them.

"One room called the Vatican is filled with whores dressed like nuns, men dressed as priests . . . and those with loftier ambitions can even fuck a Pope."

"Very imaginative," snapped Santino dryly. The men laughed.

"Greece contains the homosexuals—younger boys, who sell themselves to the depraved Britishers. *Managghia,* those blokes really ring the cash registers for Greece. Me? I personally like France and Japan, where a man is a real man. Succumbing to the passions aroused in him he can be taken care of like a sultan." He leaned in and whispered in Fidelio's ears. Genovese's eyes lit up in amazement. "*Managghia!* Three women at once? How—how do you do it?"

"I don't have to," replied Terranova kissing his fingertips. "It's heaven, I tell you. Heaven."

Young Pietro Gagliolo, listening with both ears intent on the conversation, stroked the hard lump forming in his crotch. "Can we go there?" he asked his brother Uccidato.

The men laughed uproariously at the lad's excitement. Never mind that they, too, also felt the warmth of the erotic conversation. Across from them, Santino shook his head in mild amusement. Calo Azzarello, the flute-playing shepherd who considered most of the men, especially Terranova, highly immature, poured himself a cup of wine and, picking up his guitar, began to strum a tune, *Marching Son of the Bandits,* written by Athena. His melodious voice filled the grotto and echoed warmly throughout the air: "*It has been told there's a legend of one who comes from the mountains to the sea . . . In the dark of night, in eagle's flight, he fights to set his country free . . . Some call him the bandit, some call him the law; He's a renegade to the enemy, a hero to one and all he loves. He protects the rights of his countrymen. He received his guidance from above. Some call him the bandit . . . some call him the law. . . ."*

Santino entered into his log, this day in February, 1945:

Salvatore's idealistic views have altered considerably in two years. He discusses little with his paladins, never asking, "What shall I do?" He feels that a leader who consults his subordinates is weak, ineffectual, and regarded by others with contempt. He's more than a man to his men. He's like a god, with the power of life and death in his grasp. He's not hesitant to use force or terror in enforcing justice. No one can say of him his word is thin.

Yet in this strength is inner torment and conflict. In quiet meditative moments the youth, Tori, stands in awe of this larger-than-life Salvatore, almost as if his accomplishments had been attained by another—not he. I've heard him ask himself, "Who am I to command so many men? Who am I for the world to suddenly take notice of? More important, how much longer can I keep my men unified? How much longer will they continue to follow me, with the rigid discipline I enforce upon them? How much longer can we live as outlaws?" Those who know him best believe that Salvatore wishes for little else than to settle down, be granted amnesty for his crimes, which he justifies as expedient acts committed in time of war, and continue with his own personal future plans.

The idea of pardon obsesses Salvatore, now. Through the counsel of older, somewhat distinguished men, wealthy nobles who've become enamored of him, and men in whom he places too much confidence at times, he's come to believe that such a pardon can only be achieved politically in these trying times. That if he offers his services to some rising political party, the freedom with honor which he seeks zealously will be inevitable. It's been a period of great frustration for this young man, who begins to resent leading a life unlike the one he'd chosen for himself long ago.

Power, influence and wealth mean very little to Salvatore unless they can be used to help his

311

people. Lately a change has come over him. Gradually, without having spoken a word, he has stopped being an intimate friend to the men and has become their commander. They no longer walk up to him and joke, as they once did in the past. He's become a different man entirely.

Some call him the Bandit . . . Some call him the law. . . .

The next afternoon, February 4, Tori entered the Grotto d'Oro, one of the many caves they used when jockeying about the mountains with such ease.

"I've been looking all over for you," declared Santino. He handed him an envelope bearing the seal of the Duke de Gioia. "This came by special messenger. Our station in life shows some improvement, eh, Tori?"

Salvatore glanced at the seal, raised an eyebrow in playful speculation, and grinned. "The Duke de Gioia, no less?" he walked outside in the dazzling, crisp sunlight and sat propped up against the whorled trunk of an ancient olive tree. Opening the envelope, he read the contents three times, then, without expression, he replaced the letter into its envelope and tucked it into a breast pocket of an American general's uniform he wore. Noting the lateness of the hour on his gold watch, he picked up his binoculars and scanned the countryside.

There was no movement in the far distance—no signals either from Palermo or the Castellammare Valley. Scurrying over the rocks and craggy boulders with the agility of a lizard, he moved to a higher point on the slopes waved to the sentries. Their voices bounced back at him, "No one yet—nothing from across the mountains." Their upraised hands saluted him.

Tori half-heartedly waved back, and came off the rocks slapping his muscular thighs with impatience.

"Any signs of Vincenzo or the others?" asked Santino.

"No. They're long overdue," he replied, trying to suppress his concern.

"They can handle themselves. Don't worry, eh?"

"I should have gone with them. It was my affair," Tori replied cryptically.

"What's with the Duke de Gioia? Why does he contact you?" asked Santino.

"Tonight, at dinner, I'll tell you all."

Santino frowned. "I was planning to go to Palermo. There's talk of the new movement. It seems the Separatists

312

are about to be sanctioned by the USA. I'm interested in learning why."

"The Americans plan to back the Separatists? But, why? Why should they?" It was Tori's turn to frown with puzzlement.

"I intend to find out in Palermo. There's been talk of a communist takeover in Italy. The Americans, gravely upset over this news, would prefer Sicily as an ally if trouble with Russia springs forth."

"Ah." Tori nodded. "That seems reasonable. Listen, before you go, I want you to post a letter for me."

"They want you—eh?" Santino smiled knowingly.

"Who?" he played dumb.

"Who? You know who. Why wouldn't they want you? You're their only hope."

"Why the hell do you ramble, *padre?* Stop talking like a woman."

"Say what you will. My guess is de Gioia's men will court you. There's talk of insurrection in the east," he cautioned.

Tori caught his glance. "How can that be? The Allied Control Council just transferred to the Italian government most of its authority in the liberated regions. They've been permitted to conduct foreign affairs, make diplomatic appointments, and enact legislation without the ratification of the Allies. Isn't that an indication the war will soon end?" he asked desperately—a bit too desperately.

"It would seem so, *amico.* "But don't build your hopes on it," he said quietly sensing Tori's despair. "There's much to be decided. It will take a long time before peace comes. Even then, peace won't end everything magically. You may have to remain the savior to our people for a long time to come. You're still the government in our province."

"What you're saying is that nothing's really changed in two years?"

Santino shook his head. "Only in our province, where you've been the law, are things better for the people. All over Italy and most of Sicily, the people are destitute."

"Are you telling me, *padre,* that I should spread out and promote my ideals to others?" Tori scowled darkly.

"Who, me? What would the mere historian to Salvatore know of such things?" he smiled irresistibly. "Too bad you can't light a fuse under the Big Four."

"Listen, *padre,*" said Tori in a fit of agitation. "I can only handle the matters that are Salvatore's. Let the Rome government tend its own business."

"It's you who appears most impatient," Santino said quietly and calmly.

"All right. All right! Impatient or not, if they don't hurry and correct things, the people will have lost their Salvatore."

Fifteen minutes later, Tori handed Santino a reply to the letter from the Duke de Gioia, sealed and addressed. "Make certain it leaves Palermo, today."

"To Francisco Bello. . . ." Santino read the name and address aloud.

"You know him?" asked Tori in mild surprise.

"He's the Duke de Gioia's man. Head of the new Partionist Party to replace Canepa, eh? What a laugh! Hah! Monarchists, Socialists, Separatists, what does it matter? They're all Monarchists hiding under the guise of Partionists. Mafia feudalists! It's still the same dirty old barn with a new coat of paint. The stink will return when the paint wears thin."

Salvatore stared quizzically and intently at the former Jesuit.

"What's it all about? Can you say, Tori?"

"Tonight, when you return from Palermo, come to my house. We'll talk. *Va bene?*"

Satisfied or not, he said, *"Va bene,"* and, once mounted, Santino rode off with a loud, *"Ciao!"*

The sound of gunfire exploded the air about him. He heard their wild cries. Tori ran out of the grotto and, through his binoculars, he saw his men herding hundreds of horses into the meadows below. Overhead, the sentries signalled an all-clear with ox horns. It was nearly sunset. Tori mounted his horse and headed into the draw below him to greet them.

"Where the hell did you find this bonanza of horseflesh?" he called.

Vincenzo grinned. "Go ahead, Duca, you tell him."

"No. You tell him," replied Duca with a hint of modesty.

"Someone better tell me!" said Salvatore, appraising the chestnuts, sorrels, mares, stallions, and geldings corraled behind the makeshift fencing with rapt astonishment and total bewilderment.

"We requisitioned them. Finished with our business in Mt. Erice, with time to kill, we ventured along the docks in Trapani. We saw American corpsmen loading and unloading equipment. Duca spotted these horses en route to Sardinia. Knowing our needs for such fine steeds, he simply requisitioned them. One look at the signature and the dock steward was so excited he threw in six cows, ten pigs, and his heartfelt thanks. Told us to make sure we gave his regards to the general."

"What general?"

"This one. "Vincenzo handed him copies of the expertly forged documents.

Salvatore glanced at the signature and burst into laughter. "General Patton! Didn't the fool know Patton left Sicily two years ago?"

"No, and I wasn't about to educate him, cousin."

It seemed that suddenly the fireballing sun exploded into a burst of blinding lights. And through the center of explosion came the most magnificent white Arabian stallion Salvatore had ever seen. Adorned with a silver-studded black saddle, it glittered and dazzled with such intensity that Tori was forced to avert his eyes.

With the sun at his back, Arturo Scoletti rode towards him on a most exquisite piece of horseflesh; a superb, powerful and compelling animal the color of muted pearl, with snow-white mane and tail, flaring pink velvet nostrils, and candy-glazed eyes the hue of anthracite.

"Just like the picture!" exclaimed Tori hoarsely.

"Just like the picture," agreed Vincenzo. *"Buon compleanno!"*

Tori couldn't believe his eyes. He always imagined owning such a piece of splendid horseflesh ever since he'd seen a painting of the mounted Napoleon by the artist Jacques-Louis David. He'd cut it from a book once and hung it on the wall of his bedroom.

"But, it's not my birthday——" he began, flushed with excitement.

"Well, we couldn't wait," replied Vincenzo. "Men like us have to act fast when the situation presents itself," he added. But Tori had already spanned the distance between him and the horse, and springing to the saddle, he spurred the animal into a wild gallop, wheeling him from side to side and putting him through a few fast-paced and expert maneuvers. The stallion obeyed implicitly. They blended, horse and rider, into a magnificent rhythm as one powerful unbroken force. After several moments, Tori rode back into the draw and flung himself breathlessly from the horse, pausing to stroke the animal's head lovingly. He handed the reins to Arturo and embraced his cousin affectionately. He couldn't recall such excitement and fulfillment—such a glowing happiness.

"Thank you, Vincenzo, for all the thoughtfulness. Tonight you'll come to my house for dinner."

"Each night for two years I came to your house for dinner. Now, suddenly I need an invitation?"

"This is different." He waved the letter bearing the Duke de Gioia's crest under the other's nose. "This may be the good news I've been expecting, cousin."

"*Va bene*. I'll be there. *Allora*—news reached me in Trapani that Martino Belasci has been appointed Minister of the Interior in Premier de Aspanu's cabinet. He's moving fast, that one—eh?"

"And why not? My Godfather Matteo Barbarossa promotes him."

"You know this for a fact?" Vincenzo's mouth fell open in amazement.

"There's little I don't know, cousin. What's more, soon we will pay my Godfather a visit." He accepted the cigarette and match extended him. After he lit up he exhaled the smoke. "Did you handle that small matter in Mt. Erice?"

Vincenzo's smile disappeared. "I hope you know what you're doing, Tori. I've never seen a more sinister face than that *mafioso*'s," he cautioned. "*Managghia*, It took all my courage to put on a brave face and walk out of there when I finished. He's a fork-tongued viper, that Don Pippinu. You'd best steer clear of him."

"I know what I'm doing," said Tori. "I'm going to talk with my new horse while you clean up. I'll see you later at my house, *capeeshi?*"

"What will you call him?" asked Vincenzo, indicating the horse.

"What else? *Napoleono*." Tori winked broadly at his co-captain.

Watching Tori ride off Vincenzo hoped the letter contained news to elevate Tori's spirits. Lately Tori had begun to evince an inner erosion of discontent with the life they were leading. Whatever it was that had been eating away at him had caused him to become more daring and audacious in coups against the *carabinieri*. Moreover, he'd become stricter with his men. The super-policing of the outlaws had begun to cause dissension among the men for the first time since they had organized.

The men had wondered what Tori expected of them, arguing they couldn't be the celibates Tori seemed to be. "We're virile men with healthy manly appetites. Why should we live like priests, without women?" They had lamented to Vincenzo as they burned under the rigid discipline and strict enforcement of morality imposed upon them by Tori.

If he lived to be a hundred, Vincenzo would never forget the humiliation he himself had received from his cousin Tori, recently. He'd suffered a *bastinada*, the pains of which had long since been erased, but the humiliation and the memory of his stupidity still lingered in his mind. Vincenzo, no angel, loved his sex life equally as much as, if not more than, the other men. God had endowed him with the virility of ten stud bulls. He wasn't ashamed to admit he loved to fuck. After all the abstinence imposed on him at Terra Diavlo he had a lot to make up—and he went at it like a champion, almost as much as Terranova.

Tori had warned him repeatedly to be careful, to play outside the province, and to take care that he told no one his identity or occupation. He'd been warned to be economical in his sexual relations because of his pressing health problems, but it had been to no avail.

Vincenzo had pretended to go along with his cousin outwardly, but inwardly never hearing a word spoken to him. His mind had centered on a particularly juicy morsel named Filomena, who had made him crazy over her, crazy out of his mind. Besides, Maria Angelica Candela had become so uppity with him she'd refused to tumble in the hay with him without benefit of a wedding ring. Vincenzo wasn't ready for marriage yet, so he had turned his attentions on Filomena. He had mentioned the girl to Terranova and his companion's expression had been one of farcicul disbelief. "That one has four legs, barks and says oink oink," the other Lothario had said. "I thought you had better taste."

Nevertheless, despite Tori's warnings that she was a known consort to *carabinieri,* Vincenzo couldn't get out of his head how *fantastico* she was in bed. And then one night it had happened. Irresistibly drawn to Filomena and her inventive ways, he had defied Tori one time too many. He had walked right into a betrayal. Four *carabinieri* had been lying in wait for him, and had dragged him from the house stark naked. Vincenzo had shaken uncontrollably as the handcuffs were clasped over each wrist and all the old horrors of *Terra Diavolo* had returned to shake him and fill him with the terrors he'd once lived through. He hadn't known that Tori, having already learned of the betrayal, had been waiting outside the whore's house with a few of his other men. They had moved in just before Vincenzo was thrown into the police van.

A shoot-out took place, three *carabinieri* lost their lives, one escaped, Miguel Scoletti had rushed into the girl's room, all the madness contained in him since his nightmare at *Terra Diavolo*, and holding his .38 calibre Mauser at the girl's temple, blew her brains out, shouting as he did, "*Death to the traitors in Salvatore's army*." Something had happened that night to Miguel. Behind his dark, staring, catatonic eyes had hovered unlimited terror and violence, and a wrathful accumulation of loathing had been lying in wait, ready to unleash itself in the personality of a cold blooded killer. He'd been homosexually assaulted by Nazi prison guards at *Terra Diavolo*, and it seemed everything had come out at this particular time. Tori had had to send him away for a rest and some rehabilitation after this night.

And something happened to Tori that night. For in the senseless deaths of the *carabinieri* and the girls, which could have been avoided if Vincenzo had learned to exercise self control, he had seen what could happen if the men were permitted to go about without controls. That night he had taken Vincenzo home, tied him to a tree, and given him a *bastinada*, the likes of which his other paladins had never seen.

Later, Tori had helped Vincenzo down and nursed his wounds, with the solicitous and tender loving care he'd had given a brother. But he'd been firm. "If you ever permit your sexual passion to override caution, or place yourself or the lives of our men in jeopardy as you did this night, I won't end where I did tonight. You'll have me to reckon with, Vincenzo as you never had before." Then, as he had continued to nurse his cousin, he had grown emotionally overwrought and, speaking with a congested throat, he'd spoken with great affection and *molto dolore*, "Whipping you is like whipping my own flesh. I'd have preferred taking this punishment myself. But, you wouldn't have learned a lesson. While you are my second in command and owe a responsibility to the men, you must remember that women are our most dangerous enemies— even when they truly love us. Through them, we become vulnerable to betrayal and submission. When all this is finished, you can take all the women you want—a concubine if you will. But for now, until our roles have ended, you must exercise caution and intelligence."

Tori, who wasn't totally unreasonable, and understanding the physical needs of his men, had permitted them the companionship of women, but only under rigid rules. They could never be brought to a grotto or campsite used in their business, where they moved about or worked. Women, paid for by the night, were permitted into some sequestered place, blindfolded, where the men could partake of

318

pleasure without danger of betrayal. If the men married, it was to be within a tightly knit circle of relatives or friends of the bandits themselves, with little or no publicity given the coupling or union.

Vincenzo thought back to a night, quite recently, when something had occurred which set him to wondering about Tori. He recalled that on one of their outings, the campsite had buzzed with gay activity on a festive occasion. Men and women had danced to the wild, sensuous music, some had made love, and all had drunk to their hearts' content. Near the fires a musician had struck up a fiery *tarantella* and Vincenzo, lured by his specialty, had fallen into a dancer's posture—arched back, shoulders and hips fixed—and begun his individual improvisation. Into the center of the activity he'd began pirouetting in and out of a moving line of hand-clapping, foot-stomping dancers, and, finding a suitable, lusty companion with smoldering dark eyes, he'd begun with her an interplay of female-male attitudes, set to the frenzied accompaniment of the stimulated musicians. The couple had become seductive and aggressive, and mimed a passionate jealousy between them; then they'd feigned indifference, even cruelty. For a time they had flirted outrageously, then, in tenderness had come the surrender. They had run the gamut of romantic feelings as if they had been truly emotionally involved: it was not unusual, after such a performance, for the dancers to get together for a romantic interlude. Such a stirring exhibition, too, was contagious and inspiring to onlookers.

On and on they had danced, whirling and twirling and snaking in a circle. The campfire had become a revolving kaleidoscope of oblique shadows and abstract forms, and stirring vibrations which electrified the air. Finally, Vincenzo had fallen laughingly in total exhaustion to the ground in an effort to catch his breath.

When he looked about for Tori's face among those of the spectators, Tori was absent. Vincenzo had searched everywhere and found him later, high on a bluff, outlined brightly by a full and enormous harvest moon in what appeared to be a poignant and private moment. Vincenzo had strained to hear Salvatore's words: *"I shall be avenged, Apolladora, mia. Never shall there be another for me!"*

Startled, Vincenzo had wondered. Apolladora? Apolladora who? Avenged? Upon whom? He had lumbered off the hill bewildered and taken aback. Who was Apolladora? Having never forgotten the incident, he had promised himself he'd one day ask Tori. To this day he

319

hadn't worked up the courage to ask, but he felt he must one day soon. Was now the time?

As Vincenzo made preparations, now, to ride to the house of his Aunt Antigone he considered the letter Tori had shown him. A royal seal—no less? He chuckled and hoped it was good news. He waved to Arturo Scoletti and called to him.

"C'mon, you son of a wayward tortoise, hurry up!" Mounting his black mare, he galloped ahead of Arturo, waving to his companions in the draw.

CHAPTER 24

Dinner that night at the house of his mother had been a mixture of business and pleasure and one of startling revelations. They were halfway through dinner when Tori noticed a tenseness in the air around him as the men, and his mother, waited to hear what it was that was chafing him so.

Finally Tori asked Santino, "Whats the word from Palermo?"

"Chaos," replied Santino in a candor. "Everywhere is chaos. In the elections Allies permitted all the political parties to register, and their shock at the results has left them stunned. The swing is decidedly to the left. The Reds must have infiltrated on the quiet, and suddenly, there they were in full bloom. I tell you, *amici*, everyone is shaking."

"What happened to Sicily becoming a state or colony?" asked Vincenzo idly as he devoured the succulent veal and peppers, rolling his eyes in appreciation towards his aunt.

"Talk is all it was. Talk," muttered Santino between mouthfuls.

"In any case separation from Italy is inevitable," stated Tori.

Santino shrugged. "Information I got today indicates the Palermo Grand Council, run by Don Barbarossa, is pressing for separation and autonomy. Their intentions are to form a Monarchy naming Duke de Gioia king. They are hard pressed to beat the Reds to power."

Antigone spoke up. "Russia may be one of the Allies, but at war's end there will be a mad scramble for power. Russia wants Sicilly. I fear the consequences."

"Why?" asked Tori.

"Why? Because, my son, our people are ready for anyone who promises better things than we've had in the past. At the end of the last war many soldiers returned with different ideas of how to live. They rebelled at the feudal system and refused to knuckle down to the old ways. When they learned they couldn't combat the system, some left, others remained. Attempts to take over uncultivated lands, theirs by virtue of the laws, were foiled by Mafia *gabellotti*. Rivers of peasant blood flowed in the wake of their dissent. It's still the same. Nothing has changed. Reflect on your own behavior. Haven't you all tried to change the old ways? You think it will do any good as long as the feudalists remain in power?"

The others frowned at her words, and Tori, who believed things had to change, brooded over her words.

"Shall I tell you what will happen? Sicily's conquerors—in this case the Allies—will turn their backs on her. They've a bigger job to finish—the war. They can't be bothered with us."

For a time they all tasted the new wine, with the exception of Tori. All made comments and passed judgment on it in a ritual-like activity. Tori waited until they were finished before he addressed Arturo. "What's the word from your sources?" he asked the jovial former strong man.

"A new Partionist movement is beginning, sponsored by the Allies, I'm told, all hush hush—an undercover cloak-and-dagger type of business," he replied.

"The Allies backing the Partitionists?" asked Tori, his fork in mid-air as his food was suspended in mid-sentence. "Is this the truth?" It was easy to see this news generated a great degree of excitement. Tori himself felt a new stirring in his stomach as something came together in his mind. He had already heard these rumors, and it seemed incredible to him that America would support the movement.

"It's what I heard," said Arturo. "Whether or not it's the truth depends on many things."

Tori addressed Santino once again. "What do your friends in Palermo say to this?"

"They were more interested in the Communist political strength spreading over the land. I, too, have heard such rumors. If it's important I'll check it out."

Santino gazed up into the eyes of Athena as she poured more wine. In the instant their eyes met, he read a message in them. Color rose to his face. Quickly he averted his eyes to see if they'd been observed. Excitement surged through him, at the same time he flooded with annoyance at the implications of such a look. Still, was it possible that she could care for him? He stole another glance—but by that time Athena had moved around the table, her eyes demurely lowered. Santino was elated. Blood pounded in his brain and his heart swelled with excitement as sweat poured from every pore in his body. Since before the war when he had preached from the pulpit, he'd been smitten with her beauty. Santino didn't know it yet, but he was deliriously in love.

"It's important," said Tori. "What the hell's wrong with you? Your hands are trembling, *padre*. Are you all right?" Tori studied him intently.

Every eye was upon him and Santino squirmed uncomfortably thinking they could read the truth in his eyes. "It's the wine. It's always heady when it's new."

Finally Tori unleashed the bombshell. "It's important because we've been approached by Francesco Bello and the Duke de Gioia to attend a meeting in Catania. The Partionists want Salvatore to support their cause." His voice, quiet and subdued, hadn't fully registered on the others, with the exception of his mother, whose face screwed up into a scowl.

Tori kissed his fingertips with a flourish, in full approval of her cooking. "As usual, Mamma, everything is delicious."

Antigone didn't acknowledge his praise. Her mind had stopped at the center of his announcement. "You won't go, of course," she told him. Confused by the message in his eyes she faltered. "Will you, Tori?" She studied him inscrutably as the others grew silent and motionless.

Tori broke the tension with a gentle reprimand. "What do you think?" he asked his paladins. "Here, I'm hailed as the King of Montegatta and my mamma treats me as if I were not yet toilet trained."

The others laughed in good spirits along with Tori. Antigone said nothing. She entered the pantry and returned with a large platter of *pinolatti*—deep-fried confections shaped like pine needles, dipped in honey and sprinkled with cinnamon and topped with powdered sugar. She placed the plate before Tori. "It's a trap," she said, *sotto voce*.

Again in the silence, the men refrained from speaking. They devoured the entire plateful of confections in a reverent silence, after which they extolled praises for the delicacies. They sat back patting their stomachs, complaining they'd made gluttons of themselves.

"I said, it's a trap," Antigone persisted.

"All right, Mamma, what makes you certain it's a trap?" Having already sent his reply to *Capitano* Francesco Bello, he wasn't ready to reveal his position as yet.

"Have I taught you nothing, Tori? You can't trust the nobility," she retorted. "They've been unsympathetic to the peasants' cause for centuries. Hah! What irony! They want you, Salvatore, a peasant, to come to their aid! *Butana u diaoro!* Without you they can do nothing. They'll use you, make no mistake about it, to do all their dirty work, all the low, degrading, marauding and killing necessary to promote their cause so they won't soil their dainty hands. Yes, my son, they'll use you to be their right arm. But, clasped tightly in their left, they will keep in reserve the power to annihilate you. The entire nobility is full of duplicity, treachery—and a highly perishable loyalty. At the first sign of trouble, their loyalty to you will thin out and dissolve. Then it will be you whom they'll sacrifice on their altars of gold." Antigone's voice contained no arrogance, no repudiation, no egotism. She simply stated what she believed to be a self-evident truth.

Once again the room grew pregnant with silence. They studied Antigone, noting her great face and luminous eyes. They acknowledged her words, weighing them carefully. Hadn't history already proven them true?

Vincenzo, who used no cream or sugar, stirred his black coffee absently and continuously. Santino rolled a lit cigar back and forth between thumb and fingers, flicking ashes from it from time to time in a nervous gesture. Holding a few walnuts in the palm of his hand, Tori crushed them open and sorted out the meat from the shells, popped them into his mouth, and allowed the shells to crumble off his hands onto the dish in front of him. Arturo simply sat forward, his elbows on the table, his hands supporting his chin. They hung on to every word Antigone spoke.

"It matters not to these feudal *latifondisti* which way the votes go as long as they can eat on their silver and gold encrusted plates, as long as they can sip their wines from imported crystal and are permitted to keep their bellies fat and their perverse concubines intact. For these pleasures, they would sell their souls!" She continued in an articulation not lost on the others.

"Do you really believe it matters to them whether the peasants who till their lands starve or die? Do you think

323

they care if the less fortunate remain ignorant, without education? Haven't these past few years proven my point. They are obtuse and insensitive where the problems of the peasants are concerned. Who among them released their hoarded grain? None of them!"

"As usual, *Signora,* you speak with Solomonic wisdom," said Santino. He turned to Tori. "What, in your opinion, is so special about the Partitionist movement? Doesn't it breed monarchy? Haven't we had our fill of monarchy, the empowered nobility and their corruptive practices?"

Vincenzo spoke up. Been silent for the most part, his Vincenzo, been silent for the most part, his mind on other matters, spoke up. "They want you, Tori? All these land barons want you? These *pezzenovanti,* high in government want you on their side? Bandits, no less, to become their allies?" He couldn't handle the convoluted logic of diametrical opposites forming a symbiotic relationship.

Tori raised a gentle brow and shrugged imperceptibly, an enigmatic smile playing faintly across his lips.

"What's so surprising in that?" asked Arturo. "Even Garibaldi, while employing a strategy aimed at unifying the two Kingdoms, found it necessary to make deals with men he'd normally been repelled by—those *mafiosi,* that 'honored' brotherhood."

Tori's eyes snapped open. Without moving his head he fixed stern, disapproving eyes on the former carnival man. The room became electric. Suddenly Arturo, realizing what he'd said, flushed and squirmed under Tori's cold eyes. Antigone took her cue. "What Arturo just said reinforces my earlier statements. The defense rests her case."

Vincenzo, nonetheless played with the idea. "It's a great honor to be summoned by such men of stature, no? They must respect you substantially, cousin." He nodded as if to himself. "Power such as ours can't be ignored. With it comes respect, no matter who controls it. It carries a great deal of dignity which God knows you've deserved by all the deeds you've masterminded. "Listen, cousin, I'm not as smart as you or the *padre* here, but, I think it's an honor to be approached by such men. At least hear them out."

"No! No! Not if they want my son to clean out the septic-tank conscience of their minds!" snapped his aunt, with fiery eyes blazing at him. She turned to her son, imploring him. "No." She took a new tack with him.

"I know how you must feel. Resplendent and bursting with pride to have been called upon by these titled landlords to help solve their problems. You, with the red blood

324

of peasants running through your veins, with only a limited education, must feel exhalted and puffed up with a deceptive feeling of importance to have been called upon by these titled men of dubious worth. But mark my words, Alessandro. It is you who are the important one—not they. Here in our world, which you command and control, is where you belong. Here, you reign supreme. I ask that you consider my words before making your decision. Then I'll be satified you've used your own will to guide you.

"I can't confine your thinking only to what I've learned in my lifetime, for you were born in another time. Let me only impart to you this wisdom, as old as time itself, which hasn't been altered by generations of distorted thinking. Once you agree to do their dirty work, it will be you, labeled with their crimes and deeds, who shall pay the penalty, one way or another. And it shall be you whom they'll dispose of, at their convenience. Each time these noblemen look upon your countenance and see, reflected upon it, reminders of their own vile and contemptible deeds, you shall be marked for death; these grand feudal lords can't tolerate constant reminders of their own malevolent and iniquitous crimes. I beg you, my son, stay here where you're a king among your people. Here, you know at all times what the highest of peasants think, for you are superior to him in knowledge, education and intelligence. If you choose to walk among barons, dukes and princes and condescend to become their puppet, forever, you shall be to them, the lowest of low. . . ." Antigone wasn't finished. "They boast of generations of knowledge, intelligence and royal breeding in their blood and bones. Yet, among them is more immorality, more duplicity and cunning—more irreverence to God in one noble head, I say, than in the minds of ten thousand peasants."

Tori laughed at the concern in her articulate eyes. eyes.

"Why such a sad face, Mamma *bedda*? Don't you know they'd have to get up very early indeed to fool a man who never sleeps?" He laughed again, trying to infect the others with a gayer spirit, even though his heart wasn't in it. "Besides, I've already sent my reply to his *elegance*, the Duke de Gioia, and to his puppet, Francesco Bello."

They were stunned—all of them. They looked expectantly at him. Antigone knew the look on his face. Now, she waited to hear the words.

"I informed his excellency that the city streets are too slippery for my horse!"

325

"Bravo, Alessandro," cried Antigone.

"Bravo!" the others echoed her words.

In the excitement, Santino hugged Athena, who stood at his side watching her brother, anxiously waiting for his reply. The room filled with shocked silence. Every eye was upon Santino, and he blushed a cherry pink.

"Forgive me," he apologized to the mildly astonished matriarch who exchanged glances with her daughter. "I meant no impertinence. I was carried away by the good news. . . ."

Athena lowered her thickly fringed lashes, so the delight in them wouldn't show. *He must feel something for me,* she told herself. *I hope. I hope. . . .*

Tori observed both Athena and Santino in silence. "Are you feeling any better, Athena?" he expressed his fraternal concern.

Blushing at the attention, she muttered. "I'm fine. It's nothing."

"What did the doctor say?"

"He says it's nothing!"

"Nothing!" exclaimed her mother. "This nothing causes her to bang her head against the door when the pain grows intolerable! These doctors aren't worth their salt. Nowadays they dispense aspirins if you can't have a good bowel movement."

"Padre, take Athena to Palermo," Tori said. "Make sure she sees a specialist. Talk with him. They won't double talk you. I want to know what ails my sister. You tell him, she's the sister of Salvatore. Spare no expense. I want her well." He leveled his dark eyes on the former priest.

"It's difficult to find good doctors," said Arturo.

"We'll find out what's ailing you, what's causing so much pain" Tori told his sister. He was astonished when Athena angrily spun around and left the room.

A loud piercing scream interrupted further comment. Athena rushed into the room, breathlessly. "Tori! Mamma! Someone come quickly! There's a giant beast in our back yard!" she exclaimed.

Guns drawn, the men ran towards the rear of the house. Tori first to reach the door, opened it, peered into the darkness, turned, and grinned impishly. He beckoned the others and slipped his Browning back into its holster. "Come, Mamma! Athena, come see the giant beast," he said smiling.

Napoleono had jumped the side fence, entered the yard

and stood contentedly nibbling leaves from a huge, spreading fig tree at the rear of the terrace.

"Look, Mamma. Isn't he beautiful? Vincenzo and the other men gave him to me today. He is like the one in the photograph, with Bonaparte." He stroked the stallion's head, nuzzled his own face close to him.

Vincenzo turned on the courtyard lights illuminating the stallion. Antigone froze. The words—those irrevocable words flashed across her mind: *It shall be a white horse reined in silver profusion. His horse and bridle must be protected by the sign of earth and fire."*

Donna Sabattini's voice pierced her consciousness; she paled and felt faint, as tiny bubbles of perspiration erupted on her face. There was no mistaking the *strega*'s prophecy, she told herself in those next few moments.

"Don't you like my horse?" asked Tori grasping her arm to steady it. "Mamma, what's wrong with you?"

She averted her eyes. How could she tell him. Everything inside her wanted to blurt out the whole story, but all she could manage when she regained her composure was, "Yes, Tori. It's a fine horse. *Cento anni*. May you both live a hundred years." She walked to the stallion's side and stroked its mane with trembling hands; then, turning quickly, she fled into the house. At any other time she'd have been ecstatic over the Arabian, for her love for horses was known to her family. Knowing this, the others exchanged bewildered glances.

"What will you call him?" asked Athena nuzzling the horses head.

Tori grinned. "Napoleono."

"I had to ask," she replied knowingly.

A few moments later Antigone returned to her son's side. She raised the Eye of God amulet and positioned it around his neck.

"What's this? What's this, Mamma? An amulet from you?" He winked at the others and, holding it away from his chest, he examined the disc carefully. He was partially amused and a bit irritated at the incongruity of her act, so opposed to her general lack of belief in such things.

"Don't ask," she retorted with unmistakable petulance. "Just wear it for me and don't take it off." She ran back inside the house, hoping he wouldn't question her. Moments later, when she heard the commotion outside, she ran out to investigate, and found the men huddled about the lone figure of a boy.

"Tell me what you're doing hiding in the bushes?" demanded Tori.

"I'm here because I admire you and want to join with your gang," replied a young lad, Danillo, the son of a war widow—himself a petty thief, with the slick ability to squirm in and out of scrapes.

Everyone but Tori laughed at the youth and gave him courage. "There's nothing for me with the other boys my age. I want to be near the great Salvatore!"

Tori stared at the lad with the proper amount of menace. "Go home, Danillo. Don't let me catch you where you don't belong again." Not for one minute did he believe the lad. He boxed the boy's ears, led him off the property, and gave him a playful boot in the butt. "If I ever see you here again, I'll use my gun. You hear?"

Since Tori's affection for children was such, his men thought it strange that Tori should be harsh and punitive with the lad. Their silence was an indictment. Danillo, thinking he'd put one over on Tori, left the premises. He didn't take the threat seriously and convinced himself that it left the door open for his next try at gleaning information for which he was to be paid a considerable sum.

Staring after him, Tori let his face grow implacable. Hard lines set in around his lips, and they drooped somewhat in brooding. "Now, they send babies to spy on us," he told the others. "Has he ever been around here before?" he asked his mother.

"I'm not sure—" Antigone shook her head.

"From now on, try to remember anyone you might see around the house who has no business here. No matter what reason they give to you, let me know who they are."

"Yes, my son," she replied dutifully. *Now it begins.* she told herself, trying to control the squeamishness that wrenched at her stomach.

An hour later, Tori stood in solitude at the Temple of Cats, aptly named by the ancient Romans who'd brought snow leopards and mountain lions to the area to guard their women during summer retreats and vacations away from Rome. Long after the Romans had abandoned Sicily to her next conqueror, alley cats had begun coming from all the neighboring villages to congregate at this spot around midnight. By morning they'd disappear as mysteriously as they'd appeared. The inability of anyone, including the proficient storytellers who had perpetuated the tale, to give a satisfactory reason for the continuing phenomenon gave rise to a superstitious belief that the small alley cats came in search of the spirits of their "ancestors,"

328

the lions and leopards who once had prowled the area in dignified majesty.

As Napoleono roamed the temple floor, unrestricted, Tori smoked a cigarette, seated on a boulder, staring out at the villages below. The presence of Danillo, spying on him, had provoked a bitter despair in him. When would the treacheries end? There seemed no relief in sight.

The new government formed recently in Rome had dissolved in a twinkling. What Tori had started two years before had stretched into a long, arduous task, filled with constant dangers, violent jealousies, hatred and disagreements which he'd kept in check only by employing an iron-fisted discipline. What he'd embarked upon, thinking it would only be a temporary expedient, had already consumed too much of his time. How much more could he endure of this demanding role into which he'd eased himself? Where could he go from here? His people were well fed. Crime had dropped to its lowest rate in the history of his province. What more could he do until the war ended? He was overwhelmed, considering these dilemmas.

But, there was more provoking excitement in Tori. For two years he'd been secretly considering an important move, and finally he'd made the decision to meet with his Godfather, Don Barbarossa. He'd planned what he'd say and do, and now that the decision had been made he grew apprehensive and trembled with an inner excitement, much like the one he had felt when he'd received Napoleono. How many tims he had contemplated the encounter, only to tell himself that he didn't dare present himself to so powerful a dignitary until he himself had attained a certain degree of importance! Would the Don know him? he wondered. Had he recognized the name *Salvatore* in the papers? So many men in Sicily shared the same name and bore no relation to each other, it was possible that the Don wouldn't associate the name to that of his own Godson.

God Almighty, how exciting it would be for him to meet so fantastic a man of legend, he told himself. In any event, it was time for Tori to bring to fruition certain carefully laid plans, and he needed his Godfather's influence to harvest his meticulous strategy.

His thoughts trailed to his mother's indignation earlier at supper and he concluded that, as usual, she was correct in her assessment. But Tori also concluded that she didn't understand his thinking, nor the intricacies of politics. Couldn't she understand that for Tori to secure the amnesty he sought, he had to align himself with a powerful political party? Who could be more powerful than the

329

former Monarchist, who'd formed a new coalition under the Partitionist banner?

Tori felt that he'd employed superb strategy in declining Captain Bello's initial proposal; it would only make him appear to be more vital to their plans. Besides, he'd become enough of a warrior to know their plans would fail without the support of a powerful guerrilla army—and the only such phenomenon in Sicily was Salvatore. He smiled and moving forward on the boulder, the amulet around his neck bounced about on his chest.

Tori caught it and, holding it a few inches away from his eyes, he struck a match on the stone so he could examine it better in the glow of light. What the hell had possessed his mother to give him this chatelaine? He removed it from around his neck and peered at it in the light of the full moon, and for no reason at all fastened it on Napoleono's bridle paraphernalia, allowing it to rest on the horse's forehead between its large eyes.

That night riding back over the twisting roads to his house, Tori wondered how *Capitano* Bello would react to his message. Surely, he'd be outraged, incensed, and filled with the usual mortification any of the land barons felt in having to consort with a mere peasant. He laughed aloud, knowing full well that the class-conscious constipation suffered by those men in the baronial circles would grow increasingly unpleasant when they read the reply they got from a mere peasant. He felt a sense of exquisite amusement as he pictured the fatuous nobles poring over his letter.

CHAPTER 25

"*'The City street is too slippery for my horse!'* Indeed!" roared Captain Francesco Bello aloud to himself. "Damn Salvatore! Damn the Duke de Gioia! Damn the whole Partitionist party and their muleheaded myopia!" Offended by the bandit's impudence, he slapped Salvatore's letter furiously against his thigh and paced the floor of the magnificently appointed, Moorish-influenced salon like a tiger at bay. He moved with the pretentious *panache* of a Nutcracker Suite soldier, dressed in his spanking new, royal blue serge uniform with mirror polished buttons and gold braid. Pausing momentarily before a roaring fire in the open hearth fireplace, he attempted to ward off the chill of the rainy night as he awaited the arrival of his host, the Duke de Gioia.

Outside, torrential rains splashed noisily against stained glass windows and the blustery winds, rising in ferocious intensity, denuded nearby citrus and filbert trees in its wake. Startled by the mighty force of the elements, Bello paused to listen to the eerie sounds. He asked himself, as a sinking depression engulfed him, why he had accepted this role. What minor flaws in his own character had induced him to subject himself to all the travail meted out to him as the new head of the Partitionist party?

Stuffing the offensive letter into his tunic, he reached for a nearby brandy decanter, poured himself a stiff drink, and quickly gulped it down. The blazing trail of warmth, shuddering through him, felt good. He dragged a high-backed Emperor's chair closer to the fire, plunked himself down in it, stretched his long legs, and allowed his arms to fall slackly over the arms of the carved rosewood. For a time he concentrated on the fire, fascinated by the myriad designs reflected by the flickering firelight on his black shiny boots, Mellowed by the brandy, warmed by the fire, and still despondent over his involvement, Bello became reflective.

He thought back a few months to a time shortly after New Year's in January of 1945 when there had gathered in his baronial estate in Caltagirone, southwest of Catania, a distinguished brood of politicians—influential Monarchists, representing a cross-section of the new movement favoring Sicily's separation from Italy who wanted no part in the growing threat of communism. These men, loyalists, considered themselves patriots; above all, however, were feudalists who staunchly wanted to cling to what had been theirs for centuries. They were men who'd continue to hold back large areas of Sicily from cultivation if it meant littering the street with corpses of all the peasants who dared buck their system. Having turned a profitable trick with Fascists and all previous conquerors for centuries, these breed of men, out of greed, would secure themselves, in the uncertain future, by grabbing the power wherever and from whomever they could.

An underground guerrilla movement, fostered by the Allies and later abandoned by them due to the swiftness in which politics fluctuated daily, had attracted the attention of many politicians who held high hopes in the mad scramble for power when Sicily became an independent state. Leadership in this movement changed periodically and would continue to change. Due to the unsettled conditions and chaotic state of Sicily's future, countless ambitious men, prepared to outguess History, were also prepared to shift loyalties from party to party, depending on which side showed the greatest potential and wielded the greatest power.

These men, a portion of them, had gathered in Bello's drawing room that day, having appointed as their spokesman a certain Baron Ermano Mattinata. He was a dark-skinned, ferret-eyed man whose black and piercing eyes seemed constantly to calculate a man's net worth. With all his wealth he always appeared dowdy, in a crumpled suit with a vest that rode up on him and always needed to be jerked into place, despite his thin, scrawny frame. This penny-pinching noble, well known for his niggardliness, spoke with supercilious pomposity. Like every man there, the Baron ruled his lands with a savage despotism and maintained a tenacious hold on his lands. They'd do anything, these landowners—anything, just to keep the status quo. To keep their bloodied hands manipulating the levers of their locomotives of oppression was all they lived for.

Tugging primly at his vest, Baron Mattinata had set aside his wine glass on that eventful day, stood up, and cleared his throat. His fists, balled tightly at his sides as he addressed Bello, should have given the lawyer insight into his perennial plea of penury. "My dear Bello." He had raised his voice to a high falsetto and unballed his fists. He slipped them into the high pockets of his pants and parading like a stiff-backed ostrich before his companions, winking cagily at some, nodding to others in a conspiratorial manne, he then showered his attention on their host.

"We've come to you out of respect *Avvocato* Bello," he began in a fawning manner which irked Bello. "You seem to have found a magic formula in keeping an orderly estate. Since you control your peasants well, you know what our problems are. It's simply marvelous, my dear Bello, how you've kept your peasants from claiming uncultivated lands. You see, we've been watching you."

Francesco Bello, a tall, slim man cut an imposing figure as he stroked his drooping moustache and nodded in silence. He swelled with pride at the formidable gathering of nobility under his roof. That they'd collectively seek his service for some small business venture impressed him

332

increasing his feelings of self-worth. He kept his eyes on the manipulative Baron nonetheless.

"You're well known to us," the Baron said, "respected for many shrewd business manipulations and, of course, for your political successes. All of which qualify you, my dear Bello, for the honor my associates and I intend to confer upon you." The Baron enumerating the salient points of his proposal. However, his duplicity and guile were so obvious to Bello and in a way insulting.

Too many compliments unnerved him and Bello braced himself. He took a good look at the distinguished gathering and he knew for certain they wanted something more than a mere favor. He wondered what it might be just as the Baron's voice sliced into his thoughts again.

"A month ago, Canepa, a feisty, silver-tongued orator whom you've no doubt heard of . . ." said the Baron, wiping the dry corners of his lips with his fingertips. "As scandalous as it is to speak of, this former leader of the Separatists was recently exposed as a communist! A communist, dear Bello," he blustered on tactlessly.

"Canepa a communist? No!" Bello feigned astonishment.

"Dear Bello, how we all wish your words were true," wailed the Baron. None of us were aware of his shady background. We gave him free rein to do as he wished to promote our aims. Money! Supplies! Information! We backed this traitor to the end! What we were prepared to do for him! You wouldn't believe!"

"I've heard many things about Canepa," said Bello vaguely. An eccentric—But it's definite he's a Red? It's certain?"

"Certain? Dear Bello, it's past history now. All the time he planned to do us in! Imagine? He used *our* money, *our* backing, just to get himself fixed up good with the Reds!"

"Where's Canepa now?" asked Bello pointedly . . . and with good reason.

"I can't answer you, my dear Bello. It's none of my doing. . . ."

"Nevertheless, *my dear Baron*, he's dead! Is he not?" he asked cagily.

"Then, you know? . . ." The Baron's eyes darted towards the others.

"It was an excellent hoax to keep his death a secret so as not to split up the factions, my dear Baron. But it was bound to leak out." Bello, a professional lawyer, knew the cat-and-mouse game well.

"It's none of my doing, believe me, Bello. I don't involve myself in such lowly acts," said the Baron. "I only handle diplomatic matters. . . ."

"How was it that none of your associates detected the truth of Canepa's politics? *We* recognized his leftist leanings long ago. Weren't you aware this man Canepa was once certified insane and locked up in an asylum? Didn't your people check into his background?" demanded Bello with dripping sarcasm.

"We knew he'd been with British Intelligence in 1943, and that he'd carried out a successful sabotage mission against the Germans near Syracuse. He parachuted to Northern Italy and organized the Canepa Brigade against the Reds! Even the Americans were favorable to Canepa! And with sixteen guerrilla bands ready to follow his orders—wouldn't you have been impressed?"

Bello shrugged. "The man was born of insane courage!"

"Insane courage? *Managghia!* He had to be insane to think he could fool the British, the Americans, *and* the Sicilian land barons! His plans were to seduce the Sicilian land barons, then, demand their lands or their heads! What a catastrophe! Oh, what a catastrophe that would have been!"

"Managghia!" exclaimed Bello. "What a special brand of guts that took!"

"Guts? You just said the man was insane! Demented—no? No one in his right mind would play three sides against the middle! Satan finally caught up to him!"

"You're telling me the Sicilian land barons had nothing to do with his death?"

"My dear Bello, between the British, Americans, and Russians, we Sicilians are lowest on the totem pole of worth. Canepa's communism didn't conform to Communist party lines. A separate Sicily, they felt, would be dominated by the Allies, and of necessity would be Anti-Russian and Anti-Communist. Canepa's treachery was leaked out through the Ministry of the Interior. We assumed that many red faced officials had decided it was best for all concerned if Canepa were eliminated. . . ."

Bello suggestedly knowingly. "That he was—wasn't he?"

Baron Mattinatta glanced uneasily at the others. "I repeat it wasn't *our* doing."

"What happened to the sixteen guerrilla bands?" asked Bello abruptly. Are they still available?"

The Baron's eyebrows twitched nervously. He shrugged. "It's my understanding they scattered, fearing the same betrayal as Canepa's."

Bello stroked his moustache thoughtfully. "This is a most difficult and weighty assignment you wish upon me," he began with noticeable reluctance.

"If we didn't consider you capable we shouldn't have come this great distance to pay you our respect. . . ." The Baron's hopes accelerated.

Bello shook his head dubiously. I'm afraid this will require considerable thought and study. I'm no military man. You all know that, don't you?" He didn't wait for an answer. "I can see the merit of Canepa's plan to employ guerrillas. It's the only way of demolishing government troops and *carabinieri*. . . ." Bello strutted before his captive audience in his elegantly tailored grey suit. He expounded pompously, as if he possessed the experience of a commander in Caesar's Legions. "Victory could be achieved using Pacino's bandits in the east and employing the strength of—what's his name—in the west? . . . Ah, yes, Salvatore! And mind you I'm no military strategist. . . ." Bello was impressed with his own reasoning.

"We want no common criminals to fight our cause. . . ." argued the Baron.

Palermo's Mayor Tedesco spoke up and, with perhaps the most prophetic statement of his career, he declared, "Salvatore's no common criminal! He's one of a kind!" He received scathing looks from most of the men. "You must admit—he's most unusual. There's been no one else like him. . . ." his voice dropped and he sat back, recoiling from their coldness.

Why a man of wealth and talent as Francesco Bello, a reputable landowner and lawyer with a successful practice, should abandon his professional leanings and expose himself to the perils presented as head of the Partitionist party was a mystery to his closest friends. Bello, certainly not the man Canepa had been, knew nothing of guerrilla warfare or military stratagems, but he possessed a special brand of courage, talent as a persuasive orator—and a driving ambition which dimmed his perspective. His insatiable vanity, and a superego that doted on the attention given him by these class-conscious, arrogant feudalists and Mafia Dons brought him to accept his role as captain of the Partitionist Army and plunged in valiantly to promote this venture.

There followed moments of sobriety when Francesco considered he was daft for permitting himself to be seduced by these crafty serpents. The months following his acceptance had proved trying and frustrating. There were too many people to be pleased in his pupet role as yes-man to a baronial circle of eccentric, petulant and irrational politicians. A man oriented in military protocol might have been more forceful, and less inclined to put up with their childish demands. Unfortunately for Bello, he was to learn, soon enough, that these bird-brained men whose heads soared above the clouds of reality wanted expedients for which they weren't prepared to pay.

"My dear Captain Bello," Duke de Gioia's voice interrupted Bello's reverie. "How good to see you again," The corpulent noble entered the salon on the arm of his mistress, *Principessa* Gabriella Rothschild, a slim, fashionably dressed, disdainful blonde, whose presence infused the air with fragrant perfume.

Bello rose to his full height, forced a pleasant smile on his face, clicked his heels together and bowed. He kissed the *Principessa*'s hand and embraced the Duke with the proper decorum. "My pleasure, Excellency."

The amenities over, Bello lost no time in explaining his mission. Reporting Salvatore's reply gave rise to his annoyance that this uncouth upstart of a bandit should have answered his five-page communique with a one-line sentence.

"My dear Bello, why do you fret? Relax. You don't find *me* upset by the antics of this *contadino*, do you?" The Duke moved laboriously towards his mistress, seated next to him on the silk damask sofa, he lit her cigarette and smiled at her in a secret way that annoyed Bello.

"Why do I fret?" asked Bello. "I'll tell you why. Look at this!" He tossed Salvatore's letter to him angrily and watched as the Duke fastened his *pince-nez* glasses onto his bulbous nose.

The Duke glanced disdainfully at the crude foolscap paper and the one-line reply and permitted the letter to flutter to the floor. He sighed with an attitude of boredom. "Why do you let yourself be inconvenienced by this lowly peasant? Why you need this arrogant, publicity-seeking plebeian, this son of a common sheepherder, is beyond me." The Duke, puffing on his thin cigar, dabbed at a few ashes on his vest.

Gabriella avoided eye contact with either of the men. She sipped her drink, appraised the diamonds on her fingers and wrists, and kept her thoughts to herself. Reflected in her azure eyes was an obvious boredom of long standing, one she didn't bother to obscure on occasion.

"You don't mean that the way I think you do, excellency," said Bello with narrowed eyes.

The Duke exasperated. "I meant it exactly the way I

said it. Wherever I go the subject of this peasant Salvatore monopolizes the conversation. I tell you, I'm bored with him. Bored—bored—bored!" He was panting noticeably. The Duke was fastidiously dressed, sporting elegant jewels that were somewhat offensive to good taste in wartime. This indolent noble had been courted by Don Barbarossa into thinking he'd be the ideal king in the future monarchy of Sicily, unaware that the Don considered this laughable lump of a man, with his outlandish white wig, only as a front; an ideal puppet to sit on the throne and disguise the *real* monarchy of Matteo Barbarossa. Earlier when he had confessed to Bello that he was bored, bored, bored, he meant exactly that, for the enticement of reigning as King of Sicily had been stretched over too long a period of time. He'd lusted after the throne, but it had become too elusive. He had tasted its heady elixir for so long and it had grown flat, and he needed continuous doses of flattery and reassuring praises to revitalize and rekindle his interest.

When he had first received Don Barbarossa's *communiqués*, the Duke had been in Switzerland, sitting out the war. He'd met Gabriella there in a Swiss chalet. Having considered the Don's proposal, he concluded it was only fitting that if he were to occupy a throne, he should have a princess at his side to reign as queen.

The two years in which the Duke had been forced to play a waiting game before he could be crowned King of Sicily, had grown tedious and too exacting to him. Recuperation from Canepa's treachery, painfully slow, had resulted in damaged pride—and in untold shame. Ridicule had been hurled upon him by his colleagues. Now, they weren't ready to fully trust another man. He had become cautious in his dealings and jaded in his attitude towards Bello, and an invisible barrier of hard-nosed skepticism had sprung up to disconcert the Captain. This finite comparison to Canepa, totally unfair to Bello, had greatly encumbered her progress. Having given him *carte blanche* to promote the Partitionist plans, the Monarchists now set up obstacles detering the former lawyer at every turn.

Bello stood before the floor-to-ceiling fireplace, staring glumly into the embers, sullen and downcast. Watching him, the Duke felt his temper abate. Perhaps he'd been too harsh on him. After all, it hadn't been his fault that the Kingdom had proved too slippery to grasp for the time being. Every monarch in history had kept at his side a faithful captain, a personal paladin in whom he confided.

Why wouldn't Bello be such a man, to inspire me, thought the Duke. He expressed himself in modulated tones, and addressed his captain.

"Try to understand, Bello. I come from a long line of nobles used to consorting with kings, emperors and presidents." It's degrading to be constantly reminded that some pubescent, publicity-seeking peasant, a depraved and immoral brute with no respect for law and order and who probably copulates with animals, is a man with whom men of our calibre must deign to deal with. . . ."

Gabriella's usually expressionless eyes, a pale azure, smoldered into angry sapphires. Across the room, her eyes met Bello's. They both flushed hotly, but for different reasons. Swiftly, she lowered her gaze, broke eye contact with him, and discreetly once again kept her thoughts to herself. Not Bello. He burned. He took umbrage at the Duke's insipid, double-domed, and thoughtless remarks. Bello, himself the son of peasant stock who had wisely turned into merchants when they could no longer tolerate the despair and suffocation of spirit brought on by oppressive nobles, felt insulted. Having only recently become a part of this political clique, he knew, despite the wealth he'd amassed, that he'd never be fully accepted as one of them. *Well, fuck it*, he told himself. *I'll have my say and if his fucking excellency doesn't like it—he can stick it!*

"He may be that and everything else you say, including a filthy degenerate, although I'd consider it most unlikely, Excellency," said Bello with the bit in his teeth. "But this pubescent, publicity-seeking plebeian, as you see fit to call him, controls the western section of our country! The sooner you and the other noble Monarchists recognize the fact that we need the strength of this powerful young Sicilian, who champions his people, the sooner our cause will be victorious! Are you aware that Federal officers no longer go through Salvatore's territory? That an *entente* exists between the security police and this unique bandit? Whatever remains of the *carabinieri* are under his rule and protection!"

"My dear Francesco, don't upset yourself," suggested the Duke. There's plenty of time. Relax. Pour yourself a drink. Brandy?—*Strega?* Help yourself. . . ." He gestured apathetically towards the glittering sideboard of sparkling crystal decanters and opalescent Venetian glass. "Then we shall sit down and discuss this situation like civilized men. . . ."

Resolute to the point of bullheadedness, Bello clenched his teeth and bit back the desire to tell off this overstuffed popinjay. Damned pretentious nobles! All alike! No concept of reality lodged in their antiquated brains! They're more ludicrous than any breed of men I've met, he cursed inwardly.

Principessa Gabriella Rothschild, a German Jewess who had escaped Hitler's wrath by fleeing to Switzerland, glanced at Bello in mock amusement. She could read his mind, for his thoughts draped his face like a week old laundry hung out to dry. She smiled internally. Children! All of them! These Sicilians played games that children would have abandoned long ago. She turned her attention to the ornate music box placed gracefully on the carved rosewood table next to her. With her long red-lacquered fingernails, she toyed with the switch and finally pushed it into motion. She languidly watched the small figures of cupids and dancing maidens revolve below a figure of Venus, curtsy, and whirl about on a track to the accompaniment to the habañera from *Carmen*. Her sardonic and amused eyes met Bello's and held.

Sharply annoyed by this intrusion into his thoughts, Bello cast a meaningful glance in her direction, then walked to a sideboard to pour himself a drink and refresh those of his host and hostess, wondering still as he did why he had let himself get talked into this thankless position.

"I'd hoped we could settle the matter of Salvatore," began Bello, crossing the room and seating himself opposite the Duke. "If we don't encourage his participation, we may as well abandon our plans."

De Gioia sighed heavily. "You won't permit me to enjoy your company without talk of this infernal bandit! Very well, tell me what you have in mind. . . ." The Duke's eyes never wavered from Gabriella.

"Since the stubborn billygoat refuses to come to us—I propose we go to him!"

Reluctantly, de Gioia removed his eyes from the girl. Glancing sharply at Bello he said imperiously. "Are you mad, my dear man? Are you positively senile? We'd be the laughing stock of Sicily!" The Duke tried in vain to lift himself out of the deep-cushioned sofa. After several attempts, Bello moved in and pulled him to his feet. Once erect, the grossly obese de Gioia, suffering from a malady called pure, unadulterated gluttony, paced painfully and laboriously about the room, fired by Bello's proposal.

"*Allora*—we shall have to become a laughing stock if it will win us Sicily!" Bello said firmly. "The establishment of a Sicilian monarchy, with full autonomy, will take all the military strength we can muster! Without it we haven't a whisper of a chance! None at all! It's obvious we need Salvatore more than he needs us, and I advise you to keep that fact uppermost in your mind!" he said with enough innuendo to cause the Duke to stop dead in his tracks and glance swiftly at him. Bello grew bolder. He added, "Regardless of what Don Matteo Barbarossa tells you!"

Their eyes locked and held, in duelistic silence. Watching them, Gabriella felt a rush of admiration for Bello whom she had considered to be a fatuous and over-ambitious marionette, nauseatingly condescending in his earlier poses. What a revelation! She felt like saying, *"bravo!"* Of course she didn't.

"We'll have to get full approval for this insanity!" said the Duke testily.

"Why? Why can't we tell them *after* we've effected a meeting with Salvatore? No one need know. If he refuses—there'll be no bitter vetch to swallow from our associates. If he agrees, we'll have cause to celebrate . . . *Pero*—I think we have the honey that will attract this pesky *zanzaro*, this mosquito who seems to irritate you to distraction," said Bello craftily.

In the silence, only the tinkling sounds of the music box permeated the room. 'Trust me, Excellency. With Pacino and his men in the east working in coordination with Salvatore in the west, we'll control the vote and rid ourselves of the Italian military police and government soldiers." Bello sipped the rest of the brandy and smacked his lips as his old confidence returned. The gouted Duke, with his swollen ankles, waddled about the room, wiping the perspiration from his cherubic face and pursing his lips in thought. He stopped at the ornately carved oaken table, opened a humidor, and offered a Havana to Bello, who accepted it with aplomb. For an instant Bello held his hand in the air, listened to the music and moved it rhythmically like a conductor in accompainment to the Bizet time.

"It's been a long time since I've enjoyed one of these, Excellency," Bello sniffed the cigar appreciatively and bit off one end; then he removed a candle from its holder and lit first the Duke's and then his own cigar. Outside the storm had risen; the rain and winds could be heard swooshing through the nearby trees.

"I love the rain—don't you?" Bello's voice filled the room. "Where was I? Oh, yes; Salvatore. We shall make him an enticing offer. Full commission as Colonel in the Partitionists' army, and complete amnesty for himself and his men if we emerge victorious. I understand this alone would be inducement enough. You see, he's obsessed with the idea of a pardon. I promise you, Excellency, Salvatore shall become a willing participant in our plans, a facile tool we can manipulate in any direction we choose. All bandits become as asses tied to the sun, once impressed with their own authority." His meaningful eyes shaded with subtleties only a crafty serpent could understand.

The Duke's grey eyes hung low in their sockets and grew heavy-lidded. He understood perfectly the treachery couched in Bello's words. It now became the Duke's pleasure to refill Bello's drink. Now they understood each other. He handed the glass back to his guest.

"To us," said the Duke, flushed with diabolical glee.

"To us!" echoed Bello, swelling with pride.

"By all means, to us," muttered the *Principessa*, who wasn't a princess at all, and had adopted the title in Switzerland to impress the other class-conscious prigs. She raised her glass towards them and smiled complacently. Inwardly she filled with contempt. *They're both idiots! They talk as if they have cotton brains! If this man, Salvatore is half the man they say he is, he'll see through their deceit before they flick an eyelid. . . .*

In recalling the photos she'd seen of Salvatore, and reading of his exploits and sheer daring she thought; *Now, here's a born leader! A real man! Just for once, I'd like to meet a real man! Just once. . . .* Her eyes lit up with such bright intensity that she caught the Duke's attention.

"Well, Captain Bello, it appears the *Principessa* must agree with our plans; see how the anticipation of such a proposal has stimulated her. . . ." Beaming with pleasure, he waddled to her side, bowed stiffly from the waist, kissed her hand, and patted it affectionately. "What a pleasure you are to me, Gabriella. . . ." His eyes filled with desire.

She would have liked nothing better than to clear his impression of her in that instant; instead, she lowered her eyes reservedly.

Captain Bello frowned. Discussing such vital plans in the presence of a third party, and a woman at that, left him disturbed. He sipped his brandy in silence, and kept his thoughts of her to himself, however benign or malignant her influence with the Duke might be.

Later that night, after Bello had retired, Gabriella sat at her dressing table, preparing for her hour of intimacy with the Duke. In her early thirties, she looked twenty two. Attractive, slim-figured but with ample bosoms, she had soft full lips which could turn petulant, even cruel on occasion. Her expressive eyes turned mysteriously blue or green at

341

random. Staring at her image narcissistically, she wondered why, of all the men she'd met at that Swiss chalet near Zurich, had she permitted herself to be seduced by Duke Federico de Gioia. Of course she knew the answer to her own question. She sighed deeply and considered it.

Twice her age, dazzled by her withdrawn charm, the Duke de Gioia had considered her, at first, to be a whorish bitch with insufferable airs of grandeur that somehow satisfied a masochistic quirk in his nature. On her he had showered costly gifts and extravagances that would have delighted a Lucretia Borgia, and through the art of costly persuasion he encouraged her to accompany him to Sicily, where he confided, he would soon be crowned king.

Carrying forged papers, her rapidly diminishing funds nearly gone, Gabriella, in a moment of black despair, had been forced to make a quick decision. It wasn't until she had been carefully tucked in the Duke's villa in Catania that she had revealed she was a German Jew who had escaped her homeland before Hitler had murdered six million of her kind and another six million other humans. The Duke had had his personal reasons for not caring what she was, of course.

Repulsed at first, by this giant of a man, she had later temporized and convinced herself she could have done worse. Anything was better than encountering Hitler or his dreaded SS men, she had reasoned. Now she suddenly found herself at the center of what promised to be a hotbed of political insurrection, in a foreign land, led by bloody nincompoops! She had never quite fathomed what the Duke's politics really represented. One day they were Monarchists, the next day Socialists. Then then became Separatists, now they were Partitionists. A late rumor, however true it might be, was that America was committed to back the Partitionists in their break from Italy, the Italy that had suddenly become an abomination to the Allies and had sprouted Communist horns—a fact which didn't set right either with the American, British and French, or the Sicilian feudalists.

Exposure to Hitler's brand of politics, she felt, qualified her to pass judgment on these hotheaded Sicilians, who by comparison to the Nazis were ridiculously naive. It would have accomplished nothing if she had deigned to tell Federico her views, for she learned long ago, a woman was sensible if she kept her thoughts to herself—particularly in Sicily, where she discreetly concealed any display of brain power. A glance at her five-carat diamond solitaire and her platinum and diamond bracelet convinced her she hadn't fared too badly. What the hell—

If she bided her time, she was thinking, the Duke would soon be dead. His overweight condition, his overtaxed heart, and the ills that plagued a man besieged with gluttony were horrendous. It was a miracle he'd lived this long. Not that she cared. If she had had her way, she would have preferred him dead. She hated him; she hated him in the same way she hated all men. But for Federico she reserved a particular loathing.

Wistfully she disrobed, slipped into a black sheer peignoir, and mentally prepared herself for the coming ordeal. Thank God, she only had to please Federico once a month. Thirty days each month she spent in dread of the moment to be spent in intimacy with him, and prepared herself as one might for an execution block or a chamber of horrors. At sixteen Gabriella had been mistress to a sadistic and cruelly inclined man; that had lasted until she was twenty-one, when finally she had worked up guts to escape his brand of torture—nightly torture, with her limbs tied to the bed, spread-eagled, whipped and beaten, burned with matches around the vagina, where the odor of burnt hair had sent her lover off into spasms of orgiastic pleasure. Nightmares, grotesque nightmares, she had taken in her stride until she had numbed herself into insensitivity. Lash marks had criss-crossed her body constantly; even now, after all these years, she bore faint scars. She'd never seen her youthful breasts without gnawed teeth ruts or purple weal marks until after she escaped the German's house. After that nothing a man did to her, or requested she do to him, had fazed her. Having been through the worst of it with the Nazi sadist, anything short of sadism had become a blessing. She had numbed herself to the grotesque sexual aberrations of men.

The first time of intimacy with the Duke, he appeared at her bedside without his toupee, wearing a stocking cap. Very well, she thought, some men wear socks to bed. What's wrong with a stocking cap? Due to his monstrous obesity, the only manner in which sex was possible with him was to mount him, or to engage in oral sex. Oral sex, because of its expediency, suited Gabriella. She could finish him off, drain him sufficiently, and cease contact with him, all in less than three minutes. Warned by doctors that his heart couldn't stand too much strain, Federico tended to space his sexual activities far enough apart to allow him to recuperate from the exertion.

On that first night, as she had moved her hands expertly

343

over his limp penis, she learned that by swearing at him, calling him vile names, she could excite him more readily, she had complied with his request, and when he had called to her, *"succhiare a' mi . . . succhiare a 'mi . . ."* she had obediently buried her head in his crotch and commenced her oral manipulations. Just a moment before ejaculation, eyes glittering maniacally, he'd torn off his stocking cap and pulled out tufts of hair from his head and stuffed them into his mouth! . . . .

Gabriella, who had thought she'd known every form of sexual perversion and all manner of deviants, had nearly choked on the yellowish, pale viscous substance that had spurted from the Duke's penis. Violently appalled by the scene she had vomited convulsively, and it hadn't been until the next morning that the dry heaves had ceased. His candy, perfume, messages, and other baubles had been rejected adamantly, and instantly returned to him. She had refused all communication with him and kept to herself in the Swiss Chalet. Finally, he had sent her a magnificent diamond and platinum bracelet and pleaded with her to listen to his story. The costly gift had weakened her resolve. She had permitted him to come to her suite, where with tear-filled eyes he had related his tale.

The Duke, it seemed, suffered from a form of trichophagia—an abnormal desire to break off one's hair and eat it during sexual release. It had all begun, he'd told her, when he was a small impressionable child. His mother, an Austro-Hungarian, with whom he had formed an abnormal attachment, had missed city life, her own Budapest, and the gay life of northern Italy. The Duke's father, away from the estate for so many long months of the year, had caused a terrible restlessness in the Duchess. She'd fondle her son during his bath, caress him and stimulate him more than a ten-year-old should be stimulated, and force him to watch him masturbate on occasion. Just before she climaxed, she would reach out for young Federico, grasp his head and hair with clutching fingers, and pull tight until she satisfied herself. Once, she had noticed his penis had erected from the erotic stimulation. Angry at what she deemed his indecent reaction she had grabbed at him and actually pulled out chunks of his hair. Whatever had caused him the further excitement—pain or whatever—he ejaculated. Further excited by seeing her son's semen, the Duchess had begun to copulate orally with him. At the point of her own arousal, before orgasm, once again she had pulled out chunks of his hair, and it had become his sad pattern of sexual fulfillment for life.

Tears had rolled down his punchinello face, and he had wept with bitter shame at his confession to Gabriella. He had begged her forgiveness, and promised her the world, if she'd tolerate this quirk in his sexual nature. She took her time deliberating, and, after weighing the factors, she had reasoned that the world was full of lunatics and madmen whose brains were scrambled, and as long as he didn't harm her—what could she lose? Once assured that she'd be rewarded amply for her attention and services, with priceless baubles, she had relented on the ground that she empathized with his problem. Coveting the gifts, she had begun with fierce determination to set them aside, and, as they accumulated, she had found herself waiting for the day he died, for he had provided generously for her in his will. Or, if that took too long, she'd told herself, she'd soon have enough set aside at war's end to go anyplace and live however she chose in luxurious comfort. . . .

"Ah, there you are my sweet, Federico," she purred seductively as the enormous blob of a man entered her boudoir, dressed in an elegant robe of Chinese silk with a stocking cap to match. "Come, I've been waiting anxiously for you, my sweet," she said in a deep, throaty voice, and, floating about the room like a graceful dancer, she began to dim the lights so she barely saw him. It eased the trauma. So did the champagne.

"My dearest," he began. "Would you mind if we put this off until tomorrow night? This chap Bello has tired me. His insufferable suggestions that this peasant, Salvatore, has so mesmerized his people that we are now dependent on him has filled me with such repugnance. . . ." He patted her head affectionately. "My dear you look positively ravishing tonight," he whined. "I had so looked forward to this night with you." Visibly petulant, he stuffed a chocolate cream into his mouth, from a small dish she kept at her bedside for him.

Loathing every moment spent with him, she dreaded the thought she might have to reenforce her courage for another twenty-four hours. Her belly tightened with revulsion. No! By all that was holy, nothing would deter her from getting the disgusting ordeal over with.

She reached out under his fat belly, pulled his limp sex organ from beneath his robe, through his pyjama fly, and began to knead it gently. Rewarded by a slight tremor, she felt more encouraged. It should be easy tonight.

"You mustn't allow this social frog, Bello, to interfere with your pleasure, my lord." she purred, leading him to the oversized bed, by his penis. "Why must you endure all this depressing nonsense? It's you who'll be King! You allow him to croak at you too often! You have needs which must be satisfied—no?" She pushed him down on the bed, where he sighed heavily and lay back, cooing, contentedly.

"My little pigeon, only you understand me. Oh, lucky was the day we met. . . ." He reached to squeeze one of her breasts, a small gesture of compensation for her service.

"Lie back, you fucking prick, and do as I say!" her voice rose and grew dominant and scathing. "You vile son of a whore! Bastard son of an oversexed whore!" she rasped like a raging fishwife.

"Yes! Yes!" he cried, his penis springing urgently to life. "Tell me what I am! I'm all those things you say! I'm no good! I'm a sow-fucking male whore, a craven and depraved humpbacked whale! Fuck me! Suck me! Shit all over me!" His voice was frenzied, his stocking cap falling off.

Gabriella knew her craft well. "You're so rotten the vultures turn away from you! I shall order six of my most disgusting slaves to defecate on your enormously fat belly, pee over you, make you eat their cunts, you screeching son of a bitch, lower than the whores of Satan. . . ." For an instant her voice was muffled by a gurgling sound as she finished him off. It took three minutes.

She helped him to his feet, coaxed him out the door, and accepted a small jewelled box. "Thank you my little pigeon," he said in a dazed breathlessness, with a dopey expression in his gazed wild eyes. He looked perfectly ridiculous with his stocking cap angled rakishly, but his heart, beating too swiftly and his breath, coming in short gasps prevented him from lingering. She closed and locked the door behind him.

Thank God! It was over for a month. She ran to the bathroom, washed her face and hands, and rinsed her mouth out with lemon and water in an effort to rid herself of the taste and feel of him. She turned on the bath water and bathed, scrubbing every inch of her skin until she felt cleansed. In a warm woolen robe she felt better. She had shut her eyes when he had pulled at the tufts of hair. It was less traumatic for her. She couldn't stand the sight of that billiard-ball head, with its small patches of fine hair growing sparsely and at random.

Reaching for a comforter, she dragged it across the Italian provincial bedroom and spread it on the chaise longue.

She'd never sleep in the bed in which she seduced the Duke until after the servants changed the linens.

Gabriella lay back on the damask lounge, under the glow of the lamp light gazing appreciatively at the ruby and diamond earrings the Duke had bestowed upon her. *Not bad for less than five minutes of work,* she told herself. She fell asleep admiring the gems, filled with curious thoughts of this man Salvatore, who, with his spectacular panache, had unknowingly upset the wealthiest man in Sicily, without knowing it.

This Salvatore must be some man! . . .

She stared at a photo of him she had clipped from a newspaper and slipped into the small book on the table in which she made little notes to herself daily. What was there about him that made him so vital to his people? He was a mere man—wasn't he?

Just a mere man. . . .

CHAPTER 26

It had taken three weeks of careful and meticulous planning before Tori was able to go to Godrano. And then one day he was there. He and Vincenzo arrived at the spacious villa of his Godfather, and were met by a slouched-over, aged peasant caretaker who eyed them suspiciously when they stated they had business with Don Barbarossa.

"Park the machine by the stone wall," he muttered, gesturing with his hands.

Tori glanced about the estate with admiration. "This Godfather of mine lives like a baron," he said to Vincenzo. He was glad he'd thought to bring a special tribute befitting so important a man—a man from whom he had to elicit a higher tribute in return. The matched ebony Arabian stallions, with their sleek velvety coat and flashing coal black eyes, would be perfect. Tori had discreetly said nothing to his mother about this encounter, now he wondered how he'd go about effecting a meeting with a man he knew only through her eyes.

"Rumors are that he's richer than any of the *latifon-*

disti—and more powerful," said Vincenzo, holding his awe in reserve. "I believe it. I believe it," he added.

They parked the jeep, and walked towards the dome-covered walkway at the side entrance as directed. Their eyes busily assessing the lush citrus groves, ancient olive trees, and other crops in the meticulously farmed lands.

"You think he'll like the Arabians?" asked Tori.

"Are you crazy? What's not to like? You said he once bred horses, no?"

"Yes."

"Then, calm down. *Managghia*, I've never seen you so excited. He's only a man like you and me. And while we're at it, don't forget who you are. You're not a no-body—you're Salvatore!"

"Yes," said Tori, as if he needed this to reenforce his courage. He tugged at his jacket. "Do I look all right?"

"Perfect," replied Vincenzo shaking his head in tolerant amusement. "Especially in your general's uniform. He'll be impressed, you'll see. *Porco Dio!*" he exasperated. "All this preparation for a Godfather!"

"He's not just any Godfather. He's Salvatore's!"

"That's more like it!" Vincenzo grinned. "And don't you forget it!"

Tori grinned self-consciously and felt better.

Shuffling toward them came a large-framed man in his sixties, with snowy white hair and alert black eyes behind dark tinted glasses, dressed in shirtsleeves and dark trousers held up by a pair of cheap suspenders. Don Matteo, looking tired, somewhat lethargic and older than his years, his face slightly jowled with excess flab, turned toward them without expression or acknowledgement. He walked with a royal posture and, despite his obviously paunched stomach, moved with considerable ease. In his hand he carried a slender stick, which he poked into a profusion of rose bushes bordering the villa, giving the impression he was looking for something. Annoyed at the sign of guests, he moved forward toward the young men, busily engaged in his chore. He'd planned a short holiday and rest away from the busy Palermo duties, but now, with their presence, he abandoned all hope. Preoccupied with the roses, he made alternate grimaces of approval or disapproval, depending on what he found as he inspected the foliage. Within a few feet of the Montegattans, the Don straightened up and demanded with polite aloofness.

"Who are you?"

"We're waiting for Don Barbarossa," said Vincenzo imperiously. He disliked the old geezer on sight.

"I asked—who are you, not what you wanted," snapped the Don.

About to tell the old man what he could do, Vincenzo was held back by Tori's restraining hand. He faced the Don with dignity. "You will tell Don Barbarossa, that I am Salvatore, here to seek audience with him," he spoke with measured politeness.

Don Matteo spat into the ground. Livid at the obvious insult, Vincenzo made a rash move for his gun. Instantly Tori moved to deter his cousin from making the most foolish mistake of his young life. No bodyguards were visible, but he felt instinctively that dozens of eyes were upon them, with perhaps even more guns aimed at their hearts. He was right. At least six guns, hidden from sight, were trained on them at that moment.

"Salvatore *who?*" asked the Don, with noticeable disdain. None of the silent interplay was lost on him.

Vincenzo's anger boiled over. He tensed and glared hotly at the *capomafia*.

"Alessandro Salvatore, Godson to Don Barbarossa," said the famous brigand with aplomb. "Now take me to him and be done with it, old man."

Don Barbarossa took a long hard look at the youth through his bifocals. "Alessandro Salvatore—eh? Huh," he grunted. "Come with me."

Without courtesy, friendliness or recognition, and with an air of decided boorishness, the Don turned abruptly and led the way along the tiled loggia into the villa proper. Vincenzo made a lunge for him with an appropriate facial grimace. Tori stayed him and shook his head in warning.

Neither had ever been subjected to such total lack of respect. The King of Montegatta and his Prime Minister, treated worse than the lowliest of lowly peasants squirmed hotly, their Sicilian pride damaged. Through a series of facial grimaces and hand gestures, Vincenzo conveyed his disgust. Salvatore winked and urged him forward, keeping his own indignation to himself.

They walked through long corridors under domed archways, past diamond-shaped panes of color-stained windows, alongside tropical plants and saintly religious shrines, over the gleaming tiled floors. Their boots clacked with the rhythmic cadence of a tiger beetle's death dance. Somewhere an old Caruso record played "Vesti la Giubba." They were finally ushered into the Don's office, and the two young men gazed about in fascination.

Three walls were covered by a profusion of photographs of high-ranking British and American officers, personally autographed to Don Barbarossa. An American flag, draped carelessly over the bright yellow flag of the Mafia and the tricolored flag of Sicily, stood at the center of a collection of distinguished brass plaques and citations honoring the Don. On the fourth wall, incongrous to the decor, hung a portrait of the most astonishingly beautiful woman with pale blue eyes Salvatore had ever seen. The signature intrigued him: Marco de Leone. The Lion of Sicily was a painter? More remarkable was the fact that the art work should appear in the house of a *mafioso*.

"*Managghia!* What a beauty," whispered Vincenzo appraising the oil.

Tori agreed. His attention turned to the desk—an elegant hand-carved piece with four lion heads supporting each corner and the body of the beast forming graceful legs to support the desk. On it were scattered stacks of papers and a white onyx inkwell with plumed pens. Nearby stood an elegant art object, a snorting bronze bull with flaring nostrils and ferocious eyes, its head sharply angled, displaying curved and pointed horns. Tori stared at it in rapt fascination. He was so absorbed in the deep, coppery, blue-green-hued metal that he failed to hear his host's words until Vincenzo tugged at his arm.

"Sit down," said the Don, without finesse. "Sit down—"

Irritated, yet curiously fascinated by this iceberg of a man, his guests sat in stiff, high-backed chairs opposite the messy topped desk seemingly untouched in a years accumulation of clutter.

"My Godfather's servant, no doubt," whispered Tori.

"*Porco diaoro*," hissed Vincenzo. "I'd like to give him a taste of my hospitality. Pig-eyed rhinoceros."

The Don poured three glasses of wine and lit a cigar without offering one to his guests. He puffed furiously on it until it was well lit. Through the cloudy mist of blue-white smoke, he stared critically at Salvatore. Behind his dark sun glasses, the probing black balls of his eyes studied the bandit with a fierce intensity.

So! This is Salvatore. Reports hadn't lied. Amazingly handsome chap with the charisma of a film idol, he told himself. What was it he had said outside? He is my Godson? *My Godson? Mah,* how the hell is he my Godson? *Managghia!* This is the surprise of all surprises. Who would have thought that the upstart King of Montegatta would turn out to be my Godson? The Don smiled internally, with delicious amusement. Wait until Martino Belasci hears of this! And that *fanatico*—Archbishop Voltera! Phew! With so many godsons, he had lost count.

Don Barbarossa placed the wine glasses before his guests. He raised his glass in a toast and muttered, "*Salute.*"

Salvatore and Vincenzo were thoroughly confused.

"What's wrong? Don't you drink—either of you?" asked Don Matteo.

"We're waiting for my Godfather, before we drink," said Salvatore, containing his rage. He drummed his fingertips against his thighs.

"All right—what are you waiting for?" The *capomafia* raised his glass to his lips and drained the contents. He sat back in his chair and belched.

Salvatore's face turned beet red. A sidelong glance at Vincenzo confirmed his thoughts. Vincenzo had paled excessively. In the uncomfortable silence, Salvatore thought, was it possible this man was Don Matteo Barbarossa? *His Godfather?* He felt sick. Where had the glorified concepts of his illustrious Godfather gone? The dashing libertine? The daring renegade? The flamboyant bandit of Mazzarino? The legend of the man disintegrated before his eyes. Never had he felt so let down!

"*I'm* Don Barbarossa," the Don said finally, removing all doubts.

"Yes, of course. I didn't recognize you," muttered Tori.

"People changed. They grow older. Pictures in the papers are twenty years old," the Don found himself apologizing—and it angered him.

Vincenzo, blustery and red-faced, moved to the door. "I'll leave you both. You must have much to discuss. If you need me, chief, I'll be outside the door." He appeared to be unaffected by the *capomafia;* inwardly his guts writhed. "*Piacere,*" he said to the Don mechanically, and left abruptly, closing the door behind him.

Outside, in the corridor, Vincenzo leaned heavily against the door and drew a long hard breath. Whore of the devil! So, this was Tori's Godfather? He shuddered. The Don, to Vincenzo, was the embodiment of everything evil he'd ever heard of the old Mafia. Why, he wondered, does Tori get involved with these vile *mafiosi?* What was so important they had to come here? *Mafiosi* chilled his blood. Their power-saturated stares could reach inside a man, twist his guts, and render him impotent of courage and life. Quickly he walked outside to where the stallions were housed. He unloaded them, tied them to hitching posts, and stroked their manes compassionately.

"There you are, you black beauties. Breathe fresh air while you can. I don't envy you your new master," he told them. Suddenly he wondered about many things. Why his cousin found it necessary to keep this visit a secret from his mother. Why, after his apparent dislike of *mafiosi* in his village, did Tori confer with the biggest *mafioso* of them all? Godfather or not? His speculation mushroomed. How in hell had his aunt and uncle selected Don Barbarossa to be Tori's *Padrino* in the first place? Sensing eyes upon him, he glanced up as two—four—six armed guards came into his focus from various points. Uneasy, for the first time in a long while, he merely touched his head in a salute and retreated to a nearby *pergola*, where he sat smoking a cigarette in reflective silence.

Godfather and Godson studied each other in silent appraisal. "Who was he?" asked the Don, with obvious dislike for Vincenzo.

"My cousin, Vincenzo de Montana. My co-captain."

"Hah! *Si tiene molto superbo!* He's too impressed with himself. Too arrogant! Hot-headed. A whoremaster."

"He's a good man. Loyal. He knows how to get along," countered Tori.

The Don shrugged indifferently and chewed his cigar, and, for a time, made small talk. "How's your mother?" he asked, at a loss for what to talk about.

"*Bene, grazie.*" Tori's tone matched the Don's in cool aloofness.

The Don's brows shot up. *Now he mocks me,* he thought. "And your Papa?"

"Dead these thirteen years."

Barbarossa made a half-hearted gesture of sympathy. "We all must die—no? Only this we know for sure. *La morte e sempre vittorio.* Death is always the victor." Driven by a natural impatience, the Don asked abruptly, "Well, Godson, is there something you wish from me? Money—a job? What can I do for my Godson?" He scratched his ear, stuck a stubby finger in it, and shook it vigorously, still perplexed at their relationship.

Salvatore sulked internally. *Bastard! He doesn't even know me. Damned if I present the Arabians to him. He leaves me no opening. Very well, I'll talk in terms he'll understand.* He crossed one leg over the other and patted his thigh, deliberating. "No," he said through clenched teeth. "I want no job, no money." He gazed about the room idly. "You have a beautiful place here in Godrano."

"Va, va," began the Don impatiently. "You didn't come here to praise my house."

"En route we saw one of your richly laden caravans."

"Nor have you come to speak of my caravans, eh Godson?"

He fixed a defiant eye on the other and stated simply, "I came for a favor—a special favor."

"A favor?" A faint, smug smile moved across the Don's thick lips, and he lowered his eyes on the sheaf of papers on the desk. "What is this favor?"

"Don Pippinu Grasso."

Barbarossa glanced up. "What about Don Pippinu?"

Tori swallowed hard. He locked eyes with his host and replied firmly, "I want him killed."

The *capomafia* didn't bat an eyelash. He removed his dark glasses, cleaned the lenses with a handkerchief, and gazed into his Godson's eyes. Tori felt the impact of those eyes as many men before him had, and he trembled inwardly; yet he held firm with his own steady gaze.

The Don, seething inwardly, broke the contact by barricading his burning orbs with the glasses once again. "Why come to me? From what I hear, you're perfectly capable of handling your own contracts."

"Because you can do it in such a way that it won't be traced to me," said Tori nonchalantly, irking the Don.

If the *mafioso's* astonishment was pronounced, and if he was grossly insulted by such obvious lack of respect shown him in these past moments, he contained himself superbly. "If, in my younger days, I had dared to be as impertinent as you young, overinflated cocks are these days, I'd have been tossed out on my ass and made into feed for vultures." He sighed resignedly. "Times have changed, no?" Behind those camouflaging glasses, his black eyeballs chafed with indignation, and his blood boiled at the audacity and pure gall of the man, Salvatore.

"I'll waste as few words as possible. There was no way I could have approached you before, Godfather. As it is, I've waited two years before coming to you." Tori himself grew bolder, for the Don with his earlier statement, had led Tori to believe that he wasn't totally unknown to the *mafioso.* "You see, I know you've been a busy man, and I, also am not without responsibilities."

Seated in a leather upholstered swivel chair, one elbow propped up on the arm, with a hand placed meditatively over his lips, the Don controlled himself remarkably well. His eyes were on the cigar he rolled between the fingers of his other hand.

"What injustice has Don Pippinu done to you that you ask his life in return?

"What injustice? Shall I list them all? *Va bene.* He cheated my mother and family out of money justly due us. He murdered my bride—an innocent flower in the bloom of life—without compassion. He violated the code of silence, by falsely reporting me to the *carabinieri* on trumped-up and false charges. Because of him, I killed a man needlessly. And because of him I embarked on a life of crime."

"You killed one man? Hah," grunted the Don. "Only one man, eh? Salvatore," he said in a patronizing tone, "I've heard tell there is more than one scalp strung to your belt of victories."

Tori's eyes flickered in amusement. He was right: he *wasn't* a stranger to this conspiratorial old devil. *His bags flow to overflowing with countless tricks. Va bene,* thought Tori. "What I've done was forced upon me by the vile and contemptible acts of this worthless son of a pig-eyed whore, Don Pippinu," he declared, innocence and naivete in his voice.

The Don countered skillfully. "You, Salvatore, have the gall to come to me? You, who've been like acid to our intestines for nearly two years? You've no respect for authority—only your own. You confiscate our goods, kill our guards, cut into our pockets, robbing us of profits—and now you come for a favor! You who've taken the law into your own hands have the *fegato* to come to my villa and demand the life of a brother?" He smirked contemptuously and spat into a nearby spittoon, with apparent disgust. He sat back in his chair, a leer on his face, indicating he held the trump card. "If I so desire, I'd have but to press a button and my men would immobilize you, finish you off if necessary—and no one would be the wiser."

Tori's eyes were fixed in fascination upon the bronze bull, taken by its powerful form. He appeared impervious to the Don's threats.

"You don't believe me?" The Don was both annoyed and favorably impressed with Tori's cool manner. His hands moved over a panel of buttons on the desk.

"If you were serious, Godfather, you wouldn't have taken time to warn me first." Quicker than the eye could follow, he whipped out his Browning, laid it on the desk. "But—you'd have to be faster than me."

In that instant, Tori chanced to see several newspaper clippings, with photos of himself, staring back at him from

354

a corkboard on the wall behind the Don's chair. His courage mounted.

Don Matteo looked at the gun as he might a fly. New respect shone in his eyes for the young man. He listened with fierce intensity as Tori spoke.

"Between actual facts and the reported words stand miles of disparities and untruths. In my province, before I took charge, babies died before taking their first breath because their mothers were sick and diseased from lack of food. Would you suggest I turn my back on the graft and corruption imposed upon my people by foreigners? How can you—who profess to love Sicily—turn your back on your own people? You permit the land barons to grow fatter by aborting the land and squeezing it dry. You claim to be father to the peasants? Hah! Instead, like a judas goat, you lead them to slaughter. I tell you, Godfather, you'd best look to the future instead of the past if you care anything for this great land of ours."

"Slaughter, you say?" The Don nodded. "Perhaps. But isn't that what one usually does with animals—especially sheep? Lead them to slaughter?" he mocked his guest. The Don thought, if I didn't have more vital and far-reaching plans for this *capo de cazzi*, I'd fix his balls for good. Furiously chewing his cigar, he wondered why he was permitting this impertinence and this dialogue.

The insult hit home. Tori's fists clenched, but he was damned if he'd let the Don know it.

"Ah, Salvatore, Salvatore," lamented the Don with special theatrics. "You haven't learned, yet. Peasants are no better than animals. They live in filth, worse than the stinking Bedouin across the sea from whose bellies most of them sprang. They've no guts to assert themselves. Look at me! The son of a man considered the lowliest of peasants. Did I remain in filth and squalor? No. I rose above my fellow men to become *numero uno*. It's true. I killed, murdered, and robbed to make myself important in a land where the peasant has no chance." He snorted. "I learned a long time ago the peasants are content to flounder about in their own shit."

"They are uneducated—"

"You think I was educated? My schooling came from the hard knocks I got from trying to survive. Now I survive the way the *latifondisti* survive."

"We're not all cut from the same cloth—"

"Ahhh," grunted the Don making guttural noises deep in his throat. "My sentiments, precisely. Some men are leaders. Others are content to follow. Should the leaders

355

continuously provide for the followers? Let them eat bread from the fat of the land gained by another's sword? *Porca miseria!* That's crazy thinking. You breed communism as sure as the seasons change each year. Peasants have to learn to take orders and work—"

" 'For slaves' wages? Oppressed by your *gabellotti* and indifferent landlords, who consider them so much cattle fodder? Where is it written that Sicilians must be slaves of the Church and the feudalists forever? Is there never to be a Utopia for them?" retorted Tori hotly.

The Don's patience wore thin. He wanted to argue and enlighten this brash young man, but, knowing it would be useless, he remained silent.

Tori remained adamant. "Since the inception of time, Sicily's been a refuge for slaves and the downtrodden serf. The status of the peasant, the real backbone of Sicily, remains the same. He's unable to work for a decent wage. No one has done a thing to elevate him from his misery." Annoyed by the direction of the conversation, Tori thought to end the subject. "Certainly their grievances can't be solved here and now by either you or me."

The transition in the *capomafia* was instant, immediate. "Don't be too sure of that, my boy. Do you know who it is to whom you speak? The most powerful man in all of Sicily—that's who," he boasted. "Do you really know who I am?"

"Do you know who I am, Godfather?" asked Tori, reining in his anger.

"I know who you are. What we can do for each other is more important."

In that split second Tori experienced a peculiar sensation, one so inexplicable and profoundly disturbing to him by what he saw reflected in the Don's mannerisms, that he was left shaken for a while. It was all there, the well-modulated, power-saturated glance and voice, the eye movements all of it. It was all too familiar to Tori, as if he'd held a mirror up reflecting himself. . . .

Irked because he'd been somehow driven to boast before this Godson of whom he had no recollection except from newspaper reports and the data supplied him by his network and spies—and those raving idiots on the Palermo Grand Council—he tugged at his memory, wondering how in hell it was that he had come to be Godfather to Salvatore. He knew very few people in Montegatta. Now how in the name of a bloated frog had it all come about? How? He tried a new approach. "You say you've not touched one of our caravans?"

"I've had no need to, yet, Godfather."

"You've a slick way with words."

"Why should what I do explode your corpuscles?" He took time to light a cigarette.

"Besides," added Tori, "my time has been taken up maintaining law and order in my village. The law of Salvatore prevails now."

Tori manipulated the conversation, designed to impress the Don with the dual purpose of letting the other know where the real power lay in the west and that of letting him know that Salvatore's name carried much weight. Meanwhile Don Barbarossa, in his unique manner, permitted Tori to ramble. He listened, and by listening with all his senses he learned more than Tori intended him to perceive.

"Since you are so all-powerful, why not handle Don Pippinu yourself?" A gleam of diabolical cunning sparked for an instant in the Don's eyes.

"Due to the vast space of emptiness that's existed between us over the years, I've wondered how far the bond of Godfather and Godson stretches," Tori temporized, then added cryptically, "A man must close the books on bankruptcy and go forward."

"What the hell does that mean? Listen, I don't appreciate riddles. And don't be clever with me. I don't like clever men," blurted the Don tightly.

Tori, taking the bull by the horns, argued, "If I slay Don Pippinu, it would add another crime to the formidable deeds already attributed to me, one which couldn't be argued as an involuntary act in a court of law. It would always sting as a premeditated crime, done by my own volition. Don't you see? Don Pippinu remains the only creditor to be paid off before I can move forward. I believe in closing all the doors after each bit of business, Godfather."

The Don heard him, but he didn't believe his ears. Too many contradictions stuck out in the lad already, like a swollen jaw. What a strange man is this who speaks of courts and law. What the hell's wrong with him? What the *capomafia* didn't understand, he dismissed by a wave of his hand and insults. "Bah! Sicily's no place for cowards and malcontents, certainly not for men afraid to piss in daylight."

"To be called a coward by anyone else would have brought instant retaliation," Tori said evenly. "I'm sure you didn't mean those words." It struck Tori that the Don's education was limited, that he didn't understand words with double meanings, so he proceeded on a differ-

357

ent tack, measuring his words carefully and employing a sprinkling of guile. "I, also, have found people to be foolish. Peasants, for that matter, can be more wanton than landlords and as capricious as lawmakers—"

"Ah!" exclaimed the Don. "Marvel of marvels. Then you are learning." The Don sat back in his chair, smug in his conceit, while Tori said nothing. After a moment the tight-lipped Don said quietly," "And if I should comply with your bidding?"

"I shall be forever indebted to you."

Don Matteo's head angled sharply. His brows shot up in amazement and his eyes locked with Tori's. Moments passed. Neither moved a muscle or spoke a word. Across the room a small yellow bird flew in, circled once, and came to rest on an open window sill, chirping audaciously, demanding attention. The Don averted his head, pleased.

"Ah, there you are, little friend." From his desk drawer, he removed a small box filled with bread crumbs, and, walking towards the bird, he asked cooingly, "Where've you been, you little rascal? I miss you when I don't see you. . . ." The bird took a crumb from between the Don's fingers and chirped his little head off. "See how I've trained him? When I'm away, the servants feed the little beggar—but he sings only for me." The Don laughed in a surprisingly gentle manner. When the bird flew away, the Don returned to his desk and picked up on the conversation as if there'd been no interuption.

"Among us, young man, words of honor are not spoken or taken lightly. You've uttered some heavy words, here. There may come a time when, called upon, you must return the favor done for you. . . . You've asked me to turn against my own kind, a political associate with whom I find no quarrel. In the brotherhood we are all brothers of a unity—of one strength. . . ."

"But, I'm your Godson! An injustice has been done me!"

The *capomafia* stared sullenly. *Godson! Che Demonio!* How the hell did I become his Godfather? He felt plagued by the question, disgraced to admit he couldn't remember his own Godson. Certain things were considered sacred and the Don wouldn't think of refuting him in the matter. This situation certainly put a different slant on the plans he had had in store for this cocks o' the walk, he admitted sourly. He watched the splendid young man sit down.

Mistaking the Don's silence for encouragement, Salvatore found himself relating the full story of Don Pippinu's treachery, of the subsequent fate of Apolladora. Still the Don made no comment. No indication of his feelings, one

358

way or the other, were visible on his face. When Salvatore finished, he redirected his plea.

"You'll see that justice is done, Godfather? That Don Pippinu pays for his deception? That I, your Godson, shall be avenged?"

Silence permeated the room. Salvatore could hear the savage beat of his heart bursting through his chest. His words had evoked a series of mental images and he felt himself reliving the horrors following Apolladora's death. He could feel the sweat roll off him, the dampness of his palms, the rising excitement, as he waited for an answer.

Barbarossa shook his head dubiously. "I agree to nothing—yet. Don Pippinu is an influential man, with many important friends. He controls the vote in Trapani, Marsala, and Mt. Erice. What do you control? What can I get from you in return for so special a favor?"

Tori got the picture all right. He squirmed uncomfortably and slapped the side of his boot, crossed over one leg, lightly with his fingers.

"Do my words shock you?" the Don said. "Offend you? If so you'd better learn the gut level of political manipulations. Nothing is for nothing in this life." On his feet, the Don paced the floor, chewing his cigar thoughtfully. "You say the weights and measures were established in the time of your Grandfather?"

"Si. The Naxos family held the license."

"Naxos. The Naxos family. The Don dug into his memory. "Naxos?" He had come to a complete stop before the portrait of the young beauty, when suddenly it all came together for him. He spun around, stared at Tori as if for the first time. "You are the son of Antigone Naxos?"

"*Salvatore*. Antigone Naxos *Salvatore*," Tori emphasized.

"The son of Antigone Naxos," repeated the Don. *Son of my heart!* He stared with wonder, at the strong jaw line, the unmistakable handsome features, the clear-sighted eyes, sparking with life, the even white teeth, the full lips, the shape of which he hadn't forgotten in two decades. The look of wonderment on his face dissolved his previous icy detachment. He returned to his chair, stalling for time. Color rose to his face, and he tried to subdue the pleasure shooting through him. "Tell me, how is your mother? Are your two older brothers in your organization?"

"She's as well as one can be in these troubled times. My brothers were killed in the war. Only a younger sister and I remain at home." The alteration of the Don's personality wasn't lost on Tori; before him the precious icy wall of reserve had suddenly melted away.

"The son of Antigone Naxos," the Don muttered.

Tori wondered at his sudden loss of guile, at the sentimental melancholy he detected when he spoke the name, Antigone Naxos.

"When do you come to Palermo?"

"With a price on my head, I don't court trouble. In my territory I roam with ease. Outside my domain, if a curious policeman spots me it might prove embarrassing for me, lethal for him. I provoke no such encounters without good reason."

"That's the only reason?"

"It's enough. . . ."

The Don opened his desk drawer, selected six cards, and scrawled his signature across them and handed them to Salvatore. "Passes signed by the Minister of the Interior, countersigned by me. Now, you can travel anyplace without fear. If accosted, stop. Show your passes and the *carabinieri* and security police will not dare touch you."

"You control the *carabinieri* like you do the security police?" Salvattore gave him a cynical, speculative glance.

The Don smiled enigmatically. "Its luck you found me here in Godrano. I spend little time here. I'm always found at my *apartamento* in Palermo, where I work with the Grand Council and act as chief advisor to AMGOT . . ."

"Work? I understand you *are* the Grand Council!"

The Don fairly glowed under the compliment. He nodded. "It's important that we prevent the spread of communism. God help us if Russia conquers us! She'll control the Mediterranean for sure, and in no time—the world! Sicily must be free. Separate from Italy. We must govern ourselves. With full autonomy."

Salvatore shrugged. "I leave that to you politicians," he said shrewdly. "I've little interest in politics. At least not until I've studied law, and earned the degree which qualifies me to be a lawmaker. . . ."

Don Matteo glanced up from his desk with a look of profound interest. Was the lad mocking him? Was he expressing sincerity, or was he playing a game? What? His last two statements had been as provocative as hell—but were they true, from the heart, or deliberately designed to deceive? The crafty and cunning politician put Salvatore to the test. Scowling darkly he snapped with marked irritation.

"Being a Sicilian, in itself, qualifies you to become a lawmaker, Godson! I hope you aren't the idealistic dreamer the papers print you to be. Experience in life and a knowledge of your people qualifies you—not what you learn in books!" He snorted contemptuously. The reaction on Salvatore's face puzzled the Don, and he continued to assess the true nature of the young renegade.

"Tell me, are you making jest with me with this apparent naivete? How could you have risen to such power, thinking asinine thoughts?" For a moment, the Don suppressed an internal smile. Was it just possible Salvatore wasn't fully aware of the power he wielded? Was it? Son of a bitch! This brigand was either a paradox or a simple phenonemon. Which? He decided to pursue the issue.

"You should *be* interested in politics. You, who command over five hundred men and influence thousands of people, should be vitally interested! What happens to our people shall effect you forever!" he insisted. Suddenly the Don, faltered. He stopped himself from projecting the role of father to son, and wondered at his having such a reaction to the bandit whose antics had caused him considerable distress among his peers. The ambivalence shook him.

Salvatore replied. "With such formidable politicians at the helm—like you—why should I interfere? How could I hope to know what it's taken you a lifetime to learn?"

Why do I feel that he mocks me? wondered the Don, who suspected most men. Having been taught the ropes early in life, the hard way, he couldn't accept a compliment without suspecting the motive behind it. Despite his feelings he found himself extending the lad an invitation which, later, upon reflection came to baffle him. In a sudden mad impulse he insisted, "You'll come to see me at the *Albergo-Sole* in Palermo. Use the passes and you'll be admitted without question. Hear?"

"The *Albergo-Sole?* At Allied Command Headquarters? Isn't it off limits to civilians?"

"Off limits to anyone but me. Not even Nick Gentile or Vito Genovese has been accorded the privileges given me. You'll come. At the noticeable reluctance he saw in his Godson's face he hastened to add, "When you come to Palermo next week, I shall show you how politics are born and give you my reply to your request concerning Don Pippinu Grasso . . . *va bene?*"

"I can't make a definite appointment, Godfather," replied the cagey bandit. I promise I shall come one day soon . . ." He rose to his feet.

"Smart lad!" nodded the Don. "You remind me of myself in my Mazzarine days when, I, too, trusted no one. . . ." He shuffled his feet along to the front of the

361

desk and did the unexpected. He embraced the young man affectionately and fairly glowed with charm. "You'll give my warmest wishes to your Mamma . . . *allora* . . . until we meet again. *Ciao.* . . ."

Tori holstered his gun casually. Earlier, when the air between them had been filled with venom, he had decided against giving the Don the matched Arabians, now he had better thoughts about the matter.

"*Managghia*, Godfather! I clearly forgot!" He tapped his forehead in a significant gesture. "I've brought you a tribute. A small gift, to help erase the long years of silence between us, with hopes we may restore the closeness our families once enjoyed.

As overwhelming curiosity overtook him, the Don set aside the countless plaguing questions with mixed emotions, he followed the youth outside. He did this only after he pressed a button under his desk, which signalled to his bodyguards outside the villa.

When Don Matteo first saw the breathtaking sight of matched horseflesh, he stopped in his tracks. Actually, he trembled with excitement at the sight of such perfect specimens. Stunned by the unexpected generosity, he couldn't find the words to thank his Godson. He didn't have to. Having already experienced such joy when Vincenzo had presented him with Napoleono, Tori knew his Godfather's thrill must be double that of his.

Several of the Don's men, standing in the shadows with poised guns, retreated at the silent signal they received from their Don. Watching Godfather and Godson, Vincenzo de Montana sensed a distortion. There was something wrong in this picture before him, he thought, despite the bond which appeared to have sprung up between them in his absence. He watched as they embraced in parting, and this display of questionable affection, no matter how sincere it appeared on the surface, didn't ease the cold terror in his heart.

Long after the Montegattans left, the Don remained with the stallions, bursting with pride to be the possessor of such magnificent beasts and wondering how Salvatore could have been persuaded to part with them. That *"the great Salvatore"* had, in the manner of a vassal, honored him with such a fine tribute assured Don Matteo that his position as the greatest of Sicilian overlords was indisputable. To be held in such high esteem brought a glow of satisfaction to him.

Back in his study, the Don reflected upon the events of

their encounter, and admitted he was awed by this young bandit leader who had caused a furor among the *latifondisti* and created a cult of hero worshippers among the noted journalists of the land.

Managghia! This Salvatore knew how to make himself remembered! Who could forget such a tribute? At least, the first step in the journey of many miles had been taken on this day, he told himself as he poured himself a cup of *espresso* from a pot a servant had brought in. In the future, they would become better and better acquainted, he promised himself. The *espresso* was hot, bitter and strong. He made a wry face and retrieved a bottle of anisette from the tray. He poured a spurt into the murky steam, recapped the bottle and sipped the hot liquid. He smacked his lips and uttered a loud, "Ahhhh." He spun his chair about and gazed out the window in a reflective mood.

Reacting to all men at a gut level, Don Barbarossa knew instinctively if a man was honest or dishonest; if he should be trusted or feared; if he was friend or foe. With Salvatore he was sure of nothing. Something complex in his nature, something with which he couldn't identify, left him feeling unduly excited. This was no ordinary young man. Behind the cool manner, polite self-assurance, he sensed a shrewd brain, a dogged refusal to be intimidated or impressed or detered from any but his own point of view. He reflected.

Porco Diaoro! he thought. *How the hell does he come to be my Godson?* He spent several moments trying to recollect all the Godsons he'd baptized during his reign as *capomafia,* and quickly abandoned the project. There had been too many. He proceeded, then, to the next logical step, he hoped might unravel the mystery—Antigone Naxos Salvatore.

Antigone Naxos Salvatore! What could she have been, then? In her early twenties? How could he forget?

Away from Palermo, on a holiday doing a little *caccia*—hunting—on the estate of a friend near Porto Tommaso, the Don had been riding without a bodyguard on this brusque day in February in 1922. Through ancient Greek ruins and prolific orange and lemon groves ripe with winter harvest, past *pagliai,* straw storage huts, he rode, spotting a nearby well, the *capomafia* had wheeled his horse about to sate his thirst. Curious, and cautious, and ever on the alert for his enemies, the Don dismounted, and with drawn guns searched the *pagliao* for interlopers. He peered about the shadowy interior, satisfied his fears were groundless; until suddenly, he chanced to see the huddled form of a young, frail woman, with haunting dark eyes, hugging her two small sons to her bosom.

When asked to identify herself, she first comforted her two sons and instructed them to remain inside, while she accompanied the stranger into the glaring sunlight. She had blinked her sensitive eyes at the brightness and shielded her eyes for a time. She begged his forgiveness for intruding on his property and, with quivering lips, explained she had no place to go. She had fled her village, fearing for her life and of her sons' lives, in the wake of Cesare Mori's holocaust. Mussolini's chief executioner, in his sworn attempt to liquidate all *mafiosi* in his all-out war on the Mafia, had invaded Sicily and was killing everyone in sight, *mafioso* or not. "Lined up like animals, the peasants have been shot indiscriminately in a mass murder by Mori's men. Everyone in Piana dei Greci, Villalba, Corleone, Montelepre and Montegatta has already taken to the hills!"

Had the stories been true, the Don assured her, he would have heard. His stern reprimand left Antigone dumfounded. His lack of concern sobered her. Hysteria was replaced by self-assertion. Noting his country-squire hunting habit, she presumed him to be owner of the estate she'd trespassed upon.

"I'm not demented, Excellency. I tell you I was witness to the depravity. I saw men and women and children, even priests, lined up in a row, while Mori's *squadristi*, with machine guns opened fire and massacred them. To cover their butchery, they dumped bodies into deep mountain crevasses to remain forever lost to their loved ones." She implored him not to return to the city. "There'll not be a Sicilian left in our land when this most obscene of obscenities is through. Only the powerful *latifondisti* have escaped his wrath." Antigone shivered in the cool breeze.

He studied her smooth, tanned face with its high cheekbones smudged with dirt, and looked deeply into her deeply concerned dark eyes. Beneath the veneer of nervous self-consciousness he saw a stunning woman. Having instructed her to stay well hidden, he promised to return later with food for the children and blankets to keep warm. He directed her to the nearby well, should they need water. She confided that she was uncertain of her husband's whereabouts. In the confusion they parted, and when she didn't find him at their house, she had taken to the hills to protect her sons.

He removed his jacket, insisted she wear it, and begged

364

her not to worry in his absence. From his saddle holster he removed a *lupara*, loaded it for her, and handed her a chamois pouch of pellets. "Use it if you must," he told her, swinging to his saddle expertly before riding off swiftly into the hills.

At the Duke's estate, the Don immediately dispatched a courier to Palermo to learn what, if anything, had transpired. He returned to the woman that night after dinner, with a basket laden with foods and supplies. Her face had been scrubbed clean. A thick shock of black hair hung loosely, like coils of ebony, about her shoulders, and she moved about with a certain unique majesty. He watched her feed the lads and taken not of the bond of love and devotion between them. After supper she wrapped them in blankets and put them to sleep.

Outside the *pagliao*, they had walked about in the early twilight in the beam of light cast by a full, silver moon. Already a canopy of stars glittering like chipped ice had appeared above. Antigone became awkward and self-conscious under his fixed stare. She thanked him for his generosity.

"You are a beautiful woman, *Signora*," he told her. "You speak unlike most woman I have known—more like the nobility." She acknowledged the compliment, and noticed that the words didn't come easy to him.

"What will you do, now? You can't remain here for long. The workers are in planting. Its likely they'll be working this section tomorrow. You'll be seen. I am concerned for your welfare. Come with me and I will protect you," He found himself telling her. "I myself shall return to Palermo as soon as I learn what is happening."

"No! I beg you. You mustn't go. You'll be killed. Stay away from the city until this madman Mori and his villains return to Rome. This barbarian kills at random—without mercy!" she insisted.

Matteo Barbarossa, moved emotionally that a stranger should show such concern for his welfare, hadn't been able to restrain the desire rising from the pit of his stomach to engulf him at that moment. Something intangible stirred his senses; something reminiscent of the only woman he'd ever loved in his Mazzarino days. Something about Antigone had reminded him of his former mistress, Diamonte, and he thought despairingly of his empty, loveless life of recent years. His wife, with whom he'd rarely coupled, he'd loathed. Her ugliness and uncouth manners had forced him into a life of quiet desperation. Three years of marriage—and the three times he'd been intimate with her had produced three daughters. He'd simply not been interested in other women until th ismoment with Antigone, who in an instant had become the *one* woman most men meet in a lifetime, and live to regret they hadn't taken more time to cultivate.

He turned to her, took her work-worn hands between his, and said, "Mori wouldn't dare touch me. Not one hair from the head of Matteo Barbarossa would he have courage to disturb," he proclaimed imperiously.

The color drained from her face. "Matteo Barbarossa?" The name alone evoked paralytic fear. Being in his company had had an even more staggering effect. She moved away from him, stared in disbelief. Her hands flew to her lips, loath to have spoken his name. *"Barbarossa?* The Mazzarino?" She continued to back away from him. The shock of meeting this legend face to face, the trauma of her frightening adventure, her weakened condition from lack of proper nourishment, or the combination of all three— had caused her to fall faint.

Matteo caught her as she fell, and laid her upon the ground. Quickly removing his jacket, he rolled it up and placed her head under it. He rubbed her hands, smoothed her forehead, and pushed aside silky strands of hair. She hadn't been the phenomenal beauty Diamonte had been— but what a great face. Strong, compelling and filled with love. One who saw her couldn't forget her, he'd thought.

"I don't mean to startle you, *Signora,*" he apologized when she'd begun to stir faintly. "There is nothing to fear from me." He astonished himself with such gentleness. The need and desire to be tender had long since left him. "Will you believe me?" he asked, helping her to her feet.

"You must think me to be an imbecile. I've never fainted before." She grew reserved when she saw desire in his eyes. "I can repay your kindness by imploring you not to return to Palermo under any circumstance. You, especially will be murdered on sight. This Mori is psychotic—sick in the head. I've learned one thing in this life, you don't reason with insanity. That's why I fled my village when I saw such random killing." Her composure had returned slowly in bits and pieces.

"Thank you for your concern," he said, smiling a rare smile. "I'm too important to be touched and they know it."

Antigone in full admiration shrugged imperceptibly. "Do what you will. But, remember Mori is a madman. In his fantasy, all of Sicily is Mafia!"

They walked the full length of the path to the well and back, pausing to inhale the sweet heady aroma of the fertile earth and the fragrant scent of orange and lemon blossoms. They talked a bit; she spoke of her heritage, told him her ancestors came from the Island of Naxos, named for her forefathers. She spoke of her grandfather and father, who owned the weights and measures in Mt. Erice. Not once did she stop to look at him, or note the effect she had been having on the notorious Don Matteo.

"You really don't seem concerned about this Cesare Mori?"

"Non é importanto ora. It's not important at this moment," he'd said.

She tried once more to impress him with the gravity of the situation. "Under the direct orders of Il Duce to exterminate the Mafia, he performs mass murder on countless thousands of innocent people. In Palermo, warrents for every known *mafioso* have been issued. Village dons, their followers and hired killers are being shot on sight. I was told most had fled into the hills to escape this lord high executioner. You see, he means to liquidate all of us. The Mafia is just a pretext!" she said bitterly.

"It's not important, now," he had repeated quietly, as they strolled under the enormous moon.

She'd shrugged. *The man is fearless,* she'd thought. *Very well, at least I warned him. If he doesn't wish to believe me. . . .* She looked about her and inhaled the sweet smells of the night. "When the silver moon and bonanza of winking stars overhead light up these nights and the ruins of ancient civilizations come to life to stir your senses to remind you of long-ago empires and conquerors, you know it's time for planting," she said breathlessly. "Next to harvest, it has to be the most romantic time in Sicily. And did you know that in certain areas close to the gulf of Castellammare, legend has it that if you stand still long enough and set your mind to it, the sounds of far off trumpets heralding the approach of the glorious Roman Caesars and their centurions, who came to Sicily to frolic several months out of the year, can be heard?" Antigone had paused a moment to look at him.

He laughed easily. "In Sicily anything is possible."

She nodded. Suddenly they looked at each other in that marvelous, unique way that transcends all worldly affection, politics, religions, philosophy, and government—and all else that is but pure adornment. They met and touched at the depths of their emotions, felt a power greater than personal will, and stood suspended in a moment borrowed out of the time of man and both experienced an inexplicable miracle.

Neither had anticipated such an explosive encounter.

When it was over, and they no longer felt as shaken and breathless and full of wonder, Matteo left reluctantly for the villa, with the promise to return the next day. He thought of nothing else for the balance of the night. When he returned the following day, Antigone was gone. She was no where to be found. No trace of her or her sons had remained. For a time, the Don wondered if he had dreamed her. When he'd relived those moments in which he'd headed for infinity during their sexual embrace, he'd known she'd been for real. For a long time she had remained in his mind—a vivid reality. How could he forget his Grecian goddess in the moonlight with the soul-stirring name of Antigone Naxos, with whom he had made love against a background of ancient Greek ruins?

In Palermo, chaos existed. Many of the brotherhood had fled in the night, booked passage, illegal or otherwise, to other parts of the world, mainly America. Others had sworn allegiance to fascism or went underground.

Arrested by his own hand and knowing that prison would be the safest place for him, until the *fascisti* cooled off, he had spent a few years in the Mafia prison at Ucciardone, much like a rest home for erring executives. One day, two years later the Don had walked out into broad daylight, the entire file of his criminal activites tucked safely under his arm, never to be heard of again for twenty years.

Don Matteo poured himself another cup of coffee, lit up a fresh cigar and continued to reflect. He'd never seen Antigone again. Yet this outlaw boldly claimed him as Godfather. Why had the woman filled her son with such deception? Why? Why? Why? More peculiar to the Don was why he himself hadn't set the lad straight? He was never ever hesitant or vague with others. Surprised and annoyed at himself, he wondered why he'd been so benevolent.

Don Matteo's soul retreated in confusion to the inner security of his usual craftiness, guile and treachery. In a few days he'd dispatch his trusted bodyguard, Mario Cacciatore, to locate Salvatore's mother and arrange a meeting to discuss the situation with her. He wondered—would she still remember him?

He swiveled his chair around, faced the wall containing the newspaper clippings, and stared at the photographs of the young outlaw. Sonofagun! This Salvatore was mercurial—perhaps as impossible and unmanageable as he'd

368

heard. But, like himself, he was a living legend, a man who had killed as many *carabinieri* as he himself had, if not more. No one had been able to stop him. Ambushes and traps set for him failed, and he always fought his way out of the tightest situations with uncanny insight. With no real military training of any kind, two solid years at fighting off these crack military police had earned him the name of Salvatore the Invincible. How incredible it was that Salvatore won coup after coup with unshakeable *panache!* Sonofagun! It was marvelous, how he had captured the imagination of over four million people! Don Matteo had to give him that much.

Images rushed at him, and suddenly he saw himself as he had been in the old days, as the redoubtable bandit of Mazzarino. These images alternated with those of Salvatore, and, superimposed over each other it became difficult for him to separate them. *Managghia!*" he declared. "It's like looking at a reflection of me in my younger years." Somehow, though, no suspicion entered his mind that he could possibly have sired this incredible phenomenon.

He poured himself a tumbler of wine now and flipped through a few pages of reports he had requested from his aide in Palermo. In moments his thoughts dwelled on Don Pippinu Grasso. How much of Salvatore's story could he believe? With two sides to each story, he promised himself he'd look into the matter, and resolve the issue.

Don Pippinu had grown influential and valuable to him these past few years. On the other hand, Salvatore's strength would be invaluable, in the days ahead, in his plans to control Sicily. Weighing the matter in his mind, he was surprised to see the scales tipped favorably to Salvatore. His mind made up, he summoned a servant. "Pack my bags. I'm returning to Palermo. Tell Mario Cacciatore to meet me there. I have a special job for him."

CHAPTER 27

No one had to tell Don Pippinu Grasso that Salvatore would retaliate in the unwritten law of vendetta for the death of Apollodora. What stuck in the Don's craw was

369

the fact that no money had been found on the bastard. He hadn't considered that the *carabinieri* might be holding out on him, only that Salvatore had somehow gotten away with all that money. That Tori had become a branded fugitive who couldn't show his face for a time didn't pacify the Mt. Erice Don, or avenge the shame and disgrace he felt at having been duped by so young a man. A convoluted logic ate at him like a malignancy. Never mind that he'd been the wrongdoer and perpertrator of the first evil.

Six months after the culmination of the distasteful and shameful affair, newspapers carrying bits of information about the amazing feats of Salvatore caused the Don to regret the injustice he had inflicted upon the son of his third cousin. Extra guards posted around his villa, and at the countless business interests he owned, kept a sharp lookout for treachery. When a year passed and no troubles arose, he dismissed thoughts of retaliatory action with a boast, "Salvatore wouldn't dare touch Don Pippinu!"

Two years later strangers began to frequent Naxos Weights and Measures. Always courteous, respectful and with authoritative manners, these men, dressed like dandies, would ask, "Which one is Don Pippinu?" The clerks would point to their employer. "The fat one? The one who stinks like swine?" Flushed with embarrassment, the clerks, casting furtive glances in the Don't direction, would not. "Yes, the one who stinks."

Thereupon the strangers would study the *mafioso* inscrutably for a time, as if committing him to memory. They'd exchange secret grins before departing. Many people came to gape at the formidable Mafia Don, who'd grown powerful and despotic through his association with the reestablished Mafia. So, at first, the clerks thought little of these incidents, until one day, when they began comparing notes, and felt obligated to inform the Don of this curious group of strangers and their subsequent inquiries.

It never occurred to Don Pippinu that any of this might be Salvatore's doing so long after the fact. During his rapid growth in the war years he'd made many enemies. Many were jealous of his power. In lieu of these developments, however, he chose to confine himself within a small stall and barred windows resembling early day postal booths where dollars were exchanged into lira—and where guns were kept secreted in the event of a holdup. A rigged alarm could be activated by a clerk instructed to pull a cord under a counter if and when some stranger appeared making inquiries about Don Pippinu. Automatically a small light would blink on and off beneath the

Don's counter in the cage, affording him first view of the strangers. Off the premises, he was constantly accompanied by at least two imposing brutes.

Two years to the date of Apollodora's savage death, Vincenzo de Montana, Turridu Nuliano and Dominic Lamantia entered Naxos Weights and Measures. They walked directly towards the small money cage where the Don sat confined. A clerk pulled the cord. Instantly the light in the stall blinked on and off alerting the Don. He reached for the gun and was about to press another alarm summoning his personal bodyguards.

"I wouldn't do that, *Signore*," said Lamantia coolly. He stood at the side window, a gun aimed at the Don's head, some six inches from his temple. He grinned wickedly when the Don, startled, turned in his direction. Vincenzo and Turridu stood facing them at the front window.

"Don Pippinu," Vincenzo paused a moment. "I've a message for you." He went through a lengthy ritual, placing his gun on the counter, next to which he placed a sharp stiletto, a *garrote*, a smaller hand pistol, brass knuckles—and an envelope.

Watching him stealthily through lidded eyes, Don Pippinu maintained a well practised calm. Vincenzo took the small box from Turridu's outstretched hands and plunked it on the counter.

"Here, this is for you." He shoved the box towards him. "Go on—open it."

Shaking visibly, the Don fumbled with the wrappings. Opened, he removed a glass jar containing what resembled a human heart. He read the accompanying note: *"The heart of Apolladora never forgets. Neither does Salvatore!"*

Don Pippinu fell back in his chair, the sweat pouring off his face. The sound of their laughter echoed through the store as the bandits left Don Pippinu to mull over his surprise package and wonder at his ultimate fate. It didn't take long for it all to come together for the Mt. Erice Don.

The next morning, accompanied by four trusted guards, Don Pippinu took the first charter boat to Palermo. By noon they arrived in the capital city, hailed a taxi, and went to Nunzio's *Birreria* to meet with Don Matteo Barbarossa.

The Mafia figureheads embraced in brotherhood fashion.

"Don Pippinu. . . ."

"Don Matteo—I kiss your hand."

"You look good," remarked the *capomafia.*

"You say that when I've lost much weight over a calamitous affair that needs your expert counseling. . . ." He bleated like a crusty mountain goat.

After a lavish dinner in the usual custom, and after the amenities were finished, both *mafiosi* retired to the small office kept only for the *capomafia* to conduct special business in. The Don selected two or three bottles from a lavish sideboard of special wines, to which only he and Nunzio held a key. "What do you prefer, my friend? *Vino bianco, or vino rossa?*" asked Don Matteo graciously.

"I prefer red wine today," stammered Don Pippinu, wiping the profusion of sweat descending on his brow. He placed his grey fedora on the chair next to him and watched the *capomafia* decant wine from one bottle to another, then pour it into a crystal goblet for his pleasure.

"It displeases me to bring this matter to your attention," began the harrassed Don Pippinu. "With so many things on your mind, Matteo—" He raised his glass in a silent salute to the Mafia chief. He sipped the red wine, and Don Matteo relished the *strega*. Don Pippinu smacked his lips together appreciatively and, with a winning smile, he asked, "Is this new wine? Delicious."

Don Matteo shook his head. "Three years old. Now, what complication brings you into my presence? I am flattered you seek counsel from me."

"A favor. I ask a favor of you."

"Ask."

"The death of Salvatore!"

Don Matteo bit off the end of a Havana *Sigaro*, proceeded to light it without flinching a facial muscle. Through clouds of smoke he noticed the nervous drumming of Pippinu's fingertips on the table. Only four days had passed since Salvatore had met with him in Godrano to ask for the liquidation of the Mt. Erice Don. *Annunca*—things were boiling, eh?

"Why?"

"Why? What do you mean—why? I must give you reasons? Is it not enough I came in respect to ask this favor be done?"

Behind his dark glasses, Don Matteo studied the man who ranted as one in fever. He maintained his silence. However, Don Pippinu was incensed.

"When you need a favor, do I question my *capomafia*? I didn't follow in blind faith in the matter with the Allies?"

"You've become a wealthy man, Don Pippinu," stated the *capomafia*, simply.

"Are you weighing me on the scales of merit?" Don Pippinu was aghast. His dry voice hissed when he spoke.

"It's a request I can't grant without prudent deliberation. I suggest you reconsider. Is there no way to settle your differences with Salvatore?"

"Are you crazy? Since when does the brotherhood suggest embracing an enemy?" Don Pippinu, driven by some inner goading, grew incautious.

"Salvatore," said Don Matteo, "has suddenly become a resource of considerable power, one which could prove vital to the brotherhood."

"I don't believe my ears!" Don Pippinu shook his head as if to clear it of confusion. "Do I hear you straight? Are you siding with my enemy?"

"Anyone else but Salvatore and it would have been done," Don Matteo shook his head regretfully. "It's possible we'll need this bandit in the coming days. I am pledged to the brotherhood, Don Pippinu. Not to personal ambitions."

"—And I am not? Is that what you say? Haven't my actions spoken for me?"

Abject humiliation struck and stunned him. He remained in a near state of paralysis as Don Matteo temporized.

"Were you not aware of Salvatore's rise to power? Didn't it cross your mind that, with his indestructibility, the brotherhood might need him? We're desperate for his support, now that Canepa's proven traitorous. To employ the power of this peasant is the only way we can advance our plans for a separate Sicily. Reconsider, Pippinu. I beg you. Is there no way to make amends?"

"Are you telling me you deny my request?" Don Pippinu jumped to his feet, red-faced and swollen. With reckless fury running rampant through his body, he became uncontrolled and stupid. "*Allora*, don't heed my request," he challenged. "I shall withdraw my support. With it goes Trapani, Marsala, and the villages between." He snorted like a mad bull. "You side with Salvatore over your own kind?" He proceeded to grow more stupid. "I've not been sleeping these past few years. I, too, have grown powerful, more than you imagine. The Reds have courted me. I've but to nod and I could become more prosperous than you. Have I made one disloyal move? No! I've waited with a loyal heart beating in my breast until your dream of full power was realized, like a true *amico de amici*, a true friend to you and yours. And this is the gratitude I receive?" He mopped his dripping, sweating face.

"You jump to conclusions, *amico*," said the *capo* quietly. He offered him a cigar, and proceeded to relight his own, puffing on it until it was well lit, again.

"Then tell me what you intend, so we'll both know," retorted his guest, waving aside the mist of smoke.

Don Barbarossa, the picture of serenity, purred like a benevolent father. "It would grieve me, Don *Pippinu*, if I felt compelled to take your threats seriously." A hint of compassion flickered in his eyes as he calmly watched the other loosen his necktie.

"Listen, the word, *Don*, before my name permits me to kill—not be killed. And if you don't dispose of this brigand—he'll kill me." Don Pippinu belched without apology, and patted his stomach agitatedly.

"Why is he such a threat to you?"

"I've nothing to hide. He cheated me. That sonofabitch cheated me out of six thousand American dollars! Me—Don Pippinu! While I was in the process of trying to recover my money, some cheap little slut of a prostitute was killed for refusing to tell us the information we needed."

"How did the six thousand dollars get into Salvatore's possession?"

Don Pippinu paused to sip more wine. He wiped his face and neck again.

"I paid it to him—after he threatened me, mind you. . . ."

"How long have you leased the weights and measures from his mother?" asked Barbarossa easily.

Don Pippinu glanced sharply at the *capo*. His pig eyes narrowed in suspicion and his manner grew stiff and formal, as he fought for control. "Is there nothing that escapes you?"

"No. Nothing." Pouring more wine from the special decanter into the other's glass, Don Matteo glanced with tilted eyes at his guest.

Don Pippinu coughed and hawked up a mouthful of phlegm, which he hurriedly spit into a nearby spittoon. He wiped his lips. "He told me he was your Godson, that you had a buyer for the weights and measures, and he forced me into making a deal—on the spot!" He protested.

"You could have refused him until you checked with me. Instead you chose to remain greedy. You wanted the business and the money too!"

"Ahhhhh. . . ." uttered the suddenly enlightened Don *Pippinu*. No one had to tell him the *capo* had already taken a position. His eyes furtively glanced about the room. *How am I to get out of this place, gracefully, with-*

out further inciting the Capo? he thought. He attempted to disarm the other.

"*Allora*—the young goat *is* your Godson, then?"

Don Matteo filled with a restless impatience. "Who can deny a *Godson?*" He made a gesture of helplessness.

Don Pippinu, it appeared, couldn't halt the increased perspiration. While his nervousness increased, he continued to mop his brow. "I was a fool, I should have attended to the matter personally. . . ."

"Instead you went to the *carabinieri,* Pippinu. . . ." Don Barbarossa purposely averted his eyes. He didn't want to witness the demeaning, caged expression on the other man's face as he tried to squirm out of this. "This distresses me the most. Your purse has always lain too close to your heart!" His words seemed lost on Don Pippinu, who, before his eyes, began to change rapidly.

His face engorged to a purplish hue, his eyebrows twitched, and his loose dentures rattled incessantly. He slowly deteriorated. "My stomach feels upset. I should have taken bicarbonate of soda. Why am I sweating like a stuffed pig?" He asked aloud. His right hand darted to his heart in an effort to still the tachycardia, and he gulped at the air about him.

"Did the *carabinieri* give you your justice?"

"They gave me *cazzu!*" retorted Grasso stroking his underchin with the back of his fingers in typical gesture.

"They even kept your money—*pezzo de feci.*"

"They kept—*my*—money?" It no longer seemed to matter to him. He removed his jacket with considerable difficulty. Soaked, his shirt clung to his body like the wet diaper on a baby's buttocks. "Goddammit! It's too fucking hot in here," he muttered. Abruptly he stopped. "*Who* kept my money?" His eyes screwed up questioningly.

"When Salvatore was arrested, they took the belt from him containing the money."

"But they found no money!" he protested.

"And you believed them? The *carabinieri?*" Barbarossa spat into the spitoon in a gesture of contempt, and followed it with a suitable hand gesture.

Don Pippinu couldn't stop the profuse sweating. His head fell forward as if he'd been mortally struck. In the ensuing moments, he turned a sickly yellowish color as if stricken with jaundice, and he appeared to have aged ten years. He raised his head laboriously, opened the collar of his shirt, and stretched his neck above the collar. A strained, waxy glaze appeared in his eyes. He coughed in

375

frenzied agony, waved his hands in the air, apologetically for this confusing behavior.

Don Matteo's eyes contained polite and genuine concern for his guest's discomfort. He said softly and with compassion. "A true man of honor never weakens his position, or arms his enemy by an outburst of passion or fear. He fights his own battles, keeps his mouth shut, and he never—never—goes to *the carabinieri*." Barbarossa continued to smoke with a nonchalance that maddened the lesser Don. He removed his dark glasses.

"You believe—Salvatore!" he accused.

"I—*don't* believe the *carabinieri*."

"Matteo!" he shouted frantically. "I have never asked a favor of you!" He grabbed the *capo's* arm and pleaded, full of anguish. "You must get rid of him before he kills me! I came to you in respect—you must do me this honor!"

"It's not possible. . . ."

"This is your final answer?"

Don Matteo removed his gold watch from his vest-pocket, snapped it open, and set it on the desk before him. Slowly, with deliberate movements, he raised his heavily lidded eyes and stared into the eyes of Don Pippinu without expression. At that moment, Don Pippinu knew. At that moment he read his sentence. At that moment, Don Pippinu realized he had been marked for death.

. . . *Misericordia!* And I, like a—*pezzo de shekko*—didn't realize this old judas goat was leading me to slaughter, he told himself.

Don Pippinu knew he was lost—that in a matter of moments his life would end. Yet, for some reason known only to himself, in a furtive movement, he carelessly reached into his pocket. Instantly, two men sprang from the shadows.

One man moved in swiftly and struck Pippinu Grasso in the face with a powerful fist. He went down like an ox under a hammer. Blood spurted from his face and nose.

"*Basta! Basta!*" ordered the *capo*. "He's done for, anyway. The poison will finish him off, soon enough." He looked down at the motionless form of Don Pippinu, who could still hear, for the poison hadn't begun to affect his senses. He shook his head in a gesture of resignation.

"No malice intended, old friend. It's like I said, for now we need Salvatore. But—if it will make you feel any better as you prepare to meet your maker, know that Salvatore's days are also numbered. What I've done is for the good of the brotherhood." He grasped Don Pippinu's shoulder firmly as if to give him heart. "You tell God, that Barbarossa says you are a first-class man. You hear? Barbarossa says you are A-one O.K."

Don Matteo picked up his gold watch, clicked the cover shut, slipped it into his vest pocket, and tossed his cigar into the spittoon. He put on his dark glasses, nodded to his men, and walked out the back room.

In the restaurant, he beckoned to Don Pippinu's men who stood guard near by. In an instant, tears flooded his face. He blew his nose and shook his head sorrowfully.

"Your boss has just had a heart attack! *Meskino— Povero meskino!* You will see to his funeral needs. . . ." He raised his dark glasses, shoved them back on his head, and wiped the real tears that streamed down his cheeks.

"We were such good friends," he lamented. He reached into his pocket and pressed a wad of lire into the hand of one of the men. "Give my respect to his family. And buy a large wreath of flowers in my name, *capeeshi?*" In a gesture overcome with emotion, he walked away.

"How fortunate Don Pippinu was to have a friend like Don Matteo." There goes a prince of a man!" The men disappeared into the back room to attend the fallen Don Pippinu.

CHAPTER 28

In Naples the *Carabinieri* High Command, having reached the limit of their endurance in the outrageous war declared upon them by the Sicilian, Salvatore, dispatched to Montegatta a man familiar with the area—a man with an axe to grind. The former Lieutenant Giovanni Franchina, now raised to the rank of *Maresciallo*—Marshal, the highest grade of non-commissioned officer, entered the shabby quarters of his new office and eyed the sorry mess with hypercritical eyes. The place, already a dump two years ago, would deteriorate the morals of a lizard, he told himself, containing his rage. Tossing his briefcase on the makeshift desk in the corner of the shambles of a room, he snapped on the desk lamp. He removed his uniform

377

tunic and hung it meticulously on a wooden wall peg after first blowing the dust off the peg.

Earlier he'd met the skeletal remains of a highly demoralized squadron of officers who hadn't a full uniform among them. He had asked himself how this swarm of mice-like men could claim kinship to the glorious *carabinieri*. How could they have permitted themselves to fall into such utter disrepute? Two years before, the *carabinieri* in this province had shown some spunk; gusty, feisty men who knew their business and took pride in their professions. How could one peasant have intimidated them and created such a shambles of the men? How? Sonsofbitches! Those men had better shape up, or he'd send for a battalion to combat this indolence and inertia among these counterfeit military policemen.

Marshal Franchina removed from his briefcase a bottle of whiskey and a glass and poured himself a tumbler full. He disposed of it in two gulps, smacked his lips together, and waited to feel the whiskey's fiery warmth pervade his spirit. He inhaled deeply and studied his reflection in the mirror, before resigning himself to the business at hand. He removed from the brief a thick scrapbook containing an accumulation of data and personal notes collected over a two-year span on the brigand, Salvatore, sat down at the desk, scanned the contents.

At forty-one, despite his war injuries and those which he had sustained on his last stint in Montegatta, he was still in prime condition. Fierce dark eyes, suspicious and calculating, lurked behind dark-tinted glasses, and a sharp Roman nose dominated his features.

For some reason, he couldn't concentrate on the subject matter. His mind kept seeing images of those idiots outside. Earlier he stood before the police barracks in the village of Montegatta, a temporary shelter a short distance from the *questura* and the headquarters of the security police, unable to restrain his feelings when he addressed the men, who stood at attention.

"You're a disgrace! All of you!" He told the twelve men. "Why aren't you wearing the proper uniforms? Who's in charge here?" he demanded.

"Me, *'Tenente'* Paterno. I'm officer in charge," declared a slim dark-skinned man, better known as Birdeyes. He pointed a grimy finger at himself.

"*'Tenente'* Paterno, eh?" Franchina had glanced scathingly at him. "Do you and your men always dress so disgracefully? And where are your horses?"

"The bandits confiscated them."

"The bandits confiscated them." mocked Franchina. "Just like that, you tell me! Have you no pride? Damn the devil! How do you expect to catch the bandits if you're so disorganized? What the hell's wrong with you, eh?"

Lt. Paterno's gaunt face burned with humiliation. "There's a war on, *Maresciallo*," he managed with thinning courage. "Things have been hard on us."

"So! You've permitted yourselves to be corrupted instead of honoring your uniforms. Is that it? It's all a part of Salvatore's deviltry, and you fell for it."

Glowering fiercely, the Marshal, in his spanking new uniform which drew envious glances from the officers, paced disgustedly before the staggered row of twelve motley men who, through a quirk of providence, had been supplied with the uniforms of perhaps six Indiscriminately distributed amongst them, the uniforms allowed six men to wear the trousers, while the remaining six wore the tunics with improper accessories. Six men wore left-footed boots, six wore the right. None wore a complete uniform. Another time, this grim-faced perfectionist might have found the scene hilarious, but only if the unsightly platoon belonged to another officer's detail.

"Impossible!" exploded Franchina. "How does it happen you haven't the proper uniforms? . . . I know . . . I know. There's a war on, and everything is scarce. Couldn't you have requisitioned them?"

"We did, *Maresciallo!*" Birdeyes held up three fingers. "Three times. Each time the bandits confiscated the shipments. Besides, for the amount of work we do nowadays, Salvatore told us we didn't need them. . . ."

"So! Salvatore's become your commander? . . . I should have the lot of you court-martialled! You hear? Court-martialed!"

"*Managghia*," whispered one of the men to Birdeyes. "This new Marshal means business. He's not like the other fleet-footed chickens they sent us from Naples before . . ."

"*Attenzione!* . . . Attention!" barked Franchina. "Hear me well. I want you to know I'll not stand for gross dereliction to duty! In my entire career I've never seen such a shambles! You're a blot, a stigma on the very word *carabinieri!* If I had any sense I'd take the next boat back to Naples and let you rot in your own dung!" His shark-like teeth ground together and his drooping moustache twitched noticeably. "I'm here to do a job, and by Lucifer, the job shall be done! This arrogant bandit's days are numbered. No longer shall he bring dishonor to the Italian

379

Military Police. The *carabinieri* shall not be subjected to the contemptuous role of subordinate in this fiasco between peasant and law enforcement. *Capeeshi?* . . . All right, for now, you're dismissed! But, I warn you. Shape up or I'll send you to the stockade in the Palermo jail, where you can sit to your hearts content and contemplate this bandit whom you've permitted to heap destruction upon your heads. Tomorrow when you report for duty, you'll arrive—all of you—with clean uniforms! Boots and buttons polished like mirrors!" His booming voice, echoing through the *piazza*, was heard by inquisitive and bemused shopkeepers who clapped their hands gleefully at the distress of their enemies.

Eager to break rank and leave the Marshal's company, the men made haste only to stop and glance at Birdeyes with puzzlement in their eyes. Birdeyes understood their dilemma. "Uh—*Marasciallo*, how? We've only six uniforms between the twelve of us. . . ." He waited for a reply, standing rigidly at attention.

"Simple, stupid. Six of you come fully dressed. The others will wear their regular clothing until new uniforms arrive," exasperated the Marshal.

"If I may suggest," said Birdeyes listening to his disgruntled men, 'It's best you assign the uniforms. It may not seem a big thing to you. . . ." he moved in close to the Marshal and whispered confidentially. "The men love the uniforms. You'll cause dissension if they can't wear a part of it. Even a mere shoelace makes them feel special like they belong. . . ." Birdeyes squinted and blinked his eyes rapidly, trying to read Franchina's eyes behind those dark glasses.

Marshal Franchina, fascinated by the unusual eye movement watched him. "What's wrong with your eyes? Why are you squinting? What is it, do you need glasses?"

Birdeyes nodded. "I can't see far off, only close up."

"Son of a toad-mouthed vulture!" snapped Franchina with scathing irony. "Now I find these half-assed marionettes led by a blind man!" He strutted before the others, hands on his waist, challenging. "Go on. While I'm here you may as well point out the deaf and dumb."

They all understood the insult. What remained of their self-respect hung loosely by a slim thread. Only their stubborn pride had seen them through these trying times. Trapped in the area, they had been forced to accept Salvatore's law—which they had found to be fair. Their unconcerned government hadn't taken time to bail them out of the circumstances and misery they had endured, and hadn't even paid them liveable wages. Salvatore had kept a roof over their heads and fed them well. What did this overstuffed peacock expect? What could he know of the perverse conditions they'd endured? How dare he hold these men up to ridicule? Having stripped them of the last vestiges of their pride and self-respect, he had left them nothing. They were frustrated and angry when they strutted past him. Arrogant popinjay! Cockroach! Who does he think he is? One thing was certain, they concurred, he was different than all the others who had attempted to take command in Montegatta.

"We'd better not fool around," said Birdeyes to a few of the more disgruntled. "This one's a real adder, but we'll know in a week if it's real venom he keeps stored in his serpent's tooth—or mother's milk."

The bombastic Marshal, who'd made his first mistake when he insulted these diehards, retreated to his makeshift office to reflect on the insanity he had demonstrated in returning to this land of crazy buffoons and bandits.

After the near-fatal tragedy of the second bandit attack at Rigano Pass on his previous hitch in Sicily, Marshal Franchina had spent, long, painful months of recuperation. After devoting nearly half his life to his country, he had little to show for it, and now, he wanted to live— really live—not simply exist in hospitals for the balance of his days. But how? How could he make up for lost time? For the long, agonizing days spent in hospitals under the care of doctors and nurses? He had to begin all over again.

In two years he had nearly lost touch with the Sicilian scene. Technically the war had ended, but its devastating effects were all around him. Naples was a shambles, destroyed by both German and Allied bombs. Yet, through it all, Franchina marveled that the people had something else to occupy their minds, to set aside their misery, to allow hope into their drab and dreary lives. Some bright star on the horizon had made their lives worth living. The story of Salvatore, printed in the newspapers like some romantic love story in serial form, his exploits, his brave daring and audacious behavior had become the talk of the nation. And the people, secretly in love with him, actually prayed for him. Imagine!

Giovanni Franchina, no different than others who needed hope and inspiration, judiciously followed the printed articles, dimly aware that the name Salvatore belonged to a scoundrel he might have once captured if he hadn't been caught up in that vortex of human misery in which a man wearing a *carabiniero*'s uniform was doomed.

Two months before his arrival back in Sicily, while lunching at Alfredo's on the Via Veneto in Roma with friends in Army Intelligence, he had overheard a chance remark. "Whoever captures the bandit Salvatore will make an international name for himself," said one of the officers. "And I daresay the bloke, without contest, will be able to write his own ticket, anyplace—any time."

This brief statement had set the ball rolling. At that moment, Giovanni Franchina knew his destiny. What a snap it would be! Who else but a man bent on vengeance—and familiar with the area and its people—should qualify for the honor? Franchina further bolstered his ego by deluding himself into thinking the task would be simple.

Marshal Franchina was back now, a different man: harder, tougher, more cynical with fewer scruples—armed for bear. Shocked to learn how much the area had become the dominion of Salvatore, and how different from the place he had remembered, he confessed the changes had alarmed him. Yet, hadn't he, too, changed? More exacting and less principled, only victory became meaningful to him. Promotion, higher pay, ample residuals, and an arsenal of retirement benefits were his ultimate goals. What better way to attain these than through national acclaim?

On March 15, two weeks after his arrival in Montegatta, the Marshal, who'd already shocked his platoon of incompetents by remaining in the village longer than they'd wagered he might, was about to make his second mistake. He dispatched two of his men to the Salvatore house to bring the women, the *Signora* and *Signorina,* to the jail for an informal chat.

Before the matriarch had left her house, signals sent from house to house had reached the edge of town and proceeded, with the aide of mirrors, ox horns and whistles, used by farmers, shepherds and merchants to arrive at the bandits encampment. Homing pigeons, released earlier, had swooped into their wooden cages alongside several grottos with pellets tied to their legs, containing the following message: *"Mother and Sister arrested by carabinieri. Come at once."*

Slowly, from house to house, man to man, woman to woman, a whistle, to the tune of a funeral dirge was heard, sounding much like the Bandits' Marching Song: *"Some Call him the Bandit . . . Some Call him the Law!"*

The hot afternoon sun scorched and bleached everything in sight to a blinding, eyeball-charring chalk-white.

Sparrows on overhead tree branches, struck by the abnormal silence, craned their necks, blinking nictitating eyelids as the Salvatore women passed under them. Both women, mother and daughter, with proud heads held high and impassive faces cast like stone, expressionless eyes fixed straight ahead, marched with a certain majesty, as if summoned by royalty, giving no outward indication of the inner dread they experienced.

Leaving their sanctuaries, the villagers came from all directions to trail behind at a respectful distance as the entourage made their way to the jail with their military escorts. Oh, the shame of it all! How dared this son of a loose-tongued idiot, Marshal Franchina, subject *Signora* Salvatore to such lack of respect? Wait until Salvatore hears of this disgrace. Herded into jail like common criminals! Tori will fix their tails!

The officers escorting the women found themselves sweating profusely. Having heard the signals, and aware of the increased tension among the people who followed, they braced themselves against the angry snorts and caustic remarks hurled upon them from all sides.

"You undersized pricks—you forget who puts food into your mouths! I wouldn't give a fig for your lives when Tori learns of your treachery! Bastards! He gave you enough rope, but don't be surprised if when the time comes your feet don't touch the floor!"

The policemen tried to remain cool even when a flowerpot came crashing down from an overhead balcony, missing them by inches. A growling dog, egged on by an irate mistress, charged at them chewing and snarling at their pantlegs. From another overhead balcony, a woman shook out rugs filled with dust and debris on them. Choking and coughing at the flurries of dust, the *carabinieri* brushed at their uniforms, their eyes flaring. One of the men turned around and, in a voice filled with supplication, shouted, "Don't you understand we're only doing our duty?" They quickened their steps and hurried the woman along. *"Avanti! Avanti!"*

So, thought Marshal Franchina as he watched their approach through the open grilled windows in his office, I've struck a sensitive chord, have I? In two weeks he hadn't seen one tenth the number of villagers that now gathered outside in the *piazza*. He smirked and seated himself at the desk, occupying himself with trivia by the time the women entered the room.

He rose to his feet, bowed slightly and slipped into his bright red tunic and with a bright smile tried to disarm the women. "Please, *Signora, Signorina,* be seated. What a pleasure it is to see you both again."

Antigone and Athena searched his face keenly. Neither remembered him. Two years was a long time.

"—And you, *Signorina,* I've never forgotten the heart-stirring beauty of your person." He picked up Athena's hand and kissed it lightly. Athena withdrew it from him instantly, flushed, and lowered her indignant, startled eyes. She had no immediate recollection of him at the moment.

"I am Maresciallo Franchina, at your service," He clicked his heels, bowed once again. "You don't recall me? I was here two years ago—"

No recognition shone in their eyes. He moved back to his desk and sat down. "I thought it might suit all our purposes if we became better acquainted. Right off, believe me when I say I have no personal animosity towards you or this beautiful daughter of yours, *Signora* Salvatore. I have made it my business to learn all about you, and I know you are both good women, possessed with high moral principles and the normal seriousness with which you protect the family circle. Law-abiding and God-fearing women who, through circumstances not of your own choice, find yourselves pressed like stone weights, by the shabby antics and criminal tendencies of your son. My dear *Signora,* how could this have happened to you? An erring, misguided son must be a terrible cross to bear. Let me assure you, with my guidance, your son can be reformed. I'm well qualified to rehabilitate a criminal, help steer him to live a decent life, you see."

Franchina rose to his feet, slipped his hands into his high pockets and swaggered about the room. "I want you to feel free to talk with me, as if I was your confessor in Church—eh?"

On and on, in boring repetition, he rambled, boasting of his conquests, emphasizing that he captured criminals solely for the purpose of rehabilitating them and not purely for punitive measures. Forced to listen to his bombastic *braggadocio,* both women suffered indignities at the disrespect hurled upon Tori. Neither questioned, acknowledged, or repudiated Franchina's statements.

Beginning to show his marked annoyance, the Marshal sat down behind the antiquated desk, in an atmosphere incongruous to his flamboyance. Removing a cigar from the brass humidor on his desk, he lit it and puffed thoughtfully for a time, filling the room with blue-white smoke. His dark, glittering eyes studied the women critically. Imperious lowly peasants! He wagered they hadn't heard a word he'd spoken—and this infuriated him more.

"Understand, I mean no personal effrontery in asking you here to chat with me. But, I've a job to do, and by God, I'll leave no stone unturned until this dastardly son of yours is caught and properly punished for placing himself above the government. He was earmarked for trouble in 1943, I should have stopped him then."

The women gave no outward indication that they were affected one way or another by the Marshal's words.

"Very well, play your game of silence, if you will. I've presented myself to you in friendship and in respect—without malice, mind you, and in all humility."

The women maintained their stoical silence, without reaction.

"I beg of you, as a devout follower of Our Lord, and a good Catholic, if you care for your son's soul, plead with him to surrender himself to me. My promise to you is that I'll see he receives only a short sentence. Otherwise he shall face, not only the wrath of a stern government, but also the wrath of God. His outrageous crimes, the lives of the innocent men he's taken, and the countless riches stolen from the *latifondisti* and the government are enough to keep him in jail at hard labor for eternity. Unless—I intervene and beg the court's mercy. They'll listen to me."

Maresciallo Franchina stared at the unreceptive stone statues seated in his presence and lost his control.

"Do I have before me—illiterates? Mutes who can't hear or speak? Last time we met, you had no vocal impairment. Has your son's crimes rendered you both shame-filled and silent?" His voice boomed loud and clear. "Very well, refuse my friendship! When all hell breaks loose and your son is behind bars, where he rightfully belongs, don't come begging at my feet, crying, 'Have mercy! Have mercy!'" Franchina's speech fragmented, and, growing animated, he bellowed louder, "You're either made of iron or have no tongue! Which is it?"

No reaction flickered in either woman's eyes.

Franchina jumped to his feet, flung his cigar from him savagely, stomped noisily to the door, and, with glowing menace in his eyes, he jerked open the sticky door and held it open in curt dismissal.

Antigone touched Athena's shoulder lightly with her hand. They rose to leave. Dressed in perennial black, they adjusted black mourning shawls over their heads and prepared to depart. In passing him, she permitted Athena to walk first. She raised her dark eyes, glanced at the swollen face of the Barracuda staring stonily ahead, and paused momentarily.

"When the dust settles," she said calmly, "we'll see if you ride the stallion or the ass. . . ." Taking her daughter's arm, she walked out of the decrepid, bare-walled room, where broken water lines creased each ancient wall.

Outside the villagers cheered and shouted, "*Viva viva Salvatore! Long Live Salvatore!*" when they saw the women leave the jailhouse. They swarmed around the two women and several men instantly formed a guard around them, parting the crowd, making way for them to pass.

Through the open grilled windows of his office, Franchina watched the scene of his momentary defeat as the pressing crowds moved in to champion the Salvatore women. He wasn't so crestfallen that he wasn't made aware of the tight network of protection afforded Salvatore and his men by all the villagers.

"Whoring sons of Satan!" he exclaimed bitterly. "So, that's how it is?" He moved away from the window and sat down behind the desk. From a drawer, he removed the large scrapbook he had kept on Salvatore and for a time thumbed through it, searching for something which would give him more insight on the woman, Antigone Salvatore. She was no usual peasant, this woman. He made a note to learn more about this matriarchal power who couldn't be intimidated. Finally he slammed shut the scrapbook, reached for his tunic, and decided to make an inspection of the arms and ammunition reserves.

Nothing was as appalling and disgusting to the Marshal as his unit's puny display of antiquated revolvers and rifles, many of them rusted, broken and unkempt and totally useless. He picked up a revolver based on a Colt .45, a weapon made in the late eighteen hundreds, and watched the weapon come apart in his hands. Angrily he tossed it aside on a crude wooden table, and picked up a carbine that resembled a child's popgun. Thoroughly repulsed by it, Franchina tossed it quickly aside, as if he'd been contaminated by the shabby weapon.

"Where are the supplies I sent before I arrived?" he asked Birdeyes who watched him from a short distance in the supply room.

"Oh, those?" Birdeyes scratched his head thoughtfully. "Salvatore confiscated them. . . ."

Right then, if *Maresciallo* Franchina had had any sense, he'd have taken the next boat back to Naples, permitted the Montegattans to live as they chose, and thus preserved his sanity. But the hardnosed *carabiniero* hadn't been called the Barracuda for nothing. He had had two failures in Montegatta, and didn't relish thoughts of a third. He blinked hard, turned on his heels, and left the room, lips tightly clenched. Striding across the dusty courtyard with giant steps, he paused momentarily at the sounds of bleating oxhorns. His face flushed beet-red. A knowing frown creased his brow. Swearing under his breath, he scaled the last few steps, disappeared through the entrance, and slammed the door shut behind him. "Fucking bandits! I'll get 'em all!" he vowed aloud, more grimly determined now than before.

By the time the Salvatore women arrived back at their house on Via de Grande, Santino Siragusa and the Scoletti brothers were there, concerned over their well-being. "We received word of your arrest," he began unable to take his eyes off Athena's flushed features. *What a beauty,* he thought. *An angel. . . .*

"We're fine," replied Antigone, preparing the coffee for them. She walked to a sideboard and returned with a plate of *biscotti* and a bottle of *vino rosso*.

"This Maresciallo is not like the others they've sent," she began with a note of solemnity to her voice. "He's well educated, less inclined to intimidation. Athena recalls him now. He was in Montegatta the night Vincenzo's father was killed. He was the one who came looking for Tori after Nino Marino was killed." She poured the wine. "Please tell my son, this one will bear watching."

"Allay your fears, *Signora*," Santino smiled before he sipped his wine. "What can one man do, eh?"

"What can one man do?" Antigone rubbed the knuckles of her fingers to stimulate their flexibility. "You ask what one man do, Santino? Some men in high positions have asked that same question about Tori. And I say to you—one man can move mountains, if such is his destiny."

Their eyes locked. Santino raised his glass in a toast to her. "I defer to your wisdom—as usual, *Signora*," said Santino.

The Scoletti Brothers, nodding, sipped their wine. "You needn't concern yourself, *Signora*," spoke up Arturo wrinkling amused brows. "The *carabinieri* have no arms, no ammunition, not even horses," he laughed. "Not even shoes with which to chase us. More important, the villagers, all loyal to Tori, will continue to protect us. They know Tori is a dedicated man."

Antigone studied them quietly. "How much longer will this loyalty last? The Montegattans haven't been put to the test yet" Their silence inspired further words of caution

387

from her lips. "Despite what you think, please inform my son that this Marshal is different. He's a man who could sway many for such is the power of his oratory and conviction. This *Marasciallo* is *also* a dedicated man—dedicated to his own cause."

They understood.

"*Va bene.* We shall see each other then," said Antigone.

Both women watched the men depart through the rear terraces where their horses were hidden. Athena entertained a secret rush of hope at the thought of spending time with Santino.

". . . You want me to put *these* up, *Maresciallo?*" asked Birdeyes squinting closely at the *Wanted Dead OR Alive* posters for Salvatore and his men. He swallowed hard and read aloud: "*Reward: $5,000.00*"

"Is there anyone else here? Of course I want you to do it. Take some of the men and make sure they are displayed conspicuously throughout the village."

Birdeyes shrugged. There'd be hell to pay, but he didn't relish being chewed out by the Marshal nor did he appreciate the threat of court-martial. He picked up the posters and saluted his superior officer, smartly.

"*Aspetta!* While you're at it, stop at the post office and check to see if the supply of guns has arrived from Palermo. And for God's sake, be discreet! No one's to know the shipment contains guns . . . *capeeski?* I'll show these stubborn mules! All of these hard nosed, tough-assed peasants shall learn how the word of Marshal Franchina weighs heavy."

"*Sicuro, Maresciallo.* For sure!"

"Now we'll see some action! Pretty soon this village will take full notice of Giovanni Franchina! With no cooperation from the security police, I accomplished what no other *carabiniero* accomplished in two years. After this Friday they'll not forget the name of Franchina!' he boasted. "Are you still here? Be gone, *'Tenente!'*"

Birdeyes saluting, scampered quickly out of the office.

Marshal Franchina buttoned his tunic. Studying his reflection in the cracked mirror next to a wooden coat rack, he stroked his beard thoughtfully. "Marshal, you need a shave and a haircut," he told himself aloud.

Outside, in the brisk, cool, mountain air, he drew up the collar on his overcoat and headed towards the barber shop across from the Norman tower in the *piazza.* As busy as a squirrel storing nuts for winter, the Marshal had, quietly and without fanfare, made several trips to Palermo, where he had succeeded in obtaining over two hundred warrants for the arrest of Salvatore and his men, who along with a number of villagers were charged with murder, conspiracy to commit murder, aiding and abetting outlaws, robbery, theft, and the confiscation of government property.

Franchina had revealed to no one, not even his men, what he had planned for this coming Friday, and wouldn't until the last minute to ward off any possible betrayal or treachery. Oh, did it ever pay to grease the palms of these money-hungry, half-starved peasants. His affair with the widow Grissi, a willing paramour, had opened the door for him. Silent and unassuming, he had simply kept his ears and eyes open and his lips sealed. And it was all about to pay off.

Just as Marshal Franchina made way to enter the barber shop, he caught sight of Birdeyes running towards him. He reported that the weapon shipment hadn't arrived. Franchina, swearing under his breath, ordered the *'Tenente* back to the jail with instructions to go to the stage office and check with them on the arms shipment. He watched Birdeyes salute and depart.

It was 9 A.M. The Marshal glanced about the *piazza,* where some of his men were tacking up the *Wanted* posters. He noticed that several villagers were staring with inborn curiosity at the activity. Franchina, smiling inwardly with a smug conceit, nodded to a few villagers. Most stared defiantly, while others ignored him. Very well, he told himself, we'll see how they react to my authority after Friday. By Friday night they'll all taste Marshal Franchina's brand of justice.

CHAPTER 29

"Buon giorno, Maresciallo," called Gaetano the barber.

"Buon giorno." Franchina entered the barber shop.

"I'm ready for you," announced the short, stocky man with the red moustache, brushing off the first chair in the two-chair tonsorial parlor which filled in for the office of a dentist, a doctor and a chiropractor on occasion.

Franchina removed his overcoat, slipped out of his immaculate tunic, and carefully hung it on the wooden peg provided on the opposite wall. He unbuckled his cartridge belt and gun holsters, placed them meticulously on another wooden peg, and moved with ease and agility across the small rustic room, unbuttoning the top of his long johns. He nodded to Ignazio, the second barber and son-in-law to Gaetano, who worked on a client, buried under a steaming towel.

"A little chilly out today—no?" he asked Gaetano, making small talk.

"You northerners find it difficult to adjust to our violent climate! . . ."

"That's what it's called? A violent climate?"

"The Lord punishes us with inferno in the summer and flood in the winter. What else can you call it?" Gaetano poured hot water into the Marshal's personal shaving mug from the kettle on the pot-bellied stove, and whipped up the lather. Only the rattling sounds of a wooden brush handle, knocking about the crockery, were heard. Gaetano placed a towel around the officer's neck, lowered the chair to a horizontal position, and reached into a steaming container for a hot towel, wrung it out, and twirled it in the air about him. He tested it, then placed it on Franchina's face, leaving only a space for him to breathe. He proceeded to hum an ethnic ballad.

"I'm going to buy a radio one day, to soothe my patrons," said the barber, looking toward the second chair nervously. He nodded. Instantly Ignazio removed the towel from his customer's face and Salvatore, rising, flung the sheet from him. With the agility of a cat, he leapt soundlessly from the chair, and moved across the room. He slipped the Marshal's cartridge belt over one shoulder, removed both guns from their holsters, and in seconds had positioned himself a few inches away from where Franchina lay, comfortable and without suspicion. Tori, in a careless pose, one leg up on a chair, leaned his shoulders forward, one elbow on his knee, a gun grasped firmly in each hand and aimed at Franchina. Behind him, Arturo Scoletti took his place at the rear entrance and flipped a *"Closed"* sign into place in a window pane and locked the door. Vincenzo de Montanta guarded the back entrance. Tori nodded to the barber, who on cue commenced to play his part.

"*Allora, Maresciallo.* How are you coming with the bandits?" Gaetano removed the towel and applied a foamy coat of lather to the Marshal's face.

"Can't complain. Soon, now, I'll have them all in my coat pocket."

Nervously the barber swiped the Marshal's nose unintentionally with lather. *"Mi scusa, Maresciallo,"* he said apologetically, wiping the soapy foam from his nose. He shrugged helplessly at Tori in a gesture of apology.

"What if I don't fit into your back pocket?" asked Salvatore quietly.

"What's that? Speak up, man. I can't hear you," muttered Franchina.

Gaetano paused in his work to wipe beads of sweat from his brow. Alerted by the lag in conversation, the Marshal's black eyes snapped open. From his horizontal position he saw the barber's lips weren't moving. Yet, the same voice persisted.

"What if I don't fit in your pocket?"

Suddenly, as it registered, Marshal Franchina bolted up right in his chair, whipped off the barber cloth—and stared solemnly into the face of the young bandit and into the barrels of the guns aimed inches from his heart. Franchina recognized Salvatore instantly. With little time to reflect beyond the fact that the brigand had grown more handsome and matured in two years, he was shrewd enough to know that his life hung in the balance of this moment of truth. Since no flicker of recognition passed Salvatore's eyes, he chose to treat his obstructor with the cool indifference accorded a stranger. "Who are you?" he asked icily.

"W-who is *he?*" stuttered Gaetano with trembling lips. *"Maresciallo,* this is . . ."

"Silence! This isn't your affair!" ordered the Marshal.

"But *Maresciallo,"* insisted Gaetano.

"Sta zitto! Be still!" commanded the officer. All the while, his fish eyes hadn't left Salvatore's face. "I suggest you put those guns where you found them, young buck, before they get you into trouble you can't handle," he said.

Salvatore grinned. Aiming the hair-triggered automatics at a neat row of leather strops hung on individual pegs, suspended from a wooden beam nailed to one stucco wall, he squeezed gently.

Ping! Kapowee! Bang! Ping! Baroom! He shot each strop at dead center. Ricocheting bullets bounced aimlessly off the walls. Terrified, the barbers fell flat on the floor on their bellies and covered their ears protectively with their hands. Marshal Franchina didn't move.

"Fine guns, Marshal. Better than I expected. Since I'm a collector of sorts, I might just keep these."

"Whoever you are, don't incur my wrath. Just lay the guns aside and walk out the door or I shall arrest you."

"Bravo. Bravo!" Tori forced a tight-lipped laughter. Which?" Tilting his head in mock amusement, his eyes suddenly caught sight of the officer's new boots. *"Managghia!* Such fancy boots. Please, you will remove them."

"Now, look here, boy, set aside the guns and I'll make nothing of this foolish encounter." Franchina's courage took flight. He turned his back on the brigand. "Hand me a towel, Gaetano," he addressed the barber.

A swift bullet whizzed by Franchina's ear. Before the sound stopped reverberating in his ears, Frenchina glared angrily at his obstructor. His beady eyes on Tori, he reached up, touching his burning ear and felt the warm blood ooze between his fingers. He stared at the crimson splattered on them.

"You crazy, punk kid! *Tu si pazzu!*" he shouted angrily. The pain or fear he might have experienced easily turned into shaking outrage. He snapped a towel from the petrified barber's hand and placed it against his injured ear. It hurt like hell, but he wasn't about to indicate this to the arrogant, cocksure Sicilian.

"And now, if you please, the boots!"

"I refuse!"

"I only miss a target when I wish to—" Another bullet grazed Franchina's other ear.

The Marshal reached up and, found it, too, was bleeding. His courage slowly disintegrated. *Punk Bastard! I'll fix your hide!* Both his ears throbbed painfully.

"Now, the boots!" Tori said without amusement.

Red-faced, and livid, Franchina complied. He sat forward to ease the boots off, one at a time. He beckoned to the barber for help. Gaetano moved in swiftly at a nod of Tori's head and removed them.

"Perhaps we understand each other now?" Tori slipped the guns inside his belt, pulled himself up straight and tall. "I am Salvatore," he proclaimed in his usual panache.

"Fancy that. Next you'll say you're king of Sicily." the Marshal affected boredom.

"Not yet," replied the handsome Sicilian. "But the Marshal shows himself to be not without foresight. Consider yourself fortunate that you have found Salvatore in a charitable mood. Otherwise you'd have been dead. Consider this also. You will never show such lack of respect to the mother and sister of Salvatore again, or I will replace the flagpole at Bellolampo with your body until your bones bleach in the broiling sun and the vultures feast on your entrails. Without Salvatore's protection you and your bloodsucking, thieving *carabinieri* are nothing!"

"Nothing—like Gucci and Molino?" Franchina was a brave fool that day. When Tori glanced sharply at him, trying to recollect the officer, Franchina spat at him. Tori's indulgent smile evaporated. Arturo moved in swiftly with drawn guns. Vincenzo's dark eyes froze, and he moved in towards the Marshal, filled with menace. Gaetano and his brother backed away from the activity; their eyes bugged from their heads as they watched first one, then another.

"Vincenzo, the Marshal's boots are of no use to us without his uniform. Do your stuff," said Tori, a wicked gleam in his eyes.

"Remove your trousers!" Vincenzo ordered.

"You wouldn't dare!"

Tori removed his Browning from its holster and shot over the Marshal's head nearly parting his hair down the center. Franchina, aware he'd reached the limit—both his and Salvatore's—stood up. He unbuttoned his fly and let his trousers drop. Laughing at the ridiculous figure of the officer in long johns with drop-down bottoms, Vincenzo moved quickly and collected all the clothing, including the ornately decorated tunic and overcoat. Stripped of his impressive uniform, Franchina appeared as silly as most self-conscious, disconcerted men might in such circumstances.

"*Ciao, Maresciallo!*" Tori bowed lightly and gave him a mock salute.

"Don't be smug. We'll meet again. I promise, I shall bury you."

Tori turned to him questioningly. "Would you care to make the appointment now, or another time?"

Franchina replied. "There'll be plenty of time, Sicilian. Since you took my clothes, what say you leave me a smoke at least?"

"Give the man a smoke," he said to Arturo. Sonofabitch, how he hated such men—yet this one had guts. He made the connection in that instant. "So! It's Lieutenant Franchina!" Everything came back to him vividly in his mind now, all the events of those bitter September days in 1943. He bowed grandly.

"You know, Salvatore, one of us must die. I've vowed to capture you."

Tori took a moment to light a cigarette. Through the inhalations of smoke he studied the man. Both Vincenzo and Arturo stood like statues. Was the man daft to talk such boldness? Why didn't Tori finish him off? Vincenzo eagerly fingered his gun. Arturo's gun was still in his hand and his grip on it tightened firmly. The barbers, petrified with fear, huddled in the corner of the room.

"Let me finish him off, now, chief," said Arturo a bit too eagerly.

"No, we're not murderers." Tori stopped him.

"Hah!" Franchina's snort evolved into contemptuous laughter. "Not murderers? What happened to all those officers your weapons destroyed—an act of God, I suppose?"

"So, you're the skunk they buried in my mountains? The stench has been unbearable, *Maresciallo,* but at least now you've been sniffed out." Tori had learned much in two years. Most important was never to let your enemy know your intent. And Tori knew this man would be his enemy to the end. Not for one moment did he consider Franchina a fool. A man who'd return to this territory, after two years away from it, had to be as dedicated as his mother had suggested.

"And now that my enemy has declared himself, we shall leave you to contemplate your own fate, *Maresciallo.*" Tori tossed a roll of money to the barbers. "For the damage. *Va bene?*"

"You should have disposed of him." Vincenzo told him outside as they mounted their horses. Arturo concurred with him.

"He's just lucky he didn't call me a son of a whore! I'd have had reason to kill him, then. But we're too close to our goal, cousin. I want no more problems. Especially not from a dedicated *moffetta,* a skunk."

They swung to their saddles and waved to all the villagers who cheered them as they rode out of the square. "*Viva! Viva* Salvatore! *Viva!*"

Inside the shop, the dedicated *carabiniero* stood watching the bandits through the large picture window, one towel held up to each bleeding ear. The barbers craned their necks to watch the activity, unable to conceal their glee, as the villagers tore down the "Wanted—Reward" posters. In thinking Salvatore had displayed a gutsy manliness, the barbers ignored the fact that the Marshal had also showed bravery in defying Tori. Turning from the window they caught the cold hostile look in the eyes of that foreigner, Marshal Franchina. No fool, this Marshal had seen through their sham earlier. Now, in his eyes was the fury of Vesuvius.

I'll fix their hides, Franchina swore to himself in those

394

moments. *We'll see who has the last laugh! Arrogant peasants! Bastards! They'll all feel the bite of my bullets one day.*

"Go fetch *Tenente* Paterno!" he commanded the youngest of the barbers. "Tell him to stop at my quarters and bring me suitable clothing. If either of you repeats what happened here today, I'll personally hack off his balls and let a jackass mount him! *Capeeski?*"

Two days later Tori and Vincenzo eased their horses off the ridge near the Grotto Esmeralda, one of the highest and most remote of the caves they used, and broke into a wild gallop across the buckwheat terraces as they prepared to descend the mountains. A blinding flash of light, directed at them, caused Tori to pull up sharply on the reins of his horse with terrific force. Napoleono protested, reared, and whinnied painfully at the bit in his mouth and snaked until his master comforted him. Tori glanced questioningly at Vincenzo. Both searched the area for the sourch of the mirror signals. A paint bleating of ox horns followed.

"What is it? Who's signalling?" Tori brought the binoculars to his eyes.

From the South came a single rider at breakneck speed.

"I've been searching all over for you!" called Arturo Scoletti breathlessly. He unscrewed an oxhorn amulet from a chain around his neck, removed a coded message from it. "Santino sent me, said it was urgent."

Salvatore studied the message. Decoded it read: *"Friday night, this week, Marshal Franchina plans a surprise for you and your men. Use caution. Warrants have been issued for two hundred men including you."*

He handed the note to Vincenzo. "It seems the *Maresciallo* wants blood. Ours!"

"So—the skunk already sprays the air with his stink!"

"It makes him easier to track down—no?" grinned Arturo.

Tori didn't take the matter as lightly as did his paladins. He wheeler *Napoleono* in closer to his co-captain. "Very well, cousin, the Marshal means business. And for business we ride to Palermo. To the *Albergo—Sole*." ·

"Your Godfather?" Vincenzo tried to hide his dismay. Mere mention of the *mafioso* produced a black cloud over his mind.

"First, we go to my house, to change our clothes. Arturo, you ride back to the grotto. Tell Santino to meet me at my house at eight o'clock. By then we shall return.

395

Not a word about our mission—*capeeshi?* Not even to Santino."

Arturo nodded dutifully and rode off in the opposite direction.

CHAPTER 30

For a time early in 1944 there had been widespread belief that the war in Europe was nearly at an end. Allied armies expeditiously zoomed through the warring arenas, almost unopposed, to the Rhine. The optimistic and confident American War Department issued orders to divert supplies from Europe to the Pacific theater. Denuding the European front in Sicily and Italy meant the army would have to depend on partisan forces and those involved in guerrilla warfare. It also means that these flourishing bandits would be furnished a larger quantity of weapons to make their work against the Germans more effective. These anti-fascist, anti-Nazi guerrillas began to show a marked inclination towards communism, a fact which served to disquiet the British and American Allies.

Faced with a dilemma if aid was given exclusively to communist partisans, America feared this would insure for them control of the nation's most important industrial and agricultural regions once the fighting had ended. America couldn't, and wouldn't, tolerate such a situation. Disguising U.S. outrage behind a mask of efficiency, the Office of Strategic Services formulated a plan. This plan, including a critical analysis of the Sicilian political involvement and the communist threat, was presented to the Joint Chiefs of Staff and General Eisenhower. Shortly thereafter, the OSS approached the Allied Control Council with the idea of placing the right man into a key position to indirectly oversee and direct the fate of Sicily. If Italy should swerve to the Left, a closer alliance with Sicily was imperative, a fact Don Barbarossa had perceived long before the Allies had considered the implications involved in such a move.

It was agreed that this unique and very special man would have to be exceptionally bright, tough, and highly skilled in political skullduggery; preferably a law school graduate with a political science background. He'd have to be a dedicated officer who'd carry out orders—a stickler in following a set rule, yet elastic enough to know when to make a right decision on his own. He'd have to be a colorful person, one who could fraternize with and win the confidence of an exceedingly shrewd and manipulative group of Sicilian politicians, yet remain a bulwark of strength against the opposition, not be intimidated by them. A man with a touch of Sicilian in his heritage, a fact the Sicilians would find appealing, would make him more enticing.

These requisitites, described to General George Patton one day by General O. Bagley, added to the qualifications the following: "This special officer would, of course, be responsible for performing a threefold mission; to secure accurate intelligence on the political faith of each partisan group, to prevent the communists from building an army with American weapons, and to build a strength of non-communist resistance forces."

"What you want is a combination of Flash Gordon, Superman and God," retorted the feisty, fire-tongued Patton. "Too bad I'm unavailable. You see I've a prior commitment to go fox-trotting with Hitler," he chuckled without a hint of modesty. He then proceeded to suggest the name of an extraordinary officer who "served me damned well in the North African campaign against Rommel."

The extraordinary man turned out to be Colonel Stephen Modica, a strapping man in his late thirties, a well-built, handsome man who possessed uncompromising standards, great personal integrity and high moral character; even more important was his strong background in Intelligence work.

There was no question that the Allies had miscalculated and underestimated the power and lure of communism on a defeated warring nation, and they soon awakened to the jarring fact that the plodding, well-organized communists had industriously planted seeds of discontent in the minds of those who had come to despise Mussolini's ideals and held no truck for the doctrines of Hitler. If they had been more aware of the enticements communism offered, the course of history might have changed drastically.

But, then foresight is a privilege only the gods enjoyed, thought Colonel Modica as he settled himself in the confines of his comfortable office at Allied HQ in Palermo, Sicily. He'd been pulled off the Trieste detail, where he had made extensive use of the indigenous underground resistance movements to sabotage the activities of the German and Italian armed forces in the occupied nation where he and his men had continued to stir up national unrest; these same skills were now to be employed against the communist forces in Sicily. In his capacity as advisor to the Palermo Grand Council, he served as a channel for communication and support from Allied powers.

From the beginning, however, what appeared to be a matter of routine operations began to evolve into a hopelessly and grossly complex situation. Trieste with its mushrooming network of international spies and double agents, now seemed like nursery school to Colonel Modica by comparison to the continuum of intrigues and counter-intrigues that greeted him in Palermo.

For over a year all the Colonel heard was talk, talk, talk! Very little action followed. His days and nights were consumed by endless arguments and drinking soirees with British officers and Sicilian patriots, while he simultaneously tried to uphold the intricate and clandestine duties to which he was sworn to support. The pattern was endless, unprolific, and discouraging. Why had he agreed to direct this comedy of errors, with its unusual cast of volatile and highly emotional players who, if viewed in another light other than in the tragedy of war, could be characterized as laughable? The elaborately framed plots and counter-plots, designed by characters lifted out of the Middle Ages—characters whose philosophies defied the imagination and boggled the mind—thwarted the American colonel continuously. The senseless and ceaseless activity of these men appeared to be geared for the utter destruction of order—namely Colonel Modica's order.

The way he looked at it, Colonel Modica had a problem—a big problem. It wasn't the communist threat, or the countless resistance groups with their underground army of drones, or the continuous uprooting of disloyal partisans who intimidated the formidable Modica. Nothing so simple. His was a whopper of a problem! Don Matteo Barbarossa. Code name: *Redbeard*.

The business of war wasn't frustrating enough, he had to be provoked to exasperation by this enigmatic and dynamic powerhouse, this streamroller with political clout, a Machiavelli and a subtle, ever-constant thorn in Colonel Modica's butt—Don Barbarossa.

Colonel Modica hadn't been in Palermo ten minutes before he had learned that Matteo Barbarossa was the big gun. Not the princes, barons, dukes, the politically-oriented Cardinal, the Archbishop, or the government officials—none of them wielded the power. The real political clout and muscle belonged to this aging, nondescript Mayor of Godrano, an outgoing, outrageous peasant, a fearless dynamo who had masterminded the art of pulling the right strings at the right time to orchestrate life and human emotions to march to the tempo he prescribed.

The Don's formidable presence, and his astute contributions during Grand Council meetings, had stirred Colonel Modica to intense curiosity. Modica's advisors hinted at Mafia relationships. They spoke sparingly of the Don's absolute powers before the Mussolini era, and assured the American officer that, whatever else Barbarossa might be, although there was no documentation to prove it, he was emphatically anti fascist, anti-Nazi, anti communist, anti socialist, and so anti-everything that it followed he could only be pro-Mafia and pro-Barbarossa. In 1944 the word Mafia meant little to Modica or the world. Sicilians who had lived under its iron-fisted dictates, however, were far more affected by the word.

How, wondered Modica, was he to learn anything about this mysterious Don Barbarossa with no supportive data to guide him? Goddamn war and all its complications!

For better than a year all his attempts to secure an appropriate file on the *capomafia* proved futile. The crux of Modica's problem was that he didn't know the kind of man with whom he was dealing. He found it worse than attempting to consummate clandestine relations with an angel in the dark of night—and awakening in the light of dawn to see reflected, on her countenance, the putrefying mass of sickness on the face of a diseased prostitute.

No doubt existed in Col. Modica's mind that these Mafia-Feudalists in the Grand Council intended keeping secret from the American Officer, what they knew in advance; who would control Sicily, and how.

"All I want is something—anything—whatever you can find on the man Barbarossa," pleaded Modica to his friend Captain Matt Saginor at the Rome office for USA Army Intelligence. For the better part of the past year Captain Saginor's apologetic voice had come over the horn. He hated to disappoint the colonel, but, he hadn't been able to locate anything on this apparent ghost who held the Sicilian sceptre in his tightly clenched, greedy fist. It had been a snap to locate a make on Vito Genovese and Nick Gentile, but, on Matteo Barbarossa he hadn't been able to locate a goose bump; not even a birth certificate or baptismal record—nothing!

A few weeks before, while he was in Palermo on business, Captain Matt Saginor had suggested to Colonel

Modica that he get assistance from the brass. Modica, having already taken that tack, had replied in all candor that he didn't appreciate doing business with the deaf, dumb and blind. Everyone of whom he'd inquired about the Don had seemed afflicted by the inability to hear, perceive or see. He had then showed Captain Saginor a sheaf of papers which he had removed from a desk drawer—communiques on the subject directed to the Army brass, including his former mentor General George Patton. Modica took the time to read a few of these gems to his friend. "This is from old Iron Jaws himself!" he nearly snarled at Saginor: *"Give Barbarossa whatever in hell he wants and let's get on with the fucking war! We've still got Hitler to cut down to fucking size!"*

Col. Modica flung first one, then another and another of these messages, all with similar instructions, at his friend. Saginor, a fiery redhead with a spattering of freckles on his face and arms, was unable to contain his amazement. His concern grew more obvious than his west Texas drawl.

"Good buddy, I hope you aren't headed for a courtmartial. Look, Steve, off the record, let me advise you legally. It just doesn't pay to be a maverick when the brass tells you to bleat like a sheep. According to the terms of the North Atlantic Treaty, we're supposed to give 'em what they want. It makes no difference what you want for them. They gotta want it first. Heah? If none of them has the guts to give a holler and a hoot for what they want—it isn't your responsibility."

Watching his friend bridle with frustration, Captain Matt Saginor downed a few swigs of Scotch and found he couldn't hold back his concern. "Why are you making it a personal crusade. You've got no choice in the matter, buddy."

"You mean I'm damned if I do and damned if I don't?"

"Listen, you won't be here much longer. Why get so steamed up?"

"You know something I don't?" Modica had asked him, alerted by his remark.

"The President is dying. When he does, you'll be pulled off the Sicilian detail. Concentration's gonna center on Berlin. I've already got you keyed in to A.C.C. there. Our info is that before the month ends, Hitler and his supermen will be saluting Old Glory. Keep this on the QT. All the Chiefs of Staff are being hustled off to prepare a possible confrontation with Russia. We've gotten feedback, Steve, that Russia's negotiating a peace with Hitler."

Modica snorted. "Now it begins! No one listened when

news reached the French underground, nearly two years ago, that a possible Russian-German Alliance was in the offing. They called us crazy! You know how many good men died in that operation? Goddamn them anyway!"

"You and I and a helluva lot of guys knew we should have invaded France first. Why rehash it, Steve? Does it make you feel better to know you're right—*after* the fact?"

"Why rehash it? Why? Because goddammit, there's the devil to pay! We've stayed too long in Italy! Meanwhile Russia advanced in Yugoslavia, took over Bulgaria, and reigns supreme in Warsaw! Bastards! They have the gall to boast they did it by themselves! Russia's so swollen with self-importance, she'll tell the world she won the war singlehanded. You think America has the guts to tell her to go chase herself? Oh, no. The brass will find another excuse to play down her arrogance. 'We'll need Russia to fight off the Japs,' they'll tell us. And we'll go on playing the patsy, while the big wheels continue to make their power plays! Man! Who the hell knows what goes on?" he exasperated.

"Yeah," sighed Captain Saginor. "Who knows?"

"Meanwhile Sicily goes down the drain," reflected Col. Modica, crestfallen. "I told them there'd be an insurrection—that the Sicilians would annihilate each other. Somewhere, not from me, they got the notion that America stands behind them in this strategy. Now, we're going to let them down."

"The spoils of war, good buddy. Some win—others lose."

Just before Saginor prepared to leave to fly back to Rome, he voiced his regrets in not finding the time to stay for dinner. They were interrupted by the Colonel's military aide, Lieutenant Destro.

"Sorry, sir. I've been asked to remind you the Grand Council is waiting for you."

Modica nodded, grabbed his jacket, shook hands with Saginor, and embraced him affectionately.

"Stay cool, buddy," said the Captain noting the strained expression on his friends face. "Figure it's all in a day's work. By the way, I hear your hands are full of this Sicilian Robin Hood, eh?"

"Sicilian Robin Hood?" Modica frowned in thought. "What the hell are you talking about?"

"You haven't heard of the shoot-em-up guy right in your own backyard?" Saginor laughed and poured himself a stiff drink for the road. "Headquarters is going ape with all the press-pass requests. We're deluged with requests for interviews with him. Right square in the middle of a fucking war, this *bandito* takes over like gangbusters! Like gangbusters, buddy! Word's out that a motion picture company is seeking a permit to shoot a film about him! Is he one of the resistance groups?"

"Oh, yeah. Yeah, him," muttered the Colonel. In seconds he came alive. "Yeah! Him! Salvatore! Why the hell didn't I think of him before?"

Halted in his tracks at the pure look of fiendish delight on Modica's face, Saginor's face clouded with concern. "Steve! Look, man, don't do anything foolish. There's no time to defend you in a military trial, pal. And I'd hate for you to sit out the war in the brig!"

Colonel Modica waved him off. "Have a good trip." He shed his jacket, loosened his tie, and commenced shuffling through the drawers of his desk fully preoccupied.

Captain Saginor bit his lower lip and stretched it over his teeth, in reflected thought. "Steve, Gina's in Rome."

Modica glanced up. His heart flipped over, and color rose in his cheeks "How is she?" he managed with some hesitation.

"As well as can be expected. Any message for her? She knows I'm seeing you this trip." When his friend grimaced with annoyance, Saginor added, "Sorry, buddy, it slipped."

"I've nothing to say." muttered Steve, already lost in the project at hand.

About to protest, Saginor saw it was useless. "*Ciao*, good buddy. Maybe you could save one of those little Mamma Mias for me next time I see you. . . .

For a few brief moments after Saginor left his office, Colonel Modica indulged in a few whimsical reflections of Gina O' Hoolihan. Thoughts of her, and the love they had shared, brought a wistful sigh to his lips. *Goddamn the war!* he thought. Everything had been so perfect for them, but with the war what could he have done? He had to break it off. Just as he did then, and would continue to do until the war ended, Stefano Modica turned his mind off all thoughts of romance—the lasting kind, anyhow—and turned it to the business at hand.

He forced himself to concentrate on the newspaper-clipping file previously compiled on the brigand, Salvatore. He ordered his aide to cancel the meeting of the Grand Council on any pretext, and didn't wait for Lt. Destro's sputtered protests. He thumbed through the clippings recalling what he'd told Matt Saginor earlier in his frustration.

"The fate of a country and its people rests on my conscience and all I see around me is crap. Deals upon deals are born every second of the day. Everybody's wheeling and dealing for Sicily except Sicily, herself. The people aren't represented in this fiasco. If only one of them, just one lousy Sicilian, came off the streets to tell me he either agreed or disagreed with these antiquated prima donnas of the Grand Council, I'd jump for joy. This Don Barbarossa stacks the cards, deals from any position in the deck, and always comes up smelling like roses. Damnit! He holds more trump cards than a boll weevil lays eggs."

Colonel Modica believed these words, despite their seeming futility. Studying these news clippings, Modica felt a stir inside him. Was it possible the answer might have been within his grasp all the time? That this Salvatore could be the voice he had wanted so desperately to hear? Why hadn't he come forward?

He read and reread the newsworthy items, which he had meant to read long ago and had kept tabling until he could find the time. Finally, now, he made the time. . . .

All this had taken place a week ago. Since then Colonel Modica's time had been consumed with petty annoyances and disconcerting problems, all of which centered around the inimitable Don Barbarossa. A curious twist of events had evolved since the last meeting of the Grand Council last Friday which had stymied the American. At that time, Don Barbarossa had stated with confidence that he controlled all the outlaw bands in Sicily. He promised he would personally assume their leadership in any possible confrontation with government forces. The instant it became evident that Sicily might have to fight for her independence, the Don stated that he objected to plans for an

Long ago Colonel Modica had pegged the Don for a insurrection on the basis that no one could predict the outcome of a revolution. He was one for keeping all things under control—*his* control. He had cited the Canepa *fiasco* as evidence of what lack of control could reap.

man who'd play three or more sides against the middle if it were to his benefit. Playing his hunch, he had put a tail on this redoubtable power broker. Two days ago, his spies had brought him puzzling information. Following the last meeting on Friday, Don Barbarossa was followed to the office of Chief Inspector Semano, where he had astonishingly revealed in detail a summary of secret Council business, presumed to be highly classified information. In addition he betrayed plans of the proposed insurrection planned by the newly formed Partitionist party. Colonel Modica was flabbergasted at the contents of the report.

True, the scope of their projected plans *was* broad and somewhat nebulous in these embryonic stages of development, but, *why* the Don had seen fit to bare the plans mystified the American officer. It was to have been a mock insurrection in which the real bandits, disguised as Sicilian patriots and college students, would be prepared, should the government troops create unexpected violence. This staged insurrection, tantamount to revolution, would in no way be as perilous or unpredictable as the real thing, the Don had explained to the Chief. "You'll kill two birds with a single stone. Catch the bandits whom you've had no success in capturing, and break up what appears to be a real revolution. Think of the feathers in your cap—eh?"

Colonel Modica wondered what the hell this sonofabitch was trying to pull off. If Modica had harbored any illusions, before this, that his own varied experience had taught him how to sniff out the skunks, the diabolical schemers or the scurrilous plotters, he now came to realize he had met his match. If he lived ten lifetimes, he'd never understand such a man. *How can a man get to know another,* he thought, *when his past history, swallowed by the jaws of deception, disappears like the thief in the night who comes unseen and unheard and leaves behind only a vacuum as evidence of his past?* It would have made no sense for the Colonel to report his findings to his superiors. He'd been made too cognizant of the broken record playing endlessly in his mind, *"Give the Don whateverinhell he wants!"*

Very well, thought Modica, I'll play as dirty or crazy a game as is needed. As a temporary expedient, he cancelled all Grand Council meetings at which his presence was needed. Concerned that his feelings might betray him, he simply stalled for time. Meanwhile all political machinery had slowed down to a halt. Harried calls placed to his office were ignored. He wanted no locking of horns with Don Barbarossa, not yet.

On this Wednesday, April 2, 1945, Colonel Modica sat at his desk, hip-deep in newspaper clippings of Salvatore. He had reread all the articles until he had formed a vivid impression of the renegade in his mind. What had impressed the American officer was the detailed account of all Salvatore's victories, and if you could believe the press, the bandit had had no failures. That was what made it so marvelous! Incredible to imagine. No wonder he'd appeared in print as an arrogant, self-assured young prince.

Only a man who'd never known defeat could assume such a posture. God! He was beautiful! To have burst on the scene with such spectacular verve and *panache* was short of miraculous in this way and age! But why had *he* been kept from Salvatore? Why?

Modica lit a cigarette with his lighter, and for several moments he continued to click it open and shut as he pondered the situation. Was it possible that Salvatore was a part of the plan Don Barbarossa had so laboriously embroidered to stage the coming insurrection? Modica's mind lumbered back to the first meetings of the Grand Council when he first arrived in Palermo. . . .

Click, Click. Don Barbarossa, without preamble had made their position quite clear. "It is the ardent desire of all loyal Sicilians that their nation become a State annexed by America," he had stated firmly. Or if that wasn't possible, would it please the Colonel to personally speak with the British Government to see if they might consider Sicily as a British Colony?

Click, Click. Alarming revelation at the registration of political parties in Rome, that the trend was pro-Left, had brought immediate reaction and a turnabout in their previous objectives.

Click, Click. "If it pleased the American Colonel, the Grand Council urgently presses for the immediate separation of Sicily from Italy. We further must insist upon full autonomy. Does the American Colonel understand Sicily will not permit the Reds in their land? Does he know the full extent of their displeasure if the Reds rear their ugly head in Sicilian politics? In lieu of all that's happened, the Colonel must understand the Grand Council's dilemma. Would it not be more beneficial to the Allies, if Italy swings to the Left, to keep Sicily as a friendly ally? With Sicily goes control of the Mediterranean." Control indeed!

Click, Click. Shortly thereafter, Colonel Modica had received a communique from Rome, substantiating the pro-Leftists leanings. In addition the message, crystal clear, left no room for conjecture. "Italy—pro-Left. Encourage Separatists and form coalition of all parties under one strength—the Partitionists. Imperative that you cooperate with Barbarossa. In case of trouble with Reds, we'll need friendly Allies. *Redbeard* is the only one who can pull it off." Signed, Gen. O. Baglev, Chief of Staff, OSS (*Redbeard Papers Detail*).

Click, Click. Another message followed. "OSS advises you Canepa affair backfired. Reorganize resistance groups.

Procrastination must cease. Full and complete data to follow. Get cracking!"

Modica tossed aside the lighter. That had been three days ago. All Modica had to do was tell Don Barbarossa to forge ahead with his plans. The U.S.A. would back him completely. It was that simple. Why couldn't he bring himself to issue these directives? Why the reluctance on his part? Why should he continue to give a damn? Saginor was right, he told himself. If the Sicilians didn't give a fig about their fate—why should he? Soon, with all this trouble brewing with Russia, he'd be immersed in another cause, too busy to concern himself with an apathetic people. No rationalization on his part could sufficiently ease the pain of conscience he felt. His thoughts were interrupted by the impatient buzzing of an intercom. He leaned over the desk, flipped the switch. A look of annoyance flickered in his eyes.

"Colonel Modica—what is it?" he snapped absently.

"A call from the lobby, sir. We've got a visitor," came Lt. Destro's filtered voice.

"Well?"

"It's the brigand, Salvatore, sir."

"Damnit, Lieutenant! You know the *Albergo-Sole* is off limits to civilians. Why do you bother me?"

"He has a pass signed by the Minister of the Interior. Demands audience with the Mayor of Godrano, Don Barbarossa."

"Who does?" preoccupied with his thoughts, he hadn't caught the name.

"Salvatore, sir."

"*Salvatore?*" Modica's eyes swept over the clippings on his desk. "Salvatore is here? At headquarters? Well, I'll be damned!" A look of ineffable delight crept into his eyes.

"Tell you what, Lieutenant," said Modica in a conspiratorial manner. "I want you to divert Salvatore to my quarters. You are to tell no one he's here. *Especially* Don Barbarossa. Got it?"

"Yes, sir."

While he waited for Salvatore, Colonel Modica's mind raced ahead excitedly as a plan formulated in his mind. Having come to look with great disfavor at the man, Don Barbarossa, Modica would have liked nothing better than to emulate Pontius Pilate, by washing his hands clean of the Sicilian affair. But apparently it wasn't to be. And now—this! The infamous bandit Salvatore walks into the *Al-*

406

bergo-Sole and demands audience with the very man who plans to betray him? Was this to be believed?

If the Don planned to seduce the bandits, how did he dare bring them into such formal surroundings? Modica couldn't begin to comprehend the complexities in either the man or the situation. A sharp rap at the door sliced through his thoughts.

Lieutenant Destro entered, saluted, and announced, "Colonel Modica. *Signore* Salvatore is here."

Modica glanced up. "Send him in, please," he said, acknowledging the salute.

Before he reached the door, it pushed open easily. Salvatore stood poised on the threshold, his dark eyes expertly scanning the room. Then he fixed on the well-tanned officer whose friendly blue eyes widened in astonishment when they took into focus the handsome, well-dressed youth in his dark tailored suit with his white shirt and tie, carrying a briefcase. He could have been a young lawyer or business man, but certainly too young to have attained such status, thought Modica. Damn, he was something!

"I am Salvatore," he said quietly.

"I am Colonel Modica," he said rising from his chair, with arm extended. "Please be seated, *Signore.*" Modica spoke Italian with a tinge of a Sicilian dialect and tried to remain aloof as befitted his position. It wasn't easy.

"Piacere, Colonnello," replied Tori. He sauntered casually by the adjoining bedroom and bath in an attitude of silent appraisal, while he checked all exits and entrances for possible entrapments.

"You desire to speak with Salvatore, *Colonnello?*" he asked pleasantly.

"Yes, as a matter of fact I do." The Colonel extended his hand towards a chair.

Tori sat down stiffly and struck a pose of polite reserve.

"May I see your passes? It's a matter of protocal. You understand." Modica set aside his fascination.

Tori leaned forward slightly, removed the documents from his hip pocket, and handed them to Modica. "You may speak English. It comes easier—no? If I don't understand, I'll make it known."

Modica nodded, impressed. "Did His Excellency, the Minister, sign these passes for you personally?" he asked, scanning the passes.

"Not in my presence."

"I didn't mean that. Did the passes come from Belasci, or second-hand?"

"Your Sicilian isn't too clear. But to reply—yes."

He removed a thin brown *cigarillo* from a slender box. "Permit me to smoke, *Colonnello?*" His easy smile covered his nervousness.

Modica nodded, extended his lighter across the desk. "How *did* you come by these passes?" he persisted.

"*Managghia!* You *are* relentless. My Godfather gave them to me."

Modica lit his cigarette. "Godfather?"

Tori hedged deliberately. "Please put to me precisely what you wish to know. I can shorten this interrogation." He spoke slowly, carefully.

"That's considerate of you. Please state your business." Modica found it hard to be formal with the Sicilian.

"My business—with your permission—is with Don Barbarossa."

"I'm sure. But, with *your* permission, please state the nature of it."

"With *your* permission, it's private," he replied tactfully.

"You realize I can restrain you, instantly? You took a chance, coming here with a price on your head," Colonel Modica snapped.

A thousand thoughts crossed Tori's mind. Tense, he tried not to indicate his discomfort. Had he been so blinded by his Godfather's importance that he failed to exercise simple caution? "You saw my passes. Are they not in order?" Tori moved slightly in his chair to feel the security of the gun strapped to his inner calf.

"You are an enemy of the State. Presently, I *am* the State—over and above any jurisdiction enjoyed by the Don."

"So—I am at your mercy." Tori felt sweat pop on his forehead. Under his arms it ran in streams to his waist. "Is it your desire, *Colonnello,* to shoot me up? Before you reach that button on your desk, you'll be dead. I promise. I will take my chances with those three *soldati* who work outside your door and those three by the elevator. Make no mistake, you will not live to see my fate, if such is your intent." He smiled tightly.

A glimmer of astonishment crossed Modica's face. "You're concealing weapons, also?" He shook his head tolerantly. "I shall have to reprimand my men for such gross carelessness."

"Have no fear, Colonnello. It's not my intention to contest you in a duel. My feelings are that you didn't bring Salvatore to your office to arrest him," he said, exuding an outward glow of confidence that belied his inner

408

feelings. Tori would have liked nothing better than to leave these alien grounds.

For reasons they both were later to wonder about, their communication was as instantaneous and mysterious as it was unmistakable, Modica found it difficult not to praise the young man whom he still couldn't reconcile in his mind as being the same one written about so glowingly. Finally, and with an irresistible impulse, the Colonel managed to express himself.

"You're everything that's been written about you and more. Your perception, which is astonishingly accurate, amazes me. You're right, I've no interest in detaining you or arresting you. My business is far more important."

"What sort of business does an American *Colonello* have with Salvatore?" Toni smiled.

Modica got to the point. "Why haven't your people come forth to voice their concern for the future of their country? Don't they care what happens in their lands?"

"With so many political jackals braying at your feet in the Grand Council, you need more to drive you crazy?" Tori shook his head temporately.

Colonel Modica laughed. "Political jackals, eh? You may be right. Perhaps that's why I question their qualifications as well as their aims." He fell into a more serious pose. "Doesn't the fate of Italy matter to you or your people?"

"Sicily—yes. Not so much, Italy."

"One goes hand in hand with the other, no?"

Tori shook his head thoughtfully. "Italy, to us Sicilians, was once a big love affair. In the beginning she was a goddess, someone to revere. A long time ago we came to see her as she's always been—a whore. She was never pure, never saintly, never perfect. She took too much from us—our hearts, our blood, our sweat, even our lands, and she has squeezed us dry. What can Sicilians do—run away? To what, another land? Another love affair to dissillusion us? We have been a lost people too long. We who remain in Sicily do so because we hold hope for her future. We thought, *America has come to her aid. At last there is hope for Sicilians.* But time opens our eyes. We see nothing is done. Nothing will be done. Perhaps it's because for too long our lands and our leaders offer us nothing but oppression. We have grown accustomed to it. . . ."

"There's a chance to change all that, Sicilian. You aren't forsaken, yet!"

"How? For centuries we've been a people with no voice in government. We're a conquered land. Always Sicilians are subordinate to the conquerors. Others in government, foreigners, dictate our policies.

"And you don't question them? Challenge them to make certain they do what the people want and need?" He extended an ash tray to his guest.

"But no. How is this possible? Only in a democracy are such things possible." Tori flipped his ashes in the metal container.

"Men like your Mayor Tedesco can authorize the regimentation of mankind, promote his antiquated and insufferable ideas, and you Sicilians sit back and take it like the serfs of old?" disdained the Colonel.

"The mayor can promote all he wishes. Whether the people accept such stupidity is another thing. We have our ways of dealing with such foolishness." Tori boasted with schoolboy defiance.

"Why elect such men to office in the first place? Wouldn't it seem sensible to stop them before they spread such insanity?"

"Perhaps he represents the lesser of other evils. You think we have a choice? The Church pushes its candidates upon us. If the people wish to eat and keep their jobs, they vote the way the Church tells them."

"And you permit this?" Modica was appalled.

"But—what is this? You blame *me*? I have no control in the elections. Only in these extraordinary circumstances of war have I been able to intervene for my people." The young Brigand indicated his annoyance.

"I'm sorry, Salvatore." Modica faltered, confused. "What I've read and what I heard is all to the contrary. Are you not fighting the cause of your people? Are you not rebelling against an unjust government?"

"*Si!* Against starvation, graft and corruption—inflicted upon us by those men you Americans hired to enforce your laws. *You* made it a felony to transport food from one province to another thus making felons of every decent Sicilian. It's an unjust law, *Colonnello*." He put out his cigarette and leaned back in his chair easily.

Salvatore spent the next half hour explaining the ways of the *carabinieri*, their oppression, and treacheries. "You created a nation of hunted criminals whose guilt was only to feed themselves and their loved ones. That's why I release prisoners from jail and burn their records—so they can live in peace without fear of reprisal. It was for no other reason. I, too, was forced into a life of crime by your unjust laws." He paced about the room easily.

"Is it therefore, not your concern to prevent leaders in

410

government from taking and taking from the people and never allowing them to live as human beings? Man was born free, to determine his own destiny. Shouldn't he have the right to elect his own leaders? Leaders who echo their voices? Such a cause should be wholly supported by all those close to the soil, the masses of the oppressed, for they are the ones who stand to gain." Modica watched Tori glance curiously at the maps strewn about the room.

Tori, no fool, grew silent and reflective. This wasn't strange talk to his ears. These words were like the cherished dreams of his childhood, when he'd been filled with idealistic hope. Angered at first, by the accusatorial tone, he retorted, "But—this is not my affair—" He stopped in mid-sentence and stared at the American, temporizing. "Are you saying that a mere peasant could choose a president—a Ruler?" His words, spoken softly, just above a whisper, were hesitant, unsure. "Someone like me?"

Modica nodded. "Right now you control your territory. You lead some five hundred men who do your bidding. Has it occurred to you if your people united for a worthy cause you could create the Sicily you dream of, the kind of government you desire? Even a democracy—for the people, of the people, and by the people? Yes, Salvatore, why not you? This is your country, your home, your people."

Unable to restrain himself, Colonel Modica didn't realize how far-reaching were these ideas he had implanted in the mind of this Sicilian. Later, much later, he wondered how he an American on foreign soil, despite the Occupation, dared suggest such inflamatory politics to a native. Yet, Goddamnit, it *was* his job to stir up unrest, wasn't it? Wasn't that his posture in this damnable war?

In the ensuing silence, Tori studied the American Officer with whom he felt such mysterious affinity. After several moments in which he drew his own conclusions, he asked Modica, quietly: "You mean . . . a revolution?" His eyes burned into Modica's, and he stiffened suspiciously at the direction in which the conversation was directed. Tori recoiled. He was in unfamiliar territory and this could very well be a trap, he reminded himself. These Americans were too disarming, too generous in their praises.

When he heard his words played back without guile, with unmasked innocence, Modica almost backed off. Fully committed and deeply entrenched in his work, he pushed on. "Damnit, Salvatore! How else can you help keep your country out of the hands of the communists? You don't want the Reds to take over your lands, do you?" He paused a moment. "Do you believe in destiny?"

411

The American leaned forward, his blue eyes fixed on the Sicilian.

"Does a Sicilian believe there's a sun?" Tori gave him the shadow of a smile.

"When I heard you were in the lobby, I moved swiftly. I had to meet you. If anyone represents Sicily—it's you. If anyone can tell me how Sicilians feel, what they think, what they need, it's you!" he said, impassioned. "I'm certain destiny had a hand in our encounter." Modica walked back to his desk and poured two Pernods. He handed one to his guest, flushed with excitement. Salvatore, with USA aid, could rise and conquer!

"Tori shook his head. "Grazie, *Colonnello.* I do not drink."

"Nothing?"

"Nothing." Tori explained. "I learned that the Great Alexander once killed his best friend under the influence of alcohol, and lived to deeply regret the act. If such a man was disposed to commit an act against his nature—what chance would I, a lesser man, have in keeping my faculties under control while under so potent an influence?"

Pleasantly surprised at the sobriety of his words, Modica pressed. "Ah, but then that raises the question: which nature is the true one? That which is inhibited, or that which becomes free of inhibitions when relaxed by an intoxicant?" *He's sharp and at least he's a thinker,* the Colonel told himself.

Silence. . . .

"You speak in . . . how do you say . . . *astrazione*—abstractions. I have no use for such talk. Who can prove there is anything but one nature in man? Wine or no wine?" A marked disturbance creased his face.

"Come now, Salvatore, you're Catholic, no? The Church itself speaks of the God in Man and of the demon, or devil, within, that refutes the urgings of God. That shoots your theory, doesn't it? There's your duality." He sat down heavily in the chair behind his desk.

"I don't understand—*shoots* your theory?" He was perplexed.

"Blows up. Disintegrates. In short, it renders your theory of a singular nature in man, incorrect. Theologians should know. It's their racket."

"With your permission. Translate in Italian. I do not understand your idioms."

Modica complied, and explained himself as best he could. "You see, we Americans don't really speak English, we use considerable slang, as you do in your dialect. You

412

know, you are something special? Terrific! Did you study formally? Here or abroad? What made you take up the cause of the peasant? Did it intrigue you? What?" He wasn't prepared for the subtle change in the brigand.

Tori appeared instantly withdrawn. He glanced swiftly at the officer and drummed his fingers nervously on his thighs, working up to a controlled anger.

"I, *Colonnello*, am a peasant, with no formal education. Tutored by my mother, a former school teacher, I was inspired to become a reader of books. I do not find it intriguing. I found it a bitter necessity to take up our cause. Each day I hope you law makers accelerate your labors and bring a much needed peace and prosperity to our people in their desperate struggle for survival."

"Now, hold on a moment, Salvatore. I meant nothing derogatory. The hell of it is, I find myself speechless at your accomplishments and the manner in which you speak. To say nothing of your command of my language."

"With your permission, what does the word *terrific* mean" asked Tori.

"It means what it means in your language, except, we Americans use it in the vernacular, meaning something unusually great, intense, extraordinary."

"Then, you did not mean to suggest I was a frightening, dreadful or appalling person?"

"Never!"

He relaxed and spoke the word several times. "Terrific. *Te-rrific!*" I like that word. You, also are *te-rrific, Colonnello*. Is that correct?"

"I thank you for the compliment. But, it is you who is more suited to such a word. You still amaze me."

"Why? You expected an inarticulate, lowly dog?"

"Certainly not that." Modica shoved the news clippings towards him. "I also read extensively. From what I've read here, your letters will one day become collector's items."

Tori shrugged off the compliment.

He felt inescapably drawn towards the American. They entered into a dialogue in which Tori spoke of his youth, his dreams, those of his people, conditions before the war, and what his plans for the future included. He discussed his fiery resolve to seek amnesty for his crimes.

Listening to him, the American grew more aware of the complexity of Salvatore's nature. Modica perceived easily the "larger than life" figure of a hero as it attempted to shrink into a smaller shadow of the man Tori wanted to be. He was puzzled. For a time Modica couldn't reconcile the bandit, Salvatore, with the youth, Alessandro, as if

413

they were two separate people in one body. He found himself wondering which of the two would emerge victorious in the desperate battle that raged in him. Nearly two hours later, Modica expertly directed the conversation back to where it nearly exploded earlier. Totally without guile, he asked. "What do you know about this man, Don Barbarossa?"

"My Godfather?" Tori picked up the globe paperweight from Modica's desk and bounced it in his hands. "He is some te-*rrrific* man, no?"

Stunned, Modica hardly believed his ears. "I don't understand. Barbarossa's your Godfather?"

"Yes—Why? Does it surprise you?"

The Colonel was appalled. What madness is this? he asked himself. Barbarossa plans to betray his own Godson? Recovering momentarily, he thumbed through the manila file, oblivious to the curious glances cast upon him by his guest, until he located the report which had trailed the skillfully deceitful *capomafia* to the Chief Inspector's office. He scanned the contents to assure himself there was chance for error. There was none. It was all there—every slick and cunning trick Barbarossa had employed.

The change in the American became too obvious. Tori felt uncomfortable. "Something is wrong?"

Modica hardly heard him. A fucking three-year-old dummy could have seen through the acrobatics of this cagey Sicilian mongoose, Barbarossa! Disgusted, Modica slammed the file shut. He reached for a cigarette, and, finding his pack empty, he crushed it into a ball in annoyance and tossed into a wastebasket nearby. Tori leaned in, a pack of Camels in his outstretched hand.

"Accept one of mine and I shall be honored."

The Colonel nodded absently, and reached for it. He lit it and puffed thoughtfully on it. Snapping out of his reverie, he waved his hands in the air about him apologetically. "Sorry if I seemed rude. Something struck me—nothing to do with you," he lied and changed the subject. "I mentioned earlier that I should like to become better acquainted with you. I feel in my bones that something important will come from our meeting. You understand?"

"I understand. Only our native tongue separates our thoughts from time to time." A polite smile played about his lips as he lit his own cigarette.

"I mean no offense," He liked Tori immensely.

"None taken." He spun the globe in his hands and gave it his attention for a short time.

414

Modica began to ramble. He spoke of his experiences with the Sicilians, how the intrigues annoyed him and provoked his integrity. "They amend their minds constantly, shift and change their ideals as promiscuously as a whore changes bed partners."

"Credit that idiosyncrasy to the constant changes forced upon us by our conquerors. I doubt that Sicilians can ever be what our hazy ideals tell us to be. But, one thing is certain: the allegiance and love Sicilians feel for Americans is irrevocable. Your leaders cannot accept what Sicilians feel in their hearts? That they desire to be a part of America?"

"If that was my dilemma, there'd be no problem. *My* problem is communism. In a matter of time your lands will be infiltrated with communists. Sicily, courted and wooed by them, will once again be raped by a conqueror and turned out to whore for them."

"Yes, it's true. Russia seeks control of the Mediterranean. We've known this for too long. Incredible that America permits her this vice."

"Russia has made giant strides in the past year. It's natural she wants to spread her spheres of interest," replied the American blandly.

"Why does she pluck such power from the United States? Why?" queried Tori.

"We cannot afford to offend Russia, since Hitler remains to be reckoned with. You forget we still have a date to go dancing with Tojo." Modica stared at the smoke curling from his cigarette.

Tori found this incredulous. "You risk the spread of a malignancy by not cutting out a small infection?"

Colonel Modica remained silent as he studied the noticeable changes in his guest. The color left Tori's face, then slowly reentered it, flushing crimson.

"So! Once again Sicily becomes a pawn, to be betrayed. America with a short memory, forgets her friends too quickly." Tori jumped to his feet agitated. "As long as there is breath in me, *Colonnello*, the Reds will not rule my country!"

"What would you have her do? Become a Monarchy once again? A republic? A democracy? Is she ready for any of these? Would you favor separation from Italy with full autonomy A regional Parliament set up here in Palermo?" Modica's eyes blazed blue fire. "I want to hear what the 'people's man' has to say! God Almighty! I want to hear! . . . Well—tell me. I'm waiting!"

Tori backed off. The waters were getting too deep. He didn't know the Colonel, knew less about his motives, and, as most Sicilians were prone to do, he suspected double-dealing of sorts. Salvatore smiled easily.

"I'm no *politico*, to tell you what is best for my people. They want what any man wants—freedom, a chance to live decent lives without being robbed of respect. To work and support their families. The things morally due to humans. At war's end, I shall complete my education and study law, then perhaps I can tell you the kind of government my people need."

"What qualifies you to be so positive they don't *need* communism? Moments ago you were on fire, blasting the Reds! You don't make sense, Sicilian! How can you be so adamantly opposed to one issue and tepid on others?" He wanted to inflame the young man as he had earlier.

"Everyone says communism is bad! You yourself admit it. Why is America so against it? Our lawmakers are against it because it's always the same with new conquerors. Russia will break all the promises she now baits us with."

Colonel Modica realized at once he had a neophyte on his hands. Terribly let down, he sighed with abject futility. In the next half hour he learned why Salvatore had hedged. This unusual, complex youth who had become a national hero had somehow psyched himself into believing that he was nothing without a formal education. He was wrong. But, as long as he believed it, it would remain his truth.

Almost as if he read the Colonel's mind, Tori explained. "I've become what I am through the circumstances of war. Do not mistake yourself about my importance. I told you, half the stories written about me are grossly distorted, over-exaggerated. The other half are fanciful products of highly imaginative writers."

Modica disagreed. "A formal education makes neither the man nor the politician. It helps, but it's not the prime requisite. Don't delude yourself into believing such trivia, for God's sake. In the two short years of your career, whether chosen by preference or through circumstance, you have *become* Sicily."

"No, no, no, no. You give me too much importance. I am presently nothing more than an outlaw with a price on my head—some say a bandit, a murderer chased by the law, who seeks to collect on unpaid accounts."

"That might be true—but there's more you must take into account. Unless you, yourself, recognize and face your own potential, nothing will come of your talent. What you've done—what you've accomplished—is so stellar that nothing you can say will dull the deeds you performed."

"Did you go to college, *Colonnello?*" he asked with interest.

"Yes."

"What about this General Patton. Him too?"

"Him, too."

"And *Generale* Eisenhower. What of him?"

"Yes, but—"

"You see? Every man who hopes to lead men must be more knowledgeable than those who follow. It is his duty to know more than his men."

Modica exasperated, "There is a man warming up in the bull pen right now, who never had a college education. Soon he'll be President of the United States. He was a farmer—a peasant, like you, who believed in certain principles, and became a politician. Elected to the U.S. Senate, he supported President Roosevelt and became a Chairman on a special investigation committee where his fairness and integrity came to light. He was later nominated Vice President, and elected to office with President Roosevelt. Because of the President's failing health, he will be Commander in Chief—all without a formal education. There are many others like him throughout history. Not all leaders graduate *Summa cum laude.*"

"With your permission, *Colonnello,* I will take some coffee. It is strange to hear my name spoken in the same breath as that of a future American President."

Modica barked into the intercom. "Lieutenant! Send some coffee and refreshments to us."

"Yes, sir," came Destro's filtered voice.

Tori gazed with great interest at the box on his desk.

"So, Salvatore doesn't recognize the extent of *his* power?"

"It's plain to see I haven't the power of that small box. You talk into it and it brings you coffee?"

Colonel Modica smiled. "It's plain to me you don't know. Let me tell you, you pack plenty of power. Such influence, if channeled correctly, can move mountains!"

"I have no interest to move mountains, *Colonnello.*" Tori wagged a hand in the air.

"Don't misunderstand. I'm not speaking in the literal sense, only figuratively." The American officer moved towards the window and glanced outside.

"Then, speak in the literal sense so I understand."

Modica smiled. "I'll put it this way. If I were a betting

417

man, I'd put all my money on you." He turned from the street scene below, his eyes on Tori.

"*Your* money on me? I don't comprehend such words."

"What I mean is, I'd promote you, push you forward, permit you to speak on my behalf. For instance, if you ran for public office, I'd back you with all I have." He groped for the right words in Italian.

"Ahhhh! *Capeeshu!* You'd buy all the votes for me."

"Buy all the votes? I don't mean that at all."

"How else would I win the election?"

"This is the way your officials get elected?"

"How else? Here the priests and nuns go from house to house with food and small cash donations. They even promise jobs if you vote for the men they promote."

"I assure you that isn't what I had in mind. Col. Modica took time to explain himself, while Salvatore listened intently as a student might listen to his teacher.

Finally, Salvatore understood. He sippped a glass of water and temporized. "You'd back me with money, eh? If the *Colonnello* should do such a thing, he would be backing the wrong man."

"Again you underestimate yourself—"

"If the *Colonnello* were to back a man such as Matteo Barbarossa, in my humble opinion you'd be backing the proper person. Be clever, put your money on him." Tori tapped his forehead with his forefinger. "He is one *furbo*—smart man."

Colonel Modica held his breath. Time, and a totally disarming congeniality, had lured Salvatore into his lair, where had he proceeded to methodically and intentionally, yet unobtrusively, exact certain information, heretofore elusive to him. If Colonel Modica had spent ten years compiling a dossier on Don Barbarossa, he couldn't have uncovered such explicit information.

Salvatore resorted to what amounted to hero worship as he guided the American officer through the legendary Barbarossa's life and his spectacular climb from those early Mazzarino bandit days to the uncontested high position of *capomafia* of all Sicily. Tori led the Colonel through the countless coups and the terrorizing of his enemies to which Don Barbarossa had subjected any obstructors who stood between him and the coveted role of head of all heads in the Mafia hierarchy. He afforded Modica a bird's-eye view of the national political climate that spawned such a power broker. He posed a comparison between Barbarossa and his predecessor, the former *capomafia* Don Calomare,

418

and described the shame, and humiliation he had endured during the reign of *Il Duce*.

"Very little is known about Matteo Barbarossa's activities during his twenty year exile underground," continued Salvatore. "He wasn't heard of much until you Allies landed in Sicily. You must be aware of the cooperation he extended the Allied forces at that time. What a man, eh?"

The Colonel had listened in rapt silence. Through it all, he was visibly disturbed by recognition of the fierce pride that oozed from Tori as he spoke of the *capomafia*. His first comment was spoken with brutal candor.

"It seems to me that you intend emulating this Godfather of yours, eh, Salvatore?"

Tori's expression froze. Momentarily puzzled, he thought over his words and wondered where the Colonel got such a notion. A flicker of annoyance crept into his eyes. Just as quickly, it vanished. "You overestimate me, *Colonnello*. No one could imitate the bandit of Mazzarino. Barbarossa, the most powerful man in Sicily, dethroned by Mussolini, returns to power twenty years later, to be recrowned as uncontested leader...."

For fear of losing ground already gained, the American didn't bother to argue the point. They both sat sipping coffee, brought in moments before by Lt. Destro, and dunked a generous assortment of Sicilian cookies.

"The twentieth century, stillborn for half a century has a chance to come to life, Salvatore. But, first the feudal tyranny has to be excised—cut out. You understand?"

"And you think I can revive it? Restore life to my country?" asked the outlaw quietly.

Colonel Modica smiled. "Precisely."

They were interrupted by the buzzing of the intercom. Colonel Modica glanced at his watch, and snapped on the switch. Tori, flushed by the conversation, was taken by the box. He leaned in to listen to the gadget, a look of marvel in his eyes, as Lieutenant Destro's voice came through the "magic box."

"Sorry Colonel. It's Don Barbarossa. He's furious. Wants to know why you've seen fit to detain his guest. He's hot as a pistol, sir. What'll I tell him?"

Tori grinned amiably, his eyes twinkling in amusement. "You see, *Colonnello*? It's best you put your money on him. He knows everything—misses nothing."

Colonel Modica scowled. "Tell the Don—" he began,

"*Uhhhhhhuhuh,*" Tori wagged a finger at him and shook his head playfully.

"Tell the Don," said Modica with visible restraint, "his

419

guest hasn't been detained. He'll leave momentarily." The Colonel, annoyed by the interruption, hadn't finished his conversation with the Sicilian outlaw, not by a long shot. He wanted less, however, to give the Don any insight into any plans he might be formulating, those in which Salvatore might play an important role. He moved swiftly. "Have dinner with me on Saturday or Sunday, Salvatore?"

Tori expressed mild pleasure. "Here?" he waved his hands about.

"Yes, of course. Unless you'd prefer some other place."

He smiled graciously. "It would be an honor if you would come to my house in Montegatta. I assure you safe conduct to and from my house," he added at the momentary hesitation he read in the American officer's eyes.

Colonel Modica suppressed a smile. "My concern wasn't for myself. Is it safe for you?"

"Salvatore goes where he desires—with little effort or problems."

"Very well, Sunday. What time?"

"You will come early and remain late. I shall show you some true relics of antiquity." Tori grew expansive.

"I would like that very much." He stood up and shook hands, and with an arm around Tori's shoulders, he walked him to the door. For an instant, he paused and faced the young man. His face grew somber.

"Be cautious, my friend. Trust very few men, in these times." He wanted to say "beware of Don Barbarossa," but didn't.

"Does the Colonel mean what I think he means?" Tori's dark, compelling eyes bore into the American's. "Perhaps if you were more explicit—specific—?"

"No. I can't be. But it might be wise to weigh every proposal with respect to its long-term influence. What I mean is—oh what the hell! You're a prodigious reader. Bone up on Machiavelli!" exclaimed Modica.

"Bone up?" Tori's eyes twinkled again in merriment. "What are you telling me? What is bone up?"

"Refresh your memory—familiarize yourself with a subject—"

"Ahhh. *Si.* I understand. My, my, what strange idioms you Americans use." He smiled, tucked the brief case under one arm, then said quietly.

"Throughout our conversation, I sense you wish to tell me something more than your words convey. Permit me to say, I am safe. My enemies are few. No one would dare harm Salvatore."

"It's not among one's enemies that treachery usually

420

springs," cautioned the Colonel. "I suggest you use discretion about our encounter. Until Sunday—"

"Unless I decide to start a revolution before that—eh, *Colonnello*," he laughed.

Colonel Modica's blue eyes froze into a fixed look of concern. He grew edgy.

"Never fear, *Colonnello*, I was making a joke on you. *Ciao*."

Long after the young rebel left, Colonel Modica contemplated him. He found it incredible that so young a man could have come to world-wide prominence in these troublesome times of war. He glanced through several of the news clippings, picked one out in particular and with interest reread the item:

"Alessandro Salvatore, inspiration to the young, represents immortal youth in a decaying old world. Young, idealistic, imbued with a quiet power never credited to youth, he stands opposed to an ancient feudal system which for centuries has kept his people ignorant, subjugated and confused. Before Salvatore appeared there was disunity, starvation, lack of pride, and a loss of hope among his people. This reporter, having spoken with the rebel leader, found him to be the embodiment of a modern day Robin Hood, but one who practices the doctrines of Aristotle, conquers in the manner of Alexander of Macedonia, and employs Nicomacean ethics. He demonstrates small patience with those learned men, who, proficient in knowledge and education, use these tools to break the backs of the less fortunate. In these troubled times, to have brought strength and unity to a broken, helpless people is short of miraculous. He announces to the world, in the same manner he announces himself: 'I am Salvatore, world. Wake up! Help my people to become whole!' "

Every article about him bloomed with glowing accounts of the flamboyant brigand. His had been a popular cause, picked up and given worldwide recognition by an adoring press. Most correspondents continuously stressed, like advocates pleading his case, that Salvatore's crimes had been of an involuntary nature, forced upon him by devastating circumstances and intolerable conditions in a country prostrated by defeat and occupied by numerous alien armies.

Most articles referred directly to his quest for justice, his intent to strike at the oppressors of the poor—the *carabinieri*, the feudal land barons, the insensitive government, and, of course the Mafia. In one article Salvatore was quoted as saying, "The Mafia, the enemy of the people, is a corrupt institution that has kept them bound in near-slavery to the feudal landlords."

Colonel Modica, his forehead creased in frowns, sat back in his chair apparently disgusted. He read that statement several times: "The Mafia, the enemy of the people. . . . ?"

Yet the biggest *mafioso* of all time was Salvatore's Godfather!!! Barbarossa was Agathocles incarnated, the Praetor of Syracuse, the King of Syracuse who intrigued with the Carthaginians and ended up in full control of Sicily! And Colonel Modica sought to challenge such a man? He shuddered, then grew irate as he mulled over the situation.

"Sicilian intrigue be damned! Fucking Sicilian logic! Nothing but contradictions and intrigues upon intrigues! All of it be damned!" shouted Colonel Modica, in a voice loud enough to fill his quarters.

While he sat stewing over the countless intrigues and counter-intrigues, more intrigue, hatreds, jealousies and vendettas were brooding in the political gardens of Sicilian despots like a blood-red flower waiting to burst into nightmarish bloom out of the corruption, evil and malevolency of an ancient system that refused to lie down and die and give up the ghost so that civilization could progress.

CHAPTER 31

By the time Salvatore arrived at his Godfather's penthouse he found the *mafioso* seated behind his desk, trying not to show his displeasure. As soon as the amenities were over, the Don asked, as if it didn't matter to him, what Tori had experienced in the American officer's company: "Did the *Colonnello* cause you inconvenience?"

"He was *simpatico*," said Tori unruffled. "Most cordial."

"You were there a long time. What did he want?"

"No—not long. Perhaps thirty-forty minutes—"

"Precisely one hour and forty minutes," the Don said abruptly.

"So long?" Tori smiled tersely. He disliked being questioned. Having been his own man for a lifetime, he

422

strained in a subordinate role. He crossed his leg over the other and tapped the side of his boot. "The time flew."

"What did you speak about?" The Don grew impatient with such evasiveness.

"He inspected my passes. Asked how I came by them."

"And, you told him?"

"Naturally. Was it unwise of me to have done so?"

The Don wagged a hand. "It matters not. No one questions my authority." He strutted about the penthouse in his typical attire, shirt-sleeves and trousers held up by suspenders. He waved his arms about the room, expansively. "You see how they treat me, your Godfather? All this at their expense, for Don Barbarossa! Because he is *importante*—to the Allies." He moved back behind the ornately hand-carved oak desk, picked up a fancy humidor, and offered a cigar to his guest.

Tori accepted one. The Don helped himself before replacing the box. Each man lit his own smoke. The room filled with smoke spirals. Don Matteo shuffled to the window, pushed it open, and took several fresh breaths of air. Patting his stomach contentedly he returned to the desk.

"What else did the American discuss?" He pushed his dark glasses up on the bridge of his nose. Beneath his polite mask was a raging anger.

"We spoke of politics."

"What did you tell him?"

Tori shrugged indifferently. "I told him I was no politician. That he should speak of such things to a man more qualified, more experienced and far more astute than I—you."

"That's straight? You told him that?" he expressed his surprised pleasure.

"I told him when I graduated from law school, I'd be better qualified—"

"That nonsense again? Listen, you'd better learn quickly you can't remain a rabbit among foxes!" he snorted. "What else did you discuss?"

The *Colonnello* was surprised you are my Godfather."

"You told him that, too?"

"Was I wrong to have told him?"

"It's no business of the Americans!" He stopped when he saw a curious strained expression in Tori's eyes. The Don waved his hands apologetically. "No, it wasn't wrong. I have no reason to conceal the fact the famous Sicilian bandit is Godson to Don Barbarossa," he said acidly.

He was sharp. He was hard. He was cunning. He was

capomafia, not a cheap imitator of the dime-a-dozen *mafioso.* He was the original. The stamp of an absolute monarch was on all he said and did, surmised Salvatore as he watched the man. And he *was* exciting.

"Certain things are better left unspoken. If it's known you are my Godson, with a price on your head, it might prove difficult to grant you a favor. Be it as it may, nothing shall happen to you as long as I sanction your protection. *Capeeshi?*" He shuffled through a few papers on his desk.

"Might I point out, Godfather, I've done quite well—without your protection." It was the special look the Don gave him that made Tori wary. Godfather or not, he saw something in the older man's eyes which bordered on hatred and envy. He had no desire of letting that enmity grow, so he grinned and said glibly, with a forced sparkle to his eyes. "Unless that good fortune I've enjoyed has been extended under the invisible protection and shining shield of power by the noteworthy Don Barbarossa?"

"You'll never speak truer words," replied the Don, relaxing a bit. *"Allora,* how is your Mamma? You gave her my felicitations?"

"Not yet. I've had little time to see her, since we last talked. I hadn't planned on visiting you so soon. A matter has arisen which needs the guidance of a person of your experience to steer me properly."

A rush of conflicting emotions surged through the Don. He felt, at first, the same inescapable feeling he had felt when, as a youth, out of necessity, he had mastered the art of flattery and persuasiveness for gain. He felt as if he was being had and nurtured for another man's benefit. It was this continuous push-pull, a strange compulsion to refrain from dealing harshly with Salvatore which unnerved him and placed him continuously on his guard.

"Talk. Tell me what it is you want." He sat back in his chair like an Oriental potentate.

"To my province has come a certain *Napolitano,* a *carabiniero, Maresciallo* Franchina who caused me much discomfort. There is no real problem, yet. Word has come that Franchina plans an ambush on Friday night, two days hence. He's issued two hundred warrants for me and my men. How he has learned the names of these men baffles me, for it has been a secret, well kept for two years. Perhaps he has the employ of many spies." Tori glanced at the ornate silver service on the roll away cart. "With your permission, Godfather, I should like a cup of coffee."

"Help yourself. Why don't you take care of this Marshal, yourself? It would be an easy task to dispose of him?" he tilted an eye at Tori.

"With conditions as they are, it doesn't seem appropriate at this time to promote unnecessary bloodshed, just because some overly ambitious *carabiniero* wants to promote himself at my expense. This is a critical time for Sicily, and I wish to do nothing to bring unnecessary publicity upon my affairs." He poured hot coffee into the bone china cup and allowed his eyes to travel about the splendor in which the Don lived.

Don Matteo hardly noticed Tori sauntering about the room. His brain roiled with thoughts of this audacious Marshal Franchina. A complication of this sort would prove more devastating to his plans than any of Salvatore's. All he needed was a self-appointed, promotion-minded *carabiniero* to throw a monkey wrench into his plans! And why hadn't he been informed of these warrants? For him not to have been informed there must be some diabolical plot underfoot to undermine his own efforts. Burning inwardly he wondered who was behind Marshal Franchina?

"How did you learn of the proposed ambush?"

"I have my spies." He motioned to the room and its trappings. "The Americans respect you tremendously, Godfather," he said tongue in cheek. "There's not a newspaper account of your deeds, I haven't committed to memory," continued Tori.

Tori sat down opposite him. "By the way, Godfather, I notice there are no pictures of my baptism. Don't you have any? My own mother seems to have misplaced ours. I'm sure you have a token of that special day?" He studied his Godfather through casual eyes.

"You took the words from my lips. I, too, misplaced the photographs. Times were hectic. I jailed myself after Mori's trail of death struck Sicily, and I remained at Ucciardone prison for three years. By then my wife had vacated our villa in Monreale and we returned to Godrano. After her death, I had no desire to uncrate the boxes. They are in Godrano. I promise, one day I shall have my men uncrate the boxes and locate the photographs." He avoided Tori's penetrating eyes.

Unwittingly the Don had already told Tori what he wanted to know. As soon as he'd checked the dates involved he'd know the answers to the questions which plagued him since he met the Don. He hardly heard the Don's next words.

"Leave Franchina to me. Carry on as usual. The burr shall be removed from your saddle."

Va bene. Grazie."

"It's not necessary you thank me. It is now two favors done for you out of respect. Remember, when the time comes, a favor shall be expected from you." It was the look in his eyes that jarred Tori.

"Two?" Tori was puzzled. "I don't understand—" It suddenly came to him. "What I spoke to you about in Godrano? The matter of Don Pippinu. . . ."

". . . has already been done."

"Already?" Tori was impressed. "But, how? When?"

"Not important. What matters is you've been avenged. Don Pippinu was a cheat, a disgrace to the brotherhood."

The Don savagely tore the cigar from his lips and flung it into a spittoon. "We don't earn our respect through dealings with such a fool, a common gangster who would bring us shame, dishonor and disgrace."

"What would you have done in his place?"

Almost against his will, Don Matteo found himself responding to his Godson's question, and, in so doing, taught Tori a lesson he'd never forget.

"I'd have struck a fair bargain with you. No doubt you'd have settled for a lesser figure than the one you quoted—no?"

"Perhaps."

"Allora, with gentle persuasion, I might have encouraged you to accept even less. But—it would have been a bona fide deal. A deal in business is a deal, one which cannot be broken. If a man's word is like water, no one will trust him. If loss is suffered due to a man's inability to bargain wisely—it's his misfortune and must be erased from mind as a bad experience from which a wise man would profit. To be cheated is unpardonable. The test of a real man is at the center of bargaining. Don't you see? It's no different than the results in a prize ring. It isn't always the most powerful man who wins. The best trained fighter, using special techniques, who knows his opponent's weakness, more often emerges victorious."

Struck by the Don's words, Tori experienced a peculiar sensation as if for the first time he had been given insight into the extent of his Godfather's power. He spoke politely. "I am deeply indebted to you for having helped me avenge a terrible and inhuman act." As he spoke a tremendous weight lifted from his shoulders, gave him peace. Apolladora's death had been avenged. Tori rose to

426

his feet, prepared to take his leave, but the Don didn't acknowledge his move.

"How many men are in your command, Godson?" he asked softly and portentously enough to cause the hairs on Tori's neck to stand up. . . . *Two favors done of you. Favors will be asked in return.* . . .

Sensing what was coming, he shrugged noncommittally. "I have no figures at my disposal." He brightened and tried a new tack. "I forgot to ask. How are the Arabians? Have you named them, yet? Will you breed them?"

"Don't be clever. Just answer." He cleared his throat. "How many?"

"Two—perhaps three hundred. Why?"

Don Matteo grunted. He knew the figure exceeded six hundred. "If you are needed for a special job, how long would it take you to prepare your men?"

"A *special* job?" Tori's throat constricted. "Salvatore works for no man."

"No one but me. How long?"

"You are attempting to solicit the services of Salvatore as if he was a common criminal."

"How long?" insisted the Don as if he hadn't heard Tori's words.

"Less than a week," he replied against his will. "Four days if necessary." He balled his fists tightly.

"Two—perhaps?" The Don suggested with cunning, as he padded over to the silver service and helped himself to coffee and a plate heaped with *biscotti.* "You didn't taste these, Godson. Help yourself. *Sonnu delizioso.*"

Salvatore stiffly declined. He wanted out. Uncomfortable and seething with anger at the obvious lack of respect, he wanted to leave before he said anything to destroy their relationship.

"No?" Don Matteo shrugged. "*Allora*—before you leave, you'll be contacted soon, by—uh—uh. . . ." He placed the coffee and cookies on his desk and searched his trouser pockets for some article. "Ah—here it is." He sat down in his chair and read the name aloud: "*Capitano* Bello. That's it. This new leader of the Partitionist Party will contact you shortly. He's empowered to make you a proposition. Complete amnesty for your crimes and those of your men. In addition to the rank of *Colonnello* in the Partitionist Army, he shall offer you a political appointment, one to your liking, I'm sure. If the Partitionists prove victorious in their new government, you'll be handed the double post of Chief of Police and Minister of Justice. *Va bene?*"

Tori's face drained of all color. *How the hell does he know? Did he also know that Bello had already contacted him?* Was he needling him for information? Tori drew on all his resources to keep silent and listen. *You don't play games with this deadly viper unless you know all the ground rules,* he told himself, as his sixth sense came into play, alerting him.

"What's wrong, Godson?" The Don peered through his bifocals, noticed the pale face and tightly drawn lips bordered by a thin white line.

"Nothing. I missed lunch today. Perhaps I'll take a *biscotto*." He used the next few moments to compose himself.

"You will accept the appointment. Check with me all orders you receive from anyone in authority. *Capeeshi?*"

"If I decide against the offer?" Tori posed the question, prepared for the reply.

"You won't." Don Barbarossa slurped the coffee noisily. "No one tells Salvatore which decisions to make."

"Except me." The Don dunked his *biscotto* in the coffee and brought the soggy confection to his lips before it disintegrated. He reached for a serviette to wipe his lips.

Tori measured his words carefully and spoke evenly so as not to be misunderstood. "I move only upon my directions. No one else's. Salvatore is puppet to no man." Godfather or not, *capomafia* or not, the man must be set straight.

The Don finished his coffee as if he hadn't heard a word. He pointed to the chair. "Sit down. Let's talk man to man. Peasant to peasant. Eh? Between us shall be no manure." He shook his head and reflected. "You know, you're a stubborn, mule-headed ass."

"The first lesson you must learn is never to turn down an offer until you've examined every angle. There's always time to refuse. Always leave yourself open for negotiations. Look to the future, to long term benefits. The difference between the nobility and the peasants is that peasants live only day to day. The nobility looks to the day, but plans also for the future. *Capeeshi?*"

Tori's mind blocked at the indignation he felt. "How dare you speak to Salvatore as if he was an ignorant child?"

The Don suppressed a twinkle in his eye. "You told me you wanted to end this career of banditry?" The Don played his trump card. "Well, to get something you must part with something. In this case you work for the Partitionists and earn your freedom. When victory is obtained, you shall enjoy an exalted office in the administration." The Don continued to dunk and eat all the *biscotti* on the

428

plate. "I can never get enough of these. They are my death. My death!"

"You make it sound uncomplicated. From whom would I take orders?" asked Tori, dropping his anger, a notch.

"Whoever issues the orders, you will not make a move until you clear it with me. That way I can keep my eyes and ears open for possible treacheries."

"Treacheries at your level? My, my, I thought only the savage peasants resorted to treacheries."

Their eyes met and held for an instant. "You've made many enemies, Salvatore. Many enemies," said the Don, evenly.

"Along with many friends," he retorted with marked irritation.

"Ah, si, friends," snorted the other. "Friends whom you've bought with generosity and kindness, who would sell your friendship in a moment to the highest bidder."

"You know all the answers, don't you, Godfather?"

"All the answers. Questions, too. When I led the Mazzarini we were real bandits, not this child's play which converted you to a national hero. Tell me—of what are you a hero? Of the reporters who seek your favors so they get rich writing about you? You are a hero on paper. You know what it means to be a paper hero? *Cazzu!* That's what! You know what they do with yesterday's newspaper? That's right. They wipe asses with it. And don't you forget it. I never set out to be a hero—dead or alive. You must take chances, *Capeeshi?*"

Don Barbarossa picked at the anise seeds stuck between his teeth and glanced slyly at his mercurial Godson, knowing he had snared his prey. "Don't answer me today. By next week, if you can find two good arguments against accepting the commission, come talk with me." His deceptive voice sounded placating.

Tori endured the scathing soul-ripping to which the Don subjected him to in complete humiliation. Never had he been spoken to in this manner. There had been no strong male figure in his life to excoriate him and peel back his defenses as this man had done. He also recognized the psychology behind the words and felt himself drawn to several half-truths the Don had brought to bear. A deep silence fell between them. They looked at each other without blinking; Salvatore, hostile and stonelike in features; Don Matteo, with the inert expression of a preying mongoose before the strike.

Don Matteo broke the connection. *"Va bene.* Come, we'll drink a toast."

"You have a short memory. I don't drink." Tori's words came dangerously close to severing the cord.

"Perhaps if I didn't drink as much, my memory might be as long as yours." The Don's meaningful glance left little to the imagination. "But you're right." He forced a light laugh. "You young bloods are far sharper than old codgers like me. If we don't keep in step with the times, we'll be put to pasture."

Godson or not, this young punk would be taught a lesson. The Don's eyelids grew heavy with displeasure. Whatever other plans he might have for this impertinent cock would have to wait. The political plans he held for Salvatore superseded his own personal displeasure. "You'll be contacted shortly, Godson."

Tori's fists were clenched so tightly he found it difficult to open them and shake hands with the Don before he departed. When he did, he was disgusted to find the handshake limp and without character.

He found Vincenzo at the whorehouse, Neptune's Daughters, a place overrun with soldiers and sailors, properous prostitutes, and pimping waiters, all busy making deals faster than an auctioneer calls for a bid. They left and had dinner at Angelo's on the Via Maqueda. Tori was unresponsive to conversation. He kept replaying Colonel Modica's conversation and that of Don Barbarossa's over in his mind.

"It's not among one's enemies that treacheries spring. . . ."

Weigh carefully the proposals made to you. . . ."

"Bone up on Machiavelli. . . ."

On the trip back to Montegetta, these words of caution cut into his memory, too sharply for comfort. He wasn't so naive that he didn't know the Colonel had tried to tell him something about his Godfather. What?

In recollecting how insulting his Godfather had been and how he boldly and with confidence had overstepped his position with him, he grew fiercely indignant.

"Botta de sanguo! You'd think I was his son, the way he spoke to me!"

"What the hell you talking about, Tori? You're acting like a crazy man!"

"On the contrary, cousin. For the first time in my life, I'm probably sane. I'm beginning to see things in their proper perspective. And you can bet one thing's sure. "I'm going to bone up on Machiavelli! *Capeeshi?"*

"You're crazy! That's what. You're crazy! You know

what I think cousin? I think you need a woman! A real woman—and bad! What do you say we turn around and go back, eh? *Managghia*—I found me some woman tonight. Phew! What a woman! She makes all the others look like amateurs.

"*Te-rrific!*" said Tori laughing aloud. "*Te-rrific!* Stop the car!"

"You mean it?" said Vincenzo, his eyes sparking with excitement. He braked the car to the screeching sounds of burning rubber.

"Go back to Palermo, Vincenzo, but not to Neptune's Daughters. To the Library, cousin. To the Library."

An hour later, armed with as many books as he could find on the subject of Machiavelli, they returned to Montegatta. That night, Tori poured over *The Prince* by Niccolo Machiavelli, and a whole new world opened up for him. So, he thought, the end justifies the means, eh?

More than any other precept contained in the book was the amazing insight his own mother had into Machiavellian politics—almost as if her words had been uttered verbatim from the text. She was some woman, he told himself.

CHAPTER 32

Athena sat primly in Dr. Colassamo's waiting room, wringing her hands, unable to shake the feeling that surged through her. She hadn't meant to eavesdrop, but the door was ajar and the nurse had left the outer office. When their voices, Santino's and the physician's reached her and she heard the verdict, she felt a sensation of helplessness surge through her at first, then, relief to have confirmed what she'd guessed for a long while.

Inside the doctor's office Santino sat rigidly erect, his face considerably pale. "A brain tumor?" His voice above a whisper grew thin and distant. "A brain tumor. Is that what you suspect?"

"Yes. yes!" retorted the brusque young doctor, who'd been pushed into revealing more than he intended. He strode a few feet from his desk and stared down out the window into the crowded streets below. "There's no point in either alarming the family or minimizing the situation until we're certain."

"A brain tumor!" Santino repeated the alien words.

"*Allora, Santino, basta!* Don't work yourself up. You insisted on knowing my suspicions. If it proves true that she has a tumor," he said returning to sit behind his desk, "Allow me to stress a caveat. We won't be able to determine if it's benign or malignant without proper tests."

"Doctor, you don't understand. She's the sister of Salvatore."

"I don't care if she's the sister to God! I can do nothing in war time."

"He'll spare no expense to see she gets the best of care."

"*Managghia!* Money's not our problem. War's our problem. Our biggest obstacle is that we have no equipment for diagnostic study, no specialized medical men, and fewer medicines. The Allies bring in their own medical staff and paraphernalia for use on their own men. I've been promised new equipment. . . ."

In her attempt to tune out the doctor's words, Athena vaguely heard him instruct Santino to take along a prescription for pain and to be on the lookout for the various symptoms he'd described earlier. There was something said of an electroencephalograph to study her brain waves. But he didn't have to say more. Right then she knew her time on earth was measured.

Santino's voice cut into her thoughts. "What can we do *dottore?* We must save her."

"What's the sense in my talking? You haven't heard a word I said!" The doctor returned to his desk and began to scribble on a desk pad.

"This is a prescription for medication. She is to take it once every four hours—and only when necessary! Understand that! I caution you to be on guard for other symptoms—any changes contrary to her usual nature. Promiscuity, careless morals—foul language—you know."

"*Dottore!* This is a fine, decent woman of whom you speak!" he glared angrily. "A fine, respectable woman from a moral family! Not what you think!"

"*What I think?* What the hell does what I think have to do with brain tumors and their varied symptoms?" Dr. Colasamo wagged his thumb and fingertips, held together in typical gesture. "I'm telling you a person's behavior alters considerably with the slightest pressure on the brain! Inhibitions disintegrate gradually in some instances, and patients will do and say things they normally wouldn't do. Symptoms vary with the location of the tumor. . . ."

The doctor resumed his writing. "We need an electroencephalograph to study her brain waves. We haven't the equipment! Now, if this Salvatore can conjure up an EEG machine, we'll be that much closer in discovering what causes the *Signorina* such *maldolore!* He tore off the sheet from his pad. "And mind you I said, we'd only know what it is—not find a cure! A cure is something else!"

"Through the Americans—perhaps?"

"That's your best chance! Someone at AMGOT Headquarters or through the local ministers in the Defense office. . . ."

Santino Siragusa left the doctor's office with the weight of the world on his shoulders and Athena at his side, unaware that she'd heard the doctor's words. She attempted to elevate her spirits and coax his into a more gayer mood.

"We don't have to return so soon, do we, Santino? I'd like to walk for a spell along the Corso Vittorio Emmanuale. We're but a short distance from the Garibaldi Gardens. Let's go and see the fountains and flowers. Perhaps a walk along the waterfront will inspire us. I see so little of the ocean."

He nodded numbly, hardly seeing anything or anyone. As they approached the Quattro Canti, the picturesque crossroads of the Via Maqueda and the Corso Vittorio Emmanuale, the heart of Baroque Palermo, Athena glanced all around her, and remarked, "We're either the most religious people in the world or the most wicked. Do you realize how many churches there are in Palermo?"

Santino, absorbed in his painful thoughts, said nothing. But he took time to look at the cluster of antiquity around them. To the south of the main thoroughfare stood the Royal Norman Palace, with its seventeenth-century courtyard where a magnificent staircase led to the *Capella Palatina*, a jewel of Arab art of colorful mosaics on a golden background that glittered in the mysterious halflight above the royal apartments, all decorated in a Baroque and neoclassic decor. The red domes and luxuriant tropical vegetation of the enchanting cloister of the Church of *San Giovanni degli Eremiti*, also built by Roger II, evoked a delicate image of some distant corner of the Orient. Close by the twelfth-century cathedral, majestically arrayed in fortress-like dignity with lofty Gothic towers which some late restorer had bastardized by incorporating upon it, among other monstrosities, an 18th Century dome.

"It's all so breathtaking," whispered Athena. "Although I've seen it all before, it still takes my breath away."

Santino took her hand and led her through the *Piazza Pretoria*, past the Tuscan Renaissance Fountain where flocks of doves cooed and fluttered in a mad clatter, then, they continued on past the facade of the Town Hall and the *Palazzo del Municipio* until they arrived at the *Piazza Bellini* where the breathtaking Martorana Church stood with its Norman bell tower and a huge mosaic of Roger II. It was the most magnificent Arab-Norman structure in all of Palermo, and Athena's favorite spot.

"May we go in for a moment, Santino? I'd like to offer a prayer for my brother," she said.

He stared at her with a peculiar sadness, nodding. Better she should offer a prayer for herself, he thought. Inside, they both blessed themselves and genuflected before a glittering altar. While Athena said her prayers, Santino offered his and lit a candle for her life. Watching her quiet, solemn figure kneeling, Santino's throat constricted. The doctor's words echoed through his mind, and he felt himself go weak. He was almost harsh with her when he took her small thin hand in his and went back outside into the brilliant sunshine.

A *potpourri* of all that ever was and is, Palermo greeted them on all sides. No matter where they walked, inside or out, in these creations of previous civilizations were to be found specters of a glorious and in some cases, a bloody, tortured past. Once they were back on the Via Roma, Athena asked him a question he'd never explained to anyone. "Why did you abandon the priesthood?"

"I left, that's all there is to it," he growled at her.

"No secret love—no paramour?" she persisted.

"Is that why you asked?" He smiled in spite of himself. "Sorry to disappoint you."

"I'm not disappointed. I'm glad," she giggled.

Santino said nothing. They passed hordes of street urchins, American Soldiers, British Tommies, and shabbily-dressed old men who talked with animated gestures and stopped periodically to stare with inbred curiosity at the American soldiers. Even as they unbuttoned their flies and urinated into the gutters they would tip their caps with a free hand and with toothless grins shout out their greetings, *"Buon giorno,* Joe!"

Standing on the corner waiting for the jeeps to pass, Santino caught a glimpse of Athena; she was so beautiful it took his breath away. She turned and catching the strange look in his eye, she baited him.

"What's wrong? Surprised to find I'm a woman? You always treat me as a child," she said pouting. "Look at me. Am I not desirable to you?"

Santino walked on ahead of her, red-faced and somewhat embarrassed.

"*Aspetta!*" she called after him, tugging at his arm to detain him. She was out of breath. "See?" She turned her head in profile from side to side. "See—I am a woman!" Athena smiled provocatively as though she had no cares. She twirled about for him, and the soft folds of her simple cotton frock billowed, whirled, showing trim legs. Amused, curious onlookers paused to watch them. "Really! Look!" She allowed her hands to outline her trim figure and caress her waist and hipline in a voluptuous manner.

Filled with awkward embarrassment, Santino avoided the all-knowing, smiling eyes of the more permissive libertines, who winked playfully at him. He grabbed her unceremoniously by the arm and yanked her alongside him. Made ill at ease by the emotions that sprang in him, he grew more flustered.

". . . I'm really a woman!" she laughed at his self-consciousness.

"I never thought otherwise!" he blurted, angered by the attention given her.

"Then, why haven't you talked with me? Do you find me attractive?" She pouted with the petulance of a seductive barmaid. "How stupid of me. Perhaps you don't share my feelings?"

"*Managghia!* These Americans drive worse than the Italians!" he shouted and held on protectingly to her as a jeep sped recklessly by them. He made a facial grimace at the driver who shouted an obscenity at them.

"No! It's nothing like that. If you want the truth, I've been enamored of you for a long time. At *Terra Diavolo* I thought of you, constantly. . . . Thought about you? Hah! I couldn't take you off my mind!" His face turned shades of pink.

They both stopped in the middle of the sidewalk to stare at each other in that glorious excitement of new lovers.

He told her. "I wondered about you, and I thought, Athena's growing into womanhood. . . . You are the most beautiful woman I've ever seen. . . . Your dark eyes of fire burned into my soul, and I believed with conviction that you had bewitched me! Took possession of all my senses. Then, I'd remember, I'm ten years your senior, and I'd dismiss you from my mind." He took her arm and steered her on.

435

"Holy Blessed Mother incarnate! Imagine! Ten years older than I!" She mocked him and made a clucking sound with her tongue. Her dark teasing eyes lit up in merriment.

"In truth, Santino, sometimes I think you act ten years my junior!"

She slipped her arm through his and walked to the *Piazza Marina* with the Garibaldi Gardens at its center, where they both walked in silence for several moments. To the right of the *Piazza*, the *Palazzo Chiarmonte* was visible in all its 14th-century splendor. Opposite, from Palermo Harbor, the fresh ocean breeze refreshed their senses and they simply walked about in appreciation of the fertility of greenery they seldom saw in and about Montegatta. For Athena it was all paradise, a Utopian setting, and she basked in it.

"Hello baby," said a few American soldiers in passing. They appraised Athena's beauty with open-mouthed expressions.

Santino glared at them. *"Allo bebee!* What is this?" he retorted angrily. "Go on. *Vatini!* Get lost!"

"No offense, *paesano,*" they called and rushed on, about their previous business, filled with the exuberance of soldiers on leave.

"Bastards! They have no respect! What do they think you are?"

"A woman." she said simply. "Which is precisely what I am. Only you seem blind to the fact," she replied. "They are just lonely soldiers looking for a friendly face. There are so many of them," she said glancing about the busy *strada* filled with milling crowds of the military who occupied their lands.

"It's difficult to believe the war is still on and has turned into such a terrible one. We're lucky, I suppose, we didn't experience the genocide that's occurring in Germany—so many Jews meeting their death in those reported atrocities. Do you think it's true—what they say? Or is it propaganda?"

"At this point no one knows what's true or untrue. At war's end, when all the powers begin to divide the spoils; when they are forced to take an accurate inventory, the world will separate fact from fiction. . . ."

"You mean like the stories about my brother?"

He was noncommittal as he led her to a nearby bench, several feet away from the statue of Garibaldi. She was so beautiful, thought Santino. His spirits soared, and for a moment it seemed nothing could dampen this day. Again the doctor's words echoed through his mind, though, and he felt a quiver through his heart.

"What do you think of all the publicity Tori receives from the world," she repeated interrupting his mood.

"In what way?"

"Every way."

"What's more important, Athena, is *his* reaction to this concentration of spotlights focused on him. . . ."

"I'm gravely concerned," she said quietly.

"Why?"

"It frightens me, how he basks in it. This kind of attention can intoxicate a man worse than alcohol. It can fill him with a false ego and deceive his judgment. History has been written with the blood of such great men who surround themselves with *yes* men, who scatter and run the other way at the first sign of trouble. Invariably the hero falls to shame and disgrace, having been betrayed by those same men for whom he fought. None of his virtues is ever remembered. . . ." She glanced at him in a premonitory manner.

"Promise me, Santino you'll always remain at Tori's side! Be that solid foundation he can come to depend upon, to help him uphold his true philosophies and remain true to his ideals. . . ."

He saw the frantic concern in her eyes; felt the tightening grip of her strong slender fingers upon his arm, as she implored him. He wanted to tell her—no one told Salvatore what to do. Salvatore was his own man, and she shouldn't fear for him. But he couldn't. Instead, he nodded resignedly, gently took her hand from his arm and clung to it with both his strong hands.

Birds twittered overhead in the poplar trees in the well-manicured garden and the traffic from the street seemed muted and distant.

"For so young a woman you have remarkable depth." He felt a surge of pride as he spoke the words.

"Am I not my mother's daughter? Santino," she said suddenly, "Marry me!"

His face turned berry-red, and he was momentarily at a loss for words.

"Don't think about it. Let's go and get married. Perhaps at St. John's we'll find a priest who'll marry us today!"

"Today? Now? This very instant?" He composed himself and smiled at her impulsiveness. "You'd break your mamma's heart. It's a day every mother looks forward to, Athena . . . you should realize that."

"Then, let's rush home to tell her. . . ."

"Aspetta, bedda, lets talk about this. Listen, to me . . . I've nothing to offer. I'm not even the right man for you. You deserve a man of substance, a wealthy man who can give you things, make your life easier, shower you with perfumes and luxuries a great beauty like you should have. . . ."

She laughed a zany kind of humorous laughter. "Oh my dear Santino! You aren't impulsive at all—are you?" She plucked a nearby rose and smelled it.

"Athena!" Suddenly he recalled Dr. Colassamo's warning. "This isn't like you at all! In the past two years we've hardly exchanged a dozen words between us. Now, you're chattering like a silly cuckoo-bird! You're a different person entirely!"

"I *am* different, you silly ass! I'm in love with you. For so long, I've ached for you and I've never found the opportunity to tell you. You've been so occupied with Tori and the others. If I wait any longer for you to come forward and declare yourself—I'll be dead!" She twirled the rose in her fingers.

"Athena!" he reprimanded. His heart felt strangled. "Don't talk such foolishness!"

"Foolishness?" It was her turn to stare at him. "What—that I love you? Or that I'll be dead?"

In a sudden movement, he reached for her and pulled her close to him. He held her so tightly she could hardly catch her breath. They could hear the other's heart pounding furiously, unmindful of the smiling, gaping, and several shocked passersby. Flocks of pigeons hovered close by, ruffling their plumage and cooing incessantly. The multi-shaded pink to ruby roses, genuflecting in the morning sun, shed tears of early morning dew from their velvety rolled petals, and the world continued to move for the lovers.

They parted slightly and gazed into each other's love-filled eyes. Taking courage, Santino kissed her gently, until the response in his manhood stirred and became erect with desire. He sprang back away from her body, so she wouldn't guess how deep his desire for her could be. His face grew tell-tale, and when he found courage once more to look at her, she smiled in an all-knowing, feline exaltation, to mock him.

"Athena!" He reprimanded in embarrassment.

"Si," she purred softly.

"You're shameless."

"I know. I know."

"It's time to take you home."

438

"No. Not now. I'm having such a good time. Besides, you didn't answer me. Will you or will you not marry me?" She paused. "There might not be enough time for us," she whispered.

"What's that supposed to mean?" He felt a sting of anguish.

"I heard the doctor. The door was open." She turned away. "Is that why you won't marry me?"

Santino felt limp. His heart nose-dived. He turned to her, cupped her lovely face into his hands, and turned it towards him. His soft voice cradled her. "The doctor said nothing to influence me against a decision of marriage."

"Then you will?" she grinned happily. "You will? Santino—you will?" She took his hands in hers, pulled him to his feet, and turning in a circle, they danced a jig. He fell into her mood of wild and gay abandon with a youthful exuberance that spurred him into cartwheels of ecstasy. Her lustrous and clean dark hair swung freely about her shoulders as prisms of sunbeams danced on her anthracite tresses like iridescent star points. In those moments she became the embodiment of her favorite Grecian goddess, Psyche. Graceful and lithe, with dark exotic eyes filled with the spirit of eternity, she gazed at Santino, bursting with happiness, because, like Psyche, she had found her Cupid.

It was love! Every breathless, numbing, heartfelt moment catapulted them into that world of perfection reserved only for lovers.

And now to break the news to Signora Salvatore and to Tori, himself. . . .

While the lovers were discovering each other, Tori arrived home, at the house of his mother, where he had planned to meet Vincenzo to prepare offensive tactics against Marshal Franchina's planned coup that evening.

Antigone placed a hot cup of coffee before him on the table as she watched him devour a thick slab of *ricotta*, freshly made by the cheesemaker down the street. She stroked his forehead and pushed back a loose curl from his face.

"What are you doing home this time of day? I see something unusual reflected in those brown eyes of yours," she said quietly.

"I've never been able to fool you, have I?" He wiped his lips with a napkin, opened a fresh pack of cigarettes, lit one, and puffed thoughtfully for a time. He leaned forward in his chair, crossed a leg over the other and watched the smoke from his cigarette curl upwards. "I'm waiting for Vincenzo. We have business in Monreale." He sipped his coffee. "Before he arrives, I wish to ask you several things." He set the cigarette in the ash tray his mother provided. "Why is there no baptismal picture of my Godfather and me? You have one of Filippo, Marcos, even Athena—where's mine?"

"Why do you ask now, after so many years?" Her face became colorless. "Why are you curious?"

"Nothing. It's nothing," he said. He didn't want to hurt her in any way. Then, as if he couldn't resist, he asked. "When did my Godfather baptize me? What date?"

She glanced sharply at him, and sipped her coffee.

"Well, I might as well tell you, Mamma. I met my Godfather—the other day. . . ." He searched her face for some tell-tale sign—something.

Dying inwardly, she reached for the bottle of anisette. She steadied her hand, poured a little into her coffee cup, and recorked the bottle.

"What did he have to say, after all these years?"

"He sends you his respect and best wishes for your continued health. . . ."

"He—uh—remembered us?"

"Why wouldn't he?"

"I mean—uh—after all these years. Some twenty-four years. You'll be twenty-four pretty soon . . ." She stirred her coffee. Her throat constricted.

His features remained impassive. "Not for six months. . . ."

"Of course. I'm not thinking." She picked up her mending basket and began nervously to sort some of his socks.

"When was I baptized, Mamma?" he asked gently.

"*Managghia!* Alessandro! Is it necessary that you know right this moment?" she snapped irritably. Her face filled with color. "I'm sorry. Forgive me. I'm nervous and worried about Athena. She's in Palermo with Santino at the doctors!" Anything to change the subject, she thought.

"Alone, with Santino?" he scowled. "That's a fine thing! My sister, unmarried, in the company of a single man!" He was outraged. "How could you have allowed her to go? *Mizzica!*" he wailed at her obvious lack of discretion. *"Me fa scomparire!* You bring embarrassment to me!"

"Stop being a fool. *Che se testardo!* She's in good hands and you know it! I never knew you to be so old-fashioned! Now, let's get back to you!" she looked unwaveringly at him. "You were nearly a year old. It was sometime in

1923. I'll have to find your baptismal certificate for the exact date. Do you have to know right this minute?"

He shrugged nonchalantly. "Did my Godfather play an important role in my early life? I don't really remember him—not at all."

"Why?"

"It's uncanny how much alike we are. I didn't notice it when I visited him at his villa in Godrano—"

"His villa?" She grew unduly excited and set aside the mending basket.

"Vincenzo and I went to Godrano on business. Then two days ago I met him at the *Albergo-Sole* in Palermo. That's when I noticed the similiarity. . . ."

She jumped to her feet. "What business do you have with the *capomafia?*" Her whole body trembled with a rage, a violence he'd never seen before.

"Mamma!"

Her face contorted angrily. "What business? Tell me!"

"Mamma!" he grew alarmed. "Stop! Why are you working yourself into such a frenzy?" He grabbed her shoulders and shook her gently, at first, then more vigorously. Finally he broke her mood. Her dark eyes, fixed, stared as one in shock. She inhaled long breaths until she calmed down.

"What business do you have with a *mafioso?*" she asked.

"None," he lied and averted his head.

"Do you know what it means to get involved with these 'men of respect'?"

"But . . . I am involved with the greatest of all, aren't I? My Godfather?"

"But . . ." The protest died on her lips. How could she tell him? "Because he is your Godfather doesn't mean you must emulate his ideals or share in his politics. You have a well developed mind of your own, a brilliant one with great potential, my son. I beg you do not permit anyone or anything to persuade you to change your ways."

"What makes you think I'd do that?"

"Oh—I don't know. I don't know," she retorted. "What business do you have with the *Mafia?*" she asked again, sharp and unrelenting.

His reluctance to reply accelerated her fears. This approach to her son was all wrong. She brushed aside a few wisps of gray hair from her face. "Tori, perhaps it's time we have a serious talk," she began. "I see I've neglected a portion of your education. It never occured to me they'd be reborn again. Let me explain about these men. Then, like everything else you've accepted from me, I know you'll weigh my words and come to your own decision in whatever you are involved in." She held back a rush of tears.

"The *Mafia* is unlike anything you've ever studied in the countless books you've read. The *mafiosi* are a breed unto themselves. Once you take or give anything in their name, you belong to them for life. If you accept an ounce of flour they will exact from you, a ton. Give them a thimble of your blood and soon they'll demand your entire circulatory system, veins and arteries included. One never wins with them."

"Now, you tell me! Why pick a *mafioso* in the first place to be my Godfather?" he asked testily.

Their conversation was interrupted by Vincenzo's arrival. He came charging in the rear door of their house, bringing with him the Salvatore mail he'd picked up in the village post office. If he noticed any tension between them he gave no indication. After kissing his aunt affectionately, he sat down at the table next to Tori and accepted the coffee his aunt placed before him. He sniffed the air gingerly. "Do I smell fresh bread?" he asked.

While Vincenzo and his mother extolled the virtues of fresh bread and *ricotta,* Tori brooded over his recent involvement with his Godfather, aware that the situation took on a more ominous significance than he'd bargained for. He fell into a pit of uncertainty. Oh, he'd been avenged all right, but, at what price? How naive he'd been to think the Don had performed such a special service for him because of the Godfather—Godson relationship. *Porca Miseria!* What an *embroglio!*

Tori's men were waiting for him at the Grotto Bianca. He faced them with a wry smile and a terse voice. "Tonight you'll all do what you usually do on a Friday night. Should anything unusual occur, you are to drop everything and ride swiftly to the Grotto Persephone—not here. Take all usual precautions that you aren't followed."

He broke the men into squads, giving these men detailed instructions for stripping the Grotto Bianco of all traces of their occupancy. "Transfer all supplies and the arsenal to Persefone." He directed his next words to Gambo Cusimano his armorer. "I dislike giving you this extra work, *amico,* but, until we know what this *zanzaro*—mosquito—is up to we shall have to endure these small inconveniences."

To the Nuliano and Gagliolo brothers, whom he instructed to guard all entrances to the Grotto Persephone,

442

he said, "Shoot to kill anyone who comes within shooting distance, if they fail to give you the coded password."

The men moved swiftly and silently to carry out his orders, filled with brooding and conjecture. This had been a first! The first time since they organized that any *carabiniero* had signed warrants for any of them. Franchina's recent activities had left most of them numb and shaken. Their criminal records had long since been destroyed. Who then, who had submitted the names of the four paladins of the Inner Circle, and the names of the men stated on the warrants? Their names, well guarded, had been known only amongst themselves. It followed then, that someone among them was a spy! It was cause enough for each of the men to view their associates with grave suspicion.

"Allay your fears," Tori told them. "I'll find out how Marshal Franchina suddenly got so lucky! And when I do—" He paused, looked at each of them gathered about him in the light of the bright sun, and removed his Browning from its holster. He pulled out the clip and held it up for all to see. "This gun clip is reserved for our betrayer! I promise! I, personally, will empty all fourteen shots into his guts!" he shouted dramatically.

Not one man among them disbelieved the sincerity of their leader, for Salvatore always kept his word.

Maresciallo Franchina, preparing to annihilate Salvatore and his men in those lonely hours just past midnight, preferred capturing them alive. With this consideration in mind, he had secretly procured the cooperation of the Monreale, Borgetto, and Partenico offices of the *carabinieri*, swelling his own squad of twelve men to nearly fifty well-armed horsemen.

His plan was straightforward and neat. The men were to meet under the Norman Tower in the *piazza*. There he'd break them down into small squads and progress to the proper locations, disarm the rebels, arrest them and jail them.

Maresciallo Franchina was no fool. He gave his men no information in advance. He knew that, for the sum of money he paid spies to report activity of the bandits, another man could pay that much and more for knowledge of the Marshal's plan. It wasn't without reason he kept the proposed coup, quiet.

At a quarter to midnight, nearly fifty strong, the mounted *carabinieri* converged quietly in the *piazza*, where in view of the Norman tower, Marshal Franchina instructed his men in their duties. Hardly finished detailing their orders, Marshal Franchia paused in mid-sentence, cocked his head to listen. Before he reacted to the sounds of motorized vehicles approaching the village square, his men reacted with puzzled expressions on their faces. Their horses, skittish, danced about nervously. Headlights shone first. Suddenly, they were surrounded by a horde of security police; some in jeeps, others in police vans, and a few mounted on horseback had arrived from Palermo and converged upon the village, locking the *carabinieri* into the square. Against the background of shocked faces and a pandemonium of honking car horns, spooking horses, and disgruntled, protesting military police, the bandits, expecting some unusual activity, jumped out of their warm beds and escaped to a predestined rendezvous.

The bedlam in the village square grew uncontrollable. In the melee, a special courier dispatched from the Palermo Central Office of the Italian Military Police searched frantically in the mob for Marshal Franchina. Caught at the very center of the tumultuous hordes, the Marshal, locked in tight, was unable to move his horse. Apparent on his face was the frustration he felt over this unexpected development.

"Maresciallo! Maresciallo!" called the courier loudly hoping to be heard above the din. He wheeled his horse into the turbulence, waving his orders in the air over his head. "I must see you, *Maresciallo!* It's urgent!"

"Yes! Yes! I'm over here, shouted the Marshal catching sight of the courier. "What is it?" Caught like a fly in a tangled web of irate horsemen, he strained to maneuver his horse about. A ghost couldn't have squeezed its way through the hundreds of men that spilled into the confined *piazza*, preventing any escape.

"Important message from headquarters!" called the anxious courier a few horses away.

The Marshal managed to sidle his mare in closer to the messenger and, stretching over the horse of another *carabiniero* he snatched the communique from the other's outstretched hands. Saluting halfheartedly, the courier was more concerned in finding avenues to unweave his way back through the congestion.

Even before Marshal Franchina glanced at the communique, he knew. By damn, something was amiss. At that moment with the message unopened in his hands, he sat in his saddle, a sinking sensation at the pit of his stomach and he knew. Somehow, someway, his plan of capture had been betrayed. A mule's brain could have discerned the treachery. He glanced at the artfully planned congestion, his eyes narrowing to slits. Burning with anger deep inside him, his face remained expressionless. Finding a small opening in the tightly packed horde of men and animals, he backed up, wheeled his steed around and headed towards a flickering lamppost at the edge of the square.

As the dim amber glow of the lamplight barely lit up the message and the contents were made apparent to him, his face contorted into a mask of fiery emotions. His black eyes burned like live coals, his jaws jerked in spasms, and murder flooded his heart. If anyone had seen this Barracuda gritting his teeth, they would have recognized his fierce and relentless dedication to a cause to which he'd become addicted.

Contained in the message was the order for his immediate transfer out of the territory of Salvatore, to a new post in Messina, across the island. The order, dated two days prior, invalidated his present commission and subjected his activities to strict regulations which would, if he persisted, be construed as performance conducted against orders, he would then be subject to fine, imprisonment, demotion, or all three.

Marshal Franchina stuffed the message into his tunic and stared dispassionately at the thickly congested mob, who looked like ants converged upon a plate of honey. He quickly dismounted, tied his horse to a hitching post, and propelled himself through the skittish horses and motorized vehicles crammed in tightly around him, and, amid the raucous shouting of men, the impatient beeping of car horns, and the intermittent protestations of high-strung horses, he snaked his way towards his office.

Inside the sanctuary of the small working quarters, the Marshall, trembling with livid rage, removed a whiskey bottle from a desk drawer and, pulling out the cork with his teeth, he spat it across the room. He lifted the bottle to his lips and gulped the fiery liquid greedily until his senses were shocked and he felt its burning inner glow searing his intestines.

In that moment, Marshal Franchina swore another oath to capture the bandit Salvatore, regardless of the power he wielded and despite the protection he received in the hierarchy of the provisional government. It didn't take a scholar to realize such cooperation, given to Salvatore by the security police, came from a highly placed politician. Who it was—that was another matter. One day he'd learn.

He moved close to the open-grilled window and surveyed the fiasco of the tangled knot of men. He shouted irrationally. "Fuck you! You all took orders to get into this mess! Now, go find the same runted prick of a sow's whore to get you out of it!" He paused to guzzle more whiskey.

His eyes fell upon the thick scrapbook compiled on the activities of Salvatore. "Fuck you too, you King of the peasants' scrapile!" he shouted. "Just remember one thing. Franchina never loses! One day, somehow, someway, someplace, I'll get you, Salvatore! You hear? Franchina will tie your ass to the sun!" He swilled more whiskey and launched into a fist-waving lecture on courage, loyalty to the nation, and determination. He was still ranting when a bullet exploded through the window and tore into his shoulder.

No one knew exactly what had happened or how, or even why. But when the other *carabinieri* saw Marshal Franchina come raging out of the office, shouting the battle cry to commence firing, they drew back, stared around them, and wondered how in the hell they could raise their arms against the security police, formidable and imposing as they were.

"*Avanti! Avanti!* Fire, you miserable stinking cowards!" screamed the Marshal. He ordered his men to shoot anything that moved. They didn't.

But by then, the security police had begun to back away and out of the *piazza*, and in moments the area cleared.

" '*Tenente* Paterno!" shouted Franchina. "Get your miserable sons of whoring turtles to give those devilish dogs a round of bullets, or I'll have the lot of you court-marshalled for disobeying orders!"

By then, the *carabinieri* stood silent, down to the last man watching the antics of this bullet-crazed officer, with the gleam of a madman shining in his eyes. He had collapsed in a rage, and was carried off by four of his men, still raving maniacally. "Sound the call to arms, Bugler! Fire, men! Fire faster! Faster! I'll have the whole lot of you court-martialled!"

"Poor creature," they whispered among themselves. "The man's gone crazy! Absolutely, crazy! Some bullet must have deranged his brains!"

'*Tenente* Paterno dismissed the men and told them to return to their posts and not to worry about Marshal Franchina's threat. "The Sicilian sun has fried his brains, you can be sure. Marshal Franchina is in no condition to resume this command. My report will indicate, you all followed orders *perfettamente.*"

He winked at his men and disappeared inside to observe Marshal Franchina's behavior. What a report he'd make!

CHAPTER 33

"Welcome! Welcome *Colonnello!*" shouted Salvatore. "Today's a special day for all of us," he commented, grinning broadly. "Besides the honor of your presence, we celebrate the forthcoming nuptials of my sister Athena." He greeted his guests warmly and introduced them to his family, his paladins, and the rest of his entourage, who, eager to talk with the Americans, pulled Lt. Destro aside and, plying him with wine, directed a thousand questions at him.

Colonel Modica apologetically asked Tori if there was someplace they could go to talk where they could be alone and undisturbed. "Unfortunately I won't be able to enjoy your hospitality and stay to dinner as planned. Something urgent has arisen."

At the strained urgency in the American's eyes, Tori's smile evaporated. He excused himself to his family, picked up his camera, and climbed into the American jeep with Modica and his aide. Moments later, followed by his trusted paladins on horseback, the pair arrived at the Temple of Cats.

Colonel Modica was concerned about many things that Saturday morning. What with the unsettled conditions in this suffocating nation, bogged down by the strangling yoke of antiquity, Sicily was struggling and straining to become a part of the twentieth century, and the disturbing realization that he hadn't begun to do enough for Sicily distressed him. However, more disturbing had been the coded message he'd received only that morning containing the morale-shattering information:

"President Franklin Delano Roosevelt died on April 12, 1945. Harry S. Truman succeeds to the Presidency. Hitler barricaded in the Reichs chancellery. All Chiefs of Staff are to embark immediately for Rome."

Palermo had gone crazy. All but a skeletal staff had already moved out, and the airport was jammed beyond its capacity. Colonel Modica had stuffed the communique into his uniform pocket and in moments he was in a staff car enroute to Montegatta, with his aide.

"Sir, what'll happen now?" Lieutenant Destro had asked his chief anxiously.

"The world will mourn FDR. A new man will sit at the helm, and the world will continue this stinking war until more men die. What else?"

"What about the orders, sir? They were explicit." Lieutenant Destro pressed.

"As soon as I attend to this business we'll conform to orders, Destro. Simmer down. I can't leave without seeing Salvatore."

"But, sir, the orders stated, fly immediately to Rome."

"Destro."

"Yes, sir?"

"Shut up!"

"Yes, sir."

"Lieutenant—" Modica had paused effectively for a moment. "Look," he said, "It's enough to have to explain the bloody Sicilian mess without you on my back. We'll get there soon enough to go waltzing around with the Jerries. We've got to beat the Russians to Berlin—and we will. Hear? Or they'll try to take over the fucking world! Goddammit Destro," he said fully incensed. "We're gonna fuck up again, and there ain't a bloody damned thing we can do about it," he said glumly.

"Yes, sir. I mean, no sir. I mean—I don't know what the hell I mean, sir. It's all so damned frustrating."

"Yeah, Destro, I know. I know." Colonel Modica had ended the conversation, and through the rest of the long arduous ride into Montegatta he had remained silent.

Now, standing at the center of the most breathtaking, awe-inspiring and spectacular panorama he'd ever seen, Colonel Modica gazed about the Temple of Cats, moving about the broken floor of the hand hewn temple utterly stunned by the natural beauty of the place.

"Terrifico, eh *Colonnello?"* said Tori with unmistakable pride.

The American nodded as he continued to view the spectacle of nature. "Yes, *amico,* terrific. I've never seen this face of Sicily," he admitted candidly as he turned and wheeled in a full circle. Struck by the broken columns jutting high above him, some stunted, others in near-perfect condition, most lying in a tumble of decaying majesty, he felt a shiver coursing through him. "God! It takes you back centuries in time. I suppose with a little effort I could see the legs of gods and goddesses hanging from the clouds."

As Salvatore moved about the temple floor, taking pic-

448

tures of the American officer with his camera, he enthralled Colonel Modica with stories of the legend of the temple. By the time Tori finished, the American officer close to the parapet of the temple, cocked his head to listen. His startling blue eyes impulsed in every direction darted here and there about him. "What's that?" he asked Tori. "That sound—what is it?"

Pivoting first, on one foot, then the other, he glanced in the direction of the Tyrrhenian Sea and strained to listen. Stefano heard a distinct sound of ancient trumpets echoing remotely in his mind; a strange, muted, cacophony of triumphant battle cries of another era. Puzzled, he looked in the direction of the plains below.

Watching him, Tori smiled good naturedly. *"Colonnello,* my friend, you're home at last!" Tori told him about the friendly demons of *Siculi.* Although he listened, Colonel Modica didn't seem to hear anything of earthly matters.

The American felt a strong gravitational force which compelled him to walk dangerously close to the broken parapet of the temple. Tori made no move to warn him or pull him back. And when his aide broke away from the others in an attempt to warn him, he was silenced by Tori, who indicated he was safe from harm. The Colonel, enchanted by what was happening to him stared out at the vast vista at a scene to which only he seemed privy. He watched ancient warriors materialize before his eyes; he listened intently, with a pang of dismay, as the sound of trumpets faded dimly in his mind. When it was over, Colonel Modica said softly, "This could very well be the very place where the Cartheginians did battle with the Greeks for control of the Island."

"Bravo! You know your history. The rest is vivid imagination."

"Don't tell me it's my imagination. I can still hear the trumpets!"

"It's the only logical explanation I can give you, unless you believe in reincarnation."

"Do you?" The American still stared at the fading scene in an effort to recapture it. It was incredible what he's seen and heard. Damnit! He wasn't imagining things—was he?

Tori angled his head sharply and studied the Colonel with a reserve of cynicism. "Your American journalists compare me with conquerors of the past. They say I'm the reincarnation of this man or that man; Alexander, even Napoleon. And I have yet to do real battle! The principle might explain our friendship. Perhaps we knew each other in another time in history? Is it possible our spirits transcended earthly appearances in recognition?"

Tori smiled as he watched the rise of awe in the American as he gazed about at their surroundings. "You Americans are not only *te-rrific* with your praises, but you are also enthralled with antiquity—no?"

"There's nothing like this in America. No glorious reminders of memorable and past civilizations staring at us each day. No remnants of previous cultures—except for the Indians to whom I don't relate much. But, my friend, it isn't for this that I've made a special trip to see you today." Modica sighed heavily, then, on a more somber note, he explained. "Salvatore, President Roosevelt is dead. Truman has just stepped into office."

Tori gave a start. "That's why you are leaving so soon?"

"I shouldn't be here now. I received orders to shove off today."

"What happens now?" Tori sobered at the implications.

"Who can tell? Rome's in a helluvan uproar. It's rumored that Hitler has locked himself in the Reich Chancellory. The Russians advance towards Berlin at an alarming rate of speed. I've a hunch the war will soon be over."

"Then, you'll not be able to stay for dinner?"

It took several moments for Stefano Modica to realize this day meant more to Salvatore than the status of war or the death of a foreign president. But, then—why not? This was Salvatore's life, and his world was Sicily. Twenty-three years old, and he hadn't begun to realize his true potential. Colonel Modica glanced over at his aide, who gave him the business with his eyes and pointed to his watch.

"I know. I know," he muttered to Lieutenant Destro. To Tori he apologized. "He's like a watchdog—an indispensible watchdog, however."

"About dinner—" interrupted Tori.

Colonel Modica shook his head. "There's no time. I couldn't leave without speaking to you again." They both lit up cigarettes and for a time stood in silence.

"This is a difficult posture for me," began the American. "I've never interfered in the destiny of another man. What's more I've argued with myself, telling myself that what you do is none of my business. What compels me to offer my two cents' worth of opinion is even more of a mystery to me, *amico*." He shook his head, suddenly confounded by his actions. "But, I'd feel worse leaving Sicily without taking time to tell you of the greatness I see in you. No, no, don't interrupt me," he wagged his hand at

Tori. "It took two days of courage to arrive at this decision. There's a role in all this that only you can play. Why or how you've been chosen by this mysterious force who propells our destiny is not clear. I'm certain only of what I've observed. You possess certain charismatic qualities, which, despite your protestations, have already marked you for a certain greatness, a destiny you can't escape." Modica paused. "Somewhere I read something by Shakespeare—*"There is a tide in the affairs of man, which taken at the flood leads on to fortune. Omitted, all the voyages of their life are bound in shallows and miseries. . . ."*

Tori shook his head and interrupted almost apologetically. "I fear you give me more importance than I deserve. In Palermo, I suggested that if you bet on me— you'd be making a mistake," he avoided the colonel's eyes and subtly changed the subject. "When you leave—who replaces you?"

"I had hoped it might be you," said Modica straight out.

Salvatore exploded. *"Managghia u diaoro!* Damn the devil! Again with that talk! You are some crazy man, *Colonnello!"* He studied the American officer, and cooled down, flushed with self-consciousness. "I can see by your face, you mean the words you speak. But still, I. . . ."

"I've never been more serious in my life."

Didn't you implant in the minds of your men, your basic philosophy of justice for all—an end to the gross inequities dealt your people? Isn't this the premise, the spark, which ignited the flaming heartbeats of your nation and brought you into world prominence?"

As Tori listened to Colonel Modica, it appeared that he tried to convince himself he was capable of being the creature the American painted so vividly with words. He felt the push-pull, the hesitancy, the insecurities rush at him. "But—we are a few dozen men. . . ."

"With many cooperative followers, Salvatore. This is no time for modesty."

"All right. All right, then, with many cooperative followers, but. . . ."

"Go a step further. Spread the same ideology to the people of your village and to those in surrounding villages. Do it in the same manner the corupt clergy teaches them to believe that poverty's a blessing," urged Stefano.

Tori observed him through tilted, indulgent eyes. "A revolution again?"

"Off the record, damnit it, yes! If it takes a blasted revolution to awaken your people. Well, if it—" He couldn't bring himself to say what he really felt, for reasons his military status didn't permit. It was frustrating. "Damn-it, Salvatore, no one has to tell you what must be done!"

Demonstrating great restraint, Salvatore flushed self-consciously, still unable to picture himself in the role the American had cast him.

"Again I say, I am simply an outlaw with a price on my head. I am no politician. My powers are limited only to my province. One day when my government returns to normal, I shall be a lawmaker—"

"No! *Now* is your time. Your life is at full tide—*now!* Recognize it and go on. What if your government doesn't return to normal? Sicily and your people will be lost. Stronger nations will gobble her up—and think what a waste! America will stand behind you if you oppose the Reds!" Modica tensed, he had to convince the Sicilian.

"America will stand behind Salvatore?" Such an incredible thought shook the Sicilian and sent tremors coursing through his body. Awed by both Modica and his words, Tori walked alongside of Stefano in silence as they paced the open aired temple. Inwardly he felt a rising excitement.

"Russia, eh? You think Russia will take over?"

"Who else? Red banners fly triumphantly in Rome right now," Modica retorted bitingly.

"Why? Who gives Russia this strength?" he cried softly. "Why does America give her this latitude—this liberty?"

Stefano understood his dilemma. He tried to explain.

"Until the Japs blew up that paradise in the Pacific, Hawaii, we were only allies to Great Britain, with little say about anything. Invading Italy meant we had to cut down on provisions to Russia. Soviet-Western relations suffered consequently. Our failure to open what Russia considered a necessary second front until late in the war caused a serious rift between us to widen."

Tori, considering the growing threat of communism, observed, "America will experience great difficulty when this ambitious nation decides to carve the spoils."

"No question," agreed Colonel Modica as he harked Tori back over Russia's enormous victories and brilliant military coups in the previous year. "Our actions in Sicily and Italy set a precedent in that a nation which liberates another determines that nation's political and economic future. Now, Russia watching with ferret eyes what other nations will do, is determined to capitalize on that precedent. You see, Tori, where America prefers a nation to rule itself—Russia doesn't. Hasn't she already dispatched her communists to infiltrate Italy! Hasn't she already seduced the people with unrealistic promises? After the *fiasco* of fascism, the Italians will try anything. In stages of negotiation it's easy to promise the moon. Delivery is another thing. I fear for Sicily! She is too vulnerable."

Tori realized how shrewd was his mother's thinking after all. The *Colonnello* had echoed her words, practically verbatim.

"That's why I persist in trying to make you come face to face with your potential. You must assert *your* wisdom and strength, now, at this crucial time in your nation's history. She needs you! No matter how inadequate your strength appears, it is more than enough. What you consider to be inadequacy in your mind is simply the lack of experience. Experience without theory at times can be more practical than theory without experience. Given time, they both work. Can you see this, Salvatore?"

"*Colonnello,* I could never take your place with the Grand Council! They'd laugh at me. They'd say, 'look at this *contadino,* this mere son of a lowly sheepherder trying to be a politician!' You forget, I am a peasant!"

Colonel Modica saw his dilemna. "I didn't mean that at all. God forbid you should take my place. I was forced to sit like a frozen statue while the combined forces around me plotted for Sicily's death, not life. But, so that you don't mistake my words, let me set the record straight. It'll take the courage and suffering of the peasant to lift Sicily out of her bondage—that, and the aid of a powerful nation—America."

Tori studied this man who stood in profile next to him. His visored cap was pulled down over fierce blue eyes. He had a generous face, in which was read many things. There was a candor and ferocity in it, and a respectful reverence that literate men often express for their superiors. Yet, it was a face that would commit murder and throw his life away for a friend. Strange, the affection Tori felt for this man whom he'd known for so short a period of time. Different than the closeness and affection and love he felt for Vincenzo, yet almost the same. He felt as if he'd known him forever. Tori spoke in perfect Italian.

"Please understand me, *Colonnello—*"

"Call me Steve, or Stefano."

"And you may call me, Tori. *Va bene? Allora*—Stefano, deception and shaded subtleties, calculated to influence my thinking are an insult to me. The convoluted logic of these three-a-penny politicians bore me. You think I would have patience to listen to their empty words? I would not be so patient, and I would not appreciate any-one to vote against my word if I believe I am right. For two years—I've brought no failure to my men. We've had few casualties. All this because I stand by my word. I am aware of my limitations, and know I am politically naive. Those crafty, two-tongued vipers, those sophisticated politicians, would crush me and scatter my forces to the four winds before I knew what struck me." He laughed easily. "I regret, Stefano, I am not this great man of power you see photographed in your mind. Not even with America's support."

They had walked the length of the temple several times and paused now next to the staggered scattering of pancake-shaped boulders stacked on each other, precariously. Modica glanced anxiously at his watch. Time was his enemy on this day. He despaired. "How can I reach you? How do I make you understand that this point in time belongs to you. The brass ring rests within your grasp. How do I convince you of your destiny, which I envision so clearly in my mind, and which remains a distant dream in yours? A man who's become front page news the world over? A man who controls half his nation? You, leader to an army of well over five hundred men, stand here trying to convince me you aren't qualified to lead your people, with or without the power of America?"

Tori's eyes lit up like blazing tourmalines glittering in the sun. "I can see, *amico,* you'll not let me off the nail."

"Hook, *amico.* Hook." Stefano slipped out of his uniform jacket.

"Si, hook. You will not repose until I am committed."

"If you don't, I can't leave Sicily in good conscience." The officer pushed back his cap, fanned himself and mopped his brow with a handkerchief. "How the hell do you tolerate this bloody sun? Damnit! You don't even wear sunglasses."

Tori laughed. "A Sicilian without sun would wither and die."

Stefano had removed from his jacket pocket a small box, which he thrust at Salvatore. "Before I forget," he began. "Something I bought especially for you. Accept it in the spirit of friendship and wear it in good health with my wishes for your good fortune and a long life, whatever you decide to do with it. Perhaps, Tori, one day after this war of the devil ends I'll return to Sicily and we'll both have a laugh over my emotional zeal. Your birthday is November? The papers mentioned it."

Tori, flustered and uncertain of himself, was about to

454

refuse the gift. He stared at the open box, containing a solid gold scorpion amulet suspended from a thick gold chain. He turned the amulet over and read the inscription: "To Salvatore; May the King of Montegatta rule Sicily wisely. 4-12-45 Colonel Stephen Modica."

"Truly I do not deserve such adornment. You give me too much importance, I tell you." Tori squirmed awkwardly and flushed uneasily.

Stefano craned his neck to bask in the slight breeze that whispered across the mountains from the sea, in relief from the inexorable sun. He opened his shirt, loosened his tie, and said simply. "I can only tell you what I see in you, Sicilian, what I know to be fact, regardless of your modesty. But, unless you recognize these things in yourself, all my talking won't move your mountain. When I get to where I'm going, I will write to you. Keep in touch with me, Tori. If you need me write me in care of Captain Matt Saginor, USA Army Intelligence." He scribbled the instructions on a small white card. "If you decide on revolution, I guarantee my government's support."

"I can say *te-rrific,* to such news?"

"Stefano smiled. "You can say terrific. Now, before I leave, I am forced by conscience to tell you that I know of your involvement with Don Barbarossa—his plans for you. I urge you, exercise caution in your dealings with him. These members of the Grand Council are not to be believed. Collectively they are an insidious force, damned near impossible to reason with, and dangerous."

"All of them?"

"All of them. Its a damn shame we didn't meet a year ago. God Almighty, this procrastination would have ended abruptly. Now, I leave, having done less than I intended. Listen, Tori, drive back to Palermo with me, and I'll requisition this jeep to you, to be used however you see fit. It's a shame to leave it behind, where the scavengers can pick it up for nothing."

"You have such authority?" Tori was impressed.

"I can do whatever I deem important for Sicily. You'd make more frequent trips to Palermo with a jeep at your disposal—no?"

"You won't give up on me, Stefano." Tori was immensely touched.

"Now I'm leaving, I have to abandon such thoughts."

Colonel Modica signalled his aide, in a gesture of departure as they walked towards the other men.

Ten minutes later as the AMGOT Jeep spiraled in its ascent towards Rigano Pass at the summit, Tori mentioned

Athena's physical condition as Santino had explained it to him. A fleeting image of Athena entered Modica's mind, with a flash of compassion. He'd met her earlier at the Salvatore house and remarked ardently over her incredible beauty. He indicated his heartfelt sorrow to Tori as he scribbled the name of an officer with the Medical Corps. "Don't delay getting Athena to see him. I'm not sure how much longer the Allies will remain in Palermo," he urged.

Tori, grateful for his suggestions, thanked the American. Then, feeling more secure with Stefano, he laughingly told him of the proposals made to him by the Partitionists and what they offered him if they were victorious.

The Colonel listened attentively, even as his eyes darted about the changing landscape. "And if the Partitionist plan fails, Tori? What then?"

"Exile in Brazil," replied Tori with exaggeraged eye gestures.

"So that's it! That was Barbarossa's trump card!" exploded the American. "He already had you wrapped up. What the fuck's his game?"

"Who tied Salvatore? What are you saying, *Colonnello?*"

"Wrapped up, *amico.* Wrapped up. Don Barbarossa—that's who. You already had a deal with him, but he plans to do you in—double-cross, *Capeeshi?* To shaft you, *amico,* is what he plans to do. Probably to annihilate you," he said acidly, scanning the arid mountains. No wonder his plans had been foiled!

"No." said Tori quietly. "No deals have been made with Don Barbarossa. What means this *double-cross?* This *shaft?* Annihilation I understand."

Colonel Modica explained graphically. As he did, Tori saw the doubt reflected in the officer's eyes and he repeated himself. "I promise you, no deals were made with my Godfather. No agreements. My communications have been solely with *Capitano* Francesco Bello."

A variety of mixed emotions charged through Stefano Modica in those next moments. Searching Tori's eyes, his inclination was to believe him. Yet, it didn't subdue the fires burning inside him as he recognized the diabolical machinations Don Barbarossa had implemented without his knowledge. It took him a few moments to unravel the Don's revolting schemings and plottings.

"Sonofabitch! Listen, I mean no disrespect towards your Godfather—I know how you feel about him, but—" Stefano was boiling made. "Goddamnit! You'd better know your Godfather pledged your services to the Partitionists, and guaranteed the Grand Council full control of all guerrilla forces, including all the bandits and brigands, in the coming years of insurrection. Due to my official involvement, I was unable to be more candid when we first met. Now, I'm officially off the Sicilian detail. I owe no loyalty to Don Barbarossa—or the others. It's best you know the kind of people with whom you intend to have an affair."

It was a far different Salvatore who sat, grim-faced and tight-lipped, engrossed in the American's words, his thoughts roiling turbulently.

Colonel Modica rambled. "So the Partitionists made their move towards you? You know, of course, Canepa's a communist. A hard-core Red. No matter what he appears outwardly, and he's fooled a great many, believe my assessment. He's a Red agent. Be sure you tread carefully."

"*Allora*—you don't know?" asked Salvatore, his dark eyes clouding over.

"Know what?"

"Canepa's dead."

Modica's astonishment was instantaneous. He stopped chewing gum, rolled it into a ball, and tossed it out the window of the jeep. He turned his full attention on Tori. "When? How?"

"It's suspected he was liquidated by those higher-ups who felt secure in his death. Surely you knew?"

"The hell I knew!" he retorted angrily. "And *why* I didn't know is what nags at me now! Fucking Sicilian intrigue! I'll never understand it!"

"Yet, you desire for *me* to stand at its center?" Tori forced a cynical smile. "If a man with your credentials feels at sea with such politicians, what can a baby lamb do among such predators?"

"You've got the edge on me. You're Sicilian—one of them. You all think alike." He made a gesture of apology when he caught the wilting glance Tori tossed him. "Well-almost," he added. Inwardly Colonel Modica fumed.

"They kept it secret so as not to split the factions," mused Stefano.

"*Bravo, mi Colonnello.* Sicilian logic isn't so complex."

Modica's next gesture defied classification and produced a gale of laughter by Salvatore.

"That *sonofabitch* Canepa, playing three sides against the middle. Aided by both Allies and the Reds, while courted and spoon-fed by the Sicilian land-barons, the bastard was bound to emerge victorious." Modica concluded the man was a double agent, a fact he'd known for sometime. That the man's death hadn't been reported to him is what disturbed him.

"What happened to the sixteen guerrilla bands?" he asked.

Tori grew silent. "What else? They split up and disbanded."

"And all this without my knowledge or sanction," blurted the colonel. He methodically brought it into the open. "Well—it's happened, without me. The Monarchists and Separatists formed their coalition and under the guise of Partitionists, led by this man, Francesco Bello, they've made their next play. You, my friend, are next. They want you. Only with the aid of your guerrilla army do they stand a chance at victory. You see what I've been trying to tell you? You can't escape your destiny. I only hope, my friend, that you'll know how to handle these greedy vultures."

While Tori pondered the weight of his words, Colonel Modica's mind shifted into high gear. Now, he understood why Don Barbarossa had done an about face when Italy's politics swung to the Left. Any new government assuming control of Sicily, including the Reds, could conceivably pass new land reforms and pose a serious threat to the ancient island's feudal laws, a move neither the nobility or the Mafia could afford to let happen. The American and British allies were lax, but, not Russia. She'd never assume the pacifistic role of her predecessors. Pushing for separation from Italy, and demanding autonomy with a regional Parliament would insure that Sicily would remain in the hands of the Mafia-feudalists who had kept her in bondage for centuries.

Torn between the uniform of the U.S.A. and a peculiar loyalty to his unique Sicilian, who, if guided properly, could raise his nation out of the middle ages and break the chains that kept her shackled to its unholy past. Colonel Modica stewed uncomfortably. Loyalty to the American uniform won out. How could he possibly disclose confidential matters of his government entrusted to him as Top Secret, highly classified data? He'd sworn to uphold his allegiance to America, not Sicily.

Until the jeep arrived at Rigano Pass, where Tori dismissed his paladins who had followed on horseback, and kept only Vincenzo at his side, both men remained silent, each engrossed in their personal dilemmas.

Once past Bellolampo Barracks, where *carabinieri* saluted the official AMGOT jeep, unaware that it transported the infamous Salvatore, the passengers were greeted

458

by the constant clamorous pealing of church bells. Faint at first, the sounds increased in volume the closer they got to Palermo.

"The news is out. By now the entire world mourns the death of our President," remarked Colonel Modica with an edge of sadness to his voice.

"All except for America's enemies," said Tori candidly.

Modica glanced sharply at him, then nodded at the intelligence of the remark.

As they approached the City of Palermo, Lieutenant Destro was forced to gear down in the abnormal traffic jams. City streets were congested with crowds of weeping pedestrians mourning Roosevelt's death. Allied staff cars whizzed past them in the other direction towards Palermo Airport. Pandemonium existed on all sides. The deafening sounds of the discordant church bells numbed their eardrums. Car horns bleated incessantly. People shouted incoherently and wailed like banshees. In some areas traffic had slowed down to a standstill. Civilians sobbed as they waved farewell to their G.I. friends. "So long, Joe!" "Cheerio, limey," they called to the British soldiers as they drove out by the truckload. Official flags and standards drooped in fatigue as lovers embraced tearfully and parted in sorrow. Women clung tearfully to the men in the trucks as they passed. Even the whores at *Madama* Neptune's, seldom seen by the public, were framed in the shuttered windows, waving and tossing flowers to the best customers they'd ever had and would probably never have again.

Lieutenant Destro eased the jeep into another stream of traffic and wormed his way past the Quattro Canti onto the Via Roma. In moments he pulled up before Allied HQ.

Colonel Modica suggested that Tori remain in the jeep until he returned with the proper official documents that assigned the jeep to him. He ordered his aide to scrounge up a staff car and both men snaked through the crowds who pulled at them, and fired countless questions at them. Colonel Modica waved them off politely and disappeared into Allied HQ.

Lieutenant Destro was the first to emerge. He made his way back through the pressing crowds to Tori's side and handed him the packet. He saluted the brigand and left. Several moments later, Colonel Modica emerged from the building and snaked his way towards the jeep where the Sicilians waited. Spotting him, both Tori and Vincenzo alighted from the jeep and headed towards him. They shook hands and embraced. It was impossible to be heard over the boisterous shouts of the crowd. If the Colonel had known it would be the last time he'd ever see Tori, he might have taken more time with him. But the war, a greedy mistress, had placed too high a demand on him. He moved towards the waiting staff car amid a shower of confetti and multicolored serpentine. He turned with marked hesitation on his face, as if he had more—so much more—to discuss with Tori. Glancing somberly at his friends, he waved and boarded the auto.

Salvatore, waving back to his American friend, experienced a sinking sensation in the pit of his stomach. Enveloped by inner depression, he failed to notice he'd become the object of attention among the hordes of people who began milling around him. It wasn't until he felt himself being touched and grabbed at that he realized what was happening.

"It's him!" shouted a bystander peering inscrutably at him. "It's Salvatore!" The people caught up the cry. "It's Salvatore! Salvatore! *Viva* Salvatore!" they cried and rushed at him like a giant tidal wave. Filled with adoration for their hero, they forgot their temporary woes, "Salvatore! *Dio de benediggi!*" They shouted. "God Bless you!"

Was it possible these accolades were for him? he asked himself. Infected by their contagious emotion, Tori stood up straighter, squaring his shoulders and nodding to them with the majesty and forebearance of a young prince, as confetti covered him like mounds of pastel snowflakes.

Watching him with amusement and a peculiar delight, Vincenzo was unable to measure the enthusiasm of the crowds as they closed in around his cousin. In those moments he seemed to have grown in stature, thought Vincenzo. He was struck by the nobility of his cousin's profile, by the bold manner as he strutted before the host of admirers waving to them, nodding and acknowledging their praises. In an agile move to protect Salvatore from the threatening mob, Vincenzo rushed to his side, ran interference, and steered his cousin to the safety of the jeep, before they could tear off his clothing.

"*Managghia!* cried Vincenzo breathlessly. "Did you see the way they grabbed at you! They couldn't get enough!" The gears ground raspingly and he managed to steer the vehicle away from the hordes of people, who having heard the cries, "Salvatore!" rushed at them from the *piazza* across the way. It took twenty minutes for Vincenzo to move out of traffic and snake his way back towards the narrow road through the Conca d'Oro valley.

"If I never hear another church bell in my life, it will be too soon!" said Vincenzo covering his ears. "This *Colonnello* Modica really gave this jeep to you to use?" Vincenzo thought the whole affair totally incredulous, the gesture too magnanimous to be sincere. "For nothing? What did you have to do in return?" He coughed slightly.

"Just promise I'd use it," replied Salvatore quietly as he gazed at the rich fertile valley of the Golden Shell. "He thinks I should get to Palermo more often." He glanced at his watch. "C'mon, cousin. Step on it. I'm dying of hunger. With all that good food waiting for us. . . ."

Coughing again, Vincenzo nodded and floored the accelerator, much to Salvatore's discomfort. He clung to the door handle in panic. Nothing shook him as much as his cousin's wildcat driving! By the time they arrived at the summit, Vincenzo's cough had become so intense, he stopped the jeep, got out and leaned against the vehicle until the convulsions subsided. He didn't let Salvatore know he'd coughed up an excess amount of blood. Totally drained of color he walked to the passenger side and forced a smile.

"You drive, cousin," he said weakly.

"*Botta de sanguo!* If you don't see a doctor, tomorrow, I'll personally knock you down, tie you and drag you there myself! Hear?" exclaimed Salvatore. "If I've told you once, I've told you a dozen times. If you want to be my co-captain, you've got to be well!"

"I promise. I'll go," replied Vincenzo too weak to argue.

Salvatore started the jeep and driving slowly, he filled with great concern over his cousin. He wanted to talk, to help him ease the discomfort, but he couldn't. He still entertained a terrible feeling of emptiness at the departure of Colonel Modica, as if a part of him had gone with the American. His mind filled with Modica's words, and his usual ambivalence grew deeper. And when his thoughts centered on his Godfather, Tori's features turned stony, his jaw set like iron. He could feel the strength of Hercules in him, but what to do with this strength? What?

461

Shortly after dinner, Tori lost interest in the conversation in which the guests at his house were engaged, so without a word to either his family or his paladins, he quietly slipped away to the Mountain of Cats.

In the sun's final curtain of the day the mesa had transformed into a fiery copper sea of shifting bronzes, taupes and velvety-brown shadows in an effort to give light to the full moon soon to rise against a midnight blue sky. Star points lit up intermittently, clustering overhead like a comforter of lustrous diamonds so close he could almost touch them. It was times like these that he missed Appolladora most, and times like these when he found the memories of her fading more each day. Since her death had been avenged, it was almost as if the books were being closed on the subject, and he was helpless to do anything about it. Tori struck a match on a boulder to light a cigarette. The instant burst of orange-blue flames lit up his face to reflect a myriad brooding thoughts.

Was it possible, wondered Tori, that he could be the man Colonel Modica described? Was he truly blind to his own potential? When Stefano spoke to him, he felt like a Hercules. But, did he really possess such attributes of leadership? He blew out the match before it burned his fingertips. Instantly his imagination took flight. Like a camera, his mind began to absorb the images, and he saw himself dressed in judicial robes, walking tall and proud among his peers. Seated next to the imposing men in government, he saw himself treated with reverence and respect. People asked questions of him and hung on his every word. There he was, riding in an open limousine, the streets lined with crowds of admirers shouting *"Viva Salvatore!"* just as they'd done in Palermo. In another split-second fantasy he saw himself seated in Parliament, complimented and lauded by Minister Belasci.

Managghia, he thought as his mood broke and he laughed aloud at the absurdity of such thoughts. Just as quickly Tori sobered. There it was again, that deep voice inside him trying to shake him awake as it had so many times in the past:

Wake up, Tori. You heard the American Colonnello. Now is your time! If you don't take hold, Sicily will be lost. You've been a savior to your people these past two years. You can be the man Stefano sees. You are that man!

He reached into his pocket and pulled out the golden amulet, studying it in the bright moonlight as he dangled it a few inches in front of him. *"Il scorpione, eh?"* he muttered aloud. He opened the clasp and slipped it into place around his neck, allowing it to dangle freely on his bare chest under his open-necked shirt. On this night Tori found himself at the crossroads of his life, stirred by Stefano's words and disturbed by his Godfather's. His mind, burdened by confusion, wrestled for a time with both opinions, and he knew instinctively that this night would change the course of his life. He didn't know how he knew, only that he knew.

Colonel Modica'a attempt to warn him of Don Matteo's treachery, which at first he had found hard to believe, had caused him to reconsider his Godfather. Recalling with vivid clarity the expeditious manner in which he'd disposed of Don Pippinu and the swiftness with which the security police had sent Marshal Franchina packing, he now took another look at this illustrious Don Barbarossa. He recalled his first encounter with him, and carefully considered the cold, inhospitable treatment extended him until the name "Antigone Naxos" was mentioned. The instantaneous reaction by the *mafioso* was inescapable. Tori's thoughts spiralled and he grew visibly troubled.

It just isn't possible, he told himself, feeling the cold sweat break out on his forehead. As the thoughts jelled in his mind, every nerve and fiber in his being tried to deny it. He told himself to stop the wild imaginings, that, if he permitted his thoughts to continue in this vein, he'd destroy his mother by bringing shame and humiliation to her house. But, no matter how he tried to shake the feelings his mind refused to firmly deny the truth.

For a time he forced his mind to think of his meeting with *Capitano* Bello. He instructed himself to be certain to examine all proposals. Once again his mind drifted to Don Barbarossa's recent words. "You will accept Bello's proposal and report to me," he'd told Tori. Those words burned in Tori's mind, coupled with a powerful resentment. What right did his Godfather have to demand this of him? What right? He considered who had sent the Trapani newspaper to his house. It had to be the Don's way of showing the job had been completed.

The unfortunate part of this was that the article had fallen into his mother's hands, or she might never have learned about the death of Don Pippinu Grasso. A few days ago, on Friday, just before Athena had arrived home with Santino to announce their intention to marry, Antigone had been sorting the mail casually when her attention had been captured by the sight of the Trapani newspaper. Not until she'd placed the article before him, with the photo of the dead *mafioso* staring up at him, had he understood what had caused her face to blanch. His eyes had scanned the article. Only a few words stood out: "Former proprietor of Naxos Weight and Measures from Mt. Erice dead. Heart Attack. In Palermo on business with an old friend and colleague, Don Matteo Barbarosa. . . ." At that moment Tori's eyes had met his mother's, and she had known how compromised he was with Don Barbarossa. He could see it in her eyes. She had left him alone with Vincenzo and gone outside into her unprolific garden, moving mechanically from one lifeless plant to the next, muttering, "Everything in Sicily is dead. Why do I bother to restore life to these sterile, unyielding plants that get little help from the barren earth?"

More than the recent association with his Godfather, Tori suspected that something more profound disturbed his mother, but before he had time to sort out bits and pieces in his mind, Tori gave a start.

It happened so quickly that at first he was baffled. He peered about the moonswept temple thinking a joke had been played on him. The Siculi demons, perhaps? A few stray cats had begun to gather in their nightly ritual, their cries and near-human moans growing more abundant. Still he saw no one or nothing. "Who's there?" he called out feeling for his gun. Damn! He'd left his gun at home! He slipped down behind the boulder, crouching out of sight and felt along his inner calf inside his boot for the knife he kept secreted there, while his eyes pierced through the shadows at the perimeter of the temple. He heard a voice call to him—not the voice of the playful Siculi's, for sure. Now he moved behind the huge columns, retiring into the shadows. His sensitive ears listened for unnatural sounds, and his intent eagle eyes fastened on a moving dark form who approached, seemingly unmindful of any lurking dangers.

It seemed that every cat in the province had converged upon the temple, uttering near-human cries as they swarmed together for whatever mystic rites they embarked upon each night. In the cover of this activity and these distracting noises Salvatore moved effortlessly until he was upon the interloper. With sudden agility he leaped forward, took his captive unaware, and with his knife aimed menacingly at the other's neck, he pulled back his other arm into a brutal stranglehold. In the struggle the black scarf fell from his mother's head and he found himself staring into her terrified eyes. He released her instantly. Panicked at the close call.

"Mamma!" he shouted. *"Dio Buono!* I could have killed you! What are you doing here? I could have killed you!" he repeated. "I could have killed you!'" He was shaken considerably.

"Well, you didn't. So relax! Calm down!" sighed Antigone. She appeared more interested in the congregation of cats and the eerie sounds emanating from them. *"Allora,* my son. They really *do* come here at night? I thought it was just another fanciful tale of folklore." Absorbed by the mass of cats, she wondered, "Why do they choose *this* place, in all the valley?" Shrugging, she turned to her son, dismissing the phenomenon of the cats. "What are you doing here all alone?" she scolded. "You left a house full of friends to come here by yourself. . . ."

"I came to think on some matters. By tomorrow I must make several decisions. It's best you return to the house, Mamma. You shouldn't have come by yourself, unaccompanied? Come, I'll take you home."

"Tori," she restrained him. "We must talk." Her voice was firm.

"Si, Mamma."

"Don't tell me, *si Mamma.* It's time to talk. For a long time I've not felt the closeness we once shared. Did the *Colonnello* give you cause to worry?"

"No. He suggested that I take a more active part in Sicily's politics."

"Bravo Colonnello! Mark my words, he has sense."

Tori broke out in a sudden burst of temper. "Why does everyone insist that I have such exceptional potential? That they see powerful forces in me? They ask too much—"

"Because it's true. . . ."

They stared at each other in a total silence, for several moments.

"You think I enjoy this dedication of yours to our country and our people?" began his mother solemnly. "These past two years, I've been both proud of your brave deeds

465

and paralyzed with fear that something would happen to you. That at some time you might not return to Athena and me. Daily we offer prayers to God for your protection. From the first, when I saw you take command over those men in the *maquis* I knew no words I could offer would prevent you from doing what you believed you must do. I convinced myself not to interfere, not to act maudlin, not to press on you like a stone weight, for it would belie every principle I'd taught you to believe in all your life. On the day destiny became your mistress, I knew not to compete with her, for mothers and mistresses are as incompatible as oil is to water. My days of tutoring you ended on that day. . . ."

"Oh, Mamma," cried her son sitting at her feet. "I'm not sure of my destiny! The *Colonnello* filled my head with so many pictures of what he sees in me. I'm confused. For the first time in years I don't know my own mind. I'm twenty-three, not fifty-three—I'm not a sage. What do I know?"

She stroked his head tenderly. "The chaos will settle. Like the swirls of dust that rise in the confusion of battle and fall into place, the answers will come."

"The American stirred feelings and images in me that in my wildest dreams I dare not believe possible." His anguished voice trailed off.

"Haven't I taught you from infancy—nothing's impossible? Give your youthful emotions time to catch up to a maturing mentality. That's all that's troubling you."

"I wish it were only that. What disturbs me are the blatant contradictions between what *Colonnello* Modica sees in me and what my Godfather tells me I must do . . ."

Antigone stiffened. In the moonlight her face turned to a sheet of colorless glass. "Your—uh—Godfather? What contradictions? What does he tell you you must do?"

"He makes me conscious of my station in life. Dictates my responses. Whom I should trust—whom I shouldn't! He assumes too much authority for a mere Godfather!"

Antigone swallowed hard. The moment had arrived to give her son the answer that would steer his course for the rest of his days. Difficult as it was, after hedging for several moments she couldn't put it off any longer. "Just where is it written on destiny's tablets that Don Matteo should direct your action in this life?" she asked imperiously. "You owe him nothing! It's been years since we heard from him! Now, suddenly, you permit him to dictate to you?" She glanced at him suspiciously. "He holds nothing over your head—does he?" The dreaded question was out.

Salvatore rose to his feet and paced about the mesa. He lit a cigarette and puffed on it thoughtfully. For a time he studied the burning cigarette. Anything to keep from looking at his mother. "Why do you ask?"

"Do you want me to keep silent? Continue to think the black thoughts I've not been able to rid myself of these past two days?"

He didn't reply. He knew she was referring to the death of Don Pippinu.

"I won't ask again, Tori. I will only repeat what I told you then. If they own you—you'll never be free of them. You owe them a favor? They won't stop at one, or two, or three. If you don't comply with their requests—even their slightest whim—they will dispose of you. *Capeeshi?* That's all I have to say."

"You should have thought of that twenty-three years ago, Mamma *bedda*," he whispered, half afraid of her response. The words were out, and Tori was more surprised at his own daring, his lack of anger.

She turned to her son, gazing upon him in the moonlight with a majestic dignity, and sensed instantly that he regretted his words. No matter, it was time for Antigone to unburden her soul. It came to her—to continue the deception —but she lacked the strength, and desire to do so. Besides, if Tori had gleaned any of her teachings, he'd see through any further chicanery. "You know," she said, relieved that the dreaded secret was out.

Tori felt terrible—dead inside. Thinking it was one thing; hearing the truth was another. "Then it's true, what I've sensed intuitively?" His voice, barely above a whisper, tried to conceal his terrible inner trembling.

Antigone nodded.

"You could have told me before this."

"I had no idea he was alive until you brought home the newspaper headlines." And because he was silent, she told him of the circumstances of their meeting, of the troubled times, how hungry her sons were when the Don found them.

"I was only the seed of a passing interlude—not loved, not wanted." He was reasonably hurt, angry and humiliated, suffering countless imagined indignations.

"No. No, you're wrong, Tori. I loved you more than the others. No, no; it wasn't intentional, I assure you. You were all of my flesh, babes of my womb," she reflected. "Something about you was special, even from the start.

467

I gave more to you than I did to your brothers, because you demanded it of me. Deep within you, even as a child, was an intense craving for love, knowledge and attention. You took whatever I had to impart—don't you remember what an active mind you had and still do?" She paused a moment to brush away an errant tear that had spilled on her cheek. "Since I assumed your real father to be dead, why would I tell you his real identity? What purpose would it have served? After my husband died, your need for a father was even greater than in Filippo or Marcos, so, I invented Barbarossa as your Godfather. Was that so bad? I never dreamed there'd be a day of atonement," she agonized.

Her words only vaguely entered Tori's consciousness. His mind had ground to a halt when he realized that Don Matteo was his *real* father. It was a paralyzing thought, numbing his senses—too much for his confused mind to grasp. For several moments they sat in silence, each filled with personal torment to which the other couldn't relate.

"It would be frivolous, Tori, to confront him with this news," she said. "You don't propose telling Matteo?"

"I don't know." He waved his hands despairingly. "I don't know. I just don't know. To suddenly awaken and discover I'm not who I thought I was all these years."

"Tori! I implore you. Don't bend your mind to this moment. You are exactly who you've been all your life. A name doesn't modify the fruit. You are what you are and who you are, regardless of the name you're called. The greatest men in the world have been born out of wedlock."

Tori remained uncompromising in his silence. Unintentionally, he had tuned his mother out. He sat there interminably, shrouded in tormenting silence. When he snapped out of his debilitating thoughts, he was surprised to find no one next to him. Antigone, unable to communicate with her son, had left him and returned to her house. His rejection had filled her with shame and remorse. It had been difficult to face Tori in the dark of night. How, she wondered, could she face him in the light of day?

Tori didn't recall how long he sat under the rising and fading moon. As the stars disappeared into the pale light of dawn he experienced emotional upheavals, more torment and agony than he had since the death of Apolladora. *Goddamnit! If only I could get stinking drunk—it would help ease the pain.*

At first, Tori sensed an inner revulsion towards his mother, for bringing him to these ends—a malice that grotesquely twisted his inner tranquility and rendered him beyond reason. As common sense set in, he attempted to reconcile the disastrous thoughts fermenting in him, and much of the destructive emotions abated. What the hell was wrong with him? He must be losing all reason. Apolladora had been a prostitute, whom he had willingly forgiven and had been willing to marry. His mother made one mistake—and here he was, ready to crucify her! *Dio Mio!* he thought. *What hell she must have endured to keep me.* She could have aborted. God knows how many women used the poisonous method of stuffing parsley into their vaginas to abort! Not his mother! *Damnit, Tori, grow up! These things can happen. Who needs a father, eh?* Hadn't he done well enough without one all these years? Why cry over the lack of one—rather, the acquisition of one, now? He commanded himself to cease in this schoolboy's display of foolish emotion.

It was nearly 5 A.M. when Tori left the temple. The vagrant cats had already vanished as he made his way to the Grotto Persephone. Enroute, he admonished himself over the treatment he'd given to his mother. What was more, he came to an important decision. The secret his mother had carried locked tightly in her breast all these years would remain just that—a secret. He vowed he'd never tell another soul—not even his father, Matteo Barbarossa.

"Alessandro Barbarossa," he toyed with the name over and over on his tongue. "No! It can never be," he shouted aloud at the alien sounding words. "I am Salvatore! I can be none other!"

Tori never made it clear to himself why he intended to conceal his identity from his father, not even to himself. Perhaps it was a punishment of sorts he wished to inflict on the Don for not caring enough about the woman he had impregnated with his seed. It might have been punishment directed against his mother, both for the act and concealment of his father's identity. It might even have been punishment directed against himself, for being the bastard son of an arrogant blackguard. Whatever, Tori resolved to dismiss the episode from mind—erase it completely as if his mother's words had never been spoken.

Moroever, Tori grimly determined to pursue—and find—total autonomy from Don Barbarossa, regardless of the consequences. Never, as long as he lived would he willingly involve himself in any business with the redoubtable *capomafia*. By the beard of a whale's whore, he wouldn't!

He rode swiftly through the hills and reaching the Grotto Persephone, he dismounted and stroked Napoleono's mane, nuzzling him for a few tender moments. He thought of Appolladora, then of Maria Angelica whom he hadn't seen in a long time. He promised himself to visit with her one day soon. But, in his mind was riding something more important than the image of another human being.

The early morning sun had already spread a blanket of heat on the scorched earth. Tori walked to the edge of the grotto and saluted smartly to an invisible being somewhere out in the vast open spaces spread below him.

"Perhaps, *Colonnello* Stefano Modica, I will become the man you see through your futuristic eyes, after all."

He moved over the rocks, scaled the steep incline and headed for the shadowy caverns of the grotto, the only refuge from the raw lights of a devastating, colorless sun. This day promised to be a scorcher in more ways than one, he told himself, and disappeared inside.

470

BOOK IV

BOOK IV

As political pandemonium erupted in Rome following V-E day on the eighth of May and the Eternal City became a hot bed of intrigue, a mad scramble had been precipitated into a free-for-all in which ambitious political lions scurried frantically about in fierce competition for control of the government. A King had abdicated, the son had been denounced, and the House of Savoy had come tumbling down into a downpour of total chaos. A dozen political parties vied for supremacy, and, as Colonel Modica had predicted, a people ravaged by war and infected by widespread starvation and misery—a people fully disgusted with the circus theatrics of Mussolini's dictatorship—were ready for anything. Never had the nation been more vulnerable.

By then, Salvatore had provided for his people by adhering basically to the fundamental principles of a long-ingrained feudal system in which anyone who could seize power had the right to govern and make laws to meet the situation at hand, without concern for permanency. According to feudal law, the ruler was unrestricted in his right to judge or interpret law, and those subject to his law had to obey regardless of other circumstances.

Guided by these simple, fast rules, Tori had saved his people. But now the war had ended. Caught on the one side by the still-growing needs of his people and on the other by the growing demands of his own morality, Salvatore found himself bordering desperation. Conditions had grown more intolerable, and he had made himself heard through frank and outspoken letters to the press, on the platforms open to him. "I had thought at war's end, my work would have finished. Instead I find conditions more appalling. We are enmeshed in a chaotic situation, with an ineffective government who cares nothing for its people and does little to resolve the problems besetting them. Unless measures are taken to ease the suffering, I shall be compelled to enforce my own laws just as I've done for the past few years."

Well, things didn't get better. And it seemed no one heard his loud voice echoing across the mountains and sea; nor were the voices of Sicily, coming from the Palermo Grand Council, heard as storm clouds of rebellion loomed on the horizon. Once again the voice of Salvatore arose, and was heard again in the press, "Sicily weeps at her own seduction, and, like a tender and compassionate whore, she permits herself to be used without compensation. When will she learn? When will she rebel against such treatment? Must she enforce so high a fee on her services that no one will dare molest her?"

If any one heard his cries, they paid no heed to these warnings. In the tumult and confusion as his nation underwent massive and reconstructive surgery at a snail's pace, Tori stood in his lair at the top of his golden mountains, watching with eagle eyes the silent panic that suffocated him and his people, and decided it was enough. It was finished. He had had enough. He would no longer wait.

This was the time of Salvatore. Now! The tide was in, and he had to move. It was a new Salvatore who became a willing participant in the seduction aimed at him by the Partitionist Party. Now, all was in readiness. He had finally agreed to rendezvous with *Capitano* Francesco Bello.

As the crusty, uniformed driver of an old, dusty prewar Mercedes limousine approached a cauldron-shaped meadow surrounded by four hills, thick with undergrowth and scattered with craggy boulders and desert sisal, he scanned a hand drawn map alongside him on the seat. "We're almost there, *Capitano*," he told his illustrious passenger.

"There it is, up ahead. The bridge. See it?" Captain Bello strained to see through the dusty windshield. All but prostrated by the intense heat, he mopped the sweat balls rolling down his face annoyed that he sweated at all. He squinted behind dark glasses at the sun-scorched, bleached countryside, finding the raw wilderness an abomination. He glanced behind him through a rear view window. "They're right behind us, Mafalla. You just go ahead, the car will follow."

In the car behind Bello's sat the financial power of the Partitionist Party, Baron Mattinata, that miser, that money-grubbing Shylock, that wretched skinflint whose purse strings were too close to his heart—a man who had made Bello rue the day he had formed an alliance with him. He sat stiffly with his two aides, glancing about the rugged terrain with marked scorn. The things he had to do for the Party! The people he was forced to associate with were repugnant to him, and he showed it.

Vincenzo de Montana, seated astride his horse at the top of a lone hill, watched the limousines approach until they disappeared behind rock formations. He turned in his saddle, lowered his binoculars, and signaled Salvatore who stood nearby on Napoleono. Tori nodded, shaded his eyes, and scanned the nearby hills. A total of three hundred men on horseback remained motionless behind clumps of bushes and boulders on the three hills surrounding the ruins of a Greek theater, awaiting a given signal. Below them, positioned at either side of the bridge, the Scoletti and Genovese brothers, dressed in combat fatigues, held their trusty Beretta submachine guns in hand. The sweat poured off them profusely as their eyes scanned the roads up ahead.

Vincenzo raised himself in his stirrups, adjusted the binoculars, and, squinting into the sun's glare, called to Tori, "They're almost at the bridge." Tori raised his arms into the air. The sound of bleating oxhorns pierced the air. The men on the bridge, alerted, gripped their weapons firmly in hand and turned in the direction of the sounds. Lookouts signalled from hill to hill until the all-clear signal reached Tori.

Captain Bello, hearing the horns, leaned forward in his seat, peering expectedly about the area on either side of him. The occupants of the second car, like Bello, peered about and saw no movement except for the men on the bridge flagging them down. The autos geared down and came to a full stop as Miguel and Arturo Scoletti stood in their path, guns held in menacing postures.

Captain Bello conforming to the cloak and dagger procedures, was somewhat reluctant to slip the catch on his gold belt buckle and place his gun and holster into Miguel's outstretched hands. He tried to suppress his indignation when searched by Marco Genovese, by asking in near contempt, "Where is your elusive leader?"

"In due time, *Capitano*," replied Fidelio, handing his .38 calibre Beretta to his brother. He hooked the grenade, palmed in his left hand, onto his belt and proceeded to search Bello more thoroughly than his brother. Satisified he nodded the *Capitano* on ahead. "Go on. Up ahead," he nudged him.

Miguel Scoletti, slipping the wooden end of a match stick between his teeth, eyed with noticeable envy the fancy uniform worn by the Partitionist, as he and Arturo made their way up the hill.

Captain Bello, gazing about this *terra incognita*, found

himself bottled in a mesa surrounded by three hills. He saw no one in his approach to the point of rendezvous. But in the blinding white glare of the sun, he felt a thousand eyes upon him, watching him, sizing him up. He wondered about them, as they might wonder about him. He was unable to detect any movement anywhere. It was too still—too quiet—too awesome. Only the sounds of his footsteps on crumpled rocks crunched as he moved forward. He wondered at the extreme measures taken by Salvatore to rendezvous in such a God-forsaken place with heavily-armed desperadoes enforcing his wishes. Were these measures of pure desperation—or of solid strength?

Bello was led to a petrified plateau of antiquity—a theater carved from the rocks of centuries past. He gazed up at the two smooth pillars of stone marking the gateway to the ancient arena, marvelling at their incredible longevity. A colorless sun, expanded to its zenith, filled the arena with pulsating hot light. It was difficult for Bello to see beyond the radiations of heat rising off the broken clay floor. Even the dry, parching heat, bore the unmistakable stench of the ages.

"You will walk to the center of the arena and wait, *Capitano*," instructed Arturo.

Bello nodded and strutted pompously to the center of the blinding sun spot whiter than the bleached stones of a skeleton. The staggering effect of the sun made him feel faint. *Porca Miseria!* Why the hell meet in such a savage setting—in this devil's inferno? He began to grow impatient at what he considered child's play. His dark eyes darted about the area trying to locate movement. Staggered about the circumference of this open-aired pavillion, stood runted stone pillars, like broken rows of teeth, spaced four to five feet apart, that once had zoomed skyward some thirty feet high.

In this dramatic setting, Captain Bello felt like an actor, spotlighted by a brash, cruel sun at center stage—without his lines. Where are the other players? he wondered, as the sound of oxhorns bleated again, much louder than before. His eyes were impulsed around him.

All at once the hills came alive. He saw hundreds of horses come into view at the upper level of the amphitheater. Bello turned slowly in a semicircle, his eyes darting all around him. He heard the crumbling sounds of horses' hooves as they struck against small rocks, shattering them into many fragments that bounced down the incline of rocky steps scattered along the side of a hill. A horde of men, converging on horseback, approached the arena from every direction.

God! What a picture, thought Captain Bello. He saw the glaring whites of their eyes; of both horse and rider reflected in the sun's brilliance. Salvatore's men were everywhere. *Managghia!* What a show of strength! If he hadn't seen it with his own eyes, he wouldn't have believed such an army existed. What a magnificent, awe-inspiring sight! Goddamn the devil—Salvatore was truly something else!

Under the deceptive glare of the fireballing sun, three hundred men had multiplied to three thousand in Bello's eyes. Within moments the horseback soldiers had descended the hills and come to a full halt, standing in a full circle around the outer perimeter of the theater, between broken pillars like a guard of honor. A silence fell over the ancient ruins. It was the most dramatic scene Bello had ever seen.

Salvatore, dressed in the beige uniform of a U.S. Army general worn under a white trench coat, came riding swiftly down one hill to the west of the tableland in a streak of blinding white light, like a lightning flash, on his spectacular white Arabian. He came at Bello galloping across the mesa, and stopped short a few feet away from the impressionable Partitionist leader. He sprang flamboyantly from his horse, and for a time the two men regarded each other in testy silence: one, the elegantly uniformed lawyer and wealthy landlord, the other, the virile young peasant with the uncannily dramatic flair and the formidable reputation.

"I am Salvatore," he finally announced.

"I am Bello," declared the other in the same authoritative manner.

Tori studied the colorful, uniformed politician and felt an instant, keen distrust of the man. Bello, simultaneously studied his host inscrutably and smiled internally at the general's uniform, polite mockery in his eyes.

Approaching them at a tranquil canter, a white scarf tied about his forehead, Indian-style, to catch perspiration, Vincenzo de Montana guided his ebony mare to a spot nearby. He stopped at a respectful distance, sized up Bello within the periphery of his gaze, and without obvious reaction formed a snap judgment, *this man is nothing!* Hunched forward in his saddle, he indolently crossed one leg over the saddle horn while his eyes actively skimmed the area, filled with dust and smells of sweating men and horses. Amid muffled sounds of squeaking leather saddles, clanking bridle apparatus, and of men and riders squirm-

477

ing uncomfortably in the stifling heat, Vincenzo strained catlike ears to hear the words spoken between Salvatore and Captain Bello, both of whom struck poses of nonchalance.

"We meet at last, eh, Salvatore? You can't imagine how pleasant it is to do business with a man so pleasing to the eyes. Most men in your profession are barbarians, *caro mio*. Uncouth barbarians," exclaimed Bello seemingly against his will. "I've waited so long to meet you. Now, finally we can make our plans known to each other. Speak freely, my dear man."

"Try one. They're American," said Tori, offering Bello a Camel. *God spare me from these supercilious fops and incessant talkers,* he thought as the slightest flicker of annoyance crossed his eyes.

Bello accepted one and flourished his lighter, lighting Tori's smoke first, then his own. He puffed on it and inhaled appreciatively. "Milder than Turkish, no?" After a moment's pause he continued. "Only last night I had a vision. Mind you—I'm not superstitious. But, I tell you, I saw this giant white eagle descending from heaven, holding in one claw, the sun. In the other—Sicily." He sucked in his breath dramatically. *"Allora*—can you imagine what went through my mind when I saw you descending those hills in a whirlwind like the white eagle of my dreams? Will it be you, Salvatore, who'll bring Sicily and the world to our feet?" Bello paused to watch the effect of his words on the bandit leader. Spurred by the astonishment he read on the face of his captive audience, he continued with added pomp and *panache.*

"Yes—I see it now, written—*blazed* across the sky! Destiny has brought us together for a purpose. To conquer Sicily. God willing, it shall be ours. The Partitionists shall become invincible!"

It was a foregone conclusion that from the beginning the temperaments of these two men, from different backgrounds, would be too incompatible. Each of them felt hardly anything but repugnance for the other. But, on Salvatore's part, this was quickly developing into hostility and gross displeasure. Bowled over by the man's gilt-edged oratory, Tori collected his wits. He did not smile. Generous praise and unnecessary flattery weren't the tools to exact his loyalty, especially not when employed by a man like Bello, who wore his feelings of superiority on his face as a leper wore his lesions for the world to recognize.

"If your gun's as mighty as your tongue, Bello," said Tori, tight lipped, "your victory is assured. Let us not waste time in guileful talk. You didn't travel such a distance to speak to me of visions. We are both practical men. Let us, then, speak of practical things."

Bello's fixed, fatuous smile dissolved. *Impertinent upstart!* He nodded curtly. "It's best, as you say, to dispense with the usual amenities to which the barons and dukes are afflicted. What insufferable boors they can be. *Allora*—I am prepared to offer you and your men unconditional amnesty for your crimes if you swear allegiance to the Partitionist party and secure victory for us. For you, a full commission as colonel, and, when victory is ours, a position of high rank in government."

"And if you lose?"

"My dear Salvatore—how can we lose with you on our side?"

"That's true. It's good we both realize that victory is possible only if Salvatore supports your revolution." He suppressed a smile. "But, as realists, my dear Bello, we must provide for that eventuality."

"Yes. Yes, of course." Bello bridled stiffly. "What do you propose?"

"One hundred thousand dollars—American currency, banked in advance of the revolution in my name in the Bank of Sicily. If we are victorious, you retain the sum. You do realize if the Partitionists lose I'll be forced into exile in foreign lands with my men. The sum is necessary to allow us to re-establish ourselves."

Bello was stupefied, stunned by the audacious terms. As quickly as he lost momentary composure, though, he regained it. "You're being a pessimist, aren't you?" He laughed unconvincingly and, fumbling with his watch fob, fingered it nervously. "The Partitionists won't fail. They can't fail." Dropping his voice to a confidential whisper, he added, "You see, my dear Salvatore, America fully endorses our plans. She's fully prepared to aid us with supplies and ammunition—all we need. Troops if necessary. As long as we keep Russia out of Sicily."

Although Tori heard Bello's words, his mind was sorting out the facts Colonel Modica had discussed with him recently. Despite the American's vehement protestations over the infiltration of communism in Italy, he never had admitted America's full endorsement of the Partitionist movement. Modica had stressed that caution should be exercised in any affiliation, due to the Leftist leanings of the former Separatist leader, Canepa. Hadn't he told Tori the U.S.A. would personally back *him* in a revolt? Was it now possible that at war's end America fully supported the

479

anti-Red movement? Tori paced the area between them, thumbs hooked into his belt, coat wide open, boots, scuffling in the dry dirt, sending up mounds of dust behind him.

Decisions changed so quickly in these crazy times of international chaos, he couldn't be certain that what he accepted as gospel one day would hold true the next. With this in mind, he stopped short, pivoted on one foot, and glanced at Bello through tilted eyes. "You speak the words of a man possessed with great authority. How do I know you are empowered to make me such grand promises—let alone insure them? Tell me the foundations for these offers. Whom do you represent?"

Captain Bello stroked his drooping moustache thoughtfully as he studied the spectacular display of horsemen standing at attention like a well-trained army contingent. He felt a pang of resentment, bordering on jealousy, that so many men showed devotion to a lowly peasant. That a man less worthy than he should inspire such loyalty from his men confounded him. When he got over his first reaction, and in the spirit of objectivity, Captain Bello's estimation of the guerrilla spiralled upwards. Not long ago Bello had insisted to the Duke de Gioia that victory for the Party was possible only with Salvatore's support. Now, he believed it with more conviction. Without further ado he replied to the young Montegattan.

"I represent the Duke de Gioia, Martino Belasci, the Cardinal and his Archbishop, Prince Giorgio Oliatta, the Honorable Bernardo Malaterra—" On went the star studded galaxy of Monarchists, Feudalists, titled nobility, high ranking political lions, and Mafia Dons—men whose names Tori recognized as the monetary and political influences presently pulling the life strings of Sicily. "And," continued Bello with an air calculated to inspire wonder, "although it's not official, Don Barbarossa stands among these notable men."

"What the hell kind of bullshit are you trying to feed me? *Not official!* Hah! Barbarossa *is* the Partitionist Party. He conceived it, promoted it from the resurrected ashes of the former Separatist party. Now you're saying he isn't part of it?" Tori, wary, flushed angrily.

"I tell you, Salvatore, I contacted him. Don't think I wasn't perplexed when he replied to my communiques stating resolutely he could do more for the Party by remaining detached from it for the time being. Look, my friend, I insisted that he, Barbarossa, declare his loyalties. Well, he declined. Absolutely declined to endorse the movement. Can I tell you what he told me? His involvements left little time for national politics, that he left its gross complexities to younger, hardier men, such as myself. Chew on that, *caro mio!*" Men like Don Barbarossa were obviously a sore spot to him.

Tori ground out his cigarette with the heel of his boot. His mind spot-lighted the conversation when Don Barbarossa had spelled out his exact duties in the Partitionist party. What the hell was that shrewd manipulator up to?

Witnessing the consternation on Tori's face, Bello continued in frustration. "I tell you, dear Salvatore, that *mafioso* doesn't fool me! Not for a second. He's laying the foundation for some future treachery, believe me." Captain Bello paused. Equally disturbed by Salvatore's sudden wariness, he grew cautious. "Does it matter to you if Don Barbarossa is involved in our movement?"

In the testy silence between them, Tori strutted pensively about the cracked floor of the arena where scrubs of weed sprouted between the flat stones. He hadn't counted on the Don's neutrality, and found it difficult to deal with such drastic changes. "Who feeds you orders?" asked Tori laconically.

"The Duke de Gioia. Once the insurrection commences, I, naturally, will be the commander in chief. But, first, answer my question, does Don Barbarossa's lack of participation make a difference to you?"

"Listen, Bello, if you intend to win, everything makes a difference." Tori stared at the cigarette in his hand. "Do you have enough experience to command guerrilla armies? A war is not like the guarding of an estate," he temporized.

"I'm asking you—does it matter if Don Barbarossa endorses our Party?" pressed Captain Bello.

"What Barbarossa does or doesn't do is of no consequence to me," he lied. "I'm only interested in who pays me, and who gives me orders."

"I'm telling you straight, *amico,* Barbarossa doesn't officially sanction us—all right? When your forces join mine in the east, you go on the payroll. Your salary, that of an Army colonel, begins when our talk is finished, today."

"A Colonel?" Tori laughed good naturedly and shook his head regretfully. "It would be foolish for me to accept a demotion. I will be a full general, with general's pay," he retorted flatly. "Now, then, tell me how many men you have. A thousand, at least, to match mine? All as well trained as mine?"

He was evasive. "I can't answer you. At my estate thousands of men are being recruited. Volunteers from the entire province. College students, the first to arrive, are all imbued with the spirit of nationalism. Oh, it will be grand—simply grand!" Now, he spoke with uncontrolled enthusiasm. "As to your men, since I've not observed them in action I can't make an intelligent assessment, uh—General." Bello spoke with a tinge of seduction in his voice.

Tori glanced swiftly at him, scowling in annoyance. "Why do you call me General? You're premature, Bello. Before I consider your proposal, vital issues must be settled."

Bello's face fell. "I took for granted—"

"Don't take anything for granted—least of all Salvatore. I'm here to listen and consider your proposals, not to be taken for granted."

"Very well, then, listen. You and your men shall come to my estate, and from there we shall both devastate the government forces and scatter them back to Italy where they belong."

He is incredible! The man's incredible, thought Tori. Then because he found it irresistible that the man was so horribly naive in such matters, he laughed good-naturedly as he might at a joke, and wagged a finger at him.

"No, no, no, no, *Capitano*. Salvatore doesn't move from his territory. You and your men handle the East of the island, and Salvatore will handle the West."

Bello disagreed. "United, our combined forces will melt the enemy to nothing. *Managghia!*" Bello exclaimed in a moment of annoyance. Prostrated by the intensity of the sun, he implored, "Is there someplace we can retreat to, to discuss these issues like civilized men instead of sweltering like swine in this inferno?"

"Do you ride a horse?" asked Tori glancing with disdain at his immaculate and garish uniform, with its glittering gold accessories that dazzled the eye like a marching brass band in the sun.

"Do fish swim?"

Tori signalled Vincenzo. He came at them in a swift gallop and pulled on the reins. "Fetch a horse for the *Capitano*. Meet us in Monreale at Antonetta's *Pasticceria*. Sequester the place."

Vincenzo nodded, saluted him snappily, and, wheeling his horse about, returned in moments with a chestnut mare for Captain Bello.

Overhead electric fans had cooled the temperature by a few degrees inside the *pasticceria*. The men drawn to an alcove, an extension of the modest room, seated themselves under a grape arbor, *al fresco,* overlooking the edge of a mountain village with a panoramic view of the Tyrrhenian Sea in the background. Sipping lemon ice and Marsala wine, Bello plunged into an earnest protest over Tori's refusal to endorse his military strategy.

Salvatore tolerantly tried to explain. "Right now, *Capitano*—Salvatore controls the west. What do you control? How large is this army of yours? Is it equal to mine in all ways? How many men do you lead?"

"Well, I haven't the exact number," he hedged.

"No? I control nearly two thousand. Perhaps more have joined my forces from the south. Why don't you know the exact number of your men?"

"They were still recruiting when I left Caltagirone," stammered the Easterner. Seething inwardly, Bello glanced about the quaint cafe. *Cocky, arrogant, insufferable peasant!* "Students arrive daily by the hundreds. How can I count?" Salvatore smiled tightly, leaned back, and crossed one leg over the other.

"When your regiments are as effective as mine, I suggest you demonstrate against the *carabinieri* in your province, capture their barracks, men and weapons until you control the East as Salvatore controls the West. Then we unite and synchronize our movements across the Island. Meanwhile I continue to crush resistance in the West. . . ."

"It's more expeditious for you to come to Caltagirone, now," urged Bello who knew nothing of guerrilla warfare and less about running an army. Unrealistically he had counted on Salvatore to personally train recruits and conduct all the atrocities himself. He wanted no stain on his hands.

"And in my absence, who would defend what I've already conquered? Ghosts? No, *Capitano.* First, you develop your stronghold of men, equal to mine in all ways. Then we unite. There's more logic to a division of forces, equalized in strength across the island, who fight as one. Just as the Allies did during the Occupation." Tori paused effectively, then spoke of more relevant issues. "Tell me, are your people prepared to pay the cost of such a war?"

"My dear Salvatore, multimillionaires are behind this movement."

"Please answer my question. I make no moves unless I'm paid fifteen million lire, in advance," asserted the young outlaw.

Bello's face turned purple. "Fifteen million? Are you insane, man? This, in addition to the one hundred thousand—?" He could hardly contain his rage.

"For *our* participation only. What you request for your work, to keep your soldiers well fed and properly clothed and furnished with excellent weapons and ammunition, is your business." Tori was firm.

"Fifteen million, now? *Now?*" He shrieked at the preposterous demand.

"In addition to the terms we discussed, I seek a position of importance in the new government. Say—uh—*Senatore* in the new Parliament."

Bello's face drained of color. "What we had in mind was Minister of Justice, chief of the policing forces in Palermo. . . ." The impertinence of this outrageous renegade stuck in his craw.

"Senator," insisted Tori, gently.

Trying not to show his rage and humiliation, Bello said, evenly, "In the auto, following me, is a man prepared to make such a commitment. Your last request shall have to be taken up with the senior members of the Party. You understand? By the way, I wouldn't mention the escrow demand to Baron Mattinata. Let me handle that directly with the Duke."

"My, my. You mean you aren't empowered to deal with me?" Tori inclined his head mockingly. "Tch, tch, tch," he clucked scornfully.

"If you'll have one of your men fetch the Baron we shall put the question to him." Bello's face colored to a red-purple hue.

"We shouldn't have kept so important a man waiting."

"When it comes to talking money, I leave it to the extortionists," snapped Bello. Tori laughed and signalled to one of his men, to bring the Baron into the *pasticceria.*

Baron Mattinatta's hands shook as he wiped his swarthy features with a large handkerchief; his eyes tried to adjust to the dimly lit interior of the shop, and he gazed apprehensively about the shabby premises. Earlier, en route to this place, a few bandit tricks, designed to stimulate a large army, had been employed to churn excitement in him. Thirty or forty horsemen, galloping swiftly at either side of the sedan and dragging brush in the dust, had given the impression of thousands. This skinflint feudalist was impressed by what he calculated to have been at least two thousand bandits on choice steeds.

Prostrated by the oven-like intensity of the weather, he affected a look of long suffering and fell saggingly into the chair Bello held out for him. Even his dignity had dissolved.

"Excellency," began Tori in a placating manner. "Had I been informed of your presence earlier, you wouldn't have been subjected to this Turkish bath of a day. I'd have seen to it that you were brought inside instantly."

The Baron sent Bello a withering glance. Bello burned inwardly, amazed at the silky manner in which the bandit poured it on.

"What devilish heat! *Dio Maledetto!* The machine was a sweat box!" panted the Baron. He dipped a napkin into the pitcher of ice water and splashed his face and neck, unmindful that his shirt was dripping wet.

Bello got to the point. "Salvatore demands fifteen million lire up front," he said flatly. "Right now."

Tori delighted in observing a centuries-old arrogance and disdain creep into the Baron's bony face in a matter of seconds. His inborn, inner loathing of all peasants became instantly apparent. *"Demands?"* screeched Baron Mattinata. He pulled in his neck and craned it stiffly like that of an ostrich, casting Salvatore a scornful look. "Demands?" he repeated with hostility.

Bello had the good grace to blush at Mattinata's overbearing manner. "Requests, Excellency," submitted Bello weakly.

"Uh—*demands,*" corrected Salvatore.

"What the hell do you want with all that money?" asked the Baron angrily.

"War's expensive," stated Tori flatly.

"Nonsense, young man. For your country's sake, you'll be honored to contribute your services, free of charge." He spoke condescendingly as one might to a serf and smiled cunningly, employing animated gestures.

Tori laughed raucously. "You didn't tell me the Baron was a comedian, Bello." He sobered and turned to the Baron. "Salvatore encourages neither war nor insurrection. The services of my army come high. With me, it's purely business."

"Just what the hell is it you do in the west—dance a *tarantella?*" scoffed the absurd Baron. "If that's not war or insurrection—what the hell is it?"

Tori stood up and kicked back his chair. "You should have indicated this was a social visit, Bello. I would have worn my mourning suit!" His features were cold and implacable.

"Excellency! Salvatore!" Bello, the mediator, tried to soothe both men. "For the sake of the Party, let's not get emotional!" He moved swiftly to Salvatore's side. He picked the chair off the floor and set back into place. "Let's talk this over like responsible men, not hysterical women." He implored them.

"Fifteen million is too much! *Two* million," spat the Baron, beginning the negotiations. He picked up Bello's Marsala and sipped it gingerly.

"I'll order you some wine, Excellency," said Bello disdainfully.

"No, no, no. I only wanted a sip. I have wine cellars full of it. Why should I pay someone to serve me inferior wine?" He wiped his thin lips with his grubby fingertips. "Eh," he said insufferably. "This is *la Morte de Garibaldi?* For *this* wine it is said that Garibaldi fell in love with Sicily?" He made a few disparaging grunts and groans.

Salvatore seated himself again. He lit a cigarette and stared into the flame of the match before fanning it out. He leaned back in his chair, shoved it against the wall, and propped his boots on an empty chair, making no effort to haggle. In the uncomfortable silence, Bello squirmed uncomfortably.

"Five million. Not a cent more." The Baron's moustache twitched. "Listen, brigand, why don't you kidnap some of the wealthy nobles in your province, hold them for ransom, then you'll have money to fight *your* war."

"Uh—*your* war," corrected Tori.

Sickened by the Baron's Shylock tactics, Bello intervened. "He wants fifteen million lire. Without that sum he'll not give us the services of *two thousand men!*" Bello gave Salvatore the business with his eyes.

So, thought the penurious Baron making a mental calculation, *he does have two thousand men—some of whom I saw with my own eyes!* He scratched his head through his thinning hair and smoothed the strands back into place with one hand as he hastily totaled a few sums in a small black book with the other.

"Porca Miseria! That's a little under a million lire for each man!" he shouted in gross outrage and disaffection.

"Correction, please," said Salvatore coolly. "That's fourteen million for me, and the balance to be divided among my men." He challenged them both contemptuously. By now he had had enough of this perfidious and odious man. He rose to his feet, signalled his men. Instantly they converged, flanking him on all sides. Tori flipped his cigarette expertly into a nearby spittoon, bowed curtly to Captain

Bello and stated flatly, "If for nothing else, our talk is terminated."

Salvatore was in the courtyard, one foot in the stirrup.

"Now, see what you've done!" cried Bello. "There goes your revolution!" Bello was furious. Exasperated, he threw his hands up and let them fall heavily to his sides. "Without him, you've got nothing!"

Baron Mattinata, sensing his *faux pas,* jumped to his feet excitedly and ran like a mother hen scurrying after her baby chicks. "Hey!" he called. "Hey you!" He reached Salvatore and fairly pulled him off his stallion. "All right. All right! You win!" He reached into his pockets and removed the required sum in large bank notes, flashed them before Tori's cool and impassive dark eyes. His hand gripped Tori's arm as if to drag him back inside.

Disengaging the Baron's hand from his arm, Tori's voice purred with menace. "I wouldn't do that, Baron. My men get touchy when they see another man's hand on me."

Baron Mattinata dropped his hands to his side as if he had touched fire. He glanced quickly at Salvatore's paladins, who with drawn guns had him covered. Their deadly faces expressed their earnestness.

Inside Tori gave Bello a triumphant look, as the whimpering noble bellyached. "You must think I'm a fountain of gold. All you have to do is pump my arm and gold coins spew forth from my mouth," he lamented. "They'll kill me for spending so much money. You'd better give us value for our money, brigand, or it'll be curtains for me!" He drew an invisible line across his throat from ear to ear, then pulled his pockets inside out in a gesture of poverty.

In that instant, Salvatore's loathing for the Baron increased tenfold, for he was suddenly reminded of Don Pippinu Grasso. He picked up the money, folded it, and stuffed it into his jacket pocket with a nonchalance that unnerved the Baron.

"Aren't you going to count it?"

Salvatore grinned wickedly. "If its not all there, I'll know where to find you." His voice was loaded with inneundo.

"But," insisted the Baron. "I need a receipt—for my records. . . ."

Salvatore bowed curtly to Bello. *"Capitano,* I suggest you instruct this—uh—" He feigned inability to decide what to call the baron. "This—uh—landowner," he said finally with a flourish of hand movements and abstract facial grimaces. "Perhaps this . . . *landowner* should be

487

schooled in the rules of war. Partisans never sign receipts! Nor do collaborators or instigators, for at best they are all garbage collectors, desirous that no one discovers who among them stinks the most. . . ."

Bello and Mattinata, both inflamed with indignation, stiffened noticeably.

Smiling at their discomfort, Salvatore further instructed Bello to remain in Palermo for a few days where they could meet and together draft a plan of action in an effort to coordinate their activities.

"Va bene," replied a totally crestfallen Bello. Watching Salvatore take his leave, he thought things hadn't gone the way he intended. Why hadn't he been able to persuade Salvatore to return to his estate and command the entire Partitionist forces? Suddenly Bello felt put upon, with more responsibility and pressure than he'd bargained for. Perhaps after he returned to his estate things would look less grim, he told himself, Deflated, his heart wasn't in the project, for reasons inexplicable to him at the moment.

"Oh, yes, one more thing," called Salvatore from the doorway. "Be sure to get the hundred thousand set up while you're in Palermo. It will save us considerable time. . . ." He mock-saluted the red-faced Bello and left him to explain this to the astonished Baron Mattinata.

"One hundred thousand?" sputtered the Baron. "What the hell is he talking about Francesco? Certainly not—dollars!"

Salvatore heard their loud voices of protest outside the *pasticceria*. He laughed aloud and rode off with his paladins in pursuit, feeling smugly satisfied. This Mattinata was a frugal, thick-skinned sonofabitch who reeked of hatred for the peasants. He didn't give a damn if he antagonized him. They needed Tori more than Tori needed them in this damned business of insurrection. That sonofagun, *Colonnello* Modica, must have known all along there'd be a revolution. Oddly enough, Tori never really knew the extent of Colonel Modica's true duties with the OSS until much later.

Tori recollected all that Colonel Modica had told him with clear insight. *If only I had been ready then,* he told himself. But he never looked back. There was plenty of time to contact Colonel Modica, to insure America's aid, if he should decide it was time for revolution.

Managghia! Who would have thought that Alessandro Salvatore would become a revolutionist? Goddamn—it was some role to play in history, no?

He burst into a benevolent laughter as he indulgently reflected on the stunned expression on Baron Mattinata's face as he had left the *pasticceria*.

What were the words spoken by Colonel Modica that burned in Tori's heart?

"Every revolutionary begins his mission on the winged ideals of a utopian world. You, Salvatore have the advantage of standing on solid ground, without illusion."

Managghia! A revolutionary! The thought tickled his fancy.

CHAPTER 36

They rode swiftly through the countryside. At the entrance to his village Salvatore pulled hard on the reins and wheeled the rearing stallion about; he waved his men on through shouting, "We'll see each other later tonight!" To Vincenzo he called, "Come with me!"

Anxious as he was to arrive at his house on this the eve of Athena's wedding, Salvatore's confrontation with Captain Bello left him filled with disquiet and he felt the urge to talk. Together both horses and their riders scaled the rocky incline until they reached the Temple of Cats, and, nosing their panting steeds onto the stony ridge overlooking the villages, they sat in their saddles for a time, motionless, like statues outlined against a fiery sunset.

In the wake of intolerable heat, Salvatore stripped to the waist; his skin became the color of tawny copper in the amber light. Rocks and boulders turned a fiery bronze. Sand and pebbles became like crumpled topaz. Nothing moved in this blazing world of rock and sun and desolation except for the dark rider sitting a few feet from the Montegattan Prince. Vincenzo sighed inwardly when he caught sight of the brooding melancholy in Salvatore's profile and he turned and stared somberly at the vast silence in which nothing in nature moved. Not a bird, not a lizard or a cricket could be heard.

Recently Salvatore had saved Vincenzo's life by sending a large sum of money to America for the purchase of the new drug Aureomycin to relieve the tuberculosis infecting him. Vincenzo's loyalty had multiplied, and the two had

489

become inseparable. A few days later Salvatore and Vincenzo had each cut a finger with a sharp stiletto and when the blood had flowed freely they pressed their fingers together, they had become blood brothers, pledged to die for each other should the occasion arise. Salvatore had never questioned Vincenzo's loyalty, love or devotion, and it was only to his cousin that he could open up and talk freely with ease and genuine honesty, since both were fundamentally simple in their ways of life. Circumstances often forced Salvatore to employ subtleties, craftiness and cunning when dealing with men who understood only these affectations. Finished with the two Partitionists, Tori knew a burning need to ventilate his feelings with an honesty few men knew and understood.

Studying his cousin for a time, Vincenzo reached for his goatskin bottle and gulped a swig of the wine in a final salute of farewell to their adolescence, for he noted the youth of Salvatore had left him forever.

Tori, stunned by the intense heat, sat hunched over in his saddle, staring out at the vast lands he'd conquered and despaired. "Do you know what I'd give to walk the streets a free man? I'm tired of our thankless jobs. Tired of having to live by my wits. I'm even tired of riding Napoleono over this accursed land just to keep ten jumps ahead of the *carabinieri*. I want my freedom, cousin."

Vincenzo had heard the words before, but never colored with such desperation. "This *Capitano* Bello had much to say?"

"Yes."

"*Allora*—"

"Conditional amnesty if we join the Partitionists."

"To receive these gratuities—what must the army of Salvatore do?"

"Mobilize against the government forces. Drive them back to Italy—*carabinieri* and all. Then set up our own government."

"And if we choose not to side with the Partitionists?"

"We'll be where we've been for the past two years. Stagnant as we are at this moment. Until the Rome government is settled and peace terms are agreed upon, we can't move. Time is against us, cousin. Soon, more and more *carabinieri* will arrive to attempt to annihilate us."

"The Partitionists stand a chance of winning?"

"They will if I cause them to win. I control the West. Bello assures me he controls the East."

"How does the situation really stand?" He wanted to hear it straight.

490

"Bello is the biggest ass ever foaled." Tori suppressed a laugh.

"And you trust him?" he asked incredulously.

"I trust no one—save you, cousin." The golden scorpion around Tori's neck glittered in the amber twilight and caught Vincenzo's appreciative eye.

For a time they both puffed on their cigarettes in silence. Vincenzo, admiring the golden amulet, asked quietly, "What else do they ask? What more do they want from you?"

"Besides the blood of Salvatore? Hah! The usual pound of flesh; what else, cousin?" He related Bello's absurd proposal. "That peacock wanted me to unite with his volunteer contingents in Caltagirone."

"Leave Montegatta—the west?" Before Vincenzo could expound on the insanity of such a move, Tori crossed his right leg over the saddle horn and asserted their position. "If I learned anything from history, *caro mio*, it's never to depart from my own territory. Napoleon's journey to Russia, for instance, more recently, Hitler's troops in Stalingrad."

Vincenzo countered playfully, "The Great Alexander couldn't have conquered Persia, Egypt and half the world if he had remained in Macedonia—"

"I'm not Alexander, and this isn't 356 B.C." Tori interrupted savagely.

His cocaptain's smile dissolved instantly. "How long do we fight before we can secure our freedom?"

"Until the Partitionists emerge victorious."

"Listen, Tori, no matter what we do, we're still considered criminals by our government," moralized Vincenzo. "They don't recognize the good we've done."

"We were made criminals by the war—and don't you forget it!" Tori told him hotly. "We weighed the consequences of our action many times before we mobilized. We had no recourse. Now I grow weary. It goes too long. I tell you, cousin, I'll do anything to secure our amnesty."

"We saved our people from death and starvation—"

"—And the price on our heads grows larger. How tempting to spies and bounty hunters!" spat Tori bitterly. "No matter how we may justify all we've done, we're hunted by the law. The war in Europe is over. Our country is no longer at war. Technically there's no justification for what we do. We can't continue to violate the laws of our nation. We must look to our future for survival. Don't you see, cousin? To escape prosecution we must align ourselves as partisans to a victorious political party. America

491

promises aid to help us secure our separation from Italy because they fear a communist takeover. If this proves correct and we associate ourselves with the right party we shall be indemnified—exonerated from any and all crimes performed during the war—and with this comes our freedom."

"You're willing to fight for the Partitionists, knowing they will again reestablish the old grievances that led us into banditry from the first? Truly, cousin, if a Monarchy is reestablished, all hope for Sicily dies. . . ."

"You don't understand—do you? Don't you want your freedom? A chance to go on to bigger and better things? Well, I do! Even the men grow weary of the lives we lead. You know my dreams, Vincenzo. I won't repeat them again. Because the feudalists used the brains with which God endowed them to educate themselves, they know more than the peasants. They control Sicily and the government because they possess knowledge."

"It seems to me that a man with no education at all controls Sicily. Your Godfather!" observed Vincenzo.

Salvatore flushed with annoyance at the mention of the man who was his father. He said sternly, "We'll cooperate with the Partitionists! It's our only answer. . . ."

". . . And there'll be more killings! More destruction! And the price on our heads will soar!" Vincenzo had never been a yes-man. They disagreed often. When Salvatore committed himself to a cause he felt suspect to, he didn't hesitate to tell him.

"But look at the rewards when we emerge victorious. . . ."

"Rewards? Bah! Weigh the costs, cousin. Weigh the costs!" Vincenzo butted his cigarette against the sole of his boot and flicked the remains into a ravine. "You said, 'when we emerge victorious?' Tell me, what happens if the Partitionists lose?"

"Lose?" Salvatore laughed thinly. "You forget, I'm Salvatore! We can't lose!" He chose not to mention for the moment the enormous security payment he had shrewdly bargained for.

"I forget nothing! Nor do I forget *Zia* Antigone's words about the land barons who care only for the fulfillment of their own selfish gratifications. I'm outraged that you wish to aid these fat, overfed pigs of men, who with their diseased bowels and minds lust and eat prodigiously, then philosophize over lofty ideals and matters which cannot touch them!"

Surprised at the outburst, Salvatore turned in his saddle

and watched Vincenzo wipe the sweat off his brow as he continued the tirade.

". . . They converse with scholars and with priests, but are loathe to speak humanely with the peasants. Their bellies sag with fat and their feet, as puffed up as their bladders, can't navigate their bloated bodies. They don't relate to any of us. Not to you or me or to the real backbone of our nation—our people! Tori, if you give aid to these *porche cane*—our people will be truly lost. Is our freedom so important that we would annihilate the future of our people by aiding these indolent dogs in establishing a corrupt monarchy?"

"Listen, cousin," countered Tori. "In the new monarchy we'd have a voice—a position of respect. We could change things if they didn't go right." He caught sight of Vincenzo's grim disbelieving face and he sat forward, heavily in his saddle as if the weight of the world had been thrust upon him. "Vincenzo," he said quietly, "Tell me, if you can, how *our* deaths or *our* imprisonment would help Sicily?"

Vincenzo's gut constricted. Recalling everything he had suffered at *Terra Diavolo*, he knew he could never endure such confinement again as long as he lived. "*Va bene*, you made your point."

"With every breath I take," continued the brave eagle, "I want freedom. The war has ended. *Va bene*. Can we lay down our arms? Can we return to our homes and pick up where we once left off, like the soldiers do? No. The government will send their forces to shoot us up, or arrest us. I refuse to believe that destiny had this in mind for me when she whistled me up to help Sicily. Not after what we've been through. We've too much to offer Sicily to be shuttled off to jail and subordinate our lives to fancy needlework or hard labor in the sulphur mines or rock piles." Tori swatted his boots with the leather bindings around his knees listlessly.

"There must be something else for us."

"We must move forward—to the right side, to secure our amnesty. Become freemen? It's our only hope."

Vincenzo reflected. "I became a deserter in the army because I didn't believe in Mussolini, Hitler or the war! I became a bandit because of what happened to my family and to our people. It was my choice and I believed in what I did!" He moved about in his saddle and faced his cousin quizzically. "But, you—I don't understand! You don't believe in the Partitionists or their cause, yet you're willing to aid them! Do murder for them! Commit more illegal acts, just to *possibly* win amnesty for us? Tori—Tori, this self-imposed celibacy of yours makes you think like a crazy man."

Salvatore exasperated. How could he make him understand? And why he tried baffled him. *"Managghia!* It's time you all awaken to the skillful manipulations of politics. I've not been idle these past few years, and I tell you, these *illegal acts* as you call them, when performed under the protective umbrella as partisans of the government, are *not* considered *illegal!* Not by our government, or by the world, *Capeeshi?"*

In the ensuing silence, Vincenzo, vaguely confused and somewhat cynical asked, "Are you telling me we wouldn't be considered criminals after such an insurrection?"

"Bravo!" exclaimed Tori. *"Bravo!* At last you understand. Laws are subject to interpretation every time a case is tried in a courtroom. I tell you, cousin, no law is eternal—none absolute. *Sporcaccione* worked with the partisans in Trieste no? Ask him. All his former associates earned pardons after they killed Mussolini and a dozen or more top *fascisti.* Now the guerrilla forces from the north live as respectable citizens."

"Because they were on the right side?"

"Because they were on the winning side! The world belongs to the educated man. Men in the know pull the strings. Working around the letter of the law, they stretch it, shrink it, and reshape it to perform miracles for themselves. The peasant, ignorant of the law, conforms to enforceable laws. He pays his taxes, minds his own business, and abides by the law as best he can. And if he but spits on the sidewalk or walks where it's forbidden, he remains in a paralysis of fear of being found out and dealt with by the authorities. That's justice, Vincenzo? *Managghia,* haven't you seen enough inequities to make you wonder why the law works for some and not for others?" He struck the bridle reins against his thigh in nervous vexation. "By now you should know that justice will never benefit man from the podium of a peasant." He ground out his cigarette on the heel of his boot and flipped it into the ravine below them. "What difference does it make how we attain our freedom, as long as we accomplish our aims? The end will justify the means—"

"You risk holding a seven-headed serpent by the tail. . . ."

"I'd make a pact with Lucifer to gain our freedom," snapped the eagle.

Vincenzo inclined his head. "I'd be most cautious in these dealings. . . ."

"Va! Va!" exploded Tori. "You sound like my mother!"

"When has she been wrong?"

"I've already made my decision!" said Tori.

Vincenzo hid his dismay. "Then, what the hell are we talking about, eh? As usual your orders will be complied with."

"Don't concern yourself, cousin. I make no move until all parts of the pact are observed. I made certain demands on that eunuch Baron Mattinata—and he paid, didn't he? All fifteen million lire! I didn't tell you about the security I negotiated for, without which I don't make a move? One hundred thousand American dollars!"

Whatever uneasiness Vincenzo, the *treasurer*, felt, quickly dissolved at the mention of so staggering a sum of money. His dark jubilant eyes envisioned rewards far more opulent than just their freedom.

"I'm not sure Francesco Bello will fare as well," continued Salvatore. "He is some talker, he is. But, what a dreamer! Phew! Too many idealistic aspirations. Truly, I fear he'd not the man for the job! *Pero*—he's not our worry! Keep this in mind, Vincenzo, unless Bello's army in the East matches mine in the West, we don't join them! With or without America's support!"

"America's support?" Vincenzo's ears perked up. *"Allora,* what Santino told us, is true? America backs the Partitionists?"

"No, no, no, no," protested Tori. "They supported the Separatist movement under Canepa, before his treachery with the Reds was uncovered. Whether or not they back the Partitionists remains to be seen. There's more to this movement than meets the eye. Something I can't put my finger on at the moment. . . ."

"Ah," exclaimed Vincenzo. "That changes the picture. If the Americans support the movement we can't lose." He raised the goatskin into the air. "This calls for a drink!" He guzzled the wine and it spilled over his lips and onto his chin. He laughed aloud, pleased with the outcome.

About to correct his misconception, Salvatore chose to say nothing when he saw relief registered on his cousin's face. Dismayed he realized most men believed only what they wanted to believe, giving little credence to facts. It was disappointing to learn Vincenzo, was such a man.

"We couldn't ask for better insurance than to have America on our side," said Vincenzo, fully satisfied.

Fixing his dark eyes on his cousin's face, Salvatore saw no care or concern of weighty problems wearing him down, only an expression of jubilance, one intent upon his

495

own ridiculous pleasures. "Let's go," he called, slipping into his khaki shirt.

"What do you say we go back to Monreale?" suggested Vincenzo. "Arturo tells me there are two sisters—*very* special—who can melt troubles and transport us through soft, fleecy clouds until we make contact with heaven. Eh? What do you say, cousin?" His excitement was infectious.

"Managghia!" admonished the eagle. "Have you forgotten what night this is? You'll have to keep those *sisters* in the cooler and let them do their job on you another night. Tonight belongs to Santino! Tomorrow is the wedding, remember?" They wheeled their horses about.

Vincenzo tapped his forehead forgetfully. *"Botta de Sanguo!* All I'd have to do is forget this night and I'd be forever banished from entering the gates of heaven!" His good-natured laughter rang out clearly in the dusky twilight. "You know—it's time for *me* to think of marriage, I'm in my twenties. If I wait too long, I won't be able to satisfy a wife. They say a man loses his virility by the time he reaches thirty . . ."

Unable to contain his laughter, Tori shouted, "If you lived to be a thousand—you'd never lose your virility." They began the descent to their village.

Stripped, his body immersed in a wooden tub, hot water to his waist, Tori relaxed listening to the lively chatter and music coming from his house. The bathhouse, a newly installed addition to the Salvatore house, had become a welcome luxury which Tori used as often as possible. Later this night Tori would drive to Palermo to attend a bachelor party given for Santino Siragusa, and tomorrow was the wedding of Athena. He should be happy for her—but how could he, knowing what he knew?

The night Santino and Athena had arrived home to announce their betrothal, Tori had been totally surprised and somewhat annoyed. After Athena and his mother had retired to an upstairs bedroom to get the traditional view of her mother's wedding gown, Tori turned hotly to Santino, demanding to know why they both insisted on a quick wedding date.

"It's not for the reasons you might be entertaining," the former priest had said, flushing at the implication. Then, sadly, he had explained Dr. Colassamo's diagnosis, commenting further that Athena, overhearing the conversation, had been fully aware of her fate.

Tori had felt as if a sharp knife had cut through his heart, leaving a gaping wound of bleeding desolation.

496

Dumb disbelief and horror set in for a time when he'd realized the reality of Athena's death was at hand. Collecting his wits after his stomach had digested the hard lumps of sorrow churning erratically in his stomach, Tori had made Santino promise to withhold this information from Antigone. "Sainted Mother of God, she mustn't know. Another death in our family would kill Mamma."

With this locked in his heart, Tori had listened numbly as Santino related the urgent need for the EKG tests. He had arranged for them immediately through the U.S. Army doctors suggested by Colonel Modica. When the results of those tests and the doctor's words had labeled her case terminal, Tori had hardly been able to continue the forced bravado.

"I'll be forever grateful to you, Santino, if you allow Athena to bask in happiness in the days to come. I promise to reward you well for this special attention."

Santino, understanding the spirit in which Tori's words were spoken, replied simply, "I want no rewards, Tori. I already have mine in Athena. It is I who am grateful to Athena for the happiness she's brought to me. The joy of it all is that we both share the excitement of love."

The conversation had ended with Antigone none the wiser. Three full weeks had sped by without Athena suspecting that he knew. She seemed so radiant—so lovely, and as excited as a baby chick discovering a fresh worm. . . .

Tori's eyes were closed, his body fully relaxed as a euphoria came over him. He sensed it first, and felt someone's presence. Before he could move, someone bent over him, her golden-brown hair falling on his face as she placed her moist feverish lips over his. Tori's eyes snapped open, but he couldn't make her out—not at close range. His hands reached up to hold her soft shoulders, pushing her slightly away from him so he could make her out.

"Maria Angelica!" He sat up swiftly, his eyes darting to the door of the wooden frame house. "Are you crazy, coming in here? You'll be seen—and then what will your family say?" He flung her arms off his neck.

"I don't care! You won't come to me, so I must come to you. Haven't you missed me even a little bit, Tori?" she pouted, her red lips full and inviting. She picked up the soap and began to soap his back, neck and chest.

If Tori hadn't been concerned that at any moment someone might come crashing through the door, he might have enjoyed the moments more.

"What will Vincenzo say to all this?"

"A pox on Vincenzo," she said stubbornly. "It's you I want. I've always wanted you. *Managghia*, Tori! You know how I feel. You just want me to beg, don't you?" She paused and came around the tub to face him, her blouse slipping off her shoulder to reveal the high curves of her breasts—breasts he knew by heart. Her alluring green eyes, so vibrant and tempting, were hard to resist.

"So! It's me you want, is it?" he said savagely, in a voice that never failed to excite her. He reached for her and pulled her in close to him; their eyes met. They held their breath. Their lips parted and came closer, closer, until they met and clung together. Tori kissed her with pent-up passion as he rose from the tub in all his nakedness. He stepped out of the tub and clung to her, their bodies fused together as one. Maria Angelica had never seemed as passionate. Her breath came in gasps and he could feel her heartbeats as her breasts quivered against his bare chest. She reached down and held his manhood in her hands, filled with exquisite delight. She still had her magic—the magic that could turn him from a stone statue into a living, breathing, lusty man of unquenchable passion. She felt Tori sweep her up into his arms. Just as Maria Angelica reached up to curl her arms around his neck, she felt herself dropping.

Before she could catch herself she fell into the tub of water unceremoniously. She blubbered and sputtered in a mixture of astonishment. Each movement she made to get up only caused her to fall back in the slippery, sudsy water, where in moments she resembled a limp, drowning, rag doll. Over all this, Tori's good-natured laughter filled the air adding insult to injury. He wrapped himself in a towel, drying himself off. Quickly he slipped into a pair of trousers and blew her a kiss.

"Better not let your parents see you in such a state, *appassionata*," he said teasingly.

"Oh, you—you—you insufferable ass!" she sputtered and blubbered.

"There, that's more like my Maria Angelica," he said slipping out the door. "Remember, *cara*, not to let anyone see you like that."

"What will I do, Tori? What?" she wailed, finally on her feet, looking down at her soggy, spoiled clothing, crestfallen and full of remorse.

"You should have thought of that before you grew so brave. *Ciao, carissima! Ciao!*"

Maria Angelica picked up a soggy slipper and threw it

at him furiously. But, Tori had already left the bath house, his laughter echoing after him.

Tori was grateful that the heavy branches of the pomegranate tree, clustered with late blossoms, hung thickly between the narrow passageway leading to the bath house to conceal it from view. Now, if he could only slip into the house without being stared at by gawking females who overran the Salvatore house helping with the baking, cooking and decorating, he'd have it made. . . ."

She should have known it was Tori when audible gasps of delight escaped the lips of the women in the kitchen. Antigone glanced up at her son's exposed upper torso as he snaked his way through the tight kitchen. Some of the women kept their eyes averted; others more daring made no effort to turn from him. A few flirted outrageously with Tori until their mothers forcibly turned their faces away from him.

"Tori! Have you no shame? With these young virgins present?" reprimanded Antigone with a twinkle in her eyes. She watched him enter the kitchen and strut through the congestion of admiring women, sniffing the sweet and intoxicating aromas of the kitchen.

He nodded discreetly and passed on through to the next room, leaving many blushing young women with palpitating hearts beating wildly in their breasts.

Antigone hardly heard their expressions of ineffable delight as the older women gazed lustily after her son. Into her mind was etched a burning after-image of the golden scorpion amulet around Tori's neck.

She left the chattering women as they craftily appraised their daughters, wondering which one among them would be lucky enough to capture the heart of this gallant young prince, Salvatore. Musical refrains of Sicilian folk songs, played on mandolins, guitars, flutes and pipes, wafted through the house from where the men had gathered to drink wine and make music and toast the future bride and groom. Antigone nodded to them in passing and continued on her way to Tori's room.

She knocked first and entered. She began to pick up the towels and soiled clothing strewn about the room.

"What's that around your neck?" she asked.

"This?" Tori paused in his dressing and gazed at his reflection in the mirror over the chest of drawers. "A gift from the American Colonel Modica."

"What is it?"

"The sign of Scorpio. My birth sign."

Antigone tensed visibly, sucked in her breath and

grasped the bed post for support. *"The Double sting of the scorpion gives flight to the eagle."*

The *strega's* prophesy flashed before her eyes.

Tori knew his mother too well not to detect the alarmed concern in her comportment. No Sicilian woman would have left her kitchen and the opportunity to reign as queen during a *festa* unless something was amiss.

"What's wrong, Mamma?" He continued to dress.

"What sign was *Colonnello* Modica born under?"

"I didn't ask. Why?"

"How did he come to know yours?"

"Perhaps the newspapers. Why?"

"Nothing." She studied her son in a breathless silence. "It's nothing. Did you see Maria Angelica, Tori? Did you recognize her? She's turned into some beauty—no?"

Tori smiled. "I recognized her. *Managghia,* she's grown up."

"She has eyes for you, that one. Isn't it time you think of settling down." She talked only to get her mind off the scorpion amulet.

Tori smiled and removed a white envelope from the bureau drawer. "You know I can't consider marriage in these times. I need no further troubles. Here, give this to Athena. Her wedding present. Enough to buy her house. You give it to her. I don't want to make a big thing of it in the presence of the others. It's not necessary that any one know, Mamma, outside the family. And here is five thousand dollars for you to keep—"

"Tori! Where did you come by all this money?" Her eyes widened in speculation.

Tori laughed at her wide eyed astonishment. "It's all right, Mamma. It's my salary. The rest goes into the treasury to pay the men's wages. We received the first installment by the Partitionists."

Antigone sank to the bed, dejected, "You joined them? You finally joined with them? Despite our talk—you formed an alliance?"

Ordinarily he might have taken time to explain. Today he was firm, his word, final.

"Yes. I joined with them. I'm tired. We're all tired. The war's over and my men want to quit. But can we? Daily the government strengthens its military forces. How much longer before they send some eager military police to end my career by riddling my body full of bullets? The price on my head grows more tempting. How much longer before someone in our village becomes enticed by the rewards?"

500

Antigone, defeated, still offered contest. "Is it the only way? Must you join with these fatuous monarchists? Are they the only ones who can help you?" She knew the answer, and trembled at the outcome of this unholy alliance.

"No one else has come forward to make a better offer."

Antigone sighed heavily. Her eyes clung to the golden scorpion around his neck. "In America is it the custom to make a gift in the sign of one's birth?" she asked *sotto voce*. "Where is the Eye of God amulet?"

"It's right here." He picked it up off the bureau top, on his watch chain, where he kept it. He had made a duplicate of the one he had placed over Napoleono's bridle regalia and kept it on a key chain, ever since his mother had learned he hadn't honored her request to wear it and evidenced undue concern over his actions.

Athena burst into the room, breathless, filled with an inner radiance, and did a *pirouette* or two in her shimmering satin wedding gown with its serpentine train wound about her arm to keep it off the floor.

"You like it, brother dear?"

Tori was stunned. For several moments he stared at her beauty, as lumps formed in his throat, too thick to swallow. "Like it?" He swept her up into his arms, kissed her and held her dearly. "Like it? You're the most exquisite beauty in all the universe, *cara mia*." He gazed at her flushed, rosy cheeks and tears welled up in his eyes. The love between them was immense.

"Now don't you start, Tori, or we'll all cry."

"Where is it written that a brother can't shed tears of joy for his sister's happiness?" Then, he remembered— more than he wanted to remember—and reached quickly for a clean handkerchief. There would be no future for her. He coughed to disguise the sorrow in his breast. Athena watched him somberly.

Antigone handed her daughter the envelope containing the money. "It's your wedding gift from your brother."

"Why so much, Tori?" asked Athena. "A thousand dollars buys the house. Here, you take the rest of it. You might need it for something important."

"Nothing is as important as you and Mamma. Keep it. I never need money. Everything that comes into the treasury goes to Vincenzo, who pays everyone off. We draw salaries. What do I need, outside of food, clothing and ammunition for my gun? I give Mamma most of what I earn. Isn't it enough? You need more? I'll requisition it. After all I am the leader. Perhaps I should have more, eh? You know what I'd like? A gold watch like the one *Colonnello*

501

Modica wore—one that tells the day, month and the hour," he said wistfully.

"Then, buy it!" retorted Athena sharply. She glanced uneasily at her mother. "Buy anything you want! Don't deprive yourself of anything! Look at the risks you take!"

He slapped cologne onto his face and neck, glancing from his mother's concerned face to Athena's smoldering dark eyes, and knew he had to ask.

"*Allora*—what's troubling you? Both of you. . . ."

"It's nothing," murmured Antigone. I'll get you some coffee." She rose to leave.

"Mamma! Come back," called Athena. "He has a right to know. . . ."

"It can wait until after the wedding, *cara mia*."

"No. We've never had secrets. Tell him, now."

"Tell me what? What's the mystery?" demanded Tori.

"I'll go to my room and get it. Don't say anything until I return," said Athena.

In her absence, Antigone sat quiet and reflective. Tori walked to her and said gently, "Come, Mamma, this isn't like you to keep secrets from me." Then remembering the one secret she had, indeed, withheld from him until recently, he flushed, removed a tie from a rack, placed it under his shirt collar, and began to tie it.

"How much do you trust Vincenzo?" she asked quietly.

"We're blood brothers!" He confronted her, startled by the question.

"That wasn't my question. How far do you trust him?"

"With my life."

"Perhaps, my son, you should guard your life more carefully."

Tori was thunderstruck. "What are you saying? I've never known you to talk such foolishness. He's like a brother—another son to you. You'd question a man who'd die for me?" He tied and untied the necktie as if he'd sprouted ten fingers on each hand, and finally abandoned the attempt. He reached for a cigarette, placed it tremblingly to his lips, and lit it with shaking hands. He fanned out the match and flung it into a nearby ashtray.

"Don't be angry with Mamma," said Athena standing in the doorway, in a dressing gown. "How much do you pay Vincenzo?"

"He gets what I get. We're equal in everything. What's going on?"

"I said, don't be angry with Mamma, Tori. She defended him as you've done—until this came." She handed him a letter. While he read it, Athena continued. "You've

502

been so good to him. Cared for him so tenderly. Oh, Tori! He's *my* cousin, too. Even I found it hard to believe. But read for yourself."

Tori studied the letter and official documents. There was a Deed of Trust for 100 acres of land near Tucson, Arizona in Vincenzo's name, plus a contract for land in Mexico.

"Mamma's second cousin in New York sent us the document to make sure he'd receive it. Where would Vincenzo get fifteen thousand dollars in less than six months? Did you ever take time to examine the books of the treasury?"

"You realize what you're saying?" began Tori, stunned. "What you are accusing him of doing?"

"Ask him," said Athena coolly. "If he's done nothing wrong, we forget it."

"You risked having it rain on your wedding day by telling me this?"

"Rain is incidental, Tori. Hurricanes can prove devastating. I'd not forgive myself if I didn't warn you. A man who robs a brother is a man who'll bargain for his head."

"Preposterous!" Tori exploded. "Vincenzo will explain this. You'll both regret your words. I'll not listen to any more slander."

"For your sake and his, I *hope* we have reason to regret our thoughts and words," countered Athena.

"Athena! Alessandro!" pleaded Antigone. "Stop this at once." She turned to Athena. "On this, the eve of your wedding day and what should be the happiest moment in your life, don't let spoken words between you be the cause for future regrets."

"Why not, Mamma? It's plain to see your son has judged us the wrongdoers. He's shown his colors. He believed Vincenzo before he believes his mother and sister."

"Vincenzo doesn't stab you in the back without giving you chance for an adequate defense."

"When have *we* given cause for backstabbing? What suspicion have *we* brought upon ourselves?" Athena had never shown this side of her nature, and her mother, stupefied, pleaded for an armistice between them.

She turned to her son. "Make your peace, now, Tori."

"Why should I apologize?" he countered stubbornly. "It's you two who owe an apology to Vincenzo."

"If that's the way you feel, your lordship," said Athena bitingly as she thrust the envelope containing the money at him. "Take this, which you so generously gave me as a wedding gift. I needn't tell you what you can do with it! Hire an accountant. Let him tell you where your money

503

goes!" Her dark eyes ablaze with tears, Athena ran from the room.

"Tori! Athena!" Antigone was unsure of whom she should attempt to soothe first. Turning to her son, she said, "In twenty years there's never been a harsh word between you and your sister. Why tonight? Whatever anger you feel towards me could have been directed in another way—another time. Did you have to bring this down on our shoulders tonight of all times?"

"You blame this on *me?* It wasn't I who began this conversation!" Baffled and outraged, Tori grabbed his suit jacket, stuffed the letter and deed of trust into his pocket and ran out the door cursing, *"Camoria!"*

"Yes! Yes, I took the money to buy property! Someone has to think realistically about our future. I did it for both of us!" shouted Vincenzo defensively.

Tori had encountered his cousin at his house, and he stood over him now, a figure of menace. One hand gripped Vincenzo's lapels, the other formed a fist dangerously close to his face.

"Who has a better right to the money than you and I? We both risk the most! If you'd pull your head from out the clouds you'd know we can't stay here forever. One, day, for certain, we'll both face exile."

Tori relaxed his hold. "Whore of the devil! Don't you see what you've done? How will it look to the world if they learn the treasurer of Salvatore has embezzled money to buy foreign land? Who will believe your story—that I knew nothing of it? Our esteem will nose-dive to zero! I ought to let you taste the bite of my bullets and end my shame! It isn't the first time I've heard such rumors! Is it necessary to scheme and plot against me?"

"I put the property in my name so one would connect you. I was careful to make sure no one discovered my tracks."

"Mighty careful!" snorted Tori. "That's why Mamma and Athena learned of it!" He released his grip on the other, disgust apparent on his face.

Vincenzo paled. *"They* know? But—how?"

Tori explained.

"Managghia! What did they say?"

"Allora, what do you think they said, eh? You should be boiled in oil! That's what they said!"

"They said that?" Vincenzo flushed, squirmed uncomfortably and adjusted his necktie.

"You still don't understand, do you? The recklessness of

a moment has annulled the merit of a lifetime. This one selfish act, this thoughtlessness, can erase all the good we've done. I've tried not to appear as mercenaries to the world, so that on that day of reckoning our acts can be justified as acts of war. *Managghia!* This is our home—our land—our country. Sicily has been raped long enough by outsiders. What would be left if her own people ravaged her? I want Sicily to survive. I want us to survive!"

"That's why you joined the Partitionists—so she won't be raped again? Hah!" spat Vincenzo taking courage. "I've done nothing less than what your feudalists have been doing for centuries—and you take umbrage with me?"

"Why don't you ever listen to what I tell you? Do you hear only what you want to hear?" Tori, afflicted with a sudden sadness, threw his hands up into the air in disgust and motioned him into the jeep. The doors slammed shut and they drove to Palermo in silence.

Three times now, Father Grassini had been instructed to delay the wedding an hour. A power failure, nothing new in Montegatta, had taken place and Antigone had brought out the candles. Tori and Vincenzo hadn't arrived for the nuptials. There was tenseness, a desperate silence in the air. In the flickering candlelight, Athena looked spectacularly beautiful. Even her eyes swollen and red-rimmed from the tears shed over the spat with her brother, couldn't mar the beauty. She had told her bridegroom, nothing of the misunderstanding. When neither Tori or his cousin had appeared, Santino had begun to fear the worst. They could have been intercepted someplace, captured and jailed. He paced the bedroom floor in his tuxedo waiting for some word that the ceremony would commence. It wasn't like Tori to be late—certainly not for his own sister's wedding! In the past few weeks, the widespread rumors that all the *carabinieri's* efforts were to be trebled if necessary to capture the bandits had disturbed him, as had the abnormal quantity of spies sent by the security police to infiltrate their encampments. He had mentioned it to Salvatore last evening at the bachelor party, but his chief wouldn't listen to talk of business at such a festive time. "These are not thoughts a bridegroom should entertain," he had told his historian. Santino had smiled, said a silent prayer, and deferred further comment.

Four o'clock came and went. The priest in attendance grew impatient. Twice the lights had come on, and Athena could stall no longer. Reluctantly she consented to commence with the ceremony.

Finally the priest began the litany. Musicians struck up the stirring music Tori had written especially for the ceremony. Fluttery bridesmaids took their places in the floral decorated room that hung heavy with orange blossoms. A moment before the vows were spoken, Tori stepped forward out of the shadows to officiate as best man. Tears of exquisite joy splashed down Athena's cheeks as she hung desperately to Tori's arm. Antigone blew her nose and brushed the tears from her eyes. Santino relaxed considerably, breathing in relief.

Immediately following the ceremony, Athena rushed achingly into her brother's arms and kissed him amid a torrent of tears. "Oh, Tori! Tori!" she cried passionately. "Mamma and I have been miserable! We must never quarrel again. There are only three of us left!"

In a touching family reunion, Mother, son and daughter avowed their closeness with tears of joy. Several moments later, when he could break away from the happy circle of well-wishers and wedding celebrants, Salvatore pulled Vincenzo into the pantry and, in a quick movement, he pulled back his arm and connected with a swift uppercut to Vincenzo's jaw that sent him reeling. Just as quickly he reached for and steadied the astonished Vincenzo, who cried out defensively through painfilled jaws.

"Why the fuck did you do that?" he rubbed his jaw gingerly and glowered sullenly at his cousin. "Pig of the Devil!"

"Just to stay in practice—should you persist in making more stupid blunders!" Tori grinned, held on to him and brushed him off lightly.

Tori had to admit, watching her from a short distance as she swished about in her blue taffeta bridesmaid's dress, that two years had worked wonders on Maria Angelica. She was lovelier than he had remembered, he thought with a peculiar nostalgia. She had pointedly avoided talking with him. He could see the anger in her from the dousing he'd given her the day before. Finally, as the wedding feast commenced with friends, relatives and well wishers dancing to waltzes, mazurkas, and *tarantellas* in the gaily decorated garden that was magically transformed into a floral paradise with cut flowers and a profusion of potted plants rented for the occasion, Tori moved to the edge of the terrace, gazing out at the panoramic view of the verdant Castellammare Valley spread out below like a magnificent painting, feeling more alone than ever before.

"I should be very angry with you, Tori," she said softly.

He glanced over her head, searching for Vincenzo. She'd been the object of his attention all afternoon. He'd no intention of causing any strife between them.

"I must apologize for yesterday," he began with a sheepish expression on his face. "At the time it seemed the only remedy for an impossible situation."

Maria Angelica lowered her lashes demurely.

"You've grown up these past two years."

"Then, you *did* notice," she whispered breathlessly, her eyes darkened to the color of shamrocks as they reflected the colored lights hung festively overhead. "Since you've become famous, I hardly see you. I read about you all the time."

"Don't believe all you read," he said easily.

"There are so many stories," she said plucking the petals from the rose she carried. She did her best to flirt outrageously with Tori, but the benevolent look he gave her discouraged her. "Were they all your lovers, Tori? Have there really been so many women in your life? The balladeers sing of nothing else." Her gaiety was forced for the moment.

"I said, don't believe all you read."

"Then, why not me, Tori?" she said anxiously. "If you court so many others, why not me? Didn't we have something special? Am I so hard to take?"

Tori glanced about anxiously, hoping she wasn't overheard. Many eyes were upon them, including those of her parents and those of other, envious women with whom he hadn't had the time to exchange amenities.

Maria Angelica caught Tori's arm, she looked into his eyes imploringly. "Just say the word, I'll be yours again. If you don't let me back into your life, Tori, there's no telling what I'll do!" Her voice bordered hysteria.

Color rose to his cheeks. He took her hand firmly in his and removed it from his arm. "You don't know what you're saying," he said sternly. "There can be no woman in my life—not until I've finished with this role destiny has chosen for me. I told you before." Tori knew, as he'd known in the past, there was no way for him to be friends with this young vixen. She expected total and unconditional commitment from him, something he was unable to do even if he wished. He was grateful when Vincenzo glanced in their direction and hailed them. "Ah, here's Vincenzo. It's best you respond to *his* affection, *cara mia*," he said softly.

Dismayed, Maria Angelica lowered her eyes so he

wouldn't see the hot stinging tears threatening to erupt from them or the hurt buried in their depths.

"Maria Angelica! Come!" called Vincenzo. "The musicians will play a fancy *tarantella* and we shall dance for them." Clapping his hands in tempo, he came at her dancing an exuberant, shuffling cakewalk.

With a forced air of bravado and a fraudulent expression of gaiety, the girl tossed back her head, blinked away the rising tears, and joined him.

Tori laughed congenially as musicians struck up a cord and the wildly emotional dancing began. He watched them for a time, then, feeling a sudden emptiness he went inside the house and walked about aimlessly thinking as he did, about jade-green eyes and copper-colored hair and a skin of white velvet.

"Appolladora, Appolladora," he sighed heavily.

That night, the aroma of sweet roses and garden scents of orange and pomegranate blossoms wafted into the modest bedroom of the newlyweds. A romantic medley of music played by five serenading musicians, especially for them provided a portion of the inspiring setting. It was difficult for him to see her fully. Athena's black hair was invisible in the darkness. Even the pale shaft of moonlight filtering through the partially open shutters prevented him from making her out in the dark. But he was certain that on her face was a glow of satisfaction lit by the fires in his heart.

Perhaps if she'd been plain, dowdy, and possessed with the temperament of a shrew, he might have been able to handle it. But she was none of these. In addition to her remarkable goddess-like beauty, there was within her the tenderness of a wood nymph, the innate sweetness and goodness that one imagines in the nature of an angel. Santino shuddered inwardly. He never wanted to sleep again. There wasn't enough time for them, and he was jealous of every moment he couldn't spend with her.

"You see what you missed these past two years?" she whispered shamelessly. "You should have married me sooner, beloved."

"*Mi amore,* I'm not the wise man you think I am. Else I should have carried you off, long before this." He tried to generate some gaiety, but each word constricted his throat. He reached for her and held her tenderly in his arms next to his emotionally charged body.

The newlyweds had coupled as if they'd been born to it, without shame, without embarrassment, without the awkwardness of a first union. He'd been gentle with her, and marveled at the depth of her passion—and at his own.

For a time they lay back on the pillows of the nuptial bed, feeling the close intimacy of their bodies. Her dark eyes showed carefully deliberate thought going on somewhere within her. For a time she'd been silent, her face expressionless, then, she began to express her views.

"Promise me, Santino, you'll not think of our tomorrows—that we'll only live moment by moment. It's the only way I'll be able to cope—understand?"

"Yes, my love. I understand," he replied in a display of ardent devotion. He buried his face in her breasts.

"We must both face reality, *caro mio*." She said it easily, but he noticed a catch in her voice in this show of bravado. "There is no tomorrow for me, and today is half gone. So, we must make something very special of what's left for us."

Santino turned his face from her, unable to swallow the thickness in his throat. He sat up in bed, swung his legs over the side, and reached for a cigarette on the night stand, his back to her. Athena sprang to her knees, her soft satiny arms entwined about his neck, her feverish body pressed close to his. She lay her moist face on his shoulder. He couldn't take this kind of talk.

"I talk too much," she whispered.

"Yes, *cara mia*." He inhaled the smoke and blew it out through his nose and found himself shaking involuntarily. How could he face a life without a future for her? Was he an iron man? No. He was merely a man with normal frailties who had waited so long to find such happiness.

"Please understand. It's all so new for me. For me it's like opening enormous doors and peering into a labyrinth of darkness. Each moment I live is like taking a step into the unknown, never knowing when another door will open, admitting me to a land of strangers. For me it holds a strange fascination. I forget another person might not view it as I do," she whispered.

"I'm supposed to give *you* courage, *Carissima*. Not the other way around."

The bitterness in his voice alerted her. "If you prefer I don't talk of death—" she paused. "I was always taught to speak in truths—"

"Death is so permanent. Only until I get used to it. You understand? It's new for me, too. I mean in this instance. I feel so helpless, knowing I can do nothing. Not even prayers can assuage God's decision." He stopped. "Athena, this

509

is madness. We are talking about death—as if it were an everyday occurence."

"It is, my silly *chu-chu*. It is." She moved around him and snuggled into his arms. He set aside the cigarette and held her tightly, cradling her in his strong arms.

He tried desperately to push from his mind everything except for this moment. He didn't have to wait long for God to mercifully allow his emotions to take hold and obliterate all thought except for the touch, taste and feel of his bride.

Oh, God, what ecstasy! What a glorious, wonderful feeling of wholeness! Together they were the embodiment of a very special love, one so unique that it transcended wordly affectations. *Just for today*, he told himself, over and over again. *Just for today*.

Later, when they snuggled close, just before the early predawn hours when the eastern sky pulsated with light, Santino glanced down at her still, relaxed face and brushed the long, silky strands of hair from her face. He whispered, "My beloved, I feel the need to be deluded. I'm not as strong as you. When the truth is ugly and unbearable, only a lie can be beautiful and endurable. I must believe our love's eternal, and will be lived to its fullest."

"Yes," she said sleepily. "Our love is eternal. . . . To its fullest. . . ."

CHAPTER 37

Twelve horsemen, crouched low in their saddles and covered by full rain capes pulled tightly about their necks, galloped swiftly through the rain-soaked countryside, glancing cautiously about them in the steady downpour. Not from fear of ambush, but out of inborn and well practiced caution did they appear to falter.

The storm was rising.

The moon, at intervals, burst forth from behind vagrant ambuscades of snorting black clouds flung into other ambuscades, and for fleeting instances reflected the tight, hard expressions of Salvatore's men, and, leaving their faces, plunged them once again into the thick of darkness. Rain lashed their faces and the bodies of the horses, increasing their exhaustive pace. Every heart quickened. Hands felt for the security of their guns.

Suddenly the rocks and stone walls blazed with light. The wet, dark air was torn asunder by gunshots. Terrified horses reared and plunged their forelegs into the air, striking at each other with their hooves. Another blaze! Another crash of gunfire! Explosions! Confusion burst all around them. It didn't take but a moment for Arturo Scoletti and *Sporcaccione* to realize they'd been betrayed! They had been expected! The *carabinieri* lay in ambush for them a mile the other side of the barracks.

Whizzing, whistling bullets screamed and tore at them. Shouts and screams of the horses pierced the night air. Cries of both the ambushed and the ambushers intermingled, and in the black of night it was difficult to see one's enemies. In the mad exchange of bullets and gun fire, Salvatore's men, the more expert of the two forces at ambush, retreated to the pass, encircled the prematurely jubilant *carabinieri* and within moments the military police, all fifty of them, were trapped. On each side of the slippery, slick, stone-walled pass, Salvatore's men enclosed them, preventing their escape. The *carabinieri* could neither advance nor retreat. They were stuck in the small confine, unable to wheel their horses about. A few fell off their excited steeds and rolled in the mud.

Some of the more prideful officers opened fire with automatic rifles, only to be cut in two by a swifter discharge of missiles from submachine guns.

"Dismount!" ordered *Sporcaccione*, with pent-up anger, his face drenched with rain.

"Take their horses!" commanded Arturo Scoletti.

Reluctantly, the *carabinieri* dismounted and, upon orders to remove their rain gear, they grumbled loudly and glowered at their assailants, but kept their curses under their breath. The brothers Nuliano and Genovese relieved them of all weapons and outer garments and shoved them forward into a line.

"Bastards! Stupid, ignorant, incompetent imbeciles!" snorted Fidelio Genovese to Santino Siragusa. "They could have wrecked the entire operation. Good thing Tori chose the alternate plan!" He was striving to control himself. "That man intrigues with Satan! How could he have known? How could Tori have known of such a betrayal?" He yelled to the captives, "Move! Goddammit to hell, Move!" He pushed the horseless riders on ahead with a smart slap on their shoulders.

511

Two *carabinieri*, having fallen unseen behind a boulder, poised their automatic rifles and opened fire at the mass of indistinguishable activity several yards ahead of them. Instantly the darkness came alive as blasts of scarlet light burst forth from all directions, ripping the night apart. A hot searing sensation tore into Dominic Lamantia's shoulder and upper arm. He spun about and fired with his submachine guns. Red-haired Pietro Gagliolo felt his right leg buckle as he hit the muddy ground and, rolling onto his side, he hurled a grenade towards the *carabinieri*, struck them full force and killed over a dozen men.

Those *carabinieri* who remained alive were frozen to immobility, unable to move or flinch a muscle. They fell silent, certain their enemies had eyes which penetrated the darkness like animals.

"Bastards!" shouted Uccidato, running to his brother's aid. He aimed his gun at the frozen men and squeezed the trigger. Another ten men dropped to their knees and fell sackily into the muddied ground.

"No!" *Sporcaccione* shouted. "Salvatore said to let them live!" To the *carabinieri* he yelled, "Now, get going, or every last mother's son will be cut to ribbons! Go! Move!"

Scrambling for the open road, the pitiful military police slipped and fell and picked themselves up from the rutty, rain-filled trenches, stumbling upon each other in their mad effort to depart. None entertained thoughts of becoming heroes.

Rain and wind whipped furiously at Salvatore's men as they doggedly herded the skittish cavalry of horses and headed them back towards their encampment. In one of the active areas at the far end of the draw, eight dead *carabinieri* were strapped on to three saddle horses. Once secured, *Sporcaccione* slapped their flanks and headed the horses in the direction of the weary, trudging officers who had a long way to go before they reached their barracks.

Santino Siragusa checked Lamantia's wounds and inspected those scratches sustained by Pietro. He instructed two of the men to tend them. He swung to his saddle, accompanied by Arturo and Miguel Scoletti, who only recently returned from a short rest, where he regained some sense of normalcy. The trio followed the three horses laden with the dead men until they caught up with the surly-faced *carabinieri* trudging valiantly through the torrential rains. Keeping out of sight, yet in full view of the lead officers, the three outlaws watched as the officers ordered their men to take the dead men off the horses.

"Throw their bodies into the ravine! The dead have no need of horses," ordered their Captain.

Three officers mounted the barebacked, overburdened horses and moved forward over the corkscrewed roads towards the basin of civilization in the distance. The rest of the company made their way on foot, sloshing knee-deep in mud through countless water pools forming in the steady down pour.

The violent storm had erupted in all its madness. Lightning darted across the black sky illuminating the dark, foreboding mountains. Horses spooking, rearing and sliding in the mud, whinnied in protest, spilling their passengers down the craggy slopes and puddled roads. Then bolting suddenly, they galloped with hell-bent fury into the wet darkness.

Watching the scene, Santino Siragusa and the Scoletti brothers laughed grimly; satisfied they headed back to their encampment. Riding swiftly and expertly through the raging elements, all three paladins were occupied with their own thoughts. Santino wondered who had betrayed them at Castellammare. Arturo wondered at the wisdom Tori had exercised in permitting their enemies to live and later when the men aired their feelings over this leniency, Miguel Scoletti, the most candid, spoke out bitterly.

"It's a shame Tori learns nothing. One day it will mark his downfall. The very men Tori forgives and permits to go free will one day betray him. Mark my words." His words, prophetic as they were, were ill received by his own brother, who reprimanded him sternly.

"Are you crazy to say such things?"

"Pray you're wrong," interupted Santino.

Miguel, who hadn't fully recuperated from the slight mental breakdown he'd had after killing the girl who had betrayed Vincenzo, mulled sullenly over their words, and within six days, along the coastal road along the Gulf of Castellammare, six *carabinieri* were dragged from their saddles with a lasso and hacked to death with a knife. To mark his handiwork, Miguel, according to a story perpetuated by his companions, cut the letter S—the initial letter of Tori's surname—on the forehead of each with a dagger. Once again Tori banished him from the others.

By December more than three thousand men had been recruited in General Salvatore's Western Partitionist army. Due to his shrewd strategy and the clever alliances formed with several other bandit leaders, nearly every *carabinieri* barracks west of Palermo had been wiped out. The bandits, Barone in the South and Valeriani in the south-central sector of Sicily, in synchronization with Salvatore's plan of attack, consumated victory after victory until the illustrious Montegattan and his army uncontestedly controlled the entire West.

General Salvatore grew gravely concerned that Captain Bello's Eastern Army boasted no such conquests. Further, he needed no lectures on what might be transpiring at the estate of the flamboyant Captain. And when the second payment due him for services and supplies didn't reach him, he grew concerned. Nothing tangible had arrived from Bello except for a few sketchy, unsubstantiated reports that the Eastern Army continued to swell to phenomenal proportions.

At Caltagirone, Captain Bello's hopes had unrealistically accelerated into thoughts of commanding an army far superior to Salvatore's in the West, and when he saw thousands of impressionable recruits arriving daily at the estate, his spirits had soared beyond the realm of reality.

Unfortunately, the best among them, far worse than Tori's most inexperienced lackey, ridiculous were as soldiers. Not only couldn't they shoot firearms properly, they felt less the inclination to do so. Having lived quiet, respectable lives in the past several months, this gentlemen's army grew indolent and uncooperative. Supplies grew short. They refused to comply with Captain Bello's orders to raid the wealthy landowners' estates to augment their supplies. Moreover, they felt above confiscating supplies and weapons in the name of the revolution.

The men balked. They argued they'd been misguided at the outset and, fearing the consequences and later reprisals if they continued to commit crimes which might not set well with government authorities after the insurrection, they began to manufacture countless alibis for not participating in the revolt.

Wealthy landowners who had conceived the insurrection now paid lip service to the cause and couldn't be induced to part with the vital funds needed to finance the war. In mulling over the shrewd bargaining Salvatore had demonstrated with Baron Mattinata, he realized his lack of wisdom in not having read into that scene a silent warning, a portention of the niggardly ways of the multimillionaire landowners who wanted their rebellion and victories without having to pay for them.

As food supplies diminished and his men, fearing stiff jail sentences for their part in the planned revolution defected, Bello became confused and disoriented. If Captain Bello had become aware of the growing number of defectors, he gave no visible outward show of this apparent sapping of strength and loss of morale in his camp, and he gave less importance to the fact that he was held up for ridicule by his men for believing he could outclass Salvatore's army.

It was such a climate of disintegrating morale and conspiratorial discontent that General Salvatore and Colonel de Montana arrived and remained for a time camped at the outer perimeter of the Captain's Bello's lands, engaged in clandestine observations of the comings and goings of the Eastern Partitionist Army.

The Montegattans studied the immediate area with discontent. They watched the forlorn and pathetic recruits engage in senseless military drill for hours on end.

"Tori!" called Vincenzo. "Come. See this. Follow me."

In a stony-faced silence, Salvatore guided Napoleono behind Vincenzo's mare until they reached a clearing in the woods. For an instant, his face lit up when he took notice of a stout armored tank parked boldly where it was bound to produce awe from any impressionable passerby. His hopes swelled until he dismounted and examined the imposing vehicle. The motor was missing! Firing pins from the turret guns, absent, made them inoperable. What the hell was going on? Nothing worked. The tank served no functional purpose.

A montage of curious animated glances, exchanged in silent speculation ensued between them as the two young warriors moved silently through the area. Strutting about in his colonel's uniform, Vincenzo drew the general's attention to a few suspect areas in the thick shrubbery, which at first glance appeared to be fortresses housing heavy artillery. Closer inspection found them to be a sham. In moments they uncovered wooden cannon painted to look like the real thing.

"Is this to be believed?" asked Vincenzo.

Their first impulse was to explode in laughter. They did, until their sides ached—and until Tori, brooding and filled with contemptuous scorn, sobered, his jaws set like concrete and his dark eyes smoldered angrily. *"Amonini*—let's go. It's time we come down off the hills to take a closer look at Bello's farcical encampment."

The moment his eyes caught sight of the temporary barracks and surrounding buildings wrapped with barbed wire, Tori knew the story immediately

"Bello's men are deserting," he said grimly, seething at the fiasco. "What the hell's he trying to do—win a war with a bag of tricks?"

515

"The man's out of his head—*pazzu*—crazy."

From where they sat on their horses, in a thicket, overlooking the entrance gates to the estate, from the side of the hill, they noticed a flurry of activity as a dust laden limousine of pre-war vintage geared down through the narrow road, stopping at the gate. Two guards gave them an exaggerated salute and waved them on through the small building to the right of the compound.

Through binoculars, Salvatore saw Captain Bello emerge from the building and approach the sedan, buttoning his tunic. With the aid of the nattily dressed Bello, the enormous figure of the Duke de Gioia emerged from the back seat of the car, followed by the *Principessa* Gabriella Rothschild. Not since Appolladora had Tori been as affected by a woman. Wearing breeches, boots, and a leather jacket in monochromatic beige tones to match her golden beige hair, coiled sleekly at the nape of her neck, she accompanied the Duke on his rounds. Salvatore's heart quickened with excitement. A soft, audible gasp escaped his lips, loud enough for Vincenzo to have heard it. Training his glasses on the other's point of interest, he made his observations known.

"*Managghia! Che bedda!* What a beauty—no?" Vincenzo exclaimed aloud.

"Perhaps it's time we pay our compartriots a visit, eh, Vincenzo?"

"*Amonini!* We're there!" shouted Vincenzo, glad to see his cousin aroused.

By the time they traversed the thicket, to reach the entrance to the encampment, the Duke and Gabriella had departed for Bello's villa, accompanied by escorts in a jeep.

Captain Bello's attention was trained on the flurry of dust kicked up as the two riders descended the hills. The stark white stallion and his rider stood out like a blinding sunspot against the dark forested hills and his breath quickened in recognition. Salvatore! There could be none other like him. His spirits shot up. He waved excitedly to reinforce his own courage. Hardly able to contain his excitement, Captain Bello greeted them both with gracious and genuine pleasure, and in so doing, momentarily disarmed both hostile visitors by subjecting them to excessive hugging and back slapping and a whiff of his alcoholic breath.

"What a pleasure!" repeated the bombastic Bello over and again. "So you're Colonel de Montana—eh? What a honor to see you here; a mission long overdue, my dear

General. "Come, let me look at you. What a sight for sore eyes! Come, my valiant comrades. Let me show you what wonders have transpired here at Campobello."

The westerners, revolted by the exaggerated display of false affection and alcoholic excesses, grew introverted. Tori lost what little respect he had entertained for Bello as they walked about the military complex, listening with polite interest as Bello explained.

What a shame you didn't advise me in advance of your visit. Hundreds of men, out on maneuvers in the nearby hills training zealously, will be disappointed they didn't meet with the great Salvatore," he lied with conviction. "They'll return in several days. You'll stay of course?" he asked with mounting nervousness. "Less than a hundred men are in the complex today—not even enough to honor you militarily in a dress parade, *caro mio*. An honor you truly deserve. Perhaps next time we'll arrange such a parade in your honor." Bello rambled incoherently for the most part. "New recruits by the thousands arrive daily." It was the same broken record played endlessly.

Salvatore observed with inscrutable eyes the changes in Bello; thinner, with dark circles under both eyes, he had a marked air of dissipation since their initial encounter six months before; it was too startling not to compel attention. For a time he listened as the demented man raved.

For a torturous hour the foolish display continued until finally it was capped by the most ludicrous display to which Tori had ever been subjected.

Their attention was directed to a group of four men leading two blindfolded men through the compound. One of Bello's men shouted loudly to his companions. "Pietro—tell the driver to place all artillery in the storage unit provided for them to the west of the stables. Instruct the men to ready the tanks and prepare them for the dress parade tomorrow. How many did you say arrived today?"

The man named Pietro cupped his hands around his mouth and shouted, "Fifteen tanks, six cannon, and more arms and ammunition than was used by the Nazis! You betcha my life!" It was easy to tell he'd had exposure to the U.S. Army.

Animated, and full of vitality, they appeared to be acting out some monstrous joke on the unsuspecting, blindfolded victims.

"Where are the tanks?" called the first man, playing the silly game.

Pietro shouted. "What the hell's wrong with you? Are

517

you blind? Over there on the side of the hill, you blind son of a ground hog's whore!"

"Ah—I see. I see." retorted the other. "There were so many shining in the sun, I couldn't see at first. *Managghia!* What *magnifico* machines. Phew! A thousand dollars one of these cost—eh?"

"Are you crazy? *More* than a thousand dollars! You betcha my life."

So convincing were Bello's men that his two guests turned in the direction indicated, eager to see such a show of strength. They saw nothing! Thinking he might have missed seeing something with the naked eye, Vincenzo employed his binoculars, to survey the area.

Recalling the incident of the motorless tank and wooden cannon, Tori cynical and contemptuous, turned to his host and muttered angrily. "Bello, I only pray what's happening is not what I'm thinking—"

"Isn't it brilliant?" grinned Bello with idiotic delight. "They are *carabinieri* spies caught nosing around our compound. My men, instructed to keep them blindfolded, will hint continuously of the redoubtable show of military strength we have in our possession. They'll be released later to return to their leaders consumed with false reports. They won't dare attack us if they think we are in possession of such power."

Salvatore heard it, but, he didn't believe it. A strained silence fell upon the trio. Giving each other the business with their eyes, the two Montegattans could hardly believe that this well-educated man, who by his own words had just labeled himself a jackass, was really the long eared fool he appeared.

Mistaking their silence for an inability to see through his clever strategy, Bello hastened to explain. "Don't you see? When the government forces receive reports from their spies—assuming of course, that we're far superior to them and better armed, they'll think twice before provoking an attack."

Salvatore wanted to shake the Captain into sensibility. He wanted to shout, "Stupid imbecile! It can work the other way! The government forces can gear their attack to accommodate this falsely reported strength. With reinforcements, they'll return to annihilate you and your poor excuse for an army." But he said nothing.

They walked, he and Vincenzo, to their horses, and mounted in haste, anxious to depart from this insanity before they exploded at this last incredible sham.

"Stay to dinner, at least," begged Captain Bello,

wounded at their lack of cordiality. "The Duke de Gioia arrived moments before you. It would pay you to know him better, General."

"Sorry—give the Duke my regrets. We're expected in Catania."

Tori didn't have the heart to confound the man by asking the poor fool when he expected this "army" to rise to the standards of his army in the west. Bello wasn't the same man he'd met six months ago, and Tori feared the worst.

"Either he deludes himself or his mind has snapped. Whatever—he's engaged in a game of mental masturbation concerning the revolution," he told Vincenzo candidly later, as they warmed themselves before an open fire in a cozy tavern near the village of Caltagirone, while the proprietor prepared dinner for them in the next room.

"What do we do about this comedy, now?" asked Vincenzo smelling perfume in the air. He tried to locate its source; some woman.

"Obviously the Partitionist cause is a lost one. It's good we came. Else we'd still be waiting for him to capture the east." Tori mulled over his Godfather's slick strategy. *Sonofagun!* He must have forseen in advance what might transpire at Bello's hand. No wonder he hadn't endorsed their plan!

"If we brought our men here, we'd be in control, no?" suggested his Colonel, eyeing a dark-eyed woman across the room in the dimly-lit tavern, with open seduction.

"It's over," reflected Tori, somberly. "We go home and wait until the Eastern front collapses. I'll not be a party to a useless revolt.

"Where did I get the idea you wanted to meet that tasty dish back at Bello's estate?" asked Vincenzo, all the while exchanging meaningful glances with the girl opposite him.

"I do."

"When?"

"Tonight."

"Why didn't you accept the dinner invitation?"

"And sit through a boring evening until the others fall asleep?" For a time Tori watched the interplay of seduction between these two. He smiled to himself. Vincenzo had lost all interest in Tori. Having given full endorsement to the girl's suggestive and silent promises, he strode valiantly across the room without thoughts or concern of an irate father, a jealous husband, or a vindictive brother.

The night was without light. A slim crescent moon hid

temporarily behind drifting clouds. Tori tugged up on the fur-collared jacket of his uniform and stood up in the stirrups to gaze upon the Moorish-influenced villa of Francesco Bello. Having already located the apartment occupied by Gabriella Rothschild and established that both Bello and the Duke had retired for the night, he guided Napoleono closer to the dimly-lit balcony where he had seen her pacing before the open window.

He dismounted, tied the stallion to a nearby tree and crept cautiously towards the strains of soft music emanating from her apartment. Inhaling the sweet scent of orange blossoms wafting to his nostrils from the nearby orchards, Tori paused to gather a few sprays of the blossoming *pyrus japonica* that hung over the garden wall next to the fountain in the courtyard.

His heart quickened when he saw a shaft of light from between the partial opening of damask draperies and casement silks fluffing and billowing in the wind. He moved in closer, sure and lightfooted, his fingers grasped an edge of the hanging silk and he drew them apart, his dilated, glittering eyes, anticipating, fixed themselves upon the pale blonde woman. He gasped, unable to take his eyes from the statuesque beauty.

Having just emerged from her bath moments before, Gabriella had slipped a sheer black peignoir over her nude body and sat now before a gilded Italian provincial dressing table over which hung an ornately framed mirror. Gazing narcissistically at her reflection for a time, she commenced to brush her long, pale gold hair and let it fall softly about her shoulders, a tangle of gold and platinum threads. She appraised her reflection and paused momentarily to critically search for tell tale laugh or frown lines, which she proceeded to smooth out as if in so doing she could stop the aging process.

Whatever else Gabriella Rothschild had been, she'd never been frightened of men—except those dressed in the German SS uniforms, and members of the Gestapo. Very little else intimidated her, and when she caught sight of the unnatural movement reflected in her mirror, she knew instinctively that someone was watching her. Her first thoughts credited the wind with the movement; but as the feeling of being observed persisted, she calmly lay aside the gold enameled hairbrush, picked up a perfume atomizer from the dressing table, stood up, and began to spray her hair and body with the alluring scent of musk.

She conducted a small scene in which she admired her reflection, stepped back away from the mirror, and allowed her hands to sensuously caress her body until she had backed away sufficiently and paused in close proximity with the French windows. In a sudden, swift movement she reached up, pulled back the drapes, and came face to face with the grinning manliness of the unabashed Salvatore, who bowed and extended the makeshift bouquet.

"Well!" she asked icily. "What have we here—a *voyeur?* Wouldn't the view be better from inside?" she snapped sarcastically ignorning the outstretched hand and flowers. Inwardly she trembled with excitement at the beauty of the man.

Tori bowed majestically and, with bold *panache,* strutted into the room, glanced about in appreciation and moved towards the inner bedroom door, where he nonchalantly turned a golden swan-shaped door handle. It was locked. Noting that there were no other obvious exits or entrances, he made his way back to her and set the flowers on her dressing table.

"You're right. The view is better from inside." Indolently he allowed his hand to caress the silken coverlet on the oversized bed. He glanced suggestively through tilted eyes at the cool and distant woman who observed his every move. Their eyes met in instant recognition of the animal magnetism that lay between them, a compelling force from which there was no escape. But the enormous ego in each of them, became a cumbersome obstacle for either of them to surrmount.

"I am Salvatore, my lady," he said with a flourish.

"I see. And just who is Salvatore?" she asked imperiously, covering her nervousness, for she had recognized him instantly. Brushing past him, before he could respond, she resumed her position at the dressing table and continued her earlier ritual with all the poise she could muster, hoping her heaving heart would quiet down. "There'll be the devil to pay if your master discovers you trespassing on the privacy of his guest." She spoke in a harsh German accented Italian, condescending as a noble might to a serf.

Tori, neither contemptuous or amused, sniffed the musk-filled air and made an appreciative sound in his throat. In this moment he spotted an enormous diamond solitaire on her finger, glittering brightly in the reflection of light from her dressing table. Such a gem would pay for a portion of the expenses incurred in this ridiculous insurrection, he told himself.

"It seems an unlikely story, Duchess—that you've not heard of Salvatore." Fascinated by the brilliant diamond, his eyes locked on it. "I'm astonished by your lack of sophistication on current events."

"Presumptuous is what you are, *Signore*. I am neither the Duchess de Gioia or *Signorina* de Gioia. With your permission, I am *Principessa* Gabriella Rothschild."

"*Principessa?* A real princess—a blueblood?" he mocked playfully as he picked up a spray of the *japonica* and twirled it about the air. "Really?" His eyes assessed her appealing nudity beneath the sheer negligee. Desire flooded his body. "Imagine that." He sniffed the fragrance with animated eyes.

"Yes. Really!" she snapped curtly. She flushed under his close scrutiny. She went through the illogical motions of drawing her sheer peignoir closer about her body. Nudity had never bothered her before, but at this moment she couldn't account for the terrible embarrassment she endured under his lust-filled, probing eyes. "I'll summon the guards unless you tell me what this is all about."

"I doubt you'll do that, *Principessa*. This is only a friendly visit."

"Friendly! Hah! What a comedy. Like a common thief you enter my boudoir to delude me into thinking this is a friendly visit!" Her green eyes narrowed when she caught him openly admiring the diamond solitaire. She withdrew her hand and grew uneasy.

Tori bowed politely. "With your permission, I ask the questions." He picked up the discarded hairbrush and studied the name engraved on the handle. "Gabriella eh?" He tilted his head at her, smiled, then asked with seemingly puritanical candor, "Are you de Gioia's mistress?"

She flushed hotly at the brutally frank question. "You insufferable Sicilians! You'd think you never heard the word, *fornicate!*" She tossed her head defiantly. "And if I am his mistress—what concern is it of yours?"

"What a shame!" He clucked his tongue woefully. "What a waste! The thought of wasting someone like you on that bloated behemoth makes my stomach turn."

Gabriella's pale skin, a creamy porcelain, turned a fiery pink in the soft lighting. "Look Salvatore—or whatever your name is—Let me persuade you, only a fool would attempt anything dishonorable towards me . . . I am betrothed to the Duke!"

"Dishonor you?" He chuckled disdainfully in a manner that infuriated her. "*Principessa*—you flatter yourself!" He stared into her blueish-green eyes, fired greener by increased anger. Then, Tori threw his head back in genuine amusement as laughter crashed through his throat—laughter filled with sardonic contempt. "That fat old goat! He'd be dead before he reached the marriage bed!" he goaded.

Her icy eyes narrowed at the obvious insult and continued ridicule. "I didn't know you were related to him," she began, armed to the teeth with insults. "You see that's what he calls you. The adjectives are changed from old to stupid and murderous, but its clear you're both considered goats!" she smiled with revolting sweetness.

Salvatore reached for his Browning automatic and his smile disintegrated.

Gabriella's contemptuous eyes fell to the gun in his hand and she goaded him. "Ah! To dispose of me, the brave *bandito* needs his gun?"

"Once again, madam, you flatter yourself. My motive in addressing you is simply to relieve you of the diamond solitaire. I've grown exceedingly fond of it in the past few minutes."

"My ring!" Gabriella glanced covetously at her diamond. "You wouldn't dare!"

"Wouldn't I?" He moved in close to her as she whirled about trying to escape him. He held her firmly in his arms as she struggled against him.

"Not my diamond!" she screamed hoarsely. "Anything but that! Anything!"

An insecurity of long standing reached out and engulfed her. Her only passport to freedom, away from the Duke, were the costly baubles she'd managed to set aside, and the thought of losing one of the keys to her freedom shook her violently.

"Anything?" he taunted her. Slowly he released his grip on her. The struggle subsided.

"Yes! Yes!" she grew insistent. "Anything!" She slipped out of her frothy negligee and, standing naked in the softly lit shadowy room, she appeared to be offering herself to him sacrificially.

Never in his entire life had his desire for a woman dissipated into nothing so quickly. Angry that she'd allow herself to be sold to him, he turned from her in disgust and paced before her. First to the left, then to the right, he surveyed her like a critical and shrewd buyer of cattle.

"Let me see the ring!" he ordered gruffly.

Fully confident, she removed the solitaire and handed it to him. For all his gentlemanly qualities and the reputation earned for his extreme politeness to women of nobility or otherwise, Salvatore felt a sudden, inexplicable desire to humilate and castigate her beyond all reason. He strutted before her, a proud young cock, holding the diamond from him at various angles, appraisingly. He cast alternate looks at her, taking considerable time to deliberate his choice. Gabriella's confidence began to melt. She felt like livestock at auction, as she watched him testily through humiliated eyes. He slipped the ring on his little finger, glanced at the diamond from different angles, then announced with finality. "I choose the ring. The diamond by far is more precious."

Gabriella lunged at him, swinging her arms wildly as Tori caught her by the waist. She became a tangle of intertwining arms and legs, kicking, scratching, punching, trying to get back at him for the embarrassment and humiliation to which he had so artfully subjected her. She fought to keep the tears in check.

"You son of a bitch! Fucking bastard!" she screamed. "You won't get away with this!" Her accent grew thicker.

"A real high-bred princess, eh?" laughed Tori, loosening his grip on her.

"Mother-fucking son of a whore!" she screamed. "Incestuous bastard!"

He turned on her fiercely, slapped her without restraint and sent her reeling across the bed. His dark eyes flashed with menace and he uttered a low cry. "Don't ever say such things about my mother! Filthy cunt!" he snarled, burning with violent rage.

Stunned by the forceful blow, her face smarted. Tears watered her eyes. She wasn't sure her teeth were intact or that her jaw wasn't broken. She felt numb from her neck up. Having found his Achilles heel, she wouldn't let up.

"Oedipus! Son of a fucking whore! Whore!" she yelled hoarsely, cowering on the bed like a wounded tigress. Suddenly she sprang at him, sank her teeth into his neck like a weasel at the throat of a wolf. Tori flung her from him angrily.

When she saw his facial muscles contort and recognized the tremendous effort he employed to keep from striking her again, Gabriella grew instantly repentant at goading him. As they stalked each other like animals, she felt an inner tremble heave through her body. Her facial expression changed from one of anger, as blood rushed achingly through her veins, to a look of pure lust, and her stomach fluttered curiously in a manner she hadn't experienced in many years. His ruthless savagery revolted her, but simultaneously excited the primal instinct in her.

For all his anger at the bitch, Tori wasn't brutal by nature, and the scene became a distortion to him. His gentle, well modulated nature, always under control, had become unruly. Moreover he was angry at the spoiled piece of baggage for provoking him into losing control. Watching Gabriella he saw the transition on her face. He remained wary of her; the dilated pupils of his eyes shone like animal's, savage and inhuman.

It was an awkward moment. They stared at each other in silence, unsure of what to say. Suddenly, Salvatore's manhood sprang to life, stirred by this strange and perverse feline before him, who appeared to have enjoyed being struck. Before he could examine his response to her, Gabriella, a woman who knew men, sprang across the bed, held on to his waist and whimpered apologetically.

"Forgive me, please," she begged with tears spilling down her cheeks. "When you're frightened of life you say and do crazy things." She looked craftily at the diamond on his little finger and wrap herself about his body.

Despite himself, he gathered her in his arms and kissed her. Pain rose unbearably in his loins and he shuddered as Gabriella's expert hands searched his body. Again they kissed, and suddenly Gabriella heard the chimes of Venus. She felt the explosion of Eros, as his well-aimed arrow pierced her body. She shivered involuntarily, pushed him away from her and searched his smoldering eyes.

"A real blueblood?" he whispered Huskily. "Don't you know that blue blood is infinitely more enriched when mixed with red blood?"

Lost in each other they let the tentacles of erotica suck them both into sexual ecstasy; Tori was achingly aware of the need buried deep in his loins. For the first time, since Appolladora, Tori didn't think about her while satisfying his biological needs. It marked his return to the present, no longer shackled by the past and the memory of Appolladora.

Time and again the lustfilled couple soared to the heights of exquisite orgasm, and by the time the predawn lights had appeared on the horizon, Gabriella was packed and ready to ride to wherever in the world Salvatore was headed.

"At last I've found a real man!" she cried triumphantly. "I'll never let you go!"

"You want to give up all you have for—just me?" He was mildly amused.

"I have nothing, and leave less—to go with someone extra special."

"I have no time for a mistress, Gabriella," he said soberly. "I could never love you."

She winced. "Does that matter? I shall have you. When I call you'll come to me. You'll see. It's better than what I have. At least I'm *alive,* now."

"At least write His Excellency a note. Tell him you're with me."

"It's best we leave without telling him. I'm not sure what he'll do to you when he finds out...."

"The Duke?" Salvatore laughed heartily. "What can that pig of a whale do to Salvatore?" He pondered a moment. "To leave you here would be like placing spring in the lap of winter. Not fair to you."

She smiled and flushed at the compliment.

Pen in hand, he sat at the ornate *escritoire* and wrote the Duke a note. "Excellency—Do not be concerned with the safety and well-being of the *Princepessa.* She is with me safe and sound," He signed it with a flourish, "Salvatore ..."

He put her up in a modest apartment in Palermo, left her some money to purchase a few necessities with, and promised to return as soon as possible. They embraced in the company of Vincenzo de Montana, whose shocked appraisal of the newly developed situation generated more respect in him for his cousin than ever before.

"Managghia!" he exclaimed when Gabriella waved from the balcony. "Wait 'til the others learn what a cocksman you really are!"

"It's best they learn nothing of this—understand?" warned Tori.

Vincenzo shrugged, but on his face was a broad grin. En route to Montegatta, they stopped off at the radio shack and found Santino Siragusa, the new bridegroom, seated with earphones on his head, deciphering meaningful words out of a jumble of sounds coming over the radio, with a flush of pleasurable excitement scrawled on his face. Finished writing, a look of amazement in his eyes, he glanced up to address his leader,

"The Duke wants to know—how much?"

Salvatore stared quizzically. "How much? Which Duke?"

"The ransom! The ransom ... what else? De Gioia— Duke de Gioia."

"What ransom?" In an instant, Tori burst into a paroxysm of laughter. He slapped Vincenzo's shoulders, embraced the bewildered Santino, and all three spun about the room like small children. Only Salvatore understood the reason for his sudden elation. He stopped abruptly,

read the message aloud, unable to contain his amusement over the developments.

"Name your price. Make certain the Princess isn't harmed." It was signed, the Duke de Gioia.

About to light a cigarette, Vincenzo's hand, holding a burning match halted mid-way to his lips, his lips fell open in astonishment, the cigarette fell to the floor and he hurriedly fanned out the match. "The Duke—he thinks you—"

Tori interrupted him, waving a hand in a gesture of silence.

"So he thinks I've kidnapped her, eh?" Tori paced the confines of the radio shack, which in addition to the short-wave equipment contained crude wooden chairs and a desk. "I think I've found a way for the Partitionists to pay us the money due us for this insurrection *fiasco*," he exclaimed mischieviously. He addressed himself to Santino. "Send this message to His Excellency. Simply say, Fifty million lire sent by messenger to the Shrine of Santa Rosalia at Monte Pellegrino by December 14 at four in the afternoon."

"Fifty million? That's a lot of money. Will he pay such a sum?" asked Santino scribbling away on a tablet. He glanced skeptically at Vincenzo.

"Don't worry, *padre*. Your brother-in-law knows what he's doing." Vincenzo laughed gleefully in admiration for his cousin's cleverness and urged Santino to continue with the message. "It should compensate us for the foolishness to which Bello subjected us," he added ruefully.

"What foolishness?" inquired Santino, pausing briefly.

They told Santino the whole story of their encounter in Caltagirone and what had happened later. Santino, obviously troubled, set aside his tablet, and ran his fingers through his hair nervously before addressing Tori.

"If Bello is defeated in the East—where does that leave us? You're a general in the Partitionist Army, we are officers of lesser rank. Are we to be executed by the government—hanged as revolutionaries?" He eyed Vincenzo, recollecting how earnestly the captain had demanded to be shot if ever they were caught escaping *Terra Diavolo*. Vincenzo, like many others, had vowed never to spend time in prison again.

"Are you worried, Santino?" asked Tori gently.

The former priest sighed. "We're tired of playing soldiers. There've been too many attempts at betrayals of late. It would grieve us all if anything should happen to you."

527

"Don't concern yourself," Tori reassured him. "I am not without wits or plans. Even if the Partitionists melt into nothing in the heat of political expediency, another party will rise to need Salvatore's strength."

Tori accepted a light from the lighter in Vincenzo's outstretched hand and listened as he interposed his disappointment over America's seeming reluctance to come to the aid of the Partitionists.

"I tried to tell you not to take stock in such promises. But who can blame her? Her apathy came about due to the self-serving, quarrelsome nature of those Italian politicans. They wanted too much, refused to bend, and produced several gray hairs on the heads of the officials. Even a fairy Godmother grows disenchanted with a bellicose stepchild," said Tori.

"If we only had access to information at a higher level—through someone like *Colonnello* Modica," began Santino. "Speaking of Americans." he paused to search the pockets of his leather jacket. "Some international press correspondent has requested an interview with you. I have it here someplace, already cleared with the Minister's office in Rome."

"Another one?" Tori shook his head in amusement.

"This one's American. Name of O'Hoolihan or something."

"When?"

"Whenever you say."

"Make it next week sometime—Friday . ."

"I'll notify him." said Santino. "Oh yes, one more thing. The men have left their reports on the plans effected by your officers. Barone left the Western Division and returned to his territory for a rest. When you need him, he says to whistle him up."

Tori laughed good-naturedly.

The sacred Shrine of Santa Rosalia was staked out in advance of December 14. The Scoletti brothers met with the Duke's courier, handed him a letter as soon as he had turned over the required moneybag. The courier, a frightened little man, took courage and protested vehemently at such goings on.

"I am to deliver the *Principessa*—not a letter!" insisted the scarecrow courier. "I dare not return empty-handed."

"You dare call a message from Salvatore, *empty-handed*? Go!" ordered Arturo Scoletti, scowling. "Give the Duke this letter and await instructions."

The scarecrow jumped into his Fiat and, traveling swiftly, he reached the Duke's estate, delivered the letter and retreated hastily.

The Duke de Gioia laboriously paced the study. For the fifth time, now, he read Gabriella's letter and engaged in the histrionics of a broken-hearted suitor. "*Carissino* Federico," began the letter. "Be the first to wish me happiness. I've found the one love to which every woman is born. All I need in a man—love, patience, attention, adoration, wit, intelligence, and bravery—I have found in your magnificent ally, Salvatore! Truly, he is a prince among men. My very dearest friend, thank you for the generous wedding gift. How sweet of you to be so kind." It was signed, "Affectionately, Gabriella."

"The shame! The humiliation of it all!" screamed the spoiled, immature nobleman, flinging the letter from him. It fell to the floor, where he stomped and trampled it with his feet. Difficult as it was to move his gouted foot, he managed a small ceremonial rite. He spat at it, raised his fist and shook it menacingly in the air about him. His face contorted venomously and, in his highly emotional state, he began to hyperventilate. He clutched at his breast, pounding furiously upon it until the tantrum subsided. Following the cessation of his uncontrolled rantings and ravings, he shouted aloud, "I'll kill him! I swear I'll kill him!"

He broke down and sobbed. "Gabriella, my Gabriella, I loved you so much. You left me and everything in the world for a lowly peasant, a sheepherder's son!" With the provoked petulance of a spoiled, spurned suitor he shrieked, screamed and picked up several art objects, flinging them about the room at random where they fell crashing in hopeless ruins. The elaborate music box that had so enchanted Gabriella came within his grasp. He picked it up savagely. A moment before he flung it from him, he paused to assess its worth through a monocle that hung suspended around his neck. He thought better of it and carefully replaced it. He vented his spleen on a newspaper, which he tore to shreds, then he flung the bits and pieces about him. He succumbed to his superficial desire to be maudlin and whimpered, aloud, "Why to me? *Why?*" He poured himself a goblet of wine, knowing it would only increase his pain, and drank it, masochistically. "All this could have been yours. How much longer do I have—three—four—perhaps five years?" He sobbed loudly. "Couldn't you have permitted me the peace I needed? And you, Salvatore, master cocksman! I'll see to it you don't live to enjoy the erotic delights of my sorceress! If it takes my entire fortune, I'll see you burn in hell for what you've done to me!"

The enormous blob of a man continued to drink and to fill himself with delusions and perverse fantasies until he fell into a restless slumber, knowing full well he could not confide his ego-shattering heartache to anyone for fear of being held up to ridicule. But there burned deeply in him something more than fantasy—the desire for Salvatore's blood.

"What the hell is *that?*" cried Captain Francesco Bello at the loud groaning sounds coming from the earth itself. He awoke at the crack of dawn to a persistent inner trembling and looked outside the compound.

Five thousand Federal troops had descended on San Amauro Hill with full armor and artillery support, surrounded Captain Bello's encampment, and proceeded to bombard the Partitionists' stronghold.

Exactly as Tori had predicted, Bello's flimsy trick to deceive the spies had backfired. All that remained of Bello's deserting army to fight off the five thousand soldiers commanded by three top military generals, were less than fifty men. Last night alone more than half the compound had deserted and through the dark hours Francesco Bello cried like a baby. Now, fully excited, and braced with a bottle of brandy, Bello regained his bravado and determined to win this skirmish or die in the attempt. What could he do with this handful of stalwart defenders? Bello never stopped to weigh the odds against him. He seemed to have lost all sense of reason. Stupidity, spurred by a fantasy of unrealistic hope, nearly did him in. Or was it sheer insanity?

In a moment of sublime inspiration, that crazy Bello approached the Federal Army as he might have approached a personal gun fight. He wanted only to encounter this enemy and crush them, just to show that peasant Salvatore his superiority against such odds. This ludicrous, alcoholic-crazed madman, it seemed, cared for nothing else.

True to his ridiculous strategy and ludicrous principles of trickery and deceit, Bello manically persisted in the imbecilic farce and attempted to resist the imposing army commanded by three generals to know his enemy.

On the lower slopes of San Amauro Hill, Captain Bello set up five machine-gun nests and stationed the skeletal remains of his crew at strategic positions, each armed with ample supplies of ammunition.

At dawn on December 11, Francesco Bello opened fire on his enemies and continued until noon. By then, the Federal troops, forced to abandon their tanks in the wooded mountainous terrain, resorted to artillery fire, followed by a temperate cavalry charge. Bello's Partitionists made use of numerous irrigation ditches along the lower slopes of the mountains to continuously shift their machine guns in a scheme which served to convince three Italian Generals that Bello's strength was far greater than they originally believed. This false evaluation promoted a different strategy than what was first intended by the combine.

An infantry attack spurred forward against the Partitionist army caused them to beat a hasty retreat when a fusillade of machine-gun bullets whistled through the air around them. At that moment, Bello, flushed with various shades of victory, shouted, "More! More!" He tossed one man quickly aside, grasped the machine gun firmly in his hands, and began to shoot the thing around and around in an arc, aiming at nothing in particular.

"Bello looked like a man in the throes of sexual orgasm," one soldier was to report later. Hypnotized by such erratic behavior, his men stared, frozen, at his madman's expression: bulging black eyes, centered in a sea of milky white, popped from his head. No one dared to talk with him, or interfere in his activity, until gratefully the machine gun jammed as a result of the uninterrupted firing and overheated trigger mechanism.

On December 12 the trio of Federal generals renewed their offensive with mortar fire, followed by a cannonade from antitank guns placed into position the night before. Bello, like a toy soldier it seemed, played the game simply for the glory of shooting off ineffectual missiles. For two more days these grossly imbalanced forces held each other off. Captain Bello entertained some bird-brained idea that he could retard the attack of Federal troops while a special detail sneaked into enemy camp and made off with enough ammunition to replenish his rapidly diminishing supply. Failing to stimulate his men enough to effect such a brazen raid, he was forced to make do with enough ammunition to see him through another day or two.

Three days later, on December 15, Captain Bello, dressed in a spanking new, colorful royal blue uniform with dazzling brass buttons and braid, took his position on the lower slopes of the mountain, and enthusiastically fired two hand guns alternately until both guns jammed. Unwilling to be deterred, he ran to a machine-gun nest, took over the gun, and continued his random firing until all ammo was exhausted. Bello seemed determined to keep his men firing until all ammo had been expended, as if in some curious way the expenditure of ammunition would determine the victor.

Suddenly out of touch with reality, in his distorted and feverish mind he reasoned that he couldn't be defeated now, not by these five thousand men whom he'd held off for five days. He grew more fanatical. His glazed eyes popped from his head, swollen like the unnatural brilliance of a drug addict's eyes after a fix. He kept the defecting soldiers at their posts at gunpoint, where they all remained until a grenade knocked them out and ended the fiasco. Bello and five men were captured. The remaining men, perhaps forty or less of them, vanished into the hills.

Described in newspapers as a "desperate and bloody battle fought with the latest, most sophisticated weapons, exacted with brilliant military technique," the fiasco at San Amauro Hill proved highly embarrassing to the shame-filled Partitionists when it was learned that after five days of fighting with thousands upon thousands of shells expended from a wide range of pistols, firearms and heavy artillery, each side claimed a total of six casualties and one dead man. Oh, the shame of it all! What disgrace and dishonor had been brought upon the feudalists.

The capture and imprisonment of Captain Bello sent shock waves throughout the lands of the millionaire sponsors of the insurrection, who suddenly found themselves in the most awkward and untenable position of having conspired against the federal government. Sounds resembling pure, unadulterated fear echoed throughout elegant halls in the sumptuous villas of the Mafia-Feudalists. Speculating at their present status with the central Rome government as a result of the foiled revolt, these long-eared landbarons feverishly tried to remove the egg of defeat from their overfed jowls. They sequestered themselves behind heavily guarded doors fearful of every knock at their door.

Few, if any, gave thought to Salvatore's fate in the west; whether or not he survived or received the same treatment meted to Captain Bello. Secretly, however, in the mind of the Duke de Gioia, the notion grew that God in his wisdom would reduce Salvatore to nothing, if for nothing else than daring to conspire against the noble personage of the Duke.

Pen in hand, stimulated by fires of revenge, the obese Duke sat at his desk and scribbled a list of directives to Don Matteo Barbarossa. He explained the plight of the Partitionists in the east, made suggestions as to what might be done with Salvatore in the West in order for the former Monarchists to emerge unscathed and blameless in the recent foiled revolt. Enclosed with the message was a sizeable bank draft drawn on the Banco de Sicilia, "for expenses" incurred in this unfortunate mess. The Duke further intimated to the Don that other feudalists might be encouraged to part with a like sum, if Don Barbarossa in his "infinite and patient wisdom" could find means to absolve them of any and all blame. "Your efforts will not go unrewarded, my dear Matteo," He added for emphasis. "I shall leave the disposition of that insufferable outlaw to your special brand of justice."

CHAPTER 38

Santino Siragusa received the alarming news first. He lost no time in leaving the radio shack and, after galloping wildly through open country, he climbed the rocky incline and arrived at the Grotto D'Oro, where he sprang from his saddle and ran breathlessly towards Salvatore shouting,

"Government troops are coming to wipe out the army of Salvatore!"

He handed him the message. Tori glanced up from charts he'd been preparing, and scanned the contents. The others moved in closer.

"Not the Partitionist Army, eh?" he smirked. "It's the army of Salvatore they want. When?"

"Before the week ends."

"Terrific," said Tori dully. "How many?"

"Three thousand strong. Word came from our sources in Palermo."

"Only three thousand? Does the government consider Francisco Bello's army more formidable than Salvatore's?"

The men laughed and broke the rising tension. Arturo Scoletti and Santino did not smile. They exchanged concerned glances, wondering how the guerrilla army would fare against armored columns and heavy artillery. None of them really knew much of real army warfare. Salvatore, unperturbed by the information, addressed himself to Santino.

"Which generals do we draw? All three?"

"Generals Montello and Castella. Sarroni returned to Rome."

Tori chewed on this for several moments. Top men, these. Both, skilled in Rommel's tactics, had served with the Italian forces in North Africa. It would prove interesting, to match skills with these two desert jackals.

"I don't know about the rest of you," said Tori, glancing at his gold calendar watch. "I'm going home to eat a hearty dinner."

Flushed by victory at San Amauro Hill, the government's armored division, moving with incredible swiftness, arrived in the west on December 19, prepared for an all-out attack on the army of Salvatore. Before the day ended, Salvatore's mountains swarmed with government troops and the additionally recruited *carabinieri*. Forced out of their armored vehicles and onto their feet by the very nature of the rocky terrain, Generals Castella and Montello griped at the incompatibility of their conveyances with the steep, perilous mountain terrain and retreated to Bellolampo to plot their offensive against both Salvatore and the inclement weather.

Unable to employ their personal artistry in the coming confrontation with the western Partitionist Army, the generals were forced to fight with tactics unfamiliar to them. Their skills, however, and long experience in warfare gave them a slim advantage. Having been taught by the master, Rommel, the desert fox, how to be devious and cunningly methodical, they had tasted sweet victory once and now wanted more. Briefed at length on Salvatore's spectacular invincibility, they resented the ignominy of having to tolerate the humiliation to which Tori had in the past reduced the *carabinieri* and other government forces. Was it just possible that damned Salvatore could bring them to their knees? By the balls of Lucifer—no peasant would make fools of them! If his strength was anything like that of Francesco Bello's he'd be eradicated in minutes. Why the man had no military training! Imagine! None at all.

General Castella—pudgy, short, fatuous, a fiery personality in khakis, far from a fool—was a professional who knew his business. Gen. Montello—tall, slender, shrewd, a coat of theatrical pomposity—was a brilliant tactician in warfare. These two had planned their strategy well in advance and picked the field of battle carefully. In addition to the purchase of willing spies for a price, they had been handed a worthwhile document—*"The Partitionists' Plan of Action in the West."*

534

High up in Tori's mountains it had been raining for days; not a soft, gentle rain, but one of those torrential downpours that wash out roads and uproot trees on hillsides, causing landslides and noisy, rushing streams to turn into lakes. Early the morning of December 21, two hundred soldiers disrupted the serenity of Montegatta, arresting in excess of five hundred citizens on charges of conspiracy, collaboration and the aiding and abetting of bandits. Next, with premeditated planning, they broke into a deserted farmhouse filled with a large cache of weapons and ammunition stashed secretly by Tori's men. Confiscated arms and prisoners alike were herded off to Bellolampo Barracks. Had the phenomenon of Salvatore been foreseen, this *caserne* and hundreds like it might have been built to accommodate a battalion rather than a platoon. Bulging with prisoners, the military outpost was kept under constant surveillance by reenforced details of armed soldiers.

Unquestionably, Generals Castella and Montello had taken time to learn something about their opponent, a man they intended to crush in a stinging defeat. They had paid attention to his vulnerability and had made it a point to study his psychology. But, neither had paid heed to these mountains, from whose loins Salvatore had sprung, the mountains which had sheltered and exalted him these past years.

Thousands of sweating, demoralized soldiers, unaccustomed to the gruelling marching of infantrymen, compelled to leave their vehicles and horses on the lower slopes of the limestone mountains, searched vainly through the honeycombed caves for Salvatore and his men. Slipping, stumbling and falling in the soggy, slogging, skin-drenching downpour of early winter rains, in mud up to their hips, the government forces felt the stinging humiliation and embarrassment of the hounds unable to sniff out the fox. Day after day they returned to their encampment, empty-handed, with unfullfilled souls. What mortification was this—to be outfoxed by a peasant who knew nothing of military strategy! How degrading! How positively humiliating to be shown up by a mountain guerrilla!

Then came the word!

The day after Christmas, filled with reinforced courage and a day's rest, these government troops thundered up the mountain on the tip that Salvatore and his men were nestled in the comfort of Grotto Persephone. While they were thus engaged in searching all the grottos in the honeycombed mountain, Salvatore deployed some men along the lower slopes, to make off with the armed vehicles, tanks and horses. Then they bombarded the invading troops from behind, in a continuous barrage of missiles which staggered the government army and stunned them, felling them by the hundreds, littering the hills with blood. The air shrieked with the blasting of artillery fire. In the valleys down below, sounds of gunfire, artillery fire, and mortar fire shook the windows and cracked the walls of many houses.

Meanwhile the main thrust of General Salvatore's Western Partitionist Army was many miles away from these mountains, staging counter-offensive blows on all military outposts manned by Federal soldiers in Borgetto, Montelepre, Alcamo, Partinico and Castellammare del Golfo. They confiscated all arms and ammunition. The Federal soldiers tossed into jails by Salvatore's guerrillas, never knew what hit them.

Nothing had demoralized the soldiers more than the abnormal downpour of rain, which jammed bolts on their rifles, dampened their spirits, and soaked their clothing to the skin. More than once they cursed the name of Salvatore. Realizing they had been duped, Generals Castella and Montello, at the news of Salvatore's activities miles away, ordered their men off the mountains, unaware they'd be trudging wearily off the rocky slopes into a waiting ambush of skilled guerrillas. Nearly four hundred of their men were sacrificed in this altercation—shot up by their own artillery, charged at with their own cannon, as wave after wave of Tori's horsemen surged forward at a fast gallop to mow them down in their descent. Surprised and surrounded, the Federal soldiers fell under the heavy fusillade.

The earth exploded in flames. Through the rain came white balls of fire and streaks of light erupting from the guns of the guerrilla fighters. Time and again they charged the soldiers and picked them off with grenades as other men covered their action with machine-gun fire. The fierce blows inflicted upon their enemies had been enough to force the soldiers into retreating panic. Their flanks collapsed, the beaten soldiers dropped their weapons and scattered in wild retreat. Meanwhile Miguel Scoletti's mounted guerrillas followed in savage pursuit, cutting their enemies in two. The awesome guerrilla fighters were determined to take no prisoners.

By midnight of the third day, injured soldiers, overwrought, pain-filled and sorely embittered, managed to escape the guerrillas. They straggled back to Bellolampo, only to learn that five hundred Montegattan prisoners had been released and their records burned, all federal arms had been confiscated by their liberators. The barracks, frighteningly deserted, proved a temporary refuge for General Castella's pathetic remnants, who collapsed in the antiquated military *caserne*. General Castella's 3000 soldiers had dimished to 500. Reinforced by an additional 2000 *carabinieri* hastily summoned from Palermo, all proved unequal to the 1500 Partitionist guerrilla fighters.

Watching his own men fight the government soldiers, Tori noticed that the trained military specialists had no aversion to killing, but, they did it as if it were a distasteful and unpleasant duty from which they derived no joy. They'd defend themselves diligently, and retreat instead of fighting to the end. His own men, by contrast, took triumph with them into battle. They fought with wild enthusiasm and died upon occasion without regret. Tori learned from these observations that chivalry and trained agility defended themselves poorly in the face of recklessness and ferocity. A gentleman was no match for a fighting machine. Cornered, he'd fear, more than death, the sharp sting of steel in his guts; the anticipation of a bullet's instant bite would sicken him, make him withdraw and give up without fight. This alone elated Tori, gave him additional courage for what he knew he must next do in his strategic warfare.

The Battle of Bellolampo, about to commence, would prove the bloodiest massacre, second only to the Sicilian Vespers, in the history of Sicily.

That early winter morning, in the cold, pouring rain, soldiers in the military *caserne* were stunned to see Salvatore's entire army of guerrillas thundering through Rigano Pass, heading towards Bellolampo. The alarm was sounded. Bugles rasped the call to arms. Had they known in advance what would follow, they might have sounded a retreat. Generals Castella and Montello, forced to attack half prepared, never caught up. For three days and three nights, the sounds of gunfire echoed through the stony mountains from all sides. It came alive like fire from the jaws of dragons, like thunderbolts crashing across the sky.

Salvatore's offensive slashed the enemy's advance guard to pieces, thinned down the main column by feigning retreat, then doubled back to annihilate them. When this tour de force ended, the battle was identified as *Strage di Bellolampo*—Slaughter at Bellolampo. One thing was certain. From this day forward the name Salvatore wouldn't be forgotten, discarded, or sloughed off as being that of a

537

mere *contadino*—a peasant, or a simple sheepherder's son.

Shortly before dawn on the morning of December 31, flanked on either side by his paladins and his inner circle of loyal men, Salvatore climbed the backside of the mountains to the summit, galloping through Rigano Pass and descending the frontal slopes, his troops in a V-formation. The rains had ended: the sky was still overcast. Slivers of eastern lights broke on the horizon. The roads, resembling small lakes, hadn't begun to absorb the overabundance of rainfall.

From their position on the mountain slopes, in full view of Bellolampo Barracks, they could see the broken remains of a dejected government army sagging with defeat. Crews of workmen, summoned from Palermo, piled the dead into nearby trucks and pulled out in the heavy mud towards the city while behind them sloshed the straggling remains of the more able-bodied soldiers; the vanquished, the overwhelming remnants of men who had lived to retell the amazing saga of the indestructible Salvatore.

As pitiful a sight as it was to watch the inner disintegration of a beaten army, Salvatore's men, laughed triumphantly and, with good cause, slapped one another playfully on the back at their smashing victory, thanking God that they weren't the unlucky ones. Turning to their remarkable leader for his mark of approval, the ultimate reward in battle, they shouted, *"Viva! viva Salvatore! Viva! viva!"*

They saw a stony faced Sicilian, dressed in a white trench coat astride his white stallion, cold, implacable as granite, staring at the scene below him.

"What's wrong? Why no burst of pride at such sweet victory?" asked Vincenzo.

"Sweet victory? Hah! We've been betrayed. If I hadn't ordered a counterattack and come in from behind, we'd have been slaughtered like pigs at market." Tori turned at the activity coming from another direction. *Sporcaccione* and four men came at them, riding hard, winded and obviously enraged. They pulled up sharply on their reins, a few feet from Salvatore.

"What happened at the radio station?" he asked.

"Just as you anticipated," shouted his lieutenant. "We were expected! Taking only the skeleton crew you ordered we arrived to find a hundred security police waiting in ambush. If we hadn't used the alternate plan we'd have been screwed for sure—hanging by our necks as vulture's bait."

Their horses danced a bit and strained as their riders moved in closer to their leader. Noticing the dark storm brewing in Tori's eyes, the men glanced uneasily at each other. Santino Siragusa moved in on Tori to ask, "What's wrong. Something's amiss—no?"

"The 'Partitionists' Plan of Action' was known to our enemies. They knew we'd be camped in the grottos for six days. Confident in their ability to annihilate us, they would have succeeded—if I hadn't switched plans. Bastards! My spies assured me the Federal soldiers went directly to our weapons stronghold, knowing in advance what they'd find. The five hundred villagers arrested were all relatives of the men of Salvatore. Suspecting our plans to overtake the radio station had been sabotaged, I deployed *Sporcaccione* to simulate what had originally been planned. He was anticipated. Who betrayed us? Who?"

Victory paled in the light of suspicion. Flushed with triumphant jubilation earlier, the men deflated instantly, besieged with torments of mistrust and suspicion. Aroused by overwhelming feelings of betrayal, brother silently questioned brother, cousin viewed cousin, friends grew uneasy, and none dared ventilate his thoughts. Who among these apostles was the Judas? Who among this tightly knit group of *cameratti* was the vicious and vile enemy?

Victory suddenly felt shallow; empty. None had received as much as a blister, a cut or suffered an injury these past ten days. None had felt the bite of a government bullet. Cries of *hallelujah* should have escaped their lips—praises, shouts of glorious triumphs, the satisfaction of a job well done. In silence they squirmed in their saddles, unable to slice through their worst suspicions and point a finger of accusal at anyone.

To compound matters, Salvatore wheeled his horse about and galloped off towards Palermo, without another word to any of them. Because he asked no one to accompany him, the men were deeply hurt. They could tolerate much, but not indifference or disregard from their leader. Their victory, dimmed and tarnished, had lost its luster, and, feeling this rejection, they they guided their horses back over the route towards the summit, with vague pictures of a possible Judas superimposed on their minds. Tori's paladins, however, trailed their leader at a respectable distance.

Salvatore calmly laid his Browning on Don Antonio's desk inside the *Banco* do Palermo. He presented a draft for collection of one hundred thousand American dollars.

With one eye on the Browning, the banking deputy indicated slight resistance. "We don't carry such large sums readily on hand." He faltered stalling for time. Don Antonio. May I suggest if you desire to sit at supper with your family tonight, you start counting out my money," he said softly with a diabolical grin on his face. "Sixty of my men and I have you and your employees in our gun sights, my dear deputy. Would you prefer I take *more* money than I'm entitled to? I could—with little effort."

"No. No!" cried the frustrated banker. "I'll get it. I promise."

"Don Antonio . . ." purred Salvatore. "Don't try anything foolish with Salvatore."

"Salvatore?" Sweating profusedly, the banker glanced at the demand note, nodded, turned his back, and walked the few steps into a caged vault. He returned in moments with a satchel and handed the bag to his obstructor.

"Why do you shake, deputy? It's a legal transaction, no?"

"Yes. No. I mean, they'll kill me," he moaned. "They'll kill me."

The insurrection had ended. The Partitionists couldn't survive, thought Tori. More than this amount had already been expended in wages, supplies and ammunition sorely needed by his army. Before payment was withdrawn and someone thought to dissolve the planned agreement, Tori aimed to collect the sum due him. Now that he had what he came for, he could afford a little levity.

"All right, all right, my dear deputy. Calm down. Listen to me. If they should do such a thing as kill you, you come to me, eh? You tell Salvatore all about it and he'll make short order of them. Va bene?"

"*Va bene. Va bene,* Salvatore," replied the frenzied Don Antonio, watching him leave. Only after the outlaw left the premises did the Don realize fully what the outrageous renegade had told him. Glowering darkly, he glanced about the ornate and Baroque-influenced bank. No one had even taken notice of what had transpired. It had happened so swiftly, there had been no time to press an alarm button.

Moving swiftly to his desk, he gave the operator a telephone number. The affectation of fear had dissolved from his jowled face.

"Don Matteo?" he hissed into the mouthpiece. "He was here moments ago. How much did he ask for? *Disonarato! Disgraziato!* More than he was entitled to take! . . . I could do nothing, nothing, I tell you. With hundreds of his men, he held me up at gun point. All our assets gone! Nearly a half million in cash! I can't tell you how many bonds and certificates were taken until I inventory!" he exclaimed with a wicked gleam in his eyes. "A half million in cash! *Butana u diaoro!* Mascaratti, malodetti!"

The phone at the other end hung up abruptly, with such a loud noise, the Don quickly jerked the receiver from his ear. Rubbing it gingerly, he attempted to suppress a perverse smile that formed on his lips as he mentally calculated how much he could siphon off into his personal vault, charging that Salvatore had made off with it. He moved swiftly into the vault to set about his intended task.

Across the room, behind a wooden cage where the offices of the bookkeeper and cashiers were herded together, th phone rang at one desk. A bookkeeper named Andrade answered. His dark eyes darted instantly across the room, beyond the cages towards the desk of Don Antonio. Andrade appeared perplexed and shook his head negatively. "One hundred men? Who has spun such a web of fantasy on you, Don Matteo? I've seen no one. Certainly, it would be my pleasure to meet with you. I will learn what I can."

Banner headlines in the local paper, *Il Popolo* appeared the next morning:

BANK DEPUTY DON ANTONIO SCOLESSI
ROBBED AT GUNPOINT BY SALVATORE
AND HIS BRIGANDS! $250,000 TAKEN.

Two days later, buried in the Obituary column, was the discreet announcement of Don Antonio's death. Nothing else. It was simple, direct and replete.

"How do you like that?" asked Vincenzo reading the paper. "We get some reputation for merely tending to business—eh?"

New Year's Day. The beginning of a new year with new hope.

Tori set up temporary headquarters in the old abandoned mill off the *piazza*, in Montegatta, free of any threat of *carabinieri* or soldiers, to re-group his forces and welcome all the released prisoners and to pay off the southern members of the Partitionist Army whom he temporarily disbanded. He expressed his thanks, and slapped the backs of his comrades and all those belted, gun-heavy men from the south who had joined him to defeat the Federal troops. Now Western Sicily was unmistakably Salvatore's.

Outside, hordes of favor seekers, admirers, well-wishers and reporters crowded about, hoping to touch the hero of the hour—General Salvatore. News of his brilliant victory against that formidable stronghold of government soldiers and their generals, licking their wounds in retreat, had flashed the name Salvatore around the world. He was the biggest news since Pearl Harbor.

Meanwhile Tori hadn't forgotten the betrayals of his men to Marshal Franchina's plot. He asked Bastiano Terranova, his double agent what he'd learned of the treasonous act.

"You won't like it, Tori," said Terranova, testily.

"Talk."

He moved in closer and spoke in hushed whispers out of range of inquisitive ears. Tori stiffened imperceptively, his eyes clouded in disbelief and narrowed in anger. He grabbed Terranova's lapels. "You better be sure of those words, *caro mio,*" he said evenly.

"I'm sure," said the other without flinching. You said the clip of your gun was reserved for this traitor—all fourteen bullets. Will you keep your word?" He handed Tori the photographs.

Turning from him, heartsick, he wondered, how could he empty fourteen bullets into the body of a young lad who had not yet become a man? Young Danillo had been warned. He glanced at the photographs; the indecent posture of Marshal Franchina in bed with the widowed mother of the boy, Danillo, in the throes of sexual embrace. Another photo showed Capt. Franchina paying the lad a substantial sum of money; the third—Franchina stood embracing the youth.

"It will be done," said Tori, sadly. "The word of Salvatore is not like water."

The village square at dusk, normally empty, was filled to capacity with somber Montegattans, standing about in huddled groups waiting, watching, wondering if Salvatore should do such a thing. Execute a young *picciotto* whose cumsacs hadn't filled with manhood? It was unthinkable, no? They watched as Salvatore's men brought the lad, Danillo, into the center of the *piazza*, under the Norman Tower.

Danillo's mother, the widow Grissi, penitent and filled with remorse was dressed in widow's weeds with a shawl about her head. She had followed her son from their house, where he'd been plucked from her arms during supper. She screamed, sobbing, begging for mercy. Spotting Salvatore as he rode into the square and dismounted, she broke

542

away from her companions and threw herself at Tori's feet, clutching at his legs, tears streaming down her face, much in the pose of Mary Magdalene.

"For the love of God, spare my son," she sobbed hysterically. "He's but a mere youth—a child—a baby whose diapers still need tending. He didn't know what he was doing. He merely wanted to be a man!" she lamented.

Tori leaned forward and pulled the woman up gently to her feet with a look of compassion on his face. He nodded to some of his men to take the woman from him with a kindness in his voice that gave her hope. His sunken eyes, however, bore the results of his two-day-and-night meditation. The weight of this problem had burdened him heavily. Having examined the photos time and again, he had to admit that the preponderance of evidence pointed the finger of guilt right at the boy. Hadn't he been warned before? Not once or twice, but several times? His heart had turned cold as he'd weighed the consequences of Danillo's treason. They all could have been killed.

Sternly he confronted the lad now. "Is it true—what your mother tells me? That you're a mere boy, a child, a baby whose diapers need tending? That you didn't know what you were doing?" Tori unholstered his gun and checked the bullet clip. He shoved it into place, accompanied by a metallic click that chilled the onlookers. Tori stared at the lad, hoping to find a trace of fear in him. There was none.

"Ask for forgiveness, Danillo," cried his mother. Salvatore is a just and fair man."

Displaying an insane brand of courage for his age, Danillo spat into the dust.

"*Va bene*. You've nothing to say?" asked Tori.

"Fuck you, you sonofabitch!"

"You make it easy on me," said Salvatore.

"Danillo! Beg, my son. Beg for forgiveness!"

The lad looked at his mother with a hard, cold, and disdaining expression. "*Sta mincha*, I'll beg!" he told her. "I can speak for myself. I need no whoring witch to be my voice."

Friends held the hysterical woman in check. The people stood transfixed like statues, afraid to move or speak lest they miss the unfolding of the melodrama.

"All right," said Tori. "You were warned. You know the fate of all traitors to Salvatore." The boy's attitude towards his mother was unforgivable.

The crowd stiffened imperceptibly. Their eyes lit up

543

with a terrible excitement, as Tori slowly raised the gun and carefully aimed at Danillo's heart.

"No!" screamed the widowed mother. "No! No! No!" came the slow agonized screams from her throat as she sank against the crowd.

Danillo didn't flinch a muscle. Tori waited. Oh, how he waited to to see some sign of contrition, an apology, a desire to make amends. There were none.

"Still nothing to say, eh?"

"Fuck you again! May your balls dry up and fall off!"

"Listen, don't be stupid, Danillo. You've got some guts, you know? Tell me how you were seduced and I'll let you join up with me. You've always wanted to, haven't you?"

His eyes lit up. He had fooled Tori in the past, could he do it again? Mistaking Tori's words for a sign of weakness, Danillo grew insufferably bolder. "Fuck you again! One day I'll be bolder, a bigger man than you!" he spouted with total ego.

Salvatore pulled the trigger and shot fourteen bullets into the traitor. There was little left of him when it was over. He turned to Danillo's mother, who stood staring in agonized shock, in the unbelievable silence that prevailed in the piazza.

"One thing, *Signora*, he was *molto bravo*—a brave young man. His mistake was in placing his loyalties with the wrong side."

He holstered his gun, mounted Napoleono, and rode off with his paladins.

"He was just." The villagers coming out of shock nodded in full acceptence of the act. "You must admit Salvatore was just," they told Danillo's mother in an effort to console her.

The widow stared at them with a look of idiotic insensibility and, watching the Genovese brothers pick up the broken and dead body of her son and place him in a nearby lorry, she felt dead inside. Fidelio reached into his pocket and pulled out a roll of bills which he pressed into her hands. Marco handed her the donkey reins.

"As is the usual custom, *Signora*, my chief Salvatore wishes you to know he holds no malice towards you. The crime of treason against him has been paid. He wishes no further animosity from your house to his. You understand?"

They bowed and took their leave. Emotionally drained and still stunned by the rapid order of events, the widow Grissi took the dead body of her son to her house to prepare him for burial. Slowly, bit by bit, the *piazza* emp-

tied out after her, leaving a chilling sound of emptiness—
and the crimson bloodstains of the traitor Danillo, for all
to see and remember.

A week after the burial of her son, the widow Grissi,
unable to remain in Montegatta with any degree of respectability now it was known she had consorted with Marshal
Franchina, packed her belongings and stole out of the village in the dark of night to make her home some fifty
miles distant in the village of Castelvetrano, where she
hoped never to see either Marshal Franchina or Salvatore
as long as she lived.

Every night for the next five years, until that early
morning on July 5, 1950, Giulietta Grissi prayed to be
avenged for the death of her only son. Both Franchina,
the man who had betrayed her and used her son for his
devilish scheme, and her son's executioner—just or not—
Salvatore remained at the center of her hatred and thirst
for vengeance.

CHAPTER 39

In Rome, after two more Premiers had failed to form effective governments, the newly formed Committee of National Liberation offered the Premiership to Alfonso de
Aspani, a man who wisely merged with the ecclesiastical
princes of the Church and the Christian Democratic Party
(sponsored by the Vatican). After polling over eight million votes in the national elections, the CDP, it had become evident, would be the new political power in the
land. In Salvatore's territory, Partitionists who'd remained
loyal to Tori had polled only a few less votes than the
CDP, thus indicating to the shrewd politicians watching
from the sidelines the young renegade's potential power.

Suddenly, in the still-disorganized political fight in
which anyone could and did participate, the influence of
Salvatore as a weapon of immense political significance
was considered by all major political parties. What followed was an extravagant display of courting rites aimed
at Salvatore. His time was suddenly oversubscribed by
men in certain echelons, who found it to their benefit to

545

include the name of the superluminary young Sicilian to their dinner lists. There followed dinners and secret meetings and galas where the heroic Salvatore appeared, always in the company of Vincenzo de Montana. The pair frequented the splendid villas of prominent and power-addicted feudalists and government officials. They were even on a first-name basis with the hierarchy of the Church and the titled landowners. They even mingled freely with the potent Dons, both of the old and the new Mafias.

Proposals came to Salvatore like a hailstorm of praises to a hero flushed with victory from every political arena with the exception of the communists—a fact which remained an enigma to Tori and later colored his hatred of them. However, those men who opposed communism became gravely concerned that the Reds might get to Tori with the right proposal, and so these men conspired with Tori's most trusted men to whom they paid handsomely for guarding against such a possibility.

After listening to all their offers, Tori, preferring to play the waiting game, made no hasty decisions. However, during this period in his life, he began to acquire amazing insight into the enormously complex vista of Sicilian politics. Colonel Modica had been correct in his assessment; experience was teaching Tori more than he'd get out of books. Tori had yet to learn that these politics would one day create a stranglehold upon him from which there'd be no escape. At the time he considered these proposals it seemed that destiny caused him to wait for the most important proposal of all to materialize; the one brewing in the mind of Don Barbarossa.

The inimitable Don Barbarossa, unique unto himself a man who continued to manipulate and control the most powerful political machine in Sicilian history, remained unequaled in that nation's politics. No other man other than this superhuman genius, this Machiavellian wizard, could have performed such a masterstroke of genius in the months following the foiled insurrection in the east when Bello had fallen to disgrace and imprisonment.

There had never been any intention in the Don's mind to ignore Salvatore. Early in the game he recognized that no aid would be forthcoming from America. It was for this reason that he'd failed to declare his support to Bello or show any allegiance to the Partitionists' cause.

Busily engaged in watching all arenas of activity—that ludicrous fiasco of Bello's in the east: the incendiary imbroglio between Church and communists, in the snake pit of politics in Rome; the phenomenal victories of his Godson in the West; and the power structure of the new Premier, de Aspanu, at the hub of the government—Don Barbarossa had set about to systematically manipulate the seriously untenable positions and crumbling politics of the former Partitionists into positions of strength.

Convinced that the political party destined for victory would be the Christian Democrats, who had won the full support of the Church, Don Barbarossa committed an act of betrayal by submitting to Chief Inspector Semano, the *Partitionists' Plan of Action in the west!* Here was Salvatore's *betrayer!*

It was by virtue of the Don's betrayal that Salvatore's men had found themselves expected when they had attacked the *carabinieri* barracks at Castellammare. This same betrayal had foiled their plans to capture the Palermo radio station. By virtue of this betrayal, Salvatore's cache of weapons had been uncovered and confiscated. However, through the effort of the Don Barbarossa, word of the betrayal had reached Salvatore in time for him to change his strategy, regroup his forces, and convert what might have been devastating defeat into brilliant victory.

There had never been any intent on the part of Don Matteo to bring about the destruction of Salvatore or his forces. Don Matteo's strategy had been aimed only towards the conversion of ex-Monarchists, ex-Partitionists, and former Socialists into a coalition of immensely strong and unified Christian Democratic Party.

Since time was of the essence, the conversion had to be effected swiftly, at any cost, before the situation became totally unsalvageable.

It was not for nothing that this connoisseur of good wines, cognacs, and men had become undisputed overlord of Sicily. His attempts to insure his brood of nobles, whom he adroitly controlled with the manipulations of a master puppeteer, against any and all charges which might be levelled at them for plotting insurrection against the government, were successful. The catastrophic defeat of the deluded, vainglorious Francesco Bello would shortly, under the political alchemy of Don Barbarossa, be transformed into a remarkable victory for these Mafia-feudalists.

In response to the Don's urgent directives, the baronial circle of politicians, soon to form a coalition of the strongest political forces in the nation, reluctantly left their villas en route to the capital city of Palermo to convene with their benefactor, Don Barbarossa, the modern-day machiavelli.

Martino Belasci, Minister of the Interior, first to arrive at the Don's suite at the *Albergo-Sole*, was perhaps the second most powerful man in the Italian government, second only to the Premier. Apart from several vital general administrative duties under his direct control in the Ministry, a number of highly complicated and delicate duties of a highly sensitive nature relative to the maintenance of law and order and public security fell under his jurisdiction. Minister Belasci was at the head of all the law-enforcement forces in the nation.

Martino Belasci always dressed impeccably. His poise and carriage were regal and his voice well-modulated, his speech always carefully deliberated before he uttered a word, like a painter preparing a canvas. No question, he exuded the aura of a power-saturated man.

On this day the Minister arrived at the penthouse suite of Don Barbarossa at the *Albergo-Sole* through a private entrance.

"Excellency!" exclaimed Don Matteo, rising from his chair behind the desk with the air of a proud father. "How good to see you." The two political lions embraced affectionately.

"Amico," replied the Minister warmly. "Each time I see you you look better and better."

"Sit here, Excellency," suggested the Don, flushed with pleasure. "What may I offer you? A drink? Coffee? Something to eat?" It seemed he could never do enough for his distinguished friend.

Belasci raised a slender, well-manicured hand, flashing a diamond solitaire, restraining the Don. *"Grazie mille;* I had lunch with the Premier in Rome before flying here to Palermo." He patted his stomach significantly and sat in the chair before the desk.

Don Barbarossa virtually fawned over this ambitious protege. He worked feverishly to elevate him to the future post of Premier of Italy. He always accorded him the respect and dignity of one so high in public office despite the fact that Martino had been seduced, bought and paid for by the Don. It was no secret that Belasci's soul was in hock to the *mafioso,* but so far he'd been charged no interest, and no demand had been placed upon him for payment except in the matter of a few vital political appointments that were necessary to insure the structure of the Mafia's present and future strength.

In this encounter, a somewhat hush-hush affair, Minister Belasci got to the point. "What a wonderful fertilizer—money. The Premier reacted favorably to my suggestion.

The smell of such a sum instantly converted that doubting Tommaso."

"How much did the nobility pay for these special services you procurred for them?" he asked the *capomafia.*

"One hundred thousand apiece."

"*Managghia!*" exclaimed Belasci gleefully. "How many in all?"

"Sixty—at that price."

"And we split this three ways?" He did some quick calculating. Instantly his eyes lit up with amazement and keen respect for the Don. "You never cease to amaze me—you know that? You're incredible! Absolutely incredible. Only you could have handled such a successful coup. Not Genovese. Not Gentile, Vizzini, or Russo! Not even Malaterra, with all his brain, has what you have up here." He tapped his forehead significantly. "It's a special talent you have. A very special talent. Not even I could have pulled this off."

Bypassing the flattery, the Don pressed. "Everything is in order? Did you register Christian Democrat, to let it be known you fully endorse the party?"

Minister Belasci nodded his head. "My support will be announced as soon as you settle matters here."

"They'll do as I instruct," said the Don, pouring his favorite wine, a light Marsala. "What about Francesco Bello?"

"There'll be no complaints from him. Already he prepares to run for the Constituent Assembly. At election time, upon his victory, his pardon will come automatically. From then on he can't be touched by the law. An elected deputy is immune from prosecution, as you well know."

Noting the brilliant strategy behind the move, the Don nodded approvingly. "And what of Salvatore?"

"Ah, yes," sighed Belasci. "What of Salvatore?" He inhaled smoke through his holder and exhaled gently from between his lips. He craned his neck, jutted his jaw, and pulled down on the binding shirt collar. "What do we do about Salvatore? . . . For the time being, we do nothing."

An eyebrow raised skeptically behind the Don's glasses.

"It's best we keep him on ice. In the *communique,* Premier de Aspdnu justifiably asks for several scalps, Don Matteo. I allow you the privilege of selecting the right ones. You move Salvatore in ways to suit our purpose. We may need him to fight off the communists. Mark my words, if they present a problem now, shortly, it will grow worse. The Reds won't give up until they suck the blood from our veins. Because I'm known as anti-Red, they've

singled me out. That Commie cocksucker, Senator de Casselli, is out to get me. He's one Communist that will bear
watching, hear my words."

Belasci rose to his feet and nervously paced the floor.
Mention of de Casselli's name upset him beyond reason.
There was more than political enmity between these two,
thought Don Barbarossa; however, he kept his silence along
with his subservient comportment. It suited his needs.

"The man is crazed with power. And, with the communist press behind him to serve as his vocal platform, he's
permitted too many liberties. Those darts he aims at me
do more than annoy me, Don Matteo!"

Don Matteo, occupied with more pertinent things than
the ravings of a communist Senator, wasn't a man to accept explanations instead of achievements. Neither was another young man whose name was on the lips of every
Sicilian in the land—Salvatore. He made this known immediately to Belasci.

"Salvatore expects amnesty. It was promised him, despite
Bello's failure," temporized the Don.

"Who promised him amnesty?"

"Bello and the Duke de Gioia."

"Well? Where's the problem?"

"*Allora*—explain."

"Did—*you*—promise amnesty?"

"Ahhhh, *capeeshie, capeeshie.* I understand. Since it
wasn't I who promised him such rewards, he has no recourse to demand it from me."

"Precisely."

"If I do not pacify him in some way, we will have lost
our—Salvatore. He is no ordinary peasant."

Minister Belasci had never seen the Don falter before.
He paused reflectively. "He's become a hero—in Rome."

"He's a hero, here. He controls western Sicily, now. Imagine. What can he be—23, 24 years old?"

"If he announced *his* opposition to the Reds—he'd influence many votes, no?" Belasci talked off the top of his
head.

"Yes, it's true."

"Then you sway him to favor the Christian Democrats—away from the socialists, separatists, activists, and
what's left of the stragglers, who haven't a prayer to begin
with. Keep Salvatore as your ally, Don Matteo. Promise
him anything he wants. Be sure he knows your word is
your bond. Convince him of that above all. Assure him
that if he had come to you instead of Bello or de Gioia,
you'd have done your best to secure his precious amnesty."

The Don shook his head, dubiously. "He's stubborn. Proud. A self-possessed young stallion. Bright. Very bright. He's proven his ability more than once. It's always the same story; military posts raided, supply columns assaulted, not a *carabiniero* barracks remains that isn't under his rule. Did you hear what he did to Generals Castella and Montello? *Managghia*, he made them evaporate!" The Don flushed pleasurably at the thought.

Belasci smiled tightly. "You've altered your opinion of him—eh? Nevertheless, in your hands, he will be like putty, just as I've been."

The Don's eyes grew skeptical. "There's a difference. *You* listen to me. Salvatore is a *mule*."

Belasci shrugged tolerantly until he heard the Don's next words. "What if our young rebel follows Bello's example and decides to run for office?"

Belasci's eyes were fixed on the gold cigarette holder he rolled between his fingers. "Run for office?" his voice cooled considerably. "Run for office—you say?"

"Rumors. Only rumors. Perhaps you can speculate on such a possibility even better than I. You met him a year ago at Calemi's villa in Castellamare. What did you think of him?" asked the Don easily.

"You know about that, too?" Belasci's astonishment turned to fierce respect. He leaned forward to deposit ashes into the lead crystal ashtray. "I suppose we never did speak of the encounter, Matteo. We met all right. Nothing planned, mind you. Prince Oliatta took me to a banquet held in his honor. As long as I was there, I asked His Highness to arrange a special meeting with the guest of honor. I sequestered myself in Calemi's study, away from the babbling politicians who swarmed the villa that night, and was occupied glancing at our host's enviable book collection when the door opened and there, walking into the room in formal attire, dressed as handsomely as that clotheshorse Prince Oliatta, came this impressive young man.

" 'Excellency,' said the intruder, bowing to me.

" 'I'm sorry *Signore*,' I told him. 'I'm waiting for someone. I suggest you find another salon for whatever business you might have.' Imagine my surprise when the next words he uttered were, 'Excellency, I am Salvatore.'

"I was speechless, Matteo. I expected someone far older, you see. I collected my wits and managed something trite like, 'Salvatore? *You're* Salvatore?' He smiled tolerantly and I managed to say, 'Yes, yes, of course, you're Salvatore.'

" 'I need a man like you, Salvatore.' I said. 'One who's on my side.' It was easy to see he was overcome by the praise he received from the *Minister of the Interior*. I outlined my plans to be Premier of Italy—superficially, of course. 'Communists breathing down our necks waiting to overthrow our glorious government. We cannot permit this, Salvatore,' I told him. 'We need the strength of your army to keep Sicily free from foreign rule.' I saw right off, he lacked experience and the political shrewdness to assess the validity of my promises. I made many promises in exchange for his devotion to the cause of Martino Belasci. Most important, he seeks amnesty for all his crimes, National, unconditional amnesty. You know what this means?"

"I know what it means. Go on." The Don was intent on his protege.

"It was obvious he held me in high esteem, and stood in awe of the office I represent. Instantly, in an outpouring of patriotism, he pledged himself to my cause. But—wait, that isn't the end of it. He then said something I've never forgotten, something which angered me at first."

" 'As long as your ideals correspond to mine and we both seek only glory for Sicily, I stand behind you to the end. Count on this. So there's no misunderstanding, know well in advance, if you ever betray our cause, or my trust in you, I will kill you. As long as that's perfectly clear in your mind, Excellency, I pledge myself, my life, my gun and my army at your disposal.' Then, Matteo, he smiled a smile that spoke more than his words."

"He said that to you, the Minister of the Interior?"

"He said that to *me*—Martino Belasci, the man. It was no subtle threat. He came out straight with what was on his mind. At first I burned with outrage, but, as I collected my wits, I laughed and muttered, 'Thank you, my friend.' The office of Premier comes before any personal feelings and, knowing I might need this insolent brigand, I covered my irritation. Thank God we were interrupted by Prince Oliatta, who insisted that others were clamoring to meet the guest of honor. For a time I remained in the background, observing Salvatore as he circulated amongst the crowd of fawning politicos, who treated him like a young god. Fickle bastards—all of them. I knew then how naive he was politically. No politician in his right mind would have threatened me straight out."

As if the Minister hadn't mentioned the episode, the Don repeated his earlier question. *"Allora*—what do you think of him?"

"Today? A year later?" Belasci grimaced. His words

were soaked with pure envy. "Salvatore could run for King—and win."

The Don grunted.

"Politically he's useless to us." continued Belasci. He picked a rose from a vase on the Don's desk and twirled it absently between his fingers. "We need him as he is—a genius at guerrilla warfare. Without his aid in this capacity, we can't hope to win. If we kept all the bandits under our protection and used them, they'd be ineffective. There's no one like Salvatore." Belasci drew the rose to his nose and inhaled its sweet fragrance, allowing the velvety petals to stroke his cheek as he struck an attitude of contemplation.

The Don continued in his passive role by remaining silent.

"Salvatore's political future must remain subordinate to mine," insisted Belasci. "When I control the government we can find a suitable place for him—but only if he plays ball; according to our rules. He must be taught, Matteo, that the sun doesn't rise because the cock wants to crow!"

"He won't buy it," said the Don wisely. "Not when Bello gets off the hook. Bello also killed a few *carabinieri, caro mio*."

Belasci grew thoughtful. "Ah!" he said with a burst of enthusiasm. "I think I've solved the problem. When he first became a bandit—did he kill anyone?"

"Yes. Some *carabiniero*, I think."

"Was he jailed, apprehended or brought up on charges? What?" Before the Don replied, Belasci continued. "Contact Inspector Semano. I'll have a warrant issued for any such offense. We'll move for trial, then proceed to try him in *absentia*. The judge will convict him of a felony. He'll then be ineligible to run for public office. You see how easy it is to plot against him?"

"*Va bene. Va bene*, Martino. Very good. It will apear that I had nothing to do with such a legality. Only then can he be approached properly." He glanced up from his preoccupation with the cigar band and tossed it from him. "You think he's easy to plot against?" he asked in a voice loaded with innuendo.

"I've known you a long time, my friend," said Belasci unwilling to be assuaged. He plucked the petals from the rose, "I've never seen you reluctant to deal with a man. What's wrong? Where's the *capomafia* who tore the Archbishop's theory to pieces?"

The Don made a disorganized gesture. "If I don't understand my own actions, how can I explain them to you? I, too, am confused by what happens. When we meet— sparks fly between us. He irritates me, talks to me with a total lack of respect. He is impudent—yet I detect no malice. Anyone else—I would have erased long ago. What's another life in this world, eh? In my company, he's incorrigible. I've done him favors out of respect to his family, as polite and gracious as it is within my character. More so on occasion. He mocks me, and I'm not sure why. That he does all these things, and I permit him these liberties, baffles me. Even you took no umbrage when he threatened your life—why?"

"Isn't it obvious? We need him." Belasci had never seen the Don so vulnerable, so human—or less like a *capomafia*. The metamorphosis was baffling to Martino.

The Don nodded. "He came to see me in Godrano before the war's end. What a handsome tribute he paid me. Phew!" He made appropriate hand gestures, described the matched Arabians, extolled their praiseworthy aspects, and expressed his astonishment at such homage paid him. "Truly, I thought I had reached him. I invited him into my confidence . . . but later he reared like a wild stallion and kept his distance."

"He sounds like my son, Cesare—a complete incorrigible. Ah, the things we take from our loved ones, eh Don Matteo?"

"Salvatore is *not* my son—or a loved one." The Don's subdued voice dropped off in contemplation, but only for a moment. "Goddammit! What the hell's wrong with me? Why do I speak of him with such *simpatico?* I've handled enough upstarts in my day, and I can handle him!" The Don cleared his throat and wet his lips with a sip of wine, and continued. "Your suggestion of an *in absentia* trial is perfect. When it comes to the law—you're a genius, excellency." He slapped his thigh resoundly. "Salvatore will respond to my command. He may be everything and all the people say about him, but he'll have to go far to outwit a man of my stamp."

"You're sure you can handle him?" Belasci pondered a moment. "Salvatore is one prince who has laid the foundations of his state solidly. Perhaps he will not be easily deceived, after all."

Both political lions were silent and meditative for several moments.

"Did I tell you he is my Godson?"

"Godson, Don Matteo?" Belasci's brows shot up in surprise. "You never mentioned it."

"Who can remember all the baptisms one is forced into? Before Mussolini, I was in church a dozen times a week officiating as Godfather. Somehow—sometime, some way—I became Godfather to Salvatore. Is that a kick in the ass?"

"You want Don Vizzini to handle him directly? Familial ties can get sticky . . ."

"No. He's my problem. I need no one to take my responsibilities."

"I only meant—"

"I know what you meant." The Don glanced uneasily at his watch. "It's best you leave, Excellency. We don't want the Reds to get wind of your contribution to the Partitionists' effort." He opened the rear door. "A private elevator will take you to the Via Roma exit."

A glance at his watch stirred the Don into activity after the Minister's departure. He was late. He washed his face and hands in the bathroom and, as he brushed his thick white hair, he pondered the curious rumors circulating about his protege and Prince Giorgio Oliatta, which suggested more than a casual relationship between them.

The Don had rejected the malicious gossip as vicious rumors inspired by Martino's enemies. In his sudden rise to power Martino Belasci had made many enemies, namely the communists who stopped at nothing to discredit and undermine the powerful influence the Minister held in high places.

"Bah!" the Don flung the hairbrush from him. "No one will make me believe that Martino is a powder puff," he muttered aloud. Thoughts that his protege was anything but a real man—repelled him. He slipped into the jacket, laid out for him by his valet, then attended some last minute business on his desk before entering the other room.

Noticing the small pile of rose petals left in a cluster on his desk, he recalled how delicately Martino had toyed with the flower. *Va! Va!* he thought. *I can't permit myself to think such things. Yet, he did say in parting to ask the Prince to call him in Rome as soon as possible—didn't he?*

Lucky was the day *he*, Martino Belasci, had placed his career in the able hands of that inimitable power, Don Barbarossa, he told himself as he descended the freight elevator of the hotel. In those few moments, Belasci reflected on their relationship. From the first each man had struck sympathetic chords in the other.

Belasci's father, once a vigorous, high powered *mafioso*, had schooled his son well in the pragmatic ways of the Mafia; how they thought, how they worked; how intricately the network of their minds functioned; that it didn't matter how they acquired power, only that they knew how to use it to their advantage. Under the gag of fascism, the reality of the Mafia had become a thing of the past; a bygone fantasy which older men whispered about in secret for fear of their lives. Now, the war had come and the Mafia was back in the harness, in all its glory. All his former teachings came back into focus.

Martino's small law practice, having gone by way of the bombing during the Allied Invasion had brought him to Palermo in an effort to negotiate a desperately-needed loan until reparations could be made by the government. There he had encountered a former classmate, Giovanni Russo, appointed by the *capomafia* as special assistant to the advisor of the Allied Military Government. Rossi had promptly invited his dapper friend to a small dinner party given in the Don's honor that evening, where he had been introduced to the guest of honor. Martino, with loquacious panache paid him the proper respect due him for his courageous effort on behalf of the Allied War effort.

"To have exposed yourself to the enormous dangers likely to befall a man who shows loyalty to the Allies in a country still occupied by his enemies, is a praiseworthy deed, Don Matteo. You are to be greatly admired and respected." Martino spoke with a profound sincerity, and marveled at the fact that the Don was over sixty years of age.

Such a commendable speech by a comparative stranger, spoken so eloquently, hadn't gone unappreciated by the Don. In the course of the evening, he'd got a complete run-down on the Siragusan from his aide Giovanni Rossi. He listened intently as Rossi related that Martino was the son of Don Alfredo Belasci, a proud *mafioso* of the hierarchy of the brotherhood, unfortunately a victim of the genocidal holocaust that swept the island free of many *mafiosi*.

"Martino graduated with top honors at Syracuse University; he argues one hell of a case in criminal law, and has been lauded by the president of the courts in which he defends his clients," Rossi told the Don, tapping his forehead significantly. "He has plenty up here, my Don."

Later Don Barbarossa gravitated towards a group of men to whom Belasci was speaking. He glanced up as the

Don approached, extended his arm, and drew him into the group. "Ah, Don Matteo." He flashed an ingratiating smile. "I was telling these gentlemen, you have to be the most fearless man in the world. Yet, I'm intelligent enough to know no man is without some fear or another. There *has* to be something the Don fears—even if it's a fear of the dark—or heights."

"I fear no one and nothing," the Don said, hooking his thumbs behind his suspenders, under his jacket.

"We are all afraid of something at one time or another," Martino said tactfully.

"No. A man who shows fear is no man. He's a boy. A child. A baby. A real man claims what's his by God given rights. Fear isn't a right. It's an enslavement."

"Ah, dear Don Matteo. If a man knew his God given rights, he could claim his inheritance right off. But, tell me, who among mankind knows the answer to that universal riddle?" Belasci laughed tolerantly, and found it odd that the group of men around him had suddenly vanished, leaving him alone with this professorial-looking man.

The Don studied Martino through inscrutable eyes behind those tinted lenses that had become his stock in trade. "You're Don Alfredo's son?"

"He was my father, *buon armo.*"

"Hah!" the Don spat contemptuously. "And he never taught you to claim your rightful heritage?"

For an instant he'd been incensed. How dare he mock the memory of his father? Then Martino relaxed. Like his father, this Don Matteo had to be another Sicilian day-dreamer; a spinner of fantasy. After the brilliant *coup* he had pulled off against the Italians and Germans, he was entitled to a little indulgence, Martino thought benevolently. He found himself being led by the arm to a remote corner of the elegant suite of rooms away from the well-wishers and party goers.

"Tell me, Martino Belasci," the Don said after they lit up cigars and puffed for a brief moment. "What's your ambition? What goal have you set your sights upon? Which star lights your path? Which of the many millions in the heavens have you named your very own?" At the marked hesitation and stupefaction in Martino's eyes, the Don urged, "Come, come. You must have some ambition. What is it?"

Compelled to respond by those piercing black eyes, Martino said the first thing that popped into his mind, absurd as it might sound. "To be Premier of Italy," he said defiantly.

The Don studied the younger man without a trace of emotion—without surprise or ridicule, with no indication of scorn, no stifled titter, no attempt to shrug off the statement with a realistic, "Choose something more reasonable." Finally he spoke. "That's straight? You wish to be Premier?"

"Yes." Belasci said, thinking, *now he'll let me off the hook.*

The Don did nothing of the sort. He puffed on his cigar thoughtfully and appraised the young lawyer. "What's your speciality?"

"Political Science."

"What will you sacrifice to become Premier?"

"I have no money. Since the war—"

"Who speaks of money?" The Don cut him off. "I talk of *fegato*—guts!" He pounded Martino hard in the gut.

Caught unawares, Martino jackknifed forward and uttered a low, "Uggggghhh!" He straightened up quickly—and caught the wicked smile on the Don's lips.

"You're too soft. Toughen up." He slapped his own stomach, hard, with thumping sounds. "See? Hard as steel." He removed the wet cigar from between his lips. "I talk of time. How much time can you devote to becoming Premier?"

Thinking the joke had gone far enough, the eastern lawyer had searched for an avenue of escape. "Presently no time at all. I'm in Palermo to borrow money to reestablish my practice. I have a wife and two sons to support."

"Your wife's family—no cousins or relatives will help."

"I wouldn't ask." Belasci glanced idly about the room.

"Too much pride, eh?"

"Perhaps," he'd replied airily, bored with the scene. He was about to excuse himself when he heard the Don's voice, muffled, inaudible. "I'll lend you the necessary money to support your family until—"

"With your permission. I didn't hear you—"

The Don repeated his words and puffed away on the soggy cigar.

"I'll make you Premier. You will remember two things only. *One,* you are to follow my orders to the letter. *Two,* you will never forget it was I who made you the highest power in the land, for what the Lord giveth—I can also take from you."

Martina laughed loudly and with good humor. *The whole thing's a joke,* he thought indulgently, *including*

558

the biblical misquote. The Don's had too much wine. In the morning, when his head clears and he reexamines his words, he'll find adequate excuses to kiss me off.

Morning came. Actually it was before dawn when Don Matteo called to awaken him.

"*Porca miseria!* If you wish to become Premier, you cannot spend your life in bed?" the ball-busting Don bellowed.

"It's not six o'clock yet," Belasci lamented sleepily.

"Meet me at Nunzio's in one hour. There are people you must meet—"

"But—" his protest made no dent in the empty sound at the other end of the phone. Don Matteo hung up.

It was a crazy, insane feeling, this. *Goddammit! What have I gotten myself into?* Belasci thought. Thirty-five minutes later, against his will, Belasci arrived at the famous eatery. Astounded by the flow of traffic and bustling early traffic, he was even more astounded to see nearly every influential politician, including several American officers, partaking of *latte e cafe,* with *pane e burro* and *biscotti.*

Approval and pride scrawled across the Don's face when he recognized Belasci. He pulled him in protectively toward an empty chair reserved for him. Members of the impressive group glanced up in mild interest, paused a moment from their breakfast, and then resumed eating until they heard the Don's prophetic and immortal words: "My dear friends. It's my honor to present a man who will one day be Premier of Italy. Martino Belasci."

Miniature bombs of resentment exploded in the minds of the conspiratorial politicians gathered there, some of whom already aspired secretly to become the Don's fair-haired choice for the highest office in the land.

For the rest of the morning, Martino saw only a blurred sea of faces, heard only vaguely the names of super-powered luminaries—those figureheads in the present political hierarchy he had read about. He became dimly aware that Giovanni Rossi embraced him warmly, extended his best wishes—and was astonished as Belasci himself at the sudden turn of events. The dazzling names of the Cardinal, the Archbishop, judges and local ministers staggered him; the handshakes left him exhausted, through it all, he wondered how, in the name of Lucifer, Don Barbarossa had managed to recruit the star-studded entourage of nobles at so early an hour, when the sleep balls hardly dissolved in his own eyes. Belasci soon learned that the whole of Palermo moved only to the tempo prescribed by the titan who became his mentor. From that moment Belasci's soul, placed in escrow had been held in full title by Don Barbarossa.

That morning, whether motivated by curiosity, jealousy or hatred, every envious eye leveled upon him appraised, conjectured, disapproved and ultimately felt resigned to accept this political maneuver of the Don's. Hardly a man present at breakfast knew the name Martino Belasci. By evening, everyone there had made it their business to know more about this dark horse whose sights were pointed at the highest office in the land.

Oh, they all knew full well the Don was bent on controlling the politics of the nation to make up for the *"years of the locust."* But, was Belasci the man to implement such praiseworthy ambitions? Such a neophyte? What did the *capomafia* see in him?

Apparently he'd seen the necessary requisites in Belasci, for in the days following, the Don had meticulously instructed his stunned protege that it would take careful grooming and adherence to a strict and systematic code of procedure to insure that after developing the proper political protocol, all steps up the ladder would remain in Mafia control. By the time Belasci acquired the Premiership, every important office under him would be controlled by Mafia feudalists and the political party they sponsored.

Belasci, a quick study, soon discovered that of the many politicians who compromised with the Mafia, most were unprincipled men who at election time involved themselves in swift encounters and bought votes for cash, food or jobs, exchanged in countless tangibles. "You scratch my back and I'll scratch yours," was their credo. They coldbloodedly exploited anyone and everyone and engaged in double dealing of all sorts. Most would, although opposed initially in ideals and principles, acquiesce to anything to promoting themselves. There wasn't one among such men, whom the Don didn't control directly or indirectly.

To make Martino Belasci the Premier of Italy would therefore become a mere feat of simply moving the rooks, castles, knights, even the bishops, in a slow, deliberate manner, at the right time, in the right way—known only to him—for ultimately, control of the game and board would remain with the un-checked King.

This then, had been the beginning for Martino Belasci, who only recently was appointed Minister of the Interior in the cabinet of de Aspanu; a man who was soon to become so saturated with power, he'd be ripe target for the communists. He would need all the strength and backing his friends could assemble to counter the Red threat. Through his efforts and, of course, those masterminded by the Don, the recent Partitionist nonsense was offset by Premier de Aspanu. By this afternoon, he felt certain Don Matteo would remove all traces of that ridiculous insurrection promoted by those indescribably senile Sicilian millionaires.

There was more. The Belasci-Barbarossa alliance had proved exceedingly effective. There wasn't a place the Don didn't reach—one way or another. Reparations forthcoming from the Americans, who sympathetically pledged themselves to aid in the restoration of Italy, guaranteed the brotherhood that millions upon millions of dollars would be made by them in these coming postwar years. In the years since their alliance was cemented, Belasci came to appreciate the redoubtable Don Barbarossa's political skill and knowhow. Having observed this power in action countless times, Martino discovered that the secret to the Don's success lay in the fact that he never revealed to another person the sum total of his intent. Retaining both the master plan and blueprints to any proposed action, the Don farmed out only that specific portion which an individual was responsible for performing. "It's safer this way," he'd say if anyone countered with an objection. His real intent was that no one should learn the key to his thinking.

Don Barbarossa didn't understand the meaning of the word "psychology," he could hardly pronounce it, let alone spell it. But it was obvious that life had made of him a master psychologist, and Belasci, the perfect student, followed to the letter the teachings of this skilled master craftsman, who knew men well.

Belasci's first instructions, when appointed Minister of the Interior were terse and to the point. "You will not acknowledge relationship to me or others in the brotherhood. You will conduct your affairs as discreetly as does Premier de Aspanu. Get close to him. Make yourself valuable to him, and remove as many responsibilities from his shoulders as you can without making it appear you are eager for his job. You will endorse only the political party I advocate, and remain loyal to its policies until I advise you differently."

Always the efficacious politician, calculating and cautious, Belasci never offended a *mafioso*. They understood if he didn't overly fraternize with them. But this in itself didn't matter, for in secret, he attended many functions in which he could revel in their companionship. He loved their ethnic anecdotes, never failed to laugh at their brand of humor and wit and felt perfectly at home with most. Inwardly, Martino realized that it was some deficiency in his own nature that curiously compelled him towards these audacious men, who lived by their wits, committing acts of violence in utter defiance to the laws as if they'd been singled out—given preferential rights—to defy God, country and fellowmen.

It was the same way with Salvatore. From the moment he'd met the Sicilian, he had taken to the lad and followed his career with vicarious interest. Oh, how he envied the bandit's independent streak, his boldness—and the adulation given him!

Minister Belasci shared a sumptuous villa in old Rome with his wife. Two young sons were in private school in Lausanne, Switzerland. His wife, Giuseppina, renamed Daniella because it sounded less peasantlike, had, under the tutelage and professional guidance of an impoverished baroness skilled in social and political graces, emerged a fragile, frivolous blonde who involved herself in countless charities and social functions—matters which necessitated the services of a personal secretary and two private consultants, three social satellites who added strife and strain to the life of a bewildered Sicilian waif by grinding out more commitments than Daniella was capable of handling in the short interim of her conversion to high society.

The Belascis came to live the regimented lives most political aspirants are forced into when guided by an ambitious thirst for power. Here they were two reasonable people caught irrevocably in this controlled power structure, allowing themselves to become desensitized to personal commitment and mesmerized into thinking they must conform—without personal choice—to the mold prescribed by some heartless sonofabitch more ambitious than Belasci himself. It bewildered the couple when they could find time to assess the situation. With subordinates constantly nagging at them on matters of protocol and decorum, filling their appointment books as if they were competing in a popularity contest, they were doomed to fail miserably in their private lives. It followed that Martino and Daniella would drift apart.

Divorce was out of the question—Daniella took on lovers. The Minister did likewise. Only those close to him guessed—weren't really sure—that there was something unusual in the Minister's relationship with Prince Giorgio Oliatta; something not purely platonic. The utter masculinity of both men seemed to belie the possibility of such attraction in the eyes of man. Don't they both fence with a passion? Play polo competitively and fiercely? Ski dangerously, taking chances only men with real *maschiezzo* were wont to do? Didn't both men take pride in their bodies and exercise only the way *real* men did? Why—it wasn't possible that a homosexual relationship existed between two such he-men. Was it?

Minister Belasci stepped out the freight elevator, now, and headed for the street. Don Barbarossa had mentioned Salvatore was his Godson. Why hadn't he mentioned it before this? They seldom had secrets from each other. The Don had given him the go-ahead on the *in absentia* trial, hadn't he? It was a perplexing situation, yet, knowing the *capomafia* as he did, he knew that the Mafia and its responsibilities came before anything else in his life. There was no doubt that his loyalties were stoutly in the brotherhood's favor. He felt pleased with the outcome of their talk. If things continued to progress as they had these past three years, the Premiership was a heartbeat or two away from his grasp.

Minister Belasci stepped outside in the Palermo sunshine and made his way to where his secretary, Marcello Barone, held the door open to the waiting limousine Don Barbarossa kept at his disposal on his trips to the Conca d'Oro.

"First, we stop at the chief inspector's office, Gerardo," he instructed the driver and entered the vehicle followed by the slim, sun bleached blonde haired secretary. Once seated, he confided to his aide, "I want to pick up the file on Salvatore—his entire criminal file."

The driver glanced at his passenger through the rear view mirror and smiled internally as he skirted about the early afternoon traffic. Salvatore's man, Calo Azzarello, the musical shepherd, had made a deal with the real Gerardo to escort His Excellency about Palermo on this day. And when, later, Minister Belasci departed for Rome, the criminal file on Salvatore had conveniently disappeared from Minister Belasci's belongings.

CHAPTER 40

Feudalism, an ancient system, a way of life, a substitute for government, and in some instances a system of organized anarchy had found roots in Sicily, since versions of this dehumanizing system had come in with all its many conquerors. The Greek system of *colonate* had bound agricultural workers to the land they worked; the Roman practice of *concilium plebis* had exchanged agricultural labor for protection; the Persian idea of *clientage* offered poor citizens the protection of wealthy landowners and patrons; and in all systems was found the marked subordination of the people to the directives of the *latifondo* and its wealthy land-barons, the *latifondisti*.

Emphasis on the acquisition of land has always been the basis for wealth and social prestige. Because feudalism marked the decentralization of political authority and because the right to own property became synonymous with the right to govern, local officials have always wielded considerable power in Sicily.

The system of the Mafia found its roots in such an ancient abomination, which was promulgated by its select circle of millionaire land barons and the Church—owners of the greater portion of land. As renegade bandits hiding from the law, their first dedication had come as a resistance group to champion the poor, the desperate, the sorely abused peasant from the fierce and violent oppression of the French Bourbons. Later, these bandits, evolving into a form of vigilante group to protect landowners from invading armies, became a brotherhood of honorable men performing an honorable work. Over the years, the more enterprising of these men took lessons from their feudal overlords and began a slow, insidious acquisition of land from their indolent, uncaring landowners, and, through shrewd and skillful manipulations—and in most cases crooked deals with dishonest banking firms—came to control most the land.

Mafiosi began to enjoy a social life of refinement, gentility, urbanity and sophistication that for so long had belonged only to absentee landlords who preferred the gayer life of Europe and northern Italy. In the subsequent leasing of lands from the titled nobility, Mafia Dons assumed obligations of the *suzerain*. They provided protection to the people, guaranteed them justice and exercised the rights of escheat and forfeiture—and became the only persons with whom the peasants could deal in any contest.

Mafia rule became so saturated with power that they not only controlled the people, land, trade and commerce centers, it followed that they'd also infiltrate politics. With the assumption of political power they became the second government in Sicily. Except for a brief span in time—during fascism—nothing happened in the land without the sanction of the *Mafia*.

The most integral part of this ancient order were the Feudalists, those monarchistic landlords, who for the preservation of this tenacious, bloodsucking system, had risked their necks to establish a monarchy in Sicily. Men of such stamp had intrigued with every ancient order since Sicily's inception to promote their autocratic machine, and once again they were prepared to scheme with the new powers of the government, knowing in advance it was highly hazardous—that though the stakes were high, the reward could be greater.

Sixty millionaires had been induced to leave the sanctuary of their well-fortified villas to gather in Palermo in the penthouse suite of Don Matteo Barbarossa, wondering what magical tricks the *capomafia* had up his sleeve. Could he continue to preserve for them what they had enjoyed for so long—or was this to be the end? Despite the fact that these same men had paid dear sums to the Don to save their necks from being wrung by the Rome government, they remained gravely concerned until an official verdict could exonerate them from charges of plotting against the government.

Only once in the past had the *capomafia* failed them. When Mussolini had swept the *mafiosi* out of Sicily, these perfidious land-barons had condescended to the abandonment of their gay and frivolous living habits. They had been forced to don their country-squire corduroys and tend to their own estates without help.

Don Matteo Barbarossa, a master at pleasing the insufferable and imperious feudalists, knew how to feed their ravenous, demanding egos to allow for total dependency on him. He had hired a lavish display of music and festivities in their honor. Standing on an elevated platform dressed in the livery of a fifteenth-century court page, a white wigged majordomo stood prepared to announce the names of the illustrious guests. In the lavishly decorated Baroque salon, graced with an elegant buffet of gourmand dishes and a cellar of rare vintage wines, a hush of expectancy filled the room.

Mario Cacciatore, the most feared of the Don's entourage of enforcers, stood off to one side of the salon, studying the guest list inscrutably. Cacciatore, a solitary figure with a middle-aged paunch and the same frightening, malevolent and scarred features that had once terrified an entire countryside, knew every man and servant in the salon. His dark hair, dyed to cover a white growth and considerably thinner, was worn parted low and slicked to one side as he'd worn it twenty years before. A ghastly scar on the left side of his face remained livid and roped on the folds of his aging skin. Black agate eyes darted in all directions under thick lids, seeing everything, missing nothing. He constantly fired his tongue against his lips in short staccato bursts to rid himself of small bits of tobacco stuck annoyingly to his lips.

Cacciatore dated back to the days when he and Don Matteo had been members of the Mazzarino bandits, a fierce and awesome band of cutthroat murderers, who thrived long before the days of *Il Duce*, when the Mafia was the controlling authority. After World War II, when *mafiosi* were reinstated to positions of power as mayors and political ministers, Cacciatore had made it known through the Mafia network that he'd consider it an honor once again to work for the Don. They had originally separated, only at the Don's insistence, thinking their chances of being recognized as *mafiosi* would be minimized.

Don Barbarossa's reluctance in sending for Cacciatore, at first, had stemmed from the distaste he had felt at having the most ruthless and cold-blooded of murderers he had ever encountered in his career of crime, join him in his present involvement. It was necessary that the Don maintain an air of aloofness, yet, be more friendly and outgoing with the Allies than his nature allowed. Don Barbarossa feared that the Allies might misconstrue Cacciatore's presence, for in his devotion to his Don, Cacciatore had been like a silent, dangerous animal, watching, waiting, casting suspicious eyes on all who came near his Don, whom he venerated openly. Cacciatore, never one to be concerned with what others thought of him, hadn't cared that his reputation intimidated others, or that his overly protective manner of the *capomafia* might offend the Allies or cause them to suspect the presence of such a vile animal. He cared nothing for such trivia. All that had mattered to him was the *capomafia* and his protection.

Whatever else Cacciatore had been, his loyalty to the *capomafia* had been unequaled by any man's. It was for this that the Don had welcomed him into his confidence again.

Against a background of chamber music, the court page announced the new arrivals.

"The honorable Mayor of Palermo," came the dull, monotonous voice.

Cacciatore glanced up and checked off the Mayor Tedesco's name from his list as the short, rotund butterball of a man entered the salon and, pausing here and there, shook hands with his acquaintances, seemingly unaffected by the fizzled-out insurrection. This capricious and outdated *mafioso*, who advocated the regression of the peasant to Roman times, was a man upon whom the harsh realities of the moment failed to touch, for this braying bird kept his head buried in the past.

"His Excellency, Duke Federico de Gioia dec Cantania . . ."

Dressed in an immaculate white suit, the Duke arrived dramatically, seated in a wheelchair piloted about by his manservant, a dark-eyed, Moorish-skinned man whose bright eager eyes glanced about at the impressive gathering of nobles. One foot, infected with gout, remained in a horizontal position on a leg extension of the chair before him as the Duke was wheeled about the room nodding and waving a limp hand to those in his path, as if he was loath to touch them in a handclasp.

"Excellency," called Don Matteo, bowing graciously to the corpulent giant. "It displeases me to see you ailing. Had it not been that this meeting is vital to all of us, I'd have spared you the trip."

"Yes, yes." muttered the Duke with a look of long suffering. "Such trying times, my dear Don Matteo," he said waving his lace-edged hanky and leaning towards the other in a confidential manner. "Would you believe some of Bello's uncouth bandits attempted to hide out on my estate after that disgraceful embarrassment at San Amauro Hill?"

"No!" The Don affected to be aghast. "The nerve of them."

"Yes, it was incredible. I'm astounded by Bello's lack of taste. My men ran them off the property. What a misguided lot we were, my dear Don."

And the Don was superb. "Precisely what I explained to

the Premier. We were all duped, Excellency," He had the decency to lower his eyes, as heads turned to their direction, surprised at first, then nodding in assent.

Yes, that was it. Hadn't they all been taken in by Bello, that skilled lawyer who possessed the ability, duplicity and cunning to bend another man to his will? Such a manipulator, with an artistry which could convince St. Peter to turn over the golden keys to Paradise, could easily seduce lesser men. This idea spread throughout the room.

"What a tinhorn exhibitionist, that Bello. What did he know of revolution? The idea that he should present himself as a knowledgible military strategist! The shame of it all, coming so close on the heels of the Canepa fiasco!" . . . They had all forgotten that it wasn't Bello who had sought their favor, but the other way around.

Their questionable loyalty to Bello had disappeared, buried in his defeat at San Amauro Hill. For them, Bello no longer existed.

Having already convinced himself that Bello alone should be held accountable for the fiasco, the Duke de Gioia was delighted to see that his contemporaries shared his feelings. Now, if they could be turned against Salvatore, his revenge would be a sweet one.

"His Excellency, Baron Girolamo Mattinata."

This cold, unfeeling, penny-pinching old fart, whose face screwed up in perennial complaint over finances, arrived with a companion. Don Bruno of Caltagirone, who in Captain Bello's absence represented his voice. Both men entered the salon heatedly, discussing the frenetic claims to uncultivated lands made by those incorrigible, lowly peasants, this past week.

"And where were you, Don Barbarossa?" the Baron shook hands begrudgingly with the *capomafia,* and before the amenities ended, his high voice cracked raspingly. "Where was your protection? Peasants—not bandits, mind you—broke into our granaries and relieved us of all corn and wheat stores!" He scowled darkly at the Don, whose patience, pushed to the limit by this braying jackass of a man, was about to end.

Don Matteo checked the burning impulse to put the Baron in his place. *Demonio!* If this meeting didn't have to serve as a unifier for more spectacular news he yet to pass on to this gathering. His eyes caught Cacciatore's most casual glance, and he quickly averted his head, lest his bodyguard misconstrue the message contained in his eyes. The baron continued.

"I tell you, Don Barbarossa, while we all sit here, doing

568

nothing, with the faked revolt going up in a cloud of dust, the *real* storm clouds of rebellion gather in eastern and central Sicily, aided by the Communists. If you listened to me, you'd agree they'll have to be reckoned with. We should have taken measures to eliminate all of them right after we discovered Canepa's treachery!"

"You mean . . . *murder*, Baron Mattinata?" The Don said, feigning to be aghast at the thought.

"Don't twist my words, Don Barbarossa. I'm no fool. So, don't treat me like one. Communists can only spell trouble for us."

"You're absolutely right!" replied Don Matteo with sugar-coated words. "Exactly what I've stressed. We'll get to it later, you can rest assured."

He gave Rossi the eye, and his aide quickly moved in and steered the Baron and his companion towards the re-freshments. Baron Mattinata's waxed moustache twitched nervously until he saw the Duke de Gioia. He hastily made his way towards the other, anxious to tell him of the revolting developments.

Cacciatore, who had observed and heard the rhetoric, wondered at the *capomafia's* patience. In bygone days the man would have been dead for speaking so disrespectfully. Baron or no Baron!

". . . *Don Calogero Vizzini . . . Don Ferruchio Albano . . .*"

Two of Sicily's most redoubtable Dons, second in power only to Don Barbarossa entered and embraced their host cordially with marked respect. These two powerful post-war figures had, under the tutelage of Don Matteo expanded highly lucrative black market operations and made fortunes in olive oil. They were presently involved in brilliant attempts to stunt the growth and spread of newly formed labor unions, currently organizing in Villalba and central Sicily without Mafia sanction; it was reported that Don Vizzini alone had held fifty such rioters at bay and gunned them down in the village square for refusing to obey his dictates. Don Vizzini had been over sixty when this occured.

Rossi watched them circulate among the others, stopping here for reverence and homage, and there for respectful acknowledgements from others.

"His Eminence, Cardinal Rumalino. The most Reverend Archbishop Voltera."

Sicily's most imposing figures of the Catholic Church were greeted with the reverence and respect due them as they sauntered through the crowd, which parted to make way for them. The Cardinal, having recovered recently from an illness, repeatedly ignored the unrest he caused daily among the anticlerics, who published their literary dissent with the unfairness of his political activities. *The Church has no business in the affairs of State*, contended the Reds through their explosive articles in the communist press, aimed at breaking the ties between Papacy and government. And the Cardinal would vociferously discredit the Reds as being anti-God. Between these two ecclesiastical princes of the Church, Rumalino and the flint-eyed Archbishop Voltera, there was more corruption than in the entire Mafia or Communist party, concluded young Rossi, watching them.

"...*The Honorable Bernardo Malaterra*..."

"... *His Highness Prince Giorgio Oliatta of Pantelleria* ..."

These two elegantly dressed men, both influential *confidantes* of Minister Belasci and politcally astute in the current scene, entered the salon and were immediately fawned over. Bernardo Malaterra, another of the *capomafia's* fair-haired men destined for political prominence, was soon to be elected Deputy in the Constitutional Assembly. At an early age, Malaterra, son of a penniless day laborer, had shown promise and became fully supported by a large landowning family with Mafia connections, who had put him through law school. Once qualified to practice law, he had become active in the Catholic and Popular Party activies. He had been brought to the attention of the Cardinal, who had waved his magic political wand and started him in his career.

Malaterra, a complex man who controlled more than a dozen Mafia projects at different levels of operation, possessed excellent organizational ability and manipulated a select staff of election propagandists, whom he repaid for their procurement of votes wtth jobs in banks, key positions in the post office, or state employment in regional administrations. This man, of medium build with steady brown eyes and a square, jutting jaw, was later to become Undersecretary to the Minister of Transport in two later cabinets. After Belasci became Premier, he had become Minister of Foreign Trade, or Transport, and of Agriculture. From the inception of Malaterra's political baptism, his career had also been guided by Don Barbarossa. As Belasci had been advised to do, he later would deny all Mafia associations in his ascent up the political ladder.

Prince Giorgio Oliatta, a tall, slender man of excellent breeding exuded sex appeal and charm. His features were fine and delicate, with a well-bred flare to the sensitive nostrils of his long, slender nose. He was grey at the temples mingled with coal-black hair worn longer than the current mode. Pleasant green eyes and a forced polite smile masked his inner feelings. The Prince's family were land-rich in Sicily, Italy, Germany, Brazil, Mexico and Guatemala.

He'd met Don Barbarossa and become intrigued with the intricate workings of this man's complex mind. Strange that a man with his Oxford education had become irresistibly drawn to the multifarious activities of the Mafia, but for whatever else the relationship served, it, in addition, had satisfied an exaggerated quirk in him for adventure. No longer a mere observer, he had become an active participant in this free for all to control Sicily and had momentarily backed several political aspirants, among them Martino Belasci. At these meetings, he basked in the fawning reverence the world paid to an ego-starved, blue-blooded noble.

Prince Oliatta, a confirmed monarchist, along with the others, represented an ancient feudalism that kept large areas of Sicily from cultivation through the organization of a slick and effective system, which suffocated growing outbursts of despair among the peasants—mainly by meting death to all who opposed the system.

The last to arrive, Don Santo Florio, Cavalier to the Crown of Italy, was a man who'd grown so obese over the years that it took two men to prop him up on either side. Don Florio partook prodigiously of the gourmand refreshments and spoke with measured, sparing words from time to time. The effort it took to speak took more strength than this corpulent blob of a man could muster. Here was a *mafioso*, who over the years had earned a reputation for being an impartial mediator between the warring factions of the brotherhood and all other hostile families engaged in *vendetta* in his territory.

Don Santo Florio was no Don Barbarossa—but at least the people were willing to listen to him. His word carried weight. During the fascist regime, his reputation as a stabilizing influence among his people had enabled him to maintain a position of enormous respect, despite the fact that he was a heartless, diseased, self-satisfied old lout whose impassive features belied a larcenous, deceitful nature. He was one of those crusty old men who "knew" all about everything. Few men who ever crossed this *mafioso* had lived to boast of the feat. No one ever heard a threat pass his lips—and this in itself perpetuated fear and respect.

All these men and more, personal supporters of the foiled revolt, would be personally affected by the outcome of this meeting, no one more so, however, than the one man who was conspicuous by his absence—Salvatore. Only Salvatore's disinclination to join the aborted insurrection had prevented the fiasco from blowing up beyond the point of salvage. Premier de Aspanu had made it perfectly clear to Minister Belasci that Salvatore's indescribable victory over the government forces had been the deciding factor in hastening negotiations with the Sicilian land-barons to resolve their differences. Minister Belasci had related this enlightening fact to Don Barbarossa; but it was evident the *capomafia* had no intention of revealing to Salvatore just how secure was the brigand's position, or how valuable he might be to the Don's future plans.

What a let down Salvatore's absence had proved to be to those feudalists who had anticipated meeting the young rebel, this brilliant prince among men! Never mind that a year ago, and longer, Salvatore had been a thorn in their sides, a man who had audaciously raided their warehouses and become the "voice of the peasants" in land disputes. Now he was their champion, a military strategist who had outfoxed and out maneuvered two of the nations' most heroic generals. *Managghia!* Was Salvatore to be another Garibaldi? Would he shake the nation and make the Italians dance to his tune? Just where did his future lie?

The most disappointed of the men gathered was the Duke de Gioia. Still smarting from the blow to his vanity over Gabriella's abduction, he had taken to carrying a pearl handled revolver, and had vowed to shoot the impudent man on sight. In his distorted imagination, the gargantuan nobleman saw himself included in the ballads immortalizing Salvatore as the jealous, estranged cuckold who slew the vainglorious lover in a matter of honor.

In the small anteroom off the main salon, alert musicians had been playing softly, with one eye peeled on Cacciatore, awaiting their cue for what was to come.

Don Barbarossa signalled to his *consigliero* to take his place next to him behind the impressive oak desk, away from the banquet array. The others took their places in the chairs assigned them. A chair to the Don's left remained unoccupied for the time being. The Don glanced at Cacciatore and nodded. It was the signal for the music to cease. The Don began to speak in his usual uninhibited dialect, accompanied by a repertoire of colorful hand gestures.

"My friends, I'll begin by talking straight, without wasting any time. We've all had our share of troubles recently. It is for this that we meet here today, to reassess our thinking, to examine present issues candidly. From the first I didn't sanction insurrection. I didn't fully endorse the plan despite objections from Francesco Bello. Always, I've had your welfare in mind. Remember, back in Grand Council Chambers—*my* objections were waived. Could I have persuaded you from your plans—eh? You wanted blood."

The men sat forward in their chairs, tense and anxious. Some sipped wine. Others smoked their cigars and cigarettes until the room hung heavy in a pall of misty smoke. All of them were, by the power and glory of their money, the controllers of Sicily. Prideful, wanton, lust-filled men, indolent and self-serving, possessed with a curious bent to indulge in their own warped egos, all had banded together now to save their necks at any cost. Now, painfully quiet as they listened to Don Barbarossa, they felt their loyalties wax and wane as they had with every crisis in their monstrous lives—as they had when they hadn't backed Bello with money, they'd promised him to promote their cause, they now squirmed uneasily, wondering what the Don was up to. Was he whitewashing himself? Sonofabitch! Hadn't he told them he controlled Salvatore and the other bandits? Where had Salvatore been when Bello had needed him in the east? Hadn't they paid the renegade enough? All right. All right. It was true the *capomafia* hadn't endorsed the resolution. But, how the hell else could they save face after that misbegotten son of a she-goat, Canepa, had betrayed them? They had been laughingstocks long enough after *that* insufferable Red Agent had exploited them so adroitly. They were committed to the cause, if only to ease their embarrassment. If the insurrection had succeeded—well, they wouldn't be seated here, forced to swallow the snide insults of this peasant, *capomafia* or not.

Don Barbarossa saw their innermost feelings written on their faces. Smiling internally, he continued with a flair for dramatics. "How did we permit things to progress so far out of hand? It's true, we were all taken in by the extravagant promises of a mountebank who responded to our needs with exorbitant assurances of victory. Francesco Bello beguiled us. We were duped."

What the Don implied by a crafty twisting of words was

grasped instantly by their cunning minds, and their hopes soared. Their momentary distrust dissolved.

The outspoken Baron Mattinata, who'd been twisted out of fifteen million lire by Salvatore, interrupted—out of order. "Surely, Don Barbarossa," he whined in his nasal, congested voice. "You don't expect this General Brancuso to be a wet nurse? Do you·expect Premier de Aspanu to view us as innocent victims of a half-assed revolution lasting these many months? If you can convince these two shrewd operators that we were duped by our own colleagues—" he rolled his eyes.

Don Matteo gave him a withering glance. He would have liked to put this repulsive Baron in his place for the second time this day. Again he ignored the ignominious creature.

Don Calogero Vizzini grunted loudly, sipped his wine, and declared dispassionately. "My trust is in you, Don Matteo. You have my full support. If you say we were easy marks for Bello, that we were deceived—*allora*, we were deceived." His black beady eyes darted about the room towards his supporters. If this redoubtable *mafioso* decided that the sun should be called the moon, henceforth the decree would be followed.

"I thank you for your support, my friend," said Don Matteo respectfully. "You'll be happy to learn that through my foresight and expert manipulations, I've succeeded in saving all our necks from the government hangman's noose. It's true America has foresaken us and we must look to oursevles for our future. It's imperative we forget our political differences and unite together in one strong unified party—the Christian Democrats. This party, endorsed by the Church, has taken the lead. The Vatican has the full support of our Allied friends."

A questioning murmur arose among the others, their faces screwed up with puzzled frowns. They glanced at the Cardinal and Archbishop, who nodded favorably at the Don's words.

"Having been fully compromised by the Partitionists and their partisan forces only recently," continued the Don with slower emphasis, "we shall have to make sacrifices to indicate our good intentions to the Premier."

The landowners glanced at one another uncomfortably. Rossi got the picture instantly. So! *It's to be Salvatore that will be sacrificed! That's why he isn't here!* He was filled with dismay.

The Duke de Gioia's eyes turned a smokey dull sap-

574

phire. He also got the picture. Justice at last! He drummed his fingers excitedly on his fat thighs.

"Va bene! Va bene!" cried Baron Mattinata, who bore Salvatore malice for besting him in their negotiations.

"Why?" asked Prince Oliatta, glowering at the others. He happed to be fond of Salvatore, as were many others who had intrigued with the young bandit and were now too embarrassed to show their true colors.

"Why? . . . Because his have been the most daring coups! Without word from Bello, he carried on a meaningless war. He blew up *carabinieri* barracks, massacred policemen and soldiers, and disrupted traffic by road and rail in the west. He gets rich and lines his own pockets. He's undisciplined and will not obey orders," snapped the Don impatiently. "In addition, he makes public all his deeds—informs the newspapers, as if he owed *them* loyalty."

"My dear Don Barbarossa," began Prince Oliatta. "Salvatore acted strictly in accordance with the Partitionists' Plan of Action, as agreed upon by Francesco Bello, the Minister and yourself. Why wouldn't he be entitled to the same immunity and privileges granted to us?"

Giovanni Rossi concurred with Prince Oliatta and Bernardo Malaterra. "As partisans, how can Salvatore be held more accountable than any of us?"

Don Matteo gave Rossi a look that struck terror in his heart. His eyes met those of his other two cronies. They didn't like this at all. Like the others who were in this up to their necks, they couldn't chance antagonizing Don Barbarossa. They retreated into their shells.

"The Partitionists no longer exist—or will be crushed soon enough," continued Don Barbarossa. "If it hadn't been for my quick action, Salvatore would have been caught when his men attempted to take over the Palermo radio station. I saved him from that embarrassment, at least."

So there had been a betrayal? A double one, at that, the Prince told himself. He sat woodenly staring at the smoke spiralling up from his cigarette. What will Salvatore say to this when he learns it? he wondered.

Salvatore is to be the sacrificial lamb, thought Bernardo Malaterra, glumly. There will be hell to pay! *Managghia!* Would the young buck put up with this kind of treatment? *Che demonio!* He shuddered inwardly.

"Negotiations have been under way for some time with the Premier in Rome. General Brancuso will arrive shortly

575

with the final disposition in the matter," said the Don blandly.

Two doors opened behind the semicircled seated consortium, and two waiters, pushing carts of shaved ice, with magnums of champagne buried in them, entered. Hollow-stemmed crystal goblets, packed in tinted ice, were arranged in the design of the Christian Democratic Party emblem: a gold cross with wings at either side of it. Waiters wheeled it to the center of the room and stood at attention behind the cluster of millionaires and *mafiosi*.

"What happens to *Capitano* Bello? What about him?" asked Baron Mattinata.

"He runs for political office in the coming elections—and will win. Thus he becomes immune from prosecution for his part in the revolt. Already he had renounced his Partitionist ideals and declared his loyalty to the CDP."

Murmurs of astonishment swept through the group. A few nodded knowingly. Others speculated, squirming at their earlier disloyalty.

"We always take care of our own," said the Don firmly. He popped a thyroid tablet into his mouth and washed it down with a sip of water. "Always."

It took General Simone Brancuso twenty minutes to travel through Palermo's traffic to get from his office at Carabinieri HQ to the Don's penthouse suite. He didn't look the part of a ruthless, military man who had risen in the ranks, the hard way, through dedication and political skullduggery. He could have easily passed for a doctor or a lawyer or a professor, with his alert and eager-eyed expression. Rosy red cheeks and wavy black hair took a full twenty years off his fifty-five. For some time the General had been burning the midnight oil, making secret trips back and forth to Rome, where he had sat with his superior officers and the Premier mulling over this insufferable *fiasco* in an effort to resolve the truancy of the Sicilian millionaires. There was no doubt in the General's mind that his talent as mediator would net for him a fancy, well-filled purse. This alone provided an excellent incentive for his participation.

He knew all the men present in the Don's suite by name, if not socially. By the time he had arrived and deposited his two aides outside the Don's door, he was all business. Greeted affectionately by Don Barbarossa, he exchanged a few pleasantries and got right down to business. Nodding to the others until every eye was upon him, he cleared his throat and removed with a flourish from his brief case, a letter from Premier de Aspanu.

"With your permission, Don Barbarossa, I'll get right to the letter." He dropped his eyes to the sheaf of white papers before him and commenced reading:

"My dear General: All communiques sent to Minister Belasci concerning the recent insurrection in Sicily, reached me intact and were taken under advisement. I agree with Minister Belasci that there is no supportive evidence of participation by any of the distinguished gentlemen cited in your brief. Certainly there is insufficient proof to initiate any arrests in connection with the Partitionist movement."

Expressions of intense relief and a general feeling of ease swept through the penthouse suite. Mayor Tedesco popped a belladonna tablet into his mouth and washed it down with water. A few of the others smoked nervously and sipped their wine, trying to read the results in the General's facial expressions.

General Brancuso continued: ". . .You are to expend all efforts to restore normalcy to that great land of Sicily. Whatever aid you may need shall be immediately dispatched to you. You are hereby authorized to deal leniently with those persons who were misled by the hapless instigators of the foiled revolt. At your discretion please put it to the cavaliers who wish to withdraw from the untenable position they find themselves in, that we in Rome no longer hold them responsible, since their position in the unfortunate incident was fully explained to us . . ."

A loud murmur of approval swept through the room. General Brancuso wet his lips with water. "However," He lifted his voice above the mutterings and waves of excitement, and held up a restraining arm. "—However, make it perfectly clear that those persons responsible for loss of life and damage to property shall be held accountable and prosecuted under the extreme penalty of the law—as enemies of the State."

Instant silence pervaded the room. Eyebrows shot up. Scowls formed on many faces, lips tightened grimly. Glances of concern were exchanged. *Mafiosi* and feudalists, squirmed in their chairs. *What's this? What's this? Strings attached? What did it mean?*

General Brancuso paused dramatically to look at the sea of faces and, in a slow deliberate manner, he said, "Sicily has been granted full regional autonomy within the framework of the Republic."

There was pandemonium. Cacciatore gave the musicians the signal to play the *Sicilian Freedom March*. The millionaires jumped to their feet.

577

"Bravo Bravo!" they cried. They shook hands with one another, embraced, cried aloud, dabbed at joyful tears, clapped their hands, stomped their feet and whistled like children at a circus, keeping tune to the music.

Don Barbarossa raised his hands for silence. He rapped a gavel hoping to restrain the feudalists. "*Aspetta! Aspetta!* There's more," he shouted, flushed witht he pride of his victory. Cacciatore silenced the musicians by wagging his hands in their direction.

"Because the Italian Government recognizes the extremely sensitive social problems of the Sicilian people," continued the *carabiniero* chieftain, "no land reforms shall be amended, or new ones formed over the heads of the present landlords."

What ensued was tantamount to V-E Day around the world. Without restraint, the gathering of nobles and *mafiosi* went wild. Cacciatore gave the signal for the harried band to start up again. Barons, Dukes, Princes and Dons—all of them whistled as giant crocodile tears of patriotism and relief streamed down their expressive faces. Four waiters on cue popped champagne corks and poured the pale amber sparkling wines into hollow stemware and served the jubilant celebrants.

Managghia! Once again the *capomafia* had attained a victory for them! And what a victory! Again he was their invincible protector! Again their hero! What fools to ever doubt him. They wanted to kiss, hug and smother Barbarossa with fraternal accolades and they would have if they hadn't been restrained by the excited, somewhat frustrated General Brancuso, who shouted and waved his arms in an effort to be heard. He had jumped on the desk. "Providing—" he shouted. He couldn't make himself heard.

"Providing—" he tried again. Don Barbarossa rapped the gavel.

"Quiet, please!" shouted Giovanni Rossi. He glanced at Cacciatore.

Once again the music was cut off. It took moments to restore order.

"Providing—" The booming voice of General Brancuso echoed through the room in the sudden silence. Red-faced, he dropped his tone a few notches, as he commenced to read: "Providing the landowners guarantee Sicily will remain in the hands of the Right. If Sicilian voters should swing to the Left and the Reds assume power, I shouldn't have to explain what this might mean to all of us. It would nullify all previous agreements."

This last proviso meant little to the satisfied land-barons. "Communism is a small nuisance Don Bararossa can handle as easily as swatting a fly," they declared. Once again their voices arose in rejoicing.

"On behalf of Premier de Aspanu and the Italian Government, I welcome you all back into the fold," toasted General Brancuso when a champagne glass was thrust into his hand.

"To the genius of Don Barbarossa!" toasted Duke de Goia.

"To the Christian Democratic Party!" toasted Don Barbarossa, tactfully.

On and on poured the champagne, with the celebrants toasting everyone they could think of. The frustrated musicians were cued again to commence playing the Sicilian Freedom Song.

Turridu Nuliano and Pietro Gagliolo, both members of Salvatore's Inner Circle, had traded jobs for the day with two waiters in exchange for a handsome bonus and a bit of gentle persuasion and presently circulated among the jubilant nobility. They smiled, poured champagne freely and joined with uplifted spirits in the momentum of the celebration. More than once they came under the acute scrutiny of Mario Cacciatore, who stared intently at them, then cross-checked his list of waiters and other hired help for the occasion. Instinctively he reacted, and he knew they didn't belong. Turrido, more brazen of the two, anxious to get a closer look at this legendary Cacciatore, whose name was more respected as a killer than Don Barbarossa, moved in with a tray of champagne glasses.

"*Sciampagna, Signore?*" He flourished the tray with expertise.

"Who are you?" growled Cacciatore suspiciously.

"I am Rico, cousin to Calo." He pointed to his throat. "He had a sore throat, *molto male*." In a sense it was the truth. Turridu had been forced to slip a *garrote* about Calo's neck before he had agreed to change places with him. The waiter still occupied space in a linen closet on the floor, tied up with another companion. Cacciatore was about to challenge the bandit when Don Matteo beckoned to him.

"*Cameriere*! Waiter, bring champagne."

"At once, *Signore*," he exclaimed, grateful to have escaped Cacciatore's clutches. Something sinister about this killer caused Turridu to shudder.

In a corner of the room, Don Matteo, speaking in confidential tones to General Brancuso, thanked him for the splendid cooperation shown his people. In a gesture of appreciation he handed him a deed to a 1000-acre land parcel and villa near Castelvetrano, for "the days of his retirement."

The General, affected to be stunned by the grand gesture. "In good conscience I can't accept this, for simply being an intermediary. You were the brains behind this coup, Don Matteo."

"Nonsense." Don Barbarossa shoved the deed into his tunic pocket. "We take care of our own."

Brancuso bowed politely. "A million thanks, Don Barbarossa."

In a burst of patriotism, the Don raised his glass in a toast. "To Italy!" The others chimed in, "To Italy," came the cries as they drank.

"To Sicily!" cried Giovani Rossi. *"To Sicily!"* came the cries.

"To Don Matteo!" toasted Don Vizzini. *"To Don Matteo!"* echoed the others.

"To General Brancuso!" hailed Baron Mattinata. *"To General Brancuso!"*

"To the Vatican! To the Pope!" exclaimed the Cardinal. *"To the Vatican! To the Pope!"* shouted the gathering.

"To us!" shouted Duke de Gioia. There was unrestrained laughter.

"Let us not forget *God!"* chimed in Prince Oliatta, wryly.

"One moment, Don Matteo," interrupted General Brancuso with a noticeable frown on his face. "The Premier has ordered normalcy to be restored without delay. With over fifteen guerrilla bands still at large, how can this be effected?"

"Leave it to me, General." Don Matteo winked playfully at Rossi, and made his way across the room to where Don Santo Florio, the obese *mafioso*, sat on two chairs to support his gross weight. Instantly Cacciatore moved in behind him, protectively.

For a quarter of an hour the formidible *mafiosi* engaged in repartee. The *capomafia* talked, the corpulent Don listened and nodded dutifully from time to time until Don Matteo had finished. Only then did the gargantuan Don Santo Florio, a man with an apparent pituitary dysfunction, speak reservedly.

Prince Oliatta approached Don Barbarossa with measured warmth and politeness, champagne glass in hand. "Baron Mattinata tells me there's trouble with the communists in the East. In lieu of such a present threat and danger, you can't mean to sacrifice Salvatore, my dear Don Matteo."

"Who said anything about sacrificing Salvatore?" asked the Don, rising.

"With your permission, earlier you said—" The Prince lost his poise momentarily and seized the Don's arm. He hesitated unsure of the sudden icy look in the *capomafia's* eyes. Slowly he released his grip. "You said—"

"What I say and do are as far apart as night and day, your Highness," The Don glanced at him from behind those dark glasses that veiled his thoughts.

"Then, Salvatore isn't to be pawned?" His relief didn't escape the Don. "It would be a grave injustice if he were to be expended in this political game. I've met him, and consider him to be excellent material as a political aspirant."

Don Barbarossa raised an eyebrow imperceptibly. "What the hell is this? Everyone has become so protective of Salvatore? You've all intrigued with him, promised him the world behind my back. Now you try to rub salt in my wounds?" He enjoyed watching the Prince squirm a bit. "Perhaps I had better set you straight, Highness.

"Salvatore has become a political embarrassment to the Party. Constantly I must apologize for his actions to those high officials in Rome. His actions irritate the Italian Government, who insist he must be held in check, taught better manners, and schooled in the principles of good politics."

Watching them, Don Santo Florio, without moving his head, permitted his eyes to bounce off one, then the other, as if they were contestants in a ping-pong match. He stared in rapt fascination, listening with sharp ears.

"Before it slips my mind, Highness, Martino asked me to convey a message to you. You are to call him when you arrive in Rome."

"Martino spoke with you."

"He was here earlier—with me."

"Here in Palermo—with you? He didn't tell me—"

The Don raised his fingertips to his lips, confidentially. "It's not for curious ears to hear. The Reds, you know. I suggest, Highness, that you compare your ideas with those of the Minister's. I doubt Martino's plans for Salvatore include that he should be a political aspirant. Let there be no conflict of interests—or questions where your loyalties lie."

"You make quite a point in declaring you take excellent

care of your own kind, Don Barbarossa. I'm interested. Do you not consider Salvatore one of your own kind?" Prince Oliatta sipped his champagne delicately.

The Don shrugged noncommittally and gave him a look that could have meant anything.

"Nevertheless, you are to be congratulated. This is some victory you've masterminded. I doubt my colleagues appreciate your unique political strategy. The fox has outsmarted the hounds without leaving his scent."

"That's true. How kind for you to speak it."

Prince Oliatta bowed stiffly and walked away.

"Some victory," muttered Don Matteo. He hadn't grasped fully what the Prince implied, only that it wasn't complimentary. Subtle innuendos and the stinging wit of the intellectual were something the Don hadn't come to terms with in his lifetime.

Watching the scene with inborn curiosity, Don Santo Florio cocked an eyebrow, and when the Prince took his leave he remarked with pointed caution, "One day those princely sparks will ignite into dangerous fires. Use precaution, Don Matteo. Extinguish them in advance."

Don Barbarossa simply grunted. His devious mind, having already transcended the matter of Prince Oliatta, was already centered upon Salvatore and how he'd take this jarring news when he heard it. He allowed his eyes to travel about the room until they fastened themselves on Salvatore's men, who continued to pour champagne and mingle readily about the noted guests.

Well aware of the fact that they were Salvatore's men, he reached for Cacciatore's arm to restrain him when suddenly the identity of the two brigands became apparent to the bodyguard. Masking his surprise at the knowing glance he received from his Don, he exclaimed softly, *"Managghia*—you know who they are?"

"I know," replied the Don. "Won't it be an interesting reunion when they return to their leader and report the results of this meeting?"

"Sons of whoring Satans!" muttered the embarrassed killer, burning silently. No matter how these brigands fit into the *capomafia's* scheme of things, he cursed himself for not identifying them sooner. Whatever the reason Don Matteo had, he never mentioned this *faux pas* to his bodyguard, and Cacciatore wasn't about to apologize for the moment. Searching the Don's eyes for some clue to the scenario, this well-seasoned and fully indoctrinated *mafioso* bowed reverently to his superior. No one was, to Cacciatore, as exceedingly inventive as the *capomafia*, and

582

he wondered what diabolical fires sparked in the Don's brain as he observed the two skillful brigands blend capably into their surroundings. Now he also found himself wondering how the young Montegattan prince would take this news. Phew! There'd be some hell to pay—no?

CHAPTER 41

"No amnesty for Salvatore!" Tori's eyes fixed on the words until fireworks exploded inside him. At that moment he felt as if his world had burst and fragmented into a million irreparable pieces. He crumpled the message in his hands. Was there no one who kept his word? Were the words of all men like water and shifting sand—unreliable? He turned to face his men, as they entered the grotto, to hear it from their own lips.

Turridu Nuliano and Pietro Gagliolo took turns telling Tori and the others what had taken place at the meeting of the millionaire insurrectionists. "Don Barbarossa *revealed* the *Partitionists' Plan of Action* in order to save the necks of the feudalists. At the same time he sent word to you to warn you of the betrayal so you'd cover yourself."

"It can only mean the Don is protecting us, Tori," suggested Vincenzo, with a noticeable sigh of relief.

"Yet, at the same time he signs my death warrant? Some protection," snorted Tori. "Turridu—you mentioned a letter. Did de Aspanu actually write my name in the letter? Did he list me as one of the men who should be held accountable? What did Don Barbarossa mean when he told Prince Oliatta I was a 'political embarrassment' to him?"

"*Aspetta!* one question at a time." Turridu Nuliano held up one hand and winked at his leader. Reaching into his jacket pocket, he extracted a handful of costly cigars swiped from the coffers of Don Barbarossa, and passed them around. Pietro Gagliolo displayed a case of champagne, grandly with panache.

"We also intend to celebrate Sicily's new status, *mi Generale.*" He also winked broadly at his chief and flourished a letter he had expertly lifted from General Bran-

583

cuso's briefcase. "Not only did we mention a letter from the Premier, *mi Generale*, but here it is. Now, there can be no doubt in your mind what is contained in it. *Va bene?*" Pietro's eyes sparkled mischievously.

"You cub of a fox! I could kiss you!" Tori reached for the letter and hugged the younger man.

Tori embraced the lad and then, moving to the fires, hastened to read the Premier's letter. His hopes soared! There was no mention of Salvatore specifically or in a punitive way. Only the vaguest reference had been made concerning the participation of the brigands. He took heart. He summoned Santino, gave him the letter with instructions to make up two copies—one for his file, one for Tori. The original was to be kept in a safe place where no one might have access to it.

Tori was both amused and prepared when the message came from Don Santo Florio demanding audience with him. He waited five days, then, accompanied by his paladins, presented himself to the corpulent Don who lived like an oriental potentate in his sumptuous villa in an area of verdant splendor at the edge of Partinico.

They found him at the center of a tropical garden, fully concealed from prying eyes by a high wall of stone overrun with exotic greenery, pomegranate trees, citrus and fig trees, and prickly-pear cactus, seated on a sturdy oak chair the size of a love seat—a chair well constructed to accomodate his more than three hundred pounds of massive flab.

"We talk alone, eh, Salvatore?" puffed the giant, laboriously.

Tori nodded, signalled his men accordingly. The Don nodded in a like manner to his ominous bodyguards. Together with Salvatore's men they moved out of hearing distance, crossed the terrace and stretched out under a yawning fig tree, laden with a bountiful crop. An elderly caretaker served them red wine, over which Tori politely expressed his regrets that he didn't drink.

Several dogs barked with playful ferocity; hounds, mongrels, and other mixed breeds, numbering nine in all and all trained to kill, were fenced in a shelter at the end of the courtyard. Somewhere, someone played the Bandit's *Marching Song of Victory* on a mandolin. It brought a smile to Vincenzo's face. He winked at the others and picked up a deck of playing cards and dealt a hand to Santino. Arturo Scoletti watched them for a time, but his dark apes' eyes were trained on Salvatore and the Royal Cavalier.

A magnificent aviary lined one wall of the house, containing some of the more exotic birds Tori had ever seen.

What an incongruous touch, thought Tori. Here a man known to his people as the wielder of power of the gang and gun variety actually collects warm living birds. Yet, wasn't there something brutal, something truly sadistic about someone who imprisoned that much beauty for himself alone? The very melodic sounds of the feathered creatures were lilting and pleasant to the ears. Parrots squawked raucously and chattered in Sicilian as they craned their multicolored necks. A few swarms of black flies congested in patches here and there in the lush atrium; otherwise it could have been paradise.

A young woman, with lowered eyes he couldn't see for the moment came in to the area, freely swinging her hips. Her full gathered skirts did a little jig as she moved towards them carrying a tray of fruits, wines and glasses.

Tori, as any red-blooded man would, glanced appreciatively at her, nodding in a gesture of respect. She was a bewitching wench, her face wearing the cosmetics of a city girl; her dark luminous eyes, when she glanced at him, flirted outrageously with him. Tori glanced sharply from her to Don Santo Florio, who he knew had caught the look. He didn't expect the *mafioso's* next statement. "You want Selina, eh?"

Against his will, Tori found himself flushing. Just as quickly, he recuperated from the awkwardness. "It's my understanding you have a message for me. I'm here on business. I've no time for the procurement of services you offer." His steely eyes caught and held the *mafioso's* tiny black cobra eyes, hanging low in the pouches of his puffy lids.

The Don grunted. "I have a message from your Godfather. He wants to assure you that he holds you in no contempt." He breathed laboriously. "Not for the insubordination nor the lack of respect you've accorded him."

Tori, a study in silent concentration twirled a match stick in his fingers, as the girl, on a nod from Don Florio, turned and, with a capering whirl, went into the house. Tori's eyes fell on the bowl of freshly plucked figs. He selected one, split it in half with his fingers, and popped a section into his mouth, rolling his expressive eyes with appreciation.

"*Mangi. Mangi,*" Don Florio pushed the bowl towards him. "You'll never taste figs like mine in all Sicily. Pure nectar. Ambrosia of the gods, believe me. No one grows them like Don Santo Florio. My *figgi* are to Sicily what Diego Rallo's wine represents—the best."

Tori shook his head in refusal and pushed the bowl back towards the Don. For a moment he imagined the basket of figs presented to Cleopatra containing the deadly asp. "Once I get started on them, they are my death," he said significantly, unsure if the Don had ever heard of the Egyptian queen.

"Don Matteo insists that if you had been in the east, the Partitionists wouldn't have come to the disgraceful end that befell them at Bello's hands."

Tori stared at him in silence.

"Due to the untiring efforts of that great Don Matteo, your illustrious Godfather, Sicily has been granted autonomy. What a man! What a genius! He is someone special—that one. I hope you appreciate the fact that he's your Godfather. Not too many men can be proud of such distinction."

Visibly annoyed with this one-man rooting section, Tori scowled. "You haven't called me to your villa to discuss parentage, or to tell me what I already know. Do get on with it, Don Florio," he requested tersely as he took a moment to light a cigarette. He fanned out the match and tossed it on a nearby spittoon.

"I put to you a proposition," said the Don impassionately. "Cooperate with Don Barbarossa. Persuade the electorate in our district and surrounding areas to vote the Christian Democratic ticket and he will use his persuasive powers in Parliament and with Minister Belasci to obtain pardons for you and your men." He spoke with labored effort.

This was the proposal Tori had been waiting for. Now, he understood why the *capomafia's* men hadn't put the proposal to him—the time hadn't been right. Tori tried to subdue his inner excitement.

"There are three stipulations," the Don coughed apologetically as he toyed with a fig on the table, spinning it in one direction, then to the next. You are to assist in the elimination of every rival guerrilla band in Sicily. Cease in your harassment of landowners; let them proceed in their business as they see fit. And contribute all your strength and resources to drive the communists from Sicily."

After a moment, Tori said with mocking contempt. "That's all?" His eyes bore into the Don's.

Don Florio ignored the remark, wiped his sweaty neck and face with a cloth, and swatted at the pesky flies

586

swarming around him. "You know the Premier granted you no amnesty."

"You say that too pleasurably, Dòn Florio. I detect a hint of gloating."

The Don affected to be dismayed. "*Mah*—no. How can you think that? Don't you know what I think of you? All the good you've done for our people?" He sucked his teeth, shook his head and remarked, "I'm saddened you should think me as anything but an ally." He avoided eye contact with his guest, for fear the duplicity in them would speak more truly then his lips.

Salvatore studied the diamond solitaire on his little finger. He didn't trust this conspiratorial Mafia Don, not for one moment. He turned the diamond until it caught the sun's rays and became too bright to focus on.

"Your Godfather insisted that I respectfully remind you of the two special favors done you—without question. Cooperate with him, and he'll compromise with de Aspanu on your behalf."

"What assurance do I have that the Christian Democrats won't fall, as previous parties fell?" Tori danced with him a bit, lightly, trying not to step on his toes, or reveal too much to him.

"What assurance, you ask? What assurance? Why, the word of Don Barbarossa is enough!" He snorted. "But why are you concerned? You did well, financially—no?" He was brutally candid, lacking in finesse.

"You stroll along the bottom of the sea as easily as you'd promenade in a rose garden, Don Santo Florio," said Tori evenly, leveling his eyes on the fat man. "I had their word last time. It crumpled to dust and blew away like sand on the sea."

"You had Don Barbarossa's word?"

Tori frowned. No. He'd never had his father's word in the matter. He rose to his feet, strutted about the courtyard in deep thought, hands clasped behind his back. Moving about the area, he stopped before an aviary containing exotic birds of rare and beautiful plumage; ciaques, cockatoos, Jobi Lorys, etc.

"Once there were many birds," puffed the Don. "A careless servant left the doors open one night. *Ppppffffttt!* By morning only two were left. Now, I have six rare birds. I lost eleven to those malevolent predators—the cats. My heart was broken, I tell you. Broken. Birds have little chance for survival among those dwarfed tigers, *aquilo bravo*." His host said ominously.

"Birds might succumb to dwarfed tigers, but, not

587

eagles," said Tori unable to resist a reply. "But, enough of this. It's time to talk business. You will instruct Don Barbarossa to put into writing what he promises Salvatore. Why he desires such services, and what he expects done. Such a document is to be signed by him, Martino Belasci and General Brancuso. Only when the document is delivered will Salvatore become a partisan of the Sicilian government and help restore normalcy to our nation. Only then will he assist in the butchery of its enemies, as you and the *capomafia* suggest."

"You want I should say such a thing to your Godfather?"

"Precisely."

The only exterior clues to Don Santo Florio's makeup lay in his capacity to ascribe a status and self-importance to himself that was purely deceptive. He could never be wrong. Those who disagreed with him or his ways were the wrongdoers, the culprits. He wasn't used to any other way of thinking but his own. Those men whom he was unable to convince with his brand of logic always tasted his vengeful wrath. Any man who'd just made a proposal to him, as Salvatore had just done, would have been laughed out of his villa. To convey such an outrageous proposal to the *capomafia* would have disgraced him in the brotherhood.

However, he was merely a messenger in this contemplated *entente*—not a mediator. Taking all of Salvatore's indisputable victories into account, he reasoned, this was no ordinary peasant he could browbeat into submission. All in good time.

"I am at your service, General Salvatore," he said a bit too graciously.

Only when Don Barbarossa's swift response came in full accord with Salvatore's request did the young rebel have any indication of the true strength of his position. He read the document, studied the signatures, and feeling more secure about the forthcoming amnesty than he had felt in the past, an ineffable grin of delight lit up his face. He handed the letter to Santino Siragusa with instructions to reproduce three copies of the document; the original to be kept in a safe place with Premier de Aspanu's letter; the second, framed and placed over his desk at home; the third, to be included in his biography.

"This time there can be no mistakes—no room for errors. We act as government partisans. *Then*, let them tell us there'll be no amnesty for Salvatore or his men!"

588

"There's still a price on our heads," said Vincenzo, quietly.

"A mere technicality, cousin dear. Soon it will be rectified."

Vincenzo and Santino exchanged concerned glanced. Santino moved about the Grotto D'Oro and busied himself with the large scrapbook he kept on his brother-in-law. He sighed deeply. "Enter a new chapter in the life of Salvatore. One, pray God, which will give him more peace," he murmured to himself.

Salvatore, exhilarated, proud, and happy, filled with hope. Suddenly life was becoming more than a day to day existence. There would be a future for him after all. With the power of his father and of the Christian Democrats behind him, he might soon reflect the image of the man Colonel Modica had envisioned him to be.

CHAPTER 42

What ensued in the months following was likened to mass murder performed with the art of skilled surgeons. Don Barbarossa suspended the code of silence—*Omerta*—and the black tentacles of death spread like uncontrolled malaria, drenching the Sicilian countryside. Chief Enzio Semano, the *carabinieri*, and an army of Salvatore's men cleaned up what remained of all rival guerrilla bands.

In *Gela*, the swarthy, bandy-legged Volpe, a man with a perpetual grin on his face, fell exhausted in a drunken stupor on the bed of his mistress. She hung a yellow scarf in her window. In moments the room, beseiged by police, left a trail of carmine blood in their wake. Both Volpe and his mistress: that treacherous, protesting whore, riddled with bullets, fell; betrayed and betrayer together in a heap.

In *Camporeale*, the sleepy, rabbit-eared bandit Edoardo Valone, former ally of Salvatore who had broken away from his band and continued to lay endless siege to property, found himself betrayed. He paid a visit to a reluctant landlord who protested a large penalty imposed on him. The landlord, did a turnabout, and agreed to meet his demands—and when on Valone's arrival they shook hands, the landlord held tightly to his hands as a knife was thrust into the culprit's back rendering him helpless. Valone, a crafty, vindictive renegade who had lived by his wits was ultimately unable to outsmart that new breed of police schooled by Mafia specialists. As he lay writhing on the floor, he was riddled to death by police guns.

Another bandit, Gruppo, in the *Corleone* area, had been sent a handsome new gun, a collector's item, in the name of an old and trusted friend. The first time he tried to shoot it, it exploded in his face. Two of his corrupt companions in nearby *Piana dei Greci* found an abandoned Jeep by the roadside. Excited at their good fortune, they jumped into the car, found the keys in readiness and didn't think to question such coincidence. On went the key, down went the starter and both men were blown to kingdom come.

Several illiterate bandits in *Castellammare*, had looked forward to keeping an appointed rendezvous at the beach near *Scopello*, a natural phenomenon, where wind, water and other elements combined to carve unusual shapes and forms of man-beasts on the stony cliffs facing the sea, had been convinced by their loved ones they'd be taken by boat to Palermo and transported to Brazil and freedom. God! Anything was better than to remain in Sicily, where their friends were being destroyed by the hundreds by the professional guns of the Mafia.

Over fifty fleeing renegades congregated in the early morning hours. Against a background of the tears and wailing cries of their loved ones who waved at them from the shore, they began boarding the allocated boats. Close to a hundred mothers, father, sisters, brothers, wives and children waved farewell to their men, as the overtaxed motors laboriously putt-putt-putted them into deeper waters. Suddenly out of the shifting fog banks came two high powered Coast Guard cruisers bulging with *carabinieri* and seamen heavily armed with machine guns and automatic rifles. They opened fire, ripping apart both men and boats with a hail of bullets. Many jumped into the swirling, murky waters of the open harbor in an attempt to swim to safety, only to be machine-gunned as the boats' gunners strafed the waters in a continuous fusillade.

In the wake of silence, the Coast Guard boats turned about and retreated into the shifting mist. Only the broken debris of the escapee boats, piloted by death, floated on the waters. When the open-mouthed spectators realized what had happened and that they had been inadvertently used as instruments of death, their screams shrieked through the air endlessly, in sickening torment.

Days and nights followed, filled with the treacheries of the old Mafia, who ordered that no bandit possessing information of an intimate nature concerning Mafia business was to be taken alive. Mafia henchmen and young *picciotti*, anxious to make themselves known for the glory of the brotherhood, came to life under the expertise of the *mafioso*, Cacciatore, whose skills in malevolent torture were second to none in the land.

In the south, the bandit, Russo, a former *Terra Diavolo* escapee, a man almost on a par with Salvatore's reputation, continued pillaging and kidnapping long after the order to cease and desist had been issued. He received, one day as a gift, a pair of elegant, hand-crafted leather riding boots made especially for him. A quick evaluation of the mass murders and untimely deaths of his compatriots told him he had one choice: leave Sicily. A quick attempted escape by boat to the North African coast by Russo and several of his men found them on deck as the fishing scow sailed southwards, watching as their island nation turned to a tiny dot on the horizon. In a poignant gesture of farewell, Russo gallantly saluted his country snappily, and from force of habit clicked his heels together—and blew himself and the entire boatload of men into a sea of Neptune's Hades. Contained in the hollows of his new boots which he wore for this special occasion was enough nitro to have wrecked three ships.

By the end of 1946 order had been restored to Sicily. Only one band of brigands remained—Salvatore's. The country was his.

Awareness of the word *power* was taking its effect on Tori. Having tasted its intoxicating nectar for a time, he came to enjoy its heady sensation. He savored the adulation of his people and the drugging sweetness of victory and he grew addicted to such vainglorious feelings. The past year's involvements had caused him to seriously consider Colonel Modica's words of wisdom and encouragement to take a more active part in politics. No slouch, this king of all brigands—an avid reader and a master strategist, with the strength of a loyal army behind him—he kept abreast of all political and historical happenings, and came to one conclusion. It was time for Salvatore to enter politics.

A careful appraisal of the situation brought several things into clear focus. No question in his mind existed that with the granting of autonomy, the industrialization of Sicily would follow. People would develop a political consciousness and a sense of responsibility. Impressed indelibly in his mind were the powers to be given the legislative body of ninety deputies to be set up in Palermo with its own cabinet ministers. Because this legislative body would be invested with complete control over vital areas of agriculture, mining and industry, in addition to their control of communications, public order and other phases of public life, Salvatore felt it would be wise to begin as one of these influential ministers.

Aware that one vital offshoot of autonomy provided for a special grant by the Italian government to reimburse Sicily for the inequities dealt her in the past, Tori realized it would place the taxable income lower than the national average. He had heard many of the feudalists delight and rejoice over this fact. However, the rapid growth of communists and socialists, outnumbering any present political party, and the fear they might capture the regional government and carry out drastic social reforms greatly disturbed the Mafia—Feudalist combine.

For these very reasons Don Barbarossa had taken extreme precaution to unify the Monarchists and several straggler political parties into one strong Christian Democratic Party. The Don, as quick as Salvatore to recognize the importance of controlling the party which would ultimately control the building permits, import licenses and contracts for public works, did some swift calculating and readily ascertained that regional autonomy and regional budgets automatically opened up lucrative horizons, and those who got in on the ground floor would become the richest, most powerful heads of state. The eternal race and insatiable greed for power and money was on, and to the victors would go all of Sicily.

Considering all these factors, Tori listened to the high-powered politicos who predicted so phenomenal a future for Sicily. On no one's counsel but his own, he dared try to make his dreams come true. When he finalized his decision to run for the position of Deputy in the Constitutional Assembly, he took a lesson from the example set forth by Francesco Bello, just as his *Godfather* had balefully predicted he might. He paid the corpulent Don Santo Florio a visit, and instructed him to advise Don Barbarossa to place the name of Alessandro Salvatore on the slate of candidates for local assembly in the coming election.

Informed by his spies of a plan to deter his political aspirations when the Court moved to try him *in absentia* for the murder of Nino Marino, Tori was able to protect himself from such political skullduggery. While the rats were sniffing out the cheese, he took measures to remain one step ahead of the diabolical plotters.

In strict accordance with Sicilian laws, Salvatore paid a lump sum of money to the family of the deceased *carabiniero*, Marino, and was subsequently exonerated from the guilt of his death. This restitutive gesture to the family provided that he couldn't be convicted of the felony, and thus swept aside his technical ineligibility to running for public office, to the chagrin of Minister Belasci and Don Barbarossa.

Yet, despite this clever strategy, despite all precautions and carefully laid plans, the day came when the slate of candidates was officially announced—and Salvatore's name had been omitted. The insult done him, coupled with his disappointment and all the previous betrayals and broken promises was too much.

How many times in those days did Tori wish he could drink—get blind drunk and forget his cares and worries the way Vincenzo and his other men did. Once Tori had laughed, sung, and enjoyed himself as other men might. How long had the weighty responsibilities pressed upon his shoulders, preventing him from being as easy and carefree as the others? How much longer would he not be permitted to enjoy the pleasures of men?

Drop by drop, bit by bit, day by day, Tori tasted the bitterness of being spurned by his father. He grew morose and sullen and he calculated every move. "Fuck them! Fuck them all!" he told Vincenzo. "I'll show them they can't treat Salvatore like the lowest of all obscenities! One day they will need the power of Salvatore. Then we'll see how Salvatore responds to this insult! We'll see."

Meanwhile, Salvatore filled with decision. Considering the fact that Don Barbarossa was his real father, he told himself, *one day the Don will wake up to discover that the man he intrigued the hardest against is his own flesh and blood.* And like many an outraged son, Tori's resentment and hurt mushroomed out of proportion. If he knew one thing, he knew for certain that as sure as the sun rose in the east, he wouldn't lift a finger to persuade the electorate to vote the Christian Democratic ticket in the coming election.

In the sparring corners of the political arena, the Christian Democrats employed every means at their disposal to influence voters in the election of the Sicilian Regional Parliament on April 27, 1947. As Don Barbarossa laid the groundwork by persuading the Right and Center to stand firmly behind the Christian Democrats against the communists in what he felt would be a landslide victory, the Church promoted their usual psychological persuasion by threatening to take away a man's work permit unless he voted as they instructed. In addition, Mafia thugs, fierce-faced and menacing, hung about polling stations and, behind benign glances they telegraphed their terrorist messages to any would-be opposition.

It came as a severe blow to the Christian Democrats, and most especially to Don Barbarossa, when, after taking every precaution to insure votes, they met defeat by a substantial majority. The fear of a real revolution and a communist takeover loomed threateningly in the minds of the Mafia-Feudalists.

Salvatore, that self-satisfied, political neophyte, sat back contentedly, thinking he'd taught his Godfather a lesson in respect. What did he care if his name hadn't appeared on the roster? There'd be other times. He was young and had a lifetime to fulfill his political inclinations. For now he got his satisfaction. He would be respected for the power he wielded—or else. He was exquisitely delighted to learn that his people, upon no instruction from him, had voted against the Christian Democrats. That would show that high and mighty father of his! Wouldn't it?

But Tori's joy was short lived when he learned the results of his self imposed neutrality had created a severe breach in the Christian Democratic Party, and through the loss of the majority of votes to the Reds, communism had gained a strong foothold in his beloved country. How quickly the sweet taste of revenge turned to bitter vetch.

Little did Tori know that this one act, done with a schoolboy's attitude of adolescent petulance, had succeeded in throwing a monkey wrench into the plans of a redoubtable political machine comprised of Church, Government and Mafia and would nearly bring about the collapse of a nation. His contempt for those two-tongued, lying vipers and their broken promises, his damaged ego, and the Cold War combined to play havoc with Rome's central government, and would soon lash back at him with the fury of a devastating tornado.

In Rome, on June 28, Premier Alfonso de Aspanu, that puritanical patrician and Christian Democrat, regarded with undisguised horror the mess those insane Sicilians had created in the south. Hadn't he instructed them on the perils of communist infiltration? The political structure of the Party was shaky enough without their idiotic playacting! Well, by God, there was only one thing for him to do. A complete purge! He reorganized his cabinet with a coalition of the three leading parties, and totally excluded the Reds. Immediate retaliation came in the form of loud protests headlined in the communist press. That crazy de Aspanu! Refusing the Reds a voice in government! He'll not get away with it! There followed a steady barrage of irrevocable and damaging statements denouncing Church and State.

The can of worms, disturbed when the crisis of the Cold War was at its worst, brought about irreconcilable differences between Christian Democrats and the communists, and gathered momentum daily. Communists charged that Papal rule influenced the formation of the CDP; the CDP countered, accusing the Reds of being influenced by Soviet policy. They danced a *tarantella* with each other, accusing and counter-accusing, until the friction between them threatened to burst into uncontainable flames. Suddenly, in a surprise move, the socialists joined with the communists in attacking Premier de Aspanu's policies, until his government showed signs of decline. There was no doubt in the mind of the stately, well-bred politician that the amalgamation took place with the stated objective of taking power.

In January, 1947, Premier de Aspanu, on a quick trip to Washington, D.C. obtained fifty million dollars in payment for purchases by U.S. Forces in Italy, plus a credit for one hundred million dollars from the Import-Export Bank of the United States for the immediate shipment of vital foodstuffs, plus pledges of additional aid. During his absence, the socialists, reflecting a widespread trend on the issue of collaboration with the communists, split into two groups. The leader of the pro-communist factions resigned and the entire cabinet withdrew.

The pressure on de Aspanu grew intolerable. On February 2, he formed another coalition including the communists and socialists. Once again all hell broke loose. This time the flak came from his own party. How dare he permit the Reds a voice in the government? That Sicilian Marsala he'd imported from Sicily must be dimming his vision. He was crazy—Simply crazy to do such a thing!

While Premier de Aspanu, that incurable pacifist, tried to appease all sides, other forces were constantly at work stirring up more cans of worms. In the mounting diplomatic struggle that came to be called the Cold War between western democracies and the Soviet Bloc, the political parties in Italy took sides according to their ideological orientation.

In February the Paris peace treaties were signed and, despite loud protests, the treaty was ratified by the Italian Constituent Assembly, with the communists and socialists abstaining. On September 15, the terms of the treaty took effect, and the Allied Occupational forces withdrew shortly thereafter, leaving the Reds a free hand to promote their ideologies. The Italian people who generally opposed the treaty, were encouraged by the firm attitude of the Americans which helped frustrate demands for harsher terms, and pleased by what they believed were friendly intentions towards Italy, became a bulwark for a time against communist infiltration and for a time deterred the Red menace.

But the constant state of turmoil caused a festering of boils to swell on the backsides of most conspiratorial politicians to agonizing proportions, and they soon began to gather in sequestered hideaways to discuss and seek means to further retard the growing threat of communism.

Observing the goings-on in Sicily with a modicum of disgust and frustration, Don Barbarossa viewed the scene in Rome with great concern, as a storm brewed inside him. To the layman's eyes it would hardly seem feasible that one man—*that incorrigible bandit, Salvatore*—could have so inordinately influenced politics that an entire nation trembled while suffering the consequences of his ill-fated and stubborn act of neutrality.

Goddamnit! What the hell was that young punk thinking of? The *capomafia* raved in the many hours of contemplation he spent pacing the floor of his study. Had Salvatore unwittingly brought about tremendous gains for the Reds and a sharp decline in Christian Democratic support? Or had it been a part of a cleverly planned game? Had Salvatore sold out to the communists? Had he? After the elaborate plans made by the Don to offset such a possibility.

To make matters worse—those insufferable ecclesiastical princes raved and ranted of nothing else! Hadn't they warned the Don? Hadn't they warned the entire Grand Council years before? No one listened! No one paid them any heed when they disclaimed Salvatore as anticlerical! What more proof did the *capomafia* need to believe that Salvatore had joined the communists, with the full intent to undermine the Church and seduce all of Sicily for Russia? Why else had he so cleverly manipulated the electorate to vote in favor of the Reds?

596

Martino Belasci had screamed all the way from Rome. "I thought you had Salvatore all sewed up! Promise him anything, I told you! What happened?" When the Don explained that the *in absentia* trial had backfired, that Salvatore was sulking like a petulant schoolboy, Martino was fit to be tied. Even he couldn't believe the truth. He was certain that something more devious in Salvatore's nature, perhaps a plot with the Russians had planned this political embarrassment.

Having swallowed all the indigestible goings on with an ample dosage of bicarbonate of soda, the Don decided the time had come to promote a direct confrontation with his Godson. Goddammit! The power of Salvatore loomed larger and and more devastating than ever!

Whatever prevented him from taking drastic measures against that stubborn mule, that obnoxious and arrogant donkey, unnerved him more than the political unrest and recent upset at the polls. Salvatore's action—or rather his lack of action—at the polls was unforgivable. How to bring this obstinate peasant to his knees. How?

To Don Barbarossa, who demanded rigid discipline from all men, there was no excuse in Salvatore's disrespectful, unmanly and deliberately treasonous attitude. Why, it wasn't the Sicilian thing to do!

So? How does Mohammed make the mountain come to him? All men had weaknesses. Even the vainglorious Salvatore must have an Achilles heel. But—what? A man who didn't drink? A man who was no carouser of women? A man who seemingly had no vices? What?

For a time he forgot national politics and their erupting volcanoes, and concentrated, instead, on this fact-finding mission. The very idea that one man's thoughtless actions could affect national politics was simply incredible. Incredible and immoral! And highly objectionable!

What to do? What to do?

BOOK V

CHAPTER 43

"Steve! . . . Stephen Modica!" . . .

He heard the memory-evoking voice and spun about to see an American jeep come to a screeching halt on the *Elssholzstrasse am Kleistpark* in the *Schoeneberg District* of Berlin. Modica had just emerged from the offices of the Allied Control Council; an impressive North German Baroque structure, which, prior to the occupation, had housed the highest German appelate court, the *Kammergericht*. He shaded his eyes in time to recognize the pale orchid eyes of a young woman dressed in a G.I. jumpsuit, carrying a camera slung about her neck and a gadget bag slung over one shoulder. She jumped clear of the vehicle and ran towards him. Her face, scrubbed clean of makeup except for a red lip gloss, contained a few dirt smudges and an excitement of shocked disbelief.

"Gina? . . . Gina O'Hoolihan!" His jaw fell open in astonishment. "My God! What the hell are you doing here!" shouted Modica. He picked her up in his strong arms and swung her about in a complete circle. He kissed her. Instantly he recalled a host of images of the last time they'd been together in London, during the early stages of the war. Feeling the offshoots of a deeply-rooted pain, Modica, suddenly remembering, held her away from him, and studied her for several moments.

They stared at each other, eyes searching eyes for some sign, some indication of forgiveness for not having made it all work the way a storybook dictates.

"Ten minutes away by car, in London, we couldn't find each other! Now, thousands of miles, on the other side of the fucking world we run into each other! Tell me, is it kismet—fate?"

"Hello, Steve," she whispered in a throaty voice, remembering everything good that had passed between them. They fell into each other's arms amid the ruins and rubble of a majestic city, once fiercely proud, now razed to the ground in a deplorable shambles with mounds and mounds of broken debris all around.

For an instant, Stephen Modica dared raise his hopes. Her fragrant scents evoked fond memories and stirred responses that never really left him. He felt the same old urge to possess her. Gina felt the swelling of his body against hers and drew back. When Modica searched her soul-stirring eyes, he knew the past was over. In them, he saw a depth of emotion he couldn't fathom, guarded by a gate of reserve, that communicated "look, but don't touch me again." Modica hid his disappointment and grew politely cordial.

"If I act stunned—I am!" He pulled her off to one side of the entrance of Headquarters and steered her closer to the *strasse* where they wouldn't be interrupted or annoyed by wise cracking G.I.'s.

"What are you doing here?" he offered her a cigarette and lit it for her.

". . . Two things. Nuremburg Trials and looking for you."

"How did you know I was here?" Before she replied he asked, "Are you all right, Gina? I mean really all right?"

"Don't I look all right?" she quipped with false bravado. She did a quick *pirouette*. "Look, dad, no scars!"

Steve felt a tug over his heart, and a thick lump settled in his throat. Color rose to his face, and in split seconds, mental images of their relationship replayed themselves in his mind. They had met in Washington, D.C.; she, a news correspondent, and he with U.S. Army Intelligence, back before he transferred to OSS with Patton's Seventh Army. The impact of their love had been so intense that when he had left for London two weeks later, Gina had coerced her editor to send her overseas as a War Correspondent, to get the "woman's angle" on the bombing of Britain. She had joined Modica and for six weeks they had been inseparable; they had formed a love in which each had unwittingly become dependent on the other for mere survival. Transferred suddenly to General Patton's command, Steve had tried to find Gina before his company shoved off—but couldn't. He had left a note for her before he shipped out.

It had been a night Gina would never erase from her memory. She had missed him by five minutes. She read his note and left instantly for the air terminal, only to be caught in a barrage of bombs and antiaircraft missiles. She had been seriously injured and, in addition, aborted a three month pregnancy of which he'd had no knowledge. She hadn't wished to worry him or add to his burdens.

Her physical injuries, a green-stick fracture in the upper

left thigh and an overriding fracture of the lower limb had healed in time. But she'd developed what doctors call emotional insulation, an ego-defense mechanism in which the reduction of tensions and anxieties of her needs occured by a withdrawal into passivity. Progressing into a state of disordered consciousness, Gina had performed acts of which she later had no recollection, she became a vegetable for a year and a half. Then suddenly one day she was well again, ready to work.

The story of Salvatore broke in the press through an American correspondent, whom it seemed had stirred up a hornet's nest of international controversy by being branded an American spy by the Communist press. Gina's boss got the idea she'd be perfect to interview the swashbuckling bandit, to get the "woman's angle" on him. She set about the task with careful deliberation when she learned that interviews with this Sicilian legend were viewed by the Italian Government with much apprehension.

"Look, Steve, can we go someplace to talk? I've come a long way to talk with you about Salvatore," She removed her helmet, shook out her long dark hair, and rubbed her neck gingerly. "Damned helmets!"

Colonel Modica stared at her, wondering. "Salvatore? How did you know we knew each other?"

"Matt Saginor. I met him in Rome. Since the previous press interviews with Salvatore turned to dynamite, they're being damned fussy about who they allow in Palermo."

"Why do you want to know about him?"

She explained the assignment. Colonel Modica listened—and observed the changes in Gina. No longer was she the girl he had known and loved. Several moments passed before he spoke. He took her hand between his—and noticed how expertly she slipped out of his grasp. When she saw astonishment turn to hurt in his azure blue eyes, she said simply, as if it explained everything. "You didn't bother to write. Not one letter came from you."

"In the middle of a war—there's no time for *anything,* Gina. We were—" Stefano paused. There weren't sufficient excuses he could offer to help either of them. He sighed deeply, hoping some of the pain could escape his lips.

"Honey, blame it on the time, the circumstances, death and destruction, the constant shelling and barrage of bullets we tried to duck every fucking minute! Death in the morning! Death in the afternoon! Death at night! Death all around us. Who the hell had time to think of life in a world centered around death? In war, life is at the other

603

side of the moon," he said bitterly. "What about you? What were you doing while I played soldier?" He tried to make light of it. He had no other place to go. Once they had been inseparable, two lovers with an impact on each other like nothing Steve had ever experienced and probably ever would. Now, they were like strangers with dangling umbilical cords, looking for some life to plug into, so they might restore life to their warped souls.

"What's the point, Steve?" she asked softly. "No sense rehashing the bad memories." *Of what use would it be to recreate the bombing, the accident, the unborn child?* "Why go over the agony of the past? Why load either one of us with guilt? I don't hate you—never that. Neither of us are to blame for what happened. We met. We loved. For a time we shared the priceless gift of love. Now, it's over. Simple as that." She injected a frivolous tone to her voice. "Now, tell me, how did you come to meet this famous brigand? Tell me about him, will you?"

"Can we go someplace to talk? Suddenly I'm annoyed with the whole goddamned war and all it's come to mean." He watched a truck load of POW's bounce along the rutted road, followed by a truckload of engineers; road crews working around the clock to clean up the ravaged, war-torn city.

"I've only forty minutes before my plane leaves," she replied glancing at her watch. "I'm due back in Rome." She had just about given up hope of ever seeing him when by chance she spotted him coming out of ACC headquarters.

"Where—Templehof?" he asked. "Need a lift? Listen, I'll drive you back. We can talk en route."

"Would you?" She glanced apprehensively at the abandoned jeep.

"I'll take care of it," insisted Stefano. "Whose is it?"

"Name's on the visor. Some trooper relinquished it to me."

Col. Modica tipped his hat and disappeared inside the impressive stone building and, in moments, returned with an aide alongside him. They piled into a gleaming staff car, with flags waving, and drove off towards Templeho.

"O.K. shoot. With luck we'll make it in time for your flight."

Gina smiled. He hadn't changed much. Always on the run. She asked him to tell her as much as he could about Salvatore.

"As much as I remember?" He nodded wistfully. "I wished to God I didn't remember him. No, No, nothing like that! He wasn't a thorn in my side." He told her as best he could what he thought about the young man, explaining the differences in their cultures, and, with every breath he uttered, Gina saw fierce admiration, a bond of respect, and a breathless excitement in the word pictures he painted. "I'm dearly fond of him, Gina. He's probably the best thing that's happened to his country. I pray only that he knows how to handle himself in that sea of political *piranhas* down there. He's so young, almost naive, at their brand of political skullduggery—"

The U.S. Army staff car turned left on Columbiadamm and passed through the heavily guarded gate at Templehof Airport, saluted smartly by armed sentries. Milling crowds of army personnel congested the immediate area. Glancing at either side of him through the open windows, Colonel Modica asked casually,

"Whom did you see in Palermo?"

"Who didn't I? I was tossed between hostile *carabinieri* and irritating security police." She glanced out, idly at the congested traffic in the streets.

"Wouldn't cooperate, eh?" Colonel Modica smiled. "All right. Tell you what to do. You drive from Palermo to his village in Montegatta. Ask anyone, they'll tell you where his mother lives. When you arrive, you tell *Signora* Salvatore you're a friend of mine. I won't guarantee the conditions, honey. It's been over a year since I was there. You do speak Italian?"

"Even Sicilian—a little."

"You won't need it with Tori. Sonofagun speaks English fairly well, considering he's self taught." Steve fumbled in his wallet and pulled out a card. "Here's a special pass. Use it. It might help."

The staff car eased its way through the compound and came to a halt a few feet from a waiting U.S.A. transport.

"I can't thank you enough, Steve," Gina said softly, her violet eyes swimming in the faint suspicion of tears welling up in them.

"Listen, Gina," he began hoarsely. He took her hands in his. "I thank God you're safe. I worried about you—I really did. I thought about you—dreamed about you— needed you more often than I wanted to let myself. Your image, and my memories of our love, sustained me through some frightening times. The very hell of war became the catalyst that converted me into an automaton—a mechanism of war. It'll take time before I become a normal human being again. Perhaps someday when all this is over with," He gestured abstractly in the air with his hands, "well, maybe we can meet again and patch up our differences."

"Perhaps, Steve. Perhaps."

No longer the people they were at the onset of the war, they embraced and kissed as good friends. The American officer stood at the gate silently, and hunched over, a sad and forlorn expression in his dull blue eyes until the plane took off into the sky bound for Rome. Colonel Stefano Modica, that bulwark of strength and dedication, experienced a sudden jolt of depression as he walked slowly back to the waiting staff car.

Ten minutes later, in a bombed-out section of Berlin, Stefano was so absorbed in memories of Gina that he accidently stepped on a mine. Following the explosion, he was hospitalized for a year until the trauma of losing a leg had subsided.

CHAPTER 44

Gina had spent nearly three hours with Antigone and Athena, interviewing them, enjoying their company and taking pictures of the Salvatore house. Watching her, Antigone expressed her concern.

"My son might object to the photographs, *Signora* Gina. We do nothing without his approval."

"Then, I'll leave the undeveloped film here with you until he gives his approval," she said pleasantly. She didn't want to risk losing an interview with Salvatore.

"Approval for what?" asked a deep and sensuous voice behind her.

Gina turned and looked into the dark smiling eyes of the most exciting man she'd ever met. His skin glowed a coppery bronze under a sleeveless tank top he wore. He towered over her even as he leaned lazily against the door. His appraising eyes took in every detail of her voluptuous figure hardly camouflaged by the fatigues she wore.

Athena jumped to her feet and ran into his arms in a warm burst of affection, hugging him and kissing him profusely; then, tugging at his arm she led him closer to where Gina stood awkwardly fumbling with her camera.

"Tori, this is Gina Hoo—ooli," she stammered. "I'm sorry it's difficult to pronounce."

"O'Hoolihan," she volunteered extending her trembling hand.

Tori bowed and kissed it, noticing the Captain's bars on her shoulders. "I'm Salvatore, *Capitana.* I had expected to see a man."

Noticing the devilish sparkle in his eyes, she grew flustered. As if she couldn't tell he was Salvatore. Every inch of him exuded a male sensuality. Instantly he was everything Stefano had described. In the brief instant their eyes met and held, Athena nudged her mother playfully as they both recognized the impact each had on the other.

Gathering all professionalism, Gina managed to stammer, "At last we meet. For six months I've looked forward to this moment, and only recently when I spoke with Colonel Modica—"

"Stefano?" he interrupted. "You know Stefano?" If Tori had maintained an aloofness moments before it immediately evaporated in a sunshine of smiles. "Where is the *Colonnello?* What's he doing now the war's over? *Mannagghia,* what a fine man. See?" Tori held up the golden scorpion amulet. "He gave it to me as a token of our friendship before he left Sicily." he exclaimed with pride.

"What a coincidence," retorted Gina as she held the golden chain out from around her neck. "Me too. I'm a Scorpio, also. Stefano gave this to me a long time ago."

Watching this small scene, Antigone stood very still. Her eyes jumped from one amulet to the other. Her heart pounded fiercely.

The double sting of the scorpion gives flight to the eagle!

Would she never escape the prophecy? She had yet to fully interpret it, but each word was committed to her mind, indelibly. Could this be coincidence—too? She held on to the chair next to her to steady her.

"She wants to write about you, Tori," began Athena.

"Apparently you've won my family over completely," said Tori. He smiled as he unstrapped his Browning and lay both gun and holster on a sideboard. He washed his hands and face and dried them on the towel provided by his mother.

"How much time would you need?"

"How much time can you spare?" she asked flushing with excitement.

"Do you always answer a question by asking one?"

"Sometimes." She flushed under the gaze of his penetrating eyes.

"When do you wish to begin?"

"When would you—" she stopped.

Tori smiled teasingly. "How about now?"

"I must return to Palermo to call my office in Rome first."

Va bene. I'll escort you. I have an appointment there in a while. We'll talk en route." He strapped on the gun, checked his ammo clip and replaced it.

Gina thought, how easily he does that. How calmly the family accepts it as ritual. She watched him turn to Athena with concern in his eyes.

"How are you feeling, beautiful?" He stroked her face and traced lightly the areas of her face that had altered. "What does the doctor say?"

Athena flushed and glanced quickly at Gina like a guilty child caught in a lie. She felt easier when her mother busied herself clearing away the table.

The reason for this strange look that passed between Athena and Gina was that earlier, Athena had had a slight attack, and recognizing the symptoms, Gina had urged her to seek medical attention. Because there was no time to explain, she had exacted a promise from Gina not to indicate her condition to her mother. Now Tori's solicitous questioning unnerved her. "Why do you persist in asking me how I feel, all the time?" she scolded her brother. "You're worse than Santino."

Tori held her close for several moments, deep affection written in his eyes. *He knows,* thought Gina. *He knows.* She tried to avert her eyes so her feelings wouldn't give her away. But, their eyes caught and held. Tori felt a stir in him. *This reporter—Gina—whatever her name, knows about Athena. I see it in her eyes.*

His expression changed abruptly. He smacked Athena soundly and spanked her playfully on her rump. *"Allora*—your husband's outside. Go tell him I'll take Vincenzo and Arturo with me tonight. He's free to be with you."

Athena grinned wickedly. She said goodbye to Gina. "We'll see each other soon. I'm sure," she said suggestively, with an eye on her brother. She kissed her mother and breezed out the door.

Antigone tried to conceal her stupefaction at the two golden scorpions, and found herself gazing from one to the other. The only reason no one saw the dismayed expression on her face was that they were all busy preparing to leave. Sighing resignedly she walked to the front door with them, and waved as Gina and Tori departed, asking the girl politely to return to dine with them before she left Sicily. She watched them until the jeep faded from sight, then slowly, she padded back into the kitchen to finish her coffee.

In the past three years of Tori's prominence, Antigone had aged visibly. Worry lines creased her forehead, her mouth drooped unhappily. From the night she had confirmed Tori's suspicions about his real father, things between them hadn't been the same. She should have lied to him. Yes, that was it. Who would have known? Now, it was too late to rectify that gross error in her judgement.

She began to putter about the lonely house, and she recalled vividly the strange visit she had had a few days before when the colossal mayor of Partinico, Don Santo Florio, had come to call. He had spoken of nothing but Tori. He'd raved with loquacious fervor, extolling the virtues of so thoughtful and benevolent a warrior who was so committed to his people. What were his words? Ah, yes it all came back to her. "How proud you must be of such a splendid son, *Signora*. . ."

In his sly cunning he'd asked how often she saw her son. Did he spend much time at home? Who were his closest friends and confidantes? Was it true that the reporter—the American who visited him recently—was a spy as the papers rumored, sent by President Truman? Had Salvatore formed an alliance with America? Between the subtle questions had come mountains of flattery, and valleys of deceptive concern for her welfare. Through it all Antigone had remained her usual polite and silent self. When he told her the *capomafia* had sent his profound respect and his good wishes, she stiffened with suspicion.

"Only the other day I met with him in Palermo. He told me personally and in private to inform you he would one day pay his respects and visit you. As Godfather to your son he feels the length of time since he last saw you has been for too long a duration."

Upset by her prolonged silence, the Don added, "I see you are not much of a speaker, *Signora*. Strangely enough, I've been led to believe the contrary. Your political views, outspoken for a woman, have long reached my ears . . ."

"I've learned, Don Florio, that the tongue resembles a lion. When well chained it merely watches you. If allowed to be loose at will, it will tear you to pieces." She stared mutely at the obese and panting ox of a man and wondered how much he really knew, and why he had made such a visit. It was well known throughout the village that

609

this lionized *mafioso* never left his abode for anyone. People usually paid homage to him at his own villa.

The knowledge of such a man and all he represented filled her with a silent terror and for days she brooded with premonition. Perhaps it was time she pay Donna Sabattini another visit. Three years had passed since the prophecy was placed in her hands. Was it possible for spirits to change their minds as mortals did—and no longer predict, perhaps, so mysterious a fate for her son? She had to know. Perhaps the *strega* would explain the prophecy once and for all? Antigone's reluctance to visit the *strega* was not pride any longer. Stark fear of what the old sorceress might reveal was what held her back.

Later that evening, when Maria Angelica Candela brought Antigone some *pane de Pasqua,* specially decorated bread and *biscotti* with hard-boiled eggs buried deep inside them, a special Easter treat, she asked softly, "Who was that woman driving away with Tori in the jeep?"

"An American woman journalist," replied Antigone.

"*Signora,* do you think Vincenzo would make a good husband?" she asked abruptly.

Antigone smiled brightly. "Vincenzo and you? Is it serious?"

"I'm not certain," she replied lowering her amazingly green eyes demurely. Then, suddenly, she grasped Antigone's arms, anxiously, and spoke imploringly. "It's really Tori I love. I've always loved him ever since we were children. But he doesn't know I exist. What am I to do?" she pleaded as if her heart would break.

Antigone clasped the girl's hands between hers. "He knows you exist, Maria Angelica, truly he does. Unfortunately Sicily is a jealous mistress. He belongs to her and the world. There's not much we can do in the face of such competition, *cara mia,* except to pray."

Maria Angelica felt worse than she had before she unburdened her heart. There was nothing left for her in Montegatta. She was fond of Vincenzo, but she didn't love him the way she loved and adored Tori. That night in the privacy of her bedroom, at her house, she gave thought to leaving Montegatta. She wasn't certain where she'd go, but one thing was certain. She couldn't remain in this village much longer.

CHAPTER 45

"Why such dedication to write about me, Gina?" he asked.

"The world is always eager to learn of heroes," she smiled easily.

"A hero. Me? You Americans are too generous with your praise."

"And you are too modest. You occupy the minds of people the world over. You've dazzled their senses, excited them in a way no one has for decades."

"I've done only what was necessary for a people who couldn't do for themselves." Tori poured her a glass of wine and set the bottle aside. They were in a picturesque *trattoria* off the Via Crispi near the waterfront, against a background of fishing boats and pealing fog horns. Glittering standing lights on the vessels reflected on the water, adding a romantic luster to the occasion. Tori had paid the proprietor to close down to the public for the night, while he and Gina enjoyed a light supper of prosciuto and melon. Music, soft and romantic, was kept alive by the proprietor's daughter as she sat behind a bamboo screen changing records on an antiquated hand-cranked victrola, and alternately embroidered linens for her hope chest.

"You don't drink?" asked Gina, noticing that he poured none for himself.

"I don't drink."

She nodded. "Stefano mentioned it among other things. I didn't believe him, thinking perhaps it might be a publicity gimmick."

"What is this *publicity gimmick* of which you speak?" he turned to her questioningly and gave her a half smile. "Your English, like Stefano's, isn't easy to understand."

"Never mind, it's not important. I'm more interested in you. I'm afraid my praise of you will border on flattery," she began as she sipped her wine and looked into his eyes. Her stomach flopped over, and in those moments she became acutely aware of her unfeminine clothing; GI fatigues and a wrinkled bushjacket! *Just* the thing to wear, when for the first time in three years her heart was beating with the fury of stampeding elephants.

Tori, sensing her discomfort, broke the connection. "How long will you remain in Sicily?"

"As long as it takes for me to get to know you well enough to write about you." She felt a lightheartedness creep through her.

Tori picked up her slender hand and held it in his. "I could arrange to make that a long time," he said, suggestively, and, as he did, he wondered at his own audacity with the American.

In the candlelight, Gina's amethyst eyes, framed by a border of thickly fringed lashes, shone like precious gems. She lowered them demurely, like a sixteen-year-old with her first crush. With a sudden change of mood, Gina slipped her hand from his on the pretense she had to remove a pad and pencil from her bag. "Do you mind if I begin the interview with you?" she forced a professional attitude with him.

Tori sat back in his chair, aware of the brushoff. If he felt rejected, he said and did nothing about it, except to sip his coffee, quietly.

"How, why and when did it all begin for you. What were conditions in your province like? It was September of 1943—wasn't it?" she began.

"1943? September—October—November? I suppose it was. It seems so long ago, and yet it was only yesterday." Tori closed his eyes and continued.

"Yes—1943. This life thrust upon me is a life far removed from one I had planned. I wasn't twenty-one when the course of my life changed. It was a time when death stalked us morning, noon and night. She stood on every corner dressed in frothy black veils, wispy, fluttering robes like a malevolent whore staring out at us, beckoning some, seducing others, curling a long sinewy finger of enticement at the rest. She hovered over us in every dark alley, littered street and impoverished house in my village. Death spread her villainy like a plague, and it seemed my people were too tired to care. Their voices no longer screamed in protest, shouted in supplication, or pleaded in anger or fear. The very heart of them had been rooted out by conditions forced upon us . . ."

Two hours later, holding her hand in his, Tori guided her over the rocky incline until they stood on the temple floor above Montegatta.

"This is the land of Salvatore!" he announced, and

made a sweeping gesture with his hand. "It's a place where sunsets were born and twilights remain eternal; where the influence of such a moon gives baptism to the stars. No matter how many times I've tried to capture these breathtaking miracles through photography, nothing can capture the true phenomenon reproduced by nature. I come here when I need to come to terms with myself."

Everything was one enormous silence, in which she could hear their hearts pounding. She gazed at the ceiling of glittering stars, shuddered at their breathtaking nearness, and became awed by the pale moon light illuminating the Temple of Cats.

Tori studied her silhouetted against the pearl moon and thought, how lovely she is. He found her more mellow than Apolladora, more worldly; softer than Gabriella—yet, unreachable. The protective shield she'd built as an invisible deflector to ward off unwanted advances stood in his way, retarding any and all advances he might have wanted to make towards her. Perhaps it was this very thing—this elusiveness—that made him desire her more.

"How did you learn about Athena?" he asked quietly.

"She suffered a mild attack at your mother's house."

"You're familiar with her malady?"

"My sister died as a result of a similar ailment."

"How easily you say it." He was both appalled and astonished at her attitude.

"It was over ten years ago." Gina accepted a cigarette offered her, leaned in to him as he lit it. Tori lit his own on the same match, then extinguished it.

Sensing his disturbance with her, she changed the subject. "In most of the articles I've read about you, there is considerable reference to your love life. Ballads written about your romantic prowess have stimulated women, young and old, the world over. You've become an idol—"

Tori smiled tolerantly. "I thought you'd get to that subject," he replied knowingly. "If all the stories written about such escapades were true, what time would I have to devote to my people? I'd have accomplished nothing." He talked easily with Gina, brought her up to date on the happenings in his life. He spoke reservedly about Apolladora in this, the first time he'd spoken of her to anyone.

"Is she the reason you became an outlaw?" she asked motivated by more than professional curiosity.

"No," said Tori without further explanation. In a sense, he gave Gina the usual, stereotype interview he gave to the press. He used extreme discretion, never mentioning the Mafia-related and internal affairs. If, in her writing she should allude to the honored brotherhood, it would make her too vulnerable. For reasons unclear to Tori at the moment, he felt a sudden overprotective feeling for her.

"Your life must be hard on your family," she began.

"Being the family of any man hunted unjustly by the law presents hardships to them."

"Your mother's a solid wall of strength. I found her well educated, versed well in politics, and not in the least impressionable."

"She taught me all I know," he said tightly.

"Why not tell her the truth about Athena's condition?"

Tori turned to her, aghast at her suggestion. "Are you crazy? It would break her heart. No, its out of the question," he added quickly as if he'd given it thought.

"They could say and do things oftentimes left unsaid before death—"

"Would you wish to know if a loved one was terminal?" *She was incredible!*

"Yes. Wouldn't you? Why not?"

"There you go, answering a question with a question!"

"Well—"

"No!" Tori puffed on a cigarette furiously. "It's a terrible burden to bear—knowing and not speaking of it. It's out of the question," he insisted repeatedly.

Gina grew somber. "It would mean a time of closeness—of love—a time to express your love for the other, and thank them for enriching your life. Most people act as if they're eternal, never really caring, never giving of themselves." Gina reflected, as if she were adding insight into her own recent behavior.

Tori fell into a deep silence. She noticed a peculiar isolation hung over him. Later, she would notice that, even in the company of others, Tori always remained engulfed in a privacy tuned into higher spheres of thought.

"Why does a woman like you become a correspondent?" he asked finally. "Do you enjoy the risks you take to get a story? Strange, you seem the type to settle down and raise a family," he told her.

Gina sighed resignedly. Here it comes again, the same old questions asked by every man who entered her life. "Perhaps at another time—in another century—yes. Not now. War brings about many changes."

"How do you come to know Stefano?" he asked lightly.

"Stefano? Oh, Stefano Modica. I call him Steve. I was in love with him once." She couldn't lie to Tori.

"Once?" he searched her face in the moonlight. What a strange woman.

"Yes, once. It's been over for a long time. We were both victims of the war, you know." She felt the inner trembling come over her again.

"Why don't you love him anymore? Was he bad to you?" He couldn't fathom such fickleness. "You Americans are incomprehensible!"

"Who knows why?" Gina disliked the reopening of a deep wound. "You live with a man, think you know him, then, one day, when you need him most, he isn't around to support you with his strength. You awaken, and realize you didn't know him at all—and he becomes a stranger to you. Before you know it, time melts into years. You meet one day, and find a high wall has sprung between you, preventing you both from ever recapturing a love you both cherished deeply. It's part of life, isn't it?"

"It's some wall, Gina. Why should it be there for me?"

She stammered, suddenly vulnerable to his tenderness. Tears brimmed her eyes. Angry at herself for evidencing such weakness, she became momentarily disorganized. Tori reached out for her, laid her head on his shoulder, and cradled her affectionately. Before she knew it she had blurted out the story of her relationship to Stefano—about the bombing, the accident, the unborn child—all of it.

For the first time since she left London, Gina, at the end of the catharsis, felt an immense sense of relief. She had unburdened her soul upon the strong and compassionate young savage, that crudely beautiful, sensitive young man who at the moment seemed the antithesis of the very word *bandit*. All resistance towards him melted, and with it her resolve.

Tori understood the defensive shield she had built around herself. Her soft voice, anguished, had touched his emotions. There was no doubt he felt for her an animal's passion at first which only sexual release could appease. His groin ached for her, his heart went out to her. Confusing to him was the sudden revulsion he felt, in her presence, at being an outlaw.

Against his primal instinct, he made no advances towards her. He courteously drove her back to her hotel that night. The following week he met with her as often as possible to answer her endless questions. Then, for two weeks, he didn't see her at all. She had brought out a nesting instinct in him, one to which he found himself inescapably drawn. Aware in advance that such an attachment might prove destructive, Tori deliberately avoided more encounters with her. He didn't know it then, but he'd fallen hopelessly in love.

During this time, he was impossible to be with. The influx of disturbing emotions and stormy conflicts within him made him miserable to all he encountered. One day at the end of his patience, Vincenzo remarked hotly. "What the hell possesses you, eh? Are you sick or something?"

"There's nothing wrong with me. I'm fine!" he glowered and shrugged his cousin off.

"Yeah, sure, you're fine all right! For a man who has a *Principessa* waiting for him in a romantic boudoir of fantasies—you act like a eunuch!"

"Gabriella!" Tori spun around and faced his cousin. "*Managghia!* I forgot all about her." Since Gina arrived on the scene, he hadn't concerned himself with her nor had he the inclination to further the relationship. It had been Gabriella's idea to follow him—an idea he cautioned her against.

"Vincenzo, the war's over. Convince her to return to her country—eh? See that she has enough money to live comfortably for a time. She'll manage after that. She's a resourceful woman, *capeeshi?*"

Vincenzo thought for certain Tori had taken leave of his senses, but he returned from the mission successfully and made his report.

"*Managghia!* What a hellcat! She stormed, ranted, and raved like a whore who yells *rape*, and threw the furniture at me. When I gave her a sizeable bundle of money, I'd all I could do to prevent her from seducing me," he boasted.

Tori glanced at him through amused eyes. "That would be the day you'd pass up a dish like her." He laughed in an all-knowing, good-natured way. Vincenzo blushed and gave himself away. Then on a more serious note, he asked, "Is everything else all right? The men are content?"

"The American reporter has taken many pictures. You think it's wise, all this exposure?" Vincenzo sobered.

"She'll print the story in American magazines. The President will read about us and learn the truth. Then he'll come to our aid, you'll see. I've been composing a letter to him, to make sure he takes no offense at my boldness. You know, from one statesman to another."

Santino Siragusa glanced up from his position at the short-wave radio when Tori and Vincenzo walked into the farmhouse a few days later. He called to Tori solemnly, "You'd better take a look at this mesage."

Tori picked up the communique and read aloud:

"Three hundred villagers arrested. Charged with conspiracy, aiding and abetting outlaws."

"Another message," said Santino, searching the papers on the crude makeshift desk. "Ah—here it is. Gina O'Hoolihan left for Rome and will return in two weeks."

Both Santino and Vincenzo noted the disappointment on Tori's face at this. In a sly, conspiratorial manner, they both winked at each other and suppressed smiles. Then on a more sober note Santino explained. "They told me Candela, the cooper, was picked up in this last raid, Tori. You know he's been ailing and this incarceration will aggravate his failing health. The family is frantic."

Tori lifted his eyes from the cigarette in his hand and looked soberly at his paladins. "So—It begins."

CHAPTER 46

The agile, well-tanned, fierce eyed Sicilian hurled himself from the snowy white Arabian stallion and crept past the crudely constructed shack protruding conspicuously from the center of a barren expanse of desert land, splotched here and there with cacti and sisal. Dressed in khaki shirt and trousers with black leather boots, he wore a short shoulder length *cuffiah* about his head to shield his face from the whipping sand that blew in gales about him, from time to time. His piercing dark eyes searched the skies. The horizon was an unbearable pulsing crimson, bitten into by miles of black mountains like sharks' teeth. To the east the heavens were a dim spectral pink. The western sky flamed alone in frightful isolation, illuminating the sky, but giving no light to the earth.

Tori pulled his *cuffiah* across his nose and mouth. Now, only his electric eyes peered through the aperture as he prepared for the onslaught of the descending *sirocco*. He crept up the slopes to the rise.

Through a pair of high powered binoculars, he saw a horde of mounted *carabinieri* leaving *Setti Dolore* barracks a quarter of the way below the summit of the mountain. Nearby, swirls of white sand piled into peaks as the howling sounds of vast invisible hordes assaulted the earth.

The Sicilian's eyes scanned the hills in every direction for as far as his eyes could see. He reached into his jacket and pulled out a World War II walkie-talkie. Lying on his belly atop a small sand dune, he tugged at the antenna. Static interference and feedback whistled and shrieked back at him, until finally the signal came through clearly.

"Calling *Terra Diaoro. Terra Diaoro*—can you read me?"

"You're coming in loud and clear, Generalissimo. . . ."

"Are your men ready, *Terra Diaoro*?

"All ready and waiting!"

"Allora—they just left *Setti Dolore . . ."*

"Our men are positioned at the pass as planned. How many are coming?"

"Approximately fifty. Perhaps more, give or take a few."

"Va bene! We're waiting for them!"

"See you in a few minutes!"

At the summit of the mountain at both the entrance and exit to El Passo del Morte, two dozen well-armed bandits, wearing U.S. Army combat fatigues, stood in readiness for a counter-offensive move against the *carabinieri*. Several machine-gun nests, placed strategically on the pebbly slopes of two mountains, stood in readiness as Salvatore's men, armed with Beretta submachine guns, crept into position for the ambush as the enemy approached. Through howling winds, the sound of horses' hooves could be heard like muffled thunder. The men shielded themselves from the stinging dust whipping wildly about.

Only Vincenzo's dark, scowling eyes peered through the aperture in the *cuffiah* wrapped about his head as he signalled the men to remain out of sight.

"Remember your order!" he shouted to Miguel and Arturo Scoletti.

The brothers, nodded. Their eyes were on the four truckloads of prisoners.

From a distance, fifty armed *carabinieri* rode into the entrance of the pass and continued on until the last rider had entered. Instantly, both the entrance and exits were hit with grenades. Horses whinnied and reared! Their frightened large eyes flared in terror. The riders wheeled their horses and tried to calm them as particles of dirt congested the air about them. Visibility was nil. Smoke grenades screened the atmosphere thickly. Rider ran into rider, knocking each other over, causing more chaos and bedlam! Aimless bullets zinged through the air!

As pockets of dust cleared, the blinded, coughing, *cara-*

binieri began to see through the congestion. Here and there they saw men with carbines and submachine guns aimed at them. No matter where they looked, on slopes, bluffs, rocky ledges, all over the pa,ss, they stared into machine-gun nests and armed men. One by one, the chargrined *barabinieri* raised their arms into the air above their heads, and dropped their weapons.

"Dismount!" ordered Miguel Scoletti. "And keep your hands over your heads!" he yelled as he rode among them. *"Demonio!* I said, *up!* Take their guns! All the weapons they carry! Round up their horses!" he ordered the men. "And take over the trucks loaded with our villagers."

Tori came down off the slopes of the mountains mounted Napoleono and galloped swiftly to Vincenzo's side. He pulled up abruptly on his reins. "Anyone hurt?"

"No," shouted Vincenzo.

"Tell the men to head off the trucks and return here."

Humiliated and enraged, the crestfallen *carabinieri*, who had been forced to disrobe, lined up in single file. Salvatore commenced to gallop up one side of them and down the other. He wheeled his horse about and cantered spiritedly to the center front and stood before the red-faced, indignant military police.

"Atten—*tion!*" called Arturo Scoletti.

Reluctantly the police stood at attention. It was as still as death in the draw. The winds abated slightly and left only an echoing silence.

"I am Salvatore!" he announced to the awkward, shuffling *carabinieri*. "My men and I could have killed all of you—with little effort. Because we are not murderers, I allow you to return to your command post at Bellolampo instead of *Setti Dolore*, so you can leave our country without wasting time. We shall, of course, keep your guns, clothing, and horses, and the prisoners."

Seated astride his stallion, Tori walked the animal slowly up and down the line to study his captives' faces. "If you are wise, you'll give up this insane fight against me and return to your homes and families. We ask only that you allow us to live in peace. You, foreigners in our land do not understand our problems. Go—leave with your lives. If you are foolish enough to provoke a second encounter, you'll have time only to pray to your maker before you keep an appointment with him. *Capeeshi?* You understand me?"

He spurred Napoleono, rode swiftly to Vincenzo's side at the far end of the draw, and nodded to him. Vincenzo gave Arturo and Michele Scoletti the proper signal.

"*Allora*—march! commanded Arturo. "Move into the trucks—all of you!"

Single file, more than fifty disrobed, smoldering *carabinieri* climbed into the waiting trucks that would transport them to within a mile of Bellolampo. There they'd be discharged to make their way back on foot. The motors revved up, and the ancient trucks laboriously moved in line, transporting the outraged prisoners from their sight. Salvatore's men, sober-faced and brooding, watched the spectacle with mixed emotions.

"You should have killed them," hissed Miguel Scoletti, his dark eyes sparked with hatred. His statement drew murmurs of agreement from the rest.

"There's plenty of time for that. We don't need to spill blood needlessly. We have their weapons, their clothing. What can they do?" Tori smiled and waved to the villagers he had spared from jail sentences.

"Viva Salvatore!" cried the grateful men.

The winds howled through the canyon and rose to the roar of thunder. The men drew their clothing closer to them, turned up their collars, shielded their eyes.

"*Amonini!*" shouted Salvatore. "Get the equipment and the villagers into the trucks and head them back to Montegatta," he told the Scoletti brothers. "We've a long way to go!" Napoleono reared on his hind legs and clawed the air with his forepaws, and, wheeling him about, Tori headed across the canyon up the slopes, away from Castellammare, his men following him closely.

An hour later he spotted Bellolampo in the distance, and he felt more secure in knowing they were nearly home. He heard his name called and turning in his saddle, he saw Vincenzo riding swiftly to his side.

"Candela sends his heartfelt thanks. And I forgot to tell you, cousin, the American is back. She has returned to the land of Salvatore." He grinned.

Tori's face broke with smiles. He waved to his cousin and felt a quiver of excitement shoot through him. Gina was back. Imagine that. She had returned to him. He spurred his stallion and galloped back along the trucks filled with cheering, singing men, jubilant and filled with bravado.

Tori suddenly pulled up on Napoleono, alerted by a dull pounding in his left ear. He glanced all around him with an air of caution. In a quick signal he halted the train of trucks and galloped ahead of the vehicles a few yards before the entrance to Rigano Pass. His men pulled up on their reins, filled with puzzlement. *What the hell's wrong? Why stop here?* they wondered.

All at once, a loud explosion rocked the countryside, spewing forth craters in the road ahead. His men took cover in the swirls of congested dust. The men coughed and sputtered and covered their noses with kerchiefs. The villagers jumped clear of the trucks and took cover as another explosion burst in their path. In the pandemonium that followed, the frightened horses reared, bolted and whinnied in wild-eyed frenzy, protesting the dangers underfoot.

Tori, followed by his men, galloped towards a cluster of boulders at one side of the trail. He flung himself from his horse and scrambled up the side of the rocky incline to the top of a craggy ledge, where he peered cautiously about the area. From his position he saw squadrons of *carabinieri* laying in ambush at the other end of Rigano Pass, with six Breda machine guns set up in visible positions, cutting off the entrance to Montegatta.

"They're learning, eh Tori?" scoffed young Pietro Gagliolo, who'd been on Tori's tail all the way to the top of the ridge. "Now they use your tactics!"

"They haven't learned enough, Redhead," replied Tori with a smile of bravado. In truth, he was deeply concerned. How long could they hold off before reinforcements arrived from Bellolampo to attack the rear? They were, in fact, sealed off. If Tori penetrated the blockade, it meant sure death for them. He could only retreat, send a squad of men to Bellolampo to attack the barracks, pick up reinforcements, return, and blow up the mountain side, sealing his village off from civilization forever. Or he could plow right through to instant death. The dilemma had to be solved instantly. There were no other alternatives.

"There's only one way," he told his co-captain as Vincenzo climbed the boulder to his side. "Listen. I'll send in two men who'll wave the white flag of surrender. Once inside the *carabinieri*'s lines they'll have to use their wits to harass the enemy from within as we attack as a unit."

"I'll go," volunteered Pietro.

"No. Let the older men go."

"Please Tori," begged the lad. "I'm good. *Sporcaccione* says I've become one of the best at *Lotta Salvatore*. Let me go. I'll handle those *villiachi.*"

Tori smiled tolerantly at the young man and turned away from him and continued to outline his plan of attack to Vincenzo. "There's only one way this will work. Listen carefully. Take approximately six dozen villagers, waving white flags. Uccidato, *Sporcaccione* and I will mix among them. Once inside the lines, we'll take care of our obstructors in good time. Got that?"

"Are you crazy? Why must you go? If anything happens to you, what will the rest of us do?" countered Vincenzo. "No. Choose someone else. You are too important."

As they argued the point, neither had seen young Pietro slip away to the other side of the boulder, where he paused to prepare himself. Quickly he tossed aside his submachine gun and removed his gun and holster. Several grenades, expertly pocketed into his shirt, trousers and jacket, were hidden from sight. He tied a white handkerchief to a twig picked up from the ground and buried a grenade in the palm of his left hand. Twirling the white flag overhead he approached the enemy blockade.

"Tori! Look!" cried the men. "There—it's Pietro!"

From where he lay on his stomach, high on the rocky ledge, Tori remained in full view of the action. He grabbed the binoculars from Vincenzo's hand in a sudden spurt, focused them on the redhead and watched in momentary panic as the young man moved forward. Tori trembled fearfully for the fiesty Pietro.

"Goddammit! That little fox will be torn apart and swallowed by those evil hounds!" Tori broke into a sweat as he peered below him at the scene in the basin. He saw Pietro glance cautiously about him as he neared the blockade. The *carabinieri* approached him apprehensively.

Pietro, trembling inwardly, with sweat drops the size of hailstones rolling off his freckled face, told himself he'd be at the center of the arena in moments.

"He's unarmed," shouted a wary *carabiniero*. "Keep your hands above your head," he commanded the redhaired youth. "Just keep walking towards us, nice and easy. No funny stuff—hear? It's smart of you to surrender. You should have convinced your friends to do the same," snickered the officer.

Scattered intermittently on the slopes of the mountain, Tori's men held their breath and solemnly watched the daring of young Pietro. What had he been thinking to surrender himself? Most puzzled of all was his brother Uccidato who sat frozen like a statue, gripped with petrifying horror for what might happen to his baby brother. Despite their differences the family bond was like iron.

Pietro neared the center of the blockade, where eight *carabinieri* gathered in a huddle waiting for him. Peripherally he saw all six machine guns aimed at him, plus another eight men leaving their stations in wonderment at his presence. Curious and filled with unendurable excitement the *carabinieri* marked this as the first time a white flag of surrender had been brandished by Salvatore's men. Hah! Was it possible they were breaking his resistance without knowing it? It was about time the bandit cracked.

Pietro maneuvered himself about slightly, enabling him to glance in Tori's direction and grin that inescapably warm, self-conscious grin. Then, faster than the eye could see, he pulled the pin from the grenade in his hand.

"Goddamnit! It's a trick! Shoot him!" cried the *carabinieri* squadron leader who had waited too long to make his move, to shout the order. All hopes for the *carabinieri* ended abruptly, for as six officers aimed their carbines at Pietro, fired and riddled him with bullets, they, themselves were blown to bits as each grenade, struck by bullets, exploded. Upon impact from each successive explosion, the blockade was wrecked.

Pietro having booby-trapped himself had killed more than twenty-five *carabinieri*. Those who might have escaped were savagely and expeditiously gunned down by Tori's men.

Tori, white faced and livid, scrambled to his feet. A terrible hardness came over him. Swiftly and silently he slid down off the boulders, swung to his saddle, and in moments he had galloped into the draw at the site of the holocaust. He was sick. What remained of his favorite young red-headed companion was scattered about the area, totally unrecognizable, in broken bits and pieces.

Slowly he walked his horse through the congestion of rocks, loose gravel, and dusty debris, his dark eyes murky pools of anger. He sprang from his horse and ran to where Uccidato had already reached the bloodied mass that had been his brother and was kneeling on the ground holding one freckled arm and hand with bleeding tendons at each end, stunned with disbelief and incomprehension. Tori gripped the older brother's arm firmly, and both men stared in mute silence at the gold ring shaped like an eagle which Pietro had worn to honor Salvatore. Behind them converging wildly came the rest of Tori's men, their faces taut and grim and horror-struck.

In the silence, as the dust cleared, Tori tugged at the kerchief shielding his face to reveal a stony-faced mask of mind-bending malevolence. His dark eyes burned with black hatred for this unspeakable atrocity. He said to Uccidato, "For whatever this means to you—your brother dies a hero. He's the most courageous of Salvatore's men.

He had more guts than Salvatore himself. He did this on his own to save us and three hundred villagers."

Mounting swiftly, Tori signalled the Scoletti brothers.

"Take the villagers on through to Montegatta. Have the men clean up this mess, so no traces remain. I'll join you later!" He leaned over his saddle and swept up a submachine gun from the hands of his quick thinking armorer, Gambo Cusimano, who tossed him two magazines of ammo. Tori slung them over his saddle bag and moved forward at a fast clip.

"Where are you going?" shouted Vincenzo.

"I have business," called Tori, riding towards Bellolampo in a trail of dust.

Galloping swiftly to Uccidato's side, Vincenzo commanded, "You and *Sporcaccione* go after him, in case he needs help. In his mood—no telling what he'll do. I'll attend to things here. We'll meet at Grotto D'Oro."

Dazed, but in control of his senses, Uccidato and that mountain of strength, *Sporcaccione*, mounted their steeds and rode swiftly into the clouds of dust left in Tori's wake. It was difficult to catch up to a stallion who'd suddenly taken on the spirit of the winged horse, Pegasus.

By now, the fifty, weary and nearly naked *carabinieri*, having arrived at Bellolampo after their earlier encounter with Salvatore's men, fell prostrate to the ground, exhausted from the tedious trek. A few new recruits, fresh and alert, stood gaping at the fatigued and defeated troops, rifles in hand, unsure of their moves. A few laughed and poked fun at the scantily-clad and sorely humiliated lot, while a few more vigilant recruits, having heard the explosions in the vicinity of Rigano Pass, gazed off in the distance as if they expected a signal of sorts.

Salvatore stood up on the bluff behind the military *caserne*, a short distance from the dejected, unsuspecting lot, with a fireballing sun at his back. All traces of the earlier dust storm in the valley, behind him, had evaporated.

"Here I am! Up here, you motherless bastards!" shouted Tori with an expression of diabolical hatred etched sharply into his hard features.

Those sorry, worn and disheveled military police, forced to shield their burning eyes from the blinding orange gold sun, turned in a body, attempting to pierce hazy, glaring lights in an effort to make out the shadowy image standing, gun in hand, aimed at them. Before any of the startled police could scramble for cover, Tori opened up with the Beretta, blazing hotter than his emotions, and blasted away at every last one of them, cutting them in two. From behind him came additional help as Uccidato and *Sporcaccione* riddled the mass carnage with their submachine guns and felled every last one of them.

"Kill an innocent child—will you?" shouted Tori hysterically. Even after the *carabinieri* lay dead he continued to shoot at them hysterically until Uccidato, observing him solemnly, moved in quietly to release his frozen grip from the weapon. Tori's glazed, unseeing eyes, in a trancelike state, bore into the scene at his feet. *Sporcaccione* called to his chief.

"One minute. I've a job to finish." He snapped another magazine into his gun and ran forward in the direction of the two-story, white stucco structure with its red tiled roof that had housed squadrons of their enemies from time to time. Aiming his machine gun at the building wall that faced Montegatta and Salvatore's mountains, he commenced firing round after round of ammunition, shoving in more magazines as he needed them and blasting away interminably. He stopped abruptly, apparently satisfied.

Only when the firing ceased and the dust of the crumbling stucco and cement dissolved and the air around them cleared from the assault of missiles, did Salvatore, accompanied by Uccidato, move in to see what devastation their companion had wrought. On the wall of the military *caserne,* spelled out in bullet holes, was an epitaph to be long remembered.

"In Memory of Pietro Gagliolo, who died a true hero!"

Uccidato in a gesture of humility brushed away his tears. "Wherever Pietro is—he'll like that," he said.

Tori's eyes brimmed with tears. Turning from the others he leaned his head against the coolness of his saddle and sobbed bitterly. Young Pietro, like a younger brother to him, had touched Tori deeply by his profound devotion and unimpeachable loyalty. His one act of bravery and unselfishness was one which both shamed Tori's men and made them fiercely proud. Long afterwards, they spoke with unmistakable pride and bravado for the youth they'd seen fit to bedevil for so long.

CHAPTER 47

Tori, turning to her and staring at the overflowing love in her upturned face, said quietly, "You're in love with me."

Gina, prepared to deny it, was unable to when she saw the truth reflected in his smoldering eyes. There was no room for denial—no time. "It's crazy," she said. "I suppose I'm a fool, but, I'm too old to play silly games."

"You're in love with me," he repeated softly, his dark eyes smoldering. "I like it—to know you love me."

She turned from him. Tori quickly reached in and, holding her chin, turned her face to him. Their eyes met and held in a moment of swollen desire which threatened to erupt at any moment. "You're written in my heart— you know it, don't you?" he told her.

"Yes," she said finally without apology.

"Yes. From the first, something about you. *Different* . . . I felt you deeply. . . ." he admitted, reluctantly.

"Why? Because I'm American?"

"Perhaps. . . . But there is more, *cara mia.*"

"Different than the *Principessa*?" she avoided his eyes.

He broke into a devilish grin, "That's unworthy of you. . . ." He raised his eyebrows slightly in seeming surprise. "You know about her? I hardly know her. . . ."

"That's not what the police report shows. . . ."

"Do you believe everything you read?"

Gina angled her head and smiled mockingly. "*Nooooooo.*" she stretched the word. "I was warned against that. Tell me, did you actually kidnap her?"

Unable to hide his astonishment, he turned his head and looked out at the blue Tyrrhenian sea. They were outside in the sun-drenched patio of the villa belonging to his young *Mafia* friend, Calemi, overlooking Castellammare.

Tori sprang to his feet and walked to the shaded enclosure, wearing only white swim trunks. He filled a bowl with water and told her, "Sometimes we are forced to do many things in the line of duty—" He poured the water over his head, neck and shoulders to cool off. Across from him, Gina stood, dressed only in a scant swim suit she'd

626

picked up in Paris, which at first had shocked Tori by being so abbreviated, but which drew his appreciation now that he enjoyed the fringe benefits it afforded him. She was so lovely, so feminine, so warm and endearing, he thought.

Gina thought, *God, how beautiful he is*. His brown hair became a mass of curls in the wetness and his skin had become a burnished copper in the sun. Staring at her, his eyes filled with golden topaz flecks in the bright sunlight.

It was hot! Below them, in the harbor, where no boat lay at anchor due to a westerly wind that had brought with it angry, swollen waves, the colorful fishing boats were being manually hoisted onto the sandy beach out of the water, by strong, muscular fishermen.

Sicily, plagued by a *sirocco*, had caused them to seek refuge from the intense interior heat of the land. Gina breathed the sea air deeply and appreciatively. She dreaded the thought of leaving. The past week with Tori had been paradise. She had had him to herself for the first time in a long while, and nothing, not even the prostrating heat, could dampen her spirit.

She walked towards him, towel in hand, outstretched to wipe around his neck. That was as far as she got. He pulled her in close and kissed her. Gina melted in his arms. In a matter of moments, they submitted to each other in sex without that awkwardness lovers often feel at first. Gina found Tori to possess enormous sexual depth, an erotic passion the likes of which she hadn't experienced even with Stefano.

Hours later, when it was over, they lay still in each other's arms, loath to move, until the ecstasy of their love leveled off. For a long while, Tori, wide awake, stared down at her as if committing her to memory.

She stirred, lazily at first, then wide awake, she snuggled closer to him, filled to overflowing with love for him. She felt him stiffen and pull away. Quick as a flash, Tori jumped to his feet and strode out onto the balcony overlooking the sea. He could see the ruins of the Saracen Fort guarding the harbor, feel the warm sea breeze dry off his moist body. His nude body, firm and muscular, moved with athletic perfection as the pink glow of sunset caressed it, giving it a velvety, glowing hue. He took a cigarette from the pack on the balustrade, lit it and stood with both feet implanted on the terrace, hands clasped behind his back, a fierce angry look on his face.

"I must be crazy! Out of my head crazy! I can't afford to fall in love! What kind of a life would it be for you?—For me?" He shouted aloud to himself, to Gina, and to the world with whom he felt at odds in that instant.

"Yes," whispered Gina coming up behind him. She had wrapped a towel about her body. "I understand. I really do." After a moment, she added. "You have great control, Tori. You won't let it happen." He could talk all he wanted, but Gina knew. One hundred orgasms unaccompanied by the act of love couldn't be equated with one orgasm accompanied by love. She knew the difference, felt it, was touched by it. Their sexual encounter had been very special, committed with and motivated by love—even if Tori refused to accept it. It was frustrating to her, but she had no power to deny him.

"You know if I permit myself to fall in love—our lives would be over," he protested weakly.

"I understand," she whispered.

He turned to her, stared intently at her as if he could never be done devouring her with his eyes. Only inches from each other, their eyes locked compulsively. Tori sighed, reached for her, pulled her close to him, and closed his eyes briefly. He could feel her warm trembling body shudder next to his. In the next few seconds, everything he had said was negated. Gina felt his lean body grow rigid and tense as he swelled with passion and desire.

"*No*," he cried in muffled anguish. "It's not fair to you." But he clung to her, wouldn't let her pull away from him. Through the euphoria of love, they both tried to recall his earlier words, but these dimmed and faded from their consciousness. Again they kissed, again and again, until the strength that made him Salvatore drained from him and he could only be what he was—a mere mortal with desires and needs any man might crave.

"God!" he supplicated aloud. "God—why can't I be permitted a life of my own? Why must I make such sacrifices?" In his misery he clung to her with supernatural strength. Gina could barely breathe.

In those few moments when he had bared his vulnerability to her, Gina became afraid. Thrust outside the picture as a third eye, suddenly, she concluded that if she didn't become the stronger of the two, she could very well cause his destruction. Tori was right. Earlier he had told her it was hopeless for him to fall in love. Hadn't he pointed out what had already happened to his family as a result of his own vulnerability as a bandit? She wasn't so obtuse that she couldn't discern how dangerous it might be for him if he had to concern himself with her safety while she remained in Sicily.

A wave of fear swept through her. . . .

She shivered noticeably. "I'm cold," she told him. When Tori went inside to fetch the coverlet from the bed, Gina checked back the tears welling in her eyes and tried to swallow the thickness in her throat. *He can never belong to me*, she told herself. *He's too dedicated to his cause, to his country.*

He returned with a towel draped around his waist and draped the coverlet around her tenderly and drew her close to him. "You must forgive my outburst a few moments ago; I was not myself, Gina."

"Yes. I know. Please light a cigarette for me."

He nodded, reached for her English Ovals on the balustrade, and lit two. They turned their eyes to the fading sunset.

"You mentioned Apolladora once," she began.

"That was an eternity ago," he said closing the subject. Moments passed. "A few years ago—should I say a lifetime ago?—I had a dream. To study law, get married, raise a family—all the usual things. To be favored thus by the gods, I would have wished my wife to be someone like you. You understand what I'm saying, Gina?" he asked softly, stroking her face gently.

She turned to him, cried aloud. "I can't be strong. Not if you talk like that."

Startled, he flipped the cigarette down onto the rocks below and pulled her towards him. Gently he lifted her face to meet his and wiped two giant tears from her cheeks. "*Carissima*," he whispered tenderly. "I wouldn't hurt you for anything. The strength will come from me. When I felt my heart melt towards you, I pushed you from me. It was easy before desire stirred in my loins. But, now, all those emotions I've buried for so long are too overwhelming. You understand what I'm saying, *cara mia?*"

He stood before her, looking into her eyes, until Gina had no strength to resist. She sank to her knees, her arms clung to his body. The towel around his waist fell to the floor and she laid her feverish face against his groin. Tori shivered. He felt in the throes of violent ecstacy. His manhood sprang to life and, in his desire for her, he swooped her into his arms and carried her into the bedroom.

The effect of such passionate union, essentially menacing to Tori, represented something of which he could never be a part, something he couldn't fully experience, except in such stolen moments. Something in his brain gave way. All stops were pulled and in these moments he exposed himself, bared his heart to her.

"Gina. Gina, *mi amore*. I love you, *mi amore. Mio cuore, te amo moltissimo*," he repeated over and over until the very words intoxicated her and sent her spinning into soft tumbling clouds of ecstasy. For hours they took their fill of love like two love-starved children.

Later, while Gina slept, exhausted by their all-consuming lovemaking, Tori sat in an overstuffed chair watching her. *If I just said the word, she'd be mine eternally. But how long could she endure this life?* There wasn't a question about this relationship that he hadn't already examined microscopically before he asked her to drive to Castellammare with him. In the month she had been gone, Tori had missed her as if a part of him had been severed. Constant badgering and knowing glances from Athena had maddened him, even if he knew it was all in fun. He shouldn't have been so obvious about his feelings for Gina, he had told himself time and again. He sat down heavily, one arm drooping over the back of the chair, as an attitude of remote contemplation created a desolate wretchedness to come over him. He leaned forward and dropped his head into his hands. It was then that his eyes caught sight of the article Gina had written about him. A glance in her direction confirmed the fact that she was asleep. Picking up the sheaf of papers, Tori padded out of the room, along the halls to the kitchen.

The exhilarating aroma of fragrant roses wafted in from the *loggia*, off the kitchen of the splendid villa. After he prepared a fresh pot of coffee and set it percolating on the gas range, Tori entered the patio and cut several blood-red roses, placed them in a glass of water and inhaled their sweet aroma.

He set the glass on the table before him and while he waited for the coffee to brew, he read the Article scrupulously:

"*SALVATORE, by Gina O'Hoolihan. . . .*

Periodically Tori smiled as he read the article. Essentially a complimentary work, it was as dangerous to Tori as a betrayal. Gina's love-filled eyes had clearly perceived his modus operandi. Such information, read by the wrong persons, could prove to be his swan song. With a thick black pencil he found in a kitchen drawer, Tori slashed through those portions in which Gina had unwittingly revealed much of his strategy.

Gina, following the invigorating scent of freshly brewed coffee had trailed him to the kitchen where, she stood for a time, poised in the doorway, watching him abort her labor of love. "You didn't like it at all," she accused, walking towards him.

Tori glanced up, a warm, loving smile forming on his lips, as he held out his arms invitingly for her to walk into. Her pale orchid eyes smoldered darkly as they focused on the heavily pencilled areas on the edited papers. His eyes followed her line of vision and he knew she had taken umbrage at his editing from the expression on her face. "*Cara mia*," he said softly, "If I permitted you to print the article as it was, my days on earth would be numbered."

She didn't understand until she examined the article carefully, noting the portions he eliminated. When it came together in her mind, she flushed with a pang of remorse and held a trembling hand to her moist forehead.

"I wasn't thinking. Forgive me—I didn't think."

"What's to forgive? You wrote with love-filled eyes . . ."

"When I think of what might have happened. . . ."

"Don't. It was caught in time. . . .".

They drank coffee and made small talk for a while. As they talked, Gina sensed something was disturbing Tori. His attention wasn't focused on her, and she knew he was in another world. When a shudder passed through him and he began to rub his left ear lobe thoughtfully, a frown creasing his forehead, Gina had to ask him, "What's wrong? Something's wrong, isn't it?"

Tori rose to his feet as the throbbing persisted and paced the floor momentarily lost to her. He came out of it. "What—oh," he said. "I'm not sure.".

"Are you in pain?" She watched him tug at his ear.

"Oh, this?" Instantly he released the lobe. "No," he forced a faint trace of a smile. "Didn't I mention my built-in radar? The dull throbbing in my ear when trouble approaches?"

"Is that what it is?" she asked, smiling. "You must admit these premonitions are a bit much to swallow, love."

In his sudden preoccupation, her words were lost to him, and when he abruptly suggested they leave for the interior, Gina agreed even though she felt curiously alienated and bewildered by this sudden detachment. It was as if she were suddenly transported thousands of miles from him.

They rode in the jeep to Palermo, in a silence she couldn't penetrate. In the shadows of the Via Cavour, he kissed her ardently and apologized for his mood. He thanked her for her company with such detachment that Gina was left unnerved and more perplexed than before. Then, Tori confessed to her, that this past week had been the most memorable time in his life. "I shall cherish the memories forever, *cara mia*. I'm not sure when we'll see each other again. Perhaps I'll send word—if I can. *Va bene?*" He begged her forgiveness for the abrupt manner in which he had to leave her, then swiftly boarded the jeep and sped homeward to Montegatta immersed in premonitory thoughts. He left behind him, a mystified lover, pondering his strange and unorthodox behavior.

Miguel and Arturo, standing guard outside the house of his mother alerted Tori at once by their presence. Inside he found his mother prostrate at Athena's bedside, where Santino had brought his wife at her request. Santino, pale-faced, tight-lipped and red-eyed from crying, sat by the bed, his agonized eyes on the still figure of his beautiful wife. Vincenzo stood in the door way of the room, a pale, drawn expression of sorrow on his face, nervously picking at his nails.

Athena, excessively pale and motionless, lay on the bed in the candlelit room, surrounded by religious icons, totally unaware of their presence. Her dark eyes fluttered open and through the drugged haze, she recognized one face, her brother's, and she moaned softly, forcing a shadowy smile.

"They had to summon you, Tori? *Allora*—it must be time."

Tori sat on the edge of the bed, stroking her moist, feverish face, smoothing her long black hair off her face where it fell like lustrous bands of silk against the snow-white pillowslip.

"What's wrong, *cara mia*? What's happened?" He leaned in, kissed her forehead. Her eyes fluttered gently open and shut in a drugged stupor.

"Tori," she whispered. "Tori," Athena tried to speak. "I love you, my dearest brother," she said finally with great effort, in a voice barely above a whisper. "Tori—don't go. Don't leave me," she sank back, unconscious.

"Let her sleep, my son. The doctor gave her morphine to dull the pain," said his mother softly. She sat staring at the form on the bed, unable to believe her eyes. Her fingers worked the rosary beads in her hands. Santino sat hunched over, full of wretchedness, his hands hanging between his legs like dead weights.

Later, in the kitchen under brighter lights, he searched his mother's distraught face and felt a pang of dismay at the marked change in her. Strain and heartbreak etched deeply on her face. Tori experienced pangs of guilt for having deceived her over Athena's illness. Gina was right.

These past few months should have been a time of extreme closeness between the family.

Antigone dragged herself heavily about the kitchen, preparing coffee for the others. No matter how the others tried to keep it from her, she knew. She knew Athena was going to die. Earlier, when Santino had brought his wife to her house, she'd seen the truth written on his face, and right then she'd been struck with another portion of the prophecy which the *strega* had predicted with such alarming exactness. *"The children of one father shall soon cease to be!"*

What more would it take for Antigone to accept the prophecy as gospel? More strife? More unhappiness? More tragedy? Wrapped up in her thoughts, she failed to notice the men had retired to Tori's room to talk. In their absence she broke down and sobbed with heart-rending sounds. Finally taking hold of herself, she walked to Athena's side, knelt down and bowed her head in prayer.

"Is there nothing we can do but sit around and watch her die?" asked Tori savagely, once the men retired to his room behind closed doors.

Santino, unable to speak, simply shook his head in a woebegone expression.

Vincenzo, carrying a bottle of whiskey and two glasses, poured some for Santino and a stiff one for himself. "Go on, *padre*, drink it down. It will dull the pain."

In a rare burst of temper, Tori shoved his balled fist through a wardrobe door. Grasping his pain-filled wrist with his free hand, he cursed aloud, gasping at the pain, *"Figghiu de Butana.* Son of a whore!"

Vincenzo, startled at sounds of splintered wood and Tori's loud expletives, glanced at his cousin nonplused. *"Va bene,"* he said dryly. "Fine—real fine. That's smart of you, cousin. What the hell good does it do for Athena, eh?" Annoyed by his cousin's brash, immature action, he grabbed Tori's bleeding, cracked hand and led him into the kitchen as one might lead a small child. Santino followed them, a disconsolate figure of abject misery.

"It's all right, I tell you," Tori muttered hoarsely. "I knew what I was doing. Goddamnit!" he lamented sorrowfully. "Why her? Why not me? First, Filippo, then Marco, now Athena! It's a sign, I tell you. My time is coming soon. Isn't it obvious the Salvatore family has been marked for death?"

"God moves in strange ways," Santino sighed, blowing his nose. "I've seen too much of his handiwork to question his motives." He watched as Vincenzo rubbed butter on Tori's hand. "Is it better now?"

"Don't concern yourself with me, *padre*. Say some powerful prayers to that God of yours, to spare your wife—hear? If you've got any influence with Him, promise him anything to keep her alive, you hear—anything." Tori's voice in a stifled whisper was clear and distinct. His eyes burned as one in fever. "Goddamnit, Santino, she can't die! She can't!" He loved his sister more than life and couldn't bear the thought of her dying.

A knock at the door startled them. No one could have been more astonished than Salvatore to see Gina O'Hoolihan breeze into the house. Her eyes were on Santino. "I came as soon as I got your message. Why didn't you let me know sooner?" She smiled wanly at her lover.

The message she read in Tori's eyes caused her to run swiftly to Athena's side.

"What can I do to help her, *Signora*?" she asked Antigone when her eyes had adjusted to the darkness illuminated only by the dim glow of flickering candles placed before religious icons. The room was heavy with the scent of paraffin and antiseptic. She placed her hand reassuringly on Antigone's arm.

"What's wrong with my daughter, *Signorina* Gina?" she asked. "Why won't they tell me she's dying?"

Before Gina could think of an answer, she saw Antigone stiffen and grow alert. The older woman cocked her head, held a finger to her lips to restrain Gina from speaking as she listened. Faintly, in the far off distance, came the sounds, the warning signals, the whistles. . . .

The sounds drew closer and closer. Antigone rose to her feet just as the Scoletti Brothers ran into the house calling to the others. The men came alive and moved methodically and swiftly. Before Antigone and Gina reached the kitchen, downstairs, the men, guns in hand, had disappeared at the end of the terrace, through cactus and underbrush. Mounting their horses, they faded into the shifting cover of night.

Inside, Antigone's demeanor changed instantly. She quickly wiped off the kitchen table, removing all traces of the men's presence. Gina stared in amazement at the instant transition in the older woman, the instant resourcefulness.

"What is it? I don't understand. What's happening?"

"The *carabinieri*. They'll be upon us in moments. Ever since Tori refused to cooperate with certain politicians, they come to harass us. Recently my son released three hundred prisoners from jail. Yesterday they came, the *squadristi* and *carabinieri*, to arrest five hundred more." She poured two cups of coffee. Suddenly the front and rear doors were kicked in, crashing against the walls, nearly shaking the house from its foundation, as two armed *carabinieri* entered at the rear door and four more burst in on them from the front, rifles aimed menacingly at the two women.

Before Gina knew what happened, and before hardly a word was spoken, the men scattered like mice throughout the house, searching every nook and cranny. One of the police officers addressed himself to Antigone. "*Signora* Salvatore, you are under arrest for aiding and abetting the enemies of Sicily. You will come with us at once."

Behind them one of the officers was carrying Athena down the stairs.

"No! You can't take her. She's in critical condition!"

"You can't move her!" cried Gina. "She's under heavy sedation. The poor child suffers a brain tumor," she blurted unthinkingly. "My God where's your decency? Is there no morality in Sicily? Are you all the disgraceful animals I've been led to believe?"

She was unaware that Antigone's face had blanched and she had sunk down into a chair heavily, stunned by Gina's revelation. Then it was true what she'd suspected about her daughter's fate. "Dear Sainted God, Athena is dying," she muttered aloud.

"Oh, my dear, I'm so sorry," apologized Gina. Then, turning her wrath on the *carabinieri* who stopped for no one and continued about their business like automatons, she cursed aloud. "Bastards!" she screamed at them. She attempted to use what little clout she might have as she tried to dissuade them from their task, but they paid her no mind, and soon the American found herself alone in the Salvatore house. Antigone and Athena had been whisked away in the police van.

Frightened, bewildered and thoroughly shaken by the rapid order of confusion, she waited for a half hour after they departed certain that Tori would have returned. It was nearly 10 P.M. when she approached the bright lights of Palermo, a time when in most cities of the world things were coming to life. Here, in the backwoods of a hostile country among an alien herd of which she could never hope to be a part, she hadn't begun to get the story she knew was here waiting for her.

If Gina found herself confused at the course of events that happened at the Salvatore's house, it was nothing compared to the utter astonishment and resentful anger she felt when, before she arrived at her hotel, she was unceremoniously dumped into the office of the Security Police in Palermo and stood facing Chief Enzo Semano.

"I'm astonished, *Signorina* O'Hoolihan, that you've compromised yourself with a criminal of the calibre of Salvatore." He was an egg-shaped man with an oval head as hairless as the storybook Humpty Dumpty, and bore a remarkable resemblance to Mayor Tedesco.

Gina was fit to be tied. For an hour she argued her right, as an international correspondent, to be in Sicily where she had pursued an interview with Salvatore. More irritating and rankling to her than the circumstances in which she found herself was the paternal rancor with which the man spoke with her. No matter how many times she showed him her credentials, reminding him she was a member of the fourth estate, he countered with reminders that she was in his territory and under his full jurisdiction.

"Aiding and abetting a criminal is punishable by fine and imprisonment."

"You wouldn't dare!" she countered.

"Try me."

"Call my office in Rome for verification of my status! You can't touch me without serious repercussions—and you know it."

"Don't push me, *Signorina.* I'm not a long-eared, brainless fool."

"Then stop acting like one!"

"We were deceived once by a spy feigning to be a reporter—"

"Don't blame the ineptness of your staff on *me*—"

"—a reporter, who like you, had no difficulty reaching Salvatore when our own law enforcement agencies can't locate him."

"Look, you can arrest me and detain me over night, but, ultimately you'll have to release me. Too many people know where I am. You've seen my credentials. Just remember when I return to America the light in which I characterize you will be viewed by millions. I shouldn't have to remind you of the power of the press."

"Ahhhh," he growled low in his throat. "I detect a threat in those words." Humpty Dumpty flipped a gold and enamel letter-opener from one hand to the next.

"Not at all," she replied in syrupy tones. "Just the promise of a glowing account of a most chivalrous police inspector, who extended every courtesy and kindness to a

636

poorly misguided and somewhat inept American journalist."

"How generous of you, *Signorina* O'Hoolihan," said Humpty Dumpty, feigning pleasant surprise at her words. "However—with your permission, I must do my job, and detain you overnight. I promise you a minimum of discomfort—as little inconvenience as possible."

Stifling her anger, and knowing she'd been bested by this butterballed comedian, she forced a revoltingly saccharine smile and, in English, had let loose a string of American cuss words which brought a flush to his cheeks.

"You forget we were recently occupied by the Americans. . . ." The Chief Inspector rose to his feet, pressed a buzzer on his desk to signal an aide to his office. "You will show *Signorina* O'Hoolihan the hospitality of our jail," he told the harried officer who scurried into the room. "Unless—" he turned to his irate guest. "Unless you cooperate and tell us the location of Salvatore's hideouts."

About to tell Fatso where he could go and what he might do *en route*, Gina became highly resourceful, grateful for having done her homework on Salvatore. She instructed the Chief to get rid of the aide. Chief Semano fairly pushed the officer out of the room. His fat face filled with gloating satisfaction until Gina's next few words gave him a temporary face-lift.

"What you ask of me is impossible, Inspector. . . ." She waved off the beginning protest she saw forming on his lips. "Only because my report must be made to—uh—" she glanced about and whispered confidentially. "His Excellency, *Martino Belasci. . . .*"

How could Gina have known she'd just stoked a hive of killer bees?

"The *Minister of the Interior?*" Semano's face became expressionless.

She gave him the business with her eyes and handed him the "special pass" given her by Stefano Modica, signed by Belasci, himself.

"You know how rarely His Excellency issues these passes. . . ."

Semano stood the card up on his desk, propped up by the letter opener. He shoved a nasal inhalator in each nostril to clear his sinuses and inhaled lingeringly as he scanned the card with his lidded, inert eyes. Slipping the recapped inhalator into his pocket, he lifted his eyes to hers.

"You know I can check on this instantly. . . ."

"Please do!" Gina picked up the telephone from its

cradle and shoved the instrument at him. "It would end this harassment instantly. Tomorrow your post would be filled by your successor. . . ." she smiled sweetly.

He grabbed the phone from her and slammed it back into its cradle and glowered at her.

"I'll tell you this much, Inspector," she lied with remarkable agility. "After the last *fiasco* with the journalist whom the communists labeled an American spy for Truman, the Minister refused to take chances. You can understand his position. I report *only* to him. I repeat—*only* to him!"

In seconds Gina was escorted to the door by an overly polite and obsequious Inspector Semano. Before taking her leave she whispered in a more confidential manner. "You'll make sure *General Brancuso* doesn't learn of my presence here as emissary to His Excellency. . . ."

Suddenly it all jelled for him. The extra nudge about the *carabiniero* general made her story more credible. His face filled with an expression of total complicity.

"Ah, *si*. Now I understand. Not a word! I promise they shall learn nothing of your mission," he assured her in outright honesty. Flushed with the secret he harbored, he bowed curtly, even kissed her hand in parting.

Gina's next two weeks were spent recuperating from the forcible attack and rape done to her person as she left the office of Chief Semano. Gina had crossed the narrow street, heading in the direction of her car, when suddenly she had been caught from behind, gagged and dragged into an alley. She'd been held down, raped by two men, then beaten to within an inch of her life and left to die.

When consciousness returned to her, it was nearly dawn. She had picked herself up and winced at the excruciating pain she felt. Every bone, muscle and nerve in her body felt crushed by a steam roller. Dazed and unable to think clearly, she managed to get to her rented car. Luckily the keys had been in her pocket and not her bag, so she was able to start the car. That was when she noticed her bag had been tossed in casually in the front seat. She'd opened it, and found everything intact except for the money. That was missing.

How she managed to start the engine and drive the few miles to the Catholic Hospital was a feat she never dreamed could be accomplished. Flashes of the abominable scene kept flashing into her mind. What tore at her and pained her the most was the savage manner in which they'd dragged her arms and legs apart, spreading them until she felt her limbs would tear from their sockets. The memory of the way they ravaged her and the degradation to her spirit and mind had been worse than her physical injuries, for, God willing, it would pass. But would her memory of this nightmare cease? Between her thighs was a crusty and sticky coagulation of blood and semen. What Gina would remember most of all was the vicious, animal-like grunts and the pure lust in their eyes.

The darkness had prevented her from ever identifying her assailants, and if that wasn't enough, the savage blows to her head when she tried to cry out, had brought about a curtain of forgetfullness. The only souvenir of this despicable act was a handful of black straight hair which she'd pulled from the head of an assailant. Slowly, painfully and with agonized movements, Gina had managed to get out of the car and walk into the hospital, where she had promptly passed out.

She left the hospital a week later and remained in bed in her hotel suite, wondering why there'd been no news from Tori. Had he known about her terrifying experience? Why hadn't he sent a message? In addition to the rape and trauma she'd undergone, there were more things to disturb Gina. She'd already guessed her *accident* had been inflicted by Chief Semano. Oh, not directly, but she felt sure he'd oredered it. It was too pat—too slick—and happened too coincidentally with her obstruction. Later, Gina was more concerned with the monstrous lie she'd told Chief Semano regarding Minister Belasci. If checked out, her eviction from Sicily would follow. She had experienced doubts as to what might greet her in Rome. Her paper's influence, plus aid from the U.S. Embassy, might be required to help her squirm out of the predicament.

She had no intention of leaving Sicily now, as she had faced the fact she was overwhelmingly in love with Tori.

After the second week of silence, she grew gravely concerned. Her health had improved and the bruises and swelling abated. Purple and yellowish bruises were still apparent around her eyes and jaws where she'd been struck. She hardly noticed her appearance; her thoughts were of Tori. It wasn't like him not to send word, or contact her in some way. She began reading the newspapers two and three times through, searching for some sign, some word, some hint that might tell her what was happening with him. Nothing. There was nothing to indicate Tori had met with foul play. The silence devastated her. She was forced into making the decision to leave Sicily. She was overdue in Rome. But how could she leave? She *had* to see Tori once more, to feel his arms around her, to love as they had loved at Calemi's villa, she had told herself as she packed her belongings.

The morning of the twenty-second day, just as she prepared to leave Palermo, Vincenzo arrived with word that Tori wanted to see her. If he noticed her bruises and the discoloration of her skin on her face, he gave no evidence. All the way to Castellammare, he remained aloof and uncommunicative. To an occasional question from Gina, he'd nod or shrug his shoulders indifferently.

Unable to endure this unnatural behavior or his pose of inordinate silence, Gina pressed him. "You don't like me, do you?" she asked straight out.

He was forced to reply. "I make no judgment of people. I leave that to Tori."

"At least you're fond of him."

"We're one and the same—blood brothers."

Impulsively she asked, "You think he'd ever leave Sicily?" She was dreaming aloud. If Gina was surprised at herself for asking, she was more astonished at his reply, which he did in a stern, reproving voice.

"Ask him—not me."

"I'm asking you. You know him well enough to know if he'd ever leave."

"It's best you ask no such questions of me, *Capitana*. Don't involve Vincenzo in your intrigue."

"*Intrigue?*" Gina turned in her seat and fastened her amethyst eyes on him. "I don't understand, Vincenzo. What intrigue?" She stared at his leonine profile. The grim tightness around his lips, without humor, should have alerted her and told her something was amiss. She turned from him and gazed out at the white-capped waves of the Tyrrhenian Sea and scanned the scenic panorama along the coast, feeling the agonies of the past three weeks vividly. Perplexed and bewildered by this silent Jekyll-and-Hyde treatment, she wondered what would greet her at the Calemi villa.

She found him seated on the balustrade of the upper balcony, next to a wall of cascading bougainvillaea, staring absently at the sea glittering in a crystal and distracting brilliance. Flowers in earthenpots were everywhere. A shaggy English sheepdog, lying at his feet, raised his head and growled as Gina opened the Dutch door. Tori glanced up and stayed the dog as Gina ran into his arms.

"Tori," she cried softly and clung to him fiercely. "Oh, *Caro mio*, how much I've missed you. I couldn't leave without seeing you first. I felt certain something terrible had happened. . . ."

Gina stopped. It was like holding a stone image. She backed away from him, her violet eyes searching his cold, hostile face. He looked terrible. Shadows under his eyes accentuated harsh, tight lines around his lips. He was a stranger to her—this cold, unfeeling man.

"What's wrong? Something has happened—hasn't it?" She placed a slender hand over her mouth in panic. "Nothing's happened to Athena—your mother?"

In the next instant she saw another side to him, a ruthless, savagery which revolted her and alternately excited her. He opened the door to let out the dog.

"You work for Belasci!" he said with a vitriolic tone, returning to her side.

"I—what?"

"You managed to fool me completely. Me! Salvatore!" he snarled. "I, who never allowed myself the luxury of closeness to any woman for fear of betrayal, walked into your trap." He paced the pebbled floor of the roof garden and stormed at her angrily. "*Managghia!* Never would I have guessed it of you. Never!" He exploded with the emotions of a spoiled and petulant child.

In the unmerciful confusion which followed, Gina's emotions, in no shape to be trifled with, were forced into a state of numbness. She couldn't believe her ears, much less believe what Tori was accusing her of doing. She was dreaming all this. The past three weeks had been an unholy nightmare. She'd awaken and find it all a sham.

Gina did the unexpected in those next few moments. She turned her back on Tori and moved away from him through the potted fern and palm fronds, as if he didn't exist. She paused to watch as a few bees hummed drowsily over the flowers in their cross-pollination. Above them, a fiery blue sky pulsed like a passionate heart, but, Tori, seeing none of this, had been infuriated by her cool gesture of detachment. For a time as Gina watched the shimmering waves slap up against the shore as colorful fishing vessels reminiscent of the early Phoenicians bobbed up and down in the bay, she tried desperately to fit the pieces together. It was obvious he didn't know, or care, what had happened to her.

"Look at me when I speak to you," he snarled tyrannically. When she failed to respond to his black mood, he grew more furious. He grabbed her arm and spun her about to face him.

"Make sense and I will." She glanced coolly at his hand,

grasped like a tight vise about her upper arm. She lifted her eyes to meet his until he released his hold on her.

It was then that Tori noticed the faint discolorations on her face. He peered at her closely, but wasn't ready to acknowledge them or inquire as to their origin. "What a consummate actres you are!" He spat in a fit of temper.

"Will you stop this nonsense and tell me why you're in such a steam?" she implored, losing patience.

"You deny you've been sent by the Minister of the Interior to spy upon me? Tricked me into falling in love with you, so you could betray me?"

The incredible shock registered on her face at the accusation was instantly replaced by a spontaneous, unguarded laughter which increased Tori's suspicions. His eyes grew colder, the icy wall between them more threatening. For all he cared she could have been 3000 miles away. Then it registered.

"You didn't believe that idiotic story I concocted to keep that insipid Inspector Semano off my back, did you?" Suddenly it was her turn to grow wary. "But—how did you know?"

"There's little I don't know here in Sicily."

"Then, you should have known I was 'politely' detained by the security police and charged with complicity, aiding and abetting a bandit! The Inspector wanted to incarcerate me unless I gave him information about you!"

"He did that for *your* protection."

"*My* protection?"

"So the *carabinieri* wouldn't get to you first."

"You give orders to the Chief Inspector of police? It was he who told you about Belasci, or whatever in hell his name is."

"The less you know, the safer it is for you."

"And you *never* really gave me the true story of Salvatore? I know as much as the ballad makers know? What a fool you must have thought me."

"The real truth would place you in too much danger—don't you see?"

"I see only that you believed the worst about me!" Her heart broke in two. "You condemned me before hearing my side. I thought you were known as the prince of justice—my king!" she cried acrimoniously.

She wouldn't let go. "You really believed I betrayed you?" She shook her head in dismay. "You think only Sicilians hold a patent on intrigue? We correspondents live by our wits ninety percent of the time. I saw what happened to your poor mother—how they took Athena, ill as she is, off to jail. I feared the worst when Inspector Semano intimidated me. I used whatever guile and information I could muster." She riffled through her bag until she found the special pass. "Here," she pressed it into his hand. "A special pass signed by our mutual friend, Stefano Modica! Your Chief Inspector was so astute, so discerning, he didn't notice the doctoring done to the date!" Sarcasm dripped from her lips.

Tori studied the pass. The corners of his lips turned up. He, too had enjoyed such a pass in the recent past. He had to admit the date had been cleverly altered. "*Managghia*," he exclaimed. "You're beginning to think like a Sicilian." He saw the truth in her eyes and eased up a bit.

She took the pass, tossed it into her bag and couldn't resist asking, "You're close to the police? You know what they're up to at all times?" she asked testily.

"We have an understanding." Tori avoided her imperious eyes.

"I see. Then you know the rest of it, is that it?"

"The rest of what?" He searched her eyes carefully.

"Or better yet, perhaps it was *you* behind the atrocity!"

"Make sense, woman. Stop prattling like an old crone."

"Like you made sense when I arrived and you attacked me without giving me the benefit of a doubt? Hah! All right! I'll tell you!" She searched her bag and pulled out the bill she'd paid the hospital on her release, and thrust it at him. "Either you, or your friends the Security police, or their villainous henchmen, attacked me as I left the police station, raped me, beat me up, and left me for dead!" There, it was out, and with it came the pent-up emotion she'd held inside her these past weeks. She watched the shock and incredulous expression on his face.

Tori studied the hospital bill, white-faced, his face set like ice, as Gina told him the whole story, eliminating nothing. She just didn't give a damn anymore—about anything! She had made an important decision and told him.

"Don't concern yourself with me," she fired at him, even as she noticed the confusion, and self-recrimination rise to surface in his eyes, "or with what I may have learned about you or your activities. I'm packed, ready to leave. I waited to hear some news of your mother and Athena. I've been worried sick about them ever since the night they were arrested." Gina wouldn't tell him the truth—how she had longed for him, and ate her heart out fearing the worst, even as her own life hung in the balance.

When she became silent, Tori spoke gently. "I am too stunned by your words, appalled at the attack on your person. Further, I'm humiliated and so outraged that I can't find words to express my deepest feelings. I'll get to the bottom of this *infamita*, and when I do, be assured the guilty parties will pay with their lives, I promise." He felt awful. "*Cara mia*, what you must have endured. God, God!" he exclaimed, too ashamed of his doubts to look at her.

She was silent and unmoving.

"I've offended you," he said quietly. "To have flaunted my stupidity is unforgivable." He tossed his arms into the air and let them fall heavily to his sides. "You see? I told you I'm no good for a woman. With so many treacheries underfoot I become vulnerable. My mother and sister were jailed because they are related to me." He clenched his fists and struck at the iron railing along the cement wall. "I've died sixty times a minute thinking of that night they were arrested. Now I learn you've been ravaged and mutilated. How well they aim their treacheries! Wherever I'm the most vulnerable."

Gina looked at him without speaking.

"When they told me you were a spy sent to betray me, my world collapsed. My mind went over every second we spent together. Nothing made sense. You see, my mother is drawn instinctively to you. Even Athena adored you. What I felt—what I thought—only increased my dilemma. I refused to believe Chief Semano. How I insisted he was wrong. But, no. He told me he'd put you to the test. The moment you felt threatened, you confessed."

"Anyone would confess to a wild story to save his neck," she said. "Even then, it didn't save me."

"Why the preposterous story about Belasci? The story became credible only when you mentioned his name."

"He believed me, didn't he?"

Tori put out his arms, pulling her close to him. "Gina," he called softly, nuzzling his face in her thick, clean-scented hair. "*Cara*, will you forgive me? Understand my cause for alarm. A precedent for the elimination of spies has already been set in the Salvatore camp. I was afraid for you."

Gina wasn't listening. Something nagged at her. The echo of his earlier words came crashing through her mind. "Tori—what did you mean when you said, 'Athena *adored* me?' Why do you speak of her in the past tense?"

She sensed his inner torment and deterioration, the hurt surfacing in his eyes which he tried to conceal. He averted his face and dropped his arms heavily to his sides. "Athena died over a week ago," he told her in a wavering voice, trying to blink away the welling tears in his blurred eyes.

Gina was stunned. "You should have sent for me—" she began. "I mean, who took care of her—I mean—Oh, I don't know what I mean! She told Tori how she had inadvertently betrayed the trust, how Antigone had learned from her lips Athena's fate. Watching him in his dark agonizing torment, Gina felt helpless. "And I complained over that minor altercation—"

Tori reached for her again and held her close. "Please, please, Gina, don't mention that abomination again. I must put it out of mind or I'll go mad. The thought of you being abused and raped by strangers makes my blood boil. I told you it would be handled—*my* way. Now, for the love of God, for as much terror as it struck in your heart, erase it from mind."

For several moments they clung to each other, unmoving and silent, each feeling the beat of their hearts against the other's body. Tori began to talk—to pour out his heart to her. "None of us could attend the funeral services— They wouldn't permit my mother to attend her daughter's funeral. For that, I'll never forgive them. Not for that or for taking Athena in the brutal manner they did." Tori's voice cracked. He couldn't go on with the details. "They'll pay for this disgraceful *infamita*. God Almighty, will they pay!"

Putting himself in order, Tori asked her forgiveness for expressing himself so candidly. "Someone tries very hard to get at me. Only through the hardships inflicted on my family can they weaken me. I begged them to move away—to America. They refused. Too many conplications are involved. It's best you know very little. If it's known you possess knowledge or information concerning me, or that we're close, your life as well as mine would be in danger."

For a moment, Tori stared off at the boats in the harbor, contemplating the attack on Gina. Who could have provoked such a dastardly aggression? It wasn't the way his people settled differences. To attack a woman was a sign of sickness—not strength. He turned to her, forcing her eyes to look into his. "*Cara mia*, you are to tell no one that we are lovers, understand? *No one.*"

"I've told no one," she replied.

Tori agonized. "I've made myself believe things that couldn't be true."

Gina leaned heavily against him, feeling the shudder

passing through them. "Tori," she said with a sudden inspiration, "Come to America with me."

Startled at the proposal, he pushed her gently from him, searching her face, thinking it might be a joke or a light matter. "America? Me, go with you? Why, whatever for?" he asked incredulously, as if it were the most preposterous suggestion to pass her lips.

"Yes. Yes, I'm sure it could be arranged, somehow, someway!" The more Gina considered it, the more plausible it sounded. "Yes. Why not? I'll speak to someone with political clout. We can pull it off, I'm sure!"

Tori's eyes devoured her. For a wild second, he projected his mind forward into another life, another world filled with impossible dreams and he smiled tolerantly. "Gina, Gina, Gina! My sweet, wonderful, American princess. Destiny would never relinquish her hold on me. This is *my* country, *my* people. I was born at a special time, in a special world, to do a special service to my country. Leaving Sicily wouldn't be the answer. My destiny hasn't been fulfilled, yet."

It took Gina several moments to completely understand him. Even then, it was doubtful she comprehended him fully. She wanted to tell him he was fighting a losing battle, that he alone couldn't possibly help a nation whose political complexities had baffled American military intelligence. She wanted to point out that millions of men had immigrated to America, adopting it for their own. But she couldn't form the words on her lips. He had spoken to her not as a human man with frailties, but as a powerful, ancient god might, shouldering the responsibilities of his world.

"Perhaps," temporized Tori, wistfully, "if I'd met you before it all began. . . . It's too late, now. I know too much. Shortly, I'll know even more. They'd follow me to the ends of the earth to erase my image, just like that." He snapped his fingers smartly.

Gina said nothing. She knew her words were futile. They spent the rest of the day together. Later, when they made love, Tori was gentle with her, and she sensed that he was thinking of the way she'd been violated by the two assailants. "It's all right, Tori," she whispered to him. "It's all over. I felt nothing with them. I gave them no satisfaction—whoever they were."

Tori, overcome with compassion, made love to her feverishly, frenetically, as if he couldn't be done with loving her. Music from the Palermo radio station warmed the villa with romantic and soulful music, stirring their emotions to a high pitch. Neither would face the fact that this might be their final time together.

Tori's passion, more violent than in the past, increased. Yet once, at the moment before his orgasm, he paused with supreme control as a wild-eyed, crazed expression entered his eyes. He whispered hoarsely. "I never stopped to consider, what you are doing to prevent conception?" The thought of such negligence, plus his concern for the girl cooled him for a few moments.

"Why, *caro mio*? You object to children?" she smiled enigmatically.

"I love children! . . . It's just that I wouldn't want anything to complicate your life. . . ." He stopped abruptly and stared into her smoky, amethyst eyes. In the flickering candlelight he could see the answer written in her eyes.

"Dear God, Gina, you're not. . . ." He moaned and turned from her for an instant. Then he gripped her arm tightly. "Why didn't you tell me?"

". . . And give you more problems than you have?" she whispered softly, stroking his upper arms. Touching his warm skin became an erotic sensation that caused her to tingle with excitement. He exuded so warm a body heat that contact with him set her on fire.

Tori, his emotions raw nerve ends, gasped audibly and buried his face into her full, firm breasts which seemed already swollen maternally. "*Amore mia*—my love," he murmured over and again, expressing his profound feelings. "*Quanta se bedda*—how lovely you are. When I loved you less, I could content myself with less. Now, that I love you more—I'm in constant torment without you."

He gripped her tighter, his desire overrode all else. He blotted from his mind the thought that her pregnancy might have been incubated by either of her attackers. But when she told him she was entering her third month, Tori was delirious with happiness. She abandoned herself to him and he to her, forgetting everything except these moments. God, what passion they endured as they drove each other to the brink of madness! They were two people alone in a conspiracy against reality.

As Tori descended that exquisite plateau of sexual euphoria, returning to the mundane, the thought of losing Gina, after becoming addicted to her, tore at him. He felt helpless and impotent as he watched her cuddled in his arms like a frightened waif. *She carries my child*, he told himself. The thought, exciting, yet more frightening than anything he'd contemplated, caused an ambivalence in him. How could he feel such happiness and feel terror for Gina at the same time? If anyone were to learn of this—?

He shuddered at the thought, for he knew she'd be dealt a worse fate than the one to which his mother and Athena had fallen prey to. It was in this moment's reverie that it came to Tori that Don Barbarossa—his father—had been behind the diabolical incarceration of his mother and sister. He didn't know how he knew, only that he knew, and no one could dissuade him from this truth. He reached for a cigarette and lit it with a lighter, and for a while he lay in the darkness, thinking hard on the matter. His thoughts echoed his earlier suspicion with such clarity that he knew he'd have to pay his father a visit, shortly.

Tori, so intent in his thoughts, had not noticed that Gina had slipped from his arms and sat up on the bed next to him, devouring his nakedness with her soulful eyes. It was only when she lay her cool, feverish face against his upper thigh and kissed him with soft, moist, fluttery kisses, until power surged into his genitals, did he focus his attention on her. Glowing with the intoxication of their love, the feeling surged through his body like the effects of a stimulating and elevating drug that once again sent him into the weightlessness of ecstasy. Her hot, velvety tongue caressed his swollen manhood. His senses pyramided higher—higher, until finally he grabbed the thick strands of her fragrant dark hair, twisting her face gently upwards towards him. "I'll never be done with the wonder of you," he whispered in a strained, lusty voice. "What are you doing to me, *strega*?" His dilated eyes glistening in the dark and shone like black onyx.

"Enslaving you as you've enslaved me. Let the memory of our love burn in your heart and memory, my love. Come to me, Tori, where I'll be waiting forever with *our* son." She buried her head in his groin.

"Sweet beautiful, precious God!" He trembled violently against her body. Every nerve in his body had been set on fire by her ardent skill. His eyes grew wild and frenzied, his body bursting into tiny bubbles of hot and cold sweat. When he could no longer endure the erotic sensations, he tensed, contorted wildly, twisting, writhing on the bed until the inner explosions shook him to the core.

Tori would never forget Gina O'Hoolihan. She had made certain of it. Indelibly etched into Tori's face, so that all strangers would see it, would be their love, like the bright, dazzling image of an invigorating sun.

CHAPTER 48

"The power of the Mafia—if such an organization ever existed—was pulverized by Mussolini long ago, and can be of no political worth to the Christian Democratic Party." These words, articulated by Premier Alfonso de Aspanu, in what was perhaps the most foolish and incautious moment of his life were viewed by the man to whom they were spoken with contempt.

Don Barbarossa seated opposite him in the austere offices of the Premier in Rome, Italy couldn't believe that this idiot, a man with the brain of a pygmy, could have risen to such high office. "With all due respect, Excellency," began the Sicilian power broker politely, "recall please the April 27 convention, when the vote was three to one in favor of a Republic."

"Yes, yes, of course, I recall," snapped the Premier, annoyed by this uncouth upstart of a Sicilian peasant who presumed too much. The impertinence of demanding audience with the Premier! Indeed!

"Well, Excellency," continued the Don impervious to the Premier's obvious disdain, "Due to a foolish error, and much to his regret, His Royal Highness dealt with the wrong man. Before Vittorio Emmanuel had realized his gross error, the House of Savoy fell. You see in some circles it was rumored that Nick Gentile controlled the *Societa Onorata*." The Don wagged a finger before him. "Of course he didn't. Without *my* support, the House of Savoy couldn't survive—with your permission, *didn't* survive."

Premier de Aspanu sat in a red velour chair in his gilded Baroque chambers like a stiffly arched bow, unyielding, wondering at the audacity of this Sicilian barbarian, who in his brazen, outspoken, and outrageously loathsome self-assurance was a bit too much for this well-bred, refined and dignified Chief of State.

The Don, who wanted no Reds in his beloved Sicily to complicate matters for him, had taken it upon himself, in an act strictly against his custom of maintaining political anonymity, to go to Rome and demand an audience with the Premier, to contest the recent appointment of communists to de Aspanu's government. Never had such a crushing blow been dealt the Christian Democrats as this blundering unthinking act. How could the Premier not have known that the admission of Reds to his cabinet would spur a hotbed of political intrigue among all Christian Democratic spokesmen?

Hadn't these men strenuously voiced their objections over this coalition ministry, already? Their vain cries and stout protests had met deaf ears.

Very well, thought the Don. Only one voice really mattered in Sicily, his. His voice would shake the Premier, awaken him before it was too late. The chance had to be taken before this hot-eyed, yeasty old man, the Premier, crumbled their world with his shocking ideas.

The Premier, grossly offended by the Don's presence, couldn't contain himself. The nerve of this peasant, to step foot in Rome and alight at the center of the political arena, where enemy spotlights trained on them could report this incident to the world. Those damnable Reds! Their curiosity over the Premier's activities had unnerved him of late, causing him innumerable problems. Now this! The sum total of what Don Barbarossa represented increased De Aspanu's hostility, firing his agitation against this unwelcome southerner. He listened for an hour behind a forced mask of politeness; then, indignantly made his point. "I refuse to be influenced by outside forces."

When word reached Don Barbarossa of the Premier's steadfast refusal to alter his original stand, he couldn't believe his ears. In considering the insult done to the Mafia, the Church and the baronial circle of millionaires whose money had helped place the Premier in office, the Don convinced himself he was duty-bound to by-pass heads of state and personally meet with the Premier to protest the political suicide towards which de Aspanu was headed.

These two political lions were at an impasse only because the Premier had no true estimate of the Don's power, something the *capomafia* attempted tactfully to explain to the other, with little results.

To say that the Premier sadly underestimated the power of the diabolical *mafioso*, who at best resembled a simple peasant amidst the elegant splendor of the Roman dignitary, is putting it mildly. At one point, the Premier had sniffed distastefully, rose to his feet and bowed curtly—and for the second time that morning had become irresponsibly foolish. "I have no more time for you, *Signor*

650

Barbarossa," he said impatiently with a tone of curt dismissal. His expression of offended dignity grew more pronounced when the Don remained seated, unruffled by the obvious brush-off.

Peering inscrutably at the small man, whose features were dominated by bushy, curly hair and a receding hairline, a man dressed impeccably in a dark suit and vest—who disdained him through pince-nez glasses—the Don simply grunted low in his throat and spoke economically. "Before the end of May you shall come around to my way of thinking." He spoke matter-of-factly, confidence oozing from every pore in his body. He took his time rising to his feet, picked up the scrolled briefcase, and nodded curtly. Then, in a voice the Premier later compared to the effects of a spinal anesthetic, slowly freezing the vital organs, he continued. "Unless you desire to receive the same fate inherited by your predecessors when they were forced to resign their posts, I suggest you reconsider the matter."

Don Barbarossa had the pleasure of watching de Aspanu's oval face transform into a circle of anger. His eyes, bloodshot with fury, turned red. The Don nodded, bowed stiffly and left the blustery, arrogant Chief of State to his fate.

Before Premier de Aspanu instructed his secretary to usher in the volatile communist delegation who waited in an outer office, he shouted acidly. "Get Minister Belasci on the phone!" He snapped off the intercom and paced the room furiously in a nervous, bird walk, flapping his arms wildly in the air in a waddle that resembled a Jackass penguin, a special breed of penguin whose mating call resembles the braying of a jackass. Even his voice resembled the braying penguin's mating call.

"You must have given the Premier cause for alarm," purred Martino Belasci with a wide grin on his face. "My office received a frantic call from de Aspanu, requesting a complete dossier on you."

"You spoke with him?" asked the Don airily. They had gorged themselves on costly viands and tossed off bumpers of sparkling wines at Belasci's villa while he had described the Premier's disinclination to amend the recently formed ministry. Archbishop Voltera had left for the Vatican on business, leaving the Don with the Minister, Prince Oliatta, and the Don's bodyguard, Mario Cacciatore.

Belasci nodded. "I gave the Premier an education he won't forget. I explained exactly who you were, how influential you were with the Allies, and I even detailed your involvement in the war effort. You see, Don Matteo, here in Rome your participation in the Occupation was considered top secret; as a result, few people know the essence of your true involvement."

Belasci mimicked the Premier's braying voice. "But, my dear Belasci, this man claims to be the *capo de tutti capi* of all Mafia elements in Sicily! I've been assured there is no such organization!" He wrung his hands in the Premier's inimitable manner, and laughed. "He wanted to know what influence Nick Gentile had in your affairs. I set him straight—told him who's who."

"'Pray that when I finish with that insipid mule, he'll never forget the name Barbarossa." The Don strutted about the elegant room puffing his cigar.

"Here, Don Matteo, *un bicchierino de Strega*?" smiled Prince Oliatta handing him the delicate, thimble-sized glass. "It will calm your nerves."

The Don peered through his tinted glasses, smiling internally. Royalty waiting on Don Barbarossa? How about that, eh? he told himself. He gulped down the viscous fluid and got to the point. "I've little time to waste, Martino. We must work swiftly. "Uh—this Red Senator—the one who fires your ass—de Casselli, that's the one? He will speak at the May First celebration at Portella Della Rosa?"

"He'll be there all right. Fuckin' bastard! Ready to welcome the peasants into the Reds' barn. There'll be speeches, the usual mumbo-jumbo to fool and mislead those simple minds. I tell you, Senator de Casselli is out for blood—mine! You'll just have to accept the fact that Salvatore must be sacrificed. They're getting too close to me!"

Prince Oliatta glanced up sharply. He focused first on the Don, then the Minister, displaying a keen interest in the subject matter.

"No. Salvatore can't be sacrificed." The Don looked directly at the Prince when he spoke the words. The Don had made his point; the Prince understood. "I have plans for Salvatore that do not include his capture, *caro mio*," continued Don Matteo.

"Why?" demanded Martino Belasci. "The Premier needs appeasement. Salvatore's capture would give him the needed prestige to keep the Reds off his back. Only in this way can he keep those vicious tigers from feeding on us. The freedom Salvatore enjoys is the talk of the nation. Daily the Red Press alludes to the protection Salvatore enjoys under the auspices of *my* Ministry! They say, 'Two years have passed since the war, and Minister Belasci makes no move to touch this outlaw!' Mark my words, Don Matteo, the Reds will use Salvatore as a stick to break our backs. Because they want more of a voice in government, especially in Sicily—they continue to persecute Premier de Aspanu and Minister Belasci! 'Bring me the blood of Salvatore,' cries Premier de Aspanu, 'and we'll get the Reds off our backs!' " Belasci mocked the Premier. "And I shout, 'bring *me* the blood of Salvatore, so *I* can have peace from both de Aspanu and the Communist leeches!'."

Belasci accepted the tall, cool *creme de menthe* highball from the Prince. They smiled at each other in a *knowing* way.

"Allora—it's come to that, eh? They all want the blood of Salvatore? Including you?" snorted the Don impatiently. "Do you forget, Martino, when you were calmer, and less distraught, you stated that the party, and you, needed Salvatore's guerrilla army? His strength?" He paused for proper effect and wagged a finger at his protege. "But—never mind. I have a plan."

Don Matteo gave the Minister the business with his eyes, a silent signal for him to get rid of the Prince. Belasci understood. So did His Royal Highness.

"I'll be happy to wait in the adjoining room until you two finish your business," he said discreetly. Bottle in hand, Prince Oliatta bowed flamboyantly. Between these two there flashed an expression of long-suffering, which neither the Don nor Cacciatore missed.

The sounds of shouting and laughter, the tinkling of bells resounded from the streets below mixed with the bellowing sounds of a villainous brass band and the loud thumping of a drum. Cacciatore shut the window against the celebration.

"*Carnivale*," he said almost apologetically.

The Don resumed his composure. "We both know that Salvatore is violently opposed to communism, for whatever idealistic reason is buried in his rebellious young head. So—we recruit him and his men to stage a protest demonstration at the Portella Della Rosa Festa, where your enemy de Casselli plans to make his communistic speeches. *Capeeshi?*"

The Don removed a pencil from his pocket, and, using the white table cloth for a sketch pad, he cleared aside a few dishes and roughly sketched something resembling two mountain peaks with a pass in between. He labeled one peak, Mt. Cumeta, and the other—Mt. Pizzuta. The pass he labeled Portella Della Rosa. He spoke of a possible assassination—the Senator's.

Martino Belasci couldn't conceal the pure hatred he felt for Senator de Casselli. The thought of a probable assassination lit his blue eyes with strange, supernatural lights. Clearly, as the Don described the outrageous scheme, Belasci saw the entire bloody scene reflected in his mind, and he was moved to excitement.

"You really think you can pull this off, Don Matteo? What makes you so certain Salvatore will comply with these orders? Why not just ask him to assassinate the Senator, straight out? Why so elaborate a design? You maximize the danger of a betrayal by involving so many." Belasci's joy was short-lived as he assessed the factors and weighed the consequences of such action.

"*Aspetta.* One question at a time. First, I'm certain Salvatore will now do *anything* I request of him. It took a while, but I found his weakness. *La famiglia!* His family. Already he strains over their incarceration. Believe me, he'll do anything to secure their release. Touch one hair of their heads and he goes insane. Secondly, Salvatore is no assassin! He will not kill for the sake of killing. He is no *sicario!* He had judiciously kept accounts of all deaths and executions accountable to him in preparation for his day of reckoning in court. In his mind, understand, he sees himself as a government partisan."

Belasci, particularly interested in these facts, mulled over the Don's words.

"That warrior has planned well for his amnesty," began the Don, his voice trailing off as he struck a contemplative pose. "There's a unique quality in him. . . ." Jerking himself out of the temporary reverie, the Don grew silent.

Belasci, in reexamining the crude sketches on the tablecloth said with traces of guile. "You're setting him up—aren't you?" It was almost a whisper to which he added, "He's going to know instantly that you betrayed him."

The Don's voice droned on as unemotional as a cook reciting a recipe. "Understand, the others are to be hand-selected, and must be trustworthy men who can be immediately transferred out of the area. Their instructions must be letter-perfect. There can be no slip-ups. Everything must be synchronized to the second. They will wear masks, to prevent recognition and to insure no one can identify them later. Finished, they must remove all traces of their presence. You will instruct Inspector Semano in his participation. When it's finished, the communist de Casselli will be dead; one less pain in the ass to interfere with you. The blame will be Salvatore's. *He'll* know he is innocent, and *we'll* know he is innocent, but the world will point the finger of guilt at him, and the accusation of this infamous act will make him beholden to us for as long as we need him."

Mario Cacciatore, that legendary butcher of men who killed without conscience had listened in silence to these two political tigers. Finally, unable to contain himself, he ventured an observation. "With all due respect, my Don, a fool might fall into such a trap, but not Salvatore. If he doesn't suspect foul play immediately, he'll put two and two together soon enough like the Sicilian he is. He'll know. *Managghia*, you've seen how he retaliates! Those two men, the ones hired to do the job on the American to scare her off? You heard how they were found? Not with birds in their mouths, my Don. Their *cuglione!*"

Belasci agreed with Cacciatore, perhaps too quickly. "He's right, Don Matteo. You've said yourself, Salvatore is no ordinary man. I'd say he's every bit as crafty and resourceful as you."

The Don's eyes glowered behind his dark glasses. He chewed savagely on his cigar, the only evidence that Belasci's words had touched a sensitive chord. The Minister pressed on, as soon as he drained the *creme de menthe*.

"How will you explain the massacre of innocent people to him?"

The Don shrugged. "I wouldn't—until he asks. When he does, blame it on a leak, an informer—anything. Must I draw you a picture of the obscene rivalry between *carabinieri* and security police?" He was all business. "You will reinforce my plans by cautiously instructing Chief Semano to call you two hours after the incident takes place, and report to you that Salvatore was the instigator behind the blackhearted mercilous assassination—that his hatred of communism was so highly pitched that, he took vengeance on them." The Don hawked up phlegm from his throat and spit into a nearby spittoon. "And you, Excellency, will make sure it's reported to the Rome newspapers as soon as the call comes through. Not you personally, understand. Let it circulate through the Office of Propaganda so no one points the finger of guilt at you, *capisce?* Understand?"

Belasci, unable to see the logic behind such instructions, asked the Don to explain. The Don bowed, pleased that his mind was so complex that a man like Belasci needed explanation. "Inspector Semano, by knowing such details before the *carabinieri* complete their investigation, you will stir the press into questioning the facts. Even Salvatore will wonder at this, and come to believe the treachery couldn't have been from our end. That once again the fierce competition between his enemies, with the aid of spies, was attempting to incriminate him. It will be simply one more of those dastardly things, done by others under the guise of Salvatore, that have prompted him so many times in the past to write to the newspapers and declare his innocence—*non e mia culpa.*"

The Don continued. "He'll never think to blame me. Not after I secure the release of his mother and sister from jail, which I shall do by phone to you, in his presence. Nor will he blame you after such a generous gesture on your part. *Capeeshi?*" The Don tilted his head and raised his brows.

Martino Belasci never ceased to be amazed at the massive talent encapsulated in the *mafioso's* labyrinthian mind. "You can spin more webs of intrigue than a trained army of Intelligence spiders," he admitted.

"In addition to the Portella demonstration," said the Don ignoring the Minister's compliment, "I'll encroach upon Salvatore to demonstrate against every communist headquarters west of Palermo. The east, too, if necessary. I know he feels badly over the recent mess he caused by his obstinate behavior at the polls. Oh, he'd never admit this to me. My spies have reported his remorse. Understand, Martino, after he razes the communist headquarters by any means he sees fit, bombs, fire, artillery, whatever, there'll be no question it was his work at Portella."

The real reason for Don Barbarossa's concentration on Salvatore's strength came out. "Then we'll see how fast de Aspanu changes color!" He said with glittering black eyeballs slashed with vindictiveness. "He'll receive so much pressure from the Reds, he'll agree to anything to eliminate them from Italy."

"Two birds with a stone—eh?" said Cacciatore.

"From where I sit, it looks more like a hundred birds with a single stone," said Belasci in all candor.

"Listen, Excellency, I know Salvatore's weakness now. I will modestly mention my powerful influence to him—as if he doesn't already know, eh—and convince him that ridding ourselves of the communists in Sicily will place the Premier in my power. I'll convince him that as soon as this is done I will secure this accursed amnesty for him." Pleased at such thinking the Don drained his wine glass and smacked his lips.

Rolling his wine glass between his slender fingers, Martino Belasci stared absently at the scrolled egg-and-dart molding at the baseboard of the Baroque-influenced room. He'd found Salvatore a most unusual man, and he felt a certain fondness for this rebel. However, as he had clearly indicated to the Don so often in the past, the bandit Salvatore had to be sacrificed if it came to a showdown. Belasci's future was more important than that of a subordinate peasant. He was too close to wielding the golden sceptre in Italy to have it elude him over the likes of that lowly peasant, that big wind from the south.

"When we finish uprooting the Reds, we shall toast to the government of Belasci!" cried the Don as he poured drinks for them.

"To Prime Minister Belasci," toasted the *capomafia*.

"Long Live Belasci," chanted Cacciatore.

The ambitious minister smiled. He flushed pleasurably and drank with them. "Once we win effective power, we shall proceed to alter the rules of parliamentary game procedures to guarantee ourselves, by law, a permanent majority," declared Belasci. "Then, we'll no longer need the services of a Salvatore."

The Don bowed his head in appreciation. Yes, he'd picked the right man to become Premier. He'd always known Martino Belasci had what it took. He was some politician—but, of course, not quite another Barbarossa.

"To you, Don Barbarossa. Long may you reign," said the Minister joyously.

"To Don Matteo," said Prince Oliatta in the adjoining room in a mock toast. He had overheard most of the conversation. Never had he underestimated the cunning and outrageously brilliant mind of Don Matteo, but at times he found this paradox too incredible to be real.

"Too bad, Salvatore," he muttered to himself. "You never had a chance, *caro mio*." He sighed wistfully.

CHAPTER 49

"It changes nothing if you go. You are my woman, now, before and always," he told her. "You hear? Always."

"Nothing is for always. Nothing is permanent except

death," said Gina. "Ask the dead—they know. When the shooting ends and the dead are buried and the politicians take over, it will add up to one thing—a lost cause." She could never make Tori understand, make him see the futility in all he undertook.

"If I believed that, *cara mia*, I couldn't have done all I've done. You make it sound so hopeless, so futile. You speak no soothing words like those spoken by Stefano Modica."

"Stefano Modica isn't in love with you." Could she make him understand that his dream was so close that he failed to grasp it?

They stood on the broken floor of the Temple of Cats in these, their final moments together, beneath a magnificent, orange-gold, harvest moon in a breathtaking awesome sight of a valley flooded with color. Gina looked so beautiful, with her dark hair hanging loosely about her shoulders and her violet eyes taking on the translucence of sparkling amethyst gems. Tori held his breath, afraid she'd disappear if he but touched her. He had longed to hold her tightly, to hear her heartbeat as she said *I love you, I love you, Tori.* Until now he'd confided his love for her to no one—although a few close to him suspected it—for fear he might place her in jeopardy. And he didn't confide to Gina his real reasons for hastening her journey out of Sicily. In a sense he hadn't had to tell her, for love had given birth to an affinity between them, making her sensitive to his thoughts. Besides, hadn't she seen the change in him since the incarceration of his family, the death of Athena—the inner deterioration and the self blame?

For a while he hadn't sought physical contact with her and she knew his mind was occupied by the directives of another mistress; the one of whom Gina was violently and passionately jealous—destiny. They had spent their last weekend together, during which time he was strained and edgy, moved by some inner spirit, some turbulence she was unable to circumvent. Now it was time for them to part. Tori had given her his *Eye of God* amulet, upon which he had inscribed: "Until the Gods reunite us, all my love, your '*aquilo bravo.*' "

"*Carissima*, rarely has a woman been permitted entrance to my heart, and I promise there shall be none other. If the gods favor us, we shall be together one day. If not, we've exchanged a precious gift of life and love which many never experience in a lifetime. Love beckoned; we followed in ecstasy, joy, fulfillment, even pain and sorrow until we both quivered and bent to its will. I tell you, it fills my heart with *molto dolore*, Gina, so hear my words. I can leave nothing to you or my son except the legacy of life and the love of a man who wishes now, more than ever, that he'd taken a different course. My life, without personal will, was ordained long before I was born. I attempted to introduce you to the *Siculi* demons, once as I did to Stefano Modica. I wondered why they didn't show themselves to you as they did to him. Then, one day I knew. Stefano wanted me to fulfill my destiny. You didn't. They knew, Gina. They knew you wanted to pull me away with you, so they showed their displeasure by not revealing themselves to you. It was then I knew for certain I could never leave these lands until the *Siculi* release their hold on me." Tori smiled wanly. "And that, *cara mia*, doesn't seem likely."

"Forget this affair with destiny, Tori! Your love and devotion is all we need. Destiny isn't flesh and blood. I am. So is your son, whom I carry in my belly. What loyalty do you owe her—that faceless power—that omnipotent, yet, nebulous nothing whom you empower by naming it destiny? I don't understand destiny, Tori. Who will hold you at night? Comfort you when you need comforting? Destiny? How does she feel, *caro mio*? Is she warm? Tender? Highly passionate? Does she intoxicate your senses as I do? Is she—can she ever be—my equal, Tori?"

Rebellious tears encroached themselves upon her cheeks and she brushed them aside.

He gathered her in his strong arms, held her close, inhaled her perfume, and listened to her heart beating furiously against his. After a few moments, when her hysteria subsided, he pulled away from her, wiped the tears gently from her face and stroked it tenderly, lovingly.

"We've had some fine times together, *cara mia*. They've been *molto te-rrrifico*, no?" The way he said 'te-*rrif*ic' and rolled his r's had always brought a smile to her lips. This time was no exception, and she giggled through her tears to her own annoyance.

"Tori, oh, Tori," she stammered. "How can I leave you?"

"You must go, my love, without looking back, without regrets, without tearing yourself in two. Remember, for some there is a lifetime; for others, only hours, a few hours in which to love a lifetime. You've given me love, a warm, rich love. I know now that there is more to life than just duty."

"I love you, Tori, and you love me."

"Completely."

Gina shuddered involuntarily and wept a profusion of

659

tears at his gentleness. "I can't be brave when you speak such sweetness to me."

"You can. You must. There's my girl, yes, brush away these tears. This is my *carissima, bedda*. My Gina, *mi Capitana*, with whom I fell in love. Strong, brave and possessed of infinite courage. The only gift I can give . . ."

She placed her finger over his lips. "Shhhhhh. The gift you gave me beats inside my belly. Nothing could be more precious than this gift," she blubbered.

They clung to each other until the face of time fell upon the world and reflected upon the dial on his watch. They had made many plans, spoken of the future as if it might not be impossible for them. Later, when dawn actually broke in the east and Salvatore stood alone at Palermo Airport dressed in his white trench coat in the light rainy drizzle watching as Gina O'Hoolihan left Sicily with the best part of him locked into her womb, Tori wept unashamedly. In his wretchedness and aloneness, he watched the U.S. Army transport wing skyward, silently vowing he'd join Gina as soon as he could convince himself to relinquish this fierce dedication he felt to his country.

Salvatore left the airport followed by his faithful paladins who, keeping their distance, were watchfully alert for any signs of trickery or deception around them.

Tori, for a time, remained enmeshed in the darkness and emptiness she had left in his life. Because she was still fresh in his mind's eye, he saw her in each door and window and in each passing face. His mind conceived Gina every waking moment, and his senses, registering her three-dimensionally, made him feel as if she'd never left. But time, that invisible surgeon, reminded him he must set aside his memory of her and return to the world of reality.

Salvatore, that chosen son of the world, continued upon the path towards his appointed rendezvous with destiny. Immediately following the arrest of his mother and sister, just prior to Athena's death, Tori had written open letters to the *carabinieri*, demanding their release.

To think he'd helped countless people escape jail, and he couldn't lift a finger to have aided his sweet sister and mother in their time of need! What irony was this? he asked himself countless times. All avenues of negotiation for their release had been closed to him, for reasons he failed to grasp at first. He watched, waited, sent out feelers through his spies and agents; but all reported an unnatural

silence among those very men who, in the past, had cooperated fully with them.

Now, after Gina's departure, his own excruciating pain
over Athena's death caused a noticeable change in Tori.
Colder, more impassioned, he threw himself into his work
and became a driven man, with a firmer resolve and
fiercer dedication, a man whom no one could dissuade. A
combination of many influences choked him like a garrote
around his neck. The more constricted he felt, the more
audacious became his coups against the *carabinieri*. Revenge, his by-word, unchained a force of destruction in
him, aimed at the core of his enemies.

God Almighty, how they multiplied! The more enemies
he disposed of, the more *carabinieri* swarmed the streets of
his village. Montegattans no longer recognized their
paesi—their village. Sicily had suddenly become the land
of *carabinieri*. To make matters worse, there came from
the authorities, through the Office of Propaganda, a mass
of bad press concerning the outlaw's unfeeling nature for
the families of the *carabinieri* who had lost their loved
ones in the daring raids inspired by the injustice done his
own family.

To these charges and rapier criticisms, Salvatore responded by writing another of his increasingly famous letters to the press. The letter addressed to *"Lo Specchio"*
proved to be a loving memorial for Athena. His guts,
ripped wide open by her death, poured forth as Tori explained the untold indignities and multiple sorrows he had
suffered. The letter, published, read:

> *My friends:*
> *Upon the incarceration of my mother and sis-*
> *ter, I appealed to the authorities to leave the in-*
> *nocent out of the misunderstandings I've had*
> *with them. I gave them six days to release my*
> *sainted mother and precious sister, who was al-*
> *ready near the state of extreme unction.*
> *My sister, innocent and beloved, who never*
> *harmed a soul, was dying from the effects of a*
> *brain tumor when our enemies plucked her from*
> *our house in a manner they wouldn't treat an*
> *animal. The* carabinieri *removed her from her*
> *deathbed and transported her to jail. Without*
> *medication, without care or concern for her wel-*
> *fare.*
> *My mother, appalled by such black-hearted*
> *tactics permitted a law enforcement agency,*

begged them in God's name to permit my sister the right to remain in her own bed until God took her in peace.

Through this letter, I inform you, my people, that those unfelling stone statues not only failed to honor the laws of God, but they violated the most inviolate of God's laws; the right of the spirit to transcend back into the bosom of God in peaceful serenity.

And they accuse me of having no feelings for the families of our enemies! It isn't Salvatore who trespasses on foreign soil!

Now, I ask openly, how can a moral government condone such action by its policing forces? How can Italy, enriched by centuries of civilized inheritance, fall into such depths of immorality? What will the world think of the barbarous actions of such a nation, which puts itself above God—of a nation who respects neither man or his Creator?

I'm an outlaw; yet I've never used such inhuman methods. Yes, I've been a killer in these glorious mountains, fighting against thousands of our enemies, against armored tanks and massive weaponry. When the battle has gone against our enemy, I've treated them with respect. If they surrendered, I've even dressed their wounds; a kindness and consideration they didn't deserve.

Now, I swear an oath. My people—hear me well.

I, Salvatore, who fear no reprisal from either Italy or the countless troops she may send, will open hostilities on our enemies. Even if I die in the attempt—you'll know I've been just. For on my grave shall be written: Here lies a Hero.

I no longer intend being chivalrous. I shall be without mercy—I shall repay our enemies in their own currency. I am not impressed with armored vehicles, or the entire Italian Army for that matter. My recent victories against them should exemplify that I will not be intimidated.

So, to the families of the polizia *and* carabinieri *who defy me. I give fair warning—leave while you can! From this day on I shall show you no mercy. This war ends only when our enemies no longer arrest the families of those they cannot capture, and only when they leave our country and permit Sicily to be for Sicilians.*

Salvatore.

Bitter, vindictive, and outraged, Salvatore had ample reason to be critical of the injustice shown him. Injured emotionally, Tori had licked his wounds like a bruised and offended tiger, and if he now spearheaded storms of protest that erupted throughout the land by indignant citizens, he was delighted. The cry of indignation pealed throughout the land, and the people tightened their bond with their beloved Salvatore. It also strengthened the determination of the *Carabinieri* High Command to capture this letter-writing cancer and rid Sicily of his irritating exhibitionism.

It also lit fuses under the tails of pepper-hot communists in Rome, who demanded to know why, of all the outlaws assassinated *en masse*, only recently, Salvatore's band remained intact.

"Who protects Salvatore?" came their loud protests.

Who indeed?

"It's detestably malicious, overly brazen, and melodramatic to say the least," said Minister Belasci, laying down the paper.

"The worst thing about it is that it's true." murmured Prince Oliatta. "He says things which need saying which none other has had the courage to say. At times those *carabinieri* do get out of hand, you know, my dear."

"Dear Giorgio, if I didn't know you better I'd think you were more than fond of Salvatore."

"Do I have to be fond of a man to feel compassion for him? To admit it was a loathsome and disgustingly inhuman thing for the *carabinieri* to do to his sister?" sighed the Prince. "Despite all else, he's still a remarkable young man."

The vicious lion hunter smiled tolerantly, but he wasn't listening. He was thinking of another time in the not too distant future, as the expected events of the May First *festa* played over in his mind. He came out of his reverie enough to respond to the Prince's words. "But, *chere*, if he weren't so remarkable he'd be of no use to us, *n'est ce pas, mon ami?*"

"*Oui*, it is so." Prince Oliatta prepared to leave the Minister's villa for his own in Sicily. He had work to do.

Two weeks later the prince addressed himself to Tori.

"Take my word, *amico*, go see your Godfather if you wish to secure your mother's release from prison," said Prince Oliatta firmly. Then, on a more gracious note, "You're certain I can't offer you some wine? My, it's incredible you're so disciplined that you'll not even taste the wine of Diego Rallo's Vineyards. *Managghia*, Salvatore, you're a cruel taskmaster to yourself."

"Why only Don Barbarossa?" asked Tori soberly. "No one else can help?"

"It's enough we both place ourselves in jeopardy by suggesting such a thing. There are some things men of honor, referring of course to Bernardo and myself, cannot reveal." The Prince rose from the elaborate dinner table where he and his two guests had engaged in a filling repast. "Come," he said, stretching his body and patting his stomach contentedly. "Let's retire to the study for coffee and liqueurs. I'm getting too old to allow myself the luxury of indulging in such exquisite food," he laughed. "But, you see, I've no willpower—none at all."

"Nor I," said the tall, angular man, dressed as meticulously as the Prince. Bernardo Malaterra smiled at Salvatore and extended his hand, permitting the outlaw to pass before him into the room.

Tori laughed good-naturedly at their excessive vanity. "Come spend a week with me—and learn how to be grateful for each meal you eat, when you consider it might be your last."

"Oh my dear, I'm not cut out to live such a life. I'm too much of a coward," shuddered the flamboyant Prince.

Settled in the comfort of his elegant den, surrounded by tastefully decorated furnishings including hand-bound first editions, priceless art objects from Brazil, an enviable collection of Inca artifacts, and pre-Columbian art, the amiable feudalist and his guests sat back and languidly smoked imported Cuban cigars. They made small talk, and listened to recordings of the newly hailed "American Caruso," Mario Lanza, and raved over his incredible voice.

Salvatore, anxious to get on to the business at hand, had learned that amenities meant everything to such men. He waited patiently for an opening, and when it came he dove right in. "I'm curious why you suggested that I see my Godfather concerning my mother's release from prison, Excellency."

"Giorgio! Please call me Giorgio. Excellency makes me

feel *so* aged and crotchety. My dear Salvatore, I'm only fifteen years older than you," he smiled, revealing gleaming white teeth. "Bernardo and I have watched your career constantly, *caro mio*. We both think you are excellent political material. So does Minister Belasci. Believe me! Poor Martino takes *such* abuse from the Communists. One day they'll push him too far."

" '*Poor Martino Belasci*' plans to do me in," retorted Salvatore with mocking contempt.

"Not true," said the Prince defensively. "Believe me, he'd never willingly harm you—"

"—Not unless I stand in the way of his ambition."

."He needs you, Salvatore. He needs true friends, men who believe in him, who'll join him in crushing the Red menace that threatens to strangle our nation."

"He needs me?" Tori laughed outrageously. "With a nation of soldiers behind him—*he needs me?*"

"Mere soldiers can't carry out the kind of orders the Minister must shortly entrust to someone very special. Certain things in government must remain highly covert—confidential. You should know—if anyone is to know. I tell you the Reds must be eliminated from government if our nation is to survive, especially in these perilous times of the Cold War. You think America will continue her aid if the communists take over? Never, *caro mio*. Never." The Prince exchanged glances with Malaterra, as if to reinforce his own position. "That special person is you. Salvatore. Only you can succeed in so daring a plan. You are the real power in Sicily—make no mistake. You know who you are—what you're capable of accomplishing. That's why Martino needs you."

"I'm the power all right!" snorted Salvatore bitterly. "That's why I can't get my mother out of jail—and why my sister died in prison?"

"That was an unfortunate, inhuman thing, my dear. Why do you suppose I suggest you make peace with your Godfather? Listen, Tori, we both risk a great deal by taking you into our confidence. But it's important that you know the chain of command. Don Barbarossa is the keeper of the keys to Martino Belasci. Recommendations made by the *capomafia* to the Minister take priorities over all else. It's for your good, as well as Martino's, that I lay my cards on the table, open and above board. You both need each other. One day, Martino will be Premier of Italy. Take my word, *he will be Premier*. It's best you remain in good graces with him. He has what you need."

"He gave everyone amnesty except me, after the Partitionist fiasco."

"Only because he needs you—"

"He needs me? *Mah*—what are you telling me?" Tori glanced at Malaterra for added clarification. The *mafioso* simply poured himself another cognac. Tori puffed on his cigar, inwardly perplexed.

"Think, *caro mio*, think. Don't permit the bitterness of the past to spoil the sweetness of your future. Listen, dear man, if Martino had given you the amnesty you so rightfully deserved *before* the job was finished, you'd never return to the fold for him. Believe me, he has kept your fate in abeyance until his plans come to fruition. You are the only man who can pave the way for him."

"I believe you." A slow smile tugged at the corner of Tori's lips.

"When he's Premier, it will take only a stroke of the pen to grant you what you so ardently desire. At that level of government the pen is mightier than the sword. *Capeeshi? Allora*, help Martino rid the nation of the Reds, and he'll turn the world upside down for you."

"I would be most uncomfortable in such a position," he said airily.

"My dear Salvatore, don't look so shocked. One hand always wipes the other. The story has been the same ever since God made his first covenant with Adam. Man has been making deals ever since.

"I confess Giorgio, I follow not your reasoning and less your logic." Tori stopped short. Suddenly it all came together. His eyes narrowed in thought. "*That's* why they refused to place my name on the slate of candidates?" It came together all right, but Tori didn't like what he saw—or what he felt.

"Exactly. Your skills in battle, your guerrilla forces are invaluable. Why do you think Salvatore and his brigands are the only outlaws permitted to exist in Sicily—?"

"I know why Salvatore exists! No one can capture him," Tori said bitingly.

"My dear man, can't you see that as a politician you'd be of no use to the Minister? Thrown into that pit of conniving, cabalistic political tigers, you'd be devoured in no time. Believe me, I know of what I speak. Bernardo?"

"Exactly," said Malaterra, on cue. "He knows his politics, Tori."

"Why doesn't the Minister contact me personally to convey such matters to me? Why do his words have to come through you—or anyone else for that matter? Heads of state communicate with heads of state, not through go-betweens," he snapped caustically. "No offense meant, Giorgio."

"None taken, *caro mio*. Understand, however, that at times heads of state communicate through couriers. In this instance I am that courier."

All this was new to Tori, and presented countless complications. Why couldn't they have told him all about this long ago? Being a reasonable man, he might have been encouraged to bide his time. He'd never taken time to measure his worth to the Minister of the Interior—or to anyone else. At their initial meeting at Calemi's villa, when Belasci spoke of his ambitions, Tori had gone along with the officials' vainglorious rantings in the true spirit of Sicilian jocularity, speaking only those words expected from a rebel in such circumstances. Now, to suddenly be told he figured prominently in the Minister's career was jarring to him. In hindsight he saw how many obstacles had presented themselves in view of his insubordination to the Minister's political future, and he raged internally.

There was no question that his insatiable desire for amnesty had occupied his senses, and it was true that for a time political office had enticed him; but the recent snubbing he had gotten from Don Barbarossa before the elections had caused him to dismiss the thought from mind, temporarily. He could wait. Immediate gratification wasn't necessary to his manliness.

But now, to learn that his future had been methodically plotted and planned and schemed by a coterie of shrewd, manipulative and ignominious politicians, and that the Prince had characterized him as a vital and integral part of Minister Belasci's political future, altered his thinking immeasurably. What the Prince had referred to earlier as the chain of command hadn't settled in his mind, and it wasn't until much later, when he reviewed both the countless implications and complications presented by Giorgio's words, that his earlier thoughts were reinforced. He now knew that Don Barbarossa, his father, had been at the bottom of his mother's and Athena's incarceration.

Following Tori's departure, Malaterra, who'd been silent most of the night, made a sad commentary to his host: "Salvatore has learned nothing. Nothing at all. He's doomed to a fate that will inevitably lead to his downfall—unless someone intervenes to steer him in the right direction. You'd think his political naivete would have evaporated after all the betrayals, eh, Giorgio?"

Malaterra rolled his cigar between slender, well-manicured fingers and stared at it. "Tell me," he said changing the subject. "Why do you stand on a soapbox for Martino? You think he'll approve of your intervention?"

"I know only that I have to bring Salvatore and Martino together before that crafty old serpent, Barbarossa, disposes of him and leaves Martino holding the bag by sacrificing him for some worthless, personal *vendetta*."

Malaterra sighed. "Too bad you aren't a true Sicilian, Giorgio. You might understand the *capomafia* better. Shafting Belasci is the furthest thing from his mind. The Don is aging. He lives vicariously through Martino's accomplishments; that's why he guides him so carefully. Friends always fight you the hardest, and exact more from you than those who smile and offer no criticism."

"Now, why don't *I* see those stellar qualities in Don Barbarossa?"

"Because you were never a stupid, lowly peasant. Giorgio, you are as corruptible, as predictable, stubborn, proud and greedy for power as the rest of us. You only see that portion of yourself reflected in men like Don Barbarossa. You suspect him of the same treachery of which you are capable. Perhaps you are being a bit overprotective of Martino, at that." Malaterra continued to study the cigar in his hand with fascination.

"You have a damned good education yourself, Bernardo. Don't look down that long nose of yours and condemn my Oxford background," he smiled.

Malaterra laughed. "But, don't you see, Giorgio. I was born a peasant. Those instincts will never leave me. Your instincts have had generations in which to dry up and cease functioning. Your actions are a bit too cerebral, lacking in instinct. Don't you see that's what makes Salvatore so special? There's a quality of goodness in him, a sensitive rapport with humanity, that's grossly lacking in our circle of men."

"If I didn't know you better, Bernardo, I'd swear you've become a sentimentalist. Since when does a man with heart and conscience *ever* rise to hold the highest office in the land?"

"I wasn't aware that I imparted such a suggestion."

"That's true—you didn't. But what *are* you trying to say in all this?"

"I thought we both agreed that Salvatore might be worthwhile political material?"

"We do."

"Then, for pity's sake, why sacrifice him? One day Don

Barbarossa will go the way of all flesh. He's not eternal, you know. We should be setting our sights on worthwhile young men whom we can cultivate and train to be beholden to us, so that one day we'll control the future. Salvatore's got the stuff heroes are made from. With him in our control, we can manipulate the political machine of the nation."

Prince Oliatta laughed good-naturedly. "Bernardo, oh my dear kind Bernardo. Don't you know that heroes *are* heroes because they *never* take orders. They march to the tempo of some strange and compelling force that the rest of us cannot hear or perceive. Destiny, perhaps? Tell me, *caro mio*, who wishes to contest destiny?" He laughed again, more tolerantly. "Promoted to the rank of hero long ago, Salvatore has not slipped, yet. He has not fallen, therefore he is not hailed as an impostor—yet. But, let his foot slip—let him fall, just once—and then, I'll know destiny no longer favors him. Only then can he be had, like the rest of us mortals."

"And you intend to hasten that eventuality—is that it?" prodded Bernardo.

"My loyalty is, as you know, to Martino Belasci."

"Listen, Giorgio. In this game of Sicilian roulette we play, although no chambers are loaded in the gun, we may all come to wish they had all contained powerful bombs." The Honorable Bernardo Malaterra, candid to a fault on this night, sniffed at the stale and oppressive air. Earlier it had tingled with a stir of fresh winds, with the excitement which came when it was fed with new men, new ideas and the release of energy which he felt in the presence of Salvatore. Now, deflated, he sat back, bogged down with the intellectual ferment of centuries past.

With the incurability of a Sicilian politician in love with his own voice, Malaterra repeated, "It's not impossible that the chambers *might* contain such devastating bombs, you know. . . ."

CHAPTER 50

The meeting between them was cool.

"I see the prodigal son returns." Don Barbarossa, polite and a bit restrained. Quick to notice the flush of displeasure on Salvatore's face, he quickly added, "I should be very angry with you. You've been most incorrigible." He extended an arm towards a seat opposite his desk in the penthouse at the *Albergo-Sole*.

Tori, true to his usual custom before taking the seat offered, moved about the room, checking exits and entrances for possible signs of treachery. Next to the Don's desk stood a sizeable table covered with a scale model of western Sicily, specifically the Partitionists' theater of action. Blocked into the lower right corner of the scale was a replica of San Amauro Hill with tiny white flags to indicate where the defeat had taken place. In Salvatore's territory, the west, the honeycombed mountains were exact to the last detail—including the grottos, properly named. Toy soldiers in brown signified the *carabinieri*; those in gold represented the government forces; the third, green for the army of Salvatore. A white horse and rider represented Salvatore himself. The generals were in black. Miniature tanks, cannon, artillery and round black balls were placed strategically on the model, with colored flags denoting victory or defeat for each side. Tori marveled at the lavish display. He took this time to needle the Don. "For a man not officially declared a Partitionist, I see you were greatly interested in their plans, eh, Godfather?"

"Something I picked up from the Allies, who always knew where their men were during battle."

"—And the Partitionists were *your* men?"

"I'm interested in anything that pertains to Sicily."

"I'm sure," said Tori tightly.

"I don't understand you. Why are you such an ingrate? You asked a prohibitively large favor of me—which I granted to you out of respect, without hesitation. Not once, but twice, against my better judgment," exasperated the Don, pacing the floor in his shirtsleeves. "When I ask your cooperation in a matter of great consequence, you forget I exist. What have I done to you to make you treat me so disrespectfully?" The Don picked up a cigar from a humidor, barely lit it in his excitement, and fanned out the match impatiently as he blew on it. Match in hand, he pointed with it for emphasis as he spoke. "To this day, I marvel that I've not taken retaliatory action against you. You have your beloved mother to thank for that, I tell you." He tossed the match into a spittoon.

"*Cazzu!*" said Tori without expression. "You don't have me eliminated because, number one, you need me. Number two, your *mafiosi* wouldn't dare touch me." He studied his father's posture, and with an obvious sullenness.

"Something highly personal flares in your outspoken foolishness—something which doesn't measure up to Salvatore's reputation for wisdom," the Don said testily, unable to take his eyes off his rebellious Godson.

"You sent Don Santo Florio to me with a proposition guaranteed in writing," Tori scoffed. "Since when does the *capomafia* send written guarantees? You need me as much as I need what you can offer me, so, let's cut the bullshit. About respect to my mother, that's another load of crap! You hardly remembered me as your Godson."

"A lot happened between those many years. It was fortunate that I even knew who *I* was, after that period in my life." So, thought the Don, he hadn't fooled him at all. He sat down and puffed on his cigar.

"Why did you refuse to place my name on the ballot for Deputy?" asked Tori quietly. "You permitted Bello to put the insurrection behind him, but, for Salvatore there's to be no amnesty, eh? Salvatore remains invincible—yet he's to be the sacrificial goat."

"It wasn't my decision. The Premier ordered your capture. I did all in my power to prevent it." The *capomafia*, that superb actor, was about to stage a most electrifying performance. He rose to his feet, padded over to the scale model, and pointed to an area near Palermo.

"When your men attempted to take over the radio station, didn't my people warn you of the betrayal?" He wagged a tobacco-stained finger at him.

Tori bridled. "A service for which Salvatore pays handsomely. I don't quarrel with that." He reached into his pocket and produced a copy of Premier de Aspanu's letter. "Show me where it says Salvatore must pay for the crimes of the revolutionary Partitionists." He locked eyes with the Don.

Slowly, very slowly, the Don disengaged his eyes from

his Godson's. They fell to the letter before him. He picked it up, scanned its contents, and pushed his tinted glasses up to his forehead. A foxy leer transformed his face into one of cunning. He hadn't counted on the light-fingered touch of Tori's men. Caught in a lie, he didn't bother to squirm out of it.

"*Managghia!* How did you come upon such a letter? How clever of you to come into possession of so important a document." He stalled a moment, then proceeded on a new tack. "It's too soon for you to get into politics. You said yourself, you wanted to go to a university to earn a law degree."

"I've changed my mind."

From banditry to the legislature, eh?" the Don rejected the thought with aloof contempt. "Impossible! You need more experience. All those Rome politicians would have to hear is that the Sicilian bandit becomes a politician! *Porco Diaoro!* Pig of the devil, you're something else!"

"I was a general in the army for a year—not a bandit!"

"How the hell could I put your name on the ballot? Godson or not—I hardly know you. Did you follow my instructions? No! How was I to be sure you'd be right for public office—any office?" The Don paused to take another look at his Godson. He'd grown far bolder, more impertinent, and exceedingly powerful in the past year. Even he, Don Barbarossa, had secretly admitted to the phenomenon of this Montegattan whose power was sought after by every *politico* in the land. If only the young whelp understood better the complexities and subtleties of more shrewd and conniving politicians, he'd need no one, including Don Barbarossa, he told himself. The Don sidled over and picked up a toy soldier in the vicinity of San Amauro Hill, from the model.

"Francesco Bello, a university graduate, a shrewd lawyer, slick in political fronts where it counts—better than me at times," said the Don, as if he were reading a man's resume. "But—as a military leader. . . ." He snapped the toy in two. "*Cazzu!* A total disgrace!"

Tori, as if he had no volition of his own to control his words, countered savagely. "Yet, without a formal education, it's Salvatore who controls the West. He's not lost one encounter—has been victorious from the start!" Tori cooled a bit. "If you had permitted my name on the ballot, *Godfather*," he spoke the word with contempt, "your defeat at the polls could have been transformed into one of the greatest triumphs in the history of Sicily for your Christian Democrats!"

"—And if you'd reported to me during your reign as *Generale*, perhaps the Partitionists would have won!" exploded the Don in an unguarded moment. He was seething. He wondered why he didn't pin back the ears of this stubborn mule, and why he didn't frustrated him further.

"*Va! Va!*" goaded Tori. "You must be in your dotage. The Partitionists lost the war because those millionaire delinquents wouldn't pay the price for their fanciful revolution. Gilded scoundrels! Parasites! Fools! Plotters, and all corrupt. Impractical dreamers who do nothing but talk. They play the games of children."

Moving towards the scale model, he fell into a fit of forced laughter. "*Managghia!* You don't win a war with water pistols, wooden bullets and cardboard tanks. You don't fight a war with toy soldiers who wear no clothing and eat no food, or with horses who need no water and eat no oats!" With a wide sweeping gesture he flung aside all the miniatures from the table. Some fell to the floor, others scattered in every which way across the table top. "It takes money to win a war! It takes the courage and conviction of a worthwhile leader, who gives his men something more substantial than empty promises. No wonder America gave up on your insipid puppets! Your precious land-barons are nothing but a pitiful brood of chickens—bird-brained poultry, with no guts! As stupid as the barnyard fowl who stagger about the yard after they've been decapitated." Blisteringly he continued, "Don't you tire of playing wet nurse to those scatterbrained, overfed capons? Is their blood money so enticing that you have no pride? You—a man of respect, who demands respect from all men, have none for himself!"

The door to the next room was flung open. Blustering, redfaced and fully out of control, gun in hand, Cacciatore barged in, murder in his eyes. Tori reached for his gùn, but, it was too late. A wild bullet grazed his forehead, causing him to spin back off balance. A second struck his hand, knocking the Browning to the floor. Behind Cacciatore, on the threshold, stood four shirtsleeved companions wearing holstered guns. Tori took in the picture instantly. By the surprise registered on their faces and their hesitancy to draw their guns, it was apparent they were all startled at the goings-on, as was the Don who moved quickly toward the tempestuous Cacciatore.

"You'll show more respect to Don Matteo—or I'll kill you!" snarled Cacciatore, his black eyes bulging from their sockets, grotesquely.

"No!" shouted the Don. "Stop!" He obstructed the bodyguard.

Another shot went wild. Moving with the swiftness of a tiger at the kill, Don Matteo struck the .45 from his bodyguard's hand.

"*Porco Diaoro!* What the hell's wrong with you?" he growled angrily.

"Let me at him!" cried Cacciatore, struggling to free himself from the Don's grip. He struggled valiantly against his Don, losing all sense of proportion.

"No!"

"I'll kill him!" The killer was panting, breathing heavily and sweating.

"No!"

"I'll teach him to have such lack of respect! He's had this coming!"

"No!" The Don nodded to the other men, who moved in abruptly to hold back the demon.

The shots echoing through the outer hallway, heard by Tori's men, brought them running, with guns drawn. They kicked in the door; the Genovese brothers and the Scolettis, ready to open fire, stopped short, unsure of what was happening. They glanced expectantly at their chief.

Tori felt—he almost knew—that something in all this didn't ring true. He touched the ripple of blood trickling on his forehead with his fingertips, glanced at the crimson, sticky blotches for a moment, then wiped them off with a clean white linen handkerchief, removed from the breast pocket of his suit. He pulled himself up to full height, held back his men with an upraised hand and leveled dark unsmiling eyes on his would-be assassin, Cacciatore.

"Not since the day you were born have you done anything so foolish as to raise your gun against me," he said evenly, with a deadly calm.

The men on either side stood frozen, watching the scene like players on a stage, awaiting their cues from the principle players.

Cacciatore held his ground for a moment; then he shrugged off the hands of his companions, and backed away with narrowed, reflective eyes—but not because his chief reprimanded him or saw fit to humiliate him publicly. Something in Salvatore's words had transported him back to a time years before, when as a Mazzarino bandit he had come into momentary conflict with Barbarossa. These same words—the same threat, spoken to him by the Don—stimulated his memory. He got the distinct impression the outlaw was someone he'd known intimately in the past.

The Don moved in swiftly. "Cacciatore, you will apologize to my guest, my Godson! This insult to him is an insult done to me! In my house he will be protected! *Capeeshi?*" He turned to his Godson. " I pray you aren't seriously hurt." He couldn't apologize enough.

Tori picked up his gun, holstered it and pulled a handkerchief from Arturo's vest pocket to wrap around his injured hand as he motioned his men out the door."It's all right," he assured them. "Everything's under control. I'll continue my conference with Don Barbarossa." He handed his gun to Fidelio Genovese. "The Don and I will attempt to talk once again. But should the incident repeat itself, you have my permission to empty my cartridge clip on the *capomafia* himself."

Hearing this, Cacciatore lunged at the cocksure brigand, only to be held in check by his companions' strength and Don Barbarossa's words.

"I'll issue no such orders to my men," said the Don containing his personal indignation at the entire scene. "There'll be no repetition of such disrespectful behavior in my house. Should such an incident occur, I personally will shoot Cacciatore, myself, alone, with no help." His burning eyes penetrated through his dark glasses and transferred more than warnings to his sullen bodyguard.

Cacciatore, lips tightened in a grim line managed to nod. "*Scusa, scust,*" he said brokenly. With colorless face, grey lips and shaking hands, the ruthless killer bowed, and backed out of the room, as one would in the presence of royalty.

Alone together again, the Don apologized profusely. "I deeply regret this disgraceful insult done to you under my roof. Cacciatore had no orders, no business to interfere. Pray, find it in your heart to forgive him. He's an old fool. Loyal and trusting to the end. He's used to the old ways. He can't tolerate any lack of respect shown to me. I try to tell him the young bloods are different. They desire to assert themselves before having paid their dues. It was different in the old days, and he hasn't made the adjustment. You're sure you're all right? Nothing serious?"

meticulously picked up the scattered toy soldiers, repositioning them on the scale model as he collected his

Before acknowledging Tori's indifferent shrug, the Don thoughts. He took umbrage at Tori's personal attack earlier, but what he'd seen beneath the snide remarks and raw effrontery disturbed him. Salvatore hadn't spoken to him as man to man, as enemy to enemy. No. Something of a personal nature eroded his guts. Whatever festered in Salvatore's bowels had something directly to do with him personally. The Don, who knew men well, pondered this very thing.

"Salvatore," he began. "Nothing is more tedious than performing an autopsy on past grievances. The past is over, finished, done with. My concern is for the present and the future. We must put our personal differences aside and unite for a common cause. Sicily is more important than our differences. The Reds are our enemies. On this we are agreed—no? We cannot permit them to prevail in our nation. Immediate demonstrations must be effected against Leftist groups. Their powers must be thinned—or we shall all be lost."

Tori gave him no quarter. "What of our amnesty?"

"You shall have it. I promise."

Tori laughed snidely. "You say that as easily as if I had asked you for a cup of coffee."

"It's that simple."

"Then why has it been denied me in the past?"

"I denied you nothing."

"But—"

"—*my* promises were always kept. Did I ever promise you amnesty? Never. Matteo Barbarossa's promises are not like water."

"I'm sick of promises—yours or anyone else's. You permitted that murderer of men, Bello, to run for Congress. Me, you rejected. You refused my name for the regional parliament. Why?" He wouldn't let the issue rest. It stuck in Tori's craw, and he needed an answer he could understand.

"All right! I'll tell you. Your crimes are worse than Bello's! You, with your goddamn letters written to the press, have drawn too much attention to yourself. You can't piss on the street without writing to them to tell them why you did it! By basking in the glory of all your crimes and all your acts, you've drawn world-wide attention to yourself! *Dio Malodetta*, Salvatore! You're even accused of crimes in which you took no part! Don't you know that much?"

"I read the papers," Tori grew sullen.

"Everything you stand for is against every principle in which I believe!"

"That makes me wrong and you right? Because I bask in the spotlight of truth?" Sardonic laughter crashed through his lips.

It was marvelous how the Don controlled himself. Determined to stick to the issues, he would not permit his Godson to trigger him off again. "Bello was no outlaw—no criminal. He killed the *carabinieri* in an act of war."

"You mean an act of revolution against the government. Not war! You're so expert at twisting words to your advantage, *Godfather*." Tori's heart turned to stone. There would never be amnesty for him unless he outwitted this black-hearted adder—his father. The Prince was right. Only through the efforts of this self-satisfied old cock o' the walk was there any hope for him.

Wouldn't he like to tell him the life he plots against is his own flesh and blood? Bitter resentment scathed Tori's insides. Even if he killed the bastard, he couldn't be assured his freedom. He'd have to play along with the treacherous mongoose, he told himself. One day—*one day*, he told himself. Now wasn't the time. There were important things to do. On this they both agreed.

A deep silence fell between them. "Let us work a truce, Salvatore. But, even if you cooperate, the best I can offer for a time is exile to Brazil. Now—hold on a minute. Don't get your ass in a sling! Hear me out. In a short while—I can't tell you the exact date, for these things take time—Martino Belasci will be Premier of Italy. By *my* hand, mind you, he'll be elevated to the highest position in the land. Then, it will be a simple thing to grant you full and unconditional amnesty for your crimes. And he will! You have my word—the word of Matteo Barbarossa! But—no more of this junk to the newspapers, eh? Lay low. Bring no attention to yourself. *Capeeshi?* Then you can fade away into a quieter life, where no one will take notice of your comings and goings."

There it was, straight from the horse's mouth, Prince Oliatta had played it straight with him after all. Imagine that. Truth—from the nobility?

"You control Belasci, too?" asked Tori.

"Everyone."

"Everyone?"

"Without exception."

Tori filled with irritation at the Don's smugness. "What about my mother?"

Posed behind a mask of innocence, the Don asked benignly, "Your mother? What about your mother?"

Tori's eyes narrowed in suspicion. Hah! "Don't play innocent with me! She's been in jail for two months!" His fists clenched together tightly. "As if you didn't know."

"Whore of the devil!" exclaimed the Don. "At whose hand?"

"At whose hand, eh?" snickered the young prince. "Now you try to insult me by insinuating you know nothing of this?"

For answer—Don Matteo picked up the phone, shouted a number to the operator, then asked to speak with General Brancuso. He handed an extension line to Salvatore, as he attempted to control himself.

"*Pronto . . . Pronto . . . Generale? Si, qui Don Barbarossa. Comè si va?*"

"*Ah—Don Barbarossa,*" came the General's voice in recognition. "*Molte bene grazie.*"

Tori listened and watched the stellar performance by his Godfather. As he listened, he realized he was witness to the unraveling of an intricate political embroidery to which he'd never been exposed. What was Tori? Twenty-four years old? Even at this age, with all his past experiences, he realized he was still an innocent baby lamb in the den of black-wolf politics in which Don Matteo was king. Colonel Modica has been right. *This* was Machiavelli.

"Aren't you the sly one, General," purred the Don. "All these months, you've kept it a secret, knowing you'd smoke him out and the glory would be yours. You sly fox. How imaginative. My, my."

"What exactly do you refer to, Don Barbarossa? I'm not sure why you praise me," the General said after a long pause of uncertainty.

The Don winked slyly at Salvatore. Tori didn't return the congeniality.

"I refer to Salvatore's mother."

"Salvatore's mother? You have me at a disadvantage—"

"Who else but you skilled *carabinieri* would have thought of this? Every bandit loves his mother, but, Salvatore adores his! Excellent, General. Good thinking."

"*Aspetta,* Don Matteo. There must be some mistake. We don't have her in our custody," came the nervous response. "Your sources are wrong."

The Don and Salvatore exchanged glances.

"Come, come, General. I understand. I can understand that Premier de Aspanu put the screws on you to clean up this mess."

Not for an instant did Tori believe the Don's performance. *To hell with him,* he thought. But goddamnit! Why such a farce? Why?

"I tell you we don't have her, Don Barbarossa." Brancuso grew excited.

"Then who does?"

"If that gutless dandy Chief Semano took it upon himself to do this, I'll crush his balls!"

"What jurisdiction does the Chief have in this matter?" asked the Don.

Tori began to doubt his own sanity. Could the Don be so consummate an actor so as to fool him completely? he wondered.

The Don's voice snapped him out of his reverie. "It will be most enlightening, General, to learn the truth," he said in a deadly tone.

The General's voice grew muffled and incoherent as the *mafioso* replaced the phone in its niche.

To Tori, he evidenced a profusion of apologies, astounded that such a thing could have happened. He promised the guilty parties would be dealt with severely.

"It's been reported in the papers for the past two months, and you still say you knew nothing?" Tori wanted to believe his father—he really did.

"Who believes such garbage printed in the papers? Listen, you'd best know that Barbarossa believes only what he causes to happen. My word makes news."

Tori, having replaced the phone in its cradle, gave his host a look of disbelief.

"*Botta de Sanguo!* You try my patience! What is it with you, eh? Are you bent on causing blisters to fester on my ass? What? Why this ridiculous business?"

In a black cloud of silence they regarded each other as mortal enemies. The Don had an advantage. Only he knew the outcome. He exploded, "Be a man for Christ's sake! Tell me what's stuck up your ass! Why this insufferable lack of respect for me? Clear the air between us. Earlier, you said we needed each other. *Va bene*—it's true. But hear me, young mule. I'll have no relations with a man, who like Truman's bomb, is unpredictable!"

Tori drummed his fingers impatiently against his thighs and bit his lips contemplatively, reluctant to speak. How could he tell the Don what was eating away at him? How could he accuse him of planting his seed in the belly of Antigone Salvatore, in a fleeting moment of passion and indiscretion—tell him that Tori himself was the result of that impregnation? God Almighty! What—how—could he open the subject? He brooded inwardly and said nothing.

Nagged with impatience, Don Barbarossa now made a call to Rome, the planned call to Minister Belasci. The seduction was subtle, and designed to make short order of Tori. The dialogue between these superluminaries was terse and to the point. The Don, humble and extremely respectful in his conversation, came to the point. He informed Belasci that the mother of Salvatore had been imprisoned during his absence from Palermo. "We can't permit such disrespect to Salvatore. Please assure him we took no part in this *infamita*." he instructed his protege, avoiding Tori's inscrutable eyes.

After a few incidental words, the Minister complied, stating he was appalled to hear such inflamatory information. He assured the Don, in a politician's voice dripping with sugar that if the *Signora* Salvatore had been incarcerated, he'd find out who had spearheaded the ill-advised move; that she'd be released before the sun set that same evening. Minister Belasci made one mistake.

"What about the May First celebration?" he asked confidentially. He was either unaware that Tori was listening in on the extension or it had slipped his mind.

The *capomafia*, quick to pick up on the *faux pas*. "Salvatore joins with me in thanking you. I assured him his worry is for nothing. *Ciao*, Excellency." He hung up the phone instantly.

Confusion swallowed Tori, and for a time he stared off at nothing in particular, absorbed with his thoughts, after he had hung up the phone. He took time to light a cigarette and puffed solemnly on it for a time, avoiding the Don's eyes.

"You heard him. Your mother shall be released by sunset. I know none of the particulars about the arrest, but, you can bet your balls I'll find out whose stupid blunder this was."

"If I had come sooner, perhaps the life of my sister might have been spared a little longer," said Tori economically, watching his father. His gut instinct told him it was all a sham. But, in these moments, the release of his mother from prison was all that mattered, and his joy was uncontainable.

"What are you saying?" the Don's eyes narrowed. He hadn't been informed of *this*.

Tori explained about his sister. Listening, the Don grew testy. He feared the rebels' retaliation. He took the offensive.

"You should have come sooner, then, snapped the Don. "You still don't believe me—do you? Is there nothing I can do to prove I am your friend? When will you cease in this foolishness? Whenever we meet, you succeed only in making me feel anxious, Salvatore. And I do not like feeling anxious." He popped a pill into his mouth and washed it down with a glass of water from the carafe set on his desk. "You want coffee—something?"

Tori shook his head. He paced back and forth, nervously.

"*Allora*—we get back to business. We must grow bolder in our efforts to show Rome we mean business. Premier de Aspanu has pussyfooted long enough. Imagine organizing his cabinet with communists! *Che vergogna!* The shame of it all! *Che Demonio!* And thanks to you, your enraged ego and whatever else caused you to sacrifice the election, young *galletto*—"

When he saw the sparks gather in Tori's eyes, he coughed to clear his throat and wagged a finger at him. "*Allora*—bygones are in the past, *va bene*? Only the future is, to us farsighted men, the important consideration. We are the true strength here in Sicily—you and I. And if it's really amnesty you desire, you'll be forced to follow orders, no matter how painful it is, or how badly it goes against your principles."

"*If* it's amnesty I desire?" Tori sat up wildeyed. "You secure it for me and I'll show you how fast I become a gentleman of leisure."

"*Allora—basta! Basta!*" Once more the Don found himself in a position quite maddening to him. In all encounters, he invariably fell to pacifying the outlaw. *Managghia! He acts like the first-born son of a monarch! A curse on his mother for wishing the role of Godfather upon me! Demonio!*

"We must rid ourselves of this Red pestilence which threatens our lives and most especially our way of life. Tomorrow you'll be contacted with orders to demonstrate at the May First *festa* at Portella Della Rosa. Senator de Casselli, that *disonorato* communist, will speak at the *festa*. We must put the fear of Lucifer into the peasants' minds, make them understand they pay no allegiance to the Reds. *Allora*, Salvatore, come closer here to my desk. Let me show you what has been proposed."

The Don proceeded to sketch the same diagram he had done for Martino Belasci, on a sheet of paper—two mountain peaks, with a pass in between. These he promptly labeled Mt. Cometa, Mt. Pizzuta and the pass between—Portella Della Rosa.

He demonstrated his plans animatedly. "You, Salvatore, will ride with twelve of your most trusted men to Mt. Pizzuta and station yourself on the lower slopes, here," he indicated on the drawing, "at precisely this point. For ten minutes only, you'll fire repeatedly, demonstrating, over the heads of the people. At precisely the end of ten minutes' firing, you'll cease, and leave the area instantly. Make certain none of you are spotted. You'll be furnished guns through Chief Semano's office. Instructions will come from another source."

Tori, like a general taking orders from the high command, listened and studied the plan intently. When the Don finished talking, he shook his head.

"It's best I station my men on the ridges of Mt. Cometa. At closer range it's easier to control missile fire. You see, there's a crosswind between these mountains, and at certain times in the morning the winds whistle up a mazurka. I'd wish for no interference from such enemies. Bullets could easily go astray and miss their marks in such circumstances." He punctuated his words by tapping the crude drawing as he made reference to the areas. Then, in reflection, a quizzical expression crossed his face. "Why do you find it vital to use Salvatore's men for so simple a demonstration? Such a task doesn't merit the participation of experts." He frowned in thought.

"It's because of your skill that we need your expertise," the Don said hastily. "We want no accidents. Just as you say, a stray bullet or two might cause grave embarrassment." He was astonished at Tori's knowledge of the area.

"To say nothing of a life or two," Tori assured him. "Very well, but I insist the demonstration be staged from Mt. Cometa."

"No. It's not feasible. Access to and from the area without chance of detection is easier from Mt. Pizzuta. Hauling the guns to Mt. Cometa isn't only difficult, it's out of the question. The terrain is too rugged," argued the Don. "And make certain your men wear masks to prevent recognition. I want no one to entertain the faintest suspicion that Salvatore's men were inculpated."

Tori wasn't satisfied. "Why must the guns be furnished by the Security Police?"

"So the shootings won't be traced to you. Bullet casings are tell-tale."

There were a thousand reasons why Tori didn't like the smell of this scheme. Skeptical of nearly everything, he hated the necessity of using unfamiliar guns most of all. The plan sounded too simple, like child's play, and far too smooth to suit him. Nothing he'd ever done or involved himself in had gone without unexpected kinks to ruffle him up and keep him on his toes. For the time being, Tori kept these thoughts to himself.

"You'll follow instructions to the letter. There must be no deviation from our plans. Things must go smoothly. You understand?" insisted the Don.

Considering the great favor done on behalf of his mother, Tori nodded and said, "I understand." He thanked the *capo* for the effort expended on his mother's behalf.

"Rest easy. She will reach her house in the manner that should be accorded the mother of Salvatore."

"Ah—one other thing, Godfather. What about the other activity in Montegatta? The daily arrests? *Carabinieri* crawl the streets like geckos. It's tedious to have to shoot them up." He spoke easily and watched his host cagily.

"Now that you've agreed to cooperate, it will cease," said the Don through a tight lipped smile, with a look on his face that conveyed his thoughts.

Salvatore didn't smile. He got the picture all too well. *Bastard! Sonofabitch!* He subdued his anger, forced himself to swallow the words that wanted to leap from his throat. First things first, he told himself. First his mother's release; then he'd think on the Don's plans. Prince Oliotta had laid it all out to him, all right. What control had he over his life? What a laugh?

"You were excellent, Cacciatore. Superb! I couldn't have done better myself." The Don took the wine glass from the tray and dumped two eggs into the wine and drank it down. "Ahhh." He expelled his breath and patted his stomach contentedly. "He didn't suspect a thing."

Cacciatore stood by in silence, unable to share in the Don's apparent triumph after Salvatore left the penthouse.

"Don't say it. I see by your face you are trying to swallow your tongue."

"I've said nothing." Cacciatore glowered inwardly.

"When the eyes speak so loudly—who needs a voice?"

Cacciatore moved towards the window, opened it wide, and tried to assist the smoke out of the room by fanning the air about him with his two manicured hands. The scar on his face looked like a slash of pink fire when he expressed anger and his eyes were balls of ebony coal.

"You smoke too much. You forgot the doctor's orders? Only one cigar a day!" He stared distastefully at the large stumps of floating tobacco in the putrfication of the spittoon. "Not ten!"

"If we didn't need him, Cacciatore. If we didn't need him—"

"Just make certain when you're ready, you give him to me. I want the pleasure, my Don."

"I thought you admired him?"

"Your enemies are my enemies."

"What makes you certain he's my enemy?"

"Would a frlend speak to you with such disrespect? Listen, my Don, in our day he would have been past history by now. Why do you permit him such liberty?"

"Why do you yell at me? I can hear you."

"Something about him reminds me of someone I knew long ago. Such impertinence! When he spoke to me—"

"Yes—"

"It's nothing. Before I forget, I've been advised that the villa in Monreale is prepared for your occupancy. Whenever you decide, all is in readiness."

"*Va bene.* Since the Allies left Palermo, I get little pleasure from this suite of rooms. I prefer being in my old villa. At my age, a man grows sentimental and has need for his family," he sighed.

"Yes, my Don."

"Cacciatore."

"Yes, my Don."

"Does Salvatore remind you of *me* when I was his age?"

"Yes, my Don."

"Strange, I get the same feeling. He will never measure up to the red-bearded Mazzarino bandit—will he?"

"Never, my Don."

"You're as foolish as you are loyal. He has surpassed my greatness."

"Never, my Don."

The Don grunted and shooed him out the door with both hands.

After leaving the penthouse, Tori instructed his men to return home. He promised to meet with them later that evening. Meanwhile, he and Vincenzo drove to Mamma Rosario's to dine on their favorite dish, *Perciatelli con Melanzane alla Siciliana.* For this baked speciality, pierced pasta with eggplant, Tori would have traveled far.

He went to the restroom to unwrap his hand and hold it under the cold water tap. It was only a skin rupture, nothing to see a doctor about. He stretched the muscles and flexed them. It was fine. He wiped the small traces of blood from his forehead, combed his hair, and walked back through the quaint little *trattoria* off the main thoroughfare, where the owners knew him well and were discreet about his patronage.

When he returned to the table he caught sight of a

square jewelers' box at the center of his place setting. "What's this?" he asked his cousin.

"For you. Open it. Go ahead open it," urged Vincenzo grinning.

Tori was astonished at the contents. Nestled in a velvet-lined box, staring up at him, was a solid gold, heavily encrusted belt buckle with an oval hole at its center. To the right of the oval stood a carved lion on its rear legs, its forepaws draped over the oval. To the left of the oval, a proud, fierce-eyed eagle stood firmly perched on olive branches. Clutched in one claw was a world globe with the word, Sicily engraved on it. Ornate scrolls bound both bird and beast together to frame the outer perimeter of the buckle.

"For me?" He grinned affectionately at Vincenzo. "I admire it very much—but it's too costly for me to wear—"

"Too costly, my ass! Look—me, too!" He opened his jacket and revealed a duplicate buckle on his belt. In the oval hole an enameled miniature photograph of Salvatore was embedded. "You like it better than the gift the American *Colonnello* gave you?" He asked sheepishly.

Surprised at the question, the eagle laughed easily at the transparent lion. He'd been totally unaware of the extent of Vincenzo's envy of his relationship to Stefano Modica. "*Cafone!*" he said affectionately and cuffed him good-naturedly. "I'll put it on at home."

Later that night, at the Grotto D'Oro. Tori announced his plans to his men. His decision to aid the Christian Democrats brought polite and concerned reaction from his men.

"You're sure you've declared your support to the right party?" Santino, gaunt and haggard from mourning Athena, appeared apprehensive.

"All the other parties have merged to form one strong coalition; the power is in the hands of the Christian Democrats. Only the Communists and a handful of Socialists remain in opposition." Tori paused a moment. "Come to think of it, only the Communists failed to approach us for a deal, eh, Vincenzo?"

Vincenzo flushed, and for a few awkward moments avoided Tori's eyes. His eyes darted towards Terranova, who in turn averted his head. Tori, missing none of this, said nothing, but he waited for some answer from his cousin.

"If you're wise you'll have nothing to do with these *schifosi*—these *mafiosi*." Vincenzo faltered a bit, ignoring Tori's earlier question.

"What about our amnesty?" asked Dominic Lamantia, honing a blade in the corner of the grotto. "These same men promised us amnesty a year ago. When have they kept their word? We cleaned up a a nation of "unsavory" characters, men like us," he said pointedly with scorn. He showed his displeasure.

Fidelio Genovese, smoking a thin cigar, in a stony silence, said imperatively, "I'm not certain we should trust them again."

"Trust them? Who says trust them?" spat Tori. "Not one of them is worthy of the word—trust. But, goddammit, they have something we need! Our amnesty! Without it we can't survive! So this time we proceed with caution. Remember," added Tori fairly, "it wasn't all one-sided. I didn't complete my bargain with them, either, when I refused to influence the electorate in the last election."

"We got a good swift kick in the balls last time," declared *Sporcaccione* sourly. "This time they'll castrate us. You're too easy on them, chief." His black eyes knitted together in a scowl.

"That may well be," said Tori with a note of finality, "but it's the only way I can see to gain our ends."

The conversation ended on a sour note. Disgruntled, the men felt a sense of frustration and a disinclination to trust the men who had betrayed them in the past. What's more they didn't understand Salvatore's willingness to intrigue with such backstabbing vipers. No longer did they understand his mad desire for amnesty. Why couldn't he accept his fate, as the others had done? Destiny had made outlaws of every last one of them. *Very well*, they thought, *then outlaws we shall be—all the way!* The Genovese brothers and the Nulianos endorsed kidnapping for high ransoms, and emigrating as wealthy men to another country. Sicily wasn't the only place in which they could hang their guns and holsters. Difficult as it was to emigrate to America due to the quota restrictions, there were ways they could be smuggled into the country. The men began to seriously consider these possibilities, in the days to come.

Antigone had come home, such as it was, to find the place a shambles. For the past months, her house had been occupied by *carabinieri*, who had had unrealistic hopes of capturing Salvatore. All her possessions had been tossed into crates and left in a state of neglect behind the house. What a mess!

There had been no one there to greet her, and when,

suddenly, the walls shook and a wailing, screeching sound, so loud she was forced to cover her ears, came at her, she thought the place was under bombardment. Glancing in the streets, to learn the cause of this deafening siren, she saw her neighbors scurrying into their houses as truckloads of *carabinieri* approached the village.

Bewildered, Antigone tried to fathom the reason for this assault on her village. Then she remembered hearing the police had imposed a curfew in Montegatta. The people, by day, were to be confined to their houses, permitted to leave only between the hours of 1 P.M. to 3 P.M. and one hour in the evening between six and seven. Anyone caught in the streets at any other time was arrested and thrown into jail.

She quickly bolted her door and, peering out into the shadowy twilight, she felt her heart sink. With all these police crawling about, she despaired that Tori would come to see her. Resigning herself to his absence, she set about restoring her house to its former order.

For the next few weeks she kept herself busy between house and garden, and the lonely hours alone gave her ample time to meditate. Even in jail she had spent most of her time in meditation. Blessed Lord, if a person could know in advance which path is marked by destiny, how easy it would be to avoid the pitfalls! Which of the many voices that come in meditation should she listen to? Which was the voice of God? *Was* there a God any more? Or had that, too, been a hoax perpetrated on man to keep him in fear of the unknown? Only the *strega*'s prophecy had contained any substance. Only those words written on frayed and yellowed paper, those inevitable words had come to pass.

The single greatest factor that had diminished her faith in this omnipotent God had been the death of her daughter Athena, and her own inability to bury her. Without question she entertained the actuality of the devil in her mind. Truly the devil seemed more powerful than this God whom she'd been taught to revere all her life. Hadn't Satan been all but invincible in his battles with the Lord? The God she'd known and made supplications to—he had never presented himself to her in times of stress. She hadn't been able to confide in priests, or place her faith in the Church, had she? *Priests!* The very thought of such men made her blood run cold. Her memory sparked vividly.

How would she ever forget that day in jail when she had received the shock of her life? In all this time she'd had no visitors. Food parcels had come from Tori and Vincenzo, but they dared not visit her in the prison complex. It had been shortly after Athena's death when, in her self-imposed purgatory, she had felt the burning coals of hell, that she had been told three priests were waiting to speak with her.

That day she had smoothed the folds of her black cotton shift and pushed her graying hair off her face before leaving her cell, and, with her head held high, had entered the visitors' cubicle, puzzled by the three Holy fathers in attendance. It took a few moments of polite conversation before she realized that these were her three brothers, Francesco, Tommaso, and Pietro. After a storm of emotional greeting subsided, she sat with them and filled them in on her life. She asked countless questions—where they'd been, why she hadn't heard from them for so long, etc. . . .

Her brothers aghast to see the end to which she'd come, had informed her that they were on a special mission from the Holy Fathers in Rome, who had contacted them, begging them to intervene on their behalf to persuade her son Tori to cease and desist in his continuous haranguing and violent living to which he'd been propelled. "The Holy Fathers in Rome are greatly disturbed and feel that somewhere Tori has met with bad influences. Naturally, as your brothers, we are obliged to try and save the soul of a worthwhile soul," said their spokesman, the youngest brother, Pietro.

Antigone, outraged to think they'd even consider that she'd be a party to a corrupt pact inked with the blood of her son, had stared incredulously from one to the other, unable to believe her ears.

Tommaso, a Jesuit scholar, white-haired, heavily jowled, with an influential paunch, confessed his shame when he learned that their flesh-and-blood sister had permitted her son to oppose the Church and Government. "We can hardly hold up our heads."

Francesco, an archbishop from a northern diocese, wailed aloud, asking her "What's happened to make you lose faith in God and us?"

Monseigneur Pietro hushed his brothers. "I'm certain our sister has suffered enough. Why rub salt in her wounds?" He said, "She's learned her lessons by now."

After an hour of such talk, Antigone drew herself up imperiously. "What lesson, Monseignieur?"

"You see," the archbishop said. "She's still willful and stubborn. It's your fault, Pietro, for urging our father

688

to send her to school. Now, she and her seed bring disgrace upon our heads."

Pietro, irked, suggested that his brothers control themselves while he attempted to reason with Antigone. "Convince your son to turn himself in to the authorities," he'd pleaded. "The Holy Father promises a light sentence to pacify the braying Red jackals. In a year, when he no longer commands front-page headlines, he'll be released and expatriated to a land of his choice where he can change his name, complete his education, and settle down with a woman of his choice. Could the Vatican be more fair or compassionate?"

"Do you believe them, *caro fratello?*" she asked.

"The world of the Holy Father is like the word of God!" he retorted, somewhat taken aback by her boldness.

"Is this why you came—to bargain for my son's life? You gave no thought of me, your sister, or what we've endured. You're doing only what's been ordered of you? Is there no concern in your hearts for our people, and what has happened to them these past few years? Of the grave injustices they endured until my son championed his people? He stood and fought for our rights—the rights of human beings."

"But he's a communist—an enemy of God!" the Jesuit had retorted.

Oh it all was so crazy and mixed up, thought Antigone. They insisted, since Tori had been in command of the province, people no longer attended Church as they had in the past. "Insurrection against the Church is insurrection against God!" Pietro retorted.

Antigone, no longer able to contain herself, set them straight.

"Perhaps, if you tell the Holy Father to put his own house in order, the people might return to the Church. Put worthwhile men on the pulpits and have them preach the true gospels of love and kindness and understanding, instead of corruption, immorality and subterfuge. Tell the Holy Father for me, to remove politics from God's house; to stop threatening God's children with the loss of jobs if they don't vote as the Church subscribes; and to stop bribing the people with false promises of eternal splendors; then His Eminence will find the people will flock back to the fold. My son tells no one to stay away from the Church. He bribes no man. He gives them no false hope. He feeds them, and consoles their despair, defends their human rights. You tell me—Pietro, Tommaso, Francesco—if you weren't so hypnotized by the hands that feed your bellies and minds with maggot bait, who would you believe?"

The visit had lasted two long hours, in which they had warned her of the drastic measures which would be employed if Tori didn't surrender himself.

Antigone had argued again, "I've no jurisdiction over my son's life. He's a man who does as his conscience dictates. Why do you come to me, here in jail, thinking I can help you? Am I not here at the very hands of those men you wish me to aid? Why should I have compassion for their problems, when they've never considered mine? You come to me now, telling me I must see the light, accusing me of indulging in his reckless games, of consorting with criminals. Is this what I need or deserve from three brothers who should be my strength? Where were you when my husband died? When Mamma and Papa passed away? Where were you when the war swallowed up my two oldest sons—or Athena, only recently. Our government—our Cardinal—refused me the Christian right of burying my daughter. Why didn't you intervene on your sister's behalf? You say you were all over the world doing God's work? Well, am I not one of God's children? Am I not to be considered by his emissaries with the same love and compassion they show a stranger?" Antigone had been cold. "It's too late, my dear brothers. Too late for anyone's intervention. Tori is on the road paved by destiny, which no mortal has the power to change. Not you—not the Holy Father—not the Government—not even the God you claim you represent. No one, not even his mother, has the power to change what has already begun."

She had risen to her feet to face these strangers who had once been her brothers. If there had once been a bond between them, no traces had existed by now. They had tried speaking with her, but it was too late. She had tuned them out.

Now, as Antigone worked in her garden at home, she thought of her brothers, wondering what they'd say if they knew it had been Tori who had demanded and got her release from prison. The son they had wanted her to betray. *Oh, Tori, my son, where are you?* She was dying to see him, but with all those infernal *carabinieri* milling about in the streets, the thought that Tori would appear to visit her was remote.

The shrill scream of the curfew whistle split her eardrums again. She dropped her work and ran inside the house, where she hastily bolted the door. Tremblingly she reached for her medication, and in moments she fell asleep on the day bed.

She awakened in a shadowy twilight, rubbed her eyes, and glanced at the clock. When would her son come to see her? When? She made some coffee, without bothering to turn on the lights in the dismal kitchen that somehow lost its cheeriness long ago. Suddenly Antigone gave a start. She cocked her head to listen.

"Mamma. . . ."

Antigone turned around, trying to pierce the interior shadows with her eyes.

"Mamma, over here." A dark figure moved toward her.

"Tori!" she cried softly, as a rash of emotions erupted between the fiercely devoted mother and her son. She listened as he explained he couldn't stay long. He handed her a packet of money, a substantial sum, which he cautioned her to guard dearly. He told her to make preparations to leave Montegatta, that he couldn't take the chance they'd arrest her again.

"I can't endure watching you suffer, Mamma. It also makes me vulnerable to the forces opposing me."

"I won't leave you, my son, no matter what they do to me," she insisted stubbornly. They had been over this countless times. Each time Tori had been unable to make her understand the gravity of the situation.

"Daily the government sends reinforcements, just to complicate my life."

He led his mother back into the kitchen and showed her a new secret tunnel, built during her incarceration that led from the kitchen, under the house, to the rear of the terrace and out through the side of the hill behind their property to a grotto. "When I leave, I'll close the head latch. You place the carpet over it and slide the table back into place," he instructed.

Vincenzo's head bobbed up through the opening. "*Zia! Zia bedda,*" he called climbing into the kitchen. He gave her a bear hug, smothered her with kisses, and tried to make light of a grim situation. "The vacation did you good, eh?"

Antigone asked, "How did you manage to secure my release, Tori?"

Before he could reply, Vincenzo spoke out. "His Godfather took care of it. *Managghia!* That's some Godfather you gave him. He comes in handy at times, no?"

Antigone paled, reached for a chair to steady herself.

Why did she feel so suffocated? she wondered, as an invisible rope pulled tighter around her neck.

"Come, Vincenzo, we've got to leave." Tori kissed his mother.

Vincenzo pouted and lifted up the white cloth placed over the food that the neighbors brought earlier. He helped himself to some cookies, leaned back against the cupboard, and hooked his hands into his belt.

That was when Antigone Salvatore first saw the golden belt buckle. It glittered in the soft candlelight and caught her eye.

"What's that?" she asked filled with curiosity. Her throat constricted.

"The buckle? You like it? Tori has one too! I bought it for him!" boasted the virile Sicilian. "See—Tori is the eagle, holding Sicily in one claw, and in the other, the sign of fire! And the Lion is me! It's my birth sign! *El leone*, the sign of Leo. We are brothers to the end!" he mumbled with a mouthful of *biscotti.* He winked at his cousin, then he peered cautiously out the window.

Months spent in prison had given her an ashen pallor, but it didn't compare with the colorless mask that formed on her face when the blood drained from it. In the sudden giddiness that came upon her, she felt the room sway and spin about, until an abrupt curtain of blackness fell before her consciousness. She fainted.

"*Mamma! . . . Mamma! . . . .*" she heard the voice in a far off distance. When she revived, both Tori and Vincenzo were seated next to her on her bed, concerned with her welfare.

"I can't leave her alone like this. I must find someone to remain with her . . . *Mamma?*" He saw her eyes flutter. "*Mamma*—are you all right?" Tori smoothed her moist, pale forehead and patted her face affectionately. "What's wrong? Don't you feel well?"

"I'm fine," she replied weakly. "I think I may need glasses. My eyes aren't as strong as they were." She strained to look at Vincenzo's gold buckle. *There it was— an eagle and a lion.* . . . She didn't need glasses at all.

"Vincenzo, go see if you can get Maria Angelica to stay with my mother tonight!" said Salvatore.

"But—how? I can't bring her through the streets at this time. . . ."

"No, my son! I'm fine! Don't disturb anyone, you hear. The curfew's bad enough. Really, I'm fine." She rose unsteadily to her feet and moved towards the kitchen. "You go ahead, both of you! And don't worry over me. I'll be all right. Come when you can. I love you both, now, go with God."

"I love you, too, *Mamma, bedda.*" He held her tightly to him before he moved to leave.

"Me, too," Vincenzo kissed her again.

"*El leone—eh?*" said Antigone, staring at the belt buckle.

"You forget I was born in July, just like Filippo—seven days apart."

She nodded mechanically, watched as they disappeared through the opening. She replaced the braided hooked rug and pulled the table back into place.

The Double Sting of the Scorpion Gives Flight to the Eagle—Power to the Lion. Power to the Lion. POWER TO THE LION!"

Never had Antigone felt as desperate as she did at that moment.

Power to the Lion.

What did it mean? Dear God, what did it all mean?

CHAPTER 51

Santino never got over his desperate ache and longing for Athena. For a time he'd been obsessed with guilt and an unendurable melancholy over her death and the circumstances under which she had been buried, without her loved ones in attendance. That he hadn't confided the nature of her illness to Antigone gnawed at him. In recent days he felt as if the very life had been drained from him, and, in addition, a recurring bout with chills, fever and low abdominal pain annoyed him. He knew that, despite the tango of death that made itself known into the lives of all men, he had to go on living. But on this day, April 30, the anniversary of Athena's birth, his spirits had been dampened. *Just think, today she'd have been twenty years old*, he told himself.

But there was more, much more. Rumors that Antigone had begun to show signs of senility, that her behavior of late was inconsistent to her behavior in the past, had brought him out of a self-imposed exile of solitude. He'd dressed in the garb of a cleric and went to her house.

When he arrived at the Salvatore house, he found her in her garden at work, scolding the barren earth as if it were a human who understood her laments. Her feet planted firmly in the ócherous earth, her bony scrubwoman's hands anchored at her waist, she vented her spleen at a scrawny, and unprolific rosebush. She snapped up a dry twig, inspected it critically, and, flinging it from her in disgust, she'd unleashed her venom.

"Why don't you grow? I feed you, tend to you, water and nurture you every way I know how—and all you produce is death." She'd scooped up a handful of the yellowish grey dust and allowed it to sift through her fingers like a talcum. "Once you must have been as productive as the plains below. Are you so dead that nothing stirs in your womb? Is there no hope at all for us?"

It was then that Santino, remaining in the shadows, saw what he termed aimless behavior, for suddenly, gripped by some inner compulsion she began moving rocks from one end of the garden to the other with no obvious pattern to her movements. One at a time she deposited them, as she shuffled along the dirt, kicking up tiny swirls of dust behind her.

"Mamma," he called when he was no longer able to contain himself. If she heard him, she gave no indication. Even when he fell into step along side of her and picked a few rocks as she did, and deposited them when she did, she paid him no mind. Santino kept this up for a few turns about the garden, then, suddenly, flinging the rocks from him with a burning impatience, he took her two hands in his and led her to the bench under the sprawling fig tree. "It's time we talk, Mamma," he said quietly.

There were roses to grow, rocks to move. "I've no time to talk," she told him. In her eyes he had seen a nameless terror.

He quietly assured her that nothing was as important as talking with him, and that it was time that she talked about the real trouble eroding her guts.

"Trouble? What trouble?" she cried aloud with a rising hysteria. "All my family is dead. What trouble do I have?" Tears welled up in her eyes and her trembling lips tried to ward off the surge of self-pity that swept through her.

He saw how she struggled against being maudlin—how her iron will directed her every thought; but he also saw a new vulnerability in her that he hadn't seen before. Watching this tower of strength shake in its foundation was as disconcerting and upsetting as it was baffling. Then suddenly before his eyes she became her old self.

"You said talk. Very well, we'll talk."

If Santino knew what was about to erupt from her lips, he might not have invited the catharsis as willingly. What came out was a garbled mass of disjointed bits and pieces that had something to do with omens, *strega*, prophecies, and a mumbo-jumbo quite alien to Santino's ears. Oh, it wasn't that he hadn't heard of such mysticism before, it was just that he'd never dwelled on it. He vocalized his astonishment and scoffed at her for giving credence to such foolishness that she herself had always denounced, laughed at, and repudiated in the past.

"You see," she said, "I shouldn't have spoken. You told me to talk—and when I tell you what's eating at me you laugh and tell me you expected better intelligence from a woman of my stamp. I have no one I can confide in. Then, leave me in my misery."

Santino felt awful. She was right, he wasn't a good listener. Finally he coaxed her into telling him the whole story. The woman needed a sounding board, he thought, and it might as well be him. He'd been trained professionally to listen to confessions, hadn't he?

Once she began the story snowballed, and Santino couldn't believe that this astute and sagacious woman now sat before him, talking of omens and prophecies and witches. Sensing the doubt in him Antigone contested him, and began to speak in a more calm manner.

"I, who was educated, believed in no such powers—for twenty years I scoffed, even though the *strega*'s reputation for prophecy was uncanny. It began when things started to go wrong for the Salvatore family—the war—well, *you* know, Santino. The day Tori ran home to tell me his Godfather was alive, the bottom fell out and I had to return to Donna Sabattini. I had to. Don't you see? She told me the children of one father would die and they did. Filippo, then Marco, and finally Athena—" she stopped in mid-sentence.

Antigone stared dumbly at him as if the answer to her dilemma lay in him. It didn't. She repeated, "The children of one father—" She stopped again and rising to her feet, walked to her rose garden. For Antigone it seemed that as soon as anything jelled in her mind, it eluded her just as quickly.

Watching her, Santino feared the worst. He'd never seen her in the role of a raving housewife who put credence into the mystic ravings of an embittered *strega*, a reclusive and obviously embittered old crone. "Mamma," he called to her, reluctant to open the wound, "What did she mean, the children of one father shall die?" He went to get her, and led her back to the bench.

"You said earlier I have no more troubles. You were right. My worries have been for naught," she replied rocking to and fro.

For all his Jesuit teachings, his formidable education, and his knowledge of life, Santino would never be able to fathom the minds and ways of women. They were a breed unto themselves.

"You don't understand, do you," she sighed as an enigmatic smile played on her lips. "It means, *caro mio*, that Tori will live after all. Don't you see? He isn't going to die."

He was about to tell her that all people must die—that no man was immortal—but as the impact of her words sliced through the sluggishness of his brains and he realized the full significance of her words, he came alive. He mopped his forehead of the increased beads of perspiration that drained off him. Stunned at the revelation, he tried not to show his concern, and for a time his eyes had followed the trail of a fig leaf, falling from the tree and landing on his knee before falling to the earth. He picked it up and twirled it absently, between his fingers, his eyes fixed on it in rapt fascination. "Does Tori know?" he asked huskily.

"Yes."

"How long has he known?"

"Since the night of your engagement to Athena."

Inside the house, as she fixed coffee for them, she retrieved the prophecy and showed it to him. "As long as Tori wears the Eye of God amulet, he'll be safe," she told him.

"The superstitions and rituals of our people are varied and profuse. They should believe in God with the same conviction and strength they place in amulets and religious icons," Santino reprimanded.

"If you won't listen, I'll stop talking!" she snapped with annoyance. When he nodded, with a recalcitrant grin, she continued to explain how she had thus far interpreted the prophecy. Listening to her, Santino had felt she had ample time to give it considerable thought. "You take the first line. 'The double sting of the scorpion gives flight to the eagle.' Very well, Tori, born under the sign of Scorpio, is the scorpion. He's also the eagle, which is another sign of Scorpio. It wasn't until I met the American, Gina, and learned that she, too, was born under the same sign, that any of this began to make any sense. *Allora*, it means that the power of their union would make the eagle soar—take flight,

696

capeeshi? Then when I remembered that Vincenzo was born under the sign of the lion—it was when he brought those accursed belt buckles, don't you see—"

Santino was baffled. "You've lost me. What does Gina have to do with all this?"

Antigone wasn't about to discuss Gina with Santino, and she replied, "Nothing! Nothing. The eagle on the buckle represents Tori and the lion, Vincenzo. There, you see!"

"No, Mamma, I don't see. I admit only to a profound confusion."

Again she explained, meticulously going over each detail as she saw it. Then seeing that some of her words, however incredible they might appear, were making some sense to her son-in-law, she had leaned in closer, "Now then, my son, tell me what sort of power does Tori, the eagle, give to Vincenzo the lion?" She spoke in ominous tones. "It's important to know, since two more portions of the prophecy remain yet unfulfilled."

Santino pulled back away from this *embroglio*. For a moment she had him believing in all this nonsense. "Coincidence! You can't believe this—this—trivia," he said for lack of a better word.

"Trivia, eh? What about *your* vision, Santino? Vincenzo's? Even Arturo's?" she reminded him. "Was *that* coincidence? When you all saw me in a vision and returned here and through me you met Tori, was that also coincidence? What about the white stallion reined in a profusion of silver? Listen, *caro mio*, I had the prophecy long before the stallion was presented to Tori. . . ."

What could he tell her? What could he say that hadn't already been said? She wanted to believe the prophecy, and somehow that damnable prophecy was coming to fruition. Antigone poured their coffee and patted his hands in a gentle, patronizing manner, with an *I know what I'm doing* attitude. Then as her eyes wandered off into a far-off look, she added, "It's been four years since I received the prophecy. According to its contents Tori has three more years in which he needs protection."

"And then what?"

"And then—and then. . . ." Antigone faltered. "I don't know. The *strega* didn't tell me." She placed the coffee pot on the table with trembling hands. "She didn't say, Santino. What does it mean? *Ah*," she'd said heaving a sigh of relief. "It must mean that after seven years, he shall receive the amnesty for which he struggles."

Santino considered this and wondered if it might mean that after seven years something even worse might happen.

Of course he had said nothing to her; but judging from the look of consternation on her face, Antigone was mulling over this possibility. He saw she was trying to suppress a rising hysteria when she walked to the sink and placed a wet cloth on her forehead. Santino moved to her side and brought her back to the table, where he helped her into a chair.

"Look, Mamma, you worry too much. Tori's no fool. Because he's your son and you taught him much, you fail to see the real depth of his character. He makes no move unless he examines an issue from all angles. He's destined for greatness this son of yours. I saw it that day in the *macchia,* when he moved hundreds of discouraged and desperate men to follow him. Why do you think I am so dedicated to him? You know how many people are loyal to Tori? How many have gone to jail falsely accused of aiding him? Have *they* betrayed him? No! The *carabinieri* are fools. They can accuse the whole island of harboring outlaws, yet no one will betray Tori."

"Only this morning I paused at the Temple of Cats to meditate on my destiny," he continued, wiping his eyes and taking a firmer grip on himself. "As the early morning sun began its rise, I saw my destiny as clearly as if I saw an architect's drawing. My destiny is to stand alongside Tori. I, who've been his historian, shall one day document his life. Am I not the most qualified? One day Tori will be proclaimed—the man who is Sicily."

In her eyes loomed a vast shadow as she listened to Santino. Her dark eyes took on a jewel-like brilliance, as if she envisioned a parade of worshippers shouting accolades to her son.

"He's sought after by powerful men. If he were a nobody, the world wouldn't acclaim him their hero. He has genius in him, Mamma. It's still too soon to tell where destiny guides him. But I tell you this. He's already left his mark on this earth—but not like the one he will soon leave."

"I know, I know. The knowledge of this has driven me mad. He's just like his father. Strangely enough Tori himself was quick to recognize the similarities between them, the first time they met." Antigone's hand shook as she poured more coffee.

"*He's met his father?* He tried to hide his astonishment. "Really?"

"Because you will write the truth about Tori, I will tell you. But there are conditions. Accept the burden of this knowledge as if I had told it to you in the confessional.

No one must know unless Tori himself approves—or until after we are all dead. Tori guessed the truth, or, you see, I might never have told him." Her face had grown pained as she explained what happened—the enormous lie she concocted when she thought him dead, and what subsequently happened when Tori had learned his Godfather was alive. She had continued: "One day in Godrano, Tori studied his Godfather with curious eyes and noted their similarity in characteristics and traits. Hah! Why *wouldn't* they be alike?"

"Jesus, Mary and Joseph!" By now, Santino's mouth hung agape in stupefied silence. Several moments passed before he could manage to express his thoughts. "*Don Matteo* is Tori's real father?" He still couldn't believe it. Blood rushed through his body searing him like fire. He studied Antigone, whom he placed on a pedestal with saints, and literally shook. To learn of her indiscretion didn't color his image of her, except to give it more importance in his own mind. Men of Barbarossa's calibre—despite his colorful, bloody past—were on par with the greatest statesmen in the world. Hadn't most of these men killed on the battlefields in war? Barbarossa had killed in cold blood on his own battlefield—what was the difference? Time and place? Hah! He wanted to say a thousand things now, but there had been more serious complications and implications surrounding this despot and his career of malevolency as it intertwined with the life of his champion. Salvatore. He was about to say, "I have but to examine the career of the father to know in which direction the son is destined." Of course, he hadn't. He felt as if he were in fever, and had wondered why.

"Does Don Barbarossa know of this? He must be told, you know."

"No! Tori made the decision. He refuses to permit his father to know. I must respect his word. You are not to reveal this to another soul, Santino."

"Does Vincenzo know?" Once again, searing hot pain had shot through his body.

"Despite the fidelity they've sworn to each other—no."

"But Tori hates the Mafia—Don Matteo—everything to do with it!"

"Why should that disturb you? Do you expect Tori to become a *mafioso* because of a curious twist of fate?"

Santino grew silent and reflective. The first two years of banditry, Tori had been decidedly anti-Mafia. Until the meeting with Don Santo Florio, the Mafia had been something Tori had deliberately avoided. But lately—lately, it had seemed, things were twisting, turning in a new course.

A lot would bear watching, he told himself. Tori's biography was taking on new dimensions. A host of complications of a highly provocative nature had presented themselves. Certainly it was nothing he could have discussed with his mother-in-law. His attention was diverted by the arrival of Arturo, who arrived with an urgent message from Tori, so their conversation ended. He came away from volatile information and an inner dread for what was to come. . . .

What Santino didn't know was that Antigone had watched them both leave and returned once again to her rose garden, where she had sat down to her cumulation of thoughts. The mention of Gina's name had brought to her mind that she's learned Tori had given the American his *Eye of God* amulet. Fearful for her son, Antigone decided that tomorrow she'd ride the bus to Palermo to have another amulet struck for her son in gold. Yes, tomorrow would be May First, the celebration of *Sante Crocifisso*, the Holy Crucifix, a day of celebration that peasants throughout Sicily looked forward to. She had crossed herself and said a silent prayer, noting she'd have to wait until Monday before she could get to a jeweler in view of the celebration.

"Please, God, watch over Tori until I can restore to him the protection of the *Eye of God*," she had said.

CHAPTER 52

April 30, 1947
Salvatore's Encampment

Santino was handed a communique on Prince Oliatta's stationery. He opened it and commenced reading: "*You are to proceed with the demonstration against the Reds at Portella Della Rosa, as directed in Malaterra's instructions to you. The hour of liberation is at hand! All is in readiness. I join with Bernardo in wishing you every success. We shall rid the island of the Reds forever. Take a deep breath, amico, amnesty is around the corner—Giorgio.*"

"*Allora*, this is it?" Santino asked Tori folding the message and slipping it into his jacket pocket. He dabbed at the sweat on his face.

"What's wrong, *padre?* Don't you feel well?" Tori

searched the other's face. "Look, have some wine. It will pick you up."

"A fever," he muttered searching Tori's face with a curious and intent expression. But Tori, miffed about something, had no time to be concerned with what it was Santino was thinking or feeling. He moved on and for a time talked animatedly with Vincenzo and Gambo Cusimano, his armorer.

Tori, in a rare moment of irritation, had exploded. "Why the hell have these idiotic guns been forced down our throats? No wonder the *carabinieri* can't win a battle!" He glared contemptuously at the 8mm Breda machine guns brought to him moments before and punctuated his remarks by slapping various sections of the guns.

Gambo Cusimano explained, "There are too many nuisances caused by the cartridge cases reinserted into the chamber before the feed tray is ejected. I tell you, chief, it's laughable. An empty cartridge case to a machine gun crew at the height of battle is like a flying machine with no wings—useless. Better we should use our own guns," he cautioned.

Tori snorted angrily, insisting it was too late in the day to change their plans. As he moved away, brooding and grumbling with obvious displeasure over the several irritating episodes that had cropped up to increase his annoyance in this half-assed operation, not too far away from him, across the mountains, a seemingly unrelated incident was taking place.

Lieutenant Lodovico Greco, in charge of the anti-bandit squad in Piana dei Greci, approached his commanding officer on this April 30, and, addressing himself to Marshal Franchina, he expressed his concern over the possibility of taking extra precautions for the May Day *festa* at Portella Della Rosa. The Marshal, who'd recently been transferred back to the west again, listened to the officer and finally replied.

"There's no reason for your concern, Greco. We've no indication of trouble. However, I commend you for your diligence. I plan to leave for the weekend, and won't return from Palermo until Monday. Responsibility for the area is yours."

"Yes, sir." Lieutenant Greco saluted smartly. He was an extremely bright and ambitious man, as Marshal Franchina had learned when they had first met the day after Gucci and Molino had been shot in Montegatta.

He walked along the *strada* of the Greco-Albanian inspired village, complete with mosques and Greek-speaking inhabitants, smiling at some, nodding at others, but unable to subdue the disquiet nagging at him. Only that morning he learned that Marshal Franchina was going on to bigger and better things. He'd put in for a transfer to Naples for further schooling and promotion in rank. Lieutenant Greco had ambitions, too. Wasn't he some expert on ballistics? Then, why had he been relegated to the fringes for so long? Wasn't there something he could do, something worthwhile to bring attention to himself so he could be promoted in the ranks? He moved about the sleepy village square filled with perambulating old men, walking arm in arm, taking their daily *passeggiata* and talking animatedly amongst themselves.

Lieutenant Greco paused at the fountain in the *piazza* and glanced about the area. Having learned never to oppose a silent protector inside him which guided him in his work, he gave in to this intangible sixth sense that provoked and alerted him. Acting on his own initiative, despite Franchina's assurrance, Lieutenant Greco cancelled all leaves and confined his men to their quarters when he returned to the barracks.

On May 1st, Portella Della Rosa, the name given to a tableland on the summit between two mountains, was in readiness for the May First *festa*. Mt. Pizzuta was a high, rugged cone-shaped tor to the north, and Mt. Cometa was the bare bleak stony cliff to the south. The celebrations of the religious feast of the Holy Crucifix promised to be more than a religious feast for the people of San Giuseppe Jato and Piana dei Greci, two interior villages located some seven miles apart on either side of the pass, Portella Della Rosa.

Three days before, the peasants of both villages had won the largest political victory in their history at the election polls against the invincible Mafia-Feudalist combine, the Christian Democrats. Their victory and their elation wasn't the result of their politically astute manipulations, for none of the villagers of either place were politically sophisticated enough to know whether they were voting communists, socialist or Christian Democrat. Their lack of education—their total illiteracy—precluded their comprehension of the intricacies of party politics.

The fall of the House of Savoy had reinforced their courage to unite at the polls, and when the election was over they were unaware they'd unwittingly caused a victory for the Reds. In their minds they'd voted for the right to claim uncultivated lands. This marvelous victory, the basis for their future security, was the focal point of their happiness—the cause for their celebration.

Managghia! Wasn't life beautiful? Everything was fine at last. There was hope for them—the little people—after all. *Listen—listen to the happy laughter,* cried the people. Everywhere were sounds of gay and spirited mandolins, strumming guitars, accordions, flutes, as musicians played their music, seated on mule-driven, gaily-painted Sicilian carts of legend. Why, it was enough to make you want to sing and clap your hands for joy!

From both sides of the pass came literally thousands of people, some walking, some riding brightly colored and gaily adorned mules and horses conspicuously covered with *malocchio*—amulets—to ward off the evil eye. Tinkling brass bells on bridle regalia of every description were garishly displayed. Women wore ox horns, *fica*, Medusas, two-tailed lions, sea serpents, even crosses; some of which were prominently displayed on their animals and children.

Those gaily painted Sicilian carts of legend, painted artistically with scenes of knight errantry from the crusading adventures of the Normans and the Song of Roland, the pride of every Sicilian, had been readied for this occasion and driven to Portella Della Rosa much in advance of the festivities, to be displayed in competition for prizes that ranged from a six-month supply of pasta to a barrel of homemade wine. Emotionally charged jubilation appeared on the faces of every man, woman and child on this May First.

"Look," cried the children. "Over there, at the colorful booths!"

"Mamma *bedda*, can I have some confections? Look at all those sweets! I've never seen such cakes and cookies and *torte*! And are those candy-covered almonds? The ones filled with sweet liqueurs? Oh, Mamma, can I have some, please? I will work very hard to help you pay for them."

"Papa? Why are those people dressed up so funny over there?"

"Fortune tellers, my son. They will tell your fortune, tell you what destiny has planned. Do you wish to have your fortune told, my son?"

"No, Papa. I am too afraid. I like better to spin the wheel of fortune! See over there! Look how many people wait to spin the wheel. And look at all those prizes! Wheeee!"

The children begged, the parents declined, and some,

unable to say no, spent their hard-earned coins for the pleasures they'd saved for all year. Exuberant lovers, walking at a polite distance and followed by chaperones, paused before the palmists, wanting their fortunes read; but the older, wiser chaperones advised them to save their hard-earned money for their future. Why did they need their fortunes told? Already they knew their fate. Marriage, babies and death? What else was there?

Religious items—statues, *scapula*, ornately decorated prayer missals, and other eccesiastical extravagances were marketed to help fill the coffers of the *mafiosi* who manufactured these items. Precious icons and momentos, declared to be authentic parts of dead saints, were found everywhere for a price.

Off in the picnic areas, the women had already begun to light the fires under the cauldrons in which pasta would later be cooked. The air invigorated the senses with enticing aromas of tomato sauce, wines, and sweet confections. Oh, what a glorious day! What a marvelously inspiring time for all Sicilian peasants!

No incidents, either before the celebration or after the recent election, had occurred to alert the people—or hint at what might come. If the people had been witness to anything unusual, they'd have hardly noticed at such an auspicious time in their lives, when all minds were filled to overflowing with thoughts of *festa*—festival. It wasn't until later, much later, after the tragedy had struck, that they soberly recalled several things which might have tipped them off, had they been less infected with the fever of festival.

Shortly after dawn that morning, after ailing most of the night with high fever and searing hot pains, shooting through his lower right side, Santino Siragusa was rushed to the Palermo Hospital for an emergency appendectomy.

By 9 A.M. Salvatore and twelve of his most trusted men took their positions on the lower slopes of Mt. Pizzuta overlooking the *festa* sight, several hundred yards away. Tori's planning had been faultless. Careful precautions taken to defy detection, by wearing trenchcoats and masks were enforced against the men's protests. They had taken the back roads, out of sight of normal traffic, to reach their destination, again against protestations.

Tori patted Napoleono's mane affectionately as he watched the Scoletti, Nuliano, and Genovese brothers, with *Uccidato*, Lamantia, Gambo Cusimano, and, of course, Vincenzo, set up the Bredas into firing position. He removed his binoculars from their case and strung them around his neck, by the strap. For a time Tori gazed about the area, with a genuine feeling of disquiet.

Several things disturbed Salvatore. The choice of guns continued to nag at him. Since they were only to demonstrate over the heads of the celebrants, he convinced himself it didn't matter if the guns were worthless. The attitude of his men rankled him. They made it known to him that they didn't like this business of involving themselves in anything against their own people. Many had relatives attending this celebration. They offered the same arguments he had offered his Godfather. Complaining bitterly, they asked: "Why come this far just to empty cartridges over the heads of the people? Couldn't just anyone do such a simple thing? Why should men of *their* talents involve themselves in child's play? All this was irrelevant to their real mission. These were *their* people! What if something should happen? It wasn't uncommon for a stray bullet to go wild, was it?"

Scowling blackly, Tori moved easily over the boulders, positioning himself at a point between volcanic rocks where an overhanging rocky ledge formed a shadow for cover against the sun and its reflections.

He watched Vincenzo creep to the top of another boulder, lie on his belly, and scan the area with his binoculars barely ten feet from him.

In the ominous silence, he heard the hoarse whispers of his men, the click of rifle bolts, the metallic sounds as gun clips were checked and re-checked, the brash metallic clicks of magazines fitted into the Bredas. Cautioned against smoking, for fear the smoke could be spotted at a distance or that evidence might be carelessly left behind, the men busied themselves taking more than usual precaution with their weapons. It was 9:30 A.M. by Tori's watch. He reached up and, in annoyance, worried his earlobe. He grew tense and agitated. A worried frown creased his forehead as a wary alertness flushed through him. *Now what the hell's wrong? Damnit!*

Crowds, gathering at the picnic site, were swarming about the speaker's platform, determined to get a good location where they could see and hear everything. The red banners of communism fluttered defiantly in the soft breeze as standard bearers hoisted them high into the air and lowered them securely into their special belts. Mothers, with bare, brown breasts exposed nursed their infants, scolded other children for playing too roughly near by, then settled back to listen to promises of a better future for them and their offspring. Exalted politicians, dressed impeccably in tailored white suits with white shirts and red ties, gathered their entourage of excited hangers-on while flustery program aides prepared microphones for the guest speakers. Busy, little ant-like men clustered about the stage, annoyed at the slow pace of things and urging the workers to speed things up.

At 10 A.M. Salvatore's men made final adjustments on the Bredas. Tori, peering through binoculars, observed several politicians climb the garrishly decorated, red and white crepe-papered platform as program planners skirted about the stage, positioning speakers and issuing last minute instructions. Tori squirmed uncomfortably and his left ear, throbbing unmercifully, refused to let up. He rubbed it gingerly, his scowling eyes everywhere. A lizard scurried over the toe of his boot, then darted like a shot behind a boulder. The bandit chieftain noted the absence of usual laughter from Vincenzo, who'd been coughing heavily, and from the other men who had never appeared more serious in their lives than now, bracing themselves at attention next to the machine guns.

Tori, less confident than he'd been yesterday, rechecked his Browning, holstered it, and resumed his surveillance. Damned ear! What the hell could it be? Hadn't he gone over every step of the planning meticulously? Had he overlooked something? He searched his brain. Damned if he could find a weak link. Usually if he slipped, which was rarely, one of his paladins would catch it. He raised his glasses again and directed them across the pass towards Mt. Cometa. *What the hell was that?* He gave a start and retraced his path. He was certain he'd seen an unnatural movement among the rocks. Try as he might, he was unable to locate it for the second time.

"Vincenzo!" he called. His cousin didn't budge. He whistled at him. Vincenzo finally turned to him. "What do you make of it—on Mt. Cometa?"

Vincenzo raised his glasses back into position and saw nothing out of the ordinary. "Nothing," he called out. "I see nothing."

At 10:15 A.M. the fluttery, pear-shaped Secretary of the Popular Bloc from Piana dei Greci stood up before the crowd and raised his hands high in the air to declare the ceremonies open. A small, uniformed brass band played the *Communist Freedom March*. Already the sun's blistering rays had begun scorching the earth. Only the high cross-winds provided an escape from the burning heat.

The crowds, effervescent and excited, cheered, shouted and applauded. At the end of the musical interlude, the Secretary held up his hands, gesturing for silence, until the chattering, cheering crowd quieted into a hushed silence.

"My brother workers," he began. "Today we celebrate the feast of *Sante Crocefisso* and the Workers Festival, united as comrades."

Senator de Casselli, the communist hated mortally by Minister Belasci, was a burly man, tall with an acrobat's strutting stance. Dressed elegantly in a white linen suit, and having arrived later than expected to, he now began preparing himself, speech in hand, and together with his entourage of political workers climbed the platform and waited next to the podium for his introduction. He waved and smiled animatedly at the sea of faces cheering him on.

Salvatore, on the crest of what might prove the only blight on a spectacular career—Salvatore the unconquerable saviour of his people, the King of Montegatta—raised his white handkerchief in the air above him, twirled it twice, and gave the signal to open fire.

Below him, in the pass, the speaker hesitated a moment, turned his head in the direction of popping sounds nad squinted his eyes. *What the hell is happening?* he wondered. Those fireworks aren't supposed to begin until *after* Senator de Casselli speaks! He shrugged and commenced speaking. Before his eyes, crumpled red flags fell unceremoniously upon the bodies of the standardbearers, who had hit the dust. Here, a small child clapped gleefully at the popping sounds—until his hand was shot off. There, another child gave a sudden start and fell limp across the breast of his father, shot through with bullets. Still another scrambled to the top of the platform to locate the source of the noise. His face was shot away. A horse was hit. Several mules fell, their legs riddled with bullets. A young lad, running to his mother, fell into her arms; his left arm, shot off, dangled from bloody tendons. There followed insane pandemonium: screams, shouts, yells, warnings!

The speaker dove off the platform, fell to the ground, and broke his leg. Other dignitaries fell flat to the platform, shielding their faces and crawling for cover. Crowds screamed and scattered wildly in all directions. Parents fell over their children in an effort to shield them from inherent dangers. Animals cried in protest, reared and strained at their ties to break loose. There was screaming, confusion, babbling mayhem on all sides, and most were possessed with unspeakable horror at the terrorism all around them.

Watching the growing madness through his glasses, Tori, momentarily confused, shouted a cease-fire. No one heard him. Running down the length of the narrow concourse between the rocks, he yanked first one, then another man off the machines. His men, more bewildered and confused than their chief wondered what had happened. "What's wrong," they shouted. "What the hell's wrong with Salvatore? Goddammit! He's acting like a crazy man!"

"Get down!" Tori shouted. "Down on your bellies!" he screamed at them. All around them ricocheting bullets struck the rocks and made those familiar sinking sounds; *Ping! Zing!*

Tori crept back into his original position and through his binoculars, he detected gunfire from the ridge overlooking Portella from Mt. Cometa. Small puffs of smoke clung about the area of action.

"Arturo!" he called. "Miquel! Marco and Fidelio! Ride the hell over there and find out who the crazy bastards are, shooting in a crossfire!" The men moved before his instructions ended. To the others, he commanded, "Quick! Pack the gear and move your asses! Move *Amonini!*"

Tori wasn't certain what had caused him to glance at his watch, but in doing so he noted they had fired for approximately three minutes. Later, much later, he would find that such awareness was to prove helpful in helping to solve the mystery of this malevolent infamy.

At 10:15 A.M. Lieutenant Greco had just left the barber shop in Piana dei Greci when he heard the popping sounds of distant gun fire. He, too, thought at first, fireworks! But the steady *rat-a-tat-tat*, all too familiar to him, alerted him. Running to the water fountain across the *piazza*, he stood up on the raised tile wall and shaded his eyes. Hordes of people were running down the mountain road from the summit, screaming and wildly waving their arms.

Lieutenant Greco ran across the *piazza* to his office, called the Palermo office, and asked for reinforcements. He instructed his men to ride swiftly and cordon off the area. He would later report to a Tribunal, although Palermo was only twenty minutes away by auto, it took the Palermo contingent five hours to arrive.

He mounted his horse and rode to the upper mountain, past all the wailing, moaning people, too frightened to stop and report what had happened. The gravely wounded men and children came off the mountain on the backs of mules

708

which drew carts loaded with the dead. Moaning, groaning, sobbing, hysterical mourners, distraught with shock and grief over a bloody day long to be remembered, walked about like zombies, totally dazed, anxious to get away from the holocaust, yet powerless to move except at the tempo of a funeral dirge.

By 11:00 A.M. Lieutenant Greco and his men moved in and about the pass, combing the area for clues. After receiving statements from several eye-witnesses, who testified they were caught in a crossfire, he dispatched two squads and several volunteers to search the ridges.

Where Salvatore's men had been positioned, he found nearly a thousand empty shells. These were carefully packed and kept in his possession until he completed interrogating the witnesses. Many swore they saw the gunmen in profile on the ridges of Mt. Cometa. When Lieutenant Greco searched the ridge, he found no evidence of any shooting, no clues at all. Whoever had committed what appeared to Lieutenant Greco to be a synchronized attack had cleverly erased all traces of their presence. Why? It was one of many things which made no sense at all to him. Would one side, if it had been a unified attack, leave traces of its presence while others went to deliberate means to dispose of the evidence? Lieutenant Greco had much time to ponder this avenue of thought, and a few days later, when the evidence of the casings found on Mt. Pizzuta disappeared from his office, he was greatly provoked; he delved into the situation with bulldog tenacity.

Less than an hour after the incident at Portella Della Rosa, Chief Inspector Semano placed a call to Minister Belasci in Rome, naming Salvatoré as the prime instigator and villain of the massacre. Minister Belasci, having duly noted the time of the call in his daily log, in turn notified the Office of Propaganda, who in turn released the information to the national and international press. So far it had all gone according to plan, hadn't it?

Later, when a few sharp reporters reconstructed the facts, a question arose, among many others. How could Chief Semano be so positive in his identification of Salvatore in the space of less than an hour, when the investigation of the crime didn't officially begin until May 2? Hundreds of witnesses, having given their statements, had been unable to identify the assailants.

Chief Semano smiled enigmatically at the dozens of reporters who flocked to his office, demanding an answer. With unshaken confidence, he stated that he had spies among Salvatore's men. He knew, for a fact, Salvatore had been on Mt. Pizzuta, shooting at the celebrants.

On that same day of the shooting at Portella, early in the afternoon, the Scoletti and Genovese brothers arrived at the Grotto Persephone to report to Salvatore that they had arrived at Mt. Cometa too late to find anyone. They had found several tracks at the bottom of the ridge and had managed to pick up a few empty shell casings, which had either been dropped or overlooked. When examined, the shells had been identical to the ones he and his men used.

His face like granite, Tori shoved the casings at his co-captain and glowered angrily. "The guns you brought us from Chief Semano's office were also supplied to the murderers!"

Tense and worried about the predicament facing them, the men sat about the grotto exchanging sullen and worried glances, growing concerned by the moment over Tori's possible retaliation. Livid at the revolting results of the demonstration and at the full implications of the embroglio, Tori, unable to speak, mounted Napoleono and galloped swiftly to the Mountain of Cats, where for better than five hours he sat, silent and brooding, overlooking the valley. Through a dull sunset and a murky twilight that drifted into a dismal evening, his brains roiled as he dissected the entire operation from beginning to finish.

It was more than a stinging defeat—it was the ruination of his highest hopes. Worse, for Tori, it brought untold grief. The sight of those children, broken and maimed and in some instances probably dead, would never be erased from his mind. What had gone wrong? What had he failed to take caution against? Whose diabolical scheme had placed another group of killers in the mountains across from him? More important—*why?* Someone had planned it this way from its inception. Who were they after? One man? Several? Certainly not all those innocent children and women and poor peasants!

There would be no "Viva Salvatores" now. The dastardly affair, painted vividly in the minds and imaginations of his people, would turn them against him. In his abject misery and black despair, Tori hadn't counted on the hard-nosed, dedicated efforts of a sworn enemy, a *carabiniero*, Greco, to gather up a whirlwind of controversy, and prove to him that the hand of God moved in strange ways.

For two days, Greco had diligently examined the positions from which the machine guns were fired. At Mt. Pizzuta—Salvatore's position—the *carabinieri* played a hunch. He assembled a Breda 8mm, took aim, and opened fire at the target, the speaker's platform below in the pass. From such a distance the range, better than half a mile, was too far for accurate shooting, he observed thoughtfully. Yet, in the estimated ten minutes of rapid fire, eleven were dead and sixty had been seriously wounded. A curse on the gods! Nothing made sense to the methodical and meticulous lieutenant. *Certainly if it had been Salvatore's men shooting from Mt. Cometa, which he seriously doubted, in ten minutes of rapid-fire shooting, experienced gunmen would have been more accurate. No?* The same test, performed from Mt. Cometa, met with far more exacting results. Not only did the gunfire hit its targets, but, he reasoned, men shooting with any degree of accuracy could have knocked off even more victims. There had to be more, much more, to this hornets nest of intrigue.

Further investigation forced him to conclude that there'd been a special target at which the alleged killers had aimed. It would be fully two months before Lieutenant Greco would ascertain that the lethal bullets had been aimed at the communist Senator de Casselli; that some of the shooting had camouflaged the assassination attempt. Meanwhile he continued to reconstruct all the facts in the case.

A flurry of reporters, dissatisfied with conflicting reports released through Minister Belasci's office, traveled to Piana dei Greci to confer at length with the dedicated *carabiniero.* Most of these pro-Salvatore newsmen came away to proclaim, through the media, that the situation stank of such treachery they had to wear gas masks, while sifting through the flimsy facts.

Their statements, supported by personal sleuthing, brought out certain indisputable data: *First,* convinced that the massacre didn't conform to Salvatore's usual methods, they pointed out that, for four years now, the bandits' attacks had always been aimed at the *carabinieri,* never at women and children. *Second,* they reinforced Greco's contention that experienced gunmen wouldn't have expended so much ammunition for so small a casualty list. *Thirdly,* they affirmed that if cold-blooded slaughter had been his intention, Salvatore would have finished them all off, and not quit in less than ten minutes. *Fourth* the printed photos of Greco firing the Breda guns contained his supportive statement, "The distance was too far to have connected. Whoever shot from Mt. Pizzuta had no massacre in mind."

Fifth, the preponderance of evidence collected, and amassed from the countless formal interviews with people of both villages, had revealed that they were caught in a crossfire between the two mountains; they all, to the last, had insisted that the firing from Mt. Pizzuta had halted long before the firing ceased from Mt. Cometa. Other witnesses, presumably on an outing, had reported seeing a dozen masked men descending the slopes of Mt. Cometa, engaged in a violent quarrel over something gone wrong— something concerning a high dignitary who had escaped their line of fire—other witnesses had sworn they had seen a dozen men riding off the slopes of Mt. Pizzuta. *Sixth*, when Chief Semano declared with such authority that it had been Salvatore's men who had fired from Mt. Pizzuta, it stood to reason that he also knew the identity of those who'd shot from Mt. Cometa. When interrogated on this very point, Chief Semano claimed he was under high orders not to discuss the case until all the facts were in.

Assassination attempts to the ruddy-faced communist Senator de Casselli, a man of powerful political persuasion were nothing new. His life had periodically been threatened since 1943, when he had openly declared his allegiance to communism. When the Reds uncovered the facts behind the attempt on his life at the Portella Della Rosa *festa*, a storm of controversy erupted in Communist HQ's in Rome, with the radical activists demanding immediate action. The Senator hurled charges at Minister Belasci, accusing him on intriguing with Salvatore over his attempted assassination. He charged not only the Minister, but his barbs included the Premier, the Vatican and even America.

"They're all in league with the outlaw," charged the Red Senator. "And they even furnished him the arms with which to do the dirty business."

Their inability to intrigue with Salvatore had colored their hatred of him, and the communists targeted all their wrath at the Sicilian brigand. Labor Unions called for an immediate general strike throughout the nation and came close to crippling de Aspanu's government. There was hell to pay in the national crisis that exploded. Goaded by the Premier, Minister Belasci was forced to formally declare his innocense in the matter, and he publically placed a price of five million lire on the head of Salvatore. In a synchronized thrust aimed to rid the island of Salvatore, thousands of *carabinieri* were instantly dispatched to the island to rid Sicily of the bandits and end this scourge once and for all.

Newspapermen, for the most part, were outraged. On paper, they had proven Salvatore innocent of the charges leveled at him; yet no one, it seemed had heeded their findings. What the hell kind of business was this? they wondered. They countered against the Communists, declaring "The Reds scream for blood, but don't give a damn whose it is—as long as it isn't theirs!"

On May 10, Tori roamed aimlessly about the Grotto Bianco. He had become an inconsolable figure of wretchedness in the days following Portella, as indescribable conflicts, battles and inner struggles raged within him. For days he had refused food. He'd grown thinner and more haggard, the dark shadows having grown more pronounced under his eyes. A cryptic expression had formed and remained fixed on his face, and in this time he had communicated with no one, not even Vincenzo. He poured over the newspapers' accounts daily, over each story written about the Portella affair. For a time he even took heart over the dogmatic sleuthing of Lt. Greco and the staunch support given him by the press, but it didn't pacify the guilt he still felt over those innocent women and children.

On this early evening he moved about an open fire at the mouth of the Grotto, listening to his men grumble at the label of *assassins* pinned on them for a crime they didn't commit; a crime against their very nature, and one they protested vehemently. Which man among them would have willingly engaged in the mass slaying of his own people? It was different with those marauding foreigners who kept them suppressed, now—they deserved to be shot.

Betrayed again! Who had turned into Judas? They promised each other they wouldn't accuse anyone among them again, since in the past the culprit had been outside their group. But this time it was different. Any one of them could be suspect. Their campfires had never been dampened by the blood of innocent people. Never! Fired by solemn remorse for their participation in this outrageous, inhuman act, they could get no satisfactory answer for the countless questions that remained unanswered. If only Salvatore could tell them how in God's name the situation could be righted! How could he justify this *infamita* to the men who believed in him? they wanted to know.

Because Tori remained unreachable, it was to Vincenzo that the men turned for solace and for an explanation of this inescapable blunder and blight on their careers. Vincenzo, unable to pacify the men, urged them to be patient. One day he moved away from them fully exasperated and walked to Tori's side displaying enormous compassion. He placed his hands on his cousin's shoulders and said solemnly, "I know how you must feel."

"No, you don't," retorted Tori bitterly. "Or you'd want to go out and kill somebody right now." He moved away from Vincenzo and the others and walked out along the edge of the grotto.

No amount of laughter or light talk could elevate Tori's spirits. He was deeply troubled. He could make nothing out of the infamy at Portella except that a plot had been formulated to make him appear as the instigator of a cold-blooded and heartless slaying—one that an amateur, in his most demented moments, wouldn't have committed. He smoked for a while and moved back along the rocks, and sat close to the men again, listening idly to their conversation as they tried to unravel the mystery behind the hapless demonstration.

"It has to have been the Reds who wanted to discredit Tori," said Fidelio.

Arturo glanced up from his insatiable whittling. "*Only* the Reds failed to make a proposal to Tori for his services," he said, hoping to shed light on the affair.

"It's not that cut and dried," hedged Vincenzo artfully. "The Reds wouldn't have attempted to assassinate their own man. If you ask me, we're caught in the middle of a political issue." His tongue darted to the corners of his lips.

Over the years Tori had noticed that a nervous habit—this business with the tongue—would manifest itself in Vincenzo whenever he wasn't being altogether honest, just as it was doing now as he spoke with his friends. Tori also knew that all the cunning on earth would simply bounce off Vincenzo's slick exterior if he pressed him. Watching his cousin's comportment, he knew that if he simply waited for the time and place to press, he'd get the truth from him. As he sat smoking, gazing out at the panorama with mixed thoughts about his cousin, it all came together for him.

It came as a real revelation when all the facts dovetailed. Except for a few minor details, still unclear in his mind, he knew the identity of this incredibly ingenious devil who had forced him into so untenable a position. He not only knew who—he knew why. Earlier, he'd drawn a line through Don Barbarossa's name on a list of would be betrayers. Now, he drew a thick black circle around the name in his small black book and punctuated it with several exclamation marks.

Treacherous liar! Didn't he, Tori, know the extent of the man's treachery by now? Or was it because he didn't want to believe it of his own father? *Sainted God! And I the biggest fool of all for continuing to trust him, for having believed the lying words from his black tongue! What other devious plots has my father devised for me? He made me appear guilty of the Portella affair, so he can have some monstrous hold over me in some cunning future plan, some future entrapment. What?*

What had begun as a simple, uncomplicated mission had exploded like an atom bomb, showering enormous consequences on him and his men. Tori, honing his memory, went over every microscopic detail of the Portella operation repeatedly, in hopes of discerning what motive lay behind the betrayal. Orders to shoot over the celebrants' heads had been synchronized with other orders to shoot to kill. Why? To discredit Tori with his people, naturally. That had to be it. He asked himself whose purpose would be served if Salvatore's men were discredited and placed in a bad light. In rolling back his memory over his past involvements, he found himself stopping abruptly as he recalled the *in absentia* trial. He would've been convicted of a felony if he hadn't moved swiftly to rectify matters. He asked himself why the trial had been rigged. Were they afraid if he ran for office, he'd win? What Prince Oliatta had told him was the only possible explanation of all those time consuming obstacles. It figured. But how did the Portella incident figure with what the Prince had told him? He pressed further. Discredited by the Portella massacre, he'd be hunted worse than before. What had occurred at Portella was not, and never could be, construed as an involuntary act before a court of law. Not a massacre! Besides, the war was over. In addition if the charges leveled against him ever brought him face to face with a magistrate in a court of law, where he might be asked to name the instigators of the Portella Della Rosa affair, he'd be dead before he opened his mouth."

"I'd be dead before I opened my mouth!" Tori repeated aloud, "before I ever had a chance to reveal the instigators of the Portella affair." He was cowed by this revelation.

"No truer words were ever spoken," said his co-captain, who'd followed him and stood watching him close by.

But, Tori, riding an avalanche of thoughts, continued his tirade as if Vincenzo didn't exist. "The real instigators are Martino Belasci and Don Barbarossa. Prince Oliatta and Bernardo Malaterra are only the errand boys!" He glanced up at Vincenzo and seeing him for the first time, exclaimed,

715

"You know where you are? In the presence of a fool! A complete fool! I heard Belasci ask my Godfather if everything had been set for May First. With these ears I heard him. Whore of the devil! And I didn't make the connection. Bastards! All of them! Now it takes form! Both men are motivated by their personal and selfish desires to suppress communism, but for different reasons. Belasci has to rid himself of de Casselli before he can grasp the Premiership, and my Godfather dares not permit communism to infiltrate Sicily to upset his status quo with the millionaire feudalists!"

Tori paced in agitation, a few feet to the left, a few to the right. *"Caspita!* They both need me!"

"Whatever made you believe they didn't?" Vincenzo lit up a *cigaro*.

"Amnesty dangles before me like the temptation of the apple before Adam. And I let myself fall into their ball-crushing machinations! *Botta de Sanguo!*

Enraged at his own naivete, disgusted at his gullibility and sickened by his idealistic contention that honor existed between men at his level, he slapped his thighs with continued vexation. "They've got my nuts in a vise and are squeezing me dry! What a fool I am. A first class fool!" he berated himself. "No wonder my Godfather permitted my insults to roll off his back. What cunning! So that's the way the game is played? Not one truthful sonofabitch among them! Neither he nor Belasci wish me dead. They need me, all right! There's only one Salvatore! Dead, I'd be of no use to them! They need me, Vincenzo! They need me! And I'm the last mule to know it! The Prince was right!"

Tori continued to verbalize the many thoughts that had fermented in his belly these past two weeks. "Why didn't I realize this sooner? I've been riding the crest of our victories too long! There's nothing like the bitter taste of defeat to stir up the *cuglione? Allora!* The white eagle begins to soar after all, cousin. They will have to seek me out—not because they own me and can use me at their discretion, but because my influence shall be formidable. I shall have both Sicily and the sun in my hands! A revolution, by God!"

Suddenly, Tori came back to himself and became aware of Vincenzo's presence. Flushed in anger, he reached out and grabbed Vincenzo's lapels and pulled the completely surprised co-captain close to him.

"All right, cousin dear, talk!" he snapped gruffly with sufficient menace in his smoldering eyes. "What's the story with the Communists?"

716

Taken off guard, Vincenzo blurted the truth. "They paid me off. I only took the money because I knew how you felt about them!"

"What the hell are you saying?" Tori's heart hit rock bottom.

"Chief Semano paid me to keep the Reds from you. The Christian Democrats, ready to intrigue with you, wanted to make certain the Reds wouldn't deal with you first. They felt you might sell to the highest bidder."

Sickened, Tori released his grip. "You did a good job."

"So—I took their money. I knew how you felt about them and wouldn't deal with them. What's wrong with that?"

"What other jobs have you done so well without my knowledge, cousin?"

"Nothing. That's all. Don't you believe me? *Managghia,* we're blood brothers. Together to the end—no?"

He studied his cousin's face in the shadowy twilight, pondering the unexpected, surprising revelation and astonished by the flood of bitterness he had to suppress. He observed Vincenzo with forced complaisance. "Who else was paid?" he asked tersely.

"Bastiano Terranova."

"—And?"

"No one. Just us."

"How much did you get?"

"Enough to buy more land for our future."

Overhead came the noisy squawking of avaricious falcons returning to their nests. Both young men observed them for several moments.

"Who gave Chief Semano orders about the Bredas?"

"The Secretary of the Party, Don de Matteis. Orders came from the top—as usual. Your Godfather."

Salvatore snorted contemptuously. Only because he hadn't been schooled in their deceitful ways had it been possible for him to have been so unflatteringly seduced by them. "Very well, we'll see, soon, who rides the stallion or the ass. At times you prove yourself to be quite resourceful," he smirked, much to Vincenzo's discomfort.

"Everyone knows you loathe the communists, Tori. You must believe me. It's the only reason I cooperated."

"They do, eh? Everyone knows how I loathe the Reds? Well, not as much as they'll soon learn. Not as much!" He kept to himself the strategy he planned, in the recesses of his mind.

In the privacy of his room, later that night, after he explained in detail to his mother his full involvement in the Portella Della Rosa affair, Tori spent that night and the better portion of the next day familiarizing himself with the Truman Doctrine until he felt he knew them better than their author. He then began to draft what to him became the most important letter of his life—a letter to President Harry S. Truman. He had toyed with the idea long enough. Now was the right time for action.

The next six weeks found a lull in the Salvatore camp. He sent no letters to the press to affirm or deny the charges hurled at him by the Communists. He made no comment on the price on his head. This self-imposed silence, and the findings of Lieutenant Greco, and the subsequent absolution given the outlaw by members of the press—these only added to the mystique and adoration given Salvatore by the people of the nation, who declared, "It's all part of a horrendous plot to discredit Salvatore in our eyes."

Taking heart, Tori began to lay the foundation for plans that would complicate his life, more than he expected. He confided to no one the fact that he'd written to President Truman. He gave no further indication that he'd been victimized at Portella Della Rosa, or that he was being influenced by the glowing denials of his involvement printed by an adoring press. With dogmatic perseverance, he continued to work out a plan, orginally proposed to him by his Godfather, to wreck all communist headquarters in western Sicily. The single deviation to the original plan was that Tori planned to do everything—*his* way.

From this moment on, his actions were geared to reinforce his future plans aimed at total and unconditional amnesty—which couldn't fail, he told himself. To Tori, there had been something false in all that happened which he still didn't fully understand. For a long time he wrestled with amazement at the curious chain of events that had befallen him. And one day, quite suddenly, he came to terms with the accumulation of four years' hostility and a priceless experience to guide him in the next phase of his life.

After the Portella Della Rosa disaster, there came times when Tori became confused and resentful, when others upon whom he passed early judgment failed to justify that judgment at some future time. And so in his usual way, he became conditioned to put his faith only in himself. He knew his own capabilities and knew that he'd never betray himself, he'd lived too long under a standard of rigid discipline. In due time, a ferocity of awareness in Alessandro Salvatore became as implacable as stone, as cruel and impersonal as death. He had yet to glut his vengeance on his enemies. But when he did, he promised himself he'd do it with a Sicilian's instinctive flair for melodrama, with the theatricality of an an actor reaching for a sensational climax before a spellbound audience.

CHAPTER 53

Rome, Italy
May 30, 1947

Premier de Aspanu solemnly watched the Sicilian scene. Tired of plucking the spiny darts aimed at him by the Communist press, he decided he had had enough. In a surprise move, he dissolved his Ministry and formed a new one of Christian Democrats and non-party specialists, one from which he excluded all communists and socialists. Once again the Reds roared in anger and dissatisfaction, but, the Premier donned blinders and earmuffs and remained impervious to their protests.

News of Premier de Aspanu's capitulation, conveyed through Minister Belasci to Don Barbarossa, caused the Don to grin like a Cheshire cat.

"Didn't I predict the Premier would see things my way?"

"Yes, you did. You crushed his balls, Don Matteo. What a genius you are—a real genius!" Belasci lauded him with genuine sincerity.

In Sicily came an immediate purge of all communists from public office. Salvatore's brilliant strategy, commencing the last week in June, was aimed at the efficient devastation of communist headquarters in every village and town west of Palermo and as far south as Castelvetrano.

Trade unions were demolished by hand grenades. Fires were set at socialist headquarters. Before the Communists awakened on June 23, all traces of their previous existence were eradicated. In addition, thousands upon thousands of anticommunist leaflets were distributed in the wake of devastation. Painted slogans appeared on the wall of all available buildings in Palermo. Salvatore had declared himself to his people, as anticommunist! In the space of one day, Salvatore had crippled every Red control center of operation in Palermo Partinico, Borgetto, Montelepre, Montegatta and on through to Castellamane.

His mass assault on the Reds proved a military masterpiece worthy of great comment, and was praised by every member of the Right. And why not? Wasn't he Salvatore, the general who'd outwitted the government army? Who else had been such a warrior? Very well, perhaps Garibaldi in his day. But this was the twentieth century—a time when a brave, enterprising warrior swept the land with a new voice, one of hope and promise, one steeped in the future, not anchored in the archaic past. *Salvatore!* Salvatore, the voice of a whirlwind. . . .

Reactions to the *Straggi de Portella,* the Portella Massacre, had been immediate and pandemic, but mild compared to what erupted in Rome after the hazing of communists in Sicily. A tirade of angry and indignant protests arose from the hordes of Reds in Rome, to cause many a sleepless night for those high officials in government who blistered under the acerbity of the attacks via the communist press. As usual their accusations were aimed at Minister Belasci, who, under the brunt of their continuous bombardment, almost broke. Immersing himself in the dulling effects of heavy drinking, he was able for a time to withstand the turmoil, but the effects of his alcoholic excesses finally began to alarm his close cohorts, who feared for his sanity.

"Minister Belasci scoffs at Senator de Casselli's charges. the foiled assassination of his mortal enemy, Senator de Casselli. More devastating to Minister Belasci were the effects of de Casselli's daily litany, via the Red press, and the accusations led to political mayhem. The communist press granted de Casselli license to air his grievances, and he became unrelenting in his demands upon the Minister to bring the guilty parties of the Portella massacre to justice. In a mad exchange of vindictive verbosity, both parties ventilated their opinions via the press.

In a final rebuttal to all the Senator's "insane and unfounded accusations," the laying of guilt in Belasci's lap for the attempted assassination of the Senator, Belasci's office had this to say:

"Minister Belasci scoffs at Senator de Casselli's charges. *The Communist Senator is a mental incompetent if he continues to labor under the delusion that the unfortunate incident at Portella Della Rosa was politically motivated."*

Senator de Casseli retaliated by printing a copy of Minister Belasci's official report, made to the Italian High Commissioner on the Portella affair, in which Belasci pointedly declared:

"The Portella Massacre was the result of the combined effort of the Sicilian Mafia and the outlaw Salvatore, strictly for political purposes."

The Office of the Ministry of the Interior had no comment on this.

The Communists picked up momentum, gathered their forces, and, guided by a battery of expert lawyers, commandeered a thorough investigation which triggered off a series of incidents that, blown up out of proportion to the actual deeds, paved the way for a national scandal. This scandal would inculpate many men in high places upon whom the shadow of suspicion had never before fallen.

The strikes continued. Mass demonstrations by the People's Bloc proliferated. Continued attacks upon Premier de Aspanu's government hammered away without letup, until every branch of the government, ministries, and law enforcement agencies came under the full scrutiny and rapid-fire criticism of the communists. A purge followed, as a necessity.

The *carabinieri* and security police, whose rivalry transcended the boundaries of decency, were accused of corruption, ineptness and collusion. Just why hadn't they been able to rid the island of that outrageous, bloody bandit, Salvatore? Eh? *Answer that if you can,* they demanded. *Thousands of carabinieri have been dispatched to Sicily for the capture of one man. One man! And they've failed!*

The Reds scoffed, "Such power in one man! Bah! Either you bring Salvatore to justice—or liquidate him—or we'll bring the walls crumbling down upon Premier de Aspanu's government!"

Premier de Aspanu pressed Minister Belasci. "Bring me the blood of Salvatore! And I'll take no excuses this time! God Almighty! He's a mere man!"

Minister Belasci pressed the *carabinieri* and the security police. "Take all the men you need and bring me the blood of Salvatore—or I'll have your heads!"

In Montegatta, innocent people, treated worse than animals, were jailed—and were immediately shipped out of the province to offset any attempt by Salvatore to free them. Two thousand people, men and women alike, filled the jails to overflowing in less than a week. Every known relative of Salvatore's men was either jailed or held incommunicado; in some cases these were brutally beaten and deprived of food and water for days on end.

Antigone Salvatore, jailed again, argued her own case. When charged with associating and harboring bandits, she pleaded with the presiding Magistrate, "What choice does a poor mother have, Mr. President? After all, Salvatore is my son." Wisely, the magistrate set her free to return to her house, where she tended her rose garden, prayed and bent her head in daily supplication. Although Tori had explained the Portella massacre and assured her of his innocence, she continued to experience a nameless terror in her heart. How many times she made the decision to tell Tori about the prophecy and couldn't. Now she hardly had the opportunity, for she saw her son less and less in these hectic, unpredictable times.

In Rome, a powerful stench continuously permeated the communist headquarters, and a loud bellowing roar was heard daily as Senator de Casselli used his oratorical persuasion to hammer away, with deadly menace, at those anticommunists, de Aspanu and Belasci. A powerful storm of Red clouds were gathering and at their center this loud voice accused:

"You think we don't know that Chief Inspector of Police Semano is in league with Salvatore? We have the proof! Why does Minister Belasci take no action against Semano? And why doesn't Premier de Aspanu take action against Minister Belasci? The blame begins with him! But they deceive no one! Behind them all stands the insidious shadow of the Vatican! The Church—which should not enter politics—is behind this unrest and mass unemployment. And now, our spies have uncovered a more diabolical plot! None of these people, who continued to defy the laws of their country and tailor them to carve out their personal ambitions, would be so smug if it wasn't for that capitalistic monster—the United States, which sponsors this unholy behavior of corruption among de Aspanu's government! In tomorrow's paper you will read the proof, comrades. Then, we'll take action!"

And the next day, it seemed that all hell broke loose! The communist paper carried these headlines:

"U.S.A. BEHIND SALVATORE! ARMS AND AMMUNITIONS SUPPLIED HIM BY AMERICAN COUNTER-ESPIONAGE"

The letter sent by Salvatore to President Truman was printed under the headlines. Once again Salvatore became the most exciting and controversial figure in Sicilian history, for the letter was not only published in Italy, but got full coverage around the world. Prominence directed upon this twenty-four year old phenomenon, and speculation about his importance, heightened the legend. *In league with President Truman, is he? My, my. What next?*

The Mafia and their emissaries met to assess the Salvatore phenomenon. Minister Belasci was instructed to stand pat and not panic under the pressure from the left-wing press. "Ignore that sonofabitching Red, de Casselli!" commanded Don Barbarossa in stern tones. "And stop all this stupidity with the booze, Martino. Goddammit! I hear stories every day!"

In response to public outcry, prodded by the left-wingers, Chief Semano was removed from office. In the six months following, four men, well qualified for the position, were to be removed from office before their chairs were warm, because they showed favoritism to Salvatore's cause.

A new Chief of Security Police in Palermo made his appearance on the scene: Enrico de Verde, a tall man in his forties, with dark brown hair and green eyes, a cocky man with an arbitrary nature who seemed a somewhat reluctant recruit. This former lawyer, a refined and dignified man whose temper, once triggered, reduced him to a blasphemous, fiery devil, was a friend, former classmate and confidante of Minister Belasci. Offered the position with the express purpose of trying to resolve the differences between the Minister and Salvatore, it was soon reported, that an *entente* existed between him and the famous outlaw.

While the communist jackals in Rome brayed and added fuel to the fires of sabotage against the de Aspanu government, Salvatore enjoyed a social prominence, never before experienced. Each past glory dimmed in the brilliant light of newer conquests, and each victory thrust him higher and higher, until it seemed he could go no further than the pinnacle upon which he rested. Wined and dined more sumptuously than in his earlier days, Tori, on the surface, appeared to have buried the hatchet for all past betrayals.

Treated like royalty, Salvatore, through it all, maintained an attitude of remote aloofness, never trusting any of them as he had in the past. God, was he learning! Perhaps in those early months of 1948, Salvatore became privy to more than he should have known. He stored much away in his memory. But, as soon as he returned to his house after such festivities, he would meet directly with Santino Siragusa, where he reported with perfect and accurate recall who he'd been with and what had been discussed. The compilation of facts began to shape into an explosive biography.

In Rome, the communists wouldn't let up. They would leave no stone unturned to sway Italy to the communist cause. The Reds denounced the United States and Premier de Aspanu's approval of the European Recovery Act. On October 1, 1948, reflecting hostility to the Italian Government, the Soviet delegate to the Security Council vetoed Italy's application for United Nations membership.

The Italian Communist Party founded Cominform, the Communist Information Bureau to combat American influence in Europe and extend communism. The situation between communists and the papacy grew so acute that on March 10, 1948, Pope Pius XII sanctioned anticommunist activity by the clergy.

Premier de Aspanu, under terrific pressures, accused the USSR and Cominform of directing the Communist bid for power in Italy.

In Palermo, Don Barbarossa once again suspended the code of silence until "the Reds are purged from Sicily's shores."

On March 18, 1948, in Washington, D.C., Secretary of State George Marshall warned that *no aid would be extended to any nation under the European Recovery Program* (ERP) *in the event of a communist election victory within their boundaries.* This announcement brought a scurry of activity to Premier de Aspanu's chambers with the heads of the various ministries, and resulted in a mass attempt to suppress communism. In lieu of Secretary Marshall's edict, Italy couldn't chance the loss of America's billion-dollar aid promised them. With the situation grim, much had to be done before the coming elections in April.

In Sicily, activities commenced instantly. Meetings with the Mafia Dons, both old and new, took place with each man making his own personal evaluation of the Red menace, then forwarding the information by special courier to *capomafia* Barbarossa.

In Rome, Premier de Aspanu, in conference with Minister Belasci, made himself perfectly clear on the eradication of communism in Italy.

"We can't afford to jeopardize the American alliance or we'll be in desperate straits. You must insure that *no* communists will gain a foothold in Sicily, Minister Belasci," he said decisively.

"You know what that means, Excellency?" Belasci was stunned by the order.

"I know what it means. Promise him anything—in secret of course," said the Chief of State, unable to look Belasci in the eyes. He waved his hands apologetically in the air about him before he dismissed the red-faced minister.

Martino Belasci called his two trusted couriers, Bernardo Malaterra and Prince Oliatta, for an immediate conference and hastily related the Premier's instructions. "Between you two, Don Barbarossa and myself, we must promise Salvatore anything. Victory for the Reds in the coming election will mark our annihilation. If America withdraws her support under the ERP, our plans can be kissed off. I will never be Premier! Submit this to Salvatore. Tell him I personally request his attention in this matter. Publicly, to appease the Reds, it will appear that a price remains on his head. We'll ease up a bit in Sicily," he urged. "Tell him he'll be handsomely rewarded for this marvelous effort he does on behalf of Sicily."

What a situation! What intrigue! Monumental ramifications skyrocketed the emotions of all concerned. Pride was set aside, and egos redigested, and by the time Minister Belasci's directives were assessed and pondered upon and submitted to the *capomafia,* the Don had skillfully drafted a simple proposal to his prodigal Godson. The plan, made readily apparent to Salvatore through the usual emissary, Don Santo Florio, was capped with a special handwritten note in childish script from Don Barbarossa.

> *"Guarantee the Christian Democrats victory at the polls. Drive the Communists from our shores and you shall realize your dream, Godson."*
> Don Matteo Barbarossa.

As much as the oceans, winds and temperature combine to make up a storm, so did the nature of a proud man. Salvatore's total contempt and distrust of the Mafia-Feudalist combine, the Christian Democrats and the Church, and his delay in responding to Don Santo Florio's directives, gave the communists additional time to dig more spurs into Martino Belasci's backside.

In addition Gina O'Hoolihan's articles, published and syndicated, appeared in Europe as well as America. Release of her sentimental writings, placing Salvatore in heroic profile, and endearing him to everyone in the world, had swollen the legend to even greater proportions.

No one knew for certain the true nature of Salvatore's position with President Truman, and Tori deepened the mystery by remaining silent on the subject. Articles printed by Gina O'Hoolihan fed fuel to the Communist press who ridiculed Belasci's office, labeling them incompetent buffoons.

"One journalist," they claimed "has been able to do what thousands of *carabinieri* failed to do—find Salvatore! And a woman at that!"

There was little doubt that the prominence given Salvatore by these articles intensified the attacks leveled by the Reds. Then one day, the investigative committee formed to scrutinize the Portella massacre published their findings. Headlines screamed across the front page:

THE RIDDLE OF PORTELLA DELLA ROSA—EXPLAINED

The massacre at Portella Della Rosa has been uncovered as a vast anticommunist plot. Salvatore is anticommunist. Martino Belasci is anticommunist. Both men, Sicilians, haven't proven themselves in league with all anticommunists, namely the U.S.A. In Sicily, Salvatore's army, dressed as *American* soldiers, carrying *American* arms, destroyed communist strongholds. The law enforcement agencies of the government take orders from that anticommunist, Belasci. All are in collusion with Salvatore—and we've proven Salvatore is working for the United States!

American spies, disguised as reporters sent by President Truman, constantly intrigue with Salvatore. Why do they have access to the outlaw's camps while for years our law enforcement agencies complain they can't find him? Recently we published proof that Salvatore is an American spy. Why hasn't he been apprehended? Why hasn't that anticommunist Belasci arrested Salvatore? We'll tell you why!

Belasci and his underground association of *mafiosi*, that brotherhood of murderers and bloodthirsty killers who purged Sicily of every other outlaw band except for their fair-haired boy. Salvatore, are in collusion—as one body. Permit yourself no delusion about this corrupt government. In a letter that arrogant and appalling killer wrote to his "boss" in America you will find proof of our charges. Read it. Fellow comrades, the following is proof of the alliance which exists between Salvatore and the United States—that capitalistic gargoyle who swallows a world of people for an appetizer, before they fill their bellies with the wealth and power they so easily manipulate from the unsuspecting lesser nations.

May 12, 1947

Dear President Truman:

Although we are oceans apart, after reading your Truman Doctrine, I have discovered we are not apart—at all! In our minds there is no separation, and most especially on the subject of communism.

First, if I may, let me introduce myself to you. My name is Salvatore—Alessandro Salvatore. There are many schools of thought as to my true role here in Sicily. Newspapers aren't sure whether to call me a legendary island hero—or an outlaw! Therefore your impression of me might be distorted by the fanciful tales written about me. Permit me to background my true role, Mr. President. If you will indulge me for a few brief moments.

Before I turned twenty-one, in November of 1943, because of an act falsely perpertrated against me and a subsequent act that led to the death of a military policeman who apprehended me, I was forced by betrayal to become a fugitive.

I've detested oppression, but under fascism one dared not remove the gag placed on his lips. At the time of the Occupation I was privileged to witness the political freedom initiated by the American Allies. Only then did I realize that perhaps the time had come to bring my dreams to fruition, my dreams of a free and separate Sicily.

I joined with members of the Sicilian independence movement, who advocated a separate Sicily, and was later raised to the ranks of General in the Partitionist's Army. Unfortunately the movement was dealt a crippling blow due to lack of funds to continue the fight. Our leaders dissolved the movement, to join in a coalition with the Christian Democrats.

Daily the communist threat reaches out in a stranglehold, and I fear if you do not lend us your moral and financial support, Russia shall own us body and soul!

With the war lost, we are drowning in a sea of hopelessness. It is easy for a people without hope to reach out and grasp at anything to survive! Russia longs to control the Mediterranean, and I shouldn't have to explain to you what this would mean. . . .

Whoever controls Sicily could easily control the Mediterranean!

Our main reason for wanting to serve all connections with Italy is because Sicily has always been treated as a misbegotten cancer at her feet! We have remained impoverished and treated most despicably for too long, and do not wish to be tied to a nation who sucks our blood dry and is deaf to our cries.

My organization, prepared and well trained, dares to fight the Bolsheviks only with the thought of eliminating the communists from our shores.

I tell you, Mr. President, daily it becomes increasingly difficult to put up with the spread of Red tumult. Stalin sends millions and millions to court us and win our hearts—with the usual tactics based on falsehood—and has managed to win, in a way, the people's favor. Fortunately, most of us cannot in conscience believe the picture of a heaven projected to us by the communists, therefore, every waking moment is spent in ridding ourselves of this threat. Freedom, for the Sicilian, is the most precious element of life.

If, as you state in your Truman Doctrine, you will help and assist in any way, any country opposed to Communism, Mr. President, hear our cry for help, coming from hundreds of thousands of men waiting to be liberated.

Allow me, then, sir, to remain, humbly and with great respect for a man as honest and sin-

cere as you, I pray for your good health and
success in the enormous role you play in America. . . ."

Respectfully,
A. Salvatore

Minister Belasci angrily tossed aside the newspaper and
sat back in his chair behind his desk, gulping down drink
after drink. Grim-lipped, livid and fermenting with black
passion, he reviewed what he'd read. These increasing accusations by that communist obscenity, de Casselli, were
beginning to cause boils to fester in his ass. In addition,
his verbal diarrhea was causing trouble with the American
Embassy. In a recent address to the Italian Legislature,
Senator de Casselli accused President Truman of sending
spies in various disguises, including those passing for international correspondents. The profuse apologies from his
office to the American Ambassador's office were no longer
enough. Even they demanded action be taken. *Porco
Diaoro*—Damn the devil!

Belasci asked himself questions his brain had distorted
into silent, personal threats against him. Salvatore, with
the power of the United States behind him he'd be untouchable! Sonofabitch! Was it just possible he could be
another Canepa, that commie double agent who had not
only fooled the Americans, the Italians, and the Sicilian
millionaires, but had bamboozled the Mafia, too?

Belasci blew the matter out of proportion. Who the hell
was this fucking peasant anyway? How much did any of
them really know about him? Archbishop Voltera had
predicted his power, hadn't he? What was it he said? 'Salvatore speaks of Aristotle and Plato as if they were his
constant companions.' *Porca Miseria!* The cleric had been
the only one who'd done extensive research on that Sicilian
—and they all scorned him.

Suddenly, looming in Belasci's alcoholic crazed mind,
Salvatore represented a danger to him. He couldn't escape
the feeling of impending doom. If it were true that Salvatore was a tool of the American government, he knew too
much to be permitted to live. Salvatore knew too damned
much about them *and* communism included!

It wasn't enough that Minister Belasci's convoluted
brain worked against him to provoke unintelligent
thoughts in his mind, but, to increase his growing
paranoia, a rash of communist-inspired articles unceas-
ingly peppered the daily papers, reinforcing his concern
over this mysterious apparition, Salvatore. These highly

729

imaginative writings were directed at the Minister by his enemy, Senator de Casselli.

As intelligent and knowledgeable a man as Belasci was reported to be, it seemed strangely ironic that he couldn't escape the seduction aimed at him through the expertise of communist press propagandists.

Reaching for one of the stacks of newspapers piled high on his desk, he glanced at several headlines and articles appearing in the Communist paper. An open letter written to him by the Red Senator grabbed him immediately. He read: *"Martino Belasci, you pious head of massive corruption posing under the guise of sanctimonious justice, hear this—"* Belasci tossed the paper aside angrily and picked up the next.

An intercepted letter allegedly written by Salvatore to the *"Concerned American Friends of Sicily"* followed: *"My friends; War with Russia is inevitable. We need more heavy artillery, weapons and ammunition to protect Sicily from the Reds. Advise in the usual manner when and where we can expect to receive our desperate needs."*

Belasci discarded this and reached for another paper: *"Salvatore Fights Dual War!"* declares Senator de Casselli to Parliament. "One to eliminate communism, the other aimed at breaking up the government so he can establish his own government under the democratic standard of America!" De Casselli alludes to numerous surreptitious plots in which Salvatore allegedly schemed against Italy, the Premier and Belasci. "Is it truly possible our astute Minister knows nothing of these subtle machinations, which appear to be commonplace? Is Belasci so naive? Then, I put it to him—confront the American Ambassador concerning this international espionage that breeds mutiny and provokes a hot bed of revolution under his very nose. I challenge him—confront the Ambassador. Force the White House to answer our charges. I, as a loyal citizen who loves his country, wanting the best for his comrades, insist that Minister Belasci takes action against such treachery, aimed at breaking Italy into irreparable pieces."

By adding factual information to a mountain of fiction embroidered with skillful dexterity, de Casselli's seduction, aimed to incite and provoke the Minister, succeeded. Belasci's peers, who had heard the Senator's powerful oratory and read the same articles, became susceptible to the communists' witchery. The imaginations of less astute men were stirred and fed well. But more discerning men, the more stable conservatives, readily observed the subtle pattern of intrigue woven into de Casselli's clever prodding and knew immediately it was aimed at some devious end.

One of the most patient, discerning titans, Don Barbarossa grew weary of having to appease his protégé. In his constant attempts to pacify Belasci, the Don reassured him he had nothing to concern himself with in the matter.

"But you don't have to take what I'm forced to take from this Red bastard!" he screamed in his daily laments to the Don. "I tell you I *have* to take action against this gun-toting, smug Sicilian *sonofabitch!* I don't trust him! He's a spy! I know!"

"Listen, Martino. You must exercise the patience of Job. Can you not think of more pleasant things than this prick de Casselli? Why do you permit him the luxury of disturbing your balls, eh? You let this dirty business soil you. Now, listen, tread softly in the matter of Salvatore, hear? This letter to the President is a bunch of junk. Have I ever been wrong? You know what's happening here in Sicily? Here, the thought that America supports us against communism is the best fuel we've had. The peasants are content to wait for their promises, believing that their hero works for America. Now, I ask you—is that crazy?"

"But, if it *is* true, Don Matteo, that Salvatore is subsidized by America do you realize the position we're in? He knows too much about our operations. I say get rid of him, now! No wonder he's been so patient waiting for amnesty. Oh! I boil when I think of the way he's manipulated us!"

"Martino. Martino—listen. We are in no position to rid ourselves of his fantastic services, yet. *Managghia!* Can't you see it? Patience is all we need. Patience! After the April elections we can decide on his fate. We need Salvatore to guarantee us victory at the polls! What does it matter who sponsors him, if he suits our purpose, eh? You puzzle me by such shortsightedness. What's happening to you up there? Can't you realize, that *once we, the Christian Democrats, have won effective power, we are in a position to maintain a permanent majority!* How many times must I tell you to convince you of this? Take courage my boy, don't let de Casselli creep under your skin and fester like a boil. After the April elections, Salvatore will only be a brief memory in the minds of the Sicilians—and I guarantee, one they won't wish to recollect. Now take hold of yourself. Stop letting de Casseli use your ass for a dart board. Each time you panic, you only add more venom to their darts. Haven't I taught you anything?"

On this day the Don studied the noticeable change in

his protege, the pallor, the puffiness around his eyes; even his nose was swollen from the alcoholic excesses. He grew disturbed. He had moved into his former villa in Monreale, at the outskirts of Palermo, the same one he had lived in before he was forced underground during Mussolini's reign. Now as he watched Martino pour himself an ample glass of cognac and gulp it down much too swiftly, he spoke softly without reprimand.

"You give Salvatore too much importance. *Managghia!* This peasant son of a sheepherder must be laughing at you, for Christ's sake. I'm surprised you believe all this bullshit you read about him. Did you forget you once worked in the Office of Propaganda? You forget how it all works? But, then, you wouldn't be the first diplomat to be fucked by the communists! You're letting them squeeze your balls dry!"

They drank in silence.

Both figureheads knew Salvatore better than to discount anything they heard or read about him, for he was a miracle man. And both men, weighing the possibilities of Salvatore's American alliance, were not surprised in the least when Salvatore accepted their proposal to intervene in the coming April elections to insure victory for the Christian Democrats. The only thing they questioned was what would be on his mind, *after* the elections.

News had already reached the Don that Salvatore had accepted their last proposal, a fact which both shocked and pleased him, yet left him mildly agitated in a sense, trying to outguess the young man's intentions. Not that the Don was intimidated by Salvatore or the wild rumors circulating about him. He just didn't think that Tori, after being set up as a scapegoat, would agree to any more intriguing with the same men who had foiled him in the past. This fact made the Don all the more aware that Salvatore planned something diabolical in the event of another betrayal.

Salvatore surprised himself when he stood before the whale-sized Don Santo Florio and gave his word to work on behalf of the CDP once more. There were no usual pleasantries in his attitude. Cold, formal and business like, Tori made himself clear.

"Immediately following victory in the elections, I will demand payment in full. And since you, Don Florio, are the intermediary, it had better be who you presents me with my long deserved reward—total and unconditional amnesty, in writing, from the Premier. I suggest you instruct both Premier de Aspanu and Belasci to prepare such a document and entrust it to you for safe keeping, for I shall be here at the close of the polls to enforce payment."

CHAPTER 54

Managghia, came the cries of the people. *Is he to be believed? That Salvatore, that spectacular whirlwind, that white eagle of power who swept up the people of the land and gave them hope, that prince who made them breathe to his own heart beat, has won again! Is he to be believed?*

Those two peacocks, Don Barbarossa and Martino Belasci, were far from surprised when on April 27, Salvatore handed them a smashing victory at the polls. On the contrary they knew perfectly well what they were doing. Only one man could have catapulted the Christian Democrats to the head of the political roller coaster—and Tori had done it! What a triumph!

In the three months of silent thunder which passed, May dragged by slowly, June provided a painful revelation, and, when July burst into bloom, Tori, unable to contact specific party members, forced a meeting to learn exactly where he stood—as if he didn't already know.

Tori faced the gargantuan Don Florio and that obsequious, plotting snake, Don de Matteis, secretary of the CDP, with an inscrutable face. He literally sniffed treachery in the air as he stood listening to their lame excuses and disdaining remarks. He couldn't believe they'd attempt another betrayal—not again. Finally, they spoke the words he half dared them to utter.

"No amnesty," panted the corpulent blob of a man. "You didn't really think they'd honor the low-class son of a sheepherder after what you did. All this big bluff, being sponsored by President Truman! Hah! It's time you took that arrogant nose of yours out of those crazy books and stopped filling your head with fairy tales!"

Tori's presence in no way ameliorated the deep-seated enmity between them. Once again the mountain peasant had been outfoxed and outclassed. Tori, burning with mortification, gave both *mafiosi*, in their own measure, a power-saturated glance that would have wilted the Sphinx. His silence, distressingly effective, left them considerably shaken.

When Salvatore and his two paladins left the villa of Don Florio, the two agitated *mafiosi* moved swiftly. Don de Matteis summoned a covey of bodyguards and left for his own villa like a sneak in the night, while Don Santo Florio, smug in his own conceit, maintained that he had nothing to fear from the impertinent outlaw. In the presence of the Party secretary he' put on a brave front; however, once de Matteis had taken his leave, the 'fat man summoned his own men, and placed a double watch on his estate. He sent to Palermo for the the sharpest *sicario* money could buy. Something about Tori's cool silence, the black menace in his eyes, caused the *mafioso*, for the first time in his long life, to feel threatened enough to hire a professional killer.

Tori faced his men at the Grotto Bianco in a brave but crestfallen silence. Crushed by what seemed an irrevocable blow to his fondest dreams, he disclosed this final humiliation to them.

' "I see it in your face. Once again they do the job on us," shouted Dominic Lamantia in a voice that would boil the hump off a camel.

The others tensed as they studied Tori's face. It was true—they saw humiliation in his eyes.

"They told me there's to be no amnesty for Salvatore and his men," Tori said quietly, thumbs hooked into his belt.

"I knew it!" exploded Fidelio Genovese. "I just knew it would happen." He had been cleaning his Luger when Tori gave them the news. In a gesture of violent anger he flung the gun from him. It struck the side of the cave, deflected, bounced back and struck Lamantia's temple. Injured, Dominic winced and jumped back, holding the side of his head.

"Goddammit!" shouted Vincenzo, reprimanding Genovese. "There's no sense losing your head." He turned solicitously to Lamantia. "Are you all right?"

"I can't help it," snarled Genovese. "I'm mad. Fucking mad!" He trembled with rage. "Only a fool would have trusted those vipers so many times. If anyone of *us* had been as treacherous and betrayed you as they have, Tori, we'd have been planted in the ground before spring sowing. You think they care for us? Hah! We're stupid, stubborn peasants. You, Tori—for a time you frightened them, puzzled them, and, because you were invincible and held such a tempest of power in your hands, they led you along, carefully, like a chained tiger, parading you as their possession." Fidelio stepped in closer to Tori, wagged a finger at him and his voice deflated. And because he could feel the spur of fear against his ribs, he barely spoke above a whisper.

"You've just given them Sicily, Tori."

"*You've just given them Sicily!*" These words reverberated in the minds of all the sober-faced men, and in the silence that followed, they all stared at Tori with dumfounded expressions on their faces and sinking sensations in the pits of their stomachs. Fidelio's voice cracked noticeably as he dared speak the words his companions were thinking. "You've been castrated, Tori." Another hush fell upon the men as they fidgeted awkwardly.

"By turning over the power of Salvatore to them you've made them omnipotent. Shall I tell you what the end will be? More treachery. *Si, amico,* in the dark of night will come the silent, swiftness of a blade or the sudden sting of a lethal bullet. Go ahead, laugh. Laugh, like the rest of our compatriots did before we took a hand in their destruction," Fidelio brought the men back to the recent past. "Barone laughed. Russo wouldn't believe it when he heard we'd raise a hand against our own kind. He laughed so hard he blew himself up right out of the water—remember?"

"Bastards!" shouted Lamantia rubbing the angry swelling at his temple. "Why did you trust men whose word is like diarrhea?"

Salvatore couldn't have felt worse. "If you wish, it's clear for you all to emigrate to Brazil. Prince Oliatta assures me you'll all be safe there. As for me, I plan to remain here in my own country. I have a score to settle."

"We'd all like to remain, Tori," said Arturo Scoletti, his deeply compassionate face wrinkled with perplexity. "But—how?"

They all understood Arturo's words. Under the perilous strain of recent events, with so many *carabinieri* crawling about their mountains, it had become increasingly difficult for them to move in and about their territory without encountering those graft-filled mercenaries, who forced them under threat of arrest to pay handsomely for the privilege of sauntering about their domain.

"Listen, Tori, the way things are, we're outnumbered and haven't the money to pay for the tickets or privilege of dancing around with those whores of Satan," said Marco Genovese. The men nodded in agreement.

Tori, listening, filled with an inner turbulence, wondering how things had come to such an end. Yet, it wasn't as if he hadn't anticipated such an outcome. Not once, not since the infamy at Portella had he for one moment believed that amnesty would be forthcoming. He'd gone along with the formalities of complying with orders, once more, hoping for some miracle to reinstate his belief in mankind. Yet, all the while, he had secretly prepared for another eventuality. In this, the final deceit, the naivete had been stripped from his eyes, once and for all. Never again would he trust a man against his own instincts. Never would he permit himself to be used by such men. Now, by God, he'd press. God Almighty, would he ever. He'd wipe out every traitorous son of a devilish whore—obliterate them. He'd show them no mercy, give no quarter. They'd showed their sinister stripes, stunk up the countryside with fetid and false promises. The time had come for Tori to teach every last diabolical son of a bitch the virtues of keeping his word.

Salvatore knew what must be done. He'd tested the thinking of his men only to determine who'd stand beside him and those who'd fall by the wayside. In a steady, authoritative voice containing no desperation he commenced.

"We must insist that these *gentlemen* keep their word." The others agreed. "But, how?" they queried.

"I'll tell you how." He addressed himself to Fidelio Genovese. "You, Arturo, and Miguel, go to Castellammare and kidnap Bernardo Malaterra."

The men couldn't have expressed more shock. They became disorganized.

"Are you crazy? Have you lost all your senses? That's the most foolish statement ever to escape your lips, Tori," cried Vincenzo.

"Is this really Salvatore speaking—" asked Fidelio, "—or some whirlwind of unreality that threatens murderous folly?"

"You intend to take on the Mafia?" asked Lamantia incredulously.

"Haven't we taken enough of their lies?" retorted Tori. "Well, no more! They'll have no opportunity to break their word to me again. I had misgivings when the Nuliano brothers left for North Africa a few weeks ago. But, they were right, just as you were right, Fidelio, when you predicted that amnesty was never intended for us. Very well, our Christian Democratic friends shafted us, good. Now, we'll see whose ass feels the pain—theirs or ours!" He flipped a cigarette from between his fingers in a gesture of exaggerated menace.

Standing with his thumbs hooked into his gun belt, Tori addressed his men. "Listen," he told them. "Salvatore has accepted his final betrayal. He will assert himself once more. This time, he'll trust no man, forgive no crime, and leave none of his enemies to laugh at his trusting nature. His bitter heart will show no mercy and he'll become a stranger to the cries of compassion. In showing contempt and loathing for our enemies, Salvatore is prepared to match them grave for grave, to repay each atrocity with more atrocity."

His men stared long and hard at him, unmoving, motionless. They weren't sure of this new side to Salvatore, Never had such vindictiveness shown in his nature. The silence in the grotto grew menacing and threatened each of the men in a new alien manner; their stomachs grew queasy and their heart beats accelerated and the aridity in their throats constricted them. Before any of them could articulate the fear in their minds, Tori quickly snapped orders.

"When you pick up Malaterra, let it be known the same fate awaits Don Santo Florio, Don de Matteis, Mayor Tedesco and both the Cardinal and Archbishop. Tell them none of Salvatore's betrayers shall be exempt from his retaliation." Tori's eyes narrowed, he fingered his gun. "Let it also be known that the same fate awaits Don Matteo Barbarossa."

"*Your Godfather?*" His face blanching, Vincenzo turned in desperation and exchanged concerned glances with the frail, emaciated Santino Siragusa.

Momentarily lost in the confusion of developments, Fidelio Genovese moved across the floor of the grotto to pick up his Luger. At the mention of Don Barbarossa's name, the gun slipped from between his lean hands and fell with a dull thud to the earthen ground, inches away from where Tori stood. Their chief leaned over, retrieved the gun, examined it disdainfully, and with a tight smile on his lips, he asked, "When are you going to get yourself a real gun, *amico*?"

He handed the weapon back to Genovese and permitted his eyes to travel casually to the strained expressions on the faces of the others. Most avoided his penetrating eyes and shuffled nervously on their feet. They wiped the sweat from their faces, lit cigarettes—anything to keep busy and avoid paying allegiance to their leader until they had time to seriously contemplate this crazy scheme of Salvatore's.

"It's not enough for you that we're treated like animals?" asked Tori softly. "Have we secured their mattresses, filled their coffers with gold, only to be treated like swine—to be ignored—to be shown no respect?" He began to pace the grotto like a savage beast, his eyes, fierce pulsating points. "Allora—for what do we wait, eh?" Tori spoke for another half hour. By then the spell was upon them, and they too felt stoked by the fires of vengeance. "You all know what must be done—you know the plan. Each kidnapped man is to be held in separate locations and treated with our most cordial hospitality. It will not be an easy task, but, we cannot—will not—lose this time. Remember only kidnapping with substantial ransoms. . . ." He hesitated, then added quickly, "If they resist, shoot them."

Miguel Scoletti, only recently having returned from Castellamare and a needed rest, grinned diabolically and holstered the gun he'd been cleaning.

It was a different Salvatore who spoke to them this day. Tori had never been one to kill for the sake of killing. But that all changed now. He would keep death in stock, as a merchant might keep on his shelves sacks of flour for which he might have a call at any given moment. Now, that it became necessary to kill or be killed, he would kill with little emotion, get the matter over with as little fuss as possible. He would kill any man who was dangerous to him, or who had injured or betrayed him, as he might kill a *zanzaro*—a mosquito that annoyed him. The distinction between such men and mosquitoes would be hardly worth considering, and he would kill both insects with the same indifference, he promised himself.

The wheel, set in motion, wouldn't stop. Word of Salvatore's retaliatory action spread through the underground of outraged, haughty Mafia Dons and feudalists who met in conclave to pronounce the "kiss of death" upon him. Those ecclesiastical princes, afraid to venture far from home, confined themselves to their quarters and squawked their indignation to the Dons. When one daring kidnapping after another took place, rendering *Mafia* protection ineffective, the old Mafia, target for most of Tori's vengeance, spread the word—*Salvatore is a dead man!*

And Salvatore, equally determined not to be a deadman, instructed his men: "Only one course is open to us now. Strike like lightning! Demoralize our enemies! Catch them off guard! They'll taste Salvatore's power, by God, and be ground down for pig's feed! We've nothing to lose and all Sicily to gain!"

And that was how it went.

If Tori's enemies had heeded the signs, there might have been hope for them. But, in their conceit, he was still that peasant from the hills, that sheepherder's son who could never outsmart or outmanipulate *them*. How many times had they outsmarted him in the past? Phew! Such a simple ignorant fool to match himself against those odds! A pushover—a real pushover.

In issuing its ultimatum, the old *Mafia* encountered its first obstacle: the new Mafia, the young bloods, men more educated, and less inclined to follow the old traditions of obsolescence perpetuated by their elders. They made it known they'd take no part in the destruction of Salvatore. The old Mafia couldn't—wouldn't—believe that Salvatore had been bright enough to have exercised the foresight of a victory by aligning himself with the young blood *mafiosi*.

Indeed Tori had played his cards well by becoming an indispensible ally—a staunch friend—to most of these contemporary college graduates and professorial men, whose diverse opinions and modern ways of obtaining wealth had aggravated the older, more staid *mafiosi*. Through these men, Tori maintained contact with Chief Inspector D'Verde, when the need for *detente* appeared. Through these men and his own double agent Terranova, Tori leaked what he wanted known of his operations. To the new Mafia, Tori would turn for protection in the months ahead.

Only a few knew the real truth—that Tori never intended an out-and-out war on the Mafia, that he considered most *mafiosi* antiquated old men with rusty hinges for brains, and wanted them only to feel the hot breath of the hunter on their necks: to know, in a word, the feeling he and his men experienced twenty-four hours a day.

Mafia Dons, surrounded by well paid guns, maintained around-the-clock protections for themselves while hatching several plots to assassinate Salvatore. Don Santo Florio, that gastric nightmare of a man, took courage at Tori's threat and let it be known he'd suffer no intimidation by the Montegattan prince. He threatened horrendous retaliation if a hair on his head was damaged. A week after he aired this burst of insane courage, he was found dead in the exclusive company of the secretary to the CDP, Don de Matteis. The two men, shot through the head, were found with two of Don Florio's pet birds in their mouths.

The deaths of these high-powered *mafiosi* sent shock

waves through the island. How dare Salvatore strike at the Mafia? Had he lost all signs of intelligence? Didn't he realize the true power of the Mafia? Before they could wipe the astonishment from their faces, the deaths of three more *mafiosi*—men Tori had discovered were involved in a plot to do him in—were made public. At this, the most infamous of all insults, the Mafia gathered storm clouds and prepared to meet in secret to determine the ultimate fate of that "brash, gun-crazy son of a demented idiot!"

After accumulating successful coups in his acts of *vendetta,* and with the passing of several weeks, Salvatore's fiery temper abated. However, the hatred of his father increased like an unchained madness; an incurable sickness that possessed his every waking moment. In his rash of kidnappings where millionaires were held for enormous ransoms, paid without delay, Tori had hoped to seriously undermine the protective system provided wealthy landbarons through Don Barbarossa's association of hired killers. It was one of the ingenious plans he had devised to provoke his Godfather, who now symbolized all his betrayals and at whom he indirectly aimed his revenge. So successful had been his operations that, taking courage at the deaths of those who'd betrayed him, Tori threw all caution to the winds.

There could be little doubt that in losing that last vestige of hope for amnesty, he'd been subjected to an excoriating betrayal, which of necessity forced him to sustain a violent resentment at those responsible. At last he clearly saw these newly empowered Christian Democrats for what they were: malevolent, deceitful, serpent-tongued vipers, venomous snakes fraught with ambition. He saw in them all the rotten viciousness of mankind—lust, cruelty, treachery, degradation, ingratitude, savagery, and a contempt for anything less direct and brutal than violence.

Tori felt a wild sense of outrage to think that he belonged to the same species as these, and a wilder shame that he had allowed himself to believe in their immoral objectives and loathsome cupidity. He was seized with a vast hatred for these men, more profound than the hatred he felt for the *carabinieri,* and in this hatred, because he hated his father most of all, he felt an enormous liberation in himself.

In moments of incurable insanity, when, possessed as he was by a rush of wild thoughts, nothing seemed impossible to the aroused Salvatore, whose head was already giddy with the fatigue of success—but whose heart alternately sank in profound desperation. Incubating in his mind, maturing, was perhaps the most daring and insane plan he'd ever concocted. Why not, he asked himself, why not rid the island of these treacherous snakes altogether? Better still, why not seize the *capomafia* and hold him for the highest ransom of all—total amnesty?

After what Don Barbarossa had caused to happen, why should *he* be accorded any special treatment? If that didn't work, thought Tori, plotting his insanity a step closer to madness, one could always kill him, couldn't he? Father or not, what did it matter? What was another life, now?

Tori confided this plan to no one. They'd have called him crazier than he'd been in his recent plots against the old Mafia. It took a peculiar brand of madness to attempt such an audacious and skillful abduction. Yet, who but a king had the right to take another king? With this thought bursting inside him, Tori made his plans.

A wan, spectral light, glimmering with uncertainty, lay over the earth, as hesitant clouds moved silently over the face of the moon in an atmosphere of shifting darkness and night. Salvatore, feeling unnatural in this role, approached the Villa Barbarossa alone, while a slow, steady burn, churning in his heart, arose in him in a choking sensation, searing his insides. Perhaps it was the bittersweet scent of flowering almond trees that nauseated him. Combined with the overpowering sweetness of honeysuckle and the pungent aroma of carnations, it was an odor Tori would recall to the end of his days whenever he brought this incident to mind.

Forced to set aside his inner turbulence, Tori crept in closer to the villa, scanning as he did various areas of the sprawling estate. A few guards, scattered aimlessly through the area, tended their duties indolently. Tori felt that they posed no immediate danger to him, so secure was he of his own power. He approached the villa proper on the balls of his feet, careful not to make a sound in the thicket and gardens surrounding the house. Judo techniques, taught him expertly by *Sporcaccione,* enabled him to dispose of three guards *en route* to his destination.

Standing at the edge of a rear terrace where a bricked courtyard separated him from the main *casa* and where several yawning olive trees afforded him protection behind a rim of latticed rose bushes, he suddenly flattened himself against the trunk of a gnarled olive tree. A pale shaft of light shone through an open door, and the shadowy figure of a man emerged. The figure paused momentarily to inhale several breaths of fresh night air before he moved silently over the brick flooring of the court in a *passeggiata,* a short walk around the ground. Don Barbarossa, in a courtly pose, with his hands clasped behind him, appeared to be pondering the problems of the world.

Tori strained to see in the shifting shadows and only when the man was upon him did he recognize his father. The Don appeared to be walking straight towards him, and staring right at him.

Salvatore's gun, raised, was aimed directly at the Don's heart. His hand shook involuntarily. He caught his lips between his teeth and bit down violently, stopping only when he felt a warm trickling of blood running at the corner of his mouth. Fierce hatred and a frenzied accumulation of his anger and a turbulent humiliation shook him uncontrollably. In this state of acute anxiety and overwrought passions, Tori blinked, as the Don's image blurred. He rubbed his eyes with a free hand, blinked them once again and reinforced his courage. How easy it would be. Squeeze the trigger—end the hatred.

Suddenly Don Matteo stopped, unprotected, motionless and unmoving. He stared out into the darkness until Tori felt the fierce black eyes boring holes into his soul. In the dim shadows he saw the arrogant expression of inquiry on his face, the animal-like sensitivity that warns of approaching dangers, followed by a slight sardonic smile.

Tori, seized by a wild thought, felt his father knew he was there, that he had seen him as clearly as if he stood in the blazing rays of a spotlight. His hands felt moist. Hot and cold chills churned his stomach into a sea of nausea as he fumbled for the trigger on his automatic.

Shoot! Shoot goddamnit! Shoot and get it over with! It's now or never! Forget the abduction! Shoot! Shoot! Shoot! His mind commanded him into action, but his finger and the rest of Tori was gripped in momentary paralysis.

Don Matteo cocked his head and asked. "Is that you, Cacciatore?"

"Over here," called Cacciatore, approaching his Don from the opposite end of the courtyard.

Don Matteo's eyes peered out into the night for a moment longer. Then, he turned, walked towards his bodyguard, and the two of them disappeared into the villa. Their voices grew thin and faded into nothingness.

Tori reeled against the tree trunk. The ground swayed beneath his feet and large drops of sweat rolled off his face. His throat swelled with unbearable thickness, and he ran swiftly to where he had hidden Napoleono. He

742

leaned his hot face against the coolness of the leather saddle and stood spent for several moments until the violent turbulence in his stomach erupted. He moved quickly, and vomited into a nearby ditch until the bitter spasms ceased.

When it was finished, Salvatore thought, *I must have been truly demented to think I could kill my own father! What madness afflicted me to presume I could murder him?*

At the deserted Grotto d'Oro, Tori lit a fire and sat hunched over, wrapped in a blanket, staring stonily into the hypnotic flames. He tried to convince himself it had all been a terrible nightmare. No one in his right mind would have attempted such folly.

"*Aquilo bravo*—is it you?" hailed the arthritic old Giacomo, limping towards him. "What are you doing here?" He peered about the area and, seeing no one else he studied Salvatore's pale face in the flickering firelight. He said nothing further, but moved in closer to his chief and placed next to Tori's side the Browning automatic he'd been working on and approached his young master.

"You look ill. What is it, *caro mio*? What can I do for you?"

Salvatore shook his head. "Go leave me to think."

Giacomo nodded obediently and took a position several feet away from his beloved leader. Wrapped in a poncho-like shawl, the old man leaned against a rock and kept vigil on his heavily burdened leader. Possessed of the provincial and native-born wisdom of mountain people, Giacomo who had noted a marked change in his "brave young eagle" for sometime, would have liked to have helped ease his burden. But there was no opening in Tori's imposed silence and no penetration of the armor he'd encased himself in of late. What alarmed Giacomo was the recent haggard features, the hard lines that had erased all of Tori's youth. His laughter, so infectious and so marvelous at one time, had long since disappeared. It was a hard life, this, thought Giacomo. It was bad enough on men who had little brains and existed from day to day. But, it must be torture on a man with the intelligence and clear sightedness and inspiration possessed by his *aquilo bravo*. Things would never be the same he told himself. He closed his eyes and relived all those early moments in the young outlaw's career.

Tori never felt more miserable. He was relieved that old Giacomo didn't inflict his usual gift of loquacious oratory upon him. He must have sat before the fire fully two hours, in silence, before he moved enough to notice his gun lying alongside him.

As the flickering firelight danced on the gleaming blue steel barrel of the gun, Tori slowly reached for it and tilted the weapon and leaned forward so he could read the fresh engraving: "*Beware of Enemies—once. Of friends a thousand times.*"

The irony of the inscription ate away at him.

"I'll say one thing in your favor, Reverence. You've got guts in coming here. More guts than I credited you with," said Salvatore to Archbishop Voltera. "You know I vowed to shoot up you and your kind. And Salvatore always keeps his word." He winked conspiratorially at his cousin Vincenzo, who stood a few feet from him in the deserted, shabby and run down farmhouse near Monreale, where they'd congregated to keep a requested rendezvous with the "black prince" of the Church. Tori swaggered before the small, prim man seated in a stiff, high backed chair that had seen better days. Dressed in clerical garb, *biretta* in place, the wiry man spoke solicitously to his host.

"I came, because I've never forgotten that young man I met in San Guiseppi Jato—a youth who preached to me of love—"

"That was a century ago, *padre!*" snapped Tori with considerable rancor.

"You've changed a great deal since then, Salvatore. You don't appear—"

"*You* haven't changed, I suppose?" countered the caustic voiced rebel glancing sardonically at his co-captain. "The arm of the Cardinal—this 'black prince' of oppression tells me calmly, 'you've changed.' Hah!" Turning to the Archbishop, he demanded, "Tell me, did you expect me to remain the same innocent, idealistic fool I had been after exposure to *you* and *your* kind?" Tori lit a cigarette, fanned out the match and flung it savagely from him.

"Preach all you will, Francesco, from all the pulpits in the land, including my village where, it is told, you and the Cardinal attempt to infect my people in the hopes of swaying them to betray me. But, I tell you, don't concern yourself with the status of my soul. Don't implore the cooperation of my people under the guise of saving me from mortal sin. You can no longer encourage them to consider a life hereafter to be more glorious than life on earth. They no longer believe you."

"I was led to believe you were religious—"

"Oh, I was, once. A long time ago the innocence of my

744

religious beliefs was stripped from my eyes and I saw you men of the cloth for what you are—not as the champions of spiritual justice and paladins of Christ you pass yourselves off to be. . . .!"

"Don't talk blasphemy, Salvatore! You're much too intelligent to spout cheap, communist-inspired rhetoric."

"You sanctimonious men of the cloth always have a label for people who don't conform to your way of thinking! Communists! Atheists! Nonbelievers! What's the difference! The Inquisition should have put an end to the tyranny of the Church—*pero*, it didn't. My faith in God is undiminished, Francesco. I fail to see the necessity for an intermediary between God and myself. I communicate with him on a one-to-one basis and avoid the confusion of a third party. You see, I believe I've as much right to act in the name of God as you or any member of your disreputable and corrupt clergy."

The Archbishop bridled haughtily. "I refuse to listen to such rubbish designed to bring the power and glory of God into the mud, where the muck raking communists have seen fit to chuck it in their anticlerical war against the Papacy. You, as a proud Sicilian, should be the first to oppose the disease of their minds. . . ."

"Perhaps they are gifted with more insight than we Sicilians are, eh, Francesco?" smiled Salvatore testily.

"*Allora*," snapped the Archbishop. "I didn't come to argue the communists' case. I came to argue yours. The Cardinal assures me, if you present yourself to him under the laws of Sanctuary, he'll do all in his power to secure a pardon for you. If all else fails, he can guarantee a lighter sentence. The powers in the government will listen to him. Believe me, Salvatore, you may not know it—but you have many friends who want to help you. Many friends!"

"Friends, eh?" Tori whipped out his Browning automatic.

Archbishop Voltera's face blanched. His nervousness increased, and his trembling hands reached up to wipe the pops of sweat that beaded across his forehead. His eyes never left the gun. He couldn't have been more astonished when Salvatore turned the gun around and handed it to him, butt-first. "Go ahead, read the inscription on it."

Reluctantly Archbishop Voltera lifted the gun from Tori's hand. Holding it gingerly between the thumb and forefinger of his left hand as if it was something utterly detestable, he read the inscription.

"*Allora*, now talk to me about friends." Tori's bitter laughter, accompanied by Vincenzo's raucous roar, told the story of their contempt. Tori holstered his gun. His smile dissolved and he continued to deride his guest.

"Tell the Cardinal for me that it's impossible to respond to his appeal. The judicial system that would try me for my crimes is neither Christian nor impartial. Since it exists only to try people in my position, it wouldn't recognize the greater guilt of the government for sending bloodthirsty-*carabinieri* to our lands in the first place. And since it doesn't recognize the corruption existing in our government and the Church, or the immorality of men like you, the Cardinal, the Premier and all his men including that Philistine, Martino Belasci! How could I expect justice—eh? Furthermore, I suggest you direct all your religious appeals to that conspiratorial cabal of your political peers, for their souls, in greater jeopardy than mine, need saving. Now, I suggest you depart my presence before I change my mind and execute you here and now. You came in faith; good or bad matters not. I, in good faith, respect your courage for having dared face me. It is that *courage* I respect with honor—not the garments you wear. Therefore, I ensure your life until you return to the safety of your house. Next time we meet, I may not be so generous—do you understand?"

"I'll always regret not taking more time with you that day in San Guiseppe Jato, after the death of Apollodora. It might have been different between us," said the Archbishop, with real concern.

"Go! Now—while you can," said Tori sternly, his eyes growing cold.

"You wouldn't consider his proposal?" asked Vincenzo as they both watched the Archbishop's jeep dissolve into balloons of dust in the distance.

Tori turned to his cousin with a look of mild astonishment on his face. "Are you crazy? If I gave myself up to the Cardinal, I'd be dead in a fortnight. Too many hunters, with baited breath, seek the scalp of Salvatore and would slay him at the first sign of defection. . . ."

"You think it was wise to let him go?"

"Why not? What can Voltera do? Besides, the death of an archbishop isn't one in which I desire to be inculpated at this time," he said tersely.

"*Si*. What could he have done?" said Vincenzo. He studied the grim line of tightness about Salvatore's unsmiling lips. All sensitivity and reflection had long since evaporated from his handsome face, replaced instead, by a hard line of bitterness that turned down the corners of his lips and veiled his eyes with glints of ice.

746

"Va, amonini . . . let's go! We've a lot of work to do. We're due in Castellammare to meet with Solameni and some of the other young blood. . . ."

They walked to their horses.

"What's with you and Maria Angelica?" asked Tori.

Vincenzo shrugged. "Nothing. It's cooled. . . ."

"Why? I thought you were going to marry her."

"With *our* life? What kind would that be for such a flower—eh?"

"Vincenzo—if you want to quit, leave the country, anything—just tell me. I'll get D'verde to help you. Just say the word. This is *my* cause!"

"Oh—no, cousin. *E cosa nostra!* It's *our* cause!"

"Look! I speak with sincerity! Anytime you think you've had enough—like the others—just say so! There'll be no hard feelings!"

"Will you stop talking about it! I said, *no!* I'm with you to the end! Who cares about the others? You and I are blood brothers! To the end, *capeeshi?*" Vincenzo glowered angrily, but more at the mixed feelings within himself.

"Things are going to get very rough from here on in! With the Old Mafia against us, I can't guarantee our safety, cousin. I can only live from day to day. . . ." Tori seemed to be convincing himself more than his cousin.

"At least you told me. Now I'll live each day as if it were my last, so if the end comes sooner than I expected, I'll have no regrets!" grinned Vincenzo playfully.

"You're an incorrigible bastard! You know that? But I love you, cousin! I love you!" They both rode off with elevated spirits. . . .

CHAPTER 55

The hills surrounding Montegatta were alive with thousands of *carabinieri*. The King, Salvatore, still rode his snow-white Arabian stallion through the vast lands he'd conquered, stopping here and there to give orders to his men. Many of the original band had left him; many more had joined with him, and followed in strict obedience, as in the past, without question. Salvatore, ruthless, inexorable and turbulent of nature, was still regarded with superstitious awe by his people, and with the passing of each day believed more and more in his invincibility.

In his domain, on his splendid Napoleono, he cast a giant shadow which reached all the way to the territory of another invincible monarch, also a legend in his time who reigned supreme in his own sphere of existence, a man who wasn't about to turn over the keys to his kingdom to his enigmatic Godson, despite the spectacular penumbra of power that surrounded him.

Don Matteo Barbarossa looked beyond his domain, past the mountains and arid country that had become known as Salvatore's country, and knew his enemy. Both men faced each other across the mountains and crevices, beyond the golden land of the Conca d'Oro, like the leaders of two silent armies preparing for combat.

On this day, late in March of 1948, at his villa in Monreale, Don Matteo awaited the arrival of his *amici* to discuss the most significant subject in the life of the brotherhood—the death of Salvatore. From the leading cities and villages and towns came the *mafiosi*, with their armed bodyguards.

A meeting of *mafiosi* necessitated no unusual appointments of the kind expected by the spoiled landbarons. *Mafiosi* needed no festooned affairs and gourmand foods. A good glass of wine and a fine cigar were their requisites. To them, only the word was vital.

The *capomafia* lost no time and wasted few words with members of this special consortium, for most were immune to flattery and fancy rhetoric. The ritual of their first drink over, Don Barbarossa got to the point.

"*Allora*, what do we do about Salvatore?" he asked without preamble.

"Bury him," growled Don Calogero Vizzini, a Mafia titan who had once delighted in Salvatore's bold audacity before the brigand had committed a final outrage against the brotherhood. He raised his heavy arm with a thumbs-down gesture, with less emotion than it took to swat a fly.

"First, exterminate somone close to him, then bend him to our will in a message he won't mistake as a gesture of friendship," negotiated the hawk-like Don Ferro of Jato, more punitive and sadistic in his approach.

"He has some gall to threaten us," thundered the harsh voice of Don Bruno of Caltagirone. He passed a swift sentence upon Tori with his thumb down.

Don Abruzzi, a dapper man in his sixties with white hair and a black moustache, had inherited Don Pippinu Grasso's territory in Trapani and Mt. Erice. He was younger than his contemporaries, more articulate, and was considered one of the new breed of *mafiosi*. "Listen to me, *amici*," he began expansively. "First, we encouraged Salvatore. We praised him and showed him our ways, and now that he's become a god to his people whom they adore and follow, we protest. That whelp who served us well, whom we treated with love and affection when it served our purpose, suddenly bares his fangs like a tiger—" He paused under the inscrutable stares, to wipe the perspiration on his forehead, as a few of the Dons coughed and lit up cigars or sipped their drinks. Undaunted, Don Abruzzi continued.

"We, who boast we take care of our own, have suddenly found ourselves confronted by a tiger of our own creation. Only the most foolish of men permits a tiger to go forth to kill and devour everything in its past. Can we ignore Salvatore—deny that we had any part in the creation of this menace? No. It's too late. Our very existence is threatened. *Allora*, we must unite in opposing him. I say—annihilate him before his ferocity can't be subdued." His thumb went down.

The *capomafia* listened and watched, noting readily that none of them really wanted Salvatore dead. In the past they had delighted and marveled at his daring and praised his virtues highly. But Don Matteo saw written on their faces the desperate ache for survival innate in each man. It was simply a matter of *get him before he get us*.

When Don Vizzini, second to Don Matteo in the power structure, spoke, his words were accepted as measured gold; brilliant, scarce and highly precious. The oldest man in the room was looked upon as an advisor in the hierarchy; consequently he was approached with an appropriate degree of respect.

"What are your thoughts, Don Calogero?" asked Don Matteo.

Electric black eyes, vibrant under puffy lids, shifted about the room aimlessly. He spoke with labored breathing from an overtaxed heart, his face bland.

"To declare open war on him is foolish. Bait him. Inch by inch, slowly to a point where he'll understand. *Allora*, first, obstruct his power. Destroy his influence. *Mah*—not at first. Limit it. Make him think we are only without patience. Gently, gently, softly—then *pow!*" The Don smashed his fist against the arm of his chair. "Crush him! But only after he's been made aware that we caused it to happen. By then we'll have him where we can keep an eye on him—buried in concrete in a mausoleum."

Don Matteo's lips curled contemplatively. "How do we instill fear into the fearless? Threats? Hah! I can see him now riding the infernally magnificent beast, laughing at us."

"He made us a laughing stock with his letters to the American President and to the press," snorted Don Ferro. "By aligning himself with the youngbloods he has as much as told us we should be put out to pasture."

Cacciatore thought it strange that none of the room's occupants could be more definitive in their suggestions. Would it take a specialist such as he to provide their solution? He sipped his wine, and held his little finger arched in the manner of a dandy, his diamond solitaire glistening brightly. "With your permission," he said with some reluctance. "Every man has his price. With treachery infiltrating his camp, he'll be reduced to ashes in less time than an earthquake devastates."

Each of the fourteen Mafia Dons swiveled about to scrutinize the repulsive *mafioso*. In their glittering dark eyes were reflected visions of the far-reaching effects of such treachery.

Don Vizzini nodded. "Seek the cooperation of his four horsemen. If they are immovable, try the inner circle of paladins. But, if like the mountains, they prove immovable, begin with the outer circle and move in, bit by bit." The demonstrative Don snapped his cigar in two for emphasis.

"It may take time," added Cacciatore, "But, we've learned patience. The patience it took to wait while the *fascisti* evaporated."

"With a few pieces of silver we sow the seeds of discontent, suspicion and greed among them. The communists would rejoice to melt his hide."

"No, no, no, no," protested Don Barbarossa wagging a finger at the others. "Not the communists. With them you work a two-edged sword. They can't be trusted. *Pero*—the idea is intriguing."

"He wraps the nobility around his finger with his talk of personal war on the Reds! You'd think he was the only one who had sacrificed to eliminate the Reds!" Don Bruno sipped his wine and wiped the ashes from his vest.

Don Matteo puffed thoughtfully on his cigar, his thoughts locked in about Salvatore. If there had only been some way to meet Salvatore half way! Now, it was too late. Having been cheated so many times, Salvatore wouldn't believe him if the Don offered him amnesty in a golden chalice. And, who'd blame him? As *capomafia* he

750

was committed to the elimination of Salvatore. The death of those five *mafiosi* had taken on more significance than any other act in his life—for this Salvatore was doomed. He took his time, now, to select his words carefully.

"Salvatore's men are loyal to the last one. *Pero*—several of his men, no longer preferring the precarious life have emigrated to North Africa. It is only to his cousin that he confides, and that only very little. Since our spy system is no longer available to him, he has devised his own. He uncovered Don Florio's treachery—what makes you certain he doesn't know of this meeting? He may already have taken measures against us."

The *mafiosi* squirmed in their chairs, exchanged uneasy glances, and cleared their throats uncomfortably.

"You see—the thought stirs your stomach," observed Don Matteo.

"How did we become such fools?" muttered Don Ferro. "We hired him to protect us from the Red menace; now we must mobilize to fight off his growing menace."

"It isn't my desire or habit to malign a man, without first giving him an opportunity to speak for himself," began Don Vizzini, leaning forward in his chair, grimacing at the heartburn he endured. "But, you've said very little, Don Matteo. Since it's *you* he calls Godfather—"

Don Matteo's dark eyes snapped open behind those dark glasses. For an instant, his eyes met Cacciatore's over the heads of the others. He waved his hand in the air in a gesture of annoyance. His voice took on a tone of long suffering.

"I don't know how the rumor began. I don't recall the family, clearly. One day, bold as you please, Salvatore visited me in Godrano, a young *picciotto*, hardly dry behind the ears in those early days of the war. I was busy with the Allies then, and didn't spend much time with him. We met again when the Partitionist movement neared the gallows." Don Barbarossa paused. Once a hornet's nest is disturbed—who can guarantee the outcome?

Don Vizzini wanted answers to questions that for so long remained unanswered. It was time to lay his cards on the table and play them open. His position in the Mafia heirarchy gave him that prerogative.

"What about Don Pippinu Grasso of Mt. Erice?" he asked quietly, avoiding the *capomafia's* probing gaze.

The others, visibly moved, nodded in agreement. They had waited a long time to hear this indictment.

Don Barbarossa addressed these men, whom he had reinstated to power as mayors and *capi* in their territories,

751

without apology. "Don Pippinu was unworthy of the title of Don. He broke the code of silence and brought into his affairs the *carabinieri*. For the betterment of the brotherhood, certain measures had to be taken. A man of respect looks after his own causes. *Sonnu cose nostre*. The same way Salvatore is *our* problem. His life has now become our concern. Because he chose to do murder upon our brothers, he dishonors all of us. In the matter of Salvatore, all other considerations remain secondary to his elimination. *Allora*—it is ended. Salvatore's days are numbered. It will take time, but rest assured my friends, the measurements for his tomb have already been taken."

The *mafioso*-emeritus, that crafty, grizzled, Don Vizzini, wasn't finished. There was more. "Uh—what is this 'special portfolio' of Salvatore's that has been whispered about in the underground, Don Matteo?" he asked testily.

"*Managghia!* You believe that communist propaganda, Don Calogero?" Barbarossa asked pointedly. Then aghast, he said, "And that letter to the American President—you think he *wrote* such a letter?" Don Matteo forced a light contemptuous laughter. "It would take a college graduate to construct such a letter. . . . I, myself, believed it for a time, so don't feel badly, if you fell for this bullshit."

Don Vizzini, astonished by his skillful manipulation of the real issue, listened as the *capomafia* gracefully extricated himself. The uneasy and subdued laughter of his comrades told him the story. They'd all fallen prey to Salvatore's eloquent rhetoric. Slowly his frog eyes darted about the room, this formidable Don permitted a chuckle low in his throat. Inwardly, he knew better than to believe the *capomafia's* words. A second cousin of his wife's had once belonged to the coterie of Salvatore's inner circle. Often in the past he'd speak with unmistakable praise of the renegade's amazing intelligence. Before the press had gotten wind of that letter written to the American President, Don Vizzini had heard of it. He glanced up through lidded eyes that had seen plenty in his lifetime now, and heaved a heavy sigh.

It was over. An imperceptible nod, the slightest flickering of a power-saturated eye, a barely discernible movement in an upraised hand had decided it was time to put an end to the legend, Salvatore, and bury his bones among the skeletons of the past.

This consortium of powerful political clout and muscle left Don Barbarossa's villa in a most unusual assortment of vehicular conveyances that belied their formidable positions in the redoubtable secret brotherhood; a far cry from their usual mode of transportation. Two of the Dons boarded the rear of produce trucks, disguised as laboring peasants. Another rode in a colorful peasant cart. Some put on coveralls and left in delapidated lorries, so old they looked as if they might collapse in a gust of wind. A few of the Mafia Dons changed transportation twice before they arrived at their destinations. And there were those who stood at a respectful distance until their personal drivers stepped on the starters of their Fiats and Alfa Romeos—to make certain no bombs had been planted—before they boarded the autos. They were all guarded by strong-armed, pistol-packing gunmen of the brotherhood. And none were about to take unnecessary chances.

Smug in their own conceit, that they'd taken measure to dispose of this cancer in their bellies, not one of these Mafia moguls guessed that a slight distance from them, Tori was getting ready to throw a monkey wrench in their machinery.

Following the 1948 elections, after the bitterness and disillusionment of his betrayals had subsided, Tori had remained in the sidelines as an objective observer, hoping to learn more and more about these men who'd become his mortal enemies. He watched the deadly games they played, listened to the accusations and counter accusations hurled by each upon the other, and observing the stakes for which each man worked, Tori came to one conclusion. None of them could be trusted, for they were all addicted to the blood-sucking drug called power. The Sicilian politicos, a frustrated lot of desperate men, would sell their souls for power, all of them.

Out of necessity alone, Tori was forced to devise a thick coat of protection against these adversaries, these power-crazed men, as insulation to immunize him against their ambitious and manipulative power plays and avoid being used as a pawn by them.

Never—never in his wildest imagination—had he envisioned, when he instructed Santino Siragusa to compile a personal memorandum of documents for his historical biography, that these vital papers would one day transform themselves into life-protecting instruments that would afford him unsurpassed bargaining power.

These highly inculpating papers took on a dual purpose. As historical data they were invaluable. But when they suddenly took form as life insurance to protect him and his men from possible assassination, they became priceless.

Santino had kept his records as religiously as corporate

meetings, with the names, places and dates of encounters with every key politician, land-baron, *mafioso*, and precise data on each and every event, including all involvements meticulously recorded by his own hand. There were photocopies of correspondence, and communiques, and of all directives issued to the renegade. No seemingly irrelevant factor had been eliminated, and, when weighed in its entirety, there was hardly a VIP in the upper echelons of government, Church and Mafia who hadn't involved himself in some way in the life—and the personal records—of Salvatore.

And so it was that one day, when the knowledge of the weight of these documents unfolded in Tori's mind, he let it be known through his staunch friends in the new Mafia that he kept such insurance to offset any further betrayals. "Should anything happen to me or my trusted paladins in the days to come, these highly inculpating documents shall be made public through the efforts of my countless friends in the press," Tori explained patiently to them. "Included in these documents are the secrets of Portella Della Rosa, in which I painstakingly describe the political motivation behind the dastardly affair, with precise explanations and a truthful assessment of why Salvatore was doublecrossed by these Christian Democrats who needed his services."

What Tori didn't tell them about this report, which would one day become the most sought-after document in the nation's political history, was that he named the instigators, beginning with Minister Belasci, the feudalists, the Mafia Dons, and all others involved in the affair, omitting only the name of Don Matteo Barbarossa from this indictment.

Tori got his feedback almost instantly. Word came through his friends, "Salvatore can't be touched! He's not to be captured, dead or alive, unless these private papers to which he refers are confiscated beforehand!"

The Cold War between Salvatore and the Mafia, having commenced, was about to boil over.

Santino Siragusa was being primed for another role, one quite alien to anything he'd ever done. Seated in his house, in the dark of night, where Tori had insisted they rendezvous, he listened carefully to Tori's instructions.

"You are to guard this portfolio with your life, Santino. As long as these papers are in safe hands, there'll be no further attempts on the lives of our men. While you're in America, try if you can, without being obvious, in case your identity is known, to locate *Colonnello* Stefano Modica. Tell him to contact me by writing to the P. O. Box in Palermo. The number and address is in your case. Who knows, perhaps if things don't go well here, I may join you there—or in South America—or Mexico. You understand all my instructions?"

Nodding, Santino slipped the precious "insurance policy" into his brief case. He experienced a terrible sense of foreboding when he embraced Tori in those final moments of farewell that brought hot stinging tears to his eyes.

Sobbing, he muttered, "I go only because you order me to go. My heart and my life are here with you and Athena and Mamma. Before I go, I should like a few moments alone with her, to make her understand I don't leave voluntarily. You and Vincenzo go on ahead. I'll meet you at the Grotto Bianca. *Va bene?*"

Tori nodded and left the house with Santino's luggage.

"It's time you tell Don Barbarossa he is Tori's father," said Santino straight away. He sat on the edge of her bed where he'd awakened Antigone in the early predawn hours.

Rubbing the sleep balls from her eyes and blinking harder at his words, she sat up in bed, looking at him as if he were some idiot from a faraway land.

"Are you mad, Santino? I'd lose Tori for certain if I did so foolish a thing." She reached for her robe and slipped into it, stretching and yawning.

"You'll lose him if you don't!"

"Why?" She glanced at him anxiously. "What's happened?"

"You know better than I what happens to men who defy the Mafia."

"Don't talk to me about such things," she said acidly. "How many times did they promise amnesty? Is it justice, what they did to him?"

"You look to the Mafia for justice?" Santino was aghast.

Antigone, brooding, said nothing. She led him downstairs into the kitchen, where she put together the contents for a pot of coffee. Watching her, Santino told himself he had to make her understand the gravity of the situation.

By now," said Antigone, you should know it does no good to worry over Tori. He's been his own man for too long. I no longer influence his thinking."

"I'm asking you to influence the *capomafia's* thinking—not Tori's."

She shook her head as she placed cups on the table.

"There's a contract out on him," he said above a whisper.

"How many times have I listened to that rumor?" she asked scornfully. "I've lived daily with such threats for the past four and a half years."

"The name of the man instructed to do the job on Tori is Mario Cacciatore, "said Santino solemnly.

The percolator slipped from her hands and fell crashing to the floor, water and unperked coffee grounds spilling on her robe and slippers.

Oblivious to the mess she had made, she let her burning eyes lift to meet his. She felt her heart roll over in her breast as terror gripped her.

Santino quicky retrieved the coffee pot, threw a towel into the puddle on the floor to absorb the water. He finished in time to catch Antigone as she fell faint in his arms. He seated her in a nearby chair, rubbed her wrists vigorously, and reached for a vinegar cruet. Pouring some onto a napkin, he held it to her nose.

"My medicine . . . there on the drainboard," she gasped.

Moments after taking the heart stimulant, she came back to normal.

"Are you all right? Mamma, I shouldn't have alarmed you like that. I wanted only to impress upon you the seriousness of this dirty business. It's not like before. They say he's too dangerous—he knows too much. I have my orders, and must obey him. It rests with you to tell his father." He dared not tell her his real reason for the trip to America.

"It will do no good to warn Tori," she despaired.

"Go to his father and tell him the truth!"

"No! I can't!" Stark terror possessed her and she shook her head vigorously. "I can't, Santino. God Almighty, don't ask me to do it!"

"Before they continue their retaliation in vengeance, I beg you, go to Barbarossa. Tell him it's his *son* he plots against. Mamma! It's up to you to stop this wholesale slaughter. It's Tori's only hope!" He glanced at his watch. It was time for him to depart. But—how? How in God's name could he leave unless he made her promise to do his bidding?

"I can only do what Tori instructs me to do, don't you see?"

"No, Mamma. You must do as I instruct you this time. Preserve his life and those of the men. In God's name, understand the importance of my words."

"My duty is to my son," she said without expression.

756

"Always in the past, I've admired your good sense, never contested your word. Not in this. This time you're wrong," he said sadly. He took another long look at the house that once had held so many fond memories for him, knowing now that it would never be the same again. Now, ghosts occupied the premises, and specters of death and destruction waited in the wings for their cue to take over. Shoulders drooping and tears brimming his eyes as visions of Athena swam before him, he walked sadly out of the house.

In the sterile solitude of her aloneness, in this desperate self-imposed isolation, Antigone, seated at the kitchen table in the unlit shadowy kitchen, listened as the motor started up in the jeep and grew faint in the distance. Outside, cicadas became increasingly noisy. Croaky sounds of static from a neighbor's radio attempted to pierce her world, as broken segments of a news broadcast permeated the room. Antigone heard none of this. Inside her raged a different world of doubts and faded dreams and deteriorating hopes. In all this excitement about Santino's departure for America, she had failed to tell Tori he'd become the father of a fine son named Gino. In a letter couched with ambiguities, in a prearranged simple code planned between them in case the letter was intercepted by their enemies, Gina had placed the burden of telling Tori of their son's birth directly into Antigone's hands. It wasn't that she didn't want to tell her son. •It was simply that each time he came to see her, more infrequently of late, he was always in a hurry and could hardly remain for anything more than a greeting and departure after seeing she was all right.

Santino's words echoed in her mind. It seemed highly improbable to her that Cacciatore should be given the contract to kill her son. There was a feeling of unreality connected to such a story; that it could happen to someone else—not Tori.

In the days to come, Antigone, a lonely figure of wretchedness and introversion, would attend Church each morning. Twice daily she'd pass before Donna Sabattini's house, pausing momentarily as vague, disconnected thoughts rushed at her. She was reluctant to make the last effort of conferring with the *strega,* for fear the old crone would reaffirm the same pictures that played over in her mind with vivid clarity and continuously struck fear in her heart.

The pictures, always the same, were dim and undiscernible, except for the faces of Tori and Matteo Barbarossa.

Tori, the dominant figure in her dream, looming larger than life, would begin to shrink in a gradual metamorphosis through a haze of misty apparitions until he disappeared, as the form of Matteo Barbarossa exploded clearly in its place. There was always the same diabolical leer on the Don's face, that same powerful countenance which reeked of tyranny and power. Not absent from these visions, either, were the symbolic eagle, lion and bull to increase her belief in the *strega*'s prophecy. The prophecy? Oh, yes, it was never far from her these days. . . .

CHAPTER 56

Minister Martino Belasci, stress-laden and alcoholically bent, sat in his chambers, mulling over the catastrophic events that threatened him. Two solid years of nerve-wracking harassment; the on again, off again relations with Salvatore, ordered by the Premier and other Christian Democrat heavyweights who demanded that action be taken to gag the left-wing press, had drained him completely. Pressures from his superiors, traumatic and chaotic as they were, couldn't match the repeated jackhammer blasts leveled at him by those hot-headed, viper-tongued communists. To ease their own frustrations, they'd made Belasci their daily dart board—a target who epitomized all the communists loathed and feared in an enemy.

Caught on all sides by the CDP, the Mafia, the Premier, and the Vatican—to say nothing of Salvatore—Belasci, ignoring his own disintegrating morality, found himself caught in a lethal stranglehold by these political pythons. They had squeezed him, inch by inch, until he could no longer take a full breath in peace. He had reached the breaking point, unable to take the emotional blows, the hailstorm of pressures, inflicted on him.

God, how he needed sleep! He continued to drink to excess, raving and ranting to his PR men that he didn't give a damn if his undisciplined drinking did bring frowns from his followers. What did *they* know? Did *they* have to take the daily stoning of enemies—the poisonous sting of their arrows? Prince Oliatta, having taken Salvatore's threats to heart, had made himself scarce. There was no one in Rome to whom he could turn. Not even his wife Daniella, to whom he had gone to unburden his soul one night after her lover had exited, would permit her heart to melt for this ambitiously poisoned, and crumbling, idol.

Around Martino Belasci flickered a confusing sea of nameless faces, men whose ambitions he had crushed in his fanatic pursuit of the Premiership. Half-remembered faces and names, floating about in the recesses of his mind, men who had snapped to his orders and bowed to his office, then faded away at his directives. So many of them. In this murky floating of his mind there came a voice, austere and quiet, simple and direct, to repeat time and again, 'As long as your ideals correspond to mine and we both seek only glory for Sicily, I stand behind you to the end. Count on this. So there's no misunderstanding, know well in advance, if you ever betray our cause or my trust in you—I will kill you. . . .'

"Whorish swine!" cursed Martino Belasci. "How did I ever permit things to evolve to such catastrophic proportions?" He slammed his fist hard on the desk in his plush office and winced as the pain shot through his hand. Grabbing hold of it, he blew on it gingerly as if that would erase the pain, then he exploded angrily. "That trigger-happy, letter-writing Sicilian sonofabitch!" Shoving back his chair, the Minister arose and, crossing the room to the liquor cabinet, he shook his hand until the pain subsided. He poured himself a stiff bracer of brandy, gulped it down, and carried both decanter and glass back to his desk. He paused a moment to inhale the fragrant aroma from a vase of blood-red roses, and, laying his feverish face against the cool velvety petals for a moment, he sighed heavily. Seated behind the desk, he poured another short drink, gulped it down, and patted his stomach as the warm glow flooded through him.

Belasci removed his tortoise-shell glasses, wiped his tired, swollen and bloodshot eyes with a clean handkerchief and replaced them resigning himself to the task at hand. He shuffled through a thick sheaf of newspaper clippings with bored detachment. Didn't he already know what they were? Always *Salvatore. Salvatore. Salvatore!* If he heard that fucking name again he'd explode. The headlines were the same—only the names varied:

"*Duke of Palalardo Kidnapped*—Salvatore *demands* thirty thousand ransom."

"*Duke of Verona*—Fifty Thousand ransom. *Salvatore demands.* . . ."

"Baron La Tasco—Forty Thousand. . . ." Salvatore demands. . . ."

"Prince Augustino—" Salvatore *demands! Demands! DEMANDS!*

He tossed aside the clippings disgustedly. Why did he bother with them? They were all the same. He lay back in his leather chair and, closing his red veined, burning eyes he reflected on the chaos of the past few months. Images rushed at him. Sounds pierced his eardrums, sounds of disapproving voices raised in recrimination. From every corner of the nation came comments, excoriations—and verbose accusations of the corruption in his office. He knew them by heart, having heard them day after day after day in monotonous repetition.

"Martino Belasci, that alcohol-crazed dandy wobbling from the overconsumption of booze, reminds us of that crazy Emperor Nero who let Rome burn," came the cries of those cherry-pink commies who spouted poisoned bullets from their lips.

"Tell us, Mister Minister, if you can, why you permit the kidnappings, ambushes, holdups and train robberies, eh? When will you halt the assault on the *carabinieri*? Can you answer us?"

"Belasci can do nothing," came the whispers of his enemies. "He'll never stop Salvatore. He'd sooner cut off an arm. Those two anticommunists are inseparable. Belasci can bleat all he wants. What a big *chooch*. He declares with angelic innocence that he's on the side of law and order. Since Salvatore defies the law, there can only be one end for his lawlessness. Ho-hum. So, what else is new, Minister? What else can you say that you haven't said a thousand times? What does it matter, only lies spill from your deceptive lips."

"Belasci is the most corrupt man in politics!" came the *pronounciamento* from Salvatore, from his usual platform in Sicily.

"Phheeeewwww! That crazy Salvatore. That lovable, sweet man. He'll crush Belasci's balls. He will, you wait and see."

"Salvatore promises to call off his war on the carabinieri in exchange for the amnesty promised him. He demands the release of his mother from prison. Three times now she's been incarcerated. . . . He demands the release of all the innocent villagers who are dragged to jail by the hundreds each day."

"What's wrong with those imbeciles in Rome?" cried the Sicilian press. "Don't they know by now, Salvatore always keeps his word? If that *ubbriacone*—Belasci, had sense he'd give those concessions to Salvatore. Then, those pesky *zanzari*, the *carabinieri*, could go home."

"Belasci offers five million lire for the capture of Salvatore!"

"Big deal! Salvatore offers *ten* million for Belasci's capture."

"Managghia—who can laugh any more?"

"Salvatore challenges Minister Belasci to a duel! Adding insult to injury, the Sicilian declares he'll face Minister Belasci and the entire Ministry singlehanded. If he wins, he'll take over the running of the government. If he loses, he promises to give himself up to the authorities, with the proviso that his mother is to be released from prison."

Minister Belasci's eyes snapped open. It was too much! Too much to bear! All around him he heard cries championing that outrageous rebel, that thorn in his side. The accolades were for the Sicilian bandit, who supported the poor and destitute. All Belasci got were boos and jeers and uncomplimentary remarks and criticisms. It was enough to drive him mad—mad! Worse—nothing eased up.

Recently, the communists, up in arms and moving swiftly, had filed suit against the government on behalf of the families of the poor, unfortunate victims of the Portella Della Rosa Massacre. *Allora*, that dirty business again, lamented Belasci. They won't leave that can of worms alone. It wasn't enough that Lt. Greco had proved Salvatore innocent of the charges. Those Reds were up to no good. Belasci had to agree, there was a rotten stink in Rome these days—all emanating from communist headquarters.

They insisted on going to trial. Bah, thought Belasci, what will a trial prove except to cost the government too much money? He had to hand it to the Reds, they moved to try the case in Viterbo, Italy—away from Sicily. What a field day the Sicilian press had had with this news! They had blasted the newspapers making folly of such activity.

"It's not safe to hold the trial in Sicily because Salvatore would march right into court and release the men held for trial! Sure, he'd do that, and why not? Aren't they all innocent? Why waste time with a foolish trial? Those Italian politicians always complicate things. What insanity to try the innocent."

Va bene, thought Belasci, smiling contentedly. Only recently he had retaliated by setting up a Parliamentary Committee of Inquiry to investigate the bandit, Salvatore. Now we'll see who has the last laugh. Belasci could almost hear the whispered innuendos in the Salvatore camp, the advice and words of caution spoken to him. *"Listen, Tori, watch your step, eh? Those idiots in Rome mean business. What kind of business? Eh,* caro mio, *it can only mean one kind, dirty business. Trickery, deceit, treachery and betrayals. What else,* amico? *Be careful,* caro mio. *Keep your ears and eyes open. Keep your guns handy, you hear? Don't let them kill you off,* paesano beddu."

For a time the voices from Sicily had grown subdued.

Very well, the overture had ended. It now remained up to Martino Belasci to orchestrate the entire libretto; the entire score from middle to end became his responsibility. And upon his artistry, his entire career hung in the balance. The question was could this conductor control the percussionist, the bass drummer, the loud, clanging cymbalist, the kettle drummer and that other artist who marked time to his own tempo, Salvatore?

Belasci, returning to the moment, shut out the inner dialogue and gulped down another fiery drink. This morning, August 26, 1949, the Parliamentary Committee of Inquiry had announced the results of its three-month probe and he had called for the organization of a new anti-bandit unit, aiming for the immediate destruction of Salvatore and his savage brigands. This special squad, answerable only to Minister Belasci, *Il Corpo Delle Forze Per La Repressione de Banditisimo* in Sicily, would come to be called the Forces to Suppress Banditry (FSB).

Feeling the effects of the drinks, Martino Belasci glanced at his watch at precisely the time an intercom sounded. He snapped on the switch.

"Colonnello Cesare Cala and *Capitano* Giovanni Franchina have just arrived, Excellency," announced his secretary.

"Allora—admit them!" snapped the Minister impatiently.

Belasci wove his way to an adjoining dressing room, where he washed his face and hands lightly. He dried himself with a monogramed towel then sprinkled Hermes, Eau de Doblis cologne on his hands and face and patted himself briskly. He closed his burning eyes briefly, inhaling the scintillating fragrance, and hedonistically drinking in the stirring aroma. Admiring his reflection in a gilt-edged mirror, he smoothed his hair into place and returned to his chambers. Out of habit, the Minister removed a carnation from a bouquet on an ornate *credenza* behind his desk and slipped it into the slit of his lapel. By the time his two distinguished guests entered the room, he was ready for them. He shook their hands and bowed with decorum and gestured to the chairs opposite him.

Colonel Cesare Cala, a quiet, soft-spoken man in his early fifties, wore a perennial look of concern etched into his light-skinned features. Apologetic, compassionate blue eyes, behind which lay a steel-like strength, had caused him to be dubbed the "Italian Lawrence" among his peers. Captain Franchina, the former Marshal of Montegatta who'd once been relieved of his uniform, firearms and dignity by that persuasive Salvatore, a man whose drooping moustache, like that of British Lord Kitchener, gave him a savage look, had been chosen by Colonel Cala to be his assistant, due to his fanatical absorption with the life of the bandit, Salvatore. After his disgraceful departure from Montegatta, Franchina had continued to compile data on Salvatore, determined some day to promote his enemy's downfall. Both officers had arrived to secure Minister Belasci's approval of their plans.

Belasci, blunt and to the point, asked, "What assures you of victory in capturing Salvatore when so many before you have failed?"

"Because we have a plan," replied Colonel Cala. "At the end of one year, when our plans come to fruition, I promise you Salvatore."

"One year, Colonel Cala?" Belasci's face fell in disappointment. "That won't do. That won't do at all. I demand swifter results. You hear? In a year a man could conquer a nation!" He was aghast.

"Nevertheless," replied the Colonel firmly. "I'll need a year. Consider that a firm assessment."

The Minister considered it all right. He didn't like it at all. He paced himself. "And you, Captain Franchina, you are certain this plan of Colonel Cala's will work?"

"I'm certain. I, personally, have reasons to pluck the talons from the claws of this haughty eagle, Excellency. We contend that to ensnare this rare bird, we must penetrate the weakest link in his organization."

"—And that is—?" asked Belasci fitting a cigarette into his gold holder.

"You're certain it's wise to speak in these chambers?" asked Captain Franchina, glancing about the room apprehensively. "Wasn't it recently that Red bugs were discovered in the American Embassy?"

Flushed with impatience, the Minister snapped. "Go on."

"We intend to zero in on Vincenzo de Montana."

Once over the initial shock, Belasci burst out in uncon-

763

trolled laughter as both officers exchanged uneasy glances and squirmed a bit in their seats.

"Vincenzo de Montana? *Va fa Napoli!* What crazy talk is this?" scoffed the Minister. "De Montana is Salvatore's blood brother—they are first cousins. Those two would die for each other. Even a street urchin will tell you that," he ridiculed. "Never has a bond existed between two men as strong as the one between these two." He gestured with his holder and the cigarette fell out. He picked it up and, giving the Colonel a look of long suffering, he reinserted the cigarette into the holder and painstakingly lit it.

Captain Franchina insisted. "Despite your objections, I contend that we should feed de Montana well, ply him with vintage wines, supply him with ample whores to sate his hedonistic nature, and gain his confidence by painting for him a landscape of power that stretches from one end of Sicily to the other. Then, we promise him total amnesty; that tempting bait you dangled for so long before Salvatore and never gave him, together with more money than he's dreamed about—well, I can't begin to tell you how cooperative he'll be. Do all this and I promise you a ready betrayer. De Montana will turn traitor if he believes he's saving mankind and his own neck at the same time."

Belasci, wondering at the Captain's sanity exploded. "You're crazy! You know that—crazy!" He addressed himself to Colonel Cala. "Where the hell did you find such a crazy man, eh? Those two are as inseparable as is a man to his own shadow. Now, speak intelligently or I'll appoint others whose brains aren't scrambled."

"You must trust me in this, Excellency," insisted Captain Franchina with the patience you'd extend a child. "In this unfolding melodrama, I know the actors very well. I know Salvatore better than he knows himself. He's a true genius—in his specialty, believe me. Because I admit to his genius doesn't make me laughable. I must admit to his unique talent, else I couldn't dissect him and know him as I do. By himself, Salvatore's invincible. He's already proven that. But no man is an island unto himself. There will always be a Cain to Abel, a Brutus to Julius Caesar."

"Yes, yes, and a Judas to Christ," snapped Belasci. "Get to the point."

"As I said, I've studied all Salvatore's men microscopically, and I maintain the only approachable man is Vincenzo de Montana, although he appears the least likely to betray his cousin."

The polished, sleek and tedious dandy, reeking of alcohol, sat back in his chair, affecting a tiresome manner of disagreement. He wagged a finger at Captain Franchina. "I'd hate to speculate what might happen if you're proven wrong in this matter." He had long since sobered entirely.

Displaying enough confidence for an army of men, Captain Franchina assured the Minister he was never more sure of anything in his life.

"Ah, then, you're personally acquainted with de Montana?"

"I don't recall ever speaking with him," he replied stroking his drooping moustache.

Wholly outraged, Belasci glared at the bent forward figure of the Colonel, whose gaze had remained hypnotically fixed on Captain Franchina throughout his speech. "How do you dare speak with so positive a manner and tell me nothing? It's an insult that you waste my time like this! Colonel, unless you come up with something more tangible . . . and, make no mistake, that's what you'll need to capture Salvatore! Tangible tanks! Tangible ammunition! Tangible manpower! Goddamnit! *Planes*, if you need them. High explosives to bomb him out of those insufferable goddamned mountains that cradle him to their bosom like some protective mother-suckling whore! *Misericordia!* What pressures I've endured over this one mortal. He is but one man. Why can't the *carabinieri*, the army, or the *polizia* make short order of him? Tell me why?" Belasci's performance of innocent outrage was superb, as he paced the floor, making dramatical gestures in the air.

Colonel Cala turned away from his assistant. In his inimitable, unassuming manner—which had often deceived his opponents who underestimated his genius and dedication and ultimately fallen prey to his resolute persistence—he fastened his complacent azure eyes on the Minister. "Why? Because he's more than a man, Excellency." He disengaged his glance and nodded to his assistant, in a silent gesture urging him to commence with his assessment of Vincenzo de Montana.

Captain Franchina took the cue. "De Montana led more than six hundred prisoners out of *Terra Diavolo* in the fall of 1943. Inspired by his able resourcefulness and leadership, the men, handicapped by severe malnutrition, debilitated health, and the irrevocable damages done to mind and body in some instances, escaped. Shortly after, Vincenzo, in a period of less than two hours, obliterated an entire convoy of German soldiers—hundreds of them. This former army corporal and deserter left Italy with over five hundred men under his command and returned miraculously to Sicily at a time when the surrounding waters were alive with Allied warships and soldiers."

The Minister shook his head regretfully as if he were in the company of dolts. "Despite all this—which I find irrelevant to the issue at hand, I tell you—de Montana basks in the glory of his cousin's shadow, to whom he's fiercely loyal. Don't you see? He's Salvatore's satellite." Belasci, in a fit of impatience, removed a rose from a vase on his desk, inhaled the fragrance and for a time began to twirl it absently in his hand, and sat down again.

"De Montana's a tough, determined young man," continued the FSB Captain, ignoring Belasci's chafing manner. "A highly sensual libertine, who drinks to excess, carouses with women, Vincenzo was publicly whipped by his cousin for disobeying orders to stop consorting with the village whore."

Belasci listened, his attention on the rose in his hand as he plucked each velvety petal, slowly, caressingly, then, placing each ruby slip in a pile on his desk, meticulously, as if he were constructing some marvelous edifice.

"De Montana is impressed by three things only," continued Franchina. "Freedom, money and women, in that order. His Achilles heel is his insufferable vanity. He thrives on flattery. Insulated by a thick and crusty ego, he displays his superior attitude; he is characterized by a provincial arrogance which sets him above his people. But he lacks the unique charisma of Salvatore to be an effective leader." Franchina rose to his feet and crossed to the window overlooking the busy courtyard below, looking down at the waiting limousines.

"You contend, Excellency, that de Montana basks in the glory of Salvatore. I don't deny this. Outwardly, this is true. Yet his very nature belies this adoration. He could turn into the most powerful enemy every contemplated by Salvatore." He turned back to the others in the room.

Minister Belasci studied Franchina, pausing momentarily in the denuding of the rose. He glanced at the Colonel, whose eyes were frozen on Franchina, and shrugged.

Captain Franchina continued, as he walked back and sat down again. "Where Salvatore is a loner, de Montana is not. When he's not in the company of his cousin, he is constantly surrounded by a circle of admirers."

Using the denuded rose for emphasis as he spoke, the Minister wagged him silent. "This farce has gone far enough. I disagree totally. De Montana is a *yes* man. He has no influence whatsoever. He's soft, spoiled and arrogant, in the same way all Sicilian boys are. True, he's a

766

prima donna. He dresses a bit gauche—like cinema stars." He waved his hands in the air about him impatiently. "He may be all the things you say, but, I've seen them together. I've spoken to them. I know people who know them intimately. Besides," blurted Belasci in annoyance, "he'd never betray Salvatore. You see, my uninformed friends, he'd never get the chance." He tossed the flower stem on his desk next to the pile of petals, suddenly revolted by it.

For the next fifteen minutes Captain Franchina argued with the Minister, sticking to his guns, as he broke down every facet of Vincenzo's personality and indicated where the weakness lay—and where his strength could be used against Salvatore. For every pro, Belasci rebutted with two cons; still Captain Franchina persisted. "Don't be taken in by what you term to be softness in the man, excellency. Just bear in mind that he led all those hopeless dying men out of prison, and destroyed a German convoy—"

"How many times must I be reminded of these *heroic deeds?*" snapped the Minister, resentment creeping into his voice.

"For as many times as I must repeat them to burn them into your memory. Look excellency, if you stroke this seemingly tame lion the wrong way—sparks will fly. Beneath his courteous, soft manner lie smoldering fires of a proud dignity stroked by an arrogant ferocity, ready to ignite if his free spirit is threatened."

The Captain paused to wet his lips with water. "I don't deny Salvatore is the keystone of this powerful cabal. No question. Even so, before he became so powerful, back in the early days of his career, I could have captured him, easily. Two weeks in Montegatta, and I had settled on a plan for his capture. In two years of his outlawry, I was the first *carabiniero* who got so far as to have one hundred warrants sworn out for him and his men. But, you see, I wasn't permitted free rein. On a night which might have proven successful, I was transferred out of the area. It was my contention then, and now, that Salvatore is protected by higher-ups in the government."

"Is that so?" Belasci affected to be amazed. He leaned forward, opened a humidor of slender imported cigars to his guests. They declined. Belasci selected one, and took his time lighting it. While he inhaled he studied Captain Franchina, burning his image into his mind. *Sonofabitch is more intelligent than I gave him credit for,* Belasci told himself. *But he knows nothing.* He graciously offered the officers a drink. Again they politely declined. Belasci

767

shrugged, removed another rose from a vase, and proceeded to play with it as he puffed delicately on the cigar held between his white teeth.

Both FSB officers watched this activity of Belasci's with rapt fascination, until the Colonel instructed Franchina to get on with it.

"I didn't mean to digress. We were discussing Salvatore's organization. Uncannily, Salvatore has chosen his subjects extremely well. Sometime in his young life, he learned the secret of men. You know—which duties would suit which man best. Take de Montana. Salvatore feeds his ego handsomely. He gave him equal title, wears the same silver star of valor—" Franchina reached into his portfolio and passed several glossy photos of both Salvatore and de Montana to the Minister.

"Study the photographs, Excellency. Notice how de Montana emulates his spectacular cousin. See—he even hooks his thumbs into his belt in the famous pose of Salvatore. The same corduroy jacket. Solid gold watch and diamond ring. Identical belt buckles—the Golden Eagle and Lion."

Consumed with interest, Belasci pointed out. "There are a few discrepancies that don't follow your theory. There's no photo of de Montana in Salvatore's belt buckle. What does that mean in your psychological evaluation?" He punctuated his words with the cigar.

"It means nothing except that Salvatore is total ego."

"Where's the dandified appearance in Salvatore's mode of dress?" He attempted to puncture holes in Franchina's theory.

"Since when does a king have to resort to superficial subterfuges? A king is king. People fear only the friends of kings, for by their association with power they develop deceitful facades to cover their own fears, and, therefore, can't be trusted. A look in the pages of history will prove my point. More men feared Cardinal Richelieu than they did the King of France."

"To hear your overtures, Captain, I get the feeling you envision Salvatore as a great heroic legend, one worthy of praise and glory and I can imagine how many hallelujahs—instead of the fate I've entrusted you two fine officers to administer him." Belasci's hatred and loathing was apparent.

Colonel Cala made his move. He removed his eyes from his assistance and leveled them on Belasci. "Don't you see, Excellency, that's the point." Salvatore *is* remarkable. The fact that he is *sui generis*—one of his kind—is precisely why no man has captured him. He's no cheap imitation, this man. Not the ordinary run-of-the-mill bandit. It takes more than strategy and military genius to capture a genius of Salvatore's calibre. If he were not so special, his legend couldn't have been furthered beyond a few raids. In five years, he's made no mistakes. He turns betrayals into successes."

"No mistakes, eh? What about Portella Della Rosa!" snapped Belasci.

"Ah, yes. Portella Della Rosa," replied the Colonel. "That was a mistake all right, Excellency. But, not Salvatore's."

Belasci and Cesare Cala locked eyes. They understood each other instantly. The Colonel spoke with carefully measured words, articulate and emphatic in a well-modulated voice. He placed his visored hat and gloves on the small table at his side and opened a box of English Ovals. He selected one, lit it, and slipped the box back into his jacket pocket. He puffed thoughtfully for several moments, then continued.

"Captain Franchina was brought to my attention due to his respected works on the psychology of the criminal mind. I read his published thesis, "Psychology of Criminal Genius" with great interest. When you commissioned me to head the FSB, I naturally wanted only the ablest and qualified men to work with me.

"Then, Excellency, when I learned he had compiled a dossier on Salvatore over the years, I knew my hunch was right. Let me assure you, this man is more qualified than I to bring about the demise of the great Salvatore." Cala paused. "You, above all, should know we aren't dealing with a common criminal. Weren't you associated with him once, Excellency? I believe you belonged to the Separatist Party? And later in the Partitionist's party, wasn't he commissioned as General of the Western Army? As I recall in reading the account, his troops suffered no losses—against the government forces?" Colonel Cala's eyes were fixed on the growing pile of rose petals on the Minister's desk.

Belasci's face tightened in a controlled rage. "Many of us were misguided in those early days of the war. What has all that to do with our present situation?"

"Only to make a point. I was in Yugoslavia in those days, so I can only reflect hearsay. To continue, without a formal education Salvatore has risen to incredible heights. Given a few advantages, he might very well have been sitting at the head of our government."

"Colonel Cala!" shouted Belasci. "I haven't requested a

memorial to the man! I've requested a funeral! If you think he is so all-fire god-like, perhaps I had better commission another officer to head these forces to supress banditry!" Such insufferable impertinence from these boors!

Colonel Cala raised his hands in a gesture of apology. "If you refuse to see Salvatore as he really is—and not what the papers mistake him to be, or what the Balladieers have immortalized him as—you'll never conquer him. If you view him as a lesser man than yourself or the Premier—or President, we are bound to lose. He'll never be captured. We may as well bury the FSB before it embarks on a hopeless mission."

Martino Belasci glared with marked hostility at these preening peacocks. His foot tapped out a nervous staccato under his desk, while his face screwed up in egotistic confusion. How insufferable! What indignities he had to endure by lesser men! To be told that a common outlaw—a lowly peasant—was as worthy a man as he was sufficient cause to have thrown both these glorified asses out on their rears. It was one thing to ensnare Salvatore, but not at the cost of his pride. But were they saying anything he didn't already know? Goddamnit! The curse of high office! Belasci poured himself a snifter of brandy; once again he pantomimed an offer to his guests. They refused.

"Whore of the devil!" he exploded. "I am committed to the FSB. If I don't follow through in this, the Reds will make sure I'm removed from office. They won't rest! They haven't let up on me. Bastards! All of them! Including de Aspanu! I must sink or swim under this jacket of responsibility they have buttoned on me. Very well, I'll see it through to the end. It's my ball game now. The important thing is to keep the goddamn Reds off my back, you hear?" He was finished with the flowers. He scooped them together and deposited all the petals into a waste container. "You see what this sad affair has done to me? I pick on these poor flowers. Forgive me. You were saying—"

"Only that when Salvatore is captured it will have been through the invaluable efforts of Captain Franchina's dedication. Nothing contributes to a victory more than knowing your opponents well. His dossier is the magic key that will unlock all doors to Salvatore."

"Hah," muttered Belasci, and drained his brandy glass.

Captain Franchina nodded to the Colonel and continued. "Beneath this display of outrageous vanity and puffed-up ego, de Montana fears that he has no courage at all. But in a crisis, he'll rise to the cause every time. Under great pressure, weighted by increased anxiety or even impatience, de Montana asserts himself and roars like a lion. Concentrate on him, and it shall be through him the others will fall. Through him we'll get them all including Salvatore. A limiting factor—to a small degree—is that he suffers from a tubercular infection in one lung. However, we can deal easily with such a man."

Two hours had passed swiftly. Time in which the FSB officers diagnosed the Salvatore affair with such theoretical expertise, Belasci capitulated. "Very well, *Colonnello*, you have my approval to pursue this operation in your own way. You've done your homework. You can expect full cooperation from any and all departments." Belasci paused a moment in reflection.

"You're certain you'll need a full year?" he asked with a pained expression on his face. "You've no idea what I'm suffering at the hands of this insufferable communist Senator de Casselli. They're breaking my balls—I tell you."

"Yes, you've taken a great deal of abuse. A lesser man would have collapsed long ago." Colonel Cala, at once compassionate, stood ready to depart.

"Then you understand my predicament? The pressure is not to be believed. *Managghia!* Too bad they didn't finish him off, at Portella," he blurted in an unguarded moment.

Both officers flushed with polite reserve and shuffled about on their feet uncomfortably. Catching their reaction through the beginning haze of the alcohol, he apologized in a blustery, ineffectual way. "Not meant literally, of course." His words were slurred.

"Of course," said the diplomatic Colonel. "Ah—yes, Excellency. One more thing. The Reds contend that you hired Salvatore's men as government partisans to fight communism. Is there any truth to this statement?"

"Certainly not! I don't deal with outlaws! Everyone knows how much that hotheaded Sicilian hates the communists! Here, take a look at this." He shoved a copy of Salvatore's letter to President Truman under the Colonel's nose. "I have every reason to believe he intrigues with the Americans, despite protestations to the contrary."

Colonel Cala's eyebrows raised subtly. "Do you have documented proof of this, Minister Belasci? Anything tangible we can sink our teeth into? What does Italian Intelligence report? Does the *Guardia* mention this in their files? You realize the implication if your assessment is correct?"

The Minister rose to his feet, and shut the file on the desk before him. He handed it to the Colonel. "It's all in the file. Have it photostated and return the original to me." He inflated his chest and with official decorum skirted past the questions.

"You understand I will accept no excuses this time. You will bring me the blood of Salvatore—or I will have yours. We understand each other?"

The officers nodded. "The blood of Salvatore—or ours," said Colonel Cala. They took their leave, leaving Minister Belasci to face himself.

Even though he headed the policing forces in the nation, his instinctive dislike of them was complete. "Bastards!" he mumbled. "Too fucking smart for their own good." He staggered slightly as he walked to the liquor cabinet, but he wasn't too inebriated to realize that Salvatore's death would give him a double-edged sword to continue to carve out his selfish ambitions. The thought provoked an internal flush of pleasure. Taking a fresh bottle of brandy from the liquor cabinet, he returned to his desk and poured himself an ample snort. It might turn out that these supercilious popinjays would demonstrate remarkable ability and end this nightmare of Salvatore once and for all, he told himself.

Seated again behind his desk, Belasci's eyes fell upon the photographs left behind by Captain Franchina. He lit another cigar and fanned at the smoky mist that obstructed his vision with a well manicured and jewelled hand.

"Too bad, you stupid bastard," he said aloud, addressing himself to the photo of Salvatore. "You could have gone to Giorgio's estate in Brazil and lived a splendid life. I hate losing you as a friend, but remember, it was you who chose this path—not I. You refused the role we created for you, and now you've become a danger to me. The game is over, *caro mio*. Just remember—you dealt the hand."

Belasci reached for the phone. "*Pronto. Pronto.*" He gave the operator a number and waited.

"*Caro mio?* How soon can you fly to Rome? I must see you. I have good news." Belasci laughed wickedly. "I miss you too." His smile dissolved. "What?"

He listened. "*What* portfolio?" As he listened his face went through a series of changes. "Calm down, Giorgio and tell me so I can understand. Salvatore's portfolio does *what?*" His hands shook visibly. "Fly up here immediately, and we'll talk when you arrive. No, don't worry. Things are under control. I'll call Don Barbarossa as soon as you ring off. *Ciao.*"

"*Che me c'e schiacciare le cazzi a Salvatore!*" he cursed aloud in a moment of black anger. "May the powers that be crush his balls!"

The very thought of what this portfolio might mean shook Belasci and the very core of the Mafia. When threatened in this meaningful manner, they had to protect themselves, forgetting that they were, to begin with, the malevolent and dishonored ones in this contest.

The Cold War between Salvatore and the Mafia, Government, and Church, having reached a momentary impasse, had geared down, waiting to accelerate the respective sides to victory.

BOOK VI

"Master! Master! Lend me a Horse. I must flee to Shangri-La."

"But, why? Why must you go? What frightens you?"

"Death just pointed her finger at me."

The Master confronted Death—who hovered near.

"Is this true?" he asked. "Why do you point to my servant?"

Death replied, "I merely pointed to him because I was surprised to see him here. You see, I have an appointment with him in Shangri-La."

—*Oriental Fable*

CHAPTER 57

Palermo, Sicily
August 29, 1949

The Palermo newspapers carried the following headlines
and story.

MARTINO BELASCI CALLS FOR
SUPPRESSION OF BANDITRY

*Colonel Cesare Cala, head of the FSB, has
mobilized an army of a new breed of carabinieri
who presently surround the hills of Montegatta
and surrounding villages searching for the bandit
Salvatore. Thousands of dedicated military police, concentrated in the outlaw's territory, conduct the largest manhunt in history.*

*The Office of Propaganda, under Minister
Belasci's orders, issued the following news bulletin to the international press:*

*"Minister Belasci approves the use of shock
troops and reconnaissance aircraft to be employed at Colonel Cala's discretion. A squadron
of Spitfires, plus two American-donated helicop-
ters and an additional contingent of special security officers, highly skilled in the use of
automatic weapons, have been dispatched to join
the anti-Salvatore army. Jeeps, armored vehicles,
and tons of ammunition have arrived at the out-
lying breastwork and surrounding fortifications
of Montegatta, sealing off thousands of bandits
from outside communication. Flame throwers
have burned every grotto and connecting cave in
the honeycombed mountains. It's impossible for
Salvatore to survive this heavy concentration of
manpower and ammunition. Momentarily Salvatore and his band of audacious renegades will be
smoked out of their mountain sanctuary."*

All this published before Colonel Cala had even arrived in Palermo! Such falsely blatant and unwanted pub-

licity angrily annoyed the military man of ethics and served to hinder the progress of this highly secretive officer who was used to more confidentiality in performing his work. Preferring total anonymity to the voluminous pack of contrived and laughably misleading information, Colonel Cala found his burdens had increased enormously when he arrived in Palermo, to find himself a laughing stock before he'd set foot on Sicilian soil.

When he learned that Minister Belasci had engaged in the concoction of a wide range of false and highly contrived information geared to deter the left-wing press from further embellishing on his former relationship to Salvatore, which included providing the FSB with the widest publicity coverage ever expended in a government effort, Colonel Cala was furious. He might have even turned around and returned to Rome, to tell Belasci what he could do with so outrageous a task, if he hadn't already been challenged by the festering situation he found in Palermo.

Not only had Colonel Cala's arrival been anticipated, but he soon learned his presence was grossly resented by the local law enforcement agencies. They should have been grateful for his intervention, if indeed the country wished to be rid of the incorrigible Salvatore. Colonel Cala, a slow, plodding man whose brilliant strategy was feared by his enemies, had much to learn, in the battle of wits about to take place. Salvatore was one thing, but, in his attempt to survive, the rivalry existing between *carabinieri* and the Security Police, both factions were about to drive him to the brink of madness and retard his progress on Sicilian soil.

Between the two law enforcement agencies there had always been an inbred hatred, a fierce jealousy that exceeds pure and simple rivalry. Trained meticulously under rigid military discipline, the *carabinieri* viewed the security police with enormous disdain and felt they had a comparatively soft time of it. Often the duties of the two bodies overlapped and the rivalry turned to pure unmasked hatred. Neither force was particularly welcome in Sicily; however, between the two, the security police were regarded as the cream of the police hirarchy. Extremely thorough, they were highly unprincipled and diabolically unscrupulous in their methods. Neither of the two agencies cooperated in the least with the FSB, much to the officer's disgust.

The arrival of Colonel Cala and Captain Franchina in Palermo, simultaneous with an oppressive North African *simoon* whipping up pulsating clouds of blinding dust accompanied by torrid, dry heat, didn't deter the FSB officers from asserting themselves. At the office of the Security police, their demand of all criminal records and a list of offenses with which Salvatore had been charged in his career met deaf ears. There were none, they were told.

They next tried the office of the *Carabineri* and met with the same bland replies; their probing questions incurred convenient lapses of memories.

It just wasn't possible that both factions could fail to produce the needed documents, concluded Colonel Cala, as he observed the goings-on and politely kept this lack of cooperation stored well in his memory bank. This was the first of many continuing complications which swelled the animosity and increased existing hostilities between the two existing police factions and the new interlopers, the FSB.

Forced to begin at point zero, the FSB's detailed and systematic probe into bandit activities in the province failed to provide the dramatic impact needed to string together a list of crimes that made sense or would hold up in a court of law. The FSB officers, incensed at the lack of cooperation and total disregard for their professionalism displayed by these uncouth Southerners, viewed both factions, and these ridiculous men, with comtempt and disgust.

"Now, you begin to see what I had to put up with, Colonel," Captain Franchina lamented bitterly. He wasn't as self contained as his superior officer and more often than not, he stated these people should be held in contempt for interfering in their progress.

"Listen, Captain," replied his superior. "We are going to be here at least a year. They'll get used to us before long, and one day, they'll open up. Meanwhile, when in Rome—"

Their next stop was the office of Chief Inspector D'Verde of the Security Police. Colonel Cala got straight to the point. "I wish to make a tour of Salvatore's territory."

"On such an intolerable day?" protested the large-framed Chief Inspector, sniffing at a menthol inhalator shoved into each nostril. He took two aspirins from a vial on his desk, chased them down with a glass of water and made his discomfort known to his guests. "Fighting a bout with the flue—nasty," he said.

"Would tomorrow, or the next day, afford a change for the better?" asked the Colonel, who found such people more intolerable than the weather.

Chief D'Verde lifted himself out of the chair with an

impatient scowl on his face and swaggered out of the room. He returned in moments with a look of long suffering on his craggy face, wiping sweat from his face with hasty movements. He reached for his jacket from a peg on the wall. This confrontation had just sent his blood pressure soaring and besides, he felt like hell. Of all times they could pick to arrive!

"It never rains but it pours, Colonel. Looks like you get your wish. We'll accompany a train of reinforcements to Bellolampo. Salvatore has just launched a successful attack on the *caserne* there. In addition he's vented his spleen in Castellamare, Borgetto and Alcalmo in retaliation for the incarceration of his mother again. "D'Verde, a man with the twitching and pulsating face of a perennial schemer, filed out of the office with the FSB officers behind him. Colonel Cala and his aide made no comment.

He joined the Chief Inspector in the rear seat of the Fiat, and Captain Franchina slipped in alongside the driver's seat just as the ruddy-faced driver jockeyed the car into second position in the troop train, leaving behind an aroma of burned rubber and a pasty-faced expression on the faces of his passengers.

At Bellolampo the FSB officers emerged from the auto and began to silently observe the damage done by the marauding bandits. In this shambles of an ancient military *caserne* standing among sun-scorched fields and silent desert cacti, nothing escaped Colonel Cala's scrutiny. He was introduced to Major Carrini. Captain Franchina hardly recognized the one-armed man wearing a patch over one eye. The battle scarred Major pointed out the mass damage done that morning when they came under attack.

"What's all this on the wall?" asked Colonel Cala, his attention drawn by the bullet-riddled message scrawled so expertly by *Sporcaccione*'s submachine gun in honor of young Pietro Gagliolo. "It spells out some message," added the FSB chief studying it. When the explanation came, he was incensed. "Have it repaired immediately," he ordered gruffly. "When I return tomorrow morning I expect to see a bare wall, not a monument to an outlaw! And do something about the rest of this mess," he commanded crisply gesturing to the litter and rumble strewn about as a result of the recent shoot out.

Colonel Cala left behind a pack of red-faced, sputtering, grumbling military police who had given him no guff only because his reputation had preceded him. The "Italian Lawrence?" With such a tag after his name they'd give him the benefit of the doubt.

En route to the barracks, Inspector D'Verde's condition having grown worse, was accompanied by coughing, sneezing and throat-clearing seizures. He complained of hot and cold chills, with little apology to his illustrious guests. In lieu of the man's obvious infirmity, Colonel Cala cut his visit short, stating tersely he'd visit Montegatta another day. He instructed their madcap driver to return to Palermo.

On the return trip, the FSB officer exchanged autos with several injured men. Because there had been no incident en route to the barracks, their car took the lead position as they manuevered the steep descent into the Conca D'Oro basin. At one point, as they approached a particulary rocky terrain, Inspector D'Verde, due to his rapidly increasing fever chills, requested the windows be closed—this despite the prostrating heat and increasing discomfort of his fellow passengers. His request was complied with.

And then it happened! There came a clatter of deafening explosions, one after another, bursting all around them. Bullets *zinged!* Bullets *pinged!* Bullets splattered all around them, In a thundering of unguided missiles, in the unexpected ambush! The car's driver swerved the wheel wildly; the car careened, skidding into a tailspin, hidden for a time by the clouds of dust erupting all around them. The second, third and fourth cars, carrying more than two dozen injured men, struck with grenades and bombs, exploded in the air as they rounded the last bend in the road. A carelessly hurled incendiary bomb struck the closed windows of the first car, bounced off the vehicle, and didn't explode until it had struck the boulders off the road, missing the officers completely. Due only to the fast reflexes of the quickwitted, daredevil driver, who accelerating the vehicle heavily, and shot the auto ahead, dodging both bullets and bombs, the FSB officers and the Police Inspector escaped with their lives.

As the bouncing, swerving auto shook rakishly from the continued impact of explosions in the nightmare of terror surrounding them, the driver, skillfully zig-zagging the auto, managed to speed away from the danger zone. All the others had been instantly killed.

High up on the crest of the mountain, Salvatore's men watched the near perfect ambush with keen disappointment on their faces. Miguel Scoletti, lowering his binoculars, cursed aloud in angry frustration. "Godamm the devil! How the hell could we have anticipated they'd change autos at Bellolampo!" The men watched the car containing their enemies disappear in clouds of dust.

The all-out war between Salvatore and the Forces to Suppress Banditry had commenced. It was war! Out-and-out war!

Colonel Cala's retaliation came the following week. Five hundred Montegattans, arrested, were transported immediately to the Island of Ustica, north of Sicily, to the penal colony, to allow Salvatore no attempt at rescuing them.

Salvatore countered by successfully attacking four of the anti-bandit headquarters, denuding them of all weapons and locking them in the local jails. In the next few weeks countless attempts were made upon the lives of both Colonel Cala and Captain Franchina; open bursts of machine gun fire came at them from behind thick trunked trees, huge boulders, and stone walls along rutted roads. In the shifting shadows of night came attempted assassinations. In other places where no camouflage sheltered a man there came repeated attempts. In all this time the FSB officers escaped them all. Franchina had suffered a mere scratch from a grazing bullet. Truly, the outlaws believed, these two snakes led charmed lives.

The civil war accelerated. Conditions grew deplorable. Salvatore's men could barely move about their territory with former ease. These new recruits, a new breed of *carabinieri*, proved incorruptible, and lacked the greedy, graft-filled consciousness demonstrated so keenly by their predecessors. Montegattans, greatly inconvenienced, were jailed without cause, their homes broken into and their property destroyed while police subjected them to illegal search and seizure. Their gardens were raided, food supplies stolen, all under the guise of confiscation. Nearly all the close relatives of Salvatore's men were imprisoned. Despite these intolerable afflictions, no one came forward to betray Salvatore. This in itself was remarkable, since the rewards offered by both the government and the newly empowered FSB were staggering.

In these hectic, trying times, a newcomer arrived on the scene, a man named "Satan's Ghost;" an imported, well-paid assassin, hired to exterminate Salvatore. The ironic twist to this situation was that "Satan's Ghost" resembled the former *carabiniero* Gucci enough to have been his identical twin. Thick-set, short, muscular and swarthy, he even wore the identical garb Gucci had trademarked; summer khakis, desert forage cap with neck flap, knee socks, and mountain boots. It was astounding how much alike they were, complete with hooked nose and owlish eyes.

"Satan's Ghost," a shy, introverted man, occupied a lone room at Bellolampo barracks, where Colonel Cala had kept him secreted, surrounded by an enviable collection of cloak-and-dagger weapons. A variety of unique one-shot weapons had originated in the OSS underground, but the one weapon he concentrated upon, which occupied most of his time, was a highly refined, deadly accurate, miniature machine gun designed by an expert at Belgium's *Fabrique Nationale des Armes de Guerre*, an exact replica of the Vigneron M-2, only miniaturized.

This unbelievable weapon, toylike in appearance, when properly employed could kill a dozen men in less time than it took the full-sized weapon to operate. It was incredible! Simply incredible.

"Satan's Ghost" would appear periodically wherever Salvatore was rumored to be. His attempts to stalk the bandit leader with his bulldog tenacity resulted in failure. These failures to nab Salvatore turned the Gucci lookalike into an even more determined assassin. Every spare moment was spent perusing Captain Franchina's thick file on the bandit, searching for some vulnerability in Salvatore's life where he might strike successfully. The more he read and learned, the more elusive became the Montegattan to this predator. Conversely, "Satan's Ghost" became more fiercely dedicated; his reputation was at stake.

Salvatore, never too far away from all the activity, observed many of the FSB goings-on without humor. Rumors of paid assassins weren't new to Tori. His spies, however, had thus far turned up no one and nothing to support these stories.

On September 3, 1949, Tori stood, undisguised and undetected, on the top of the Norman tower overlooking the piazza in his village, solemnly watching another massive arrest of his *paesani* and wondering how much more his people would endure the severe hardships inflicted upon them, before one or more of them broke and betrayed him. Loaded onto trucks like wild animals, pushed, shoved, and treated inhumanely, they were handcuffed and driven off for an immediate exodus to a penal colony.

One thing is certain, thought Tori, *the FSB know their business.* Colonel Cala had taken the time to know his enemy well. Very well, the time had come for Tori to take steps to end this fiasco.

On September 6, the following letter from Salvatore to his people appeared in the Palermo newspaper, *Lo Specchio:*

*I, Salvatore, hereby request an open plebiscite. I
leave it up to the people of Sicily if I should be
treated like a hero or an outlaw. I hereby
promise to abide by the electorate's decision. If
they consider me an enemy, I'll submit myself
immediately to the authorities. However, unless
this fight against me is called off and the release
of my mother and other people falsely accused is
effected, I shall spearhead a campaign of war
against the FSB, more devastating than the one I
fought against government forces two years ago.
If these atrocities continue there is nothing left
but to further this civil war.*

By order of Colonel Cesare Cala, this would be the last
open letter the press would publish on Salvatore's behalf.
On September 7, he enforced a restraining order against
every newspaper to close this platform of expression to
Salvatore. Was this Colonel Cala some tough cucumber?
The Sicilians waited with bated breath for the next developments to come.

On September 8, as dawn broke over the sleeping city
of Palermo, hundreds of Salvatore's workers had completed their handiwork, and by the time early risers
swarmed the streets, hundred upon hundreds of placards
greeted them from every available nook and cranny in
town. A direct appeal from Salvatore to his people
brought cheers and "bravo's" from their lips.

"Cala uses the tactics of a chess player," the placards
read. "He moves his pawns carefully, but he will never
capture this King! I am not eager to kill *carabinieri* or
anyone for that matter, but, those two bloodthirsty Pharisees, de Aspanu and Belasci, those self-seeking Christian
Democrats who have lied and cheated me and attempt to
use me as scapegoat, now hunt me as a wild beast. What
men are these who conceive death with each stroke of the
pen? They degrade their people through injustice and ineq-
uity. They dishonor the dead—how then, can they honor
the living? With such men running our government with
their foul, loathsome and corrupt practices, I swear to you,
my people, that I would die before I surrendered myself to
such base, underhanded and immoral men!

"FSB—be warned! *Carabinieri*—be warned! Leave the
territory of Salvatore! Go home to your families, desist in
your efforts against me, for I swear once more I shall not
end this war between us until my mother and my people

are set free!". The signature of Salvatore ended the communique.

That afternoon, the moment news reached him, Colonel Cala rode up and down the streets of Palermo surveying Salvatore's handiwork. Seated beside him in the offical police car, Captain Franchina assessed the effect of this brilliant coup. Both FSB officers were grim-faced and silent as they watched the hordes of people glued to the posters reading and cheering and shouting ecstatically, *"Viva Salvatore! Viva Salvatore!"*

Back in his office, Colonel Cala issued orders for the instant removal of all offensive posters, and the recruiting of a contingent force of auxilliary police, who along with the *squadistras* were to police Palermo around the clock and arrest anyone seen attempting to put up such posters. A new ordinance was enforced requiring a special permit by the FSB to display any posters.

The following day, the city was littered with graffiti elaborately scrawled: *"Long Live Salvatore!"*

Colonel Cala ordered it removed and doubled the guards throughout the city.

September 10. Eight *carabinieri*, held up at gunpoint in Montegatta, were relieved of their guns and ammunition. Tori explained his leniency when he permitted the men to go free. "You who are my enemies, I set free because you don't deserve to die. You all have families who need you. Knowing you are only following orders, I take only your weapons, and allow you to leave my province. I know all your faces, now. And I promise that if I see you in Montegatta again. I shall show you no mercy." He glanced significantly at their identity cards as if committing them to memory, and slipped them into his breast pocket for further acknowledgement, with sufficient menace in his eyes to make them believe him.

Newspapers printed such newsworthy happenings. Public sentiment arose in favor of Salvatore. Colonel Cala's efforts to prohibit such newspaper coverage was vehemently opposed. They could understand his trying to ban Salvatore's letters, but they refused to conform to his stifling the news.

September 12: An urgent communique from Minister Belasci to Colonel Cala "Suppress that impudent outlaw immediately. I will accept no excuses. I must have something to appease the Premier." Confirm, M. Belasci.

September 13: Memo from FSB to Minister Belasci: "My word still stands. One year from the date we began. You can count on that." Colonel Cala.

September 30, 1949: The following article appeared in *Lo Specchio*, the Palermo newspaper, and was forwarded to Minister Belasci "FSB announces the capture of thirty members of Salvatore's band. A crippling of forces destroyed the outlaw's defenses. A tough fight ensued. All were captured alive, due to the brave, undaunted efforts of the FSB. Forty hand guns, concealed grenades, and an arsenal of heavy weapons were confiscated. Acting on a tip by FSB spies who've infiltrated Salvatore's camp, they were all caught off guard."

The truth behind this announcement was: three men apprehended were fringe area outlaws who had never been a part of Salvatore's group. One man carried a snout-nosed carbine, the others had none.)

October 7, 1949: A newspaper story. "Two bandits were instantly killed in a FSB planned ambush and eight of Salvatore's most valuable men, jailed instantly, were sent to Viterbo to await trial for the Portella Massacre."

(There was no truth to this story. It was simply a plant by FSB propagandists, a complete fabrication.)

October 14, 1949: Another newspaper story: "Amid the wind whipped rain of an early storm, indefatigable FSB officers and *carabinieri* sloshed about the mud and courageously battled twelve of Salvatore's key men to emerge victorious. They caught rare prizes when they nabbed Dominic Lamantia and Ross Rizzuto. The names of the eleven remaining men, key figures in the rapidly diminishing band of renegades, have been withheld at the request of the bandits, who fear reprisal. Under the able direction of Captain Giovanni Franchina, an arch enemy of Salvatore's who has sworn to capture the outlaw, his anti-bandit squads broke into and confiscated an arsenal of weapons, rifles, and heavy duty artillery, enough to keep an army at bay for a year."

(The truth of this statement: Six *carabinieri* accosted an old peasant en route to his house carrying two concealed weapons, *lupara*, in his cart. Coincidentally, as often happens in Sicily, many people share the same name. The old peasant's name was Dominic Lamantia—no relation to the famed outlaw member of Salvatore's Inner Circle. The old man attempted to explain, his wife's maiden name was Rosa Rizzuto. . . .)

November, 13, 1949: Another Newspaper story: "Four bandits attack police in a double ambush under a hail of pistol and rifle fire on a Montegatta road. Courageously inflamed over the death of six comrades, Officer Brunelli escaped the burning auto by jumping into a nearby ditch,

786

where he hastily reassembled an overturned machine gun and opened fire, killing all four men. Officer Brunelli will be awarded a special medal for his bravery."

(The truth: All reports concluded this actually happened as reported—except that the bandits captured were *not* members of Salvatore's invincible warriors.)

December 1, 1949: Another news item: "Antonio Gagliolo, *avvocato* for a family of bandit members and, distant cousin to Giovanni ("Uccidato") Gagliolo, was arrested by the FSB as an accomplice, charged with aiding and abetting the outlaws. Highly incensed at the treatment accorded a member of the court, Gagliolo has called for a general strike of all lawyers to protest this travesty of justice. "A lawyer-client relationship, must not be attacked by unlawful procedures!" insisted Antonio Gagliolo. "It is sacrosanct, as inviolable as the relationship between man and priest in the confessional! Does the FSB set itself up higher than the Ministers of Justice?"

These incredible stories multiplied. Fact, difficult to sort from fiction, became totally swollen with distortions and half-truths and served only to instill the people with more hostility towards the FSB. However, one thing was factual. The Forces to Supress Banditry grew increasingly troubled. Five months had passed, and the enigma, Salvatore, had remained just that—an enigma to his enemies.

The war between Salvatore and the Forces to Suppress Banditry entered its most violent phase in the last months of 1949. Despite a number of successful arrests, Colonel Cala found himself no closer to capturing Salvatore than they'd been at the outset of the campaign. On the other hand, Salvatore had been equally successful in committing daring holdups, in kidnapping for high ransoms, and in the utter demolition of *carabinieri* barracks. In addition he had found many willing and loyal new recruits to join his rapidly fluctuating inner and outer circle of men. Constant ambushes took the police off guard and erased their existence in some areas. Clashes with the *carabinieri* continued. More troops arrived daily to replace the dead and injured.

There was no end to the false reports emanating from Belasci's office declaring the amazing headway made by the FSB. The laughable disproportion between the opposing forces was a matter of great amusement to Salvatore and his men. Opposing three thousand, well armed soldiers, Salvatore's real army never exceeded fifty in these last months. According to propaganda, the only weapon not employed against Salvatore had been the atom bomb!

Salvatore's army had never been organized like a battallion of men who could stand abreast of each other and be counted off. Once when Colonel Cala asked Captain Franchina, "How many men are in Salvatore's army?" Looking down from the slopes of a mountain, Captain Franchina with a wide sweeping gesture of his hand, stated bitterly, "Every man, woman and child down there in the valley is in Salvatore's army!" He was right. Salvatore's army consisted of the mass of peasants across two plains in western Sicily, who on a given signal would lay down their work and flock to Salvatore's side. They mobilized whenever needed. Many were paid on a regular basis from the ransoms he collected; some received specific sums for special jobs performed, while others were given gratuities and benefited handsomely from his generous redistribution of wealth. Never did Salvatore mobilize to the swollen numbers of the Partitionist Army again, but these people became an integral part of his defense.

From the moment the Mafia withdrew its support, everything changed for Salvatore. Even the elaborate spy system for which he had paid handsomely was withdrawn, and no longer became available to him. Many of his men, who felt the lack of protection, declared to Tori that they'd had enough, and insisted upon emigrating immediately. Saddened by their decision, Tori, nonetheless understood. It was then arranged for several of his men to emigrate to North Africa through the combined efforts of Inspector D' Verde.

In the sudden shifting of alliances that had come about in these last months, many people wondered why the Mafia had taken so long to exact their vengeance upon Salvatore for the deaths of those five *mafiosi*. Others were piqued with insatiable curiosity as to what had delayed Salvatore's retaliation upon the hierarchy of the Mafia. Both sides felt as if they sat on a time bomb, ready to explode at any moment. But Salvatore, despite the apparent setbacks visited upon him, learned the most valuable of lessons—that of patiently waiting and watching.

In the final months of 1949, of the nearly 75 men who had left for North Africa, 20, betrayed by the Mafia, were caught and extradited back to Sicily, where they were quickly whisked away to Viterbo to await trial. There was no doubt that, in what promised to be the scandal of the century, the Portella Della Rosa Massacre, blown up beyond proportions by communists, would be the instrument through which the Reds intended to pry Belasci out of office.

Meanwhile, Salvatore, against all predictable odds, continued to exceed all bounds of popularity. Heralded throughout the globe as the lone adversary of Italian communism, he was more in demand for press interviews than at any other time in his amazing young life. The Reds hated him as passionately as the world championed him. In all probability, the King of Montegatta could have continued to oppose the FSB and anyone else Belasci might dispatch to drain his blood for as long as he desired to oppose them.

But, Salvatore was growing weary. It didn't placate him or salve his ego in the least to know he couldn't be captured. His conscience ate away at him and eroded his guts of late, and he began to feel the weight of the daily hardships, the welter of inconvenience, and the brutality inflicted upon his people. (Many were to later testify that they'd sustained severe injuries resulting from the third degree, the *bastinada,* and the cruel punishment they'd received for the alleged offenses for which they'd been unjustly accused.)

The rearrest of Antigone Salvatore and her deportation to the penal colony on the Island of Ustica was what crumbled Tori's strength and resolve. His inability to negotiate for her release sparked the inner deterioration of his hopes. She had paid him no heed when he had repeatedly begged his mother to leave Sicily. Now, her incarceration, and the growing reality of the hardships inflicted upon his people, ate away at him like a spreading cancer, causing him to reassess his position. When he did, Tori came to many startling discoveries and conclusions.

It became painfully clear to him what the FSB intended, when, after so many months, they had come nowhere near capturing him. Obviously they couldn't defeat him at his own game. Despite their obvious expenditures of men and ammunition, the FSB with their anti-bandit squads, stood no chance of besting him at guerrilla warfare. Ignorant of the principles of ambush and guerrilla tactics, they took means to divert attention from this fact by keeping up a sham on the fighting front, while their real tools of destruction chipped away at Tori's people—and his mother.

"Bastards!" he cursed to Vincenzo one day. "Cala has taken time to know me well, and has aimed his darts at my most vulnerable spots. Their only hope to get me is through a betrayal. Before they get to any of my men, I shall beat them at their game. I'm not Sicilian for nothing!" he declared hotly.

Tori spoke to no one, not even to Vincenzo, of the

plans formulating in his mind. Soon, through the cooperation of the new Mafia, there commenced a series of clandestine meetings; a going and coming of various VIPs in the Mafia network, government officials and secret police who traveled to Rome and back negotiating on his behalf for the release of his mother and other innocent villagers from prison. Huge sums of money were negotiated as rewards for the efforts expended by all concerned, in exchange for Salvatore's promise to exile himself from Sicily.

By the end of 1949 it became apparent to the general public that the countless feats attributed to either side of the warring factions would have no actual bearing on what would ultimately decide the future of this contest between the FSB and Salvatore. All sides, busily engaged in a snake dance of surreptitious intrigue, had caused a spiral of fantasy and conjecture as to the final outcome of this pandemic controversy that had rocked a nation and tickled the fancy of the people.

However, none of the countless intrigues embarked upon were as complicated and as far-fetched as the dedicated melodrama, fraught with total disorder, that Captain Franchina strove to bring to fruition.

CHAPTER 58

"*Campamo cente anni!*" said Dominic Lamantia raising his wine glass in a toast. "Pray we all live to a hundred years." His bloodshot eyes were tell-tale of a long drinking spree.

Inside the overcrowded *trattoria* Nunzio's *Birreria* in Palermo, seated at dinner, the men raised their glasses and exclaimed almost in unison. "*Si cento anni.*" They drank the Valpolicella and contentedly inhaled the exquisite aromas of the food being served to them. Vincenzo de Montana smacked his lips together at the sight of the baked, stuffed *rigatoni* casserole heaped with gooey *mozzarella* and *marinara* sauce placed before him. The others, Marco and Fidelio Genovese, made up the foursome. They all began to make short order of their food as they called, "*Buon pranzo.*"

Lamantia, his tongue loosened by wine prattled on, "I've stored up a bundle in my gut to talk about."

Lorenzo, their waiter, approached Vincenzo with a bucket of shaved ice and a magnum of champagne. "*Signore* de Montana," he addressed himself to Vincenzo. "Compliments of *Capitano* Giovanni Franchina," he said, grinning.

With a forced nonchalance the men felt for the security of their weapons. They exchanged meaningful glances under heavily lidded eyes. Vincenzo, ill at ease, turned his suspicious eyes on the room of crowded people, peering through the smoke filled, dimly-lit *trattoria,* searching for a face that vaguely resembled the FSB officer. "What insanity is this?" he muttered to his companions. To Lorenzo, he said, "You must be joking. What *Capitano* Franchina, eh? Why does he send me *sciampagna*?" His face had reddened. His companions stiffening noticeably stared stonily at him.

Lifting his voice above the sounds of mandolins and guitars, Lorenzo tactfully told the bandits, "It's for all of you, *Signore*."

Vincenzo relaxed and sighing heavily, understood the gesture less. "Where is this Franchina?"

The waiter pointed to a table a section away from them and they all turned in a body to glance in the direction he indicated. However, they couldn't make out the man's features in the shadowy room.

"Return the *sciampagna* to the *porco cane*," instructed Vincenzo sourly. "Tell him de Montana and his companions do not drink the wine of a sworn enemy." He made a sweeping gesture with the back of his hands to remove the offending wine from their sight. They resumed eating with undisguised gusto.

Distressed, Lorenzo scurried back to Capt. Franchina's table with the champagne and the message. Over the waiter's head, Captain Franchina watched as the bandits laughed animatedly. The FSB officer impassively scribbled a note and instructed the waiter to take it to Vincenzo de Montana.

Vincenzo removed the napkin from his vest with a flourish, wiped his lips, and with dramatic overtones read the message to them:

"The *Capitano* says, '*We may be enemies, but, it doesn't preclude my admiration for four brave men. I would enjoy speaking with you. I promise I am not on duty. In no way will I endeavor to entrap you. Besides, what can one* porco

791

cane *do to four courageous men of Salvatore's Inner Circle?'* "

Dominic Lamantia laughed the loudest. Glints of wickedness shone in his green jade eyes. "What harm would it do to talk with him, eh? We haven't had much fun of late. What do you say—eh?" He patted the bulge under his jacket, significantly.

Vincenzo exploded. "Are you crazy?" He glanced at the others for approval.

"Why not?" asked Marco Genovese, his blue eyes full of bedevilment. "Lamantia's right. We get little opportunity to laugh these days. What harm can it do? Tori intrigues with those *mafiosi* and security police; why can't we do a little intriguing ourselves?"

"He may have something to tell us," suggested Fidelio.

Vincenzo was outnumbered.

In the remarkable and highly unusual political climate which existed in Sicily at the time, opposing forces were permitted to enjoy *detente* with law enforcement officers at odd times of the day and night. At a time when hostilities were at their apex, the FSB, under strict orders from the *Mafia,* confined all aggression and/or heroics to the battlefield. Promptly at 6 P.M. each day, in an act reminiscent of when knighthood was in flower, hostilities ceased. It wasn't unusual to behold opposing forces dining in the same restaurant or attending some social function together, if the purpose suited them. Of course, they all took the usual precautions in the event of possible treachery.

Captain Franchina carried the champagne in a nest of ice to their table, personally. After a few awkward moments in which both sides were uncomfortable, he put them at ease by saying to Vincenzo, "You're dè Montana." He stretched his arm out in a friendly gesture.

Reluctantly, Vincenzo shook hands with him.

"And you're Dominic Lamantia," he addressed the handsome, cynical outlaw. Lamantia expressed only mild surprise.

"—And you," he said to the last two "are the Genovese brothers." Franchina smiled amiably. "Don't tell me—I'll tell you." He gazed into the dark compelling eyes of the eldest. "You are Fidelio. And that leaves only Marco—the youngest, no?"

"Bravo!" said Vincenzo, clapping his hands at the pace of a funeral dirge. The Genovese brothers weren't elated at the instant recognition. Vincenzo indicated to the waiter to bring another chair.

"Aren't you concerned with your reputation? To be seen

in the company of Salvatore's men might give others the wrong idea," began Vincenzo, controlling his obvious dislike for both the man and the situation in which they found themselves.

"Because we are enemies on the battlefield doesn't mean I don't respect your heroics and brilliant strategy of your remarkable leader."

"You defend your position with exquisite finesse, *Capitano*," said Vincenzo, uncomfortable at the man's tone of voice and his compliments. They were on guard every moment.

"*Allora*, if you think so much of us, perhaps you can encourage your FSB's to leave Sicily," suggested Lamantia teasingly. "You know you don't stand a chance against the skill of Salvatore."

"You'd like that—wouldn't you?" laughed Franchina taking no outward offense at the barbs hurled at him. "But, alas, *amico*, to ensnare the great white eagle one must first get close enough—"

"Perhaps if you, once, sent manly men to fight, instead of snot-nosed simpletons you'd stand a chance," grinned Lamantia.

Captain Franchina, representing the establishment, and Lamantia representing lifelong oppression by such men, clashed immediately, while playing the game in which Captain Franchina knew all the rules. He accepted the brunt of jokes hurled upon him with constrained, but good humor, knowing well the spirit of youth, accompanied by the mellowness of wine, would ultimately lower inhibitions. He wanted to disarm them.

"To catch an eagle one doesn't parade with a military band, to the crashing roar of cymbals and the beating of a bass drum," temporized Fidelio Genovese, a master in the art of intrigue.

"I agree wholeheartedly, Genovese," responded the FSB Captain. "But that nonsense was none of our doing. Like you, Colonel Cala and I take orders. If the Minister of the Interior orders a certain course of action, we must humbly obey. We are soldiers just as you are."

The outlaws relaxed. They boasted of victories and ridiculed the bumbling tactics of the *carabinieri*. Capt. Franchina countered by playing up his victories, careful not to overstep the boundaries where personal effrontery and scathing insults might interfere with the relations he attempted to cement with them. It was a dangerous mission upon which he embarked. In the past his own ego had been a stumbling block in this type of encounter. He fought valiantly to refrain from putting Lamantia in his place. Soon the four gentlemen outlaws were turning to putty in his hands. He drew them out with subtle and unobtrusive praise, lauding their accomplishments.

"I would have never taken you for Salvatore's men, if I didn't know in advance who you were. You make a handsome foursome."

"You high and mighty Italians have always considered Sicilians mere animals—haven't you? Take another look, *Capitano*, we have two eyes, two ears, a nose and mouth like you. We even relieve ourselves as you do. We get indigestion and expel gas with as equal ease as you Italians." Vincenzo paused, then added, "If you cut us—we bleed. If shot, we feel the bullets' sting." He leaned back in his chair and flung one arm over the back of it, indolently.

At that moment, Captain Franchina caught sight of the solid gold belt buckle on his belt. He leaned in closer and asked confidentially, "Tell me, which one are you? The eagle or the lion?"

"Now why do I get the feeling that you already know?" said Vincenzo, patting the belt buckle. He grinned easily, to mask a deep-seated annoyance.

Franchina didn't press. He laughed with Vincenzo. "Too bad we're on opposite sides, my friends. I'd give anything to have such loyal men working for me."

"Work for the FSB?" Marco Genovese expressed his contempt. "I'd rather be dead first. Your men are far more corrupt. Besides they stink worse than us!"

"That depends by which barometer you measure the fact?"

Lamantia, who grew more surly by the moment, muttered, "Mother rapers! All of them! Incestuous bastards! Tell me, Franchina, is it true all Italians rape their mothers and sisters?" He'd never forgiven the *carabinieri* for the fate of his family. His bloodshot eyes glared testily at the Captain.

Vincenzo and Fidelio exchanged tense glances. Lamantia, having imbibed too heavily was in no mood to accept appeasement.

"Lamantia's a prodigious reader, *Capitano*," said Fidelio, slapping his friend's shoulders, trying to get a smile from him.

Captain Franchina, his face a fiery scarlet, sipped his champagne with a forced indifference, ignoring, for the moment, the impudent *contadino's* insults.

"Perhaps you're right," he said easily. "I understand the

Romans picked up many delightful habits from you savage Sicilians in the days they visited your shores as a vacation-land." He nonchalantly poured more champagne from the bottle filling all the glasses.

Vincenzo placed a restraining hand on Lamantia's arm when he lurched towards the FSB officer. Grateful that Bastiano Terranova had chosen that moment to arrive, he called out, "Ah—Terranova! Just in time to drink with us."

Terranova smiled to his friends. At the sight of Captain Franchina, he stiffened imperceptibly. Behind his bland expression, his mind roiled suspiciously. What would Salvatore have said to witness this *tete a tete?* he wondered.

Recognition became an instant wedge of animosity between Terranova and Captain Franchina. As if on cue, the FSB officer excused himself gracefully. He had wanted to establish an easy relationship with Vincenzo, one that would further the conviviality of the occasion at a future date and guarantee after he left that Vincenzo would say of him—*that Franchina is not a bad sort after all.* But in the presence of the double agent, he felt stifled.

"It's been a pleasure speaking with such fine men." He glanced at Lamantia. "No offense meant, young man, it's all in good fun." He prepared to depart.

"Fine men?" Marco laughed. "Can we quote you on such keen powers of observation?" he teased.

"Perhaps we shall all have the pleasure of meeting socially again, before the final curtain of this drama—no?" He bowed stiffly and exited.

"Thanks for the champagne," called Vincenzo after him. "*Allora,* the best men shall win—no?"

"That's the spirit, de Montana. A real civilized attitude!" He waved as he returned to his table.

Lamantia made an obscene gesture behind his back and scowling darkly muttered, "Cocksucker! That pig was weaned on his father's cock! I don't trust him!"

"He's not a bad sort after all," muttered Vincenzo, just as Franchina had predicted he would.

Back at his table, Captain Franchina observed them, thinking, *Damn! What I'd give to eavesdrop on that conversation.* He sipped his coffee.

"What was that snake doing here talking with you?" asked Terranova suspiciously. "He's not to be trusted." His green eyes were narrowed slits.

"If anyone should know, it's you," muttered Lamantia.

"What the hell's that supposed to mean—eh? Salvatore

chose this job as a double agent for me. You think I like it?" he glowered angrily.

"You could always quit!" Lamantia instinctively disliked anyone who wore two or more faces.

"*Va! Va!*" shouted Vincenzo. "Cut this nonsense. Fighting among ourselves isn't helping us!" He rose, and shut the double doors to the alcove.

"Don't worry about Franchina," said Fidelio. "We told him nothing. You forget we're Sicilians." He unwrapped the foil from a cigar, bit off the end, and lit it. "What do you say we get down to business?" He turned to Vincenzo who propped his feet up on an empty chair, much in the manner of Salvatore.

"For a long time, now, we've been disenchanted with Tori," began Fidelio, the most malcontent of all. "Daily the risks increase. We are kept too much in the dark. The antibandit squads multiply, and Salvatore isn't in the least affected."

"We feel we've reached the end of our journey," said Marco, his eyes avoiding contact with Vincenzo. "We don't appreciate the indiscriminate manner in which Tori changes the tide to suit his whims. In the past we faced starvation, fought for survival—even sanctioned war against the *carabinieri*, the communists. . . . but war against the *Mafia?* It's insane. You know it. We know it. Only Salvatore doesn't seem to agree."

"Very well, he attacks Belasci, the Premier, the Cardinal—even the Archbishop! *Mah—Porco Dio*—the *Mafia?*" Lamantia, sobering sensibly, picked his teeth with a toothpick. "And we're caught in the middle."

"Too many broken promises," insisted Marco, as he broke the seal on a package of Camels. "The other day, Fidelio and I were offered jobs in Naples with Luciano. We're foolish to remain here and be at odds with the only men who can help us. The young bloods talk about profits in narcotics that make our heads spin. They could use men like us."

"What makes you sure it isn't a trap to lure you away from Salvatore, so they can betray you and clap you into prison?" queried Vincenzo. "Think, *amici*, Lucky Luciano and Don Barbarossa are as thick as minestrone! I don't ask from where the offer came, *mah*, give it plenty of thought before you accept, *capeeshi?* As for me, I prefer taking my chances with Tori."

"He still trusts the same men who've betrayed him so many times in the past. He is a fool! He executes spies and double dealing vipers! Why hasn't he executed those *schifosi—mafiosi*, like we did Don Florio and Don de Matteis and the others?" Fidelio spat out the tiny tobacco fragments that clung to his lips. "Word's around that something peculiar goes on between him and that Godfather of his. You must know something, Vincenzo."

"I know nothing—and that's straight," replied Vincenzo quietly.

"You admit there *is* something, then?"

Lamantia prodded Terranova. "What about you Casanova? What does that crazy head of yours say about Barbarossa and Salvatore?"

"About what?" Terranova blew on his espresso to cool it.

"About what? Oh, boy, are you some stupid peasant. Phew! You know what, goddammit! Are you always going to be a man who lives for his purse and his projectile?"

"Of course. You think I'm crazy? What else is there? I leave the intrigue to you."

"No, no, no, no,!" exploded Fidelio wagging his hands animatedly. "You aren't gonna get away with that. You know more than you're telling us. *Allora,* give us some straight answers—or to hell with you!"

"Listen," protested the double agent. "Don't try to peel back my skin in hopes you can arouse me. The *capomafia* is who he is, the only real *pezzonovante* in the land. How do I know why Salvatore doesn't kill him? It's not my affair. Why the fuck don't you make things easy, eh? Ask Tori."

Terranova's unique position with Salvatore, the security police and even at times with the *carabinieri* permitted him the freedom to travel within the confines of all policing factions with a modicum of ease and still leave him time to engage in his sexual promiscuities. In his line of duty, he siphoned off to the police exactly what Tori wished him to reveal and vice versa. His redeeming qualities, however dangerous was his position, were his cold-blooded attitude, icy detachment and objectivity coupled with his crafty, ingenious methods of compelling Tori's enemies to wholeheartedly believe in him. Deeply loyal as he was to Tori, the bandit leader's trust in Terranova as a necessity was greatly limited. On this night, he was exasperated as he addressed himself to the others.

"Listen," he said confidentially. "You blockheads should be cautious in dealing with that *birbante,* Franchina. Words around that he's perfecting some devious plan to nab Salvatore through the betrayal of one or two of his men." Terranova instantly became the center of attention.

797

The men were dumbstruck. "Who? Who'd betray Salvatore?" asked Fidelio Genovese. "Who?"

"No one knows yet at whom Franchina aims his seduction." The double agent sipped his espresso.

"Bah! It's only talk," snorted Fidelio. He sipped his *creme de menthe frappe* with gusto. "*Allora* lets get back to the important issue. I've openly disagreed with Tori. He still refuses to take us into his confidence. We must assert ourselves. Either we have a voice in all future decisions or we leave him." He picked up a cookie.

"I agree," said Lamantia.

"Me, too," agreed Marco.

"Salvatore knows what he's doing," insisted Terranova, glowering.

Marco's blue eyes widened in astonishment. "How can you say such an insipid thing? First, the Separatists fucked us good. The Partitionists seduced him and raped the rest of us. We got *cazzu* from the Christian Democrats—and his own Godfather strips him of his balls! I won't mention the utter disrepute we've endured from the Portella Della Rosa fiasco! We should have taken all we could and run the hell out of Sicily."

Lamantia spat venomously, as he tried to remove a slither of tobacco from his lips. "Now, that ludicrous cream puff, Belasci, that *cornuttu* who loves the milk of men, makes overtones. 'Wait until I become Premier,' he tells Tori. 'I'll pardon you all!' His eyes, the color of green fire, glowed like gemstones. "Hah! By then, we'll all be dead!" he snorted angrily. "—And buried six feet under."

"Believe me," interjected Fidelio. "None of them can be trusted. *Brutti fittusi maladetti!* Dirty, filthy malevolent scum! Now, Tori intrigues with the young blood *mafiosi* who say they'll back him to the end. What the fuck kind of Sicilian is Tori that he doesn't know that blood is thicker than water?"

"That Belasci's a real *citrollo!*" exploded Vincenzo. He's behind the granting of licenses to Luciano so that drug production here can be on a legal basis. If you join with this Lucky Luciano, this Don Salvatore, you'll get yourself into the same pot of boiling oil, *compare.*"

"Belasci is in with Luciano too? *Butana u' diaoro!* Is there nothing sacrosanct!" Fidelio glanced at Terranova for confirmation. "Is it true?"

"About Belasci? "The other nodded. "That's the word in upper circles."

A silence fell upon the men for several moments.

"If only Tori would stop clinging to that idealistic non-

798

sense of amnesty!" sneered Lamantia. "You know what we'll get—" He clasped the inner elbow of one arm with his free hand and made a loud smacking sound. "*Cazzu!* We'll get *cazzu!* They'll murder us!"

"There'll be no pardons for us," said Fidelio prophetically.

"Swallow your tongue!" snapped Terranova. "You don't know what's going on. Haven't you learned anything from your years with Salvatore? Think positive!" he encouraged the others.

"You know what, Terranova? If your brain wasn't buried between your loins, you'd be pretty smart. Wake up to what's happening! If we had any sense, we'd kidnap millionaires and *keep* the ransoms, instead of redistributing the wealth to the poor as our generous leader has done, then, get the hell out of Sicily and live like royalty the rest of our lives!" said Fidelio Genovese. "Marco was right, all along."

More silence hovered over them, distilling Vincenzo's indignation. Throwing caution to the winds, he ignored the warning look from Terranova, and spoke up.

"It may look like the sky's falling, what with these lice, the FSB crawling around our lands. These fucking mercenaries must make noise to appease those soft bastards in Rome. Vital negotiations are under way. Soon something big will break. Tori knows how you feel. But he cannot sacrifice his ideals for your *and* accept the consequences if tragedy befalls us. Soon the trial begins at Viterbo. The newspapers scream, 'Salvatore and his men are innocent!' Yet, someone in power tries to convict us. Look what the Mafia has done to those of us who chose to leave Sicily! Betrayed, they were returned here to rot in jail where they'll encounter more betrayals in Viterbo. I for one prefer taking my chances with Tori."

"I see Tori's fever has infected you, *caro mio*," said Lamantia sadly. "How much longer before a *paesano*, tempted by the large reward offered for us, betrays us, eh?"

"And I wouldn't blame them," added Marco. The rewards increase daily. *Managghia*, even I'd turn myself in if they'd pay me what they offer for my head."

No one laughed. Lamantia pressed. "Things change too rapidly, even if they're only playing games until Belasci and Tori come to terms. Bastards! Every day more *paesani* die, and more are imprisoned just so the FSB can save face. It's too dangerous a game they play!"

"Since when have you been intimidated by danger?"

scoffed Vincenzo, nudging him playfully in the ribs in an effort to dispel his irritation. It didn't work. He turned to the others and crossed his fingers. "Salvatore is like this with D'Verde. For nearly a month he's been in process of securing our exiles to Brazil. His portfolio gave him excellent bargaining power. The idea is—we leave Sicily well-cushioned financially. Who knows what we find in a strange land? When Belasci becomes Premier, our amnesty is guaranteed. With unconditional pardons, we come home as heroes. Be patient. Nothing is decided in a night. Tori asks no one to stay here with him. If you choose to leave, he'll do all in his power to help you. But, *amici,* bear in mind what happened to the others. To the Nuliano's and those who thought they were wise in leaving us. The Mafia won't rest until they betray all of us. Our only hope lies in negotiation." It was like talking to stone statues, thought Vincenzo, glancing at his companions.

"Come with us, Vincenzo!" pleaded Fidelio. "If you remain, you'll go under with Salvatore. I see a madness in his eyes ever since the Portella Massacre! He seeks personal vengeance! Why should we be a part of his *vendetta?*" Never had he been more in earnest.

"Ever since Portella he murders and executes with dispassionate violence!" exclaimed Marco. "Fidelio is right! He's not the Salvatore we joined up with to protect our people!"

"Goddammit!" cursed Vincenzo losing patience. "Who among us is the same as we were seven years ago? A lesser man would have broken long ago! He's always guarded our interests. Knowing you want to defect, he risks his own neck to save yours. Hasn't his own mother suffered, shuttled from jail to jail—and in her condition? How can I leave such a man who has the concern of his people foremost in his mind! Cousin or not, Salvatore is un *maschiezzo molto bravo,* the bravest of all men! And all together you aren't worth the paper he wipes his ass on!"

"Are you so blind you can't see? No one questions his manliness!" said Lamantia more sober than anyone could recall. "He lusts for power! He no longer thinks of Sicily! He'll betray her before all this is over because he wants amnesty on his own terms. He's been puppet to four different forces, all of whom have thrown him on the sacrificial altar! It's the peasants who adore Salvatore—and he turned his back on them long ago. He should have organized them, all of them, like he did us! And, by God, caused a revolution that would turn this island upside down!"

"Are you looking to die before your time, Dominic?" asked Vincenzo, lethally fingering his gun. His face swelled with anger and his black eyes dilated fiercely.

"Vincenzo! . . . Dominic!" shouted Fidelio restraining both men.

"Hard as it may be to believe," said Lamantia, undaunted by Vincenzo's threat. "The backbone of Sicily *is* the peasant. And the peasant has been betrayed! You and I, Vincenzo, have been fast friends these past seven years. I respect Salvatore. I really love him like a brother. But, face it, he hasn't championed the people in a long while."

Vincenzo dropped his troubled eyes to the table and stared at the dregs of his coffee cup. He suddenly recalled what his Aunt Antigone had said before Tori accepted the Partitionist's commission.

"The land barons can't be trusted. They'll use you to do their dirty work. You'll be their right arm, but, clasped tightly in their left, will be the power to annihilate you. They are full of duplicity, treacheries and highly perishable loyalties!

How prophetic were her words? Tori loved his mother passionately but he hadn't sought her counsel for a long time.

Fidelio's words sliced through his thoughts. "Perhaps it would have been better if the Reds *had* taken control. If Tori had sided with the communists, we might have had our amnesty and our victory."

Vincenzo and Terranova glanced anxiously at the other, and felt traitorous. As Fidelio's words sunk in, Vincenzo wondered if the money they'd received to keep the Reds away from intriguing with Tori had been worth the betrayal. What might have happened had they listened to the Reds was only conjecture now. They won Italy over *without* the help of the Mafia—hadn't they? If Tori hadn't retarded the Red influence they might have been in control of the island—and, who knew, perhaps proven best for all concerned. They'd shown marvelous organizational ability. The control they exercised over labor unions was power! *Managghia!* Who knew the right thing to do? Who, between the Mafia and Communists, were the lesser of both evils? It was too late for second thoughts.

Dominic Lamantia exploded. "Goddammit! Why didn't America help us form a democracy? From the days of the Occupation we fought a losing battle. America left us to the mercy of men like Don Barbarossa. Did President

801

Truman express faith in Tori's proposals? Hah! Up your ass! No one heard our cries. Only the Reds promised our people a decent life, with the right to till their own soil—and we shut the door in their faces!"

"It's not as easy as you make it sound," insisted Vincenzo. "None of us knows the extent of communist control. If it's so big a deal, how come America fights against the Reds so hard?"

"In what way are Sicily and America twins?" challenged Fidelio. Sicily has no rich, overflowing purse to lay next to her heart like a cheap whore. We aren't capitalists."

"Forget America," snapped Marco Genovese. "Belasci and the Mafia oppose communism because they're afraid the common people—us peasants—will grow too strong and usurp their corrupt powers. New land reforms, which are bound to result if the Reds took control, would shake the Mafia-feudalists off their asses and decrease their revenues.

Genovese butted his cigarette in his coffee cup. "We've all been betrayed, *amico*. The quicker we leave Sicily, the better off we'll be! There can be no further victories for Salvatore!"

Numbly, the men stared at Marco and felt the impact of truth in his words. Vincenzo filled with noticeable annoyance, arose to leave.

"*Allora—amonini!*" He peeled off several bills from a sizeable roll of money and tossed them onto the table. He felt drained and stunned by the acid-tongued frankness of the men. In the six years of their alliance, he'd never known the depths of their feelings. When things had gone well, all they'd thought about was wine, women, song and money. And now. . . .

Awareness of the seriousness and meaningful responsibility of their actions came about when they learned they had been set up as a part of the Portella Massacre. Although they lacked the slick sophistication of Palermo politicians, their provincial intelligence and animal instinct taught them they'd been done in by the same forces who hired them. What's more, they discovered why! The way of this disturbed them more than anything, for it made them suddenly aware of their own power. It gave them a false sense of security against pitfalls none of them had been prepared to combat.

The men had reassessed their positions. Justifiably, as they discussed the events following the Portella Massacre, concern for their own safety mounted. No matter how

Salvatore loomed as their remarkable leader, they had concluded that like them, he was made of flesh and blood and none possessed immorality. Because they hadn't been as subjective and as emotionally involved, nor as possessed with strict codes of morals, as Salvatore, they all saw how vulnerable he had become. Earlier Vincenzo had asked Fidelio Genovese, "Tell me one thing straight. Are we such a danger to Belasci that he should deny amnesty to us so many times?"

"You tell me," insisted Genovese. "You're the smart one."

Vincenzo nodded dully and answered his own question. "Why *should* he grant us amnesty? Free, we'd be of no use to him. Only shackled to him would we do his bidding. So, Belasci dangles the keys to our freedom before us, bit by bit."

"See—I told you you were the smart one," said Fidelio with an edge to his voice.

The handwriting on the wall had appeared to these men, in much bolder print than it had to Salvatore. Shaken into a stark reality, they knew they had reached their zenith of power and glory; that what followed now could only be a downhill momentum. Unable to grasp the growing complexities and political intrigues in which they found themselves slowly drowning, the last of Salvatore's men, brooding at the state of affairs in which they found themselves, expendable in a game they couldn't understand, left the restaurant grimly determined to escape their untenable positions.

Stunned at first by the astonishing resemblance "Satan's Ghost" bore to the dead *carabiniero*, Gucci, Salvatore stared at the man as if he indeed saw a ghost. But the expression of amazement and rapturous delight on Tori's face when he examined the marvelous weapon, this extraordinary miniature machine gun, presented to him by this stranger promoted the first incaution on his part in many months. Disarmed totally by the intricate machinations of the weapon, Tori became most anxious to demonstrate the marvel to his men.

The overhead sun split through rain clouds in the lapis lazuli sky to light up portions of the dismal countryside as Tori rode through the slogging, muddy mountain roads accompanied by this thick-necked man in summer khakis covered by a dark rain cape. A desert forage cap, with neck protector flapping in the wind was tugged fiercely down over his black eyes, veiling secret exhaltation in "Satan's Ghost."

For months his attempts to assassinate Salvatore had met with failure. Unaccustomed to failure, this crafty, paid assassin had devised a plan to infiltrate Salvatore's tightly knit coterie of men. Through the use of outer fringe bandits in whom he implanted the idea that he wanted to bring to Tori's attention this extraordinary special weapon, word got to Salvatore. It took months of lengthy intrigues and ample payoffs to effect a meeting with Salvatore.

What a glorious day for "Satan's Ghost!" Not only would he end up assassinating Salvatore, but he'd already framed a design in his mind to dispose of the entire band of brigands. His deal with Colonel Cala had provided for terms to enable him to retire for life, the dream of every hired assassin. Once he'd gained the confidence of the remaining men—the rest would be simple.

Noting all the back roads taken, off the beaten path where *carabinieri* crawled about in profusion, "Satan's Ghost" grew increasingly impressed by Tori's intricate system of signals as they approached one of the honeycombed grottos. Dismounting near the mouth of a cave, where they hitched their horses, Tori led the way through the darkened interior, taking a series of bends and curves too swiftly for the assassin to record in his mind. Continuing through an endless laybrinth of interconnecting caves, they finally emerged outside on a rocky ledge where the entire Castellammare Valley lay stretched out at his feet. But he was fully confused as to how they arrived at this place.

Voices came at them as Salvatore's men hailed him in greeting. They stopped short, stared at "Satan's Ghost" suspiciously. Tori drew the men together to allay their suspicions and prepared them for what would follow. He nodded to the gargoyle and instructed him to proceed with the demonstration.

"Satan's Ghost" opened the clarinet case he carried with him, glanced about the area, and, choosing a select spot, began to assemble the parts of the weapon, much to the amazement of the bandits who moved in closer, moved by a profound curiosity. Gambo Cusimano, more stupefied than the others at such a remarkable innovation, stood by flabbergasted as "Satan's Ghost" deftly snapped the .32 calibre cartridge case into position, ready for action.

Selecting a flat boulder at the approximate distance of 100 yards, he asked several of the men to set up cans or bottles strewn about the mouth of the cave. "Satan's Ghost" commenced firing away at the targets.

Cusimano picked up a few bullets, the size of a pea, and shook his head in amazement as he bounced them up and down in the palm of his hand. *My, my, what will they think of next?* he wondered, and as he glanced up at Tori, he caught the same silent wonder in his chief's eyes.

"Satan's Ghost" took aim at a hawk circling overhead and let loose a volley of shots, felling the bird with bullets, they barely saw. One of Tori's men retrieved the dead bird while the others professed their amazement.

Goddamn! This was some machine! The men ogled it in awe.

While Tori and the others examined the bird and lauded the merits of such a *fantastico* weapon, "Satan's Ghost" snapped a fresh magazine into the chamber, swiveled the gun around, and squinted one eye through the sights. Salvatore stood at dead center.

What would it take? A slight squeeze—and mission completed. "Satan's Ghost," every inch a skilled professional, knew he'd be a dead man before he ever left the grotto. Even if he succeeded in killing all the men—and he could, with this amazing gun, he'd never find his way out of this infernal place. No. His plans were to create an excitement in Salvatore, take orders on the gun with a promise of delivery. The next time they met, Tori would be off guard—without suspicion. Then—a slow squeeze—a gentle caress of the trigger . . . instant eternity.

Even the sound of fast riding hadn't broken the men's concentration. Terranova had sprung from his horse and made his way through the grotto to the upper level, filled with a rising excitement, anxious to impart to Tori what he considered earth-shattering news. He'd been made privy to information concerning an assassination plot against his chief. Moved to annoyance at the lack of attention given his arrival and wondering at the commotion created by the circle of men who chattered incessantly, and blocked his vision, he moved around them, wrapped in his own curiosity, until he caught sight of the heavy set figure lying prone on his belly aiming what seemed to be a toy gun at Salvatore.

What the hell is this? A toy? What's going on? Terranova craned his neck to observe better. Suddenly he tensed—instantly alert. Where had he seen this stranger before? Those outrageous, laughable shorts—hairy legs—the fierce profile of a hawk? When it came together, the stranger was no longer a stranger, the toy not a toy. Gun

805

grasped firmly in hand, and wondering at the insanity of permitting this hired assassin within the confines of their camp, he moved swiftly and silently out of range of his companions. Taking deadly aim, he emptied his gun on his target. Bullets *pinged* and *zinged* loudly as they hit their mark. The unsuspecting body of "Satan's Ghost" jerked into the air, twisted and doubled over under the impact of the missiles.

Everywhere there was instant bedlam as the bandits dove for cover. They pulled out their weapons and aimed at nothing in particular until, somewhat mystified, they saw Terranova, with gun blazing, acting like some crazy man.

Vincenzo had lept into the air, tackled Tori, and knocked him into the dust where they both landed unceremoniously. The Genovese brothers half stood, half crouched, with drawn guns, looking dazed, expressions of total incomprehension on their faces. Lamantia would have emptied his gun into Terranova if *Sporcaccione* hadn't already tackled the double agent and knocked him down a few feet from where "Satan's Ghost" had rendezvoused with his maker.

Sporcaccione eased off him, Terranova stared dispassionately at the dying assassin. One arm bleeding profusely, blood spurting from wounds in his head, "Satan's Ghost" turned to face his killer, a glimmer of recognition swimming through blurred eyes. On his initial arrival at Bellolampo, Terranova had been present when he had demonstrated his remarkable weapon to the FSB officers. The recognition in the assassin's eyes melted into a glassy-eyed death stare.

"What the hell's wrong with you?" stormed Tori, dusting himself off while collecting his composure. "You just lost us the finest invention ever made!" he glowered moving towards the professional assassin.

"I just saved your life," said Terranova without expression. He inserted a full clip into his gun, holstered it and slapped the dust from his trousers. "Perhaps the lives of all the rest, included," he added wryly. He proceeded to explain his mission as the men collected themselves and juggled their nerves back into place.

They listened to Terranova's story and glanced uneasily at one another. Only that morning Terranova had accidentally been made privy to the assassination plot. Even when he'd first seen the weapon, he'd never made the connection that it was to be used against Salvatore, he told the others. "Imagine my astonishment when I ride in and find that sonofabitch, lying a few feet from his target as calm as a cucumber. Who's the stupid *chu chu* who let him come here?"

"I'm the stupid *chu-chu*," admitted Tori calmly. He held up his hands to ward off the apology formed on Terranova's lips. "It's true. I'm the dolt who led him right up here."

Salvatore, listening to Terranova sobered instantly. He'd been nearly done in by his own carelessness. He wondered, had the charm of Salvatore been broken? His left ear had failed to warn him; he had received no customary throbbing sensation to warn him of impending dangers. More than his gross carelessness, it was this anatomical failure which shook him to the core. Was it possible God had abandoned him?

It was time for introspection, he told himself. Leaving his men he rode to his sanctuary at the Temple of Cats, where in his secret grotto he fell into a state of meditation for three days and nights. He emerged on the fourth day, unshaven, slovenly in appearance, somewhat emaciated from lack of food—but his glassy, compelling eyes burned bright with decision.

CHAPTER 59

"You want to meet personally with Colonel Cala?" Bartolomeo Calemi's cigar fell from his thick lips and he stared dumbly at his famous guest.

"I want to meet with him," said Tori firmly. "It's my life at stake."

Calemi's face, scarred with pitted craters from a bad bout with small pox as a child, was beetle-browed over dark eyes filled with a natural menace. Despite an engaging sense of humor which endeared him to the most robust of men, Calemi, a young blood *mafioso*, could turn into a lethal monster of destruction. This *mafioso*, whom most men avoided encountering was the man Tori had trusted with his life.

"You've gotta be crazy," insisted Calemi tentatively, retrieving his fallen cigar. Then it came to him. "Ahhh," he said knowingly. "You're worried about the betrayals of your men in North Africa. Well it's not Cala's doing. He's nothing without the big guns of the Mafia," he said impatiently, relighting the dead cigar.

"My concern is the bad blood between the FSB and the security police. I don't wish to be caught in the middle of their idiocy."

"D'Verde won't like it."

"Fuck D'Verde," countered Tori.

"I've instigated many intrigues, but this one stinks worse than Solameni's fish." Greed showing in his black lizard eyes, he pressed," Will Cala have to be cut in on this?" His eyes cut across the room to the third man, seated opposite them in the elegant study, munching on chocolates, as he listened to the conversation.

"Listen," said Tori impatiently. "The money issue is between you and Belasci. All I want is to insure the deal against collapsing from internal causes. Who knows what the hell Cala contemplates—what goes on in his complicated mind? He may already be on to what's happening and waits to pull another surprise like 'Satan's Ghost'."

" 'Satan's Ghost?' " Calemi's heavy brows knit together darkly. "What the Hell are you talking about—'Satan's Ghost?' "

Tori filled him in on the incredible man with his even more incredible weapon.

"*Bastard*," glowered Calemi. "What the fuck's wrong with Belasci, permitting Cala such a free hand? How come he hasn't given orders to that toy soldier to lay low? A paid assassin is news to me. What about you, Natale?" he addressed himself to the third man another youngblood.

It was apparent that Natale Solameni worshipped Salvatore—with certain reservations, of course—by the way he fairly glowed in Tori's presence.

"He may be right," muttered Natale, chomping noisily. "It wouldn't hurt to meet with Cala. Get some idea what's on his mind—eh? Look, we don't mention the deal until we're certain Salvatore's right, *capeeshi?*"

"I know I'm right. You think I don't know my enemies?" retorted Tori.

"Who can argue with your success?" Solameni unwrapped the foil from another chocolate with gusto, devouring it instantly.

"From the first," added Tori, "D'Verde put the FSB in a demoralizing light. If I was Cala and discovered a plot to bring disgrace on my head I'd protect myself, by God."

"*Va! Va!*" A simple bullet or two will remove all cause

for concern," Calemi offered his usual remedy for ending a troublesome situation.

"Why bring problems to the picture if we can handle it through polite persuasion, eh, Calemi?" Tori studied his friend's evil face and smiled gently. "I admit it's a daring plan. Should I fail to bring these rival forces together to work jointly on my behalf, I may inform the Colonel of a few interesting facts to encourage this 'Italian Lawrence' to disband his forces and return to Rome gracefully."

"*Pe d'avero?* Really?" muttered Calemi, evidencing interest.

"True, all this is risky and highly speculative. But, have I a choice?" asked Tori. "In the rivalry between these men, dangling in a precarious balance, almost by a thread, hangs my life. The stakes are high. But—don't you see I have no other way to go? I do as I must!"

Natale Solameni, an affluent *mafioso* who made a fortune in construction in post war Sicily before he was thirty, rose to his feet, wiped his pudgy, candy-stained hands on a handkerchief. "*Allora*, you want to meet with Cala? Consider it done." He glanced at Calemi for his approval.

"It's your life," retorted Calemi, sourly. "Do with it what you will."

Assured in advance there'd be no attempted treacheries or foul play, Colonel Cala braved torrential rains that inundated western Sicily and arrived at Calemi's villa for the clandestine meeting with the famous bandit.

He found Tori standing before an enormous floor to ceiling fireplace, dressed casually in well-tailored beige shirt and trousers, topped by an olive drab pinwale corduroy jacket. His thumbs were hooked into his belt as he stood in a careless pose. Tori's dark eyes reflected brilliant lights; even his hand-crafted leather boots glistened lustrously in the glow of the crackling fires burning brightly on the hearth. At the sound of the door opening, he glanced up to see Colonel Cala, standing on the threshold in a stiff pose, still chilled by the foul damp night.

Slowly, Tori straightened up and smiled politely. After a terse introduction by Natale Solameni; the redoubtable enemies were left alone to regard each other in silence. A musty aroma of ancient timelessness clung to the air.

For all his worldliness, the Colonel couldn't subdue the excitement he felt when he stood at last face to face with the volatile young man. Totally unprepared as he was for the youth and the manly good looks of the brigand, the incongruity between his personal expectations as opposed to what he encountered in the flesh left him speechless for several moments.

In moments his eyes swept over him, taking in the well-dressed, relaxed picture of what could easily have been a member of the nobility. The brilliance of the large diamond ring that graced the little finger of his left hand; the solid gold watch, known by millions to have given him pleasure; the golden scorpion around his neck; the famous solid gold belt buckle; even the Eye of God amulet looped on a chain through the button holes of his vest—all of it transformed the legend of Salvatore into a living, breathing man before his very eyes. Cala, like any other human, wasn't immune to the excitement generated by such a man.

"Please, Colonel, make yourself comfortable."

"Yes. Yes, of course. He removed his visored hat and shook the rain off it, placed it right side up on a chair, and walked with an arched back to the fireplace, rubbing his hands together. His appraising eyes assessed the tasteful furnishings of the villa in silence. *Porca la majorca!* It's really coming down out there!"

"This will warm you," said Tori, handing him a snifter of brandy.

"You don't drink?" he asked, then answered his own query. "That's right, you don't," he added, recalling Captain Franchina's report. "A very commendable habit," he muttered as he raised his glass in a mock salute. He gulped the fiery liquid as the warming effects surged through him and until the chills abated. Unable or unwilling to remove his eyes from Salvatore for a time, his eyes clung reflectively to the scorpion amulet.

"You seem preoccupied with my amulet," said Tori.

"Yes," he muttered absently. "Strange how the mind works. You see something and suddenly a door opens in your mind and out comes a drawer full of memories and accumulated trivia. You're Scorpio—eh? Once a sorceress told me about those born under your sign. Stubborn, rebellious, passionate, overbearing, shrewd, logical and extremely private. A 'brave eagle' who can lead men into battle, into the very face of death without a tremor." He smiled tightly. "And in addition you turn out to be disarmingly handsome."

Tori bowed slightly, amused by the man's expression. "Some schools of thought believe reality exists only in the mind," he said bypassing the flattery. "But I am certain,

810

Colonel, you are only interested in the reality of the moment—no?"

Cala nodded.

"I respectfully asked to meet with you because your reputation is that of an honorable man; a dedicated man with integrity rarely found in this day and age. Described to me as a man who scrupulously performs his professional duties with a moral dignity and respect for the rights of others, I—"

"Show me a man who isn't swayed by the compliments of so worthy an opponent," interrupted the officer tilting his head, indulgently.

"I meant no compliments," Tori cut him off. "I submit merely a statement of facts as reported to me by my sources."

"Nonetheless you flatter me. In all honesty I must disillusion you. I confess to being as ruthless and as dedicated as you in the pursuance of your duties. I am known to be as underhanded, deceptive, savage and as outrageously crafty as is needed in my profession." His clear blue eyes displayed a pride of consciousness and superiority, however, his manner was not offensive.

"Is that so?" The corners of Salvatore's lips drooped in an affectation of dismay. "That's a shame. I've heard so much about your unimpeachable character. That as a man of high calibre, your capacity for moral integrity greatly surpasses that of your employer."

"I'm not certain who it is you refer to as my employer, but the rest is true," he said immodestly. "That is, over and above my professional involvements."

"*Allora, Colonnello, basta.* We have no time to play games."

"Fair enough."

"It's best you know now, I will never surrender to the corrupt government you represent. Above all, you must understand that. Repeatedly I stated in my letters to the press, before you cut off that platform of expression, that I'd never turn myself over to an immoral government, and I reiterate the same to you."

Cala glanced up from the drink in hand mildly surprised at the outrageous declaration. Questions formed in his eyes, but he made no move to agree, add to, or refute Salvatore's statement.

"With your permission, I'll outline a plan to put an end to this useless bloodshed that claims the lives of so many of your men."

Colonel Cala, without resentment or hostility at the au-

811

thoritative manner in which Tori had taken charge of the situation, moved away from the fireplace and took a seat nearby. As yet he hadn't noticed the object on a nearby table, which Tori had covered with a large dinner napkin.

"We both know there can be no amnesty for Salvatore. Four promises and four betrayals stripped the veil of naivete from my eyes." Tori lit both their cigarettes and replaced the graceful urn-shaped lighter to the marble-topped coffee table. He strutted before the Colonel.

"To commence, my first consideration is for my mother's welfare. I will not leave Sicily until she's released from prison and I'm assured by your word she'll be free, never to be molested again. Only then will I agree to go into exile." Tori glanced swiftly at Cala and laughed in a meaningful way. "No, *not* to North Africa, *Colonnello*."

A faint trace of a smile appeared on Cala's lined face. It was a face heavily lined with character wrinkles, of a man who appeared to overflow with compassion.

"I'll need passports, immigration papers, money—" Tori paused.

A vast silence fell between them, a silence in which the howling winds and turbulent rains whipped against the villa, accompanied by the sounds of trees and bushes groaning in the assault of the elements. Here and there a flower trellis came unhinged and banged loudly against the outer walls of the villa. Ocean swells rose to incalculable heights, and the entire seaside village trembled under the force of westerly gales that shook the northwest shores of Sicily. Inside the fire snapped and spat cracklingly and, mingled with the exterior sounds, served only to heighten the silence between them.

Out of this loud silence, Colonel Cala turned to his host and with official restraint and a cool reserve asked, "Whatever gives you the idea, Salvatore, that you can bargain with me for your life?"

Turning away from the French doors where he stood for a time peering out at the dark, raging night, Tori fixed his dark eyes on the officer. He felt the color rise in his cheeks as he moved closer to the fire.

"What are you telling me?" he asked soberly. "You promised no games."

"Only that I have no authority to enter into such negotiations. My orders are to destroy you—not mediate for your salvation," said the Colonel quietly.

"I'm well aware of your intentions, *Colonnello*," replied Tori, tearing the napkin off the bulky mass on the table where Col. Cala's eyes were instantly impulsed.

Barely a flicker of disturbance stirred in Cala's blue eyes as he stared at the exposed, miniature machine gun belonging to "Satan's Ghost." Tori thought, *he's superb. It's absolutely marvelous how he keeps his emotions in check. You'd think he was innocent of this act against me.* He smiled tightly.

"If you haven't guessed before this, you must be aware by now that your assassin has been expended."

"I don't understand any of this," said the officer, feigning ignorance.

"It couldn't be that I'm wrong twice in an evening." Tori's eyes narrowed. "Didn't Belasci make it clear to you I'm not to be captured or killed?"

Col. Cala's face drained of color. He placed his brandy glass on the table, collected his composure and cast a bland look at his host. "I don't follow you."

"*Managghia!* You really *don't* know?" Stunned, Tori paced the floor. "You really don't know—do you? You know nothing of my *insurance?* My 'personal portfolio'?" He slapped his thigh gleefully. "*Allora,* I can see where they might not want you to know. Not a man as highly regarded as you, *Colonnello.*"

The doors to the adjoining room swung open to admit Vincenzo de Montana. Both men turned to him; however, preoccupied in their immediate conversation and thoughts, neither spoke.

"The weather slowed me up. Roads washed out to the south," apologized Vincenzo, glancing awkwardly from one to the other.

Tori was the first to come out of the silence. He glanced at his watch. "Ah, cousin. Finally, eh? What took so long? Well, never mind. Here, meet our worthy opponent, *Colonnello* Cesare Cala. And this, Colonel is my co-captain and dear cousin, Vincenzo de Montana."

The introductions over, they shook hands and sized each other up. *So, this is the man upon whom Captain Franchina builds his hopes,* thought Cala.

"You hear, Vincenzo? The *Colonnello* knows nothing of my personal portfolio. What do you make of this?" Tori laughed as he glanced at his cousin, who, turning from the fireplace where he stood warming himself, observed them both in silence and expressed his disbelief with an enigmatic smile.

"I regret not seeing the humor in all this," said Cala. "Perhaps you'll enlighten me?"

"Delighted, *Colonnello*. Delighted." He took time to explain as he carefully outlined highlights in his spectacular career, dropping names, places and dates which obviously upset the FSB officer despite his excellent control. Tori continued.

"I trust you can see how these highly confidential incidents might prove politically embarrassing and lethal to the careers of our—uh—respectable and highly placed government officials. If anything should happen to me before I reach the age of sixty—either to me or my associates, I might add—the contents of the portfolios will be published instantly, regardless of how many heads roll in the wake of truth."

"What has your portfolio to do with me?" said Cala finally. I am not inculpated. I have not intrigued with you."

For a moment Tori was thunderstruck when he saw the information seemed to be of little consequence to Cala. "Perhaps you had better discuss the matter with Minister Belasci, since you work for him."

"Correction. I work for the Italian Government. I simply *report* to Minister Belasci," he said coldly, his eyes in a continuous assessment of Vincenzo de Montana.

Tori exchanged meaningful glances with his co-captain and walked back to the fireplace, where he casually flipped the butt of his cigarette into the flames and watched as the fires consumed it. This was a tough bloke, all right. "Either way, it's best you inform the Minister that you've been told of the portfolio's existence."

Colonel Cala leaned forward in his seat, and from his pocket he removed a letter bearing the seal of the Minister's office. He tapped it lightly on his knee. "Before I agreed to rendezvous with you, I naturally contacted his Excellency." He glanced apologetically at his host. "I wasn't sure what you wanted of me. "Normally, I'd not meet with an enemy like this."

"You consider me your enemy?" asked Tori.

Vincenzo tensed and, without being obvious, felt for his gun. Filled with instant distrust, his initial dislike of the man was reinforced. His eyes were on his cousin.

"You are the enemy of the government—my government. Therefore you are *my* enemy." Cala held the letter in his outstretched hand. "His Excellency sent this communique to you."

Tori studied the letter, made no move to accept it.

"Look here, Salvatore. I want no part in this sort of thing. I'm here only as emissary of Minister Belasci. Normally this is business for Captain Franchina. I, personally, frown on intrigue. Had you not stated unequivocally that only I should come, he would have been here in my stead.

814

Now, I'm here, I'm at your disposal." He offered the letter again.

"You mean like the last wish of a condemned man?" scoffed Tori, ignoring the letter.

"No." Cala sighed heavily. "Difficult as it might seem to you, I have profound respect for a man of your calibre and achievements. I find it distressing that you were so misguided in your youth. A man of your potential could have reached untold heights if you'd retained your morality and remained incorruptible."

"Incorruptible?" Salvatore laughed aloud. Vincenzo grinned in disbelief at so inane a remark. "You hear what the Colonel tells me, cousin?" They both had a good laugh at Cala's expense. Then, sobering, Tori proceeded to enlighten the FSB officer.

"If I had retained my morality and remained incorruptible, eh? Tell me how such a thing is possible when the very government we should look up to is structured on the words immorality and corruption? Go ahead, tell me. I'm listening. You can't offer an explanation, can you? Very well, let me tell you what I learned as I grew up. I saw my own people, hungry and starving, treated like animals by the gross inequities of antiquated laws no one has bothered to amend, because in the past when they had tried—they were tortured or murdered, or both! . . . With my own eyes I saw foreigners—the *carabinieri*—my enemies, cheat my people, falsely imprison them, steal and take bribes and cause serve hardships on a hard-working people who asked no more than to be able to support their families. . . . You know what I learned when I saw it was impossible to live under immoral conditions imposed upon my people? . . . When I saw immorality and corruption in every bend of the road; in every hostile eye of the *carabinieri;* on the sanctimonious faces of those bloodsucking priests and nuns who preach piety and praise poverty to the peasants, while they sit down to feasts and break every commandment in the scriptures; and in the greedy avaricious eyes of scheming politicians who make false promises and break their word with each breath they take for self seeking gains. I'll tell you what I learned—morality is on the side of the heaviest artillery!"

In those moments Colonel Cala saw reflected in Tori's eyes the bitterness of all his betrayals, an idealistic and youthful anger at a system more ancient than his youth could perceive, and a disenchantment in those people in whom he placed his trust.

"You don't *really* believe our government and their politics are untainted, without corruption—do you?" asked Tori with incredible disbelief.

Cala remained noncommittal. "I haven't made myself aware of the contents of this letter," he began as if Tori had said nothing to influence him in any way. "I deliver it to you from Minister Belasci, sealed with his signet."

Noticeably annoyed by the other's cool indifference, Tori moved towards the letter, then, changed his mind. He winked at Vincenzo.

"You read it to me, Colonel."

Vincenzo grinned wickedly.

"I prefer not to read it—"

"Then, I will not accept it."

Under knotted brows, Cala's irritation flared. He inhaled a deep breath and tapped the letter nervously on his knee, deliberating. He glanced from one to the other and scowled. Drawn by the crackling, spitting noises of the fire as rain dropped through the chimney, he finally rose to his feet, donned a pair of horn-rimmed glasses and walked towards the fire, breaking the seal on the letter as he went. He held the letter up to the firelight and commenced to read:

"*Carissimo Salvatore:*" He cleared his throat and coughed embarrassedly, at the familiarity in greetings. Salvatore smiled subtly, with ironic eyes. "*It's unfortunate that matters have taken a turn for the worse. Once we were on the same side, fighting for a worthy cause. Now, suddenly, we are in opposing camps. The strong bond that once existed between us has been shattered by forces over which I have no control. You could have waited a little longer, until the power of your life was in my control, before attacking me publicly.*"

Cala's voice broke. He glanced at Tori in a peculiar, studied look as if waiting for an explanation. Tori gave him a taste.

"The Mafia's support for revolutionary governments are always followed by a stab in the back. Belasci's alliance with the Mafia is stronger than his word to me as a loyal human being, who assisted him for a time in his political future."

Cala's eyes returned to the letter and continued:

"*You understand I'm not alone in this. I, too, take orders, just as you took them from me.*"

Unhappy in his role, Cala stopped reading. "Look here, Salvatore, I have no business reading this. It's not my affair! It's a matter between you and Belasci." He showed increasing signs of irritation at the precarious position into which he was sliding.

"It's not your affair? The man who promised my blood to Belasci? Are you so blindly devoted to your job you'd murder an innocent man for an executioner like Belasci?" Once again his ironic laughter was joined by that of Vincenzo's.

"It doesn't disturb you that the situation may not be as described to you by Minister Belasci?" asked Vincenzo.

"Like you, I also take orders. I don't question the character or qualifications of my superiors, I leave it to the electorate to choose their leaders."

Salvatore clucked his tongue against his teeth. "Ah, *Colonnello,* you disappoint me. Are you as regimented in your duties as the Gestapo who blindly followed orders by that madman Hitler? The Nuremburg trials didn't interest you? Are you a man who accepts orders to murder for his government, and salves his conscience by convincing himself it's for a worthy cause?"

"Now, see here, Salvatore. I didn't come here to be insulted! Who are you anyway? The pot calling the kettle black!" he exploded. "Indeed! We both took orders from our government—so don't pull that sanctimonious—"

"Hah!" cried Salvatore triumphantly. "Exactly!"

Colonel Cala stopped abruptly.

"I couldn't have said it better, Colonel. So—tell me, why do you walk the earth a free man, and I cannot? We both followed orders—from the same man. Where's the justice in that? Don't tell me the difference is this!" He reached for and placed Cala's hat on his head. "Is the difference in the uniform we wear?" He saluted Cala smartly. "We're both on the same side, fighting for the same government—yet, why am I the hunted and you the hunter?"

"I'm on the side of law and order! You're on the side of corruption and violence!" he snapped in irritation.

"But, how can that be?" We both take orders from the same man. Unless—" He cocked his head, removed the cap, and replaced it as he ran his fingers through his curly hair. "Something smells in such a set up—no?"

"You became a pawn of the Mafia." said Cala icily.

"—And you haven't?" Tori's patience thinned. "I earned my reputation by courage and skill and a belief that oppression in my country should end. I became a partisan to earn my freedom. Furthermore, I was naive enough to live by a strict code of ethics and morality while my government reorganized itself. I thought my efforts to help my people and maintain law and order during a time of intolerable lawlessness would be lauded by a grateful and concerned government who'd grant me amnesty for my contribution during those trying times."

He slapped his thigh as he paced the floor. "After four betrayals I woke up. But why do I defend my actions to you? I've not betrayed my people. I made one irrevocable error when I permitted the Christian Democrats to become so powerful. I made Belasci omnipotent. If I'd been politically astute, wiser in the ways of cunning and deception, they'd be taking orders from me!" He pounded his chest with fervor. "Salvatore gave them the power they needed to guarantee Italy to them and through the manipulation of the law they will control this country for many years. This is my crime, Colonel Cala! This the most terrifying crime of my life—to have made it possible for these bloodthirsty beasts to control my beloved country. This is my *peccato*, my shame! I will never live such unjustifiable actions down for the balance of my life. It will be the cross I must carry."

The room grew silent. Tori filled with anguish. These words had been heavy enough to carry locked inside him. Now they were out. Worse, they were the truth! To have let the Christian Democrats take the power was his blackest shame. Vincenzo stared at his cousin and tried to swallow the lump in his throat. Colonel Cala said nothing. Vincenzo started up the conversation again.

"This Lieutenant Greco, from Piana dei Greci, proved Salvatore couldn't have committed the May First atrocity at Portella. Still you seek out our men, betrayed by the *Mafia*. Now, you compound the injustice by incarcerating them at Viterbo!" he said snidely.

"I'm not empowered to determine the criminalty of a man. Your efforts to include me into the administration of justice are to no avail."

"In other words, you are simply a puppet of Belasci's? A wooden puppet, without heart, feelings or a mind of your own to determine right from wrong. You don't bleed—eh?"

"I meant I have no legal authority or power to hear or decide cases. And I assure you, I bleed as readily as you if cut or wounded."

Salvatore sipped a glass of water, poured from a carafe on the sideboard. "Please continue, *Colonnello*. Perhaps its best we wait to hear what else Belasci has on his mind."

Cala put out his cigarette in the ashtray before him, spit out a few tobacco fragments, and resumed his reading:

818

"Exile awaits you on Giorgio's estate in Brazil. You will comply with the following: Submit a letter in your handwriting to the Chief Magistrate of Viterbo, taking full responsibility for the Portella Massacre, thereby eliminating any further investigation. That should satisfy the Reds. Hopefully the trial will cease. By your admission, you'll state you took it upon yourself to assassinate Senator de Casselli; that no one ordered or suggested that his life be taken; that your personal hatred of communism inspired your action; that you feel it should be eliminated at any cost. State specifically that all that rubbish about a crossfire in which many people stated they were caught was a figment of someone's overactive imagination. (What Matteo was thinking about is still beyond my comprehension!)"

It became increasingly difficult for Colonel Cala to conceal his feelings. He paused periodically to wipe the microbeads of perspiration that burst on the surface of his skin. His voice droned on in monotone.

"That of your own free will, your hatred of communism and your love for Sicily compelled you to blow up communist headquarters and reduce their quarters to rubble. You will make no further reference to the Christian Democrats or to any involvement or activities you entered into on their behalf with me, Don Barbarossa, Malaterra or Prince Oliatta. In exchange for these personal favors to your government and to me, the release of your mother from prison will follow. You have my sincerest and official assurance she'll never be molested again. My endeavors to exculpate your former associates incarcerated at Viterbo is forthcoming. (You are to make two copies of the letter, seal them, and give one to Colonel Cala, and mail one directly to the Chief Magistrate, Presidente Ginestra, at Viterbo.) I shall endeavor to do all in my power to assist your arrangements and through Colonel Cala, will provide you with all the necessary documents, passports, and visas to enable you to begin a successful life abroad.

"I regret things couldn't have been different. I, too, have had my share of disappointments, caro mio, and like so many before us, we must take our turns in waiting for our dreams to come true. Be patient. I repeat what I have always promised. When I become Premier, I shall provide you with the amnesty you justly deserve. With great affection, Martino Belasci. P. S. Destroy this letter as you have done with the others."

The FSB officer flung the letter from him in disgust. It landed on the floor a few feet from Vincenzo, who leaned over to retrieve it. He glanced at it superficially, then slipped it into his jacket pocket. Both he and Tori watched the prim officer pace the floor in a state of mild agitation.

Colonel Cala was used to treachery in high places. His work in Intelligence had uncovered voluminous cases of this nature, but never with *him* as scapegoat! At worst he thought, Salvatore could be labled a misguided partisan, bamboozled by slick politicians who twisted him into a tool for their corruption. Three political parties, plus the Mafia, had abused his power to elevate themselves to near omnipotency and now his usefulness served no further purpose. They wanted to exterminate him. But—he'd been too smart. Since he knew too much and wisely sought to insure himself against their treachery, Belasci had formed the FSB to make him appear sincere in his effort to quash banditry. *Hah!* he thought. *What a laugh! The press will have a field day at my expense! I'll be the one labeled* jackass! Grossly offended at the obvious conspiracy, Cala struggled against the impulse to ventilate his true feelings. The military confidentiality of his work precluded this.

"Did you know Colonel, at this very moment, Inspector D'Verde plots behind your back to secure my escape?" said Tori watching him closely for reaction. "Did Belasci alert you to the fact that the security police seek to discredit you?"

"Very little escapes me on assignment," he said.

"You didn't know about my portfolio—that I wasn't to be captured . . ."

"No. I didn't." His face reddened.

"Two months ago, before many lives were needlessly expended in this fiasco between us, I attempted to talk with you. Captain Franchina intervened. He told us the only talk between us can be with machine guns! So, my people contacted D'Verde. I place more confidence in you—not the *carabinieri*, but you."

Cala seethed inwardly. Did he now have to concern himself with treachery from within his own organization? Franchina had been mute on this revelation.

"Franchina never brought this to my attention. I can see much hasn't been confided to me," replied the Colonel with a mixture of resentment and apology.

"You see how easily it is to play into their hands? You've permitted the Mafia to help you betray us. Soon you'll be sucked under, become useful tools to them just as we were before I realized what took place." Tori's eyes grew distant. "They have a peculiar talent for bending people to their purpose and, making it appear *they* are the ones doing the favor. I can see your feathers have already been preened in preparation for their courtship rites."

Cala judiciously kept his inflamatory thoughts to himself as Tori continued.

"They forgot *they* were outlaws before me. *They* called Mussolini's government unjust because he arrested *their* families and considered *them* outlaws. I wisely protected myself and they dare not touch me. Now they call themselves pure, and frown on me. These paragons of injustice! It's best you know what you're up against now, Colonel, and save yourself walking the pirate's plank later. You won't win in this encounter. You'll never succeed in bringing the 'blood of Salvatore' to your superiors. Worse— you'll be left without face! They will say of you when its over, 'Cala was incompetent!' Belasci will take full credit after making you the ass. He'll say, 'I banished Salvatore and his kind from Sicily! I ended this bloody war and saved the lives of innocent men!' You know what? He'll be hailed as Premier—and his graft and corruption will continue on and on. *You'll* probably be demoted and sent off to some foreign outpost, to be buried in obscurity." Tori clicked his tongue against his teeth apologetically as we walked to the sideboard and poured two drinks. He handed one to the officer, and, when Vincenzo shook his head in refusal, kept it himself.

"No hard feelings, *Colonello!*" He raised his glass and sipped a bit and made a wry face. "Will you believe this is only the second time I've tasted wine? I've missed nothing."

Salvatore walked to the large double oak doors, turned to the FSB officer, and bowed slightly. "And now if you'll permit me." He opened the doors wide, leading to another room where several men milled about. Among the young blood *mafiosi*, Enrico D'Verde stood relaxed with a smile on his lips, talking with Calemi. At the sight of Salvatore he became buoyant, and walking towards him a warm greeting forming on his lips, he stopped short at the sight of Colonel Cala, like a fox who just barely escapes the jaws of a trap.

"Come. Come in, Inspector," smiled Tori, pleasantly. "I'm certain you two know each other." He winked at Calemi and Solameni, who stood off to one side, watching with great interest the discomfort in each man.

The rivals each bowed curtly to the other, hostility apparent in their eyes. D'Verde spun around and glared hotly at the two *mafiosi* and muttered hotly,

"What's the meaning of this?"

"I take full responsibility, Enrico," said Salvatore. "I realize this encounter proves awkward to you both. Long deliberation on my present status caused me to reevaluate the situation to offset the possibility of treachery. Your unending hostilities as rival forces places me in an untenable position—caught between the two of you. I decided then, it would serve me best if you *both* involved yourself, jointly, in Salvatore's business. I cannot permit your incompatibility to cause my downfall," smiled Salvatore in his wisdom. "You do understand my thinking—no?" He paused briefly.

"Now that you both know the rules—tell me if I can accept your cooperation. If not, I shall be forced to make other plans."

D'Verde was a mess. He fumed inwardly. His livid face, a dead give away, marked both his humiliation and disappointment. He had hoped his stay in Sicily would have ended by now. Having worked diligently on this special project, he didn't relish having to share the spotlight with anyone, most especially not a glorified FSB *carabiniero*.

Colonel Cala inclined to be more generous towards the man guilty of blocking his progress so effectively. Lack of cooperation from the security police had impeded his progress, but to find D'Verde had been plotting behind his back infuriated him. If only he'd been more discriminate before accepting the task of coddling this accursed brainchild of Belasci's! *The Forces to Suppress Banditry*, indeed! What a fiasco!

"*Allora*—is it agreed?" Salvatore glanced expectantly from one officer to the other.

D'Verde scowled fiercely at Calemi. He shrugged, threw his hands into the air in a helpless gesture, and nodded condescendingly. Without expression Colonel Cala nodded. The *mafiosi* breathed in relief. Salvatore moved with agility towards the fireplace and winked at his cousin.

"*Va bene*. You will inform Minister Belasci no agreements shall be reached until my mother is set free. It is already 1950. Under the provisions of the Holy Year Amnesty, she can be pardoned. She is also to be provided with all necessary documents whatever it takes to join me at some future date—"

As Salvatore continued to stipulate his intentions Colonel Cala became more convinced that an *entente* had existed between D'Verde and the outlaw for some time. To think he'd been taken in by these strange and complex people! Never had Cala experienced the likes of Sicilian intrigue. No set pattern existed, no logical explanation could be articulated. There existed only a mass of voluminous threads like those used in intricate embroidery, leading to and forming a complex pattern which appeared to have no beginning or end. Colonel Cala forced his thoughts to trail back to the situation at hand and heard D'Verde, a former lawyer, agree to draft the memoranda on Portella Della Rosa.

"Since I'm familiar with his requirements, I'll handle it. It would please me if we could get these arrangements out of the way as soon as possible," said the Inspector. "My term of office expires legally on December 31. I've remained here simply at the request of the Minister—"

Colonel Cala burned hotly at this revelation.

"It is not I who holds the mother of Salvatore in prison, unjustly!" retorted Salvatore.

"When the release of your mother from prison is secured, you agree to call off all hostilities against all authorities?" suggested D'Verde.

"Salvatore never breaks his word. That's more than I can say for you high officials, eh, *Colonnello*?"

The meeting ended. They shook hands, assured each other of *detente* for the sake of resolving the Salvatore matter.

Salvatore walked Colonel Cala through the marble-floored foyer of the villa. His voice, grew hushed and apologetic. "I regret being the instrument to shatter your illusions, Colonel. You must understand that we Sicilians are a strange breed. Our way of life, over centuries of oppression, has been a constant refinement of all tools necessary for survival." Tori paused reflectively. "Oddly enough, we are alike, you and I—in many ways—each dedicated to our causes. It's a pity you've been infected with fraudulent hope—and it was I who had to instill your vision with hoplessness. But, if you, as a servant of your God and government, have used five thousand warriors to destroy me, a solitary servant of God for my people, then, pray tell me, who shall be remembered in time—you or me?"

Colonel Cala, stoop-shouldered and heavily weighted with monumental problems for the moment, said nothing. He stared at the burning cigarette in his fingers.

"Go, Cesare Cala, go. Leave Sicily while you can. There shall flow no more bloody rivers at Salvatore's hand. Nor shall you have the blood of Salvatore to sweeten your victory. Should you delude yourself further into thinking a laurel wreath awaits you in Rome, as glorious as the one which graced the head of Caesar, take caution, my friend, for it shall turn into a wreath of thorns to fill your life *con molto dolore*, with many sorrows. *Allora*—go! Now."

"What difference should it make if I go or stay?" asked Cala.

"It makes a difference to me."

"Why?"

"You are not my enemy. You have never harmed me. You are simply an arm of my enemy. So I tell you, go. Save yourself before you are plagued by a legion of satanic devils for all eternity."

Colonel Cala smiled tightly. "Besides being stellar at guerilla warfare, you seem to have a penchant for psychological warfare as well, eh? *Va bene. Piacere de conoscere*. If nothing else, it was a pleasure meeting you."

"*Piacere*." The invincible one nodded curtly and opened the door. He stood for a time quietly watching the FSB officer struggle against the violence of the wind whipping rain as he made his way to his car, and driver.

All the way back to Palermo, Colonel Cesare Cala wondered why? Why all the fuss, loss of lives, gross expenditures, and loss of sanity in this overt war against the outlaw? For show? For faded glory? God Almighty! with what *fiasco* had he become impregnated? The FSB were doomed to perform a more outrageous abortion than the one Francesco Bello pulled off at San Amauro Hill. Why had he permitted himself to be seduced by that whore, Belasci? Why? In God's name—why?

Cesare Cala left Calemi's villa with several distinct impressions. He felt no disgust at Salvatore, no hatred of an enemy, no vindictiveness. Not even the challenge between sworn enemies on a battlefield. Should Cala win in this contest between the Sicilian champion and the State, Salvatore was right—there'd be no sweet victory. None at all. Overriding his personal conclusions about the outlaw was the bitter knowledge of the grossly infuriating, underhanded, double dealing of that snake, Martino Belasci, and of the lack of confidence placed in him as head of the Forces to Suppress Banditry. One thing was certain in Colonel Cala's mind as he approached Palermo's environs: after devoting a lifetime to an honorable and impeccable career, achieved by hard work and a spotless integrity, he wasn't about to be made a laughing stock by some limp-wristed *finocchio* in government.

Long after the warring chieftains left Calemi's villa and Tori was left with his co-captain, Vincenzo, and the two sat watching the fires burn low, the famed Sicilian's eyes were fixed compellingly upon the bright flames curling in a variegation of colors.

"There are times, cousin, when I feel the power of words inhibits my action. I feel inside me a power that words would despoil, a power of conquest, far greater than words."

"But—without words, where would man be?" queried Vincenzo.

"Perhaps a lot better off than we are, now."

In those few moments, Tori felt a peculiar sensation, as if he were part of a spiralling circle within a circle moving towards infinity, where he observed the world from afar, and feeling a part of an enormous cosmos where the petty gripes of mankind meant nothing—nothing at all, he sensed a strange and incredible feeling, a marvel of weightlessness, a sensation that from this moment on, nothing would really matter. He no longer smiled with usual dark cynicism.

BOOK VII

"In these final hours before my exile, I feel compelled by a force more powerful than I to explain these seven tumultuous years of my existence. I know not where the future lies—or how history will document my life on earth. But, since God keeps accurate records, should I do less?

"In the spirit of candor and consultation I have often raised my face upwards and gazed through sun split clouds, high above the wind kissed mountains of gold above my village, which sheltered me and I have grown to love. Higher and higher I searched until I came face to face with God. He wasn't an angry God; neither wrathful nor disappointed. Yet, I saw upon his countenance, a profound sadness, a mournful melancholy.

" 'I did the best I could with the little help you gave me,' I said. 'You expected the impossible and I almost succeeded. But, God,' I hastened to add, 'When it all began, did you forget I was a mere mortal?' " . . .

A. Salvatore

At the end of January, 1950, Antigone was released from prison in accordance with the Holy Year amnesty provisions. In Montegatta where she retired to her house to become a recluse, the steady staccato of gunfire had ceased. From Salvatore there came no further ambushes, no offensive action, no more kidnap victims, no more retaliations. The villagers, unused to the unnatural atmosphere, asked themselves what was happening. They grew tense, frustrated, and apprehensive wondering of this was the lull before the storm. Not knowing heightened their anxieties.

The role of Colonel Cala in this period became a strange one to observe. To the more sophisticated observer, it became apparent that as he engaged in a series of contrived activities seemingly geared for the purpose of occupying newspaper space; frenzied actions slanted solely to relieve himself of any possible embarrassment when Minister Belasci's plans with Salvatore were finalized. Still, it was a crazy way for this stellar military man to behave.

Bandits who served Salvatore in his early days, and were later granted amnesty when Italy became a republic and had settled down to farming and a peaceful existence, were uprooted from their homes, arrested, and jailed—only to be systematically released hours later. One by one, their bodies were discovered dead on lonely waysides. In photographs that the FSB demanded be published, the poor culprits, invariably shown sprawled face down on the ground or in a gutter armed to the teeth with grenades, machine guns, and a host of weapons they couldn't possibly have toted about, caught the attention of several crime reporters who saw through the contrived photography, perceiving instantly the false manner in which the weapons had been planted around the corpses. It took a tribunal to learn that it had been part of a plan to undermine the remainder of Tori's men, who were at large, to give them an idea of what they might expect if they didn't surrender.

Because there was no longer an enemy to fight, it appeared that the FSB conducted warfare on their own initiative; Cala constructed his own opposition. Had he suddenly begun to learn to play the game according to Sicilian rules, those very same rules that once offended his morals? People in the know laughed at him. Others continued to watch his antics with brooding curiosity. The *mafiosi* in particular watched with singular interest and continued to ask themselves why Minister Belasci hadn't disbanded the Forces to Suppress Banditry in lieu of the clandestine negotiations underway with Salvatore. This provocative point of debate became a disquieting factor to all sides.

For the next few months, the foreboding gray mountains of Montegatta, fanged and chaotic, stood like silent specters of the past gazing down at the land of Salvatore like some imperious diety, waiting, watching, certain something spectacular was going to happen. The question on everyone's lips was the same: Where is Salvatore? North Africa—Brazil—Spain—America?

Rumors and speculations mushroomed and varied according to the source. He was in Spain raising an army to return and conquer his beloved country! Don't you know that? shouted his staunch supporters. You're crazy, shouted the undaunted Reds. He's in Russia enlisting her aid, for he's finally realized Communism is the only answer for his people! You're all crazy, shouted those in the know. Salvatore is in America to confer with his good friend President Truman! Whatsa matter, you can't see the handwriting on the wall? America has been behind him all the time! They won't let him down! If you had any sense, cried the skeptics, you'd know he's in North Africa on the run. But, he won't last! The Mafia will catch up with him. They never lost a contest before, did they? Oh, boy, are you all some crazy people, cried those who had lived a little longer and had seen the beginnings of this phenomenon Salvatore. Right now, while you are all stirring up wind with your stupid voices, Salvatore is secreted in Viterbo. He will rescue all his men from jail, like he's done so many times in the past. Shouldn't we know? He saved us from prison!

To support this last theory and make it plausible, the rumor spread about that Salvatore felt he couldn't trust his former companions to withhold the names of the high officials who instigated the Portella massacre, and whom Tori promised to protect in exchange for his freedom. But the rumors stirred by all these voices were false. No one guessed that in the nearly six months that sped quickly by, Salvatore had remained close to Castellammare and Monreale, shuttling back and forth between the Calemi and So-lameni villas. As often as he could he would visit his mother, and the bond between them grew stronger. His closest companion who was constantly at his side, was his cousin Vincenzo. Officially speaking, only Vincenzo, the Scoletti brothers, and Bastiano Terranova remained at large. The whereabouts of the Genovese brothers and a few others wasn't specifically known at the end of May.

Don Matteo Barbarossa was immersed in highly lu-crative business dealings that occupied most of his time. When news of Salvatore's highly explosive personal *port-folio* reached him, he grew disturbed because it threatened most of the men he'd placed in high office. Of all those in-culpated, in the portfolio, the Don had the least to lose. He had only to deny any participation—who wouldn't ac-cept his word? Because those men he'd supported politi-cally were involved and the scandal if made public would cause a breach in his carefully designed plans, the *Capo* had to concern himself.

He had meticulously posted, in chronological order, on a large bulletin board in his office, everything in print plus daily reports on the progress of the FSB. Reconstructed to scale on a large table next to the bay window overlooking the rear patio of the enormous Monreale villa was sprawled a relief map of Salvatore's territory, complete with toy soldiers, horses, and tanks similar to the one he had kept in his former office at the *Albergo-Sole*. On this model, depicting fields of action between Salvatore and the antibandit squads, both sides remained in the positions they'd been in before the neutralizing action of the Janu-ary pact, when Salvatore agreed to end all hostilities. In a sense, Don Matteo had long since considered the Salvatore matter closed. More vital and highly profitable issues com-manded his attention.

Involved in the business machinations of an interna-tional cartel, the Don ingeniously utilized America's Economic Aid program to implement the amassing of a sizeable fortune by diverting strategic Cold War supplies to Communist countries for a dear price. Through Mafia-controlled government officials, in nearly every Ministry office the extensive falsification of vital documents and forgeries ran rampant, and the political chain of command put into force by this redoubtable *capomafia* paid off handsomely in a highly complex plan that baffled the brightest Intelligence and Treasury agents from both the USA and Italy for many years. In addition to these lu-crative involvements, several of his colleagues had recently involved themselves in the transporting and sale of narcotics in the Luciano combine.

Despite the extensive involvements in these richly rewarding activities, Don Matteo was drawn inexplicably toward the matter of Salvatore. Soon after the last meeting with Mafia potentates, his own spies began infiltrating Salvatore's inner circle to bring about a demoralization of key figures who later defected to North Africa. His spies had succeeded in splitting the factions in Salvatore's camp with the lightning speed of a deadly serpent turned loose in a nursery of unsuspecting babies. Later, it was through his own organization that the defectors, tracked down and arrested, were extradited and shipped off to Viterbo in Italy in a manner no law enforcement agency could have initiated as expeditiously.

News of the existence of Salvatore's portfolio had called for an immediate halt to further skullduggery. Conferences with Martino Belasci brought about the cessation of any and all surreptitious activities aimed against Salvatore, and a regrouping of forces took place. Belasci couldn't risk the publication of the portfolio, knowing the communists would use the incendiary material to oust him from office. He assured Don Barbarossa he could handle the matter and from that moment on he personally took over the Salvatore matter.

Now, as the Don understood it, they had come to terms. Antigone Salvatore had been released from prison, and in a matter of time Salvatore would leave Sicily. The complicated negotiations with the principle powers had entered the final stages. It had been agreed that the other bandits awaiting trial would be exonerated. Vincenzo de Montana's freedom had been agreed upon in a satisfactory manner to all concerned.

However, through an oversight, the only project not terminated by the *capomafia* had been the search in America, by his associates, for Santino Siragusa and the personal portfolio of Salvatore. Don Barbarossa hadn't forgotten the portfolio, or Santino Siragusa—he had simply kept the information tucked into a corner of his mind and went about his business in the last six months giving little thought to his big-wind bandit from the hill who for a time had appeared on the scene with clashing cymbals and the roar of a loud, booming drum.

One month before the date of his departure, Salvatore entered the final stages of the preparations for his exile. He had held himself in readiness for a move to the New World, where he intended to lay the foundation for a new life and perhaps repair the old dream that had taken a circuitous route. He experienced an exaltation as if he stood on the crest of a magnificent mountain, upon which he alone remained untouchable and impregnable. So lofty were his last minute involvements, and so intricate were the ramifications surrounding the negotiations, that he hadn't noticed that the strong foundation he once took such pain and effort to carefully construct was being dismantled stealthily, stone by stone, layer by layer, until there remained only the keystone. Its removal could cause the utter destruction of the Salvatore empire—if not the legend.

One final task remained before Tori could bring himself to leave with a clear conscience. So on this day, one month before his scheduled departure, the soon-to-be-exiled King of Montegatta sat at the *escritoire* in his suite of rooms at the Calemi villa in Castellamare by the sea and he wrote one final letter—a letter that would prove to be the most significant act in the whirlwind tenure of his seven years of glory. The world would never know about this letter addressed to Don Barbarossa, his father.

Old Giacomo rode alongside the driver, Bartolomeo Calemi, in the Fiat en route to Monreale. In the old man's pocket was the letter written by Salvatore to be delivered to Don Barbarossa with the express orders that he was to guard it with his life. Giacomo, grateful for the opportunity to once again serve his *aquilo bravo*, assured him only death would separate him from the letter until it reached the proper hands. How little did he know how prophetic those words would be!

On this trip to the Villa Barbarossa, Calemi boiled with curiosity. As he considered the animosity between the old and new Mafias and the accumulative troubles the youngbloods had suffered to protect and defend Salvatore, the singular thought of secret messages traveling to the *capomafia* gravely disturbed him. He interpreted it as a total lack of trust on Salvatore's part. He questioned Giacomo, subtly, from time to time, but the old man had given him no quarter. As a true Sicilian who knew the importance of sealing one's lips in the presence of the Mafia, young or old, he remained silent, implcable, and immovable.

Giacomo hadn't understood the reason for all the secrecy and protection afforded Salvatore. His brave young eagle whom he'd come to worship these past seven years could take care of himself any day! When word came summoning him to Tori's side, his feet, crippled and slow, took wings. After expending a wealth of emotional greetings, the old man listened as his Chief stressed that the contents of the letter were of so compromising a nature, it must no get into anyone else's hands other than Don Barbarossa.

"Yes, brave eagle, I understand," he had reverently replied. Then, because his brave eagle looked pale and wan under the strain of the past several months, Giacomo asked Tori if he was all right and if he needed him.

Tori had embraced the old man, slapped his back with gusto, then gripped his arm in the old familiar gesture that brought many memories and tears to his eyes.

"*Va bene*, old friend. Besides Vincenzo, you are the only one I can trust. All around me are men who call themselves friends, but as you so aptly engraved on my gun butt once, *Beware of enemies, once. Of friends a thousand times!* I continue to view these . . . friends . . . with extreme caution. *Allora*, when you've delivered the letter to Don Matteo, return here; I shall have a letter for you to take to Mamma. *Va Bene?*"

"*Va bene, aquilo*," said the old man, and he left to join the awesome Calemi.

Now, they continued to drive in silence, each man absorbed in his own thoughts. Concerned that something could go wrong and affect the lengthy negotiations expended on Salvatore's behalf, Calemi made a quick decision. Without a change in expression, or advance warning, he pulled the car off the road and stopped on the shoulder. With split second timing he removed his gun from its holster and shot the puzzled old man through the head.

The tired, old body sagged forward. Even then he made a last attempt to serve Salvatore by reaching for the letter as if he might destroy it before Calemi could lay his hands on it. "*Aquilo . . . Aquilo*," he murmured, as blood spurted from the hole in his head.

Calemi took aim, squeezed the trigger again, and shot off Giacomo's face. Blood and flesh splattered in all directions. Now there was no doubt Giacomo was dead and beyond identification. He expertly searched his pockets for the letter and proceeded to remove all identity from the body of his passenger. He pocketed the tidy sum of bills Tori had slipped into the old arthritic's pockets. Glancing cautiously in all directions, Calemi dragged the body out of the auto and dumped it over the rocky cliff to the sea below with less emotion than it took to blow his nose.

Back at the car, he released the bonnet of the Fiat and

834

jiggled the radiator cap until steam escaped. Working gingerly to avoid being burned by the hissing vapor, he unglued the flap on the envelope. He lay the letter on the seat of the car, then moved about to remove all traces of blood stains. He found an oil cloth behind the front seat which he dipped into the radiator to soak. Twirling it in the air about him to cool, h ethen meticulously cleaned his hands and rubbed the blood stains from his jacket and those left on the seat of the car. Satisfied, he tossed the bloodied rag behind a boulder and sat behind the wheel of the car, inscrutably studying the contents of the letter.

Calemi's eyes widened in astonishment as his nervous eyes raced back and forth over the lines. His excitement, increased to a feverish pitch, caused his whole body to tremble at the implications contained in this explosive missive. His shaky hands, holding the letter, fell sackily on the steering wheel as he forced himself to gaze out at the panorama of the sea below him. He couldn't breathe.

"Botta de Sanguo!" he muttered aloud. "I don't believe it!" One hand flew to his face, covered his lips, then slid off to one side where he slapped his cheek in a gesture of stupefaction. He reread the letter, to convince himself he wasn't dreaming, slipped it back into the envelope, and, when it wouldn't reseal, tapped it thoughtfully on the empty seat next to him. After considering the volatile implications, he came to a decision. He slipped the letter into a jacket pocket, started up the motor, and drove to Monreale, where he stopped at a small shop to purchase a bottle of glue to reseal the envelope. Patching his shattered composure as well while his brain roiled with the possibility of presenting himself to the *capomafia*, he drove off toward the Villa Barbarossa.

Shortly before Giacomo had arrived at Calemi's villa to run Tori's errand. Natale Solameni had stopped by for a friendly chat with his famous friend.

He mentioned in passing that he was en route to the Villa Barbarossa for a meeting. "One of my cousin's friends, Luciano, wants to cut us in on the business." He shook his wrist in a rapid motion. *"Managghia,* Salvatore, too bad we couldn't have worked something else out for you. We could all become millionaires in a hurry!" he told Tori.

"Aren't you satisfied with what you already have? You own the west coast of Sicily—and with this new contract, you'll soon own Palermo!" teased Tori playfully, knowing Solameni liked to be reminded of his wealth. It was the only way the *mafioso* could combat the inner frustrations he had endured at being considered an outcast by his father, a formidable *mafioso* of the old Mafia.

Solameni grinned self-consciously. He wore his compliments like one would show off jewelry. "*Allora*, I've got to leave. I wanted only to pause and tell you to keep your courage. How much longer, three . . . four weeks or so?"

"Or so," laughed Tori. "*Aspetta*, Natale," he called. "Do me a favor, eh? Give this note to Barbarossa." He sat down, scribbled a few lines, slipped it into an envelope, sealed it, and scribbled the name *Don Barbarossa* across its front. He handed it to his friend.

If Solameni was surprised by the request, he refrained from showing it. He crammed the envelope into his pocket, shoved a chocolate tidbit into his mouth, and waved Salvatore off.

Solameni hadn't earned his reputation or his fortune by being a nice guy. Despite his affable ways, he knew every trick in the book. The stocky, young man with a predatory face even controlled the tuna fisheries on the west coast in addition to the wealth accumulated in the post-war construction business. He was a driven man, a hustler personified, who dipped his fingers into every pie thrown his way and managed somehow even to get a piece of the action on those pies withheld from him.

Like Calemi, Solameni grew concerned over Salvatore's sudden interest in Don Barbarossa, whom the new Mafia considered to be Tori's arch enemy. He didn't wait until he boarded his car before he peeled back the flap on the envelope, removed the letter, and read it with a conspiratorial air.

"Godfather," it began. "*By special courier, my trusted old friend Giacomo will bring a letter to you, meant only for your eyes. Should it arrive by any other means than through him, use your discretion in what must be done. Respectfully yours, your Godson, Salvatore.*"

Natale Solameni shrugged, refolded the letter, slipped it back into the envelope, and resealed the letter. He tore the wrapper off another chocolate, popped it into his mouth, got into the car, and drove off.

Watching him from the upper balcony, Tori smiled to himself, then laughed aloud. He returned to his room where he put the finishing touches on the letter he would later entrust to old Giacomo to deliver for him.

Don Matteo's reaction to the note delivered by Natale Solameni was one of apathy, then annoyance. He tossed it aside on his desk only to pick it up and reread it several times. Noticeably agitated, his usual confidence faded as questions formed in his mind. Why all the intrigue over the delivery of a letter? And why did Salvatore wish to communicate with him at this late date, after an interminable silence? He was not amused.

His thoughts were interrupted abruptly when Mario Cacciatore knocked at the door of his study and entered the room.

"Bartolomo Calemi is here. He says he has a letter for you. Only to you will he deliver it."

"From who?" asked the Don, suddenly alert. He knew his Godson lived at the Calemi villa until time for his departure.

"He wouldn't say."

"First, bring the letter."

Noting his hesitation, Don Matteo shoved the note toward his bodyguard who read it and then asked, "What do you wish done?"

"Bring me the letter—*first!*"

"*Va bene.*"

Absorbed in watching an assortment of lovebirds and canaries in the aviary, off the foyer of the villa, Calemi didn't hear Cacciatore's light footsteps until he was almost upon him.

"Don Matteo wishes, first, to see the letter," muttered the swarthy bodyguard indifferently as he studied the youngblood.

"No, no!" Calemi waved his hand in a negative fashion. "I can't do that. This letter must be delivered personally from my hand to Don Barbarossa. I have my orders . . ." Calemi paled at the sudden, queasy feeling that surged through him. *Something's wrong,* he thought. *I should have brought along some insurance.* The side of his face screwed up in a scowl and the deeply pitted craters looked more grotesque, as his eyes flared wildly for a few seconds.

Cacciatore stared with brutal openness at the disfiguring scars on the youngblood's face. His own scars were frightful, but he learned long ago not to smile or exaggerate any expressions that may cause hideous distortions to his features. He shrugged and raised his eyebrows impatiently.

"I, too, follow orders. It's best you let me deliver the letter first."

In a stupid, blundering move, Calemi reached for his automatic, but wasn't fast enough for the formidable Cacciatore, who shoved a blade into his gut quicker than the eye could follow. An expression of shocked surprise followed by disorganized emotion registered on his face before he doubled over in muffled agony and fell heavily into Cacciatore's arms.

Calmly the Don's bodyguard dragged his body along the tiled hall and propped it onto a high-backed throne chair of carved oak. He searched Calemi's pockets and retrieved the letter. He called out in a throaty voice,

"Samuzzo! . . . Samuzzo. . . ." He held the sagging, dead body up against the wall and beckoned to a flashily dressed *piccioto*, who appeared at the other end of the long hallway. With a jerk of his head, Cacciatore silently indicated he should dispose of the corpse. "Leave his identification on him."

Don Barbarossa examined the letter under the glare of his desk lamp, noting the seepage of extra glue oozing from the flap. He lifted it gently, observing readily that it had been tampered with. Filled with curiosity he donned his reading glasses.

Caro Papa:

The Don froze. Every life-producing force in his body stopped cold. His eyes quickly re-read the salutation.

"*Mah, che cazzu!*" he muttered aloud. "What the fuck is this?"

He thumbed through the pages and found the last page of the letter and his eyes rested on the signature. A hot flush swept through his body. He paused a moment to wipe the sweat beads on his forehead. His hands trembled and the letter shook uncontrollably. He set it down on his desk. Reaching for the wine decanter, he poured himself a glass full, and drank it down.

Now, he picked up the letter and began to read:

> *Caro Papa*:
> *The most difficult thing in my life has been the ordeal of sitting down to write this letter to you. Soon, I'll be leaving my Sicilia, but I couldn't leave without clearing the air between us. It wouldn't be fair to either of us.*
> *When we first met, I knew nothing of our true relationship. Not even at the second or third encounter did I suspicion that we were bound together by flesh and blood.*
> *The American Colonel Modica at our meeting urged me to involve myself in politics. He saw something in me, something special, which*

*convinced him I should be a leader of my people.
Had I known then what he envisioned in me was
that part which is you, I might have understood
him better. Each time he described certain attributes of mine I couldn't recognize in myself, it
was as if he painted a word-picture describing
you—your past and your numerable accomplishments.*

*As the similarity between us became more ob-
vious to me, turbulent conflicts continued to distort my senses. I knew instantly in my heart what
my mind tried to deny; that I was of your flesh,
the son of your seed, the issue of your loins. My
mother didn't deny the truth! . . ."*

Don Matteo's hand containing the letter fell with a
heavy, dull thud to the desk. He could feel the blood drain
from his body as he sagged forward, limply. He made constant dabs attempting to mop up the profuse perspiration
on his face and neck with his handkerchief. Reaching for
a vial containing phenobarbital tablets he washed them
down with a glass of water from a carafe nearby. *So this
is to be my penance? Salvatore is my son! My son! What
witchery is this?* After inhaling a few deep breaths of air,
he picked up the letter again:

*Oh, how I resented you for cheating me out
of a life I've dreamed of since childhood! Your
empty promises, the manner in which you continuously manipulated me, the numerous traps
and intrigues, all these were abhorrent to me,
because I am your son. Because I am your son
and too much like you, I saw through all your
schemes aimed at my destruction—a bit too late
to design retribution.*

*As Godson to the much heralded Barbarossa,
I stood in awe of you all my life. Can you imagine how I felt when I learned you were my real
father? The conflicts, resentments, and self-tor-
ture I endured are beyond calculation to anyone who's never experienced my dilemma.*

*Because I refused to be owned by you, or any-
one else, I couldn't come to you with the revelation of this truth between us. I, too, grew up
trusting in myself, feeling what you must have
felt in your youth, when you were forced to bide
your time—waiting for the moment you could*

shoot to the sky and conquer the earth, the sun, and the moon! By attempting to subjugate me to your will, you would have robbed me of my destiny. It wouldn't have worked. We're too much alike.

Perhaps under your auspices, I might be sitting where Martino Belasci sits, close to the helm of our government. Or where Bernardo Malaterra sits, in the Assembly. Both are sons of mafiosi—but not on the scale of your worth.

I regret that we've both expended spies, plots of treachery, hatred, and vengence against each other. This useless fiasco with the FSB has been an abomination to me! To have killed so many innocent people and caused such untold hardship upon countless others just so the FSB saves face is reprehensible!

Allora, the bandits of Salvatore are no more! They'll soon settle down into obscurity. So shall Salvatore be gone from his beloved Sicilia. Would I have done anything differently in my life? Destiny wills what she will. All I did has been done and history shall record it so.

Pero, there's a matter of which you should be made aware. News has reached me, totally inaccurate, that my brother in-law, Santino Siragusa, was apprehended in America: that the portfolio was confiscated and destroyed. What utter nonsense! More of Belasci's absurd propaganda! I personally spoke to Siragusa two weeks after the purported abduction took place.

The letter sent to the Chief Magistrate at Viterbo has been received by the Tribunal, I'm told. Hopefully it will put an end to the ridiculous and trumped up charges against my men, who were jailed and bound over for trial. When the story of Salvatore is told, those men of the press who suspicion the truth will know the intent behind the letter. The whole of Sicily would have to be annihilated to stop her people from knowing the real truth.

It's unfortunate that you and your associates underestimate the common man. They aren't as easily beguiled as you choose to believe. The day will come when you men, who've looked backward for so long, will come to realize you've been guided by sure death—not life! Sicilians

*will awaken one day and move forward to the
spirit of freedom and insist on the right to expect humane treatment by their government.
They're a good people who deserve more than
meager existence foisted on them by a handful
of arrogant and insufferable baronial delinquents!*

*Perhaps the spirit of Salvatore who is Sicily
shall be the spirit who moves them. My last wish
is that it could have been different between us,
my father."*

*With respect from your son,
A. Salvatore, Barbarossa.*

*P.S. Somehow I feel the urge to be candid with
you so that my soul will rest better. One night, on
the night of July 7, 1948, I came within six feet
of you, at your villa in Monreale. You were in
my gun sight. I tried with all my strength to
pull the trigger, to kill you. I couldn't do it. How
in God's name could I have killed my own
father—even though you were my mortal enemy?
Adieu, Salvatore.*

For the next five hours Don Matteo read and reread the
letter, losing all semblance of time. "Salvatore is my son,"
he muttered over and over, as if in repetition the fact
would become more real to him. It took time to fit the
pieces together, to fully acknowledge that the sperm of his
manhood could have conceived so splendid a son. The
more he considered the more real became the truth.
What's the matter with me, he asked himself. *Salvatore
can be the son of no other man than Matteo Barbarossa.
Such a magnificent son I fathered—a truly handsome
prince of a man! He's a proud, manly, king of a man. He
is my son. My son!* Figghiu de mi cuore! *Son of my heart!
Goddammit! He's the son of Matteo Barbarossa! Son of
the* capomafia! *From me he inherited all that I am plus
that which God endowed him with to have made him the
miracle he is. Is he some* maschiezzo! Managghia! *He believes in himself as only the son of a real* capo di tutti capi
*does. Oh joys of all joys! My son is the man who could be
king of Sicily!*

The Don wanted to shout the news from the top of the
world to anyone who'd listen. But, to whom could he tell
this marvelous news? To whom? Dejected, he sat back in
his chair, the very life drained from him as he read the
letter over and over, mulling over its contents. From time

to time, he wrung his hands in desperation, then, alternately as a rush of adrenalin flushed through him, he'd pop barbituates into his mouth. Nothing helped to ease the brutal but exquisite pain he felt. Was this why he hadn't been able to take punitive measures against his son? How could he have known that such a tie existed between them? Still, he should have known, for Salvatore was the image of him in his youth.

He considered what Tori had written in the postscript—that he'd come close to killing him one night nearly a year ago. He couldn't even recollect the events of that night, but, never mind. He believed his son.

Only once in his life did Matteo Barbarossa break down and cry real tears, when his first love Diamonte had died. This moment marked the second time. A genuine feeling of sorrow shook his composure and he felt as if a part of him was dying and he had no control over it. "Son of my seed! Son of my life!" he sobbed unashamedly. "Why did you let this happen, God? Why? What irony have you conspired against Matteo Barbarossa?"

The enormity of the truth after such close examination bowled him over. Emotionally overwrought and utterly destroyed inside, the Don finally sat down after pacing the floor and sank heavily into his chair behind the desk. The tears had left him. Once he'd been the personification of a timeless evil and all that was violent in mankind, now he sat hunched over in a simple portrait of a mere mortal mourning his son. His chin hung down to his chest in prostrated defeat.

A series of mental images raced through his consciousness. Mental images of his son as he was when they first met in Godrano. He recalled Archbishop Voltera's perceptive observation of Salvatore when his name came up for discussion in the Grand Council meeting. He saw Salvatore riding Napoleono through the lands and recollected all their conversations with painful accuracy. How boldly he'd asked for the life of Don Pippinu Grasso! And why not?

Everything came back with such vivid clarity and seemed so alive to the *capomafia* that he suddenly realized it was the only place his son would remain alive for him—in the cradle of his mind.

Realization struck hard at the core of him! There was nothing he could do to save the flesh of his flesh! The order had been given!

Or, had it? Was it too late? Salvatore had denied it in

his letter, but news reached Don Matteo that Santino Siragusa had been caught in America and the explosive portfolio destroyed. He pounded the top of his desk with his fist until it ached.

"Managghia u' diaoro! Am I bound to be so helpless in this?" he shouted aloud. The peculiar irony of the situation tore him to shreds. Again his head dropped into his hands and he sat hunched over his desk a pitiful, old man.

The role of a father was new to him. His role as *capomafia*, nearly of lifetime duration and more a part of him, compelled him to think as a *mafioso, primo de tutti,* first of all. The more he considered the Siragusa case, the more he realized he'd been right from the beginning, especially now that he learned Salvatore was his own son. His mistake in never giving Salvatore credit for thinking as the son of a *mafioso* struck at him and he considered why Salvatore, despite his political naivete, had been more shrewd in many things than his enemies. Why not? He had the blood of the most redoubtable *mafioso* of all in his veins. In the Don's mind it followed that Tori wouldn't have been careless and allowed only one copy of his portfolio to exist. There had to be another, for insurance, no? Hah! Perhaps the portfolio never even left Sicily. Was it possible Salvatore had sent Siragusa to America to distract everyone?

An enigmatic smile crossed his lips and he began to feel a lessening of the burden he endured earlier. He continued to explore the matter on a different tack.

For hours he extolled the virtues and wrongdoings of his son, equated myopically with the moralities of a *mafioso.* He reflected on the caution used by Salvatore in sending the letter to him. Even at the end he protected me, thought the Don. The letter in the wrong hands would not only cause embarrassment, but might serve to promote irrevocable breaks in the shaky structure and present status between old and new Mafia. It was bad enough the youngbloods caused a weakness in the heirarchy that split factions considerably. If it was learned that Salvatore was Don Matteo's son, the youngbloods would think nothing of murdering their fathers, or vice versa, for profit. A precedent would have been established, one that could easily destroy the bond of father to son. Who would ever believe the *capomafia* of Sicilily couldn't recognize his own flesh and blood? Oh, the detestably exquisite shame of it all!

Don Barbarossa berated himself for not having learned the truth before this. As plans formulated in his mind over new possibilities presented to him by this stunning revelation, the anguish in his heart abated temporarily. By 6 A.M. he finally dozed off on the sofa, more from the sedation of so many tranquilizers than the need for sleep.

Cacciatore knocked repeatedly on the study door. He got no response. Gravely concerned over the *capomafia*'s welfare, he used a set of skeleton keys to gain entrance to the room, only to find the Don sprawled out in a restful pose of drugged sleep, the letter still clutched in his hand.

The heavily sedated sleeping form of Don Barbarossa didn't budge, even after several attempts to awaken him. Cacciatore removed a blanket from a nearby closet and covered his body. He picked up the letter from the floor, shook his head tolerantly, and was about to place it on the desk when something caught his attention. The salutation, "*Caro Papa*" wasn't something he could ignore easily. Arrested by the words, curiosity got the best of him and he read the letter. Later he wished he hadn't. He glanced again at the Don's sleeping form, placed the letter on the desk, turned out the lights, and exited, closing the door behind him.

Misericordia! What a mess! Only today the death order came for Salvatore because Luciano's friends in the States claim they destroyed the portfolio of Salvatore! What a *commedia* this will be! *Managghia!* As he sipped his coffee, a curious glint entered his dark, brooding eyes. *Managghia!* Salvatore is Don Barbarossa's son! His mind exploded into disorganized conjecture. He could think of nothing else! Was it possible for the man who knew everything in Sicily not to have known about his own son?

CHAPTER 61

Natale Solameni compulsively stuffed another of a rapidly diminishing mound of chocolates from his desk into his mouth. Chomping noisily on it, he glanced up as Nero Giotto, a trusted companion, entered the office, his features a relief map of boiling frustration. "Goddamnit!" he shouted. "Look at this, will you." He tossed a copy of a death certificate he just received from the new Chief Inspector of Police, Zanorelli, at Nero. "Calemi's dead," he snapped.

"Calemi dead?" Nero, a cold-blooded killer—a short man with closely cropped, black hair, wiry as nails, and the finely chiseled features of a Botticelli saint—glanced stonily at his boss as he shoved a stack of orders at him, taking the certificate from the desk. "Sign these," he told Natale. As he scanned the official document, his hand swept the flat top of his brush-cut hair. His nostrils flared slightly and his cat eyes, yellowish green, narrowed thoughtfully. "Who did it to Calemi?"

"Can't these papers wait until tomorrow?" asked Natale, flipping through them with obvious annoyance.

"Your foreman says today. Who did it? You know?"

"Sonofabitch! 'Who did it? You know?'" he retorted mockingly. "*Mah* how the fuck do I know, eh? I just got the fuckin' report. "Solameni's black eyes perused the orders before signing them. "You better find out something, Nero. We gotta know, ya hear?" He continued the business with the orders.

"Where's Salvatore?"

"Calemi's villa. The usual place."

"Maybe you should move him, fast." He gestured with his hand for emphasis.

"That's what I'd be expected to do, if it's part of a plot. He's safest exactly where he is. Fuck! Only a few more days and this has to happen. I thought we figured all the angles."

Nero, who received his name because he carried a sub-machine gun in a violin case like his American counterparts had been rumored to do, was dissatisfied. He slapped the report in his hand, exclaiming his feelings. "*Mah*, who could have done this? There's no order for Calemi's death. No rumors, nothing. There would have been rumbles, *capeeshi?* I don't like this, Natale, not now. Not at this late date."

Afternoon shadows lengthened, dimming the interior of the office. Outside, the raspy, impatient whistles of tuna boats, announcing their arrival with the day's catch, were greeted by loud, brittle voices shouting orders to prepare for unloading. A strong fish odor clung cohesively to the air, permeating the office interior with the pungent stale smells both men were used to.

"Sonofabitch! I'll be happy when this dirty business is finished. Everyone's fucking guts have been wrung out and hung up to dry in this Salvatore affair."

"Who could have done it to Calemi?" asked Nero,

watching his boss chew his fingernails to a frazzle. "Where the hell were his bodyguards?"

"Fucking report says his face was slashed beyond recognition. Not the work of youngbloods. Maybe in Corleone, *amico*, but not here," Natale said tersely, trying to fathom the riddle of Calemi's death.

"Maybe the FSB, eh? To save face they'll have to change color like the gecko's. Phooh—they'll look like asses when Belasci announces Salvatore's exile."

"Fucking bastards! You're right! Whole fuckin' mess begins to smell of the fuckin' betrayal Tori tried to warn us about right from the start of this dirty business." Obsessed with the four letter word he learned from American GIs during the occupation, he used it to express himself with boring frequency.

"Read the report again, boss," suggested Nero. "Where it says, . . . 'such underhanded double dealing annoys the FSB and moves them into defensive action.' "

As Solameni scanned the report, he chewed his nails voraciously. Periodically, bursts of awareness alerted him to what he was doing to his fingers, he'd clench his fists angrily and slam the desk with them until he stopped the compulsion that turned him into a nervous wreck. He lit a cigarette, puffed two or three times, then snuffed it out savagely in the ash tray piled high with candy wrappers.

Nero dumped the ash tray's contents into a waste receptacle and replaced it on the makeshift desk. He watched his boss solemnly and, feeling a surge of overwhelming compassion combined with mixed feelings of disgust for the man's inability to control these compulsive obsessive habits, wisely kept his thoughts to himself. His cat-eyes fixed intently on the other as if he could read his mind.

Solameni reached for another chocolate and munched on it thoughtfully. He and Calemi had involved themselves in a tempest of dealings and double dealings these past few months, orchestrated by Minister Belasci. Fifty thousand dollars was the price offered them, if they'd pull off Salvatore's exile without further incident. One half that amount had been paid them. However, the negotiations finalized in conjunction with Inspector D'Verde had caused a deviation from the plan formulated by Tori to include the FSB in the final settlement to offset treachery. Both Calemi and he had felt it totally unnecessary to include the FSB in their dealings and had no intention of sharing their spoils with those greedy hawks. He suddenly saw the wisdom in Tori's judgment.

"*Porco Diaoro!* Pig of the devil!" exclaimed Natale.

"Salvatore was right! He predicted that the rivalry between the *carabinieri* and the security police would be a factor to consider!" Not for a moment did he connect Don Barbarossa to Calemi's death. At this point there was nothing to indicate such foul play.

He angrily snatched the pen from his desk and proceeded signing orders.

"*Butana u diaoro!* Whore of the devil!" he cried out in pain. He had accidently bit his lip with such ferocity to draw blood. He angrily tossed aside the pen, rose to his feet, and crossed the room to the streaked mirror over a messy wash basin in the corner of the bleak room of peeling wallpaper, cracked walls, and blistered paint, sadly in need of renovation, where he inspected the cut critically. He washed his hands and scrubbed his fingertips with a stiff brush, wincing at the pain on the tender areas. Almost in a ritualistic manner he applied a styptic pencil to the cut, and at the bleeding around his finger nails. Shaking his hands gingerly and wincing now and again at the pain and destruction done in the wake of such fierce nail-biting, Solameni returned to his seat behind the desk. From a drawer he removed a roll of adhesive tape, pulled out a portion of it, and cut off the required amount. Cutting the tape into smaller strips, he proceeded to tape the tip of each damaged finger.

Nero Giotti glanced from the empty candy dish to his boss's taped fingers and shook his head with solemn compassion. "Natale," he said quietly. "What about the old man, eh? You think he could've had a hand in all this?"

"What the hell you trying to say, eh? What about the *old man?*"

"Only what a few have been saying. You know, a rumor here, a whisper there, a lifted eyebrow, yet no one talks."

"Look, you got something to say? Say it! Go on, spill it. Stop the old woman act. Fucking bastards! All I got around me is old women. Nagging old bags."

Nero Giotto shrugged evasively and shifted his eyes around the room. "I'm asking. You think he could've had a hand in this job?"

Solameni glared at him. He tossed the pen aside, kicked at an empty crate, and glowered angrily. "Go on! Get the hell outa here. Leave me alone, eh!"

Nero tossed his hands up in the air and made a gesture of helplessness as he retreated towards the door. Before he departed his boss shouted, "Go get some more candy for Christ's sake!"

Solameni slammed his fist hard on the rickety desk, causing it to tremble under the impact. The telephone jiggled off the hook, the empty candy bowl spiralled rakishly within its circle several times before wheeling to a halt, and Natale, incited further by this instant confusion he seemed unable to circumvent, glumly restored order to the desk top. He sat back meditatively.

What about the old man, eh? You think he could've had a hand in all this?

Those two questions stirred his guts and stoked a cauldron of bad memories in Natale. The bad blood between him and his super-powered *mafioso* father, Don Nitto Solameni of the old Mafia, was a touchy subject—one very few men every brought up in Natale's presence.

Under the complicated system of protecting Salvatore, it had become increasingly difficult for anyone to contact Tori directly. The route, devised by Solameni and Calemi, was tedious, long, and involved and most circuitous even for his paladins and those who remained of Tori's Inner Circle. Betrayals were feared on every front. Regardless of how Tori felt in the matter, once he placed himself in the hands of the new Mafia for protection, he was obliged to abide by their stringent rules. Unknown to Salvatore or Natale Solameni for that matter until it came to his attention a few weeks before, many traps had been expertly set until one by one the inner circle of Tori's men had been spirited away without publicity so that Tori wouldn't learn of the incidents. Arrested by the FSB and speedily flown to Viterbo to await trial, most of the bandits didn't know what struck them. They had been instructed to lay low to escape prosecution until Salvatore's negotiations had been finalized. Restless and tired of the inactivity, they had all at one time or another attempted to contact their chief, making them exceedingly vulnerable to capture. Only Vincenzo de Montana and the Scoletti brothers remained at large, so to speak.

This of itself had been of no earthshaking importance to Natale Solameni until he learned through the new Mafia spy network that his father, Don Nitto, had spearheaded the treacheries. Shaken, Natale had rushed to Calemi's villa to assure Salvatore this had been none of his doing. That day, he found Tori shaving in the bathroom. Unable to contain his distress he had unburdened his soul to the outlaw. Tori, calmly continuing his toilet, had replied compassionately, "I know, Natale. I've known for sometime you've had no part in the old man's deviltry."

More astonished than relieved, Natale asked, "You know, already? What will you do?"

"There isn't much I can do," Tori had replied. "Is there?" Tori had told the *mafioso* nothing of what he knew to have transpired at the hands of Don Nitto. He was certain he'd know soon enough. Applying a hot towel to his face for a moment, he had patted it dry with a fresh one and walked back into the bedroom with Natale following at his heels like a faithful hound dog.

"At the end of June or the first of July perhaps," Tori had told him, "I'll be gone, and if Belasci lives up to his bargain, my men will be pardoned. The Tribunal President has already received my statement. *Annunca*, Natale, take courage. It's just a matter of time before I'll be out of your hair."

"What do you mean *if* Belasci lives up to the agreement?" he had asked.

"Natale," Tori had said patiently. "If you knew them as long as I've known them, you'd take what politicians say with a grain of salt."

Natale had agreed with Tori and said so, muttering something about honor between thieves being the only trustworthy kind. Tori had laughed and, patting the heavily paunched *mafioso* on the belly, advised him to lay off the sweets. "Your *panza* hangs out like that of a pregnant cow," he had chided.

"I'll come see you tomorrow," said Solameni, ignoring Tori's words. "And Salvatore, no hard feelings about the old man, eh?"

"None," remarked the young man who watched him depart.

That day early in May, before Solameni left the villa, he had ordered a double guard around the clock to protect his infamous guest. At his own villa he placed men on day and night surveillance and doubled the shifts of bodyguards at the fisheries and construction company offices.

Coming out of his reveries, Natalie asked himself how the hell Salvatore would take the death of Calemi? Fuck! Now he'd have to tell him about their double crossing of Colonel Cala! Damn the devil! Damn! Damn! In a short while it would have all ended.

He left his office, surrounded by three bodyguards, got into the Fiat, and drove toward Castellammare to see Salvatore. En route he was absorbed with black thoughts of his father, Don Nitto Solameni. Could the old bastard have had a hand in killing Calemi? The m.o. had certainly been old Mafia. Fucking bastard! Why had such a man been wished upon him as a father? Solameni's dark, twitching eyes, glittering, rolling, jerking at times, inspired distrust and wariness in others, but hadn't in Salvatore, who was moved to profound compassion because he knew how much Natale needed love and got nothing from the man who should have given it to him—his father.

In the Monreale area, no more awesome man existed than the *mafioso* without a face, as Don Nitto was known in his territory. His ability to control his inner thoughts so skillfully resulted in a continual, frozen, masklike facial expression that became his trademark. Not only did Don Nitto disagree with his son's youngblood affiliations, he considered all connections to the new Mafia a slap in the face to him, something for which he never forgave his son.

Having grown up under the umbrella of his father's mighty and insufferable power, spoon-fed to him in doses that suffocated him, the neurotic Natale finally broke away from the old man's clutches and managed to assert himself in ways that might have provoked pride and praise from any normal father. None was forthcoming from the soured, loathesome, tyrranical old man whose arrogance and self-inflated ego bordered the erratic behavior and grandeur illusions of an antisocial psychopath who attempted to make his family accept him at his own self-evaluation. He was an absolute despot, a black-hearted sonofabitch of a man!

Don Nitto, a powerfully built man in his fifties, bald as an egg with a hairy chest and arms to make up for the lack of it on his head, looked ten feet tall. Actually he was five feet nine inches. He had the fierce, black-eyed look and appearance of an early Ottoman Turk. His nose was sharp and hooked, his lips thick and full with a cruel twist. No one had ever seen Don Nitto smile, laugh, cry, frown, or give vent to any emotion in the act of everyday living. Absolute control of his facial expressions had evoked fear from everyone including his son Natale, who had had occasion to witness his savage brutality and overbearing, dictatorial ways with his children, all of whom left home the moment they had saved enough to escape his tyranny.

Natale had been the recipient of his excoriating, ego-destroying, vicious tongue lashing all his life. To this day father and son only saw each other when necessary, for no love existed between them.

This highly respected member of the old Mafia, along with his hindsighted cronies, had perpetuated their hate and contempt and the jealousies of all the younger *mafiosi* and did all in their power to retard their progress. It stuck in their craw that the young cocks hadn't been made to pay their dues before receiving enormous benefits.

Recently there'd been more to rankle Don Nitto, a man who struck terror in the hearts of men who might have business with him.

Only a modern-day psychiatrist could explain the complicated syndrome of so warped a personality and why the embodiment of his hatred and contempt should focus on Salvatore, a man he'd never met. Often in the past, Don Nitto had voiced an outspoken loathing for Salvatore's flamboyant comportment. More revolting to the Don had been Tori's highly lauded letter-writing to the press. He had detested the uncanny flair for publicity demonstrated by the outlaw throughout his colorful career; something against the grain of most *mafiosi*. The Don was a man possessed by hatred and envy, and churning through his arteries was a violent and passionate jealousy when he considered that he, a powerful *Mafia* Don, hadn't achieved the status or reverence paid Salvatore. He despised most of all the renegade's generosity to the poor. It repelled him, insulted everything for which a man of respect stood. A man of respect took and took from the people, bled them dry, and kept them subjugated through fear. It was the only way. Not what this fool was doing. You don't gain respect by being too good to the people!

When Don Nitto learned that his son and the youngblood Mafia had elected to protect Salvatore against the wishes of the old Mafia, he tempestuously opposed him, berated him for such gross stupidity, and denounced him, bellowing "No son of mine would commit so dishonorable an act!"

All his life, Don Nitto despised ostentatious exaggerations of wealth. He lived his life in a hovel, generously called a farmhouse, out in the country, doing without conveniences or luxuries he could well afford. Daily he tended flocks of sheep and lived in virtual squalor. It remained an enigma to all, including his children, why such a man, respected and devoutly feared as Lucifer himself, should choose to live as primitively as he did. It certainly heightened the mysterious aura that clung to him and he continued to reign as the most awesome man in the hills surrounding Palermo. Deep inside him, although he feared no man, remained the innate doubt, that if he should give up the craft of his fathers, shepherding, his wealth would disappear.

When Captain Franchina learned about the legendary

mafioso and the bad blood existing between father and son, he felt certain he discovered the connecting link to bring their plans of capturing Salvatore to fruition. He had no idea, when he embarked on the mission of making contact with Don Nitto, that the *mafioso* had already turned down tempting offers by the security police and *carabinieri* to betray his son and Salvatore.

At about noon on a day late in April of that year, Captain Franchina had finally located Don Nitto high on a hillside tending his sheep. Watching the approaching peacock dressed in fine plumage from a distance, the Don made no move until he was within a hundred yards of him. Then, swinging his *lupara* into place, he took careful aim and held the strutting *major domo* in his sights until Franchina hesitated and stopped abruptly.

Frozen-faced, Don Nitto demanded bluntly. "What's a fancy dressed rare bird like you doing so far from his roost?"

"Don Nitto Solameni?" Franchina's voice filled with caution, as he mopped his sweaty brow.

"Talk!" ordered the man with no face. The *lupara* never wavered.

"Put the gun down and we talk," said Franchina.

Slowly, the gun was lowered. The effect of his black eyes nearly shattered Franchina's resolve, but, he held firm.

"I said . . . talk."

"I want your assistance to help me catch Salvatore."

"You ask, just like that?" snorted the Don. "You ask for a man's life like you ask directions to an outhouse?" He spat on the ground, expelled gas without apology at Franchina's request. His eyes, burning black balls, stung more than a bullet's bite.

Franchina came unhinged, and nearly urinated on the spot. How many times had he faced danger? How many times had he nearly lost his life? His breed of man was fearless—and he, the most fearless. Then what was it about this man, this satanic being, this demon out of the dark ages, that shook him to the core? He was a mere man, this *mafioso*—wasn't he?

Having already forgotten the usual amenities, of respect demanded by these men when soliciting their favor, all he could manage was, "Can we go someplace to talk?" He swallowed hard and followed the older man toward a massive, gnarled, old olive tree high on a knoll overlooking the village of Carini. Miles away from civilization with an iceberg of a man who could kill him in a second, while the world remained ignorant of the deed, became a grim reality that Franchina had failed to take into consideration when he chose to make the trip to the interior alone.

In the shade of the sparse olive branches, out of the sun's warmth, Don Nitto donned a sheepskin hip-length vest and removed his stocking cap to reveal a glistening sheen of baldness. The man's savage appearance, the raw animal magnetism, struck the FSB officer, and the barbaric stench about him nearly knocked him out. Losing no time, he hastily outlined his intentions, careful to mention the sizeable rewards involved, if they emerged victorious.

"First, we get the men close to him, and last, but not least we get to the key—Vincenzo de Montana. With him in our clutches, getting Salvatore will be child's play."

"I see," snorted Don Nitto. "Ensnare the dogs who guard the rooster from the fox, so you can wring the chicken's neck, hang him up to bleed, and when the smell of blood lures the fox, the blood of both will be your wine of triumph and you'll be acclaimed the victor!"

Scowling, Franchina held back his fury. "The way you put it, you make it sound reprehensible and brutal! Nevertheless, its my job."

Don Nitto spat into the ground contemptuously. And when, after an hour of such talk, Captain Franchina was about to forget the whole matter and consider himself fortunate to escape with his life, no one could have been more flabbergasted and relieved when the Don agreed to aid the FSB. The twenty-five-thousand-dollar reward had been a persuasive factor. After making several arrangements and an appointment to meet and discuss their plans, Captain Franchina took his leave.

Watching him make the long trek back to the auto at the foot of the mountain, Don Nitto's eyes became veiled in thought. He sat back and leaned against the trunk of the tree and swilled wine freely from his goatskin *botta*.

The real motivation for his intervention had been a battle for supremacy between father and son. Don Nitto believed with conviction that his son Natale, whom he considered an oaf, could never match his inimitable superiority or take away the glories of his past, so he grasped at this chance to teach his son a bitter lesson and to impress Natale that he could never overshadow his father's formidable reputation. Competition between them had always been fierce with an unrivaled hatred.

Also behind this act of betrayal by Don Nitto lay the eternal threat made by the older *mafiosi* to each generation of youngbloods who screamed their wrath, "You youngbloods fuck around with us, the older, more seasoned men of respect, and we'll show you who's boss!" It had never been in the role of a loving father to a son, rather that of a marble institution against the inherent dangers of the young with daring ideas that might threaten its very existence.

Ah, the irony of it all! To think that between a son's earnest desire to rise above his father's prestigious position and become an entity of respect in his own right, and a father's vengeful determination to pin back the ears of an incorrigible, thankless offspring who didn't measure up to standards, the fate of one great man—Salvatore—hung in the balance, was a revolting, uncalculated development not even Salvatore could have foreseen.

CHAPTER 62

Don Nitto's well-oiled machinery and craftiness, set into motion, succeeded in luring nearly all of Salvatore's men, who were speedily apprehended and deposited where Captain Franchina wanted them for the time being. Only the Scoletti brothers blocked his path to Vincenzo de Montana, the man whom he'd cast to play Judas in the unfolding melodrama.

At the end of May, Arturo and Miguel Scoletti, bent on seeing their leader, had been subjected to the complex system protecting Salvatore. Guided to Don Nitto's men at a point in Monreale and carefully hidden in a produce truck, camouflaged to prevent detection from the FSB, they had no idea that by the time the truck made its final stop they'd be outnumbered by *carabinieri* holding automatic weapons aimed at their hearts. The truck had driven them directly to Bellolampo barracks. Arrested, they were flown immediately to Viterbo to await trial. Now, only Vincenzo remained to be seduced by that whore, Captain Franchina.

As difficult as it was for his men to reach him, Tori, in these last few months, had maintained a degree of freedom, even with the new *mafiosi* guarding him. He moved about with little effort. One week after the entrapment of his last two paladins, Destiny intervened, placing both Salvatore and Vincenzo in Monreale, sauntering along the Via Napoli, past the orphanage where Arturo and Miguel were raised.

By chance they had encountered an old friend, the aging Father Andrea walking along the outer perimeter of the Church grounds reading his missal. After the warm greetings subsided (Tori had been a generous contributor to the orphanage), the priest made a chance remark that he hadn't seen the brothers since Don Nitto's truck transported them to see Salvatore.

Yes, he was certain of the date, one week to the day. "You see, they had just delivered playground equipment to the children earlier. God Bless them. They never forgot us. Arturo apologized because they couldn't stay longer, because of their plans to see you. They bade me farewell," said the kindly old priest. "I watched them walk down the street and get into the waiting truck." He recalled another matter. "In fact, Salvatore, they left their horses and saddles with me until their return."

Salvatore and Vincenzo exchanged concerned glances.

"You're sure, *padre*, the truck belonged to Don Nitto Solameni, and not his son, Natale?" questioned Salvatore explicitly.

"Listen, *caro mio*," retorted the priest in reflection. "I've seen that broken-down truck long enough to know it on sight. He keeps it down the street." He pointed his gnarled old hand toward a small building in the sad state of neglect with an adjoining courtyard. "Arturo's other friends came to see you in the same manner, now that I recall." He told Tori how he'd seen the Genovese brothers, Azzarello, Gambo Cusimano, and many whose names he couldn't recall take the same means of conveyance to see their chief. "There's no trouble, is there Salvatore?" asked the priest at the growing concern in both their eyes.

"Don't concern yourself, *padre*," comforted Salvatore. "If something was wrong before, things will be set right, shortly." *Va bene, padre?*"

Salvatore shoved several bills into the pries's hands and gripped his arm firmly in a gesture of affection.

"God bless you both!" called Father Andrea watching them walk away.

"What will you do first?" asked Vincenzo when they discovered the truck in the deserted courtyard just as the priest indicated they would.

"First, we find Don Nitto, to settle a score!"

"Let it go!" urged Vincenzo. "In less than a month everything works out for you. I say, let this go. Forget it for now. If they've been betrayed, the men will be turned over to the FSB for trial, then they'll be released according to the terms you agreed upon with Belasci."

"How can I let this go? Why is this happening, cousin? So close to the end? For the last two months, I've sensed things aren't right, but I've put it out of my mind. Now, this! I'll have to teach Don Nitto some manners."

They found him asleep, snoring loudly in his decrepit, rat-trap lodgings. Vincenzo shook him vigorously and when Don Nitto awakened he sat up and stared into the barrel of Tori's Browning. Slowly, he raised his sleep-filled eyes and scowled darkly in recognition. It was their first face-to-face confrontation. Don Nitto knew him instantly. He grunted with marked disdain, scratched his crotch, and in his stoney-faced expression looked upon his obstructors as if they were insects. Vincenzo lit a candle and placed it on the table.

"All right, old man, talk," commanded Tori in temperate voice.

"I am called Don Nitto, peasant. Why do you come here to trespass upon my house?" he growled full of menace. "Where's your respect, eh?"

"I ask once again, old man. Talk. Where are Salvatore's men?"

The Don's jaws tightened, his lips pursed together stubbornly. Only Tori and Vincenzo had come to confront this *mafioso* but, understanding the ways of a *mafioso* well, Tori gave the impression that Don Nitto's *casa* was surrounded by more of his men.

"Very well, you tongue-tied viper, keep your silence," he suggested easily. Turning to Vincenzo he snapped out a few orders. "Instruct the others to round up all the sheep in the fold. When I give the command, slaughter them— all of them"

Don Nitto sat as rigid as mortar without a trace of expression. Tori goaded him superbly, but the Don gave no indication he was touched by the threat.

"Very well, Vincenzo, and when you finish with the sheep, deploy six men to kidnap Natale Solameni and his family. You will then set fire to the Solameni Fisheries. And send a dozen of the men to dynamite the construction company. If that doesn't grease this viper's tongue into action, line up his family and shoot them, including the children." He snapped the orders rapidly.

The Don, against his will, found himself admiring this

bandit. Sonofagun! He was all they said about him—proud, powerful, and manly. Sonofabitch! Why couldn't he have sired such a strapping young *giovanotto*? All that Salvatore represented appalled this *mafioso* glacier, and his hate was so intense he wouldn't attempt to scrutinize the curious feelings that tried to ward off his resentment. Glancing from one cocksure warrior to the other, he saw much less courage in Vincenzo de Montana than in Salvatore. He, too, knew his enemy well. He had a job to do and, despite this inclination of respect he was forced to bestow on Salvatore against his own nature, he told himself to get on with his part in the unfolding drama.

What the hell is this? he asked himself. *Me, Don Nitto, a man born of undiminished and probably insane courage feel admiration for this young punk. Hah! He placed his hand on the barrel of Tori's gun and pushed it away from him.*

"Put that pea shooter away. I know when I've met a real *maschiezzo*—a manly man." He stood up in his longjohns and casually pulled on his wrinkled and soiled trousers. He proceeded to tell them of Captain Franchina's visit, how the plan to capture Tori's men had been executed, avoiding only mention of the FSB's intention to capture their Judas, Vincenzo de Montana.

Don Nitto Solameni was driven to an old abandoned farmhouse in the Castellammare valley to be kept under guard by Vincenzo until Tori further unraveled the mystery behind the FSB plans and why they continued to oppose Belasci's plan for his exile.

"Aren't you aware your son stands to collect a handsome piece of change for arranging my exile?" he asked the Don curiously motivated to understand his actions. But, the Don with no face, said nothing. Salvatore goaded him. "You, a man of respect, joined forces with the *carabinieri*?" Tori grinned wickedly. "I wonder what the *capomafia* will say to this news?"

Still, the Don remained impassive.

Tori sniffed the air gingerly, made a wry face. *"Managghia!* What smells so fetid?" His face puckered up with distaste as he peered about the shack.

Vincenzo pointed to the Don and made an appropriate facial grimace at the repugnant odor. "It's him."

Tori shuddered. He looked upon this man of ice with revulsion.

The Don still gave no reaction either to Tori's words or his behavior.

Tori returned an hour later with ample provisions for them. "You take care, cousin. Don't let him out of your sight. If, for any reason you have to leave him alone, tie him securely. Meanwhile I'll get to the bottom of this betrayal."

"*Va bene*," replied Vincenzo, who didn't relish the prospects of this job. He not only hated Don Nitto with a passion, he also held him in fearsome awe. Thoughts that he might have suffered the same fate as his companions tightened his determination to keep the old bastard in tow until Tori returned.

Salvatore hadn't been gone five minutes, before the repulsive *mafioso* made his move. "You won't get away with this, de Montana. Be smart and I'll fix it so you can walk away from this situation a wealthy man, and live like one. You'll be jailed for life. Is that what you want? You listen to me—now, while you have a chance, turn your cousin over to the authorities, to the FSB, and all your worries are over. I can fix it. I'm thick with these men." He wouldn't let up on his jailer, who blinked hard at the other's audacity.

"Do you think for a moment someone isn't watching us? Let me tell you, young cock, all this is part of the plan. It was planned that you and Salvatore come to my house to capture me. The FSB spies know exactly where I am, where we are. Those names I gave to that arrogant cock o'the walk, Salvatore, you think they were the right names? Hah! Then you're more foolish than I thought. Salvatore would have to get up earlier in the morning to get the best of Don Nitto Solamenti!" he boasted.

"Be still, old man! Unless you're looking to die!"

"Why? You think you have the guts to shoot me?" scoffed the Don.

Such was the nature of his conversation for three solid days. It began to appear, after the third day of such mind-bending innuendos and bold declarations, that Vincenzo, a mere youth of twenty-eight years, was no match for this veteran *mafioso*, whose native intelligence and suggestionary powers had broken tougher, more seasoned, brutal killers in his day. He harped on the very quality Captain Franchina confided to be Vincenzo's weakness—freedom. The Don hammered away at his captive jailer with increasing boldness in his attempt to undermine his loyalty to Salvatore.

"Because Salvatore is insane, you don't have to be insensible. Trust me, de Montana. I have powerful and influential friends who can help you. Consider the sign of the lion around your neck and on your belt. The sign of power is all around you. The power of the lion is unquestioned. Why, then do you accept a back seat to Salvatore? Eh?"

"Be quiet, old man!" brazened Vincenzo. "Next to Salvatore you have the stature of a cockroach."

Malevolent, black hatred struck a cord of terror in Vincenzo's heart, even though the *mafioso* was firmly secured. The Don's features grew sharp as though sucked together by an acrid fluid. Thick bettlebrows, like his son's, were thicker, shaggier, more savage in appearance, and his bald head shone like a slimy mirror. Until Don Nitto could subdue the violent anger and hatred he felt toward Vincenzo for the lack of respect shone him, he kept silent.

Nothing sickened Vincenzo more than to be made a part of the man's vulgarities. Don Nitto, coarse, crude, and obscene, a gargantuan eater and drinker, remained tied to the table, his hands free to feed himself. In addition to a holstered gun Vincenzo wore, a submachine gun remained by his side. Because he couldn't permit the Don out of his sight, he was forced to accompany him whenever he performed a bodily function. The most detested role in Vincenzo's life was when he was elected to cook and clean after this loathsome man. Not even his confinement at *Terra Diavolo*, where he'd been exposed to the worst of animalistic behavior, had the devastating effect of being unwillingly cooped up with so vile an animal. It was simply too much for Vincenzo to stomach. His nerves, shattered and frayed, felt as if they'd been turned inside out and sprinkled with acid. He became sensitive to the striking of a match. Any slight noise jarred him, shattering his composure.

Unconcerned by what Vincenzo felt or thought, the Don belched continuously. He farted at random, snored like a buzz saw, and his foul, repulsive breath from the result of neglected, rotting teeth, permeated the room, and sickened Vincenzo, who continuously struck sulphur matches in an attempt to kill the stench. Don Nitto picked his nose continuously and rolled the refuse into a ball between his fingers until it dried and fell to the floor. Otherwise, he'd blow the mucus from his nose onto the floor. He expectorated wherever and whenever it suited his fancy. Vincenzo guessed the old man hadn't bathed in a year.

The awesome fear he evidenced for the man at their first encounter, had disintegrated into unadulterated disgust. For a man like Vincenzo, whose personal toilet habits were pridefully meticulous, it became an intolerable nightmare to continue in the role of appointed keeper to this vile animal.

On the fifth day, Vincenzo could barely stand the sight of the Don. Whenever he opened his mouth to speak with him, Vincenzo moved away. The Don got the picture. Around three in the afternoon, Vincenzo was startled to hear his name called in the most gentle tone ever to leave the Don's filthy mouth.

"Be a good lad, de Montana, and do a man a favor, eh? I miss my sheep dearly. It's been too long for me, eh?"

It took several moments before he realized the Don had asked him to bend over to permit him to take his pleasure as his friendly sheep had done. When realization struck him, he picked up a bucket of water from the table in the crudely constructed farmhouse and gave the old man a good dowsing.

"There, that should cool you down you, hot cock!" he laughed vindictively. "Animals, no less! The great Don Nitto, the fearsome *mafioso*, hasn't got balls to find himself a good woman!" he bleated unmercifully. All the resentment, disgust and contempt he'd disguised these past five days burst forth in an avalanche of revulsion and he let the *mafioso* have it between the eyes!

"Why you pitiful old man! You, who've wrecked the lives of your fine sons, because of your sick mind! That's what it is, let me tell you, a sick, demented mind! You're all talk, no guts! No *fegato*! If your son Natale could only see you now, he wouldn't be so fucked up anymore!

"Do you realize what you've done to that son of yours? He wants love from you in the worst way! From you! An animal! He tears his fingers apart! His eyes won't hold still, because of you. He stuffs his stomach with candy until he makes himself sick, because of what you've done to him! You should be ashamed to call yourself a human being! *Capeeshi?* You hide behind the title of *mafioso!* You scare the people with your well-practiced, frozen face. But, I've seen through you, scum! These past five days have taught me a lesson. You're nothing! And at that, the most repulsive, stinking, filthy, excuse of a human I've ever seen!"

The old *mafioso*'s blood boiled. He slammed his fist on the table with such force, one of its shaky legs fell and the table, supported only by the remaining three, leaned on an angle, spilling the items from its top. He strained against his bonds with a fury that could have killed a man, if he were free to do it.

"Ah," goaded Vincenzo. "The bull is enraged, eh? He begins to roar! You want to fight, is that it?" He flung off his vest and struck a belligerent pose. "Fuck me, eh? *Schifoso moledetto!* Goddamn stinking pig! You want me to be your sow, eh? I'll fix you, you licentious old bastard! Son of a cum-crazy whore! You depraved, pitiful excuse of a man!" He kicked his chair out of the way, picked up a sharp knife from a sheath on the counter and approached the *mafioso*. Never had he been so aroused, so venomous, so provoked that poison had replaced the blood in his veins. He was ready to cut the man's bindings so they could fight, man to man.

"I ought to cut off your balls instead! Maybe you'd stop castrating that son of yours, if I taught you a lesson!"

Don Nitto's head inclined to his chest; he appeared humiliated, and crest-fallen. Was it remorse Vincenzo had seen flicker in his eyes moment before? If he had a hair on his head, Vincenzo could have pulled back on it just to peer at the old bastard's face. Don Nitto anticipated his move. Slowly he raised his head and Vincenzo stopped in his tracks. Son of a gun! He'd seen everything, now.

That frightful old man without a face, was crying real tears; tears that progressed into convulsive, shamed sobs.

"Damn! You aren't worth the effort!" snarled Vincenzo disgustedly. He threw down the knife and walked outside the farmhouse and sat on a felled tree in the early spring sunshine, smoking cigarette after cigarette until he calmed down. He dreaded the thought of having to return to the putrefaction of sickening smells. In despair he shouted aloud in a plaintive voice. "Goddamnit, Tori! Where the hell are you?"

It was dusk before he entered the house to give the Don food and water. He lit an oil lamp. The Don was asleep slumped over in his chair. Vincenzo thought, he looks like any miserable broken down old man, until he opens his eyes. He shuddered, then busied himself lighting a fire. He set a fresh pot of coffee to cook, warmed over their lunch, and set to fixing the table's leg.

Unable to any longer tolerate the man's foul odor, he shook him to awaken him, and cut the bindings from his legs.

"What is it? What are you doing?" grumbled the Don.

"Get up!" ordered Vincenzo. "You're coming with me!" He held his gun on the Don and nudged him outside.

"You decided to shoot me before your chief returns?"

"If I had any sense that's exactly what I'd do and end my discomfort! You are going to take a bath! I'm tired of the way you stink, you hear? Outside—one funny move and I'll empty the clip of my gun into your belly!"

Don Nitto was so startled by the unusual demand, he got to his feet and scurried out the door, with Vincenzo following close behind him.

"There's a water trough and soap. I want you to scrub until the stink is gone! Wash your mouth, too!"

For nearly a half hour, he made the old man scrub his body, amid protests, and when he was through, he made him wash out his clothing.

"I have nothing else to wear! I'll freeze tonight!" he complained bitterly.

"Better you freeze than me suffocate from your stink!" retorted Vincenzo.

He got an old blanket from inside the house, and ordered the Don to wrap himself in it. He was surprised at the lean, hard, muscular body, for a man his age.

"Bring in your clothing and we'll hang it up to dry near the stove." he ordered.

Inside the farmhouse, Vincenzo secured the man's bindings once again. He finished cooking and set the food on the table before him. They ate in silence, Vincenzo noticed the Don didn't eat his usual rations.

"Go ahead, eat all you want! There's more!" urged Vincenzo, politely.

Don Nitto shook his head. An errant tear sprung from his eyes. He brushed it aside quickly, as if he were annoyed by its presence.

Vincenzo turned away. He cleared away the dishes and moved about the small room, with ease. He poured water and washed himself, and brushed his teeth. Vincenzo had practiced his toilet habits religiously. The Don watched him from the corner of his eyes as he had in the previous days, when he labeled Vincenzo a dandy.

Before that afternoon's humiliation, the Don sensed Vincenzo's resistance had drained. He had appeared fretful and less sure of himself. Now, after what had taken place, he didn't feel as sure of his adversary. What Don Nitto mistook for weakness in Vincenzo had merely been revulsion at the close contact. Familiarity had not only bred contempt in this case, it stimulated a loathing in each man for the other, for different reasons.

Witnessing more complexity in Vincenzo than what Captain Franchina had theorized, Don Nitto had to change tack. Later, after dinner, Vincenzo settled down to read.

"You want to play cards?" asked the Don.

"We have none."

"De Montana?"

"*Che voi?* What the hell you want?"

"It's difficult for a man of my stature to say what he feels."

Vincenzo continued to read the translation of *In Dubious Battle* by Steinbeck, that Tori had brought him.

"Are you listening?"

"Talk," muttered Vincenzo absently.

"You don't make it easy."

"What?"

"*Porco Dio*, I'm attempting to apologize. *Me va scomparire.* You make me ashamed." He stopped. "What the hell's wrong with me? Why should I apologize?" he demanded haughtily.

"Then, don't!"

"I'm trying to say, thank you for opening my eyes to my son's trouble."

"You're his trouble. Maybe after you're dead he'll straighten up." Vincenzo gave him no quarter.

"You're a fucking bastard, you know that?"

"You're a prize, I suppose."

"Look, if we're going to be confined together for God knows how long, can't we be sociable?"

"Well it's a damned sure thing I can't read while you crow like a disgruntled cock!" exasperated Vincenzo, slamming the book together.

"I tell you straight, de Montana, I hold you in esteem. It took a real man to tell me off like you did."

Vincenzo glanced up sharply, his eyes narrowing suspiciously. *What the hell is this viper up to now?* he wondered.

"Salvatore seldom smiles," began the Don. "Did he learn of my powers and copy me?"

"Salvatore mimics no man," retored Vincenzo defensively. "He's only one of a kind."

"You admire your cousin?"

"Why wouldn't I? He's the greatest man in Sicily today. One day the world will awaken and regret they didn't honor him properly."

"I think it's you they should honor."

"What's this? The cobra teaching the asp how to strike?"

"You think I'm jesting? I am serious. Especially after today. You really twisted my balls." He shook his head in mock disbelief.

For nearly two hours the Don filled Vincenzo's head

with glowing praises and slipped into the conversation bits and pieces of juicy information he'd picked up from Captain Franchina. His change in attitude thoroughly bewildered Vincenzo and shot down his defenses until his nerves began to fray.

That night, Vincenzo coughed more than usual. Unprepared for the long stay, he had had to cut his medication in half dosages. God willing, Tori would return soon. Before he fell asleep, he reflected on the day's events. He felt a tinge of compassion for the old man, but he reminded himself of the very reason he was here, that he was still confronted with one of the deadliest men in Sicily, next to Don Barbarossa. So filled with thoughts of this obnoxious *mafioso* had he been, he had had little time to think of Maria Angelica Candela.

The last time he saw her, he had actually asked her to marry him. These plans for Salvatore's exile, the promise of pardon in the near future, had changed everything for Vincenzo. He dared dream of a normal life with her, in a little villa someplace, and then a family, eh? He dozed off filled with hopes and dreams of another life, hoping Maria would be patient for a while longer.

The next morning the Don awakened at the crack of dawn. Vincenzo slept soundly in the bunk across the room. Don Nitto blinked his eyes and glanced about the room until he noticed the knife on the table near him.

He rubbed his eyes, still filled with sleep balls, until they cleared and with one eye on Vincenzo, he moved cautiously toward the knife. Grasping it in one hand, he gripped the handle with his teeth. He placed both hands over the sharp blade trying to slice through the ropes. It took several agonizing moments, but he managed to free himself. He slashed at the bindings around his ankles, tiptoed across the room, picked up his clothing from the area of the stove, and dressed quickly.

Vincenzo stirred slightly, rolled over, and fell into deeper slumber.

Don Nitto slipped out of the farmhouse with a look of cunning on his face.

Vincenzo awakened to the fragrant aroma of fresh coffee, fried potatoes, green pepper, and eggs and the voice of Don Nitto with an unfamiliar ring to it.

"Time to get up, de Montana."

Startled, Vincenzo jumped from the bed and glanced about the room in a state of utter bewilderment that turned into suspicion. "Who untied you? How did you get free?" he asked red faced.

"You left the knife within my reach. So, I decided it was only fair that I cook breakfast for you, for a change."

Vincenzo rubbed his eyes in disbelief. "You could have escaped!" he muttered glumly. "Why didn't you?"

"Because I want to return the favor you did me, yesterday."

"I did you no favor."

"But you did. Now, come and sit down and eat your breakfast. I went to a lot of trouble to get these eggs. I stole them from the next *casita*."

"Two kilometers away?" Vincenzo grew more baffled. It didn't take long to know what Don Nitto was up to. "What kind of a favor have you in mind for me? The last feast before betrayal?"

"If I had escaped, your boss wouldn't have liked it. You'd have been in trouble!" He ignored the innuendo.

"Salvatore's not my boss! We share equally in everything! And I wouldn't have been in any trouble!" he retorted adamantly.

"It's all well and good that you defend him. That's as it should be. After all, you don't know what's really going on. You know only what Salvatore chooses to tell you." He continued to lay his foundation of treachery.

Vincenzo washed his face and hands and sat down at the table. He helped himself to the pepper and eggs. It was delicious. "Why didn't you tell me you could cook? I'd have let you take over," he grinned, irascibly. "And you're wrong! Salvatore tells me everything!"

"Everything he wants you to know."

"Everything I care to know!"

"You think he has your best interests at heart? Hah! Salvatore cares only for his skin! And mark my words, you stubborn young cock, Salvatore will never leave Sicily alive!" boasted the revolting *mafioso*.

Instantly Vincenzo's ear perked up. At some point in the conversation Vincenzo was well aware of the intended seduction. Very well, you old stinking swine, seduce me, he thought. He appeared nonchalant and remotely moved by the Don's words, knowing if he showed interest the Don was slick enough to be on to him. He played the game. He grew testy and began to goad the *mafioso*.

"That's what you think, Solameni!"

"I am Don Solameni to you!" he snapped angrily. "I demand the respect I deserve!"

"I have no respect for a man who doesn't honor his son!"

"It's not your affair! Silence!" He demanded imperiously.

Vincenzo laughed. "If you don't like it, kiss my ass!" He patted the gun.

Inside, Don Nitto's blood boiled at the impudence of the upstart. His face was a sheet of glass. Patience, he told himself. Patience.

"My cousin is more intelligent than all the FSBs, *carabinieri*, and security police put together! If you really want to know the truth, Belasci eats out of his hand!" continued Vincenzo, hoping to hear more of the Don's earlier statement.

"Hah! Tell me another fairytale! I tell you, de Montana, Salvatore will not leave Sicily alive! So, where does that leave you and the others, eh? You think Belasci intends to honor any agreement made with that big shot Salvatore? What a crazy man you are if you believe such a fabrication."

"Your son seems to think so!"

"My son? Bah, that *cafone!* What does he know? What do any of the youngbloods know? *Cazzu*, that's all! Salvatore and his personal portfolio! What a laugh! You don't know that Luciano's men took care of Siragusa outside of Chicago? Now, where's his insurance?"

Suddenly it all dovetailed for Vincenzo. Now, he knew why Don Nitto hadn't escaped when he had the opportunity. *It's me he wants! The whole fucking operation has been a trap to snare me!* His Sicilian mind went to work.

"Give it up, Vincenzo, you haven't got a chance!" insisted Don Nitto.

Wheels of intrigue spun around in Vincenzo's mind swiftly. In the next few hours, Vincenzo played a stellar role. He continued to negate the Don at every turn, building Salvatore up with each blow struck at him by the Don. Finally, he demonstrated an attitude of defeat, one of possible capitulation.

"After six days of your blunt candor, I'm beginning to think you may be right." He deliberated. "You're sure you can secure unconditional amnesty for me? They wouldn't betray me like they betrayed Salvatore so many times?"

"The word of Don Nitto is stronger than iron and steel."

"I'd really be doing Sicily a great service to rid her of Salvatore?"

"*Managghia*, what a service! You'd be hailed a hero! On top of that, there's a handsome reward! You'll split it with me, of course. It's understood!"

"What else?" asked Vincenzo in all innocence.

Don Nitto glared hotly at him, then set aside his personal animosity for future rewards. They talked for some time and it was finally resolved.

"*Allora*," instructed Vincenzo carefully, "you tell everyone that you escaped. I don't want Salvatore to suspect collusion until the last minute when I can look him squarely in the eye and say to him, 'It was I, your cousin Vincenzo, who betrayed you! I, who've been forced to take a back seat to you all these years!"

Don Nitto stared askance at him, not fully certain he had worked a miracle on Vincenzo. His instinct told him Vincenzo was not to be trusted. But, in his last speech, Vincenzo projected a black look of menace, and for an instant, Don Nitto felt satisfied. He rationalized. *I don't care what happens after I turn him over to Franchina and collect my rewards. Let them deal with de Montana if he shows treachery.* His ego didn't allow for failure.

"*Allora, amonini!*" urged the Don. "Hurry and let's be off!"

"No! You go ahead!" proposed Vincenzo. "Otherwise it won't appear that you escaped."

Filled with suspicion, Don Nitto hesitated. "If you have any sense, you'll come with me, now. From what I saw of Salvatore, he'd not hesitate to shoot you in cold blood!"

"No! It's best I remain. I've many things to do before he returns. In three days, I'll come to your house for protective custody. You make sure Captain Franchina is there and that I get the protection I'll need! Agreed?"

Don Nitto temporized. "It's better you come now."

"No!" Vincenzo was firm. "I said, later. After all, I know my cousin!"

It's better than nothing, thought the Don. *Better I leave quickly, before Salvatore returns to repair the damage it took nearly a week to perform on de Montana.* He was in a hurry to tell Captain Franchina the good news.

Long after the Don left, Vincenzo sat amid the cluttered, disorganized rubble in the yard on a felled tree stump basking in the warm sunshine collecting his thoughts, not fully certain of all that had transpired in the past week.

"He thinks I set him free to betray you," he told Salvatore when his cousin arrived. He lost no time in telling him what had transpired. "I let him think anything that pleased him so I could learn of the traps that await you. He made it clear the betrayal would come either from

Calemi or his own son, regardless of any deals made with Belasci or D'Verde."

"So! Another betrayal after all!" said Tori expelling a despondent sigh. "They couldn't even be honest with Salvatore in this very last dealing with him." He seemed thinner, more weary than usual, his face, drawn and haggard.

"There's a fifty-thousand-dollar reward on your head."

"That much?" Tori whistled appreciatively.

They both knew what it meant.

"It's enough to lure the angel Gabriel to do me in." Tori considered the situation. "If nothing else, we've learned every form of treachery known to man, eh? We've been instructed by masters."

"Why do you suppose Belasci's forces are split? You think he knows what Colonel Cala and Captain Franchina are boiling in their pot of treachery?"

"I told you at Calemi's what I thought. I did my best to bring the opposing forces together. If only those bastards had followed my orders! You see what happens when a man no longer controls a situation and has to depend on others?" Tori paced back and forth inside the farmhouse. "I can't believe Belasci is behind this. I still have my insurance. He wouldn't take the chance that I'd publish it."

"Tori," said his cousin not sure how to tell him what he'd learned from Don Nitto. "Santino's been caught. Your personal portfolio is already in Belasci's hands by now. That's probably why they intend to betray you."

Tori suppressed a smile. "Who told you that?"

"Don Nitto."

"It's preposterous."

"Listen, through Luciano's contacts in America, Santino was abducted. They've been holding him for nearly a month. I hope to God they didn't kill him."

"You believe, Don Nitto?"

"Would he have any reason to deceive me?"

"I can think of at least a half dozen."

Vincenzo grew puzzled.

"Listen, cousin. One week ago, Gambo Cusimano's cousin, the fisherman, took me to Naples. I made a telephone call to America and personally spoke with Santino. It is not true, what Don Nitto told you. Besides none of it makes any difference. Lies! They all spout lies, *caro cugino.*"

"Why doesn't it make any difference?"

"The portfolio is not with Santino. It never left Sicily."

"By the unholy black balls of Satan!" exclaimed Vincenzo. "Where is it?"

"It's best you don't know. Listen, cousin," he said with a faraway look in his eyes, "I want you to go through with this plan of Don Nitto's—"

"Now I know you're crazy!" Vincenzo was aghast.

"Perhaps, but, I still want you to play the fool with them.

"You really are crazy!" Vincenzo was outraged.

"Go through with the betrayal," insisted Tori. "See where it leads. Be smart. Get everything in writing, not by the go-betweens but by the principal parties, *capeeshi*? I want to learn where the betrayal comes from, cousin. From Belasci? D'Verde? Colonel Cala? The Premier himself? Meanwhile, you may be able to secure your position better than what I negotiated for you. My personal confession for the Portella fiasco exonerates you and the others."

"*Aspetta*, Tori. You're going too fast for me. Who ever caught Santino, if he's been caught, will think the portfolio is with him. They'll give the orders to kill you on sight."

"Not if we can leak information that another portfolio exists, here in Sicily, say . . . a duplicate?"

"And how do you propose to do that in time? Don Nitto told me that word is out you'll be betrayed before you leave Sicily."

"Then, we'll have to work fast,?" Salvatore paused a moment, and frowned. He shook his head slowly. "Wait, Vincenzo. Think clearly. It's *me* they want, not *you*. You have but to bide your time and you can live a free man. You don't have to involve yourself further in my affairs. There are too many risks, too many complications, too many treacheries . . ."

"I have no illusions about my fate, Tori," said Vincenzo, seriously. "I told you we're in this together, until the end. If they took your life, it would be the same as if they took mine. Your enemies are my enemies. Once they get you, do you think they'd ever let me go free? So, what are we talking about?"

That frivolous Vincenzo; that carefree, vivacious man who loved life and lived it as he saw fit, made light of a perilous situation that both surprised and pleased Tori. He was deeply moved for several moments.

"*Allora*, then listen carefully. Before you agree to become my betrayer, allow each man who intrigues with you to think you are happy to be on his side. *But, always, always bear in mind the rivalry between the carabinieri and security police!* For all we know one of them might have started the rumor to discredit the other side. Wouldn't the FSB find it a feather in their caps if they could discredit

D'Verde's agreement and hand me over, dead or alive, to Belasci, and collect the reward, too?"

"*Managghia*! Fucking bastards!" exclaimed Vincenzo. He understood too well. "So fucking many complications! Will it never end?"

"Not until we show them how it's done. First, cousin, you'll drop hints to all who intrigue with you, that their competitor plans to do them in. When you've gained Colonel Cala's confidence, you will slyly hint to him that Salvatore and D'Verde plan to kidnap him and later kill him. Do likewise to Captain Franchina. Tell him the new Chief Inspector Zanorelli plans to discredit him. We'll give them a real taste of Sicilian intrigue."

"*Managghia*! You'll have them dancing the *tarantella* over an open pit of vipers!" Vincenzo grinned wickedly. "I'm beginning to like this after all."

"You'll not be dealing with ignoramuses, cousin. Don't get involved with the *mafiosi*, either side. Steer clear of them. If they approach you with an offer, don't give them the time of day. Become mute, and be as slippery as a fox in a hunt. Otherwise, they'll see through you like glass. Meanwhile I shall endeavor to locate the source of the betrayal and learn why the FSB haven't abandoned the Salvatore project. It will give me time to redirect the treachery. I will remain at Calemi's villa unless it proves unsafe. My mother is to know nothing of any intended treachery *Capeeshi?*"

"You have to tell me?"

"Don't forget, let it be known that someone has made a mistake about Santino and be sure to pound the existence of a duplicate *portfolio* into their heads."

"You want me to be a regular Terranova, eh?"

"Who would be better?"

Before they left the miserable, cracked-walled, broken-down farmhouse, both cousins embraced warmly. Once again Tori cautioned.

"Avoid the *mafiosi*. Make personal contact with Colonel Cala or Captain Franchina and for God's sake avoid any traffic with Don Nitto! If it's gone too far, do what you must. God be with you, Vincenzo."

They lingered a moment before each wiped the spilling tears from their eyes and parted.

"Understand we split the reward, de Montana," said Don Nitto giving Vincenzo the business with his eyes.

"I'm not interested in the money, Colonel Cala."

"I want unconditional amnesty in recognition for my special services to the State."

"You heard him! You heard him! I get all the reward. You're my witness," rasped the greedy Don.

Colonel Cala spoke to the Don with measured politeness. "Thank you for all your efforts, Don Nitto. You are free to go. From here, it's government business. We'll contact you when the reward money is to be paid, when Salvatore is either dead or in custody."

"Oh no! No, no, no, no, no!" The Don wagged a grimy finger under the Colonel's nose. "That was not our agreement. I agreed to deliver Salvatore's men and de Montana. I've filled my contract. Now, I want my money!"

"But, that's impossible!" replied Colonel Cala a bit too sternly and perhaps too rashly. "There was no reward on de Montana's head. Only on Salvatore's."

Don Nitto drew himself up. He had bathed and dressed presentably for this clandestine meeting at the *Albergo-Sole* in Palermo. He towered over the FSB Officer. In his eyes was a black menace never before encountered by Cala. To have been hoodwinked on such a technicality didn't set well with this satanic titan. "It would have been no more effort to deliver Salvatore than his cousin," he said slowly with guarded malice.

"Don't get excited, Don Nitto," said Captain Franchina. "I'm sure as soon as Minister Belasci hears of your bravery and cooperation, they'll hurry things up and your reward will get to you. Patience, Don Nitto."

"As long as you don't mistake me for some dog-faced mule," he said pointedly in a voice that caused the fine hair on Franchina's body to stand up.

"My dear Don Nitto, you do yourself a disservice if you think we would underestimate the mentality of a man of respect such as you," said Captain Franchina in a patronizing voice that he hoped would disguise his nervousness.

Further words were unnecessary when the Don leveled his eyes of menace on the FSB officials and took his leave. Vincenzo noticed it was long after the *mafioso*'s departure before the color returned to Captain Franchina's cheeks. Colonel Cala appeared unaffected. It became obvious he wished he could get the hell out of Sicily and never return.

Vincenzo made his position clear instantly. "The business about not claiming the reward was nonsense. If I'm going to subject myself to future discomforts I positively want the benefit of a reward. That's first," he told the FSB officers. "Second, I want it clearly understood that my position is not that of an informer, rather as a full-fledged partner of the FSB, otherwise my honor as a Sicilian will not permit me to discredit my cousin or his name. In addition, I desire full amnesty for all my crimes and a firm promise I shall never be prosecuted for previous offenses. Also safe conduct, should I immigrate to another country. Is it understood?"

"I'll see what I can do," said Colonel Cala studying him intently. "I'll discuss your demands with my superiors."

"Promises are insufficient. Without written assurances from either the Premier or Minister Belasci, I don't cooperate. I'll stand for no false promises such as those made to Salvatore. Remember, only I can deliver him to you."

"I'll remember," said Colonel Cala quietly. He was so close to capturing Salvatore he could almost taste the sweetness of victory. *What then, Belasci?* he thought. You'll *think twice before farming* me *to some remote outpost.*

Both he and his associate strained to subdue their excitement. Imagine, they had Vincenzo de Montana, like Franchina had figured from the start. Oh, the exquisite delight of it all! If things fell into place as they'd planned, the whole damnable affair would be over in less than a month. Salvatore's departure was scheduled for July 1st!

All doubts and suspicion, Vincenzo's motives might have implanted in Colonel Cala's mind, were immediately dispelled when Vincenzo demanded immediate protection, insisting he'd only feel safe if he moved in with the FSB officers. Setting aside an inborn cynicism, Colonel Cala assigned him to share quarters with Captain Franchina, the man whose job it was to further break down the bandit's resistance.

Colonel Cala would never forget the meeting with Salvatore at Calemi's villa and the subsequent treatment he received from D'Verde and the youngbloods when he was squeezed out of negotiations despite Salvatore's insistence that they amalgamate. In addition to the knowledge of the treachery underfoot, Cala, a dedicated soldier who preferred others to consider him a clod if it served his purpose, never questioned Minister Belasci's reasons in not calling a halt to FSB activities. He didn't have to. The reasons became all too obvious to the politically oriented officer. If Belasci had publicly order him to disband the Forces to Suppress Banditry, the Ministry would have been inundated with protests from the communists demanding satisfaction or his removal from office.

All Belasci was doing was marking time. No word was

872

to leak out about his clandestine machinations until *after* he made a formal announcement and then, only *after* Salvatore left Sicily in exile.

When it became apparent to the FSB officers that they would emerge as fools in the fiasco, the idea didn't set well with them. Targeted to suffer the humiliations of Belasci's political indiscretions, neither Cala nor Franchina relished prospects of ending their careers in shame or disgrace or in the obscurity of some desert outpost. Together they had discussed various plans of action, some alternatives to save face in the event they were made to be scapegoats in the Salvatore affair.

Under Colonel Cala's strict orders a shrowd of mystery surrounded their activities. Only then did the FSB, who detested Belasci's craze for publicity, begin to make progress. The past six months of independent action had finally produced Vincenzo de Montana, the man who would get them Salvatore! Soon they all would see the stuff Cesare Cala was made of!

The first week in June, 1950, produced astounding results. Colonel Cala delivered to Vincenzo the letter he had demanded from Minister Belasci guaranteeing him unconditional amnesty for the part he was to play in Salvatore's betrayal. Vincenzo promptly placed this letter in a safety deposit box. The FSB officers, highly solicitous of his every whim when it appeared he had taken them into his confidence, couldn't do enough for the former bandit. Now, it was Vincenzo's turn to play their game. Having learned a stellar technique of double dealing from Don Nitto Solameni, he began to pour subtle and invidious thoughts of a possible kidnapping attempt into the mind of Colonel Cala, just as Tori had instructed him to do.

Colonel Cala had listened politely and made no comment. Nothing, it seemed, penetrated those implacable features. Although he found Vincenzo to be personable and seemingly sincere, the distinct feeling that Vincenzo's capitulation had been a bit too pat didn't linger far from the mind of this discerning officer. He remained at times unconvinced of the Sicilian's sincerity, most especially when he engaged Vincenzo into discussions about Salvatore and praise continued to spill forth from the outlaw's lips. For whatever purpose it served, and perhaps for the specific reason to determine Vincenzo's sincerity, Colonel Cala often badgered him into a defensive role. One night he goaded his guest by characterizing Salvatore in a bad light, to which Vincenzo hastily replied, "You must be insane to say such a foolish thing about Tori. Tell me, who can match him in battle? Even in anger he's the wisest of men. There's never been another Sicilian like him!"

never been another Sicilian like him!"

"Yet, you're willing to betray such a noble man?" pressed the Colonel.

"Only because I fear Salvatore has gone mad. I'm doing this for the good of Sicily. For all we may know, because of these many betrayals by our government, he may have made a pact with Russia. You know how long the Communists have attempted to intrigue with him? Phew! If that happens, if that should happen, *Colonnello*, I ask you, where would Sicily be? You know who it was who prevented them from making deals with Salvatore? Me. That's who. The prevention of communism should be credited to Vincenzo de Montana. That's right—me!"

Captain Franchina glanced up from his unending book work at the end of the declaration with a look of gloating in his *I-told-you-so* eyes.

"Well expressed, Vincenzo," said Captain Franchina. "We shall remember your words."

Periodically Vincenzo dropped hints of Salvatore's duplicate *portfolio*, hoping to get some reaction, some volunteer information of Santino's abduction. You think it phased either of them? No way. To puzzle Vincenzo even more, they were not the least concerned about the *portfolio*; further, they acted as if it didn't matter what was contained in the explosive *portfolio*, since the FSB wasn't inculpated. Vincenzo pretended to be unaffected by their lack of concern and for a time took advantage of his new environment.

The hint of a belly under his sweater at his waist wasn't surprising considering how much Vincenzo drank and ate and smoked of late and how indolent he'd become. He went on shopping sprees with Captain Franchina, was seen only in the finest of haberdasheries, where he bought a handsome wardrobe of hand-tailored suits and silk shirts with his impeccable good taste. The services of a pulmonary specialist were engaged to help relieve the pressure in his lungs. Due to the aggravating side effects of the drug Aureomycin he was taken off the medication; his eyesight had become impaired and he grew dizzy from the indiscriminate use of the drug. New medication, plenty of rest and care, and time for his body to restore itself and prevent the imprisoned germs in his body from spreading became the order of the day for him, and everyone treated him with considerable attention.

Yes, for the young Montegattan, it was time for *la dolce vita*, a time of peaches and cream and fresh *fragole*, strawberries, while he marked time.

CHAPTER 63

Colonel Cala had stormed into the hotel suite clutching the report of Bartolomeo Calemi's death in his hand. He had received the news the same day Natale received the report. His usual calm was absent as he confronted Vincenzo. "You mentioned a duplicate *portfolio* of Salvatore's not long ago. What do you know about it?" he asked right off.

"I thought it didn't interest you." Vincenzo paused in his reading.

Captain Franchina glanced up from his desk with mild surprise, his interest piqued.

"My sources tell me the word's out to get Salvatore," said the FSB head. "Siragusa's been caught in Chicago. The much talked about insurance is worthless," he scoffed as he slapped his hand with the report.

Vincenzo, tensing slightly, kept himself well in check. "But, you already knew this, didn't you? Why do you choose such a time to tell me?"

"What makes you think I knew?" Colonel Cala asked.

Vincenzo shrugged indifferently. "Don Nitto had told me about Siragusa. I assumed he had learned of his fate through you. Listen," said Vincenzo with annoyance. "I don't understand you. I've mentioned the duplicate *portfolio* to you a dozen times. Now, suddenly it's of vital importance. Why?"

The officers weren't listening to him. Between them there was some mystic form of communication and the captain, a bit more demonstrative than his superior officer, tapped his head in a sudden rush of enlightenment. "The Mafia!" he declared, as if that dreaded word answered their problems. "Who else but the Mafia, and Don Barbarossa?"

Vincenzo frowned, his dark eyes studying the captain. "What the hell does the Mafia have to do with what we're talking about?"

Colonel Cala was a step ahead of both. "*Carogna malodetta!* In the free for all. Everyone will be after him."

Vincenzo swallowed hard. "Make yourself clear, *Colonnello.* Who is everyone?"

"Anyone who wishes to avail themselves of the reward."

"After our precautions, all our carefully laid plans?" Captain Franchina showed his dismay.

Vincenzo lit a cigarette, with trembling hands. From time to time he'd gaze from one to the other, trying not to indicate his true feelings.

The Colonel's usual pacific nature had burst into restrained white rage, his customary apologetic apathy into myopic subjectivity. He handed the death report to his assistant.

"When was Siragusa caught?" asked Vincenzo trying to make conversation.

"Two, three weeks ago. I'm not certain," replied Colonel Cala. "Why?"

"And you just learned of it?" retorted Vincenzo guarded and aloof.

"Very well, it came to my attention three weeks ago."

"And you failed to inform me?" Captain Franchina looked up from the report.

"It wasn't important. The portfolio doesn't concern the FSB. But," he exasperated, "now, everything matters if we hope to fathom this *cioppino*, this kettle of fish."

"You think there's a tie-in, Cesare?" asked Franchina?"

"Ask de Montana," Cala said snidely. "He knows his people better than we."

Vincenzo grew uneasy. The courtship rites had ended. He glanced at the Captain for some explanation to Cala's abrasive statement.

"Bartolomeo Calemi has been murdered." Captain Franchina was final.

Vincenzo's jaw fell slack. Even after he read the report he found it all too incredible. His brain rolled with possibilities. *Could Tori have discovered betrayal in the man? Who could have done it so close to the end?* He shook his head, feigning astonishment. "How would I know if there's a tie-in? Being here with you two for the past many weeks has put me out of touch." He inhaled smoke from his cigarette and blew it out through his nose. "You're sure the report's on the up and up?"

"Goddammit!" Cala was beside himself. "Do I have to check into that, too? Is there nothing here in Sicily I can assume to be truth?"

"It's easy for you to verify such a report, isn't it?" asked Vincenzo.

Captain Franchina picked up the phone and called headquarters. In moments he got his answer. "It's on the up and up all right. Our own men discovered the body and made the report to Chief Zanorelli's office.

"*Allora*, then it's ended," exclaimed the crest-fallen Colonel. "It is finished. Salvatore's protection has crumbled and so shall he."

So occupied were the FSB officers with their own disappointment they took no time to document Vincenzo's reaction. If they'd taken time to scan the face of their glorified "Judas" they'd have noticed the sudden paleness, the trembling of his hands, the marked agitation as he snuffed out his cigarette.

"Perhaps, on the outside, I can learn what happened," suggested Vincenzo. He had to get out. To find Tori.

"Why? We fight a losing battle. Someone is bound to get Salvatore before we do."

"Listen" said Vincenzo taking courage. "You don't know my cousin like I know him. He's no fool. Your strength and cunning couldn't capture him. Only I can get to him."

"You say that as if you know something," said Cala.

"I know Salvatore! If he wants to remain in Montegatta, no one could get to him. Believe me. Only I can deliver him to you. The FSB offers nothing to entice him. Belasci offers freedom . . ."

"Some freedom! Hah! With Siragusa caught and the portfolio in his hands, what good are the deals made him?"

"Take it from me, Colonel," began Vincenzo with daring in his eyes. "Siragusa was *not* captured!"

Both the FSB officers turned their eyes on him.

"What do you mean he was not captured?"

Vincenzo explained what Salvatore had told him. "I tried to tell you about Salvatore's portfolio, but you wouldn't listen. You realize what bargaining power it would give you if you held it in your hands? Belasci would never permit you to be the laughing stock. He would be beholden to you *capeeshi*?"

The officers listened intently. What new possibilities this presented! Deals had been made over their heads. Their only hope had been to capture the renegade on their own. Only then could they hope to escape possible entrapment by the Minister of the Interior. But what of this portfolio?

"Did Calemi have anything to do with the betrayal of

the other bandits?" asked Vincenzo blowing smoke through his nose.

"Why do you ask?"

"Don Nitto suggested he did. Later he claimed he misled me. I thought it strange he should implicate Calemi if there was no truth to his words."

After an exchange of concerned looks between the officers, Colonel Cala shrugged. "Yes, he had a hand in it."

Vincenzo did a slow burn as he butted his cigarette. His voice was cold and curt. "That explains it, then. Someone must have got on to his double dealing and killed him."

"You mean Salvatore?"

"I mentioned no one. Who stands to lose most from Calemi's stupid action?"

"That could mean many people," exasperated Captain Franchina. "But it does eliminate Salvatore."

"Why?" asked the irate Cala. "He's been known to execute spies!"

"Execute, yes. Butcher, no. Read the report." He tossed the paper to his chief.

"Goddammit! You're right," he snapped impatiently. "It would have simplified matters if he had been Salvatore's victim. Nothing's simple in this accursed land!" He tossed the paper back on the nearby table.

Vincenzo out of curiosity leaned in to pick up the report and scanned it. What clue led them to believe the death hadn't been Salvatore's *peccato*? His eyes stopped on the line:

Body of male found with multiple stab wounds, face blown off, identity cards intact.

His face lit up. "You're right. It's not Salvatore's work. Nor the youngbloods, either. This is the old way! Calemi was killed by the old Mafia," he exclaimed in relief, forgetting for a moment in whose company he was in. *Goddammit!* He caught himself. *Why the hell am I helping my enemies?* He bit his lower lip savagely for being so incautious.

"Old Mafia, eh? Don Barbarossa? *Cazzu!* He's not out of the picture as I've been led to believe!" Colonel Cala stormed past them to the balcony overlooking the golden city and the busy *piazza* below him.

Captain Franchina and Vincenzo moved in behind him and for a time stood watching the traffic. Their sudden presence sent a covey of doves to ruffle their feathers and take flight to another roosting place.

"In all my life I've never encountered such a complication of intrigue. I'd sooner battle the Turks on their own grounds, by their rules, their choice of weapons than ever see another Sicilian assignment!" Colonel Cala made the sign of the cross in the air before him and kissed his finger tips in a gesture of finality. "*Croce e noce!*"

"*Managghia!* Such a statement, Colonel," teased Vincenzo. "The Turks are legendary savages famous for their barbarous methods of torture and killing."

"Exactly!" spat Colonel Cala with biting sarcasm.

For the rest of the evening the trio remained uncommunicative. Colonel Cala retired to his suite of rooms to contemplate the situation. Captain Franchina, while thoroughly disturbed by the developments, occupied himself in his infernal reports. Vincenzo settled down and continued to read. Behind veiled eyes, his thoughts ran rampant with these latest developments. *What the hell's going on?* he wondered. *I'm a Sicilian and even I am confused by these wild rumors, conjectures, and facts bandied about. Who of the old Mafia killed Calemi, and why? Why? What is the real truth about Santino? Is he dead or alive? Without the portfolio what could they do—just as Tori suggested? Damn! How many times had he brought it up to these two citrolli?* He glanced at Captain Franchina, and a thought struck him.

"Franchina," he called across the room. "Tell me something. How come you don't seem interested in Salvatore's portfolio?" he asked finally.

"Who said I wasn't interested?" The Captain continued in his work.

"But—" he stopped. "*Porco Dio!* All the time you've paid it no mind."

Franchina glanced up from his work. "Tell me, you think you could lay your hands on it?" he asked conspiratorially.

"Who, me?" hedged Tori's cousin. "*Managghia!* You ask a lot. Why? What would it be worth to you if I could lay my hands on it?" he asked, making a few mathematical calculations.

"Your life, what else?" said the Captain. "Listen, every man must think of himself at times. This may be one of those times. Cala has no instinct for survival."

"This may be the last time I'll see you, my beloved Sicily," said Tori moving about the vast silence of the Temple of Cats, impervious to the brash elements in what promised to be a desperately hot day. He'd been taking pictures of the area with his camera and stopped to stroke Napoleono's mane. "This may be the last time we'll be together for a while, old friend. I shall miss you most of all."

Napoleono's huge head bobbed up and down in a near-human response, his enormous coal-black eyes, glistening brightly in the sun, reflecting his master's image. He nuzzled his master, nudging him as Tori tied a kerchief around his forehead, Indian-style, to keep the salty sweat from running into his eyes.

"What shall become of you after I leave, old friend? I'll have to leave you with someone I know will care for you, *va bene?*"

The horse, glancing sideways at him, snorted and bobbed his head again. Tori laughed. He lit a cigarette and raised one leg to rest on a boulder as he glanced at his watch. He was waiting for his mother. He'd chosen the temple for their farewells with a definite purpose in mind. While he waited his thoughts strayed back to his father. He'd heard nothing from the Don since he wrote the letter to him. *It's better this way,* he thought resignedly. *Why bother to become acquainted at this late date?* He'd done what he'd felt proper and correct.

He thought about Bartolomeo Calemi and observed with fascination how the youngblood's death had shaken the *mafiosi, carabinieri* and security police, to say nothing of the FSB. Each faction blamed the other and no one had hinted in the least at the remote possibility that it could have been the work of the *capomafia.* His concern over Giacomo's fate had filled him with disquiet. He hadn't heard from his old friend and nothing had been reported, but Tori knew something had happened or the man would have moved heaven and earth to report back to him.

Natale Solameni, a nervous wreck, had called the villa

ten times a day to assure himself that Tori was safe. Solameni had personally spread rumors that Tori had already left Sicily to offset any possible last-minute treacheries, but rumors of plans to entrap Tori before he left Sicily still continued to spread.

"Mamma *bedda*," he called to her as she climbed the steep slope toward him, accompanied by two of Solameni's bodyguards. Tori ran down the incline to greet her and waved the men off. They gratefully retired to the shade of a cypress down below them.

Mother and son embraced endearingly, then, Tori with his powerful arms about her, guided her toward his private grotto. "It's important you pay careful attention to where I take you," he told her. "Look, see here between the fourth and fifth columns, right here, you turn left." He ushered her through a narrow passageway and, pausing before a large boulder, he said, "See how easy it moves? It's not as heavy as it appears."

Antigone's eyes widened in astonishment as the boulder gave way, revealing an opening in the rocks. Tori led her into an inner grotto. In the refreshing coolness of the cave she breathed easier and, once her enormous eyes grew accustomed to the dimness, stared wide-eyed at her surroundings, allowing her black mourning veil to slip off her head. "Whenever did you find such a place?" she asked staring at the memorabilia attached to the grotto walls. Photos of Tori and his men, placards portraying his colorful career were everywhere, including relics from the stint in the Partitionist Army, traces of his former campaigns, and an abundance of food supplies.

"I found it a lifetime ago, Mamma *bedda*."

He took her small, work-worn hand in his strong hands and sat down on the rock beside her.

"Mamma, it's time to say our farewells."

Tears welled in her eyes. She stroked his handsome face gently, with such a look of love on her face his heart almost broke.

"I want you to know I regret causing you such heartache and strife," he began with affected bravado. "I've always loved you deeply, even when it appeared for a while that I had no room in my heart for you. My own anger, my frustration in learning the identity of my real father, blinded me for a time. To find fault in you would have been like condemning an orange tree for bearing figs, or a fig tree for bearing oranges. I was wrong and now, before I leave, I ask for your forgiveness."

Antigone glanced uneasily about the cave, her voice

filled with caution. "*Figghiu mio*, are you certain there are no treacheries underfoot? I can't place the trust you do in these people, not even this Inspector D'Verde." She pulled out a letter from her pocket and handed it to him.

"I'll read it later."

"It's best you read it now."

Their eyes met and in that moment, he knew she'd read it. He unfolded the paper once he'd opened the envelope and studied it.

> *Information received confirms report that Vincenzo de Montana plots against you. He's held in readiness to assassinate you. Avoid any confrontation with him and be on your guard to offset any possible treachery.*

"They still try to turn us against each other," he said with a harsh edge of contempt to his voice.

Before Antigone's eyes there flashed a bright light and in the glow she saw Vincenzo with the lion amulet around his neck and the belt buckle at his waist, just as Tori wore his now. She cleared her throat and with firm resolve told him what she'd come to say and when she finished nearly a half hour later, she looked into the amazed eyes of her son. Before he could form any protest on his lips, she pressed the *strega*'s prophecy in his hands.

Tori studied his mother as if she were truly in her dotage and he tried to be temperate and understanding; she'd been through hell. But he saw he'd have to read the prophecy she described and he did.

"You wore the scorpion amulet, Gina wore one. The double sting of the scorpion. . . . Well, the two of you gave flight to the eagle, no?"

Half-disbelieving and half-filled with mirthful laughter, Salvatore suddenly sobered. If anyone had made him soar high, it had been Gina. His smile vanished.

"Tell me, Tori, how did you give . . . *power to the lion*? I have every reason to believe Vincenzo is the lion in the prophecy, whether or not you believe it."

"*Power to the Lion?*" He wanted to tell her, *I gave power to the lion, when I put my life in his hands!* But he said nothing. He remained introverted with thought.

"I haven't been able to piece together the part of the bull. Who represents the bull in your life, Tori?" persisted his mother. "If D'Verde's message is correct and Vincenzo plans to assassinate you, would that be the power given him?"

"Mamma, since I wasn't born to superstition I have never attempted to deceive the gods lest they notice me and become jealous. How can I begin now to strike up an acquaintance with them?"

"I don't know how Donna Sabattini's power of prophecy comes to her." Antigone insisted. "All I know is with my own eyes, my ears, and in my own lifetime, I've seen, heard, and lived through all she faultlessly predicted. From the moment you wore the *Eye of God* amulet, things went well. You gave yours to Gina, remember? I had another made. It took three weeks. In that space of time everything went wrong for you. Portella Della Rosa, the bombings of the communist headquarters, and all else. When I presented you with the new one, things again went well for you for a time. Did you ever remove it without my knowledge? Say in April of 1948?"

Tori's ego lost its cadence of assurance. Shaken, he felt his invincible armor crumble internally. His mother would never speak such trivia unless she truly discovered it was no longer trivia. He fought these thoughts and her words with all his strength. He shook his head slowly then it gathered momentum. "No! No," he said reprimandingly. "I refuse to think I'm simply a reed in the wind, dependent on some hidden force that allows me to do only that which is written in some dark mysterious cosmos. No! I refuse to allow myself to believe only in good luck amulets instead of my own inner resources, my intelligence, and infallible instinct. If I did, I'd be a nothing. A nothing at all, without volition, without will. I'd be nothing less than a mechanical toy who moves only on another's direction without a power of his own. Don't you see?"

"The *strega* said, 'Seven years of glory shall be his reign,' " she said sadly.

Tori didn't believe this was his mother. He thought her to be in her dotage. She saw it in his eyes when he pressed the prophecy back into her hands.

"Mamma, don't excite yourself like this." He tried to soothe her, to comfort her. He gathered her in his arms and affectionately stroked her head.

How could she make him understand and believe as she had come to believe. How? Even she had refused to believe until only recently.

"Calm yourself," he told her. "I can feel your heart beating wildly. I promise to be most cautious, doubly cautious for your sake as well as mine." He glanced anxiously at his watch. There was little time. "Come," he told her. "I want to show you something."

He walked her along to the far end of the grotto and with one hand felt along the wall of the cave. "See this flat rock? It's slightly different in color from the others—the color of Marsala wine." He placed both hands on it, manipulated it until it came loose. He removed it, placed it on the ground, then reached inside the cavity and removed a rolled leather *portfolio* wrapped in oilskin.

"These are my private *portfolios*, the memorial, the biography, and the entire diary of my political career. My writings, including my poetry, even my own epitaph," he smiled. "It's more fitting I write my own epitaph than someone who never knew me or what was in my heart while I was on earth."

Antigone filled with an unknown terror.

"In the event of my . . . well, any treachery, send the portfolio to the man whose name is on the inside cover, Colonel Stefano Modica. The instructions are in this envelope. The papers will then be published in all the newspapers so the guilty parties shall not go unpunished. The corruption must stop some time."

"I thought Santino had all these—" she was suddenly confused. "Why the necessity of sending him away?"

"It was more credible that way." He returned the papers to their niche, replaced the stone, and walked her back to where they sat earlier. "No one will think to look here."

"Yes, I understand, Tori," she hesitated unable to say what she felt to be true, that those writings were warrants for his death.

As if he read her mind, he said, gently, "Those papers are insurance that will take me to safety and later escort you to safety when I send for you. This has been my sanctuary, where I've always felt at home and at peace. From the first time I heard the *Siculi* demons call to me, I've felt a strong affinity to this place, almost as if I'll never be far, although I may be oceans away." He turned to her, took her hands in his. "No one knows of this place except you and I. Not even Gina, whom I loved deeply."

What was it she had to tell him about Gina? "Tori," her mind struggled to bring it to the surface, but there was so much more, so very much more. "There is something I must say—"

"*Managghia*, Mamma!" he exclaimed glancing at his watch. "It's time to say our farewells."

"So soon?" Tears welled in her eyes. Everything else eluded her.

He held her tightly. "I want you to know how much love and respect I hold for you in my heart. It breaks my heart that we must part, but then, we've prepared for this day these past six months, haven't we? You've been the best mother a man could ever hope to have."

"If I had been a better mother you might not be taking flight from our country, like a hunted animal."

"There are times when flight is victory," he reminded her.

"Oh, my son!" she wailed. "I did this to you! I did! The fear of losing you sealed the protest on my lips. I should have protested Destiny's stranglehold on you the moment I saw her reach out to you. I should have fought her off, tooth and nail, for your life," she cried. "At first, I told myself it's for Sicily . . . for our people. Suddenly, you did belong to the world. You fed our people, protected them, bargained for them, and became their saviour, their king! Even I deluded myself into believing what you did was right. Justified."

"Mamma! Don't get yourself worked up! It's all over with. I don't belong to the world any longer."

"No, don't stop me, Tori. I must tell you what I actually felt, what I thought all these years. If I'm not honest with you now, I'll never rest in peace. This must be the moment of truth between us. For three years, you were King—truly a king, Tori. Then, something happened. I saw it. Everyone saw it. We who loved you wondered what made you change."

He nodded as he listened as if in agreement.

"But, suddenly you became an animal—no better than the men who gave you orders. It was as if murder and killings became a joy to you!"

"Mamma!" his heart broke. "Stop! Don't let this be our farewell!"

He felt utterly prostrate at her behavior. "Now that you're against me, it's best I do leave," he said bitterly.

"It's my fault," she raved on. "All this is my fault!" There was no stopping her. "From childhood I filled your mind with the deeds of great men, Alexander of Macedonia, Julius Caesar, even Napoleon! I had to acquaint you will all the conquerors, all of them. I taught you to believe all things could be justified in the name of expediency. Because I was a woman who felt cheated at not being born a man, here in Sicily where every male child is worshipped like a god, I afflicted you with my frustrations, my disappointments, my dreams! It was I who put a sword into your hand! I, who created the tyranny of your life. I, without the courage of my own convictions, poured into you my resentments, hatreds, and animosities toward those who had treated our people unjustly. It was as if I assembled you out of the dust and ashes of the desperate men in history and molded you into the man you've become. A man who must now flee his country and his home to take his place among the vanquished!"

Antigone was on her feet addressing her son who had risen and turned from her trying to shut out her words. But she gave him no quarter.

"It wasn't God who placed into your hands the power of life and death, Tori. I am the guilty one. I must have been possessed of a demon when I poured forth into your innocent mind the poison that afflicted me." Antigone, fully spent, sank to her knees, her arms flung about her son's legs as he stood before her somber and silent. His face, set like rock, filled with harsh planes in the shadows of the grotto. He had never seen his mother without her usual tranquillity, her strength, and he filled with mixed feelings. Reduced to a mass of defenseless womanly frailties, dying inside because her son's plight had taken on such inexplicable proportions, she experienced total wretchedness in her commiseration.

Tori reached down and pulled her gently to her feet. "Why do you blame yourself for my fate? You forget there is another person who should accept the responsibility for helping to conceive me, my father. Mamma, have I been so bad a human being? Do I deserve this kind of a farewell? Am I suddenly a monster to you?"

"Oh, my God! I never seem to say the right thing. I love you Tori, with the passion only a mother can have for her son. Because I love you I've only wanted the best for you! From the very moment I recognized you to be a man of destiny, I should have seen to it that you left Sicily, before it devoured you."

"Now you speak the words of a fool! I refuse to indulge you further!" said Tori sternly. "I'm disturbed you should choose these last few moments to destroy my image of you!"

"Why, because I'm a mere woman? Not a statue to be revered?"

Tori weakened, wiped away her tears. His voice softened. "You forget I am also *his* son. I inherited much from him. It only follows I should be like him in many ways. Can that fact be set aside, ignored? If you weren't so upset, you'd recognize the truths in what I say. Please, Mamma *bedda*, try to understand I'm not ashamed of one moment of my life or of any act I've committed. I would do the same all over again," he smiled. "All except to believe those men in whom I put my faith. I regret the Portella Della Rosa tragedy, not because I wasn't inculpated, but because I should have been more wary of the deceit and treacheries aimed at me. But, it is all in the past. I leave Sicily now, because I made a deal. I gave my word if you were released from prison, I would leave Sicily. Besides, this may be the best step I've ever taken. Why all the sadness?" He hugged her once again and kissed her. "Now, Mamma, we go."

Tears welled in his eyes, tears he fought to control, and because he knew his mother would collapse, if she saw them, he brushed them quickly aside. He led her into the blinding, hot sun and replaced the boulder.

"*Allora*, don't forget this place. Between the fifth and sixth columns, to the north of the gateway. This is where the spirit of Salvatore shall remain," he winked at her and clicked his camera at her.

Instinctively like any other woman, she became self-conscious, patted her hair into place, and objected. He grinned. It broke the tension. Tori lifted the Eye of God amulet from around his neck and handed it to her. "You keep this, Mamma. I have no further use for it."

If he had known her reaction, it would have been the very last thing he'd do. She screamed hysterically. "No! No! No! You must always wear it! Always! Promise me!" Her eyes widened maniacally. "Promise me!"

"*Allora, basta! Va bene*, Mamma! *Va bene!*" Her violent reaction stunned him.

She calmed down finally and he led her to the edge of the temple floor. Once again he kissed her and waved his hand to Solameni's men below. Cautiously, they sprang from the car and scurried up the slopes toward her. He watched for a time until they reached her. His mother turned once more and stared at this god-like son etched against the sun as Napoleone galloped to his side.

"God bless you, heart of my heart, spirit of my soul," she whispered.

It wasn't until the bodyguards delivered her safely to her house that she remembered she hadn't told Tori he was the father of a one-year-old son. She had even forgotten to tell him about the contract of death placed upon him, that Cacciatore was the missionary of death. There had been too much to remember.

By the time Tori rode his horse across the plains and reached Calemi's villa, he found Natale Solameni waiting anxiously for him.

"I beg you don't hold the stupidity of my father's meddling ways against me, Salvatore," pleaded Natale, that candy-eating polar bear. "He knew nothing of the finalizing of our plans with D'Verde when that fucking FSB Captain formed an alliance with him," he said in an avalanche of apology.

"He's your father. When the time comes, you'll side with him, rather than honor a pact with me," announced Salvatore dispassionately. "If you wish to withdraw from this arrangement, I'll understand."

"What the hell are you saying? Who said anything about withdrawing? I made a deal and a deal's a deal, regardless of anything my father does or says!"

Salvatore looked at him tolerantly through tilted eyes.

"I'm serious! You know the older men are meddling bastards! I can't prevent what he does anymore than he can stop me from choosing the path I select!" Solameni was pacing furiously about the room.

"Even after the reconciliation with your father?"

Natale glanced sharply at his charge. "Fuck! Is there nothing that escapes you?"

"No, nothing." He smiled patiently. "I've no quarrel with you, Natale. Blood being stronger than water, I prefer that D'Verde replaces you for these last steps of my journey. *Va bene?*"

Natale made a disorganized gesture. In the end he had to succumb to Tori's demands, no matter how he felt.

Porca miseria! His sullen, broad face darkened. *Why the fuck did my father have to intervene, now! After so many years!* "Calemi's dead! Who do you suggest can be trusted so late in the game?" he snapped angrily, suddenly amazed at his own bravado.

"The son of Bernardo Malaterra," replied Salvatore.

"The son of—" Natale halted abruptly. "You're crazy! They won't permit it!" Solameni saw through Salvatore's strategy. *With the son of so powerful a mafioso at his side, who would attempt any foul play?*

"Nevertheless, I'll not leave Sicily unless Rudolfo Malatera accompanies me, *capeeshi?*" he announced flatly.

"I'll relate your instructions." stated the dour-faced Natale, tearing the wrapper off a fresh chocolate bar. He left to carry out the orders.

CHAPTER 65

So! It was really finally over. All behind him now: the mountains, the grottos, the sounds of horses in the darkness, the laughter of his men around campfires, the killings, the sounds of ambush and firearms, the cries in the night, the lean, frightening lonely years. The endless searching and wanting and countless disappointments in finding only treacheries and betrayals. It was done. *Basta, e finito!*

I never want to see another dead face or broken body. I never want to see treachery in another man's face. I want to forget that any of this ever happened. I want to regain my trust in mankind. God help me!

Would I ever forget it? he asked himself. *No.* But he'd try very hard to pretend it never happened. It wasn't the life or the end he had planned. Life, more important than death, had much to teach him and there was much to learn. Yet he refused to be cowed by the treacheries meted him thus far.

Tori moved about his suite of rooms planning his departure. Reality inexorably invaded his thoughts as he reflected upon his seven years of manhood. At twenty seven, Tori felt he'd been a man for an eternity. All noble reflections of the past had long since vanished, along with the naive idealism. Now, stripped of this naivete, he stood firmly against the background of a new reality, the brittle crust of delusion broken and crumbled to bits at his feet. He'd never known a life of gaiety and irresponsibility and it seemed he'd been born old. Everything had changed for Tori because he'd changed. Now, he faced a strange, new life, one filled with the unknown.

He snapped the lock. One bag packed, ready to go, was placed in a corner near the door. He turned the lock in the door and searched the apartment to make certain he was alone. From the balcony, he saw Solameni's car drive away. The courtyard was empty now and the guards chatted idly.

Tori removed the *Eye of God* amulet from around his neck, tossed it on a chair next to the bed, and smiled tolerantly as he recalled his mother's sharp warnings. *How had she allowed herself to be so seduced by the strega?* he asked himself as he continued to undress. *Black magic, witchcraft, all of it.* Even *malocchio* amulets had been something he scoffed at during his lifetime. He hung his gun belt and Browning automatic on a wooden stool in the bathroom next to the marble tub and drew water for his bath. For several moments he fumbled with a radio dial, tuning in to a station that played music, and finally stepped into the tub to bathe indolently.

Tori's mind flowed with thoughts of Gina. He realized it had been nearly two years since he last saw her. Even though his mother failed to tell him the news, he'd long since calculated the approximate age of their child. God willing, before too long they might be together. This thought alone inspired him to flush with happiness and anticipation.

Once he'd finished bathing, Tori finished his packing and, having slipped into fresh shorts, donned a pair of beige levis and slid his feet into leather-thonged sandals. He strapped on the Browning, lit a cigarette, and sauntered out onto the balcony where he stood for a time gazing at the flowers in the courtyard and the tiled water fountain below.

Here he was standing on the raw, blinding threshold of a new world, a new life. He could no longer escape this road routed by destiny. It was incredible to Tori that his enemies weren't inclined to cease and desist in their betrayal attempts. They'd do anything to kill him, even now. Nothing was sacred to them, not even their word. Only five days ago, young Jocco, his bodyguard, brought a stranger in to see him, a man he'd caught skulking about the iron gates of the sealed off courtyard. The man, under the carefully aimed gun of the guard, had insisted he could only speak in private to Salvatore. After a thorough search of his person for concealed weapons, Salvatore dismissed Jocco.

"Talk," he ordered the man when they were alone.

The man said his name was Morelli and explained he was part of a highly covert plan to secret Salvatore out of Sicily. He claimed that he was an American agent who represented Colonel Stefano Modica, that it had taken him two weeks before he finally located Salvatore at Calemi's villa. He handed Tori the sealed envelope informing him that Stefano Modica would arrive in Palermo the afternoon of July 5 at 5:00 P.M. to personally escort Tori out the country. He was instructed to prepare himself for the journey to avoid unnecessary delays.

In these final hours, Tori had been suspicious of his own shadow and justifiably so, in lieu of the intrigue exploding on all sides of him. He listened intently to Morelli, thinking as he did, *was it just possible, possible that Stefano Modica had actually come to his aid? After a five-year silence?*

"There's no time for doubt, reflection or hesitancy," Morelli had emphasized. "Too much time has already elapsed and I need a reply for Colonel Modica."

Tori had obliged. Using the code name, Scorpio, he sent a note to Modica. It was the same message Morelli handed Stefano Modica in the men's room at Rome's airport on July 5.

Tori didn't believe Morelli and put no stock in the message from Stefano. He permitted Morelli to leave the villa with safe escort, hoping the message would throw off his would-be assailants. He convinced himself that this encounter was simply one more branch off a proliferating tree of betrayal, he must cautiously avoid. To think that in five years he'd heard not one word from Stefano Modica. Now those idiots in Rome attempt to lure him into such a flimsy, glued-together trap with a half-baked plot a child could see through. What will they think to do next?

Several times after Tori sent Morelli away, the thought struck Tori that perhaps the message might have been bonafide. He reasoned, that if Colonel Modica had really been at the center of a plan to come to his aid, it would have been accomplished long before the eleventh hour in a systematic and orderly manner.

Little did he know how difficult it had been for Stefano to locate him via other channels.

He chose to forget the encounter and concentrated on more immediate matters.

What hell there'd be when Solameni asked for Bernardo Malaterra's son to escort him to safety, he thought. Tori smiled and suddenly a loud laughter rippled from his throat. Pleased with his astute planning, he considered it would serve them right for thinking they could doublecross him again.

Before the dull, pounding headache forming at the base of his skull developed into the old warnings behind his ear lobe, Tori took several aspirins. Having had no breakfast or lunch that day he reasoned the pain was due to hunger pangs. This was the first of a slew of self-deceptions he indulged in this day.

He walked back onto the balcony in time to see a gleaming, black Alfa Romeo sedan pull into the courtyard. Immediately, the two guards rushed both car and driver with guns poised menacingly. Tori sprang back out of sight and watched the goings-on from between a crack in the shutters. A dark figure, husky and without intimidation, emerged from the auto and spoke to the guards.

Tori stiffened imperceptibly, when he recognized Don Barbarossa's loathsome bodyguard, Cacciatore. He watched with marked curiosity as the guards searched, then allowed the man to pass. Subconsciously Tori's hand touched his forehead in recollection of the skull creasing given him by this gargoyle. He unholstered his gun, rechecked the clip, and shoved it back into place. Gun held firmly in hand, he moved swiftly to the bedroom door and unlocked it just as Jocco knocked on it. They exchanged concerned glances.

"Cacciatore is here with a message from Don Barbarossa." Jocco handed him a letter as they entered the room, his .38 calibre Beretta covering the *mafioso.*

Images of their last encounter burning vividly in his mind kept his features immobile. "Keep him covered, Jocco."

"My pleasure," grinned the redheaded youth, who was so awed by Tori he'd gladly lay down his life for the famous outlaw. He'd never seen the likes of a legend of Cacciatore's stature either, and he continued to gawk at both men like an impressionable youth seeing his first movie stars.

Cacciatore gazed at Salvatore through lidded eyes, with a different perspective. As he studied the bold man's comportment, his attitude measured his handsome face as he searched for the similarities between father and son. Several feet away from him, Tori stood reading the letter, his heart racing wildly.

> *Mio caro figghui*:
> Fill an old man with pleasure. Grant him the joy of gazing upon the face of his son before you leave Sicily. Cacciatore will escort you safely to my villa. You've my word you need fear no betrayal from him.
>
> *Tu padre*, M. Barbarossa.

As he fought the overwhelming desire to comply with his father's request he forced himself to remember all the spawned animosities prevailing between them. However, the invitation, so powerfully persuasive, diminished Tori's will. It suddenly became of tremendous importance to him that this encounter take place. He glanced at his watch. It was 3:30 P.M. He'd already made changes in his original plans. He paced the floor in contemplative thought as a flurry of excitement permeated his spirit.

In the next few moments, as he grew more elated, he tossed the greater percentage of caution he usually employed to the four winds. Only one thing stood out in his mind—one thing drove him—his father wanted to see him. Imagine. Twenty-seven years of his life had been spent waiting for this one moment; a moment held suspended in time for him and his real father.

By now his pulse raced furiously. The familiar throbbing behind his left ear pounded achingly and in his delirious ebullience Tori ignored the familiar signs. For perhaps the first time in his life he'd failed to heed the warnings and in so doing became foolishly incautious.

Setting aside the knowledge of who Cacciatore was and what he represented, he ignored the enmity between them and the insult done him in Palermo. *What the hell,* he told himself in a benevolent rush of magnaminity, *the old boy only took orders, and from his father at that.* Still, despite this charitable mood, Tori wasn't altogether without wits. He kept his guard up.

From across the room Jocco blinked wide-eyed at Tori's reaction.

"You go ahead, Cacciatore," he instructed the *mafioso* as he slipped into a white, sleeveless undershirt. "I'll join you there on my stallion." He grabbed a light-weight windbreaker jacket from the chair. The sudden movement caused the *Eye of God* amulet to slide to the back of the upholstered damask chair, unnoticed.

"You know where Don Barbarossa's villa is located?" Cacciatore frowned.

"Doesn't everybody?"

"It's best you come with me, not to waste time."

"I'll wager that I arrive before you," retorted Tori impulsively.

"I'm not a betting man. Be there in fifteen minutes," he muttered.

"Make it twelve," said Tori glancing at his watch.

Cacciatore reluctantly took his leave, but he didn't like this. Not at all.

Before Tori left the villa, he rechecked all documents and passports. All were in order. Opening a packed bag, he placed the papers and a packet of money into a secret compartment, and relocking the bag, he returned it to its original place next to the desk. He checked his Browning, holstered it, and, glancing about the room, he left. By the time he returned from his father's villa, Natale Solameni would be back with the information he requested. *Va bene.*

Scheduled plans to fly out of the Castelvetrano airport on July 5 had been changed. He had decided to leave that evening for the southern village, to make connections on a boat for Lisbon and from there fly to South America.

He rode through open country where peasants, stooped over, sang at their work and where paths were tangled in moist dark shades of green, heavy with the earth's perfume. He arrived at the Villa Barbarossa as a radiant mist crept over the valley. Everything was marvelous, he told himself. Cacciatore pulled into the flower courtyard just as Tori dismounted and tied Napoleono to a hitching post. The stallion kept throwing up his head, mane flowing, pawing the ground with his hooves, his eyes flaring wildly. Tori stroked the animals forehead soothingly.

"I'll be back in a short while, Napoleono. Calm down, eh?" He caught sight of the *Eye of God* amulet between the animal's eyes where he's fastened it years ago. An after-image of the one he removed just before his bath struck him. Instinctively his hand flew to his neck where he probed for the amulet and felt only the golden scorpion. Normally he wouldn't have been disturbed. But his mother's words echoed through his mind and for reasons unknown he shook with trepidation.

Damnit! If only she hadn't told me about the prophecy! Now, she has me believing in all that nonsense, he told himself. Then he laughed aloud at his own uneasiness. He patted Napoleono reassuringly once again.

"What the hell can happen to me now, am I not in my father's house?"

He moved along the flower-lined brick walkway to join Cacciatore who indicated considerable relief at Tori's presence. Driving back from Castellammare he had entertained second thoughts about permitting Salvatore to ride through the Sicilian countryside without escort. The reward on the outlaw's head was too tempting now. Phew! What if some greedy sonofabitch had taken a pot shot at him? He'd have been fish bait by now.

The Moorish-inspired villa, more luxurious than the one in Godrano, held special fascination for Salvatore. He walked through the shadowy corridor as dazzling reflections of an afternoon sun sent shafts of colored lights through the stained-glass windows of a domed skylight.

Arched, marble columns at either side of him framed the solarium of hot-house plants and tropical fronds. At the center of the foyer, he was instructed to bear to the right of the structure. Cacciatore stopped at the entrance to the Don's study, extended his hand. "Your gun," he demanded.

"Oh, no," protested Salvatore. "You don't take my gun." He moved swiftly in split second timing, whipped out his firearm, and held it firmly, descisively.

"Then, you leave without seeing the Don."

"*Va bene*. Then, I leave." Tori tensed.

A familiar voice called from inside the study. "Let him pass, Cacciatore."

"He carries weapons," came the protesting sour voice.

Don Barbarossa appeared at the door, gaunt, thinner, and heavily weighted with problems. His shoulders sagged. In Cacciatore's presence, he deliberately avoided eye contact with Salvatore. He extended his hand, permitted Tori to enter and to Cacciatore he said, "I say, it's all right." A deep pocket of lined furrows stretched across his forehead.

The bodyguard stared glumly and tossing his hands into the air in a gesture of hopelessness, he padded down the corridor, out of sight.

Inside the study, the reigning monarchs of Sicily, both legends in their time, stood facing each other. Their eyes met and held in this moment of high emotion. It was a powerful and intoxicating moment for both, one neither would ever experience again. The man who was Sicily regarded the true ruler of Sicily through calm, relaxed warm brown eyes that spelled no threat of danger.

Matteo Barbarossa, free from guile or pretense, stripped of all the facades which made him *capomafia*, stood before his son, in silence. Suddenly he clasped his hands to his chest in a gesture conveying wonder, disbelief, compassion, and futility all in one. His eyes brimmed with tears.

Overcome with emotion, he stretched out his arms to draw his son forward into the circle of a father's affection. Both men shared in the embrace, the Don more tempestuous, Salvatore more reserved.

It was all so new to him, Tori remained in a state of impervious rigidity until the sight of this giant, crying unashamedly and displaying a wealth of emotion, touched him to the core, enough to evoke a welling up of tears. Several moments of bear hugs ensued in which the Don alternately pushed him away to gaze upon his son's face, then drew him to his bosom. He repeated the process, as if by so doing he could commit his son's features to memory.

Finally the emotional storm subsided and the Don motioned his son to a chair opposite him.

"*Allora*, sit, my son. Sit." He wiped the tears from his eyes and cheeks and as he seated himself he exclaimed with fierce emotion. "You have your mother's beauty! Everything else is like me."

The study, stifling hot and sweltering as a result of a broken electric fan, had been shuttered to keep out the afternoon sun, and they sat in partial shadow as the Don fanned himself with a bamboo fan. He, himself, was in shirtsleeves and he suggested to his son, "Take off your jacket. It's hotter than the fiery furnace of hell in here."

Glancing at the disabled fan, Tori said. "If you'll give me a screwdriver perhaps I can repair the fan. You don't know I'm a mechanical wizard, do you?" Spying a letter opener on the desk, he reached for it. "Here, let me have it. It will do. Most of the time it's just a short or a worn contact that's loose." He unzipped his jacket laid it on the chair and removed the back plate from the fan.

It took but a few moments to locate the source of trouble. After splicing the wires properly and reconnecting them to the proper poles, he secured them into place. All the while the Don looked at his son as if he could never be done with the wonder of him. Pride oozed from every pore in his body as the Don watched the fascinating play of muscles rippling with every movement of Tori's arms and hands.

Tori replaced the plate, reset the fan, and switched on the motor. It responded instantly. The whirring motor at high speed began to gesticulate from side to side. "There! Like new! You didn't know I worked as a telephone lineman installing lines from Palermo to Castellamare?"

"There are not too many things I don't know about you," replied his father. "That, however, I did not know."

"Before I was eighteen, I supervised eight men under me. It wasn't easy, I tell you." Tori wiped his hands on his handkerchief. "Older men who resented me because of my youth. You know how it is with older men who feel insecure when the young—" He stopped in time. "Nevertheless, one thing led to another and here I am."

Don Matteo vaguely heard his son's words. His eyes, feasting on the young man, drank everything in while he kept repeating to himself, *this is my son. The flesh and blood of my seed, sits before me, my son.* As most Sicilian fathers are wont to do, he searched for family resemblances. He saw the beauty of Antigone Salvatore in the face and eyes of his son, continuously.

Watching him, indulgently, Tori wiped the perspiration from his face and basked in the cooling breeze stirred by the fan. He didn't put his jacket on again. Fascinated by the bronze figure of a bull on the Don's desk he leaned in to pick it up, amazed by its weight. "El Toro, eh?" he muttered. His mother's words echoed in his mind, *"Scorpio becomes impotent against the fury of the bull.*

He shook his head tolerantly as he unconsciously reached up to feel the golden scorpion.

"What's wrong?" asked the Don watching him intently.

"Nothing. It's just that I recalled once you mentioned you were born in May? . . ."

"You are an expert on the heavens, also?" asked the Don. "Next, you'll be telling me you sport an astral telescope like the nobility," he snorted.

"Nothing like that." Temporarily distracted, he too smiled at the inference.

"Are you all set to leave?"

"Yes."

"When?"

"My plane departs in four hours." His guard was up.

"They changed departure time? I thought you didn't leave for two days?"

"I should know better than to try to disguise my plans with you. My plans have been changed."

Yes, thought his father. *Your plans have been changed.*

He offered his son a cigar from his special humidor. Each fumbled with the wrappings. Tori stood up to light first his father's, then his own. Silence hung over them for several moments as the room filled with blue-white puffs of smoke, displaced only when the course of the fan cut through to separate the mist and spiral it upward toward the ceiling, where it collected in a misty blanket. For a time they regarded each other in a rush of awkwardness.

"How long have you known we are related?" asked the Don clearing a thick lump in his throat.

"It was in my letter. Five years. I mentioned it."

"Why didn't you come to me sooner?"

"It was a difficult thing for me, even now."

"Nothing should be difficult to discuss with one's father."

"It took three years to approach you as a Godfather. Imagine my reaction when I learned the truth?" He looked into his father's eyes and said quietly, "This, for me is a special moment. When I considered it might be the last time we'd see each other, I couldn't deny myself, or you, this moment."

"If it was in my power to change the past I would."

"Why bring up the past? What's been done is already history."

The Don made a gesture of impatience! "What happiness I felt when I learned my seed gave you life. Yet the same knowledge eats at me like a malignant cancer. God burdens my old age heavily with agony and ecstasy. It's as if I'd been granted all the gold at the end of the rainbow but, when I reach to grab it it crumbles to dust. Why didn't you come to me five years ago? I could have changed the course of history for you. You never believed in my power. Why?"

Tori shrugged imperceptibly.

"I'd like nothing better to stand atop the towers in every village in the land and proclaim, 'Salvatore is my son! My flesh! My blood!' Oh, my son, my pride is swollen by your many accomplishments."

Tori stared wonderously at his father. The blood coursing through his body gave rise to the pleasure of a parent's compliments. It was worth having to wait all his life to hear this moment of praise.

"But, can I?" continued the Don. "My punishment is that I can never tell a soul you are my son!" He hung his head disconsolately.

The afternoon shadows lengthened and slanted in through the blinds. Now that it was cooler, the Don turned on his desk lamp. It took a moment for Tori's eyes to adjust and when they did he saw the collections of newsclippings on the wall behind the Don's chair, and the scale model of western Sicily he'd seen at the *Albergo-Sole*.

"What can I say? That somehow I knew, sensed, something between us? I gave you more room than I've given to another who proved as disrespectful as you. Even as I followed your career, I wondered why I didn't—" He banged his fist down hard on the desk. "It wouldn't have been difficult to do in those early days, to crush you."

"You mean something like the Portella fiasco?" Salvatore smiled tolerantly and was surprised that he felt no indignation or hatred in that moment.

"You knew what had been intended?"

"Only, after the fact, unfortunately. By then, a mere child could have seen through the infamous plot. I still laugh at the absurd antics of your protégé, Martino Belasci, who made me sign a confession to the Magistrate at Viterbo. The trial has already commenced, hasn't it, some three or four weeks ago? They hold fifty men, charged for an atrocity purportedly committed by twelve

898

men, none of whom were guilty in the first place. What a mockery of justice! What folly to request a signed confession from me for a crime no one in his right mind attributes to me. Do you really think you can hoodwink the people into believing that trash? The case will have to be thrown out of court when the facts are presented."

"But, your men *were* guilty of the real crime, my son."

"I don't understand. My men didn't shoot to kill."

"The men on Mt. Cumeta, who discharged the fatal bullets, were your men. Oh, you didn't order them to kill. We did. But, make no mistake, they were *your* men."

"I don't believe you." He spoke as he would to an enemy.

"Why would I lie to you, now?"

"Yes, why would you? Who were they?"

"Does it matter now?"

"Strange as it seems, yes."

The Don rattled off the names as one would recite a prayer he'd memorized. "The Brancato brothers, Lupo Messina, Pianello, Sapienza, Delgato—you don't remember them? All these men took orders from you once."

Tori's face blanched with rage. All were fringe area bandits, never really considered his men. He'd used these tough butchers only to intimidate the *carabinieri* He'd used these unmanageable bandits to decimate communist headquarters *after* the Portella massacre. He could see how this would hold up in court.

"I can see how you might have coerced the others to betray me, but I must express surprise at the Brancato brothers."

"It was simple. Inspector Semano convinced them Senator de Casselli was responsible for denying them amnesty after the Partitionists fell. They hated the Senator so they agreed to execute him in exchange for pardons.

And instead of granting their pardons, you incarcerated them," Tori expressed sardonic contempt. "I can see how God, Himself, might betray me, once exposed to your masterful persuasion." He shook his head in stupefaction. "You're a true genius, Godfather, I mean, father. A wizard. Machiavelli himself would have envied your brand of political intrigue."

The Don, who knew little about Machiavelli, and recognized less the compliment his son bestowed upon him, didn't acknowledge what he misconstrued as flattery because he knew it to be laced with bitterness and black memories experienced by Tori in those grim hours following the Portella fiasco.

"If you had come to me sooner, do you have any idea how high you might have climbed? By next year, maybe the year after, I'll control the highest office in the land. It could have been my son who'd occupy that post."

Tori, growing weary, hadn't intended this encounter be spent rehashing old issues. He disapproved of post-mortems and grew dismayed that his father would waste their precious time flaunting his power.

"After Belasci becomes premier it might be arranged for you to return here with full amnesty."

Tori steeled himself. "It's best you don't play that broken record."

"You can't tell what the future holds. After all, you are my son," said the Don.

"Return here? The possibility of that dream has long evaporated in my mind. I dare not dream those dreams again."

"When Belasci becomes premier, nothing will be impossible."

"You're telling me I could return to Sicily, to school, and become a respected lawmaker?" He asked it straight. He had to know it wasn't a game.

"I told you. Nothing's impossible."

"Don't." Tori held up a restraining hand. He wagged the hand at his father. "Just don't. Don't give me hope." "Just don't, don't do that." He had to reject such possibilities. He had no room left for such naivete. None at all.

"You never believed in the power of Don Barbarossa?"

Tori, on his feet moved about the room seeking momentary refuge from such tempting whisperings. With all his strength he disclaimed what his brain telegraphed. Finally, he returned to his seat. Tori lifted his eyes to meet his father's His spirits spiralled and soared above the clouds and he pulled himself closer to earth where he could examine the situation in a calm, controlled manner. He ignored Vincenzo's urgings to guard against a betrayal from any direction. Here, the most powerful man in Sicily was telling his son nothing was impossible. Was this a straw for him to grasp that would support his hopes?

"You *know* what I'd give for such an eventuality."

"Your personal portfolio? The original?" The Don asked this so quietly that at first, Tori didn't hear him clearly.

Once again the idealism was stripped from his eyes. The foundation under his feet began to crumble. "My portfolio?"

"Yes, the *portfolio*."

The man seated opposite Tori bore no relationship to the emotional parent who greeted him earlier. Here was the calculating, wheeling and dealing *Capomafia*, ready to strike a bargain.

"Would you be willing to turn over to me all copies of the *portfolio*, promise never to breathe the names of the men who instigated the Portella fiasco and anything else, for that matter? Give me your word as my son."

Tori studied the crafty barracuda closely. Caught in a confrontation with himself, the peace he belatedly secured for himself crumbled slowly. It was a pivotal moment, one that assumed a quick and unexpected reversal.

"What good would that do? Did you forget I committed a cardinal sin? I am responsible for the deaths of five *mafiosi*." He tested the Don.

"There are ways to absolve you of the crimes of their deaths. There's little to fear when the law is on your side."

"A deal? Is that what you suggest?"

"I didn't know before that you are my flesh, my blood."

"You say, I can remain here, safe and secure, without threat of reprisal, if I turn over my portfolio?"

"Listen, my son, this is a new idea in my head. I have to think on it. It will take time to examine the situation. Records will have to be expunged, new records put in their place. In time people will forget Salvatore. Are you willing to forego the stature of Salvatore, and everything he represents?"

"All this for my portfolio?"

"Your portfolio, my son, is dynamite!" he replied in blunt candor. "Everything many men have worked a lifetime for can explode if the contents of your . . . *memorial* . . . are made public. You think they will stand by and let you get away with this?"

"How do you know what's contained in my portfolio?"

"How do I know? I don't know. I can only guess. Listen, a guess to many men is often more frightening than the truth. Right now, you are cloaked in a jacket marked Danger, High Explosives, which everyone has seen fit to handle with care. It's a *molto pericoloso*, a perilous position, for anyone to find himself in. Many fuses lead to your center. *Mah, pero,* for anyone to attempt to ignite one of them would be a dangerous foolhardy act. One day, perhaps, the correct fuse will be discovered and someone, when you least expect it, will light it. Then, poof!"

"Three times in the past your word turned to dust—"

"I told you, I didn't know you were my son."

"That makes a difference whether a man of respect gives his word and keeps it?" He said with snide innuendo.

Eyes burned into eyes and both returned to their former hostilities.

The Don broke first. "You see how you are? It isn't easy for a man of my stature to bend when spoken to with such lack of respect. You defy me, constantly."

"Because you treated me unjustly!" retorted Tori. "How many times does a man have to fall on his ass before you stop kicking him? Tori got to his feet angrily and made a disorganized gesture. "What a sad, pitiful farewell is this! You force me to regurgitate everything in my stomach." He paced the floor. "Forgive me. I don't mean to argue."

Don Matteo studied the cigar he rolled between his fingers thoughtfully. "As you said, let's forget the past. Let us concern ourselves with your future. Will you give up the portfolio in exchange for your rehabilitation?" he put the question to him again.

Salvatore walked to the windows and opened the shutters. Soon, it would be sunset, the time he loved most in every day, a time when special magic took place in such a way no human has been able to duplicate on canvas. Next to the miracle of childbirth, sunsets to Tori were the most miraculous of creation. His voice was soft and quiet, and remarkably without malice. "The moment I give up my portfolio, the very instant it leaves my hands, I'll be dead. You know it and I know it, *caro, papa.*"

"Let me do something for you, my son," implored the Don rising from his chair. "I can't let it end like this. I can't! I will not be able to live with myself if I don't make an effort to save you."

This slip of the tongue might have saved Tori if he'd been a little older, wiser, and better trained to perceive the workings of Don Matteo's mind. If he had looked upon what appeared to be a broken man concerned with his son, through different eyes, he might have realized that his role of *capomafia* had been of longer duration, more practiced and more a part of his totality than his newly acquired paternal role to Salvatore.

"It's too late for anything other than what's been agreed upon," said Tori wistfully. "There can be no alterations to the bargain, at least not on my part. I'm wise enough to know that." He turned to the Don and lit a cigarette, while watching his father's expression. "You know that Siragusa was not captured as has been rumored?"

For an instant the Don couldn't conceal his astonishment. "My sources differ."

"You believed D'Verde?" Tori smiled gently. "Didn't Belasci check the report properly?"

"What makes you so certain?"

"I just know, that's all." Something in the Don's attitude restrained Tori from blurting out the truth.

The entire matter now moved slowly as if to a giant stage, with a series of spotlights trained on every aspect involved. As the lights focused, other details came to life and the eminent dangers to all the Don's charges in government loomed more prominent than before. The two superluminaries took their places. Don Barbarossa sat behind his desk, omnipotent as usual. Tori sat down again and stretched out his long legs.

"You see how inexperienced you really are, my son? Once I told you to never turn down a deal until you've explored each avenue."

Tori gazed at him through scorn-filled eyes.

"*Aspetta*, hear me out," insisted the Don. "If what you say is true that Siragusa is free and in no jeopardy, what further insurance do you need? In America he holds the duplicate, you have the original here. Make the deal. Insure your future. Then we'll all be happy. Turn over the original and allow Siragusa to keep the copy for insurance."

Salvatore felt himself go numb as he lifted his dark, fiery eyes to meet those of his father's. "What gives you the idea there are two portfolios?" he asked evenly. He felt like a crustacean, out of the sea thrown into boiling water; its shell reddening and cracking. Would it split wide open?

"Aren't there two?" asked the Don easily. "I took for granted you wouldn't take chances without protection. As my son you must have inherited my thinking."

Tori had forgotten that he'd encouraged Vincenzo to circulate rumors of the duplicate portfolio. By the time he did, it was too late. The moment had ended.

"Besides," added the Don significantly, "I owe you something. "You said you didn't kill me when you had the chance. I owe you for that."

"You owe me nothing. The fact that I couldn't take the life of my own father has nothing to do with our politics. I still find yours reprehensible."

"All right. All right, you win." The Don held up a restraining hand. "It's not my wish to keep the air between us filled with poison. *Allora*, I can help you if you turn the portfolio over to me. That accursed portfolio! My stomach turns to vinegar when I think of that abomination!"

For only the briefest of moments did Tori ask himself *why does he talk of helping me when my exile is set? I've all my passports, financial considerations, everything.*

"Perhaps when I settle in Brazil, I'll write you to discuss the situation. For now, I need the insurance the portfolio brings me."

Salvatore's mind, having transcended the immediate problem, raced ahead to the future. Could he ever really become Don Barbarossa's son, in the strictest sense of the word? If he agreed to his father's terms, was it possible the orders he'd receive might conflict with his own conscience? Where would that leave them but in a continual state of conflict, on a carousel, deeply entrenched in the putrefaction of corrupt and immoral politics he had long rebelled against. It was conceivable to him he'd no longer be hailed as Salvatore the Saviour, rather, Tori Barbarossa, the butcher!

Don Matteo's eyes were intent on his son. He saw the conflicts in the lad give rise to hope, then submerge into truths, and knew he felt ravaged inside. He saw Salvatore glance at his watch, then, reach for his jacket.

"Could I ask a special favor of you?"

"Ask."

"Will you care for *Napoleono* until I can send for him?"

"*Napoleono!* Ah, your stallion." The Don swallowed hard.

"I've no place to keep him, no one I could entrust to care for him. Here, with the others in your stables, he'd be content. As soon as I'm settled, I'll send for him."

"Consider it done." The Don averted his eyes.

Tori paced the room majestically and paused to observe his father with a strange tenderness. He stroked the back of his left ear several times, stretching the crease behind it and smiled enigmatically at the dull throbbing.

"Godfather, I mean father. Thank you but, I must refuse dim my eyes to the position of esteem you hold. It's not your generosity. Because you are my blood relative doesn't my desire to involve you further in my complicated life. I never realized how much alike we are until today. It would never work out. We would argue, contest each other, and perhaps end up despising one another, the way Don Nitto Solameni and his son annihilate each other every waking day they've lived. The difference in our beliefs, too vast, can't be spanned. And when I think of the disparities of our politics—" He rolled his eyes significantly. "I was weaned on the heroics of the Great Alexander and the morals and ethics of Aristotle. You on the other hand were

904

weaned probably on the warfare of Genghis Khan and adopted the morals of a Marquis de Sade and politics of Machiavelli. There's no way we could bridge the gap between us."

Dazed by the rhetoric and wondering curiously who were these men of whom his son spoke, the Don shoved them from his mind and suggested, "You could change your ways to mine, my son."

"Or, you could change your ways to mine."

"Are you crazy? My ways are the right ways. Who can argue with success?"

"For me, my ways have been right. Can you argue with my success?"

They were stalemated.

Tori slung his jacket over his shoulder and moved toward the scale model with interest. "Thank you for allowing me this time to talk with you. Perhaps in a year or two when Sicily forgets me, I shall write to you. Who knows, time away from my beloved *Sicilia* may temper me. I might change my mind and attitudes considerably." He picked up a toy soldier, the one on a white horse, and studied it in rapt fascination. Tori's mental landscape didn't include the remotest possibility he could be betrayed at this point, especially not by his father.

Tori was so intent on the scale model, he didn't see the Don's hand move slowly, stealthily to a drawer and grasp a .45 calibre automatic with a silencer attached to it. With the gun held behind his back, gripped tightly in his left hand, he approached his son. In the dim light illuminating the Don's silent, anguished, and watchful face, it was difficult for him to focus his eyes, nevertheless he moved in closer. Somewhere in the villa a phonograph played.

"*Managghia*," marveled Tori. "Even the grottos are in scale."

"Especially the Grottos Bianco and Persephone," said the Don, forcing an elevation of spirit.

"Still, I outsmarted them. They never captured me, not once."

"*They never captured you*," echoed his father in a strangely distant voice. "Why wouldn't you outsmart them? You're my son. Once I foolishly boasted there were no greater bandits than the Mazzarinos, remember?"

Tori nodding, glanced absently at a toy truck from the table of models.

"*Pero*, I was wrong. Along came Salvatore."

Tori, mildly astonished and infinitely touched by his father's compliment glanced at him flushed with pleasure, knowing how difficult it was for the Don to compliment another, how against his character it was.

"You surpassed all my conquests," continued the Don in that same peculiar voice, in a more noteworthy, valorous, and memorable way. "There'll never be another Salvatore. Sicily will mourn you and never forget you. I will mourn you and wish eternally it could have been different between us." The Don's face had paled excessively, even as pride poured from every pore in his body.

Tori's eyes blurred with tears. He had no will or volition to refrain from a warmth of affection he showered on the *mafioso* as he moved to embrace the man who was his father, the man who held a gun concealed skillfully in one hand behind his back. "Thank you for that. The praise of a father is the most thrilling and satisfactory of any." He expelled a burst of short laughter. *"Pero,* I don't wish to be mourned until I'm dead. I'm only leaving Sicily, not entering a mausoleum."

"Allora," said the Don authoritatively. "Go, if you must, before you reduce a poor father to broken hearted despair." A sob tore through the Don, escaping his lips. "Go, now. Go with God, *figghiu beddu,* my beautiful son."

Tori, nodding, gripping the Don's arm in a gesture of farewell, ambled to the door, absently slipping the white toy soldier into his pants pocket, and turned the door with his free, left hand.

"Tori—" His father called softly, his black eyes like burning balls of fire.

"Si?" He turned his head slowly, glanced at the Don over his left shoulder poised questioningly between the door and frame.

"Forgive me, son of my heart." The Don's words fell and bounced in the darkness like a distant echo. His finger squeezed the trigger of the gun that would end all dreams for Salvatore. The deadly bullets struck the young prince below the left shoulder blade, perforating the heart chamber from the rear long before Tori saw the glint of blue steel in his father's hand.

Don Barbarossa had blown Tori's heart open, and he bled. God Almighty, how he bled. Blood rushed into his face as a look of utter amazement filled his features and a soft, almost inaudible sigh escaped his lips. His probing dark eyes etched with heartbreak fixed on his father, but he made no overt move toward his own gun. Sagging heavily against the door, his eyes blinked hard as if his vision played tricks on him. *Scorpio becomes impotent against the fury of the bull.*

In a twinkling, the Don flung the gun from him as if it had turned into a hissing python in his hand. Moving swiftly to Tori's side, and supporting his son's body with his strength, he eased him gently, oh, so gently toward the sofa. Giant tears welled in his eyes, spilling onto his cheeks, and the sound of Tori's laborious breathing as he laid him tenderly on the sofa and the silent unasked questions in Tori's eyes tore him in two."

"Why?" whispered Tori when he could. "Why?"

"You think every man who wears a lion's skin is a hero? I had to save you. Don't you see it yet? I had to save you." He cradled his son in his arms.

"Better to let the lion devour me, than the dogs," Tori spoke each word with considerable effort and when he finished blood spurted from his mouth, trickling at each sides onto his chin.

"You were marked for death, my dear son. You would never have left Sicily. Your end, at the hands of those two butchers, Cala and Franchina, was something I couldn't endure." He spat their names with vitriol. "They set a trap for you without my sanction. I had to rob them of their treachery, at the expense of your death.. Let the blood of my blood be on my hands. Only a king can claim the life of another king. I won't let them scandalize the glory of your memory publicly as they intended. At least I can promise you the greatest dignity ever afforded a man at death." Don Matteo leaned over to make certain Tori understood him. But he was talking to a corpse.

Salvatore, the greatest of all Sicilians, was dead. *Long live Salvatore!* The man whom the nation wouldn't forget had already given up the ghost.

"My son," moaned the Don over and over in a ritualistic chant. "My beautiful, brave, and gallant son. None has been more valiant. None more invincible. None greater."

Long after rigor mortis set in, he continued to cradle the dead man. The avalanche of tears long gone, he continued stroking the handsome, waxen face, pushing the curly dark hair off his forehead, whispering endearments as only an exalted father might to a son of whom he was fiercely proud, making up for the lost years between them. The gradual metamorphosis of death altered the expression on Tori's face as the angels of peace descended to release his soul from its earthly confinement, leaving his coppery, sun-kissed skin smoothed out in a glowing translucence. He appeared more youthful, more handsome than he was in life.

Don Matteo sat frozen, like a statue, drinking in and committing to his memory all he could of this beloved son who came to him too late in life.

It was 5 P.M. on July 1, 1950, when Salvatore took his last breath.

Working in her garden, Antigone glanced up as the sounds of the clock in the Norma Tower in her village tolled 5 P.M. In a state of wary restlessness, she permitted her eyes to move about her in a full circle, turning her body as she did. She uttered no cry, made no outward gesture of fright, but it was apparent she had been alarmed by something. Shuffling across the brick walk, she entered her house and noted the time on the kitchen clock. It was 5 P.M. all right.

Her dark eyes, still swollen from the tearful farewell with her son earlier, burned so she wrung out a cloth with cool water and pressed it to them. She sat down at the table, a dejected, despairing human, with her head supported between her hands. Suddenly she gave a start. She cocked her head. Off in the distance she heard Athena's voice. She could see Tori, laughing as he began playing his guitar as Athena began to sing. Mental images rushed at her of her entire family. In her imagination she saw herself rise from the table and serve them steaming *panettas* with melted cheese.

"Sing with us, Mamma *bedda*," they called to her. "Sing!" *He stands up to his men like a leader, brave, across the mountains to the sea. To those he loves he gives his life, a leader is what he'll always be. Some call him the Bandit, Some call him the law."*

The music and images faded from her sight. The room, empty again, filled only with mournful echoes of the past. The heartbroken sobs and pain wracked soul of Antigone made her nightmare reality.

In Palermo at 5 P.M. chimes rang throughout the city. Vincenzo glancing at his watch thought in less than twenty four hours Tori will have gone. He too, felt a peculiar disquiet. His eyes impulsed about the room, and, hearing sounds of shuffling feet in the next room, walked softly on the balls of his feet thinking perhaps Captain Franchina had returned and gone into the bedroom unnoticed. At the threshold, he peered in and about the empty room and, seeing nothing, retraced his steps only to stop suddenly.

"Tori! *Per larme dio,* for the love of God, what the hell

are you doing here?" He ran towards the open window where Tori stood grinning at him in his typical pose, thumbs hooked into his belt, with a peacock's strut. Vincenzo stopped short again, blinking as if he'd seen an apparition. He moved his hands about the area where seconds before he had seen Tori. There was no one, nobody there. For a few seconds he struck an attitude of perplexity. Then, he grinned.

"All right, cousin. You wanna play? What a helluva time to pick to play games with me." He reached in, pulled the drapes forward and swished them about, thinking to find Tori there. *"Managghia!* Am I losing my mind?" he shouted aloud when the space proved as empty as the area before the window.

Vincenzo, shaken, began to perspire. His heart quickened and his dark eyes, glazed, filled with supernatural lights. He moved stealthily back to his seat on the sofa, lit a cigarette, his eyes still darting about the room. He picked up his copy of *In Dubious Battle* and tried to concentrate on it.

"We'll be seeing each other sooner than you think, cousin," said a voice unmistakably Salvatore's. A series of mental images rushed at him when he jumped from the sofa and glanced about the room again. He saw Tori and he riding horseback in the hills and mountains, he saw himself being whipped by Tori when he disobeyed orders and how he cared for him, nursing his wounds later. He saw himself with Tori at Athena's wedding, when Tori had become provoked over the funds taken from the treasure. A kaleidescope of their happy times together came at him in confusion.

He jumped to his feet, wild eyed and frenzied, shouting hoarsely, "What are you doing to me? What's happening? I'm losing my mind—what?"

The door opened and Captain Franchina ran swiftly to his side. "What's wrong with you?" he asked trying to calm the young outlaw down.

"It's Salvatore! Playing tricks on me! Some one is trying to drive me crazy with tricks and games!" shouted Vincenzo irrationally.

Not fully aware of Vincenzo's genre of torment, and misunderstanding the bandit's laments, Captain Franchina grinned diabolically. "Don't worry, my friend. Salvatore's finished playing tricks on anyone. Be patient. His time on earth will soon be over."

"What? What's that you're saying?" asked Vincenzo like a madman seeing different pictures in his head. "What are you telling me?" he asked fiercely, grabbing the FSB Captain by the shoulders and shaking him savagely. "What are you saying, *cornuttu bestio* you son of a horned toad?!"

Captain Franchina geared himself for a powerful blow, pulling his arm back, and struck his captive hard, across the face. Instantly Vincenzo snapped out of his momentary madness, unaware of what had taken place.

"Are you all right, now?" Franchina's face hardened as he peered at the Sicilian.

Dazed, Vincenzo asked, "What is it? What happened?"

"You were delirious. Ranting and raving about Salvatore playing games on you! The strain's hard on all of us. But, you've got no worries. Salvatore can't get to you! You're safe, believe me, de Montana. . . ."

"*Si*, I'm safe." he echoed thinly. His thoughts were centered on Franchina's earlier statement. *Salvatore's time on earth will soon be over.*

Dio buono! How could he find out what Franchina meant? Somehow he had to learn what treachery they intended. . . .

That night, as soon as the FSB officers retired, Vincenzo stole out of the hotel and made his way back to Castellamare. He had to find out what was happening. Something was underfoot, he could sense it, feel it in his bones. He was too Sicilian to ignore the visions he received earlier.

What he needed was the feel of a woman's thighs. First a woman, then he could think clearly. That's the formula. With this in mind, he hired a brunette at Neptune's daughters, and took her to Calemi's villa to sate himself.

CHAPTER 66

The faint sounds of bells, somewhere in the far-off distance, cut through Don Barbarossa's consciousness—closer now—more distinct. He stared through tunneled eyes at the telephone on his desk until it struck him the instrument was the source of the intrusion. He removed the inert, waxen hand of his son's from between his own vein-roped hands and, trancelike, he moved stiffly to the desk and sat down. He picked up the phone. It was Natale Solameni.

"Where's Salvatore?" his brittle, high-pitched voice screeched frantically. "What did Cacciatore do with him? Are you trying to pull some fast trick on us, Don Barbarossa?" There was no trace of respect in his panic-stricken voice, only frenzy and alarm. Strangely enough, his caustic words didn't penetrate the Don's dazed state. Solameni kept repeating, "*Pronto! Pronto!* Operator, am I disconnected? *Butana de shekko!*"

The Don finally spoke, *sotto voce.* "What the hell do you want?"

"Salvatore! That's who the hell I want! What have you done with him? He never returned from your villa! Something's gone wrong and you know it!"

Don Matteo sighed heavily, despondently, as a father who mourned his son. He rubbed his forehead, stretching the furrows between his eyes, and suddenly snapped out of euphoria. "Where are you, Solameni?"

"At my villa."

"Who's at Calemi's villa?" Quickly he added. "Never mind that. I want you to go to Calemi's villa, and wait there until my man talks with you. Listen, carefully, Solameni. You are not to call or alarm anyone. Say nothing to no one. *Capeeshi?*"

Don Matteo had never given Natale Solameni the time of day. Always eager to be in his good graces, the younger *mafioso* found himself acquiescing to the *capomafia*'s suggestion. Before he had an opportunity to reply, the Don had hung up. The *capomafia* had to think things out very carefully. Already two men had died to prevent his relationship to Salvatore from being publicly aired. His fingers nervously drummed the desk top as he forced the fog to lift from his mind. He picked up the house phone to summon his bodyguard.

The sight of Salvatore's body stretched out lifeless on the sofa took Cacciatore aback momentarily. The pale, distraught face of his Don prompted him to ask, "He didn't try anything—did he? I told you he carried weapons."

The Don wagged a finger at him to silence him. "Listen, old friend, there is something I wish you to do." They huddled and the Don issued his instructions in a voice barely above a whisper.

Cacciatore nodded from time to time. His eyes quickly assessed the fact that Salvatore's gun hadn't been drawn.

"One important thing—and understand this well—so

911

you can convey it properly. Salvatore is to be buried with the highest of respect, as if they were honoring a *Capo de Capi. Capeeshi?* You are to impress this very fact upon Solameni and tell him the favor will be returned multiplied many times."

Cacciatore watched his Don remove the gold calendar watch from his son's wrist along with the fabled Browning gun and holster. He paused a moment to read the inscription carved into the gun butt:

"Beware of your enemy once. Of your friends a thousand times."

Don Barbarossa, speaking huskily through the thickness in his throat, continued his instructions: "Get a blanket and wrap him carefully. We'll leave the ring and gold belt buckle for *la Mamma*. Tell Solameni to make no mistake about these orders or he'll have me to reckon with."

He grabbed hold of Cacciatore's arm for emphasis. "You know nothing of this—*capeeshi?*"

"You have to tell me?"

The Don made a gesture of apology. "I'm not myself. You understand?"

Cacciatore nodded. He didn't understand, but, he could guess. Either way, it wasn't his affair. He couldn't help thinking, as he wrapped the body, *managghia!* His own son! That took balls! More guts than I'd have!

"Before you leave, remove the saddle from the white stallion, store it in the stables, out of sight. Then put him in a special paddock, until the other stallions arrive from Sardinia. No—put him with the brood mares."

Cacciatore nodded solemnly. He left Barbarossa's villa, cradling the blanket wrapped body of Salvatore.

Downstairs in the baroque living room of the Calemi villa, with the large double doors closed tightly to prevent anyone from overhearing their conversation, Don Nitto Solameni, the *mafioso* with no face, faced his son, Natale. His scornful and acrimonious voice continued to upbraid his son with the usual diatribe. Irate and nervous, under more pressure than he could stand, Natale's eye twitched uncontrollably. He tore at his fingernails relentlessly and walked to the radio several times, turning up the volume of music to drown out his father's raspy and caustic voice as it railed at him.

"The trouble with you—you castrated eunuch—is you never listen! *Pezzo de shekko!* All your life I've told you to stop and think before you do anything! Do you listen? No! You half-baked *pezzonovante!* Mr. Big Shot! You gotta do things your way—and see what happens?"

Natale, unable to bear up under the verbal abuse, finally exploded.

"What do you want me to do—walk around in dirty diapers all my life, waiting for you to change them? There comes a time when a man must assert himself and cut the cord!" he countered. Oh, how he rued the day Vincenzo de Montana shamed his father into making peace with him! It was better the other way!

"A man—yes! A *bobbosooni de cazzo*? No! I tried to tell you, be patient! Be cautious with whom you deal! Now Salvatore's gone and where's your reward? Up your ass—that's where it is! My way, twenty-five thousand dollars would have been mine! In addition to the sum already paid you, it would represent a tidy sum, which would have been yours ultimately! You youngblood asses have no sense!"

While Don Nitto and his son excoriated each other with vitriolic candor, and while their bellowing, castigating voices thundered throughout the house, Mario Cacciatore dogmatically completed his assignment without interference. He had bribed young Jocco to go on a short errand for him, then sent the only other servant in search of the guard. Without curious eyes upon him, he moved with freedom and transported the blanketed corpse to his suite of rooms via the back steps. Gently, he placed the body on the bed, removed the blanket and glanced about the room. His eyes fell on the travel bag. He picked it up, wrapped it in the blanket, slipped out the back once more, and locked the items in the trunk of his car. He smoothed out his rumpled suit, straightened out his tie, and walked to the front entrance, and rang the chimes.

Sweating profusely, Natale Solameni swung open the double oaken doors to the living room with such force, it banged into the wall and knocked off a painting. It fell crashing to the floor. "Goddammit!" cursed Natale. When he saw Cacciatore, his anger increased daringly. "What the hell do you want?" He picked up the painting, and tried to reset it on the wall, fumbling as he did for several moments.

"I wish to speak with Salvatore," said Cacciatore. "I have a message from Don Matteo."

"Hah! What kind of shit are you handing me? It was you who spirited him away earlier today!" His hands shook. Unable to secure the painting, he flung it from him in a violent gesture of pent-up frustration. It landed on the opposite wall where it struck loudly and fell crashing to the floor.

"Well? What have you to say?" shouted Natale. "Don't stand there like a *mammalucco!* Talk! Son of a bitch!"

A black look of menace crept into Cacciatore's malevolent eyes with such conveyance of power that even this highly incensed *mafioso* realized his *faux pas*. Sobering instantly, Natale came to his senses and apologized, never knowing how close he came to sampling the killer's wrath. "I'm sorry." He made a disorganized gesture. "I'm under terrible stress. You asked for Salvatore? Didn't Don Matteo tell you I called? That Salvatore is missing? Ever since you were here today he's been missing!"

"Me?" asked Cacciatore in affected innocence. "I wasn't here today."

"What are you telling me?" asked Natale, drawing his brow together in a scowl. "Don't give me none of that shit—man!"

"I wasn't here," he lied easily. "I don't know where you got such an idea!"

"Have you checked his rooms?" asked Cacciatore calmly.

"Are you crazy? Of course—" He paused. His face flushed with embarrassment. There had been no time to check the room. He had taken Jocco's word that Salvatore hadn't returned that day.

"Let's take a look," suggested the former Mazzarino. "Perhaps we'll find something that might tell us where he might have gone."

It was the first sensible suggestion Natale Solameni had heard all day. He led the way upstairs just as Don Nitto came out of the living room. He glanced at Cacciatore and nodded. The two men knew each other instantly.

"Where are you going?" he questioned his son.

"To search Salvatore's room."

"Why?"

"Why?" Exasperated, Natale yelled, "Come and you'll see!"

They reached the upper hallway and stopped before Salvatore's room. Natale knocked first, then swung the door open. He allowed the older men to enter first. For a moment, his vision was blocked by the two men who had entered and stopped abruptly, rooted to the spot. He followed their line of vision and moved around them. When he saw the inert body of Salvatore on the bed, his face drained of color. Refusing to believe what he read in the eyes of the older *mafiosi*, he crept in closer to the bed. Gently he shook the corpse.

"Salvatore? Salvatore?" The motionless body felt cold to

his touch. He leaned in to listen for a heart beat, knowing all the while he was dead.

"He's dead . . . Salvatore is dead!" His jaw fell open in disbelief. "He's dead," he repeated in shocked amazement. "Salvatore is dead!"

Don Nitto, educated formidably in the ways of the old Mafia, didn't have to be told what had happened. He glanced knowingly at Cacciatore through veiled eyes that barely masked his greed. Cacciatore, wearing as deceptive and expressionless a face, stared right through the man.

"Salvatore's dead!" ranted Natale like a broken record. "He's dead!" It was incredible that such a thing could have happened—after all their caution.

"*Porca Miseria!* He's really dead!" His mind raced in every direction as he tried to piece together the enigma of the unrelated deaths. First Calemi, now Salvatore! He should have been next—not Salvatore! Who had done this?

Cacciatore busied himself, looking about the room as if it had been the very first time he'd been there. He sauntered to the bathroom and scanned Salvatore's personal toilet items neatly arranged on the marble commode. He came into the bedroom room and looked about the room. His eyes caught sight of the glitter of gold partially hidden in the chair. He picked up the Eye of God amulet and examined it.

"Salvatore's?" he asked the despondent Natale who, having flung himself in a nearby chair, utterly prostrated in defeat, managed to nod.

"You sounded so crazy making wild accusations over the phone, Don Matteo sent me to help solve your problem," began Cacciatore as he walked to Salvatore's side. He laid the amulet on Salvatore's bare chest. "Since we find him, dead, the capo sent instructions he wants you to follow to the letter. *Capeeshi?* First, you are to make sure Salvatore receives a funeral suitable to his station in life. Since he was Godson to Don Matteo, you will spare no expense. The *capomafia* will take care of all expenses. Furthermore, you are to await instructions by Don Matteo before you notify the *Signora* Salvatore of her son's death. *Capeeshi?*"

Cacciatore asked Natale Solameni to repeat the instructions so there could be no misunderstanding. He left immediately, leaving father and son to their miseries.

Natale walked to the telephone.

"What are you doing?" asked Don Nitto with marked impatience.

"Call Enrico D'Verde—to tell him what happened."

Don Nitto grabbed the phone from his son's hand and slammed it back on the cradle. "And you call yourself a smart *mafioso*? Bah! Youngbloods! *Allora*—this time, *porco dio*, you'll listen to me! *Capeeshi?*" he hissed with serpent's venon in his voice. "I'm going to teach you a lesson if it kills me! Are you so blind you don't know what's happened?"

Don Nitto picked up the phone and gave the operator a number. "This is Don Nitto Solameni talking. You bring me fifty thousand dollars and I'll hand over Salvatore!" he said to the party at the other end. "I don't care where you get the money, but it must be in cash! You think I'm a man who makes jokes? *Managghia!* No, I won't tell you where I have him. You bring me the cash and I will take you to him! You have twenty-four hours to raise the money—or I'll hand him over to the security police for the reward *they* offer!"

BOOK VIII

The Trial of Portella Della Rosa

"I failed only once in life. It was not altogether a failure. I prefer to think that for a time Destiny put me to sleep until it comes time for me to suffer a rebirth."

Assorted writings of Salvatore

The stunning news of Salvatore's death had caused a temporary postponement of the Viterbo trial. Shortly thereafter it reconvened with far more publicity than the Tribunal magistrates had anticipated. A nation in shock, utterly prostrate over the sad affair, nursed internal wounds and fixed their attention on the complex circumstances surrounding the death of their beloved lionhearted hero and fate of the former bandits.

But, if a nation in mourning could be further stupefied by the bizaare happenings it had to be that day of December 5, 1950, six months to the date of Salvatore's demise, when it was reported that Vincenzo de Montana had walked boldly into the office of Chief Inspector Zanorelli in Palermo and stated simply. "I am Vincenzo de Montana. I have come to surrender to the courts of justice. I place myself into your hands."

Sent home for political reasons, he was later arrested and chained like a ferocious beast. Handsome and implacable, de Montana made lengthy statements to the local magistrates. He later repeated his words from the Stipendiary magistrates and was immediately transferred to Viterbo to await trial before the Tribunal in session there.

A nation of perplexed and wounded citizens and officials beset with a mixture of abounding curiosity and native wariness were ready for anything, including the possibility that Vincenzo de Montana would suddenly emerge on his black mare and singlehandedly promote the miraculous escape of his former comrades. After all, he had not been Salvatore's second in command all these years for nothing. He had learned plenty from his chief—no?

Shrewd, discerning newsmen, having guzzled this latest development, had difficulty digesting de Montana's statements, wondering what that crazy man was trying to prove. The former bandits awaiting trial retreated into a stoical silence. Montegattans held their breath, expecting some of Salvatore's usual magic to materialize—telling the world it was all some horrendous mistake, including the reports of his death.

Tense politicians in Rome nodding knowingly agreed it was best not to wake a sleeping tiger. Some things could remain buried—and others? Oooh, boy. Such complications. Who knew what to expect? The question on everyone's lips was the same. Why had Vincenzo de Montana surrendered? It was legend he hated prisons. How many times had he sworn he'd never be taken alive—eh? Unable to second guess this move, an entire public and his former companions view Vincenzo's move through cynical eyes.

—And then it came!

Electrifying news jolted a nation. Impossible! came the shocked cries. More lies! More twists and turns to confuse them. But—there it was, on January 7, 1951, right before their eyes in banner headlines:

"I, Vincenzo de Montana, assassinated Salvatore in his sleep. This act was done by personal arrangement with the Minister of the Interior, Martino Belasci, in the government of Premier de Aspanu."

Vincenzo's *pronounciamento*, done much in the style of Salvatore's, came in the form of a statement released to the papers through his defense counsel, *Avvocato* Luigi Basile. It set the nation against him.

*Disgraziato! Lazzarone! Carogna! Cornuto! Th*e cries of anger and disgust were heard across the nation. Wretched scoundrel! Bum! Louse! Bastard! Worst of all—*Judas!* They extolled Salvatore's virtues and excoriated Vincenzo. There weren't enough words in their vocabulary to describe their utter disenchantment and vitriolic candor at what Tori's co-captain had brought to bear.

Stefano Modica bought every newspaper available that day after court, and took them to his hotel suite where he pored over them endlessly. He couldn't believe Vincenzo's statement, not if his relationship to his cousin had been as Salvatore had described in his personal papers. Why Vincenzo's lawyer had permitted such a move stirred him beyond reason and led him to think nothing less than total insanity permeated these proceedings.

Stefano Modica continued to attend the trials as he had each day since his arrival in December 1950 as inconspicuously as possible. His mode of dress and manners blended with the local natives and he kept himself in the gallerias amidst the crowds. As he listened to the tedium of testimony, he began to question his own sanity in coming to Viterbo. To Modica it seemed the truth found no spawning grounds here. From the first he predicted justice wouldn't be served at this Tribunal. He felt that the ill-fated bandits were scapegoats bound to receive the maximum penalty of the law—life imprisonment—even death. But, not for their purported involvement in the Portella Della Rosa infamy. Simply that they knew too much and weren't talking. Their sphinxlike qualities not only amazed him, but it was simply astounding how mute they remained even under severe cross-examination by the prosecution.

Shortly after his confession appeared in the papers, Vincenzo appeared in the courtroom, meticulously dressed in an elegant black silk suit, white shirt, and tie. He kept his handsome dark face straight ahead, neither looking to the right nor left, his dark expressive eyes reflecting defiance to authority in every gesture. On his pale features, was an unmistakable arrogance of pride and self-assurance, combined with the marked hesitation of a wary animal who senses danger.

If Vincenzo found it distressing that the former bandits hardly glanced at him he kept it to himself. They gave him no importance at all; not the slightest telltale flicker of an eye, scowl or grimace passed between them. It was as if they hadn't known each other—as if he didn't exist for them and never had. Hard? Vindictive? Cold? It was more than that. It was their way of marking time, of waiting, of watching and exercising that most valuable of Sicilian virtues—patience for what was to come.

To Modica, the most significant thing about Vincenzo's confession was that he had made liars out of the FSB. It publicly denounced Major Franchina as Salvatore's killer, a fact which shook up the prosecution and negated all official stories following that event on July 5. To make matters worse it placed Minister Martino Belasci in an untenable position. Where would it all lead? He had but to wait and watch.

It was to be fully three months before Vincenzo would be permitted to speak in open court. Meanwhile Stefano did little else except to attend the trials and retreat to his second-rate hostelry off the beaten path, where he was less likely to encounter any of the trial's principal parties and thereby avoiding any detection.

One evening, feeling stifled and in desperate need of a change in his daily activities, Stefano dined at a favorite restaurant on the Via Tuscanese and after a sumptuous feast of spit-roasted venison, he toured the medieval city.

For a time he stood at the Fontana Grande watching the swirling waters of a magnificent thirteenth-century water fountain amid the graceful statuary in the old section of the ancient city, once the residence of popes. It was a beautiful warm and balmy evening and crowds milled about in the *piazza*. At one point Modica turned from the spectacular architecture and, heading towards the Via Cavour, came face to face with Major Franchina.

Dressed in a natty beige uniform, with the empty sleeve of his jacket pinned to the inside of his pocket, the Major strolled about with a few of his cronies when he spotted Modica. He stopped abruptly in a moment's reflection and by the time he speculated on the identity of that familiar face of the man dressed in rumpled khaki trousers and jacket, Modica had disappeared into the perambulating crowds, grateful that the Major hadn't had time to observe the noticeable limp of his left foot; a sure giveaway.

From inside the dimly lit interior of a tobacco kiosk, Modica saw Major Franchina peer about the *piazza* with a curious expression on his face, before he finally left with his companions. After that, Modica remained more closely confined to his quarters.

The morning of March 8, 1951, Stefano arrived at the courthouse earlier than usual, almost sensing this day would be special. Having already determined to sit downstairs instead of his usual place of anonymity, in the gallery, he gazed about the crowded Palace of Justice, smoked a half-dozen cigarettes and stared for a time at the giant placard set on a gilded tripod before the enormous Gothic-inspired doors:

PALACE OF JUSTICE   MARCH 8, 1951

COURT OF TRIBUNAL

PEOPLE VS ASSASSINS
AT PORTELLA DELLA ROSA
PRESIDING MAGISTRATE, U. GINESTRA

Court convened at its usual snail's pace as soon as the Presiding Magistrate and two adjunct judges took their seats behind the impressive bench.

Suddenly—there was bedlam! It happened so fast— without warning—no one knew what had taken place.

Modica craned his neck to see over the heads of the people in the rows ahead of him. He asked the man seated next to him what had happened. The man simply pointed to the center of the arena where chaos had erupted.

The pasty-faced, lizard-eyed Clerk of the Court, usually a calm and complacent little man, rapped vigorously for order and, momentarily wild-eyed, tried to discern what had taken place. He could have been striking the gavel against a bale of cotton for all the good it did. A flurry of excitement between President Ginestra and his two adjuncts ensued in which all these formidable men tried to contain their obvious discomfort at this disruption of protocol.

But—there he was, at the center of all their attention, shouting for the entire court to hear. Salvatore's co-captain, that snake in the grass whose name was on the tongue of every redblooded Sicilian, had risen to his feet, shouting in a booming voice, "Mr. *Presidente*! Before God and this Tribunal, I swear, that, I, Vincenzo de Montana, first cousin to Alessandro Salvatore, and his second in command, assassinated him! It was I—not Major Franchina—who committed this act to which he falsely lays claim. It was I who put an end to banditry in Sicily!"

"He lies! He lies!" shouted Major Franchina, rising to his feet from a special witness box. "It was I who hunted that vicious animal and shot him. You've read the official report signed by General Cala himself. I inflicted the *coup de grace!*" The officer's face contorted with rage and humiliation.

"Order! Order!" commanded the irate President. "I said—*order in the court!*"

The clerk of the Court had had enough. He gestured to the armed guards and, with rifles poised like bayonets, they eased forward demanding respect for the court.

"Mr. President!" called *Avvocato* Luigi Basile loudly. "I object!"

Redfaced, the Prosecutor General jumped to his feet. Bewildered by the rapidly moving disorder, he shouted in a booming voice, "Oh, no! It is I who voice an objection!"

"If anyone objects," contended President Ginestra, glowering at the courtroom spectators and the bevy of clacking lawyers seated in their stalls like disgruntled roosters, "it is I!"

The speakers could have been talking to the four winds for the good it did. Pandemonium had removed all dignity from the courtroom and in the *gallerias,* where they had crammed themselves, the people were uncontainable.

Pressmen scrambled to the nearest exits to reach phones to report to their editors. Lightbulbs popped like a strobe lighting display as photographers moved forward into waves of blinding explosions, hoping to catch the principals in a variety of candid reactions.

De Montana's statement had placed both the Premier and Minister of the Interior in a highly compromising situation, to say nothing of the discrediting of Major Franchina's heroism. The predjudicial words spoken in the presence of the one-armed military martyr drew a variety of responses from all.

From the witness cages, fifty of Salvatore's men sat in their conservative dark suits, heads turned toward their former co-chieftain and on their faces, for the first time, was a mixture of incredible shock, disbelief, and a creeping hatred toward this man who, by his own admission, had assassinated their beloved leader. Before, it was only hearsay, but now, in his own words, from his own lips, came the foolish admission of being Salvatore's assassin. In breaking the Sicilian code of silence, what Vincenzo did was tantamount to the signing of his own death warrant. And by his statement he had succeeded in blanketing the proceedings in total confusion.

In the first of many unprecedented actions which were to inevitably follow, *Presidente* Ginestra stood up. Slowly, very slowly, a hush descended upon the court until everyone present had risen to their feet and focused their eyes upon the imposing presiding magistrate, who stared out at them in stony silence. At the continued risk of upsetting judicial decorum, he maintained the stubborn silence until he had everyone's attention. He cleared his throat, reseated himself, and addressed himself to *Avvocato* Basile, his colorful judicial robes and cap like a page from antiquity.

"I'm not sure why you've objected, *Avvocato* Basile, but I suggest you had better silence your client or I shall find the legal means to gag him!" he snapped brittlely. He glanced over his bifocals, his blue eyes disapproving and reprimanding. "If there is one more disruption like this last one, I shall clear the court. Furthermore, I shall ban the public from these hearings if I cannot conduct this court as I see fit!"

Jeers and boos rocked the austere courtroom. Those spectators who knew this high and mighty peacock, Ginestra, knew that clearing the courtroom was the furthest thing from the mind of this publicity-crazy bird and made no effort to conceal this fact. It took five additional minutes to restore order.

"We shall now proceed in an orderly fashion. There will be no lack of decorum in my court!" Ginestra admonished the lawyers and directed his stinging bite at *Avvocato* Basile, who smiled artfully.

"If you had permitted my client to give evidence upon his arrival it wouldn't have fermented in his bowels," remarked the dynamic defense counsel, his challenging hazel eyes masking his arrogance. He inclined his head in a gesture of humble supplication.

"In my court, I make the decisions," replied President Ginestra.

"Then, I respectfully beg the court's permission to allow my client his moment in court. Let him present his testimony," cajoled the articulate lawyer, "or, I cannot guarantee when the need for catharsis may come upon my client, again."

"I object, Mr. President!" bellowed Prosecutor General Volpe. (In Italian courts he is comparable to Attorney General.) "I object on the grounds that de Montana was the last of Salvatore's men to be arrested. He should wait his turn to be heard." He glared at *Avvocato* Basile and turned his triumphant, beady eyes upon the President, awaiting his deposition.

President Ginestra, glancing uneasily at the spectators in the jam-packed courtroom, sustained the objection in a monotone, inwardly concerning himself with thought of those hordes outside the court. Lines of people, six abreast, waited turns to sneak into the Palace of Justice where high drama and testy emotions mingled fiercely in what promised to be the most publicized trial in Italian history. Disturbed at his growing unpopularity, the presiding magistrate experienced the shame and humiliation of opera stars who, when they miss a lyric or a beat, are readily reprimanded by an audience reading from a libretto in hand.

Avvocato Basile, on his feet, instantly disputed the ruling. "Mr. President! I strenuously object! This is an outrage!" he stormed. "Unprecedented ruling under our judicial procedure assumes that an accused person volunteering a statement indicates a desire to collaborate with justice—not obstruct it. You've kept my client waiting three valuable months! Months in which many truths could have been resolved."

From another direction came the imposing voice of *Avvocato* Bellini, who represented the people suffering losses at Portella Della Rosa. This slick communist lawyer, who resembled a caracal, a cautious cat with small pointed ears, had been hired by Senator de Casselli, the intended victim in the alleged assassination attempt at Portella and the Reds who sought to uncover any possible connection between Minister Belasci and Salvatore's bandits. Agreeing with *Avvocato* Basile, Bellini addressed the court. Speaking with dramatic overtones, using animated gestures, he attempted to put his point across.

"It appears that some subversive attempt has been made in select government circles to discredit evidence given by this extraordinary witness, de Montana," he began, spreading his arms in a wide gesture appealing to bandits, courtroom spectators, and the correspondents to whom he played constantly. "When Salvatore sent a declaration to this Tribunal denying the role of instigators in the reprehensible massacre of innocent men, women, and babies at Portella Della Rosa, it is quite possible that he signed his own death warrant—no?" he challenged the Tribunal.

Instant approval of his hypothesis swept the courtroom. People murmured in assent. The former bandits wore noncommittal masks as usual. Vincenzo's lips curled in satisfaction. *Avvocato* Basile nodded emphatically at Bellini. Magistrate Ginestra, an imposing man in his sixties with delicate features and piercing blue eyes, shuffled a few papers on his desk in an effort to hide his displeasure.

The second magistrate, a dark-skinned, hollow-cheeked man with iron gray hair slicked down in a side part, and the ridiculous name of Lord Byron Aloysius Montevecchio, twiddled his thumbs and kept his head bowed throughout most the trial, as if it were a great imposition thrust upon him to be seated on this bench of the Tribunal.

The third judge, Lord Vulcano de Verona, a fair-skinned man with a nose too small for the rest of his features, was preoccupied with the fact that the trial was taking too long. One month, they estimated at the outset, perhaps two, but three at the very most. It was already nearing one year. If it continued he wouldn't have a chaste wife to return to. Two nights ago she had threatened to take on a lover and, knowing her, she would do it—to spite him. With these thoughts coursing through his mind, he hardly heard the President's words. What's more, he cared less.

"In my court, I have my opinions which I shall exercise as I see fit. Only when I deem it the time proper shall I interrogate de Montana. Until then, he will keep his mouth buttoned up in my court. Is that clearly understood?" Ginestra's words uttered in a tone of finality were not without bitterness. He glanced at both lawyers with intemperate disdain.

"Listen," declared *Avvocato* Bellini, "if you think to find any objection on my part, forget it. I fully support the right of the accused to speak."

"Support what you will," retorted the indignant magistrate. "The accused will keep what he has to say in his belly. His time will come soon enough!"

The Prosecutor General made waves. "In this court we are trying those responsible for the massacre at Portella Della Rosa. Anything else is immaterial and irrelevant!" Tall, thin, and vinegar-faced, the public official sat down stiffly, with sufficient propriety, his eyes rotating like those of a chameleon.

Not to be intimidated, *Avvocato* Basile proceeded daringly: "I ask the court's permission to read the statement ter. (In Italian courts, the Public Minister watches brief by Vincenzo de Wontana, addressed to the Public Minis- for the state and is supposed to hold the balance between prosecution and defense.)

"I suggest you send the statement to the Public Minister by special delivery!" snapped the Chief Magistrate.

"And I suggest, Mr. President, that I shall read it!"

"No! You will not read it!"

"Article 444 of the Code of General Procedure—" began Lawyer Basile.

"I said, leave the Code of General Procedure out of this!" warned the President.

The Public Minister intervened. *"The Declaration shall not be read!"*

Bowing with exquisite panache, Basile ran his forefinger under his nose, caressing an itch, while strutting nonchalantly to the Chief Magistrate's bench where he handed his copy to the glowering President. His aide simultaneously handed a copy each to the Public Minister, Prosecutor General, and other lawyers.

Basile's voice filled the courtroom:

"To the Public Minister: Knowing you to be a man of good conscience, honesty, and utmost integrity, I entrust myself to you in full confidence. The moment has come to inform you, that by personal agreement and arrangement with His Excellency, Martino Belasci, Minister of the Interior, I killed Salvatore. I reserve the right to further explain my actions at the Viterbo trial. Respectfully, Vincenzo de Montana."

Well, there it was again! Out in the open and read into the legal records of the court. There could be no more conjecture. It was official—part of records which couldn't be stricken out at whim. De Montana's earlier statements to the Chief Inspector of Police and Stipendiary Magistrates in Palermo, had disappeared. Now no one could erase this statement.

From this point on, it was to be Vincenzo's aim to demonstrate that the bandits had always acted under orders of high government officials as partisans, and that the Portella Della Rosa massacre had been the brainchild of these same officials, all Christian Democrats who violently opposed communism.

The courtroom, once again chaotic and disorganized, showed no signs of quieting down after such disclosures. Through it all, Vincenzo stared at nothing in particular and remained impervious to the hostile glares he received from those men who had idolized Salvatore.

For nearly three months Vincenzo had feverishly paced the confines of his restrictive jail cell. Held incommunicado, he waited patiently for his day in court. With the passing of each day, he'd grown increasingly paranoid. For a time he ate only that food brought to him by Gabriella Rothschild, the fraudulant princess who had managed to inherit an Italian palace a few kilometers outside of Viterbo after she left Sicily. But soon enough he was to be denied this privilege and, concluding that someone wanted him dead, he became watchful and wary, his eyes glazed over with suspicion. He caught a small English sparrow when it flew into his cell one day and he began to test the food served to him by feeding it first to the bird.

It was not without good cause that Vincenzo considered his life to be in jeopardy; twice, attempts had been made on him to do him in. The Scoletti brothers, Arturo and Miguel, grabbed him one day when they passed each other en route to court. Intervening guards foiled the attempt. Later, the Genovese brothers cornered him in the men's room and beat on him brutally. For several days, visible welts, bruises, and contusions on his face caused much speculation in the courtroom. This hostile treatment given him by men who previously claimed love and brotherly affection for him confused and intrigued the spectators. Vincenzo took this abuse temperately, secretly knowing that once they knew the full story they'd change their opinion of him.

The one man Vincenzo steered clear of was *Sporcaccione*, for he knew full well the satanic power hidden behind stony and lidded hate-filled eyes. Taking him at his word, Salvatore's former paladins and inner circle of men believed without question he had killed Salvatore. Why wouldn't they? Hadn't Vincenzo like a fool admitted it in open court?

Speculation among the nation mounted daily. Was Vincenzo telling the truth? Or was this another act in the vengeance of Tori's death? Regardless of any and all conjectures, one thing was certain. From this point forward in time, every eye in the nation would be fixed adhesively on this star witness.

Avvocato Basile had given him the opening and Vincenzo controlled center stage, dominating the proceedings as he had intended. He told his story:

"I haven't sold my soul to Lucifer as many of you, including my former companions, think. No one captured me, as my enemies have tried to make you believe. I volunteered in the interests of justice to testify of my own free will.

"I reject with scorn the accusation of having taken part in that butchery at Portella Della Rosa. We were not bandits who robbed and stole and murdered children as you have been led to believe. I, personally, was nowhere near Portello Della Rosa on the day in question. On May 1, 1947, I was extremely ill with a collapsed lung and could not have participated in that so-called massacre if I had chosen to."

Documents, X-rays, and statements produced to the court to support his declaration were submitted along with the letter from a highly respected physician in Palermo, who attested to Vincenzo's physical ailment, and swore Vincenzo was having X-rays taken on the day in question.

He continued in a voice spoken loud enough to permeate the courtroom.

". . . I don't deny I was a member of Salvatore's army when he became General of the Western Partitionists' Army organized by Captain Francesco Bello, a man who, although he killed over eight *carabinieri* and effected bandit raids on the estates around Caltagirone, now goes free, entitled Honorable Deputy of the Constituent Assembly! We were told we were fighting for the freedom of our beloved Sicily! Hah! This was the first of many deceptions!"

President Ginestra raised a restraining hand. "One moment, de Montana. Tell us first what you know of the Portella incident, since this is our primary concern. We have sworn affidavits from Salvatore, attesting that there were *no* instigators for the Portella affair. Papers in which he accepts full blame for the atrocity."

"No! That's not true!" retorted Vincenzo hotly. "Salvatore was forced to sign those papers! In due time I shall name those instigators."

Avvocato Bellini, the people's lawyer, leaned forward in his chair in rapt attention. His dark probing eyes never left Vincenzo's face, while his right hand doodled intricate patterns on the foolscap notebook. Even the spectators hung onto the witness's every word. The room was unduly silent. Most reporters felt the truth would out eventually, but where would it lead? Impervious to the goings-on about him, *Avvocato* Basile kept cool eyes on his client.

". . . I wasn't present at the final meeting before the May 1 *fiesta,* due to my illness. But on that night, Salvatore had returned from Grotto D'Oro and announced to us that Communism must be halted at any cost. I saw the letter—of which this court has a copy—delivered to him earlier that day. Those words are etched like fire in my memory. *'My very dear Salvatore: We are on the eve of the downfall of Communism and with our combined efforts we can destroy it before it spreads to cause irreparable damage to our beloved country. Let victory be ours and you shall have the unconditional amnesty which you and your brave men so justly deserve. You are a brave patriot with whom I've been proud to have been associated. I remain your friend in victory.'* It was signed 'Affectionately, Martino Belasci.' "

Vincenzo paused to pour a glass of water from the carafe on a stand next to him in the witness cage. Sated, he pressed a white handkerchief delicately to his lips to wipe off the excess moisture. "I shall now name the instigators of the *fiasco* at Portella Della Rosa—"

"I object!" shouted Prosecutor General Volpe, waving his long wing like arms in protest. "I object on the grounds that this is hearsay!" His sour faced tightened into a puckered frown.

A hush prevailed in the enormous room. The former bandits numbering nearly fifty leaned forward in their chairs, eager to hear publicly what they had guessed. Salvatore, the epitome of discretion, had never mentioned the names of those in high offices with whom he had intrigued.

Avvocato Basile rose easily to his feet with arms outstretched in a supplicating manner as he appealed to the Tribunal, his colleagues, and the public. "Let us be reasonable," he placated. "Salvatore is dead. We have here his second in command—his co-captain, a man who can tell us exactly what happened as if it came directly from Salvatore. Is it therefore not feasible to accept his testimony

930

in the absence of Salvatore, if it proves beyond the shadow of a doubt that these men were partisans of the government under the direct orders of the second most powerful man in the nation?"

The lawyers went into a huddle with the magistrates. They voiced legal precedences pro and con for permitting de Montana's testimony. For twenty minutes court procedure was held up until the decision was reached. Wearily, President Ginestra nodded to the star witness to proceed with his testimony. Perspiring noticeably in the cool room, Vincenzo cleared his throat and continued!

"The instigators of the Portella affair were, His Excellency, Martino Belasci, Prince Giorgio Oliatta, the Honorable Bernardo Malaterra, and—" He tugged at his shirt collar and glanced about the courtroom with a look of frenzy—of stark terror. His voice dropped to a hoarse whisper. "And—" He choked, gurgled, and strained to signal his lawyer. Basile rushed to de Montana's side, catching him as he fell back into the witness cage, his eyes bulging in fright.

"Quick!" shouted *Avvocato* Basile. "A doctor! Summon a doctor! De Montana has been stricken!"

Needless to say, court was adjourned for the day.

Once again Vincenzo commanded attention in all the papers. Headlines screamed:

> "DE MONTANA STARK-RAVING MAD! He accuses heaven and hell and earthlings, too. Named in his testimony, just before he collapsed from an unknown ailment, were officials high in Premier de Aspanu's government. How many more than the three men named below in his official statement de Montana would accuse of instigating the Portella massacre is something we can learn only from the witness. Our sources indicate an attempted homicide."

Stefano Modica waded through the rest of the newspaper that morning at breakfast. Similar stories, blown out of proportion, had dominated the front pages of every Italian and foreign newspaper. It was 7:30 A.M. by the time Modica showered and dressed and finished a pot of black coffee. He arrived across town at the Palace of Justice, dismayed by the crowds pressing to gain admittance. Mobs of reporters, having previously viewed Vincenzo's confession with cynicism, had flocked to Viterbo for what now seemed more explosive than Salvatore himself.

Those former bandits who had made Vincenzo's life hell and had attempted to slay him now maintained a cool silence, eyeing him with native curiosity bordering respect for the firm stand he'd taken to denounce corruption among the high politicos. The breaking of silence— *omerta*—took considerable courage, the kind men of their calibre were forced to respect, for it broke with an island tradition of many centuries duration.

The trial commenced. The courtroom, strained beyond its capacity by those curiously excited people who wanted a glimpse of a new and identifiable hero, became a shambles when it was learned a week would pass before de Montana was well enough to endure the rigors of the trial. What are they trying to do—kill de Montana like they did Salvatore? The cries and accusations fairly crumbled the walls of justice; the people demanded some explanation.

Because it heightened suspense and kept Vincenzo in the limelight as a hero, the Defense Counsel remained tight-lipped and refused to elaborate on the nature of his infirmity. By identifying the ailment for what it really was, a collapsed lung, President Ginestra invited the ridicule and scorn of the public who didn't for a moment believe him. The credibility of the court and government hit an all-time low. Even the press took sides. Some reported it as a lung ailment. Others insisted it was an attempted homicide—a poisoning. A few of the more imaginative fed the people's superstition by declaring that the ghost of Salvatore sought retribution.

The last week in March Vincenzo returned to court, pounds lighter, dressed dashingly as usual, with his dark curly hair brushed neatly into place. Thickly fringed lashes veiled his dark, almost effeminate brown eyes, and his moustache, trimmed in perfect symmetry, never showed a misplaced hair. He was beseiged with photographers and reporters, who flocked around him desperately trying to wrangle a statement from him, but the guards kept them at distance. Fickle spectators, certain he'd been the victim of foul play, cheered him, clapped their hands, and shouted his name reverently.

Vincenzo would smile and acknowledge their cheers with the self-assured ego of the Sicilian male. But those who knew this former *bon vivant* and were used to the merry twinkle always present in his eyes, now saw only a brooding expression obscuring his former personality.

"Vincenzo de Montana."

He arose from the lawyer's table, nodded imperceptibly at *Avvocato* Basile, and flanked on either side by two court guards, walked the short distance to the witness cage.

Annoyed by Vincenzo's emergence recently as a hero, Prosecutor General Volpe, a man in his fifties with a sour disposition and a sparse fringe of snowy white hair around his bald pate, lost no time in getting on with the trial. "You recognize these men in the cages opposite you, de Montana?"

"Yes."

"They are former comrades whom you've ordered about with the equal fervor of Salvatore?"

"Yes."

"They, as you, stand accused for their participation in the Portella massacre. Now then, do you, Vincenzo de Montana, identify them as the men who took part in the massacre?" Volpe turned his back on the witness and struck a confident pose as he waited for the reply.

"I do not," came the stupefying reply.

Volpe spun about and stared at de Montana in dumb bewilderment. A hush prevailed in the courtroom. Everyone, including the former bandits were swept up in a wave of astonishment. President Ginestra, and the adjunct judges glanced up from their doodling, momentarily taken aback.

"You—*do*—*not?*" Volpe's mouth hung agape. "Explain, please."

"Those men to whom you indicated are all innocent of the crime for which they, as well as I, have been accused."

"What cleverness is this?" asked Volpe. "I remind you you're under oath."

"The real culprits have long since left Palermo with passes supplied them by Minister Belasci and are no doubt enjoying the comforts of Brazil or Argentina while this farce continues to be enacted," said Vincenzo in a voice loaded with contempt.

Numbing confusion spread like a pox over the court officials and *avvocatos* involved in the trial. The bandits, trying to shield their amazement, squirmed with joy, and tried to suppress the emotions giving rise to hope inside them. *Managghia*—this Vincenzo! Phew! Could he pull it off? Could he? Sainted God! What cleverness for sure!

"At the airport those men were received honorably and saluted by several public officials with considerable respect. Believe me, *signore* Prosecutor General, those men who sit opposite me, like myself had nothing to do with the Portella *infamita*," continued Vincenzo in a saccharine voice.

Undaunted, Prosecutor Volpe addressed himself to the star witness with a look of cunning on his face. His hands clasped the lapels of his jacket. Volpe rocked on the balls of his feet, his eyes, glittering wickedly, the expression of a Cheshire cat on his face.

"Since you've established yourself as powerful and as omnipotent as Salvatore himself, you will now furnish to this court, the names of those persons who *did* participate in the Portella massacre—even if they now live across the world on a different continent."

Vincenzo shook his head regretfully. "This I cannot do. Since I was not there personally, would I not be contributing to what you lawyers claim is *hearsay?*" he asked with wide-eyed innocence.

"Do you mean to tell me you refuse to reveal their names?"

"No, *signore* Prosecutor. Only that I cannot. It would be most unfair. Some men might have remained on the lower slopes taking no part in the actual gunfire. However—those men on Mt. Cumeta—whoever they were—those blackhearted scoundrels—those scurrilous dogs who dared fire on innocent men and women and babes—" He paused dramatically. "None of us know who they might be. Certainly they got no orders from Salvatore!"

Stefano Modica sensed the court didn't believe Vincenzo at this point. Did they sense he might be telling something contrary to the truth? The entire course of events began to irritate Modica and he wondered why Vincenzo had jeopardized himself by taking the stand. It became obvious to him that Vincenzo didn't want to incur the further wrath of his former comrades who might have given opposing testimony of which he hadn't been aware prior to his appearance. If that had been his aim in hedging he should have relied on his Sicilian intuition. Earlier in the trial all men, tight-lipped in the tradition of the old Mafia, denied all charges and each · had offered alibis which they stubbornly clung to throughout the trial. But *Avvocato* Basile would have had access to the previous testimony and would have informed Vincenzo, wouldn't he? Why, then, this? This blatant untruth? It took only a few moments for Stefano to realize that he was probably the only other person outside the *coterie* of Salvatore's men who knew the actual truth of that day. Well, he told himself, you can't say this isn't an interesting drama—or was it to be a comedy? Only time would tell.

The trial wasn't all dark and bitter and tense. There were moments of levity. At one point, Arturo Scoletti, trusted paladin of Salvatore, had been questioned at length about his relationship and activities as a member of Salvatore's band of brigands. Of course, Arturo with his apelike features grimaced with humor and denied everything, and having evaded with cunning and dexterity all questions, Prosecuting General Volpe, fully exasperated was prompted to ask if he knew Salvatore at all.

Arturo Scoletti's reply was immortalized. Shrugging his shoulders, he said, "Often we'd see each other on the street. He would say 'good morning' if it suited his mood and I would simply nod in passing."

Even the former bandits had difficulty in repressing smiles.

Avvocato Basile steered his client into other avenues of questioning, when the prosecution called a huddle after the last bombshell. "Please explain to the court, describe, if you will, the *entente* that existed between Salvatore and the police. What sort of protection was offered you and the others?"

Vincenzo hedged deliberately. "What you ask is difficult for me to relate. If this honorable Tribunal would permit me to start at the beginning and follow a chronological sequence of events building to the position we find ourselves in today, I could construct a truer picture."

"The witness will adhere only to the matters of Portella Della Rosa," insisted President Ginestra, who nursed a toothache on this day and became exceedingly abrupt with nearly all the testimony. "Instruct your client, *Avvocato* Basile, to relate only the matter being tried."

"Mr. President, I agree with *signore* de Montana's declaration. It would be simpler if he started at the beginning. It would save this Tribunal precious time and prevent tedious, repetitious testimony." Basile hooked his thumbs into his vest pockets and strutted about with a schoolboy's defiance. The spectators who agreed with him cheered him on.

"I'll make a formal objection, Your Honor," called out Prosecutor Volpe. "Tell de Montana to stick to the facts."

"Sustained," muttered the President, rubbing his jaw, He glanced over his bifocals at those who disagreed with him and leaned back in his chair with a sullen expression.

"Answer the question, de Montana," Basile instructed his client.

"We always had as many passes as we needed to circulate freely. As partisans of the government were we not entitled to such liberties?" asked de Montana innocently.

"Your Honor!" objected the Prosecutor. "I object! It's never been established here or any other place that these bandits acted as partisans!"

"Basile!" came the President's reprimand.

The lawyer held up his hand. "All right. All right, Mr. President." He turned to his client. "I don't understand your meaning, de Montana." Basile pressed on. "Explain the intricacies in their *modus vivendi*—this compromise if you will, so the people can know and understand."

The President interrupted. "It isn't necessary that the *people* understand this *entente,* Basile. It's necessary that I understand!" The magistrate when exasperated had a habit of blinking his eyes rapidly, cutting off eye contact with his adversary.

"Ahhhh," sighed Vincenzo with a woebegone look of innocence. "Mr. President, our lives were complicated daily with intrigues none of us ever understood. *You* might understand, but I doubt an innocent public would ever grasp the significance of the ultrasophisticated brand of politics in which we were forced to take part."

Basile flashed him a silent warning. Ginestra glanced at the witness, his eyes narrowed to pinpoints. His words were addressed to the lawyer.

"*Avvocato* Basile, instruct your client in the proper decorum or I shall rule him in contempt," he said icily.

Basile nodded. "Confine your answers."

De Montana interrupted. "No offense meant, Your Honor. What I'm trying to say is there is no easy way to explain. As I said earlier—it's best I start at the beginning. Explain who and what we were before the circumstance of war brought Salvatore and the rest of us into world prominence."

"Take your time, de Montana," said *Avvocato* Basile boldly. "This Tribunal has all the time in the world to hear the truth! When a question arises that regards public affairs it guarantees the administration of justice will take place. We are here to ascertain only the truth in this matter."

Thirty years as a professional magistrate in which he ascended the political ladder after serving his apprenticeship as a stipendiary magistrate, prevented President Ginestra from giving vent to his utter frustration and annoyance at the tedious delays. He refrained from telling the bombastic *Avvocato* Basile to spout his idealistic nonsense in someone else's court. But, the public had already taken Basile to their bosom, favoring him as if he, too, was on trial. Public opinion, President Ginestra's worst enemy, forced him to swallow his pride, but not the bitter bile which spouted from his mouth with acid-coated words.

"Would you mind, *Avvocato* Basile, if *I* call a recess in—*my*—court?"

"Why certainly not, Mister President," declared the unabashed lawyer. "As you've said often enough, this is *your* court. It is up to you to decide when and what will take place," Basile smiled benignly and inclined his chin on an impassioned chest, his arms outstretched in an openhanded gesture.

The pendulum had swung decidedly into the positive zones for Vincenzo. It seemed nothing could go wrong for him. And feeling this he took heart and confidence continued to ooze from him as the trial continued.

CHAPTER 68

Principessa Gabriella Rothschild stared at the name on the register of the Villa Etruria, which she had purchased from the land-rich, lira-poor real princess, and converted into a hostelry a short distance from the ancient city of Viterbo. The name: *G. O'Hoolihan* caused the small hairs at the nape of her neck to rise. Wasn't this the name of the American correspondent who had stolen Salvatore's affection from her—a name burned in her memory? It couldn't be coincidence, she asked herself, could it?

In addition to the irritation she felt at seeing the name of this recent guest to her establishment, there was more to exasperate this wordly woman whose low-boiling point was well known by her associates. On this day she'd been tactfully ordered to desist from visiting Vincenzo de Montana. It was bad enough they had denied her the privilege of supplying his food a few weeks past, but now this! What complications seemed to follow the Sicilians everywhere, she thought.

At the office of the Prefect of Police, she had screamed and stormed and threatened reprisal. But the cold and impersonal Prefect simply reminded her that her licenses came up for renewal soon and, since the Ministry which handled such business was chiefly Christian Democrat, she'd be wise not to incur their wrath by coddling an enemy of theirs. She readily recognized the subtle threat.

At one time there had been more to her relationship with Vincenzo than he'd ever told Salvatore. It wasn't in Vincenzo's nature to allow as ripe a plum as Gabriella to be wasted and the two had formed an affinity which bloomed into a torrid love affair for a time. Gabriella, a rebel at heart, having heard of Vincenzo's plight, had presented herself to him as an ally. Since he had certainly provided her with much pleasure for a time, why not help him? Now it was over. These supercilious politicians had dictated terms she was forced to recognize even though she had bridled angrily at their edicts.

Gabriella had fared well after leaving Sicily. Having ingratiated herself to an aging prince who died six months after their affair, she fell heir to a sizable estate which she quickly turned over in profit to purchase this magnificent, sprawling estate nestled in the luxurious and verdant hills surrounding Viterbo, north of Rome. The former palace, surrounded by cloisters, convents, and monasteries amid a profusion of resplendent Renaissance gardens and villas was perfect for her plans. And if anyone knew how to run an elegant establishment, Gabriella Rothschild was such a person. Smart, svelte, and financially astute, she fell into the role as if she'd been born to it.

Rechecking the signature card on file, Gabriella noted the passport was Irish, yet, after hearing him talk, she discerned the accent to be American. Stefano Modica, the man who called himself G. O'Hoolihan, had been seen in and about the Villa Etruria by Gabriella, who missed very little. She decided to keep her eyes on the man she had labeled an impostor in her mind.

Late in August, foregoing the trials for a time, Modica returned to San Francisco on a short hiatus. He had returned to Viterbo to find the medieval city in festival. This, in addition to the influx of new reporters who had converged on the trial city, had caused him to seek new lodgings a few kilometers outside the city proper and he ended up in this former palace, the Villa Etruria.

Modica had seen Gabriella several times, walking grandly in and about the lobby, speaking with several of the guests. He'd have had to be blind and insensible not to notice her imposing presence or appreciate the alluring fragrance she left in the air about her as she walked past. The thought that she'd be some very special dish hadn't escaped his mind, not for a moment. The cool, impersonal blonde with green eyes concealing a raging inferno of pas-

938

sions didn't fool him, and he knew what lurked behind such marble features. However, unwilling to be deterred from his primary concern, the trial, Stefano had donned blinders and earplugs when his manly passions stirred him. On several occasions in the past when the need for coupling couldn't be ignored, Stefano had sought the services of professionals to sate his needs. He wanted no lasting relationships, not now, not under these circumstances. Odd how he conformed to some of Tori's ideals.

Modica's suite, elegantly baroque, opened onto a tiled courtyard, as did all the suites on the main floor of the old palace. Often he could hear and see other guests moving about, talking and exchanging pleasantries. At night the air was so clear, that voices traveled distinctly. The gardens, the fragrant air, the setting including the panorama was absolutely breathtaking and picturesque.

Against this background, on the eve of October 10, the enticing aroma of roses and bougainvillea cascading over pillared balustrades drifted into Stefano's suite of rooms and lured him away from his tedious translations into the courtyard to smoke an after-dinner cigar and enjoy the final phases of a mauve sunset as it yawned into a purple twilight. Arrested by the familiar-sounding voices drifting toward him, Stefano had paused momentarily, cocking his head to listen. Elsewhere in the villa the recordings of Frank Sinatra drifted toward him. From the second floor of the villa came sounds of the operatic aria from *La Tosca*. But arising above all other sounds loud and clear, came the voice of *Avvocato* Luigi Basile from an adjoining suite of rooms.

It grew apparent to Stefano as he listened that *Avvocato* Basile, after spending endless hours reading and poring over the massive trial transcripts and studying the interrogatives and testimony of witnesses, was obviously dissatisfied with the trial's progress. He spoke at length of numerous documents and letters from high-ranking government officials presented to the court by his client, de Montana, to prove his allegations along with letters from Minister Belasci, which surprisingly had been well preserved over the seven-year reign of Salvatore.

"Despite the preponderance of evidence presented," Basile told his companions, "there's a chance we'll lose. I suggest we begin preparing an appeal to the Court of Cassation," he instructed them.

Stefano eased in closer without making it too obvious he was eavesdropping. The courtyard was deserted and he stood casually posed next to an ivy-covered pillar.

"How can we lose?" asked del Vecchio, Basile's co-counsel and associate.

"It's a gut feeling I have that my client isn't telling the truth. I must put it to de Montana that for his own good he must be honest with me."

"Hah!" retorted del Vecchio, a dapper man in his forties with shortly cropped hair like steel wool. He adjusted his dark horn-rimmed glasses and snorted. "To ask the truth from a Sicilian is like asking a stone statue to come to life. For whatever reason they have, truth is something they avoid. But aside from that, let's look at the points we've made—*punc tatim*—There is no way the Tribunal can ignore the affadavits entered into evidence. And the evidence points to a definite collaboration between bandits and Minister Belasci's forces. So—where will that leave the people? They'll have to seek redress from the government for their losses at Portella. Therefore, it will be wise for Bellini to support our contention—no? They stand to win if they support de Montana's position. What the hell can they get from the bandits?" Del Vecchio studied Basile intently. "You don't suspect any subversive behavior on Bellini's part?"

Basile shrugged. "On paper and *viva voce* you would appear correct, *amico,* but there are other considerations—"

Stefano Modica hadn't wanted to eavesdrop, but he did. He also watched them through the open doors.

"You must be aware of the fact that Presidente Umberto Ginestra is strictly a party man. His soul is in escrow to the Christian Democrats. Bought and paid for. Already, I've heard rumblings—"

"But—how can we lose? If all documents submitted are viewed in the light of their true importance—the preponderance of evidence points to their collaboration," insisted del Vecchio repeatedly. "Salvatore claimed they were partisans, de Montana reiterates—"

"Listen," snapped Basile impatiently. "If you think the evidence we've presented will weigh in the final outcome of this trial, you're crazy—or too goddamned naive!"

"You mean we should consider a deal?" del Vecchio asked, deflated.

"Possibly."

"You said de Montana will consider no deals."

"That's true."

Basile paced the room thoughtfully. "All men implicated by de Montana are top Party men. I told you I've

940

heard rumblings. If de Montana retracts his statements they might make it easy on him."

"You don't really believe that."

"No," sighed Basile. "That's the pity of it. We're up against an iron man in de Montana. No deals for *him!*" He fell into a deeply cushioned chair, his chin propped up by his hand, his elbow on the arm, in an attitude of contemplation.

Paolo Franco, a young apprentice who'd been quiet, spoke up. "We've broached the subject before. It's in the files. De Montana has rejected a half-dozen such proposals, including those made by the FSB prior to his confession. They were named in the lengthy statements made to the Stipendiary judges in Palermo. No wonder they disappeared, eh? If you ask me, Counselor Basile, I think he's suicidal. Take into account, if you will, those three attempted homicides in jail which hardly affected him. Is that the attitude of a normal man?" Young Franco cast a meaningful eye toward his superior. "Anyway, if de Montana walks out of court a free man, I'll wager he'll be dead in less than a week."

Out of the silence, Basile leaned forward, a light in his eye.

"Say that again, Paolo—about de Montana being suicidal."

"*Allora*—isn't he? It appears to me he wishes to die, but before he's done he's intent on taking several people with him. *Coute que coute*."

"Suicidal, eh? At whatever the cost? I wonder," mused Basile. "I wonder. Vendetta—vengeance—it's all part of the Sicilian syndrome, no?"

Del Vecchio rose to his feet and closed the doors against a gust of October wind. The burning sky had rapidly paled and faded. In a moment, night had fallen.

"*Buona sera, signore* O'Hoolihan," said Gabriella Rothschild, emerging from the shadows. Walking toward him, she appeared like an apparition startling Stefano. She stood very still, watching him as he nodded to her and moved across the courtyard only to disappear into his suite of rooms.

Perplexed by his rude behavior, she glanced in the direction of *Avvocato* Basile's suite with narrowed, thoughtful eyes and disappeared inside the villa.

Inside, Modica paced the floor, giving no thought to Gabriella, who she was, and whether her appearance on the terrace was planned or coincidental. His mind was elsewhere. God! How he'd like to set Basile straight on a

941

few points. He told himself, if Basile was worth his salt—and it seemed he was—he'd stumble across the truth. Or if he proved inept and if his client wanted to keep certain information from him, Stefano couldn't justify any move on his own initiative to disturb client-counselor relationship, could he? He wrestled with his conscience for several hours and finally convinced himself it wouldn't harm if he gently prodded *Avvocato* Basile a bit.

Seated at the *escritoire,* he wrote a note to the lawyer, left unsigned. About midnight, he glanced across the courtyard and noticed the lights were out. Moments later, Modica padded down the thickly carpeted corridor, annoyed to find a guard at Basile's door. Back in his room he called the *concierge,* ordered a bottle of wine to be delivered to the man posted outside the lawyer's door, with an appropriate note attached. He waited an hour. When he again returned to Basile's suite, the guard was seated in his chair, slumped over, snoring loudly. On the floor next to him was a near-empty bottle of wine and an empty glass.

Modica smiled. He moved lightly to the door, slipped the note under it, and hastened back to his suite as swiftly as his prosthesis would allow.

The next morning, bright and early, *Avvocato* Basile conferred with his client, Vincenzo de Montana, in the small anteroom away from the ornately designed courtroom. Somber of face and pensive, Basile struck a pose of contemplation with thumbs hooked into the pockets of a tartan plaid vest worn under a navy flannel suit. He paced the floor and stopped to remove an ornate gold watch from his vest pocket. He opened the lid to note the time and the brief refrains of a Sicilian lullaby played. Impatiently he snapped the lid shut and confronted his overly cocky and confident client, whose merry dark eyes were fastened on him in exquisite amusement. There was no doubt that Vincenzo liked this lawyer; that his lawyer liked him.

Watching him each day, Basile felt as if he was watching a peacock plume himself. Vincenzo was a colorful character; at times shortsighted, filled with the normal biases and prejudices against his sworn enemies and at times he expounded a needlessly argumentative verbosity. Yet there were times when *Avvocato* Basile wished he could get him to speak out more directly on relevant matters. But that was like asking the gods for a miracle. He was too reserved in his explanation of Salvatore and their relationship. Basile learned at the outset of their relation-

942

ship that to Vincenzo anything less than God, Salvatore, or himself, were subjects for mockery. No one mocked Salvatore, but no one. Not even Vincenzo.

With this in mind, the lawyer opened the conversation bluntly. "You think it's going well, de Montana?"

"I think so—no?"

Basile shrugged imperceptibly. "You're sure you've told me everything? Not holding anything back? I want no surprises in that pit of crocodiles. Up to now it's been mild. Understand what I'm saying?"

"What could I keep from you, *dottore?*" Vincenso evidenced his perennial smile of innocence. "You're my lawyer. I've told you everything you *need* to know."

"*Need* to know—eh?" Basile felt uneasy, now, more than ever. Only that morning he had discovered a mysterious note under his door, containing a curious message. Something he intended asking this spirited client of his soon enough. "Listen, *amico.* To do my best for you, I must know everything, *mi capeeshi?* If you don't trust me with everything, I can get murdered in there—and take you along with me. I'm too egotisical to consider losing. I'm your lawyer. I'd like to think I'm your friend—at least that." Basile walked away from his client. Then, turning abruptly, he glanced into and held his client's eyes compulsively. "*Allora*—Vincenzo, why do I get the feeling you aren't telling me the truth?" He paused for emphasis. "Let me advance that a step farther. If I get this feeling, what the hell do you think the prosecution thinks?"

Vincenzo shrugged indifferently. He offered Basile an English Oval cigarette. His lawyer wagged a finger at him. Vincenzo lit his and inhaled appreciatively. "*Allora, dottore*, you're the *avvocato.* How the hell do I know what they think—eh? I have enough to do to keep my own thoughts in order. You think I can concern myself with what others think? Eh?"

Again the same bland mask of innocence, thought Basile as a dull thud plopped at the pit of his stomach. He broke eye contact with his client and sighed with despair. Whenever these gut feelings came to him, he knew that something wasn't in balance—and a gross distortion nagged at him.

Basile made a disorganized gesture and moving toward the modest wooden desk upon which he earlier had flung his briefcase, he assembled a sheaf of papers, studying his client out of the corner of his eyes, noting the fastidious figure he cut with his expensive clothing and accessories. Basile, in his moderately priced suit and conservative accessories, an initialed gold ring LAB, ornate gold chain and pocket watch with its musical clockworks, felt dowdy next to his glamorous client who sported a costly diamond watch, handcrafted leather boots, diamond ring, and at his waist, always, the solid-gold belt buckle. Watching his client, Basile couldn't help feeling that a ghost stood between them; *a ghost named Salvatore*.

"Where's a Santino Siragusa?" he asked Vincenzo unexpectedly and watched for a reaction.

Taken by surprise, Vincenzo smiled cagily. "You've been doing your homework, eh, Basile?"

The lawyer didn't smile. He waited for an answer.

"In America, I suppose," he said staring at the smoke spiralling from his cigarette. He didn't ask why, so the lawyer gave it little importance.

"Where is Salvatore's personal portfolio?"

"You know where it is. I testified in court that Major Franchina has it. I gave it to him. That's why I went to Castelvetrano in the first place. The deal was to give Franchina and Cala the personal portfolio and for this I'd receive immunity."

"You haven't testified to that yet, Vincenzo. It hasn't been entered into testimony yet. I'm hoping for this, of course. Has your memory failed you, my friend? You've only mentioned this to me in passing. So far I haven't attached much importance to it. Perhaps I've been wrong?"

Vincenzo appeared agitated.

Basile pressed. "Are you certain Siragusa doesn't have the portfolio? He was historian to the bandits—no? Where do you suppose Siragusa is?"

"He was Salvatore's personal historian," he corrected a bit too quickly.

"Well, then, wouldn't he have *all* the records? I recall you told me an accurate diary of the bandit's activities was maintained. I mean apart from the politically damaging and inculpating portfolio. Wouldn't the names of the Portella participants be recorded, documented, so we could end this farce?"

"Listen, Basile, you have all the documents presented to the courts. I don't know where Santino is. I've produced all documents and communiques needed to prove we were acting as partisans of the government under Belasci's orders." Vincenzo lit another cigarette from the butt in his hand with trembling fingers as he paced the floor. "Besides, I have the only copy. Tori gave it to me." He avoided looking at his lawyer for fear Basile could see through his sham.

"You're sure? I mean there is nothing anyone can surprise us with in court, is there? Not the prosecutor or Bellini, for that matter? They won't surprise us with another copy of the portfolio?" Basile asked candidly.

"Listen, Basile, I told you everything you need to know. I was a paid assassin. *Basta e' fine*. That's all—there is no more. And you don't have to worry about the original portfolio—it's in America."

"Why are you confessing to a crime you didn't commit?" asked Basile quietly. He had the opening he was looking for.

Vincenzo glanced sharply at the lawyer with masked innocence. "What are you saying—eh? Tell me what you are getting at because I don't believe my ears, *dottore*."

Lawyer and client locked eyes. Italian and Sicilian. Man to man.

"You know and I know you didn't assassinate your cousin. *Allora*—why? Why are you doing this to yourself?"

"*Va! Va!* You're crazy, Basile. *Tu si pazzu*. Out of your mind! You think I'd admit to the slaying of a hero if it wasn't true? Would I subject myself to the dangers, adverse press, ridicule, and hatred of my countrymen and put my life on the block with my former companions if I hadn't committed the crime for the good of my country?" he insisted with rising emotion.

Basile made known his disgust. "Your words have the impact of someone breaking wind in the confines of a drawing room, de Montana. Bullshit! You can convince anyone of a thousand or more—but not this Italian."

"Look, Basile," The Sicilian's face turned beet red. "I'm paying you to defend me of the charges leveled against me by this Tribunal. I am not guilty of the Portella massacre and neither are the other men tried for the criminal assault. I want you to get me off. When the time comes for the trial of Salvatore's murder, I'll have plenty more to say. Meanwhile, all you have to know is I killed Salvatore, not the man who claims he did and received a decoration and promotion from the Republic for his efforts. What I did, I did under the full instructions of Martino Belasci and that's the truth!"

They stared at each other, eyeball to eyeball. "All right," sighed Basile with a sinking sensation. "But, if there is more you feel I should know—at any time—contact me. Meanwhile, I'll try to work a miracle for you."

"Why? I thought it was in the bag. You yourself told me I had impressed the court with my personal integrity.

Didn't I make liars out of nearly all the witnesses for the prosecution? I made them all look like long-nosed Pinocchios. What of the documents to support my testimony?"

"Vincenzo, anything can happen in there. That's why it's important that you be honest with me. It's the only way I can help you. One lie—one little white lie and that leaning Tower of Pisa you've constructed can come toppling down around us. If such a lie exists, I must know of it. You understand?"

"There is nothing more. No lies," said Vincenzo through veiled eyes.

Before they left for court, Vincenzo asked his lawyer if there was a chance he might see a woman. He handed Basile a slip of paper with the name of Maria Angelica Candela on it. The lawyer burned the name into his memory.

"Girlfriend—lover? Someone from your village?"

Vincenzo nodded expectantly.

"If the girl means anything to you, I wouldn't drag her into this. She might be subjected to further harassment."

Vincenzo reached for the slip of paper, tore it to shreds. "You're right. It was a foolish thought. *Allora—amonini.* Let's go."

"Now, de Montana," said the Prosecutor, scratching his bony cheeks, "I want to take you back to your testimony before you collapsed in court two weeks ago. You were naming the instigators of the *Portella* Massacre." He checked his notes. "You had already named Martino Belasci, Prince Oliatta, Bernardo Malaterra, and were about to name others. Proceed, please, to complete this list of alleged instigators."

Reacting with disfavor to this question, Vincenzo looked to his counselor for some sign. Basile, intent on the words he'd scribbled on his pad before him on the *avvocato's* table—*suicidal—vendetta—vengeance*—failed in this moment to see the concern on his client's face.

"Come, come, de Montana," pressed Volpe. "Who are the others?"

"Several Christian Democrats," said Vincenzo, his voice dropped to a hoarse whisper. "Don Santo Flores, Don de Matteis, and I think—uh—er—" His voice cracked and through a thickened throat he managed, "Don Barbarossa."

"What's that, de Montana? Speak up, man! Don Matteo Barbarossa, you said?" The Prosecutor's voice boomed loudly. *"You think?"* he asked dourly. *"You think? Are we now playing guessing games?"*

"I'm certain." The star witness appeared cowed by the weight of the name he'd just spoken. His voice alerted *Avvocato* Basile.

Glancing up, the lawyer noted his client had turned the color of clay and retreated into a sullen silence. He glanced also at the faces of the men in the witness cages and noted they also had reacted with marked degrees of nervousness, discomfort, and some even wore telltale expressions of concern on their faces, as if Vincenzo had suddenly lost all sense of sanity. Basile scribbled the name Don Barbarossa on his pad, underlining it heavily. He had to learn why the mention of this man reflected diabolical fear in the bandits.

Prosecutor Volpe picked up on the subtle changes in the witness, however, attributing them to something else, he changed tack and hammered away at him in a different vein:

"Earlier you stated the men who took part in the Portella infamy were well out of the country. Are you inferring the men in the courtroom are innocent of any participation in the alleged crime?"

The peculiar feeling of doom lifted when Volpe didn't press the Barbarossa matter. "I don't infer anything," he said sullenly.

"Well then, let me put it another way." Volpe pulled out a blackboard on rollers to the center of the arena, where a map denoting the physical layout of Portella Della Rosa had been drawn. One mountain peak was labeled Mt. Cometa; the other Mt. Pizzuta. "Now then, tell me where Salvatore's men congregated when they were instructed to demonstrate over the heads of the celebrants?"

"From Mt. Pizzuta."

"And those who fired from Mt. Cometa?"

"What about them?"

"Weren't they also Salvatore's men?"

"I told you—whoever fired from Cometa took no orders from Salvatore."

"Do you mean to tell this Tribunal that the men who fired from Mt. Cometa were not Salvatore's men?"

"I object, Mr. President. My client has already testified three times to that effect. I suggest the Prosecutor either rinse out his hairy ears, or at least read the transcripts correctly!" shouted Basile.

The President glanced at the Prosecutor. "De Montana has already replied to that question," he said flatly.

Prosecutor Volpe huddled with his co-counsels. *Avvocato* Bellini, the people's lawyer, huddled with his associates. The spectators were silent as they watched the activity in the arena. *Avvocato* Basile questioned his client.

"Please tell the court to the best of your recollection what makes you so certain of the fact that the men firing from Mt. Cometa took no orders from Salvatore."

"I learned from Salvatore that within three minutes of firing he ordered his men to cease. Having noticed a crossfiring from the ridges of Mt. Cometa, he ordered four of his men to ride the distance to Cometa to learn who it was that shot to kill the unfortunate celebrants. Then he quickly ordered his men to pack their gear and head back to the Grotto D'Oro. His paladins returned and reported finding no trace of the men who fired from Mt. Cometa. They brought back with them a few shell casings found below the ridge. In comparing them to the bullets used by his men, he found them identical."

The spectators in the court murmured knowingly. It had been a conspiracy after all. A conspiracy to discredit Salvatore, just as Lt. Greco admitted to the press. Now the truth will out. Now—

"Tell the court, de Montana, if you will, where did the machine guns used by Salvatore's men come from?"

"The guns were provided by Chief Semano of the security police."

"Are you then saying the security police then furnished guns to the alleged killers who fired from Mt. Cometa?"

"Since they fired identical bullets, used by the same guns furnished to us—what do you think? That was a vital part of the agreement—the guns to be furnished us.

Pandemonium broke out in the courtroom. The people's lawyer and his associates were sent flying into a huddle. The Prosecutor's staff huddled. *Avvocato* Basile smiled faintly. Bellini had to make his move pretty soon, he thought, but, there was still so much he had to bring out.

Behind him in the witness cages sat those twelve men who had fired the lethal bullets. Former fringe-area bandits once hired by Salvatore for interim jobs had been granted a reprieve by Vincenzo de Montana when he refused to identify them. Confident in their positions, they stuck to the alibis previously given in testimony of—not guilty. *Managghia!* Was it possible they would get away with their infamous deed? Was it? Would they?

"Let us clear up another point, de Montana," began Basile. "At the outset of your testimony, you told the court Salvatore had been forced to sign a confession in which he stated there were no instigators of the Portella affair."

"Yes, it was a time for terrible dilemma for me."

"In what way?"

"Salvatore told me at the end he intended to comply with Belasci's request."

"You're referring of course to the Minister of the Interior, Martino Belasci?" pointed out Basile, stroking his moustache.

"Yes."

"Very well. Please continue. Just what was Minister Belasci's request?"

"He wanted Salvatore to write to the President of this Tribunal, here in Viterbo, accepting full responsibility for the Portella massacre. And to deny the existence of any instigators. This request came through Chief Inspector of Police D'Verde as well as in a letter from Belasci—uh—Martino Belasci, the Minister of the Interior," added Vincenzo on cue from his lawyer. "D'Verde promised to send his own son with the necessary documents, passports, and monetary imbursements and whatever else was necessary to guarantee Salvatore safe passage out of the country." Vincenzo paused to catch his breath. He felt calmer today and sensed less hostility from his former comrades.

"I told Salvatore he was foolish to comply with this request. "You're not only risking your life, but that of mine and the others as well,' I told him." To make a long story short, they got to him behind my back and he handed them the document they wanted."

"To whom did Salvatore give this document?"

"Prince Oliatta and Bernardo Malaterra. I was there. Another copy was sent to President Ginestra and the other to Martino Belasci. It was after this that I approached Colonel Cala to make a deal. You see, the Christian Democrats had fixed it for Salvatore to leave the country and leave the rest of us to face the music. So—for the good of the Republic I agreed to assassinate him."

In the silence of the enormous room, no one moved, no one breathed.

"I even told General Cala of the several threats to be made upon his life—by Belasci's men. That he'd never be permitted to capture Salvatore."

And so it went; Vincenzo continued spinning a web of partial truths and half lies sprinkled with fanciful imagination, yet loaded with enough facts to make his story entirely credible. And what an actor! Phew! The best! He continued:

"A slick defense counsel was forced upon me by Colonel Cala. This same lawyer offered me fifty million

949

lire—directly from Martino Belasci himself. Yes, the Minister of the Interior," he added quickly, 'to seal my lips. I refused his services."

"Why did you refuse these services, de Montana?"

"Because they wanted to postpone my trial and this might prove dangerous to me." Vincenzo's voice cracked. He cleared his throat.

"You may take more water if you need it," said President Ginestra.

"No, thank you!" replied Vincenzo with a wicked gleam in his eye.

The courtroom broke into good-humored laughter.

"What I wish to know, Mr. President," goaded the communist lawyer Bellini. "Did de Montana really kill Salvatore? Or was this just a part of another conspiracy?"

"Yes! Yes! I killed Salvatore! You all made me kill him! You didn't dare have him alive any longer! If I may be permitted to tell the story right from the beginning, Mr. President. Here, in front of the world—"

"De Montana!" warned *Avvocato* Basile, shaking his head.

A rumble of *sotto voce* opprobrium broke out among the spectators even the Tribunal judges couldn't suppress.

"Yes, let de Montana talk," came the indignant cries. "Let him speak the truth! *Bravo* de Montana! *Bravo*. Let him speak!"

"Silence in the court!" cried the clerk. "Silence!"

"He may not speak!" cried President Ginestra, wheezing loudly from a hay fever attack. "*Avvocato* Basile, I demand order! I've warned you repeatedly. We are trying the Portella massacre here, not Salvatore's murder! De Montana may not speak without permission."

"But, Mr. President, it was the people's lawyer who asked the question, not I." Basile smiled politely and winked at a few members of the press.

The weeks dragged on. The interrogation and cross-examination of witnesses continued and the ignominious Portella massacre faded into the background as the even more scandalous story of the betrayal and death of Salvatore dominated the newspapers. Collusion with high government officials and Christian Democrats hinted at was blown out of proportion. Communists demanded action be taken against those responsible for hiring the paid assassins.

Worse, no one believed that incredible story concocted by Major Franchina and the FSB about that morning of

July 5, 1950. The constant references made by the international press to the fact that Minister Belasci had officially endorsed that version of Salvatore's capture and death, not once but many times since July 5, brought the Office of the Ministry under vicious daily attacks.

One afternoon after a luncheon recess, Vincenzo demanded that the FSB officers be made to answer specific questions. He assured the court he wasn't concerned with the countless lies promoted by the Minister of the Interior or the FSB in the past, only that General Cala be made to answer three specific questions.

Finally, after several weeks of bitter controversy, President Ginestra was forced to assuage the derogatory public opinion that arose due to his refusal to call the FSB officers to testify. He relented, but not gracefully. He first acidly accused the combined lawyers of attempting to turn his courtroom into carnival atmosphere.

"I will run things my way," he protested with exaggerated patience to deaf ears.

CHAPTER 69

"Then who do you suppose really killed Salvatore?" asked Alonzo del Vecchio, *Avvocato* Basile's colleague. There was no reply for a time.

Their voices carried clear in the night air, loud enough for Stefano Modica to hear without straining. He stood in the courtyard at the Villa Etruria, smoking his rationed nightly cigar. Throughout the trials Modica had attempted to fathom this very question. Who indeed had actually committed the lethal act? Oddly enough, Modica felt strongly that the key to this puzzle had to lay in Antigone Salvatore. Did he dare go to Montegatta to confer with her? Subject himself to the possible dangers that lay in store for him in Sicily? In lieu of all that had happened to Saginor and Salina, even the attack on his own person, how could he go there without bringing attention to himself? How? It wasn't that he feared for his life. God knows he'd faced countless dangers, even death, too often to be intimidated by the living. Yet, as committed to this cause as he was, he was Sicilian enough to know he had to operate in the utmost secrecy.

Basile's voice sliced through his thoughts. "To tell the truth, I don't give a damn at this point. I want only to insure that my client is free of any culpability in the Portella massacre. I'll cross the bridge as to his guilt of Salvatore's death and/or whomsoever else might be implicated—when I come to it!"

Stefano Modica returned to his suite. He wrote a brief letter to Antigone Salvatore and signed it with the name on his passport, G. O'Hoolihan, a name Antigone was certain to remember. Two weeks later a reply came. In it was a simple white card with the name, Angelo Duca—Master Jeweler—Bagheria, Sicily. Stefano placed the card in the secret compartment in his prosthesis.

The following morning, he encountered *Avvocato* Basile and his associates in the lobby of the Villa Etruria preparing to depart for court. For an instant their eyes met. Stefano nodded briefly and walked on past them. Basile nodded imperceptibly, then walked on toward the black Mercedes limousine that pulled up before the villa. Modica got into his rented Fiat and wheeled the auto through the rolling countryside back to Viterbo. Watching the activity from the mezzanine, Gabriella Rothschild smoked a cigarette then quickly walked into an alcove marked Private. She made a telephone call.

General Cala, dressed nattily in his beige uniform, found himself in a most untenable position as soon as he was sworn in. With the official version of Salvatore's death so completely shattered, no effort on his part could restore a shred of their original story, thought Stefano as he listened to *Avvocato* Basile's line of questioning.

"General Cala, I have only three questions for you. First, were you in constant contact with Vincenzo de Montana? Second, did you request de Montana to procure Salvatore's personal portfolio which contained factual documentation of the Portella Della Rosa participation for a reward of three million lire? Third, did de Montana ever warn you of the *entente* existing between Chief D'Verde and Salvatore—of a plot to do you in?"

"I wish to make it clear that I do not relish being here at this time," said Cala, struggling internally for the proper response. He couldn't deny Vincenzo's allegations and earn the court's respect, but he somehow had to find a way to make the stories compatible. "I cannot in good conscience reply to your questions, point blank, *Avvocato* Basile. As de Montana stressed earlier, it is most difficult to begin at midpoint in this saga." He pondered. "Where shall I begin? Where?"

"Let's see if I can be of help. What were de Montana's words to you at your initial meeting?"

"De Montana outlined a conditional offer of collaboration with the FSB. He insisted upon receipt of a letter from Martino Belasci indemnifying him from all charges leveled against him and he requested my solemn oath to intervene on his behalf should he be caught. There was no question about claiming the reward. It would of course go to de Montana. I agreed to his demands. I even provided a letter from Belasci which I, in all honesty, forged myself. In my line of work we are trained to resort to any means to get the desired results.

"In the several meetings I had with de Montana I learned that Salvatore spent much time in Castelvetrano living in the house of *Avvocato* de Meo. However, something new was brought to light. Something I doubt even Vincenzo knew about, at the very last moment, we received information that Salvatore would be in Castelvetrano preparing for his expatriation by American undercover agents."

Stefano Modica leaned in intently and, alerted by General Cala's words, he still wondered how anyone had heard of the intended expatriation. It was difficult for him to believe these rumors when the dates had never been settled. How? Who could have leaked the information to the Minister?

The voice of *Avvocato* Basile brought him out of his revery. "One moment, General. Please explain how you came to hear of such a plan?" Basile, for some reason, found this news electrifying.

"Well, I'm not sure I can reveal information considered classified information." The General indicated his concern.

The Public Minister echoed his protest. "The General *cannot* make public that information considered highly classified by Italian Intelligence."

"I withdraw the question," said Basile, waving them off. "But only until I can demonstrate a precedent, Mr. President." He turned back to the General.

"Please explain under whose protection Salvatore found himself in the last few days before his death?" He fingered his gold watch chain.

"I suppose—his friends."

"Who specifically?"

"*Avvocato* de Meo, for one, and his associates."

"Who were these associates?" persisted Basile.

Cala hedged. He regarded the ceiling with artful evasiveness.

"You will kindly reply to the question, General, if you have knowledge of these associates?"

"The youngblood *mafiosi*," he said finally, *sotto voce*.

"Names, General. Names."

"Bartolomeo Calemi, Natali Solameni, and de Meo."

"Let the record show the first two are deceased. Continue, General."

"It's true, de Montana warned me of the *entente* between Chief D'Verde and Salvatore," he admitted. "But, I know nothing of this special portfolio to which he refers."

"You lie!" shouted Vincenzo, springing to his feet. "It was part of the agreement between Martino Belasci and myself and you! It was to obtain these papers that I assassinated my own blood brother on the eve of his expatriation. With a tormented soul and heart I was forced to kill my beloved cousin. I had to put an end to this slaughter because he would have unustly destroyed all of us."

"Order! Order in my court!" cried the indignant President at the emotional outburst. "*Avvocato* Basile, you will instruct your client not to expurgate himself with such quenchless furor. He'll be given ample time to contest General Cala's remarks."

"Thank you, Mr. President." Basile motioned to Vincenzo to sit down.

"No! No, I will not be silenced!" Vincenzo cried impassionately. "Cala lies! Ask him. Ask him about the secret meeting between him and Salvatore. In my presence Salvatore told Cala he wouldn't have the chance to capture him—because Salvatore couldn't be touched. I was there when Cala was told about the personal portfolio by Salvatore."

"Who else was present at this alleged meeting?" asked a scoffing and cynical Prosecutor.

"Inspector D'Verde Bartolemeo Calemi, and Natale Solameni!" shouted Vincenzo, bringing in the names of the young blood *mafiosi* to more prominence.

Basile frowned. The prosecution was sure to pick up on it. And they did.

"Isn't it strange, de Montana, that a man the caliber of General Cala would intrigue with Salvatore in the middle of a bitter battle for his life? And doesn't it appear equally questionable that two men you name as witnesses to this highly suspect *entente* are both dead under highly suspect circumstances?" asked Prosecutor Volpe too quickly.

"I know nothing of their deaths or of Cala's character. I

know only they were all present at the meeting at Calemi's villa, when I went under Salvatore's orders and where the Inspector was also present. Cala knew six months in advance of Salvatore's death about the existence of the personal portfolio. It was Salvatore who told him about it."

"A likely story!" scoffed the Prosecutor.

"Objection, Mr. President!" stormed *Avvocato* Basile. I object to the Prosecutor General's attitude. Need I remind him of his duties of the Tribunal? I shall take time to read the Constitutional Position of the Public Prosecutor. Articles 73 and 74 of the Ordinamento Giudizario states: 'The Public Prosecutor shall watch over the observance of the law, the prompt and regular administration of justice, the tutelage of rights of the State. He is to direct judiciary policy and proceeds directly to the summary of the investigation . . .'"

"That'll do, Basile," interrupted President Ginestra, suppressing a smile. "I'm confident Prosecutor Volpe knows his functions."

"I suggest he be made more aware of these functions, for it appears he's had a sudden lapse of memory. He's not been appointed an honorable magistrate, yet," retorted the disdaining Basile.

Prosecutor Volpe and his assistants sat back with glum expressions as order was restored. The Tribunal magistrates thumbed absently through sheafs of papers. Vincenzo had grown introverted. His dark, glazed eyes stared out at the spectators and he sighed inwardly. Prison life had taken its toll. Having psyched himself into believing it would be a matter of time before he walked out the courtroom a free man, he became victimized by lengthy court procedure, red tape, and insurmountable legal delays. Almost a year had passed since that day he turned himself in and he felt less certain of himself as the days passed.

He thought of his Aunt Antigone constantly and lamented his despair. He thought of Maria Angelica more with the passing of each day and yearned to turn back the clock to when Tori was preparing his exile. Why hadn't he gone with him? He might be alive today, and what would have been wrong with Brazil or Argentina? At least they'd be alive. There was little communication from the other bandits. At least they had ceased in their harassment and antagonism. Even Arturo and Miguel Scoletti and the Genovese brothers began to smile and nod at him.

Major Franchina took the stand. The loss of one arm

couldn't convert the martyred officer back into his former role as national hero and when the stony-faced, fully discredited officer took the stand, he stubbornly clung to that ridiculous story originally given to the reporters in Castelvetrano. He took the position that as an officer of the *carabinieri* and FSB, he was always under the orders of his superiors, Martino Belasci and General Cala. He claimed he knew nothing other than what his superiors dictated to him. He denied having received documents from anyone. "I was sent to the de Meo house in Castelvetrano to pick them up and was told to inform Vincenzo de Montana that de Meo himself had burned Salvatore's portfolio. If General Cala received them, I have no knowledge of this."

"You admit, then, Major, you were sent to the de Meo house to pick up Salvatore's portfolio?" asked *Avvocato* Basile subtly.

"I never denied it!" he retorted hotly.

Avoccato Basile bridled egotistically and winked at Vincenzo. By his statement, the Major had admitted the portfolio had been part of the agreement between the FSB and de Montana, but Vincenzo wasn't satisfied.

"I delivered the portfolio to Major Franchina personally," he insisted, jumping to his feet. "From my hands to his, I turned over the portfolio. You see how they lie? Lie! Lie!"

The next morning Basile plunged ahead in his questioning of de Montana.

"While you were a fugitive from justice did you make a trip to Rome?"

"The witness will not answer the question," directed the President.

Vincenzo shrieked, "I went to Rome at the request of Minister Belasci."

President Ginestra grimaced angrily. "I insist you cease in this avenue of interrogation!" His blue eyes turned to ice under a shelf of white brows.

"Martino Belasci summoned me. He wanted to deal directly with me. They were in trouble and needed my help!" retorted Vincenzo.

"*Avvocato* Basile! I shall remove your client from my court if you do not take measures to silence him. I've warned you repeatedly we are here trying the Portella Della Rosa infamy. I shall return your client to prison!"

"Go ahead!" shouted Vincenzo. "See if I care. I shall

956

never return here again!" He shouted at the end of that trial day.

Under Italian law, no government official need subject himself to the rigors of the courtroom tribulations and during his tenure of office he is immune to prosecution unless caught—*flagrante delicto*—in the act of committing a crime. So, when Minister Belasci volunteered his testimony, many high-seated officials squirmed and shuddered at the risks. It was to appease some of the dissident Party members that Belasci even considered making an appearance in Viterbo, in hopes that his show of bravado would still the ugly rumors that continued to haunt the office of the Ministry. Dressed impressively in a gray silk suit with exquisite accessories, and carrying himself with the forbearance of royalty, he sauntered past Vincenzo without a glimmer of recognition, his face a benign mask of complacency.

Vincenzo de Montana hadn't smiled for many days, his cocky and arrogant manner had abated considerably, and he listened to each and every part of the testimony with concentrated effort. But on the day of Belasci's arrival in Viterbo, as if to taunt the Minister, Vincenzo forced an elevation of spirits. Vitality oozed from his confident, probing eyes. Periodically, he'd glance at the well-poised Minister in silent challenge. The smile of confidence returned to his face like magic. Even his clothing was on par with the ostentatious haberdashery displayed by the Minister.

Members of the left-wing press, tipped off to the Minister's court appearance, motored to Viterbo and packed the courtroom, hoping to learn some startling information that could topple this power saturated political enemy of theirs. Despite the hostile vibrations he sensed in the air around him, Belasci spoke with remarkable calm and displayed excellent control. There were no visible signs of his recent alcoholic excesses. Put through a few preliminary questions, Minister Belasci responded simply and to the point. He was then permitted, by the joint counsels, to give his statement.

"I've no reason to doubt the official story given me by General Cala and Major Franchina about the death of Salvatore," he began. "It's *possible* that de Montana *may* have been the betrayer of his blood brother and first cousin, but, there's no doubt in my mind that it was Major Franchina who inflicted the *coup de grace,* in the line of duty." Belasci looked right through de Montana with obvious disdain. "De Montana wouldn't have found the courage to pull the trigger to kill the man who'd been his best friend and benefactor," he scoffed noticeably. He treated Vincenzo as if he were some insect.

De Montana seethed internally and thought, I'd like to clout that lying sonofabitch of a *finocchio*.

"Is it true, *Signore* Belasci, that you met with Vincenzo de Montana in Rome on several occasions?" asked *Avvocato* Basile, preparing for the kill.

"Never. It is not true."

"Isn't it also true that your emissaries, Prince Oliatta and Bernardo Malaterra, met with Salvatore on many occasions and as recently as June 1950 met with Vincenzo de Montana? On June 7, to be exact?"

"Absolutely not true."

"Isn't it also true, that you bargained with Salvatore? You entered into negotiations, not once or twice, but many times with the outlaw Salvatore, who with his men were considered partisans of the government? All of whom received orders directly from you?"

"My dear Basile, I've stated publicly my position with Salvatore. I don't deal with—"

"—outlaws," interrupted Basile, completing the sentence. "We're all aware of what you state publicly. But, here, under oath, you've sworn—"

"Come now, Basile . . . I can't answer for the actions of others. Nor can I testify to their actions on certain dates. I can barely recall what—*I*—do on certain dates. . . ." He affected a smile and struggled for composure.

"I see. Then you take the position that neither Prince Oliatta or Malaterra ever acted on your behalf in any capacity between Salvatore or Vincenzo de Montana?" Basile's inscrutable eyes fixed on the Minister intently.

"Most emphatically—No!"

"Need I remind you, Excellency, you are under oath?"

"I practiced law when you were in diapers, Basile!"

The courtroom broke out into titters. The clerk rapped his gavel.

"Isn't it a fact you've maintained contact through correspondence and other forms of communication with Salvatore in a close relationship since 1945?"

"Absolutely not!" Bored for several moments, Belasci sat forward and in afterthought added, "I responded publicly through the press to the demands he made upon me. You might call that a form of correspondence."

"You're sure that's all, *Signore* Belasci?" Basile's brows
958

wrinkled with purpose and deliberation as he leaned back in his chair.

"I'm sure." He spoke with exaggerated confidence.

"Mr. President. I have here an item previously entered as exhibit Y in de Montana's records and special papers, one of a collection of many from the personal portfolio of Salvatore." He walked to the bench, identified the letter held in his hand, and paused a moment. "With your permission, Mr. Presidente." he began to read:

"*Carissimo* Salvatore: *It's unfortunate matters have taken a turn for the worse. Once on the same side of the fence, fighting for a worthy cause, we now stand in opposing camps. The strong bond that once existed between us—*"

"Mr. President! I object!" exploded Martino Belasci. Turning to the Prosecutor, he ranted, "And you too, should object, Mr. Prosecutor! Belasci's smoldering eyes were fixed on Volpe, signaling burning messages to come to his aid. "I object most strenuously to the reading of such an obvious forgery!"

Somewhat startled, Prosecutor Volpe rose to the occasion to voice a weak objection. "Until it's established if this item is or is not a forgery, I'll not allow it to be read in this courtroom!" He quickly scanned the contents of a copy of the letter read by Basile, thrust into his hands by an associate.

"Objection sustained!" said the President.

"Mr. President!" Affecting to be totally confounded by the turn of events, *Avvocato* Basile flung out his arms in an open gesture of amazement. "I'm totally shocked that the words of Minister Belasci appear to be enough to label this letter a forgery! I submit, how dare Minister Belasci claim this letter a forgery when I have *not yet* revealed the full contents or the author of this letter?"

"Now, listen, Basile. You heard me sustain the objection. You know better than to explain after I've ruled on a motion!"

"And I submit once again, Mr. President, the question of authenticity has never come before the court in this trial. I further submit, how does *Signore* Belasci assume this letter to be a forgery when in fact he has not read it or examined it?" *Avvocato* Basile stood firm and resolute.

"That'll do, Basile. *Basta!* In my court, when I say enough, I mean it! Now then, do you wish to discuss this—off the record?"

"Off the record? Absolutely not! I demand this stay in the record! My client is entitled to his rights—" Basile stopped, a deadly calm flooded his face. He smiled benignly, then continued:

"Very well, Mr. President." Confidence oozed from every pore as Basile strutted before the court. "Having anticipated such a declaration I took the liberty of authenticating the document. I submit further, the certifications of three independent specialists attesting to its authenticity, all of which are attached as addendums to Exhibt Y. Please note all three firms concur the letter was written in the handwriting and signed with the signature of Martino Belasci, on record." *Avvocato* Basile smiled with revolting sweetness. "I requested individual certifications to offset the possibility of the mysterious disappearance of the original letter from the files. Ever since the lengthy statements made by my client to both local and Stipendiary magistrafes in Palermo disappeared, I took precautions. Understand?"

"*Basta!*" exploded President Ginestra at the stunning revelation. "Enough!"

Gales of laughter split the air overhead. The court was bedlam again, as people cheered and shouted, "*Bravo, Basile. Bravo!*"

"Do you have further questions of His Excellency?" asked the Magistrate sternly.

"Of *signore* Belasci?" asked Basile with noticeable detachment. He shook his head. "Noooooope! *Signore* Belasci has given me more answers than for which I had questions." Hamming it up, Basile glanced out at the galaxy of reporters who hung onto his every word. He winked and shrugged nonchalantly. He became their champion throughout the trial.

At the end of the confrontation with the dapper lawyer, Martino Belasci exited the witness cage, having done considerable damage to his credibility. With his usual panache he stepped down from the witness cage as if he hadn't been remotely touched by the goings-on. Sure of himself, he strutted through the high-domed chamber, his movements orchestrated by the accompanied boos and jeers given to men of his stamp by the demonstrative spectators which hardly phased him. He glanced from left to right nodding with mechanical and political know-how. Then suddenly he stopped dead in his tracks.

For a split second Belasci floundered. He found himself staring into the incredibly blue eyes of Stefano Modica. He stopped long enough to bring attention to himself and noticeable unwanted attention to Modica, who cursed in-

wardly that he'd forgotten to wear his dark glasses on this
tinued out the door amid much speculation as to who and
day.

As Modica calmly averted his head and feigned preoccupation with other activity in the courtroom, Belasci con-
what had caused the Minister's temporary loss of poise.

The slight commotion and noticeable murmurs in the
courtroom caused the men seated at the *Avvocato's* table
to turn around and attempt to fathom the goings on.
Basile leaned in toward his co-counsel to ask what was
causing the commotion. Del Vecchio wasn't certain, but he
felt it had something to do with the man seated in the
third row, second from the aisle to the left of the courtroom. *Avvocato* Basile turned around matter of factly,
glanced over his shoulders, and caught Modica's well-practiced bland expression without a glimmer of response from
the American.

"Who is he?" asked Basile.

"Not sure. Whoever he is, he sure caused the Minister a
few bad moments. He acted as if his balls were caught in
a vise."

"Find out who he is," replied Basile and returned to his
brief.

Outside the Palace of Justice, Minister Belasci affected a
benign, fixed politician's smile to cover the anger and humiliation he suffered at the hands of *Avvocato* Basile. Disapproval of this high official expressed by the crowds
included an untranslatable Italian vulgarity of facial and
hand gestures. When he passed, backs were turned to him.
Flanked on either side by *carabinieri* guards, he moved
imperiously through the milling crowds and entered his
limousine as photographers captured his departure on film.
Impervious to the sneers and jeers and silent rebuke, Minister Belasci waved mechanically to the hostile crowds as
the sleek limousine crawled through narrow streets and
hastened back to Rome.

Irked by the ill treatment, he hastily poured himself a
stiff shot of whiskey from the portable bar in the luxurious
hotel on wheels. He downed it, then he poured another
and another and still another until he felt more relaxed.

Sonsofbitches! All of them! That stupid, stupid jackass,
Franchina! Hadn't he told him Vincenzo wasn't the Judas
he had pegged him to be? That he had permitted those
two clowns Cala and Franchina to talk him into such stupidity was not to be believed. Goddamnit! Goddamnit!
And if they weren't enough to gall him, that courtroom

flamingo, Basile, had done a more adequate job of blistering his ass.

What stuck in Belasci's craw more than Basile's outrageous behavior was the total lack of respect accorded him. Moreover, he was furious that neither Presidente Ginestra nor the Prosecutor General had apprised him of the existence of such an inculpating letter, or that it had been permitted in evidence. Long before this, the letter could have been removed from the files or destroyed. Now, with Basile's insinuations and the letter itself a matter of record, he'd have to pursue another avenue. Taking priority over all this was the face of a man out of his past. Those remarkable blue eyes and easily identifiable good looks belonged to a man he knew quite well several years before.

"Get me a file on *Avvocato* Luigi Basile," Belasci instructed his secretary Marcello Barone, when he stalked into his office at the Ministry in Rome. "I want to know all there is to know about this insolent upstart!"

Marcello nodded his blond curly head and bowed out instantly when he recognized the temper his boss displayed. Belasci drummed his fingers on his desk impatiently for several moments. He picked up his private phone and asked the operator to connect him with the American Embassy. "No, no, no! I do *not* wish to speak with the Ambassador. I wish extension 711."

"*Amico,* without acknowledging me, you know who this is?"

"*Si,*" came the reply.

"*Va bene.* I have special service for you to perform."

"*Si.* You have but to ask."

"I will leave a name with Julio at Ernesto's Trattoria at dinner. I will need a complete file on him. Where he is and what he's involved in presently. It is vital I know in whose jurisdiction he operates."

"*Communisto?*"

"No. *Americano.* State Department."

"That narrows it down, *grazie.*"

"I have little time. There must be files on him. Do you have access to war records? No, don't answer. If you do it would be in 1943-45 files. It is vital you get back to me, *subito!*"

Belasci hung up before the man could reply. He picked up a newspaper from a batch placed on his desk by his secretary. In headlines, the communist papers screamed:

"BELASCI TESTIFIES TODAY! *Will ghost of Salvatore shake him into speaking the truth? Or will he continue to lie as he's done so skillfully in the past?"*

Belasci tossed the paper from him in disgust. These fucking Reds! How much longer would he have to suffer their outrageous slander before he could rid himself of them once and for all?

Stefano Modica tried to remain as obscure as possible, but it was not meant to be. At luncheon recess, he was beseiged by countless reporters asking his identity and why Minister Belasci had reacted as he did. Photographers tried to take his photo and in each Modica skillfully evaded them by holding his hands to his face or glancing away from the lenses. He tried to convince them he had no idea why the Minister had gazed at him, in fact he attempted to convince them the Minister had been looking at the woman next to him and not him at all. The newsmen finally gave up thinking there might be a story there and walked away from him in a huff.

He chose a small cafe for lunch not far from the Palace of Justice, so he could hurry back to the courtroom to hear the balance of General Cala's testimony whose words had been interrupted previously. There were several things bothering Stefano besides the look of recognition on Martino Belasci's face, and knowing he would have to face the possibility of being tailed soon enough, he concentrated on the other jarring disturbances. If he had the original portfolio of Salvatore's, where in hell did Vincenzo get all the documents he presented to the court? He felt certain he had the original letter written by Belasci to Salvatore locked in his safe in San Francisco. Yet, day after day, there had been more presented one after another, all those affadavits of which he held the originals. How, then? He had been tempted to visit Vincenzo, but couldn't without bringing attention upon himself—unwanted attention. Stefano sensed that the end was coming soon. Damnit! He could almost guess at the outcome! Wishing he wouldn't be as predictable as his mind told him he'd be, he paid his check and returned to court.

Somewhere, somehow, they all got sidetracked in this court of Tribunal and although the Salvatore affair was never to have been aired at the Portella trial, the Magistrate seemed unable to control his courtroom or its players. The reconstruction of Salvatore's death took place.

"May I stress, so that it is perfectly clear to this court," began General Cala in his quiet apologetic voice, 'that I was *not* at the scene of the action when tragedy struck Salvatore. It's my understanding that de Montana had gone to the house of de Meo in Castelvetrano at approximately twelve midnight to talk with his cousin. Major Franchina waited outside in the courtyard, machine gun ready, until three A.M. Finally from inside the house came sounds of violent quarreling voices. Salvatore was heard to have shouted obscenities. Suddenly the door opened. De Montana ran outside followed by Salvatore. It's my understanding that Major Franchina permitted de Montana to pass, then he riddled Salvatore with machine gun fire. It's possible that de Montana might have wounded Salvatore, but it was the Major who inflicted the fatal shots."

When *Avvocato* Basile pointed out that this testimony differed from the "Official Report," General Cala became noncommital. He then elaborated on the appalling situation existing between the law enforcement agencies in Sicily, how both factions had been deterrants to him. His manner, one of profound regret, as if he were loath to put a fellow officer in so shabby a light, influenced the Tribunal effectively. General Cala then admitted, under oath, that he'd received reports inculpating Inspector Semano in the Portella affair—by supplying guns and amunition to the bandits whom he'd hired to perform the May 1 crime. General Cala continued: Through covert means, I was forced to protect my position as head of the FSB against all the treachery perpetrated upon us by the security police. While lives were being needlessly lost in a battle against the bandits, it came to my attention that the security police escorted foreign correspondents to Salvatore's camp to interview him. They even had the audacity to permit a motion picture film to be made of the bandit's life while we were miles away in the heat of battle. Such blatant affrontry was possible only through the *entente* existing between Salvatore and the security police."

President Ginestra appeared to be shocked at the corrupt goings-on. Having never heard such an admission by so high ranking an officer his embarrassment grew more pronounced and he was obviously flustered by the open declaration. The people were also impressed by General Cala's straightforwardness. The lawyers didn't move for cross-examination. They all felt the General was too remote and detached from the main thrust of the action, further they focused profound interest on the next witness, *Avvocato* de Meo, the Mafia lawyer in whose courtyard Salvatore's body had been found. By now it became ap-

964

parent that de Meo must somehow be involved in the demise of Salvatore.

Having already given three versions of what transpired the night of Salvatore's death, and with each version came a modification of the facts, Antonio de Meo had prepared his final and still libelous version.

"Salvatore had fallen asleep in his bedroom when Vincenzo de Montana arrived at approximately midnight. I retired to my room after admitting de Montana and fell asleep. Sometime later, awakened by the sound of gunfire, I saw de Montana run past my door shouting, 'I've killed him! Salvatore is dead.' He ran past me, downstairs and out the door. I ran to the bedroom and saw for myself, Salvatore was dead. In a state of frenzy, I, too, ran from the house in an attempt to escape, but I was halted by Major Franchina who led me back upstairs. I was ordered to clear away all traces of blood from the bed. We both dressed Salvatore and carried him into the courtyard. I went back into my house and closed the door. A while later, I heard a short burst of machine gun fire, this was followed by Major Franchina's call for water . . ."

There followed more lies and distortions followed by denials and counter accusations. What struck the reporters more than the spoken words of the many people who offered their versions of that night preceding the morning of July 5, were those words left unspoken by both Major Franchina and Vincenzo de Montana. Both these men vied for the stellar role as Salvatore's assassin, yet neither would reconstruct a detailed story of that particular night.

"You're certain you're all right, Vincenzo?" asked Gabriella during this her final visit with him, one she had wheedled and cajoled from the Prefect. "Bastards! Not only have they refused to let me bring you food, but this is to be our last visit. They say since I'm not a relative they can do nothing." She hinted how they threatened to cancel her licenses for the hostelry.

"It's a marvel they even permitted your presence this many times, Gabriella," said Vincenzo solemnly. "Listen, I don't want anything to happen to you, you hear?"

"Don't worry about me, Sicilian. I can handle myself. I know a few little *peccados* these high and mighty politicians have committed. If they get too demanding and turn their superior noses up at me, they'll find they've tangled with a feisty porcupine. How does it look for you?" she asked, concerned.

Utterly confident, he boasted, "How can they touch me?

965

The proof is before them. As partisans of the government we did as we were ordered. Do they dare touch a hair on our heads without bringing Belasci and de Aspanu down with us? Only pardons can follow. Pardons and we'll all be free."

Gabriella studied her Sicilian friend. Well tailored in a taupe wool suit and beige blouse, her presence marked by the fragrance of Chanel No. 5, she sat smoking a cigarette across from him in the small cubicle permitted a prisoner with a visitor.

"There's someone at the villa, someone I don't trust. He is inordinately interested in the machinations of your lawyer," she told him quietly.

"Who?" The tone of her voice alerted him more than the information.

"He signs his name G. O'Hoolihan. His passport is Irish, yet he is an American. Of this I am positive."

"G. O'Hoolihan?" echoed Vincenzo. "But, G. O'Hoolihan is a woman!"

"I know," replied Gabriella tightly. She explained how often she'd seen this man in the area of *Avvocato* Basile's suite of rooms. That the name O'Hoolihan, one she'd never forget, alerted her to him. She continued:

"There is something cold about this man. Cold and dangerous. I see it in his eyes. He has no friends, makes no phone calls, receives no mail, yet each day he arises and departs for the courthouse simultaneously with your lawyer and his associates. I've had him followed. It seems all he does is attend court, dines out once in a while, and keeping within the confines of his room for the most part, he does mail several bulk packages to the United States. I paid a clerk handsomely to reveal the address on these parcels. It's always the same: To Gina O'Hoolihan. So there's the full circle."

"You say he's in court each day?" He stoked his memory in vain.

"Yes." Gabriella paused. "It's best you tell your lawyer." She gave him a description of Modica, complete with the possibility he might have only one leg. "He walks stiff legged, as if he has some infirmity."

If Vincenzo had entertained any thought that the man could remotely be Stefano Modica, he dispelled the thought at the mention of an infirmity. He'd no way of knowing about Stefano's disability. "I'll look for him in court tomorrow," he assured her. "Gabriella," he said, taking her hands into his, "why do you come and risk these

966

personal dangers? Practically everyone has deserted me, you know."

"Perhaps that's why," she said quietly. "You were a friend to me once when I needed a friend. Even Tori never wronged me. It wasn't his fault if he couldn't love me."

"For not being Sicilian, you've got plenty of *fegato*—guts. You're a champion in my eyes, Gabriella."

"For what? Befriending a man when he has no one? It happened to me once and someone helped me. It's only right that I pass on the gift."

Touched by her honesty, Vincenzo laughed lightly to ease his embarrassment. "*Managghia!* What a *bandita* you'd have made. Sonofagun! Riding alongside of us—with your guts we'd have faired better than we did. You were inspired to follow Salvatore once, Gabriella. What inspired you?" he asked softly.

"What does it matter how I was inspired? For a woman there is only one way. Her man inspires her. She's fortunate if he also is inspired. If not, well then, the story ends as it did with me and Tori. But tell me, Sicilian, how was it *you* were so inspired by your cousin? Why did you stay with him all those years? You told me you retired for a time due to your health, the time you were granted amnesty after the Partitionist's movement fizzled out. What inspired you to return to a life of banditry? You could have quit, lived a quiet life . . . saved yourself from all this." She seemed totally baffled.

Vincenzo listened to her intently and as he did his eyes took on curious lights. He felt his spirit accelerate to the health at the time. One day while sitting out this amnesty, excitement of another time.

"What inspired me? I'll tell you. It's true I was granted amnesty and Tori insisted I accept, due to my failing I was riding across the basin of the Conca d'Oro, headed toward the summit, when I encountered a skirmish in progress. Shootings. Guns exploding. Bombs roaring all around me. Everyone around ran to see what was happening. Me, too. The *carabinieri* had reenforced the *caserne* at Bellolampo. Hundreds of troops had converged to fight this invincible cousin of mine. It was beautiful. I was intrigued by the odds. Hundreds of men against how many? Fourteen—maybe fifteen? Well, it went against my nature to see such unfair measures. The next thing I knew I rode my horse swiftly into Tori's stronghold, joining him and shooting excitedly at the enemies. Any man who'd oppose so many men fearlessly had my loyalty and support eternally. Like the others, I shouted my *Viva Salvatores*."

"Yes."

"That's it."

"Nothing more?"

"What more did it take? I knew from then on my place was right alongside this courageous cousin of mine who tried to help our people to a better life."

"Yet, you slaughtered him." It was a quiet indictment.

Vincenzo felt her well-camouflaged contempt as the smile and excitement melted from his features. He went through a series of subtle changes visible to her. Avoiding her probing eyes, he replied. "Yes, I killed him. I had to—don't you see?"

"I see nothing. It's neither my business to ask nor my desire to know. You did what you had to do. Pray God, it's the right thing." Gabriella continued to stare at him inscrutably. "Listen, Sicilian, between us there's been truth. I cannot believe you assassinated Tori for whatever reasons your lips mouth."

Vincenzo gazed at her, his throat constricting. He was touched by her loyalty, but he could say nothing to her. He could take no chances.

Glancing about the cubicle, Gabriella lowered her voice to an inaudible whisper. "Is there anything you wish me to tell Santino Siragusa or Angelo Duca?"

"They are here?" he asked amazed.

"For a long time. Well disguised. I told Santino about this G. O'Hoolihan whoever he is. So don't worry. They'll keep an eye on him. Duca works at the hotel as a room service waiter. He's been able to stay close to this impostor and will do so until we know what he's up to."

"Santino's alive and well?" He couldn't seem to get this through his head.

"Shall I give him a message? Anything?"

"No. Nothing. Tell him to stay away. I'm confident all the men shall be vindicated of the charges against them."

"And me?"

"And you."

"You're sure?"

"I'm sure."

Sensing something complex in Vincenzo, something she didn't and couldn't hope to understand, she embraced him, sighing wistfully, unsure of when she might see him again.

"Gabriella?" Vincenzo grasped her shoulder, soft hand in his. "Thank you, *cara mia*, for all you've done for

Vincenzo. You're a champion. Even Tori believed this." He inhaled her perfume. "You are a lovely woman."

For a brief instant, her blue-green eyes swam in pools of tears. She swallowed hard. "Thank you for that, Sicilian. If we need to communicate, it shall be through your *avvocato*." She slipped her hand out of his and left him.

A uniformed waiter pushed an elaborate service cart into his suite of rooms and when Stefano noticed a bottle of champagne buried in crushed ice with two hollow-stemmed glasses, a chafing dish, ornate canapes, etc., he protested, "There must be some mistake—I never ordered this."

"No, but I did, *Signore* O'Hoolihan," said Gabriella in her German-accented Italian as she drifted into the room gowned in a cloud of shaded pink silks and ethereal chiffons. "Compliments of the management. *Buon compleano.* Happy birthday, *Signore.*"

Modica arched his brows in good humor. "But—how did you know? I confess, *Madama,* that I had completely forgotten this anniversary." He sniffed the fragrant air about him. "Your essence is as intoxicating as it is enchanting."

Gabriella accepted the compliment without comment. "Your passport told me. We at the Villa Etruria try to make our guests feel at home."

Modica tilted his head and smiled with profound appreciation. He watched as she dismissed the waiter with aplomb and took over the ritual of cooling the champagne and glasses. "You do that as if you were born to it. But, allow me. It is truly a man's duty." He moved closer to her and took the bottle from her hand.

"Tell me," she asked, moving around to the sofa. "What brings you here from Ireland? Are you a writer? Will you write of the trial? Perhaps a correspondent?"

"Why do you ask?"

"I've seen you in court several times and you always seem to be writing. I have friends among the bandits, *Signore.* Does that shock you?"

"I'm afraid nothing shocks me. Ah—uh—to whom have I the pleasure of addressing? I've seen you about the premises on occasion."

"*Principessa* Gabriella Rothschild. I am proprietor of this establishment."

It took several moments before Stefano connected the name. This was the woman Tori had written about in his diary? It was a stunning thought. Instantly his guard went

969

up. Earlier it became obvious to him she was trying to bait him. Disguising his feelings, Stefano bowed slightly. "What a pleasure, *Principessa*."

"Call me Gabriella." She accepted the filled champagne glass from him and made room for him as he moved toward the sofa.

"I can only stay briefly. I have many duties here at the villa. While you're here can we accommodate you with anything special? A companion perhaps?" Her dark lashes lifted, then fell over her luminous suggestive eyes.

"You—?"

"No. We have dealings with various establishments, shall we say, who for a price provide companions, if such a desire should arise in you."

"Then, thank you, no. *Only* if you yourself were available would I consider the suggestion. I am discriminating in my choice of companions."

"I come very high, *Signore*. Judging from your possessions, I can see I am out of your range." She had glanced about the bare room in a premature assessment of his worldly goods.

"Now, if I had a mind to entertain such provocative thoughts, understand, and I'm saying—if—just how high would high be?" he countered seductively.

"Too high for you, *Signore*. Money can't buy me."

"What then?"

"More than you or any other man could offer, I'm afraid." She drained her glass and Stefano refilled it.

More intrigued with each passing moment, he pressed. "Name it."

"Love and all that goes with it."

"You're right. I can't afford you," said Stefano.

"You see how it is? Whenever I see someone who appeals to me—it's always the same. I can form no lasting relationships. So, I do without."

"You may be missing something quite exquisite, Gabriella. It's a shame your requisites are so unrealistic."

And so it went. They made small talk for a time. He never asked her the questions she had hoped might give her a lead into the bandit's plight. He was all she had told Vincenzo—shrewd, cool, and sharp. She sensed something sinister behind his clear blue eyes, and a brain far too complex for her to fathom. She toyed with the idea of becoming intimate with him in order to pierce that veil of secretiveness. Soon he became a challenge to her. He made no mistakes, no slip-ups, to reveal his true identity.

The champagne nearly gone, Gabriella picked up the phone and ordered more to be sent to Modica's suit.

He was about to restrain her, but he changed her mind. He got little enjoyment these days and having imposed so rigorous a role on himself, one so demanding, it left him feeling dehumanized at times, he gave in. Besides, he was intrigued by this seductress, and moved by curiosity and a need, he told himself it might be worthwhile to see what Salvatore's ex-paramour wanted with him.

She moved about the room with exquisite feline movements designed to seduce him. Was it the champagne—the desperate need in his loins or both? Whatever, she became highly desirable to him. The emptiness—where his leg had been fastened to him, loomed before his eyes and she read his thoughts.

"Don't let that disturb you, *Signore* O'Hoolihan. It matters not to me," she told him, sensing his discomfort, "if you have one leg or ten."

Moments later they were in bed together and she was laughing with enjoyment. "You were right. Perhaps my expectations have been aimed too high. This is exquisite," she said breathlessly.

Exhausted after their sexual interlude, they fell asleep in each other's arms. Stefano wakened to shadows and darkness outside. He tried to move, but the weight of her body on his arms restricted him. Gently he removed his arm from under Gabriella's head. He turned from her, swung his legs out over the bed, and sat up holding his head. God, he hated champagne hangovers. Nothing's worse than a champagne head, he muttered to himself. He reached for his robe, slipped into it, and moved across to the French doors. A slight breeze fluttered through the open doors and the casements fluttered and billowed in the movement.

Stefano stiffened imperceptibly. His sixth sense at work made him move back against the wall and cautiously peer out at the darkened room. His brain churned. He had secured the doors earlier. How then, had they been opened? His eyes pierced the shadows. Slowly, he reached down into his prosthesis, removed the gun secreted in it, and cautiously moved toward the sleeping form on the bed. Stefano recalled when he'd slipped his arm out from under Gabriella's head it felt leaden. He secured the doors and quickly returned to the bed.

He stood over her, staring at her. His eyes had adjusted to the dark. She might have been sleeping except for the rush of blood bubbling up through her mouth and nose, staining her breasts and naked body. Her eyes—wide and fixed—looked like green glassy balls. He reached for the wall light. Seeing the grotesque body under the brash lights of reality sickened him. He shut his eyes, hoping to erase the sickening sight from his eyes.

Why, he asked himself. Gabriella had been talkative for a time and mentioned Salvatore and Vincenzo. But the giddiness that affected his brain from the champagne had dulled his perception for a time. But none of this really mattered. Stefano was concerned with why she was killed in his suite. Something told him he had to think and act fast. If only he had the presence of mind to refuse her gracious birthday offering, she might be alive. He shook his head in an effort to clear his head and promote more concise thought.

He had to get rid of the body. This was the first consideration. He moved in her direction. Only then did he see a knife buried to the hilt in her back. The fact she was still warm only heightened his anxiety and self-guilt. If only he'd awakened sooner. Stop punishing yourself, Modica, he told himself. He opened the corridor door; seeing nothing and no one stirring, he moved soundlessly over the carpeted floor in the direction of a door marked Service. He tried the handle. It opened into a linen supply closet, a large room with an adequate inventory of items needed for maintenance. He saw another room beyond this and headed for it. Inside the shadowy interior he opened a door leading to a laundry shoot spiraling toward the basement.

Less than ten minutes later, Gabriella's body was placed in this cubicle and found its way to the basement with the rest of the soiled laundry. Stefano had had several bad moments. She deserved a better fate than this, he told himself. Now it was up to him to fathom her death. Back in his room he quickly made up the room with fresh linens he'd removed from the linen supply, having removed the blood-stained sheets to wrap Gabriella in earlier. Stefano showered and dressed not a moment too soon. A sharp knock came at the door.

"*Avanti*," called Stefano, seated on the sofa as indolently as he could be.

"*Me scusa, signore*," said the bell captain. "*La Principessa* is needed in her office." He craned his neck, trying to see beyond Stefano in the next room.

"Forgive me. *Principessa*—who?" Modica asked blandly.

"*Principessa* Rothschild—who else?" The scoundrel's

suspicious dark eyes were drawn together sharply over his aquiline nose.

"You must be mistaken, I know of no such *Principessa*," countered Stefano, in a thickly clotted voice.

"But *signore,* excuse me. She was here earlier with the champagne."

"Ah," said Stefano. "*La amministratrice.* The manager? But she left long ago."

Fifteen minutes later a surly bell captain had returned with two security police who questioned Stefano and looked around the premises, fully scrutinizing the neatly kept room. They asked him a series of usual questions, to which Modica answered as economically as possible. He was compelled to show them his passport and letters of credit. Everything being in order, the trio left, arguing candidly in Italian, calling the bell captain every kind of jerk imaginable.

For the next several hours, Stefano tried to piece together parts of an insoluble riddle. There was little to go on except that someone wanted him dead. Considering what had happened in the recent past, it wasn't surprising. How could he have known that Gabriella Rothschild had brought about her own destruction by claiming to be a friend of Vincenzo de Montana? One thing was certain; the affect of her death was devastating upon him. Who could cushion the shock of a murder when it happens inches away from you?

Devoured by curiosity and consumed with the unfairness of the tragedy, Stefano felt an intolerable outrage at the behavior of those who sought to destroy him. His first instinct was to run—flee the Villa Etruria. Second thoughts came to him, stabilizing his emotions, and he felt it safer to remain. He sensed the trial's end was in sight. So, grim-faced and determined, he took hold of himself and forced himself to be more alert, more on guard than he'd been lately.

He continued with the role he'd wrapped himself into these past many months. The only salvation to his sanity over this calamitous affair was that the trial moved ahead swiftly and he involved himself in its daily dramatics, hoping against hope no further complications would arise to thwart him and force him to leave prematurely.

CHAPTER 70

The pendulum swung back into the negative zones of Vincenzo's life late in October, 1951. Modica observed the carefully constructed edifice of belabored facts upon which Vincenzo had fabricated his defense began to show signs of crumbling.

Infallible as it might have seemed when originally planned, the air-tight alibi Vincenzo had submitted for his nonparticipation in the May First tragedy, blew up in his face. X-ray films taken of his lungs on that date in 1947 submitted to the court had been viewed by eleven specialists. Among them, four of the nation's most renown experts in the field of pulmonary disorders, in a scholarly debate proceeded to explain what the evidence revealed. The defense argued no one in the condition revealed in the radiographic studies could have expended the effort needed to ride horseback to Portella and back to Montegatta, or perform the rigorous duties described in testimony on that day. The experts concurred totally with the defense.

Meanwhile, out of left field, in an unforseen move, the people's lawyer, Concetto Bellini requested permission to call in their own experts, who, when summoned and after examination of the X-rays in question, disagreed with the experts on every point.

Things moved swiftly, in rapid-fire order. An old, well-respected physician, Dr. Augusto, a highly regarded old veteran with an excellent war record, was called to testify. He recalled vividly the X-rays were taken on May 1, 1947, because de Montana had arrived very ill, coughing blood in large quantities. He had attempted to take X-rays immediately, but, due to the holiday, the electric current had been weak. Therefore, he was put to taking X-rays the following day, which were stamped and dated accordingly.

General Cala had testified under oath. "In my investigations of the Portella affair, I arrived at the conclusion de Montana had been nowhere near the site of the tragedy, due to the severe nature of his illness.

"To reinforce this statement, Major Franchina had also

sworn under oath at the outset of the trial, Lieutenant Greco of Piana dei Greci told me personally that Vincenzo de Montana did not participate in the dastardly affair."

Lieutenant Greco called upon to testify had countered hotly. "Never! Never did I make such a statement to Major Franchina!"

Avvocato Bellini produced an unexpected witness and fairly shook the court. Francesco Conti, an electrical engineer on duty at the power plant at Monreale on the day of the purported ¬assacre, swore before God and the Tribunal, "To offset the danger of a power failure on this holiday, two additional transformers had been installed." This man, a hard-working, God-fearing man with no political bent, brought records to attest to this procedure. "There couldn't possibly have been a power failure on the day in question," he repeated, asserting himself with provincial sincerity, great courtesy, and respect for the Court of Tribunal.

Avvocato Basile turned to his client with blazing eyes. Blood rushed to his face. "Why didn't you tell me the truth, Goddamnit!" he hissed. "Never mind! We'll talk later!" Basile shook his head, held his breath, and waited for the volcano to erupt, with that all too familiar feeling, that sinking sensation that comes from losing a case.

Vincenzo was silent, his face expressionless. His palms grew sweaty and itchy. He watched the procedure with mixed feelings.

The courtroom rocked with emotions. All eyes, trained on Vincenzo, continued to speculate on the outcome as they listened to the puckered old figs on the bench.

Because the men shooting from Mt. Cometa had been Salvatore's men at one time, the Tribunal took no notice of the possible treachery that erupted in opposing camps. They claimed there was no difference between those men ordered to demonstrate and those who shot to kill. Even the expert testimony of Lieutenant Greco, who maintained from the beginning and after extensive investigation that the men shooting from Mt. Pizzuta couldn't have fired the lethal bullets, failed to impress the Tribunal.

Caught in this one blatant lie, Vincenzo's testimony for the most had been discredited. The lies and obvious perjuries of most principal parties including Major Franchina, who had in the year of trials changed their testimony at whim, became prime factors in influencing the final verdict. But it hadn't ended for this military snake—not yet.

Another surprise witness presented by the prosecution to

attack the credibility of Captain Franchina's sworn statements was the widow Giuletta Grissi, whom the former Marshal didn't recognize at first. Dressed in her black widow weeds, her dark hair draped by a matching shawl accented the fire in her eyes which she kept lowered. Her version of that early dawn on July 5, 1950, differed considerably from Major Franchina's version.

"I saw figures moving about the courtyard. It was dark—no moon in the sky, so I saw only shadows. But I saw this man, Major Franchina, a man I would know anyplace, moving about with a gun in his hand. I saw him shoot to kill an assistant and drag his body into the front of the yard outside the courtyard, next to the street.

"You lie!" shouted Major Franchina. "Who is this woman that she should question my authority? How could she recognize me? I've never laid eyes on the woman. I demand you charge her with perjury!"

"Silence, Major. Your time will come to contest her statement."

Avvocato Basile, who wondered why this statement was permitted at all, since it wasn't related to Portella Della Ròsa, sat back and listened intently, without objection, in hopes of what might be revealed by this woman—and why.

"You realize, *Signora*, you are contesting the words of a great hero, a fine military man?" prodded the Magistrate, leaning toward the witness.

The widow Grissi nodded. "I am sure that I am jeopardizing my own life by testifying, Mr. Presidente, but my duty as a citizen is far more important. I tell you, Salvatore was dead before he was placed in the courtyard. Major Franchina never killed him. He lacks the courage to execute a man of Salvatore's stamp. His *forte* is to kill men like Private Foti, a man who assisted him."

"How are you so certain it was Major Franchina you saw?" asked the Major's lawyer. "It was dark, no moon, and difficult to see from a second-floor window."

"This same man came to my door and knocked, begging for water. As I said, I would know Major Franchina anyplace." Widow Grissi reached under her shawl and handed the Presidente Ginestra a manila envelope.

He extended his arm, reached across his desk, and took it from her. He opened it and two photos fell out, both somewhat aged and yellowed, but quite clear. The Presidente's blue eyes scanned the contents and looked disapprovingly in her direction and coughed. Guilietta Grissi lowered her eyes demurely. How sweet is the nectar of revenge she thought.

"Let the court know this witness is fully acquainted with Major Franchina." He handed the photos to the court clerk, those intimate photos inculpating her with Marshal Franchina in Montegatta when her son Danillo was killed at Salvatore's hand. Widow Grissi had her revenge. Salvatore was dead. The man who betrayed her was about to receive his just desserts.

In those ensuing moments, Major Franchina sweated bullets. He leaned in to whisper to his lawyer. "She lies, I tell you. I've never see than woman since the morning of July 5, 1950. She lies!" he hissed.

Reaching for the evidence, after it was tagged by the clerk, he examined the photos inscrutably and, flushing a beet red, the lawyer handed them to his client. Peering scornfully at them, the Major's lower jaw fell open in astonishment, then recognition. Instantly his eyes darted to the widow in time to see the gleam of triumph in them. He flushed with displeasure and hotly contested the woman's testimony to his lawyers in hushed whispers and animated gestures.

Avvocato Basile examined the photos, shrugged, and handed them to his client. Vincenzo recognized them instantly. He stared from the widow Grissi to Major Franchina knowingly. Full recollection of the execution of young Danillo struck him and he sat back, silently marveling the avenues of Sicilian justice. He later explained the situation to *Avvocato* Basile.

However titillating and revealing this was, the episode had little effect on the trial and when the Tribunal ended session, the verdicts came as a shock to all.

Prosecutor General Volpe delivered a scathing argument at the last and concluded: "It's even possible that Salvatore himself devised the crossfire strategy for the purpose of exculpating himself. His warring talents and military tactics were widely known and respected." He sneered triumphantly at the defense.

President Ginestra, who demonstrated utter contempt for Vincenzo de Montana, praised Salvatore, stating honor should be given such a man for his discretion in not betraying the names of the instigators of the Portella affair. Communist lawyer Concetto Bellini, it was later learned, had no real interest in defending the people's rights; his aim had been directed in spotlighting the *entente* between Belasci and the bandits. For whatever other purpose the Reds had in bringing pressure to bear upon Vincenzo de Montana, other than to explode any agreement that might have existed between him and Belasci, would remain a mystery until Belasci became Premier of Italy, when his past would arise out of the depths of corruption to dim the lights of his victories.

Vincenzo's well-organized defense with the countless devastation of documents revealing that law enforcement agencies hadn't been pure in their past dealings were now viewed with skepticism. All his testimony, much of great importance, was overshadowed with the out-and-out fraud of the X-rays.

Vincenzo was dealt a blow he hadn't expected, when a very vindictive President Ginestra, in his assessment of the Montegattan, personally sentenced him and the former bandits to life imprisonment at hard labor.

Results of the Viterbo trial brought about indictments against Major Franchina on the grounds of perjury, fraud, and collusion with Salvatore's forces. Trial was set for him at a later date.

Charges brought against former Chief Inspector D'Verde for conspiracy, collusion, dereliction to duty, and others too numerous to mention were dropped when news of his suicide rocked the nation. Later, this would prove to be false, for it hadn't been a suicide after all, but an out-and-out murder by unknown assailants. Chief Inspector Zanorelli, transferred to Livorno, near *Terra Diablo* in central Italy because he'd been unsuccessful in locating Salvatore's portfolio, was of no further use to the Christian Democrats. Sent to a communist-infiltrated area, it was hoped he'd be put out of the way.

The trial ended as Modica had predicted and the verdicts were certain to be appealed to the Court of Cassation. As long as he lived, Modica would never forget the open-mouthed expressions of astonishment as the bandits gaped at President Ginestra when he sentenced them to life at hard labor. Their eyes, turbulent and defiant, grew scornful when they filed arrogantly from the courtroom.

"You bastard! You stupid, stupid bastard!" *Avvocato* Basile tore his client apart. "If I had any idea—any at all that your alibi was purely a fabrication I'd have thrown it out of the defense! We didn't need it! Understand? We didn't need it! The fact that you had been at Portella would have reinforced your testimony that your side hadn't expended the lethal bullets. The moment Bellini proved your alibi false your credibility sunk so low even Jesus Christ couldn't have resurrected it! You stupid sonofabitch! Didn't I tell you to level with me? Goddamnit! You screwed up good, de Montana!" Basile, past containment, thundered, "You succeeded in seducing me good, didn't you?"

Basile had grown fond of de Montana during the course of the long, arduous trial. Now he felt betrayed by such stupidity and lack of confidentiality on the part of his client. Pacing back and forth on the floor of the lawyer's room at Viterbo prison, redfaced and emotionally overwrought, the fiery young lawyer could only glare indignantly at Vincenzo. The Sicilian tried to effect an outer show of bravado.

"You can appeal, can't you? Listen, Basile, Cala and Franchina cooked up that alibi for me. First, it was Tori's idea, then the FSB got hold of it and convinced me it was air-tight. Since they were supposed to back my play, it seemed better than admit I was at Portella at all."

"If you trusted them so fucking much why didn't you hire them as your barristers!" snapped Basile impatiently. His impatience gave way to anger, anger to despair, as he pulled up a chair closer to his client. "*Allora*, listen carefully to me now, Vincenzo." He paused to light Vincenzo's cigarello with his slim gold lighter and clicked it shut. He sat down and spoke in confidential tones. "You realize you're in the same position as Salvatore was in before his death."

"What position?"

"You know too much. You're a threat to them."

"*Và bene. Va bene.* I want them to squirm as they made me squirm and for what they did to my cousin."

"They'll kill you," said Basile quietly and realistically.

"It's too late to think of killing me now. The truth will ruin them all."

"Then they really have nothing to lose, have they?" He tried to get his point across. "You know, I've got to be some kind of jackass to try to help you now! A man intent on suicide!"

Vincenzo stared at him for a moment, then he let his eyes look past the lawyer toward the window and out past the verdant hills of Tuscany. He rose to his feet. "*Va! Va! Non me stonare cazzi!*" he said impatiently. "Don't aggravate my balls!"

"Why? Tell me why you are letting yourself in for this kind of treatment? We both know you didn't kill Salvatore. Nothing you do will bring him back. *Allora—*" He waited for an answer.

"You wouldn't understand."

"Try me."

Vincenzo shrugged.

"What about Maria Angelica?"

Vincenzo turned to him fire in his eyes. He was shaking inside, "Don't mention her name again, Basile. I don't want her brought into this! She's suffered enough!"

"You know what she's doing, Vincenzo? Where she's been for the past year? I made a point to learn, hoping I could convince her to talk some sense into your head. You know there's still a chance for you. Maybe not here. In some other country—some place."

Vincenzo gazed around the small, barren room with cracked plaster walls and a leprous ceiling in the ancient old lock up, as if he sought some avenue of escape from his lawyer's remarks. "Where is she?" he asked finally.

"In a place called . . ." Basile glanced at the small book he removed from his pocket, "Neptune's Daughters."

"Neptune's Daughters—I don't understand."

"She works there, I'm told—in Palermo."

Vincenzo paled. Disbelief flooded his face. Behind his hot, painful eyes he could feel the mad throbbing of his brain. He felt sick.

"She could no longer remain in Montegatta. Not even her parents wanted her, I'm told. Not after consorting with Salvatore's assassin."

Vincenzo moved toward the window and pounded his fists hard on the concrete sill below the iron bars. His breath came in short gasps and the wild pulsating throb in his head increased. He buried his head in his hands.

"I'm sorry, Vincenzo. I thought you should know."

It took a few moments before he took himself in hand. He straightened up, resumed his courtly posture, and with obvious *maschiezzo*, took control of the situation. "Basile, you will see to it she lacks for nothing. If you will bring me a special form from my bank, I will sign it and give you the necessary funds to take her out of Neptune's Daughters, *va bene*? She deserves this at least."

"But—what about you? It's not too late to join her and make some plans for your future. Perhaps something can be worked out. Salvatore's portfolio for your feedom".

"It's too late. The wheels of vengeance have been set in motion."

"You're doing all this for vengeance?" asked Basile. He heard it but couldn't believe it. His young clerk had hit it on the head after all.

"You're not Sicilian. You wouldn't understand."

"I don't understand that kind of talk, de Montana. This is the twentieth century—not the middle ages!"

"Basile—listen to me. Even as my lawyer, it's best you don't know everything. I want the top man—and all those other bastards who deceived us. It's a matter of honor now. Somehow, someway, it will happen. I want several things. First, the reward money, nearly fifty thousand dollars to give to my Aunt Antigone. She's entitled to something for all the grief she's endured. Those bastards, Belasci, Oliatta, Malaterra, and Barbarossa should have taken care of her. Did they? Hah!"

"You did all this for the reward?" Basile was bewildered. "You sure as hell sell yourself cheaply."

"At least Franchina can't claim the reward. I managed to discredit that fucking bastard! Liars! All of them! You think the trial at Viterbo is what I aimed for?" He laughed. "I'm waiting for the trial of Salvatore's murder to commence. Then you'll see how the pigs slip in their own shit."

Basile looked at his client with a subtle affectation of a languid jaguar. "Take care, *amico*. You're caught in several crossfires; between *carabinieri* and security police, and between the Mafia and highly placed politicians. They may not touch you now, because they've not located Salvatore's portfolio. But, if I were a betting man I wouldn't give a *lira* for your life in the next few months, *caro mio*."

Vincenzo laughed. He should have been bitter and vindictive and he had reasons to be critical of the injustice meted to him in court that day. He was the injured party who should have been licking his wounds. Instead, he laughed. "You aren't trying to lull me into a false sense of security, are you?" he asked the lawyer.

Avvocato Basile shook his head with a mixture of regret and wonder. "You know where you go from here?"

"*Si*. Ucciardone Prison in Palermo—no?" he said in a showy, superficial cleverness with unruffled composure.

"Goddamnit, de Montana! I wish I could pound some sense into that Sicilian hardhead of yours!" He had put up with a lot that day, but Basile had to admit his client was a gutsy bastard. "All I can say is you've got an overload of guts, *amico*," he exasperated at last.

"No, *dottore*, what I've got is plenty of insurance."

Basile's head bobbed up and down like a sinker on a turbulent lake. "All right, all right, my friend. Suit yourself. But you'd better make fucking sure you keep up the payments on those premiums. Understand?" retorted Basile with an edge to his voice. He felt terribly depressed. "I detest that you have to hear more bad news to compound that in court today," he added.

"What is it? Go on, *professore*, I can take anything," he said with bravado.

"Gabriella Rothschild is dead."

The shock on Vincenzo's face turned his face white as death. His head shook in disbelief. "When—where—how?" he managed to stammer. "Who?"

Basile explained. "They found her body in the cellar of the villa. No one knows how—who—or why. But if it's an educated guess you want—"

"No. I want nothing. I know—*who*."

Basile left him seated at the wooden table and chair provided for prisoners, his hands clasped together, before him, his head inclined like a fallen bright bird.

Vincenzo came to accept the news of Gabriella's death with typical Sicilian vengeance. Shocked at first, his anger became fired with emotionalism. "Bastards!! Those filthy egg-sucking ferrets! Gabriella never hurt anyone!" He had slammed his fist against the prison wall again and again until the side of his hand was bruised black and blue. "All because of me!" It took a while before his anger cooled into self-blame and wallowing in this guilt he grew silent. There wasn't much he could do from his prison perch.

Torn between Maria Angelica's fate and Gabriella's last rewards, he felt a total desperation. "Tori," he wailed internally. "What do I do now?"

Ucciardone, a prison controlled by the Mafia, was perhaps the most unique prison in the world. Many powerful *mafiosi* did time here in the manner of the nobility enjoying the conveniences of a rest home. Fully in control of the Mafia, the governor—or warden is hired solely at the discretion of the *mafiosi*, who hire the guards and every other worker in the imposing complex.

Underworld czars, feudal landlords and felonious politicians who found life a trifle too hot on the outside from time to time, arranged for long, leisurelike sentences in comfortably furnished cells and had all their meals catered by the best restaurants in Palermo. And when needed allowed for the cohabitation privileges of either wives or prostitutes.

Profitable businesses, run from inside the prison promoted by the more enterprising, flourished readily with considerable graft passed about to the more cooperative. Oftentimes an inmate registered legally had occasionally absented himself over long periods of time to perform some nefarious activities on the outside. Later, if anything came of his involvement, his alibi was air-tight. How could a prisoner incarcerated within the walls of such an institution have committed a crime on the outside? How, indeed? Actually, Ucciardone was in a sense a Mafia university where apprentices received further refresher courses in new developments in crime.

Inmates, recipients to severe beatings, ended up with permanent injuries and broken bones when they didn't adhere to certain directives. Casualties were high. Hospital records, easily falsified, indicated a vast number of—accidents—such as slipping in wet corridors, falling down stairs, slipping on a bar of soap, etc. An excess of a hundred such cases were reported yearly.

Deposited in this den of thieves, murderers, and carnivorous villains, protected only by his newly assumed role as Salvatore's assassin, a self-imposed introversion and a general mistrust of anyone and everyone around him, Vincenzo de Montana was afforded the privacy he wanted, for most all others kept their distance. To wile away his time until the Salvatore murder trial was scheduled, Vincenzo began to write his biography. He also took up and became proficient at needlepoint. He was denied visitors and no permits were issued by the Minister of the Interior permitting interviews with the press. His only companion was the little sparrow he brought with him from Viterbo.

Here, Vincenzo remained isolated in a special wing of this unique prison set aside for the former bandits and himself. It was practically impossible for anyone to penetrate the security of this wing of the prison complex. Not only was each employee and guard carefully selected for his role, he was trained to instantly detect any deviation from normal procedure. Only priests and physicians and lawyers were permitted in the cell blocks. If an illness occurred necessitating the removal of any inmate to the infirmary, he was guarded by no less than four expert marksmen until the inmate was carefully secured inside the infirmary, again provided with tight security.

Governor Casabianco received explicit instructions when the bandits were remanded into his custody. "The spotlight of the world is focused upon us," said the Prosecutor General to the prison warden. "We can't afford to be disgraced internationally by the occurrence of any incidents until after the murder trial. You do understand, my dear Governor?"

Understanding perfectly well, Governor Casabianco tightened security instantly in the bandit quarters. He wanted no close scrutiny or investigation of his prison. The safety of Salvatore's men would prevail if it took the last breath in his body, at least until the impending trial when the disposition of all concerned would be decided.

During the next two years at Ucciardone Prison while awaiting trial, Vincenzo's life was filled with countless upheavals which daily eroded his guts. The balladmakers so terribly fond of Salvatore had written many a fanciful verse about their magnificient King of Montegatta and vented their lyrical spleen at that Judas Iscariot, that murderer, that venomous snake in the grass, Vincenzo de Montana. What a vile traitor! That bloody assassin! Would they ever fix that lowest of lowest incarnation of Judas? The streets and airwaves filled constantly with heartrending songs of passion and melodramatic torment, overwrought with frenzy and the vile treachery and black-hearted betrayal of that scurrilous dog, de Montana.

Vincenzo hadn't counted on this. The strain proved too much. His emotions were tuned to the breaking point. Each time he turned on the radio, the constant allusions to that malevolent act as reported at the trial came at him in dramatic narration and impassioned songs. Through his lawyer he brought suit against the balladmakers and recording companies for criminal libel. The cases were subsequently dismissed for no one could prevent songs from being sung on the lips of those who idolized Salvatore.

In his so-called act of honor Vincenzo had traded one reputation for another; the latest jacket had damned near strangled him. His life never seemed darker than in those years following Tori's death. Silent, alone, ignored by his former companions despite his attempt to save them from an inevitable fate, he was still shunned because they believed he had assassinated his cousin. Never has a man gone through such agony to make himself appear guilty of a crime he hadn't committed. The fact that his former companions believed the myth strengthened his resolve for that future day of reckoning.

The lonely, self-imposed life of a recluse was not one to which Antigone Salvatore took easily. However, it permitted her more peace of mind than enduring the pity of her neighbors. For so long after Tori's funeral, the daily pilgrimages to made to church each morning for mass would draw mixed reactions from small groups of women and men huddled together whispering innuendos. The retailing of her private sorrows for the purposes of small talk was unbearable to her and highly offensive. Inevitably there would appear on her face visible annoyance as she passed them.

Soon, she no longer went to church. She felt she could pray to her Maker just as effectively within the chambers of her own heart.

On July 28, 1952, Antigone, bent and stooped, working industriously in her garden, chanting her rosary, glanced up and looked about the area quizzically, certain she had heard her name called. She shook her head and resumed her hoeing. Long ago she learned to ignore these voices, just as she had ignored the hordes of reporters who clamored for interviews, and kept her curious neighbors out of her life by not taking them into her confidence. Her refusal to be maudlin in their midst infuriated them and frightened them somewhat. She had steadfastly refused to play the hysterical role Sicilian women were forced to play when they dramatized their rage against death.

Once again she heard her name called. She paused in her work, glanced about again, annoyance on her face when she saw an ecclesiastically garbed man approach her. "With your permission, *Signora,* may I have a word with you?" he asked.

Since the death of her son, the priests of Montegatta had shunned her. None came calling except when they wanted a handout. Then, they all knew her. *Che Demonio!* What new charity are they begging today? She wiped her hands on her apron and beckoned to the frocked man. "Very well, come inside."

She courteously brought forth a bottle of wine and two glasses and a plate of *biscotti* which she placed on the table.

"Are you here alone, *Signora?*"

Alerted, Antigone glanced more inscrutably at him. "What is it, *padre?*"

The small man removed his dark-tinted glasses and his *biretta* and looked into her eyes. Something—something about him seemed familiar, she told herself. Reaching for her glasses, she put them on and studied him.

"Mamma *bedda,* it's me, Santino."

She squinted her eyes, not willing to believe or trust in her eyesight or him. He'd grown plumper, his face, once haggard and drawn, had filled out considerably. His dark brown hair, dyed black, was slicked down with a side part and not permitted to corkscrew as it had in the past, and he wore a handlebar moustache, typical of the Spanish.

"It's me, Mamma. Don't let the disguise fool you."

Santino opened his arms to her and she fell into them,

tears streaming down her face. "It's you? It's really you, Santino? *Santo Dio*—they told me you were dead."

For a time they both shed tears of joy, sadness, and remorse. They talked and tried to bridge the gap of two years. When the tears dried and she regained some calm, she asked him, "But—what are you doing here? Is it safe? How did you get here without being discovered? Where have you been all this time?"

He explained he'd been in Viterbo watching the trials, disbelieving the infamous production of injustice meted to his former companions. The subject got around to Vincenzo de Montana and his blackhearted deed.

"To think—he was so despicable, so utterly without conscience that he could kill Tori! After all Tori did for him?" Santino had never been so violently worked up. "Bastard! I'd never have believed it of him! But I was there, Mamma. I was in Viterbo to hear with these ears, from his own mouth. I heard him tell the world that he assassinated his blood brother—Salvatore! *Managghia!* By the unholy hairless balls of Satan! I wouldn't have believed it. I would have accused any of the others ten times before laying any blame on that demon, Vincenzo!"

Antigone's face turned white as death. "Santino! Stop this minute! You will not speak of Vincenzo so blasphemously!" She crossed herself and whispered confidentially, as if the walls had ears. "Vincenzo is innocent of Tori's blood! God help me! Vincenzo wasn't the assassin!"

He knew it! He knew the answer lay right back here in the Salvatore house. He had never believed Vincenzo's story—not for a minute. He'd told Stefano Modica the same thing when he and Angelo Duca had saved the American's life. For two years he'd been stewing over the injustice at the trial, but he couldn't outguess that Sicilian's head of Vincenzo's—couldn't understand the direction in which his head was working in this tragic comedy of errors. Finally, Santino had tossed caution to the winds and returned to Montegatta, feeling instinctively that the answers to the riddle lay right here.

Santino had been corresponding with Stefano Modica and he felt certain that despite the dangers the American had subjected himself to and the inherent dangers they both faced in this amalgamation, the story of Salvatore couldn't be completed until they had solved his murder.

Flushed with an elevation of spirits, Santino came alive with the excitement of knowing the end was near.

"You speak with such conviction, Mamma," he said at last. "He's been sentenced to life imprisonment and you tell me he's innocent before the trial for your son's murder takes place. Well, then, tell me—who is the guilty party? Who was the bloody assassin that took the life from your son before his time?"

Antigone flushed with rising nervousness, she turned her face from him. "I—I—uh—er—can't tell you."

"You *know* and you haven't come forward to testify on your nephew's behalf?" The words, spoken slowly, were an instant indictment. Santino was aghast. He stared at her incredulously, with stern reprimand, as if her words suddenly became clearer. "You actually know the identity of Tori's killer?" he asked repeatedly.

Antigone's heart beat furiously. For so long she hadn't thought of it. Oh, she had heard the newscast on the radio, the fate of the bandits, the sentencing, but in time she'd erased it from her mind. She couldn't have lived, otherwise. How could she tell Santino what she knew? Hadn't she taken an oath never to reveal the identity of her son's assassin? She opened her mouth to speak, her lips formed words, but no sound came forth. She stifled a cry and made a disorganized gesture.

"Very well, I won't press you, Mamma. Like I didn't press you when I pleaded with you to tell Tori's father his real identity. If you had complied with my request your son would be alive today."

Antigone raised her stricken eyes slowly, dying internally bit by bit. Affected by her reaction, Santino was moved to ask. "Tell me why, in God's name, Vincenzo admitted to something he isn't guilty of?"

If you only knew, Santino. If you only knew.

Antigone clasped her hands together in a woebegone manner. "I don't know why, Santino. For the love of God, I don't know. Once, I thought I saw the guiding hand of Salvatore in all this. After Vincenzo was sentenced, it all lost clarity for me. I'm sure he didn't think it would go this far. Now, it's obvious they want Vincenzo dead, too."

"I don't follow your reasoning."

"I think he gave himself up to remain in the safety of prison until time for Tori's murder trial. That's when he intends to speak the truth and bring forth Tori's portfolio. He intends to discredit all the men who up until the very end plotted against Tori."

"They didn't honor their word even at last?"

Antigone shook her head. "There were several plots to do him in. Tori told me how his men had been abducted by Don Nitto Solameni, and how the FSB had gone against Belasci's plan and of the complicated mass of intrigue going on around the clock those last few weeks. Up until the end of the trial, I felt sure Vincenzo would reach some deal with his enemies. When I heard the sentence passed upon him and the others, my heart sank. I've wanted to visit him at Ucciardone. I am all he has left. But how would it look of the mother of the man he claims to have assassinated visit him in prison?"

"You could tell them that forgiveness is the greatest of all virtues!" said Santino sternly. "That they should all forgive the trespasses of others."

"And if I jeopardize whatever plans Vincenzo might have had for doing what he did?" she asked in her old voice.

Santino thought a moment. "Yes, perhaps you did right."

"He has no one. With the world against him, he must die a little each day. What must he think when he hears himself characterized as a bloody assassin?"

"None of this makes sense. His reasons for remaining in jail must be of powerful persuasion. You know how many times he told me, 'Santino, if I'm ever captured—kill me first!' "

"I know."

"We must help him. You must tell me the name of Tori's assassin."

"I cannot."

"You must."

"You ask too much."

"Vincenzo's life? Is it too much to ask?"

Antigone turned from him. "My life hangs in the balance," she said quietly. Relieved that he believed her, she added, "There must be another way."

"There is none," he told her.

They sat in silence, pondering the dilemma. Antigone's eyes fixed on her son-in-law. She would have never known him—not the way he looked. A thought came to her. "You could walk in their midst undetected. If I didn't know you, they will never recognize you. You could go to Ucciardone as a priest. No one would question you. Find out what Vincenzo is preparing to do. Ask if we can help him. Tell him his aunt knows he is not the assassin."

"Tell me first who is."

"Not yet. First, I wish to know his plan."

Santino appeared dubious and hesitant. "If they looked at my papers twice, they might discover the forgeries. Or they might insist I get clearance from the Minister of the Interior's office. It could mean serious trouble—even my life. Then, I could be of no help to either Vincenzo or you."

"I would die if you were caught. But—" she hesitated. "If Angelo Duca were to prepare your papers—" Her eyes lit up hopefully. "Who yet has detected his superb workmanship? You know where he is?"

"I know where he is."

"Then go to him. He'll prepare everything. Santino, do you have a duplicate of Tori's portfolio?"

"It never left Sicily."

"I know. But do you know where it is, now?"

"No."

"I gave a copy to *Colonnello* Modica and I have died a hundred deaths ever since. It was a grave mistake trusting in him. Oh, what a blunder. God forgive me!"

"No, Mamma. You're wrong again." He took time to explain the American's dedication—his anguish at the injustice meted Tori by the Tribunal. The attempt on his life and all that happened at Viterbo.

"I thought he came here under the protection of Don Barbarossa! I refused to talk with him." Antigone grew reflective, frightened. "God! What have I done?" She wrung her hands together in her frustration.

"What has he to say about what happened?" Santino's voice grew hostile.

"Who?"

"Don Barbarossa."

Antigone said nothing for a moment. Then, in noticeable transition she drew herself up regally. "If anything happens to Vincenzo, I shall make public my son's portfolio. I shall write to the American Colonel and tell him he has my permission to publish his memorial immediately."

"There've been enough tragedies over those infernal papers."

"Why should the guilty be free to continue their crimes?"

"Are they free, Mamma *bedda*? Don't you suppose they live in their own personal manmade hell?" he said quietly, drawing on his cigarette.

"Did your trip to America leave you soft in the head? So, you forget how many times they lied to you and kept you all dangling like puppets in the wind? Why shouldn't they be made to pay the way we've paid?"

"What's this? What's this?" Santino was aghast. "Vendetta was never preached from your pulpit. Didn't you teach your children that vengeance belongs to the Lord!"

"And look where it got them!" she retorted venomously.

"He'd never seen her so stormy, so rebellious. "If my return has caused a river of bitterness to overflow in your heart, I am profoundly saddened, Mamma. I had hoped to bring you comfort, not stoke the fires of retaliation and revenge. If such is your intention, I cannot, will not, be party to it. Two long years have passed since Tori's death. I beg you let him rest in peace."

She lifted her eyes to his. "Santino, the time has passed for me to see nothing, hear, feel, and think nothing. I've chained my emotions for so long and maintained a patience even the gods would have envied. Each day I grow older. How much longer do I have upon the earth? If my son's life stood for anything during his short span on earth, are my last days to be spent refuting his existence? Denying his purpose on earth and hanging my head in shame? What will this have accomplished? Oh, I know what's expected of me by Sicilian standards. I cannot live up to the ideal of womanliness by burying myself in self-pity. I cannot! Life is hard, without mercy, its limitations are rigid and demanding. It offers man few chances in life and seldom offers second chances. All I have left are memories and my honor. One does not maintain his family's honor by being noble and passive, but by being clever and shrewd. There is no one to carry on the family name of Salvatore—save one. Already he goes by another name. But one day, depending upon the direction of my deeds on this day, he shall hold his head high when the name of his father is mentioned, not hide in shame because a nation of politically diseased men choose to bury that hero's good deeds and obscure his very existence on earth. For two years, I've kept the secret of Tori's death sealed tight in a vault of my mind, with a skull and crossbones emblazoned upon it as if this knowledge were the most lethal of poisons. I was certain I would carry this secret to my grave and long since relinquished all thoughts of vengeance. I ask God's forgiveness for harboring such bitter thoughts in my heart. But my mind is made up. *Allora*—there is nothing we can do for the dead. Let us see what can be done to help the living!"

Santino was relieved to hear her speak rationally. "At least you're making sense now. You're thinking in logical terms instead of that superstitious mumbo jumbo about a prophecy and the *strega*," he told her. "Thank God Tori wasn't superstitious."

Antigone turned from her son-in-law with an attitude of

quiet desperation. "Don't talk to me of logic. If Tori had been more superstitious, he'd have been alive today," she said quietly, rocking monotonously to and fro.

CHAPTER 71

Father Serra Diego speaking his best Castilian convinced the Governor of Ucciardone that he was on pilgrimage from Madrid to examine the prison systems in Sicily. His formidable display of permits and papers and letters of introduction from the holy fathers in Spain expertly forged by Angelo Duca that defied detection.

And so it was that padre Serra Diego, *alias* Santino Siragusa, was permitted to roam Ucciardone Prison armed with a camera and tripod and a young male assistant who would help him take the required photos of the highly sequestered prison. Given full privileges under the full scrutiny of the guards whom he humored right off with a few risque stories and plied with cigarettes, he managed easily to scout the enormous complex without interference.

Fluttery and whimsical movements marked the good Father's approach. He took his time, stopping here and there to bless the convicts, or take a confession, and was careful to do so only after requesting permission of the guards assigned to him. The guards watched him continuously filled with a mixture of amusement and dispassion that bordered boredom. At the end of the week, *Padre* Serra Diego had become a fixture at the prison.

Now and then guards would glance up from their duties out of curiosity, study his movements and those of his assistant, then smile tolerantly wondering why a priest should bother himself with the contents of a prison. Periodically, the prison governor Casabianco would glance into the courtyard from his office window, watching the impoverished priest amble about the inner courtyard where he'd pause to eat a meager lunch from a wrinkled brown bag until a butterfly in flight or a new floral bloom would catch his attention and he'd take time to photograph the natural phenomenons. The Governor would go out of his way to wave to the small man whose slicked-down hair stood up in tiny corckscrews when he perspired.

As often as possible, Father Serra Diego would praise the Governor for maintaining such excellent conditions at the prison complex. "The cleanliness alone is a giant step forward, Excellency," Santino would literally fawn over this mammoth caretaker. "If you saw the deplorable conditions in Spain—" he lamented sorrowfully. "If conscientious men like you alone were hired to run such facilities—ah, what a giant step forward!"

With such praiseworthy comments he had made a devout friend of the Governor. And with this same psychology he won over most of the guards.

It took Santino a week before he progressed to the special prison block in which Vincenzo and the other bandits were housed.

Vincenzo de Montana and the other bandits whom Santino knew intimately observed his comings and goings from their windows without a flicker of recognition. In their usual passive detachment they looked upon him as nothing special or unusual. By the time he worked his way into their quarters, they simply studied him through the bars of their cells with little outward show of emotion.

Discreetly, Santino kept to himself. He went about his duties as he had in the other units. He took more photos, made pencil sketches, listed the number of men to each cell and the number of allocated guards to make his survey as authentic as possible. He asked incessant questions of the guards. Why were the men kept isolated? How often were then fed? Did thep enjoy visiting hours? How often? Were they permitted personal contact with the opposite sex? Was the incidence of homosexuality of great concern? He asked about the medical facility. What degree of medication could be given?

Soon the friendly guards who appreciated the priest's gratuities—wine and cigarettes—left him alone. They found his routine questions boring and too detailed for their lazy minds. On occasion he'd taken photographs of taboo areas. One guard protested. Santino wrung his hands, apologized abjectly asking, "How else can I photograph the cells? Unless you'd like to ask the poor unfortunate souls to step outside their cells for a moment?" No they couldn't allow that, he was told. After considering the problem for a moment, they gave him permission.

"Oh, go ahead, Father. What harm will it do? They'll probably all be dead before you return to Spain." The guard laughed heartily.

Santino clicked his tongue against his teeth and made a sorrowful supplication to God. "Don't listen to him, Lord. He only speaks in jest. We know the final judgment is yours." He then blessed the guard who laughed uproariously at his serious manner.

They approached the cell in which Vincenzo sat confined, writing industriously in a lined notebook. One of the guards nudged Santino. "Don't get too close to that animal, Father. He's a mean one. He's the vicious and voracious tiger who murdered Salvatore."

"Who is Salvatore?" he asked pleasantly, staring through his thick-lensed, black-framed glasses.

"Who is Salvatore?" bellowed the guard loud enough for the entire cell block to hear. He burst into uncontrollable laughter as the inmates moved forward in their cells to see what the commotion was about.

"That's a good one, Father Diego! That's really something! Who is Salvatore?" The guard's titillation at the priest's naivete sent him scurrying off to repeat the incident to his companions.

It was opportunity enough for Santino to slip a note to Vincenzo, who out of curiosity moved forward to the doors of his cell to gaze upon the scene in the hall. Much thinner, with prison pallor etched into his features. Vincenzo hesitated a moment, then took the note, shoved it quickly into his pocket, his eyes moving in every direction. He studied Santino without recognition in his eyes as the priest walked away with his camera and tripod in hand. After a moment, Vincenzo returned to his writing desk. He heard the priest's voice call to his aide,

"Come, Julio. There's a good lad. Set the camera up looking into the corridor from this position. I wish to get a view of the cells from this angle."

Literally shaking, Vincenzo glanced about him, turned his back on the door, lit a cigarette, puffed on it nonchalantly for a moment, then calmly opened the note. His electric eyes skimmed hurriedly over the words:

"*Terra Diaoro—Padre* Santino. Will be here a week. Without arousing suspicion, ask for a confession. Whatever you want or need, write it down. Tell me what I can do. *Zia* Antigone sends love. She knows everything."

With trembling hands, Vincenzo shoved the note between the cover of his writing pad. He sauntered toward the door of his cell again and watched the funny little priest putter about. He studied his walk—his talk—and tried to recall the characteristics of his longtime friend. Three years had changed him, *if* it was Santino. The disguise was deceptive enough. And he knew the old password. But so did the other bandits—and who knew which among them might sell their souls for a pardon? It could easily be a trap. He told himself to use caution, to be foxy and clever and artful in his dealings with the priest. Slowly, he began to whistle the *Marching Song of the Bandits*, his dark, cynical eyes intent on the priest.

Glancing up from their idleness, a germ of excitement firing their veins, the men in the adjoining cells began to whistle the tune, one by one, until they all whistled in unison. Alarmed, Santino spun about and catching the discerning look in Vincenzo's eyes, he turned back to his work flushed with uneasiness, wondering as he did, what the hell was wrong with Vincenzo to stir up everyone's *cuglione*. He hoped the guards wouldn't be alerted. Having progressed to Arturo Scoletti's cell, Santino glanced causally in his direction.

"Bless you my son," he said in ritualistic chant.

"Thank you, *Padre*." Arturo was pleasant enough, his eyes under that shelf of primal brows as friendly as ever.

Watching Santino until he could no longer see him, Vincenzo moved soundlessly to the back of his cell to reread the note. Then he burned it, with the tip of his cigarette and tossed it in the waste receptacle.

Several guards, alerted by the whistling two, stepped back into the cell, glancing anxiously about the place in a guarded manner. Seeing nothing unusual, they retreated after a moment into the monotony of their duties.

Vincenzo's brain roiled with countless questions. Was it really Santino? Why was he here? How had he managed to flee America? Had Tori been correct—that he'd never been caught? Or had he made a deal and returned as a spy? Did he work for Belasci to locate Tori's portfolio? On and on came the tormenting questions, long after Santino left the prison complex. He chain smoked most the night and paced the floor of his cell, unable to sleep. Paranoia had infected him since he arrived here from Viterbo. He could trust no one.

If it was Santino and he's trying to be of help, wondered Vincenzo, what could he do? What did he mean that his aunt knew everything? Does she think I really betrayed Tori—or that I'm not his assassin? Why now? Why after nearly three years? More important does he have the portfolio—or is he Belasci's tool? Not Santino. He couldn't work for Belasci. Of all the old gang, not Santino, he told himself. On and on came these insidious thoughts to torture him. A feverish battle raged in his mind which kept him awake most the night. By morning he reached his decision. He concentrated on the completion of his autobiography, openly ignoring the priest.

Vincenzo, like most the prison inmates in this special cell block, was permitted to make his own coffee and kept snacks available which were originally purchased or received as gifts from family members. Sipping his coffee, Vincenzo covertly watched for the arrival of Father Serra Diego and continued to observe his comings and goings without being obvious. He watched the man's daily ritual, the blessing of the guards and subordinates.

Santino had created such a stir in the bandits' quarters that one or two shouted amiably. "Hey, *Padré*, how about listening to my confession! I'll say I gotta a helluva lot to tell you—if you can stand all my sins!"

Santino turned to the guards questioningly. "I don't wish to burden you with extra work, my son, but these poor men shouldn't be denied their moment with the Lord."

"Listen, Father, don't get yourself involved with those beasts. It would take you ten years to hear one of their confessions, all right. Like they said, they've a lot to tell you, you can believe me," said Rosario, a simpatico guard.

"As a man of God it isn't for me to judge. With your permission, relate to the Governor their request for confessions. I assure you it is no strain upon me to grant their requests," he told the guards. To the men in the cells, he said, "I shall do my best *muchacos*, to see what this Spaniard can accomplish. You see, I am not of this diocese."

Arturo Scoletti heard that voice. He arose from his cot, ambled toward the bars, and peered out at the priest as something struck a harmonic chord. He rubbed his eyes and blinked several times. *I must be crazy. I'm imagining things. Phew, this place is making me crazy for sure. For a moment I was sure I heard Santino's voice. But, that fat old priest with the black moustache and black hair could never be Santino.* He moved back to his cot and continued to daydream for a while.

"He's a good old sport, that Spaniard," said the guards as they strode towards the Governor's office. "He's caused us no problems, followed our rules, and besides he brings us all these thoughtful gifts."

When the Captain of the guards approached the Governor, he found him seated in his overstuffed chair smoking one of the cigars Father Diego had brought him only that morning. He listened to the request and pondered a bit.

"Is it possible the—bandits are becoming rehabilitated?" he asked.

"It's the first time any of them have asked for *confession*, Governor."

"Even our own priests haven't been successful in reaching them."

The Captain smiled. "This one's different than our priests. Much more tolerant and less pious—no?"

The Governor nodded. "I'm told in Spain the priests are more dedicated and less attached to worldly possessions. Did you see his clothing? He wears the same habit for nearly three weeks now. Still, he thinks to bring us little remembrances. He's a cheerful little man." The Governor grew expansive. "Why not? Go ahead, let him take as many confessions as they want. It might ease the tension in those abominable quarters."

Having already ascertained that escape from this prison was impossible unless arranged by the Mafia—Santino could give no one false hope, so at this point he had no reason to reveal his identity to anyone except Vincenzo. However, he had no recourse but to continue with the confessions as requested and pray none of his former companions recognized him. With shaking fingers, he removed a purple surplice from his bag, placed it around his neck and entered the first cell where Dominic Lamantia knelt before him and commenced in ritual.

"Bless me, Father, I confess to Almighty God and to you, Father—"

Standing at the entrance of his cell, Vincenzo scrutinized every move of Santino's. He watched as Santino finished and performed seven more confessions. When finished, Santino continued in his work as if there had been no interruption. Once or twice he looked toward Vincenzo's cell only to be ignored by his former chieftain. At noon, Santino waved to the guards and inmates and he and his assistant took their lunch out on the quad where visitors sauntered with various inmates.

Santino grew concerned. In three or four days he'd have to leave. Vincenzo had made no effort whatsoever to ask for a confession, to slip him a note, or anything! He doesn't trust me, thought Santino. Probably doesn't recognize me. How could he? None of the other showed a glimmering of recognition, either. He glanced at his watch. If he hurried he could make it to Montegatta and back in a couple of hours.

"Julio—I must leave to pick up a few more supplies. You continue without me."

In Montegatta, he took no chances. He used the old underground passage to his mother-in-law's house. A knock at the trap door startled Antigone, and by the time he opened the latch, he found her holding a *lupara* aimed at him.

"Mamma—it's me!" he called softly.

Clutching her wildly beating heart, she set aside the shot gun and hugged him as he entered the kitchen. Quickly, he told her of his problem with Vincenzo.

"He doesn't trust me—I'm sure. I must have something of Tori's that will convince him that I'm sincere!"

"I have all of his possessions except for the gun, and gold watch," she temporized. *Allora!* The belt buckle! The golden buckle Vincenzo gave to Tori," she suggested with a measure of excitement.

Antigone lost no time in bringing it to Santino. She watched him remove his belt and affix the famous buckle to it. Quickly he slipped his belt on and hooked the buckle in place.

"*Va bene,*" she said solemnly. "Be careful, my son. Give Vincenzo my love."

"*Si.* I'll get back to you as soon as I can talk with him."

Santino didn't resume with the confessions on his return. Instead he set up his camera outside Vincenzo's cell, facing the east corridor. He removed his cassock and wore only the trousers, vest, and shirt of his order. On this visitor's day, the guards, occupied in the various tediums of guiding traffic, accepted the cigarettes and sweets he brought them and didn't bother with him for the rest of the day. In the bandits' quarters the halls were comparatively quiet. Only the sounds Santino and his assistant made as they whispered back and forth could be heard. Santino sat on a chair facing Vincenzo's cell, scribbling on a sketch pad, giving the outward impression of a skilled craftsman.

"Hey, *padre,*" called Vincenzo. "Got any erasers?"

"Yes, my son. Of course." replied Santino, taking hope. He reached into his case and brought out art gum erasers, and quickly unbuttoned the last four buttons of his vest. "I'll divide what I have with you."

He walked slowly toward Vincenzo's cell and made sure the buckle was in prominent display. Vincenzo's eyes caught the bright glare of gold in the shaft of light. Instantly his eyes left the buckle and searched Santino's eyes.

"Here you are, my son."

"*Si tu?* Really you?" hissed Vincenzo.

"Think nothing of it—you are welcome to share with

997

me. *"No, its a jackass! Damnit. Request a confession!"* Santino bowed. *"And be quick about it—I can't stay much longer."* He returned to his chair, rebuttoned his vest, and tugged it down over the belt buckle.

Vincenzo stared at him for several moments then returned to his desk. Two hours passed. It was almost time for him to leave for the day.

Why doesn't he ask for a confession, Santino wondered, growing angry and a bit impatient. *To think I'm risking my life for this idiot,* he glowered inwardly.

Vincenzo called to a guard. After a moment's conversation, the guard ambled over to the priest.

"Padre Diego! You got another one. This time you caught a big fish!" He jerked his head toward Vincenzo and studied the priest with interest.

Santino glanced at his watch in a short burst of impatience. "Can't it wait until tomorrow?"

Rosario, the guard, a pleasant enough sort of man, not as seasoned and as tough as most of the guards, and not as impressed with self-importance, shrugged easily. "Go ahead, *padre.* You've got nearly an hour before they eat supper. This *one* needs your services the *most!"* Rosario didn't elaborate since the priest had already assured him he never heard of Salvatore.

Purple surplice around his neck, he entered the cell. "I'm Father Serra Diego, my son. You wish a confession?"

They walked to the rear of the cell. "Kneel down, Vincenzo," ordered Santino, making the sign of the cross in the air over him.

"Managghia! It's really you?"

"No! It's the cuckoo in the clock! *Managghia,* what took you so long?" he hissed.

"Yes, my son. It will do your soul good to confess." He sprinkled holy water on him and made a pontifical blessing. "Tell me what I can do and keep talking while I pray in Latin. I know you didn't kill Tori. Why the charades with your life—eh?

"In nomini Patri et figlio et spirtus sanctus."

Hesitant for several moments as if to collect his thoughts, Vincenzo bowed his head and began to speak as in litany. "In the six months following Tori's death, I was summoned to Rome to make a deal with Belasci. They were in hot water. The facts didn't add up nor did the official version of Tori's death. The entire trial was a fiasco, set up to make it appear as if justice was being done. What a farce! I, in collaboration with Belasci, agreed to take the responsibility of Tori's death so the guilt and sus-

998

picion wouldn't fall upon the administration or its officials. By claiming to be his assassin I was promised an honorable pardon and a substantial reward to accommodate me in a foreign country." But as usual they tried to double-cross me."

"*Deo te absolvum,*" muttered Santino, crossing the air over his head.

"Now Belasci denies everything. I had to discredit Franchina, that evil crocodile who plotted against Tori's life to the very end. They uncovered a conspiracy in which America planned to aid Tori—expatriate him. That bastard Belasci knew a month in advance that *Colonnello* Modica planned to help Tori escape. Even so, Tori wouldn't have left Sicily alive. Even the pilot was bought."

"Are you sorry for your sins?" droned Santino's monotone voice. "*Who killed Tori?*"

"Isn't it obvious? Don Nitto Solameni and Natale! They claimed the reward from the FSB. He was dead long before his body was found in that phony set-up in Castelvetrano. It took Cesare Cala nearly four days to get the reward money together to pay those *mafiosi, schifosi,* for the corpse. On delivery of the specified sum, my cousin's body was turned over to the FSB to dispose of however they saw fit. You know the rest. Santino," he whispered conspiratorially, "I've finished my biography. I want you to take it out of here. If something should happen to me, publish it with Tori's papers. Give the money to my aunt—and to Maria Angelica Candela." He told her about the girl and exacted Santino's promise to get her out of Neptune's Daughters.

"*Pax hominibus. Et cum spiritu tu.*" Santino shook as he listened to the incredible tale. "Be still, Vincenzo," he warned. He caught sight of the Governor of the prison walking past the cell with two visiting dignitaries. They nodded to Santino in passing. Santino continued with his Latin litany as Vincenzo continued with his story.

"Through arrangement with Chief Zanorelli who arrested me to spite the FSB and discredit Franchina's story, I was taken into custody. Not because I really killed Tori. They all know I didn't. I promised them Tori's portfolio as soon as I'm released from prison, In addition, an honorable discharge with enough money to emigrate—if I choose. Colonel Cala fixed up my alibi for Portella, but you see how that backfired."

"I saw. I saw."

"But all that doesn't matter. At the trial of Salvatore's murder, As soon as I'm charged with the crime, Belasci will supply the court with an unconditional pardon and explain what I did was on behalf of the State, in the interests of justice, and I'll be a free man that same day. *C'e' vuole un pocco de pazienza.* It takes only a bit of patience."

"*Non te fa pigliato per fesso!* Don't let them take you for a fool, *amico!*" Santino was outraged. "You don't believe them—do you?" He continued his litany. "*Hosanna in excelsis deo. Sit et benedicto.*" Unsure of what he was saying or how it sounded, he tried to calm himself, realizing the futility of mission.

"I didn't count on it taking so long. But the longer I remain alive the better the odds. You'll make the portfolio available to me?"

"Your aunt knows where it is."

"I've been offered millions for my silence," he gloated for a moment.

"Like they did to Salvatore?"

"Listen, so far I've got most of them. Franchina won't survive. After his trial, he'll never be permitted to wear his uniform again. He faces imprisonment and fines."

Unconvinced, Santino persisted. "You're sure Don Nitto and his son killed Tori? You know this for a fact?"

A guard walked by. Vincenzo lowered his head and crossed himself as Santino sprinkled holy water over him.

"All I know is the Solámeni's produced the body after they bargained for the reward," he repeated impatiently. "I told you—"

"Where are they now?"

"Disappeared—both of them. Their bodies haven't been found. Dead—eh?"

"*Allora*—then they weren't Tori's killers?"

Vincenzo tensed, glanced up sharply. "Who, then? Who?" It was the first time this possibility struck him. "If not Don Nitto—who? No, Santino, it had to be them. If someone disposed of them it had to be someone who resented the manner in which they dealt for the reward."

"Or by the real killer to keep them from talking?"

"Goddamnit! Fucking jail cell has dulled my Sicilian head." He slapped his forehead. "*Allora*—that presents more complications—eh, *compare?*" His eyes lit up in silent speculation.

"Leave it at that for now. What can I do to help?"

"Take my manuscript, do with it as I ask. If I go down, they all go down." He shoved the notebook at him. "Hide it under your vest."

Santino literally shook as he shoved the biography under his vest.

"Where can you be reached if my *avvocato* needs you?"

"I'll leave word with Tori's mother. As soon as I leave here I shall have to destroy all existence of *padre* Diego."

"Promise me, Santino. If any thing should happen to me, if treachery lies in wait for me as it did Tori, you'll publish both mine and his memorial."

Before he replied, the guard reappeared. "Sorry, *padre*. Time's up. You'll have to finish his confession tomorrow."

"*Si*, Rosario." The notebook tucked away from prying eyes, Santino walked toward him. "You were right, Rosario. He'd much to confess." He turned to Vincenzo. "God bless you, my son. I'll see you in the morning."

"I told you this one was special. His sins weigh heavily on him."

Santino smiled faintly as he and his assistant picked up their equipment and left Ucciardone.

CHAPTER 72

The Prosecutor General insituted charges against Major Franchina and during his arraignment accused him of perjury and promoting personal, self-serving interests against those of the State. Six top officials in the *carabinieri* were also arrested and tried for aiding and abetting Major Franchina. As the new year approached, Major Franchina stubbornly prepared his defense, basing his entire case on the fact that he only carried out orders from his superior officers. He was soon to learn how far this posture could justify charges of perjury and of complicity with outlaws when he in fact took his stand against the State.

Vincenzo de Montana was formally arraigned and charged with the murder of Salvatore. At the end of October, *Avvocato* Luigi Basile arrived at Ucciardone Prison to prepare his client's case. His left arm was in a sling, as the result of a gunshot wound inflicted upon him by a would-be assassin. The two men greeted each other warmly.

"What the hell happened to you, *dottore?*" asked Vincenzo.

"It's nothing. A hazard of my profession, I suppose."

"It's because of me?"

"Who can tell? Would-be assassins don't leave calling cards."

Vincenzo brooded darkly. He apologized profusely and the lawyer waved him off. "I said forget it."

They talked for nearly four hours. Finally Basile grew serious. "I can't stress enough, Vincenzo, that you must talk with no one about your case. You understand? To no one."

"To whom can I speak here? I'm ignored by all my old friends."

"Nevertheless, I must caution you. Rumor's spreading that you intend spilling your guts at the trial."

"I've always told you I would—if they attempt to betray me."

"You insist on committing suicide—don't you?"

"Why do you say such things to me, Basile? Don't you think I feel bad enough?" exploded the prisoner. "My nerves are already raw enough."

It was the first time he had evidenced the strain of prison life and its uncertainties.

The lawyer paced back and forth in the bare-walled room reserved for lawyers and clients. He removed a pack of cigarettes from his jacket pocket, offered one to his client. Vincenzo refused but he quickly lit the lawyer's with his gold lighter. "I've smoked too much lately and my cough has returned. It's damp and cold here in the winter. They gave me some new medication which hasn't seemed to help," he complained.

"Vincenzo—hear me out. You hired me to represent you and I'll do as you request. But I'm going to tell you my personal feelings in this matter, whether you like it or not. I think you're foolish. There is no longer a cause to fight for! Salvatore's been dead over three years. What purpose does this sacrificing of your life serve?"

"I told you, Basile. If they don't try to save me, they'll go down with me. Already they've cheated me out of the fifty-thousand-dollar reward I was promised. The draft for the reward came from some big-shot banking firm. Someone in Rome claimed it was a forgery. You find that check, and I'll guarantee it's not a forgery. Read the endorsement and you'll fight a first-class thief. For fifty thousand he's gotta be first class!"

"But, this is incredible! Why didn't you tell me before this?"

"I thought you knew?"

"Mah—how could I have known? They don't tell me everything. It's your job to keep your lawyer informed. Or are you still too Sicilian to even confide in your lawyer? Where did the draft come from?"

"Some *pezzonovante* banking firm—New York Trust? Something like that?"

Basile made notes. "You should have notified me immediately. When did this take place?"

"Two—three weeks ago."

"Now let's get back to you. Under no circumstances are you to talk with anyone about the case. No one—understand?"

Vincenzo nodded like a petulant adolescent.

"Are you comfortable? Have they taken good care of you?"

"Money always talks, *dottore*."

"Yes, money talks," said Basile wryly, "and always loudly, eh?"

Vincenzo didn't get the point. Basile pulled up a chair and glanced into his client's eyes. "You know Martino Belasci is about to accept the Premiership of Italy?"

Vincenzo snorted with contemptuous scorn. "So! The biggest bandit of all takes over the reins of the government—eh? Despite all Salvatore said openly about this cancer? Despite all the facts uncovered from his double dealing—thievery, corruption, and immoral behavior in office? It's not to be believed."

"One man alone or a handful of men haven't been able to beat the system or intimidate a man with Belasci's political clout. You know what kind of a machine is behind Belasci?" asked Basile, who once a thousand years ago had been an idealist and had long since succumbed to the system he once despised and remained in a constant state of disenchantment. "You mentioned your biography, Vincenzo. Where is it? How dangerous is it to all these high politicos?"

"It's safe." He rolled his eyes. "More than Tori's."

"Here?"

"No."

"No?" Basile paused. "Where, then? *Managghia!* How the hell did you get it out of here?"

"The less you know, the better for you," he gestured to Basile's injury.

"Those words have a familiar ring to them. What about those people you've entrusted the biography to? Can they be trusted? Damnit, didn't I just tell you to trust no one! You never know who'll turn out to be the villain in the plot."

"It's in safekeeping. In hands like my own."

1003

"Let me be candid. You've made powerful enemies of both the *carabinieri*, and security police—to say nothing of the Christian Democrats, who contend your loquacious free speech has damaged the Party. They feel your future orations might jeopardize them immeasurably. They know you didn't kill Salvatore, that you're cooperating with Belasci. On the basis of that I've been approached to offer you a deal."

"You, Basile? They came to you?" Vincenzo's eyes widened in amazement. He smiled with irony.

"Look, I was approached by a member of Parliament, a Christian Democrat, far removed from your scene, who put it to me. All I'm doing is relaying the information. If it were not for the fact that I want to save your life, I'd have punched the bastard in the mouth and deprived him of a few teeth!"

Vincenzo smiled benignly. He stared intently at the sling around Basile's neck.

"They offer to grant you a sizeable amount, plus your freedom, if you'll retract the statements made at Viterbo."

"Another deal they won't keep."

"No. This time I'll be there to make sure they don't go back on their word."

"And then your life shall hang in the balance."

"I think not," said the confident lawyer. "There's a difference in the mechanics used by and between sophisticated politicians and professional men. The intricacies of the law are vast. Each man knows what the other is capable of doing."

"Providing you gentlemen play according to the rules, eh? In my circle, Basile, a bullet speaks louder than words and becomes less tedious."

"Come, Vincenzo, be reasonable. We're all civilized. We don't play cops and robbers like they do in those preposterous, shoot 'em up American films. Not in this day and age!"

Vincenzo's unconstrained laughter filled the small room and echoed through the halls at Ucciardone. He doubled over, unable to stop the waves of hysteria and laughter that rolled through his body. Suddenly he began to cough. For several moments, Basile watched him with concern. He slapped his client's shoulders and tried everything he could to prevent the coughing.

Vincenzo waved him off until control returned. He wiped at the tears that rolled from his cheeks. "You make a statement like that to a man whose entire life has been

1004

:ops and robbers and he's bound to crack up with laughter
as I just did."

"Goddammit, de Montana! So, my choice of words were
wrong! What I'm trying to say is that in legal procedures,
an uneducated man hasn't a chance—unless he's well
represented."

"What you mean is that a poor ignorant peasant like me
has no chance in a court of law. In thirteen centuries justice hasn't triumphed?"

"First, you're not poor. Second, you're not ignorant!
Third, you've got no chance in a court of law unless you
trust your lawyer. Don't you understand you're at the
mercy of men like me? Did Viterbo teach you nothing?"

"What does that mean?" asked Vincenzo, suddenly suspicious.

"Because we know the law, you put yourselves in our
hands. You realize how easy it would be to defend you
improperly? Make the wrong deal—either in error or on
purpose? Sell you out to the highest bidder?"

"*Once* you'd get that chance in Sicily. Only once," said
the Sicilian, drawing himself up. He suddenly felt very
alone and hostile. "Is there none among you who are honest?" he said thickly.

"Very few, I'm sad to say. Temptations proliferate in
our profession. Now, wait a moment, Vincenzo. I don't
want to give you the impression that I intend to betray
you—although I've received many an enticing offer. I'm
trying to tell you to wake up the world around you. Think
sensibly before it's too late. A man like you has no chance
against a super-powerful force you've committed yourself
to oppose. They'll forgive and forget—if you retract what
has already been said."

"And lose my honor?"

"Goddammit! You can't eat honor! There's only one
place I know of where the word honor is suitable—on a
tombstone. '*He died with honor!*' " said the lawyer with
contempt. "I'd rather see you alive and thriving someplace."

Silence filled the room. Vincenzo sipped water from the
carafe on the table. "What would you do in my place,
Basile?"

A surge of compassion flooded Basile's face. He ran his
fingers through his curly hair, then slapped his thighs
resignedly. "Damnit! I don't know! We aren't driven by the
same forces. So how can I tell you? Strange, isn't it? I
came prepared to show you the error of your ways, to
point out the intelligence in the saving of your life. Now

1005

that you reverse the roles, I'm stuck for an answer. Pinning me down—I think I'd have to be honest enough to say I'd want to survive."

"At least you're honest."

"What's honesty got to do with this? Be sensible, eh? If you value your life," Basile paused. "You do value your life—don't you?"

"Damn you, Basile! You're trying to confuse me. If I retract my statements, they'll kill me, like they killed Salvatore. Might as well die with honor as to die in shame. From the President on down, I trust none of those whoring sons of Satan. Would you?" Vincenzo paced the tight little room, head down, hands behind his back, striving for self-control. When he lost his temper he generally sacrificed all traces of logic. "Listen, *dottore*, everything I said at Viterbo was the truth—except for my culpability in the assassination of my cousin, Tori, and of course the X-rays. I admit—that was pure folly. I've had time to regret the folly of not taking you into my confidence. You may be right in what you say—that the politics in most countries are not ideal. Every politician has his price. How well I know that. Even in America—that wonderland of wonderlands!" he snorted with the look of a man possessed of a great secret. "How else do you think Belasci learned of the attempted expatriation of Salvatore by his old friend *Colonnello* Modica? He has friends in the White House—all the way to Washington, this Belasci. Imagine that?"

In the silence it was *Avvocato* Basile's turn to stare in stupefaction. "Colonel Modica—the American was attempting to expatriate Salvatore?" In his astonishment Basile tried fitting the pieces of the puzzle together. "Why didn't you tell me this in Viterbo, damnit? Oh, Vincenzo—you fool! You poor fool! If you'd taken time to tell me this, that Tribunal would have been reduced to rubble!" He took time to describe his encounter with Stefano Modica and the attempt on the American's life at trial's end. "The American knew something. I was certain. Else why did he trouble himself to attend your trial with such dedication. Someplace I have his card. I will write to him make him understand the importance of his testimony in the future trial."

Vincenzo's brows drew together in thought. Was it possible the G. O'Hoolihan Gabriella spoke of was *Colonnello* Modica? Mistaking Vincenzo's silence for his inability to grasp the gist of Basile's thoughts, the lawyer prompted his client.

"You don't see, do you? If we can find the leak from

Washington to Belasci—" Basile paused in midsentence, his eyes searching the confines of the small room. Instantly aware of the major complications and the enormous implications this illicit relationship presented, his voice dropped to just above a whisper. "And you're trying to fight this machine?" He stared at his client with a mixture of respect and apprehension. "*Managghia,* Vincenzo, you've got to be daft! Insane. Listen, you be careful who you talk to—understand?" Basile, growing more uncomfortable by the minute searched the room again for unseen eyes and ears, for possible eavesdroppers.

In the baffling confusions of newly posed possibilities, Vincenzo grew expansive and, flushed with a burst of bravado, he told his lawyer none of this really mattered. "I told you the deal we have. At the trial, Belasci will pardon me. It is of no further importance to me who planned Salvatore's expatriation."

"You're sure it will be that cut and dried?"

"Of course. Belasci wouldn't dare doublecross me, not now. Or, I swear, Basile, not only will both portfolios be made public, but in addition I will have Belasci torn into so many pieces only the vultures will find him."

Basile shrugged in annoyance, then he remembered. "Tell me, just how does Don Matteo Barbarossa fit into this?"

Vincenzo cringed inwardly. "Why do you mention this man, now?"

"In court, you turned green at the mention of his name."

"He's the *capomafia.* No one fools with him." He shuddered as he had in the past at the mention of Tori's Godfather.

"How does he figure in all this?"

Reining back his revulsion, Vincenzo relaxed somewhat. "I forget—you're not Sicilian. You know little of the Mafia—besides, you Italians don't believe in its existence."

"Well—"

"Don Barbarossa is the big noise here. He's behind Belasci, Malaterra, even Prince Oliatta. Some say even de Aspanu trembles at his name." For several moments Vincenzo filled Basile in on the importance and power of Barbarossa. "He was Salvatore's Godfather. Imagine that."

"Playing both ends against the middle—eh?" Basile was ahead of his client.

"Worse than that. But there was more, Basile. Much more. Something between Tori and that Godfather of his that ate away at my cousin. He would never discuss him and I was content not to hear his name." He mentioned the quasi-entente that existed between the former bandit chieftain and his Godfather and in the next half hour, as he spoke, certain factors which had either eluded Vincenzo in the past, or he had refused to examine as carefully as he did at this moment, mushroomed into mind-bending malevolence.

Suddenly, as he spoke an expression of indescribable astonishment on his face turned into a mask of forced containment, then melted into incredulous disbelief as it all came together in his mind. He was totally lost to the lawyer. His mind, working swiftly and diligently in an effort to sift through the broken pieces in his mind, suddenly spotlighted one vital factor, and in that instant Vincenzo knew the identity of Salvatore's assassin. All this had elevated him into a state of breathless anticipation in which the wildest improbabilities hinted at in his mind were dovetailing into a crystalized picture of truths and certainty.

More encouraging was the silent communication passing from one man to another. If Basile had been Sicilian he'd have gotten the message instantly. But, being Italian, and never really subjected to any dealings with so power saturated a man as Matteo Barbarossa, he wasn't certain what Vincenzo's mind had given birth to in those few moments. However, he did hear his client's next few words.

"If Belasci fails to keep his word at the trial and an attempt is made to betray me, I shall reveal the identity of the man who killed Salvatore!"

Later in reflection Vincenzo asked himself what prompted him to blurt this out and he could find no justifiable reason except to give vent to an inner compulsion over which he had no control.

Avvocato Basile turned the color of ash. "You fool!" he reprimanded. "Even the walls have ears! How many times have I cautioned you not to speak with such perilous candor?" Frustrated, Basile walked to the door, opened it, and glancing about in all directions he shut it, satisfied there were no eavesdroppers. He returned to Vincenzo's side. "If I'm to represent you at the coming trial, you are going to be honest with me. I want no more surprises like the one you dealt me at Viterbo."

"You northerners may know the law, but few of you have any guts."

"No guts eh? But we sure as hell live longer." The lawyer gathered his papers, shoved them into his briefcase, and snapped it shut. "I know it's futile to ask you to give no further importance to the identity of the real killer. Believe me, even I don't wish to know. It really has no bearing on the final outcome of the trial, unfortunately. *Allora*, I'll give them your answer. You're sure you won't change your mind and let me help save you?"

Vincenzo shook his head as he lit a cigarette and blew the smoke out through his nose impatiently. "You worry too much. What I know buys my freedom."

Observing his client with a curious mixture of tenderness and exasperation, Basile finally remonstrated hotly. "For Christsakes, don't breathe a word of what you know to anyone—you hear?"

Vincenzo laughed uproariously at his lawyer's overly dramatic concern. "You just prepare yourself for the coming trial. I'll give you the information to deal with these vipers if they suddenly develop forked tongues."

"You must have some other personal ambition greater than swinging at the end of a rope for a crime you didn't commit . . . Else this shall be your epitaph, carved into your tombstone."

Vincenzo laughed again. *"Avvocato*—you worry too much. Trust me."

"Yes, my Sicilian friend. I trust you. I trust you'll fuck up again. Trial is set for March 1, 1954. I shall return here about February 10th."

Vincenzo laughed again, only this time his laughter was colored by a forced falsetto. *"Va bene, dottore.* If I don't see you before then, *buon capitano!* Happy New Year! And don't catch any more bullets—*capeeshi?*"

"Si, amico. Happy New Year."

January 28, 1954. A new prisoner was placed in the cell next to Vincenzo's. Eight days passed before Vincenzo would speak to the man. Like a hawk circling over a hen, he watched him with wary eyes and kept his own counsel. On February 5, the man was overheard saying to Vincenzo that he felt the Sicilian was too young to spend the rest of his life in jail. "Me, I'm old and along in years. I can resign myself to such a sentence. But, you, you're too young and vigorous with a whole lifetime ahead of you. Make a deal with your enemies. Why bring about your personal destruction?"

Vincenzo simply stared at the man in his usual aloof and courteous manner, making no comment whatsoever.

The ice broken, the following day the man engaged in small repartee "I know who you are—your fame is widespread, de Montana." He offered him a cigarette. "It matters not what you say to me—I'm a dead man. They plan to hang me soon enough. But why do you put up with this

1009

life? Your trial is due soon. Why don't you make a deal? You seem to be the only one who is losing. All your other enemies are sitting pretty in the government. Be smart. It's known that you are not Salvatore's assassin."

"It is—eh?" replied Vincenzo. Hours spent in a one-sided conversation began to irk him. "Do you know who the assassin of Salvatore is?"

"Me? Mah—no. Why would I know?"

"Well, I know. That's what I intend revealing at the trial. Now, go back and tell your sponsors what information that crazy de Montana revealed to you!" He began to laugh, with the gleam of a madman in his eyes, and retired to his cell thinking—they still were trying to best him. Well! He'd show them! Plant a spy in his midst! Imagine. What will they think of next!

The recent prisoner retreated into his cell. An hour later he was heard calling the guard, complaining of severe stomach pains. He was removed from the cell and never seen again. Vincenzo's laughter echoing through the prison complex caused a few of the more curious of his companions to believe their former co-chieftain was losing his sanity.

On February 8, 1954, Martino Belasci accepted the Premiership of Italy.

On February 9th, the very next day, Vincenzo arose at 7 A.M. after a disturbing night filled with restless dreams, and made his coffee as usual. He put into the cup two teaspoons of sugar and a tablespoon of his new medication given him for his lung condition. He took the hot coffee cup to the window of his cell and gazed out at the early morning haze threatening rain. All at once he was stricken with a hungry passion for the home of his youth, a lighthearted gay and carelessness of youth full of music and laughter and his mother's soft reassuring words of love. He remembered all the gaiety at the Salvatore house with his cousins and his Aunt Antigone. He gazed at this vision with the agony of an exile knowing in this instant of intuition he'd never see that life again.

He sipped his coffee until the cup was drained, then poured another one. Suddenly he lifted his head alertly, his senses whirling in confusion. The ache in his heart extended until it seemed his whole body throbbed with a weariness and futility that assaulted him even at this light and frivolous time of day. He paced the room erratically like a wild bird irrevocably caught in the restrictive confines of a caged environment. A cadaverlike hue formed on his skin.

Two minutes later, he fell to the floor of his cell in agonized frenzy as the diabolical effects of tetanic contractions in his muscular system convulsed him into excruciating pain. He struggled to his desk, screaming tortures of the damned. "Tori! Maria Angelica! Gabriella!" His voice croaked and gasped and finally screamed, "They've poisoned me! They poisoned me!" He tried in vain to reach a bottle of olive oil from a shelf overhead, in hopes of swallowing it so he could vomit the poison in his valiant determination to fight off death's hungry jaws.

His former companions in the adjoining cells heard his violent and agonizing screams, ran to their cell doors and craned their necks to see what was happening. Those with the best views saw him rolling, writhing, and twisting convulsively in indescribable torment. Blood oozed from between his lips from chewing his swollen tongue. Rushed to the infirmary and haplessly into the very hands of the agent who administered the strychnine to his medication, Vincenzo died within the hour, subjected to the most violent torture a body could endure.

Because the autopsy showed the cause of death was due to strychnine poisoning, the entire staff of the prison complex in the bandits' quarters was changed. Prison doctor Rudolfo Reggio, a staunch Christian Democrat, was arrested for complicity in the matter.

On March 7 the Nuliano brothers and the Genovese brothers, Marco and Fidelio, were found slain in their cells. Assassins unknown. The remaining members of Salvatore's valorous band of brigands were acquitted. Those acquitted of their crimes were later assassinated by unknown assailants with the exception of Arturo Scoletti, who, with Ross, *Sporcaccione*, Rizzuto, disappeared off the face of the earth.

Antigone Naxos Salvatore had sent her son's personal affects to Gina O'Hoolihan as a legacy for Salvatore's son. In 1955, Gina married Stefano Modica and lived in seclusion under an assumed name on the property deeded over to her in Baja California where the former Army Colonel with Renzo Bellomo completed the memorial to Salvatore.

In 1959, Don Barbarossa died as a result of a cardiac arrest.

In 1964, Antigone Salvatore died of natural causes.

In 1970, in a final meeting with Stefano Modica before publication of the Salvatore memorial, Santino imparted his final notes to the American and saw him off at the Palermo airport. After the Alitalia transport took off, Santino returned to his car, stepped on the starter of his Alfa Romeo, and blew himself to instant eternity. Buried in a pauper's grave with no one to mourn him, not even Angelo Duca dared attend the shabby departure of a man who once had a close rapport with God.

Somewhere in the Temple of Cats, secretly hidden from an unsuspecting world, entombed for all posterity when another civilization might uncover them, are the remains of Salvatore's memorabilia and Vincenzo's biography.

And the Christian Democrats, and the Mafia, go marching on—and on—and on.

EPILOGUE

Twenty-five years had passed since the violence of his death. Inside the cool marble structure designed to resemble a miniature Grecian temple of antiquity, an altar and sarcophagus commanded their attention. At the center of the elaborate marble structure ornamented by carved figures and scrolled designs, recessed in an oval hollow, a fading photograph of Alessandro Salvatore curled away from its holder. On the lid of the sarcophagus was carved the epitaph Salvatore himself had written long before his death, in Italian.

> *Once I cherished dreams of love that perished in death's ashes. I chose instead to serve the world, a proud inspiring phantom who fell, was crushed and doomed to die by Destiny's defection.*

Stefano Modica, suntanned, with snow-white hair, transcribed the words into English for his wife Gina and their son, Gino. Midway through, a vagrant tear splashed on his cheek.

"Who was he, Dad?" asked Gino, the spitting image of his father, a man he'd never known. "It's certainly an impressive memorial."

"Who was he?" Stefano glanced into his wife's pale orchid eyes and squeezed her slender hand tenderly. "A brave and fearless man whom I met when stationed here in World War II," he replied. Stefano glanced at the yellowed, fading photograph of his old friend and put an arm around his wife's waist.

"Like spectres of the past, proud, inspiring, and foresworn, you were doomed to die before you were born," said Gina softly, then added, "my very dearest love." She placed a single white rose into the floral container. Her eyes brimmed with tears gave a translucence to the violet shadows around them.

"Come, son," said Stefano. "We're going to the Temple of Cats where legend claims the playful *Siculi* demons call to their own. Imagine. Once they even called to me."

A half-hour later, the three Americans stood on the Temple floor, looking out onto the vast lands once conquered by Salvatore. Both Stefano and Gina were immediately transported back in time to the days of Salvatore. They both glanced at their son, Gino, who walked very close to the edge of the parapet overlooking the valley.

Husband and wife stood hand in hand watching this magnificent son of theirs, who bore an uncanny resemblance to Salvatore. Their hands clasped tightly into the other's, they both caught their breath when they saw Gino's powerful young body tense and strain to hear only the sounds he could hear. He tilted his head from side to side and stood listening with every inch of his body. About to call his parents' attention to what he alone was privy to, Gino changed his mind, suddenly loathe to interrupt the magic of the moment, thinking, if he did, whatever it was he saw and heard might disappear. He directed his attention back to the vista below him.

Suddenly it was all there right before him, spread out in the valley below; legions of ancient warriors, hordes of mounted horsemen in colorful battle array, kicking up clouds of spiraling dust, the blast of victorious trumpet calls growing louder, more enthralling, brilliant silken colors carried by standard bearers, fluttering in the wind, came closer in spectacle. Right at the center, from a point at infinity, snowballing toward him in a cloud of blinding white mist came a fabulous rider on a snow-white stallion, galloping with the wind. Horse and rider came swiftly toward Gino, faster and faster rushing at him, then stopped abruptly a short distance from him; the horse rearing on two hind legs with forepaws clawing the air before him. In the manner of a gallant cavalier with unmis-

1013

takable panache, the rider waved his arm, then turned and rode back into infinity where he disappeared in a maze of white dust along with the other apparitions.

Startled and struck with the faintest glimmer of disbelief, Gino turned to both his parents, his dark brown eyes with violet centers blinked incredulously. It had all happened so fast he wasn't sure if it had been a vision he'd seen or a bit of fanciful whimsy.

"You aren't going to believe what I just saw," he exclaimed.

"Before you tell us, just remember you're in Sicily where anything can happen—and often does." Stefano smiled. "Let's go, son, before the *Siculis* claim you for their own." He glanced questioningly into his wife's eyes, searched them silently.

She shook her head and whispered. "Not now, Stefano. One day we'll both tell him. But not now." She filled with a nameless terror, a fear that Stefano might be right, that the *Siculis* wouldn't rest until they claimed Gino for their own as they had claimed Salvatore. "Please, not now."

The Americans left the Temple of Cats and returned to their land. But in the heart of Salvatore's son beat a curious excitement, a feeling that he had left the best part of him behind, in Sicily.

Did Stefano Modica ever uncover the name of the man who linked the White House to the Minister of Interior in Rome, the man who became Premier of Italy?

In 1957, Premier Belasci arrived in America on a goodwill tour. On this tour he was scheduled to speak before an affluent group of Italian-American Citizens of Business and Professionals at a Columbus Day Rally in Buffalo, New York.

Both Renzo Bellomo and Stefano Modica flew to Buffalo to observe this man on American soil. It came as no surprise to either of the former agents to find among those men in the upper echelons of American politics who greeted the Italian Premier, the Vice President of the United States, Roger Cutter, at ease among the most redoubtable members of the American Mafia and others connected with organized crime that weren't Italian joined together in making the Premier's stay a pleasant one.

Modica could do no more. His time was nearly over.

Bellomo *would* do no more when he witnessed the pinnacle of power in which the corruption of two nations was vested.

Destiny had other intentions for this man named Cutter. Almost two decades would pass before the tight file kept on this man erupted into one of the worst political scandals in American history. Banished from office, he retired in scandal and shame.

Martino Belasci barely finished his first term in office as Premier of Italy when the horror and corruption of his political life reached out from the countless graves surrounding him to haunt him. Unable to withstand the pressures and vivid memories of his evil deeds, he retired from politics haunted by the ghosts of Salvatore and de Montana, until his recent death.

"Truly," came the cries of the people, "vengeance belongs to the Lord!"

Or was the vengeance Salvatore's?